P9-DMW-560

"Do you not have a partner for this dance, my lord?"

"No. I do not care to dance every dance. What about you?"

"Alas, no gentleman requested my hand for this dance." Liberty's full lips pursed slightly, then twitched into a half smile. "But I *am* engaged for a waltz after supper and I am looking forward to that exceedingly."

"In order that you may tear me off another couple of strips?"

"Avon! That is *most* ungentlemanly of you." Her eyes sparkled, drawing him in, and it was with an effort he tore his gaze from hers, blanked his expression and cast a bored look over the dancers. "You did admit I was sorely provoked."

He couldn't resist another sideways glance at her, a glance that revealed twinkling eyes above pouting lips that drew his gaze like a magnet. Good grief. They were in a crowded ballroom and all he could think about was sweeping her into his arms and kissing her. His hand rubbed at the back of his neck as his inner voice of caution screamed at him to walk away. But still he lingered.

Author Note

When I decided to continue the story of the Beauchamp family with the three children of Leo, the Duke of Cheriton, I wasn't sure what to make of his eldest son, Dominic, Lord Avon. He's always (as he says himself) been the responsible one and in previous novels he has come across as pretty conventional—even a little stuffy in comparison to his younger siblings, Alexander and Olivia. In essence, he was the perfect duke's heir.

Then, in *Lady Olivia and the Infamous Rake*, Leo said something that stayed with me—

> *"...if there is one thing I have learned it is this. We cannot dictate where love will find us but, when it does, we must grab it with both hands... I now find myself watching Avon with some trepidation. I almost expect him to turn up with an actress upon his arm."*

—and Liberty Lovejoy popped into my head. Of course, she's not an actress but, with a name like that, she could be!

So, we move on five years from the events in *Lady Olivia and the Infamous Rake* and Dominic has decided it is time to find the perfect bride—a lady with impeccable breeding, the correct upbringing and immaculate conduct suitable for the heir of a wealthy and powerful duke. He even writes a list.

I hope you enjoy Dominic's battle to follow his head rather than his heart when the totally *unsuitable* Miss Liberty Lovejoy erupts into his life.

JANICE PRESTON

Daring to Love the Duke's Heir

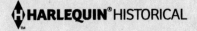

If you purchased this book without a cover you should be aware
that this book is stolen property. It was reported as "unsold and
destroyed" to the publisher, and neither the author nor the
publisher has received any payment for this "stripped book."

Recycling programs
for this product may
not exist in your area.

ISBN-13: 978-1-335-63522-8

Daring to Love the Duke's Heir

Copyright © 2019 by Janice Preston

All rights reserved. Except for use in any review, the reproduction or
utilization of this work in whole or in part in any form by any electronic,
mechanical or other means, now known or hereafter invented, including
xerography, photocopying and recording, or in any information storage
or retrieval system, is forbidden without the written permission of the
publisher, Harlequin Enterprises Limited, 22 Adelaide St. West, 40th Floor,
Toronto, Ontario M5H 4E3, Canada.

This is a work of fiction. Names, characters, places and incidents are
either the product of the author's imagination or are used fictitiously,
and any resemblance to actual persons, living or dead, business
establishments, events or locales is entirely coincidental.

This edition published by arrangement with Harlequin Books S.A.

For questions and comments about the quality of this book,
please contact us at CustomerService@Harlequin.com.

® and TM are trademarks of Harlequin Enterprises Limited or its
corporate affiliates. Trademarks indicated with ® are registered in the
United States Patent and Trademark Office, the Canadian Intellectual
Property Office and in other countries.

Printed in U.S.A.

Janice Preston grew up in Wembley, North London, with a love of reading, writing stories and animals. In the past she has worked as a farmer, a police call handler and a university administrator. She now lives in the West Midlands with her husband and two cats and has a part-time job with a weight-management counselor—vainly trying to control her own weight despite her love of chocolate!

Books by Janice Preston

Harlequin Historical

Mary and the Marquis
From Wallflower to Countess
Regency Christmas Wishes
"Awakening His Sleeping Beauty"

The Lochmore Legacy

His Convenient Highland Wedding

The Beauchamp Heirs

Lady Olivia and the Infamous Rake
Daring to Love the Duke's Heir

The Beauchamp Betrothals

Cinderella and the Duke
Scandal and Miss Markham
Lady Cecily and the Mysterious Mr. Gray

The Governess Tales

The Governess's Secret Baby

Men About Town

Return of Scandal's Son
Saved by Scandal's Heir

Visit the Author Profile page at Harlequin.com.

To Lynn.

Thank you.

Chapter One

March 1817

Raindrops rattled on the roof of the carriage that carried Miss Liberty Lovejoy and her sister Hope through the dark, slick streets of a rain-drenched London.

'Liberty. I beg you…please do not do this. Gideon will never forgive you.'

Liberty wrenched her attention from the passing streets and resolutely swallowed down her own burgeoning doubt. She didn't want to do this, but she had to. *Someone* must save Gideon from himself.

'I have to do something, Hope. Gideon is running amok and it is all the fault of Lord Alexander Beauchamp. Gideon will be grateful to me for saving him from the results of his own folly. Eventually.'

'Well, I do not think you are fair to embroil me without warning,' said Hope tartly. 'You *said* we were going to Hookham's. I would never have agreed to accompany you if I knew you intended to visit Alexander's father, of all people. He is a *duke*, Liberty. People like us do not just call upon a duke.'

Hope's reaction did not surprise Liberty—she had

given up expecting support from either of her sisters when there was any unpleasantness to deal with. They had been so young when their parents had died within days of one another and they had come to rely on Liberty and her twin brother, Gideon—just nineteen at the time—to take charge. Uncle Eustace was worse than useless…far too selfish to stir himself, even though he had been appointed their guardian. It was no wonder her entire family took Liberty for granted.

'If you are afraid to come in, you may remain in the carriage while I speak to the Duke. *I* cannot afford the luxury of fear.' Oh, but how she wished she could order Bilk, their coachman, to turn the carriage around and drive back to their rented London house. 'It is my responsibility as the eldest—'

'You are the eldest by a mere five minutes, Liberty Louisa Lovejoy, and *Gideon* now happens to be an earl.'

'His conduct is more reminiscent of an overgrown schoolboy than a peer of the realm,' retorted Liberty.

Since Liberty's twin brother had unexpectedly acceded to the Earldom of Wendover last autumn his behaviour had grown increasingly exasperating. Was it really asking too much of him to help her to secure their sisters' futures instead of careening around town and frittering his newfound prosperity on wine, cards and horses and in the pursuit of females who were no better than they should be? Besides, she missed Gideon and how they had worked together to ensure the survival of their family.

'Well, I would say that being an earl makes him senior to you, do you not? Do not forget we are all reliant on his goodwill now if we do not wish to be banished back to Eversham with Uncle Eustace. I think it is very generous of Gideon to fund a Season for all three of us at the same time.'

Liberty clenched her jaw. If Hope only knew how much persuasion it had taken for Gideon to agree to his sisters coming to London in the first place…left to himself, she had no doubt her twin would have been content for his sisters to remain hidden away at Eversham for ever while he lived the high life to which he now felt entitled.

She stared out of the window, seeing neither the grey streets they passed nor the people hurrying along beneath their umbrellas, wrapped in coats and cloaks against the dreadful dark, cold and wet weather that had assailed the entire country for the past year. If it were not for Hope and Verity she would much prefer to still be at home, running the house for Uncle Eustace—her late mother's unmarried brother who had always made his home with the Lovejoys—and living in quiet obscurity.

But Hope and Verity, at one-and-twenty and nineteen respectively, deserved a chance to better themselves in life. After their parents' deaths there had been neither opportunity nor funds for the younger Lovejoy sisters to even dream of a come out, not until the unexpected death of a distant cousin and his two sons in a house fire and Gideon's sudden preferment.

'And do not forget what Mrs Mount said.' Hope's words broke into Liberty's train of thought. 'It is bad etiquette to call on your social superiors before *they* have left their card with *you*.'

Mrs Mount was the lady they had hired as duenna during their sojourn in London. The daughter of a viscount and now the widow of the younger son of an earl, she had many acquaintances within the *ton* and was thus perfectly placed to help steer the Lovejoy girls through the mysteries of polite society. Well, perfectly placed if Liberty chose to follow her advice. Which, in this instance, she did not.

'It is a certainty that the Duke of Cheriton is never likely to leave his card for us,' said Liberty, 'so I do not see that I have any choice if I am to persuade him to control his son's wild behaviour.'

'I cannot believe that a duke will take kindly to a country squire's daughter lecturing him on how he should control his son. Libby—it is not too late. Please, let us go home and I promise I will help you talk some sense into Gideon.'

'But we have tried that, Hope, many times, and he ignores us. I fear his new status has gone to his head and that he will never be the same again.'

She was not even certain she much liked the man her twin had become. He had become secretive and thoughtless, and the closeness that had bound the two of them together throughout their childhood now felt as though it hung by the most fragile of threads.

It breaks my heart, this distance between us.

Liberty slid one gloved hand inside her woollen cloak and pressed it to her upper chest, rubbing in a soothing, circular motion, but the familiar hollow ache remained, as it had for the five years since her childhood sweetheart, Bernard, died.

Being back in London had resurrected those dreadful memories and, with them, the guilt. If only she hadn't been so selfish by accepting the offer from her wealthy godmother to sponsor her through a London Season. If only she had stayed at home, Bernard and her parents might still be alive. At the very least she would have been able to say goodbye to her husband-to-be. A knot of disquiet had taken root in her stomach since their arrival in London…a nagging reminder of her selfishness and her failure.

Well, she would not fail Gideon, or the girls. And if it meant calling on a duke unannounced, then so be it.

In an unexpected gesture, Hope clasped Liberty's hand.

'You cannot protect all of us all the time, Liberty. Gideon is a grown man. I know you miss the old Gideon, but he will come to his senses, you'll see.'

'But what if he does not? What if I sit by and do nothing and he ends up destroying himself? And that's quite apart from the damage his wild behaviour will do to you and Verity.'

Their background would be hurdle enough without Gideon casting a deeper shadow over them. Papa had been a gentleman, but Mama had been the daughter of a coal merchant—that whiff of trade would be a difficult barrier to overcome, according to Mrs Mount.

The carriage rocked to a halt.

'This must be it,' Hope said, her voice awed. 'Goodness!'

Liberty was momentarily distracted as thunder growled in the distance, a stark reminder of the most terrible day in her life—the day she had learned that not only both her beloved parents, but also Bernard, had succumbed to the outbreak of cholera that swept through their village while Liberty had been enjoying dress fittings in London in preparation for her debut. She had not even glimpsed the inside of a ballroom before receiving that urgent summons to return home.

She thrust down the memory that still had the power to bring hot, stinging tears to her eyes and peered through the rain that streamed down the window. She gulped. *This* was Beauchamp House? It was huge. Magnificent. Intimidating. It was not a house, but a mansion. Stretching for five wide bays, it would swallow several houses such as their modest rented abode in Green Street. A new surge of doubt as to her plan swept over Liberty, but she had come this far and she wouldn't allow herself to back away now. She gathered her courage, flung open the carriage door, grabbed her oilskin umbrella and, opening it, thrust it out of the door into the deluge. Lightning flickered and she braced herself for the next rumble of thunder. Was the storm getting closer? There were several seconds before the sound reached her ears—it sounded more distant than before and she released her pent-up breath. She gave herself no time for further qualms. Bilk handed her down and she hurried up the steps to the imposing front door of Beauchamp House, which remained firmly shut.

She lifted the brass knocker—so highly polished it gleamed even in the unnatural yellowish-grey afternoon light—and let it fall. Then she waited, irritation clambering over any nerves she felt at facing such a powerful nobleman. What was taking so long? 'Where—?'

'Might I be of assistance?'

She whipped around. A carriage was drawing away from the front of the house, presumably after depositing this man…her darting gaze settled on his face, half-shielded by his own umbrella, and she gasped, her stomach clenching with anger. She held fast to her courage and straightened her spine even though her knees quaked. This close, she was only too conscious of Lord Alexander Beauchamp's daunting presence—his height and the width of his shoulders spoke of a powerful man.

'I have come to speak to your father about your behaviour.'

He stiffened, his dark brows slashed into a forbidding frown. 'I *beg* your pardon?'

As she opened her mouth, he held up his hand, palm forward, effectively silencing her. 'Apart from the fact that you and I have never met, madam, I regret to inform you that the Duke is not in residence.' He brushed past her to the door.

'We may indeed never have met, my lord, but I know who you are.' Liberty set her jaw. She'd recognise Lord Alexander Beauchamp anywhere, even though she'd only ever glimpsed him in the distance as he gaily led her brother astray. 'The knocker is on the door.' She summoned her very haughtiest tone. 'That means the family is in residence.'

'A member of the family, maybe, but that member is not my father. Now, if you will excuse me? You might relish being out in such weather, but I can assure you I do not.' The door began to open. 'I suggest you put your grievance into writing. If you have it delivered here it will be forwarded on to my father for his attention, you have my word.'

The word of a rackety rakehell!

The door opened fully to reveal a liveried footman.

'Sorry, milord,' he said breathlessly. 'I was downstairs when I heard the knock.'

'No need for apologies, William. This—' Liberty stiffened, detecting the faint curl of his upper lip as His Lordship looked her up and down '—*person* wished to speak to my father. I have advised her to write to him.'

He handed his dripping umbrella to the servant and strode into the hall. Despair spread its tentacles through Liberty, squeezing her lungs. Coming here to confront the Duke had been a risk, but at least she would have had an opportunity to use her powers of persuasion. A letter could be all too easily dismissed. It was true she had never met Alexander, but perhaps if he knew who she was…? If she could appeal to his better nature…?

'Lord Alexander! Please!' She tried to dodge around the footman, who foiled her attempts using His Lordship's still-open umbrella. 'Wait, I beg of you.'

Once she succeeded in knocking aside that umbrella, she could see His Lordship had stopped and now faced her, a look of weary resignation on his face. Encouraged, she discarded her own umbrella on the doorstep and rushed towards him, darting around the still-protesting footman.

'Please. May we talk? I am Gideon's sister.'

His brows snapped together, forming once again a dark slash across his forehead. 'Gideon? Who is Gideon?'

'Lord Wendover.'

'You have my sympathy.'

Liberty bridled. 'If you think so little of him, why do you spend so much time together?'

He looked beyond her. 'William—take the lady's coat and bonnet, if you please. Ask Mrs Himley to send wine and cakes to the drawing room, and find a maid to sit with us—' He looked Liberty up and down before fixing his gaze on her face. The chill in his light-coloured eyes sent a shiver through her. 'For propriety's sake,' he continued. '*You* might have no compunction about calling upon your social superiors not only un-invited but also unchaperoned, madam, but a man cannot be too careful.'

The nerve of him! 'My sister is in the carriage out-side,' said Liberty, shedding her dripping cloak. 'She was too afraid to come in and speak to your father.'

'Too afraid or too sensible? I suspect the latter. Perhaps you would be wise to pay more attention to your sister's instincts.' His bored tone sent Liberty's temper soaring. 'Invite her to join us, William, if you please. She cannot wait outside. But I shall still require a maid,' he called after the departing footman.

He eyed Liberty again, from head to toe, and she squirmed inside. She had donned her best Pomona-green bombazine afternoon dress for this visit to the Duke, but His Lordship's impassive inspection made her feel as though she was dressed in rags. It was not the height of fashion—she had been unable to reconcile herself to wasting money on new gowns when she had a trunk full of barely worn dresses and accessories from five years ago—but it was respectable.

'One cannot be too careful.'

He means for himself! He is not concerned with my *reputation, only that I might try to entrap him!*

Liberty squared her shoulders and elevated her chin. 'The drawing room, sir?' She was proud of the haughty tone she achieved.

Utterly unruffled, he strolled to a nearby door and opened it. 'This way, ma'am.' *His* tone conveyed bored amusement.

She swept through, head high. How dare he treat her as though she were of no consequence? Although, she had to admit it was humiliation that spurred her rage. Undoubtedly, to a duke's son, she *was* inconsequential. He followed her inside the elegantly furnished room with its vermilion-painted walls above white-painted wainscoting, its high ceiling with elaborately moulded cornice and three tall windows dressed with delicately sprigged floor-length curtains.

'You are suffering under a misapprehension.'

She started at the voice behind her. She halted her in-

spection of the room and turned to find him closer than
she anticipated. Nerves fluttered deep in her belly as she
got her first good look at his pale silvery-grey eyes and
the utter confidence they conveyed. And why should
they not? Not only was he the son of one of the most
powerful Dukes in the land but he was sinfully, classi-
cally handsome with a straight nose, sharp cheekbones
and a beautifully sculpted mouth above a determined
chin. Those silvery eyes of his seemed to penetrate deep
inside her and yet they were as opaque as a silver coin,
revealing no hint of his thoughts.

She stepped back, dragging her gaze from his. His
beautifully tied cravat—how Gideon would appreciate such skill in *his* valet!—sported a simple gold pin
in the shape of a whip and his olive-green superfine
coat hugged wide shoulders and well-muscled arms.
Beneath that form-fitting coat he sported a grey-and-
white-striped waistcoat that did nothing to hide the
heavy muscles of his chest. Her eyes travelled further, skimming the powerful thighs encased in cream
breeches. He had the look of a Corinthian…the name
given to gentlemen who enjoyed and excelled at physical sports such as riding, boxing and fencing, according to Gideon.

The face of a Greek God, the body of a warrior and
a duke's son. How could one man have so many advantages in life? Her gaze snapped back to his face,
the sight of those powerful thighs imprinted on her
brain. He was watching her. By the quirk of his lips,
her perusal of his person amused him. Mortified at
being caught studying him as a sculptor might study his
subject, Liberty swallowed and then sucked in a deep
breath. That did nothing to calm her nerves. Male and

spicy, his scent filled her and those butterflies in her belly fluttered even more.

She forced a scowl to her face. This was Lord Alexander Beauchamp: the devil who was leading Gideon astray. She tilted her chin and looked down her nose at him, but the look that satisfactorily quelled the most persistent of tradesmen dunning for payment made no impression on His Lordship, judging by the arrogant lift of his eyebrows.

'Misapprehension, my lord?'

'Indeed.'

His deep cultured tones penetrated all the way inside her, stirring yet more fluttery sensations as she felt the full force of his attention.

'Allow me to introduce myself.' He bowed, the action somehow mocking. 'Avon, at your service. Miss…?'

His words jerked her from her irritation. 'What did you say? Who is Avon?'

'Alexander is my brother. My *younger* brother. I am the Marquess of Avon, hence Lord Avon.' His head tilted. 'Do you require an explanation of courtesy titles? I understand you and your brother were not raised in aristocratic circles.'

Liberty's face burned. Mrs Mount had warned them that their background would swiftly become common knowledge in the *ton*. No doubt His Lordship also knew her grandfather was a coal merchant. Without volition, her chin rose even higher than before.

'I am not ignorant of such matters, sir. If Gideon ever has a son, he will take Gideon's next highest title, Viscount Haxby, as a courtesy title to use as his own until Gideon's death, when he will become the Earl of Wendover.'

'I am relieved you have learned something since

your brother was elevated to the peerage. The fundamental etiquette of introductions appears to have passed you by, however. It is customary to introduce oneself in return.'

Infuriated that he was right, her face scorched even hotter. Lord Avon might resemble one of the marble statues she had admired at the British Museum last week, but he was as patronising and pompous as any man she had ever had the misfortune to meet.

She stiffened her spine and again looked down her nose. 'I am Miss Liberty Lovejoy.'

Chapter Two

Dominic bit back the sudden urge to laugh. Liberty Lovejoy? What parent would saddle their daughter with such a name? They had no choice over surname, to be sure—he was well aware Lovejoy was the family name of the Earls of Wendover—but what was wrong with naming their daughter Jane or Mary? Liberty Lovejoy— she sounded like some kind of actress. Or worse.

Still…he controlled his amusement and bowed. 'And to what do we owe the pleasure of your visit, Miss Lovejoy?'

He found himself scrutinised by a pair of intelligent, almond-shaped eyes. They were extraordinary and he found himself being drawn into their depths. They were the dark blue of the summer sky at midnight, with golden flecks in the irises and fringed with thick golden-brown lashes. Tawny brows drew together in a frown and her lips, soft pink and lush, compressed. He waited for her reply, controlling his visceral reaction to Miss Liberty Lovejoy. He was well practised in that art—his position as heir to a wealthy dukedom as well as his honour as a gentleman meant he simply did not indulge in idle flirtations.

'Your brother is tempting *my* brother into entirely inappropriate and wild behaviour and I came here to dem—*beg* your father to stop your brother from leading Gideon astray.'

Her velvety eyes glowed with fervour and he didn't doubt her genuine concern. His heart sank at the news that Alex might be falling back into his old, wild ways. He had already heard tales circulating about the newly ennobled Lord Wendover and his readiness to sample every entertainment available to a young, wealthy man about town, but Alex's name hadn't arisen in connection with them. The last he had heard, Alex was living at Foxbourne Manor in Berkshire and making a success of his horse breeding and training establishment— gaining a reputation for providing high-quality riding and carriage horses.

'Please be seated, Miss Lovejoy.' Dominic indicated a chair by the fireplace.

With a swish of her skirts, she settled on the sofa. Mentally, he shrugged. He would allow her that small victory. He studied his visitor as he strolled across to sit by her side—his scrutiny, his pace and his choice of seat specifically intended to ruffle her feathers. A man had to have some fun, after all.

Her gown looked new, but was outmoded by a few years, with its high neck and ruff of triple lace, and he couldn't help but notice how beautifully it clung to her curves. His pulse kicked, but Dominic controlled his surge of desire for this voluptuous woman. He prided himself on his self-control. In every area of his life. He sat, half-facing her, noting the crease of a frown between her tawny eyebrows and the tension in the lines around her mouth.

'I trust you have no objection to my sitting next to you?'

He allowed one corner of his mouth to quirk up and was rewarded by Liberty's subtle but unmistakable shift along the sofa, increasing the distance between them. The faint scent of roses drifted into his awareness—the scent of his late mother, remembered from his childhood—and all thought of teasing Miss Liberty Lovejoy vanished, swamped by a swirl of memories.

His mother had been on his mind more and more lately—ever since he had decided that this was the Season he would choose a wife. It was time to marry. Time to produce an heir. Time to fulfil the vow he had made all those years ago after his mother had died. He straightened, rolling his shoulders back. The sooner he addressed Miss Lovejoy's concerns, the sooner he could get on with compiling a list of candidates suitable for his bride.

'Tell me why you believe Alexander to be in any way responsible for your own brother's behaviour,' he said. 'Is he not his own man?'

She drew in a sharp breath but, before she could reply, William appeared in the open doorway.

'Miss Hope Lovejoy, milord,' he said.

Dominic stood. A young lady bearing a familial resemblance to Liberty Lovejoy entered the room, her cheeks blooming a becoming shade of pink. Out of habit, Dominic registered her appearance with one sweeping glance. Pretty. Golden-haired. Delicate features. Taller than her sister, with a trim figure, enhanced by the latest fashions. He couldn't resist glancing once again at Liberty and making comparisons. No. He wasn't mistaken. It would appear Liberty was a woman prepared to make personal sacrifices to ensure her younger sibling enjoyed every advantage. Was it that same trait that had driven her to come here and confront his father? That took some courage. His opinion of Liberty Lovejoy rose. Just a notch.

He bowed to Hope and directed his most charming smile at her, fully aware it would further vex the still-smouldering Liberty. 'I am pleased to make your acquaintance, Miss Lovejoy.'

Hope would prove popular with the gentlemen of the *ton*, he had no doubt. And she was fully aware of the effect of her beauty upon members of the opposite sex, he realised, as she rewarded him with a coquettish smile and a swift, appraising glance through her long lashes. A poorly stifled *hmmph* from Liberty reached Dominic's ears, stirring another urge to laugh which he manfully resisted.

'I am Avon. Please be seated.' He gestured to the place on the sofa he had recently vacated. 'Your sister and I were about to discuss the reason for this visit. Ah, Betty, Thomas, thank you.' A maid had come in with a dish of macaroons, followed by another footman carrying a tray bearing a bottle of Madeira and three glasses. 'Please be good enough to pour the wine, Thomas. Betty—will you sit by the window once you have served our visitors? You may remain until our visitors leave. Thank you.'

Liberty glowered at him, clearly irritated by the implication that her motives for this visit might differ from her stated reason. But, from a young age, Dominic had known his duty was to choose a suitable, well-brought-up lady as his future Duchess and it was now second nature to avoid any risk of getting trapped into an unsuitable alliance through carelessness.

Hope had now settled next to Liberty on the sofa and so Dominic moved to stand by the fireplace while he waited for the wine to be served.

'So. To continue with the reason for your visit, Miss Lovejoy—you lay the blame for your brother's wayward behaviour at the door of *my* brother?'

She raised her gaze from the contemplation of her glass. 'Yes.' She bit delicately into a macaroon.

Dominic frowned at her brusque reply.

'Why?' Two could play at that game.

The pink tip of her tongue as it rescued stray crumbs from her lips did strange things to Dominic's pulse rate. Irritated, he willed his body under control. Simple lust—not difficult for a man like him to resist. Yet he could not tear his gaze from her mouth as she chewed in a leisurely fashion, her fine tawny brows drawn together in a frown of concentration.

'Gideon has never been on the town before,' she said eventually. 'He is a...a...greenhead, I think is the word. He is being led astray by your brother, who appears intent on introducing him to every vice known to man.'

I sincerely hope not. Reading the earnestness of Liberty's expression, Dominic doubted she had the first idea of the full extent of the vices available in London to eager young bucks with money to burn. But he trusted Alex not to return to his past reckless behaviour. Didn't he? He made a mental note to check up on his brother's activities. If he felt Alex was in danger of sliding back into his old, wild ways, he would nip that in the bud before their father and stepmother came up to town.

'I am sure Alex is simply helping your brother to find his feet in town,' he said. 'I fail to understand why you feel he needs your protection. What would he say if he knew you had come here to speak to my father?'

Liberty's cheeks bloomed red. 'He would object, of course.'

She was honest, at least. His opinion lifted another degree.

'Then you will do well to allow him to determine his own path. No man would take kindly to his sister trying to control him. I presume you are older than him?'

'We are twins but, yes, I am the elder.'

'Twins? No wonder he objects to your interference. Heed my advice, Miss Lovejoy, and allow your brother to be his own man.'

Her lips parted as she inhaled. Her breasts rose, drawing Dominic's gaze like a lodestone. His pulse quickened and his cravat suddenly felt too tight. The room too warm. He swallowed down his reaction even as he acknowledged that Liberty Lovejoy's natural, curvaceous femininity was more attractive to him than any of the painstakingly elegant ladies of the *ton*. He could never act upon such attraction, however—as the sister of an earl and a lady, she was off limits other than for marriage. And she was definitely not marriageable material. Not for him.

He had sworn at his mother's death, when he was eight years old, that he would do his duty and make her proud of him.

Never forget, Avon—you will be the Duke one day. You must never bring your heritage into disrepute. Make me proud, my Son.

He'd spent his life striving to fulfil her expectations. He had never felt good enough for her while she was alive—other than that one hint of affection he had glimpsed from her, on the day she died—but now, this Season, he would finally prove to her that he was worthy. Besides, it was what was expected of a man in his position, and he owed his father that much, too. His bride must be perfect in every way: bloodlines, up-bringing, behaviour.

And Liberty Lovejoy fitted none of those require-ments. Not one.

Unsettled and irritated by his visceral reaction to this woman Dominic lowered his gaze to where her hands were gripped together in her lap, her kid gloves stretched taut over her knuckles. He choked back his exasperation. It was not Liberty's fault he found her so…enticing. Her distress at her brother's behaviour was tangible and the urge to comfort her took him by surprise. He softened his tone.

'What your brother is doing is not so very unusual, Miss Lovejoy. Most young men on the town for the first time behave somewhat recklessly. But they soon settle down and I am convinced your brother will, too.'

'But I must stop him before he squanders his entire inheritance.'

'Are his debts so very ruinous?' He would have thought Wendover's estates were wealthy enough, even after the disaster of last year's harvest.

Liberty's lips pursed.

'*I* am certain you are right, my lord.' Hope smiled at Dominic and fluttered her lashes. 'As you might guess, my sister does have an unfortunate tendency to imag-ine the worst. We do not know the scale of his debts as Gideon, *quite rightly*—' she cast a quelling look at her sister '—refuses to discuss—'

'He is out until all hours and sometimes he does not come home at all.'

The words burst from Miss Lovejoy as she swept her hand through her hair, scattering hairpins and leaving bits of hair the hue of dark honey sticking out sideways from her scalp. Two locks unwound to drape unnoticed over her shoulder.

'And when he does, he is so…so distant. So *secretive*.' Her voice rang with despair. 'We have always shared everything, but he will not confide in me…the tradesmen haven't been paid…there is a stack of bills awaiting his attention, yet when I begged him to pay them, all he would say is that he must pay his gambling debts first as a matter of honour. He lost two hundred pounds at hazard last night. Two *hundred*!'

Her horror at such a loss was clear, but her words convinced Dominic that she was worrying over nothing. Her lack of understanding of the ways of the aristocracy was hardly surprising when she had not been raised in such circles.

'That does not sound so very bad to me.'

'Not so very bad? *Two hundred pounds?*'

He'd intended to reassure her. Instead she was looking at him as though he'd suddenly sprouted a second head.

'Well, no. The Earldom of Wendover is a wealthy one with properties in Buckinghamshire and Suffolk, if I remember rightly. It can stand a few losses at the gaming tables. I am convinced you are worrying over nothing, Miss Lovejoy. You will see. Your brother will eventually settle down.'

'But…the tradesmen. Gideon flatly refuses to pay them. He says they can wait. He never used to be so… so careless of other people, but whenever I remonstrate with him, all he will say is that is how everyone in society carries on.'

Dominic shrugged. 'Many do.'

He did not do that himself. Neither did his father. But he could not deny that many gentlemen consid-

ered tradesmen to be at the bottom of the list of debt-
ors to be paid.

'It is your brother's prerogative to pay the tradesmen
who supply your household as and when he chooses,
just as it is the tradesmen's prerogative to cease supplying such late-paying customers if they choose. In my
experience, most tradesmen elect to continue enjoying
the patronage of their aristocratic clients for the prestige it brings them.'

'That is *appalling*.'

He agreed. It was one of the many habits of the
higher echelons of society that he disliked, but he would
not admit as much to Miss Liberty Lovejoy as she sat
on his father's sofa passing judgement. She seemed determined to believe the worst of his world, including
blaming *his* brother for *her* brother's misbehaviour.

'Can you not ask your brother to stop encouraging
Gideon? *Please*, my lord.'

Dominic passed one hand around the back of his
head, massaging the tight muscles at the top of his neck.
'Even if I were inclined to speak to him on this, I can
assure you Alex would likely do the exact opposite of
what I asked of him.'

And, now he came to think of it, that was no doubt
the exact reason Gideon was behaving as Miss Lovejoy had described.

'Perhaps if you trusted your brother to make his
own decisions instead of—how did you put it?—
remonstrating with him, he would mend his ways that
much sooner.'

Liberty surged to her feet.

'So it is *my* fault, is it, Lord Avon?'

Dominic didn't answer, distracted by her curvaceous

figure as she paced the room, her skirts swishing. She really was magnificent.

'*If* you would do me the courtesy of replying to my point?'

Her voice dripped sarcasm. Furious with himself for ogling her in such an ill-bred manner, Dominic blanked his expression and calmly met her glare. If looks could kill, or even maim, then he would be prostrate on the floor even now. The impulse to prod her further was irresistible. He raised one brow in deliberate provocation.

'You may have noticed, my dear Miss Lovejoy, that calmness, elegance and poise are three of the qualities most desired in the young ladies of our world. There is a very good reason for that and I would advise you to nurture such traits in your own behaviour.'

Her eyes narrowed. 'What do you mean?'

'Only that too much vigour and…er…*passion* are not the done thing, you know.'

He smiled kindly at her as she continued to look daggers at him.

'You, sir, are no gentleman.'

'I am merely trying to give you a hint as to how to go on in society, Miss Lovejoy.' He folded his arms across his chest, enjoying her chagrin. 'And, might I add, sarcasm does not become you. Am I correct in assuming that you and your sister will be making your debuts this coming Season?'

Liberty turned to her sister. 'Come, Hope. We are wasting our time expecting any assistance from His Lordship.' She glared again at Dominic. 'I shall write to your father, as you suggested, sir, in the hope that he possesses the conscience you so clearly lack.'

Hectic pink flushed Hope Lovejoy's cheeks as she shot a furious look at her sister. She stood and smoothed out her skirts, then dipped a curtsy as she smiled apologetically.

'Do please excuse us for invading your home, Lord Avon,' she said. 'Good afternoon.'

Dominic bowed. 'No apology is necessary. Good afternoon, Miss Hope Lovejoy.'

He then glanced at Liberty and guilt thumped him hard in the chest at the despair that dulled those extraordinary eyes. He stifled a sigh.

'I shall have a word with Alex and make sure he and Wendover are not getting in too deep, Miss Liberty Lovejoy—' and her name still made him want to smile '—but other than that there is little I can do. Alex will not take kindly to any attempt by me to tell him how to behave.'

Gratitude suffused her features.

'But I am still convinced you are worrying over nothing,' he added.

'I thank you nevertheless, my lord.'

Liberty's face lit with a more-generous smile than his offer warranted and, before he could stop himself, he found himself responding. He blanked his expression again and crossed to the bell pull. Liberty Lovejoy provoked strange emotions in him—emotions he did not care to examine too closely—but he was reassured by the knowledge their paths would rarely cross. Wendover, as a peer—even a hellraising peer—would find acceptance everywhere, but his sisters, raised in obscurity and with a grandfather in trade, would likely only frequent the fringes of society.

William, thankfully, answered his summons promptly.

'Please see the ladies out, William.'

He bowed again, avoiding eye contact with either

of his visitors, then stood stock still after they had gone, staring unseeingly at the closed door, wondering how one voluptuous, sweet-smelling woman had stirred such unaccustomed feelings within him. He had always kept his emotions under strict control, as behoved his father's heir. Alex and their younger sister, Olivia—before she had wed four years ago—had always been the lively, mischievous ones of the family, but Dominic had grown up with the weight of expectation on his shoulders. It was his duty to make his father proud, to uphold the family name and to always behave as befitted a future duke.

Also, strangely, he felt compelled to protect his father— a nonsensical-seeming notion when one considered how powerful Father was. But Dominic recalled his mother's death all too clearly, and how Father had suffered from guilt. Dominic had seen and heard things no eight-year-old boy should ever see and hear and, by shouldering the responsibility of being the perfect son and the perfect heir, he had vowed to shield his father from further distress.

He shook his head, as though he might dislodge those memories and the thoughts they evoked, clicking his tongue in irritation. He swung round to face the room. Betty hovered not five feet from him, having been unable to get past him to the door as he stood there like a mindless idiot, blocking her exit.

He frowned and moved aside, motioning for the maid to leave, his promise to Miss Lovejoy—it *had* been a promise, had it not?—nipping at him. He would speak to Alex.

'Betty?'

'Yes, milord?'

'Is Lord Alexander currently in residence?'

Dominic did not live at Beauchamp House, preferring the privacy of his own town house when staying in London. He had travelled up to town yesterday from Cheriton Abbey and had merely called at Beauchamp House to warn the staff that his father's butler, Grantham, would be arriving shortly to prepare the house for the arrival of the Duke and Duchess and to find out what day his sister, Olivia, and his brother-in-law, Hugo, were due to arrive in London.

'No, milord.'

'Ask downstairs if anyone knows where he is staying in London, will you please?'

Betty nodded and then scurried past him out of the room.

Chapter Three

That glimpse of kindness in Lord Avon just before they left almost changed Liberty's impression of His Lordship. Almost, but not quite. That one final concession was simply not enough to wipe out the many black marks against him, and Liberty, crotchety and restless after that interview, was in no mood to forgive. She clambered into the carriage behind Hope and sat down before knocking on the roof with her umbrella as a signal to Bilk to drive on. As soon as the carriage was in motion, Hope swivelled on the bench to face Liberty.

'I was never more embarrassed,' she said. 'Do you *never* stop to think of the consequences of your actions on me and Verity? Lord Avon is the most eligible bachelor in the *ton* and Mrs Mount had grand hopes that one of us might catch his eye. She told me the family estates in Devonshire are *vast*, but now you have ruined our chances because you will *never* listen to *anybody*. You always think you know best. Oh! To think! I might have been a duchess.'

'A marchioness, Hope. Lord Avon's father is very much alive and well. And do please stop dramatising everything. That man would never seriously consider either you or Verity as suitable…he was utterly contemptuous about us not being raised with the expectations of moving in high society.'

'But we have our looks on our side. Why, Lord Redbridge called me an Incomparable the other day! And, oh, Liberty! Isn't Lord Avon the most handsome, well-set figure of a man you have ever seen?'

'Hmmph. A person might think that, if she cared for the Corinthian type, but he is also arrogant, haughty, conceited—'

Words failed her but, next to her, Hope unexpectedly giggled.

'He *has* made you cross, hasn't he, Liberty? Do you not realise all those words have the same meaning?'

Liberty pursed her lips. 'Unfeeling. Rude. Superior—'

'Superior means the same again,' crowed Hope.

'Well, we can't all have a way with words like you, Hope.'

Now Hope was relieved of the necessity to earn a little money by teaching in the local school, she either had her head buried in a novel, or was madly scribbling poetry and plays, while Verity was rarely seen without a sketchbook in her hands.

They were happy to leave the practicalities of running the family to Liberty—a responsibility she had taken on after their parents died, having promised her dying mother that she would look after the family and keep them safe.

'Well, it matters not what your opinion of His Lordship may be, Libby, for I am very certain he would not consider *you* as marriageable after the way you spoke to him.'

'I said no more than the situation warranted.' Liberty turned aside and stared pointedly through the window as she continued her diatribe against Lord Avon inside her head.

How dare he look down on us? Just because we weren't raised in the lap of luxury it does not mean we are worth less as people.

She glanced down at her gown. Admittedly, it was not today's fashion, but it had hardly been worn, and surely it was wasteful not to make use of the gowns made for her five years ago.

At least His Precious Lordship can't fault Hope— her gown is the very latest fashion!

The carriage pulled up outside the Green Street town house they currently called home. Lord Avon might have tried to divert her by claiming the Wendover estates could stand such losses as two hundred pounds a night—even thinking of such a loss made Liberty feel quite faint—but Gideon's inheritance did not even include a house in London and his country house needed complete rebuilding, which would cost a fortune, so she was right to worry about money. Someone had to. She'd wager Lord Avon had never had to worry about money, with a father who was a wealthy duke. They were clearly so vastly rich and so elevated on the social scale that ordinary people's fears simply did not register with them.

Hope jumped from the carriage and scurried to the door, leaving Liberty to follow. As she shrugged out of her pelisse and handed it to Ethel, their housemaid, Hope's tones of outrage floated down the stairs.

'And, *would you believe*, she dragged me to the house of none other than the Duke of Cheriton to confront him about his son's behaviour.'

Liberty sighed.

'Thank you, Ethel. Has Miss Hope ordered a tea tray?'

'Yes, miss.'

Liberty trod up the stairs, reluctance to face her sisters and Mrs Mount slowing her steps. Of course they would all three disapprove of what she had done, but what choice did she have?

She had kept to her word to Mama, working hard to help keep their small family estate solvent. Gideon— who had inherited the estate from Papa—had left university and thrown himself into the life of a country squire and farmer. He'd never complained. She'd thought he was content enough.

Gideon and she...they had been a true partnership through those hard years. But then, last year, summer had never materialised and harvests had failed the length and breadth of the country, leaving many in hardship and the poorest starving. Gideon had become morose and withdrawn, worrying about the survival of their family home. And then had come the most unexpected news of all. Lord Wendover and his entire family—distant family members they had never even met, so obscure was the connection—had perished, leaving Gideon as the nearest male relation and thus the new Earl of Wendover.

Gideon had changed. It had been as though he had been incarcerated in a prison, and freedom had taken him and turned him from a hard-working, considerate brother into...a stranger. That familiar hollow ache filled Liberty's chest and she rubbed at it absent-mindedly, tears burning behind her eyes. Her beloved brother. The other half of her. Her twin. They'd always shared a close bond but now...she feared he was lost to her for good.

What does Lord Avon know? Supercilious, over-privileged, condescending... He seemed to think this behaviour was normal. Well, Liberty knew Gideon as well as she knew herself and this was as far from normal for him as it was possible to be. It *had* to be the influence of Avon's wicked brother.

Head high, she walked into the drawing room and a deathly silence. Before she had taken a seat by the fire, however, all three occupants spoke at once.

Hope, accusing. 'I told them what you did.'

Mrs Mount, regretful. 'My dear—how could you possibly think that a wise course? If only you had sought my advice. You know how important it is for you all to get vouchers for Almack's—this sort of transgression will do nothing to help your cause.'

Verity, condemning. 'Isn't that just like you, Liberty—charging in without a thought as to how your actions will reflect upon the rest of us?'

Liberty sat down and arranged her skirts, then folded her hands in her lap.

'If you have all *quite* finished—I did what I thought needed to be done and I shall not apologise for it.'

She sensed the others exchanging glances, but she kept her attention on the flickering flames and concentrated on keeping any tell-tale tears at bay as she hoped Lord Avon would not spread the story of her visit far and wide. She had taken a risk, but she was growing desperate and she felt so alone. Where else could she turn for help? Even Godmama was gone now, having passed away last year. The alternative was to ignore Gideon's ever-wilder behaviour and simply pray he would come to his senses. Well, that approach might have been Mama and Papa's solution were they still alive—they had always put their total faith in God and the Bible—but Liberty had long ago stopped trusting in Divine intervention. Where had God been when first Bernard, then Papa, then Mama had all succumbed to the cholera, even though Liberty had spent the entire journey home from London in desperate prayer? Nowhere, that was where.

No. It had been worth the risk to visit the Duke, even though only his arrogant son had been in residence. Lord Avon had given his word to speak to Alexander, although his warning that his brother would be unlikely to pay any heed rang in her ears, reviving her feeling of utter hopelessness.

Ethel brought in the tea tray and Verity poured the cups and handed them round. Liberty accepted hers and sipped, relishing the slide of the hot tea as it soothed her paper-dry throat.

'What did the Duke say?' Mrs Mount's tentative enquiry broke into Liberty's circling thoughts.

'Ah.' Liberty placed her half-drunk cup carefully in its saucer. 'He is not in residence. We did, however, speak to his son, Lord Avon. Lord Alexander's older brother. Do you know him?'

'Yes, of course, although not as well as his father. He and I are of an age, you know—such a tragedy, his first wife dying like that...but there! That's all in the past now. Avon, now...he is a very different man to his brother—very serious and correct. And he is the most eligible bachelor in the *ton*.' Her reproving look scoured Liberty. 'I did harbour hopes he might develop a *tendre* for one of your sisters, but that is now a lost cause. Avon's behaviour is very proper. Beyond reproach. I dare say he was shocked at a young lady having the temerity to call upon him without prior introduction and unchaperoned to boot.'

Liberty shrugged. 'Firstly, I was not unchaperoned. Hope was there and there was a maid in the room, too.

And secondly, I should not care to even hazard a guess as to His Lordship's thoughts.'

She recalled the slide of his gaze over her figure—for a split second she had seen desire flare, before he masked his expression. The thought sent a quiver of heat chasing across her skin.

'Hope,' said Mrs Mount reprovingly, 'is not an adequate chaperon for you, nor you for her. And so the visit was a waste of time and a risk not worth taking?'

'Not entirely. He did offer to speak to his brother, but he did not give us much hope that Lord Alexander will pay him any heed.'

'Is the Duke coming to town? If anyone can control Lord Alexander, it will be him.'

'Lord Avon did not say. Maybe…should I speak to Lord Alexander myself?'

'Nooo!' three voices chorused.

Mrs Mount shushed Liberty's sisters with a wave of her hand before fixing Liberty with a stern look. 'You have done what you can, my dear. I really think you must allow Gideon to come to his senses in his own time. And he will. I am sure of it. In the meantime, we should concentrate on the upcoming Season and finding you three girls suitable husbands. Once you are married off and have families of your own, you will have more important matters to occupy your thoughts.' Her grey eyes raked Liberty. 'Are you *certain* I cannot persuade you to have a new gown or two made, my dear? That one does look sadly outmoded.'

'Mrs Mount is right, Liberty,' said Hope. 'Verity and I have had so much and you've barely spent a penny on yourself. You deserve something nice. Surely you can bring yourself to order one gown?'

Liberty recognised Hope's peace offering—their

family squabbles never lasted long, thank goodness. She recalled Lord Avon's initial perusal of her. Despite Gideon's assurance that he could *'stand the blunt'*, as he put it, Liberty had been unable to bring herself to squander even more money on herself. Now, however, she found herself eager to prove to His High-and-Mighty Lordship that the Lovejoys could be respectable.

'Very well. One evening gown,' she conceded. 'But not to catch a husband. I have told you. I shall never marry. Bernard was my one and only love and I shall remain true to his memory.'

The words were automatically spoken. When Bernard died, she had sworn never to look at another man, never to contemplate marriage. But over the past year she had come to accept the truth. She was lonely. Even with her entire family around her, she was lonely.

That hollow, aching feeling invaded her again and she rubbed absently at her upper chest.

But she was still afraid to admit her change of heart out loud…afraid to fully acknowledge that she dreamed of finding someone to love who would love her in return…afraid that no man could ever take Bernard's place. It was safer to keep that daydream locked inside. That way she would not have to face anyone's pity if she failed to meet such a man. That way, she could keep her pride.

'Still hiding behind the sainted Bernard, Sis? Isn't it time you looked to the future instead of forever harking back to the past?'

That careless drawl shot Liberty to her feet. 'Gideon!' She rushed to him and grabbed his upper arms, scanning him quickly: his drawn, pale features; the dark shadows beneath his eyes; the dishevelled evening clothes. The lingering smell of alcohol and…she wrin-

kled her nose…cheap perfume and—there was no other
word for it—*bodies*. Activities she did not wish to think
of. She released her brother and stepped back.

'You have been out all night.'

He quirked a brow and a faint smile lifted the corners of his mouth. 'I have indeed.'

'You need a bath.'

His eyes narrowed. 'So I do. And I have sent word
for water to be heated. Not that it is polite for you to
mention such a matter.'

'But—'

'But nothing, Liberty. You are not my keeper.' He
moved past her. 'Good afternoon, Mrs Mount. Hope.
Verity. I trust you are all well?'

All three returned his smile and his greeting but, before he left, Hope—after a sympathetic smile at Liberty—
said, 'We do miss you when you stay out so very much,
Gideon. Will you dine with us tonight? We have no invitations.'

In truth, invitations for the Lovejoy ladies to attend
evening events were still a rarity. Mrs Mount had reassured the girls that the Season had barely begun and
that once Easter was over many more families would
come to town and the invitations would, hopefully, start
to arrive. Currently only one invitation adorned their
mantelpiece—to a rout at the home of Sir Gerald and
Lady Trent, Sir Gerald being a cousin of Mrs Mount.

'Can't. Sorry.' Gideon turned to the door. 'A bath and
a couple of hours' shut-eye, then I'm off to the theatre.'

'We could go with you,' said Liberty. 'We could hire
a box.'

His look of dismay clawed at her, leaving her feeling raw and, somehow, exposed. 'I'm not going to the
theatre with my *sisters*. Good God! Where's the fun in

sitting in a box when I could be down in the pit where all the fun is? Tell you what, Sis—if you're that keen on seeing Mary the Maid of the Inn, I'll reserve a box for you another night. Just tell me when you want to go. You've got Mrs M. to chaperon you and you'll soon have beaux flocking around you if it's male company you're pining for.'

With that, Gideon marched out of the room, leaving the three sisters—and Mrs Mount—looking at one another in despair.

'I still say it's just the novelty of it all that has turned his head,' said Mrs Mount in a faint voice as the sound reached them of him bounding up the stairs. '*Surely* he will come to his senses?'

Liberty did not reply. She returned to her chair and stared at the fire, her mind awash with ideas as plans spiralled to the surface and then sank again as her common sense scuppered them. Finally, realising she was getting nowhere, she went to consult Mrs Taylor about dinner that evening. It went against the grain but, somehow, she must control her penchant for taking action and trust that Lord Avon would be true to his word and do something to curb his own brother's wild ways.

Chapter Four

The next day was dry but cold after the thunderstorm and Dominic, following a sparring session with Gentleman John Jackson in his saloon on Bond Street, strolled to White's for a glass of wine and a bite to eat. On arrival, he picked up *The Times* and appropriated a quiet table in the corner of the morning room, hoping the open newspaper would discourage anyone from joining him. He had important matters to attend to this Season, like selecting a wife—a well-bred young lady with the poise and the correct upbringing suitable for a marchioness, a society hostess and, one day, a duchess. His purpose in coming up to town in advance of the rest of the family was to make a decision about his bride-to-be and here was as good a place to plan his strategy as any.

After being served, he drank a little wine, took one bite of the cold beef and horseradish sandwich and then settled back into the chair, holding the paper but not actually reading. He'd written a list of names last night. Seven in all. He wasn't interested in a bride straight out of the schoolroom—his Marchioness would already have some town polish with, preferably, at least two

Seasons behind her. The highest families were in no hurry to marry off their daughters—they took their time and selected the very best husbands, usually with a view to allying with a powerful family. A huge dowry wasn't a prerequisite for his perfect bride; he was more concerned with their breeding and background as well as their conduct. These were essential qualities for a lady who would, at some time in the future, occupy the role of Duchess of Cheriton and give birth to the Eighth Duke.

Seven names were too many...he must cut his list to three or four ladies, then he could concentrate on making his final choice, but discreetly; it would not do to raise expectations in the ladies themselves or in society in general. He was under no illusion, imagining himself so perfect that any female would swoon at his feet. It was not conceit, but realism...any one of the ladies on his list would jump at the chance of marrying into the Beauchamps, one of the most powerful families in the land.

He lay down the paper, hooked one hand around the back of his neck and rubbed, sighing. He would be happy when it was all over and he could get on with his life. In his mind's eye he saw his future stretching ahead of him, and he felt...nothing. No excitement. No anticipation.

Unbidden, Liberty Lovejoy crept into his thoughts and he dismissed her with a silent oath. Wasn't it bad enough she had invaded his dreams last night...erotic, enchanting dreams that had him waking bathed in sweat and in a state of solid arousal? A woman such as Liberty Lovejoy had no place in his future—to marry well was his duty and his destiny, as it had been Father's. Dominic was fortunate that *he* had not been obliged to wed at eighteen as Father had done, when his own father was in failing health and worrying over the future of the Dukedom. *Father* had put aside any personal inclination by doing his duty and marrying Dominic's mother, the daughter of a marquess and the granddaughter of a duke. The current Duchess—his stepmother, Rosalind—might be the daughter of a soldier and the granddaughter of a silversmith, but that did not affect the aristocratic lineage of the Dukes of Cheriton.

At least Dominic was six and twenty and had some experience of life, but sometimes—although he would never admit as much, not to anyone—the responsibility lay heavy on his shoulders. Almost without conscious thought, he withdrew the list of names from his pocket, unfolded it and read the names. If he could cross off three names, that would make—

'Mind if I join you, old chap?'

Hurriedly, Dominic folded the list and shoved it back into his pocket. He looked up into the bright blue inquisitive gaze of Lord Redbridge and inwardly cursed. Of all men, it had to be Redbridge. One of Alex's friends, he was an inveterate gossip and Dominic could only hope he hadn't deciphered any of the names on his list. He smiled and gestured to the chair next to his, then reached for his sandwich and bit into it. His leisurely luncheon was about to change into a hurried repast.

Redbridge had no qualms in admitting he had recognised at least two of the names on that sheet of paper and proceeded to not only tease Dominic about its existence, but also badger him about the other names.

'There must have been half a dozen on there at least, Avon.' His eyes were alive with curiosity. 'You can tell me, you know. Soul of discretion and all that. It'd do you good to talk about it. Alex is always sayin' you're too buttoned up for your own good.'

Dominic knocked back what remained of his wine and stood up. 'Your imagination is running amok, as usual, Redbridge. Now, if you will excuse me...?'

Redbridge didn't take the hint. He stood, too, and exited the coffee room by Dominic's side. 'Are you thinking of getting leg-shackled then? Oh, my life—the ladies will be in a flutter! There'll be neither time nor attention for the rest of us poor sods once the word gets out...it'll all be about Lord Avon and his list!'

He nudged Dominic with a sharp elbow and grinned hugely. Dominic stifled the urge to grab his neckcloth and slowly choke the wretch. Instead, he halted and turned to face his companion. They were close to the front door of the club by now and Dominic was damned if he'd put up with the man's inane chatter all the way to his front door.

'I'll bid you good afternoon here, Redbridge. And I will repeat what I have already said—your conjecture over that list is entirely wrong. My sister arrives in town today and she asked me to list any ladies I can think of who came out in the past two Seasons, as she will not have made their acquaintance. The truth is as mundane as that. And if—' he thrust his face close to Redbridge's '—I happen to hear *any* rumours to the contrary, I shall know precisely whose door to knock upon. Are we clear?'

Redbridge's mouth drooped. 'Perfectly.'

Dominic pivoted on his heel and strode for the door, anger driving him to reach home in record time. He barged through the front door of his leased town house, his temper frayed and his nerves on edge. He knew better than to believe Redbridge would keep such a juicy morsel to himself. Half the *ton* thrived on gossip and this, he knew, would be avidly passed from mouth to mouth. He would have to tread very carefully indeed not to reveal any preference for any of the many eligible ladies in town, but at least there were now two names he could cross off his list—the two Redbridge had read. Dominic would avoid those two as he would avoid a rabid dog and concentrate his efforts on the remaining five.

'Brailsford?'

'My lord?'

His man, who fulfilled the roles of valet, butler and footman in his bachelor household, appeared like magic from the kitchen stairs.

'Send word to the mews for my curricle to be ready for three-thirty. I intend to drive in the Park.'

'Will you require Ted to accompany you, sir?'

'Yes.' He would need a groom up behind if any of the five ladies were in the Park: to hold the horses if he got out to walk or to add propriety if he took one into his curricle to drive her around the Park. He felt heavy…his heart a leaden weight in his chest. But this was his duty; his destiny. And he would not allow himself to shirk it.

At three-forty, Dominic steered his matched bays into the Park and sent them along the carriageway at a smart trot. Ted perched behind him on the back of the curricle, ready to take charge of Beau and Buck if needs be. As Dominic drove, he scanned the walkers they passed and the small knots of people who had gathered to exchange the latest on-dits. The Season was not fully underway and wouldn't be until after Easter, but many families were already in town to attend to essential dress fittings and other preparations. He eased his horses back to a walk as he spied Lady Caroline Warnock in a stationery barouche, next to her mother, the Marchioness of Druffield. A couple they had been talking to had just walked away as Dominic drew his curricle alongside and raised his hat.

'Good afternoon, ladies.'

'Good afternoon, sir.'

Lady Druffield honoured him with a regal smile as her daughter bowed her head, her own smile gentle and gracious.

'Good afternoon, Lord Avon,' Caroline said. 'A pleasant afternoon for a drive, is it not?'

'Very pleasant, following yesterday's thunderstorm.'

A delicate shudder passed through Caroline. 'I do not care for the loud bangs or the lightning.'

Lady Druffield patted Caroline's hand. 'Such things are bound to play havoc with your sensibilities, my dear. As they would with any lady.'

Unbidden, yet again, an image of Liberty Lovejoy surfaced. *She* had not been undone by a mere thunderstorm. He could not imagine Lady Caroline standing under a dripping umbrella, nor dodging around a determined footman. He bit back a smile at the memory and he couldn't resist a gentle challenge.

'But there is something delightfully elemental about a good storm, is there not?'

He raised an eyebrow at Caroline, whose serene expression did not waver.

'Of course, my lord. You are so right—a good storm can be most exciting.'

Lady Druffield nodded in approval at her daughter's response, but impatience already plagued Dominic. He was so easily bored by this sort of dance with words...

talking about nothing…being polite and mannerly…
and females who hung upon and agreed with every
word he uttered. But it was the game they all played,
him included. And it was not Caroline's fault—she had
been raised to be the perfect lady and that was what he
wanted. Wasn't it?

'It is an age since we last met, sir,' Caroline said. 'Was
it at…?'

She hesitated, her head tipped to one side, a smile
hovering around her lips and her fine brows arched.
Dominic complied readily with her hint…it would be
unladylike for Caroline to admit she recalled their last
meeting but he, as a gentleman, was expected to remember the exact place and circumstances.

'It was at Lord Silverdale's house party in February,
if memory serves me correctly, my lady.'

'Ah, yes, indeed.' Caroline settled her dark brown
gaze on his face.

'I am delighted to renew our acquaintance,' said
Dominic.

Caroline smiled and her lashes swept low as she cast
her gaze to her lap, where her hands rested in tranquil
repose. 'As am I.'

He might as well begin his campaign. 'Would you
care to take a turn around the Park in my curricle, Lady
Caroline? With your mother's permission, of course.'

Another gracious smile. Not once had she revealed
her teeth. Nor had any of those smiles reached her eyes.
He wondered if she might show a little more life out of
earshot of Lady Druffield. Dominic directed his most
charming smile at that lady.

'But of course. It will be perfectly proper with the
groom up behind, Caroline. And I can trust His Lord-

ship to remain in the Park…he will take every care of you, I make no doubt.'

Dominic tied off the reins while Ted ran to the horses' heads, enabling Dominic to climb from the curricle and assist Lady Caroline from the barouche and into his curricle. Then he leapt aboard.

'I will deliver her back to you safe and sound, my lady.' He gave Beau and Buck the office to proceed and they set off at a trot, the vehicle dipping as Ted sprang up behind.

The first person Dominic saw was Liberty Lovejoy. From the direction of her purposeful stride he could only surmise she had been heading straight for him, presumably with the intention of interrupting him despite the fact he was already engaged in conversation. He did not slow his horses. He had nothing to tell her, in any case, because—and guilt coiled in his gut—he had been putting off his promise to speak to Alex. He hadn't forgotten it—he hadn't been *able* to forget it because, since she had erupted precipitously into his life yesterday, he had been quite unable to banish Miss Liberty Lovejoy from his mind.

Liberty's accusing gaze pierced him as the curricle drew level with her and she raised her hand, as though to stop them. Dominic tipped his hat to her, but did not slow. There was nothing to say and he did not want to say it in front of Caroline.

'That lady looked as though she wanted to speak with you,' said Caroline, looking over her shoulder at Liberty. 'I do not believe I have made her acquaintance… is she someone?'

Someone. Dominic held back his snort. What did that even mean? Well, he knew what it meant, but it did not stop him disliking that too widely held presumption that only 'their' sort of people were anyone.

'She is the new Earl of Wendover's sister.'

'Oh. I see.' Those three words were sufficient to convey Caroline's opinion. 'Mama warned me to be wary of his sisters. She said they are not really our sort of people. How do you know her?'

'I do not know her.' Officially, her visit to Beauchamp House had never taken place and Dominic had never met either Liberty or her sister. Their transgression of the rules would not become common knowledge through him. 'I know her identity because my brother is friendly with Wendover.'

'I see.' Caroline folded her hands on her lap. 'I wonder what she wanted to speak to you about.'

'I doubt very much she wanted to speak to me. I am certain you are mistaken.'

'Yes, of course. That must be it.'

As luck would have it, two of the other ladies whose names were on Dominic's list—Lady Amelia Carstairs and Lady Georgiana Buckleigh—were promenading that afternoon so, after delivering Caroline back to her mother, he endured two further circuits of the Park. Not one of the three put a foot wrong or spoke a word out of place. He should be thrilled. Any one of them would be the perfect wife for him. There was little to distinguish between them so far and once he had also renewed his acquaintance with Lady Sarah Patcham and Lady Sybilla Gratton, he would decide which one of them to concentrate on. Then, as soon as his father arrived in London, Dominic would make his offer.

Two days later Liberty stood to one side of the Trents' crowded salon with Mrs Mount, and plied her fan, sipping from the wine glass in her other hand. Although the weather was chilly the number of people packed into the modestly sized room for the rout party, combined with the heat from dozens of candles, made the room insufferably hot and stuffy. And the tightness of her corset wasn't helping, she silently admitted. When she had dressed for the rout in the least outmoded of her evening gowns, it had proved a touch too snug across the bosom, and so she had donned her sturdiest corset and ordered Lizzie—the maid she shared with Hope and Verity—to lace it as tightly as she possibly could in order to ease the fit of the dress. Now the disadvantage of that was becoming clear as her breathing grew shallower.

To distract herself from her increasing discomfort, she focused her attention on her sisters—so charming and pretty, their golden hair shining with health—and she watched with pleasure as young gentlemen vied with one another for their attention. They weren't bad girls, just a little thoughtless at times, and she knew her tendency to take charge made it easy for them to leave any difficult or awkward matters to her.

Gideon, of course, had declined to escort them and his valet, Rudge, had confirmed his master's intention to visit the Sans Pareil Theatre once again, causing dismay to ripple through Liberty. She feared she knew the attraction of that particular theatre, recalling how Gideon had waxed lyrical over a certain actress called Camilla Trace.

She leaned towards their chaperon.

'I am hopeful the girls will both attract offers before the Season is out, Mrs Mount.'

'Dear Hope and Verity…their popularity is unmistakable,' said Mrs Mount, 'but I must implore you not to risk a scandal with any more ill-advised visits, Liberty. I saw Lord Avon a few minutes ago and it seemed to me that, when he noticed you, he deliberately avoided this area of the room.'

'Avon is here?'

Her pulse kicked—surely just at the prospect of finding out if he had kept his promise? She'd spied him only once since her visit to Beauchamp House, in Hyde Park. She'd tried to catch his eye but, although he acknowledged her, he had driven his curricle straight past her.

'I wonder if he has spoken to his brother yet?' She craned her neck to try to see over the throng of people, but it was impossible. 'I shall go and ask—'

'No!' Mrs Mount caught hold of Liberty's hand, restraining her. 'Did you not hear what I said? Or perhaps you misunderstand the meaning of his action? He *turned away* when he saw you. You *cannot* approach him. He is the most eligible bachelor in the *ton*. Eyes follow him wherever he goes and tongues will always find stories to spread about him. Merely to approach him is unthinkable and if he were to *cut* you...oh, my dear, the tales would spread like wildfire and they would scorch your sisters' reputations in the telling. The gossip columns in the newssheets would not spare your blushes— the upstart twin of the new Earl of Wendover making an overt play for the Marquess of Avon...oh, heavens!' She plied her own fan vigorously to ruddy cheeks. 'Do you not understand? Your situation renders it even more imperative that your conduct is above reproach.'

Anger smouldered inside Liberty, heating her still further, and she felt as though she had a furnace inside her. She drank more wine and then tugged discreetly at her neckline in a vain attempt to allow some cooling air to reach her skin. Each breath she drew seemed shallower than the one before.

'But I am not interested in Lord Avon in the way you imply,' she said. 'You know I am not. I am concerned only about Gideon and I wish to know if Avon has spoken to his rascally brother yet.'

'I know, my dear.' Mrs Mount patted Liberty's hand without loosening her grip upon it. 'But you can do nothing about it until he decides to tell you. And he will *not* do so here—he will no more risk awakening speculation by singling out an unattached female than he would strip off his jacket and cavort about in his shirt-sleeves. Proper conduct is everything to His Lordship, particularly this Season, if that rumour is true.'

'Rumour? What rumour?' Despite her dire need for fresh air, or a chair to sit on, or both, Liberty was distracted by this titbit.

'It is said that he has compiled a shortlist of eligible young ladies who meet the standards he has set—breeding, upbringing, ladylike conduct—and that he will make his selection before the end of the Season.'

The hushed awe of Mrs Mount's words stirred resentment inside Liberty. No wonder Avon was so top-lofty with people hanging upon his every word and treating him like some kind of god.

'A shortlist? I presume you mean for a wife. Why on earth does he need a *shortlist*?'

'Avon's bride must possess the very best bloodlines, perfect manners and be of exemplary character. Only the best will do for a man in his position and to be the mother of a future duke.'

The suppressed excitement in Mrs Mount's voice irritated Liberty even more.

'You make the poor girl sound like a glorified brood mare,' she muttered.

Really! Had people nothing more to worry about? What about all the poverty in London? Children in rags living on the street while their so-called betters lived in luxury. People like Avon were in a position to help and yet, instead of helping those worse off than him, he put his time and effort into making pathetic *lists* in order that any bride he might choose was *worthy* of him.

'So you do see why it is imperative that you do not put a foot wrong in any further contact with His Lordship, do you not, Liberty?' Mrs Mount's anxious enquiry brought Liberty's attention back to her. 'Not so much for your sake, but for Hope and for Verity.'

'You are not suggesting that His Lordship might consider—'

'It is unlikely, my dear, but…one never can tell what might happen when a pretty girl catches a gentleman's eye. Avon is expected to look much higher for his bride—at the very *least* the daughter of an earl—and she will be a young lady who has been properly prepared from childhood for her role as the wife of a peer of the realm. But your sisters, especially dear Verity, are so very pretty—one never knows what might happen. A list may always be added to.'

Mrs Mount's voice appeared to fade. Goodness, it was so hot. Liberty plied her fan with renewed vigour as she stared at her chaperon's mouth, concentrating fiercely in order to make out her words.

'And the lucky young lady of his choice will be a future duchess. It is worth keeping our hopes alive for such high stakes.'

Liberty put a hand to her forehead. The room seemed

to sway and she was aware of Mrs Mount staring anxiously at her.

'Liberty? My dear? Are you quite well? Oh, dear.' Mrs Mount clutched at Liberty's arm. 'Are you sickening for something? Do you need to leave? Only, it would be such a shame...'

Liberty gritted her teeth in a desperate attempt to remain upright. She thrust her empty wine glass at Mrs Mount. 'I am not sickening for anything. I need air. Watch the girls, will you, Mrs Mount?' Desperate now to get out of the room, she headed in the direction of the door, weaving in and out of the chattering groups of strangers, until her way was blocked by a tall figure with a pair of wide shoulders in a dark blue swallowtail coat. To either side of those shoulders were people, pressed closely, clearly hanging on every word uttered by the gentleman. Liberty screwed her eyes shut, wafted her fan over her heated skin, sucked desperately at the stale air, then opened her eyes and prepared to negotiate her way around the group, for it was obvious she could not barge through the middle of them. She shuffled sideways until she spied a gap. Perspiration now dampened her forehead and she could feel it gather on her chest and trickle into the valley between her breasts. She frowned, concentrating on placing one foot in front of the other as she edged through that gap. She was close to the door now—she could see it above people's heads—and she blindly aimed for it, desperate now to get away from this crush of people.

'Well! Of all the—'

'I say! That was my foot!'

'I'm sorry.' The words came on a gasp. 'I cannot—' Horror filled her as her knees buckled.

A strong arm encircled her waist from behind. A deep voice barked, 'Stand aside. She's swooned.'

She desperately wanted to deny it—she had never swooned in her life—but all she could manage was to turn into that embrace, her head tipping forward until her forehead rested against a solid chest. She breathed in a clean smell of soap and starch, mixed with a pleasing masculine scent.

Then she knew no more.

Chapter Five

Dominic stared in disbelief at the swooning woman in his arms, her head tipped into his chest. How in hell had this happened? He tightened his hold around her as she sagged. There was no other word for it—her head lolled back on her neck and he was certain her legs were no longer supporting her. He tightened his arms again, instinctively taking note of her womanly curves and her soft flesh.

He peered down into her face and recognition speared him. Miss Liberty Lovejoy. Her eyes were closed, her golden lashes a feathery fan against her creamy skin; her cheeks were flushed pink; her lips… plump and rosy…parted to reveal small, white, even teeth. And the urge to press his mouth to hers took him completely by surprise.

He tore his gaze away and scanned the faces that surrounded the two of them, noting the various expressions.

Eager—they were the gossips! Disgruntled—the young ladies who aspired to his hand. Envious—the rakes and…well, more or less every male within touching distance, damn them. As if he would relinquish her to *their* tender mercies. Speculative—he would soon put a stop to *that*! And concerned…

He focused on the nearest of those faces. Lady Jane Colebrooke, whom Dominic had known since childhood. Jane's family were neighbours of the Beauchamps in Devonshire—she was a kind girl with not a spiteful bone in her body.

'Lady Jane, would you come with me, please? I shall need your assistance.'

He bent down and slid one arm behind Miss Lovejoy's knees and hefted her up into his arms, cradling her like a baby. He felt something inside his chest shift as her rose scent curled through his senses and his exasperation melted away. However much she had defied the conventions when she had called on him, he knew it was from love for her brother. His own family were large and loving and he could not condemn a woman who put her family first.

'Yes, of course, my lord.' Jane bent to scoop Liberty's reticule and fan from the floor.

Dominic headed for the door, slicing through the crowd which parted before him—like the Red Sea before Moses, he thought sardonically. Through the door and out on to the landing—the fingers of his left hand curving possessively around the soft warmth of her thigh. Jane kept pace with him and thankfully refrained from bombarding him with inane comments or pointless conjectures. Then the pitter-patter of footsteps behind them prompted a glance over his shoulder.

Just perfect!

Not the lady—presumably the Lovejoy girls' chaperon—he had seen Liberty with earlier, nor either of her sisters. Any one of those would be welcome at this moment. No, they were being pursued by two determined-looking young ladies, both of whom happened to be in Dominic's final five. He had little doubt that their reasons for following him had everything to do with currying his favour and absolutely nothing to do with a desire to help a stricken fellow guest. In fact, he had overheard Lady Amelia being particularly scathing about 'those common Lovejoy girls' earlier that evening.

At least with them here as well as Jane, I cannot be accused of compromising anyone.

A servant directed them to a small parlour.

'Send a maid to assist, if you please,' said Dominic, 'and tell her to bring a glass of water and smelling salts.'

He gently deposited Liberty on a sofa and Jane snatched an embroidered cushion from a nearby chair to tuck under her head while the other two hung back and stared, doing absolutely nothing to help.

'Lady Sarah!'

The Earl's daughter started. 'Y-yes, my lord?'

'If you have come to assist us, be so good as to fan Miss Lovejoy's face. She appears to have been overcome by the heat.'

Lady Sarah moved forward, but thrust her fan into Jane's hand. With a wry flick of her eyebrows at Dominic, Jane wafted the fan, the breeze lifting the curls on Liberty's forehead. Her colour was already less hectic, but Dominic's hand still twitched with the urge to touch her forehead and check her temperature. He curled his fingers into his palm and stepped back, yet he could not tear his gaze from her luscious figure. The fabric of her gown—the colour of spring leaves—moulded softly to every curve and hollow, revealing far more than it should: her rounded thighs; the soft swell of her belly; the narrow waist above generous hips; and above that…good Lord…those gorgeous, bountiful breasts…

Dominic quickly shifted his gaze to Liberty's face, uncomfortably aware of both Lady Sarah and Lady Amelia watching him closely.

Liberty's lashes fluttered and her lids slowly lifted to reveal two dazed eyes that gazed in confusion into his before flying open in horror. She struggled to sit and Dominic instinctively pressed her back down. Her skin was like warm silk, smooth and baby soft and he longed to caress…to explore…to taste… The hairs on his arms stirred as his nerve endings tingled and saliva flooded his mouth. Good God…how he wanted to—he buried that thought before it could surface.

'Lie still!'

She collapsed back at his barked command, eyes wide, and he snatched his hands away.

'Who should I request to attend to you, Miss Lovejoy?'

'Mrs Mount.' Their eyes met and his heart thudded in his chest as his throat constricted. 'She is our chaperon. Thank you.'

She half-raised her hand and he began to reach for it before recalling their surroundings. Their witnesses.

'My Lord Avon, you may safely leave Miss Lovejoy in our care.' Lady Amelia inserted herself gracefully between Dominic and the sofa. 'This is no place for a gentleman.'

Our care?

He controlled his snort of derision—he'd seen precious little care from either Amelia or Sarah—but he knew she was right. This was no place for him and Liberty *would* be safe in Jane's hands, he knew. Jane, still gently fanning, caught his eye and again flicked her brows at him, clearly sharing his cynical reaction.

'I have hartshorn here.' Lady Sarah, on his other side, reached into her reticule.

'Good. Good,' he said, retreating. 'Make sure she remains lying down. I shall send a footman to alert Mrs Mount. Jane, is there anything else you need?'

Both Amelia and Sarah shot resentful glances at Jane. Mentally, he scratched their names from his list although he would still pay them some attention, if only to divert the gossips from identifying the three names that remained.

'No, thank you,' said Jane. 'I am sure Miss Lovejoy will soon recover.'

Dominic strode for the door, every step between himself and all that temptation lifting a weight from his shoulders. He had purposely avoided her tonight. He had seen her across the room with a spare-framed woman in her mid-forties and he'd taken care to keep his distance—partly for propriety's sake, when they had not, officially, been introduced, and partly through guilt because he still had not fulfilled his promise to speak to Alex. And the reason for that, he knew, was because his innate cautiousness was screaming at him to keep his distance from Liberty Lovejoy. But, try as he might, he had been unable to entirely banish her from his thoughts and he knew he must remedy his failure as soon as possible.

For the first time he wondered if she had seen him, too, and had purposely swooned to force him to catch her. He cast a look over his shoulder. Eyes like midnight-blue velvet followed his progress from the room. No. He did not believe her swoon was faked—she hadn't even glanced his way as she stumbled blindly through the group that surrounded him and, if he was absolutely honest with himself, there had been half-a-dozen fellows closer to her than him, any one of whom could have caught her when she swooned.

Except… His jaw clenched as he reviewed his actions. He might not have consciously recognised her but, by the time she collapsed, his feet had already moved him to her side, putting *him* in the perfect position to catch her.

He paused outside the room, still thinking. His head began to throb. *Good grief…*he rubbed his temples. He hadn't even known she existed three days ago, but she'd been on his mind ever since and now here he was—the instant he saw her again—playing the hero like an eager young pup in the throes of first love. He scowled as he scanned the landing. All his life he had avoided any behaviour that might give rise to gossip or speculation. He had always been far too conscious of his position as his father's heir and the expectations he placed on himself.

He beckoned to the same footman he had spoken to before.

'Please find Mrs Mount and ask her to attend Miss Lovejoy in the parlour at her earliest convenience.'

He was damned if he'd take the message himself—the more distance he kept between himself and the Lovejoys the better.

The sooner I make good my promise and speak to Alex about her dratted brother, the better.

His enquiry as to Alex's whereabouts had elicited not only the information that his younger brother had taken a set of rooms at Albany, St James's, but also that he often frequented the Sans Pareil Theatre, on the Strand, in the company of a group of young noblemen, the new Earl of Wendover among them. He felt a twinge of envy at Alex's ability to make friends so easily—a trait that had somehow always eluded Dominic.

He returned to the salon. He had no particular urge to rejoin his earlier companions, but he must—he could not allow the other guests' last sight of him to be of him carrying a swooning female from the room. He made polite conversation for twenty minutes or so and, once he was confident enough people had noted his return, he took his leave.

Too restless to go home and prompted by the events of the evening, he headed for Sans Pareil in search of Alex, determined to discharge his promise to Liberty as soon as he possibly could. From the floor of the theatre he scanned the boxes, finally spotting his father's close friend, Lord Stanton and his wife, Felicity, Dominic's second cousin. He ran up the stairs and slid into a vacant seat behind them.

'Mind if I join you?'

Felicity's head whipped round and a huge smile lit her face. 'Dominic! Of course. We're delighted to see you. But you have missed the play, you know. There is only the farce left.' Her eyes twinkled. She knew very well that most people preferred the farce to the serious drama, which was why the theatres always showed the farce last in the programme.

'I'm not here to watch either—I'm looking for Alex. Have you seen him?'

Stanton leant forward, searching the pit below. He pointed. 'There he is,' he said, 'with Wolfe and Wendover.'

Felicity also leant forward. 'Wendover? Is that the new Earl? Oh, yes. I see—the man with the golden hair? I've never seen him before, although I have, of course, heard the gossip.' She settled back into her seat. 'Such a dreadful thing to happen—the previous Lord Wendover and his entire family perishing in that fire.' She shuddered. 'It's frightening.'

Stanton took her hand. 'Try not to think about it, Felicity Joy. You mustn't upset yourself.' Then he twisted in his seat to face Dominic and lowered his voice. 'The entire house was gutted, I hear. It is beyond repair. Wendover will have to rebuild.'

Was that why Liberty was so anxious about money? The knowledge that the family seat would need to be completely rebuilt?

'Have you heard how the fire started?'

'The bed hangings in the main bedchamber caught fire. Wendover and his lady were in bed. They didn't stand a chance—the house went up like a rocket, with all those dry old timbers to feed the flames.'

Dominic suppressed his own shudder. Fire...it was a terrifying prospect, and an ever-present danger with candles and lanterns supplying light and with open fires where an unwary soul might find their clothes catching alight and going up in flames. There were new innovations, with gas lighting now more common in London streets, but there was widespread distrust at the idea of employing the new technology in private homes.

Felicity looked at them, frowning. 'What are you two whispering about?' She narrowed her eyes at Stanton and shook her head. 'You should know better than to try to hide unpalatable truths from me, Richard.'

Her husband laughed. 'I wouldn't dare,' he said, with a wink at Dominic. 'But this is not hiding. It is *protecting*. You know the tragedy that occurred, but you do *not* need to know the details, my sweet.'

Felicity pouted, then smiled. 'You are right. As you so often are, my darling husband.'

A laugh rumbled in Richard's chest. 'If you believe that last remark, Dom, my boy, you do not know women. Or, more particularly, wives. We men might hold the titles, property and wealth, but, in a marriage, it is the wife who holds the power.' He captured Felicity's hands and kissed first one palm, then the other. 'My heart. Your hands.'

His smile confirmed his happiness at being in such thrall to Felicity and Dominic was happy for them. He was very fond of Felicity—they had worked together closely for years, supporting and funding Westfield, a school and asylum for orphans and destitute children—and he remembered only too well the traumas of the early months of Richard and Felicity's arranged marriage. Would he be so fortunate in his marriage of convenience? He mentally ran through his shortlist and doubts erupted. Not one of them, from his observations, had Felicity's kind heart and sincerity. He shifted uneasily in his seat and tried to quash those doubts.

I'm not looking for love. Nor for a comfortable wife. I want a lady suited to the position of a marchioness; someone with the perfect qualities to be a duchess in the future and capable of raising a son who will one day be a duke. Someone of whom my mother would approve and a daughter-in-law to make my father proud.

That had always been his destiny. From a young age, his mother had drummed into him his responsibility as his father's heir and his duty to marry a lady worthy of the future position as the Duchess of Cheriton. It was the price one paid when one was firstborn.

His situation was entirely different to that of the Stantons.

He dragged his thoughts away from his future marriage to concentrate on the reason he had come to the theatre. If he could set Miss Lovejoy's mind at rest about her brother, then hopefully he could move on with his plan without distraction.

Liberty's brother was easy to pick out in the auditorium below, with his hair the same shade as Hope's— a golden-blond colour, two shades lighter and much brighter than Liberty's dark honey hue. Dominic watched him. He was behaving much as every other young buck in the pit—whistling and calling at the hapless performers and, during those times the on-stage drama failed to hold his attention, boldly ogling the theatre boxes and any halfway pretty occupants. So far, no different to how most young men behaved when they were out with other young men and without the civilising influence of ladies to curtail their antics.

Alex, Dominic was interested to see, was more subdued—indeed, he looked almost bored, gazing in a desultory fashion at the surrounding boxes. He gave every impression of wishing he was anywhere but where he was. Whatever jinks the three young men were up to, Alex was not the ringleader.

Dominic leaned forward. 'What do you know of Wendover, Stan?'

'Not a great deal,' Stanton replied. 'A gentleman's son, but his mother was some sort of merchant's daughter. He attended Eton, but left Oxford early after his father died. He has three sisters and I've heard it was a financial struggle for them after their father's death. He's a lucky man, inheriting so unexpectedly. Why do you ask?'

'He and Alex were pally at Eton and I've been told that Alex is encouraging Wendover in some wild behaviour. I'm worried Alex will slip back into his old ways.'

'How old is Alex now?'

'Five and twenty. Old enough to know better.'

Alex had always been a difficult youth, but Dominic, and the rest of the family, had believed the worst of his wildness was in the past.

'I didn't even know Alex was in town,' said Stanton. 'I heard Wendover's new-found fortune has gone to his head and, looking at them now, I should say he is the instigator, not Alex or Wolfe. It is Wendover's first time on the town—he's bound to kick out. I shouldn't worry too much, Dominic.'

How perfect if Stanton was right and it was Gideon trying to lead Alex and Neville astray. Dominic would enjoy putting Liberty straight…although…there was still the effect of Wendover's behaviour on his sisters' reputations—they would face enough of a struggle to be accepted in society, with their maternal grandfather being in trade, without a rackety brother to further taint the family.

He stood. 'I'll go and talk to him, nevertheless. I think you are right, but it won't hurt to make certain.' He shook Stanton's outstretched hand and bent to kiss Felicity on the cheek.

Down on the floor of the theatre, he stood at the back until the end of the play, keeping a close watch on Alex, Neville and Wendover. As the audience began to leave, he moved to meet the three men.

Alex's eyes met his. A smile was swiftly masked.

'Dominic.' Alex nodded casually.

'Alex.' Dominic kept his nod just as casual. 'Why did you not let me know you were in town?'

He cringed inwardly as soon as he said the words. There was nothing he could have said more likely to provoke Alex into a fit of the sullens, as their aunt Cecily used to call them.

Alex shrugged. 'I don't need your permission to have some fun in my life, do I?'

Dominic bit back the urge to cuff his brother's ear as he might have done when they were lads.

'No, of course not. But if I'd known I could have let you know Olivia, Hugo and the twins arrived yesterday.'

They'd been due to arrive the day he'd met Liberty at Beauchamp House, but had delayed their journey a couple of days when one of the twins was poorly.

Alex's eyes lit up. 'Are they staying in Grosvenor Square?' Dominic nodded. 'Good. I'll call on them tomorrow.'

Dominic then turned to Neville Wolfe, a friend of Alex's since boyhood.

'Wolfe. How do you do? Are your family well?'

Neville grinned and shook Dominic's hand. 'Very well, Avon. Very well.'

Dominic shifted his attention to Gideon, Lord Wendover. Miss Liberty Lovejoy's twin brother. The family resemblance was strong—the same stubborn chin and the same blue eyes. He wondered idly if Wendover's irises were likewise flecked with gold before jerking back to the realisation that he was staring mindlessly at the man. He thrust out his hand.

'I don't believe we've met. I'm Avon... Alex's brother.'

Gideon shook Dominic's hand. 'Wendover. Good to meet you, Avon, but... I beg you will excuse me—I'm due backstage.'

His words slurred and Dominic could smell the gin on his breath, but at least neither Alex nor Wolfe appeared foxed. Gideon was quickly absorbed into the throng of people slowly shuffling out of the theatre.

Alex muttered a curse. 'I'll call on you tomorrow, Dom. I have to go now. C'mon, Nev.'

He followed Gideon but, as Neville began to move, Dominic grabbed his arm.

'Hold hard there, Wolfe.'

Neville halted, but looked pointedly at Dominic's hand on his sleeve. Dominic released his grip.

'Give me a moment,' he said. 'I just want to be sure he's safe.'

Understanding dawned on Neville's face. He'd been friends with Alex for a long time and had stood by him through difficult times and wild behaviour. 'There's nothing going on that need trouble you, Avon. We're tryin' to watch out for Gid, that's all. He's got the bit between his teeth—taken a fancy to Camilla Trace and we're trying to stop him doing anything stupid like promise to marry her when he's in his cups!'

Camilla Trace was a beautiful and popular actress currently appearing at the Sans Pareil.

'Is Alex in danger of following Wendover's path?' At Neville's startled expression, Dominic elaborated. 'I don't mean falling in love with an actress. I heard Wendover's getting in deep and I'm worried Alex might get drawn back into high-stakes games.'

'Don't worry, Alex won't lose sight of what's important to him—he values his horses too much to put his business in jeopardy.' Neville clapped Dominic on the shoulder. 'Leave it to me to watch him.'

Dominic watched the other man go, his brows knit in a frown. Neville Wolfe and Alex had been partners in crime throughout their youth—what if they *both* slipped back into their old ways? With neither Father nor Uncle Vernon in town, it was up to Dominic to keep Alex safe. So, while Alex and Neville watched over Gideon,

Dominic would watch over his brother. From a distance. Because one thing was certain—if Alex got wind of what Dominic was up to, he would just as likely dive headlong into any and every vice that presented itself to him. Simply to prove he was his own man.

Dominic sighed and made his way to the door into the backstage area. He entered and immediately spied a cloaked and hooded figure lurking in a doorway up ahead. He adjusted his grip on his ebony cane, which handily concealed a sword, but the figure did not move as he passed.

He'd taken two steps past before the scent of roses reached him, sending the hair on the back of his neck on end. He pivoted round to face…Miss Liberty Lovejoy.

Chapter Six

Liberty gasped as a vice-like grip encircled her upper arm. The thick wool of the cloak she wore did little to disguise the strength in those fingers. Heart pumping with fear, she raised her eyes to her assailant and the breath whooshed from her lungs.

'You scared me half to death. What are you doing here?'

Dominic did not answer. His fingers tightened, then he was dragging her with him, opening doors at random, muttering apologies, until he found an empty room. He whisked her inside and released her, pushing her to the far side of the small, cluttered space. A lamp illuminated the interior, revealing clothing strewn over a chair and brushes and pots of face powder and rouge scattered upon a table with a mirror fixed on the wall behind it—a mirror that reflected Dominic's furious expression as he glared at the back of Liberty's head.

She squared her shoulders and pivoted to face him. 'How dare you manhandle me?'

She strode for the door, but his hand covered hers on the handle before she could open it. She tugged her hand free and turned to face him, her back to the door.

He was close. Too close. And his expression had, somehow, transformed from fury into… Stillness. Focus.
Like a cat waiting to pounce. Heat shimmered in those
silvery eyes.

Liberty swallowed—hard—as her pulse hammered.
His body was against hers, all unyielding muscle and
spicy, musky, masculinity. Her stomach fluttered and
liquid heat pooled in her core. She could not tear her
gaze from his as he propped his hands against the door,
one either side of her shoulders, pinning her. His scent
surrounded her, sending waves of pure longing crashing through her—a feeling she hadn't experienced since
Bernard had died. And just like that, she broke free of
his spell. She shoved at his chest, ducked beneath one
of his arms and stalked to the furthest corner of the
room. Her breathing steadied the more distance she
put between them…he remained by the door and did
not follow her.

'What are you doing here?' He growled the question out.

Liberty elevated her nose. 'I asked you first.'

*No doubt he is here to visit his amour. That's what
gentlemen do, is it not? Keep company with lightskirts
and actresses and the like?*

And that's exactly what she feared Gideon was doing
here now. Wasting his time and his money on an actress
when he should be thinking about securing his new position as a peer. He would need an heir. He wouldn't
meet a suitable wife backstage at a theatre!

'I am a man. I can do as I please. My reputation is
not at stake.'

'And *my* reputation matters not when it comes to my
brother's well-being.'

His narrowed gaze pierced her. '*Your* reputation

might be of little consequence to you, but what about your sisters' reputations?'

'What of them?'

'If you are seen, not only will *you* suffer, but your sisters will be irretrievably tainted. Is that really what you want?'

Her bravado was shrinking fast. She had been unable to settle after their return from the rout, so worried was she about what Gideon was up to. She had taken a calculated risk in coming here tonight, sneaking out of the house, persuading Bilk, their coachman, to drive her to the theatre by telling him that Gideon had asked her to meet him there, and entering such a place unescorted. A scandalously improper way for a lady to behave, but she had persuaded herself she would not be noticed.

Now, though, she was well and truly caught, and her disgrace would rebound on Hope and Verity if Lord Avon chose to reveal it.

But she refused to beg for his help again, not when he had failed to keep his earlier promise.

'Well, I *have* been seen now, so I have nothing left to lose, have I?' She dipped a curtsy, intending the gesture to be ironic. 'If it is your intention to expose my conduct, I cannot stop you. If it is not, then please allow me to leave so I can find Gideon.'

His lips firmed. 'You asked why I am here. I shall tell you. I have come to see what your brother is up to and to ensure that his bad example does not corrupt my own brother.'

'Oh! That is outrageous! It is *your* brother leading mine astray.'

He raised one brow, making her itch to slap him. Smug, superior know-it-all.

'I hate to contradict a lady, but my observations thus far indicate the exact opposite.'

Their gazes remained locked for several fraught seconds until Dominic's shoulders relaxed and one corner of his lips—his beautifully shaped mobile, enticing lips—lifted.

'Liberty—'

She opened her mouth to object, but held her silence when he raised his hand, palm forward.

'It is shocking for me to call you Liberty, but acceptable for you to wander alone backstage at a theatre?'

His lips twitched. They really were fascinating lips. What would it be like to kiss him? To feel his lips moving over hers? His tongue in her mouth, sliding against hers?

Oh, dear God. Forget scandalous. I am utterly depraved.

She moistened her dry lips. His eyes darkened. A pulse in her neck fluttered wildly and, without volition, she pressed shaking fingers to it. A vain attempt to suppress it? Then his gaze lowered and her nipples peaked in immediate response. She swallowed again and tugged at the edges of her cloak, pulling it across her chest in a defensive gesture.

Dominic hauled in an audible breath, his broad chest swelling and then deflating again as he released his breath.

'Let us begin again, Miss Lovejoy.'

His tone meant business. His very stance meant business. Despite herself, Liberty paid attention. This was not a man to defy, not in this mood.

'I am here at this theatre to see what *both* of our brothers are up to.'

Despite herself, she rather liked that—it was nice to

have someone on her side, someone to rely on, if only for a short while. Although she would die before she admitted it to him.

'How did you know they would be here?'

'I asked the servants. They tend to know everything, you know—they seem to have their own methods of finding things out and of spreading the word. You would do well to remember that.'

Her thoughts flew to Bilk. She had sworn him to secrecy, but could she trust him? Liberty bit back her doubts. It was too late now. Unconsciously, she raised her chin.

'Continue,' she said.

Drat him. There was that barely concealed smirk again.

'I have spoken with all three of them—my own brother and Mr Wolfe are watching over your brother to ensure he does nothing…stupid.'

'Stupid? Like…what?'

'Like making rash promises.'

Liberty pondered his words. 'Promises? To whom?' They were in a theatre…that must mean… 'As in… promises of marriage? Offers? Oh, dear God.'

She rushed for the door, but Dominic grabbed her arm as she brushed past him. Liberty struggled to free herself.

'Let me go! You mean one of these floozies, don't you? A common actress. I have to stop him.'

A tug unbalanced her and suddenly she was in his arms, held for the second time that night against the solid comfort of his chest. She felt herself relax into him, despite her panic over Gideon. It felt good, to feel a man's arms around her, to feel protected, even if for a split second.

'You can do nothing.' His voice rumbled in his chest, vibrating through her. He gripped her shoulders and set her away from him, gazing down at her. 'Gideon will heed his friends' advice and opinions more readily than that of his sister. Leave it to us.'

'Leave it to the men, you mean. You think because I am a female that my opinions count for nothing.'

That infuriating brow rose once again. 'I think that because you are his sister, your opinions will simply drive him into contrary behaviour. Take my advice, Miss Lovejoy. Use your time wisely and channel your energies into finding respectable husbands for yourself and your sisters.'

'I do not seek a husband for myself,' she muttered. Pride would not allow her to admit her private dream of finding love again. Especially to him.

'Then concentrate on your sisters' futures, if that is the case. Leave your brother to me. It is all under control.'

She raised her gaze to his. Those silvery eyes shone like polished steel. She could see herself reflected in them, but she could read nothing of the man within. They were like a mirror. What secrets did he hide? Or maybe he had none. Maybe he was exactly what he appeared to be—a handsome, straitlaced nobleman who never succumbed to spontaneity and always behaved with utmost propriety, as Mrs Mount had said.

'Why should I put my trust in you? What do *you* care what Gideon does?'

'I shall keep my eye on your brother simply to ensure Alex does not follow him into reckless behaviour and harmful habits.'

'But you are not watching him now. You are here with me.'

'That is true, but I happen to know both Alex and Mr Wolfe are with Gideon so he is in no imminent danger of making a complete cake of himself. Now, will you allow me to escort you home, Miss Lovejoy?'

'There is no need. I shall take a hackney.'

Earlier, she'd had no qualms about how she would get home, anticipating that Gideon would feel honour-bound to escort her. Now, for the first time, she realised her predicament, but pride, again, forbade her from admitting as much to His Lordship.

His eyes narrowed. 'Refusal is not an option. *That* was not a question.'

'It sounded exactly like a question to me.'

A muscle leapt at the side of his jaw. 'I was being polite.'

'Be that as it may, I am in no need of your escort. Just think how your reputation will suffer if we are seen together.'

He sighed. 'I told you before that sarcasm does not become you, Miss Lovejoy. Your choice is twofold. Either you allow me to take you home. Now. Or you and I shall go and find your brother and see what he has to say about his twin sister snooping around the nether regions of a theatre. The choice is yours.'

'My lord... I have no wish to sound ungrateful, but you cannot simply order me around. Besides, I have no wish to disrupt your evening further than I already have.'

His sensual lips thinned into a firm line. He spun to face the door, grabbing Liberty's right hand as he did so. He drew it firmly between his left arm and his ribcage and then crooked his elbow, clamping her arm in place. He strode for the door and she found herself stumbling in his wake, unable to resist his strength.

'My lord... Avon! Stop!'

'No.' The word was gritted out. 'No more talk. Pull up your hood.' They left the room and he slammed to a halt. 'Do it,' he growled, 'or I'll do it for you. Unless you *want* to be recognised?'

The sight of a figure emerging from a nearby door spurred her to obey. She pulled up her hood, tugging it forward to cover her face and, without another word, Avon headed towards the rear of the theatre, towing Liberty behind him. She kept her gaze to the floor, avoiding eye contact with anyone they passed, then they were out of the door, into the chill night air, with raindrops pitter-pattering on her hood and, when she risked glancing up, her face.

'Keep moving and don't look at anyone,' Dominic muttered. 'Maiden Lane is no place for a lady.'

He walked briskly, rounded a corner and then another, and she recognised the Strand and the front of the theatre, where a town coach and pair waited, a coachman at the horses' heads. The waiting man whisked sacking from the horses' backs as Liberty found herself bundled unceremoniously into the vehicle. Avon leaned inside as she perched on the edge of the seat.

'Where do you live?'

'Green Street.'

He withdrew and she heard him call, 'Webster. Green Street, please.'

The carriage dipped as Dominic climbed inside. He stripped off his gloves and hat and cast them on to the opposite seat before settling next to her, his hip and thigh touching hers. She inched away from him, until her own hip was pressed against the padded side of the coach, still stiffly upright, wondering how it had happened that she had been removed from the theatre without catching even one glimpse of Gideon or discovering what he was up to. And how she was now in a carriage, alone with a man she barely knew.

'I presume you have fully recovered from your swoon earlier tonight?'

'Yes, thank you.' It infuriated her that he'd seen her behave in such a feeble way. 'I do not make a habit of swooning. It was excessively stuffy in that room.'

'It was.' His amused tone set her hackles to rise. 'I did not, however, notice any other ladies swoon.'

She had no answer to that. It was true. And the episode had undermined her determination to have only one new gown made. She had no choice now. She would need more. She only hoped Gideon could afford it.

'How can I be sure Gideon is safe?'

'You cannot be sure. Not completely. But you have to understand there is nothing you can do. You are a female. You simply *cannot* follow him around to spy on him. Perhaps you should instead learn to trust him? And besides—' Dominic swivelled on the seat to face her '—tell me truthfully. What exactly did you intend to do if you caught Gideon behaving recklessly?'

'I… I do not know, for certain. I suppose I would try to persuade him to leave and to return home with me.'

'I see.'

The simple scepticism in those two words spoke volumes. In the silence that followed Liberty began to realise the futility of her plan—what *had* she thought she might achieve?

'And your chance of success would be?'

Liberty slumped back against the squabs.

'Very well. You are right. He would refuse. We would argue.'

'And the result would be that the distance you spoke of between you and your brother would widen further.'

That was the last thing she wanted. She missed sharing things…*life*…with Gideon; missed having him to lean on; she missed his company. And she was terrified he would make some drastic mistake and blight his life. She rubbed at her aching chest while the guilt lay heavy in her stomach. She had failed Bernard and her parents. She could not fail Gideon, too.

Dominic faced forward again, folding his arms across his chest. Liberty waited for the 'I told you so' or 'How could you be so stupid?', but no recriminations were forthcoming. After several excruciating minutes of silent self-recrimination, she exhaled sharply.

'I am sorry.'

He cocked his head. 'Sorry for what?'

'My behaviour. I know it is not what is expected of a lady, but I—I could not go to bed and sleep without trying to do *something*.'

'I do understand. Gideon is your brother and your worry for him overrode everything else.' A long, quiet sigh escaped him. 'Lest you forget, I have a brother, too, and, although he is not as wild as he used to be, he is still not an easy man to understand or even, sometimes, to like.' He leaned forward, his forearms propped on his knees and his gaze on the floor. 'Our sister has been known to get herself into some difficult scrapes in an effort to protect Alex—often without regard for the consequences. In that respect you remind me of her.'

He looked at her. 'For the Beauchamps all that is in the past and Olivia is a respectable married lady now. If you will take my advice—concentrate your efforts on your sisters even if you have no wish for marriage yourself. I meant what I said earlier—if you bring disgrace upon yourself, your sisters will suffer. They will be tainted for life. You already start from a lowly position in society and there will be many who will relish any disgrace as it will reinforce their view that inferior breeding will out.'

Liberty bristled at being lectured. 'A view you yourself agree with, I am given to understand. I've heard you have a list of perfect ladies suitable for a future duke and that breeding comes right at the top of your requirements.'

'Only insofar as it affects my choice of bride,' he retorted. 'It is my duty as my father's heir to marry well, but I do not hold such views in general.'

'Because everyone below you is so far beneath your notice?'

She felt the full force of his stare. 'Not at all,' he said, stiffly. 'As it happens, I'm involved—'

Liberty waited, but he did not continue. 'You're involved…?'

'It is of no matter.'

He faced forward again and they lapsed into silence. Within a short time, Liberty felt shame creep through her. She had been unfair, needling him in that way. For all he was infuriating, he *had* been trying to help her.

She swivelled slightly so she could study him. She could just about make out his profile in the gloomy interior of the coach. As they passed the occasional street lamp, she could make out lines of strain running from his nose to his mouth.

'Do you really believe your brother can be trusted to bring Gideon back to his senses, my lord?'

He hooked one hand behind his neck, further obscuring her view of him. At first she thought he would not answer her, but then he abruptly released his neck and lowered his arm, shooting her a sidelong look.

'I believe so.' He twisted to face her then, and

touched her hand. '*You* may trust *me*, however. I shall keep an eye on both Alex *and* Gideon.'

And she did trust his word.

'Thank you. You are more generous than perhaps I deserve.'

His eyes glittered as they passed another street lamp. 'Generous?' He reached out, and touched her face with one finger, tracing her cheekbone, raising a shiver in its wake before he withdrew it. 'You needed help and I have been in a position to provide it.' His teeth gleamed as he smiled and her heart tumbled over. 'Twice. As I said, you remind me of my sister...oh, not in the way you look, but in that stubborn determination to make sure the people you love are safe. How could I not help?' He leaned forward, gazing out of the window. 'We are here. Green Street. Which house is it?'

'A little further along, on the left-hand side.'

She felt dazed. What had happened to the pompous lord she had met at Beauchamp House? Dominic rapped on the carriage ceiling and it halted. He climbed out, then turned to hand her out.

'Pull your hood up again,' he whispered. 'I will watch to see you safely inside the house, but I won't escort you to the door in case we are seen. I hope we are now agreed that your reputation is important, if only for the sake of your sisters.'

'Yes. Thank you again.'

His eyes gleamed briefly, then he raised her hand to his lips. 'You are most welcome, Miss Liberty Lovejoy.'

Chapter Seven

A sense of urgency—of events slipping out of his grasp—drove Dominic to head straight for home and for his sitting room.

'I shan't need you again tonight, Brailsford,' he said to his man. 'You get off to bed.'

'Can I fetch you something to eat before I go, milord?'

Dominic consulted his gut. 'No. I'm not hungry.' Actually, he felt a little nauseous…sort of uneasy…a churning, unsettling sensation. Apprehension, that was it. Well, it was hardly surprising when he was about to make such a momentous decision. 'But you may pour me a brandy before you go, if you would.'

Dominic crossed the room to his writing desk and, opening a drawer, he extracted a sheet of paper. He had no real need of the list—the names that remained were indelibly inscribed into his memory. There was no chance he would forget any of them. But he nevertheless carried the list over to his favourite chair—a deeply buttoned green-leather-upholstered wing chair—and waited while Brailsford poured a glass of brandy, set it on the small table next to his chair and stirred the slumbering fire into life before refuelling it. Dominic did not look at the list until the door had shut behind Brailsford, then he scanned the names before steadily working his way through them again, from the first name to the fifth. Amelia and Sarah, of course, he had taken against, leaving three. For each name—Caroline, Georgiana and Sybilla—he conjured forth a mental image of the lady in question, mentally reviewing what he knew of each one: her family connections, her qualities, her conduct. Any one of them would be suitable for the Marchioness of Avon, and for the future Duchess of Cheriton, although he hoped that last would not be for a very long time. No one lady stood out among the others, but Georgiana was, he knew, afraid of horses. Did he want a wife who was afraid of horses? And Sybilla wasn't even in town yet.

'Lady Caroline Warnock.'

He closed his eyes, recalling the sweet sound of her singing at a musical recital last Season. Her voice had raised the hairs on his arms. He opened his eyes again and mentally shrugged. She had a beautiful singing voice. It was as good a reason as any. Her attitude towards Liberty the other day had irritated him, but it was, he knew, no different to the attitude of many in the *ton* to those whom they considered of inferior breeding and upbringing. That was settled, then. Although no one but he would know—he would pay equal attention to all five original names but, as soon as Father came up from Devonshire, Dominic would make his offer. He did not doubt Caroline would welcome an offer from him—she had been raised with a view to taking her place as the wife of a high-ranking aristocrat.

The sound of the door opening disturbed his thoughts.

'I told Brailsford to leave me to find my own way.'

Alex sauntered across to the brandy decanter and poured himself a generous glassful. 'You don't mind, do you?' He raised the glass as he wandered across to the fireplace and sat in the matching wing-back chair set on the opposite side to Dominic's.

'Be my guest. Oh. Wait. You already have.' Dominic reached for his own glass, raised it in a silent toast to his brother, drank, then returned it to the side table. He placed his list next to the glass before eyeing Alex. 'I didn't expect to see you again tonight. To what do I owe this pleasure?'

'My insatiable curiosity. Saw you leaving the back door of the theatre with a woman and, if my eyes weren't deceiving me, it was Wendover's twin sister— the interfering and irritating Liberty.'

Dominic frowned. 'I didn't think you'd seen us. And I didn't know the two of you had even met.'

'We haven't...but I've seen her from afar and I recognised her, before she pulled up her hood. That description, by the by, is verbatim from her ever-loving brother.'

Sympathy for Liberty bloomed in Dominic's chest. He drank some brandy then shifted in his chair, unsettled, staring into his glass as he swirled the amber liquid around. He'd come in here determined to finalise his future and to forget Miss Liberty Lovejoy and now here was Alex, stirring up her presence all over again.

'So I was right. It was her.'

The softly spoken comment jerked Dominic from his thoughts. He looked up to find Alex watching him with a knowing look.

'Is she the reason you came to the theatre? What were the pair of you doing backstage?'

Dominic tilted his glass and drank again, considering. Then he set his glass down again and steepled his fingers in front of his mouth, his joined forefingers resting against his lips.

'It was coincidence. But I do know she is worried about her brother. I saw her there and I persuaded her to leave. That is it.' This subject needed changing. 'More importantly, what are you up to with Wendover? You're not slipping back into old habits, are you?'

'No.' Alex sipped his brandy. 'Lucky for you it was me that saw you.'

Silently damning his brother's tenacity, Dominic asked, 'What d'you mean?'

Alex's eyes gleamed, crinkling at the corners. He was unmistakably a Beauchamp, but he was the only one of the three children who had inherited their late mother's colouring—thick mahogany brown hair and golden-brown eyes that always reminded Dominic of a tiger he had seen at the Exeter Exchange when he was a boy. Now, those eyes mocked Dominic, whose jaw clenched.

'Careful you don't get caught, that's all,' Alex drawled. 'I doubt the luscious Liberty would tick many of the qualities on the list of the perfect bride for the perfect heir.'

Alex left his chair in one fluid motion and, before Dominic realised his intention, he snatched the list from the table. Dominic surged to his feet.

'Alex!'

Alex spun away and scanned the names. Then he thrust the paper at Dominic and subsided back into his chair. Gritting his teeth, Dominic folded the list and put it in his pocket before sitting back down, steeling himself for the ribbing he sensed was coming his way.

'I was hoping the existence of that list was a daft rumour.' Alex recited the five names, his voice soft and almost sorrowful. '*Really*, Dom? They're the best you can conjure up?'

'What are you talking about, you numbskull? They come from the very best families in England and every one of them has been properly raised and educated to take her place in society and to be the perfect choice for a nobleman's wife.'

Alex drained his glass and went to refill it, and topped up Dominic's while he was up.

'There's not one of 'em with an ounce of warmth or spark,' he said once he regained his seat. 'Yes, they're perfect ladies, but they're so icy and correct they can freeze a fellow with just one look.'

'Alex...you know I have always planned to marry a lady worthy of being a future duchess. I need to choose my bride carefully.'

Alex simply held Dominic's gaze.

Goaded, Dominic said, 'I never took *you* for a romantic. I should have thought you would approve of marriages of convenience.'

'This isn't about me. It's about you.' Alex scrubbed his hand through his hair, a slight flush washing across his cheeks. 'You always seem so...alone, somehow. I don't want to see you alone in your marriage as well,' he added, his voice gruff.

Dominic stared at his brother. How unlike Alex to trouble himself over someone else, even a member of the family. That thought unsettled him far more than Alex's words and he shifted uncomfortably in his chair.

'Do you remember Liv and I used to call you Lord Earnest after...after...?'

'I remember.' Dominic knew he meant after their mother's death, but they never talked about it. Ever.

He supposed they'd been too young to fully understand what had happened at the time and it had become something of an unwritten rule. He couldn't even remember his father or Aunt Cecily really mentioning it, except as a fact. They had never *talked* about it. 'Someone had to be the responsible one. I am the eldest…it was my duty to help keep you and Livvy out of trouble, as it is my duty to marry well.'

'You take care that sense of duty don't choke you, Brother.' Alex sipped again at his brandy. 'I look at you sometimes, Dom, and all I see is the perfect heir to the Duke of Cheriton—the man you present to the world. And I wonder about the man inside and about *his* dreams and desires.'

Dominic's heart pounded uncomfortably. 'You're talking utter rubbish.'

His brother might be a year his junior—and he might have spent his youth bouncing from one scrape to another—but there were times when he appeared much, much older than his years. It was all right for Alex…*he* wasn't burdened by the weight of duty and expectation. *He* wasn't the heir.

Dominic had never questioned that duty—it was the way of their world. He was destined to follow the example set by his father, when he had married their mother for the good of the Dukedom.

'The family have it all wrong, Dom. They've spent years fretting about me, watching over me. But it's *you* they should be worrying about. I don't believe any of those women will make you happy. You are allowed to be happy, you know.'

Dominic stared at his brother as those words sank in, stirring unfamiliar feelings that, somehow, tightened his throat until it felt as though he had tried to swallow a lump of dry bread. He was not used to this sombre and, somehow, sorrowful version of Alex; where was his devil-may-care brother who took mockery to new heights?

He thrust down the unfamiliar surge of emotion and unclenched his jaw. Never would he reveal how that simple comment had reached deep inside him and wrenched at his soul. He drew in a deep breath before forcing a hearty laugh.

'All this is an excellent ruse, Alex, but you won't divert me that easily.'

Alex shrugged. 'Not trying to divert anyone. Just telling it as I see it.'

Dominic straightened his spine, now thoroughly irritated with himself for succumbing to Alex's mood and allowing him to raise doubts in his mind. 'I spoke to Wolfe earlier.'

Alex's eyes narrowed. 'He said.'

'What's your game with Wendover? Tell me you're not getting in too deep. Is everything truly all right?'

'Why wouldn't it be?'

'Alex…'

Alex's eyes glittered. He tossed back his brandy and rose to his feet. 'Worry about your own future. Not mine. *One* day maybe my family will see me as something other than a boy looking for trouble. 'Night, Avon.'

Dominic sat for a long time after Alexander left, that same nervy apprehension churning his stomach relentlessly even as he reassured himself that Alex didn't have a damned clue what he was talking about.

The following morning, Dominic called at Beauchamp House, to take his brother-in-law, Hugo, to Jackson's boxing saloon for a sparring session. It was Olivia and Hugo's first visit to London for the Season since the birth of their two-year-old twins, Julius and Daisy, and he found them waiting for him in the first-floor salon. After greeting Olivia with a kiss, Dominic said, 'Ready to go, Hugo? We'll soon get you back in condition.' He jabbed at Hugo's abdomen. 'Seems to me you've gone soft since you married.'

Hugo laughed, but Olivia leapt to his defence. 'He has not gone soft, Dominic! I'll have you know—'

She stopped as the door opened again and Alex strolled in. Dominic's heart sank as their eyes met. Their conversation of the night before was unfinished and Alex, he knew, would have no hesitation in raising the subject in front of Olivia and Hugo.

'Alex!' Olivia flew across the room to embrace him. 'Oh, I am so happy to see you! *Why* have you not been to visit us for such an age?'

'Hey! Steady on, Sis! You near to knocked me flying—you're no slip of a girl nowadays, are you?' Alex held her away from him and looked her up and down, mischief glimmering in his eyes. 'But still as much a hoyden as ever.'

'Oh, do stop teasing, Alex.' She reached up to tidy her black hair, re-pinning it haphazardly. 'I'm a respectable matron now, don't you know.'

He grinned. 'I'll accept matron, but respectable?'

She punched his arm. 'I am a mother! Of course I am respectable!'

Alex kissed her cheek, then greeted Hugo and Dominic, who took the opportunity to suggest to Hugo it was time they left.

'Something I said, Brother?' said Alex. 'Or something I *might* say?'

Dominic shrugged. 'I thought you and Livvy would appreciate the chance to catch up.'

'Oh, we'll have plenty to talk about,' drawled Alex, casting himself down on the sofa. 'See you later, Dom. Don't take out *all* your frustrations on Hugo, will you?'

Dominic didn't trust himself to answer—not without causing an argument. He strode from the room and waited until he saw Hugo's tall form descending the stairs before he left the house and climbed into his carriage. Hugo settled by his side and the carriage moved off.

'Well?' he said eventually, unable to stomach the continuing silence. 'I suppose Alex told you?'

Hugo raised one dark eyebrow. 'That you intend to select a bride this Season? Yes, he did. Congratulations.'

'You might say that like you mean it.'

Hugo huffed a laugh. 'As if you care for my opinion. I warn you, though, Livvy is hell-bent on meeting the ladies on your list.'

He'd been afraid of that.

'I've warned her not to interfere, but I have no doubt you'll know her verdict once she's met them all.'

'No doubt.'

Silence fell, and Dominic gazed from the window as the carriage turned into New Bond Street, idly watching the people they passed. Then he stiffened as he caught sight of Ma Prinks, shabbily dressed as ever, carrying a wailing toddler. Dominic rapped on the ceiling and the carriage halted.

'What is it?' Hugo leaned over to peer out of the window.

'I know that woman and I know her game.'

Dominic leapt from the carriage and strode back towards Prinks, who halted the minute she saw Dominic, her scowl morphing into an ingratiating simper.

'You're a long way from your usual haunts, Ma. What are you up to?'

'Not up to nuffin, milor'. Just takin' my young nipper for a walk, see?'

Dominic studied the child, pale-skinned and red-haired, with puffed-up eyes and snot trailing from its nostrils, and then eyed Prinks's dark hair and swarthy face.

'Yours, is it?' It was impossible to tell the sex of the child.

'His pa was ginger.'

'I don't believe you, Ma. Are you up to your old tricks again?' He glanced at Hugo, standing by his side. 'Ma Prinks here has a talent for "finding" young 'uns and using them to gain sympathy and money from passers-by.'

'You never cease to amaze me by the company you keep, Avon,' drawled Hugo.

Dominic frowned as he noticed the interest of people passing them by. Fortunately, it was still before noon and most of the *haut ton* had not yet started to shop, but he had no wish to continue drawing attention.

'Did you think Bond Street might give you easy pickings, Ma?'

The woman snorted. 'So it would if certain nobs would keep their conks out of poor folks' business.'

'Did you steal him?'

'No! I never! 'Is ma's dead, in't she, and 'is father's nowhere to be found. I'm doin' him a favour, see? At least wi' me he'll get fed.'

Dominic held out his arms. 'Give him to me, Ma. I'll make sure he's cared for.'

'You got no right—'

'Hand him over, or I'll hand *you* over to the constables. I'm sure the magistrates will be even more interested than me to hear how you came by the boy.'

She thrust the child at Dominic, not even waiting until he had him securely before releasing him. 'Tek 'im,' she snarled. 'Plenty more where 'e came from.'

By the time Dominic had the boy in a secure hold, Ma Prinks was striding away. He sighed.

'She's right,' he said to Hugo. 'We do our bit at Westfield, but it simply isn't enough. There are just too many children.'

He led the way back to the carriage and, once inside, he looked down into the infant's face. Two blue eyes stared back. Then Dominic checked his limbs. Two arms. Two legs.

'At least this one appears unharmed. The last one she had was blind.' His heart clenched at the memory. '*Deliberately* blinded, to gain more sympathy and thus more alms. It's a filthy business.'

'That...' Hugo's voice choked. He cleared his throat. 'That is atrocious. He looks the same age as our twins. When I think...' Again, his voice failed him and he cleared his throat again. 'What now?'

'I'll take him straight out to Westfield. The Whittakers will take him in and then Peter will make enquiries just in case anyone *is* missing their child. I don't hold out much hope, though.' He smiled wryly at Hugo. 'Sorry. It looks like we'll have to postpone our session. But we can drop you off at Jackson's if you wish. I'm sure someone there will spar with you.'

'No.' Hugo's voice was thoughtful. 'I'd rather come with you, if you've no objection. I have a sudden urge to discover what it is you do at this school of yours.'

* * *

Three days later, Liberty sat with Mrs Mount at one end of Lord and Lady Twyford's ballroom, absorbing the gowns and the jewels, the elegant dancing and the smiling faces, tapping her foot in time to the music from the quartet sitting on the dais at the far end of the room and just...just...*enjoying* being there.

This was the first truly prestigious ball she and her sisters had been invited to attend, courtesy of the unflagging efforts of Mrs Mount to inveigle invitations for the Lovejoy sisters who were indeed viewed as upstarts by many members of the *haut ton*. Liberty hoped and prayed this ball would be the first of many. It was her sisters' first opportunity to mingle with the highest in society and they had already proved a draw for several eligible gentlemen eager for introductions. Hope—her blue eyes shining with excitement—had been led out for the first dance by the youthful Lord Walsall and Verity's card was also full although Liberty would have preferred a less...seedy-looking partner for her youngest sister's first dance. The gentleman, who had been introduced by Lord Twyford himself as Lord Bridlington, looked forty if he looked a day and there was a gleam in his sleepy-lidded eyes as he leisurely inspected Verity's person that Liberty could not quite like. Still, she consoled herself...it was just one dance.

Gideon and Lord Alexander Beauchamp were also gracing the ball with their presence which meant Liberty could relax and enjoy herself rather than fretting over what her twin was up to. The rules that governed high society, she had decided, were hopeless as far as females were concerned. Even *she* hesitated to follow Gideon to some of the haunts he frequented. But she had found an unlikely ally in Gideon's valet, who was as determined as Liberty to prevent his master from committing social suicide, and Rudge was proving a satisfactory spy, informing Liberty of Gideon's intended destination every evening. But every time Liberty was tempted to throw caution to the winds and follow Gideon, Dominic's words would echo in her memory.

It is your sisters who will suffer. They will be tainted for life.

She was infuriated at finding herself controlled by his words even in his absence but, because she knew him to be right, she could not disregard his warning. Nor had she found it easy to banish Dominic himself from her thoughts. For the first time since Bernard's death she was attracted to a man but, in a hopeless twist of fate, it was to a man who—although she could see he found her attractive in return—would never in a million years act upon that attraction. He was not only heir to a powerful duke, but he had set out a list of essential qualities for his perfect bride to help him make his choice. Liberty suppressed a snort. His choice, indeed. As if he just needed to snap his fingers and any female he selected would simply fall at his feet.

She banished Lord Avon from her thoughts. It was Lord Alexander she must apply herself to for, as far as she could see, his bad influence on Gideon continued unabated despite what Dominic claimed. Now she had seen him at close quarters Liberty wondered how she had ever mistaken Dominic for his brother. Their facial characteristics were similar, to be sure, but Alex was nowhere near as intimidating as his brother. Not quite as tall, not as solid, nor as *dark*…as brooding.

Nor is he as handsome.

The latter observation whispered through her thoughts before she could prevent it. She swatted it away and distracted herself by watching Gideon as he partnered one of Lord Twyford's daughters. Her hand rose to her chest, as though to fill the hole there…the void that yawned deeper and darker the more her twin seemed to reject her.

Again, she gathered her scattering thoughts and redirected them to Alex, who was also dancing. Gideon had already declined to introduce her to him, but she was determined to find somebody who would. Maybe a direct appeal to him might work after all? She wouldn't know until she tried. Lord knew, she'd made no progress in bringing Gideon to his senses over the past week and although she'd seen Lord Avon a few times, driving or riding in the Park, he had done no more than tip his hat to her so she had no way of knowing if he had kept to his promise to watch over their respective brothers.

She scanned the Twyfords' ballroom for the umpteenth time, searching for *anyone* who might introduce her to Lord Alexander Beauchamp. Of a sudden, her pulse kicked. Across the floor, through a gap in the dancers, she spied a face she recognised—Lady Jane Colebrooke, standing with a beautiful young woman with shining black hair and a tall, dark gentleman.

Chapter Eight

'Mrs Mount.' Liberty leaned towards their chaperon. 'Lady Jane Colebrooke is over there—I should like to renew my acquaintance with her and to thank her again for her kindness. I shan't be gone long.'

Mrs Mount nodded and smiled, then resumed her conversation with the matron sitting on her other side. Liberty stood and shook out the skirts of her new violet gown—one of three she'd had made after the disaster at the Trents' rout—before making her way around the edge of the room. She slowed as she reached Lady Jane and her companions and, as she hoped, Lady Jane noticed her.

'Miss Lovejoy! How do you do?'

'Why, Lady Jane. What a happy coincidence. I had hoped I might see you, to thank you again for your kindness.'

Lady Jane blushed. 'Oh, it was my pleasure. Might I introduce you to Lord Hugo Alastair and his wife, Lady Olivia? Miss Lovejoy is Lord Wendover's sister,' she said to Lady Olivia. 'We met when she was overcome by the heat at a party last week—I merely leant my assistance when requested by your brother, Avon.'

Brother? Liberty's breath seized as cool silvery-grey

eyes—the mirror of Avon's—slowly assessed her. Of all the rotten luck—she could hardly beg an introduction to Lord Alexander when his sister was within earshot. Liberty curtsied again, this time a little deeper. Lady Olivia, after all, was the daughter of a duke and would no doubt expect her due. And Lord Hugo must be the son of a high-ranking aristocrat, she realised, as he bowed with a charming smile.

Mrs Mount's efforts to drum lessons of aristocratic precedence into the three Lovejoy sisters had not been for nothing because Liberty now knew that only the sons of marquesses and dukes had the courtesy title of 'Lord' affixed to their Christian names, so Lord Hugo must at least be the son of a marquess. Or marquis as some of them chose to be known. But Liberty still couldn't quite fathom why sons of earls were not called 'Lord' when their sisters were afforded the title of 'Lady'. This world was still a confused muddle of rules and details that had never touched upon her or her life before, but to which she must now conform.

Lady Olivia's gaze fixed on Lady Jane. 'I am all agog, Jane. What happened? And how came Dominic to be involved?'

'Livvy.' There was a note of warning in Lord Hugo's voice. He smiled at Liberty. 'I apologise for my wife's inquisitiveness, Miss Lovejoy.'

'Oh, *pfft*, Hugo. Jane knows me too well to take offence and I am sure Miss Lovejoy will forgive my curiosity about what my brother gets up to when I'm not around to keep an eye on him.' Lady Olivia grinned at Liberty. 'Jane's family estate adjoins our father's in Devonshire. We grew up together and dear Jane is well accustomed to the Beauchamps' ways, are you not, Jane?'

It struck Liberty that, for all their high birth, these aristocrats seemed less stuffy than many of the lower ranks of the peerage she had encountered since their arrival in London. *They* did not appear to view her as a person not fit to associate with.

Jane smiled. 'I am. As to the other night, all I recall is seeing Miss Lovejoy walking towards the door and then she seemed to stumble over someone's foot before…well, her knees simply buckled. And Dominic… he was quite the hero. He must have been quick to notice something amiss because, even though he was on the far side of our group, he was the first to reach Miss Lovejoy and he caught her before she could fall to the floor.'

Liberty kept her attention on Jane although she felt the weight of Lady Olivia's silver-eyed stare. Nerves quaked in her stomach. Would she think it had been a deliberate ploy on Liberty's part? A trick to attract Avon's attention? That particular rumour had already reached the Lovejoys' ears, but Liberty knew any attempt at denial would sound like too much protestation.

'And he asked you to go with him to protect Miss Lovejoy's reputation?'

'I believe it was with a view of protecting his own reputation.' The tart words blurted from Liberty's lips before she could stop them. Horrified, she clapped her hand to her mouth but, to her amazement, Olivia laughed.

'That sounds just like Dominic—his behaviour must always be above reproach. Does your brother attend this evening, Miss Lovejoy? I do not believe I have ever met him—this is our first time in town for over two years.'

'Yes. He is dancing in the same set as your brother Alexander…the man with the golden hair.'

'Oh, he is very handsome, is he not? I can see many

girls losing their hearts over that head of hair!' Olivia grinned. 'Do you envy him? Oh! I do beg your pardon. I did not mean to be rude. Your hair is very pretty, but it is not quite so...um...eye-catching, is it?'

Liberty smiled back. 'I take no offence. I am used to my brother garnering all the attention. We are twins and when we were children people would stop and exclaim at his angelic appearance—'

'*Twins?*'

'Why, yes.'

'Hugo!' Olivia nudged her husband. 'Did you hear that? Miss Lovejoy and her brother are *twins*.'

Lord Hugo smiled indulgently. 'I heard her say so, my love.'

'Miss Lovejoy! Will you do me the honour of calling on me at Beauchamp House tomorrow? I should deem it a great favour.' Olivia's eyes shone with excitement. 'We have two-year-old twins—a boy and a girl also. I should appreciate hearing from you direct what it is like to grow up as a twin.'

Liberty was happy to accept. She liked what she had seen so far of Lady Olivia and who knew what advantages Hope and Verity might gain if Liberty and Olivia were to become friends?

'I shall be happy to call upon you, but you must realise I have no experience of growing up *not* a twin so I am not sure I can be of much help.'

'Oh, I am sure you can. Shall we say two o'clock? You must come, too, Jane. I long to hear how things are at home.'

'I am sorry, Livvy, but I cannot. Stepmama wishes me to remain at home every single afternoon in case of gentlemen callers.' She sighed, sending a rueful smile Liberty's way. 'She is determined to see me married this year, before my stepsister makes her debut next Season.' She lowered her voice. 'Unfortunately the only gentleman who ever calls on me is Sir Denzil Pikeford and my fear of displeasing Stepmama is not yet as great as my fear of marrying a drunkard with scant manners and even less conversation.'

Olivia pulled a face. 'Pikeford? You have my sympathies!'

The music stopped and the dance ended, and Liberty was happy to see Lord Alexander heading in their direction. This would save her from having to beg an introduction. As he neared, he was joined by Lord Avon and Liberty's heart performed a lazy somersault as his gaze swept over her. What would he think, finding her here with his sister and brother-in-law after their last encounter at the theatre? His impassive features gave nothing of his thoughts away and, without volition, Liberty plucked at the low, round neckline of her new violet ball gown—a neckline that exposed rather more of her décolletage, shoulders and back than she was used to. She stopped that nervy fidgeting as soon as she realised what she was doing, but she was grateful she had given in to Mrs Mount's persuasion and had some new gowns made, even though the cost had set her nerves jangling. They jangled again now, but for a completely different reason, as the Beauchamp brothers neared.

Liberty watched Olivia greet both of her brothers with a kiss...she really was very different from so many members of the *ton* with their painfully correct behaviour. Liberty found herself looking forward to her visit the next day.

Olivia drew Liberty forward. 'You have already met my brother Dominic, of course, Miss Lovejoy.'

Avon's eyes met hers and the question in their silver-grey depths prompted Liberty to elaborate. 'Jane has been regaling your sister with the story of how she and I met, my lord.'

'Ah, yes. I trust you are fully recovered, Miss Love-joy?'

'Thank you, sir. I am.'

'And have you met my other brother, Alexander?' Olivia said. 'Alex, this is Miss Lovejoy.'

Liberty found herself the object of a quizzing stare from Alex's tawny eyes before he inclined his head. 'Miss Lovejoy. We have not formally met, but I am acquainted with your brother, Wendover.'

'I am aware of it, my lord.'

She knew her tone was a touch terse and a frown flicked between his brows, but he did not respond. Instead, his eyes moved on to his older brother, his gaze mocking. 'I'm surprised you're wasting your time with us, Dom. Haven't you an agenda to follow? Important decisions to make?'

Avon's eyes narrowed. 'Not here, Alex.'

'Your list is an open secret, Brother. No need for coyness. Did you know about it, Jane?' Jane nodded, somewhat reluctantly it appeared to Liberty. 'Have you heard of it, Miss Lovejoy? Lord Avon's list?'

Finding herself the centre of attention, Liberty swallowed, suddenly as nervous as Jane had looked. 'I have heard a mention of it,' she admitted.

Alex shrugged. 'Common knowledge, Dom. They're taking bets at White's.'

'In that case...' Dominic straightened the cuffs of his black swallowtail coat '... I shall go and attend to my...er...*agenda*, as you so elegantly phrase it, Alex.'

'No! Wait!' Olivia clutched at Dominic's sleeve.

'Don't do anything hasty, Dominic. I should like to at least meet these girls before you decide.'

A smile curled Avon's lips, but there was no humour in it. 'You wish to inspect my choice of potential bride, Sis?' He swept the room with a searching glance. 'You wish me to introduce you?' He crooked his arm. 'Come, then. Let us proceed.'

Liberty watched the byplay, fascinated by this glimpse into the undercurrents that swirled around the Beauchamps. The hint of sarcasm in Dominic's tone had brought fire flashing into his sister's eyes and Liberty was aware of Lord Hugo watching intently, with the focus of a cat waiting to pounce. She didn't doubt he would intervene to protect his wife if needed. Alex, on the other hand, now stood back. It was as though, having lit the fuse, he was waiting to enjoy the fireworks.

Liberty had always imagined other families were calm and polite in their dealings with each other. It appeared she was wrong. Maybe the Lovejoy family wasn't so different after all, with their petty squabbles. But there was no denying the strong bond between the Beauchamps and she prayed the bond between her and Gideon would prove resilient enough to be repaired.

'I have no wish to meet them in a noisy ballroom,' Olivia snapped. 'How can I talk to them properly or get to know their characters?'

'Their characters are none of your concern, Olivia. It will be my decision. Not yours.'

'*Pfft!* You know what I mean, Dominic.' She bit her lip, then stepped closer to him, putting her hand on his arm, her voice softer. Pleading. 'Of *course* it is your decision, Dom, but I want to help. Let me help. Please.'

A muscle ticked in his jaw. 'Very well. I shall drive you in the Park tomorrow and make the introductions.'

'Perfect! Are they all in town?'

Olivia was all smiles again and Lord Hugo relaxed. Alex, strangely, also looked satisfied, although Liberty would have sworn he had deliberately stirred trouble between his brother and sister in order to enjoy the ensuing argument.

'Yes, they are all here. And will no doubt be on parade in the Park at the fashionable hour,' he added in a cynical undertone.

'You never know, I might find you another lady to add to your list.' A frown darkened Dominic's brow, which Olivia blithely ignored. 'You may call for me at four o'clock. Miss Lovejoy is calling at two to meet Julius and Daisy. Did you know she and Wendover are twins as well?'

'I did know, but I don't understand why you should believe that has any relevance, Liv. Neither your two nor Miss Lovejoy and her brother are identical twins and—from the behaviour of the twins I have observed at Westfield—the non-identical twins appear to be much like any other family members who are close in age—they bicker much of the time and yet woe betide anyone who dares to upset the other.'

'Pooh! You cannot compare Julius and Daisy to the children at Westfield—heaven knows what traumas those poor mites have been through. Besides, Liberty *wants* to meet the twins, don't you, Liberty?'

'I...' Liberty—busy puzzling over Dominic's comments about children and Westfield—was caught unawares by the sudden direct appeal to her. 'I...of course, Lady Olivia. I should love to meet them.'

'Olivia! You must call me Olivia, for I foresee that we shall be great friends.' Olivia turned a triumphant smile on her brother. 'There, Dominic. See?'

Dominic shook his head at her. 'I see you are as manipulative as ever, minx.' He grinned at his brother-in-law. 'Thank God she is your responsibility now, Hugo. You should get a medal.'

Hugo grinned back. 'It's as well I thank God every day she's mine as well, then, is it not? Come on, Trouble—dare you be unfashionable and dance with your husband?' He led his beaming wife on to the dance floor.

Liberty felt it the second Dominic switched his attention back to her. 'So...you are to be interrogated about what it is like to be a twin, are you? Poor Olivia. She will go to any lengths, so determined is she to be a good mother.'

Alex smirked and Liberty stiffened.

'*Any* lengths? That includes, I collect, fraternising with someone like me?'

Dominic's lips quirked, but his voice was deadly serious. 'That is not what I meant at all, Miss Lovejoy. You really ought not to belittle yourself in such a way. There was no hidden meaning in my words—I meant exactly what I said. Olivia is determined to be the perfect mother and she drives herself relentlessly. I only hope the twins will not end up spoilt brats.'

'Like their mother,' Alex murmured, earning him a frown from his brother. 'Well, you can't deny she's always been wilful, Dom.'

'And you, my dear brother, should remember her good heart. She helped you out of more scrapes than I care to remember.'

'And led me into enough, too,' grumbled Alex, before straightening, his attention caught by something behind Dominic. Liberty followed his gaze and saw a group of young ladies heading in their direction, their collective attention firmly fixed on Dominic.

'Oh, lord,' Alex muttered. 'Pack alert. I'm off.'

Dominic glanced round at the approaching pack, as Alex had called them. It was an apt description, Liberty thought—like a pack of wolves with tasty prey in their sight. Beyond the tightening of his jaw, however, Dominic did not react.

'Janey…' Alex bowed '…would you do me the honour, etcetera, etcetera?'

'Alex! That is hardly the way to invite—'

'Oh, Janey don't mind, do you?' Alex grabbed Jane's hand. 'She knows me too well—she don't expect me to do the pretty with her! C'mon, let's dance.'

He tugged Jane on to the floor, leaving Liberty with Dominic. They were very soon surrounded by the young ladies, simpering and making eyes at Dominic, who appeared to effortlessly don the guise of the perfect gentleman as he responded with consummate gallantry. Liberty, although she was acknowledged, soon found herself deftly cut out. She stood, irresolute, for a moment but, as she made up her mind to walk away, Dominic raised his voice.

'Miss Lovejoy—pray tell me you have not forgotten our dance?'

She was torn between irritation at being an excuse to escape his coterie of admirers—and how was that different to how Alex had used Jane?—and admiration of his adroit handling of his dilemma. At least he waited for her reply rather than taking her acquiescence for granted as Alex had done with Jane.

She dipped a slight curtsy. 'Of course I have not forgotten, my lord.'

He sent his charming smile around his admirers. 'Please do excuse us, ladies.' He extended his hand. The girls parted and Liberty stepped towards him, trying to ignore the poisonous glances sent her way. She put her hand in his and their eyes met. She felt the jolt way down inside, in the pit of her belly, and heat washed across the entire surface of her skin, including her cheeks which she was certain were scarlet. His eyes darkened and she felt her lips part in response as her tongue darted out to moisten her unexpectedly dry lips. He dragged his gaze from hers.

'Come, Miss Lovejoy.'

His expression blank, his tone was one of world-weary boredom. But Liberty recognised it for the act it was. He led her into the set and she found herself the object of many more envious and a few disapproving looks.

'Are you sure your reputation will survive a dance with me?'

He cocked a brow and his lips twitched. 'Oh, I am tolerably sure it will remain intact.' He placed her next to Olivia in the line of dancers and, before retreating to stand with the gentlemen, he bent his head close to her ear and murmured, 'But please do not swoon again. *That* might take some explanation.'

His breath whispered across her neck, raising shivers in its wake. She smiled, reading it as a teasing remark rather than a reproof. When they first met she'd thought him superior and pompous, but was revising her opinion after he had spoken so movingly about his sister and now upon seeing him with Olivia and with Alex. A man who cared that much for his family couldn't be all bad. She only wished Gideon would demonstrate the same caring attitude.

Among the dancers taking their places for the next dance Liberty saw Hope and Verity and she experienced a tiny glow of triumph at her sisters' shocked and envious expressions when they noticed Liberty's partner.

Now dare to tell me I've ruined your chances!

It could only help their standing in society to be accepted by the Beauchamps, but she found herself hoping their acquaintance would prosper for her own sake. She had thoroughly enjoyed being included in their circle this evening and it made her realise quite how isolated she had become since Bernard's death, when she had withdrawn into the cocoon of her family.

She still found it difficult to accept that she deserved happiness. If she hadn't come to London five years ago, might she have spotted the symptoms earlier? She might have nursed them better. Saved them. The only way to make her guilt bearable had been to care for and protect the family she had left. But how could she protect Gideon...save him...when every time she tried to talk to him she ended up pushing him further away?

The music began. It was another country dance—one with which Liberty was familiar—and while she performed the steps mechanically she set her mind to wondering how might she use the Beauchamp connection to further her sisters' chances of meeting eligible men. If she could only persuade Dominic to stand up with both Hope *and* Verity, that would be a real coup. She had realised, since their first encounter, just how many of his peers looked up to Lord Avon, mainly due to his sporting prowess, and neither could she help but notice how many ladies—both young and not so young—fluttered around him, vying for attention. She understood their interest. Not only was he heir to a wealthy duke but he was handsome, he cut a fine, manly figure and he was intelligent.

'Miss Lovejoy? Liberty!'

Startled, she met Dominic's gaze, his silvery eyes like mirrors, as ever—reflecting the world back rather than allowing the light through to his soul.

'It is customary to make at least some pretence of interest in your partner's conversation.'

'Sorry. I was... I was...'

Chapter Nine

The movement of the dance separated them before Liberty finished her excuse, leaving Dominic even more time to regret not following his instinct to avoid them when he had first seen Liberty Lovejoy with Hugo and Olivia. But then Alex had headed in their direction and he had seen Liberty's eyes light up. Her expressions were utterly transparent—a window to her inner thoughts and feelings—and Dominic's feet had carried him over to the group without a second thought. Who knew what mischief Alex might stir if he felt unjustly accused of leading Gideon astray; his tongue could be sharp and—quite why, he did not know—Dominic felt this compulsion to stay close rather than to walk away.

He'd almost forgotten she was a virtual stranger as he relaxed among his family and fell to bickering with Olivia, as they had in the old days before she had wed. But he had not forgotten Liberty's *presence*. He was viscerally aware of her the entire time, sensitive to the slightest change in her expression and the strange sensations she conjured within him. He could not shake the feeling—no, the certainty—that, somehow, he *knew* her, understood her, could feel her deepest emotions. And he felt…happy. Content.

Until those girls had surrounded them, isolating Liberty as effectively as a well trained sheepdog would cut a single sheep from a flock. Dominic had felt the cloak of his public image fall into place as he became the Marquess of Avon and unaccustomed resentment at those girls had bubbled under his skin when he saw Liberty hesitate, then turn to walk away. Before he could consider the consequences, he was asking her to dance, when nothing had been further from his thoughts or intention. But the pleasure that radiated throughout his body as she placed her hand in his banished his doubts as to the wisdom of his action. Why should he not dance with his sister's friend? Nobody else could see how Liberty Lovejoy fascinated him. As far as anyone else was concerned, it was no different to him standing up with Jane.

But the minute the dance began, those insidious doubts wormed their way once again into his thoughts, fuelled by those memories of his mother, who had been more and more on his mind since his decision that this would be the Season he chose his bride.

Make me proud, my Son. Society will watch your every move. Never disgrace your position as heir.

His attempts to quash his mother's voice were not helped by the fact that the innocuous remarks he addressed to his partner were roundly ignored. Liberty appeared more interested in her sisters than in her own partner and he questioned again why he hadn't just left her to Alex's tender mercies. As the steps brought them together again, his irritation got the better of him.

'Well? Have you a reason for ignoring me?'

Even as the words left his mouth he regretted them.

It was hardly Liberty's fault he found her so maddeningly irresistible.

Her eyes flashed and her lips thinned. 'I was debating which of those charming young misses were on that list of yours, Lord Avon.'

They parted company, then the steps brought them together again, but before Dominic could speak, Liberty continued, 'I am certain any one of them would make the perfect Marchioness—as long as they possess the requisite bloodlines, of course.'

Her words stung and he retaliated instinctively. 'None of them, for your information. My future wife will not be a female who makes her intentions so very obvious. Discretion and poise—they are the attributes I seek.'

He cringed inside at how very pompous he sounded, but the words were out there and he was damned if he'd humble himself by retracting them.

'As well as *calmness* and *elegance*, if my recollection is correct.' Hectic flags of colour painted her cheeks. 'And now *discretion* to add to your list of requirements.'

'Do not forget poise, Miss Lovejoy.'

'I have not forgotten it, sir, but I am well aware that elegance and poise are one and the same. Did you think me uneducated as well as ill-bred?'

The words hissed out at him from under her breath. The movement of the dance parted them again and he cautioned himself not to further fuel the flame of her temper with any attempt to defend his position. Liberty—as he might have guessed—had no such compunction. She continued as soon as they were close enough for him to hear her. He supposed he should be grateful she waited until none of the neighbouring couples would be able to overhear her tirade.

'I am sorry to disappoint you—although I make no doubt that well-educated is not an essential quality for your ideal wife. I also happen to have an excellent memory. Not this time for the attributes necessary for the perfect Marchioness, but for the *undesirable* traits.'

Again they moved apart and again they came back together.

'Now...let me see...it was most *definitely* no vigour or passion. I can see, however, that none of those insipid young misses would disappoint you in that regard!'

He clamped his jaw tight as the movement of the dance parted them again. What the hell was he doing dancing with Liberty Lovejoy and allowing her to provoke him? All five of the ladies on his original list, together with their families, were present tonight. He would dance with them all, even though Caroline was currently his first choice. That would keep the gossips busy and it would be a far better use of his time.

He and Liberty circled one another, with no opportunity for speech before they parted company yet again. A glance across the ballroom brought Lady Caroline into his line of sight. She was elegant and cool as she performed the steps, smiling serenely as she responded to her partner's comments. He switched his gaze to Liberty—her eyes bright with accusation, her skin flushed, her lips parted and plump, her breasts...*glorious*. His loins tightened. He could not even summon any anger towards her because every word she had said was true. But it didn't change the fact that his bride must be the perfect lady, despite the yearning of every fibre of his being for a woman who was palpably *not* the perfect lady.

Never had he felt so very enticed by any female at a society event. Or by any female anywhere.

He found himself executing a figure of eight with Olivia.

'Are you and Miss Lovejoy *quarrelling*, Dominic?'

Caution whispered through him. If Olivia had noticed, others might, too.

'Don't be absurd!'

Olivia smiled impishly as she circled around him and rejoined Hugo. Dominic and Liberty came together again and this time, before she could speak, Dominic squeezed her hand.

'I apologise unreservedly. Tell me how I might make amends.'

It stole the next wave of invective from her tongue, but the gleam in her eyes warned him that she would take full advantage of his peace offering.

'Will you dance with my sisters, my lord? Please?'

'Your *sisters*?'

Her worry was plain as she sought her sisters among the dancers before directing her gold-flecked midnight-blue gaze back to him.

'Surely that would help us to be more fully accepted?'

He could not bring himself to refuse such a simple, direct request. 'Very well. I shall dance with each of them tonight. But please do not ask me to make a habit of it.'

Her grateful smile caressed him and he cursed the fact that his list was common knowledge. If it were not, he might have delayed finding a wife until next year. But he could not, with honour, back away now speculation over his choice was rife. Or, rather, he *would not* back away. It was one of the standards he set himself as a gentleman—to be true to his word. He knew there could never be more than friendship between him and

Liberty, but he might have been better able to relax and enjoy that friendship had the eyes of the *ton* not been watching his every move for a hint as to his intentions.

'I am relieved they have achieved *some* success,' Liberty continued, 'but I cannot help worrying.' She frowned and bit into her plump lower lip, sending sparks sizzling through him. 'I know we are not fully accepted everywhere and I'm afraid that can only get worse if Gideon continues in his reckless ways. If only he would come to his senses…he still won't listen to me.'

'But he is here tonight and behaving impeccably. He looks in a fair way to being smitten with Twyford's eldest girl. That must surely please you?'

She released her lip and smiled again, her eyes crinkling—a smile that was balm to his soul. He kept his expression impassive, again conscious of too many eyes watching.

'Yes, it does. Anyone would be preferable to that actress—I pray he has given her up entirely! And thank you for agreeing to partner Hope and Verity after having danced with me. It is very kind of you.'

'It will help some people to accept you more readily, as will your friendship with Olivia if that continues.'

The dance ended and Liberty took Dominic's proffered arm as they left the floor.

'As I said at the outset, your brother is simply finding his feet in town. I've talked to Alex and I've kept an eye on the pair of them—I have seen nothing for you to worry about.'

Liberty smiled with such trust in her eyes that his heart clenched. How could she affect him so, with just one look? Again, he blanked his expression, delivering her back to Mrs Mount with a wash of relief. Resolutely, he walked away. He would approach her sisters later, after dancing with other partners…partners whose name was not Lovejoy. And, as he had already put Caroline Warnock to the head of the queue, where better than to start with her?

'Good evening, Lord Avon.' Lady Caroline dipped a graceful curtsy.

'Good evening, my lady.' Dominic bowed. 'May I say how very charming you look this evening?'

'You are too kind, my lord.' Caroline raised her fan and fluttered it, her dark brown gaze clinging to Dominic's face.

'Dare I hope you have a dance available this evening, Lady Caroline?'

'I do, my lord. It is the supper dance, if that is acceptable?'

Dominic was aware of Lady Druffield watching them from her nearby chair with a gleam of satisfaction. Lady Georgiana's mother sat with the Marchioness and was also watching Dominic and Caroline, her expression revealing no hint of her feelings, yet Dominic knew she would be loathing every second of her rival's triumph.

'That is most acceptable,' he said to Caroline. 'Now, if you will excuse me…?'

He did not wait for her response, but headed straight for Lady Amelia and Lady Sarah and secured their hands for dances. Then he scanned the room for Lady Georgiana. His gaze collided with that of Liberty, accusation burning in her eyes. Her thoughts were as plain as if she had shouted them across the ballroom—*You promised to dance with Hope and Verity.* Although such transparency of feelings was frowned upon by most members of the *ton*, Dominic was charmed and enter-

tained by them. And by her. As long as he took care not
to single her out—*or to annoy her while we are dancing! I've learned my lesson there!*—he could still amuse
himself by teasing her.

He cocked his brow and had the satisfaction of seeing
that blatant accusation darken into a glower. He would
approach her sisters in his own good time—he would
not march to Liberty Lovejoy's command. He caught
sight of Lady Georgiana and made his way across the
room to discover she was free for the next dance. He led
her on to the floor, only to find they were next to Liberty and her current partner, Stephen Damerel, damn
his eyes. The man was older than Dominic and the
second son of Lord Rushock. He was a decent enough
man, but he was a scholar and far too staid for a lively
woman such as Liberty.

'My lord? My *lord*!'

Georgiana's petulant tone grabbed his attention.
He pushed Liberty and Damerel from his thoughts to
concentrate on his own partner, but the dance seemed
never ending and, despite his best intentions, he found
his gaze straying to Liberty on several occasions. By
the time he'd seen her smiling at Damerel in that open,
guileless way of hers he was ready to punch something.
Or someone. But through it all, he chatted with Georgiana and, at the end of the dance, he felt sure she would
have no cause to label him as an inattentive partner.

*One ticked off. Three more to go. Plus Hope and
Verity, of course.*

He didn't dare to question himself as to why he was
keen to get his duty dances out of the way. He just knew
he was. He had no partner for the next and, spying Hope
close to where Mrs Mount sat, he grabbed a glass of
champagne from a footman carrying a tray, drained it

in one and headed in their direction. He arrived at the same moment as Liberty, her hand on Damerel's arm. Dominic nodded at the other man, who returned his nod, bowed to the ladies and then sauntered away.

Dominic turned to Hope. 'Would you care to dance, Miss Lovejoy? If your card is not already full?'

She glanced at Liberty before replying, 'Thank you, my lord. I am engaged for the next two, but the first after supper is free.'

'Perfect. And I believe the one after *that* is a waltz, so...' He captured Liberty's gaze. 'Would you do me the honour of waltzing with me, Miss Lovejoy?'

Her brow creased, puzzlement in her eyes. If she could have asked him what he was about—which she could not with Mrs Mount and Hope in earshot—he would not be able to tell her because he had no idea himself. What the devil had prompted him to ask her to waltz, of all things? He must enjoy being tortured. And, quite apart from that, he must now make very sure to engage his other partners for a second dance—ever since he had first been on the town he had made a point of never dancing more than once with any lady at a ball. He suppressed a sigh. How did this one woman manage to provoke him into such uncharacteristic behaviour? And why did he have to meet her this Season of all Seasons? He couldn't stop thinking about her, but it would not, could not, change the future he had mapped out.

Liberty parted her lips to reply but, before she could speak, Alex joined them, slapping Dominic on the shoulder as Hope's next partner arrived and led her on to the floor.

'Just the people I need to speak to,' said Alex. 'And both in the same place as well. Am I not the fortunate one?'

Liberty's eyebrows flicked high.

'Miss Liberty Lovejoy.' Alex bowed. 'Would you kindly do me the honour of saving the supper dance for me?'

A silent growl vibrated in Dominic's throat, not helped by the impish smile Alex directed at him.

'Why. Yes. Thank you. Both of you.' Liberty looked from one of them to the other, clearly as confused as Dominic. 'You are most kind.'

'Oh, think nothing of it,' said Alex airily. 'Livvy wanted me to ask you, so we can eat supper with her and Hugo.'

'Oh. Well…will Jane not expect—?'

She fell silent as Alex laughed. 'Lord, no. We're just friends and, besides, her stepmother has promised the supper dance to Pikeford on her behalf.' He grinned at Dominic. 'It makes you thankful we didn't end up with her as our stepmother, don't it? Thank the Lord we've got Rosalind. So, Dom…who've you bagged for supper? Livvy said I was to ask you to join us, too, but— just a hint, you understand, Brother—when Olivia said *ask* she meant *tell*.'

Dominic closed his eyes briefly, shaking his head as he suppressed a smile. Life had been dull the past few years without Alex and Olivia and their irrepressible antics to brighten his life.

'I think I might legitimately dodge that particular invitation. I'm promised to Lady Caroline and I should imagine she will wish to remain with her particular friends.'

'On your head be it, Brother. Only Olivia did say, most particularly, that she wanted us all together for supper because, believe it or not, she has missed us.'

'Oh, very well. I'll see what I can do.'

'Good man! I'll leave you two in peace.'

With a wink, Alex wandered away. Dominic had already spent too much time with Liberty that evening but, somehow, he could not tear himself away. Not yet.

'Do you not have a partner for this dance, my lord?'

'No. I do not care to dance every dance. What about you?'

'Alas, no gentleman requested my hand for this dance.' Her full lips pursed slightly, then twitched into a half-smile. 'But I *am* engaged for a waltz after supper and I am looking forward to that exceedingly.'

'In order that you may tear me off another couple of strips?'

'Avon! That is *most* ungentlemanly of you.' Her eyes sparkled, drawing him in, and it was with an effort he tore his gaze from hers, blanked his expression and cast a bored look over the dancers. 'You did admit I was sorely provoked.'

He couldn't resist another sideways glance at her, a glance that revealed twinkling eyes above pouting lips that drew his gaze like a magnet. Good grief. They were in a crowded ballroom and all he could think about was sweeping her into his arms and kissing her. His hand rubbed at the back of his neck as his inner voice of caution screamed at him to walk away. But still he lingered.

The trouble was…his interest in her wasn't confined to lust. He just enjoyed being with her, even when they were bickering. Especially when they were bickering, in fact, because she treated him like an ordinary man. Every other female—apart from his family—treated him as 'the heir'. And damned if he wasn't complicit in that…he had occupied that public position for so much of his life it had become second nature.

'As I recall,' he adopted a light, teasing tone, 'I offered you an apology without admitting fault. It is called being gallant.'

'Very well.' She sighed dramatically. 'If you are intent on making me shoulder the blame, there is nothing more I can say. But I must tell you how grateful I am that you kept your promise and are engaged to stand up with Hope.'

He read the question in her expression.

'I have not asked Verity yet, but I shall. Which reminds me—I saw her dancing with Bridlington earlier. You may not be aware, but he has a somewhat disreputable reputation—an unsuitable partner for any young innocent.'

She changed instantly from a teasing, flirting girl into a serious woman. 'Thank you for the warning. I confess I thought him rather old for her and I have noticed he seeks her out between dances, too. I shall speak to Mrs Mount.'

'Would you like me to have a word with him?'

'N-no. I do not think so. I think it is Gideon's place to do so, don't you?'

'You're probably right. But if you wish me to intervene, just let me know.'

'Thank you. I will.' They watched the dancing in silence for a few minutes. 'My lord...may I ask you something?'

'If you must.'

'Oh! You wound me. How grudging you sound.'

'I sound that way because such a request from you usually means trouble.'

She laughed. 'You barely know me and you have deduced that already? You cut me to the quick, sir.' Then she sobered. 'I realise it may be an impertinent question, but what is Westfield?'

'Westfield?'

He was happy to be a patron of the school and to help the children with their lessons and find positions for the older children in households and as apprentices but he was uncomfortable talking about it—it smacked too much of puffing off his own good deeds. He did what he did for the children, not to bolster his reputation.

'Yes. You spoke of it earlier, when we were with your sister.'

'It is an orphan asylum supported by my second cousin, Lady Stanton. I merely help her out occasionally.'

'I was intrigued by how knowledgeable you seemed about the children. And about twins.'

He shrugged, keeping his attention away from her and on the dancers. 'Much of what I said is common sense. The rest I have gleaned from Felicity…Lady Stanton, that is.' The introduction of this subject gave him the impetus he needed to tear himself away from her. 'Now, if you will excuse me, Miss Lovejoy, I ought to circulate.' He bowed. 'I expect I shall see you at supper.'

He walked away without giving her a chance to respond. He knew, from when he had first started supporting Westfield, that it elicited more questions from others than he cared to answer. Questions as to why he, a wealthy and privileged aristocrat, should concern himself with orphans and other destitute children. But to answer those inevitably led to questions about his mother and her death…and he had no wish to resurrect those memories, or to share them. With anyone. He strolled on, stopping and chatting to acquaintances on occasion, but all the time he was conscious that none of these people were really his friends. The people he wanted to be with were his family. He was looking forward to his father's arrival and that of his aunts and uncles.

He paused and scanned the ballroom, his restless gaze settling as it found Liberty. She was talking, animatedly, with her brother, who was glowering at her. Why would she not take his advice? Could she not see that the more she badgered Wendover the more likely he was to rebel?

'Keeping an eye on the luscious Liberty again?'

He gritted his teeth as Alex joined him. 'I don't know what you are talking about.'

'Come on, Dom…best to keep moving, or the wolves'll be circling again.' Alex linked his arm through Dominic's and they strolled on. 'And you know precisely what I'm talking about. I haven't seen you pay this much attention to a woman for…well, for ever, actually. What I don't understand is why you left her standing just now. I gave you privacy and you threw the opportunity away.'

'It makes no difference—I might find her attractive and enjoy her company, but you know as well as I do that she is totally unsuitable to be a future duchess.'

'Do I? How so? Her brother's an earl; you give every impression of enjoying her company.' He leaned in closer. 'And you can't tell me you don't want to—'

'Enough!' Dominic snatched his arm from Alex's. 'How about you and I meet for a sparring session at Jackson's tomorrow?'

It would give him huge satisfaction to punch that knowing smirk off his brother's face, but he could hardly plant him a facer at the Twyfords' ball.

Alex grinned. 'Not on your life, Brother. I ain't that stupid.'

'Despite appearances to the contrary!'

'Ouch! Take care! That wit of yours is sharp enough to cause real damage to a fellow.'

'Good. You deserve it.'

'Aw, come on, Dom. It's just a bit of gentle ribbing... you know I don't mean anything by it.'

Dominic scanned Alex's expression of innocence. He sighed. 'I know it's hard for you, but try to respect the fact that I am simply not in the mood for your peculiar sense of humour. Not today.'

Alex nudged him. 'We'll talk again tomorrow, then.'

He winked and strolled away, leaving Dominic to inwardly seethe. The music was drawing to a close, which meant the supper dance would be next. Battening down his exasperation, he set off to find a drink before it was time to seek out Lady Caroline Warnock—his next partner and, very possibly, his future wife.

Chapter Ten

Dominic's warning about Lord Bridlington had brought Liberty's protective instincts rushing to the surface. She watched His Lordship as he sniffed around Verity—really, there was no other way to describe it—and her disquiet grew. He reminded her of nothing more than a street dog on the hunt for a casual coupling. Liberty crossed the ballroom to her sister and drew her aside.

'Lord Bridlington is very attentive, Verity. Has he put his name down for a second dance?'

Verity flushed. 'Yes. The supper dance.'

Liberty frowned at her sister's subdued tone. 'Do you like him?'

'Not…not really. But Mrs Mount told us we must never refuse a gentleman if he asks us to dance. And, if we do, we cannot then dance with *any* gentleman. And she told me I should be flattered by his attention because he is an earl and…and he would be a suitable match.'

'Well, *I* think it would be an appalling match—*if* his intentions are honourable, which I beg to doubt. I'll ask Gideon to warn him off, shall I?'

'You mean you won't go storming up to him yourself

and harangue him?' There was a teasing note in Verity's tone, but Liberty recognised the kernel of truth in her question and felt her skin heat.

'No, I shall not. That,' she added, with a wink, 'is not how a lady should behave. You see... I *am* learning.'

But Gideon, when she caught up with him, was less than amenable to her suggestion that he pull rank as Verity's brother and partner her for the supper dance, ousting Bridlington.

'Don't see there's anything I can do if she's already agreed to have supper with the fellow,' he said, stretching his neck to peer over the sea of heads in the ballroom. 'I'm engaged myself for the supper dance, as it happens. To Lady Emily.' His wrapt expression as he said her name spoke volumes. 'In fact...there she is! I must go, Sis. Look, don't worry—nothing's going to happen to Verity in a crowded ballroom. I'll speak to Bridlington later.'

Liberty bit back her frustration as Gideon hurried away. Was it really too much to ask him to take an interest in his sister and to protect her?

'Libby.' A flustered-looking Hope grabbed her arm. 'My flounce is torn.' She pivoted and indicated the damaged lace at her hem, at the back of her dress. 'Will you come and help me fix it? Only I needs must make haste because it is the supper dance next and I am promised to Lord Whiteley.'

'Of course.' Liberty couldn't mistake Hope's suppressed excitement. It seemed she was as happy with her supper partner as Gideon was, unlike poor Verity. 'Come, we'll go to the withdrawing room and pin it up. It won't take long.'

As they headed upstairs, Hope said, 'Are you quite well, Lib? You look a little out of sorts. Was it...was it something Lord Avon said?' She glanced around, then drew Liberty to one side of the landing to sit on a window seat. 'I saw you with him earlier and I cannot help but notice how you seem to…to…gravitate towards one another.' She clutched Liberty's hand. 'Oh! Would it not be exciting if he fell in love with you?'

Liberty wrenched her hand free and stood up. 'What nonsense you talk at times, Hope. No, it was nothing to do with Lord Avon. It was Gideon.'

'Oh, *Liberty*! Have you been harrying him again? Why can't you *trust* him?'

Liberty bit her tongue, hurt that Hope assumed she was interfering when all she was trying to do was to protect Verity.

'Come.' She recalled she was due to partner Alex and that Dominic might join them for supper. Perhaps she would take him up on his offer after all, if Gideon was so blind to his brotherly duty. 'I have a packet of pins in my pocket so we shall have that tear mended in a trice and you can return to your Lord Whiteley.'

They went into the room set aside for the female guests. A maid was on duty, ready to assist any ladies who needed help, but Liberty waved her away. It would be a matter of moments to pin the flounce and then they could return to the ball. They went behind a screen placed across the room to afford privacy and Hope stepped up on to a low stool while Liberty knelt behind her. She barely registered the sound of the door opening until a haughty female voice said, 'Have you seen that lumpy Lovejoy creature positively *throwing* herself at Avon?'

Liberty froze as a spiteful titter sounded from the other side of the screen. She settled back on to her heels and looked up at Hope, who was peering over the top of the screen. Seeing her sister's mouth come open, Liberty wrapped her fingers around her ankle and squeezed a warning. Hope glanced down and Liberty shook her head, putting one finger to her lips. Hope grimaced back and held three fingers aloft.

'I declare, I don't know how he remains civil to her.' It was the same voice, one she did not recognise, but one that clearly denoted the aristocratic heritage of its owner. 'I heard that she swooned right into his arms at the Trents' rout party and, even before that, I saw her for myself in the Park, attempting to waylay him while he was driving *me* in his curricle.'

Lady Caroline!

Mrs Mount had identified Lady Caroline Warnock as Dominic's passenger in the Park that day and, since then, Liberty had increasingly heard her name touted as the front runner in the race to become the Marchioness of Avon. It was hard to reconcile this malicious-sounding female with the butter-wouldn't-melt-in-her-mouth young lady Liberty had seen in public.

'But there…what else is to be expected of such a family?' the hateful voice continued. 'The Earl of Wendover, indeed! The grandson of a coal merchant! Better they allowed the title to slip into abeyance than let such people be elevated above their station.'

'Did Avon mention her? I saw you talking with him.' A different voice this time.

'No, he did not. And quite rightly, too. She is far beneath his notice, although for some unfathomable reason his sister appears to be encouraging an acquaintance with the woman. No, Avon was too intent on engaging me for the supper dance.'

Caroline's smug self-satisfaction made Liberty long to slap her. A third voice joined in the conversation.

'Well, *I* saw Avon dancing with her and they talked together afterwards, too. They looked positively *intimate*.'

'Such a comment is beneath you, Elizabeth—' Caroline again, her voice sharp now '—and I suggest you do not repeat it, for it makes you appear a bad loser. I have not heard anyone whisper *your* name in connection with Lord Avon's list. But, then…a mere baronet's daughter…hardly a fitting background for a duchess, is it, Pamela?'

'Oh, no. Most unfitting, I agree.' The breathless adoration in Pamela's reply raised Liberty's hackles and presumably had the same effect on the invisible Elizabeth, for a soft *hmmph* reached the listeners' ears. 'My brother is certain you will win him, Caro. Oh, to think! A marchioness! Vincent told me he has a hundred guineas riding on you, so you'd better make sure you win.'

'Oh, I shall. I made sure to drop him a hint about poor Georgiana's shocking piano playing. I don't see *her* usurping me as favourite…and rumour has it Avon was less than impressed by Sarah and Amelia scuttling after him when Lumpy Liberty staged her swoon. But… let us not linger, or we shall miss the start of the supper dance. Did I mention that I am promised to Avon?'

The door opened and closed and they heard a muttered 'Yes. More than once' from Elizabeth before she, too, left the room.

'Well!' Hope's voice rang with indignation. 'How *dare*—?'

'Yes, yes. I agree, Hope, but let me finishing pinning your lace or we shall be late for the dance. We will complain bitterly about those arrogant madams later.'

'Very well. But you will take note that I am not the

only person who noticed that you and Avon seemed somewhat...friendly.'

There was little she could say to that, so Liberty finished the repair and they hurried down to the ballroom, reaching the door just as the first strains of the dance sounded. Both of their partners were standing with Mrs Mount. Lord Whiteley's face showed nothing but relief at the sight of Hope. Alex's showed...nothing at all as their eyes met and Liberty's courage wavered as she walked forward to take his hand. No doubt here was another one who disapproved of her and the thought of sharing supper with that spiteful cat, Caroline, set her stomach churning. How would she resist retaliating if Caroline was as nasty to her face as she had been in the withdrawing room?

To her surprise, however, Alex was the perfect gentleman and at no point did his inoffensive conversation cause Liberty even the slightest discomfort. Once the dance was over, he escorted her into the second supper room where he had arranged to meet Olivia and Hugo. It was one of the smallest tables, set for six, and they were the first to sit down, shortly followed by Olivia and Hugo.

'Well!' Olivia's attention was fixed on the doorway as footmen served the dishes for a hot supper. 'I know you asked Dominic to join us, Alex, for he told me so himself. And he promised he would do so. Where can he be?' She spooned up some white soup from the bowl set in front of her. 'This is delicious! Oh! Look! *There* they are...and...is that not one of your sisters, Liberty?'

Liberty looked up at the doorway to see Dominic walk into the room with Verity on one arm and Caroline— sporting a sour expression quite unlike her usual ladylike mien—on the other. Dominic looked...impassive.

But the slight compression of his lips told her he was angry. Verity looked… Liberty pushed back her chair, ready to rush to her distressed sister's aid, but a strong hand closed around her wrist, preventing her from rising.

'Don't draw attention,' Alex muttered. 'You'll find out soon enough.'

Dominic paused by a footman and murmured something, indicating their table with a nod of his head. The footman hurried away, and Dominic guided Verity and Caroline to their table. He seated Verity first, next to Liberty, and then a pursed-lipped Caroline next to Hugo. The footman brought another chair, which he placed between Verity and Caroline, and another man arrived with porcelain and silverware to set a place for Dominic. No one uttered a word until the servants were out of earshot, but Liberty could see Verity's hands gripped tightly in her lap and her chest rose and fell as though she were out of breath.

'What happened?'

Liberty's question was directed at Dominic. He saw her grope for Verity's hands and cover them, folding her fingers around them.

'Bridlington became a little over-enthusiastic,' he replied. 'Fortunately, Caroline and I happened to see what he was about and I…er…persuaded him to think again.'

Alex gestured at Dominic's hand—he saw a smear of blood on his knuckle and slipped his hand beneath the table, out of sight.

'Lord Avon was quite the hero,' said Caroline. 'Goodness knows what the outcome might have been for your dear sister, Miss Lovejoy, had he not intervened.'

She smiled warmly at Dominic, surprising him. When they first saw Bridlington trying to manoeuvre

Verity into a side room, Caroline had tried to persuade
Dominic not to get involved, more concerned about
her own and Dominic's reputations than about what
was happening to Verity. Maybe he should excuse her
immediate reaction. After all, most gently born ladies
would surely prefer to avoid any sort of altercation.

'I confess the entire event has shaken my nerves
alarmingly.' She reached for her glass with a visibly
trembling hand. 'I dare say I do not stem from such robust stock as the Lovejoys.'

Liberty's eyes glinted dangerously and her mouth
opened.

'I am sure no one was unaffected, Lady Caroline,'
Dominic interjected, quick to forestall Liberty. 'But
now I suggest we all settle down and enjoy this delicious supper and forget all about it. Lord Bridlington
has left the ball now so there is no need to dwell upon
what happened.'

'But I want to know—'

'You do know, Miss Lovejoy. I have told you.'

'I should like to know as well,' said Olivia. 'Did you
punch him, Dom? We've all seen the blood on your
hand, so you needn't bother to hide it.' She leaned across
the table. 'Are you *sure* you are all right, Miss Lovejoy?'

'I am all right now, thank you. I am exceedingly
grateful to your brother, however.' Verity smiled at him.
'He is right…can we please forget this and enjoy our
supper?'

Olivia's intervention had given Liberty time to sub-
side, but Dominic could tell her blood was still simmering and he had no doubt he would be questioned
thoroughly during their waltz. His pulse kicked at the
thought of holding her even as he again mentally slated
himself for taking the risk of dancing with her twice.

'Indeed. I suggest we forget all about that unfortunate occurrence.' Caroline raised her spoon to her mouth, and swallowed. 'This white soup really is excellent, do you not agree?'

'Excellent indeed. How fortunate it is not *lumpy*, Lady Caroline,' said Liberty in a kindly manner. 'That, I am persuaded, would quite spoil your enjoyment.'

Dominic frowned and he saw Olivia shoot Liberty a questioning look, but Caroline seemed not to notice Liberty's overtly sweet tone.

'Indeed it would, Miss Lovejoy.'

Her smile was all graciousness. Did she have any clue that Liberty's smile wasn't genuine? It didn't take Dominic long to realise that she did not. It was increasingly clear that none of Liberty's comments or opinions mattered to Caroline because she quite clearly viewed Liberty—and Verity, too, although she barely joined the conversation—as utterly beneath her notice. She was polite and respectful—even delightful—in her dealings with Dominic, Alex, Olivia and Hugo, however.

It took the duration of that one supper for Dominic to change his mind about his list. A beautiful singing voice was no compensation for such arrogance. And how, he wondered, would someone such as Caroline respond to the spouses of his father, uncle and aunt? Rosalind, his stepmother, might be a duchess now, but her father was a simple soldier and her grandfather a silversmith. Thea, Uncle Vernon's wife, was the daughter of a glassmaker, and Zach, Aunt Cecily's husband—who refused to allow anyone to call him uncle—had a Romany mother. Dominic would never risk introducing discord into his beloved family.

He was still hesitant about Georgiana and her fear of horses, which left him with Lady Sybilla Gratton.

As they finished their supper, Gideon appeared behind Liberty and Verity.

'I thought you said Verity was having supper with Bridlington, Liberty?' he said, accusingly. 'I've been searching everywhere for them... Mrs Mount didn't seem to know where they were and neither did Hope and now, after worrying the life out of me, I find she's been with you the whole time!'

Liberty's cheeks flushed. 'If you had done your duty as I asked, you would have known precisely where she was.'

Verity jumped to her feet. 'You are being unfair, Gideon.' She grasped his arm, and lowered her voice. 'I was due to have supper with him, but...but...'

She cast an anxious look around the table, then put her lips to her brother's ear. As she whispered, Gideon's face leached of colour and his gaze sought Dominic's as one hand came to rest on Liberty's shoulder.

'I am sorry, Sis. I shouldn't have sounded off at you... I was worried when I couldn't find them. And I am grateful to you, Avon. You can be sure I'll have something to say to Bridlington next time our paths cross.' He put his arm around Verity and hugged her. 'Are you all right? Do you want to go home? I'll take you, if you do.'

'No.' Verity raised her chin and Dominic recognised the family resemblance with Liberty in that defiant gesture. 'I shall not allow that...that...*scoundrel*...to spoil my enjoyment of my first-ever ball.'

Alert to the nuances of Liberty's expression, Dominic saw her pride at her sister's strength and then, as her gaze met and held that of her twin, love shone from her eyes. Then a tut and a sigh sounded from behind him and he sensed movement. Caroline, her lips thinly disapproving, was preparing to leave the table. He stood up and pulled her chair back.

'Allow me.'

'Thank you, my lord.'

She smiled at him and held out her hand. Dominic helped her to rise and then she placed her hand on his sleeve, clearly expecting his escort back to the ballroom. He breathed a sigh of relief when he returned her to her mother and then sought out Hope, his next partner. But throughout the dance he was distracted, watching Liberty, who was dancing with Redbridge—that incorrigible tattletale—and laughing up at him.

'You are dancing with Liberty next, I believe, my lord?'

The question jerked his attention away from Liberty and back to Hope, who was studying him with something like speculation in her eyes. Drat the girl.

'I am. I apologise for neglecting you, Miss Lovejoy. Seeing your sister with Lord Redbridge reminded me of a matter I must discuss with him, but that is no excuse for ignoring my partner.'

He set himself to entertaining Hope and, by the end of the dance, he thought his distraction a success. They reached Mrs Mount at the same time as Redbridge and Liberty, who was beaming all over her face. Hadn't anyone ever told her it was unladylike to exhibit an excess of emotion? He could not tear his gaze from her as he wondered who had conjured up such a ridiculous rule. And, more importantly, why?

He bit down his irritation at Redbridge for encouraging Liberty and then had to bite it back even harder when he noticed Hope looking from him to Liberty and back again. He didn't try to interpret her expression, he just concentrated on blanking his own.

It was a relief when it was time for the next dance and he could lead Liberty on to the dance floor.

'Why did you ask me to waltz?'

Liberty gazed up at Dominic, her eyes smiling although her lips were serious. Dominic's fingers flexed on her waist, holding her more securely as they entered their first turn. The truthful answer was that he did not know. The words had slipped from his lips before his brain could stop them. But he didn't regret his impulse—she felt so right in his arms. If only... He quashed that wish before it could fully form. There was no *if only*. Not for him. He knew his duty to the Dukedom. To his father. To his mother.

As ever, the thought of his mother conjured forth that feeling of never quite being good enough. If she had lived, what would she think of the man he had become? *Would* she, finally, be proud? His chest tightened as he recalled the last time he had seen his mother— the only time in his eight years he could remember any spontaneous gesture of affection from her. It was her custom to walk around the lake every day when she was at home at the Abbey and, that day, Dominic had asked if he might go with her. Rather than the brusque refusal he expected, she had smiled at him and patted his cheek.

'Mr Brockley will be waiting for you, Dominic, but—if you are good and pay attention in your lessons— maybe we can go out again later.'

Later had never come. He had never seen his mother again and the memory of that last encounter had, over the years, helped to fuel his determination to fulfil his destiny.

He wrenched his thoughts out of the past—Liberty awaited his answer...why *had* he asked her to waltz? He gazed into her midnight-blue eyes, breathed in the scent of roses...now not solely his mother's preserve, but that of Liberty Lovejoy as well. Mother wouldn't approve of Liberty, that was for sure. But it was only one waltz.

'Why not?' he countered.

'Well, now. Let me see. Maybe because this is the cautious Lord Avon who is intent on selecting the perfect bride to complete his perfect life and who appears to conduct his entire life with the sole purpose of protecting his reputation?'

He strove to keep his expression blank at her succinct summation of his life.

'So cautious, in fact,' she continued, 'that I have heard it whispered that he never dances twice with the same young lady. And yet this is our second dance this evening.'

He hid his surprise. 'You will note, however, that I have engaged several young ladies to dance with me twice this evening.'

Their gazes fused, her blue eyes knowing. 'I *also* noted that the other engagements followed mine as you sought to divert attention from your uncharacteristic slip.'

'Slip?'

'You masked it well, my lord, but I saw the shock in your eyes in the split second after you asked me to waltz. Were I a more generous person, I would have refused that impulsive offer, but I could not resist accepting, if only to see how you would manage your mistake.'

'It was no mistake. I did and I *do* want to waltz with you, Liberty Lovejoy.'

He heard her quick intake of breath and, without volition, his hand tightened on hers and his other hand slid further around her waist, drawing her closer. Caution clamoured through his brain, but he ignored it.

'You...' Her voice sounded breathless. 'You are unused to acting on impulse, I would guess.'

'A man in my position cannot afford to act on impulse.'

She stayed silent and a quick glance down revealed a wrinkled forehead.

'You are puzzled?'

Her head snapped up. 'No. Not puzzled. Sad.'

'Sad?'

He felt her shrug. 'It must be an uncomfortable existence, to be forever on your guard, wary of how you appear to others.'

Her words came close to his earlier thoughts about ridiculous rules, but they were a fact of life. His life, in any case. 'That is the world we live in. That is what it means to be part of the *haut ton*. But, to return to your original question, I asked you to waltz because it is a chance to talk uninterrupted. With no risk of being overheard.'

Her eyebrows arched. 'You wanted the opportunity to talk to me without being overheard? Why, Lord Avon...' she batted her eyelashes at him '...what can you possibly have to say to me that ought not to be overheard?' She tilted her head, her lips closer to his ear. 'Will I be shocked?'

Her breath on his skin raised the hairs at his nape. He was playing with fire. His common sense warned him to keep his distance. But something deep inside him—something older, baser, more primeval—now challenged the innate caution that had been part of his character for as long as he could remember...challenged it square on, with raised fists and a desire to knock it out. But, he reasoned, as long as he managed to keep that challenger under control, there was no reason why he could not indulge in a little flirtation.

'It depends, Miss Lovejoy, on how easily you are shocked.'

His voice sounded husky. Deep. And he felt Liberty's reaction. He *had* intended to shock her and it seemed he was successful.

She cleared her throat. 'Tell me what happened with Verity and Lord Bridlington.'

Dominic bit back a smile. For all her boldness a moment ago, that change of subject revealed much about Liberty's true character, even though she might flirt a little and take risks.

'You know what happened. I told you.'

'You punched him? Did he hit you back?'

'No. He knew he was in the wrong. He was caught before any damage was done and he will accept he has lost.'

She frowned. 'Should I be worried? Will he target Verity again?'

'I doubt it. He is an opportunist. He viewed Verity as easy prey with no father to protect her and a brother who appeared not to care less. He knows differently now. He will turn his attention to someone less well protected, especially after Gideon speaks to him, as he promised he will.'

She shivered. 'I did not realise there are such men in the *ton*, masquerading as gentlemen.'

'I am afraid there are such men in all walks of life.'

'I am so grateful you saw him and stopped him.'

'It was my pleasure.'

Her smile did strange things to him. It was the tremble of her lip—it was not artifice, he was certain—and it was the hint of vulnerability in her eyes, the deep breath she often took before replying to a comment, as if steeling herself. The truth hit him like a lightning strike. She acted and spoke boldly, but it was not boldness but bravery. She found the courage from somewhere to stand up for those she loved and for what she believed in.

He didn't want to admire her. Wasn't the ever-present lust enough for him to fight against? It felt as though his well-ordered, meticulously planned life was spinning out of control. He clenched his jaw, set her at the correct distance from him and concentrated on the steps of the waltz even as the scent of roses wove magic through his veins.

Chapter Eleven

The following afternoon Liberty was about to set out on the short walk to Grosvenor Square when Gideon descended the staircase. She took a minute to admire him—he was so handsome and he looked a proper gentleman in his blue superfine coat, cream breeches and polished Hessians. She frowned. She had grown accustomed to him staying out until dawn and then sleeping most of the day away. Since their arrival in London it seemed that the only times she'd seen him this early in the day he had been unshaven and wearing a dressing robe and slippers. But last night he had escorted his sisters home and, it would appear, gone straight to bed.

'You look very smart, Gideon.'

A faint flag of colour washed over his cheeks. 'I intend to call on Lady Twyford, to pay my respects and to thank her for last night's entertainment.'

'Ah.' Of course. Gideon had spent much of his time in a group of young men surrounding Lady Emily Crighton, Lord Twyford's eldest daughter. And joined her for supper. 'Please extend my gratitude as well—it was kind of them to invite us.'

'Well, I have no doubt the invitations will roll in

apace, now you've established yourself as part of the Beauchamps' inner circle.'

Stung by the implication she was a social climber, Liberty finished pulling on her second glove before she trusted herself to answer him.

'I hope you know me better than to think I would pretend friendship with someone simply for advancement.'

She held her twin's gaze, hating that he might think that of her. Particularly when her sole reason for approaching Jane last night had been to inveigle an introduction to Alex and the reason for *that* was standing in front of her looking positively angelic.

Gideon looked away first.

'No. Of course you would not. And I'm sorry, again, for not listening when you warned me about Bridlington. I'll be sure to speak to him when I next see him, but I trust Avon when he said Verity isn't in any danger now. But enough of that. Where are you off to? And where are the others? You're not...' His eyes narrowed. 'Tell me you are not going out *alone*?'

That was exactly what she had intended. It was such a short walk to Beauchamp House—just around the corner, really—that she hadn't even considered the impropriety until Gideon asked his question. Dominic's words whispered through her brain: *If you bring disgrace upon yourself, it is your sisters who will suffer.*

She put her nose in the air. 'Of course I am not going out alone, Gideon. I was on the brink of sending for one of the maids to accompany me but, as you are here now, you may escort me yourself.'

Gideon scowled. 'I ain't going *shopping* with you, if that's where you're off to. I told you. I'm calling on E— Lady Twyford.'

'Well, for your information, I am not going shopping. I have been invited to Beauchamp House to meet Lady Olivia's children.' Liberty snaked her arm around Gideon's and headed for the door, towing him with her. 'It is barely out of your way at all.'

'Very well.'

They were soon strolling in the direction of Grosvenor Square.

'Gideon.' It was rare lately that she had the chance to speak to him privately. She could not pass up the opportunity and, for once, he was not suffering the consequences of either overindulgence or lack of sleep. 'I *have* been worried about you.'

'I know. You've made that very clear.'

'That actress…'

He halted and frowned down at her. 'What,' he said, menacingly, 'do you know about her?'

'I am not a fool! I know you haven't been haunting the Sans Pareil for the quality of the performances.'

He growled, deep in his throat, then continued to walk. 'I cannot believe I am having this conversation with my sister. Listen, Liberty—you must stop thinking you can dictate where I go or what I do.'

'I am not trying to dictate to you. I—I just want you—all of you—to be safe. And happy.'

Gideon slipped his arm around her waist and gave her a quick squeeze. 'Lib. Listen to me. It wasn't your fault they died.'

Her heart clenched. 'I—I know.'

'And it doesn't mean it is your responsibility to protect all of us. I am a grown man and I can look after myself.'

'I know that, too.'

He raised his brows. 'Do you? Look…yes, I visit the

theatre, but…it is just a bit of fun. I am at no risk. You say you are not a fool. Well, neither am I—I am a peer now and I'm aware of my obligations. And before you complain again about me frittering my fortune away, believe me when I tell you I can afford a few losses at the gaming tables.'

If only she could fully believe him. It seemed the habit of protecting her family, especially her beloved twin, would not be satisfied *that* easily. Wisely, she did not say so.

Gideon sighed and slanted a smile at her, his blue eyes glinting. 'I *also* admit it will not help Hope and Verity to find decent husbands if I continue to set the gossips' tongues alight. So, I shall henceforth be the soul of discretion—I shall still have fun and enjoy myself, but I shall do so well away from the public gaze.'

They had arrived at Beauchamp House and the door opened before Gideon could knock, giving Liberty no chance to reply. A haughty-looking butler peered out, looking down his long nose at her.

'Miss Lovejoy. Lady Olivia is expecting me.'

The butler's gaze slid to Gideon, perused him from head to toe, then stood back and bowed.

'Please come in, Miss Lovejoy; my Lord Wendover.'

'Oh, I'm not coming in—just wanted to see my sister safely delivered. I'll see you at dinner, Lib.'

Liberty watched Gideon walk away, whistling a jaunty tune, leaving Liberty to enter alone. She paused on the threshold, remembering the last time she had called at this house, and a smile tugged at her lips as she recalled her efforts to dodge the footman.

'Ahem.'

The butler raised one brow and Liberty wiped any

hint of amusement from her features before entering the hall.

'Lady Olivia is expecting you, Miss Lovejoy. Please follow me.'

He led the way up the magnificent marble staircase to a parlour on the first floor—a cosy and informal room and not nearly as grand as the room into which Dominic had shown her. Olivia was sitting on a sofa, her legs tucked up under her, reading. She looked up, smiled and set her book aside.

'I am so pleased to see you, Liberty. Thank you for coming. Grantham, please inform Mrs Himley that my guest has arrived and she may send up refreshments. Now—' as the butler left the room '—come and sit by me... I asked Ruth to bring the twins down after we have drunk our tea—lively two-year-olds and cups of hot liquid are a poor combination.'

Liberty did as she was bid.

'I'm sorry to receive you in here,' Olivia went on, 'but the servants are working so hard to prepare the house for Papa's arrival that I could not in all conscience receive you in the salon, not when the twins will be joining us.' She grinned. 'They have the ability to reduce any room to utter chaos without even trying. Grantham was mortified when he discovered I intended to receive a guest in the family parlour, but I made sure you would not object.'

'Of course I don't object. Is Grantham your father's butler?'

'He is. He arrived in London yesterday.'

'I am rather pleased he was not here when I called—' Liberty snapped her mouth shut as her cheeks burned.

Olivia tilted her head. 'When you called...? You have been here before?'

'No. Yes. Oh, heavens…my wretched tongue! I…'

But hadn't Dominic told her Olivia had always been protective of Alex? Surely she would understand? She told Olivia of the reason for her visit to Beauchamp House and how she had mistaken Dominic for Alex. Olivia's eyes danced with merriment.

'What fun! That takes me back to my debut year—I tied myself in tangles trying to protect Alex from the consequences of his actions…but we both survived and I met my beloved Hugo, and all turned out for the best. In the end. But…forgive me, but Wendover does not seem near as wild or as…*self-destructive*…as Alex used to be. I noticed nothing out of the way in his behaviour last night. Indeed, he appeared the perfect gentleman.'

'I believe…I *hope*…that may be because he has developed a *tendre* for a certain young lady. It appears there is nothing as likely to persuade a man to behave himself as the presence of watchful parents.'

Olivia sighed. 'Oh, how I wish Alex would develop a fancy for a nice girl. I fear he will never wed—his temperament is too unpredictable.' She caught Liberty's eye and smiled ruefully. 'You and I seem very alike. As do our families. Ought I to apologise for our family squabbling last night? It's odd. Here I am, married for four years and the mother of twins, yet as soon as I am with Dominic and Alex the years seem to drop away and we slip back into the same old relationship. With me as their little sister,' she added in a disgusted tone. 'I keep meaning to resist, but it seems impossible—that role is so natural to me, it happens quite without any intent on my part.' Olivia sent Liberty a rueful smile. 'I don't know! Brothers! They spend half their life tormenting and teasing you—pretending they are so very superior simply because they are male—and the rest of the time they appear hell-bent on ruining their lives. You cannot help but try to protect them from their own folly.'

Liberty frowned. 'But…surely… Lord Avon…he, at least, is all that is proper and gentlemanly. *He* cannot give you cause for concern.'

A maid came in at that moment, with a tea tray and cakes. The butler had opened the door for her and he lingered, waiting until the maid had poured the tea and handed Olivia and Liberty their cups.

'Thank you, Betty,' said Olivia. The maid flashed a smile, then hurried towards the waiting butler and the still-open door.

'The poor things don't know what's hit them since Grantham arrived—heaven forfend Papa should find a speck of dust or a picture unaligned when he arrives.' Olivia gurgled a laugh.

'H-he sounds quite intimidating,' said Liberty.

'Oh, pooh. He gives himself airs and graces, but underneath it all he's an old softy.'

Liberty stared at Olivia, open-mouthed. Olivia returned her quizzical look, then burst out laughing. 'I meant Grantham, silly! Not Papa! Not that he's intimidating either…well, he might appear so at times, but he is not. Not really. Grantham could give any duke lessons on how to be pompous and unbending.'

Silence reigned as they sipped their tea and nibbled at slices of moist fruit cake.

'Speaking of Lord Avon—' Liberty could contain her curiosity no longer '—I was intrigued by your conversation about Westfield last night. For a bachelor, your brother appears strangely knowledgeable about twins and children in general, but when I asked him about it, he seemed to…well, to withdraw somehow.'

'Oh, Dom is never one to puff off his good deeds.

Or anything about his life, in actual fact. He is quite private. But Westfield—he's been a patron for…ooh, seven years now—since he was nineteen. It is a school and orphan asylum in Islington.'

'That seems a strange thing for such a young man to get involved with.'

'Maybe to outsiders,' said Olivia, 'but not when you know Dominic. Lady Stanton, who is one of our cousins—second or third, or some such—was already a patron, even before she married, and when she told Dominic about it he decided to help. He knows how hard it was to lose Mother and *we* still had Papa. He said at the time he could not bear to imagine how much worse it would be if your family was poor and you lost both parents. He wanted to help give those children a future other than crime and begging.'

'I remember how hard it was to lose both *our* parents and I was nineteen.'

Liberty tried, and failed, to imagine how dreadful it must be for a very young child to suddenly find itself all alone in the world. Her respect for Dominic increased—he did not have to help those children, but he chose to.

'Westfield is not just for orphans, but for abandoned children, too. There are more of those than you would care to know about. Why, just a few days ago he recognised a beggar woman on the street with a child that wasn't hers and rescued it. My Hugo was with him, or I'd never have known about it, of course. Hugo is taking me to visit Westfield soon—he went there with Dominic and he told me it is hopelessly overcrowded. He thought we might set up an establishment in Sussex, near to where we live, to take some of the children.'

'That is a kind thought.'

'I'm ashamed to admit I've never been there before,'

Olivia said. 'That makes me rather thought*less*, doesn't it?' She chewed at her lip, staring down at her hands in her lap. 'I've never considered getting involved myself, even though I know how hard it is to lose a parent. And I had every advantage in life, because of who Papa is, and we had my aunt and my uncle, too.'

'What was your mother like?'

'I don't remember her very well. All I remember is rejection and impatience. I was only five, of course, when she died—I've no doubt I *was* a constant nuisance—but try as I might I can never remember approval or affection. I will never know if that would have changed as I grew up…never know if she would finally approve of me and be proud of me.' She raised her eyes and Liberty was concerned to see tears sheening them. On impulse, she took Olivia's hand and squeezed. Olivia emitted a sound, half-laugh, half-sniff. 'Hark at me, getting all maudlin. But at least now you understand why I am so determined to be a good mother to my twins.'

'I am sure you could never be a bad mother, Olivia. You have proved how much you care and all children need is to know they are loved.'

'They know how much their papa and I dote on them, but I am still curious about them being twins and interested in how, if at all, it might make them different from other children. Will you tell me about your childhood? Were you and your brother always close? Was your relationship with him different to your relationship with your sisters?'

They chatted for several minutes about twins in particular and brothers and sisters in general—although Liberty didn't feel she offered Olivia any special insight into being a twin. She and Gideon had naturally bonded more as children, but she believed that was due more to the age difference between them and their younger sisters than simply because they happened to be born at the same time. It was hard to accept the bond she had believed unbreakable had frayed so badly, although there was more hope in her heart after their talk on the way to Beauchamp House. The time flew by, until the door opened and a nursemaid entered, ushering two infants into the room. They were followed by a footman carrying a large wooden ship which he set down on the rug in front of the fireplace. The children stood stock still upon spying Liberty, their eyes huge, thumbs jammed into their mouths.

'Ruth,' said Olivia to the nursemaid, her silver eyes brimming with laughter, 'this pair can't possibly be Julius and Daisy—I do believe you have switched them for imposters. *They* are never this quiet.' She held out her arms then. 'Come to Mama, sweeties, and meet Mama's friend.'

Before too long, Julius, still somewhat shy, was perched comfortably on Liberty's knee, patting and stroking her hair and face, while Olivia had joined her daughter on the floor to play with a splendid ark and a collection of carved wooden animals.

Julius was so soft and huggable. Liberty's arms closed around the little boy and that familiar hollow ached in her chest. She no longer doubted that she was ready to find love again, but the only man she had ever come close to having feelings for was Dominic. And he was so far out of her reach it was futile to even daydream about it.

'Liberty? *Liberty!*'

She was jerked out of her thoughts by Olivia's persistent calling of her name. Then Julius stiffened in her lap before wriggling free of her arms and sliding down to the floor.

'Well, young Julius,' drawled a deep, familiar voice, 'I see you have started young with the ladies.'

Heat scorched Liberty's cheeks as she realised Dominic must have been watching them for some minutes before being noticed. She quickly tidied her hair. Her heart, from being an aching void, bloomed with joy as his mouth curved in an irresistible smile and mischief twinkled in his eyes and she struggled to keep her feelings hidden—she could not bear it if he realised how she was beginning to care for him. How utterly mortifying that would be. She smiled a cool greeting as the twins rushed to him and he gathered them both up and kissed their cheeks soundly, blowing air against their skin to make loud noises and sending them into fits of giggles.

With blinding clarity she saw he was two different men. There was the public Lord Avon, with his proper behaviour and his correct manners—the Lord Avon who was familiar to the *haut ton* and who had attended to Lady Caroline at supper last night—and then there was the Dominic who emerged when his family were around him. His family...and her. Liberty Lovejoy. Because somehow, without even trying, Liberty had been admitted into the inner circle of people with whom Dominic felt able to relax and to reveal more of the real man inside.

But did that simply mean her opinion was unimportant to him?

A lump swelled in her throat as she watched him with Olivia's children. He would make a wonderful father... and he was a man who *cared*. How many nineteen-year-old wealthy and privileged young men would bother themselves with the plight of orphans? Not Gideon, even now he was almost five-and-twenty. Dominic was clearly a man who trod his own path, regardless of what his peers expected of a man in his position.

He was so much more than she had first believed, when all she had seen was a wealthy but shallow aristocrat who knew and cared nothing for the plight of others. Not only did he take practical steps to help those less fortunate, but his selflessness was not in order to enhance his own reputation. He was well-known in society, and often talked about, but Liberty had not heard the slightest hint of his charity work.

Her thoughts whirled with what she had learned… was learning…about him. Olivia's revelations about her childhood and the mother who had never given her the unconditional love she craved prompted Liberty to wonder about Dominic and his relationship with that same mother.

'Dominic!' Olivia regained her feet and shook out her skirts. 'You are early! We agreed four o'clock, did we not, and it is only just gone three.'

'I wanted to spend a little uninterrupted time with my niece and nephew while I have the chance.'

He hugged them both into his chest again before setting them down on the floor and strolling further into the room.

'Good afternoon, Miss Lovejoy.' He bowed. 'I do hope you will not object to my disturbing your time with Livvy? I can always go up to the nursery with the twins if I am *de trop* and you wish to gossip unhindered.'

'Now, Dom, you know very well we would not gossip in front of the children…not that we do gossip, of course,' Olivia added hastily.

'Of course,' Dominic agreed smoothly as the twins tugged at him to play with their toys. He sighed. 'Very well, scamps, but allow me to remove my coat first—

Brailsford will never forgive me if I soil my coat *before* I display my elegance in the Park.'

'Dominic! Miss Lovejoy is my guest. You cannot cavort before her in shirt sleeves!'

Liberty found herself the object of a penetrating look from Dominic. A look that set off a delicious fluttering deep in her abdomen.

'Will I offend your sensibilities, Miss Lovejoy?' He arched one brow. 'I know it is not quite the done thing, but surely we may relax a few of the conventions after our recent...er...slightly *un*conventional encounters?'

'You need not be coy, Dominic—Liberty has told me how she called here to beard Papa in his den and mistook you for Alex.' Olivia giggled as she sat next to Liberty on the sofa and nudged her. 'You should be honoured—he only ever teases people he likes and they're mostly family. Oh! I know! You can be our honorary sister. I always wanted a sister!'

Chapter Twelve

Dominic tried to ignore the tension swirling in his gut. This had seemed a good idea at the time—an opportunity to spend a little time with Julius and Daisy before Father and Stepmother arrived, when his half-sister and half-brother, Christabel and Sebastian, would also demand his attention. Besides, he adored spending time with the little monkeys.

That Liberty Lovejoy would be here was entirely incidental. Wasn't it? She tempted him like no other woman of his acquaintance and—if he was wise, which he clearly wasn't—he should do all he could to avoid her. Yet here he was, concentrating on steadying his breathing as the subtle note of her perfume weaved through his senses. That picture of her with young Julius on her lap—her pensive, wistful expression—was now seared into his brain. His heart had twitched with longing as he took in the sight and, try as he might to replace her image with any of the ladies on that original shortlist, he simply could not imagine any of them dandling a child on their knee and allowing it to fiddle with their hair.

Mother, certainly, would never have tolerated such behaviour. She had been goddess-like to her three children—

a goddess they had all worshipped and done their utmost to please, forever seeking her praise. He thrust down those memories and the weight of duty, responsibility and expectation they evoked.

'Olivia.'

'Dominic?'

'By my calculations I have now spoken to Miss Lovejoy twice since entering this room, including asking her a number of direct questions, and she has yet to reply to any of them because you have rushed in to speak for her.'

He welcomed the familiar spark in his sister's eyes. 'Well, that is entirely your fault, Brother dear, for asking her such awkward questions in the first place! *I* am Liberty's hostess and it is my duty to protect her from feeling uncomfortable. You forget, she is not used to your teasing ways, Dom.'

'Good Lord, you haven't changed, Livvy! Four years wed and you are still the fiery brat you always were.'

Olivia's cheekbones sported two bright flags of colour and he regretted the words as soon as they were spoken. What was he? Sixteen years old again? Of course Olivia was still the same spirited girl and he prayed she always would be—she would not be the little sister he loved and cherished if marriage and motherhood changed her too much.

'Liv... I'm sorry! We do seem to slip back into that same old relationship when we get together, don't we?'

The colour in her cheeks faded and she grinned. 'I was saying much the same thing before the twins came down, wasn't I, Liberty?'

'You were indeed, Olivia.' Liberty's response was calm, with just the right touch of light amusement. 'And in answer to your query about your jacket, sir, please do so. I pledge myself to remain utterly unoffended by such an action.'

Dominic saw that their little spat had given Liberty a chance to collect herself. When she first became aware of him, a soft pink blush had washed across her skin and her velvety-blue eyes had widened and darkened as her lush lips parted. Her unguarded reaction had lasted a bare second, but her joyful expression had drawn a similar happy response from him. Then her expression had shuttered and it was apparent that the woman he had first met, whose feelings shone in her expressions, had changed in the time he had known her. Her features were no longer a window into her soul. He could not blame her—society and the *ton* were enough to make even the toughest-skinned person wary—but, damn it, he hated that he could no longer read her every thought.

Olivia's words resounded through his head. *An honorary sister*, indeed. Nothing could be further from the way he felt about Liberty Lovejoy. But he could, and must, view her as a family friend, such as Jane Colebrooke was—although he had never lusted after Jane in his entire life. He could cope with thinking of Liberty as a friend…just. But in no way could he view her as his sister.

He shrugged out of his jacket and joined the twins on the rug. He was soon lost in their game, pairing up the animals and marching them up the ramp into the ark, the faint murmur of conversation fading into the background, until he realised Liberty was standing up, clearly preparing to take her leave. He jumped to his feet and collected his jacket from the chair where he had laid it.

'Did a maid accompany you, Miss Lovejoy?'

She probably came alone. I wouldn't put it past her.

'No. My brother escorted me, sir. I wonder if a maid might walk with me back to Green Street, Olivia?'

She caught Dominic's eye and raised one challenging brow as if to say, *See? I can behave like a lady when I choose to.*

He bit back a grin. 'There's no need to bother one of the maids—might I offer to drive you home?' He batted away the inner warning that he was, again, playing with fire. He was merely being practical. Being a gentleman. 'I ordered my curricle brought round for four but, unless Olivia has changed the habits of a lifetime, I cannot see her being dressed and ready to go by then as it is already three minutes to the hour. Unless, of course, you no longer wish to drive in the Park this afternoon, Liv?'

'Heavens! Is that the time? Oh, I have enjoyed our time together this afternoon, Liberty…do say you will come again.

'And of course I still want to go to the Park, Dom. How else am I to properly meet your young ladies without calling upon them…and that would never do, would it?'

'No. It would not.'

A shudder racked Dominic at the very idea. As soon as any member of his family showed marked attention to any one of the names that were thought to be on his shortlist, the news would be on every gossipmonger's lips and he would soon find himself in a corner and honour-bound to make an offer. At least any attention he paid to Liberty was unlikely to be misconstrued, firstly because of her friendship with Olivia but, more importantly, because no one in the *ton* would imagine for one moment that such an unsuitable female would ever be included on his list.

'Well, Miss Lovejoy? Are you happy to accept my offer of escort?'

'Indeed I am, my lord. Thank you.'

Olivia said nothing but, at the gleam in her eyes as she looked from Dominic to Liberty and back again, a warning trickled down his spine. His sister was no fool—he must work even harder at masking his growing feelings for Liberty. As Olivia, Ruth and the twins headed upstairs after saying goodbye to Liberty, Dominic walked with her to the front door where Grantham waited.

'Your curricle arrived two minutes ago, my lord.' The butler opened the door.

'Thank you, Grantham.'

'They are a beautiful pair.' Liberty surprised Dominic by heading straight to the horses, being held by his groom, Ted. She looked them over with clear appreciation, then removed her glove and held her hand to each horse's nose in turn to allow them to snuffle at her palm and take in her scent. 'Very well matched. What are their names?'

'Thank you. Beau and Buck—they are a pleasure to drive. Very responsive.' He was proud of his bays, which he had purchased last year. 'Alex bred and trained them. Do you drive, Miss Lovejoy?'

She smiled up at him, and his heart soared. 'I have never driven anything other than our old cob at home. But I have a lovely riding mare.' Then she frowned. 'At least, she *is* lovely, but she is also now quite old. We left her behind in Sussex.'

With one accord they returned to the curricle. Dominic took Liberty's hand to help her into the vehicle, his fingers closing around hers. She hadn't replaced her glove and Dominic had not yet drawn his on and, as he registered the warmth of her smooth, soft skin his breath seized and he had to stifle the urge to haul her into his arms. He swallowed and released her hand as soon as she was in the curricle. He pulled on his gloves, willing his heartbeat and his body under control as he climbed up next to her.

Liberty nudged into him with her shoulder—the slightest of movements, but his heart lurched again at that contact. He looked down into her innocent expression. One golden brow arched.

'Do not forget to order your groom to jump up behind,' she whispered. Her lips curved into a delicious, teasing smile. 'You have your reputation to protect.'

His throat ached with suppressed longing, but he refused to yield to his base desires. Duty was what mattered, not physical needs. He smiled back. 'With what you already know of me, Berty, you cannot possibly imagine I would overlook such a crucial matter.'

'Berty?' She sounded outraged, but her eyes twinkled.

'Liberty is such a mouthful.' His loins instantly reacted to his unintentional double entendre.

'What is wrong with Libby?' She stared up at him, innocently, clearly having missed the meaning. 'Or Lib? That is what my family call me sometimes.'

'Oh, I couldn't possibly,' Dominic murmured. 'They are far too easily confused with Livvy and Liv, and I most definitely do *not* think of you as another sister, despite what Olivia said.'

Her cheeks bloomed pink. The curricle dipped as Ted climbed up behind and Dominic flicked the reins. They set off on the short drive to Green Street.

'Maybe I should be relieved that we cannot now talk without being overheard.'

Another teasing smile filled him with the urge to simply touch her mouth. With one fingertip. To test whether her lips were as soft and luscious as they looked….to trace their fullness…to slip his finger into that hot, moist… Blood flooded his groin and different urges took him in their hold. He wrenched his gaze from her mouth to her eyes, full of teasing laughter, battling to keep his expression blank.

'A good groom knows when to turn a deaf ear,' he said. 'Is that not right, Ted?'

'Beg pardon, milord? Were you speakin' to me? I didn' quite catch what you said.'

Liberty laughed, a delightful gurgling sound of pleasure. 'Oh, that is famous! Lord Avon, you, sir, are such a contradiction—the perfect lord whose servants are as well trained as his horses.'

'I prefer to describe my staff as loyal rather than well trained.'

'Loyal, indeed. What else, I wonder, have your servants failed to notice over the years, for fear of sullying your reputation?'

Their eyes met. And held. And the naked look of… *longing* in those velvety-blue eyes matched exactly what was in his heart. His voice when he answered her was husky.

'I wish I could lay claim to a wild, exciting parallel existence to this life but, alas, what you see before you is the whole.'

'What? No hidden depths? You disappoint me, sir.'

And the thought of disappointing her wrenched at him. He cleared his throat and, this time, his words emerged light and airy. Nonchalant. Exactly as they should sound.

'Nary a one, I'm afraid.'

Liberty fell silent. A sideways glance revealed a blush on her cheeks and her golden eyebrows drawn into a frown. Had she, like him, recognised the dangerous territory into which they had strayed? He drove around the corner into Green Street and the relief that flooded him took him by surprise. He had intended a light flirtation. He enjoyed Liberty's company, but this…this flirtatious repartee… It was dangerous. *Here* were the depths his life had so far lacked and his inner voice of caution was screaming at him to take care and not to venture so far that he could not return to the shallows.

He offered a change of subject and her relief was palpable. 'I am pleased you and Olivia seem destined to be friends.'

'I like her very much. I… I have not had many friends my own age. Gideon and the girls were always enough.'

That comment alone explained much about Liberty— she had devoted her life to her family. Was that why she fretted so about Gideon? The huge change in their lives must be as unsettling for her as it was for her brother. Their lives would never be the same again.

He reined Beau and Buck to a halt outside the Love-joys' house. 'Here we are.'

Ted ran to the horses' heads and Dominic leapt to the pavement to hand Liberty down. She placed her hand— gloved this time—into his. Without volition, his fingers closed around hers, pressing. Another blush coloured her cheeks and Dominic cursed himself for a weak-minded fool. What the hell was he playing at? When-

ever he was in Liberty Lovejoy's presence he seemed
to lose all vestige of self-control.

The second she reached the ground he released her
hand as though it were red-hot. He knocked on the door
and, as soon as it opened, he bowed.

'Thank you for driving me home, my lord.'

'It was my pleasure, Miss Lovejoy.'

And he meant it. He really did. It had been—it had
always been—a pleasure to spend time in her company.
But he must take care to avoid such tête-à-têtes in future. It was simply too dangerous and it would be Liberty's reputation that suffered. Not his.

Liberty removed her pelisse and bonnet and handed
them to Ethel, her thoughts in turmoil, matching the
bubbling confusion in her belly. Did it mean anything
that Dominic had come early to Beauchamp House,
knowing she would be there? Or was her presence neither here nor there and he had told the absolute truth—
that the only reason he called earlier than expected was
to spend time with the twins? Was her imagination running away with her—envisaging a happy ever after
where there could never be one, simply because she had
discovered that he was the man who stirred her blood
like no other—even Bernard? Because she had found
that, in addition to all his other attributes, Lord Avon
was also a kind and charitable gentleman?

Why, then, had he insisted on driving her home? Had
he been flirting with her, or was she naïve in thinking
there was a special warmth in his voice when he spoke
to her? He had called her Berty and the memory kindled
a glow inside her. He found her attractive, she knew,
but was his behaviour with her mere practised flirtation from a gentleman or did his feelings go deeper? He

enjoyed her company, and he was relaxed and informal with her in a way she never saw him behave with any of the ladies on his shortlist, but did *any* of that amount to anything other than wishful thinking on her part?

She could not decide. But, increasingly, she knew what she would like the answer to be.

'Mrs Mount is in the drawing room, miss,' said Ethel.

Liberty headed upstairs to the drawing room where she found Mrs Mount having a quiet doze in a chair by the fire. She awoke with a start as Liberty entered the room.

'Where are Hope and Verity?'

'They are riding in the Park. With Lord Wendover.'

'Gideon?' Liberty sat in the opposite chair. 'Do my ears deceive me? Do you mean to tell me he came back home after calling on Lady Twyford?'

She had been certain that was the last any of them would see of her brother until dinner that evening.

'Yes. He returned in a rush to inform us he had hired two horses from the livery stables and that your sisters were to get changed and be ready to ride out with him. He was most insistent. Verity believes he had arranged to meet up with Lady Emily in the Park and Hope and Verity will provide him with the perfect excuse to ride with her.'

'Oh, that is wonderful news. Lady Emily would be a splendid match—'

'Stop!' Mrs Mount leaned forward. 'I beg your pardon, my dear, but please do not get carried away. Gideon only met Lady Emily last night and he is still young.'

Liberty sighed. 'You are right. I cannot help but be happy she is distracting him from that horrid actress, though.'

Mrs Mount relaxed back with a relieved sigh. 'Now.

What about you, my dear? You must count yourself fortunate that Lady Olivia has taken a shine to you.'

'Fortunate? How so?'

'So there will be no repercussions from your... um...*unusual* encounters with Lord Avon, of course. He could scarcely cut his sister's friend—he is far too much the gentleman—and, to think, he not only danced with you last night, but with Hope and Verity, too! I always prayed they might catch his eye.'

She beamed with satisfaction and Liberty bit her tongue against telling her the real reason Dominic had danced with her sisters.

'Well, I do not see what is so very special about His Lordship,' she muttered, even though she knew exactly what was so very special about Dominic. But she would be mortified if anyone had the slightest suspicion of her growing feelings for him.

'And that attitude, miss, will get you nowhere in society.'

A blush heated Liberty's cheeks at Mrs Mount's reprimand. She had been hired to help Liberty and her sisters learn how to behave as well-brought-up young ladies should and Liberty was aware of the flaw in her own personality that prompted her to rebel against such strict mores.

'Whether you approve or not, Liberty, the heir to a dukedom will always command respect and be fêted and courted by those lower in precedence.' Mrs Mount's voice softened. 'Now, tell me all about your visit—did you meet the twins?'

'Oh, they are delightful! Olivia is besotted with them, but I cannot think I have helped her understand how raising twins is different to raising other children. She is so determined to be the perfect mother to them.'

'Well, I hope for their sake she is a better mother than her own proved to be.'

'Olivia's mother? Why?' Olivia's confidences about her childhood had piqued Liberty's interest. 'What was she like? Did you know her well?'

'The first Duchess? Why, yes, my dear. We were close in age and we made our debut together. She was three years older than Cheriton, you know. Oh, she was as selfish as they come and utterly arrogant, especially after becoming a duchess. She had not a thought for anyone or anything beyond her own selfish pleasures. Poor Cheriton. He married young…far too young…and all *she* wanted was the glamour and acclaim of the title. She had no interest in those poor children—she spent as much time as possible in London after Olivia was born. She could not bear to be "buried in the depths of the countryside" as she used to put it.' Mrs Mount huffed a laugh. 'Ironic, really, when you consider that's where she ended up—buried at Cheriton Abbey.'

'What happened?' Liberty could not help her curiosity. 'Did she die in childbirth?' That tragic fate befell so many women it seemed a reasonable assumption. Then a shiver chased across her skin as she recalled her parents and Bernard. 'Did she fall ill?'

'No, my dear.' Mrs Mount lowered her voice. 'She was *murdered*.'

'Murdered?' That was the last thing she expected to hear. A duchess, murdered? 'But…how?'

'No one knows, my dear. They say it was probably a passing vagrant. And, much as it pains me to speak ill of the dead, it was probably a blessing for those poor children and their father. Their aunt, Lady Cecily, raised them after that and it's a wonder they have all turned out as well as they have. Well, apart from Lord Alexander…he was ever a wild youth, but it does seem he has settled at long last.

'Now, tell me all about today, my dear. Has the Duke arrived yet?'

'Not yet—only Lady Olivia and her family are in residence at the moment but the staff are all bustling about preparing the house, so the Duke and Duchess and their children must be expected soon. And Lord Avon called while I was there.' She hadn't meant to mention him, but his name slipped past her lips quite without intention. 'He had arranged to drive Olivia in the Park, but came early to spend some time with the twins.'

'The Park?' Mrs Mount clapped her hands together. 'How wonderful… I do hope he will acknowledge your sisters! He is sure to do so after dancing with them last night. Oh, I do hope Gideon has chosen their mounts wisely, to show them off to best advantage!'

'Mrs Mount!'

'Yes, my dear?'

'I do not believe you. You criticise me for getting carried away with the possibilities for Gideon and yet you insist on imagining castles in the clouds when it comes to Hope and Verity's prospects.'

'It does not hurt to have ambition, my dear Liberty. Who knows what might happen should a man like Avon lose his heart? And your sisters are exceptionally pretty.'

Liberty ground her teeth in frustration. 'He drove me home this afternoon. Lord Avon, that is. In his curricle.'

And, again, she hadn't meant to say such a thing, but the words, and his name, were battering the inside of her head, desperate to be spoken. She held her breath, awaiting Mrs Mount's response.

'*Avon* drove you home? Good gracious…such condescension! Although you are, of course, his sister's friend so no doubt he felt under some obligation. But, still, what a feather in your cap, my dear—to be singled out and driven by such a notable whip.' Then her eyes narrowed and a slow smile stretched her lips. 'Especially after such a sought-after gentleman singled you out last night, to dance. Twice! And you had supper together!' Mrs Mount's voice shrilled with excitement. 'Oh!' She lowered her voice into a conspiratorial whisper. 'Has he *said* anything to you, my dear? Has he passed any hints?'

Exasperated, because she really wished she could say yes, Liberty said, 'No. He has said nothing. And I had supper with his brother, not him. As you quite rightly said, ma'am, I am his sister's friend and both Avon and Lord Alex were merely acting the gentleman. You told me yourself about Avon's list and Lord Alexander mentioned it last night…it appears to be common knowledge and Avon did not deny its existence.

'In fact, that is precisely the reason he is driving Olivia in the Park as we speak, because she insisted she wants to meet the ladies concerned before he makes his decision.'

A surge of energy sent Liberty to her feet. She crossed to the window, which overlooked the street, and peered out.

Who in their right mind would have a list of candidates for a wife? What about the heart? What of love? That emotion clearly had no place in Dominic's plans. She thought of the time he had compared her to Olivia… that protective care each of them held for their family. That was love…a different sort of love, maybe, but Dominic clearly did not completely dismiss the emotion. Could such a clinical choice of partner ever lead to happiness? It hadn't for his father, so it seemed.

She returned to her chair. 'You said Olivia's father married too young, Mrs Mount. Why did he do so? Did he fall in love?'

'Oh, no, my dear. Many more marriages back then were arranged affairs, you know. He was only eighteen and he married to please his ailing father. Margaret was three years his senior, but she was the daughter of a marquess—very suitable in that respect. She was one of the most selfish creatures I have ever met, although she put on a good show for Cheriton and, at eighteen, I dare say he did not know enough about human nature to see the danger signs.' She shook her head. 'She had affairs. Many affairs. And not always discreetly. She even played him false with his own cousin, although I'm not sure he ever knew about that.'

She sounded an awful woman. Poor Dominic, to have such a mother.

'What about the present Duchess? Olivia seems fond of her.'

'I do not know her well, but they say it was a love match and that the Duke is very happy, even though she was only a soldier's daughter. They wed five years ago now.' She sighed. 'Now *that* was a year for romance— first the Duke, then his brother Vernon and lastly their sister, Cecily. All in the same year, all love matches and all with unexpected and, some would say, unsuitable partners.' She studied Liberty, who felt a blush heat her skin. 'I wonder...?'

Liberty leapt to her feet again. She could not allow Mrs Mount to speculate. That way lay heartache, she knew, because if someone else began to think the unthinkable she just knew that her hopes would mushroom out of control. And she could not bear that. Lord Avon had his shortlist and her name was not on it. She did not possess the qualities he looked for in a bride and to hope he might change his criteria for a woman he only met for the first time less than a fortnight ago was stretching believability a little too far, even for her.

'Please excuse me, Mrs Mount. I must consult with Mrs Taylor on dinner tonight.'

She fled the room before she could be tempted to stay and hear what Mrs Mount was going to say.

Chapter Thirteen

Bond Street, as usual, was busy with members of the *ton* shopping, Liberty, her sisters and Mrs Mount among them. Liberty's heart was not really engaged in finding the perfect hat to go with Hope's new walking dress, but she'd realised that staying at home brooding over Dominic would be even worse than being forced to exclaim at each and every hat Hope tried on, only for her to then discard it as being not *precisely* what she wanted.

As they exited the third milliner's shop, however, her attention was grabbed by a high-pitched yelp and, half-hidden in a doorway, she caught sight of a burly man, wearing a bloodied apron, who had a squirming dog tight by the scruff of his neck as he raised his other arm. The thin stick in his hand swished audibly through the air and landed on the dog's back with a resounding crack. A scream split the air, and a bloodied welt appeared in the dog's pale golden fur.

Rage surged though Liberty. She raced to the man's side, grabbing his arm as he raised it once more.

'Stop that, you rogue!'

The man paused and eyed her with astonishment.

'Get your hands off me,' he growled. 'The dog's a thief and I'll learn him a lesson if it's the last thing I do.'

He wrenched his arm from her grip and lifted it again. The dog cringed, fear in its eyes.

'Liberty! Come away. Please.' Mrs Mount took Liberty's arm and tugged her from the doorway, away from the man and the cowering dog. 'Don't get involved,' she hissed. 'People are watching.'

The whistle of the stick cut through the air once more and the dog's scream this time was even more desperate. Gorge rose to clog Liberty's throat. She snatched her arm from Mrs Mount and rounded again on the brute. He was tall and wide, his face showing no emotion as he prepared to hit the dog again. She couldn't bear it. She didn't care who saw her. She thrust herself between man and dog and shoved at his chest with all her strength.

'Stop!' Fear and rage in equal measures sent her voice soaring a couple of octaves. 'You *will not* beat that poor animal!'

'An' 'oo are you to tell me what I may and may not do? That's my livelihood, that is.'

He gestured to the ground, to a half-mangled joint of meat. 'I chased that mangy runt from my shop an' now I've got 'im bang to rights. He won't be nabbin' meat off anyone again. Not when I've finished with 'im.'

He shoved Liberty aside and she stumbled back, her shoulder and arm colliding painfully with the hard edge of the door recess. The man raised his arm again and she pushed her hands against the brickwork and propelled herself forward, again putting her body between the two in a desperate effort to spare the dog.

'I wonder what's going on over there?'

Hugo paused outside the doorway to Angelo's Fenc-

ing Academy and drew Dominic's attention to a crowd
gathering further along the street. Dominic shrugged.

'Some altercation or other, it looks like. Nothing that
need—'

He stopped speaking as he recognised Hope and Ver-
ity clutching one another on the periphery of the crowd.
He didn't know, not for certain, but something told him
Liberty was in there, somewhere. In the thick of it.

'I'll join you directly,' he called over his shoulder as
he set off at a run towards the crowd. He hadn't even
covered half the distance when he realised Hugo was
by his side.

'You don't get to have *all* the fun, Dom,' he panted,
with a grin.

Dominic shouldered through the crowd in time to
see a huge brute of a fellow shove Liberty against a
wall and raise a stick high. He took in the scene in an
instant—the pain and shock on Liberty's face as she
collided with the brickwork and the cowering, bloodied
dog, its neck held fast by a huge hand. He recognised
her utter determination as she thrust herself away from
the wall. Rage boiled and he leapt forward even as Liberty pushed herself between the dog and that stick. He
thrust his arm over Liberty's shoulder and grabbed the
stick just as it began a downward trajectory.

The brute struggled, trying desperately to free the
stick from Dominic's grip, as he glared down at Liberty and the dog she shielded. He hadn't even spared a
glance at Dominic, he was so intent on his target. He
didn't even appear to realise that, if he continued, he
would hit Liberty.

'Leggo!' Spittle flew from his lips as he roared his rage.

Seeing the other man's uncontrolled fury just made
Dominic more determined to control his own temper.

'I will take that.' The man's gaze snapped to Dominic. 'Or is it your intention to hit a lady in broad daylight, in front of witnesses?'

The man paled and gulped, and his grip on the stick loosened. Dominic took it from him and handed it to Hugo, standing to one side of him. Then he stepped in front of the bastard who had dared to threaten Liberty and he bunched his lapels in his fists. 'Don't you *ever...*' he spoke softly, '...let me see you again. Or the pain that dog suffered will be nothing to what I inflict upon you. Do you understand?'

The man's mouth twisted. 'It *stole* from me, m'lord. A man has to make a living.'

He felt a hand tug at his arm.

'Leave this to me, Miss Lovejoy.'

She took no notice, though. Almost before the words had left his lips she was nudging him aside so she could confront the brute.

'You are a despicable specimen of a human being.' She glared up at him. 'But even disgusting types like you need to make a living. Here.' She cast a handful of coins at his feet. 'The meat is paid for. Now, give me the dog.'

Dominic released his lapels and the man, with a snarl, thrust the pitiful dog at Liberty, scrabbled for the coins and then disappeared into the slowly dispersing crowd. In the absence of any means of holding the dog, Liberty grabbed its scruff, crooning to it in a low voice. Dominic placed a hand on her shoulder.

'He's gone, Miss Lovejoy. You can leave it now.'

She looked up at him, her eyes swimming. 'Look at him. The poor creature. He is skin and bone. I *cannot* leave him to fend for himself.'

'But what do you mean to do with it? It is filthy and no doubt riddled with fleas.'

'It really is not your concern, is it, my lord?' She regained her feet, but had to remain half-bent in order to keep hold of the animal, twisting her head to look up at him. 'I am grateful for your help in seeing off that scoundrel, but if I choose to keep this sweet little dog then I shall. I do need some way of securing him, though.'

She gazed around, then her eyes lit up.

'Be pleased to hold him a minute, sir, if you will.' She thrust the dog at Dominic, who had little choice but to comply. Next thing, she had removed her bonnet and was pulling at a ribbon that was threaded through her lustrous hair. 'This will do nicely, I believe.' She smiled happily as she thrust it at Dominic. 'Would you be so good as to tie it around his neck while I put my bonnet back on?'

Dominic registered the sound of a muffled snort and he relieved his feelings by glaring at his brother-in-law. But he did tie the blue ribbon around the dog's neck. It left a very short length with which to lead the dog, however. Liberty frowned as she studied the dog.

'Liberty.' Her chaperon, Mrs Mount, took Liberty by the elbow. 'We *cannot* take that filthy creature home with us.'

'Of course we can, my dear ma'am. Why ever not? Once he is bathed and his coat brushed, he will be quite respectable and he really does have the sweetest expression, do you not agree?'

'My lord?' Mrs Mount gazed at Dominic beseechingly.

Dominic looked down at the dog, who returned his look with a curl of his lip and an ingratiating grin. Then he looked at Liberty, taking in her outward bluster of confidence, but that same hint of vulnerability in her eyes that unmanned him every time he saw it.

'I cannot see what harm it will do.' Liberty's smile was his reward. 'Allow me to hail a hackney—that will make it easier to get the animal home. Hold him, will you, Hugo?' He thrust the short length of ribbon at his brother-in-law, who grinned and stuck his hands behind his back.

'*I* shall hail a cab,' he said. 'You're doing such a fine job there, Dom. I should hate to let the little ru—*darling* slip!'

After they had deposited the Lovejoy sisters and their chaperon at their home, Dominic and Hugo elected to walk together back to Beauchamp House. Dominic was soon aware of Hugo's amused scrutiny.

'Something on your mind, Hugo?'

'Just wonderin' where the lovely Liberty fits into your future plans, Dom.'

'Nowhere.'

Hugo shrugged, strolling on without further comment, swinging his cane.

'I admire the way she takes a stand for what is right,' Dominic said eventually, goaded by his brother-in-law's continuing silence and his mildly sceptical expression.

'Rushing in where angels fear to tread?'

'Not at all! She reminds me of Olivia, as it happens.'

Hugo cocked an eyebrow and his lips curved. 'Quite.'

'Are you calling your wife a fool?'

'Far from it—but you have to admit she used to act first and worry about the consequences afterwards. She has…er…mellowed somewhat in that regard. Since the twins. But she has *always* had her family's backs and still does.'

'That is what I admire about Miss Lovejoy.'

'But that, my dear Dominic, was a stray dog.'

'It is to her credit she did not ignore the suffering of a fellow creature, as so many others do.'

'Something like you and your orphans?'

Dominic's stomach clenched in warning. Oh, Hugo was a sly one…he could see exactly where this conversation was leading. He knew his brother-in-law well enough to know he would not continue to badger Dominic once he had replied to that initial question about Liberty, not like Olivia or Alexander might—questions that would inevitably lead to an argument. Hugo was far more subtle, skirting around the same subject until a less cautious man might let too much information slip. Well, he'd have no luck here.

'*Nothing* like that.'

Hugo smiled and Dominic promised himself he'd make him suffer next time they sparred at Jackson's.

They reached Beauchamp House and Dominic accepted Hugo's invitation to come in to visit Olivia. He very soon wished he hadn't, although at least Olivia didn't plague him about Liberty Lovejoy. No. *She* was far more interested in his blasted list…and how he wished he had never written the damned thing! Or at least had taken more care that nobody but he ever set eyes on it.

'Have you thought about Miss Whitlow? Why is she not on your list?'

'Unsuitable. Her father's a reckless gambler.'

'And only a viscount,' Hugo pointed out.

'Lady Elisa Critchlow? Oh! I know! Lady Frederica Sutton.'

'No and no. You're like a dog with a bone, Livvy,'

Dominic growled. 'Why can't you accept this is my business and my decision?'

'Talkin' of dogs—'

'Hu-u-u-u-go…'

Hugo opened his eyes wide at Dominic's growled warning. 'I merely thought the tale might distract my wife and stop her throwing an endless succession of names at you. It was, after all, merely a diverting interlude of little importance.' He arched his brows. 'Was it not?'

'You know it was.' But Hugo had a point…it *would* divert Olivia from the subject of his damned list. 'Your friend Miss Lovejoy rescued a dog that was being beaten. It was nothing. Over almost before it began.'

'With your intervention,' said Hugo.

'I shall ask Liberty to tell me all about it,' said Olivia, somewhat absently. 'Now, Dominic. What about Miss Fothergill?' She frowned, tapping one finger to her lips, then sat bolt upright. 'Of course! Jane Colebrooke! She would be perfect! So sweet-natured!'

'Good God, no! It would be like marrying my sister! And that thought, at this moment in time, fills me with abject horror. Olivia…if you do *not* stop pestering me I shall never call on you again. Or are you *trying* to drive me away?'

Olivia leapt up from the sofa to perch on the arm of Dominic's chair. She ruffled his hair and he jerked his head away. What did she think he was? A small boy to be humoured? He was the eldest, dammit. *He* had always been the sensible one; the one they listened to. Her arm slid behind his neck and she hugged him to her.

'I'm sorry. I don't mean to plague you. But I'm worried, Dom. I can't picture any of those women in among us. The rest of the family, I mean. I know Papa is a duke, but the thought of how some of them might behave with Aunt Thea, or with Zach, sends shivers right through me.' Her voice betrayed the strength of her feelings. 'We Beauchamps always stick together—I couldn't *bear* the thought that anyone might drive a wedge between us.'

'You're being overdramatic, Liv.'

But his anger dissipated at her words—he knew how much the family meant to Olivia. And to him, too. But that would not stop him doing his duty as he saw it and as he had promised Mother. *Make me proud, my Son.* The memories, as ever, weighted him down.

Duty. Expectation. Responsibility.

Except recently they had also brought doubts creeping into his thoughts. Undermining his determination. And he shied away from examining those doubts too closely, for fear of what they might reveal.

'You know me better than to think I would marry anyone likely to upset any member of the family. That is the reason I am taking my decision so seriously.'

'But what is so wrong with marrying for love? We did. Uncle Vernon and Aunt Cecily did. Even *Papa* did.'

'Father only married for love because the succession was already secure through his marriage to our mother.'

Olivia pouted. 'I suppose I cannot argue with that, but I still think you are making a mistake. When do you think you will decide?'

'Soon.' His spirits dipped as he said the words: 'I shall speak to Father when he arrives and, as long as he has no objection to her family, that will be it.'

His life sorted. It was what he wanted. It was what he had always planned.

* * *

'Romeo!'

A sleek head emerged from behind the floor-length curtain that, a moment ago, was being shaken with vigour, accompanied by ferocious growls. Liberty marched across the room and took her new pet by the collar. It was the day after she had rescued him and already she doubted her wisdom in keeping him. Not that she would admit that to the rest of the family, or to Mrs Mount, who were all extremely vocal in their condemnation of both her actions yesterday and her stubbornness in bringing him home. It had taken her two hours to bathe him and, by the time she had finished, the kitchen was in uproar and Mrs Taylor was prostrate on a chair in the corner, her apron over her face. It did little to muffle her shrieks. They had dined on cold meat, bread and cheese last night.

The name, Romeo, had popped into her head when Gideon asked what the dog's name was and the resulting hilarity from her entire family had been enough to stop Liberty changing her mind. Even though the name, she silently agreed, did not suit him in the slightest. He was a rascal. Up to every kind of mischief, having already chewed a rug, one of Gideon's slippers and now attacking the curtains.

Romeo gazed up at her, his brown eyes innocent and full of adoration, his head, with its two permanently upright ears, cocked to one side and his tail, tightly curled over his back, waggling his entire bottom. Liberty's heart melted. She dropped to her knees and hugged his thin body close. And then, without warning, she was crying into his soft golden coat; sobbing, her arms tightening around him as he wriggled, trying to reach her face and lick the tears from her cheeks.

'I must be cursed, Romeo. Bernard died and now there's Dominic—so far out of my reach he might as well be a prince.'

She hugged the dog closer, as the agony of unrequited love clawed at her. Twice she had loved and twice lost. And now she felt she was losing Gideon as well.

'I miss him, Romeo. I thought nothing could weaken the bond we shared, but now I don't know how to mend it. I *hate* London.' She'd been content before they came here. Numb, but content. 'I wish we'd never come here.'

'Liberty?'

She froze and desperately gulped back her sorrow as Gideon came into the room and sat on the floor next to her. He handed her his handkerchief and put his arms around her, pulling her close.

'Don't cry, Sis. You *never* cry.' She hid her face against his chest and hot tears flowed anew. 'I heard what you said. This is my fault.'

She shook her head, but he took no notice. 'Please don't cry. I know I've been selfish. I'm so sorry—I never thought how it must bring it all back to you, being in London again. Look.' He tilted her face up, his expression serious. 'I don't deny all this went to my head at first, but I will behave better. I promise. Our bond is not broken. It will never break, but it *will* change. It is inevitable. You do see that, don't you?'

Liberty nodded, then dried her face on his handkerchief.

'And I'll say no more about the dog. I promise. I can always buy new slippers and I'll make sure the others know he's welcome to stay.'

'Th-thank you.'

She bit her lip against the confession that her tears were not entirely about Gideon and not at all about the arguments over Romeo. It was no use admitting the real cause, because no one could help her and her family's pity would be far more painful than enduring her heartbreak alone.

Gideon handed Liberty a sealed note. 'Lady Olivia has sent a message—her footman is waiting for your reply.'

'Thank you.'

Liberty broke the seal.

'Olivia has asked if I would care to join her to promenade in the Park this afternoon,' she told Gideon.

'Shall you go?'

'Yes.'

Her spirits lifted even as anticipation and hopelessness warred in her mind—Dominic was likely to be in the Park at that hour, too, but he would no doubt be discreetly courting one, or more, of his contenders. Anticipation won that battle. Any glimpse, any contact, was better than none. And she did enjoy Olivia's company—she would help keep Liberty from chasing impossible dreams.

'I'll escort you there if you like,' said Gideon.

'You are not riding today?' Liberty asked as she headed for the small writing desk to reply to Olivia.

'Not today.'

'Then I accept. Thank you.' Liberty penned a quick acceptance to Olivia, agreeing to meet her in the Park at four o'clock.

'Maybe we could ride in the Park together one afternoon soon?'

Liberty laughed. 'Only if you can hire me a better beast than the ones Hope and Verity ended up with. They told me all about it.'

'I'll see what I can do,' Gideon said. 'They *were* a

poor couple of plodders…bad enough for our sisters, but hardly suited to a rider of your ability.' Gideon held out his hand. 'I'll take that to Lady Olivia's man for you.'

Pleasure at his compliment warmed Liberty as she handed over the folded note. 'Thank you.'

An hour later, Liberty walked to the Park with Gideon and met Olivia, as arranged, just inside the gates.

'I thought you might have brought your new dog,' Olivia said with a smile as they strolled among the crowds. 'Hugo told me all about it and how you rescued him from that cruel brute.'

Liberty gazed around. Some ladies did indeed have dogs on leads, or in their carriages.

'I am not certain Romeo is quite respectable enough for promenading in the Park,' she said.

'Romeo? Is that his name? Oh, I cannot wait to meet him. And don't worry whether he's respectable enough. You have every right to walk your dog here. It doesn't matter what anyone else thinks.'

Spoken like a true duke's daughter.

'Maybe I shall.'

A few paces further on they met Dominic, Lady Sybilla on his arm. Liberty's heart sank and jealousy clawed her. She curtsied, Dominic bowed and Olivia and Sybilla inclined their heads graciously.

'Such a pleasant afternoon for a walk,' said Sybilla.

'Indeed,' Olivia responded.

'Mama and I had the intention of driving around the carriageway, but Lord Avon persuaded me to walk with him instead and Mama gave her permission. Is Lord Hugo not accompanying you this afternoon, Lady Olivia?'

'As you see, he is not,' Olivia replied gravely. 'He is otherwise engaged, I am afraid.'

'That is regrettable.' A slight smile touched Lady Sybilla's lips. 'However, one cannot expect one's husband to dance attendance upon one *all* of the time, can one?'

Liberty risked a glance at Dominic. His face was impassive, but his silver eyes betrayed a hint of resignation.

'No, indeed,' Olivia agreed.

'We ought perhaps to keep moving, Lady Sybilla,' said Dominic. 'It would not do to catch a chill.'

'Good heavens, no.' She tinkled a laugh. 'That would indeed be unfortunate this early in the Season.' She inclined her head again. 'Good afternoon to you both, Lady Olivia; Miss Lovejoy.'

'Oh, dear.' Olivia tucked her arm through Liberty's as they strolled away. 'Although my brother is nothing but discreet, I do fear he is now angling towards Sybilla Gratton as first choice.'

Dominic's list was the very last thing Liberty wished to dwell on, but at the same time the subject drew her back like a magnet.

'I thought his preference was for Lady Caroline?'

'Her attitude after that business between your sister and Bridlington at the Twyfords' ball changed his mind, I believe.'

'I see.' Liberty was glad Dominic had seen through Caroline, but she knew very little about Lady Sybilla other than she was the eldest daughter of the Duke of Wragby and she always appeared perfectly poised and calm. In other words, perfect for Dominic's bride. 'You do not approve?'

'I do not. She is like a...like a statue carved out of

ice.' Olivia huffed in disgust. 'I have never seen a natural expression on her face nor heard an unconsidered word leave her lips. Not that I have known her long, for her family were late coming up to town, but still… Poor Dominic will be frozen out of bed by that one.' She gasped and clapped her hand over her mouth. 'Oops. I apologise. I should not talk to you like that. I keep forgetting you are unmarried.'

Liberty couldn't help but laugh. 'I am not so easily shocked, Olivia. But you cannot deny she meets all of your brother's requirements. She's the daughter of a duke and her upbringing, manners and behaviour are impeccable.'

'She is…oh, I don't know! She is so false, somehow. I wonder if she even knows what joy is? How will she ever make him happy?'

'I don't believe his own happiness features very highly on your brother's list of requirements.'

'But it *should*. Oh, Liberty… I don't how I shall do it but, somehow, I must find a way to persuade him to think again, even though I know very well he will not listen to me.' Olivia swished her closed parasol in a gesture of frustration. 'Not one of them is right for him, but he is so stubborn and he will not listen to sense…he just accuses me of meddling! But all I want is for him to be happy, as I am with my Hugo. But it is like Alex says…once Dominic has set his mind on a course of action he is the very devil to divert from it.'

'But…' Liberty ignored her inner voice that shrieked at her to change the subject. 'But…what if he, say, met someone and fell in love?'

'Hah! You don't know my brother and his…his… *blinkered*ness! He believes the wife of a future duke should be chosen with the head, not the heart. He will marry for the sake of the Dukedom, not for himself.'

'Could your father not talk to him, if you ask him to?'

'I doubt Papa will interfere,' said Olivia gloomily. 'His whole life, Dominic has done his utmost to be the perfect son and the perfect heir—constantly aware of his responsibility as Papa's heir. If Papa was to say *Don't marry Lady X, marry Lady Y*, Dominic would do just that to please Papa. *That's* not choosing with his heart. And Papa knows he would do it, too. So he won't risk interfering. Oh…how I wish Aunt Cecily were here. *She* might talk some sense into Dom, but she and Zach aren't coming for another three weeks at least. It'll be too late by then.

'No. I don't know how I shall contrive it, but I must try. *Someone* has to do *something*.' She lapsed into a brooding silence before adding, 'Oh, and talking of Dominic… Hugo and I are going to visit Westfield to-morrow. Would you care to join us?'

'I would love to—as long as your brother will not object to my accompanying you?'

'Why should he? Hugo is happy for you to accompany us and I don't suppose Dominic will even be there. He'll be too busy courting his blasted list of perfect brides.'

Chapter Fourteen

The following afternoon, Dominic entered the school-room at Westfield where Mrs Whittaker was supervising the children at their lessons. He pulled up a low chair next to Tommy, who he knew struggled with his reading. Westfield prided itself on teaching both letters and numbers to the children in its care—not to make scholars of them, but to prepare them to become useful members of society, able to earn their living. And that was where Dominic and Felicity were invaluable, in helping to place the older children in positions with tradesmen or in households where they had the opportunity to better themselves with hard work. But Dominic also loved to spend time helping the individual children when he could—and, just at this moment, it was exactly what he needed to take his mind off his dilemma.

The past few days had been thoroughly dispiriting. He had spent time with all five ladies from his original list and the only thing he was certain of was that he was less sure of his ultimate decision now than he had been a week ago. But speculation in society was rife and he would look a dithering fool if he did not proceed when the talk was of nothing else. And yet he still hesitated over making that final, irreversible decision.

Make me proud, my Son. You were born to be the Duke...never disgrace your position in society...the eyes of the world will be on you. Judging you. Never let them see weakness.

His mother's strictures when he was a boy. The demands he had striven to obey as a boy, desperate for her love and approval...the same demands that had driven him to follow his duty all his life, ever conscious of his responsibility to his heritage, his mother's memory and to the family name.

But, also, the gentleman in him rebelled against insulting the ladies on his list with the implication that not one of them was up to his standards. He was eager to set up his nursery—that was the one bright, hopeful thing in this mess—and he knew he'd be in a worse position if he delayed until later in the year, or even until next Season. The same names would be on any list he drew up, only now they would be aware of his reluctance. And the name he longed to include—Liberty Lovejoy—would still not be on his list. Her maternal grandfather would still be a coal merchant.

You are the Marquess of Avon. You will be Duke of Cheriton one day, and your son and your son's son. That is your destiny. Do not allow the weakness of base desires to contaminate the bloodline—it is your duty to keep it pure.

His father would arrive in town within a fortnight. By then, the decision *would* be made. That had been his plan from the beginning of the Season when he had been keen to get on with his selection and to start his own family. But now he simply felt numb as his well-ordered plans appeared to fragment around him.

He pushed his worries aside and pointed to the word *apple* written on the slate.

'Try again,' he said.

Tommy scowled down at the slate. He'd not long been at Westfield, having been referred by the magistrates' court after being arrested as a pickpocket...his first offence.

'Sound out each letter...you know the sounds they make, Tommy. Come on. You can do this. I have faith in you.'

He barely registered the sound of the door opening until he heard Peter Whittaker—who owned and ran Westfield with his wife, Jane—say, 'And this is the schoolroom.'

Dominic glanced around, then shot to his feet as he saw Liberty, her eyes huge and riveted on him. He felt the colour build in his face and he gritted his teeth as he struggled to control his suddenly erratic breathing and to keep the smile in his heart from reaching his lips.

'Good afternoon, Miss Lovejoy.' He bowed. 'It is a pleasure to see you again.'

He nodded at Hugo and Olivia—whom he had expected—and who followed Liberty into the room.

'I invited Liberty to come with us.' Olivia smiled happily. 'I knew you would not object and she is very interested in Westfield.'

Is she indeed?

He was somewhat gratified to see Liberty's blush. At least it wasn't just him who felt awkward. But he also caught a glint of surprise in her eyes...she hadn't expected him to be here? Or was her surprise that he was helping teach the children?

'Why should I object?'

Olivia crossed the room to him. 'Well, you are so very close-chested about this sort of thing, Dom, you know you are. Does Lady Sybilla know of your connection with Westfield?'

Beyond Olivia, he could see Hugo questioning Peter as Liberty listened intently.

'Why would I mention it to Lady Sybilla?' How did Olivia know Sybilla had been his favourite until his current state of indecision? He'd taken such care not to single out any one lady more than another. 'Or to anyone else, come to that?'

'Why indeed? Your Lady Sybilla has about as much compassion in her as that statue of Venus in the British Museum—I cannot see her ever sharing your interest in the welfare of these poor children, Dom.'

Dominic bit back his frustration.

'Shouldn't you go and listen to Mr Whittaker, Livvy? I thought Hugo brought you here to find out about Westfield, didn't he? Not to plague me about that dam—dratted list.'

'Of course he did, silly! I didn't even know you would be here. I'll see you later.'

With a quick smile, she returned to the others, where Peter was explaining the workings of the school and what they hoped to achieve for their children. Dominic returned his attention to Tommy and his reading.

Finally, realising Tommy's concentration was drifting, Dominic stood up and realised, with a start of surprise, that although Peter's voice had long since fallen silent and he had assumed the entire group had left the schoolroom, Liberty was still there, crouching by the side of another, younger, lad, and helping him with *his* reading. His heart lurched as she smiled up at him.

'Little Ronnie here is doing very well, Lord Avon, but I think he is growing a little weary. Would you mind…?'

She reached out to him and he took her dainty hand in his. He helped her to rise, stifling the urge to press his lips to her palm, and released it the second she gained her feet.

'Thank you. I am grateful you are here, for my legs had grown quite stiff with crouching down like that and I feared a most inelegant lurch to my feet.'

Her smile twinkled in her eyes.

'I was unaware you were still in the room.'

'Mr Whittaker offered Hugo and Olivia a tour of the place, but I preferred to remain here, with the children.' She hesitated. Then touched his arm. 'This is admirable…that both you and Lady Stanton have been involved in this place for so long. I…' She paused before continuing, 'It's not what I would ever have expected of…'

'Of a man like me?' He didn't wait for her reply. A glance at the room showed the children paying more attention to them than to their lessons. 'Come. Let us leave Mrs Whittaker to teach in peace. We are disrupting her lesson.' He sent a smile across the room to Peter's wife, then ushered Liberty out into a passage and towards the entrance hall, where the afternoon sun sent beams of coloured light through the stained-glass windows either side of the front door. 'We can wait here for the others—or we can go and find them if you prefer?'

'No.' She stared at him, a light of calculation in those beautiful midnight-blue eyes of hers. Her throat rippled as she swallowed. 'There is something I should like to say to you.'

So serious. A shiver of disquiet rippled across the skin of his back.

'I… I…'

He moved closer, breathing in her scent. Roses—they no longer exclusively recalled his childhood and his mother but, increasingly, brought the image of Liberty Lovejoy into his thoughts.

'It is not like you to be hesitant, Berty. I thought you were unafraid of any subject, or any man.'

She sucked in a breath. 'It is about your list.'

He felt his forehead bunch. 'What about it?'

'I…' She paused. Gold-flecked midnight-blue eyes searched his and then her lips set in a determined line. 'I am worried about the…the…singlemindedness of your plan.'

'My plan is actually none of your concern.' He heard the finality in his tone, sensed the barrier rise up between them. 'Do you not believe me capable of making the right decision?'

'I just feel… I am worried…' A frustrated growl rattled in her throat. 'Surely by sticking so rigidly to this list of yours, you are limiting your choice of bride?'

'But that is the idea. It is all about finding the perfect bride.'

She frowned at him. A puzzled frown, not angry. 'But why not just choose the lady you like best?'

He set his jaw, feeling his own frown deepen. 'What do you mean?'

Liberty sighed, a gust of exasperation. 'Exactly what I say. Who—do—you—like—best?'

He tensed. 'That is neither here nor there. Personal taste doesn't come into it.'

She didn't understand. How could she possibly understand? This was his destiny. His duty. He was the Duke's heir.

'But…it is madness! The lady you choose… Dominic…you will be bound to her. For ever. Surely you want to be happy?'

'That is not how our world works. Many people marry for convenience.'

'Olivia and Hugo did not. Nor did the rest of your family, from what Olivia has said.'

A suspicion seized him. 'Did my sister put you up to this?'

'No! No, of course not. Although I do know she is worried about you, too.'

'No one needs to worry about me. My life is under control. *My* control.'

Then why haven't you decided yet? Why do you still hunger after what you cannot have?

He thrust down that inner voice.

'And in answer to your question, the rest of my family are not in my shoes. *I* am my father's heir. He married my mother for the future of the Dukedom, to keep it secure for the generations to come. It is my destiny…my *duty*…to do the same. Happiness does not come into it.'

'But that is so sad. It sounds a lonely life to me.'

He shrugged and could see his indifference infuriated her. But it really did not matter to him—any one of those ladies on his list would do.

'What do you actually want from this marriage, Dominic?'

'Me?' He paused, pondering her question. 'I want to do my duty. To do what is right for the title and for my father. And I am ready to start a family. I want my children to grow up close in age to Olivia's twins and to my father's second family and my little cousins.'

'So you will choose duty over happiness?'

'There is no reason for me to be unhappy once I make my choice.'

'Dominic…' his name on her lips and the hand she rested on his chest as she gazed up at him sent his silly heart tumbling '…please…at least consider other young ladies in addition to your shortlist.'

'Like you?' His voice rasped. The unfairness of that question shocked him, but that did not stop the rest of it from spilling out. 'Or maybe you still harbour hopes for your sisters?'

She snatched her hand away and stepped back, hurt in her eyes. 'That is not what I thought for one moment. I know only too well that neither I nor my sisters match your requirements. Dominic… I am speaking to you now as your *friend*. At least, I hope we are friends?'

He raised his hand to the back of his neck and rubbed. He craved more than friendship with this woman. But it could never be. And he should have known better than to accuse her of self-interest. He had seen her passion for protecting those she cared about, from her brother to a stray dog. And she cared for *him*, too. She felt that same connection between them that he was trying so hard to resist.

Of course she would want to protect him from making what she saw as a mistake. He should expect no less.

'I apologise. That accusation was unjustified. Yes, we are friends and I value it.'

'Then, as your friend, *please* think again about your choice of bride. I don't believe any of those on your shortlist will make you a comfortable wife.'

'Comfortable?' He huffed a laugh. 'I do not seek a comfortable wife, Liberty. I seek a suitable wife. There is a world of difference.'

'And there is a world of difference between a suitable match on paper and the reality of marriage to that same person.' She laid her hand upon his sleeve. 'Please reconsider. There is nowhere as lonely as a poor marriage. Make certain you have at least something in common with your bride.'

'We'll have the most important thing in common,' he growled. 'Breeding.'

She shook her head and sighed. 'I can say no more.'

A door opened at the far end of the hall and Hugo and Olivia emerged.

'Do you go to the Attwoods' ball tonight?' Liberty asked Dominic as the others joined them.

The evening was mild for April. Afterwards, Liberty used that as an excuse for what happened at the Attwoods' ball. If it had been cool, she would never have ventured alone on to the terrace instead of going to supper. There were a few others out there, taking the air, but she did not approach them, preferring her own company. One by one, they returned inside, but she had no wish to indulge in more polite conversation. She sighed, propped her hands on the stone balustrade and gazed up at the stars. Somewhere, up there, Bernard was watching her, wishing her well. She was sure of it even though, with every year that passed, his memory faded—his features more indistinct; his voice more silent; his touch... She shivered, pushing that memory away. But that old guilt persisted. That nagging feeling she might have saved them, if only she had done more.

His scent alerted her to his presence and she turned. His features were in shadow as he stood close. Almost too close.

'I neglected to ask you earlier. How is that dog?'

'Romeo? He is—'

She fell silent as he erupted into laughter. 'Romeo?

You could not give that mongrel a more inappropriate name if you tried!'

Still shaky after her memories of Bernard, she shoved at his chest. 'Do *not* mock me!' She pushed past him, heading for the French window and the ballroom beyond. As she reached for the handle, Dominic grabbed her wrist, bringing her to an abrupt halt.

'Don't go!'

She would not look at him. 'Why not?'

He tugged her to the side, away from the window and out of the patch of light that spilled on to the terrace and into the shadow of the house wall. He turned her to face him and, his free hand on her shoulder, he backed her against the wall. The bricks were hard and cool through the silk of her gown, but she was anything but cold as her stomach flipped and heat spiralled through her. He towered above her—dark, strong, masculine—the trace of his spicy cologne mingling with the scent of wine and brandy on his breath. He moved closer, his body against hers, all that hard, solid muscle...all that strength...all that power... Her breathing hitched and her lips parted as she desperately sucked in a new breath.

His head bent towards her as his hands slid lower to settle on her hips. It was too dark to decipher his expression, but his tattered breathing punctuated the silence of the night air and his thudding heartbeat vibrated through her.

'Liberty...'

Warm breath feathered across her face and the ache in his voice tore into her heart. She reached up to touch his mouth...those fascinating, sensual lips she had fantasised about kissing. Her forefinger traced his bottom lip and she craved...oh, she craved... Her fingers splayed and her hand slipped up and around his cheek, learning the shape of that sculpted cheekbone, tracing the curve of his ear and pushing into the thick softness of his midnight-dark hair.

With a tortured groan, he slid his hands around her, hauling her away from the harsh unyielding bricks at her back, crushing her against his sculptured heat, his hands cupping her bottom, lifting. His lips captured hers, demanding as his tongue plunged into her mouth. Helpless to resist, she returned thrust for thrust, relishing every moment of that stormy kiss. Her arms wrapped around him, clinging, as that initial passionate desperation eased, as the movement of their lips slowed and gentled, as their murmurs of appreciation mingled in the night air...until the sound of the musicians resuming play in the ballroom ended their kiss.

Dominic's tight embrace eased, his hands gliding soothingly up her back as she regained her balance. He rested his forehead against hers, his chest heaving even as Liberty, too, struggled to catch her breath. Eventually, he raised his head and she caught the glitter of his silver-grey eyes as their gazes met. And held.

Frustration tangled her stomach into knots. Nothing had changed. Nothing *could* change. Not unless *Dominic* changed and turned away from what he had grown up to believe was his duty. And, unless that miracle happened, Liberty could never be more to him than...

'Just friends?'

'Friends.' His eyes bored into hers, sending waves of longing crashing through her. 'It is all we can ever be.'

Regret coloured his tone, but also resolve. Could she accept his decision, even though it broke her heart?

'I... I should not have kissed you.' His fingers brushed her cheek. 'It was self-indulgent and I am sorry.'

'I am also at fault.' The blame was equally theirs.

They were both grown-ups. He had not forced her. 'We shall forget it happened.'

She gathered every vestige of strength she could find and stepped aside, away from his warmth and his strength. She turned from him and returned to the ballroom.

She had survived worse, although it would be hell watching him with another woman. Especially when she fully believed he was heading towards disaster. Without volition, her eyes swept the ballroom until she had seen each one of his shortlist, but her worried gaze lingered on Lady Sybilla. Olivia believed she was now his preferred option—*option! How cold that sounds*—and of all of them, she was the one Liberty knew the least about. Oh, she knew the public guise, but of the woman beneath that ice-cool exterior she knew nothing. Did Dominic know any more than she did, or had he, too, only ever seen what the lady chose to reveal?

There was little she could do other than hope he came to his senses in time, but if she wanted to protect herself... her heart...she should not risk being alone with him again.

Heavens! The entire surface of her body heated at the memory of that kiss and her stomach swirled with unspent restless energy. How had she become entangled in the web of desire so quickly? So fiercely? And now, if she allowed herself to, she could easily succumb to misery, knowing there could be no happy ending. But she would not indulge herself. She had known him but a few weeks. Passion would fade. It couldn't be anything more...meaningful.

It couldn't be love.

Could it?

With Bernard there had been a slow, sweet build to love and desire over the years they had known one another. There had never been that sudden violence of passion that had held her in its thrall on the terrace.

It *couldn't* be love.

'Miss Lovejoy.' Lord Silverdale, an attractive man in his middle thirties, bowed before her. 'If you lack a partner, may I request the pleasure of this dance?'

The distraction welcome, she accepted, smiling up at the Earl. As he led her into the set, she caught sight of Dominic, with Lady Sarah as his partner. Their gazes fused and a shiver chased across her skin, desire pulsing at her core. She tore her eyes from his and directed her attention to Lord Silverdale, pushing all thought of Dominic from her mind.

Afterwards, she stayed close to Olivia and Hugo when possible and occupied herself by watching Gideon as he danced attendance on Lady Emily Crighton, and her sisters, both happy, both contented, partnered by a succession of good-looking, handsome and eligible bachelors.

'You are not still worried about your brother, are you?' Olivia asked later.

'No. He and I…we had a talk—' she would never admit to Olivia that Gideon had found her weeping '—and he has allayed my fears.'

Olivia's silvery gaze swept the room, settling on Dominic and Alex, deep in conversation. 'I wish I could say the same about my brothers. I fear Alex will never change and Dominic is still determined to select his bride before Father arrives.'

Liberty did not want to talk, or even think, about Dominic and his future wife and she soon took her leave of Olivia and wandered around the perimeter of the ballroom, trying not to catch any gentleman's eye.

She really was not in the mood for dancing. She spied an empty chair in an alcove and settled gratefully into in, partially shielded from the floor by a floral arrangement on a pedestal. She relaxed, closing her eyes, trying to dismiss that kiss from her mind and her heart and yet reliving every second of it, and relishing it. Her heart sang—he had kissed her as though he meant it—and it ached, because that kiss could never lead to what she now admitted she wanted above all else.

Him. And her. Together.

'Why are you hiding away?' Her eyes flew open at Dominic's question. 'Are you unwell?' He stood two paces away, worry creasing his brow. He lowered his voice, but came no nearer. 'Are you upset about what happened?'

Her throat ached. This was torment. Did she have the strength to see him, talk to him, to pretend that kiss had not pierced her heart?

'I am not upset, merely enjoying a little peace.'

'I cannot leave you sitting in here all alone—who knows what manner of undesirable men might corner you?' His smile slipped, becoming crooked, and she longed to soothe it. To soothe him. 'Will you allow me to escort you to Mrs Mount or to Olivia?'

Dominic held out his hand and, as she placed her hand in his, he murmured, 'Are you certain nothing is troubling you, Berty?'

The strength of his fingers as they closed around hers, and his use of her private nickname, stirred all sorts of warm feelings deep inside. They were still friends and, if she could expect nothing more from him, she would settle for that.

As she rose to her feet, she said, 'I am certain.'

Chapter Fifteen

Liberty stepped towards Dominic, her hand still enclosed in his, her midnight-blue gaze open and honest.
The silky fabric of her blue gown clung to her curves,
her décolletage enticingly framed by her low, lace-
trimmed neckline. Her honey-blonde hair was piled on
her head, leaving tendrils to frame her face and brush
her bare shoulders.

His hands twitched with the longing to stroke. To
caress.

His back was to the ballroom, blocking her from
view and, without volition, his forefinger trailed down
her arm, from the lace that trimmed her short sleeve to
the edge of her elbow-length glove. Her skin was warm
satin and his eyes charted the shiver that followed in
the wake of his touch.

He was playing with fire. Again. He clenched his
jaw and locked his feelings inside, placing her hand on
his sleeve as he turned to face the room and escort her
to Mrs Mount.

'I am engaged with Lady Sybilla for the next,' he
said. 'But I hope to see you in the Park tomorrow afternoon.'

Her face lit and her soft gasp whispered past his ears, but the glow in her blue eyes quickly dimmed. Her tawny brows gathered in a frown.

'Why?' Her whisper was fierce.

'Why what?'

'You kiss me. You say we can never be more than friends. Yet still you stroked my arm and now you "hope to see me in the Park". What is it you want from me, Dominic?'

He wanted *her*, that was the truth. And she was right to rebuke him. He was being unfair and he would take greater care from now on. But tomorrow…he was almost tempted to tell her the reason he mentioned the Park and to reveal the secret Alex had told him earlier. But it was not his secret to tell. And although he would be wise to stay away, he could not wait to see her face. Was it so wrong to indulge himself?

He told her none of that. 'I am sorry.'

He bowed, leaving Liberty with Mrs Mount, swallowing past the emotion that thickened his throat as he walked away. He had struggled to keep away from her after that kiss, knowing that all he wanted was to kiss her again. And again. But he must protect her reputation and so he had kept his distance. Until Alex had let slip that it was Gideon and Liberty's birthday the next day and that Gideon and her sisters had planned a surprise for Liberty. In the Park.

And because Dominic would never have the right to give Liberty a gift of any kind, he could not resist the chance to see, and to share in, her joy and excitement when Gideon revealed his present to her.

He did his utmost to push Liberty from his thoughts as he danced with Lady Sybilla, but it proved impossible. Sybilla was utter perfection in her looks: a beau-

tiful brunette with burnished locks and porcelain skin.
Her serene expression rarely altered and her behaviour
was correct in every way: she never displayed a vulgar
excess of emotion; she agreed amenably with every
opinion he uttered; she, quite properly, revealed little
knowledge about any subject under discussion. Dominic had spent enough time with her in the past week or
so to know she was polite to servants, but never overly
familiar, and that she never appeared to look down on
anyone she might deem beneath her because of their
more lowly birth. In short, she was the perfect bride.
She was exactly the lady he had set out to find at the
start of the Season.

And he was already bored. She was simply *too* perfect. Try as he might, he couldn't imagine her having fun, teasing him, cuddling a child, rescuing a dog,
crouching beside a child to help it read until her legs
were so stiff she couldn't rise without help. The entire time he danced with Sybilla, it was Liberty's face
he saw in his mind's eye. Liberty's lips he could still
taste. His head ached with the constant inner battles
that plagued his thoughts and, lately, kept him awake
at night.

*What would it matter if you changed your mind?
Why not follow your heart? Others have and the world
did not end.*

*But what of my promise to Mother? And how can
I abandon my duty to the succession and to the family name?*

He had spent his boyhood trying to live up to his
mother's expectations…trying to be good enough…de-
termined to be worthy of that approval he had glimpsed
just before she died. And still he chased that image of

duty and responsibility that was part of the expectations of society as well as his own expectations of himself.

Still he strove to conform.

He escorted Sybilla back to her mother, the Duchess of Wragby, the arguments still raging inside his head, which was starting to throb.

'Well, Avon?' The Duchess looked him up and down with approval. 'Do you have news of your father's arrival in town?'

'Indeed, Your Grace. He and my stepmother arrive next week.'

Time is running out.

That thought had clawed at him for days now. The time was coming when he must announce his decision and his future would be set in stone. His stomach clenched with nerves. He had always been decisive, but now he dithered, unable to take that final, irrecoverable step. And his indecision, he knew, was because, in his heart of hearts, he simply didn't care *who* he wed, unless it was Liberty.

And as soon as any such thought arose, an image of a coal merchant would materialise in his head...a man such as Liberty's grandfather.

'Never allow your base desires to contaminate the bloodline, my Son. Keep it pure. Make me proud.'

Not one whisper of his inner turmoil was allowed to surface, however. His behaviour was as correct as it had ever been. No one would suspect the whirlwind of indecision that plagued his thoughts. If Lady Sybilla was the perfect lady, *he* had always taken care to present himself to the world as the perfect gentleman.

He had only ever allowed himself to relax that perfection when he was safe among his family.

And with Liberty.

He shrugged that thought away. If he was a different man beneath the gentlemanly exterior, then Sybilla, too, might be different.

But different how? In a good way or a bad way?

He could stand no more. He felt as though he rode a runaway steed, the reins slipping through his useless fingers. He bowed abruptly to the Duchess and Sybilla. 'If you will excuse me, ladies?'

Not by a flicker did either lady reveal any disappointment in his departure. He really could not read either of them. He was sick of puzzling over his dilemma. He would speak to Alex and Gideon and check on the arrangements for tomorrow, then go to his club and banish that blasted list from his mind for a few hours.

The following afternoon Dominic met Gideon and Alex as arranged, at three o'clock by the Park gates. Gideon looked as giddy as a schoolboy, his blue eyes dancing with excitement, as he sat on his black gelding, holding a pretty chestnut mare by her reins. This was his surprise… Bella. A new horse for Liberty's birthday—one with outstanding conformation and, Alex had assured him, perfect manners. And Alex should know, because he had bred and trained Bella, using one of his stable lads to help accustom her to the side-saddle.

Alex was astride his huge grey, standing up in his stirrups, scanning the crowds for their first sight of Liberty. Hope and Verity had pledged to be in the Park by three and to bring Liberty with them.

'I do hope she doesn't suspect anything,' Gideon said for the umpteenth time.

Dominic was on foot. He wished he felt half as lively as Gideon, but his head still thumped from his late night at White's, when he had imbibed rather too freely of the brandy, and another restless night. He massaged his temples and closed his eyes briefly.

'I see her.' Alex lowered himself into his saddle. 'She's with your sisters, but they've got that dog with them.'

'I heard Liberty say she planned to walk it in the Park today,' said Gideon, 'and I *told* Hope on no account were they to bring him along. Why do sisters *never* listen?'

'I'll go and meet them,' said Dominic. 'I can steer them towards a less crowded spot, in case Bella should start to fidget.'

Gideon glanced at the mare. 'She seems calm enough—I just hope she doesn't object to dogs.'

'Indeed,' said Alex, with a wink. 'Or you'll be left holding Romeo, Dom. That won't do your image as a suave man about town any good at all.'

Dominic didn't dignify that remark with a reply. He set off through the throng of walkers and, before too long, he came across Liberty, Hope and Verity. Romeo, tongue lolling, was prancing by Liberty's side, exhibiting a showy action that would not be out of place on one of Alex's specially bred high-stepping carriage horses. His upright ears were even more highly pricked than ever, and his tail curled tightly over his back.

Dominic bowed, taking in Liberty's blushing cheeks and the hint of self-consciousness in her eyes. Her periwinkle-blue walking dress fitted her like a glove, moulding to her breasts, and the memory of their fullness softly pressing against his chest last night sent the blood surging to his groin.

He conjured up Sybilla's serene half-smile and his lust subsided.

'Good afternoon, ladies. May I wish you a happy birthday, Miss Lovejoy?'

'Good afternoon, sir, and thank you.' Liberty's lips curved in a smile as all three ladies curtsied, but her smile was strained.

'Good afternoon, Lord Avon,' Hope and Verity chorused.

Hope caught his eye, raising her brows, a question in her blue eyes, and Dominic gave her a brief nod. Yes. Gideon *was* at the Park with Liberty's gift.

'And Romeo…' Dominic continued smoothly, eyeing the hound, who eyed him back, a definite hint of arrogance in his stance. 'Well, he appears to have fully recovered from his ordeal. Anyone would think he was born to parade in the Park at the promenade hour.'

'We did try to persuade Liberty to leave him at home, my lord,' said Hope, 'but she would not listen.'

'Well, as it is your sister's birthday, I think she might be allowed a little indulgence.' He patted Romeo, who tolerated it. Gone was the cringing, fawning animal of only a few days ago. 'May I walk with you a short way, ladies?'

'We would be honoured, my lord.' Liberty was all graciousness, but, as they fell into step, she whispered, 'Your sister suggested I should walk Romeo here, but is it *really* acceptable?'

Her disquiet was unmistakable.

'Are you actually *asking* my advice? Is this the Liberty Lovejoy I… I first met on my father's doorstep?' He maintained his teasing tone, but flinched at the words he had so nearly uttered. *The Liberty Lovejoy I know and love.* It might be trite and a cliché, but those words had come from somewhere.

From the heart.

Nonsense. Friends. She agreed with me. It's lust on my part. That's all.

'I am sure it could not be anything *other* than acceptable now *I* have lent you countenance by walking with you,' he said, using his haughtiest tone.

He was rewarded with a gurgled laugh and a light slap on the arm.

It was a relief to see Gideon and Alex riding towards them. Dominic clasped Liberty's elbow and drew her to a halt. She looked at him, an enquiring frown hovering. He nodded to the carriageway ahead. Her eyes widened and her mouth fell open. Dominic removed Romeo's lead from her slack hold and nudged her forward.

Gideon slid from his horse's back and waited, a huge grin on his face, as Liberty walked towards him.

'Lib, meet Bella. Happy birthday.' He handed her the lead rein.

As Dominic watched Liberty's joy and excitement a previously unknown emotion raked his insides. It took him a moment to realise he was jealous of Gideon. *He* wanted to give her things. *He* wanted to be the recipient of that joyous smile and that unrestrained hug. For the first time in his life he cursed that he was a duke's son. The heir. He longed to break free of the shackles and expectations of society.

He concentrated on keeping all trace of emotion from his face until, with relief, he spied his cousin and friend, Felicity Stanton, driving her pony pair, Nutmeg and Spice, at a spanking trot towards him. He thrust Romeo's lead at Verity and flagged Felicity to stop, which she did with a flourish.

'Dominic! How lovely to see you… I was at Westfield this morning and Peter told me all about your visit yesterday. And what splendid news, that Lord Hugo and

Olivia are going to become patrons. Do you know any more of their plans?'

'Take me up and I will tell you all I know,' he said.

Gideon, Liberty and her sisters were all preoccupied examining Bella. They wouldn't even notice Dominic had gone. He caught Alex's eye, raised his hand in salute and then climbed in next to Felicity.

His destiny was ordained and it did not include Liberty Lovejoy, the granddaughter of a coal merchant. The time until his father arrived would pass quickly and as long as he kept reminding himself that he and Liberty were only friends all would be well.

He filled those days with activity: visits to Westfield, where he again helped the older children with their lessons; boxing and fencing sessions; visits to his clubs, where he partook in several lively political debates; and daily rides in Hyde Park, where he had yet to see Liberty out on Bella. He both longed for and dreaded seeing her, knowing his resolve would not be strong enough to refrain from riding by her side, even if the most he could hope for would be polite chit-chat.

Friends.

The evenings were trickier, but he was proud of his demeanour. He remained totally in control and even Olivia and Alexander had stopped badgering him about his damned list, although Olivia couldn't quite disguise her anxiety whenever she thought he wasn't looking.

No one, he was certain, would suspect the knot that had taken up residence in his guts and that inexorably tightened with each day that passed.

He danced with every lady on his shortlist and a few more besides, keeping up a flow of frivolous conversation. If Liberty were present, he danced with her, too, his stomach muscles rigid with the effort required to maintain his mask of light friendship. Not by a word or a look did either of them refer to that kiss.

In short, he presented the same Lord Avon to the *ton* that he had presented for the past nine years, since he first came to town at seventeen years of age.

On the day of Father's arrival it brought him no relief to realise that this strange charade was near its end and so he awarded himself one last indulgence. Olivia and Hugo were to ride in the Park with Liberty. Dominic made sure to join them.

The days since their kiss had provided a salutary lesson for Liberty.

Dominic had proved time after time that their kiss meant nothing to him even though that same kiss haunted her dreams. He was the same suave, sophisticated gentleman he had always been. Any observer would claim he behaved no differently to her, but she knew there was a faint but discernible detachment in the way he acted around her. He avoided any situation where they might speak privately and, when they danced, he no longer teased her, but merely kept up the same light, inconsequential conversation he maintained with all his partners.

She ought to be pleased at his caution, but she missed him and she missed their friendship and his teasing. Her heart sank whenever she saw him with one of the ladies on his list, especially Sybilla following Olivia's suspicion that she was now Dominic's choice.

On the day Olivia's father was due to arrive in town, she and Hugo arranged to meet Liberty for a ride in the Park. Gideon rode with Liberty and waited with her by the Park gate until Hugo and Olivia arrived. Liberty tried to ignore the silly way her heart leapt at the sight of Dominic accompanying them, telling herself his presence meant nothing. She marshalled her courage and smiled serenely as he greeted her, but no sooner had they started to walk their horses along the carriageway than they appeared to fall naturally into two pairs: Hugo and Olivia, followed by Dominic and Liberty.

'I hope you do not object to my joining you this afternoon?' Dominic said, after they had exchanged comments on the weather—which was dry but still unseasonably cold.

He grinned at her. Totally relaxed and utterly gorgeous. No hint of self-consciousness over that kiss. No tinge of regret either. It was as though it had never happened.

'Why should I?' She was pleased with the light nonchalance of her reply.

'I have been wondering how you were getting on with Bella. Do you like her?'

Liberty smoothed one gloved hand along Bella's silken mane. 'Oh, yes. She is perfect. It was a lovely surprise.' She narrowed her eyes at him. 'I collect you knew all about it at the Attwoods' ball, when you said you hoped to see me in the Park the following day?'

'I did—and now you see why I could not tell you the reason for my question. You were a tad irritated with me at the time, as I recall.'

She *had* been irritated and still was—but by his ability to sweep the memory of that kiss…of her…away. She must have tensed because Bella threw her head up and danced sideways. Liberty forced her hands to relax on the rein and settled her with a hand to her neck and a soothing word. Dominic watched her and she caught a glint of admiration in his silver gaze.

She didn't want his admiration. It made everything so much harder to bear.

'You are well aware, my Lord Avon, that was not the only reason for my irritation,' she snapped.

Her mood only appeared to amuse him and a teasing smile stretched his lips.

'Ah. So you *were* upset because I kissed you.'

His remark riled her still further, until she realised he was being deliberately provocative and that she was rising to it. She reined in her temper and aimed for a similar kind of teasing banter.

'I was not. It was merely a kiss.' She stuck her nose in the air, but kept her tone light. 'It was hardly my first! It was your subsequent behaviour that I found so objectionable, sir.'

'*Sir* is it now? You *are* in a huff with me!' He laughed. 'Very well. I apologise for taking advantage of you by stroking your naked arm.' His choice of words set her pulse racing. 'But, really, Berty…what do you expect of a red-blooded man when you present him with such temptation in a secluded alcove? If you will take my advice, you will remain close to your chaperon in future and not run the risk of leading random gentlemen astray.'

'Why, thank you so much for those words of wisdom, Lord Avon. Truly…' she placed her hand over her heart and fluttered her eyelashes at him '…I do not know how we weak females would manage without such penetrating male insight to guide us. Perhaps I should clothe myself in a nun's habit for future balls, if one expanse of bare skin can have such an undesirable effect on so-called gentlemen.'

She saw the effort it took him to bite back his grin.

'Now, now, Berty. I have told you before, sarcasm does not suit you.'

'And pontificating about the blinking obvious does not suit you, Dominic.'

'Touché,' he murmured.

They drifted into an amicable silence as they rode on, but the question that had plagued her for days bubbled in her brain, foiling her efforts to ignore it. She had to know the worst. She had to prepare herself.

'I have something I wish to ask you.'

His features blanked, a hint of wariness in his eyes.

'Go on.'

'Have you made your choice?'

He would know what she meant, no need to elaborate further. She burned to know *who* and *when*, so she could be ready to stand by and smile benignly even though she was still convinced he was heading for a cold and miserable future.

His eyebrows met in a dark slash. 'I have.'

Her heart tumbled and nausea rose to choke her. She swallowed hard. 'Is the young lady aware of her good fortune?'

His lips firmed and a muscle leapt in his cheek.

'Not as yet. You are the first to know.' He paused, the groove between his eyebrows deepening. 'I shall ask Lady Sybilla to be my wife,' he said eventually.

Her throat thickened. She had asked and now she knew. Olivia had been right. Sybilla was exquisitely polite to Liberty if ever their paths met, but she had never caught the slightest glimpse of the real woman beneath that emotionless façade. And now Liberty would be forced to smile and congratulate the happy couple.

How will he be happy with Sybilla? He'll end

*up lonely and embittered...he needs a woman with
warmth and kindness to bring joy into his life, not an
ice maiden.*

Sybilla was cold enough to freeze a stream of lava
in mid-flow.

'And when shall you offer for her?'

His silver gaze roamed restlessly around the Park.

'Father arrived today and the family will all dine at
Beauchamp House tonight. I shall inform them of my
decision then.'

'So you will tell your family before you speak to
Lady Sybilla?'

'Of course.' His chest swelled as he inhaled. He
switched his gaze to Liberty. Then the air left his lungs
in a rush. 'You know very well this is a practical arrangement. I want my family's blessing before I make
any commitment. Once I make my offer there will be
no going back.'

She knew that. Knew that his gentleman's honour,
let alone his obsession with *duty*, would never allow
him to behave otherwise. And her heart ached for him.
From everything she had learned from Mrs Mount and
from Olivia, the members of his extended family were
all happily married—every one of them a love match.
But even with those examples, Dominic still steered
resolutely on his chosen course.

'And if your father gives his approval?' She knew it
was his father's approval that was crucial. The rest of
the family were important, but the Duke's opinion was
the one that mattered.

'Then I shall call on the Duke of Wragby in the
morning.'

She had pushed him far enough. There was a finality in his tone that warned her to stop. She swallowed

again and concentrated on maintaining her posture in the saddle even though she longed to slump in defeat.

'I wish you well.'

'Thank you.'

They rode on in silence.

Chapter Sixteen

Dominic felt no relief at announcing his decision. What he didn't tell Liberty was that, until the moment she asked, he had still not made his final choice—wavering from one name to the other and back again until he was in a state of utter confusion—even though he still planned to tell the rest of the family tonight. Her question had pushed him into the final decision, but the words in his head had felt alien and they felt even worse coming from his mouth. But he said them none the less, that promise to his mother still on his mind…his promise and her expectations…he had vowed to prove to her that he was worthy. And he also wanted to please his father; he surely deserved at least one trouble-free son.

Dominic had spent his life conforming to what was expected of a man of his birthright precisely in order to protect his father from pain and anxiety. He was not about to change now.

Besides. He glanced over at Liberty. All that 'follow your heart' nonsense was just that. Nonsense. Pure, honest-to-goodness lust was the driving force behind his craving for Liberty Lovejoy. Without volition, his gaze slid over her, lingering on her full breasts, outlined by the snug fit of her dove-grey riding habit. Everything about her sent desire racing through his bloodstream, but he could rise above that visceral response. He'd done it before, often and often.

He'd made his choice. Lady Sybilla. She was twenty-one years old—no green girl on the town for the first time. He'd met her many times, during the Season and at house parties out of season, and she had never put an elegantly shod foot out of place. She was beautiful, reserved, well-mannered, a graceful dancer and an accomplished rider and she deferred to a man's opinion just as she ought.

He frowned, sneaking another sideways look at Liberty. No one could ever accuse her of deferring to a man's opinion simply because of his sex. If she thought her opinion was right, she had absolutely no compunction in voicing it. Much like the rest of the females in his family, he mused, except, maybe, Aunt Cecily…until she met Zach and had changed from the quiet, compliant lady Dominic had always known. He frowned. Aunt Cecily, it turned out, had not been truly happy all those years when she was raising her brother's children. She'd been content, but not happy. Not fulfilled. But she had never said so.

Would Liberty end up the same? A maiden aunt, quashing her own desires and deferring to her brother and sisters? He shook those thoughts away. It was her decision…there was nothing to stop her marrying if she chose to, even though the thought of her with another man sent anger spiking through his veins.

'Why do you care about my choice? Or when I intend to make my offer?'

He thrust down the voice that reminded him that she

had kissed him. Passionately. Of course she cared. Probably more than she should and more than he deserved.

'You are my friend. I *care* about you… I want you to be happy.'

'I shall be happy.' His reply came by rote.

She shook her head at him, then smiled. Her pearly teeth sent waves of longing crashing through him and he wrenched his gaze from hers with a silent snarl at his rampant lust.

'We *have* become serious,' she said. 'Come. Let us enjoy our time together for, once you make your announcement, I make no doubt you will be far too busy with your betrothed to spend time riding in the Park with me.' Was it his imagination, or did her voice hitch, just a little? 'The ride is less crowded here,' she continued gaily. 'Let us canter.'

She didn't wait for his reply, but set off and, after a moment's hesitation, Dominic sent Vulcan in her wake.

Beauchamp House was alight with chatter and laughter when Dominic arrived at six that evening. He entered the salon and paused, unnoticed for a few moments, just taking in his family…the smiles on their faces as they caught up with one another's news. The children, too, were there, together with their nursemaids who would whisk them away once dinner was announced. His two-year-old half-brother, Sebastian, was the first to see him.

'*Dominic!*'

He scurried across the room, closely pursued by his older sister, Christabel. Dominic swung Sebastian up and around, the boy's dress flaring out, his chubby legs kicking in delight as he giggled. Dominic planted a kiss on his cheek, then settled him under one arm as he scooped up Christabel with the other. Her arms wound around his neck and she pressed her hot cheek against his.

'I love you, Dominic. You're my *bestest* brother.'

'I love you, too, sweetie-pie!' Dominic hugged her close for a minute, then groaned theatrically and staggered. 'Help! Help me! I... I... I can't hold these monsters any longer!'

The conversation had paused as everyone watched the byplay then, accompanied by more laughter, Father strode forward and plucked Christabel from Dominic's arms.

'I *told* you not to eat so much, Christy—you've reduced your big brother to a quivering wreck.'

He cradled her in one arm and freed his other to tickle her. She shrieked and squirmed.

'Papa! No! Mama! Help!'

Dominic's stepmother, Rosalind, came up with a smile. As he kissed her in greeting, she said, 'I might have known you would reduce our ordered gathering to chaos as soon as you arrived, Dominic. It is good to see you, though.' She turned to Father. 'Let me take her, Leo, or Penny will complain they're too excited to sleep.'

'Yes, Your Grace.' Leo handed his daughter over to Rosalind and gave her a mock salute.

Dominic's adopted sister, Susie—now thirteen and growing up into a serious, studious girl—came over to take charge of Sebastian and order reigned once more.

'How are you, my Son?' Father's silver gaze—so like Dominic's—scanned him. 'Are these rumours I've heard true?'

Trust Father to know what was going on in advance

and to have no compunction in raising the matter. He always seemed to be two steps ahead of everyone else.

Dominic forced a nonchalant shrug. 'There are always rumours. Have you taken to listening to gossip now, Father?'

Tell him! Get it over with!

'Ah, well. I dare say I have it wrong.'

His tone suggested otherwise, but Father merely slung his arm across Dominic's shoulders and they joined the rest of the family. Dominic sought out Olivia, Hugo and Alex one by one and sent each of them a look of warning. This was his business—it was not their place to pre-empt him. Not that Alex was likely to, as he rarely voluntarily spoke to Father, but Olivia…she was a very different matter. She returned his look with an innocent lift of her eyebrows, but Dominic thought she would stay silent, not least because she had made it clear she did not approve of any of the ladies on his shortlist.

He stood to one side of the room, drinking, and he watched his family, paying particular attention to Rosalind and Olivia as they interacted with their children and their husbands, trying to picture Sybilla in that role. Then he tried to imagine her fitting in with his family as they chattered together, laughing and teasing. But he could not imagine her behaving with such informality, even in a family setting. Liberty, though…

He thrust her image away, clenching his jaw. Perhaps one of the others would be a better choice? After all, nobody knew he had selected Sybilla. Apart from Liberty and she would not tell anyone. He tried to put any one of those ladies into this scenario, but the only face that surfaced in his imagination was Liberty Lovejoy's.

'Things on your mind, Dom?'

'No.'

'Have you made your choice yet? Have you been picturing her here in the bosom of our family?'

It was too close to the truth. Dominic drained his wine glass. 'Don't be ridiculous.'

Alex leaned closer. 'Father knows. Look at him. He's waiting for you to broach the subject.'

'He told you that, did he?' Irritation with Alex prompted him to add, 'Or did you somehow let it slip during one of your cosy father-and-son chats?'

One corner of Alex's mouth lifted in a half-smile that roused Dominic's guilt. He was normally careful not to enflame his brother's hostility towards their father.

'Unworthy, Brother. You should know by now the Duke doesn't need to be told things…he just knows.'

Again, Dominic was conscious of his father's gaze on him even though he carefully avoided looking in his direction. He signalled to William, who crossed the room to fill his glass again. As soon as the footman was out of earshot, Alex turned serious.

'Dom. Listen to me. Don't tie yourself to any of 'em. Not yet. Any fool can see your heart isn't in it—'

'The heart is irrelevant, Alexander. I make decisions with my head. With logic and planning.'

'You're a damned stubborn fool once you get an idea in that head of yours, that's for certain,' Alex growled. 'Tell me, once and for all. Are you going to tell Father tonight or not?'

Dominic's clenched jaw ached as he battled with his answer. Yes? Or no? One simple word. That's all it needed.

'No,' he said finally and the relief when his decision emerged washed over him like a tidal wave, sweeping all tension and friction from him. 'No. I will not tell him tonight. There is no hurry.'

Alex grinned and slapped Dominic on the back. 'Best news I've heard in an age. There'll be a lot of anxious punters at White's, wondering what the verdict will be, mind.' He leaned in again and lowered his voice. 'I know you won't take my advice, but I shall say what I think nevertheless. Scrap that list and think again.' He walked away before Dominic could reply.

How easy it was for Alex to say that and to believe it.

He was not the heir.

He didn't have the weight of expectation on his shoulders.

He was not bound by duty.

Dominic's chest ached and his throat constricted. He had never felt so alone, even though his family were all around him. He rubbed at his chest and the action brought Liberty bouncing into his head. How many times had he noticed her doing the exact same thing? He scowled down into his glass. How many times would he continue to allow her to invade his head and upset his carefully laid plans? No matter how many times he caught himself wishing to share a joke with her, or to point out a beautiful flower or an interesting cloud formation in the sky, nothing could change the fact that the granddaughter of a coal merchant was unsuited to the position of Marchioness of Avon, let alone the future Duchess of Cheriton.

The children were shortly packed off to the nursery and dinner was served. Throughout the meal, even as the conversation ebbed and flowed, Dominic was conscious of his father's eyes resting on him from time to time, a crease between his dark brows. He didn't doubt his father knew all about the list…the question was, would he speak to Dominic about it or would he wait for Dominic to approach him? Somehow, Dominic thought he would wait. The relief he had felt had been temporary. Tension still wound his gut, robbing him of his appetite. He picked at his food.

'Are you quite well, Dominic?' Rosalind spoke softly. 'You are hardly eating a thing and you are very quiet. And drinking more than usual. Is…is something troubling you? Your father has noticed…he looks concerned.'

'I am perfectly well, thank you. I made the mistake of eating at my club earlier—I must have eaten more than I intended for I am simply not hungry now.'

The excuse slid readily from his tongue, but her face was still etched with worry. He raised his wine glass in a toast.

'Good health.'

Sarcasm laced his words and Rosalind, after another long, level look, turned her attention from him. He thrust away the guilt that stabbed at him—it was unfair to take his mood out on his stepmother, but he didn't want to talk. Not about anything. He just wanted this damned Season to be over with…for all decisions to be made and irreversible. Surely, then, he would stop this nonsensical yearning after a woman he could never have?

If that's how you feel, why not make the announcement now? This minute? The decision would be made then.

He stared blindly at his plate, unaccustomed rage battering at his chest. It was the pain from his jaw—again clenched so tightly his teeth hurt, too—that pulled him back from the brink. He concentrated on breathing steadily until he was back in control. He would not be goaded into a hasty announcement, not even by his own inner voice. He slipped on the cloak of urbanity that he wore in public and joined the conversation, but he was rattled by his uncharacteristic gibe at Rosalind. His father's frown revealed it had not gone unnoticed, but he had not mentioned it.

Yet.

But Dominic was sure it would come and he was in no fit state to verbally spar with the man who had never lost a match yet.

I cannot cope with much more of this.

He craved solitude. As soon as it was polite, Dominic made his excuses to leave Beauchamp House and Alex, to no one's surprise but to Dominic's exasperation, elected to leave with him. Dominic wanted to be alone to think through his future. Yet again. Did he need to rethink his strategy? He couldn't deny his doubts about choosing a wife from his shortlist all stemmed from his feelings for Liberty. But that didn't make her any more suitable. He could not get away from that. So, in that case, wasn't one shortlist much like another?

'Come on, Dom. A few hands of whist will shake you out of the doldrums.'

They had reached the corner of his road and Dominic glanced towards his house, further along, on the opposite side. A flash of pale skin by the area steps caught his attention and all his senses went on to high alert. He halted.

'Thanks, Alex, but not tonight.' He clapped his brother's shoulder. 'You go on. I'm for my bed. I've a session booked at Angelo's in the morning.'

And after he'd honed his fencing skills with Henry, he might very well call in next door to Jackson's—

maybe a sparring session would work off some of his bottled-up energy. Or—and his grip tightened on his ebony cane—maybe whoever was lurking near his front door might provide him with that opportunity right now.

'Oh, well.' Alex shrugged. 'I'll be off then—I arranged to meet Nev and Gid once I'd done the family duty bit. G'night, Dom!'

'Goodnight, Alex.'

Dominic watched his brother saunter away before he crossed the road and strolled along the pavement towards his house, swinging his cane nonchalantly. If it was a thief lying in wait for an unwary passer-by, he would get more than he bargained for. Dominic was in just the mood for some physical action. Something to work out his frustrations.

As he drew level with the steps that led down to the basement kitchens, a movement flickered in the corner of his eye. He gripped his cane, unsheathing the sword in one smooth movement. Then the scent reached him, curling through his senses, bringing with it a sense of peace...and a desperate longing.

Roses.

Liberty gasped as a steel blade flashed in the light from the nearby street lamp.

'It's me,' she hissed.

His face was in shadow, but she saw from the way he squared his shoulders that he was annoyed.

Of course he's annoyed! What am I doing, lying in wait for him like this?

But she had to try, one last time, to save him from himself. If she failed...well, if she failed she would at least know she had left no stone unturned and, once she returned to Eversham, she would probably never see him again. The melancholy thought weighed heavy on her, her heart aching with loneliness. She rubbed at her chest.

'What the devil are you *doing*?' He growled the question. 'Do you *want* to cause a scandal?'

He still stood on the pavement. She still stood on the steps, her face at the level of his groin. She felt her skin heat as she remembered the things Bernard had told her a man and a woman could do together. Things with mouths and...

She swallowed. Such shocking thoughts—she would never be a lady. Dominic was right not to even consider her. Although Bernard had not taken her innocence, they *had* kissed and been intimate—hardly the behaviour suitable for a society lady—and she was familiar with a man's anatomy and what it could do. She had seen and recognised Dominic's physical reaction to her more than once—and she'd felt his arousal that time they kissed. He wanted her as a man wants a woman.

And she...God help her...wanted him. She could not deny it. She was five-and-twenty now...would probably never marry...and Dominic haunted her dreams.

And though she knew she could never have him, she still wanted him to be happy. She couldn't bear to think of him unhappy. She had failed to save one man she loved, Bernard, and now she was here to try to save Dominic from this huge mistake. She wasn't entirely sure what lay in his heart, but she was damned certain it was not Lady Sybilla Gratton. So she would try, one last time, to open his eyes and his heart to the truth... to show him the difference between what he wanted and what he needed.

'Of course not.' She kept her voice to a whisper as she answered him, conscious that any member of his staff could see them if they happened to look out of the window behind her. 'But I cannot stand by and watch you make a mistake you will live to regret.'

'How can you possibly know I would regret it? And, besides, how does it concern you?'

'You asked me that this afternoon. My answer is the same. You are my friend. I want you to be happy.'

'And you think my choosing a suitable wife will make me *un*happy?' His head snapped round and he stared along the street. 'You cannot stay there. How did you get here?'

'I walked.'

'Walked? Alone? Good God, Berty…anything could have happened. You know it's unsafe for a lady to walk alone, especially at night.'

She might as well admit the worst, because he would see for himself soon enough. She sucked in a shaky breath and stepped back, away from the wall. Dominic craned his neck over the railings. She heard his spluttered laugh and, offended, she rammed Gideon's best beaver hat back on her head. It slid down to rest atop her ears, the brim half-covering her eyes.

'There is a reason females do not wear trousers.' He was using his superior voice and it set Liberty's hackles rising. 'They are entirely the wrong shape for them. At least…*you* are entirely the wrong shape.'

She didn't think she looked that dreadful…although, admittedly, her hips and legs *were* curvier than Gideon's and the pantaloons *were* stretched somewhat more thinly than they were designed for. She *hmmph*ed quietly even as she registered the change in Dominic's voice. It had turned, somehow, caressing. He couldn't hold on to all that anger, she knew he couldn't. She stared up at him.

'Did you tell them?'

He shook his head. 'No.'

The knot in her stomach loosened, just a little. She wasn't too late. If only—

'I want to talk to you. Please.'

'But I know what you are going to say and it will make no difference. Besides, we cannot stand here much longer without attracting all sorts of the wrong attention.'

'Please?'

He tipped his head back and stared up at the house. 'Stay there and keep quiet.'

He disappeared from her sight and she heard the sound of a key in a lock followed by the murmur of masculine voices and the quiet sound of a door closing. She waited…and she had just begun to think he had abandoned her there as a joke or a punishment when the door opened, spilling light on to the pavement.

'Be quick.'

Liberty ran up the remaining steps and in through the front door as quickly as she could. Contrary to what Dominic thought, she really did have no desire to be seen dressed in men's clothing and loitering outside his door. It had taken all her courage to come here, but she had come nevertheless—scurrying through the streets with her head down—because she simply couldn't bear the thought of the future that awaited him. She'd come prepared for a lengthy wait—not knowing what time he might arrive home—and had almost cried with relief when she had seen him turn the corner into his street.

Dominic ushered her into a very masculine, but comfortable sitting room. A fire blazed in the hearth. A cold repast was laid out on a side table next to a silver salver with two glasses and a full decanter. The door closed behind Liberty with a soft click and she wheeled around to face Dominic.

Chapter Seventeen

Liberty's heart tumbled in her chest, her breathing quickened and her pulse leapt, heat flushing her skin.

Dear heavens, he is gorgeous. If only...

She batted away that errant thought. There were no 'if onlys'. She clung tight to that knowledge. She would not fool herself...she loved Dominic. And she knew he...what? He liked her, certainly. They were friends. They enjoyed one another's company, they made one another laugh. But she also knew that caring for him... loving him...meant wanting what was best for him. And that was *not* to burden him with a wife who was so far removed from his ideal that she might as well be a duck.

This was not about persuading him to throw away the principles he held dear and to marry her regardless. It was about persuading him he deserved to find a suitable lady for his wife who would make him *happy*.

'Do take off that preposterous hat, Berty,' Dominic drawled as he crossed to the table and poured two glasses of wine.

She removed it with relief. Her ears were already sore from the brim chafing them. Dominic handed her the glass and gestured to the fire, bracketed by a pair of green-leather wing-back chairs. Liberty sat and sipped her wine.

'Let me have it, then, Berty.'

Dominic moved to stand in front of her, his glass in one long-fingered hand. His reflection in the gilt-framed mirror above the mantelpiece revealed a muscle bunching in his jaw as he clenched it. The firelight played across his skin, making it glow and highlighting the dark hairs that dusted the back of his hand. There was strength and beauty in that hand and she itched to just reach out and touch it.

'Best we get this out of the way. I'm tired and I need my bed.'

His bored tone didn't fool Liberty for one second. He was as tense as she'd ever seen him. She mulled over how to start.

'You do realise how preposterous your behaviour is?' he drawled. 'And what would happen if someone caught us in here? Like this?'

She jumped to her feet at that. 'You know that is not why I have come.' She couldn't bear him to even suspect she might try to entrap him. 'I would never behave in such a low, sneaky, despicable way.'

A mirthless smile stretched his lips. 'I do know it. You are doing what you always do...risking yourself for those you...those you *care* for. You are a good, kind-hearted woman, Liberty Lovejoy, but you must allow other people to tread their own path, even if you believe they are making a monumental mistake.' He raised his glass in a mock salute and downed it in one again, before eyeing his empty glass in disgust. 'I need something stronger than this.' He wheeled away and went to a side table, returning with two glasses in one hand and a bottle in the other. 'Brandy?'

Her wine glass was empty. She nodded and watched him pour amber liquid into the glasses, her eyes following him as he bent to set the bottle down on the hearth, took Liberty's empty glass from her hand and passed her the new one. She sipped. It was good brandy— the fiery spirit slipped down a treat. She'd occasionally enjoyed a glass in the evening with Bernard. They'd shared a glass the night before she left for London. It had been the last time she ever saw him.

Without warning, her eyes brimmed. She should never have gone to London. She should never have left Gideon… Mama… Papa… The guilt scoured her.

'Liberty?' The gentleness of Dominic's tone was nearly her undoing, but she blinked furiously and swallowed back her tears before facing him again, chin up.

'I am sorry. It is nothing…a memory caught me unawares, that is all.'

'Your intended?'

She nodded, rubbing at the lonely ache in her chest as she stared into the flames. What was she doing here? *Could* she ever persuade Dominic to think again?

'How do you know about Bernard…my intended?'

'Was that his name? Gideon told Alex who told Olivia. I just happened to be present.' Dominic steered Liberty back to her chair. He sat opposite and fixed her with an unwavering silver gaze. 'Will you tell me about him?'

And she did. How they had grown up as neighbours, always knowing they were destined to be married.

'You were childhood sweethearts, then?'

'Yes.'

'And no other man will ever usurp the sainted Bernard in your affections?'

She frowned. 'That is how Gideon always refers to

Bernard. It's not true. He was no saint and I never set him up on a pedestal to worship.'

'I meant no disrespect. To either of you.'

Liberty pushed her fingers through her hair and stood up. 'I am too hot.' She unwound her roughly tied neckcloth and then began to shrug out of Gideon's coat. 'Do you mind if I take this off?'

'Be my guest.'

He pushed himself out of his chair and came behind her to help, for which she was grateful. She'd had enough of a struggle getting the tailored coat on in the first place. Removing it was even more difficult. As Dominic grasped the collar his fingers brushed Liberty's neck and she gasped as tingles radiated through her body. Her arms free, she then felt him lift one lock of hair, just behind her ear. His breathing in her ear was erratic, almost harsh. Their reflections in the mirror above the mantelpiece showed his attention transfixed by that tendril as he allowed it to slip through his fingers to drape over her shoulder.

She stepped away. 'Thank you. No wonder you gentlemen need valets.'

She sat down again, avoiding eye contact, conscious of that visceral attraction between them, careful not to tempt fate. Liberty Lovejoy was still Liberty Lovejoy. Not a suitable future duchess.

Dominic placed the coat on a wooden chair near the door and then flung himself into the other fireside chair.

'So...when did you get betrothed to the s—to Bernard?'

'Two days before I left for London to make my debut. He urged me to go...to take advantage of my godmother's offer to sponsor me.' She swallowed. 'He fell ill two weeks after I left...'

In a halting voice, she told Dominic about the message that had reached her...the worst day of her life... that terrible dash back to Sussex, urging the post boys to go ever faster.

'The worst thing,' she said, at the end of her tale, 'is the guilt that I was not there. At least I saw my parents again and helped to nurse them. But not Bernard... I never said goodbye and I can barely picture his face any more.'

'There is no portrait?'

'No. He promised to have a miniature painted for me, but he never did.'

Again her throat ached with the memory, but the sorrow was distant now...almost as though it had happened to another person. Slowly, the thought surfaced that she had never felt for Bernard what she now felt for Dominic. She had loved him, but it had been a quieter love... steadier. Passion had kindled, when he had kissed her, and touched her...but it had been a slow burn. It had never been this all-encompassing fire that consumed her whenever she thought of Dominic. Whenever she was near him.

'I suppose I am fortunate that there is a portrait of my mother at the Abbey.' Dominic was staring into the fire, the orange flames reflected in his eyes. 'And I still had my father and my aunt and uncle. You suffered a dreadful blow, losing your parents at the same time, too. It must have been so hard for all of you.'

There was no answer to that other than *Yes*. Liberty sipped her brandy as she, too, contemplated the flames.

'How old were you when your mother died?'

'Eight. And she didn't just die. She was *murdered*.'

His bitterness shouldn't shock her, but it did. He sounded so...angry. 'Did they ever find out who did it?'

'No. Alex found her body. He was only seven. He didn't speak for a year and he was never quite the same afterwards.'

'Oh, poor little boy. That must have been dreadful for him...for all of you. And for your father, too, to lose his wife that way.'

His eyes glittered. 'The memories of that time are hazy now...as though a veil covers the details. I just remember feeling...disbelief, I suppose. I was upset but, looking back, I doubt I fully understood I would never see her again.' He sank his head into his hands, elbows propped on his knees. 'As a family, we never talk about it. We were too young when it happened and I suppose we all just got used to not discussing it. The past is the past and we move forward into the future.'

'And is that how you feel inside? That it's all in the past? That it cannot affect you...any of you...now?'

'Yes. No.' He scrubbed his hands through his hair. 'I don't know.'

Liberty said nothing, waiting for him to go on—sensing his battle between wanting to unburden himself and family loyalty.

'I do know it affected Father for a long time.' His words came quietly. 'He had refused to allow her to go to London. He told her she must spend more time with us. Her children. And a week later she was dead. I know he felt guilty for failing to protect her.'

She knew that feeling...the guilt of failing to protect. Dominic stared down at the rug.

'We were never enough for her.' His voice was raw. 'She used to say she was proud of "her boys"—particularly me, as I was the heir—but they were just words to her. They had no meaning—there was never any pleas-

ing her. And poor Olivia never got *any* maternal attention or affection from her.

'My memories are those of a child—at the time I
overheard things that made little sense, but as I got
older I understood. Probably more than I cared to.' He
huffed a mirthless laugh. 'I know she married Father
for his wealth and for the prestige of being a duchess.
She was never happy at the Abbey—she craved the excitement of London and the adulation of her admirers
even though we all tried hard to behave well and to be
worthy of her attention and her approval.

'But we knew no different—she was our mother,
and we worshipped her, constantly seeking approval.
Now…when I look back… I compare Cecily and how
she loved us all and I can see that all we ever got from
Mother was coldness and rejection.'

The pain in his voice wrenched at Liberty's heart-
strings, and she ached for those children.

'She wanted to be adored by us all, but she gave nothing…apart from one time…' Dominic faltered, then he
cleared his throat and dashed one hand across his eyes.
His voice hardened. 'She gave us nothing in return.
Certainly not love.'

Liberty stared at him. 'But…you…'

He met her gaze, his eyes glittering. 'But…? I…?'

His tone mocked. She tried to gather her thoughts,
frowning. It made no sense.

'I do not understand. Why are you so set on fulfilling a promise to your mother if she was as cold as you
say? Surely you owe her nothing?'

'I don't…' He emptied his glass and set it down.
He leaned forward, his head bowed, his eyes screwed
shut. His elbow propped on the armrest and his splayed
hand covered his face, all four fingertips pressed to his

forehead, his thumb digging into his cheek. 'I don't know…' he said, his voice muffled. Aching. 'Just before she died, I hoped she might…' He shook his head. 'I suppose I still want to prove I am worthy of her and to make her proud of me.'

Liberty longed to take him in her arms and soothe away his pain.

'You were eight years old, Dominic. You should not feel bound by such an oath.'

His head jerked up. 'I shouldn't be talking to you like this. Besides, there's my father to think of. He suffered, too, and Alex… Alex… Well, I don't understand, but Alex and Father will never be close. I am his heir… I cannot let him down.' His voice broke. '*He* did not shirk his duty. I want to make him proud.'

'Oh, Dominic.' Liberty went to him, sank on to her knees on the floor and cradled his face in her hands. 'I have not met your father, but how could he not be proud of you? And the rest of your family love you— that is obvious. Do you really think they wish you to be unhappy?'

He jerked his head from between her hands at that, lowering the hand that shielded his eyes. For the flash of a second, Liberty saw his vulnerability before his silvery eyes shuttered.

'Why should I be unhappy? My marriage will be no different to hundreds of others—it is the norm in our world.'

'It is not the norm in your family, from what I have been told. What is your stepmother like? Does she make your father happy?'

Dominic's eyes warmed. 'Oh, yes. She is perfect for him. We all love her.'

'And can you picture Lady Sybilla in the bosom of your family? Will she fit in?'

His gaze slid from hers. 'Why should she not?'

Liberty's hands were on his knees. Her thighs and belly pressed against his shins. A knot of emotion lodged in her throat as she struggled to find the arguments to get through to him...the words that would help him to see what a huge mistake he was about to make.

'Can you not see, though?' She slid her hands up his thighs, the muscles rock hard beneath her fingers. She captured his gaze. 'If you marry a woman like Lady Sybilla, you are asking for history to repeat itself.' Her hands moved further, up his flat belly to his chest, his silk waistcoat smooth and warm to her touch. His eyes darkened and a thrill spiralled through her. 'Is that truly what you want? Look around you, Dominic. Look at your father and your stepmother, your uncles and aunts, Olivia and Hugo. They all have love matches and are happy and content.' Olivia had told Liberty all about the Beauchamps. 'Is that not what you want for yourself?' She reached his neck and curved her fingers around his jaw, his dark stubble scratching her skin.

'Dominic...is that not what you want for *your* children?'

All her altruistic notions fled as she gazed deep into those silvery-grey eyes that were no longer cold mirrors, but deep, white-hot furnaces that blazed, sending bolts of pure energy and need sizzling through her. He needed a woman with warmth and curves and love to bring happiness to his life. He needed—if only he could see it—Liberty Lovejoy. But could she persuade him before it was too late?

She pressed closer and his knees parted as his hands

gripped her sides and lifted, pulling her almost roughly to him. For what seemed an eternity their eyes locked and held as blood rampaged through her veins like a river in flood and the heat of desire pooled between her thighs. She fancied a question formed deep in his silvery gaze—and she knew her answer.

With a sigh of pleasure, she slipped her fingers into the heavy silk of his hair and she pressed her mouth to his.

Neither the frantic attempts by his controlling inner voice nor the stridency of the warning bells that reverberated inside his head could stop him. The groan vibrated deep, deep inside Dominic's chest as he wrapped his arms around Liberty Lovejoy and gloried in the caress of her mouth. He had no strength to fight the strongest impulse he had ever known: the impulse to take, to enjoy, to wallow. To simply *feel* and not to plan…or to control…or to consider any implications. His mind might clamour all it liked for him to resist, but his body would not…could not…obey. This was what he had craved since the day he'd met her. The dam of his self-control had burst and this was what he wanted.

Right here. Right now. Regardless.

His hands plunged into her hair, shaking it loose, the heavy tresses spilling down her back as her soft body moulded to his. Her breasts—glorious, abundant, wonderful—pressed between them. Her scent curled around him, through him, drugging him…roses…no longer a smell to awaken regret and failure, but a smell to conjure forth hope and possibility. With another heartfelt groan, one hand at the small of her back, the other between her shoulder blades, he slithered from the chair, holding her carefully until they were on their knees on the rug before the fire, caressing her sweet mouth that tasted of honey. His tongue traced the soft fullness of her lips and, as they parted, swept inside, his lips sliding over hers, kissing her with a hunger that set his entire being on fire. Gently, he eased her back and he half-covered her—exactly where he had fantasised having her ever since the day she had burst into his life.

He explored her mouth at first with dreamy intimacy—lingering, savouring every moment…a kiss for his tired soul to melt into. He shifted to ease the fullness in his groin and angled his head, deepening the kiss, his tongue thrusting now with more urgency, his fingers curling into her silken tresses, holding her head still as he plundered her mouth. Her hands skimmed his back restlessly as a low moan sounded in her throat and her body arched beneath him. He forced his mouth from hers, raising himself on one elbow to look his fill, his heart pounding in his chest.

Heavy lids half-covered slumberous midnight-blue eyes. Her sweet-scented skin was flushed and her lips… oh, her lips, were softly sheening and succulent. Her breasts rose and fell with every fragmented breath, the sound intensely, intoxicatingly feminine.

'Dominic…'

Her voice low and husky, she reached for him again, her fingers insistent as they clutched at his shoulders. He brushed her hair back from her temple and took her lips again in a slow, intoxicating kiss that made his senses swim and every nerve ending pulse with life. Every thought that tried to intrude was ruthlessly quashed.

She was all that mattered. All he wanted. She…*this*… was what he needed.

Her arms wound around his neck and her fingers tangled again in his hair. His fingertips skimmed down the side of her face to her neck and lingered over the sensitive skin by her ear as a delicate shudder racked her. He deepened the kiss, plunging his tongue again and again, and she responded—each sensual stroke ensnaring him deeper in her spell. He stroked her neck, inside the open collar of the shirt she wore, tracing the delicate skin over her collarbone, then moving lower, seeking…he bit back a groan as his hand closed possessively around her breast, only the fine fabric of her chemise between his hand and the heat of her skin, her nipple a hard bud against his palm.

He dragged his mouth from hers and nuzzled her neck, searching for her pulse, laving it as it hammered beneath his tongue. His own heart pounded, sending hot blood surging through his veins, around his body, flooding his groin.

How long had he dreamed of her breasts? Conscious thought played no part in him tugging both shirt and chemise free from her waistband. He pushed both garments high, then reared back to gaze his fill at her beautiful, full breasts, the nipples and areoles a dusky pink. Each firm globe more than filled his hands. She shivered, a low moan escaping her lips as he teased her nipples into hard peaks, rubbing and tugging.

Her hands were on his jacket, pushing it open. On the buttons of his waistcoat. Again he reared back and shrugged out of both garments. She watched him, her eyes glinting.

'Your shirt,' she whispered. 'I want to see.'

He didn't think he could get any harder, but he did as he pulled his shirt over his head and saw her reaction. She reached up, and stroked her hands up his belly and across his chest, then down each arm to his hands.

'Help me.'

She sat up, took hold of her shirt and began to pull. He needed no further encouragement and the feeling of those wonderful breasts as they brushed against his chest was torture. He dipped his head and she gasped as he paid homage to them, licking, sucking and nipping to his heart's content while she explored his arms and torso—seemingly fascinated with the dark hair that covered his chest. He didn't know who initiated it, but before long they were on their feet, ripping off the rest of their clothes.

He stilled, feasting his eyes on all that glorious, naked flesh and gently, reverently, he cupped her upper arms, willing his body to be patient even as slender fingers wrapped around his length, squeezing and stroking. He removed her hand and pulled her towards him, kissing her long and deep as her body softened, moulding into his, and she moaned her pleasure.

He wanted nothing more than to lay her full length on the floor and to plunge his aching arousal into her heat, but he wouldn't rush this. He would make it good for her. So he laid her down and followed her. He took his time, worshipping her with his touch and his mouth, listening to her sighs and her gasps of pleasure, learning her, feeling her body arch beneath him, her nails digging into his shoulders, the impatient tilt of her hips, her husky 'Dominic...please...'

And when her fingers clutched harder and her head moved restlessly from side to side, when she was hot and wet and ready for him, he moved between her open thighs, positioned his throbbing shaft at her entrance, reached again for the pearl hidden in her secret folds and he pressed.

She screamed his name as she reached her zenith and, as her body shuddered with ecstasy, he thrust inside her. It took only a few thrusts for him to reach fulfilment, but he was happy. Her pleasure was his pleasure, her ecstasy, his ecstasy.

He gathered her close and settled down with her in his arms.

Chapter Eighteen

She felt so right in his arms, nestled into his chest, her hair tickling his chin.

But…

Those warnings he had successfully kept at bay came clamouring into his brain. The head-banging, gut-churning reasons why he could not even dream of marrying Liberty Lovejoy, even though his soul cried out for her. Even though he had, tentatively, begun to believe dreams might come true.

'Make me proud, my Son.'

His mother's words…uttered in that cold, demanding voice…the one all three of her children had striven to obey, desperate to win words of praise and approval. A taunting reminder of the past. Those insidious words—sneaking around his head, prying into the corners where hope had dared to germinate, marshalling his embryonic dreams together and, mockingly, dismissing them as the unworthy fantasies of a child.

'Never forget your duty—you were born to be the Duke. Never disgrace your position in society—the eyes of the world will be on you. Judging you. Never let them see weakness. You are not the same as other

men, driven by base desires. You are the Marquess of Avon. You will be Duke of Cheriton one day, and your son, and your son's son, and countless generations to follow will also fulfil that role. Do not allow your weakness to contaminate the bloodline—it is your destiny to keep it pure. Choose your wife with care and with pride and, above all, with your intelligence.'

Nausea and a deep, throbbing dread filled him. He tightened his embrace and breathed in her sweet, subtle essence—mixed now with the scent of their lovemaking. Honour whispered he must offer for Liberty. His heart craved nothing more than to spend his life with her. But duty and cold hard reasoning dictated otherwise.

He scrambled to his feet and grabbed his clothes, pulling them on hastily and haphazardly, the battle between heart and mind filling his head.

'Dominic...?'

Low, pained, questioning...her voice grabbed at his emotions and twisted. Hard. There was Liberty to think of...*her* feelings. Her future. And that tipped the balance of the scales in favour of his honour and his heart.

'I'm sorry. That shouldn't have happened...would never have happened had you not...had I not...' He was gabbling...his words sounded cold. Heartless.

'Never forget your duty, my Son.'

The scales tilted the opposite way. But he could not abandon Liberty. Not now.

'I will apply for a special licence in the morning. Get dressed. I will escort you home.'

'What?'

He looked at her then—sitting before the fire, the flames bronzing her skin, highlighting the honey and gold of her hair, her brother's shirt clutched to her breasts, her midnight-blue eyes with those glinting gold flecks, huge...searching...uncertain.

What more could he say? He could not reassure her, not properly. How could he when he barely knew which way was up? How could he, with his head churning with such conflict? Everything was in turmoil...his carefully laid plans...he barely knew what to think, let alone what to say or do. For once in his well-ordered, meticulously planned life, he was lost. The path he had followed from childhood had not only forked, it had vanished, leaving him frantically searching with no clue which way to turn.

A childhood memory surfaced of tumbling out of a tree, scrabbling at the branches, trying desperately to slow his fall. He felt the same sensation now—as though he were tumbling, ever faster, out of control.

His heart twisted in his chest at her beloved face, her doubt. The last thing he wanted was to hurt her, but he couldn't find the right words, not when he was still reeling. He needed space and time to get his thoughts straight. But he *would* make it right—explain properly— later. He just needed time to think.

He softened his voice. 'Get dressed, Liberty. I will call on you in the morning and we will put this right.'

Her eyes flashed and she bounced to her feet.

That shouldn't have happened...would never have happened had you not...

He hadn't needed to finish that thought... Liberty could read between those lines. What he meant was: it would never have happened had she not defied all the rules of proper behaviour and come here clandes- tinely, and then compounded her offence by drawing him out about his mother and resurrecting all those painful memories for him.

Humiliation burned through her as she tugged Gideon's shirt over her head and pulled on his pantaloons, wriggling to fit them past her hips.

'A licence will not be necessary, Dominic.'

Her gamble had failed. She had hoped—stupid, forlorn, immature hope—that by loving him…by showing him what he *could* have in his life…he would finally open his eyes and his heart to the truth. He did love her—he had proved that with every kiss, every caress, every touch. He had proved it every time he looked at her with his heart in his eyes.

But that was not enough. If he was only offering for her under duress—from some stuffy, ridiculous sense of honour—she could never accept, no matter how much she loved him. He might love her now, but she feared that love would never survive if he was ashamed of her. And his reaction…his words…confirmed that fear.

'I have taken your innocence. We *must* be wed.'

'You did not take my innocence.' God help her, she lied. She had been intimate with Bernard, but they had never actually made love. But the act had not hurt as she had thought it might. It had been wonderful…swept along on a tide of passion…the slightest of discomforts when he first entered her…but she had been wet, and so ready for him, longing for him. There had been no pain. 'Bernard and I…'

She had no need to finish; she read his comprehension in his eyes. And was that a tinge of relief? Her heart tore…not even in two, but into shreds. Too numerous to count.

'You need not concern yourself with me. Just promise me you will think twice before pledging yourself to

Lady Sybilla.' She couldn't help herself. She couldn't bear to think of the cold, lonely life that awaited him. She went to him, touched his arm. 'Please. You deserve better than her, whatever her pedigree might say.'

'You must marry me!' His silver gaze pierced her, filling her with sudden hope. Hope that was dashed with his next words. 'What if you are with child?'

Liberty swallowed hard. 'And what if I am not? Marriage is for a lifetime and my grandfather was still a lowly coal merchant.'

Please. Argue with me. Tell me you've reconsidered. Anything!

Dominic passed one hand around the back of his neck, then picked up his discarded coat, shrugging into it. 'We will talk about this tomorrow. But...' he paused, and she saw his throat move as he swallowed 'if you find there are consequences you must let me know.' He avoided her gaze. 'I will see you want for nothing... I will pay you an allowance. Buy you a—'

She shoved him. He staggered back a pace, taken unawares. Liberty followed him, thrusting her face close to his. *'I do not want your money.'*

She cast an eye around the room. Boots. She grabbed them and easily pulled them on as they were many sizes too big for her. Jacket. She snatched it from the chair, passed it wordlessly to Dominic. He held it for her while she wriggled into it. Hat. She bundled her hair into a rope, piled it on top of her head and rammed the hat down hard, relishing the pain as the brim folded her ears and trapped them. Any pain was preferable to what she felt inside.

She reached for the door. 'And I do not need your escort.'

He reached past her and held the door shut. 'I will not allow you to walk the streets alone.'

'I got here without mishap. I can get home.'

He released the pressure on the door and Liberty marched into the hall and out of the front door, crossing the street to make her way home. There were a few people about, but most were in carriages. She kept her eyes fixed firmly on the pavement in front of her and walked as quickly as she could. As she reached the corner, a movement caught her eye.

Dominic. Five paces behind her.

'Berty!'

She ignored his whisper and increased her pace to a trot, a stitch forming in her side at the unaccustomed exertion. He made no attempt to catch her up. Good. The less she had to do with that stubborn numbskull in the future, the better she would like it! Lord Arrogant could ride to hell backwards on a donkey for all she cared! He didn't deserve her!

As they turned into Green Street, however, he caught her up and grabbed her arm, forcing her to a stop.

'What are you doing? Someone might see us,' she hissed.

They were close to a street lamp and Dominic manoeuvred her so her face was in shadow. She supposed she should be grateful for that. She wasn't so enamoured of the lift of one dark eyebrow and the quirk of his lips that she could now see quite clearly, with the lamplight illuminating his features.

'They might indeed. But that doesn't matter because we *will* be married, Liberty. I will call on you tomorrow at noon and I shall request a private interview.'

She thought quickly. If he did that, there would be no doubt in her sisters' or Mrs Mount's minds that he intended to propose to her. Her heart quailed at the thought of trying to convince them she would refuse… they had all noticed how friendly the two of them were and her sisters had both, laughingly, accused her of carrying a torch for Lord Avon.

'Come at two,' she said. They had arranged to pay visits tomorrow afternoon…she could easily excuse herself.

His eyes narrowed. 'Are you up to something, Berty? Because, I warn you, I expect you to be at home. Or I shall come looking for you.'

She suppressed the shiver his softly spoken words aroused. 'I will be there.'

He tilted her chin with one long finger and for one wild moment she thought he might kiss her. But he merely said, 'Good.'

Anger sustained her as she crept indoors and upstairs. Safely back in her bedchamber, she struggled out of Gideon's coat—hearing an ominous rip in the process—then shed the remainder of his clothes and shoved them beneath her bed, out of sight. She would deal with them in the morning. She had the rest of her life to deal with them. She burrowed under the bedclothes and, finally, she gave way to her misery.

After Mrs Mount and her sisters left the house the following afternoon, Liberty paced around the small salon feeling like a caged animal. She didn't fool herself Dominic would give up easily—he would consider himself honour-bound to marry her even though it had been her decision to visit him and they had been swept away on a mutual tide of passion. Her stomach swooped and her skin tingled at the memory of his touch, his whispers, the caress of his lips…and of *him*. The spicy, musky scent of aroused male; the salty tang of his skin; the texture of his hair-roughened skin beneath her questing fingertips; the slide of skin over his hot, hard length as she stroked. His weight on her, between her thighs… her belly tightened at those memories and hot, sweet need pooled at her core.

They had both lost control, that was the honest truth, and she did not shy away from her own culpability—it was more her fault than his. *She* had gone to *him* with the genuine aim of stopping him from making a dreadful mistake. Had she truly believed he would suddenly discard his belief in his duty? A belief that had lasted a lifetime. How utterly foolish, to think that she—Liberty Lovejoy—could ever influence a man like the Marquess of Avon.

But then, once they were alone together…when he told her about his mother…oh, then her heart yearned to heal him. And she had wantonly indulged her own desire to make love with the man who haunted her dreams, knowing she might never again have the chance.

And because it was more her fault than his, she would save him from another mistake and protect him from marrying her out of a misguided sense of honour. It was a marriage she was afraid he would come to regret and she could not bear that he would grow to rue the day he met her.

If she allowed herself to, she could sink into a swamp of despair. But a thought had surfaced…the faintest glimmer of a hope. There was no doubt that Dominic would try by any means to persuade her to accept his offer today. And she could not, would not, accept.

But…if the possibility of a child were removed… what then? What if, by some miracle, Dominic *did* change his mind? What if her gamble had borne fruit and opened his mind to the possibility of another way… of a marriage for love instead of duty?

It was a fragile hope, but it was all she had to cling to. If, of course, he *did* love her. Last night, she had been convinced. Now, in the clear light of day, she was not so sure.

All she could do, for now, was to remain steadfast in her refusal of him. For both their sakes.

And pray she was not with child.

She was so lost in thought she jumped when Ethel opened the salon door to announce Lord Avon. Her heart hammered and it felt as though every muscle in her body turned to jelly. She hauled in a steadying breath and smoothed her palms down the skirt of her gown.

'Show him in, please, Ethel.'

She took advantage of the few minutes it would take him to come upstairs to check her reflection in the mirror on the wall by the door. Her cheeks were flushed, her eyes somewhat wild and there was a quiver in her lower lip she could not quell without taking it between her teeth and biting down on it. She patted her hair into place, then hurried to stand before the window, feeling more confident with the light at her back.

'Lord Avon, miss. Would you like me to stay?'

Just one look at him set her heart skipping and jumping—his tall, broad frame, his dark good looks, his crooked smile revealing his uncertainty over the action he intended to take.

Liberty switched her attention to the maid. 'No, Ethel. That will not be necessary. His Lordship will not remain above five minutes.'

As soon as they were alone, Dominic strode across the room and reached for her hands. She tucked them behind her back. He frowned, but he took the hint and stepped back.

'Liberty…look…' He swept a hand through his hair. 'I am aware I made a complete mull of it last night after…after we…well. I am sorry. Truly I am… I didn't think what I was saying before I blurted it out.'

'You voiced your immediate thoughts, Dominic. It is quite all right. I understand.'

'No. It is not all right.'

He moved closer again and his spicy cologne weaved through her senses as he cupped her shoulders. The warm, steady strength of his hands was nearly her undoing. How simple it would be to bow to the inevitable… to fold into his embrace, to lean into his solid frame and allow him to take control, to accept him and to worry about any consequences later. She blanked her expression and forced herself to remain rigidly upright.

'Accept me and I shall leave here and arrange the licence straight away. We can be wed by the end of next week.' He put his lips to her ear. 'We will be happy together.'

His breath tickled, but she gritted her teeth, determined not to squirm. Was he trying to convince himself as much as persuade her? It was not hard to believe and it made her even more determined to stick to her plan.

'No, Dominic. I will not marry you. You are only offering for me out of guilt, but there is no need. I am an adult, not some green girl who did not know what she was doing. There is no need to ruin both our lives.'

'*Both* our lives?' His grip tightened. 'What are you saying…that you do not care for me after all? Are you in the habit of giving yourself to random men you have no feelings for?'

She tore herself from his grasp and paced across

the room before whirling to face him. 'I care for you too much to saddle you with a wife you are marrying out of duty.'

He visibly flinched. '*Duty?* It is duty that resulted in that damned shortlist. It is my honour that dictates I make an honest woman of you.'

She stared at him, holding his gaze without wavering, willing him to say more…to speak of what was in his heart. Did he love her? Or was last night purely about lust after all? If she accepted him like this, she might never know. But of one thing she was certain—if he did not love her and he was offering purely with his honour, then he would soon grow to resent and even hate her.

She had faced heartbreak before and survived. She would do so again.

'No. You are free to continue with your perfect, dutiful life, my lord. You are under no obligation to me.'

'And if you are with child?'

She had done the calculations. It would not be long before she knew. A matter of days only.

'If I am, we will talk again.' She moved to the door and opened it. 'I hope we may remain friends, when we meet?'

He searched her face, then nodded.

'Then I shall bid you good afternoon, Lord Avon.'

If she thought he would give up that easily, she could think again. Dominic strode up Green Street, fury at her stubbornness biting at his gut. The clip-clop of hooves behind him reminded him that he had driven his curricle to her house. He gestured at Ted to stay back and he kept walking.

Who does she think she is? Doesn't she realise the honour I've—?

His whirling thoughts steadied and he lopped off his diatribe before he could finish it, recognising his sheer arrogance to even think such a thing. As his thoughts slowed down so did his pace and his tumbling emotions, and his churning gut.

Why are you so damned furious?

He halted on the corner of the street, staring blindly at the houses opposite as he strove to untangle his thoughts from his feelings.

Why *was* he so furious? Madly, rigidly, agonisingly furious?

He had what he wanted. He'd told himself, time and again, that it was lust driving his obsession with Liberty Lovejoy. He should be rejoicing. He'd had her. She'd set him free. Free to have what he wanted—the perfect Lady Sybilla Gratton as his wife. His Marchioness. The mother of his children. The future Duchess of Cheriton.

He paced onwards, his steps slow and measured, his gaze on the pavement.

And slowly the truth emerged out of that muddle of emotions and he finally accepted it with a clear head. The idea of having Liberty Lovejoy as his wife had taken hold in his brain and it felt right. He could not dislodge that image. It grew stronger and brighter with every second, every minute that passed. He didn't only want Liberty Lovejoy, he *needed* her. In his life. Always.

On the brink of spinning around to march back to Green Street, he halted.

She had refused him. And he—the perfect, gentlemanly Marquess of Avon—had managed to both insult and infuriate the woman he loved. If he returned to her now and prostrated himself at her feet, she would no doubt laugh him out of the house. And he wouldn't blame her. He'd made an utter mess of the entire thing.

He walked on.

He would make a plan.

I'll court her properly... I'll make *her change her mind.*

He halted at the next corner and waited for Ted to bring up his curricle. He felt a burning need to work off his frustration. A visit to Jackson's would help.

The next few days tried his patience to the limit. A new and different Liberty Lovejoy had emerged— coolly correct in everything she did and said. She smiled graciously. She danced with precision and with elegance. She smiled at him, but with her lips closed. And she refused to rise to any provocation, merely agreeing with every word he said. She had encased her heart and her soul in an exquisitely polite but impenetrable shell and nothing he said or did could pierce it.

If she should get with child, though, it will change everything. She won't refuse me then.

A part of him understood he was clutching at that thought in the hope it would solve this impasse for him. But that was all he had to cling to.

Chapter Nineteen

A mere six days after *that night*—the night when Liberty had gambled the highest stakes of all and lost—Lord and Lady Stanton threw a ball at their mansion in Cavendish Square. The Lovejoys, along with most of the *ton*, were invited and Liberty waited with bated breath and with a thudding heart for Dominic to make an appearance. She had a very important message for him.

At every ball since *that night* Dominic asked Liberty to dance. And, if she had a dance free, she accepted. But she avoided any hint of personal conversation, talking only of inconsequential matters and agreeing with every single one of Dominic's opinions, which grew increasingly outrageous as the days passed. He was being deliberately provocative, she knew, but she refused to lower her guard for one single second. He wanted a perfect lady? Well, she might have missed out on the strictly correct upbringing of Lady Sybilla and her ilk, but she would show him she could be a lady when necessary.

As far as the rest of the *ton* were concerned, his behaviour was still impeccable. He partnered several perfectly eligible young ladies, including Sybilla, at every ball but the announcement everyone was waiting for never came.

And Liberty knew why. And tonight she would set his mind at rest. If he was *still* determined to marry the perfect Lady Sybilla, he could now do so with a clear conscience. This morning her prayers had been answered and tonight she would reassure His Lordship that there had been no unwanted consequences from *that night* and that he was free to continue with the life he'd mapped out from a young boy.

And she was free to continue with hers. She rubbed absently at her chest. This hollow feeling was one she must grow accustomed to…unless this final, desperate gamble of hers bore fruit. But the decision must be his. She would give him no encouragement. And if *this* gamble paid off, she would *know* he loved her, even if he never actually said those words.

She gazed around the room despondently. Olivia and Hugo were absent tonight as Olivia was suffering from a slight head cold and Liberty could garner no interest in joining Mrs Mount and the chattering chaperons. A nagging ache low in her belly was a constant reminder of her news for Dominic. How would he react? She didn't fool herself that he would suddenly throw himself at her feet and declare his undying love for her, but would he…*could* he…reconsider his plans?

She was confident she had been right to refuse Dominic's offer. Although offer wasn't the right word—it had been more of a statement.

This is what we will do. I have decided. You will comply.

Her heart still ached for him. Her body still craved him. But, most disconcerting of all, she missed him— just talking to him, laughing with him, teasing him.

Being teased in return.

No one but he called her Berty.

The heart of her uncertainty was that she knew he liked her and cared for her and was attracted to her. She was almost certain he loved her.

But did he love her *enough*?

And would he give himself the chance to find out, or was he so committed to his lifelong vision of his future that he would continue along that path without considering the alternative? Without considering her?

A flurry of activity at the ballroom door grabbed her attention as all activity seemed to freeze for an instant before conversations restarted, seemingly brighter and more animated than before. Liberty knew without looking what that meant. She had become accustomed to the phenomenon since Dominic's father had arrived in town—he had that effect whenever he walked into an event.

Liberty had never been introduced to the Duke, but he did not appear to be the sort of man who would welcome someone like Liberty Lovejoy as the wife of his son and heir. As Dominic had said, on *that night*, his father had not shirked *his* duty—his first wife, Dominic's mother, had been the daughter of a marquess and the granddaughter of a duke. The aristocratic heritage of the Dukedom was intact, even though the current Duchess's grandfather was a simple silversmith. And that also confirmed Liberty had been right to refuse Dominic because, unless she knew without a shadow of doubt that he loved her and, more importantly, unless *Dominic* knew and admitted it, she was convinced he would grow to regret their union and become ashamed of her.

Only love, in all its strength and glory, would give

a union between them the chance to stand strong and withstand other people's opinions.

So. Had Dominic arrived with the Duke and Duchess or would Liberty have to be patient a little longer? She tiptoed up to peer towards the door. She could not see. There were too many people in the way.

'What are you up to, Sis?'

She smiled up at Gideon as he slipped his arm around her waist. 'Looking for Hope and Verity,' she lied.

Since Gideon had caught her crying he had become a calmer, nicer person. Lady Emily, too, had influenced him in a positive way although he still stayed out late with his friends. Liberty, however, no longer fretted about him quite so much and, surprisingly, the less she worried about him, the closer they had grown.

'You're a proper mother hen, aren't you, Sis? Don't worry about them—that's what Mrs Mount is for. You should be looking to your own future.' His blue eyes searched hers, suddenly serious. 'It's been five years, Liberty. It's time you began to live your life again. Bernard would want you to.'

Tears prickled at the back of her eyes. 'I know he would.'

It was the first time she had admitted to any member of her family that she might be ready to find love again. Until now it had felt as though she were laying her soul bare to be trampled over but, somehow, this time in London had helped all of the Lovejoys to change. They had grown closer as a family, although her sisters still complained bitterly when Romeo got up to mischief.

'You deserve to be happy again, Lib. And you will be. I can feel it in my bones. I'm on my way to make sure Verity is all right. Bridlington is here. I had a word with him, but it's best to be sure. I'll see you later.'

Gideon hugged her closer before releasing her and she watched as he made his way across the room.

'Is he still causing you concern?' The deep voice sent tingles racing through her.

It was the same whenever they met.

Whenever they spoke.

Whenever they danced—the touch of his hand pure agony with the wanting of him. And, if he could, he always picked a waltz—her hand on his shoulder, his hand on her waist, the helpless longing in her heart and the aching void of loneliness in her chest. That void had begun to fill. Before. Now, it gaped wider and blacker than ever.

She stretched her lips in a cool smile and turned to Dominic.

'No. He is doing his duty as an older brother. It seems Bridlington is here tonight. He has already spoken to him and now he is checking on Verity.'

'I'm pleased to hear it.'

A swift scan of him showed he was on edge, as he had been ever since *that night*. He disguised it well, but she could read his moods where other, more casual, observers would see nothing. It was time to put him out of his misery. And time to take that chance…to destroy that last tie that bound them together, that final strand that had been keeping her fragile hopes alive. And to hope Dominic would reach into his heart and see that the power was in his hands to forge a deeper, stronger link that could join them for ever.

'Have you a dance free this evening, Liberty?'

'I am afraid I do not dance this evening, my lord.' She would go home early, with a headache as an excuse. 'But I have news for you.'

Their gazes fused, his as opaque as it ever had been, his face impassive.

'I can confirm there were no c-c-consequences.' Try as she might, she could not control the wobble in her voice. Anguish scorched every fibre of her being. 'You need delay your betrothal no longer.'

She bobbed a curtsy and turned away, but Dominic grabbed her elbow, stopping her. 'Liberty!' His voice was low. Urgent. 'We need to talk.'

She pivoted to face him. '*We* need do nothing. *You* are free now to make your choice—and you know as well as I that not one unattached lady in this room to-night would refuse an offer from you. The choice is up to you.'

She stared up into those silvery eyes, but all she could see was her own image, reflected in them.

'Not one, Dominic,' she added softly. 'Your choice.'

She tugged her arm free and hurried away through the crowd to where Mrs Mount sat with the other chaperons. She looked up at Liberty enquiringly, her look changing to one of concern.

'You were right, dear ma'am,' said Liberty. 'I should have remained at home this evening.'

She laid her hand briefly to her lower belly and Mrs Mount gave her an understanding smile. She knew Liberty's courses had begun. She would not think it odd for Liberty to leave.

'There is no need for concern,' Liberty continued. 'I shall ask Gideon to escort me home and he will be back before you know it.'

Dominic watched as Liberty was absorbed into the crowd. He should feel released. He felt the opposite— as though prison walls were closing in on him. Ever since that night—the most glorious, wonderful night of his entire life—he had been as though held in limbo. He saw an insect trapped in amber once, at the British Museum, and that is exactly how he had felt since *that night*. But he had made a complete mull of it afterwards…talking of them marrying by special licence, speaking of *consequences*. Offering her *money*.

She was rightly disgusted with him, but no more disgusted than he was with himself. What had happened to his famed manners? His powers of address? They appeared to have deserted him at the time he most desperately needed them. He had tried everything to recover their friendship as a prelude to courting Liberty Lovejoy properly. To prove to her that he loved her. Only her. And to prove he could not give a damn whether she was the daughter of a duke or the daughter of a ditch-digger. But how could he do that when she kept him at arm's length with her perfect lady image and her exquisitely correct manners? His heart yearned for the old Liberty back…the real Liberty.

Dominic snagged a glass of champagne from a passing footman, swallowed one mouthful and then stilled.

It was not only his life that had been in limbo since *that night*. His thinking, it seemed, had been suspended, too. The family had noticed—he'd seen them watching him with concern when they thought he wouldn't notice—but none of them had mentioned his list.

Except Father.

'You may feel you have backed yourself into a corner, Dom, but there is absolutely no need to make any decisions this year. It will wait. What is your hurry?'

And he could not bring himself to admit that the hurry was the fear he might lose Liberty for good. And neither could he admit he had fallen in love. Not to Father, because he would then move heaven and earth to put things right for Dominic.

But this was *his* mess. He was a grown man and it was up to him to sort it out.

He tipped the remainder of the champagne into a nearby urn of flowers—with a silent apology to Felicity—and cursed himself for even more of a fool.

He had been waiting…hoping…that circumstance would intervene and that Liberty would find herself with child and she would *have* to marry him. A coward's hope. Her words tonight had shattered that dream, but now, picking through the wreckage of the plan that had not even been a plan but a weak, vague hope that everything would turn out all right, he understood that Liberty's news was a blessing.

Now, she had provided him with the perfect way to prove he loved her. If she had been with child, she would never believe he *wanted* to marry her. She would always fear he had been, in effect, trapped into it. Now…*now* he was free to prove to her that he loved her and only her.

With renewed vigour, he turned on his heel and went to find his stepmother. He had plans to make. Proper plans this time.

Chapter Twenty

It would be *the* ball of the Season. Everybody who was anybody would be there.

'But you *must* attend, Liberty. Tell her, Hope.' Verity looked from one of her sisters to the other. 'It is the first ball the Duke of Cheriton has hosted since Lady Olivia made her debut *five years ago*!'

The ball had been announced just four days before, much to the consternation of those members of the *ton* who already had evening events arranged for tomorrow night. They had bowed to the inevitable and many events had been cancelled amid speculation as to whether there might be a specific purpose to the ball… whether a *special announcement* was imminent.

And people had nudged one another and cast surreptitious looks at the Marquess of Avon as they did so, convinced that he had finally chosen his bride and that the ball was to celebrate their betrothal. But not even the most incorrigible tittle-tattles could pretend they had an inkling of his choice. His Lordship went about his daily life as inscrutably as ever and not one of the young ladies believed to feature on his shortlist gave the smallest indication that she harboured a grand secret.

Liberty had no more idea than anyone else. Dominic had continued to be friendly whenever their paths crossed and he continued to dance with her as well as with many other young ladies, including those on his shortlist. His provocative teasing had stopped, however, much to Liberty's mingled consternation and relief.

His behaviour to her was that of the consummate gentleman and hers to him was that of the perfect lady.

Not even Olivia had let any information about the ball slip, although that, Liberty was fairly sure, was because even *she* did not why the ball had been arranged with such haste. All she knew, she had told Liberty crossly, was that her stepmother was rushing around like a whirlwind—for, as the lady of the house, the ball was under her jurisdiction—and that Grantham was being impossibly officious. Her father, she added, had brought in an army of additional servants to help get the ball ready on time.

But Liberty's entire family appeared unable to accept that she was happy not to attend the ball. Ever since the Stantons' ball she had steeled herself for the announcement of Dominic's betrothal and now, having been forewarned it was likely to happen tomorrow night, she would be a fool to put herself through such a trial in such a public setting.

'You *must* attend.' Hope added her voice to Verity's. 'Think how dreadful it would be for us to miss it.'

'*You* do not have to miss it.' Liberty put her arms around Romeo—seated beside her on the sofa—and kissed his head. 'Mrs Mount and Gideon will be there. Nobody will even notice or care about my absence.'

'Lady Olivia will be offended if you do not attend,' said Hope. 'You are friends—why on earth do you not want to go to her stepmother's ball?'

Really! Can they not see my heart is breaking?

No sooner had that very unfair thought surfaced than it was swept aside by the reassurance that no one actually *knew* Liberty's heart was shattered or that her life was over. She hadn't felt pain like this since Bernard died. She simply could not summon the strength to stand there and smile and look happy for Dominic and the flawless Lady Sybilla and, even worse, to congratulate them and wish them happy together.

She couldn't do it.

'I have no suitable gown to wear.'

It was no lie. Liberty had worn each of her three new ball gowns at least twice and the *ball of the Season* surely warranted a new gown.

'That is no excuse!' Hope grabbed Liberty's hand, forcing her to pay attention. 'Gideon, Verity and I decided it was time to show you our appreciation for everything you have done for us and we ordered a new gown. Cinderella *shall* go to the ball!'

Despite her dejection, Liberty could not help but laugh. 'Does that make you two the Ugly Sisters?' Then she sobered. 'But the ball is tomorrow night. There is no time. I shall send a note to Olivia explaining I am indisposed. The dress will come for another night... perhaps the Derhams' ball next week?'

Hope pouted. 'I think you are being very mean, Liberty. What have you got against the Duke and Duchess?'

'Nothing!'

Other than that the Duke terrified her. She had met him just two days before, introduced by Olivia, and his silvery-grey gaze—so like his son's—had swept over her, leaving her feeling as though he knew all her deepest, darkest secrets. Including that she was in love with his son and heir and had seduced him in the hope he might see sense. She shivered at the thought the Duke might find that out.

'I simply…it will be too grand. I do not care for such huge occasions. Now, please, stop pestering me. You will be perfectly safe attending with both Gideon and Mrs Mount and once you are surrounded by all your fawning admirers you won't have a thought to spare for me.'

Liberty spent the next day at home, even eschewing a ride in the Park. She could not face the growing excitement. It was just a ball, for goodness sake. What did the reason behind it matter? The Duke would no doubt announce the betrothal between Dominic and Lady Sybilla, and then the *ton*, in all its glittering, gossiping glory, would move on to the next shiny piece of news.

Much ado about nothing.

Except it wasn't nothing. Not to her. Romeo was beside her on the sofa and she buried her face in his soft fur. He licked her ear. Although it tickled, she could not summon even a giggle. Everywhere felt so numb.

'Miss Lovejoy?'

Her head jerked up at the maid's voice. 'Yes, Ethel?'

It was early evening and, having already dined, Liberty was alone in the drawing room, waiting to see the rest of the family, all dressed in their finery, before they left for the Cheritons' ball.

The maid looked flushed and flustered.

'It's Mrs Mount, miss. She's had the megrim come on.'

'Oh, dear!' Liberty stood. 'I shall go to her at once. Ask Mrs Taylor to prepare some willow-bark tea, if you will. That may help.'

'Yes, miss.'

When she reached Mrs Mount's bedchamber, Hope and Verity were both in attendance and Mrs Mount herself was in bed, the covers pulled up to her chin and a damp cloth draped across her forehead.

'My dear Mrs Mount.' Liberty went to her bedside, ushering her sisters out of the way. 'You must tell me if there is anything I can do to help.'

Mrs Mount moaned softly, her eyes shut. 'Nothing,' she whispered. 'I just need peace and quiet.'

'Of course.' Liberty scanned the room. The curtains were drawn, blocking out the light, and there was a glass of water on the bedside table. 'I have ordered willow-bark tea and I shall send one of the maids up to sit with you, in case you require anything. Come, girls...' she waved Hope and Verity towards the door '...let us leave poor Mrs Mount in peace.'

Once on the landing, she said, 'Why aren't you dressed for the ball? I thought the carriage was ordered for half past?'

Verity pouted. 'How can we go now? We have no chaperon. Mrs Mount is indisposed and *you* have refused to go.'

'It's the ball of the Season,' Hope wailed, 'and we shall be the only ones not there!'

'Oh, good grief.' Liberty thought quickly, but could see no alternative. 'I... I must accompany you, I suppose. I can hardly expect Gideon to watch over you both.'

Verity flung her arms around Liberty and kissed her cheek. 'Oh, *thank* you. You are the *best* sister.'

Her heart expanded, knowing she had made her sisters happy. But what about her? She would have to face Dominic and, probably, endure his happy news. It was the last thing she wished to do. And yet...by staying away, would he not guess the reason why? She thought she had managed to hoodwink him so far, acting as though she could not care less, but he was no fool. Her absence would scream the truth more loudly than her stoical attendance.

Perhaps this was for the best. It would be but a few hours of her life. She had endured worse and coped. She would survive this.

'I suppose it will have to be the violet silk again,' she said. 'But no matter—no one will be looking my way, after all.'

'Oh! I forgot to tell you!' Hope's blue eyes sparkled. 'You won't need your violet silk. Do you recall that new gown I told you about? It was delivered this afternoon, but Lizzie stupidly put it in my bedchamber, thinking it was mine! She will bring it to you and she can help you with your hair, for mine is already done.'

The gown was perfect. If Liberty could have chosen a gown for herself, without consideration of cost, it was just what she would have chosen—a high-waisted gown of blush-pink crepe over a satin slip, the skirt decorated with two festoons of pink rosebuds at the hem. The bodice—with scattered seed pearls and tiny rosebuds stitched to the fabric—was cut low over the shoulders, in the current fashion, with short sleeves held up by narrow satin bands. Lizzie pinned her hair on top of her head, threading a string of pearls through her locks and leaving a few curls to frame her face. Her mother's single strand of pearls was clasped around her throat and matching pearl eardrops hung from her lobes.

Her sisters' gasps when she appeared at the head of the stairs were balm to Liberty's soul. She straightened her shoulders and raised her chin as she descended to where they waited in the hall. Gideon came in the front door.

'The carriage is waiting.' He let out a low whistle as he caught sight of Liberty and he walked to meet her and kissed her hand. 'You look like a princess.'

The line of carriages waiting to deliver their occupants to Beauchamp House stretched all the way around Grosvenor Square. As they waited, the evening dry, the sky spangled with stars, Liberty remembered the very first time she had called at Beauchamp House: the heavy rain, the thunder and lightning, the footman with the umbrella. And Dominic. The very first time they met. Little did she imagine then how she would come to feel about him. Little did she imagine he would break her heart. She swallowed, forcing down the aching mass that invaded her throat.

I will not disgrace myself. I am braver...stronger... than that.

By the time the Lovejoys entered the front door Liberty's nerves had wound so tight she could barely hear a word said to her as she climbed the magnificent marble staircase with Gideon, Hope and Verity, and then stood in line to be greeted by their host and hostess.

The Duke was resplendent in severe black evening clothes and the Duchess looked lovely in lemon gauze over a cream underdress. As they waited their turn, a quick sweep of the surrounding area revealed no trace of any of the rest of the Beauchamps and, for that, Liberty was grateful. One step at a time. Get the formalities out of the way and she could hopefully lose herself in the crush—and it truly was a crush. As they reached the Duke—Gideon bowing and she, Hope and Verity sinking into curtsies—Liberty caught a glimpse of the crowded ballroom, down a short flight of stairs. How on earth anyone would manage to dance was beyond her although, no doubt, the elders would soon disperse to the card rooms and salons, leaving the ballroom free for the dancers and their chaperons.

She rose from her curtsy to find herself being regarded by a pair of friendly golden-brown eyes.

'We have heard a great deal about you from Olivia, Miss Lovejoy,' said the Duchess. 'Thank you for being such a good friend to her...she puts so much pressure on herself to be the perfect mother to the twins, even though we keep telling her not to be so hard on herself, is that not so, Leo?'

Gideon and the girls had moved on, waiting now at the top of the flight of steps down into the ballroom, and the following guests had not yet moved forward, leaving Liberty in limbo with the Duke and the Duchess. She sucked in a sharp breath in an attempt to quell her nerves as the Duke's penetrating silver-grey gaze studied her unhurriedly.

'Indeed.' He smiled at Liberty, his eyes crinkling at the corners, and suddenly he did not look as intimidating. His gaze did not swerve from hers. 'It is a pleasure to meet you again, Miss Lovejoy. We are honoured that you accepted our invitation.'

Liberty managed a smile in return, even as she wondered at the strange phrasing used by the Duke. She joined Gideon and the girls at the head of the stairs.

Chapter Twenty-One

'The Earl of Wendover; Miss Lovejoy; Miss Hope Lovejoy; Miss Verity Lovejoy.'

Their arrival was announced by Grantham—very erect and clearly relishing his role as Master of Ceremonies—in resonant tones. They descended the stairs into the ballroom. Liberty rested her hand on Gideon's arm as Hope and Verity followed behind, and aimed her gaze resolutely above the heads of the crowd. As they reached the foot of the stairs, Gideon slipped his arm from beneath her hand.

'I see Emily over by the window. I shall see you later.'

He melted among the crowd, lost to sight within seconds. Liberty didn't even know which window he might be heading for—there were five sets of French windows along the far wall, but she had been so determined not to catch sight of Dominic or Sybilla that neither had she seen Lady Emily, or where she stood. She turned to Hope and Verity, but they were already surrounded by young men eager to reserve dances.

Liberty rubbed her upper chest, feeling the hollow swoop of her stomach as she did so. This had been her worst fear. Being alone, in the crowd, waiting for the axe to fall. She peered around anxiously, and froze.

Dominic. Two paces away, handsome and debonair in black evening clothes, a dark sapphire pin in his neckcloth. His gaze steady. On her. She swallowed and forced a smile. She would not evade this meeting. Her actions had been her own, the decisions her own. She had gambled of her own free will and it was not Dominic's fault that he still believed in duty over love.

'Good evening, Liberty.'

His rich voice sent shudders of helpless desire through her, as did the look of intent in his silvery gaze. He moved closer and she could smell the spicy, musky cologne he favoured. When she closed her eyes at night, it was that remembered scent that started the memories rolling through her head. She blinked, forcing her mind out of her feelings and into the practicalities of coping with this meeting without making a complete idiot of herself.

'Good evening, my lord.' Love—pure, despairing, eternal—squeezed her heart, catching at her breath. How could she bear this? But bear it she must. 'It is… it is a crush tonight, is it not? Your stepmother must be pleased with the success of her ball.'

He smiled. Tenderly. She blinked again, too accustomed to him blanking his emotions to believe her own eyes. But she was not mistaken. That tender smile was aimed directly at her. It reached his eyes, too—no opaque silver coins tonight, nor even mirrors reflecting the world back. For almost the first time since she had known him—other than *that night*—he appeared to be inviting her in. Inviting her to see the real man inside.

'I am sure she is.'

Her heart beat a little faster. That vice constricting

her heart eased a fraction and hope stirred as Dominic extended one hand. As though in a dream she placed her own hand in his. His fingers closed strongly around hers, warm, comforting, safe. Tears stung her eyes and she desperately swallowed her emotions down. She could not cope with comforting. Or with safe.

Her heart began to pound. Disjointed questions ricocheted around her head. *What...? Why...? How...?* Her knees trembled and her mouth dried, and all coherent thought scattered, as out of reach as the stars in the sky.

Dominic captured her other hand, bringing their joined hands together, between them, at chest height. Then, in a gesture that stole her breath, he opened his fingers leaving his hands side by side, palm up, almost in supplication. Her own hands lay on his, palm to palm, but she was not controlled in any way. She could remove her hands. She could move away, if she chose to. But she would not...could not...move. Her mind had ceased to control her body. She stood, helpless, waiting to hear what he might say. Dreading and yet hoping... yearning...*praying*.

He smiled into her eyes.

'If you do not want this, Liberty Louisa Lovejoy...if you do not want *me*...please tell me now and we shall say no more about it.'

She could not grasp his meaning, so she picked on the familiar.

'How do you know my middle name?'

One corner of his lips quirked up in a half-smile. 'Verity told me.'

Her gaze skimmed past him, to where she had last seen her sisters. Hope and Verity, beyond Dominic's right shoulder, were watching her, wide smiles on their faces. She wrenched her attention back to Dominic.

'V-Verity? Wh-why did she tell you that?'

'I asked her.'

'Oh.' Her throat ached unbearably. She still could not allow herself to hope…to believe…what his words meant. 'Wh-what is this? What are you doing?'

He ducked his head close to listen to her whispered question. His ear, his dark hair curling slightly over its rim, was tantalisingly close to her lips. He was so close she could see the texture of his skin, the faint shadow of his beard, even though he was freshly shaven. He raised his head again and she saw the glisten of his tongue as it moistened his visibly dry lips. She slid her palms over his and her fingertips found the pulse in his wrist. It pounded even faster than her own.

'I am about to propose to you.'

Her heart leapt. Her lungs seized. Her sisters were still watching avidly…with Gideon and…*Mrs Mount*? Liberty swallowed down a swell of tears as she processed his words. Propose? To her? But… 'What about Sybilla?' she whispered.

'Forget Sybilla,' he said roughly. 'It is you I love. You I need.' His chest expanded as he inhaled, then his words came out in a disjointed rush. 'Berty…if you can forgive me…if you can love me…if, when I ask you to marry me, your answer is yes…then stay here, by my side. But if you cannot, if your answer is still no, then we will say no more.'

He captured her gaze again. Heat swirled in his eyes and she could feel the dampness of his palms.

'My intention was to declare my love and to propose to you tonight—here, in front of everyone, so neither you nor anyone else will doubt my love for you is true. But I changed my mind.'

Liberty's heart had begun to soar. Now, she could not stifle her gasp of dismay.

'I changed my mind,' Dominic continued, 'because I will not back you into a corner in front of all these people. I will not put you in a position where you feel you *cannot* refuse me. You are in control, my darling Berty. Walk away now, if you wish, and no one will be any the wiser. But know that my heart will go with you.'

Her heart somersaulted. This private man—a man who concealed his heart and his emotions behind duty and obligation—was about to make a public declaration. To her!

The cacophony of surrounding voices was fading—a tide of sound receding. She sensed they now stood in a clearing and that the people around them were moving back, but she could not tear her gaze from his.

She slid her hands back until just their fingers overlapped and then she curled her fingers until they were linked with his. She smoothed her thumbs across his knuckles and put all of her love into her smile. 'I will not walk away, Dominic. I love you.'

His lips curved and his fingers tightened around hers. He raised his head, clearly seeking someone over the heads of the crowd. A gong reverberated throughout the room and now the hush of the crowd could not be mistaken.

'My lords, ladies and gentleman.' Liberty recognised Grantham's voice. 'Pray silence for His Lordship, the Marquess of Avon.'

The difficult part was over. So why did his knees still shake and why was his stomach still churning? She would not walk away. She had said so. But this was still the most important moment of his life and he was desperate to get it right. Dominic swallowed past the swell of emotion that clogged his throat and clasped Liberty's hands even tighter, revelling in the knowledge that he could hold her hands whenever he chose, from this night onwards, for the rest of their lives. He could feel her suppressed emotion in the tremble of her hands and he could see it by the quiver of her lower lip.

Then their eyes met. And she smiled and it was as though the sun broke through dark clouds and everything...*everything*...was all right. His tension fragmented and a surge of energy...of hope...of joy... radiated throughout his entire body. He hauled in a deep breath and, when he spoke, there was no hesitancy in his words or in his voice.

He had prepared what he would say—the proper words and sentiments for an occasion such as this—but he ignored all his careful plans. He gazed out at the sea of faces surrounding them and he spoke from the heart.

'There has been much speculation in the past weeks about my intentions. I arrived in town with the aim of finding the perfect wife for me and for my position as my father's heir. I have to tell you...' his gaze swept the crowd '...that I was possibly even more undecided than any one of you as to whom that lady might be.

'And then this lady—Liberty Louisa Lovejoy—burst into my life like a...like a...'

He paused, and stared down at Liberty. How could he sum up what she had come to mean to him in just a few words? What words could do her justice? She smiled, her gold-flecked blue eyes urging him on. And then the exact words didn't matter. He was talking with his heart, not his head—and if they came out less than perfect, he did not care.

'She burst into my life like a whirlwind of sunshine,

lighting my life with laughter, with love and with joy. And I had found my perfect partner in life. And, if she will have me, my perfect wife...my perfect Marchioness.'

It was his turn to smile, while Liberty looked serious.

'Liberty Lovejoy, I love you with every beat of my heart. I love you with every breath I take. You already have possession of my heart. Will you now do me the great honour of accepting my hand as well? Will you marry me?'

For what felt like an eternity her expression remained set and it felt as though his heart, too, stilled as he waited. The room around them was silent, not a sound to be heard. He concentrated on her mouth, those lush lips, willing her to answer. Slowly...excruciatingly slowly...her lips lifted at the corners...curved into a smile...and parted.

And he shouldn't have been surprised, but he was. Because she went up on tiptoes, threw her arms around his neck and kissed him, quite thoroughly, accompanied by a chorus of gasps and sighs from their audience.

And Dominic could breathe properly for the first time since Liberty had announced she was not with child and he could marry whomever he chose.

He chose Liberty Lovejoy.

And she said yes...in deed if not in so many words.

Chapter Twenty-Two

The ball was finally over. The guests, other than their families, had all gone home and the Beauchamps and the Lovejoys repaired to the family parlour for their first opportunity to discuss the betrothal. Publicly, of course, all his family had congratulated him. They had put on a good show…but was it just a show, or would they really be happy for him and welcome Liberty into the fold? The hard ball of anxiety that had lodged in Dominic's stomach over the past weeks had dissolved, leaving one tiny knot of unease, one unanswered question, behind.

Would following his heart mean a rift between him and his beloved family?

Dominic tucked Liberty close to him as they sat side by side on the sofa and the Beauchamps, Lovejoys—and Mrs Mount—assembled. Olivia, of course, piped up the minute the door closed.

'Well! I do think you might have told *me* what you planned, Dominic. Liberty *is* my friend, after all. I could have helped.'

He should have expected no less and he noticed Father and Rosalind exchange wry smiles.

'I neither needed nor wanted your help, Livvy,' he said. 'But thank you for the thought.'

Olivia pouted. 'Hope and Verity knew! And even Mrs Mount and she's not even family.'

'I had to confide in them, Liv. I wasn't confident Liberty would come tonight otherwise.'

'She was exceedingly stubborn.' Hope was sitting next to Alex, casting occasional coquettish glances at him through her lashes while Alex pretended not to notice. 'Poor Mrs Mount had to feign illness before she would give in.'

'Well, I still think—' Olivia fell silent as Hugo placed a hand on her shoulder.

'All has worked out for the best, my sweet, so you must concede that Dominic didn't need your help. He knew what he was doing.'

'Eventually,' said Alex.

Dominic frowned at his brother, receiving an innocent smile in return as Alex continued, 'You're slipping, Liv. It must be motherhood. Hugo and I knew which way the wind was blowing *weeks* ago.'

Olivia sucked in a deep breath, ready to retaliate, and Dominic saw his father getting ready to intervene, but it was Liberty who spoke.

'Are you disappointed you weren't told, or disappointed in Dominic's choice, Olivia?'

The slightest of tremors in her voice told him how much courage it had taken for her to ask such a direct question, especially when she had already confided in him how nervous she was at facing his family. Especially his father. He took her hand and squeezed.

Olivia paled at Liberty's words and she shot out of her seat and sat on the other side of Liberty, putting her arm around her shoulders.

'How could you even *think* I might be disappointed he chose you, Liberty? When I think of those haughty girls on that ridiculous list of his—no! There is no comparison. You are perfect, just as Dom said. It is just that I feel like I'm the only one who didn't know.'

'You always did want to know everything that is going on, Olivia, and you haven't changed.' Father stood and moved across to the mantelpiece, commanding the room as was his wont. 'If it's any consolation, your stepmother and I knew nothing either, not until the very first guests were already walking up the stairs this evening. That is the first time we knew Liberty's identity.'

Both Rosalind and Father had trusted Dominic when he had asked them to throw a ball for a special announcement without revealing any details. He prayed they did not now feel that trust had been betrayed. Liberty's fingers tightened on Dominic's and he heard her intake of breath.

'Is that why you said what you did to me when I arrived, Your Grace?'

Dominic stared at his father. Had he been unwelcoming?

'What did you say to her?' he demanded. He had to challenge him—he would not stand for any member of his family, even his father, upsetting Liberty. He had deliberately not revealed her identity earlier because he had wanted neither his father's help nor his hindrance. Nor had he wanted to know if Father disapproved because his approval or disapproval had been irrelevant, in the end.

Liberty was Dominic's choice and his alone.

He held his breath, awaiting his father's reply, but it was Liberty who spoke.

'He said it was a pleasure to meet me again and that

he and the Duchess were honoured that I accepted their invitation.' She smiled up at Dominic. 'Honoured! Your father made me feel welcome and that helped to give me the courage to face this evening.'

Dominic caught his father's eyes and sent him a silent apology. Father ghosted a wink in reply and that last knot of tension in Dominic's stomach unravelled.

But Liberty hadn't finished. Her cheeks turned pink as her gaze took in every person in the room, one by one.

'I was convinced Dominic was about to announce his betrothal to someone else and I wanted to be anywhere but here tonight.' She beamed then at her brother and sisters, and Mrs Mount, who had still come to the ball, but rather later than planned. 'Thank you all for not giving up on me.'

'That's all right, Sis,' said Gideon. 'We did it for ourselves more than you—how else could we get rid of Romeo?'

'Is that your dog, Liberty?' Rosalind asked, over the chuckles raised by Gideon's remarks. 'I hope he likes other dogs because there will be several around when you come to the Abbey in July.'

Liberty looked questioningly at Dominic. He hadn't even thought that far ahead. The Abbey was his childhood home and he couldn't wait to show Liberty around, although they would make their home at one of Father's minor estates.

'The entire family will all be together for the first time since Olivia and Hugo married, four years ago,' said Dominic. He lifted her hand and kissed it. 'I cannot wait for you—and Romeo—to meet the rest of them.'

She smiled at that. 'I am sure he will be on his best behaviour,' she said to Rosalind.

'Well, now.' Father crossed to where Rosalind was sitting and helped her to rise, then he led her across to Dominic and Liberty, who stood up also. 'I said it in the ballroom, Liberty, but I want you to be in no doubt... I am delighted to welcome you to our family. I can see you have made my son a happy man and that's good enough for me.'

He placed his hands on her shoulders and bent to kiss her cheek, then murmured something into her ear. Something Dominic could not hear.

'Goodnight, everyone.' He and Rosalind went to the door, then Father held it open, making it clear to the rest of the company it was time to leave. One by one they said goodnight to Dominic and Liberty and trooped out. Gideon was the last to go.

'We'll wait for you in the entrance hall, Sis,' he said.

And then they were alone. At last. Dominic wrapped Liberty in his arms, but still the question burned in him and he had to ask.

'What did Father whisper to you?'

Liberty beamed up at him. 'He said he knew it was me, from the night of Lady Stanton's ball.'

'And I was very pleased,' came a deep voice from the doorway, 'that you saw sense, my Son. After all, why spoil the Beauchamp tradition of following our hearts?'

'Why did you say nothing?'

His father never normally shied away from manipulating events to suit himself.

'Because it was your decision, Dom. It was for you to make your own choice—head or heart. I'm happy it was the right one. Eventually, as your brother would say. Goodnight.'

They were alone again. And now there were no more unanswered questions. Except... Dominic frowned.

'What is it?'

'You never did answer my question, Berty.'

'Which question?'

'Will you marry me?'

She smiled and traced his lower lip with her forefinger. '*I* thought I answered you most explicitly, Lord Avon. But, if you want unequivocal, then you shall have it.'

She slipped her arms around his neck, went up on tiptoes and, for the second time that night, she kissed him. Very thoroughly. Until his senses swam and his blood was on fire.

'Oh, yes,' she whispered against his lips. 'Yes. Yes. Yes.'

* * * * *

If you enjoyed this story
be sure to read the other book in
The Beauchamp Heirs miniseries

Lady Olivia and the Infamous Rake

And while you're waiting for
Janice Preston's next book
check out
The Beauchamp Betrothals miniseries

Cinderella and the Duke
Scandal and Miss Markham
Lady Cecily and the Mysterious Mr. Gray

𝒮 ₁

"Hey! How everybody this morning?"

Her heart inexplicably lifting at the sound of the familiar voice, Sunshine turned to see Grady striding toward them with that distinctive masculine gait, his impossibly broad shoulders clad in a windbreaker.

"Grady!" To Sunshine's surprise, her daughter let out a cry of welcome and abandoned the swing to run toward him.

When Tessa reached Grady, she grabbed his hand and gazed happily up at him. "Now you can see how high I can swing."

He glanced at Sunshine, looking slightly taken aback at Tessa's grip on his hand. "I can do that."

Willingly, he allowed her to pull him forward to stand next to her mother.

Tessa dashed for the swings. In a flash, she had herself moving.

"Are you watching?" a demanding voice called.

"We're watching!" they yelled in unison, then exchanged a glance and laughed.

The kindergartner was pumping herself higher and higher, a determined look on her little face.

"You're doing great, Tessa!" Grady's words of encouragement impelled her to pump harder, and her triumphant smile widened.

Sunshine's heart swelled with love.

Glynna Kaye treasures memories of growing up in small Midwestern towns—and vacations spent with the Texan side of the family. She traces her love of storytelling to the times a houseful of great-aunts and great-uncles gathered with her grandma to share candid, heartwarming, poignant and often humorous tales of their youth and young adulthood. Glynna now lives in Arizona, where she enjoys gardening, photography and the great outdoors.

Books by Glynna Kaye

Love Inspired

Hearts of Hunter Ridge

Rekindling the Widower's Heart
Claiming the Single Mom's Heart

Dreaming of Home
Second Chance Courtship
At Home in His Heart
High Country Hearts
Look-Alike Lawman
A Canyon Springs Courtship
Pine Country Cowboy
High Country Holiday

Claiming the Single Mom's Heart

Glynna Kaye

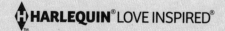

If you purchased this book without a cover you should be aware
that this book is stolen property. It was reported as "unsold and
destroyed" to the publisher, and neither the author nor the
publisher has received any payment for this "stripped book."

 LOVE INSPIRED BOOKS

Recycling programs
for this product may
not exist in your area.

ISBN-13: 978-0-373-81908-9

Claiming the Single Mom's Heart

Copyright © 2016 by Glynna Kaye Sirpless

All rights reserved. Except for use in any review, the reproduction
or utilization of this work in whole or in part in any form by any
electronic, mechanical or other means, now known or hereinafter
invented, including xerography, photocopying and recording, or in
any information storage or retrieval system, is forbidden without
the written permission of the editorial office, Love Inspired Books,
195 Broadway, New York, NY 10007 U.S.A.

This is a work of fiction. Names, characters, places and incidents are
either the product of the author's imagination or are used fictitiously, and
any resemblance to actual persons, living or dead, business establishments,
events or locales is entirely coincidental.

This edition published by arrangement with Love Inspired Books.

® and TM are trademarks of Love Inspired Books, used under license.
Trademarks indicated with ® are registered in the United States Patent
and Trademark Office, the Canadian Intellectual Property Office and in
other countries.

www.Harlequin.com

Printed in U.S.A.

"For I know the plans I have for you," declares the Lord, "plans to prosper you and not to harm you, plans to give you hope and a future."
—*Jeremiah* 29:11

The Lord Himself goes before you and will be with you; He will never leave you nor forsake you. Do not be afraid; do not be discouraged.
—*Deuteronomy* 31:8

To Jim and Phyllis Dorman, whose deep love of God and faithful ministry have greatly influenced my life. Thank you.

Chapter One

"A family legend is worthless unless you have proof."

"I'm going to get proof." With more confidence than she felt, Sunshine Carston gave her longtime friend Tori a reassuring nod. "It's just taking longer than expected."

Much longer.

She shifted restlessly in the passenger seat of Victoria Janner's steel-blue Kia compact as they searched for a parking spot in the crowded graveled lot of Hunter's Hideaway. Her own ancient SUV was in the shop—again—and out-of-town visitor Tori had agreed to take a detour while running errands Saturday morning. But Tori's willingness had swiftly evaporated when on the way to their destination Sunshine had divulged her true intention for this next stop.

Big mistake.

She rolled down her window, breathing in the soothing scent of sun-warmed ponderosa pines. An aroma deliciously indigenous to the rugged mountain country surrounding Hunter Ridge, Arizona, it was one her great-great-grandparents would have been familiar with. One she herself would have likely grown up with had life not dealt her ancestors an unfair blow.

She stared across the parking lot at the connecting log, stone and frame structures that made up the main building of Hunter's Hideaway. The vast wooded acreage had been a home away from home for hunters, horsemen, hikers and other outdoorsmen since Harrison "Duke" Hunter had—allegedly—rooted it to that exact spot early in the past century.

"*They* seem to be doing a good business this Labor Day weekend." Resentment welled up within her. "No noisy remodeling like they're inflicting on the Artists' Cooperative gallery this morning."

A cute blonde with a pixie haircut, Tori and her usual dazzling smile was nowhere to be seen as they slipped into an empty spot. "If you go in there with a chip on your shoulder," she cautioned, "you can't expect a positive outcome."

What response had Sunshine hoped to get from her friend when she'd confessed her true motive for relocating to Hunter Ridge two years ago? A cry of outrage at the unfairness of it all? Reinforcement of her plans? Encouragement to face her fear of the influential family who the town was named for?

"And don't forget," Tori added as she cut off the engine, "what the good Lord says about revenge."

"I'm seeking justice. Not revenge. There's a difference."

A *big* difference. Revenge involved retaliation. Inflicting injury. Justice had to do with revealing truth and righting wrongs. And yes, restoring of at least some of what by rights belonged to her family. To her. And to her five-year-old daughter, Tessa.

Tori cast her a disbelieving look. "Surely you don't think anyone is going to fork over restitution for something your great-great-grandfather was supposedly cheated out of. Even if you could prove it—which I doubt you can—you don't have the money to back up your claim with legal action."

"No, but I'm counting on the seemingly impeccable reputation of the Hunters to apply its own brand of pressure. That they'll be compelled, for the sake of their standing in the community, to make things right once the facts are brought to their attention."

Tori slumped down in the bucket seat. "I wish

you hadn't told me any of this. It sounds too much like blackmail."

Sunshine made a face. "Not blackmail. I look at it as an opportunity for them to live up to their good name. I don't hold it against later generations that Duke Hunter didn't play well with others."

"You could get hauled into court if one of them thinks it smacks of extortion." Tori gave her a sharp glance. "Especially now that you've decided to run for a town council seat against one of the family members."

Against Elaine Hunter, who was trying for a second term.

"Everything will be aboveboard. Trust me, okay?"

If only her maternal grandmother, Alice Heywood, were still alive. She'd recall the details of the account Sunshine remembered hearing as a kid. The vague references to "the ridge of the hunter." A betrayal by someone considered a friend. It was a story, though, which over time she'd dismissed as nothing but a fairy tale that once captured her childish imagination. That was, until her world turned upside down not long after her daughter's birth and she began pondering the possibilities.

"The din from their renovation of the property next to the Artists' Co-op," she continued, "offers a perfect excuse for a visit. You heard the racket this morning. That less-than-sympathetic contractor overseeing the project told me to take it up with the Hunters. So here I am."

Squaring her shoulders, she'd just exited the vehicle when someone stepped out on the covered porch that stretched across the front of the adjoined buildings. A muscle in her midsection involuntarily tightened.

"Oh, no, not *him*," she whispered. Wouldn't you know it? That too-handsome-for-his-own-good Grady Hunter, cell phone pressed to his ear, now paced the length of the porch like a lion guarding the entrance to his lair.

Although she'd only seen him around town, she'd heard plenty of starry-eyed feminine gossip surrounding the popular ladies' man. Having once had a personal, close-up view of what it was like to be married to a male with that reputation, she wasn't impressed.

"I wanted to get invited inside to talk to his mom or his grandma so I could look around. You know, for clues. But I don't want to deal with this guy."

"Maybe God doesn't think snooping is a good idea," Tori said.

"I have to start somewhere, don't I?" She focused again on the broad-shouldered man striding across the porch. Black trousers. Snow-white shirt. Gray vest. Black bow tie.

"Why's he dressed like that?" Tori echoed the question forming in Sunshine's mind.

Then realization dawned and any remaining courage to take on the Hunters drained out of her. "I forgot. It's his older brother's wedding day."

How had she lost track of such a high-profile event? Widower and single dad Luke Hunter was marrying Delaney Marks, a young woman who Sunshine had become acquainted with over the past summer. Obviously she'd been way too busy and much too preoccupied if she'd forgotten. So what was new?

"Maybe you'd better come back in a few days." Tori sounded relieved that her mission might be aborted.

"But by then the holiday weekend will be over, the last of the summer customers come and gone." There might soon be leaf-peepers searching for a burst of aspen gold—and hunters, of course—but the prime season to market the talents of local artists would be over until late next spring. "I have a responsibility to represent the best interests of our artists' community. And that constant din next door isn't one of them."

Torn, she again looked to where Grady had finished his conversation and pocketed his cell phone. She found big, self-confident men intimidating, but she'd have no choice but to deal with him if she ventured forth now.

Intruding on a family gathering, though, might not be the best strategy. Nor would stating the case for the Artists' Co-op to the man on the porch rather than to his civic-minded mother. But before she could get back in the car, Grady's gaze swept the parking lot and he spotted her, his eyes locking on hers.

Her heart jerked as his expression appeared to sharpen. Question. Challenge.

The decision was made.

"Ramp up the prayers, Tori." She shut the car door, cutting off her friend's words of protest. *Here we go, Lord.*

What was *she* doing here?

Grady Hunter's eyes narrowed as the petite young woman, her black hair glinting in the late-morning sunlight, wove her way between cars in the parking lot. Clad in jeans and a black T-shirt, the fringe of her camel-colored jacket swaying with each step, Sunshine Carston looked like one determined woman.

Just what he didn't need right now. Not, for that matter, what any of the Hunter clan needed while setting aside anxious thoughts regarding his mother's recent cancer diagnosis in order to celebrate today. Couldn't whatever Sunshine had on her mind wait until after the Labor Day weekend? Or at least until after the guests dispersed from his big brother's postwedding brunch, which was now in full swing?

Having ditched his tux jacket inside, he loosened his tie, regretting having stepped outside for a breath of fresh air and to make a quick phone call. He didn't know who Ms. Carston intended to see, but regardless he would halt her at the door. Admittedly, he had a reputation for being overly protective of his family. But thirty-four years of life's lessons had given him reason to be, and today would be no different.

"Good morning." An almost shy smile accompanied her greeting as she paused at the base of the porch steps, but her dark brown eyes reflected the resolve he'd initially identified from a distance.

Up close she was prettier than he'd originally thought from seeing her around town and—only recently—in church. Although his area of expertise was wildlife photography, he nonetheless found himself mentally framing her for a perfect shot. Not a stiffly formal studio portrait, though. She was far too vibrant for that.

Her glossy, shoulder-length hair, slightly longer in front than in back, accented her straight nose and high cheekbones, and a smooth, warm skin tone hinted of possible Native American ancestry. She appeared to be in her late twenties—much too young to challenge his mother or Irvin Baydlin for a seat on the town council. From what he'd heard from multiple sources—including his mom—she kept the current council members on their toes. Which, of course, wasn't necessarily a bad thing.

But he wouldn't be voting for her.

"Good morning," he acknowledged with a friendly nod. Hunters were known for their hospitality, and he'd uphold that to his dying day or risk repercussions from Grandma Jo. He stepped off the porch and extended his hand. "Grady Hunter. How may I help you?"

Doe-like eyes met his in momentary hesitation, and then she gripped his hand in a firm shake. "Sunshine Carston. Manager of the Hunter Ridge Artists' Cooperative."

Her voice was softer, gentler, than he'd assumed from her reputation. That, combined with the delicate hand she'd placed in his, contradicted the image he'd previously formed of the single mom as "one tough cookie."

She motioned to the overflowing parking lot of the property his great-great-grandparents had settled in the early 1900s. "I apologize for the intrusion. I forgot this is Delaney Marks's wedding day."

That was right, his brother's new bride was, coincidentally, an aspiring artist herself and, in exchange for jewelry-making lessons from another local artist, on occasion worked at the Artists' Co-op.

"I won't take but a few minutes of your time," she said, not waiting to see if he'd voice any objections to conducting business on his brother's wedding day. "The adjoining property north of the Artists' Co-op is being renovated by a contractor hired by Hunter Enterprises."

"That's correct."

"I realize Hunter's Hideaway caters to a different customer base," she continued, and he found himself drawn to the softly lilting voice, the expressive eyes. "But, as a fellow business owner who is impacted by visitors to this region, you know how important the months from Memorial Day weekend through Labor Day are to local businesses."

"They are indeed." Fortunately, although Hunter's Hideaway no longer offered guided hunts on their own property or in the neighboring national forests, they'd diversified through the years to not only provide camping and cabins for hunters, but also for competitive trail riders and runners seeking to condition at a higher altitude. For seekers of a quiet place to get away from it all, as well.

Those more recent additions, in fact, gave him hope that he might soon see his long-held dream come to fruition—wildlife-photography workshops and related guided tours of the forested wilderness surrounding them. But he had to convince his family that it was worthwhile. Not an easy thing to do.

Sunshine's dark eyes pinned him. "Then, you can understand how sales might be negatively impacted at a fine-arts gallery when the adjoining property is undergoing a massive overhaul on the last holiday weekend of the season."

So that was the problem. It couldn't be that bad, though, could it? It wasn't as if they were dynamiting. "No harm intended, I assure you."

"The contractor overseeing the project says he's under a tight deadline." She folded her arms as she looked up at him. "We've had disgruntled customers walk out of the gallery when the pounding, vibration and whine of power tools wouldn't let up."

Weighing his options, he briefly stared at formidable clouds building in the distance for what would likely bring an afternoon monsoon rain. "What do you say I give the contractor a call and postpone things for a few days? I imagine he and his crew wouldn't mind having the rest of the weekend off."

Brows arched as if in disbelief. Or was that disappointment flickering through her eyes? Had she expected—relished even—a fight?

"You'd do that?"

"Neighbors have to look out for neighbors."

The contractor did have a deadline, but there

was no point in making things harder for Grady's mother right now by waving a red flag in Ms. Carston's face. Although the family was struggling to come to terms with Mom's upcoming surgery—a single-side mastectomy—she insisted she still intended to run for office, so there was no point in riling up one of her opponents unnecessarily.

"Well, then…" Sunshine's uncertain tone betrayed that verbalizing gratitude wasn't easy for her in this instance, almost as if she suspected she'd missed something in their exchange. That maybe he was trying to pull a fast one on her. "Thank you, Mr. Hunter."

"Grady. And you're welcome."

But she didn't depart. Instead, she stood looking at him almost expectantly.

"Was there something else?"

An unexpected smile surfaced. "I'm waiting for you to make the call."

Oh, she was, was she?

A smile of his own tugged in response to the one that had made his breath catch, and he pulled out his cell phone. He wasn't used to not being trusted to do what he said he'd do. But anything to keep the peace, right? And to keep Sunshine smiling like that. On Mom's behalf, of course.

Under her watchful gaze he put some distance between them, then punched the contractor's speed-dial number. "Ted. It's Grady. I hear you've got your crew working this weekend."

"A deadline's a deadline," the gravelly voice responded, his tone defensive. "I've never missed one yet."

"That work ethic is certainly why you were picked for the job." Grady cut a look at Sunshine. "But what do you say we extend it by a week and let you and your boys knock off for the rest of the holiday weekend?"

It would be cutting it close, but an extra week wouldn't be a deal breaker, would it?

After a long pause, Ted chuckled. "That pretty artist complained to you, didn't she?"

Grady forced a smile as he nodded reassuringly in Sunshine's direction. "You're welcome, Ted."

"Pushover."

Was he? "Glad I could help your crew out."

The contractor chuckled again. "Be careful there, Grady. You're playing with fire."

"Sure thing. You have a good one, too, bud."

Pocketing his cell phone again, Grady moved back to Sunshine. "All done."

From the wary look in her eyes, she clearly hadn't anticipated he'd willingly accommodate her. A sense of satisfaction rose, catching her off guard, throwing a wrench in her assumptions.

"Anything else?" He needed to get back inside. They'd be cutting the cake shortly and he'd promised a toast. "I know you'd once approached Hunter Enterprises about leasing the property next door to expand the Artists' Co-op, but we've long had plans for it. We'll do our best to be a top-notch neighbor."

"It's true we could use the additional space, but it will be nice having a bookstore in town."

He frowned. "Bookstore?"

"You're opening a bookstore, right?"

"No."

"I heard it was going to be a bookstore."

"It's not."

"Then, what—" her words came cautiously, reflecting a growing dread in her eyes "—will be going in next door to us?"

Chapter Two

"Hunter Ridge Wild Game Supply."

"When you say *wild game*," Sunshine ventured without much hope, "I don't suppose you mean a place that sells video games?"

Laugh lines crinkled at the corners of Grady's deep blue eyes and she steeled herself against the engaging grin. This was Grady Hunter, ladies' man, and she'd do well to keep that in mind. He'd been unexpectedly accommodating about the renovation next door. What was he up to?

"No, I mean a store that sells equipment and supplies for processing wild game. You know, stuff for making elk sausage and venison steaks."

Okay. Deep breath. She could handle this. Her great-great-grandfather had, according to her grandmother, been a marksman who'd put food on the table with his hunting skills. She herself wasn't any more squeamish about wild game than she was about buying chicken or a pound of hamburger at the grocery store. But some Co-op members might disagree.

"Not solely in-store sales, but online, as well," Grady continued, a note of pride in his voice. "Once we pass inspection, we'll also be officially licensed to do processing demonstrations as well as process game donated for regional food pantry programs. That's what the ongoing renovation is about—to put in a commercial kitchen, freezers, the works."

She stiffened. *Processing on the premises?* Services that meant hunters hauling their field-dressed trophies through the front door? On the other hand, how could she object to feeding the hungry?

She must have hesitated a moment too long, for Grady's eyes narrowed.

"You have a problem with that?"

Not wanting to give the impression she was opposed to the idea, she offered what she hoped was a convincing smile. As a candidate for town council, she had to weigh her words carefully. It wouldn't be wise, two months before an election, to give the majority of those living in a town catering to outdoorsmen the impression she had issues with that.

She glanced toward the parking lot where Tori

was no doubt watching and wondering what was taking her so long. "I personally have no problem with it, but some gallery customers and Co-op members may."

"That's unfortunate." He didn't look concerned. "But your worries are unfounded. We won't hang carcasses in the window or mount a deer head over the front door. It will be low-key. Discreet."

"You do understand my problem, though, don't you?" She looked to him in appeal. "Our members are trying to create a welcoming atmosphere for shoppers of the fine arts. The gulf between the two worlds might be disconcerting for some."

"I know a number of hunters who appreciate the fine arts and who, in fact, are award-winning painters and sculptors of wildlife. Maybe the Co-op should expand its horizons and find a way to better serve the foundation that Hunter Ridge was built on."

"Taxidermy?" She flashed a smile. "I don't think that would go over well with local artists who call this town home."

"Then, it sounds as if folks should have researched Hunter Ridge more closely before coming here, doesn't it?" He quirked a persuasive smile of his own. "You *could* move the gallery, you know. If not to another town, there are empty buildings that I imagine would be suitable."

"Unfortunately…" Sunshine drew in a resigned breath "…the Co-op recently signed a three-year lease."

Which had been her doing. She'd been proud of convincing their out-of-town landlord, Charlotte Gyles, to give the Co-op a lower monthly rental rate in exchange for committing to a three-year contract. But look where it had landed them now. Member Gideon Edlow, who'd give anything to unseat her as manager of the Co-op, would gleefully cry, "I told you so." Being booted out of the position would mean losing the apartment above the gallery and being forced out of town before she'd had a chance to verify her grandmother's story.

She couldn't allow that to happen.

"Even if relocation isn't an option, you don't have anything to worry about." Grady tugged at his loosened tie, and she couldn't help but wonder how he'd looked in the full regalia at that morning's nuptials. "This is to be an unobtrusive, word-of-mouth and online operation. We have a good-size customer base of hunters who have been asking for this type of service for years. Word will get around without fanfare."

She couldn't help but laugh. "That's what I'm afraid of, Mr. Hunter. Word getting around."

"Grady, remember?" Twinkling eyes held her gaze a bit too long. "There's no cause for worry."

Easy enough for him to say. She'd taken a huge risk coming to Hunter Ridge in pursuit of the truth of her grandmother's tale and in accepting the nomination to run for town council on behalf of the artist community.

"Everything will be fine," he concluded. "Trust me."

Trust a Hunter? Like her great-great-grandfather had? Like she'd trusted her ex-husband to stick around after Tessa's birth? "I guess we don't have a choice, do we? That is, unless *you're* willing to relocate?"

Startled brows raised, then his eyes warmed as if charmed by her impertinence. "Not a chance, Sunshine. But if it would put your mind at rest, why don't you come out to the Hideaway this week and take a look at the architectural drawings. I think you'll be satisfied with what you see."

He was inviting her to Hunter's Hideaway?

It wasn't likely that he'd spread the blueprints out on a picnic table under the trees or on the porch, was it? Surely she'd be welcomed beyond the public areas and into the more private ones?

A ripple of excitement danced through her. Right when she'd almost given up hope of a closer look at the property, Grady had unknowingly opened the door to an answered prayer.

She nodded, hoping a carefully casual response

wouldn't betray her eagerness. "If I can find the time, I might do that."

"Don't tell me you're thinking of making more changes to those plans, Grady."

With a grin, he looked up from where he'd spread the blueprints across the heavy oak table he used as an office desk. Her silver-gray hair upswept and secured with decorative combs, eighty-year-old Grandma Jo stepped into his office. It wouldn't be long before her signature summertime attire of jeans and a collared shirt gave way to wool slacks and a turtleneck.

"No, no more changes. Sunshine Carston went into a tailspin when she found out we're opening a wild game supply next to the Artists' Co-op." She'd have probably freaked out had he mentioned bow hunters were currently combing neighboring forests for mule deer and that elk season was getting underway. "I made the mistake of inviting her to look at the plans and see for herself that she has nothing to worry about. She called a while ago to say she's on her way."

"That sounds proactive. Why is inviting her here a mistake?"

"Just is," he said with a shrug. He wouldn't admit to his grandmother that the manager of the Artists' Co-op had been on his mind more than she should be. "I guess by going this extra mile to disarm her fears, I almost feel as if I'm fraternizing with the enemy. I mean, she *is* Mom's opponent."

"Nonsense, Grady." Grandma joined him to gaze down at the blueprints. "I have the utmost confidence in you as a guardian of this family's best interests. Don't let that previous situation you found yourself in undermine you. We all make mistakes, and trust those who aren't worthy of our trust. But don't let that weigh on you. Nothing came of it."

Except his own broken heart and the humiliation of the betrayal. Not to mention letting down Jasmine's daughter when things had fallen apart, and how he'd unwittingly risked his family's reputation. *Don't forget that, Grandma.* He hadn't.

Since Hunter had grown up on stories of how his great-great-grandfather had almost lost the Hideaway due to misplaced trust, and seeing with his own eyes the repercussions of Aunt Charlotte's nasty divorce from Dad's younger brother, you'd have thought he'd have been more cautious about where he placed his heart. But he'd been head over heels for Jasmine—who'd falsely given others the impression that he and his family endorsed a controversial land-development project she was orchestrating behind the scenes. One that, had she succeeded, would have resulted in filling her pockets with a lucrative kickback. Thankfully, the ring was still in his pocket when everything came to light. But it had been a close call.

"Grady?" His twenty-year-old sister, Rio, appeared in the doorway, sun-streaked blond hair cascading down her back and her expression troubled. "Sunshine Carston's here. She says you're expecting her, but I asked them to have a seat while I tracked you down."

"Them?" Sunshine brought someone else along? He hadn't counted on a third party.

"Her kid is with her."

Tensed muscles relaxed. "Thanks, I'll go get her in a minute."

Rio departed and Grandma Jo returned to the door.

"This is a smart move, Grady, to put Sunshine's fears to rest. Don't let the past cause you to second-guess yourself."

But had his motive for inviting her been entirely untainted? Since that last disaster in the romance department, he'd rededicated himself to safeguarding the Hunter clan in both business and personal dealings—going to excessive lengths to ensure he didn't make the same mistake again. But had his invitation, ostensibly on behalf of family business, been influenced by a subconscious hope of spending time with the attractive woman?

Now alone in the room, he moved to the window facing the forest behind the Hideaway and adjusted the wooden louvers. Rearranged a chair. Straightened a crooked lampshade.

Then, tamping down an inexplicable sense of anticipation, he paused again to appraise the room—and uttered a silent prayer that his spiritual armor would remain securely in place.

"Come sit by me, sweetheart." Sunshine patted the leather sofa cushion next to her, relieved that Tessa seemed less clingy this morning than she'd been in recent weeks. She'd slept somewhat better last night, too, only calling twice for her to banish something lurking in the shadows of her closet. Now enthralled with the animal heads on the log walls, the half-barrel end tables and an antler-designed chandelier above, it was almost too much to expect her raven-haired kindergartner to anchor herself to one spot.

Maybe she should have waited to come until after Tessa was in school for the afternoon. Having a five-year-old in tow wouldn't make sleuthing for clues easy. But after the holiday weekend, Tori had had to make a quick trip back to the thriving Arizona artists' community of Jerome. Then she'd return tomorrow to help with Tessa and, somewhat reluctantly, with the historic record research Sunshine intended to do.

"Look, Mommy." Tessa pointed to a wide staircase that ascended to an open-railed landing. "Can I go up there?"

"I'm afraid not. We're not guests."

But how tempting to look the other way while Tessa wandered up the carpeted flight, then hurry up behind her to bring her back, giving herself a chance to look around. This building, of course, may not have existed at the time her great-great-grandparents had been here. Probably hadn't. But could there still be something of value to lend credence to Sunshine's grandma's stories?

"Good morning," a familiar male voice greeted. "I'm glad you could make it here today."

She stared into Grady's smiling eyes as he approached from a hallway beyond the staircase, looking at home in the rustic surroundings. In jeans, work boots and a Western-cut shirt, he exuded a commanding confidence.

She rose from the sofa, a betraying flutter in her stomach. But was that at the prospect of exploring private areas of the historic building? Or spending time with Grady? "I hope you don't mind that I brought my daughter. She won't be in school until this afternoon."

"No problem." Still smiling, he held out his hand to the little girl. "Hi, I'm Grady. What's your name?"

"Tessa." She shyly shook his hand.

"Beautiful name for a beautiful young lady." Grady looked over at Sunshine. "She looks like you."

Sunshine's face warmed. She'd heard that comment before. She'd wildly, foolishly, loved Tessa's father, Jerrel Carston. But she was grateful not to look into a miniversion of his face on a daily basis.

"Is this your house?" Tessa asked, again drawing Grady's attention.

"This is where I do business. I live in a cabin not far from here." He glanced at Sunshine. "Would you like to come back to my office? I can walk you through the plans."

"Thank you. Come on, Tessa."

They followed Grady through a shadowed hallway, Sunshine taking her time as she tried to absorb everything around her. Old photographs, paintings and sketches on the walls. An antique mirror. Faded framed embroidery work.

Up ahead Grady waited outside an open door, watching as she paused to study the faces in one of the yellowing photos.

"Is this your family?"

He laughed, and the sound unexpectedly warmed her. "Who knows? Mom's been known to rescue historic photographs from garage sales and antique shops, and they can pop up anywhere— guest rooms, cabins, hallways."

Disappointed, she gave the image a lingering

look as Grady beckoned her and Tessa forward to usher them into his office.

Inside the sunlit room, he motioned for them to take a seat off to the side, his gaze touching apologetically on her daughter. "I'm afraid I don't have any fun kid stuff, Tessa."

But as always, Tessa's eyes were wide, taking in her surroundings with interest. The book-lined shelves, wall groupings of photographs from an earlier era and striking black-and-white photos of wildlife. Elk. Deer. A fox.

"Don't worry. Books, paper, crayons. We're set." Sunshine held up a tote bag, then almost laughed at the relief passing through Grady's eyes.

"Well, then, let's take a look at the plans, shall we?"

With Tessa rummaging through the tote, Sunshine joined him at the table, suddenly aware of his height, solid build and a subtle scent of woodsy aftershave. He tugged one of the large blueprint sheets forward. "What we have here is an elevation of the front of the building. As you can see, it looks like any other shop you'd expect to encounter in Hunter Ridge."

It did, and the tension she'd harbored since Saturday eased slightly. The two-story stone structure remained true to the 1940s era in which it had been built. But it was the color rendering of the building on a laptop screen that brought its charm alive. Even with the shop's name lettered on the window, if she didn't know better, she'd think you were entering nothing more controversial than a gift shop or bakery.

"So what do you think?"

It would be nothing but stubbornness that kept her from admitting its acceptability. She raised her eyes to his, startled by the intent scrutiny of his gaze. "It appears tastefully done."

He gave a brisk, satisfied nod and tapped a key on the laptop to bring up another rendering. "The second floor is reserved for an office and stock, but this is the front interior. As you can see, it gives the impression of what you'd expect of an old-fashioned hardware store."

Lots of wood. Retention of the beamed ceiling and polished wood flooring. Indirect lighting.

"And this—" his gaze, now uncertain, remained on her as he moved to the next screen "—is the interior rear of the building."

The game processing area. But it looked as modern and benign as any restaurant kitchen with its massive stainless-steel island, vertical freezers and oversize sinks. The heavy double doors, of course, led to a graveled parking lot out back. The comings and goings of hunters and their game would be discreetly conducted away from the public eye.

"So can the Co-op live with this?"

Did it matter? He'd plainly told her it was there to stay. That the Co-op had only itself to blame if its neighbor was less than ideal for the next three years.

She stepped back from the table and farther from the imposing presence of Grady. "I can't speak for the other members of the Co-op, but I see nothing objectionable here. As you indicated, it's low profile. Nothing blatantly offensive to the sensibilities of others."

"I'm glad you agree."

She offered a coaxing smile. "Would you have any objections if I took printouts of the color designs to the Artists' Co-op meeting tomorrow night?"

He studied her for a long moment, as if hesitant to turn loose the illustrations. "Maybe I should speak with them personally. Deal with their concerns. I can rearrange my schedule."

Grady Hunter in attendance? Not a good idea.

"Thank you, but as the saying goes, a picture paints a thousand words." She didn't want the more contentious members haranguing Grady if he were there in person.

Unquestionably, the growing artists' community needed to be fairly represented in local government and she'd committed to being their voice. But they didn't need to further turn the longtime residents of Hunter Ridge against them with unreasonable demands. "I'll take responsibility for the prints and won't allow anyone to photograph or otherwise copy them."

"I have your word on that?" A half smile surfaced, as if recognizing his wasn't a trusting nature any more than hers was.

"You do. And I'll return the printouts as soon as possible." It was a good excuse to come back to Hunter's Hideaway. Maybe she could take a closer look at the old photographs in the hallway—and the ones in his office, as well.

He studied her a moment longer, as though trying to convince himself of her trustworthiness, and her face warmed under his scrutiny. Then abruptly he reached over to the laptop to press the print key for each of the illustrations he'd shown her. Straightening again, he gave her a challenging look. "Since I have your word…"

He moved to stand over a credenza, where a printer whirred its output, then removed the pages from the tray. Frowning, he held them aloft. "Looks as though it needs a new black ink cartridge. I'll be back in a minute."

As he headed into the hallway, she confirmed Tessa was occupied, then approached a grouping of framed photographs that had caught her eye. Were the faces of her ancestors captured here? If only she had time to scrutinize them. If only…

She darted a look toward the door and, before

she could stop herself, she whipped out her cell phone from her jacket pocket.

But as she raised it, zoomed in on one of the old photos, she paused. She'd given her word not to copy the building illustrations, the implication clear that she'd not use them in any way against Grady's family. Would capturing the old photographs in an attempt to find something that she *could* use against the Hunters be breaking that vow?

A muscle in her throat tightened.

Grady would be back any moment. Yes, as he'd pointed out, the photos might not have any connection to his family. But who knew when she'd again have an opportunity to examine evidence that might provide substance to her grandmother's tale?

It was now or never.

Aligning the camera lens once more, she glanced toward her daughter concentrating on the coloring book in her lap. Her daughter in whom she intended to instill the hallmarks of good character, determined that she wouldn't follow in her father's footsteps.

With a soft sigh and a lingering look at the photos, she pocketed her phone—just as Grady strode back into the room.

"How did it go?" Grandma Jo's voice came from behind him where he stood on the front porch, watching as Sunshine's SUV backed out of a parking spot.

Cutting off his apprehensive thoughts, Grady responded. "She agreed that the store design is, in her words, 'tastefully done.' So I don't think Mom will get pushback from her during the election."

"Excellent. Well done, Grady."

His heart swelled at the praise, something Grandma Jo didn't lavish unless merited. Sunshine had been cooperative, but what about the other Co-op members who'd view the renderings? He should have insisted that if the printouts went to the meeting, he be part of the package, too. But those dark, appealing eyes, the soft coaxing voice, had won him over.

Hadn't he learned his lesson six years ago?

"Ms. Carston doesn't stand a chance against your mother." Grandma's tone brooked no argument. "While the artists she represents will rally, there aren't enough to swing a vote."

"Garrett says she's not concentrating exclusively on the artist community." His pastor cousin was often privy to behind-the-scenes rumblings—aka gossip. "She's digging deep to learn what others might like to see change in Hunter Ridge and promising to represent their viewpoint, as well."

"I'm not concerned." Grandma Jo's chin lifted. "We've had Hunters on the town council since its beginnings."

"True." Aunts, uncles, cousins. One day, if he couldn't run fast enough, he'd probably get lassoed into the role, too. But hopefully that was a long way off—if ever. He had too many other things he hoped to accomplish and no taste for politics.

"Again, Grady, good job." Grandma Jo patted his arm. "We can always count on you."

She returned inside and he restlessly stepped off the porch. Grandma was a straight shooter who wasn't afraid to look you in the eye and give you her honest opinion. He'd gotten a no-holds-barred appraisal from her six years ago. She was giving him her equally honest opinion now.

She trusted him.

But, as she'd reminded him that long ago day when things had fallen apart with Jasmine, a reputation once shattered might be patched together—but people would forever be on the lookout for cracks.

There would be no cracks on his watch.

Nevertheless, why hadn't he confessed to Grandma Jo that he'd sent Sunshine off into the world with photocopies of their latest business endeavor?

Chapter Three

"Things could have been worse," Sunshine admitted to Tori as she closed the apartment door behind her Wednesday night. "Nobody stoned me, although I did see Gideon eyeing a molded concrete owl used as a doorstop in the public library's conference room."

More than once, though, she'd wished for the calming presence of Co-op member Benton Mason, her loyal supporter on about any stance she took. But he was working at his part-time maintenance job at Hunter's Hideaway tonight.

Tori set aside the book she'd been reading, her gaze sympathetic. "How was the turnout?"

"Good. About seventeen. Eighteen, maybe." She moved into the open area that served as a dining/living room to put a folder of meeting notes and Grady's printouts on a flat-topped trunk. Then she dropped into a chair opposite where Tori was seated on the sofa and proceeded to rummage through her fringed leather purse. "You haven't seen a sparkly turquoise pen wandering around here have you? I went to pull it out tonight and it was gone."

"No. That's the one your father gave you for high school graduation, isn't it?"

"Yeah." Graduation had been one of the few milestones in her life that Gordon Haynes had remembered to acknowledge. Her wedding and the birth of Tessa had escaped his radar. She sighed and set aside her purse, determined to look for the sentimental item later. Then she glanced at the closed door leading to Tessa's bedroom. "Did you have any trouble getting her to bed?"

"Not too much, although at first she insisted on waiting for you to get home. She wanted to make sure you didn't get locked out. I told her I'd make sure."

"I don't know what's made her so anxious these past few weeks. It started shortly before school started."

"Even kindergarten can be demanding. Schools expect a lot out of kids these days."

"I suppose. But at least this district seems to focus on the basics, on getting the kids grounded academically. I guess we'll wait and see how many times she comes to get me tonight." With a sigh, Sunshine scooted forward to adjust a throw pillow behind her back, then settled in once again.

"Thanks again, Tori, for helping out with her. With the gallery and all the behind-the-scenes business that goes with it, I haven't had as much time as I'd like to meet with potential voters outside the arts community. You know, to find out what their vision is for Hunter Ridge. Although I might edge out Irvin Baydlin, I know the likelihood of beating Elaine Hunter is slim. But I don't stand a chance with either of them if I can't convince others that I can adequately represent them, too."

"I'm more than happy to be here. With things up in the air between Heath and me…" She gazed down at the diamond engagement ring on her left hand.

"He'll come around."

But for reasons that weren't yet clear, Tori's fiancé had decided they needed space. So at Sunshine's invitation, she'd loaded her car with clothes and the tools of her artistic trade and come to Hunter Ridge.

"I appreciate, too, that you're willing to help me with family research while you're here. I haven't had any free time to explore the truth of anything I remember Grandma saying. Honestly, I don't know where to start."

With little time to call her own, she hadn't so

much as confirmed that her great-great-grandparents had been in this region at the same time as the Hunters whose descendants now called this area home. She had no idea if "the ridge of the hunter" her Apache great-great-grandmother had purportedly referred to was truly a reference to Hunter Ridge—or just a coincidence.

Tori drew in a breath, her expression doubtful. "About that research, Sunshine. I'm not sure that—"

Her words were halted by a knock at the door that led to small studios, storage space, a fire escape and stairs to the gallery below.

"Hold that thought, Tori. I think Candy's here to let me know she's locking up for the night." The gallery hours were ten to six, but two nights a week—Wednesday and Saturday, mid-May through mid-September—they remained open until nine. Candy had covered for her while Sunshine met with the Co-op members.

"Hey, Sunshine." Ever perky, the early-twenties brunette standing in the hall was nevertheless smiling more than usual. "Sorry to interrupt, but there's a man downstairs who'd like to speak with you."

"Does he have a name?"

Her fair cheeks flushed and she lowered her voice. "He didn't say and I forgot to ask. I guess I got flustered. He's one of those ruggedly handsome types with dreamy eyes, a yummy voice and a killer smile."

The description fit blond-haired, blue-eyed Sawyer Banks, owner of the Echo Ridge Outpost down the street. Sunshine had run into him at the grocery store that day and they'd chatted a few minutes. But as a newcomer to town, Candy hadn't yet met many of the locals and certainly not one who didn't hang out with the artsy set. But Sawyer was hardly the type to come calling to borrow a cup of sugar, so he must have something else on his mind.

"I'll be right back, Tori." She followed Candy down the stairs.

At the bottom of the steps, she didn't immediately see him as her gaze swept the open space, its hardwood floors glinting under soft, strategically placed lighting. Breathing in the faint, familiar scent of oil paints and leather, she noted with satisfaction the pleasing arrangement of the Co-op's offerings. Oils, watercolors and acrylics. Pottery. Ceramic tiles. Leather handbags. Jewelry. Embroidered pillows and clothing. As the daughter of artists, albeit one of them a mostly absentee father, Sunshine felt right at home.

Candy having hurried on her way home through the front door, Sunshine called out to the seemingly empty space, "Hello?"

"Over here," a low male voice returned and,

as she looked toward the rear of the gallery, her heart lurched.

Not Sawyer. Grady Hunter.

Dressed in jeans, work boots and a gray long-sleeved chamois shirt, the big man looked out of place surrounded by clear glass shelving and spotlighted by canister lights. Or was it that the gallery appeared incompatible in the presence of the broad-shouldered, dark-haired man?

"What brings you here this evening, Mr. Hunter?" Surely he hadn't expected her to drive out to his place tonight to return the printouts immediately after the meeting? But she'd have to turn them over to him now—so there'd be no follow-up visit to the hallowed halls of Hunter's Hideaway. She should have snapped a picture of those old photos on his walls when she'd had a chance.

His expression intent, Grady gently placed a delicate piece of hand-blown glass back on the shelf in front of him. Then he looked up at her with a proud smile, as if relieved that his big hands had successfully accomplished the feat.

"It's Grady, Sunshine. Remember?"

His blue eyes skimmed appreciatively over her as he approached and, to her irritation, her heart beat faster. Oh, yes, he was as engaging as the rumors had suggested. That disarming grin and unexpected cooperative spirit at their last two meetings had caught her off guard. But she was ready for him tonight. Armor in place.

Nevertheless, she offered a smile, finding it difficult to suppress. But she'd make him ask her for the printouts, if only to see what excuse he'd make for coming to collect them. "How may I help you...Grady?"

He nodded toward the north wall of the gallery. "I'm giving you a heads-up that there will be increased activity next door for the next couple of days."

He couldn't have phoned the gallery and left a message? "Activity, as in noise?"

"Bingo. I've discussed it with Ted and we think we can work things out to meet our deadline with only weekday disturbance."

"Thank you." Cooperative *and* considerate. And although Candy was right—he did have dreamy eyes and a yummy voice—she couldn't let that distract her.

"So..." He tilted his head. "How did the meeting go tonight?"

Uneasy about that, was he? He didn't *look* uneasy, though. In fact, as usual, he appeared as relaxed and self-assured as she'd expect a privileged Hunter to be. But hadn't there been a fleeting uncertainty in his eyes when he'd turned over the printouts to her yesterday?

"I can't say there was celebrating in the streets,

but the drawings you provided set the minds of the majority at rest. At least for now."

"Glad to hear it." But a crease formed on his forehead. "No concerns I need to be made aware of?"

How much should she tell him? Certainly not the details of a sometimes heated discussion. As expected, Gideon had pointed out that they wouldn't be stuck in this position if *she* hadn't negotiated the lease renewal for three years. Also, that by now advising them not to take any action at this point, she was cozying up to the opposition in the upcoming election. But, fortunately, most members saw the reasonableness of her counsel.

She moved away to straighten a sculpture on its pedestal, then glanced at Grady. "There were some concerns, yes. That occasional game processing taking place right next door might be off-putting to the clientele the gallery is attempting to attract. A few members were, shall we say, disturbed. There was…talk of a petition."

A petition? "It's a little late for that, don't you think? Unless you plan to use this issue to boost your standing at the polls."

Color tinged her cheeks. "I didn't say it was my idea."

"Everything was done aboveboard, out in the open. I don't know who told you that space was to be a bookstore. Maybe it was someone's idea of a joke?"

Or the doing of his aunt Charlotte, who owned the gallery space. She and her big-city lawyers not only grabbed custody of her toddler son, but just about cleaned out Uncle Doug. That was what rallied the family to pull together and form Hunter Enterprises as a future protective measure.

"We've had this plan for the game supply store in the works," he continued, "and preliminary approvals acquired long before the Co-op leased the property next door to it."

"I understand that and I did make that point to everyone at the meeting."

This kind of thing was exactly what Mom didn't need—misinformed people starting up a petition that she'd have to address in her campaign. But that was the least of her and Dad's worries right now. Despite the family's urging, with Luke's wedding scheduled for last weekend she'd postponed surgery until today. In fact, he'd just come back from the regional medical center in Show Low.

With effort, he drew his thoughts back to the present. "You said earlier that the Co-op signed a three-year lease, right? If Co-op members are so bent out of shape, why don't they simply sublet this place, find a new spot and be done with it? There are plenty of available properties."

In fact, Hunter Enterprises had bought several—like the one where the game supply store would go—to keep longtime friends from going bankrupt. But others were now bank owned or the absentee owners continued to fork over the mortgage payment until an upswing in the economy allowed them to unload the property.

Sunshine brushed back her hair. "Unfortunately, there's a nonsublease stipulation in the contract."

That figured. Aunt Char wouldn't risk a Hunter subletting one of the prizes she'd managed to wrest from them.

"Look," she continued. "I was quite firm that a petition would cause hard feelings in the community toward us—the 'aliens.' You *have* heard us called that, haven't you?"

A glint of amusement now lit her eyes.

"Aliens. Outsiders." His own smile tugged. "Just as I've heard those of us who've long made this our home labeled 'old-timers'."

"So you can see it's not to our benefit to further antagonize the community. Or at least that's my standpoint."

"Spoken with the finesse of a true politician."

"I'm not a politician. I'm merely someone who feels passionate about the arts and fair play."

"Fair play? Pushing into a community uninvited and trying to extinguish the core character of a town?" Newcomers needed to accept Hunter Ridge for what it was or move on. Even a newcomer who looked mighty attractive tonight in denim capris, sandals and an off-the-shoulder embroidered tunic.

"Look, Grady—"

"Mommy?" A plaintive voice called from the top of the staircase and a barefooted, pajama-clad Tessa eased down one step at a time. "I think there's something in my closet."

Grady caught the distress in Sunshine's eyes.

"Sweetie, there's nothing in your closet but your clothes."

"But there *is*." The girl's eyes widened as she spied him, and then she crouched down on the step.

Sunshine sent a look of apology in his direction. "Give me a few minutes to get her back to bed."

"Sure. And about those building renderings I gave you…"

"I'll drop them off tomorrow after I've looked at them again, if that's okay."

"That won't be necessary. Shredding them would be fine."

Sunshine frowned.

"There you are, Tessa." A feminine voice called from the top of the staircase and a short-haired young blonde appeared, relief tingeing her tone when she spied the little girl. "I'm sorry, Sunshine. I stepped into the bathroom for a minute or two."

"It's okay, Tori. Don't worry about it."

The other woman took Tessa's hand, her gaze touching on him curiously. Sunshine caught the look.

"Tori, I'd like you to meet Grady Hunter. Grady, this is my friend Tori Janner. She's visiting from Jerome."

"Hunter?" The name was spoken almost cautiously.

"As in our soon-to-be next-door neighbor," Sunshine supplied. "He stopped by to let us know to expect more activity tomorrow."

"I'll get out my earplugs." She tugged lightly on Tessa's hand and the two returned upstairs.

Grady shifted. "I'd better let you go trounce whatever is in Tessa's closet. Monsters?"

Sunshine gave a weary sigh. "Monsters I could deal with. Moms are natural-born slayers of monsters. This, unfortunately, is a more vague anxiety that's had her upset since shortly before school started."

"Once she makes friends and settles into a new environment, those worries will evaporate."

"That's my hope." But she didn't sound as if she believed his words.

He moved closer to look down on her with mock chastisement. "Now, don't *you* go worrying about Tessa's worrying. You know what the Good Book says about that."

Or maybe she didn't know. She'd only recently started attending Christ's Church of Hunter Ridge. Was that a politically motivated move? He'd like to think a single mom had more concern for her child's spiritual welfare than that. But God gave people more freedom of choice than he would if running the show himself.

With a sigh, she stared down at the floor and his chest tightened. This kid thing must be getting to her.

"It's just that…" She shook her head, lost in thought.

Without thinking, he reached out and gently lifted her chin with his fingertips, her startled eyes meeting his.

"Stop with the worrying, Sunshine."

She froze, staring up at him as the warmth of his fingers shot a bolt of awareness through her. An unsettling, although not unpleasant feeling. But this was Grady Hunter. A male cut from the same bolt of cloth as her ex.

She stepped back to break the connection, fearful he'd feel the pounding of her heart. "Believe me, I'm doing my best *not* to."

"Well, good, then."

Their eyes remained locked for an uncomfortable moment, and then she glanced to the top of the staircase. "Are you sure you don't want me to drop off the design printouts tomorrow?"

"Like I said, destroy them."

There went her excuse to visit Hunter's Hideaway again.

He moved toward the door, then paused in front of a watercolor painting displayed on an easel. "I noticed that several of these bear the intertwined initials ESC. Is that you?"

The subject of this painting in particular could have clued him in on the identity of the artist, as well. The child, in partial shadow and facing slightly away, might easily be recognizable as Tessa to someone who knew her. Reluctantly, Sunshine joined him where he continued to study the painting.

"The *E* stands for Elizabeth. Sunshine's always been the name I go by." Her father, who'd been around more often in those early years, had bestowed it on her when she was a toddler.

"You're extremely talented."

"Thank you."

"This is for sale?" His brow furrowed as his gaze met hers uncertainly. "A painting of your daughter?"

He sounded almost disapproving.

"It's not a portrait." With effort, she suppressed the defensiveness his words provoked. "It could be any little girl with a Native American patterned blanket clutched in her arms. Customers like that Southwestern touch."

"It's very striking."

"Thanks."

He moved to the door and she followed to lock up.

"You *will* keep me informed, won't you?" He paused in the doorway, all business now. "I mean, if there are any developments with the Co-op members I should be made aware of? I'm available to meet with them, to answer questions and set things straight."

"As I said earlier, I believe the proposed petition has been squelched." At least Gideon had backed off for the time being.

Grady looked as if he wanted to say something more but instead nodded a goodbye. She locked up and dimmed the lights. Then wearily heading up the stairs, two troubling thoughts remained foremost.

Why did Grady touching her take her breath away?

And please, Lord, don't let me be present if Grady Hunter and Gideon Edlow ever cross paths.

Chapter Four

Whoever would have thought when Grady insisted she destroy the printouts rather than returning them that another excuse to visit Hunter's Hideaway would be delivered to her doorstep so speedily?

Now, Thursday afternoon, trailing his younger sister Rio down the hallway to his office, she could hardly believe her good fortune. There was an added bonus, as well. Rio said Grady had stepped out and hadn't yet returned. So if she could manage to ditch Rio, she might not only find her missing pen, but have an opportunity for another look at the photographs on Grady's wall. On closer examination, would a face in one of them stand out as resembling her mother or grandmother?

"This is the only place I think I could have lost it," Sunshine said as Rio flipped on the light and they stepped into Grady's office. "I used it to jot down notes when I was waiting in the lobby the other day, then distinctly remember putting it back into my jacket pocket. That's the last time I saw it. At Hunter's Hideaway. And since it wasn't in your lost and found, hopefully it's in here somewhere. It was a gift from my father, so it's special."

After having thoroughly combed her apartment, SUV, tote bag and jacket pockets that morning, it had taken mental backtracking to figure out the possible whereabouts of the pen. That maybe when she'd pulled out her phone here a few days ago, she'd accidentally dislodged the pen. It was a long shot, but if it had dropped to the thick, patterned area rug, she wouldn't have heard it hit the floor. Engrossed in her coloring book, Tessa might not have noticed, either.

Rio adjusted the wooden louvered blinds to admit more natural light. "Let's take a look."

Ignoring a prick of disappointment that Grady's sister chose not to return immediately to the front desk, Sunshine gave a longing look at the photographs on the wall, then embarked on the quest for her pen.

"I sat in this area with Tessa for a few minutes," she explained, leaning over to check under the chairs and lamp-topped table, "then stood over there with Grady to look at the blueprints and his laptop screen."

She wouldn't mention wandering the perimeters of the room with a camera in her hand.

"If it's here, we'll find it."

"Thanks, but I hate taking you away from your work." *Maybe you'd better get back to it. Hint. Hint.*

"Maybe Grady found it." Rio optimistically checked out the pencil cup on the desk, then shook her head and they resumed the search.

"Aah, here it is." As tempting as it was to nudge the colorful pen farther under the edge of the rug with her toe, Sunshine reluctantly bent to retrieve it. So much for thinking God had rewarded her with an opportunity to explore. "Ta-da!"

"What's going on?" Grady's deep voice drew her attention as he crossed the threshold of his office, surprise at seeing her there evident in his eyes.

"Sunshine was looking for the pen she lost here the other day." Rio cast her a bright smile. "Her dad had given it to her."

"I hadn't realized you'd lost something or I could have looked around for you."

"No problem."

When Rio disappeared into the hallway, Grady moved to his desk and placed his laptop case on the oak surface. "You're close to your dad, are you?"

Clutching the pen in her hand, she moved to stand across the desk from him. "Not exactly."

A puzzled look shadowed his eyes.

"I don't mean to sound mysterious," she amended. "It's just that, well, I never saw a lot of him. He wasn't around much—he never got around to marrying my mom."

Grady's expression filled with sympathy. "Rough."

"But I'm over it." She slipped the pen into her purse, careful to push it securely to the bottom. "So I guess it's corny to get overly sentimental about a high school graduation gift."

"Not corny at all. I'm glad you found it."

His reassuring words comforted. Made her feel less silly for clinging to the pen for all these years. "Like I said, it isn't that he's an intentionally bad father or anything like that. He has a busy career, and has always traveled frequently."

"What did he do for a living that took him away so often?"

She trailed her fingers along the edge of the desk, remembering as a child how excited she'd be when he put in an appearance—and how disappointed when he left without a goodbye. "He's an artist. Jewelry maker. His work is featured in shops and galleries throughout the Southwest."

"Wow. So that's where you got your talent."

"And from my mother. And her mother and her mother's mother before that. I've heard stories that my great-great-grandmother had strong creative leanings, as well."

"That's quite a lineage. You should be proud of that."

"Oh, I am." Why was she telling him this? Searching for a change in topic, she glanced at one of the wildlife photographs on the wall. "Who's the photographer?"

He looked up from where he was booting up his laptop. "What's that?"

"Who took these amazing wildlife shots? I noticed them the last time I was here. I'd love to get a print of this deer for my living room."

"That can be arranged."

"You know the artist? Whoever took these has an incredible eye for detail. A great understanding of composition."

"I'll pass on the compliment."

"Is he local? Or she, I guess I should say. A focus on wildlife isn't the sole domain of males."

"He's about as local as you can get." Grady grinned sheepishly and suddenly she got it.

"You took these pictures?" She moved closer to the one of the fox. "They're amazing. I didn't know you were a professional photographer."

He came around the desk to stand by her. "Define *professional*."

"Talented. Gifted. And receiving payment for your work."

"Then, I guess I don't qualify."

She stared at him. "You're kidding. Why not?"

"Just a hobby."

"You mean you've never tried to sell anything?"

He folded his arms. "Wildlife photographers are a dime a dozen—especially with the advent of digital cameras. Go online and type in *wildlife photography* and see the results you get. There are bunches of talented people out there."

"And you're one of them."

He looked shyly pleased at her words, but she could only stare at him in surprise. "Has no one ever told you how accomplished you are? How sensitively you've captured the nuances of nature? It's criminal that you're not being paid to do this. I could—"

No, while she could easily prove her point that his work could garner sales, she wouldn't offer to take his photos to the gallery. Not only would some of the other Co-op members—like Gideon— frown on that, but why should she, a struggling artist herself, smooth the rocky road for a Hunter?

Drawn to the charismatic outdoorsman with an artistic eye, how quickly she'd forgotten he was where *he* was today and she was where *she* was because his ancestor had cheated hers.

"Photography is a private thing for me." Grady turned his full attention to the petite woman standing beside him, absorbing her evaluation of his work. He'd never talked to anyone outside the family about his photography. And seldom with family, although if he was going to get his plans off the ground to add a photographic element to the Hunter Ridge lineup, that would soon be changing. "Don't you find that yourself? That in each of your creations you've poured a piece of yourself into it and find it hard to release it into the hands of others?"

He still didn't understand how she could put that extraordinary watercolor of Tessa up for sale. To offer it to some stranger to hang on the wall of their home or office just because they forked over a credit card.

With a soft laugh, she cast him a wary look, no doubt recognizing where his thoughts were going. "A similar reluctance may have been the case for me years ago but now, with a child to support, the almighty dollar wins out every time. I definitely agree with you, though. Each creation carries the creator's fingerprint, so to speak."

He nodded. Although she'd pushed herself beyond the self-conscious unwillingness to expose her work to the criticism of others—the thing that held him back—she nevertheless understood his hesitance to go public.

Sunshine pointed at the photo of a fox he'd taken last winter. "Like this one. I don't imagine you conveniently shot it through your kitchen window, did you? While it's a moment caught in time, it's my guess you observed the comings and goings of this elusive creature, studied the angle of the sun, glare off the snow, and gave thought to composition. You knew the mood and message you wanted to convey before the shutter clicked. All three of these photos strongly reflect the artist behind the lens."

Artist. He didn't much care for that label. He thought of himself as more of an observer of wildlife who'd learned the tricks of capturing an image. One who made use of a camera's technical features to produce a pleasing photo.

They talked for some time about his current preference for black-and-white, use of focal length and the considerations made in composition. About the challenges of wildlife. It was in many ways oddly affirming to speak with someone knowledgeable about those aspects of his work.

"Oh, my goodness." Sunshine cringed as she looked at the clock on his credenza. "I barged in on your day to look for my pen, but didn't intend to take up all your time."

He smiled at her flustered movements, the appealing flush on her face. "I didn't have anything scheduled for the rest of the afternoon. I enjoyed our visit."

"I did, too." Another wave of color rose in her

cheeks. Then she abruptly turned away. "But I need to get back to the gallery."

Halfway to the door, she glanced at the grouping of vintage photos on the wall and paused. "So are these more of your mother's yard-sale finds?"

Curiously relieved that she hadn't dashed off, he moved to stand beside her. "Not these. I latched on to them when my grandpa Hunter passed away when I was nineteen."

"So this is your family?"

"Some are." He studied the photos, then pointed to a stiffly composed group of people standing outside a cabin. "Like this one."

"Do you know who they are?"

"These two are my great-great-grandparents. Harrison—he went by Duke—and Pearl Hunter. They came here on the cusp of the twentieth century. Acquired land in the very early 1900s. The youngster hanging on to the mangy-looking dog is my great-grandfather, Carson. And his sisters are next to him."

"And what about these two?" Sunshine touched her finger lightly to the nonreflective glass, noting another man and a woman off to the side. "If I'm not mistaken, the woman looks to be Native American."

A muscle twitched in his jaw. "Those people lived on the property. Friends of the family."

That was, if you could call a man who'd betrayed you a friend. Grady had intentionally placed this photo front and center in his office after Jasmine's underhandedness. A reminder that, as also in the case of Aunt Char's disloyalty, Hunters had to look out for Hunters first and foremost. Outsiders couldn't be trusted.

"Do they have names?"

"Walter Royce and his wife, Flora." Their monikers were emblazoned on his brain. "And yes, she's Native American. White Mountain Apache."

Sunshine stepped closer, her gaze more intent. Like his mom, she seemed enthralled with old-time photographs and the stories they held.

"That woven blanket draped over her arm… It's such an interesting pattern. One I'd like to incorporate in one of my paintings." She looked to him hopefully. "Would you mind if I took a picture of it?"

He shrugged. "Have at it."

She eagerly slipped her cell phone from her purse and snapped a few shots. "Inspiration sometimes comes from directions you least expect, doesn't it?"

"I guess so." Actually, he *knew* so. How many times had his eyes been drawn to something because of the texture, the shadow, the sheer beauty of it and his fingers itched to reach for his camera? Like right now. With Sunshine's dark eyes bright with excitement and natural light from the windows glinting off her glossy black hair and highlighting a soft cheek and the gentle curve of her lips.

"When do you think this photo was taken?"

"Judging from my great-grandfather's age here, I'm guessing about 1906, 1907, maybe?"

A wistful look flickered in her eyes. "It must be wonderful to trace your family back this far. To know that these pine trees on the property shaded them as they do your family now. That every single day you're walking where they walked."

"Yeah, I guess it is remarkable." Her enthusiasm was almost contagious, and he found himself smiling. "In fact, the original cabin in this picture and the one the Royces lived in are still on the property."

Her eyes widened. "You're kidding. I'd love to see them sometime."

While they weren't rotting or anything like that—his family had seen to it that they were well maintained—they hadn't been modernized. "They're nothing fancy, you understand."

"I wouldn't expect them to be. But I'd love to see buildings that hold such history."

"Well, then, sometime when you don't have to rush off, I can arrange that."

From the indecisive flicker in her eyes, for a moment he thought she might claim that getting back to the gallery was of minor importance and insist that now was as good a time as any for a tour. But when she merely uttered a thank-you, he determined the perceived wavering on her part must have been in his imagination.

Wishful thinking?

Unfortunately, that could only get him into trouble. He'd heard grumblings at a family breakfast meeting that morning about Sunshine's earlier visit to the Hideaway. Uncle Doug warned that she might be snooping around for something to use against Grady's mother in the upcoming election—although neither he nor Uncle "Mac" McCrae could come up with exactly what that might be. Aunt Suzy—Dad's sister and Uncle Mac's wife—reiterated that until more was known about her sister-in-law's health status, everyone should keep silent about it with those outside the family. As political opponents, Sunshine Carston and Irvin Baydlin didn't need to be alerted just yet.

Grandma Jo, fortunately, had put in a good word as to his "proactive" endeavors to soothe the ruffled feathers of the Artists' Co-op members regarding the new Hunter business. But how would he explain escorting Sunshine around the property to see old family cabins?

"Grady?" Sunshine's curious eyes met his, no doubt wondering where he'd mentally wandered off.

"Let me know when you're available to take a

look at the cabins, and I'll check my schedule."
Maybe he could put her off for a while. With all
there was to do at the Hideaway with the influx
of hunters and with details of the new wild game
supply store demanding his attention, he'd have
an excuse to beg off if he needed one.

She moved to the door, then paused, a thoughtful look on her face. "Your mother wouldn't happen to be around this afternoon, would she? I
wanted to ask her about—"

"No, I'm afraid not. She's out of town this
week."

"Oh? I'll get in touch with her later, then."

As Sunshine disappeared into the hallway,
Grady again studied the old photograph of the
original Hunter's Hideaway. Remembered the deceit that had severed a friendship.

Was Sunshine's request to talk to his mother an
innocent one? Or had she somehow gotten wind
of her opponent's possible Achilles' heel and today's visit was nothing more than a fishing expe-
dition to learn more?

Chapter Five

"**I** think I *may* have confirmed it, Tori." Sunshine glanced at her friend Saturday morning. "Not only is 'the ridge of the hunter' likely the same as Hunter Ridge, but I may now have proof that my ancestors knew the Hunter family just as in the family legend."

With satisfaction, she tapped the screen of her laptop computer, where she'd uploaded photos from her phone. They were the first images she'd ever seen of her legendary ancestors if, indeed, these two were her great-great-grandparents. When Grady pointed them out, named names she'd never before heard, it was all she could do not to topple over in amazement as the pieces fit together.

"A pioneer family named Hunter, can you believe it? Who not only lived in the area that one day would neighbor Hunter Ridge, but who were friends of another couple—an Anglo husband with an Apache wife. Identical to the family story related by my grandma."

Had Grady noticed her excitement?

"You said her name was Flora?" Tori inspected one of the photos. "That doesn't sound like an Indian name, but she does look like the full-blooded White Mountain Apache of family folklore, doesn't she? I can see where your jet-black hair, dark eyes and beautiful warm complexion could have been inherited from her. Do you see any other family resemblance to either of them?"

"Flora's build and facial structure is similar to my grandmother's—Flora's granddaughter—if indeed this is my ancestor. And Walter?" Sunshine frowned. "I'm not sure."

"This is wild." Tori stepped back, but her attention remained fixed on the screen. "I have to admit, I didn't think there was any substance to those tall tales you told me."

"Well, we don't know for sure." But something deep inside Sunshine bubbled up, telling her she was looking into the faces of those who'd come before her. "I never knew their names. But it's not as if I've had some pristine lineage traced back to the *Mayflower*, you know. The family on Mom's side has been fragmented. There was never an interest in documenting our ancestry. Grandma's mother died when Grandma was a teen. That's who she'd have gotten her information from, and Grandma's grandma died before that. So even though my great-grandma knew her parents' names, that wouldn't necessarily have been passed down to her own daughter."

"Gets complicated, doesn't it? I didn't even know my own great-grandparents' names until I did research."

"It's not as if my grandmother tried to verify any of this, either. I mean, the substance of the story she passed down was focused solely on the unfortunate fact that our ancestors were cheated out of property by someone they considered a friend."

Tori crossed the room to lower herself onto the sofa. "Even if these two are related to you, that doesn't mean there's any truth to the core of that story. You know, that Hunters grabbed their land or anything."

"No, but…" Stories had to start somewhere, didn't they?

"So what's next?"

Sunshine moved to a front window overlooking the road through town, then pushed aside a sheer curtain to watch the activity below. "Well, I guess I need to go online and see if those names can be verified on one of those genealogy websites."

"You know it isn't as easy as those TV shows depict, don't you? I mean, they have professional genealogists who do months of background research. Then when the celebrity shows up with cameras rolling, they tap a few keys and pull up the proof as if they'd just discovered it."

"I know, but it's somewhere to start. I'll begin with what I know about Mom and Grandma and work my way back."

"People in the olden days didn't always have birth certificates. And your Apache ancestor likely didn't."

"True." Sunshine rested her forehead on the cool pane of glass, trying to better see what was going on below. Was that Grady Hunter hauling a box out of a navy blue SUV in front of the building next door?

"What are you looking at?"

"Oh, nothing." Sunshine moved away from the window and sat down. "So has my family mystery intrigued you enough that you're willing to help me? I know you have reservations about how the story involves the Hunters."

"That's the part that I'm most concerned about. But I've researched my own family and found it rewarding. So I'd be happy to do that for you while you're seeing to the gallery, Co-op business and getting out to meet your future constituency."

"You're the best friend in the world, Tori."

But when would Tori's fiancé recognize the treasure he had in her? He hadn't asked her to return the engagement ring, so that had to mean there was hope, didn't it?

"It's the least I can do, with you letting me stay here. I couldn't stay in Jerome and risk bumping into Heath every time I turned around. Or having people ask me about him, probing to find out what's going on with us when I don't know myself."

"Have you—" Sunshine paused, knowing this was sensitive territory "—considered breaking the engagement yourself? Provoking him into working through whatever it is that's gotten into him?"

"I know it sounds stupid." Tori looked down at the ring on her hand. "But I'm not ready to close the door yet. I love him."

Ah, yes, love.

Sunshine had been there herself and couldn't point fingers at her friend now. "Whatever happens—wedding or no wedding—know that I'm here for you."

When Tori returned to her room, Sunshine again moved restlessly to the window. Yes, that was Grady down there, now talking with the man she knew to be his contractor.

He'd promised to show her those historic cabins, but they hadn't firmed that up. The likelihood that she'd make new discoveries under those roofs to confirm her grandmother's story was slim, but it would be worth a try.

She glanced down at her watch. She had thirty minutes until she had to unlock the gallery doors for another business day.

"Tessa?" she called, intending to see if she'd like to go on a walk, which would coincidentally lead past the renovation of the store next door.

But then she stopped herself.

That thinking—or rather *not* thinking—was exactly how she'd gotten tangled up with Tessa's father. And *this* guy was a descendent of Duke Hunter.

Windshield wipers beating a steady rhythm, Grady applied the brakes as he rounded another wet curve on the way back from visiting his mother at the hospital Sunday evening. She'd had an adverse reaction to her medications a few days ago, but seemed to have stabilized and might soon come home. Then would begin the long haul of postsurgery physical therapy and chemotherapy treatments.

Man, he hated to see her go through that. Dad, too.

Please, God, heal Mom. We need her.

Now, halfway between Canyon Springs and Hunter Ridge, twilight had given over to darkness, and clouds from a late-season monsoon rain hung low. The days were rapidly growing shorter and summer was pretty much over as the nighttime temperatures dropped into the midforties. Elections would soon be upon them. Would Mom stick it out or withdraw from the race?

He lowered the volume of the country tune belting out of the stereo speakers. It was a mournful love song that, for some irritating reason, made him think of Sunshine.

He'd been relieved that after their conversation a few days ago, she'd made no further attempts to visit the Hideaway or to try to see his mother. Nor had she pressed him to show her the old family cabins that appeared to have captured her imagination when he'd mentioned them. So his family's concerns that she had ulterior motives were unfounded.

Although he hadn't forgotten that she did have a reputation for stirring things up—for championing the sometimes extremist views of the local artists—he couldn't see her doing anything underhanded, such as using his mother's illness to undermine her during the weeks preceding the election.

Then again, he'd not been that good of a judge of women in the past, had he?

Rounding another curve, his headlights sliced through the dark, and up ahead he spied the flashing emergency lights of a vehicle pulled off to the side of the road. Nasty night to have car trouble.

He slowed, but he'd no more than gotten up to

it when he recognized the older-model, burgundy-colored SUV. He'd taken notice of it the day he'd stood on the Hideaway porch and watched it out of sight. Rusted out near a back wheel well, it also boasted a slightly bent bumper with a Hunter Ridge Artists' Cooperative sticker.

Sunshine.

Braking, he abruptly pulled off the rain slick road, then backed up until the rear bumper of his SUV almost kissed the front of the other vehicle. He couldn't be sure with headlights lancing into his back window, but he thought he'd glimpsed someone in the front driver's seat when he'd passed by.

He pulled up the hood of his windbreaker and climbed out, striding through the rain and glare of headlights to make his way to the driver's side window.

"Grady?" a soft, familiar voice came through the partially rolled-down window.

"You okay?"

"Yeah. It died on me. Like, it ran out of steam."

"How long have you been out here?"

"Maybe half an hour or so. It doesn't seem to be a battery problem, though. The lights are working. I'd have called for assistance, but for some reason I can't get a signal on my cell phone."

"We'll deal with your car later. Why don't you hop on out and I'll give you a ride home."

She shifted to look in the backseat. "Stop crying, sweetheart. There's nothing to be afraid of."

She had Tessa with her?

"This is our friend Grady," she continued. "You remember him? Didn't I tell you God would send someone to help us?"

He couldn't catch the child's response, but he heard another murmured reassurance from her mother before Sunshine faced him again. "I'm sorry. You're getting soaked."

"I won't melt. Let's get you both home. Do you have jackets?"

"Yes, and we'll need to take Tessa's booster seat, too."

"No problem."

In no time at all, he transferred the ladies to his vehicle, secured Sunshine's SUV, then set up reflectors to alert any passing traffic.

At last he climbed inside, his hair now plastered to his head and cold rain trickling down the back of his neck. But he hardly noticed.

"Everybody buckled in? Ready to roll?"

Upon hearing the happy affirmatives, he pulled on to the highway and headed toward Hunter Ridge.

"I can't tell you, Grady—" Sunshine leaned in closer, her voice low, he assumed, to keep Tessa from hearing "—how relieved I was to see you.

I had no idea who might have pulled up in front of us."

Like Tessa, she'd been scared.

He cleared his throat. "God was watching out for you."

"He was. Thank you."

Grady gave her a reassuring smile, acutely aware of her grateful eyes on him as the windshield wipers beat a steady rhythm. When she settled back into her seat, drawing her jacket more closely around her, he flipped on the heater.

A weary sigh escaped her lips. "Believe it or not, I got that thing out of the shop right after Labor Day. *Again.* It's costing me a small fortune."

"Fairly old vehicle, isn't it?"

"It was old when I bought it, but it's always been reliable. And the four-wheel drive has come in handy since I moved to town."

"Might be time to start looking for a replacement."

"Fat chance."

"If you'll give me your keys when we get back to town, I'll catch a ride with a tow truck and we'll get your SUV to a repair shop." There were several. He'd find out which one she'd been going to and determine if a switch was in order.

"Thanks. But I hate for you to go back out in this."

"No biggie."

"Mommy?" Tessa's query carried from the backseat.

"Yeah, sweetie?"

"I'm hungry."

"I'll fix you something as soon as we get home."

Grady lowered his voice. "I can stop to pick something up for her."

"Thanks, but that won't be necessary. I think because it gets dark earlier now, she thinks it's later than it actually is. She had a late lunch, and a big one at that. Those church-related gatherings sure know how to put on a potluck."

"So you went to church in Canyon Springs? I didn't see you at Christ's Church this morning." Should he have admitted that? Did it sound like he'd been looking for her?

"No, not Canyon Springs. A church on the White Mountain Apache reservation." Sunshine held out her hands to the heating vent to warm them. "I've gotten involved there since moving to Hunter Ridge. But with Tessa starting school, I realize she needs to get to bed early on Sunday nights. So this was our last full day there until next summer."

He slowed the vehicle as they approached the turnoff to Hunter Ridge, then headed down a steep, forested descent to the bridge over Hunter Creek. On the other side, the twisting road again led upward to the little community he'd always called home. It could be a mean route to negotiate after a snowfall. Sunshine would definitely need four-wheel drive if she intended to keep living here in the winter months.

By the time he pulled in front of the Hunter Ridge Artists' Cooperative, the rain had slackened to a drizzle. Sunshine helped Tessa from the vehicle, and he snared the booster seat, then met them under the awning, where Sunshine ushered her daughter inside.

"Keys, please." He held out his hand.

"You're sure?"

"Positive."

She disengaged the car key from her key chain and handed it to him. "I don't know what we'd have done without you tonight. I wish there was some way I could repay you."

"No need."

She scowled, obviously not satisfied with his answer. Then her gaze swept the dimly lit gallery, her eyes brightening. "I know! I can display some of your wildlife photos here. As a guest artist. I'll prove to you that your work can be a moneymaker."

He stepped back, shaking his head. "I don't think so."

"Why not?"

Why not? Because he couldn't afford to be la-

beled as an "artist" in this town. Couldn't afford
to have his friends and family snickering behind
his back or criticizing him for what might be interpreted as joining the very people in the community that had a candidate running against his
mother.

"I'm not ready to go there, but thanks for offering."

Disappointment colored her eyes, but she didn't
argue. Merely thanked him again and watched
from the doorway as he returned to his vehicle.
He called a local towing service, then headed out
to meet the guy at his garage.

Sunshine's offer to display his photos had been
unexpected. A flattering boost to his ego. Tempting, too, even if the offer had been made out of
a sense of indebtedness. Unfortunately, for many
reasons it wasn't something he could afford to take
her up on. Including the fact he had no desire to
discover—in such a public forum—that no one
wanted to buy his photographs.

Chapter Six

Thankfully, Grady had turned down her offer to display his wildlife photographs. Sunshine had already nixed the idea earlier, but overwhelmed with gratitude that night, she'd wanted to demonstrate how much she appreciated what he'd done for her and Tessa.

Now, four days later, looking lovingly at her daughter across the breakfast table, that sense of appreciation overflowed. If it hadn't been for Grady, who knows how long they'd have sat out there on the dark, rainy road? Or who else might have pulled over to offer assistance?

"So the problem turned out to be something haywire with the fuel pump?" Tori rose from her chair and started clearing dishes.

"Right." The mechanic at the shop the Hunters had long done business with was able to fix it— and she suspected the bill she'd paid was considerably reduced because of the connection to the prominent local family. "The guy at the garage says I should find a replacement vehicle before winter sets in. As if that's going to happen."

Right about now she could sure use that dreamed-of settlement from the property her great-great-grandparents had lost to the Hunters. *Allegedly* lost, as Tori always reminded. Tessa needed new snow boots, car and health insurance were coming due and annual dental and doctor appointments couldn't be put off much longer. Once she proved her grandma's tale held substance, would the Hunters feel obligated to compensate her?

"You know, you're always welcome," Tori said as she rinsed a plate, "to use my car for as long as I'm here."

"I may have to take you up on that." As Tessa scurried off to her room, Sunshine joined her friend in the kitchen. "But I need to figure out a solution for the long run. Right now money is tight."

"At least that Hunter guy was in the right place at the right time." Tori handed her a plate, which Sunshine placed in the dishwasher. "Does it seem weird to be seeing so much of him lately? You know, since you're running against his mother and want to prove his family cheated yours."

"It's awkward sometimes." She loaded two

more plates and a handful of utensils. "At other times I forget about that and we just, you know, talk as if those barriers don't exist."

Which was a danger zone she needed to be on guard against.

"He seems nice. Cute, too." Tori's tone held a probing note.

"Don't get any ideas on my behalf." Sunshine gave her friend a warning look. "He's too much like Jerrel. The easygoing, charming, never-knows-a-stranger type. You've noticed, haven't you, how the single gals flock around him at church on Sunday mornings? Yep, too much like Jerrel."

"Jerrel didn't go to church, though."

"I didn't go, either, remember?"

In fact, she'd never graced the door of a church until after Tessa had been born and her husband—the lead vocalist in a promising regional country band—had decided a child cramped his style. That was when she'd met Tori—at a storefront church in Jerome shortly after Jerrel filed for divorce.

"So what's on your agenda for today, Sunshine?"

To her relief, Tori didn't pursue further talk of Grady Hunter. "I thought I'd take Tessa to the park for a while before I open the gallery."

"When you get back, I'll pull out my sewing

machine, and that should keep us busy for the rest of the morning. Tessa wants to make a tote bag, and since my mother started me on simple things like that when I was her age, I think she can handle it. We'll begin with the safety-first basics."

Quilting was Tori's gift to the world, her artistic contribution. A labor of love. Tessa couldn't have a better teacher.

When they reached the park and Tessa had made a beeline for the swings, Sunshine was glad they'd worn light jackets. Although the sun filtered down through overhanging pine branches, it was still a cool, fallish morning. From somewhere above came the skitter of a squirrel's claws on roughened bark, and a chorus of sparrows chirping a cheerful song.

The park had only a handful of kid-friendly amenities. Swings, a merry-go-round and a trio of slides in varying sizes—of which Tessa had proudly graduated to the middlemost. But the park was treed, spacious and nestled in the heart of Hunter Ridge's business district. It was for this location that last spring she'd requested a permit approval for a series of art-in-the-park events. But she'd been turned down.

Maybe next year, if she was elected to the town council?

"Hey! How is everybody this morning?"

Her heart inexplicably lifting at the sound of

the familiar voice, Sunshine turned to see Grady striding toward them with that distinctive masculine gait, his impossibly broad shoulders clad in a windbreaker.

"Grady!" To Sunshine's surprise, her daughter let out a cry of welcome and abandoned the swing to run toward him, her oversize jacket flapping around her.

Tessa loved the variations of the cotton jacket's purple color, so Sunshine had given in and bought it from the sale table at the bargain store. She hadn't intended for Tessa to wear it until she'd grown into it in a few years, but this morning Tessa had spied it in the back of the coat closet and insisted on wearing it.

When Tessa reached Grady, she grabbed his hand and gazed happily up at him. "Now you can see how high I can swing."

He glanced at Sunshine, looking slightly taken aback at Tessa's grip on his hand. "I can do that."

Willingly, he allowed her to pull him forward to stand next to her mother.

"Okay. Now watch." Tessa dashed for the swings.

"I'm watching." A grin lit his face at the little girl's enthusiasm. "Do you need a push?"

She shook her head as she lowered herself onto the seat and grasped the swing chains, proud that she didn't need assistance. In a flash, she had her-self moving.

"Wow," he said in an aside to Sunshine. "To have that much energy."

She laughed. "I know."

"Do you think her jacket's big enough?" Humor lit his eyes.

He *would* notice. "Obviously you don't fully comprehend the persuasive abilities of a five-year-old."

He folded his arms and slanted her a look. "I have a fairly good idea. Nieces and nephews, you know."

"Are you watching?" a demanding voice called.

"We're watching!" they yelled in unison, then exchanged a glance and laughed.

The kindergartner was pumping herself higher and higher, a determined look on her little face.

"You're doing great, Tessa!" With Grady's words of encouragement impelling her to pump harder, a triumphant smile widened.

Sunshine's heart swelled with love. And regret. Seeing how her daughter openly craved the atten-tion of Grady acutely reminded her of her own ab-sentee father. The longing for a dad's attention. A male role model. As much as she'd hated having a father who wasn't around, here she was repeating history with her own child. The last thing she'd ever intended to have happen.

"Thank you again, Grady, for the rescue Sunday night."

"You're welcome.

"I—" Sunshine tensed as from across the street she glimpsed Gideon Edlow, who'd paused to stare at her and Grady. He was frowning, as though it was any of his business who she talked to. He'd been cantankerous at last night's Co-op meeting. That wasn't anything new, but it was growing increasingly tiresome. Worrisome, as well. With effort, she refocused her attention on Grady, silently willing Gideon to move on.

"Thanks, too, for getting my SUV to someone who not only knows what he's doing, but didn't request I turn over my firstborn for payment."

He looked pleased. "So you have wheels again?"

"I do. But he's of the same mind as you—that I should find a replacement before winter."

Grady's eyes grew thoughtful. "Do you have today off?"

Why did he want to know that? Surely he didn't intend to go car shopping with her. "No, I have to open the gallery at ten. But we thought we'd get some sunshine while we can. Winter is just around the corner."

"It is."

"But even with summer basically over, I have plenty to do at the Co-op as well as campaign-related things—" She caught his eye apologetically. After all, she was his mother's opponent. "And I have plans to expand the Co-op's offerings. While anyone—as your sister-in-law Delaney has done—can take private lessons with an artist-mentor, I'd like to see classes geared to those in middle and high school."

"Provide them with more hands-on exposure to the arts?"

"Exactly. Maybe painting, jewelry making, pottery and—" She tilted her head to look up at him. "Have you ever given thought to teaching photography?"

"Me?"

His expression must have looked as strained as his voice sounded, because Sunshine laughed. "Sure. Every kid in town has a camera these days, even if only the one on their cell phone."

He didn't want to lie. If he ever got his plans off the ground, she'd hear that the Hideaway had branched into wildlife photography. "Actually, that's something I've given thought to."

"Really?"

He had her full attention now. "Years ago, when I was in my late teens, I thought it would be a great idea if Hunter's Hideaway offered guided treks for aspiring wildlife photographers. You know, with workshops on the side."

"That's a wonderful idea."

He shrugged, his smile somewhat wry. "It wasn't well received by my family at the time."

"How come?"

"Well, to quote my uncle Doug... 'Look, boy, we specialize in helping hunters pack out an elk for the freezer, not take purty pictures of it.'"

He could still hear his uncle's laughter and that of Dad and Uncle Mac joining in. Even now he could clearly recall the wave of heat that had coursed up his neck and how his reddening face had egged Uncle Doug to more laughter. It had been a humiliating moment and he'd not brought up the subject of wildlife photography since then.

"That was a long time ago, Grady. Things change. I think you should do it."

"I'd like to." He let his gaze momentarily wander to where Tessa was now dragging her tennis-shoe-clad feet in the dirt, slowing herself down to a gradual stop. "But Hunter Enterprises is a family-run business, so I have to get buy-in. I'll have to prove it would attract enough business to make it worthwhile. Be a moneymaker."

"Of course it would be." She focused intently on him. "It's not as though you're suggesting the entire operation switch its emphasis solely to photography. It would be another revenue path, like the trail rides, cross-country skiing and training for high-elevation endurance riders."

"That was my thinking, too, but..." It was more

complicated than she made it sound. As an adult, he now understood that better than he had as a teen. Many decisions had to be made. Youth or adult sessions or both? Weeklong or select weekends? Which seasons? How best to advertise? And he'd have to work the program around the scheduling of the cabins and property use. You couldn't have preoccupied photographers wandering during the various hunting seasons.

"Do it, Grady."

Looking into her excited eyes, a spark of determination flared in him. "So you don't think it's a far-fetched idea?"

"I think it's a great idea."

But was it one that his family wouldn't reject the moment he opened his mouth? Sunshine was right, though. With the advent of digitals, it seemed everyone had a camera and wanted to share photos with others, even if only on Facebook or Instagram.

"I admit this past summer I've given serious thought to developing a proposal. You know, to formally present to Hunter Enterprises. I've been researching and calculating how much we'd have to charge to make it profitable."

"I *love* it." Then the delight in her eyes dimmed. "But I'm disappointed that if you do this, you won't be available to teach youth classes at the

Co-op. That is, if I could manage to sweet-talk you into that."

Sweet talk, hmm? What might that entail?

"Mommy! Grady! I'm on the slide now!"

Exchanging a guilty glance for having gotten engrossed in conversation, they turned to where Tessa had reached the top of a towering slide— the largest of the three—poised to push off. Gutsy little gal.

"Tessa! No! Your sleeve!"

At the terror in Sunshine's voice, his eyes locked on Tessa. But her mother's warning had come too late, for as Tessa pushed off, her laughing squeal turned to a horrified scream. The upper part of the loose jacket sleeve had snagged at the top of the slide and torn, jerking her roughly and pulling her over the edge.

Dangling.

He took off, thundering past the swings. Breath ragged. Heart pounding. His gaze never wavering from the child. But what appeared a short distance seemed to stretch into miles.

Please, God. Please.

"Mommy!"

The tearful whimper tore at his heart. And then he was suddenly there. Below her. His hands stretching high above his head in hopes of keeping her from falling should the sleeve tear free. The fabric of the buttoned jacket strained across

Tessa's chest, but it wasn't choking her. Didn't inhibit her breathing.

Nevertheless, she was out of reach. "Hang on, Tessa. I'm here."

Lips trembling, she nodded as she looked down at him. And at that exact moment, seeing the unwavering trust in her eyes, something deep inside him split apart. Shaken, he looked to Sunshine, who was now at his side, offering soothing words to her daughter suspended above their heads.

"Can you climb up there, Sunshine? See if you can get the sleeve loose? Then I can catch her." He glanced down at his windbreaker. "There's a knife in that pocket. Take it in case you can't get her sleeve free."

He didn't have to tell her twice. She dipped her hand into the pocket and grasped the pocketknife. Then before he'd barely taken another breath, she was climbing the steep slide steps to the ringing sound of metal underfoot.

"Mommy?"

"Your mommy's going to get you loose, Tessa." He smiled encouragingly up at her. "Then I'm going to catch you, okay?"

"'Kay." She nodded, her eyes still filled with faith in him.

Please, Lord, let me catch her.

"I can't get it out." Sunshine's strained voice came from above him. "It's caught tight."

"Then, cut it."

But before she could get the knife pulled from its sheath, the sound of ripping fabric rent the air.

The sleeve tore loose—Tessa screaming as she dropped.

Please, God.

And then…the little girl was safe in his arms.

Heart pounding, barely able to breathe, Sunshine descended the slide steps and ran to where Grady had her daughter clasped tightly to his chest. A crying Tessa had a death grip around his neck.

Sunshine stretched out her arms and, with only a slight hesitation, Tessa loosened her hold on Grady. He lowered her to the ground where Sunshine pulled the trembling body close.

Thank God, thank God.

Whatever would she have done had Tessa been seriously hurt? Or even— No, she wouldn't go there. Not while she had the most precious possession of her heart wrapped in her arms. She tightened the embrace. *Thank You, Lord.*

A sniffling Tessa wiggled loose, pulling back to cup her mother's face in her small hands. "Don't cry, Mommy. Grady saved me."

"Yes, sweetheart, he did." Wiping away her own tears with her hand, she looked up to where he was watching them silently, his eyes filled with unmistakable relief. And something more…

"Thank you, Grady." Tears again pricked her eyes as she ran her hand along the gaping hole where the sleeve had torn away. "Tessa, you know you aren't supposed to go on the big one yet. You promised, remember?"

"I forgot, Mommy. I wanted Grady to see me go down it."

Sunshine exchanged a glance with him, catching the flinch in his expression. Her daughter's desperate hope of being noticed by a father figure had spurred her to a dangerous decision. But there would be plenty of time for chastisement later.

Grady held out a handkerchief and, with a wobbly smile, she took it from him and dabbed at her own eyes and Tessa's. Then let the little girl blow her nose.

"Looks as though you're our hero twice in one week, Grady." But the word *hero* didn't express half of what she was feeling toward him. The rush of emotion that only with willpower did she keep in check, stopping herself from leaping to her feet and throwing her arms around him, seeking solace in the strong arms that had saved her daughter.

How would she ever repay him for what he'd done for her today?

Pull out of the campaign against his mother,

her conscience pricked. *Drop pursuit of compensation on your great-great-grandfather's behalf.*

Pushing aside the nagging accusations, she managed a smile. "I'll wash your handkerchief when I do laundry this week."

"No rush." He glanced behind her, his eyes narrowing. "I'll let Parks and Rec know they need to cordon off that slide until they can get it fixed. We don't want some other little kid getting clothing caught on it."

"No, the outcome might not be so fortunate." She gave Tessa another hug.

There was nothing she could do that would ever repay Grady, but surely there was a way she could demonstrate appreciation for rescuing her daughter from harm and herself from heartache. To somehow release her from the heavy weight of indebtedness to a Hunter.

Her mind raced, searching. And then, a possibility dawned.

But would he allow her to do it?

Chapter Seven

By Saturday Grady was still dealing with the impact of the rescue that left him more shaken than he cared to admit.

Too many times he'd relived—in excruciatingly detailed slow motion—that heartrending moment when he'd seen Tessa go over the edge of the slide. Again felt the fear that he wouldn't cover the distance in time to break her fall to the hard ground below.

But by God's grace, all was well.

So he should be happy, shouldn't he, that he'd see Tessa today? Her mother had called last night to ask if he could show them the historic cabins on the Hunter's Hideaway property and he'd agreed. But for a number of reasons, he was far from happy about it.

"Earth to Grady." Seated next to him, Rio bumped his shoulder with hers.

"What?" His attention jerked to the breakfast meeting underway in a conference room at the Hideaway. A roomful of curious eyes focused on him. Warmth crept into his face.

From the head of the table, his father repeated, "I asked how the game supply store is coming along."

"Extremely well." Grady met Dad's steady gaze with a reassuring nod.

At age sixty, Dave Hunter was a man who in both manner and appearance had long reminded Grady of the steady, hardworking father seen on reruns of *The Waltons* TV show. But for many years—since Luke had headed off to the army when Grady was fifteen—his father had expected more and more of his youngest son. Without fail—except for once—he'd always stepped up to deliver on those expectations.

"Even with stopping the weekend work," Grady added, "Ted and his crew are making solid headway."

"Good to hear." Dad rewarded him with a smile.

"I anticipate we'll be right on target for a mid-October opening. The security systems are being set up at both the store and the off-site storage facility. Worker bees are lined up to process online sales, including Trevor and one of his high school buddies, and a few to man the shop and demonstrate equipment. Stock is set for delivery and the website's being finalized."

Trevor, Luke's eldest child of three from his first marriage, was over-the-top excited about being a part of this new venture.

"You've done an excellent job overseeing this, Grady." Grandma Jo's eyes warmed. "We can always count on you."

"Hear, hear!" Luke, now back from his honeymoon, raised his glass of orange juice in tribute. Grady knew what effort that took. Although Luke and Dad were mending fences, it had to hurt at times that his younger brother had been running the show, heading up the enterprise alongside their father during the years he'd been gone.

"I appreciate you being my backup right now, son." His father paused, ducking his head slightly and Grady knew he was having difficulty expressing himself. "You know, freeing me up to be with your mother."

An uncomfortable silence drifted over the table.

"I'm there for you and Mom. Always." He glanced around at his extended family—grandmother, siblings, uncles, aunts and cousins. Only Mom wasn't in attendance. "We all are."

Everyone nodded. A united Hunter front.

Dad looked up again, his lips tightening as he rose from the table. "Let's get on with our day."

Once outside in the fresh mountain air, Grady

climbed into his SUV and headed to his cabin. Although it was out of the way, he'd given Sunshine directions, thinking that her arrival would create less speculation if she didn't march in the front door of the Hideaway's main buildings.

As he parked outside his cabin, he paused to look at the rustic dwelling he called home. It was a relatively new cabin. Built in the late 1950s, a porch stretching across its width lent a homey look, as did half barrels of red geraniums squatting on either side of the steps. Grandma Jo's touch. What would Sunshine and Tessa think of it?

And why should he care?

Once inside, he gave his surroundings a final inspection. He'd been up late last night after Sunshine's call—vacuuming, straightening up in the living room, cleaning the kitchen and bathrooms. Making sure his clothes were gathered up from the floor and stowed neatly in closets and drawers. Opening windows to freshen things up.

He didn't often have company these days. Certainly not feminine company. He didn't want Sunshine to think he was a total slob.

He'd just hung his jacket on a peg near the front door when he heard the slamming of car doors. Female voices. Without thinking, he hastily checked his hair in an antique wall mirror in the entryway. Then, realizing what he was doing, he grimaced at himself and opened the door to welcome his guests.

"Grady!" Tessa raced up the steps to give him a hug. Which was exactly the reason why this morning's outing made him less than happy. He couldn't get attached to Sunshine's kid, nor her to him. It was one thing to pour his heart into his nieces and nephews, but past experience proved it was better to keep other people's kids at a distance.

Sunshine had told him last night that Tessa's shoulder was sore, but she seemed to be doing okay today. No worse for the wear. When she released him, she peered around him into the cabin.

"This is where you live? Can I see inside?"

"Now, Tessa—" Sunshine cast him an apologetic look.

"No problem. Come on in." At least the house was relatively clean now. Smelled good. He stepped back and, wide-eyed, Tessa joined him to take in her surroundings.

"Oh, look, Mommy!" In a flash, she covered the ground between the entry and the far side of the living room, coming to stand beside an oversize wooden rocking horse. "Can I ride it?"

"Sure." It was sturdy enough. He'd made it for Jasmine's then-four-year-old daughter, Allyson, so she'd have something to play with when they visited. There was a swing out back, too, secured to a big oak branch.

Why hadn't he gotten rid of that stuff?

"Sorry to invade your space, Grady." Sunshine stepped inside as well, looking around with as much interest as her daughter had. "This is nice. I love the open floor plan—how the staircase in the middle divides the front living area from the kitchen and dining room. It looks comfortable."

It did look nice, if he said so himself. The warmth of the wood. Sun streaming in the windows. "Well, any of the decorative stuff you can credit my sisters for. You've met Rio, who isn't much into that, but the twins between Rio and me made sure I'm not living life with lawn chairs and a card table or a wall calendar as my only artwork."

"I noticed several of your photos here." She inspected an enlargement of a doe and fawn, then looked back at him. "I've been giving some thought to your idea to incorporate a photography element at Hunter's Hideaway. How you said you're not sure where to start with a proposal. But I know exactly where you should start."

"You do?" Not surprising. She had a reputation for always having an answer and insisting others go along with it.

"It starts by addressing the main issue your family will be thinking when you approach them about it. The same thing almost every person on the planet wonders when presented with a new proposition. What's in it for me?"

"I guess I need to figure that out, don't I? I haven't been free to invest as much time on it as I'd like."

"What if I helped? For years my mother has worked at artists' cooperatives in the towns we've lived in. Jerome. Sedona. Triumph. In fact, Triumph is where Mom helped establish and still manages the local co-op. As a result, I had extensive experience working with her—which is how I landed this job."

"And that relates to my photography idea how?"

"Mom and I've helped dozens of artists prepare proposals to get their work into exclusive galleries and shops. With tons of talent out there, the competition is huge. But the artists who can present well, who can convince people that featuring their work will be worth their while…well, they have an edge over equally talented artists who don't know how to sell themselves."

"Makes sense." The web designer for their new online store had talked about things like that. But he hadn't thought about how it might apply to his photography proposition.

"I'd be happy to help you drill down to the essence of what your family needs to know and solidify that in a proposal that will knock their socks off. So what do you say?"

From the resistance in his eyes, she'd thought Grady would flatly turn her down. But he'd said thank you and that he'd think about it.

Now, slowly bumping along a rutted dirt track that wound its way through the forest, he appeared to be giving it more thought. Asked a few questions. Grew silent. Asked a few more. So there was still hope that she could somehow balance out the debt she owed for the two rescues that week.

"Well, there it is."

Grady motioned to the left and she glimpsed an old gray cabin through a stand of ponderosas. A tingle of excitement sped through her as he pulled his SUV off the dirt road and onto an overgrown track through the trees. This was possibly the home of her great-great-grandparents. Where they'd lived. Loved. Had they started a family here? How long had they been settled before they'd lost everything to the Hunters?

When they'd climbed from the vehicle and Grady had helped Tessa out of the back, she was immediately struck by how quiet it was. An unearthly quiet, not even the sound of the wind in the trees, the bark of a squirrel or the chirp of a bird. Not so much as the distant drone of an airplane overhead. What must it have been like to have lived here over a hundred years ago, far from civilization?

An involuntary shiver curled up her spine.

As if absorbing the atmosphere of the property as well, Grady let Tessa take his hand and together they approached the weathered cabin silently.

"It's not very big, is it?" Sunshine said softly.

Likewise, Grady's voice lowered. "Not big at all."

He paused to study the cabin, then released Tessa's hand and pulled out a set of keys. Inserted them in a padlock. "We keep it locked up now. Transients found their way back here a few years ago and took up residence. They made a real mess of the place."

She didn't like the thought of someone desecrating this historic home. "That's a shame."

Tessa drew close. "Why are we whispering, Mommy?"

Sunshine smiled as Grady pushed open the door to the darkened interior. "I guess because it's so quiet here that I feel as if I need to be quiet, too."

Tessa's nose wrinkled as she eyed the open doorway with suspicion. "I don't like this place. It's creepy."

"You don't have to go inside, but stay close by, okay? Don't wander off."

Grady motioned for Sunshine to precede him into the cabin.

"Oh, wow. Dirt floors." But at least natural light came in from the small paned windows on two sides of the room, and open rafters overhead reduced the claustrophobic feeling that might otherwise have dominated. She stepped farther into the room, inspecting the chinked log walls. It was cool inside, an earthy smell mingling with the faint scent of wood smoke from past fires. She moved to the soot-stained stone fireplace, noticing the charred remains in the iron grate. "Someone's been here recently."

"Me."

She glanced at him curiously.

"I occasionally spend the night out here so I can be up early to take photos." He moved to one of the smudged windows, then looked at her again. "A twenty-or thirty-minute drive through the forest in this direction is far enough from the heart of Hideaway activity to put wildlife more at ease."

"And you said the other couple in that photo— Walter and Flora Royce—lived here? Why so far away from the current site of Hunter's Hideaway where your ancestors settled?"

He shrugged, his expression unexpectedly grim. "People needed elbow room, I guess."

She continued to survey the sparsely furnished room. A small table and chairs. Bench. Shelves.

A lantern on a side table. "I don't suppose any of this is original furniture?"

"No, that's long gone."

"So where do you sleep when you come here?" A bed frame or hammock was conspicuously absent.

"Sleeping bag on the floor." He grinned at her look of dismay. "No different than camping except you have more protection from the elements and critters in here."

"True." She moved again to the fireplace, resting her hand on its cool, natural-stone surface. Had her ancestors roasted venison here? Stirred iron cooking pots of stew? Shared intimate hours in front of a crackling fire? "If only these walls could talk."

"Mommy!"

Startled at Tessa's cry of alarm, Sunshine spun toward the door. "Oh!"

Not knowing he'd come in close behind her, she'd run smack into solid-as-a-rock Grady. Startled, he gently grasped her upper arms to steady her. Heart thudding, her breath shallow, time seemed to stand still as she stared into his eyes. At the strong jaw and slightly crooked nose. He seemed to be studying her features with equal interest. And then, as if remembering what had sent her careening into him, he released her and stepped back. After only a moment's hesitation, she rushed through the open cabin door and into the bright sunlight.

Almost frantic, she searched for Tessa. "Where—?"

"Over here, Mommy!"

Aware that Grady was behind her, Sunshine hurried to where her daughter stood partially hidden, her chest pressed against a towering ponderosa, eyes wide and pointing to something on the far edge of the clearing. "What are they? Little hairy pigs?"

Some distance away, Sunshine noticed motion down low, among the shaded clumps of tall grasses and boulders. Then, warily, two small creatures emerged and she recognized them at once.

"Javelina." Grady's low voice echoed her thoughts.

Tessa stared up at him. "Have-a-what?"

"Javelina," he repeated, amusement lighting his eyes. "And yes, they do look like hairy pigs, but they're not pigs."

Sunshine eyed them warily. "They don't usually come out during the daytime, do they?"

"Actually, they can be quite active in the mornings and enjoy sunshine. They don't usually venture into elevations a whole lot higher than the Mogollon Rim, though, so these may have gotten separated from their herd."

"Let's leave them in peace, then, shall we? We need to let you get back to work, so the other cabin can wait for another time."

"Work will be there waiting whenever I return."

"What is it, exactly, that you do at Hunter's Hideaway?" She'd been wanting to ask for some time.

"Your question would probably be better stated as what *don't* I do at the Hideaway." He reached for Tessa's hand and the threesome moved back toward the cabin and his vehicle. "You name it and at some time or another I've probably done it."

"But what do you do now?"

"I don't exactly have a title." His forehead creased as he helped Tessa into the backseat and secured her in. "I was about fifteen when Luke took off for the army, and ever since then I've been Dad's right-hand man. Dad's the eldest of his siblings, so after the death of his father, by default he became the primary overseer of the Hideaway. And by default, too, I guess, I'm following in his footsteps."

He chucked a giggling Tessa under the chin, then shut the back door and leaned against it, arms folded.

"My days vary. Overseeing property maintenance and supervising—along with Rio and our cousin J.C.—horse care, trail rides and horse and rider training programs. Helping hunters pack in their trophies. Providing support and guidance on inn and general store operation." With a laugh, he took an exaggerated breath and continued, "I order supplies. Manage employees. Keep on top of the events master calendar, provide preseason scouting tips for hunters and mingle with our varied guests. I guess you'd say I'm a troubleshooter, involved in every aspect of the business."

"I'm impressed."

"And in the midst of all that, I managed to pick up an associate's degree in business at Northland Pioneer College and rounded that out with additional online classes for a bachelor's." With a proud grin, he pushed away from the truck to pull keys from his pocket. "Give me a minute to lock up, okay? Then I'd be happy to come back to do some more bragging. It's always sweet to impress a pretty girl."

Laughing, she took a playful swat at him, but missed him by a mile.

When he returned, he climbed into the driver's seat next to her, slammed the door and started up the SUV.

"Fortunately, Luke's now taking on additional responsibilities for the Hideaway. Correspondence and paperwork to keep us legal with federal, state and county agencies. Overseeing financial investments. Can't say I'll miss doing that."

He gave her a lopsided grin and for some silly reason, her cheeks warmed.

"He'll also make sure," Grady added, "that we have facts and figures for making critical decisions."

She studied him thoughtfully, trying not to notice his still twinkling eyes. "So that means he'll be a primary person you'll need to convince that your photography idea is feasible?"

"I guess so." He frowned as he turned the vehicle in the direction from which they'd come. "Our relationship was strained when he first got out of the army six years ago. He and Dad had a falling-out back in the day. Then when he returned, here I am filling the shoes our father always intended for him to fill. We've pretty much worked through it, but sometimes it still gets thorny."

"Do you think he'll push back because he's now in a position to?"

"I don't think so." He thought a moment longer, eyes narrowing as they bumped down the rub-board road. "But it might not be a half-bad idea to bring someone on board who knows how to deal with that possibility."

He slanted a look at her. Then winked.

"Know anyone who might have that type of experience?"

Chapter Eight

It turned out, however, to be far easier to convince Grady to take her up on her offer of assistance than it was to find a time and place suitable for them to work on the project together.

Thankfully, Tori was available to babysit, or they probably never would have worked things out with their busy schedules. Which might have meant they'd have had to work via phone and email.

Considering how nervous she was after dinner Tuesday evening as she readied for the drive to Grady's place, working by phone might have been the better option.

Tori stepped back to look at her approvingly. "Pretty skirt, Sunshine."

"Do you think it's too much?" She hadn't worn the striking Native American patterned wool skirt topped by a burgundy suede fringed jacket since last winter. But mid-September evenings were cooling down. "I want to look—"

"Beautiful?" Tori's eyes glowed with approval. "You nailed it."

Sunshine made a face. "No, I meant professional."

"Well, you look that, too."

"I'm thinking of wearing this a week from Friday to that parent-teacher meeting, so I want to see if I still feel comfortable in it. It'll be the first kickoff event for the town council elections, with each candidate given an opportunity to briefly state our platform and answer questions."

"Three of you, right?"

"Right. Irv Baydlin. Elaine Hunter. Me."

"Does Grady ever mention that when you're with him? I mean, does he say anything about you running against his mother?"

"Not so far."

"Seems like an elephant in the room to me. And now with what I found online this morning, *two* elephants."

After days of diligently searching, Tori had unearthed documentation that Sunshine's great-grandmother's maiden name had been Royce. Which meant that she'd most likely confirm her parents were Walter and Flora.

"I have to admit, it's hard not to tell him that I'm almost ninety-nine percent certain the owners of the cabin he showed me on Saturday are my ancestors."

Tori folded her arms, her expression doubtful. "Do you think it's wise to withhold that? I mean, the guy saved you and your daughter twice. Now you're trying to repay that debt by spending more time with him on this business-proposal thing. Don't you think he might resent it when you pop up with a big 'reveal'? Why not tell him now? Why keep it a secret?"

Sunshine slipped her feet into a pair of black pumps. "Because until we can find unquestionable evidence that the Hunters somehow managed to cheat my great-greats out of their land, there's no point in bringing it up."

"So the elephant in the room grows ever larger."

"You're as bad as Tessa, Tori. You worry too much. See imaginary things in the closet."

"Someone needs to. And I do it because I care."

Sunshine gave her friend a grateful look. "I care about you, too. But everything is going to be fine. One more step back and you'll confirm the names of my great-great-grandparents. Then we can decide where to go from there on proving the rest of it. Are you on board?"

"I guess so. But I don't want to see you—or this Grady guy—get hurt."

"Nobody's going to get hurt." How could they? They hardly knew each other. Staring into each other's eyes when she'd bumped into him at the cabin had been nothing but awkward. Besides, it wasn't as if she intended to sue his family for what they'd done to her predecessors. She'd present the evidence and leave it in the hands of God—and the consciences of the Hunters.

But tonight she had to keep her focus on the business at hand—lifting some of the weight of indebtedness off her shoulders by doing a good turn for Grady.

The two hours flew by faster than he could ever have imagined, with Sunshine seated on one side of a corner of the dining table, him the other, so they could share a view of his laptop screen. But in presenting to her the research he'd gathered over the past few months, it didn't appear to be as compelling as he'd built it up in his mind to be. She asked good questions, though, that provoked him to think more deeply, to look at the issues from a different angle.

He glanced at the attractive woman, sweet smelling and feminine in that soft jacket, the fringe of which—like the sway of her hair—caught his attention every time she moved. "What do you think, Sunshine? Can I build a winning case?"

If she said no, what was the point in trying?

Luke, with his financial savvy, would eat him up and spit him out.

She leaned back in her chair. "If you can fill in those gaps, I think the bones of it are here."

"I can squeeze in a few hours for gap filling this week."

"When that's done, we'll group your data into logical segments, sort of how I've illustrated on the newsprint pad here. Then we'll give thought to the sequencing and break each down into bite-size, presentable pieces. You have to hit them out of the gate with a 'big promise' punch, then the remainder of the presentation will back up your promises."

"You make this sound simple."

"Simple doesn't mean without considerable thought or planning, though. I think you've done a lot of that. We need to tweak what you have."

She was probably just being nice, careful not to be overly critical of his hodgepodge of notes. But it was far better to have her punch holes in what he'd been thinking now than to have Luke go after him on those same points in front of the whole family.

"So how are you feeling about this, Grady? Have I hijacked your plans? Veered off from the direction you intended to go?"

"No, not at all." He rose from his chair and stretched. "It's as if you've taken my vague, cloudy dreams and solidified them in my own mind and, hopefully, in the minds of my family members in the future."

She looked relieved. Had she been concerned that he wouldn't care for her input? He much preferred dealing with a straight shooter than someone who only said what they thought he wanted to hear. Which might actually make her a solid candidate for the town council if she could somehow clearly reveal that side of herself to voters.

She wouldn't win, of course. Not with Mom in the race, but still…

He moved into the kitchen to look inside the refrigerator. "Would you like something to drink? A snack, maybe?"

"Thanks, but I need to be going." Sunshine stood and reached for the purse she'd looped over the back of her chair. "I want to make sure Tessa hasn't given Tori problems getting her settled down for the night."

"She's still thinking there are mysterious things in the closet? I can understand after the fall from a slide how that might add to her anxiety."

"Oddly, that didn't seem to compound the situation. In fact, she seems to be more focused on you as her hero than reliving those scary moments."

"That's good, I guess." But he didn't want to be any little kid's hero. What had Jasmine's daughter thought when he'd broken up with her mom? He'd been her hero, too, but what scars had been left when he'd abruptly disappeared from the child's life? That was when he'd vowed to never get involved again with a woman who had children.

Although he wasn't *involved* with Sunshine, he had come in contact with her daughter several times last week. Dangerous territory for a little kid's heart.

A man's, too.

As he walked her to the door, he couldn't help looking at Sunshine with regret. Too bad she had a kid. Too bad as well that she was running against his mother for a town council seat.

Sunshine's smile dissolved as she looked up at him. "Why so glum? You've got a fantastic idea, Grady. You've done your homework. All we have to do is put the puzzle pieces together to make a complete picture for your family."

"I can't thank you enough for your input tonight." He mustered a smile. "I promise I'll have those gaps you talked about filled as fast as I can."

"Wonderful." Her eyes sparkled as she looked up at him, and for a long moment their gazes locked.

His mouth went dry. She was beautiful standing there in the dim light of the entryway, her silky black hair shiny and her smooth skin appearing soft, touchable. Heart drumming against the walls of his chest, he swallowed. Then, pulling himself together, he abruptly jerked open the front door—only to find his cousin, Pastor Garrett McCrae, standing there under the porch light, hand raised to knock.

"Good evening, Sunshine. Grady." Garrett's smile was way too wide as he took in the pair standing inside the entry. "Hope I'm not interrupting anything."

"I'm on my way out." Sunshine glanced uncertainly at Grady. "I'll see you later?"

"Call me when you get home so I know you're there safely."

Her brows rose, but she nodded. Then with a smile directed at Garrett, she slipped past him and into the shadows to her car. Grady waited in the doorway until she drove off, then motioned his cousin inside.

"To what honor do I owe this house call, Garrett?"

"I haven't seen you for a while except in church, so thought I'd stop by and keep a fellow lonely old bachelor company." He plopped himself on the sofa and stretched out as Grady eased himself into a nearby recliner. "But it looks as though things may have taken an interesting turn since we last talked."

Grady grunted. "Don't go getting any wild ideas. Ms. Carston was here on business. Nothing more. You can wipe that silly grin off your face."

Garrett's gray eyes questioned, but Grady didn't feel like enlightening him any further. Although there was a four-year age gap between them, they'd long been buds, but he didn't intend to share his hopes for the photography addition to the Hunter's Hideaway lineup with him. Not yet anyway. Maybe closer to the presentation he'd call on the good pastor to offer up prayers on his behalf.

Straightening up, Garrett glanced around him, a puzzled expression on his face. Then he looked past Grady and into the dining room. "Something's different."

"Nothing's different."

"Wait a minute!" Laughter lit Garrett's features. "You cleaned, didn't you? Not just ran a vacuum and sprayed air freshener, but you picked things up, stashed the junk someplace and actually *cleaned.*"

Garrett leaped to his feet and started across the room.

"Hey! Where do you think you're going?"

"To inspect the bathroom."

In spite of himself, Grady couldn't help cracking a smile. "Get back here."

Still laughing, Garrett resettled himself on the sofa. "I can't believe this. I imagine you haven't cleaned this place much since you booted Jas—"

Grady's warning look cut him off. "Don't go there."

"Well, it's the truth, isn't it?"

Grady didn't want to talk about truth. Or have his housecleaning efforts speculated upon. "So what are you really doing here tonight, Garrett?"

The laughter dimmed in his cousin's eyes as he leaned forward to rest his forearms on his knees. "I wanted to talk to you about your mother."

Grady flipped the recliner lever and brought himself upright. "What about Mom?"

Garret looked him steadily in the eye.

"My mom—" Meaning Grady's dad's sister, his aunt Suzy. "My mom told me your dad wants Aunt Elaine to drop out of the election."

Grady's throat tightened. "Why?"

Was there something about her condition his parents weren't sharing with their kids? Last he'd talked to his mother, not even twenty-four hours ago, she was gung ho for the campaign trail. She viewed this time-out as temporary.

"He thinks it's going to be too much for her. Too much stress right when she needs to be resting and focusing on fighting the cancer."

"You should know my mother well enough to recognize that Dad spouting off his opinion isn't going to sway her. Once she sets her mind to something, just try to bar the door."

"Despite good intentions, chemo treatments can

take a toll, Grady. She's barely getting underway with it. Even in a small town like this, elections are demanding. They take time and effort, putting yourself out there nonstop in the public eye. Which is another thing—her immune system will be compromised, so she'll have to be extra careful with cold and flu season getting underway."

"This is a reelection, though." Grady relaxed somewhat. "Everybody knows her. Knows what she stands for. She could spend the next seven weeks in utter seclusion and still win."

"Maybe."

"What exactly are you hinting at, Garrett?" He didn't like this beating-around-the-bush stuff.

"This election is a little different."

"How so?"

"Irvin's doing his best to mount up a strong opposition, promising this and that to folks who pretty much are looking for a handout wherever they turn. People who'd like to see the high-and-mighty Hunters toppled. You do realize, don't you, that we've had a family member on the town council since the town's founding in the 1920s?"

"And Sunshine?" Garrett continued. "Like I told you earlier, she's been all over the place in the past few weeks since that friend of hers came to town. She's not sitting around naively assuming the artists in the community can get her elected. She knows there aren't enough of them to do that."

"I don't see how any of this will make a difference."

"Live in your rose-colored-glasses world, Grady, but my mom is concerned. Dad, too. Especially if your dad persuades your mother to give it up."

"He won't."

Garrett fell silent for a moment, and then he cocked his head, his gaze boring into Grady's. "There *is* such a thing as a write-in vote."

"Meaning?"

"If your mother pulls out, we could mount a campaign to get *you* elected in Aunt Elaine's stead. You won't be on the ballot, but you could still pull it off."

Think again, cuz. Grady resolutely pushed himself out of the recliner and pointed a warning finger at his cousin. "No."

"Why not? You don't think your lady friend can beat you, do you?"

"Sunshine is not my 'lady friend.' And I'm not much concerned about whether or not she could beat me because I'm not running for an elected office." His eyes narrowed. "Why don't *you* do it if you're worried about Hunters losing?"

"Because you have to be a resident for at least one year prior to the election. I moved back here last December and I have no idea how much longer I'll hold this interim pastor position. Besides, I have my hands full at Christ's Church."

"And my hands aren't full, too? I can't take on a four-year commitment." Grady spread his arms wide. "What do you think I've been doing around the Hideaway since I was a teenager anyway?"

"You mean besides sneaking off for a kissing fest with some cute little gal?" Garrett teased, an attempt to ease a heated moment.

Grady couldn't help but laugh. His cousin hadn't exactly been a choir boy in his younger days, either. "You should talk, preacher."

Garrett suppressed a smile. "Honestly, Grady, if you'd be willing to give this serious thought, I think it would ease my folks' minds. Uncle Doug's, too. Probably the whole family's."

"I'm not running for office." And he wasn't praying about it, either, so Garrett better not ask him to.

With a sound of frustration, Garrett stood at the same moment the phone rang. "Better get that. Your lady friend's checking in."

"I told you—"

"I know. She's not your lady friend." Garrett headed to the front door, then paused to look back. "But you'll be careful, won't you? I don't want to be the last bachelor left standing in the Hunter clan."

Chapter Nine

"This is looking good, Grady."

Sunshine motioned to the laptop screen as she pushed her chair back from Grady's dining table. This was their fourth work session over the past two weeks, and progress had been steady.

"You think we're getting there?"

"Definitely."

After what had felt like a too-close encounter right before Garrett had shown up at the conclusion of their first meeting, she'd been hesitant to meet with Grady again. But she hadn't felt ill at ease during the follow-up sessions at all. Not to say that Grady wasn't Grady. He'd probably flirted in the hospital nursery on the very day of his arrival into the world. He couldn't help himself now any more than he could back then. Which actually made for a fun and nonthreatening time together.

Tonight, though, while not awkward in that respect, Grady seemed preoccupied.

As had become their custom when they'd wrapped things up for the night, he rose to pour himself a mug of coffee and her a cup of tea, then led the way to the living room. She followed, pulling a crocheted afghan across her lap as she made herself comfortable on the sofa. He settled into the recliner and she clasped her hands around the warm teacup.

She'd come to look forward to this time to talk about various topics, to get to know each other better. Grady was an intriguing man despite being a Hunter.

"I could put a fire in the fireplace if you're chilly." He started to rise, but she shook her head.

"No, I'm fine. But thanks. The afghan's all I need."

"You're sure?"

"Positive."

He eased back down and took a sip of coffee. "I'm pleased with the way the proposal is coming together. Thanks to you. What do you think? Can we finalize it at our next meeting?"

Only one more? An unexpected wave of disappointment washed through her. "I think so. I'll polish up the slide presentation I've been working on and we can put the final touches on it."

"If my family doesn't go for this after all the

work we've put into it, I should probably saddle up and ride off into the sunset."

She leaned forward. "They'll go for it, Grady."

"I hope so."

"This means a lot to you, doesn't it?"

He set his mug on the end table next to him. "It's something I've wanted to pursue ever since I got into photography as a teenager. A dream that never died."

She couldn't help but smile as he glanced away, almost as if he'd revealed too much of himself in that simple statement.

"I can't see why they would turn this down now." She took another sip of the fragrant tea. "There's minimal financial investment. Negligible advertising expense, too, because it will be incorporated into the Hideaway's other promotional efforts—brochures and the website. It's mostly juggling around cabin availability and hunting seasons. I think your documentation proves it will be profitable."

He gave her a regretful smile. "With my family, I learned long ago not to get too excited about something until it's a done deal."

"Getting excited is half the fun. But if for some totally irrational reason they reject your proposal, that doesn't have to be the end of it."

"What do you mean?"

"Hunter's Hideaway isn't the only game in

town. Or at least not the only game in Arizona mountain country. Or anywhere for that matter. There are plenty of other outdoor-related businesses that might welcome a potential money-maker like this, one that has a business plan mapped out and ready to go."

He looked at her as if she'd lost her mind.

"Your family doesn't hold the key to your dream, Grady. God does. And if He leads you elsewhere…"

His brows lowered. "I can't imagine taking this elsewhere."

"I'm not saying you should. I'm pointing out that you have options. Don't close doors. That's God's job."

He rose from the recliner, then moved to place a hand on the polished oak mantel of the stone fireplace, where he stared into the cold grate, deep in thought. Under the surface all evening, he'd been restless. Agitated. It wasn't her imagination.

"There's something bothering you, isn't there?" she said softly. "Something that doesn't have anything to do with your business proposal."

His head jerked up in surprise, and then he nodded almost imperceptibly.

"Yeah. Something that makes this proposal seem inconsequential."

"I'm a good listener."

"I know. And it's something you'll find out tomorrow anyway. I just didn't know how to tell you." He fisted the hand he'd placed on the fireplace mantel. "It's not easy for me to talk about."

Curious—and somewhat alarmed—she set her cup aside, then pulled the afghan more closely around herself to wait. To give him time to work through whatever was troubling him.

The antique clock on the mantel ticked loudly, measuring the seconds. Overhead a wind-loosened pinecone hit the rooftop. The refrigerator's steady hum silenced.

Then with a heavy sigh, Grady looked to her again, his eyes bleak. "My mother has breast cancer."

With a gasp, she momentarily pressed her hand to her mouth. "Oh, Grady. I'm sorry."

With a guilty sense of self-incrimination, she chastised herself for the appalling first thoughts that had flashed uninvited into her mind. Would Elaine pull out of the election? Would her opponents now have a chance to win?

Forgive me, Lord.

A sad smile touched his lips, tugging at her heart. "We found out a day or two before Luke and Delaney's wedding. We didn't know the extent of it then, of course. But she wouldn't let them postpone the wedding or call off the honeymoon."

She waited in silence, praying for Grady. His mother. His family.

"Anyway, it was a family decision not to say anything to anyone until we knew more. She had surgery. Then a reaction to meds. Council members, of course, were informed in private that she'd miss a few sessions due to a needed medical procedure. But the word *cancer* wasn't shared with anyone outside the family."

"And now?"

"She started chemo a week or so ago and it's already taking its toll much faster than she anticipated. She's really sick." He pushed away from the fireplace and slowly paced the room. "So tomorrow she'll make it public that she's battling cancer. She feels because she holds a public office that the community is entitled to know."

"What a blow to your mother and your family."

He nodded. "But that's not all I need to tell you."

What more could there be?

"Mom wants to remain on the ballot." He forced a smile. "That's so typical of her. She doesn't want to let down those who voted her into office and want to see her remain there."

Sunshine winced. And *she* was doing her best to unseat his mother from a second term.

"Which leads me to inform you—" Grady halted his pacing and rammed his hands into his jeans' back pockets, his blue eyes piercing into hers. "Mom's asked me to stand in for her tomorrow night at the parent-teacher meeting. In her absence I'll present her platform, her point of view, her hopes for Hunter Ridge."

Sunshine sucked in a startled breath.

She'd be behind the podium with Grady Hunter?

"Well, don't you look dolled up and ready to dance." Luke leaned against the door frame of Grady's office Friday evening, a smirk on his face.

Grady's lip curled as Grandma Jo adjusted his tie. "Don't you have someplace you need to be, Luke? Like giving your new bride a little attention?"

"Now, boys." Enveloped in her fuzzy blue bathrobe, Mom looked up from where she sat at his desk, going through her notes and drilling him on her election platform. Dark shadows emphasized the weariness in her eyes, belying the amused smile. He still couldn't get used to her in that colorful turban she'd donned, having had her head shaved in anticipation of losing her hair to the chemo. It was all Mom could do to keep Rio from shaving her own head as a solidarity move. "I think Grady looks quite handsome."

At least he'd talked her out of a suit. Who wore suits in Hunter Ridge except when getting married or buried? But she'd insisted he pair up a tie with a tan, corduroy sports jacket and a new pair of jeans.

As he'd reminded her earlier, though, he wasn't the one running for office. It was important he make that clear after what Garrett had shared with him about Aunt Suzy and Uncle Mac wanting him to be a write-in candidate. No way.

"Yep, Mom," Luke agreed. "My baby brother looks mighty fine tonight. Even shaved. Combed his hair, too."

"Enough." Grandma Jo pointed at the door. "We have more we need to pour into Grady's head before he leaves for the parent-teacher meeting."

"Shouldn't be a problem." Luke's eyes twinkled. "There's plenty of empty space in there."

"Out." Grandma laughingly marched up to Luke, turned him toward the hallway and gave him a gentle push. Shut the door behind him. Still smiling, she shook her head at her daughter-in-law. "I don't think your boys will ever grow up."

"So how are you feeling about this now, Grady?" His mother set aside her notes to study him.

He adjusted his tie. "I don't understand why this falls to me. It's not as though this family has a shortage of members to choose from."

"You know we've always counted on you," Grandma Jo reminded, a proud look in her eyes.

Wasn't that the truth? *Luke has a tiff with Dad and bails on Hunter's Hideaway, so guess who's enlisted to take his place? Dad prefers the man-*

*ual labor and, consequently, who gets stuck with
the endless paperwork? Uncle Doug hates contract negotiations, so their go-to guy takes that
on, as well.*

Given a minute or two, he could tick off dozens
more let-Grady-do-it scenarios that had landed
on his plate over the years. Stuff that he'd never,
at the time, given a thought to as he'd taken them
on. But it had begun to dawn on him, when he'd
found it hard to fit in a few measly hours with
Sunshine each week, that his life revolved exclusively around Hunter's Hideaway.

"You've told the whole family no one related
to the Hunters is to show up there, right? It's
just me—solo." He didn't want family members
watching from the sidelines. He'd be uncomfortable enough playing politician in front of strangers—even as a stand-in.

"Yes, we got the word out."

While that was a relief, he still didn't look
forward to fulfilling his familial duties. Forty
minutes later, his brain stuffed to the max with
information from his mom, he headed to town.
When he stepped through the door of the high
school cafeteria, he couldn't help but look for Sunshine.

And there she was. Across the room chatting
with Mayor Vicky Silas, a hardworking, gray-
haired descendant of one of the earlier families

to settle Hunter Ridge. Sunshine, dressed in that eye-catching print skirt she'd worn the first night she'd come to his place, almost glowed as the high school principal stepped in to join them. The same principal who'd on occasion hauled Grady into his office for rowdy behavior.

Glancing quickly away, he spied other teachers, school board members and parents he recognized, including several members of the artisan community. It looked to be a healthy turnout.

Not far away, candidate Irvin Baydlin—who'd also known Grady as a boy—was engaged in conversation with several teachers who Grady recognized as having, at one time or another, taught his nieces and nephews. And—good grief—wasn't that Mrs. Rivers? His seventh-grade English teacher who'd constantly been on him for poor spelling and less-than-perfect grammar?

It looked as though Mom picked the wrong Hunter for tonight's assignment.

"Grady!"

He pivoted toward a gal his brother had dated in high school, relieved at seeing a familiar face that didn't remind him of his past wrongdoings. She was married and a math teacher now.

"Hey, Monica. Good to see you."

"You, too." Then the corners of her mouth dipped downward as she gave his arm a squeeze. "I'm sorry to hear about your mother."

"Keep her in your prayers." He'd expected to hear words of concern tonight, but he hadn't adequately prepared himself to discuss Mom's illness. It was too new. Too raw. He glanced around the spacious room. "Do you know where I'm supposed to go? I'm filling in for my mother tonight."

"That's what I'd heard." She pointed to the stage, where a table, five folding chairs and podium had been set up. And in front of them, on the cafeteria floor, were several dozen chairs, as well. "The candidates—and you, too, of course—will be up there."

He willed himself not to grimace. He'd hoped for a more informal setting where he could relax into a casual conversation. This was too much like a speech.

He didn't do speeches.

"Give your mother my love." Monica patted his arm, then stepped away to greet someone entering the door behind him.

He set a course for the stage as those around him began to fill the seats on the main floor, and had just reached the steps when Sunshine appeared at his side.

"Nervous, Grady?"

"Not really." Would lightning strike him for that blatant fib? "How about you?"

"Yes!" She laughed as he motioned for her to precede him onto the stage. It was easy to see how she came by her nickname with that smile warming him from the inside out. "I've never spoken in front of a group this big."

"You'll do fine."

Her expression sobered and they moved toward the chairs arranged for them. "How is your mother?"

"It's rough. But she insists if this is what she has to go through to come out on the other side and live a long, meaningful life, she'll do it without complaint."

"She's courageous. Has a deep faith."

"She's all that." An invisible fist tightened around his heart. "But she's realistically aware that faith isn't a ticket to always getting what you want. Earthly life has an expiration date. A shorter one for some than others."

They'd barely seated themselves when Irvin, accompanied by the president of the parent-teacher organization and the head of the school board, joined them. The latter introduced them to the audience then, with an encouraging smile from Sunshine, Grady rose to make his mom's presentation.

Twenty minutes later he was done and, relieved, he settled himself back into his chair. A few people had asked general questions, which he felt confident in answering. Because Elaine Hunter was the incumbent, most knew her and her track record by reputation. He'd gotten off easy.

It was rougher for Sunshine.

She'd approached the podium with apparent confidence despite her confession of nervousness. In addition to being the prettiest one on stage, she made a good showing by focusing her ten-minute presentation on issues related to the community as a whole—education, increased employment opportunities, the environment—rather than solely on the concerns of local artists.

Please get her through the questions, Lord.

That was the hardest part, not knowing what challenges might come out of left field when someone raised a hand. Friend or foe? As he'd expected, being a resident of Hunter Ridge for a mere two years and known as outspoken on behalf of the artisan community, questions directed at her were more pointed and probing than they'd been with him. But, fortunately, none were overtly hostile. When she sat down thirty minutes later, he sensed in her a relief equal to his own and gave her a reassuring wink.

Irvin, though, seemed determined to make it clear that neither Elaine Hunter nor Sunshine Carston had a realistic grasp of the needs of Hunter Ridge.

A pompous man in a loud jacket and sporting a bow tie, he didn't merely present an overview of the platform he had chosen to run on. Instead, he managed to take digs at his opponents, even going as far, under the guise of expressing sympathy at Grady's mother's "unfortunate health setback," to raise questions as to her fitness to continue serving in public office. Mom had warned him to expect that, to not react, so he was prepared to keep his expression deliberately neutral.

But when Irvin, in occasional humorous asides, focused his sights on Sunshine, it was all Grady could do not to toss the guy off the stage. Referring to her with a patronizing smile as "our junior candidate," he proceeded to poke holes in her presentation by twisting her words and leaving his listeners with the impression that what Irvin was saying she'd said was in reality what she'd meant.

Blood boiling, Grady kept his features schooled to bland indifference, but a covert glance in Sunshine's direction confirmed her mortification. Not so much in her expression, which remained pleasant and seemingly unaffected by Irvin's gibes, but by something Grady couldn't put his finger on. Something more subtle he was picking up on, having gotten to know her better these past few weeks.

After forty minutes Irvin finally shut his trap and sat down. Then the president of the parent-teacher organization said a few closing words and encouraged attendees to linger and meet the candidates in person.

"This has been the longest night of my life," Sunshine whispered as he escorted her from the stage.

But before he could respond with more than a shared glance of mutual sympathy, they were drawn off to separate conversations with potential voters. An hour later, he saw Sunshine slip out and started in that direction himself, hoping to have a few words with her in the parking lot.

Unfortunately, Irvin intercepted him. But before he could speak whatever was on his mind, Grady took the lead.

"You had some good points there, Mr. Baydlin, but wouldn't you agree you overstepped?"

"In what way?"

"This is Hunter Ridge. We can afford to show our opponents common courtesy."

"I believe voters have a right to know that your mother's health may affect her fulfilling her duties."

"That remains to be seen. Treatments have barely started. But that's not what I'm referring to."

"Which is?"

"The digs at Sunshine Carston were uncalled-for. This wasn't a forum intended for personal attacks."

"I hardly consider clarifying what another candidate has publically said to be a personal attack."

"What would you call deliberately twisting someone's words to suit your own agenda when there's no opportunity for rebuttal?"

Irvin chuckled. "It's obvious you're not well schooled in campaign strategies, young man. You have to seize opportunities when they arise. Obviously, you need to leave the politicking to your mother."

"My mother wouldn't have given her blessing to your treatment of Ms. Carston, and you know it."

"So tell me again—" Irvin pushed open the exit door and stepped into the night, his eyes narrowing as he looked back at Grady in open speculation. "Which candidate is it you're campaigning for?"

Chapter Ten

"It's been days since that parent-teacher meeting," Sunshine told jewelry maker Benton Mason as they rearranged the Co-op gallery's display cases. "Yet I can still hear Irvin's barbed remarks. The way he twisted my words."

"You knew what you might be getting into," the heavyset bearded man reminded, "when you were asked to represent the artisan community in the town council race."

She carefully lifted the sculpture of a—well, she wasn't exactly sure what it was. But it had an interesting texture and pleasing lines that drew the eye. "I suppose. But at the time I filed, Elaine Hunter was the lone candidate. She would never have publicly sliced and diced me like Irvin did. There wasn't an opportunity to challenge his assertions."

"You'll get that at this Friday's engagement with the veterans' group."

She did *not* look forward to that. "I won't play dirty like Irvin."

"You don't have to." Benton moved the heavy pedestal several feet away, under more direct lighting, and she placed the sculpture once again atop it. "My wife and I thought you did great last week. You presented your ideas well. Came across as reasonable and civic minded. Gave voters the opportunity to see that the artists new to this community aren't the enemy."

She grimaced. "Then Irvin twisted everything I said and left them with a totally different impression."

"You underestimate those in attendance." He nodded to an acrylic still life on a nearby easel and she lifted it down so he could move the tripod stand. "I sensed a discomfort around me when Baydlin starting taking potshots at you. Oh, sure, some will listen to what he said and form an opinion in his favor without examining the facts. But not all. Far from all."

"I hope you're right."

"You need to toughen up, Sunshine." He took the canvas from her and placed it back on the newly relocated easel. He knew all about toughening up, having served in the armed forces and now working through PTSD-related issues. "Only five weeks until voters hit the polls. It may get rough."

She wrinkled her nose. "I don't think I'm cut out for this."

"Sure you are. I have every confidence in you. You're passionate about meeting the needs of the community, not just the artists. You have a strong sense of right and wrong. A zeal for justice." Benton placed his hands on his hips. "Baydlin took potshots at Elaine Hunter, too, remember? About her health and how she won't keep her commitments if she wins the election. How she's not currently keeping her commitment to the town council."

"That was nasty."

"Do you think it was easy for Grady Hunter to sit there and listen to that?"

"I guess not." She reached for a feather duster and brushed the top of a glass counter.

"Of course not. But I did see him speaking to Irvin after you left. By the look on their faces, he may have been clearing the air in private. At some point you may need to do that with Irvin, too."

"And let him use that against me in a public forum, as well?"

"Hey." He touched her arm and she faced him. "When you were asked by the Artists' Co-op members to run for office, did you pray about it at all?"

"Of course."

"And the answer was…?"

"That getting elected to the town council was a long shot, but I might educate the community about the needs of newcomers to town who earn a living with their artwork."

"And has that calling changed?"

"I guess not."

"It's not about winning, Sunshine. But you know that."

She did. Despite Elaine's health being in question, Grady's mother was the favored candidate. Sunshine had known that from the start. Irvin filing to run and his less-than-courteous campaigning had caused her to lose focus, her sense of purpose.

"Now, didn't you have errands to run this afternoon? I have things covered here."

"Thank you. And thanks for the pep talk."

She ran upstairs to her apartment, paused to see if Tori had made headway on her family research—she'd sent off email queries to county and state offices to follow a few leads—then grabbed a jacket to ward off the chill. October already. That seemed impossible.

Once outside the gallery, she noticed Grady's SUV parked in front of the neighboring wild game supply store, the shop's door standing open. Unlike most days, though, there was no sound of pounding and sawing, so thankfully that phase might be over. She'd see Grady tonight—for a final review of the presentation slides—but should she stop in to say hello now?

She'd taken a few steps in that direction when a gruff male voice called her name, drawing her to a halt. A glowering Gideon Edlow, bundled up against the wind, crossed the road and came to stand in front of her.

"Hello, Gideon."

Not much taller than she was, the talented potter eyed her with distaste, a wisp of a mustache and the goatee on his pointed chin almost trembling with suppressed outrage.

"For someone who's a candidate for the town council, you sure are hard to get hold of." He rammed his hands into his jacket pockets. "I've stopped by the Co-op gallery numerous times the past several days and you're either occupied with customers or gallivanting off somewhere. Like now."

She tensed. Accommodating customers and taking time to run errands or meet with community members was unacceptable? "You should have left a message. I would have returned your call."

"I'd prefer to speak with you face-to-face."

"What's on your mind, then?"

"For one thing, you've gotten awfully cozy with your town council opponents."

"Irvin Baydlin and I are real buds."

Gideon's mouth twisted. "I'm talking about Elaine Hunter's son, not that pompous slime, Baydlin. I don't consider him competition even after that speech of his at the parent-teacher meeting."

Gideon had attended? She hadn't seen him. He wasn't a parent or a teacher, so he must have been lurking in the shadows.

Suddenly conscious of the open door to the adjacent store, she lowered her voice, hoping Gideon would follow her cue. "For a few weeks Mr. Hunter will be representing his mother at gatherings hosted for the candidates. I'm sure I'll see him and Mr. Baydlin often between now and election day. I intend to keep interactions friendly. But I would hardly call that 'getting cozy.'"

Gideon *had* seen her, though, visiting with Grady at the park the day he'd rescued Tessa from the slide mishap. How long might he have lingered out of sight to watch them? They hadn't done anything inappropriate or incriminating. Surely he didn't know of their meetings at Grady's place. Did he?

"I don't think you understand what's at stake here, Sunshine." To her alarm, he didn't keep his voice down. "You've lived in Hunter Ridge two years. I've lived here five and, believe me, people in this town have kicked me around more times than I can count. Put me down because I choose to make my way in the world by adding beauty to it. Not marching around in the wilderness with a gun, bow or fishing rod."

She winced as he jerked his head in the direction of Grady's new store.

"I'm aware," she said quietly, again hoping he'd follow suit, "that the artists in this community face numerous challenges. And I think you'd have to agree that I've taken a lead in attempting to bridge that gap, to approach the town council numerous times on behalf of our segment of the population."

Not merely bellyaching like Gideon was known to do.

The man snorted. "And where's that gotten us? Nowhere. Friday night you barely touched on our demands. I wanted to see you shake a fist and challenge the voters. Point out the prejudice they hold against us."

"You think that would win voters?"

"What I think is that you're forgetting why you were chosen to represent us." He wagged a finger at her. "Not that *I* chose you. You're too young. Too inexperienced. Too naive."

His face flushing, Gideon grabbed her upper arms and roughly shook her. Almost unbalancing her. Then, with a surprised wheeze of protest, his own arms were grasped and he was spun around to face a grim Grady Hunter.

"Keep your hands to yourself, Mr. Edlow. Or I'll stand as a witness for Ms. Carston if she wants to file attempted assault charges."

"Stay out of this, Hunter," Gideon sputtered. "This is none of your business."

"When you laid a hand on her, you made it my business."

Gideon's fists clenched, and for a horrified moment, Sunshine feared he'd take a swing at Grady. But with a glare in her direction, he stepped back. "You and your Boy Scout here think this is over, Sunshine. But it's not. You aren't fit to represent our arts community in public office and you're not fit to run the Co-op."

With a murderous scowl in Grady's direction, he charged back across the street in the direction from which he'd come.

"Are you okay?"

From the stunned look on her face, she wasn't. But that revealing expression was immediately replaced by one of annoyance.

"You shouldn't have interfered, Grady." Her words came softly, yet firmly. "I was handling the situation just fine."

She was mad at *him*?

"He grabbed you, Sunshine. He was shaking you."

"He wasn't hurting me. He was venting. He's not a happy man. Never has been. And he's always resented the fact that I was hired to manage the Co-op rather than him."

"You didn't feel threatened when he grabbed you? Your face told another story."

"He startled me. That's all." She cast a regretful look in the direction in which Gideon had disappeared. "I wish you hadn't interfered. It'll make things harder for me."

"Excuse me? I don't think it's acceptable for a man to shake a woman like that." He studied her. "Do you?"

For a moment he thought she wasn't going to answer. Then, almost reluctantly, she responded. "No. But at times my ex-husband could get a little…physical."

Something inside Grady jolted.

"Not that he ever hurt me," she quickly added. "But like Gideon, he had a temper."

"I have a temper, too, but you don't see me shaking women until their teeth rattle."

She motioned impatiently. "Look, Grady, I don't want to discuss this. My ex is out of my life. It's in the past. So let's let it drop."

She started to move around him, but he sidestepped to block her way. "Not just yet. Your ex-husband may be long gone, but Gideon is in the here and now. What did you mean my 'interfering' will make things harder on you?"

"I'll not discuss my personal life on a street corner." She gave him a pointed look, then flashed a bright smile to a woman with a toddler passing by them.

He motioned to the open door of the Hunter store. "Is that private enough? The contractor and his crew knocked off at noon today."

With an exasperated sigh, she preceded him into the shadowed interior. He closed the glass-paned door behind them, but she moved farther into the building, taking in the renovated space. He watched in silence.

Eventually she looked back at him. "Wow. The exposed brick and refinished woodwork are amazing."

It did look good. Ted and his crew had outdone themselves in giving him what he'd envisioned. Display cases would be delivered next week. He'd gone out on a limb to have enlargements made of some of his own wildlife photos. Framing would be completed before the midmonth grand opening. No, they wouldn't be for sale, but somehow the thought of putting them on the wall here—instead of a stranger's work purchased off the internet—gave him a deep sense of satisfaction.

But he wasn't letting Sunshine off the hook.

"How is it that my stepping in when Gideon was out of line going to make things harder for you?"

She looked away from him, moving to where she could run her fingertips along the polished surface of wood shelving. "You have to understand, Grady, that Gideon is a force to be reckoned with."

"Or at least he *thinks* he is." Gideon's bluster didn't faze him.

"When the Hunter Ridge Artists' Cooperative was getting off the ground, the members of the fledgling organization hired me. Gideon had wanted the position for himself but, for obvious reasons, the membership felt neither his personality nor his experience were suitably matched. He resented that. Resents me."

"So he's made it rough on you from the beginning."

"He and a couple of others who look up to him. For each step forward that I attempt to take, they push back. Fortunately, I have the full support of the majority of the membership, including our officers, but dealing with Gideon has never been pleasant."

"From what I overheard, he has a chip on his shoulder. But that's no excuse for grabbing you like he did."

"No, but I'm fine. Unhurt. His outbursts are nothing new."

"No? So what do you think he was driving at when he said this isn't over and that you're unfit to run the Co-op or run for office? That sounds like a veiled threat to me."

"I won't pretend to understand Gideon's thinking. But knowing him, he'll attempt to further slander me at the weekly Co-op meetings. Behind the scenes he'll try to win more members in whatever way he can to force me out."

"Isn't that illegal?"

"He's never been shy in letting me know that he wants to unseat me from managing the Co-op. I think the membership asking me to represent them on the town council was the last straw."

He leaned against an oak checkout counter, arms folded. "I don't like this one bit."

"I appreciate your concern but—no offense intended—like Gideon said, this is none of your business. I'd appreciate it if you'd stay out of it in the future."

Why was she so determined to make light of that jerk's behavior and chastise *him* for stepping in?

"You need to promise me that you won't meet with him anywhere except in a public place. Don't let him get you alone, not even corner you by yourself at a meeting where he could let his temper fly without any witnesses."

"I can't make that promise, but I assure you I'll be on my guard."

He raised his hands in surrender, irritation coloring his tone. "Pardon me for jumping in where I'm not wanted."

"Grady, don't be like that. I appreciate your concern. And thank you for wanting to protect me. But truly, your intervention will make him more determined to get me fired. I can't afford to lose this job. I have Tessa to support."

"I'm sorry if you think my stepping in added fuel to the fire. But in my opinion, he's a powder keg waiting to go off and his behavior needs to be nipped in the bud." Easy enough for him to say, though. He wasn't a single mother who needed a job to keep a roof over her daughter's head and food on the table. "I understand where you're coming from, Sunshine. Honestly, I do. But don't allow this guy to bully you. If he does it again, promise me you'll go to the authorities. I'm seriously thinking about doing that myself."

"Please, Grady, don't do that."

"Then, you'll promise me that if he approaches you again, tries to intimidate you, you'll report him?"

Warring emotions flashed through her eyes. Irritation. Resentment. And finally—relief? When she nodded, he could barely keep himself from reaching for her. To hug her for making that concession.

For a long moment their gazes held, then abruptly she glanced at her watch. "Look, I've got to run. Benton's covering for me at the gallery so I can do a few errands."

She moved briskly to the door and opened it.

"We're still on for tonight?" he called out. This would be their final review of the presentation. Their last evening together. He'd hit the grocery store last night, picking up cheesecake, potatoes to bake and filet mignon to grill.

A thank-you gift.

Hand on the doorknob, she paused to look at him, her expression suddenly apologetic. "I'm sorry, something's come up and I have to cancel. But I'll email the presentation to you. I think we're basically done if you think it's good to go. Take a look at it and let me know."

With a fleeting smile, she was gone.

Something had come up?

Grady groaned. He'd obviously overstepped his bounds when he'd instinctively stepped in to halt Gideon, the macho-minded rescue somehow sinking his ship.

And what ship might that be, Grady? Winning a lady's heart?

He kicked aside the betraying thought. He had absolutely no designs on Sunshine Carston. None.

Right?

Chapter Eleven

"You're coming to the Hideaway Saturday evening, aren't you, Sunshine?" Delaney Marks Hunter, her wavy, sun-streaked blond hair tumbling around her shoulders, paused at the bottom of the Co-op gallery staircase that led not only to Sunshine's apartment, but to several small studios where Delaney had started taking silversmithing lessons from Benton Mason during the summer.

Sunshine had received and responded to the invitation Delaney was referring to with mixed emotions. Elaine and Dave Hunter were hosting a gathering of current town council members, candidates and other prominent people in the community. It was hard to imagine socializing with Irvin after his ungallant performance a week ago, but that was not what bothered her most.

"I'll be there. My friend Tori is going watch Tessa."

"Bring Tessa along. Tori, too." Delaney's smile

broadened, obviously thrilled to be a Hunter now. Having married into the family a month ago, she was already comfortable speaking on their behalf. "The Hunters would be fine with that."

"I think a night of boring local politics might be a bit much for both."

"Our kids will be there. At least for the cook-out." Luke had three children, which Delaney already thought of as her own and had earlier confided her intent to adopt. "Claire—one of Luke's twin sisters—and her kids are in town to help out, so they'll be there, too. And I imagine several others will bring their children. The Hunters are all about family. You should see Grady when he's surrounded by his nieces and nephews. He's going to make a great dad some day."

He'd certainly won Tessa's heart.

The invitation had been addressed to Sunshine Carston and family, noting she could bring a guest. But with Tori busy researching how the Hunters may have swindled Sunshine's great-great-grandparents out of their property, she'd likely balk at being asked to socialize with them. And although Tessa might enjoy playing with the other kids, her obsession with Grady being her hero didn't need to be fueled further. When Tessa had spied him at church last Sunday, she'd gone running with arms outstretched to the poor surprised man. Recovering, he'd laughed, picked her up and lifted her high before setting her back on her feet. Not good.

"It's nice of the Hunters to plan something like this." Even though it was awkward. Not only was she hoping to prove their ancestor had done hers wrong, but she'd been nagged by guilt for days at having let Grady down Tuesday night—and having put him off on Thursday, as well. But after Gideon's accusations about her "getting cozy" with Grady, she'd had no choice.

She had a fine line to walk, keeping the two factions of the Co-op on speaking terms and unified in purpose. While Gideon had kept a physical distance at Wednesday evening's meeting—no doubt wary after having been confronted by Grady— he'd challenged her again and again.

She could *not* lose her job and the apartment that came with it. Maybe at tonight's veterans-hosted dinner she'd have the opportunity to clarify things with Grady. To smooth the gulf between them that she'd been forced to create.

"Well, I'll see you then!" Always full of energy, Delaney dashed up the stairs.

Over the next several hours, Sunshine waited on customers at the gallery, then got cleaned up and changed clothes for the evening's event. Would Irvin be on better behavior tonight?

The sun had set by the time she arrived at the Log Cabin Café, owner and former marine William "Packy" Westin welcoming her to a spacious back room where others were gathering for an opportunity to get to know the candidates. She'd expected mostly males, but spouses, dates and female vets were also in attendance.

A burly guy in his early sixties with a close-cropped beard, Packy's shaved head shone under the overhead lights as he helped her remove her coat and led her to her seat at the front of a U-shaped table arrangement.

Next to Grady, thankfully, and not Irvin.

Her breath caught unexpectedly as Grady's warm gaze met hers without a trace of the distancing between them that she'd feared.

"Beautiful dress, Sunshine."

Heat warmed her cheeks. Tori had loaned it to her. A black sheath that skimmed her figure, topped by a fitted ruby sweater jacket. Strappy high heels gave it an added touch of style that she didn't often indulge in. And to think she'd almost resorted to wool slacks, turtleneck and flats because the evening had turned nippy.

Now, seeing that appreciative spark in Grady's eyes, she knew she'd made the right choice.

With Packy on one side of her and Grady on the other, the meal passed pleasantly, not allowing her much time to notice the butterflies in her stomach. Then, much to her relief, Irvin was called upon to present first, then her and finally Grady.

All that worry of Irvin putting on a repeat performance at her expense had been for nothing. This group asked harder questions of Mr. Baydlin than the others had, politely but pointedly putting him on the spot a few times. That let a little of the hot air out of him. With former army vet and fellow artist Benton Mason and his wife in attendance, she more confidently presented her hopes that the old and new could work together to improve the economy for Hunter Ridge.

The evening was unexpectedly painless and, following some mingling and answering questions one-on-one, by nine thirty the guests began to disperse. She'd done it. Made it through another event. If only the remaining ones would be so effortless.

Among the last to leave, Grady held out her coat and helped her to slip it on. "May I walk you to your car?"

"If you don't mind. I parked out back and the lighting isn't that good."

"My pleasure."

Attempting to tamp down the rapid beating of her heart, she followed Grady down a short hallway. Then he held open the door and they stepped out into the night.

"Brrr." She pulled her coat collar up around her neck, wishing she'd brought along her wool scarf and leather gloves. She took note of Grady's shirt-sleeves. "Didn't you bring a coat?"

"It's inside. I'll get it after I see you to your car."

Carefully navigating the steps, Sunshine gave a silent sigh of relief when she reached the bottom without mishap, acutely conscious of Grady's hand grazing her waist at the back of her coat.

"Where are you parked?"

"Over there." She clicked a button on her car key, the SUV's taillights momentarily illuminating, but she immediately concentrated on negotiating the graveled parking lot with care. Not easy in high heels after dark.

They almost made it to her vehicle when her footing gave way. A pothole. With a startled cry, she fought to regain her balance, only to be caught by Grady. Steadied. Grateful, she turned to thank him.

But he was unexpectedly close.

Her breathing suddenly shallow, she stared up at him and in the dim light saw his eyes widen slightly, as surprised to find her in his arms as she was to be there.

"Grady—" Their gazes locked, and she could feel his heart beating where her hand rested on his shirtfront. But she couldn't voice the words of thanks that needed to be said. "I—"

He placed his finger gently to her lips to silence her.

Somewhere in the distance, as a barely there breeze touched her cheek, she could hear the cry of a night bird. The bark of a dog. The sound of muted laughter coming from one of the other restaurants along the main road through town.

And then, ever so slowly he closed his eyes and leaned forward until she could feel his soft breath inches from her lips.

He is going to kiss me. She should stop him. And yet…her own eyes closed and her lips parted in anticipation.

"Grady!" Packy's marine-tough voice barreled across the darkened parking lot.

They jerked apart. Staring at each other as if dazed.

"You out there, Grady?" Packy remained silhouetted at the restaurant's back door.

"Yeah." Grady cleared his throat, then raised his voice. "Yeah, I'm here, Packy."

"You left your jacket. Don't forget to come back and get it."

"Will do."

Packy disappeared from the doorway and they were again alone. But the moment had been broken.

Grady again cleared his throat. "I guess I'd better let you get in your vehicle and get warmed up."

From the second he'd taken her into his arms, however, she'd no longer been aware of the cold but had been flooded by a curious warmth. A warmth that now quickly ebbed. With a shiver, she took the final steps to her SUV, where she unlocked the door. He held it open as she seated herself, the glare of the interior light further stripping away the fleeting thrill of what had happened.

What had *almost* happened.

"Good night, Sunshine." Grady's tone was flat, impersonal, as he shut the door, then stepped back into the shadows.

Now trembling, Sunshine started the engine, then carefully backed out and exited the almost empty parking lot.

Once on the road to home, she pressed her unsteady fingers lightly to her lips.

"Either grab a box and help, Grady, or get out of the way." Luke, arms laden with an oversize plastic bin, elbowed his way past him and onto the patio at the back of the inn.

With a midafternoon wind kicking up, they'd delayed patio preparation until the last minute. Mom hadn't wanted to risk everything getting blown into the next county. But now, with the sun dipping below the towering treetops, calm had returned. Time for all hands on deck.

"Are you feeling all right, Grady?" Grandma Jo looking at him with concern, lifted her hand to his forehead. "No fever. But you haven't been yourself today."

Luke rolled his eyes at him as, bin delivered, he returned to the inn.

"Stuff on my mind I guess, Grandma."

She studied him with open curiosity, then, without further comment, returned inside.

He had a lot on his mind, all right. Like the fact that not only had he almost kissed Sunshine last night, but she'd be arriving any minute. What would he say to her? Should he pretend nothing happened between them at all? Apologize?

Heading into the inn, he grabbed one of the bins out of the storage room and carried it outside to where Rio was unpacking others in front of the big outdoor fireplace. Plastic table covers. Salt and pepper shakers. Cloth napkins.

"Need any help there?" he felt obligated to ask.

She looked up at him. "Thanks, but I think I've got it. You could finish setting up tables for the kids, though, and tell Luke to bring out the rest of the folding chairs. We're expecting about fifty. That's including maybe a dozen children."

Fifty. With that many packed out here, he might not have to worry too much about interacting with Sunshine after all. Besides, as a candidate for town council she'd have her focus on meeting people, making a good impression, baby kissing and all that.

Inwardly he groaned. Why did he have to think of *kissing*?

But instantly his thoughts flew to the dark parking lot behind the Log Cabin Café. Would he ever be back there again without thinking of last night? When he'd kept Sunshine from falling, she'd turned in his arms and…his mind had converted to mush. If Packy hadn't hollered out the door, well, he'd be in a bigger heap of trouble than he was right now.

"Grady?"

He jerked back to the present where Rio was staring up at him doubtfully.

"Are you going to stand there or are you going to deliver my message to Luke and get the tables set up?"

"On it."

He had to get his head out of the clouds. Fast.

"There you are!" His sister Claire, one of the twins, caught his arm just as he stepped inside to search for Luke. "I've been back home for a week and have hardly seen you."

She gave him a hug. She was so different from their youngest sister, Rio, who was a loner who'd far prefer to spend her time out in the stable with the horses than deal with a crowd of people. Which meant that after her duties here were completed, she'd pull a disappearing act.

Not Claire, though. She loved being in the thick

of things, would thrive on playing hostess at Hunter's Hideaway even if only during a visit. Since marrying and moving to Dallas, she didn't often get back once she and Del had three kids aged five and under.

"I've been around." He lowered his voice. "Mom sure appreciates your coming back to help right now. We all do."

"Flying in and out solo for Luke and Delaney's wedding reminded me how much I miss you all. Del's out of the country on business for a few weeks, so I saw no reason why I shouldn't pack up the kids and come on home to help out. Nothing to stop me."

"So," he continued, "do you think Mom's up to this tonight? When she announced her intentions on Sunday not to cancel the barbecue, you could have knocked me over with a feather."

"I imagine having something other than chemo treatments to look forward to perked her up this week. I know she looked tired when I got here, but don't you think she's seemed livelier the past few days?"

"Maybe. I don't want her overdoing it, though. And her possibly being exposed to colds or flu with all these kids running around concerns me, but she wouldn't hear of asking guests not to bring their children. I don't much care, either, that she's giving her opponents ammunition to use against her if she isn't up to par tonight."

Irv's earlier potshots still rankled.

Claire frowned. "Do you think Irvin and that Sunshine woman would do that? I don't put it past Irv, of course. He was in Dad's high school graduating class and Dad's never cared for him. But I don't know much about this Carston lady. She's lived here a couple of years, right? What do you know about her?"

Warmth crept up his neck.

What did he know about Sunshine? Well, she was a good mother. A hard worker. A fine artist. She knew a lot about marketing, which she'd been willing to share with him. Stubborn at times, but she had a smile that invariably coaxed out one of his own.

"I only recently met her, so I couldn't say." Claire didn't need to know how close he'd come to kissing her. "But I don't think she'd take advantage. I was thinking more of Baydlin. You know I'm filling in for Mom at election-related events, right? She'd hardly started chemo when he was raising questions about her fitness for office."

He glanced back through the door to the patio, noting that while he'd stood there jawing with Claire, a surprising number of guests had arrived, mingling as Dad fired up the gas grills.

"Hey, sis." He touched her arm. "Could you

find Luke for me? Rio needs him to bring out more folding chairs. I'm supposed to be setting up tables for the kids."

"Sure." Then she leaned close, her eyes twinkling and voice lowered conspiratorially. "Let's have lunch sometime next week, okay? You need to catch me up on your love life."

He laughed. "That shouldn't take long."

"No one special yet, Grady?" She eyed him with concern and, once again, heat stole up his neck. "I know Jasmine left a bad taste in your mouth, but don't give up hope. We serve a big God. It can happen when you least expect it."

"Don't think I'll hold my breath."

She made a pouty face. "You're a wonderful man, and you deserve a wonderful woman. It's a matter of time. One of these days you're going to turn around and, when you least expect it, there she'll be."

She gave him a hug, then headed off.

He stood there a moment longer, contemplating Claire's ever-optimistic words. Then he pushed open the door and stepped out onto the patio— just as Sunshine rounded the corner of the inn.

Chapter Twelve

Sunshine's breath caught as she looked across the crowded patio—and right into Grady Hunter's eyes.

More handsome than ever, he stood looking at her with an intensity every bit as potent as what she remembered from last night. Despite the many times she'd replayed those moments in her mind, wondering if it might have been a dream, maybe she hadn't made it up?

Which meant it was all the more important to steer clear of him this evening. She'd given it considerable thought—and prayer—and concluded she had no business falling for a Hunter. Her history and that of his family were too intermingled, went too far back. When the time came that she could finally prove her suspicions against Grady's ancestors, she didn't want a romantic entanglement holding her back from claiming what rightfully belonged to her and her daughter.

With considerable effort, she broke eye contact and strode purposefully into the midst of the gathering just as Elaine Hunter joined her guests. For a moment Sunshine thought she'd restyled her sandy-brown, previously shoulder-length hair, then immediately realized the sassy new cut was a wig. She'd heard a few days ago that not too long into chemo, Elaine had courageously had her head shaved in anticipation of losing her hair. She'd started chemo barely a month ago and had lost weight. Nothing drastic, but the fullness had left her face. She was looking better, though, than Sunshine would have expected from what Grady had told her about how sick his mother had been.

This image of a still somewhat plucky Elaine should dispel any hopes Irvin Baydlin had of discrediting her with voters.

But before Sunshine could make her way through the crowd to thank her hostess for the invitation, Irvin suddenly appeared at Elaine's side. Obviously fawning over her from the looks of it. But surely he didn't believe Grady hadn't shared the snide remarks he'd made about her at the parent-teacher meeting. Then again, maybe Grady hadn't, for fear of distressing his mother and Irvin was betting on that.

Looking around for other familiar faces, she spied Delaney talking to an older woman—

Josephine Hunter—and edged her way in their direction.

Delaney's smile brightened as she saw her. "Grandma Jo, have you met Sunshine Carston?" She quickly made introductions.

"I'm delighted you could join us this evening, Sunshine," the older woman acknowledged. "It's long been a family tradition to gather town council candidates for a relaxing, nonpolitically focused evening. A chance to get to know one another and each other's families on an informal basis."

Was that no-politicking comment intended as a reminder to a newcomer who'd barged her way into the town's affairs?

"I appreciate the invitation." Although she attempted to stay focused on the immediate conversation, her radar couldn't help but note Grady moving among the guests, heading to where Mr. Baydlin remained glued to Elaine's side.

A protector by nature. That was Grady through and through.

Her stomach fluttered as again she recalled how he'd prevented her from falling last night. Held her gently but securely. And when she'd looked up at him…

"I understand you have a daughter, Sunshine. A kindergartner?"

"Yes. Tessa."

"She's a sweetie," Delaney chimed in. "Black hair and big brown eyes."

Ah, good. Grady had reached his mother's side and Irvin was slinking off. But she didn't much care for the smugly satisfied look on her fellow candidate's face. No doubt he'd been pumping Elaine under the guise of concern for her health.

With the mouthwatering scent of grilled meats and vegetables now filling the early-evening air, she chatted with Delaney and Mrs. Hunter awhile longer, then introduced herself to others she didn't know, including several of Grady's family members. It was nice, however, not to be expected to discuss the upcoming election. She hadn't realized how stressful that had become this past month, feeling pressured to somehow steer the topic to her campaign and solicit feedback from potential voters.

Across the way she again saw Grady, surrounded by a group of jabbering kids as he set up card tables and his brother, Luke, brought in folding chairs. She recognized Luke and Delaney's eight-year-old daughter, Chloe. But were any of the other children Grady's nieces and nephews? One laughing little fellow, about two years old, was lifted high into the air and settled on the big man's broad shoulders. Naturally, that set off a chorus of "Do me! Do me!"

From across the patio, his gaze was drawn to

hers. But her smile hadn't even reached her lips before he looked away to give the youngsters his full attention.

As the sun dipped farther behind the towering ponderosas, adults and children lined up at a long, makeshift buffet to fill plates with hamburgers, hot dogs and veggie burgers. Potato salad. Baked beans. Cheesy potatoes. And more.

Now cast in shade, the patio was considerably cooler, although nowhere near the chill of the previous night. A fire crackled in the big stone outdoor fireplace and the strategically placed propane patio heaters were lit, offering warmth and a cozy glow, as well. Nevertheless, she was glad to have brought along a jacket.

Plate filled with food, she scanned the surrounding tables, looking for a place to sit. She'd hardly taken a step when Grady, a piled-high plate gripped in his hands, appeared at her side.

"I need to speak to you."

Please don't let him bring up last night.

But his expression gave nothing away. "Um, sure."

He nodded to one of the empty tables, then led the way. When they were seated, he poured them both a glass of iced tea and spread a napkin across his lap. Then he leaned toward her, his tone, to her relief, all business.

"I thought you should know that Mom said Irvin was trying to pin down her opinion of you."

"Why would he do that?"

"He probably figured Mom knows you better than he does, that she might shed light on something juicy he could use against you in the campaign."

She crumpled inside. "So your mother—?"

"Was on to him immediately and deflected his not-so-subtle inquiries. But she thought you should know, seeing as how he'd unfairly targeted you at the parent-teacher meeting."

She glanced across the patio to where Grady's mother and father sat, deep in conversation with those at their table. She wouldn't have expected Elaine, her opponent, to thwart Irvin on her behalf, let alone warn her of his intentions.

"Please thank your mother for me, will you?"

"I will." Then he motioned almost self-consciously to their plates. "Food's getting cold."

For an excruciatingly long span of time they ate in silence. Side by side, elbows mere inches from each other, he was acutely aware of the petite woman seated next to him. Her sweet scent. Her graceful movements as she reached for her tea glass. The way she occasionally paused to lift her cloth napkin to her lips...

He drew in a deep breath. He wasn't often at a

loss for words, but his mind roamed unsuccessfully for a topic of conversation. Maybe it hadn't been a good idea to sit down together. Had his family noticed them sitting off by themselves? Irv?

He shifted uncomfortably in his chair, suddenly feeling as if all eyes were on them.

"What did you think of the presentation I put together, Grady?"

Her soft words startled him but, relieved, he gratefully responded. "I'm ashamed to admit I haven't had a single minute to look at it. Another project took precedence."

Disappointment clouded her eyes. Had his seeming indifference to her work hurt her?

"I've been up to my eyeballs," he said quickly, "in preparations for the grand opening two weeks from today. You know the old Murphy's Law? Well, multiply that times ten this past week."

"I'm sorry to hear that."

"Yeah, it's been wild. A delay in a number of deliveries. The guy who designed the website had problems with the host server. And there were unexpected issues with obtaining final approval paperwork. But—" He managed a smile, hoping he'd convinced her that he hadn't put off reviewing her presentation because he considered it of no value. "After Herculean effort on the part of those involved, everything's been resolved. Things should settle down next week."

"Good."

Once again they lapsed into silence. Resumed eating.

This was ridiculous. Maybe he was stuck-up for thinking her thoughts were gravitating back to last night as did his. But this couldn't go on. Abruptly he pushed back his empty plate and downed the remainder of his tea. Then he clasped his hands on the table in front of him and pinned her with a determined look.

"Okay, let's stop tiptoeing around each other and get this out in the open."

Startled eyes met his, her face flushing.

"I think we both know that something happened between us last night. Or rather, almost happened. And it's built a barrier that can't be allowed to remain since we'll be seeing each other on a regular basis at political events."

After a moment's hesitation, she placed her fork on her half-eaten plate and settled her hands in her lap. Despite her wary gaze, a faint smile touched her lips. "From the looks of your mother tonight, your stand-in duties may be a thing of the past."

"Don't let appearances fool you. It's been several days since her last chemo treatment and today she spent most of her time in bed, resting up for tonight." He tipped a look of mild reprimand in her direction. "And don't try to change the subject. I think I wouldn't be speaking out of line if I said that there's an…attraction. You know, between us. And it came to a head last night. Would you agree?"

For a moment he thought she'd deny it, but then she nodded.

"I like you, Sunshine. I'm under the impression you think I'm okay, too." His eyes searched hers, but she only stared back at him, her feelings masked. "I may be mistaken, but I don't think either of us is looking for a relationship right now."

"I—" She paused. "That's correct."

He relaxed only slightly, disturbed that her confirmation didn't shoot off any fireworks of relief. "Please don't take my reluctance to get involved right now the wrong way. As I said, I like you. You're a beautiful, bright young woman. But it's tricky dating a woman with a kid. I don't make a habit of it."

She gave a brittle laugh. "You make it sound as though involvement with someone's child is something undesirable. That surprises me. I was under the impression you like children."

"I do. And that's exactly why I'm careful about who I date. I don't want to hurt a kid when things don't work out between the adults."

"Is that experience talking?"

"Unfortunately, yes."

"Well, don't lose any sleep over sharing that with me. I don't take it personally. To be honest, the last thing I need right now is another romantic entanglement."

"Because of your ex? From what you've told me, it doesn't sound like you should spend too much time mourning the loss of him."

"He's very talented—a musician in a country band. He has a great sense of humor. Works hard. Charms the socks off the ladies. Like you in those respects."

That comparison left a sour taste in his mouth. "So if he was such a great guy, what happened?"

She stared across the patio for a long moment, the flicker of light from a table candle illuminating the softness of her face. Her troubled eyes. "We were young. Or at least I was. He's nine years my senior. You know, one of those classic little-girl-without-a-strong-male-role-model-goes-looking-for-one scenarios."

"Not surprising."

She shrugged. "Anyway, we got married when I was nineteen. And things were good for several years. It was exciting traveling with him and his band. They were popular throughout the Southwest, with Nashville-bound stars in their eyes. But then…" She quirked a smile. "Pregnancy."

"He wasn't happy about that?"

"At first he was. But once Tessa was born, it became harder and harder for me to be on the road. To help with the driving, the set up and breakdown. The kid stuff I had to drag along irritated him. And the diapers. A baby crying when he was trying to sleep. No longer having me at his beck and call."

"Sounds like a selfish jerk."

"Sometimes. But he was a man with dreams— ones that didn't include hauling around a diaper bag. He wanted me to leave Tessa with my mom." Her voice drifted off, then came back strong. "Don't get me wrong. I love my mother, but she could be hard to please. I grew up with a cloud of disapproval hanging over my head, so there was no way I was going to leave the offspring of a man she'd warned me about in her care for long stretches of time. I did everything I could, though, to make things work, to stay on the road with him. But it wasn't enough and he said adios."

"Does he keep in contact with you? With his daughter?"

"Are you kidding? The band continues to struggle. They live out of cheap hotels and campers on the back of their trucks. I expect to hear anytime now that they've broken up, gone their separate ways. With only sporadic paychecks, of course, there's rarely a child-support payment. Nor does Jerrel Carston want any part in Tessa's life. Or mine."

Grady's hand clenched, resisting reaching down to take Sunshine's in his. It was that tenderhearted thinking last night that had got them where they were now. Confessing they weren't ready for a relationship.

"So you see," Sunshine said almost brightly, "why I neither take offense that you're cautious about involvement with some woman's kid, nor am I hurt by your honesty about your feelings about me. We're on the same page."

"So we're good?"

"We're good."

Then, why doesn't it feel good?

She glanced at her surroundings, where others had finished their meal and were moving from table to table to greet fellow guests. "I guess I'd better get out and mingle."

"I should do the same. Show a little Hunter hospitality. And maybe I'll grab a bowlful of that ice cream I see they're serving now."

"I want to slip over there to personally thank your mother for inviting me. And meet your father."

When she stood, he rose, too, oddly dissatisfied with the way their conversation was ending. He lightly touched her arm. "Hey, when you're ready to leave, find me okay? I'll walk you to your car."

Catching the deliberately teasing lilt in this tone, she laughed. "Thank you, but I'll pass on your gentlemanly offer this time, Mr. Hunter. I've come prepared for a trek across your graveled parking lot." She patted her jacket pocket. "Flashlight and—" she lifted her loafer-clad foot and wiggled it "—no heels."

They stood smiling at each other, neither making any attempt to hurry off to their social obligations.

Grady silently absorbed the loveliness of the woman before him. Was he being stupid about his unwillingness to get involved with a woman who had a child? Using it as an excuse not to risk loving again? But no matter what conclusions he came to on that issue, she'd been clear enough tonight that she wasn't ready for another relationship.

As if suddenly self-conscious under his thoughtful gaze, the laughter faded from Sunshine's eyes. She lifted her hand in a parting wave, leaving Grady with an inexplicable ache in the region of his heart.

Chapter Thirteen

"I'm praying everything will work out the way you want it to, Tori." Sunshine stood just inside the guest room doorway watching as her friend packed her suitcase late Saturday afternoon. Her fiancé had called a short while ago and wanted her to come back to Jerome, saying they needed to talk.

Which left Sunshine with a real bad feeling. If a man had decided in favor of reconfirming his engagement, wouldn't he show up on his fiancée's doorstep, not ask her to drive over three hours to see him?

"That's just it." Tori tucked her hair dryer into a side pocket. "I'm no longer sure how I want it to work out."

"Your feelings toward Heath have changed? Absence isn't making the heart grow fonder?"

"I love him with all my heart, but I don't want

to be his choice by default because nothing better came along during our separation." Tori checked the contents of her bag, then zipped it shut. "Guess I'd better hit the road. I'll come back and get the rest of my stuff, you know, if—"

Impulsively, Sunshine gave her friend a quick hug. "No matter what, everything is going to be okay. If Heath's stupid enough to let you go, God has something better in mind."

"I keep telling myself that." She lifted her bag from the bed. "I'll call you, whatever the outcome. And thanks for letting me stay here. Tessa has been such a wonderful distraction. You're fortunate to have her. I only wish…"

Tori shook her head with regret, as if deciding her hopes were better left unshared.

"Wish what?"

"That God would bring a special man into your life. Someone like Grady Hunter. You know, real hero material."

A prick of sadness pierced Sunshine's heart, an echo of the melancholy that had lingered since her encounter with Grady a week ago.

He might be genuine hero material, but he wasn't looking for a woman with a child. He'd said he didn't want to risk hurting a kid, but maybe, as with Jerrel, the real issue was that a kid took time and attention. Attention away from him. Even if she pulled out of the campaign and dropped the pursuit of proof that would hold his family accountable for wrongs done to hers, there would be no future there. He'd made that clear last weekend.

"It will be dark before long," Sunshine reminded as Tori departed. "Call me when you get there so I know you made it safely."

Despite the comforting sound of Tessa chatting with her dolls, the apartment seemed unbearably empty once Tori departed. Maybe she'd fix them something simple for supper, then pop in a Disney DVD to watch together. Or maybe…?

"Tessa?" She stepped to the open doorway of her daughter's room, her heart, as always, warming at the sight of the child God had given her. "How would you like to have supper at the Log Cabin Café tonight?"

With money tight, they didn't eat out often, but she had a coupon. Maybe they could split the Saturday-night burger special.

Tessa's face lit up. She loved Packy, who always brought her a special treat on the rare excursions to his restaurant. A small cup of yogurt or a piece of candy. "Can we have sweet potato fries?"

"I see no reason why not."

Tessa scrambled to her feet. "Are we going now?"

"It's a little early. I'll come get you when we're ready to go." Restless and highly conscious of Tori's departure to a future that might be decided tonight, Sunshine wandered to the kitchen and began straightening the pantry. There was nothing, in her opinion, like getting organized to chase away the blues. But she'd barely gotten started when Tori's words resurfaced in her mind.

I wish God would bring a special man into your life.

Sunshine sighed. Well, He hadn't. Maybe He never would. But the Bible said God had a good plan for her. A plan not to bring harm, but to give her a hope and a future. She had to hang on tight to that now, just as she had since Jerrel had walked out of her life.

Someone like Grady Hunter.

She plopped a can of beans on the shelf with a thud. That door was closed, and there was no point in dwelling on it.

You know, real hero material.

Nonsense. She didn't need a hero. She and Tessa were doing fine on their own. Hadn't God generously given her a job that came with housing? A schedule that allowed her time to paint in order to supplement her income and spend quality time with Tessa? And hadn't He, too, brought any number of people into her life at exactly the right moment?

Like Tori, who'd stepped in to care for Tessa when Sunshine needed more time for campaigning. And someone to assist when her vehicle had conked out on the highway at night. To help get her SUV fixed. And to rescue Tessa when she'd gotten caught on the slide.

With a growl of irritation, Sunshine halted herself before she slammed another can onto the shelf. Just because Grady happened to fill a few of those roles, that didn't mean he was meant to be *her* hero. Or Tessa's.

He'd made it clear he wasn't interested in anything like that. But could she stand to live in this town if he someday became some other woman's hero?

"I admit it surprises me, but I actually like Sunshine." Across the table from Grady at the Log Cabin Café Saturday night, Luke took a final sip from his coffee mug. Then he smiled at his bride seated next to him in the high-backed booth. "Delaney said *she* did. But until last weekend, I didn't agree."

He slid a look in Grady's direction. One intended to make his younger brother squirm.

"I like her, too," Rio, next to Grady, chimed in.

Grady looked around at the packed restaurant, animated conversations swirling around him keeping the sound volume to a low roar. Typical Saturday night. Was there any hope he could sneak out of here to escape the direction this conversation had taken?

"So what do you think of her, Grady?" Luke wasn't about to let him off the hook. "The two of you seemed to have a lot to talk about at the cookout."

"You noticed that, too?" Delaney laughed and slipped her arm into the crook of her husband's. But she was looking at her brother-in-law. "Seemed very chummy to me."

A smiling Rio elbowed him. "Have anything you want to fill us in on, Grady?"

Remembering how he and Rio had mercilessly teased Luke about Delaney a few short months ago, the tables were now turned. He pushed his plate away, conscious of everyone's eyes on him.

"Sunshine and I were talking business."

Rio giggled. "Nice try, Grady. Tell us another one."

"Maybe the three of you have forgotten, but Sunshine Carston's is Mom's *opponent*."

Luke grimaced. "There is that drawback. And the fact that she's the primary spokesperson for an artists' contingent that won't shut up."

"Now, Luke," Delaney chided, "they do have good points. I mean, why were they turned down on having an art-in-the-park event? That makes no sense to me."

"Because, sweetheart," Luke said, patting her hand in a patronizing manner that would likely get him yelled at once they got home, "they intended to bring in outside vendors—like food trucks and others who would take away from local businesses and restaurants. Summer is a make-it-or-break-it deal for most people around here. Losing ground one weekend a month for three or four months could be a significant loss."

"Or it could be—" she nudged her husband, undaunted "—that the event would draw even more business to the locals. Put Hunter Ridge on the map."

Grady grinned. "Looks as if you have your work cut out for you, Luke. Delaney's starting to think like one of them."

To his relief, the owner of the café appeared at their table before the topic could switch back to him and Sunshine.

"Anything else I can get you folks? More coffee? Water?"

"I think that's it, Packy." Grady patted his own flat but full stomach. "Great meal as always. Thanks."

"You're welcome. Have a good rest of your evening." Packy placed the bill on the table and moved on to the next.

Grady snatched up the slip of paper, but he'd barely risen to his feet and moved away from the booth when he felt a tug on his sleeve.

"Hi, Grady!" Tessa, smiling ear to ear, threw

her arms around him as Sunshine walked up behind her. He returned the exuberant hug.

"I'm sorry for the interruption." Sunshine looked apologetically at him and the others at the table. "But Tessa didn't want to leave without saying hello."

"Good to see you again." Luke nodded to Sunshine as he, too, slipped out of the booth. "I don't believe I've met your daughter."

Grady made introductions to his family, self-conscious as the little girl clung to his hand.

Tessa looked up at him, her expression reflecting awe. "You have a big family, don't you, Grady?"

"Yeah, and there are more who aren't here." As an only child, she probably found siblings a fascinating concept. "I have one brother and three sisters."

"Wow."

"Come on, Tessa. Time to go." Sunshine held out her hand.

"Can Grady walk home with us? It's dark outside."

Noting her voice was tinged with apprehension, he exchanged a quick glance with Sunshine. Was this what she'd alluded to earlier? Anxiety related to the mysterious presence in the little girl's closet?

"We'll be fine walking home, honey. There's nothing to be afraid of."

While Saturday night in town usually had lots of people out and about and they'd be safe on the way to their apartment, the gallant thing to do would be to see them safely home. But after that too-close-for-comfort incident in the parking lot last weekend, he sensed her reluctance.

As he quickly debated with himself, his family filed past him, Luke snagging the bill from his fingers.

"I'll get this. And Rio can ride home with us."

Looked as if that settled it. "I'd be happy to see you home, Tessa, if your mother doesn't mind my company."

"You don't mind, do you, Mommy?"

Tessa's eyes pleaded and, after a moment's indecision, Sunshine gave in. "Thank you, Grady."

But she wasn't happy about it.

Outside, she was relieved that the wind had died down and, although as chilly as a mid-October evening in the Arizona high country was expected to be, the walk would warm them.

She needn't have worried about making conversation. Gripping Grady's hand, Tessa chatted like a proverbial magpie, telling him about the late-season butterfly she'd seen at the park that morning, how her kindergarten teacher praised her for a picture she'd drawn and that Tori would be gone a few days.

Her daughter's enthusiasm at having this man's full attention again dredged up memories of her own childhood, triggering an ache in her heart for Tessa. Grady was right. When things didn't work out in relationships, innocent kids could get hurt. Although Grady barely hesitated when Tessa expressed hopes that he would accompany them, that concern had to have been on his mind.

As they neared the gallery door, Sunshine fished in her jacket pocket for the key, but she sensed Tessa slowing her pace, reluctant for the walk to come to an end.

"Mommy, can Grady come in and see my new goldfish?"

She should have anticipated this bedtime-delay tactic. "I imagine he's seen goldfish before."

"But he hasn't seen *my* goldfish." She looked up at him, her eyes imploring. "Please, Grady?"

He looked to Sunshine. "I have a few minutes. That is, if—"

"Okay. But we can't keep Grady long, honey. He has to walk back to the café and then drive home."

Tessa jumped up and down as Sunshine let them inside the gallery and locked the door behind them. Then Tessa eagerly pulled Grady forward, among the dimly illuminated displays and up the stairs to the apartment.

Acutely aware of Grady's presence beside her, Sunshine tensed as she inserted the key in the door.

Had she put away the stuffed animals Tessa had dragged to the living room that afternoon? Was the kitchen clean? And most of all, had Tori's research that she'd been reviewing before they left for the café been tucked out of sight?

As they stepped inside, she scanned the room. Everything appeared to be in order.

"Nice place." Grady's eyes took in their living quarters as Tessa again tugged him forward.

"My room is nice, too. Come and see."

At his questioning look, Sunshine nodded and he allowed Tessa to guide him into the diminutive space, softly lit by a bedside lamp. Big enough for a single bed, dresser and skirted nightstand, it had been decorated with secondhand and discount store finds that lent it a fashionable shabby-chic look. The white-painted furniture set off the pink floral bedspread, area rug and throw pillows. Dolls and stuffed animals lined a wall shelf next to the bed.

"There he is!" Tessa pointed proudly to the goldfish in a bowl atop her dresser. "Goldie."

Sunshine had bought the fish for her when in Canyon Springs on business earlier in the week, hoping the tiny fellow's presence might ease Tessa's nighttime fears. Unfortunately, Tessa insisted the aquatic creature was afraid of the dark and continued to keep the night-light on.

Grady leaned in to inspect her new friend. "That's a handsome-looking fish you have there."

"I know."

Then Tessa hurriedly rummaged through a dresser drawer.

Sunshine frowned. "What are you looking for, sweetheart?"

"My new jammies. The ones Tori bought me. I want Grady to see me in them." Locating them, she clutched them to her heart, a serious look on her face. "Don't leave, okay, Grady? I'll be right back."

"Tessa, I don't think—"

But Tessa wiggled past her and out the bedroom door. Seconds later, the bathroom door shut behind her.

"I'm sorry, Grady. She'll do about anything to avoid turning out the lights and being left in her room at bedtime. But I don't dare let her sleep with me and get that started."

"Don't be sorry. I'm not. She's a sweet kid."

But they both knew he didn't want to get attached to a kid. At least not one that didn't belong to him or his family.

"I've seen quite a bit of activity next door this

week." She moved to turn down Tessa's bed. Plumped a pillow. "So how are things going for the grand opening?"

She couldn't bring herself to ask him again if he'd looked at her presentation for his photography proposal, afraid it might not be what he'd hoped.

"Going good. Or as good as you can expect with it only a week away. The website is up and running and our team is processing orders."

"Wonderful."

Grady folded his arms. "So has there been any more talk of a petition to put us out of business?"

"Not to my knowledge."

"Gideon is keeping his distance?" Grady's eyes narrowed. "And his hands to himself?"

"He is." She didn't dare mention his rant at the last Co-op meeting.

"Here I am!" Dressed in her baby blue flannel and eyelet-trimmed nightwear, a beaming Tessa appeared in the doorway, arms outstretched like a miniature diva.

"Now, don't you look beautiful."

Tessa's smile broadened at Grady's praise. Then she stepped toward him and lifted her arm. "It's soft. See?"

His big hand brushed the delicate flannel sleeve. "Oh, wow, it is. I'm sure that keeps you warm, too."

"Uh-huh." She made a dive for her bed and

scrambled to get herself situated. "You can tuck me in, Grady."

His surprised gaze met Sunshine's, searching hers for direction, permission. When she nodded, he sat on the edge of the bed, looking huge next to the tiny girl. After a moment's hesitation, he tucked the covers around her, then leaned in to place a kiss on her forehead.

Not unexpectedly, Tessa cast an apprehensive look around the room. "I forgot to close the closet door. Mommy?"

"I'll do it." For whatever reason, Tessa couldn't sleep without the door firmly closed and her night-light on. "But there's no reason to be afraid."

Tessa's hand crept out from under the covers to reach for Grady's hand and his big one swallowed up her tiny one. "So you're scared of something, are you, Tessa? Something that might come out of your closet?"

She nodded solemnly.

"I understand what it's like to be afraid."

"You do?"

"Sure. I've been scared lots of times."

"Mommy says there's nothing to be afraid of." Tessa darted a doubtful look in her direction.

"You know," Grady continued, his voice sooth-ing, "there's nothing in that closet that can hurt you, don't you? Your mom wouldn't allow that and she wouldn't tell you there was nothing in there if there was. So you *know* there's nothing in there, right? But you *feel* scared anyway."

He ran a finger down the upper part of her flannel-clad arm. "And it's as if something has a hold of you right here, isn't it? Squeezing tight. And maybe your knees and your tummy hurt, too."

Tessa nodded again and he gently brushed her hair back from her face. "That's what I thought. But we both agree with your mom, right? Nothing is in the closet. So what I want you to do now is settle back on your pillow and close your eyes, okay?"

"'Kay."

But Tessa's eyes immediately flew open when he turned off the bedside lamp, leaving the room illuminated only by the light coming through the bedroom door.

He gave her hand a squeeze. "Eyes closed, remember?"

Nodding again, she obeyed.

And then, in a low, gentle voice, he began to pray.

"Father God, Tessa is scared. She knows there's nothing in her closet, but it *feels* as if there is. As You know, feelings are powerful things. You gave them to us so we can enjoy the good things You give us and so they can warn us when there's danger. There's no danger here, but Tessa's feelings are mixed up and telling her there is."

Tears pricked Sunshine's eyes. This dear man, going before his Heavenly Father on her daughter's behalf. Understanding a little girl's fears. Not telling her, as Sunshine had repeatedly done, to stop being afraid.

"So we're here tonight asking in the name of Your son, Jesus," he continued, "that You grab hold of the feelings that are telling Tessa fibs. That You will make the scary things she's seeing in her mind go away. That You will make the feelings that are squeezing her body let go. Thank You."

Eyes still closed, Tessa nodded her agreement and once more Grady brushed back her hair, his voice gentle but firm. "Now, when bad feelings try to sneak in and start to squeeze you, I want you to say in your mind or out loud, 'Jesus says, "Stop!"' Okay?"

"'Kay."

"Say it for me now."

"Jesus says, 'Stop!'" she murmured.

"Good girl. And after you say that, I want you to think about other things. Don't look at what those bad feelings want you to look at. Think about something happy. Like watching a butterfly flit from flower to flower. Or Goldie swimming in his bowl. Or your mommy holding your hand as you go for a walk. Can you do that for me right now?"

"'Kay."

Sunshine could see Tessa's features relaxing. Then, before long, amazingly, her breathing evened out and she was asleep.

Grady remained seated on the bed another five minutes, then carefully released Tessa's hand and stood. Wordlessly, they both left the room, Grady quietly closing the bedroom door behind them.

Chapter Fourteen

"You may have to do that with her nightly for a while." Grady moved to the apartment door, his own feelings of tenderness toward Sunshine's daughter leaving him unsettled and ill at ease in the presence of the little girl's mom. "You know, to remind her. To help her make calling on Jesus and thinking about something else a habit."

"I know we're not out of the woods on this, Grady, but I can't thank you enough." Her beautiful eyes reflected her gratefulness. "I'm ashamed, though, that I thought buying her a fish to keep her company would solve anything. That I never recognized that while she knows there's nothing in the closet, she *feels* as if there is."

"Don't beat yourself up. It's an easy enough mistake to make. It's helpful, though, to remember there's no wrong in a feeling itself. God gave them to us for a purpose. But we're not supposed to let them rule us—or control us—in a negative way."

Like running from Sunshine because she, like the woman who'd betrayed him, had a daughter? As Sunshine was doing because she didn't want to be abandoned again, hurt as her ex-husband had hurt her?

She stepped closer, a spark of affection clearly in her eyes. "How'd you get to be so smart about little girls and things that go bump in the night?"

He chuckled. "My baby sister. When Rio was about four, the son of one of our employees thought it would be funny to lock her in a utility closet. It was only about fifteen or twenty minutes, but after that she was skittish and had trouble sleeping without a night-light. After a few weeks of prayer and guidance, she worked through those fears."

Sunshine tilted her head. "You talked to her like you did Tessa tonight?"

"I can't take credit for that. But that's how my mother handled it, letting the rest of us know so we could reinforce it if we sensed Rio becoming anxious about anything."

"Your mother is a wise woman. But at least she could pinpoint the origin of your sister's fears. I think that would help. I'm at a loss."

"You said this began shortly before school started, so maybe it's related to that? Or something unrelated happened about that time that frightened her? Something's buried there. Maybe you can get her to talk about it now."

"She spent several days with her grandmother—my mom—the week before school started, but Mom didn't mention anything out of the ordinary when I picked Tessa up."

"Something has her rattled. Worrying. And it's manifesting in that closet."

What was he doing anyway, coming across like some renowned child psychologist to a woman who had five years of parenting under her belt while he had zilch?

Leaving the apartment door open so she'd hear Tessa if she cried out, she escorted him down the stairs, then led him through the dim gallery. He paused in front of the faintly illuminated watercolor of Tessa, more reluctant now than before to see it sold to a stranger.

"I'd like to buy this."

Sunshine's eyes rounded.

"Not right this minute. But hold it for me, okay?"

"I'm glad you like it." Her eyes met his in obvious puzzlement. "But I admit this surprises me."

"Why?"

"Because I know that you don't…"

"Don't want to get attached to someone else's kids?" He could give her a song and dance about giving it to someone as a gift, about donating it to an upcoming cancer fund-raiser for a silent auction. But the truth was, he wanted it hanging on his own wall. To be reminded of Tessa. And her mother.

Why did Sunshine have to look so beautiful tonight? Her features softly lit by a faint streetlight coming through the windows. His heart rate ramped up a notch.

"Maybe I was wrong about that." His words came softly. "You know, about the kid thing. There's more to the story and, maybe, I'm... wrong."

"More to what story?"

"The one I fed you last weekend. About the woman I broke up with who had a kid. Yeah, that left me feeling lousy. As if I'd let her daughter down. But even more..."

Sunshine's gaze never left his face.

"Even more, I got hurt because of her betrayal."

"She cheated on you?"

"Not with another man. But she used me—used my family—for financial gain."

Uneasiness flickered through Sunshine's eyes. Obviously he wasn't making himself clear. But how could he explain that mess?

"I won't bore you with the details, but Jasmine was a successful real estate agent who I'd met through an online photography club. Unbeknownst to me, she was working with clients and their big-time lawyers, wheeling and dealing to get some forest service property deeded to the county and zoned for commercial use."

He could tell by the anxious look on her face that Sunshine still wasn't following. "To make a long story short, she was throwing my name—and that of my family—around as backers of a plan to commercialize a property that we would never have agreed should be commercialized. We're an influential family in these parts, known for our interest in protecting the environment. She was taking advantage of that, playing the odds that no one would come to me for verification when she'd made certain it was widely known that we were seeing each other."

He drew a breath. "When the whole story came out, I learned it was no accident that she'd approached me online to begin with. She'd recognized my name and initiated a chat, which progressed from there. When all was said and done, I ended up feeling as if I'd let my whole family down. And her little girl got hurt, as well."

A stricken look flashed through Sunshine's eyes. "I'm sorry, Grady."

"Thanks. But when you're played for a fool, you can't help but wonder what part was your own fault. If maybe you deserved what you got because you were too stupid to see that you'd let your ego and your too-easily-led-astray heart rule your head."

"You didn't deserve that, Grady." Her words came softly. "You didn't."

"That's debatable. But the point is—" his gaze captured hers "—I've let that betrayal spook me. Let it run my life the past six years. Sort of like Tessa is allowing whatever she imagines is in that closet to control hers. And—as I suspect—how you're letting that ex-husband rule yours."

He heard a startled intake of breath and reached for her hand. "What I'm trying to say here, Sunshine, is—"

"That you," she offered hesitantly, "like the watercolor of Tessa?"

"I do. And I'd like to buy it. I'd also like…" Heart hammering, he tugged gently on her hand to move her closer, deeper into the shadows. "I'd very much like to kiss you."

Her eyes widened but, not hearing any objections, he leaned in and touched his lips to hers.

Lightly. Ever so lightly. Not daring to ask for more, but savoring the sweet sensation of her mouth on his. Sunshine. So like her namesake, a ray of warmth piercing the icy lock he'd secured on his heart, melting the frozen, off-limits regions he'd allowed to harden over time.

"Grady." Her lips moved softly against his as her hands slipped behind his neck. Drew him closer.

He'd dated a lot of women. Kissed his fair share. But never, ever, had he felt the way he was feeling now with Sunshine in his arms. This overwhelming desire to hold her, cherish her, protect her.

Forever.

Breathless, Sunshine drew back slightly. What was she doing? Not only allowing him to kiss her as she'd never before been kissed, but kissing him back with a zeal she wouldn't later be able to deny.

And she *had* to deny it. Had to convince him they'd gotten carried away in the moment. That it didn't mean anything. *Couldn't* mean anything. And yet... Again she pressed her lips to his warm, inviting mouth as his arms tightened around her.

He'd been betrayed.

Taken advantage of. Hurt deeply. Wasn't she equally as guilty as that other woman? Wasn't she trying to find a way to obtain compensation from the Hunters and, indirectly, from Grady, too?

She drew back again. Found her voice, although it came not much louder than a whisper. A breath. "Grady?"

"So sweet," he murmured as his lips brushed her cheek, obviously loath to let her go.

"Grady. We can't do this."

"Do what?" His gaze met hers, clouded with—what? Surely not love. No, not love.

"We can't—"

"Why not?"

He again touched his lips to hers but, with a willpower she didn't know she possessed, she firmly pressed her palms to his solid chest to gently push him away.

"This won't work, and we both know it."

His forehead puckered as her words sank in. "What are you talking about?"

"Us. You and me. I'm your mother's opponent for town council, or have you forgotten?"

"I can't say that was on my mind these past few minutes, no."

Offering a hard-to-resist smile, he tried to pull her closer, but she resisted, firmly removing his hands from her waist.

"Listen to me, Grady."

"Okay, okay. I'm listening."

He sounded somewhat cross. Which was fine. Maybe his irritation would provoke him into paying closer attention to what she was trying to say.

"Your mother and I are running against each other for a seat on the town council. How do you think your family will feel about me if we start seeing each other? It's a disaster waiting to happen."

Seeing the bewilderment in his eyes, warmth heated her cheeks, flaming hot as realization dawned. Grady hadn't said anything about seeing each other. About dating or love or anything of the kind. He'd only admitted to wanting to *kiss* her.

Which he'd done quite capably.

No wonder he looked confused. Almost dazed. She'd jumped to conclusions. Made a fool of herself.

"Never mind. I think it's time for you to go. I'll have Benton drop off the painting at Hunter's Hideaway. You can give me your credit card number whenever you have time." She grasped him by his rock-solid biceps, attempting to turn him toward the door. But he didn't budge.

"Wait." He held up his hand. "What's going on here, Sunshine? One moment you're kissing me as if there's no tomorrow and the next you're rambling about my family and disasters and trying to boot me out the door. What disasters are you talking about?"

"It's not important. I misspoke."

"What am I not understanding here?" He studied her for a long moment. "Maybe I'm dense, but I thought that not only is there a mutual attraction between us, but that there might be something more substantial."

"Substantial?"

"You know, important. Yeah, physical attraction, but the enjoying each other's company thing, the spiritual bond, too. Maybe something on down the road?" He looked at her doubtfully. "Did I make that up?"

It was tempting to let him think he had. But she couldn't do that to him, especially with relief flooding through her that she hadn't misunderstood the intention of the kiss.

"I do think there's a connection, Grady." As much as she didn't want there to be.

He grinned, and passed the back of his hand across his forehead. "Whew. I thought I was losing it for a minute there. So what's the deal with my family? The disaster stuff?"

"You don't think if we start seeing each other, your family might have a problem with it? And what about Gideon? He already has a target on my back for fraternizing with the enemy."

"The election will be over the second Tuesday in November. A little over three weeks. Then everything goes back to normal."

He took it for granted that Elaine would win. Which she undoubtedly would. "But don't you think—?"

His eyes smiling, he placed a gentle finger momentarily to her lips. "Jesus says, 'Stop.' Remember?"

She laughed, recalling his time with Tessa.

Of course, he was right. The election would be behind them before they knew it. But still…he didn't know about her original intention for coming to Hunter Ridge. What was the likelihood, though, that Tori would find the indisputable evidence she sought? Why not give it up? Let it go? See where things went with Grady?

A murmur of hope rose up in her spirit. Did God have a bigger plan in bringing her and Tessa to Hunter Ridge than simply chasing after some family legend?

"Hey," he whispered. "Tonight Rio and Luke both told me they like you. I think Grandma admires your spunk. Mom feels protective of you. Who cares what the rest of the family thinks?"

"So the rest of your family doesn't like me?"

"Sunshine?" He cocked a brow. "Remember, Jesus says—"

"Stop."

He reached for her hand. "We don't have to make a big deal out of this right now. Nobody has to know where we might be headed when we don't even know ourselves. A few more weeks won't matter. That will give us both time to get used to the idea. Get to know each other better."

He was making sense.

"And behind the scenes—" He wiggled his eyebrows and leaned in close. "We can sneak in a few more kisses."

Laughing, she pulled away. "I think it's time for you to go."

"Just when things are starting to get interesting?"

"For that exact reason."

He let out a disappointed groan. Was this a dream? Grady Hunter was attracted to her? Wanted to get to know her better?

He moved reluctantly toward the door. "Things are going to be crazy this week for both of us. The upcoming election. The grand opening. But I'd like to see you if we can work it out."

"I imagine we could arrange that."

"Good." A quick stolen kiss caught her by surprise.

Laughing at her expression, he slipped into the chilly night. She locked the door behind him and then, with an almost giddy laugh, she crossed the gallery to climb the stairs with a light step. But she'd barely reached the apartment door when the walking-on-air feeling evaporated.

Lord, what am I getting myself into?

Chapter Fifteen

"Your mother isn't up to doing the ribbon cutting at the grand opening tomorrow."

Grady's father rubbed the back of his neck in a weary gesture, then turned back to where he'd been hand sanding splintered wood on the seat of one of the inn's chairs late Friday afternoon. The glare of the work shed's overhead light revealed in his haggard expression the toll concern for his wife was taking.

"She'll rally." Grady adjusted a gooseneck lamp to provide better lighting. Mom had made a decent comeback so many times throughout the chemo treatments. She'd do it again.

"She should be taking better care of herself," Dad said gruffly. "Even with you filling in at the election events, she's overdoing it. Pushing herself."

"That's Mom for you."

"I want her to pull out of the race." Dad reached for a fresh piece of sandpaper. "But she won't hear of it."

"Although she hasn't been able to attend meetings recently, she loves being on the council and wants to fulfill her duties both this term and next."

Dad looked up at him, his gaze bleak. "At what price, son?"

A knot twisted in Grady's gut.

They hadn't dared let themselves consider that she might not come through this. That the chemo wouldn't work. That prayers might be unanswered.

"You know the doc is treating this more aggressively because Mom's mother died from it. There have been promising medical strides since then." The words of assurance were as much for himself as his father. "Mom's going to make it, Dad."

Dad nodded slowly. "She has to. I can't…I don't know how I'd live without your mother, Grady. I—"

His father's voice broke and Grady swiftly moved around the worktable for a quick embrace. "She's going to be fine, Dad."

"We'll be married forty years next June."

"And you'll be celebrating that anniversary together." Unbidden, Sunshine's smile surfaced in his mind. If things worked out as he was beginning to hope they would, could a fortieth anniversary be in their future, too? But loving had a price, as his father was experiencing. "So tell me, Dad, how'd you know Mom was 'the one'?"

Dad returned to his sanding, a slow smile surfacing. "I couldn't stop thinking about her. Couldn't imagine my life without her."

Was that how he was beginning to feel about Sunshine? He sure wasn't getting much sleep at night. All the praying. Wondering how she really felt about him. Remembering every word she said, how the corners of her mouth lifted in a smile, how good that kiss had been.

Dad looked up, studying Grady. "Was that a get-the-old-man's-gloomy-thoughts-diverted question? Or do you have your eye on some young lady? Like that Sunshine gal you spent considerable time talking to on the patio the other night?"

"I—" He wasn't ready to talk about how he felt about Sunshine. He was thinking about her. Spending time with her. But after Jasmine's betrayal, it was like walking on quicksand as he tried to find his footing.

"I know you got handed a raw deal with that other woman a few years back. Took it hard."

"It's not something I'd care to relive." Being manipulated for selfish purposes—left feeling like a fool for thinking she cared for him as much as he did her—wasn't something you easily got over. But Sunshine made him want to try.

"Loving takes courage, son. Risk. There are no guarantees. But don't let the past dictate your future."

The fact that he'd taken her and Tessa to a fun-filled lunch in Canyon Springs on Sunday, talked to her on the phone every night this week and couldn't wait to see her after the grand opening tomorrow had to mean *something*, didn't it?

"How would you feel, Dad, if I did start seeing Sunshine Carston?" There, he'd said it out loud. "I mean, she's Mom's rival and is a vocal backer of the artists in this town, too. There's no getting around either of those facts."

Dad nodded knowingly. "Your mother said she thought there might be something developing there between you two."

"So do either of you have a problem with that?"

He was taking a risk asking a point-blank question. What if Dad said he and Mom didn't like her, that he was making a big mistake? Would that make a difference in his feelings about her?

Dad set aside the sandpaper. "You may not know this, son, but your mother's folks didn't think much of me at first."

"You're kidding." He never would have guessed. But they'd lived in Scottsdale, and Grandma had died when Grady was just a boy, so he wouldn't have been the most perceptive of observers. "Why not?"

"Your mom and I were teenagers when we met, heading into our senior year of high school. Her father had come to the Hideaway to hunt and brought his wife and kids along." Dad shook his head at the memory, a soft smile playing on his lips. "Believe me, I found lots of reasons to hang out wherever your mother might be, which didn't set well with her parents. They were well-to-do and she was college bound. Ivy League. Some punk kid whose folks ran a hunting lodge didn't fit the picture."

"But Mom married you anyway."

"She did. We both knew our own minds. Knew deep down that God had a hand in it. But her folks made the road rocky at first." Dad shifted his weight and looked Grady in the eye. "I guess what I'm trying to say is that your mother and I, we're good with whatever decisions you make as long as you're sure God has a hand in them."

Did God have a hand in his relationship with Sunshine?

It felt right, despite the obvious barriers. But it had felt right with Jasmine, too, hadn't it? No, not like it did now with Sunshine. Sure, he'd been drawn to Jasmine like a moth to a flickering flame. But looking back, it was more of an ego thing. She was smart, beautiful—and he liked how it felt to be seen with her as much as anything. He'd been bowled over by the fact she was into him, a guy from a small town in what most might consider the middle of nowhere.

But a more-than-friends relationship with a spiritual foundation such as the one that was blossoming between him and Sunshine? No, none of that with Jasmine.

"Guess I've given you food for thought, huh?" Dad grinned.

Grady gave him a hesitant smile. "I can't be sure since this is barely getting off the ground. But there's something more there, more solid than what I had with Jasmine."

"Good to hear it."

"This could get sticky, though, you know? Sunshine representing the artists' community and going up against Mom in the election."

"You can't decide who's going to get your vote?" Dad's teasing tone prodded.

Which candidate is it you're campaigning for?

Irvin's question echoed uncomfortably in his head. Dad might find it funny, but it was no laughing matter.

"It's nippy out there, isn't it?" Sunshine shivered as Grady helped her out of his SUV Saturday night, then escorted her up the cabin steps to usher her inside. The scent of baking potatoes welcomed her, triggering a homey whisper of belonging that touched deep inside. Not only of belonging at his place but belonging anywhere he happened to be.

She smiled up at Grady as he assisted in removing her coat, treasuring that quiet, inner assurance. But was she letting her hopes get ahead of her? Despite what Grady had said earlier, she couldn't shake concerns about how she'd be accepted by his family. Their backgrounds were vastly different. She very much wanted to believe that wouldn't matter. But her mother had once alluded to the fact that Sunshine's father's grandfather had pressured him not to marry her, a girl from the other side of the tracks, and instead to wed a woman who fulfilled family expectations. Or was there no substance to that at all, but what Mom chose to believe, unable to face the truth that the man who'd fathered her child didn't love her enough to marry her?

Grady hung her coat on a peg. "I'm glad Tori's back so we could get together tonight. I've missed seeing you. A glimpse or two of you at today's grand opening just didn't do it."

"Unfortunately, she's back because her fiancé broke up with her." Sunshine was both relieved and angered by that turn of events. And no doubt tonight's uncertainty about Grady had been influenced by her friend's emotional upheaval.

"I'm sorry things didn't work out. She's a nice gal." Grady led the way to the dining table, where he had his laptop set up for a final review of his presentation. He'd told her earlier that he liked what she'd developed, so this meeting was probably an excuse to spend time together. Which was fine with her. She'd missed seeing him this week, too, even though she'd delighted in his phone calls.

Late each evening, Tessa having been sound asleep for hours, those moments of intimate conversation filled her with a happiness she'd never before imagined. They'd talked well into the wee hours of the morning, both eagerly sharing hopes and dreams and spiritual journeys. Each generously offering the other a glimpse of who they were as children, teens, young adults. So many questions and a mutual willingness to confide answers drew them closer than she would have expected in such a short time. When had she ever felt so comfortable with a man? So safe in opening her heart without fear of rejection? It was crazy. They'd just met. But in many ways it seemed as if they'd known each other forever.

"Here you go." Grady set a cup of fragrant tea on the table next to her. "This should get you warmed up, and I've lit logs in the fireplace, too. Then as soon as we finish here—I don't think it will take long—I'll throw the steaks on the grill and we'll dine like kings."

"You should have let me bring something. I could have made dessert."

"I have that covered."

"Wow. I feel spoiled."

"You deserve to be spoiled." He settled down next to her and adjusted the laptop screen. "You did a fabulous job on the presentation, putting my data into an eye-catching design."

She took a sip of tea. "You did the hard work. All the research. I got to do the fun stuff. Making it pretty."

"It was your marketing savvy that filtered the research down to something concise and comprehensible." He eyed her hopefully. "I'm thinking it might make sense to have you there when I make the presentation. Not only for moral support, but to field questions. I'll get hammered by Luke and Uncle Doug, and you know this stuff as well as I do now."

"You'll do fine without me there. This is *your* dream, your moment to shine."

"You're my dream, too." His words caught her by surprise as his gaze, smoldering with mischief, drifted to her mouth.

"Now, now, Mr. Hunter." Flustered, she reached over to tap the page-down key, keeping her eyes trained on the next slide. "Let's not mix business with pleasure."

"Where's the fun in that?" He leaned in a tad closer.

A ripple of anticipation coursed through her,

but she kept her attention glued to the laptop. "Behave yourself now."

He laughed, then settled back in his chair. "Okay, I can take a hint. Let's take a look at this presentation of yours."

She pressed Page Down again with more force than necessary. How absurd to feel disappointed that he didn't persist. That was what she wanted, wasn't it? For their relationship to progress slowly? She was older now, wiser than she'd been when Jerrel had come into her life. With a daughter now to consider, she didn't dare make any mistakes this time.

Not when she might very possibly be falling in love with Grady Hunter.

As they washed up the dishes, Grady couldn't help but occasionally sneak a peek at Sunshine. And each time he did, his heart did a funny little skip he wasn't accustomed to. While he washed and she dried, there were plenty of opportunities for his fingers to brush hers. Or to lean in close to point out which cabinet or drawer an item she'd dried called home. He couldn't remember when he'd enjoyed cleanup chores so much. Maybe he needed to rethink installing a dishwasher his mom seemed to think he should get.

"That was a wonderful meal, Grady." Sunshine looped the damp towel through the handle of the refrigerator. "A perfect ending to your grand-opening day. Were you pleased with the attendance?"

He leaned against the counter. "Actually, I was surprised at the great turnout considering that the largest volume of sales is expected to come from online orders. I guess those merchandise drawings and giveaways for adults and the balloons for the kids did the trick."

"Tessa made me go back three times so she could have one of each color. Red, white and blue."

"Is she sleeping better?" He motioned for Sunshine to precede him into the living room, where they settled in. Her on the sofa, him in his trusty recliner and the fire in the fireplace snapping and crackling and keeping the space comfy.

"It's a little early to tell, but she doesn't seem quite so anxious at bedtime. Sometimes after we've said our prayers and I've left the room, though, I can hear her saying 'Jesus says, "Stop."'"

He couldn't suppress a smile, picturing Tessa, eyes closed and blankets snuggled around her as she told the antagonistic feelings who was boss. "Has she given you any hints as to how this all got started?"

Sunshine shook her head. "None. I'm hesitant to ask if she's not ready to talk about it."

"Give her time."

They were silent for several minutes, both gazing into the flames licking at the logs in the fireplace. He sneaked a look at Sunshine, her gaze thoughtful and...troubled?

Concerned about Tessa?

As if sensing his attention had focused on her, she looked up. "What?"

"Is something besides Tessa weighing on your mind?" Gideon's face flashed into his thoughts. "That Edlow guy isn't causing problems, is he?"

"No more than usual."

"So what's up?"

She brushed the flat of her hand along the sofa's fabric. "This has been such a lovely evening, I hate to spoil it."

A muscle tightened in his chest. Had something he'd shared tonight or during one of those late-night phone calls disturbed her? They'd both shared openly about their pasts, their dreams of the future. He'd never before spoken so freely, so vulnerably to a woman, though. Maybe he'd gone too far.

He let out a slow breath. "There's nothing you can't share with me, Sunshine."

Even if she had something to say that he didn't want to hear.

"I still have some reservations."

"About us?"

She nodded. "I know you said you don't think

my running for the town council against your mother is anything to worry about. That it will all be over in a couple of weeks and life will go on."

"But you don't agree?"

"It's not that I don't *want* to agree. It's just that I'm a realist. At least most of the time anyway." She stood and moved to the fireplace, her hands outstretched to the warmth, the dancing flames highlighting her delicate features—and the apprehensive look in her eyes.

He eased himself out of the recliner and joined her, his voice reassuring. "So talk to me."

She turned, tears forming in her eyes. What had he done to make her cry? He reached for her hand. "Did I do something wrong? Say something that hurt you?"

Wiping at the tears with her free hand, she shook her head. "No, not at all."

"What, then?"

"I feel stupid talking about this." She hesitated, composing herself. "What if your parents don't want us to get involved? What if they think I'm not good enough for you?"

"Why would they think that?" He released her hand to cup her face in both of his. "My dad's already told me that he and Mom are good with whatever decisions I make in my life as long as I make sure God's a part of it. And that conversation took place only a few days ago—and in reference to you."

"You talked to them about me?"

"To Dad. So stop with the worrying."

She blinked back tears. "But...he doesn't know that my father never married my mother. I'm illegitimate. Not exactly a prize for you to be carting home to the family."

"Hey, hey." He gently brushed away a tear. "Believe me, nobody's going to hold that against you. That wasn't any of your doing."

"But—"

"God's going to lead us. He'll let us know if this doesn't have His blessing. Wasn't it you who told me that it's His job to close doors? Not mine?"

"Did I say that?"

"I believe so. Therefore, repeat after me. Jesus says...?" He raised a questioning brow.

"Stop," she finished with a giggle, and his heart soared at the sound of it.

Then, before she could avert his intentions, he did what he'd been dying to do all evening.

Kissed her.

Chapter Sixteen

Tori nodded to the envelope Sunshine clenched in her hand. "What are you going to do?"

Sunshine extracted the documents that had arrived in yesterday's mail, still trying to digest what she'd read. "I'm not sure."

"That shows your great-great-grandfather paid the taxes on the property they now call Hunter's Hideaway. I matched the description to land records. The following year Harrison Hunter paid taxes on it. Now I'm searching for a record of sale from your ancestor to Hunter, in case it was a legitimate transfer from one to the other."

"But it could be," Sunshine said softly, "that the Hunters found a way to cheat Walter Royce of his land. Just like Grandma's story."

Tori looked torn, as if unwilling to come to that conclusion. She'd been against this search, this hope that Sunshine had clung to of holding modern-day Hunters accountable. "Documentation can tell half-truths. I'll need to research further, but it looks as if that's a possibility."

"Why didn't he fight it?" Sunshine gave the papers a shake. "Seek legal help? I know Arizona was still a territory, oftentimes lawless, but land grabbers couldn't have been well thought of."

"Didn't you notice the date on the death certificate tucked in there? Not long after he paid the taxes, Walter apparently left this area. The following year he died of pneumonia. That newspaper notice implies he died deep in debt."

Sunshine eased down onto the sofa, overwhelmed by a sudden sadness. "He died and left his family impoverished."

Her family.

A poverty, in fact, that had taken generations to climb their way out of. She clenched her hands in her lap. How different life might have been for her family if Hunter's Hideaway had remained in their possession. If Duke Hunter had indeed paid a fair price for the land that would become Hunter's Hideaway, how could barely a year later her ancestor have died in debt?

"So what are you going to do?" Tori repeated, her tone unsure. "Now that you may possibly have the evidence you want."

"I don't know, Tori. I guess I didn't deep down believe Grandma's story. Didn't think I'd find proof of it anyway." Nor had she foreseen feelings for a man like Grady Hunter would stand in her way if she did find it.

But the dream of righting a wrong was a part of her before she'd met Grady. Before she'd fallen in love with him. Could she march up to the Hunters now and present evidence of their ancestor's duplicity?

A muscle tightened in her stomach. *Betrayal.* That was how Grady would see it. Another betrayal by a woman he cared for. As much as she and Tessa needed a solid financial foundation—their ancient SUV had finally bit the dust yesterday and she had no idea where the next medical-insurance payment would come from— could she do that to him?

And yet…what if things didn't work out between them? The attraction was undoubtedly there. He was a good, godly man, but had she lowered her guard too quickly to dream of what it might be like to share her life with him? To be his wife. To give her daughter a father.

Was that hope realistic? She hadn't dated much since Tessa's father had walked out of her life. A few nice guys had come and gone, but things had never worked out. What if things went no further with Grady than dating relationships had in the past?

No declaration of love. No ring. No wedding.

She glanced uncertainly at the papers in her hand. Were they a God-provided insurance of sorts? If things didn't work out with Grady, could she garner the courage to approach his family? See if they would be willing, out of the goodness of their hearts…?

No. Even if they parted ways, she could never bring herself to hurt Grady like that.

"What am I going to do, Tori?" She gave her friend a determined smile. "Nothing."

Then she crumpled the papers in her hand.

"I've got a bad feeling about this. No offense intended, Grady, but I'm afraid your mother will pull out of the race at the last minute and leave us sitting high and dry." Thin-lipped, Arlen Gifford swallowed down the remainder of his coffee and set his mug firmly on their back corner table at the Log Cabin Café Thursday evening, his expression undeniably gloomy.

Grady cut a look at his uncle Doug, who appeared lost in thought across the table from him. This wasn't the first time he'd heard a similar concern voiced recently and it wasn't surprising to hear it again, even at this impromptu gathering he'd been pulled into by some of Mom's more ardent supporters.

"You can't blame her, Giff, if that's the way it goes." Bo Briggs cut Grady a sympathetic look from under his bushy gray eyebrows. "She looks more exhausted each time I see her."

"She's left us with no options, though." Arlen's tone remained petulant. "If she'd have pulled out a month ago, we could have put someone else forward as a write-in candidate. Now we've missed the registration deadline."

"Don't blame her." Patti Ventura narrowed her black-brown eyes in reprimand. "She'd barely started treatments and couldn't have known how ill they'd make her."

"I'm not blamin', I'm just sayin'."

Bo looked expectantly at Uncle Doug, then Grady. "Are either of you getting a feel for Elaine's plans?"

"I haven't heard one way or another." Grady could honestly voice that. Dad wanted Mom to put her health first. That wasn't for him to share with others, though, not even supporters. Mom and Dad would together make the final decision but, knowing Dad, he wouldn't point-blank tell her what to do.

Uncle Doug folded his arms on the table in front of him. "Elaine won't give up unless she has no choice. I guarantee you that."

Arlen didn't look satisfied with either answer. "I wish we had options, you know? Either Elaine comes through for us, or we're saddled with four years of Irvin or that artist lady."

Dare Grady put in a good word for Sunshine? He cleared his throat to speak, but Bo launched in first.

"Hopefully we can convince her not to forfeit her all-but-guaranteed victory by pulling out of the election."

"But her health, Bo," Patti reminded. "We don't want her taking risks she shouldn't, no matter how much we want her in office."

Uncle Doug rapped his knuckles on the oak table, drawing their attention. Then he glanced almost furtively around the café and leaned in, his voice low. "What if we can get her to hang in there for the election, then resign from office at the opening council session in January?"

He arched a brow, eyes gleaming, and Grady almost groaned out loud. Leave it to Uncle Doug to have a plan. Grandma Jo said that ever since Aunt Char had divorced him, he was always on the alert to avoid being caught off guard again.

"A belated resignation," he continued, not meeting Grady's pointed gaze, "relieves her of council responsibilities to take care of her health, and the city is forced into a special election to replace her."

With a satisfied smile, he settled back into his chair. The others nodded thoughtfully, taking in his idea. Mulling it over.

Would Mom agree to a scheme like that? To deliberately not withdraw prior to the election, knowing full well she intended to resign? It wasn't illegal by any means, but somehow the proposal smacked of not quite right.

"Council rules don't allow for a permanent appointment in her stead," Arlen inserted, "nor would a runner-up from the November election automatically slide into her empty spot. So you're right, there'd have to be a special election."

"Which means," Bo added, "we'd need a candidate the town would rally around. Someone sure to trounce Irvin and that Carston woman if they'd throw their hats into the ring again."

The gazes of Mom's four supporters slid to Grady.

He held up his hands. "Hold on now. Don't look at me."

"You're a natural," Patti encouraged. "You've filled in admirably for your mother, thoroughly know her platform and people are familiar with your face now that you're not buried behind the scenes at the Hideaway. Voters will assume you'll represent them well, just as your mother would."

He chuckled uncomfortably. "I appreciate your faith in me, but—"

"There's been a Hunter on the town council as long as there has been a town council," Bo reminded. "How can you refuse to accept your responsibility to the community?"

His responsibility? Since when?

Uncle Doug rose to his feet and leveled a look down at him. "Hunters have always stepped up to the plate, Grady. Done their civic duty."

Uncle Doug had served several terms himself, but Grady wasn't into politics, wasn't interested in trying to keep an entire town pleased with him. Keeping the Hunter clan happy through the years had been hard enough.

He offered a placating smile. "I think there's plenty of family to keep the tradition going. I'm sure you could talk any one of the others into it."

Patti frowned. "But we want you in that council seat, Grady."

"Thanks, but in all honesty, I don't have time to serve on the town council."

Even with Luke assuming more responsibility, his hands were full. The new business demanded time and attention. Then there was his long-dreamed-of plan to add a wildlife-photography element to the Hideaway's venue. He didn't want to shortchange that, to risk it failing. And what about Sunshine? Would she tackle the special election, too, and he'd find himself running against her?

"We believe you can handle it, boy." Uncle Doug moved to confidently clap him on the shoulder, his voice low but uncompromising. "We want you in that special election—in the town council seat—and we won't take no for an answer. You owe it to your family and to this town."

"Sunshine?"

Grady.

She frantically closed the lid on her laptop and stuffed the folder of telltale documentation underneath it. When Tori had left to take Tessa to the middle-school musical Saturday evening, Sunshine hadn't been able to resist opening her computer on the dining table and taking another look at the photos of Walter and Flora and the burgeoning folder of documentation Tori had accumulated.

Roots. For the first time in her life, she truly had roots. Right here in Hunter Ridge.

But Candy, working late downstairs to set up a special project, had obviously okayed Grady ascending the stairs, not bothering to give her a heads-up. With a quick breath to still her racing heart, she smoothed her skirt, then opened the door to a smiling Grady, who held out a bouquet of cream and bronze chrysanthemums.

"Thank you! I love the autumn colors." She reached for them, then self-consciously spun toward the kitchen to look for a vase. She'd never received flowers from a man before.

"Tessa here?" He glanced around the apartment,

then held up a decorative gift bag. "I brought her something, too."

A contented warmth hugged Sunshine. "She'll be back in another hour. Tori was dying to see a musical she'd helped make the costumes for and borrowed Tessa for the evening."

He set the bag on the counter and watched as she arranged the flowers. "You have a knack for that."

She viewed it from all angles, then carried it to the coffee table in the living room. "So what brings you here bearing gifts tonight?"

"I hadn't seen you in a few days. Although we've talked on the phone, it seemed like a good idea to stop in and make sure you weren't a figment of my imagination." He caught her hand and tugged her toward him, his eyes dancing.

A man who obviously had more kissing on his mind.

She cast him a flirtatious smile. That was all the encouragement he needed, for he immediately stepped in to gently raise her chin with his fingertips and graze his lips across hers. A happy sigh escaped her lips, but before she could slip her arms around his neck he stepped back with a satisfied smile.

"Nope, not a figment. But now that we have that issue resolved, I have something I want to show you." He glanced toward the dining table. "Do you mind if I borrow your laptop?"

Her laptop? With Tori's research folder wedged beneath it and the photo of her and Grady's great-great-grandparents set as the desktop image.

She could explain the photo, though, couldn't she?

"Help yourself." She followed him to the table, where she picked up the laptop and nudged the folder out from under it. Then she lifted the cover and typed in her password. "There you go."

He seated himself, then looked at her with a quizzical smile. "What do you know? My great-great-grands front and center. You're as bad as my mom about old photos."

"I am. And speaking of your mother, how is she doing?"

His forehead creased as he reached for the mouse, then typed something into the web browser. "Not so good today."

"I'm sorry to hear that." She'd heard speculation around town, people wondering if Elaine would be up to fulfilling her current town council obligations, let alone a future commitment. "Do you think she'll take on another four years?"

Sunshine recoiled from her own words. Did that sound as though she was fishing to find out if she'd have smooth sailing herself with only Irvin to worry about?

"I honestly don't know."

She wanted to ask how his mother was *really* doing and how the family was faring in the wake of her diagnosis. But although her concern for Elaine was genuine, any interest felt two-faced. Intrusive.

"Okay, take a look at this." He turned the laptop so she could see the screen.

A background of subtle autumn colors set the tone, inviting the eye to explore, to take in the striking kaleidoscope of wildlife photographs. When she saw Grady's name in a bold, distinctive font, she gasped. "You have a website?"

"You like it?"

"Oh, I love it." She leaned in closer, acutely aware of his proximity. "You didn't tell me you were doing this."

"I wanted it to be a surprise." He slipped his arm around her waist. "See what an inspiration you are?"

"Your photos are for sale?"

"They are. Or at least they will be when the website goes live." He clicked on one of the links and guided her through an impressive gallery of elk shots, leaving the other links to be explored. "I've been working with the guy who did the website for the wild game supply store. He's an outdoorsman himself and I think it shows in his design."

"Oh, it does." She lightly touched Grady's shoulder. "I'm so excited that you're doing this."

"I thought you'd be pleased."

"This is why you didn't have as much time as you'd hoped to review what I'd put together for your photography proposal, isn't it?"

"Guilty as charged."

"How's it feel to step out of your comfort zone?" She was proud of him.

He squinted one eye. "Scary?"

Laughing, she leaned in for a hug but, when she straightened, her elbow somehow brushed the folder on the table, pushing it over the edge and strewing its contents onto Grady's lap and the floor.

Heart racing, she knelt to gather the loose papers. But when she stood, breathless, a frowning Grady was examining one of the documents that she'd knocked into his lap. A slightly crumpled one that she'd earlier carefully smoothed out.

Then he looked up at her, confusion in his eyes.

Chapter Seventeen

Grady's stomach lurched as he again stared down at the handwritten name on the photocopied receipt. *Walter Royce.* The ungrateful scoundrel who'd taken advantage of Duke Hunter's generosity. "Where'd you get this?"

"I—" Sunshine's gaze locked with his, her eyes wide.

"Did you get interested in the people in the photograph or something?" He motioned to the laptop. "You do know, don't you, that the guy listed on this receipt is one of the men in the picture?"

She nodded.

He looked down at the wrinkled photocopy again. A tax receipt for land right here in this county. But Walter Royce, to his knowledge, had never owned land around here. Maybe not anywhere. So was this—? It had to be. The infamous receipt for taxes Royce had been sent to pay on behalf of Duke Hunter, who'd been too ill to make the journey himself. A receipt that was written out to the name of Walter Royce.

"Where'd you get this?"

"Tori's been helping me research." She glanced at the folder in her hands.

His gaze held hers, curious. "What were you researching?"

"My great-great-grandparents."

That didn't make sense. She wasn't from around here. "What did your great-greats have to do with Walter Royce? No, wait. Don't tell me. He cheated them, too?"

"What do you mean?"

He flicked the paper with the back of his hand. "This character. He almost cost my great-great-grandparents their land. Fraudulently took out a loan on it, then defaulted." A document like the one he held in his hands would no doubt have been the evidence of ownership Royce had used to acquire that private loan and purchase a business in a neighboring county. "Did he do your family dirty, too?"

A troubled look wavered in her eyes.

"Sunshine?"

"No, he didn't cheat my family." She swallowed, her eyes riveted on his. "He was—is, actually—family."

"What do you mean?"

"Walter and Flora Royce," she said, her grip tightening on the folder in her hands, "are my great-great-grandparents."

It was his turn to stare. "Are you kidding me?"

She shook her head.

"I didn't think you were from around here. Why didn't you say something?"

For a fleeting moment he thought she might not answer. Or might bolt. But she stood her ground.

"I didn't have proof of ties to Hunter Ridge, not until you showed me that photograph and told me the names of the people in the picture so I could backtrack to them." The expression in her eyes remained as cautious as the delivery of her words. "I merely had a story to go on that my grandmother shared with me. A story handed down to her about her grandparents who'd lived in an area referred to as the ridge of the hunter."

He'd heard that phrase before. The founders of the town had adapted it when they'd named the fledgling community of Hunter Ridge in the 1920s.

He sat back in his chair. "This blows me away."

In fact, he couldn't get his head around it. The woman he was falling in love with was the great-great-granddaughter of someone who'd almost cost the Hunters their property? Did God have a sense of humor or what?

"Flora," he said softly, studying her. "She was

White Mountain Apache. Or at least that's what I was told growing up. That's why you bear traces of Native American ancestry?"

"Considerably diluted, but yes."

"And why you volunteer at that church on the rez? Why Native images play a role in your art?"

She nodded as she placed the folder on the table. "I'm proud of that lineage and want Tessa to be proud of it, too. Working at the church alongside others who share that blood bond gives me a sense of belonging. A sense of my own history, which I knew little of until recently."

"Wow." He shook his head. "I have to admit, this comes as a shock. Not your Apache connection, but your connection to Walter Royce. He's not well thought of in the annals of my own family history."

Her chin lifted. "Wrongly so."

"Why do you say that?"

"You're holding the evidence in your hand." Her words came softly, the look in her eyes a disquieting mix of apology and determination. "It's a tax receipt for the land on which Hunter's Hideaway now stands. Walter Royce owned it, but somehow Duke Hunter managed to disenfranchise Walter and Flora."

That was nuts. She'd gotten the story wrong. "You think old Duke cheated the Royces out of *their* land?"

"My grandmother told me about it when I was growing up, how they'd been swindled. I didn't know what to believe." Her gaze flickered uneasily. "Not until I came to Hunter Ridge to—"

"To what?" He gave a half laugh, trying to make sense of this. "Prove my family cheated your family out of the Hideaway?"

Surely he was misunderstanding. She'd been asked to manage the Artists' Cooperative, right? That was what had brought her here. Brought her into his life. But she didn't laugh, and something deep in his gut twisted at the guilt stamped on her pretty face.

"That's why you came here?" he said softly, an uncomfortable pressure weighing in his chest. "To prove the Hideaway belongs to *your* family?"

Under her startled gaze, he reached for the paper-stuffed folder. Flipped through its contents. Birth certificates. Census and land records. Correspondence. He looked up in disbelief. "Please tell me this isn't what it looks like."

She stood rigidly at his side, her gaze pleading, but she didn't respond.

"All this is an attempt to prove my family stole land from your family?" Having the story wrong didn't excuse the fact that she'd come to Hunter Ridge with an agenda to—what? Hold his family legally liable? To try to wrest the Hideaway from them in court like Aunt Char had attempted when she'd divorced Uncle Doug? To use him and his vulnerable heart to obtain evidence she intended to bring before a judge?

He pushed back in the chair and stood, gripping the folder. Then tossed the paperwork to the table. Hadn't she once admitted that with a child to support, the almighty dollar won out every time? He had to get out of here.

She placed a restraining hand on his arm, finally finding her voice. "Grady, please, I can explain."

"I seriously doubt it." He looked at her, as if into the face of a stranger.

Her grip tightened. "You have to listen to me."

"You're telling me you didn't come to Hunter Ridge with the express purpose of claiming your fair share of the Hideaway?"

"I didn't. Not like that. Yes, I wanted to find out the truth of the family legend, had even hoped that perhaps—"

"Your family never owned a single inch of Hunter property. I can assure you of that."

"But the tax receipt shows—"

"Duke Hunter was seriously ill, Sunshine. He sent a *trusted friend* to pay his taxes. A friend who used that receipt to fraudulently acquire a loan and buy a business. A business that subsequently failed, resulting in a default that brought the authorities and an irate lender to Duke Hunter's doorstep in an attempted foreclosure."

"I don't—"

"Believe it, Sunshine. When your friend continues her research, she's bound to find records documenting the whole thing. Of course, by the time the mess was sorted out, Walter Royce had conveniently gotten himself put six feet under."

She gasped at his insensitive remark, but he continued, "You know what's most sad about that? Duke had plans to deed over to his friend the portion of his property that he'd allowed him and his wife to settle on."

He moved toward the door.

"Grady. Please. You have to believe me when I say I would never have used any of this documentation against your family, even if it was true."

"Never crossed your mind, did it?" His voice sounded harsh in his own ears, but from the look on her face and the absence of a denial, he had no regrets. He reached for the doorknob. "That's what I thought."

"Grady, please. This isn't how it looks. I would never intentionally hurt you or your family. Never try to take Hunter's Hideaway from you. You have no idea how much I—"

"Love me?" He quirked a smile. "Nice try, Sunshine, but that's a bit more than I can swallow right now."

* * *

"Grady," she whispered as the door closed behind him with a finality that shattered her heart. Rooted to the floor, an icy cold enveloped her, leaving her shaking.

Once she'd decided not to pursue that avenue with the Hunters, why hadn't she destroyed those papers? Hadn't Tori said it would take more research to confirm what the papers appeared to reveal? She'd told Tori not to do more research. She was done. So why had she given in to looking through the information one last time—and this night of all nights?

If what Grady said was true, that he could prove her great-great-grandfather had never owned so much as a thimbleful of Hunter's Hideaway, that made this even worse.

Sunshine woodenly moved to the table and looked down at her laptop, at the solemn faces on the desktop screen of her great-great-grand-parents—and Grady's. Could it be true that Walter—a trusted friend, Grady had called him—had falsely used the Hunter property to acquire a loan? Why would he do that? And how had the story Grandma told gotten so twisted over time?

How long she stood staring down at the vintage photo, she had no idea. A few minutes? Thirty? An hour? But abruptly she was brought back to the present by the sound of feet running up the stairs.

"We're home!" Tessa sounded elated as she burst into the room, but a past-her-bedtime weariness reflected in her eyes. Tori's, too, for that matter, although it wasn't late.

"Let's get you ready for bed and you can tell me all about it."

"What's this?" Tessa, peeling out of her coat, had spotted the brightly colored gift bag on the kitchen counter.

Sunshine handed it to her. "Grady brought you something."

"I missed him?" Tessa's face puckered with disappointment.

"Grady was here, hmm?" Tori gave her a teasing look. "While the kitties are away, the mice—"

"Not exactly."

Her friend's gaze sharpened. "What's up?"

"Later."

"Look, Mommy!" Tessa lifted a stuffed goldfish from the bag, then clasped it to her chest in a hug. "Just like Goldie!"

Still numb, Sunshine knelt to take a closer look at the soft, brightly colored animal. "How cute."

"Grady thinks I'm a good girl, Mommy. Can we call him so Goldie and I can tell him thank-you?"

"Of course he thinks you're a good girl, but it's

getting late." She exchanged a glance with Tori. "Let's save that for tomorrow, okay?"

"'Kay." Tessa gave her a hug, then dashed for her bedroom, the stuffed fish tight in her arms.

"That was nice of him," Tori ventured, then tilted her head toward the flowers on the coffee table. "From him, too?"

Sunshine nodded.

"But I get the impression something's not right."

Sunshine drew in a breath and let it out slowly. Could she talk about this right now? Even with Tori? "I guess you'd say we broke up."

Tori's eyes widened. "What happened?"

"He found the documentation of our research." She motioned to the kitchen table. "So he knows everything. About why I came to Hunter Ridge, I mean."

"Oh, Sunshine." Her friend stepped forward to place a comforting hand on her arm. "After you decided to leave the past in the past?"

Sunshine nodded again. "Doesn't hardly seem fair, does it? But he reacted as I thought he might—seeing it as a betrayal. That I was attempting to use him for financial gain like a former girlfriend had."

"You told him, though, didn't you, that you weren't going to use the documentation against his family?"

"I did. But the original intent was there. It

couldn't be denied." Sunshine wandered into the living room to look down at the festive flowers. Had it been such a short time ago that Grady had swept her into his arms and playfully kissed her?

"You know what the worst part is?" She cast a bleak look in Tori's direction. "The story that's been passed down in his family is much different than the one in mine. He maintains it was the Hunters who'd been done wrong, not the Royces. That my great-great-grandfather had deliberately made poor decisions that had almost cost them their land. He says he can prove it."

"I did say that additional research was needed." Sadness filled Tori's eyes. "But I'm so sorry. I feel as if this is partly my fault."

"It's not. Don't think that. You were researching what I asked you to research. This was my own doing." All her own doing. "I should have shredded every scrap of paper the minute I decided my relationship with Grady was more important than righting a past wrong."

"You're in love with him?"

"It sure feels like it."

"Mommy! I'm in my jammies!"

"Coming, sweetheart." The ache in Sunshine's chest deepened. Not only had her foolishness driven Grady away, broken her own heart and his, but Tessa would never have the father she deserved and so desperately needed.

"I'll be praying," Tori whispered as Sunshine moved in the direction of Tessa's bedroom. "Praying that once he thinks over what you said, that he'll recognize you hadn't set out to use him."

Inside the cozy bedroom, Tessa cuddled under the flannel sheets, the plush fish secure in her arms.

"Goldie is happy to have a new friend." She lifted one of the toy's soft fins to wave at the fishbowl sitting on the dresser. Then giggled. "I wish Grady could be here to see."

Grady, who only two weeks ago had sat here on the edge of her daughter's bed and prayed with her. Who had encouraged her to say "stop" in Jesus's name to the fears that plagued her. Gradually, ever so gradually, the bedtime anxiety had lessened. Now he'd given her a furry friend to keep her company.

When they'd completed a bedtime story and said their prayers, Sunshine brushed back Tessa's hair and gazed down at her with a love that ached. "Do you want me to leave the night-light on?"

This would be a first if she didn't, but Sunshine could always hope.

Tessa thought a moment, then shook her head. "No. Grandma was wrong."

Grandma? "What do you mean?"

"There's nothing in the closet that will come and get me if I'm not a good girl."

Sunshine's heart stilled. "Grandma told you that?"

"Uh-huh." Tessa frowned at the memory. "When I broke one of her pretty cups she said I was a bad girl. And that bad things came out of the closet at night to get bad girls."

Sickened, Sunshine reached for her hand. Why hadn't she suspected something like this had occurred when Tessa had spent a long weekend with her grandmother before the school year started?

"Why didn't you tell me this, Tessa?"

"'Cause Grandma said if I told anyone, the bad things would come get them, too. I didn't want them to get you, Mommy. Or Grady or Tori."

"Oh, honey." Sunshine squeezed her daughter's hand. "Thank you for wanting to keep us safe, but you can always tell me anything. Always. Promise?"

Tessa nodded. "Why did Grandma tell me bad things are in the closet if it isn't true?"

Touchy ground here, and something she intended to discuss with Mom at the first opportunity. Although she didn't want a distrust built between Tessa and her grandma Heywood, could Sunshine ever trust her enough to leave Tessa alone with her again?

"I don't know. Maybe she was tired that day and

made a mistake. Or maybe she was trying to be funny and didn't realize you'd take her seriously."

Or maybe an active five-year-old was too much for her mother these days. Tessa had taken her valuable time and was in her way, much as Sunshine had been when growing up. Never able to keep her mother happy. *Bad girl.* The long-forgotten indictment rang in Sunshine's ears. Maybe the broken cup had upset her mother, but there was no valid excuse for telling Tessa that if she was a bad girl, bad things would get her and those she loved.

"I didn't break the cup on purpose, Mommy. I said I was sorry."

"Of course you didn't do it on purpose. You did the right thing by apologizing." Now Sunshine's mother owed her granddaughter an apology, as well.

"I love you, Mommy."

"I love you, too, sweetie." She pressed a kiss to her daughter's forehead. "So no night-light?"

She shook her head. "Remember? Grady says to think about happy things."

Grady. Their hero.

But what happy things could she possibly find to think about tonight when she turned out her own light?

Chapter Eighteen

"And there you have it." Grady motioned to the wall monitor in a Hunter's Hideaway conference room, then turned to a select group of family members seated around the table. "My proposal for a wildlife-photography addition to our offerings."

Mom hadn't felt up to attending, but Dad and Grandma Jo had joined several of his uncles and aunts. Luke and Delaney. Rio. All had paid respectful attention as he'd gone through the presentation slides. Asked good questions.

But would it be enough?

Would things have gone better had Sunshine been there, lending her support, chiming in on critical points he perhaps hadn't emphasized enough? Maybe she could have helped him refocus when a question from Luke or Uncle Doug had sidetracked him.

"Well put together, son." His father smiled his approval, but his noncommittal choice of words made Grady acutely aware he wasn't ready to deliver a decision.

"This is certainly something to think about," Aunt Suzy said. "Your proposal holds considerable merit."

"I like it," chimed in Rio. "Really, really like it."

He smiled at his little sister, but how much influence would a twenty-year-old have in the final decision making?

Uncle Doug picked up the more detailed backup materials Grady had printed for each of them. "We need time to look over your facts and figures. Luke can run some numbers, then we'll discuss this with you further."

Grady looked to Grandma Jo, questioning.

Her eyes warmed. "It's evident you've put time and effort into this. Your enthusiasm for the project is evident."

So she wanted to look over the numbers, too, think through his proposal.

"I believe it will be worth the time and effort, Grandma." And fun. Something he could sink his teeth into. He could picture the conference room packed with enthusiastic amateur photographers, attention glued to a master photographer guest speaker. Could envision himself overseeing small groups in the predawn stillness of their forested surroundings, helping them capture dreamed-of shots of elk at a watering hole. A deer stepping into a clearing. A hawk soaring overhead.

"Give us time to digest the data you've provided and we'll meet again soon." Dad rose from his chair, the meeting adjourned.

In a now-empty room, Grady shut down his laptop, then deposited it in his office before stepping outside for a breath of fresh air. November already. Fluffy flakes heralding the first snowfall of the season danced before his weary eyes. This autumn had been a season of disappointments in many ways. His mother's medical issues. A delayed commitment on his business proposal. The eye-opening betrayal by Sunshine.

He looked down as something solid bumped almost sympathetically against his leg. Rags. Luke's German shepherd. He knelt down to scratch the friendly fellow behind the ears.

How many times in the past several days had he reached for his phone, hoping that if he called Sunshine she'd tell him he'd dreamed up last week's nightmare? That it had never happened. But he'd be seeing her soon enough, at tonight's last public event before the election. What would they have to say to each other?

He'd been so sure that God was bringing Sunshine and Tessa into his life. How could he have so badly misjudged a woman's intentions twice?

And how could she have done this to him, knowing what had happened to him before and how he felt about hurting a child? He hadn't told any of his family members about why Sunshine had come to Hunter Ridge—but should he? He'd need help gathering documentation to disprove her claims if she decided to take them to court.

He gave Rags a final pat, then rose to his feet.

"Grady." Uncle Doug's hand clasped his shoulder. "I'm impressed with your persistence on this wildlife-photography pursuit. I seem to recall you bringing this up years ago. Gave us a good laugh at the time."

Grady gave his uncle a sharp look. "Not so laughable now, is it? When it could be a moneymaker."

"That remains to be seen. But if we can prevent your mother from throwing in the towel for a few more days—which I think we can—your hands will be full with council duties for the next four years. I don't think any of us would be willing to give your proposal the nod, knowing how your time will be limited. A new venture like this will take considerable oversight if it's to succeed."

"You know I haven't agreed to run in a special election, don't you?"

"You will. You'll come through for your family like you always do. We're counting on you." Uncle Doug clapped him on the back, then, before he could gather his thoughts to respond, his uncle went back inside.

Grady raked his fingers roughly through his hair. No, he hadn't agreed to run in a special election if it came down to that. He didn't *want* to be a councilman. But once again, like many times before, duty called. Family loyalties came into play.

Knowing what he knew about Sunshine now, about her deceptive ways, could he in good conscience refuse to run and leave Hunter Ridge at the mercy of her or Irv?

As Sunshine had also pointed out, with the proliferation of digital cameras, the timing for launching his business plan couldn't be better. Would it still be four years from now? Maybe. Maybe not. Uncle Doug was right—it *would* take tremendous oversight of innumerable details if the endeavor wasn't to fail right out of the starting gate. Sure, the town council only met twice a month, but, as he knew from his mother's involvement, the position involved work sessions, subcommittee meetings and volumes of reading and keeping yourself tuned full-time to the heartbeat of the community's needs and opinions.

Could he turn away from his family's expectations? Let them down? Or would serving his time on the town council somehow make up for his near-miss encounters with two women who'd seen an easy target coming from a mile away?

Was there a chance he could juggle Hunter's Hideaway and the added responsibilities of a wild game supply store, the photography venture and the town council at the same time? Do them all justice?

A heaviness settled into his heart.

Not likely.

"Four more days, folks." Irvin, having just had his last say in an organized public venue before the election, grinned at Sunshine and Grady as he stepped away from the podium Friday night. "May the best *man* win."

Sunshine managed not to grimace. Surprisingly, Elaine hadn't pulled out of the running, so maybe her health was taking an upward swing. Who'd have known, though, what a big deal a small-town election would be? Not only time-consuming, but physically, mentally and emotionally draining. Did Elaine have it in her to go into another term? And for that matter, did Sunshine have it in her to juggle motherhood, manage the Artists' Cooperative and take on town council commitments for four years?

It was almost with a sense of relief that with Elaine still in the race, she wouldn't have to find an answer to that question. Grady's mother was certain to win.

As the threesome left the elementary-school

stage, Sunshine ventured a glance in Grady's direction. He was so handsome tonight that if this were election day and he the candidate rather than his mother, she'd be hard-pressed not to cast her vote on his behalf.

Upon arriving at tonight's event, the two had awkwardly exchanged a handful of pleasantries. Two strangers with nothing to say to each other. Or at least nothing that could be said in a public place. Many times during the past week she'd almost called him to apologize again. But what more could she say to convince him of her sincerity?

She had no intention of asking Tori to research further to prove the evidence one way or another. But she couldn't deny her original plan, the wrong motives that had caused her to jump at the Artists' Co-op position in the first place.

"Sunshine?" Grady's voice drew her attention. "Mom asked me to reaffirm that she wishes you the best in this election and is sorry she couldn't be here tonight to say so in person."

"She's still not feeling well?"

"Conserving her strength for the next four years."

"Please tell her it's been a privilege to share a campaign with her, even though mostly through a very capable proxy." She met his steady gaze with a smile, hoping it might serve as an icebreaker.

But he didn't return it. "She's a fine council-woman, and the town will be fortunate to have her representing them in the next term."

"You're not hoping to win?"

"With your mother running for reelection?" She shook her head. "But it was never about winning. It was about giving a voice to those who didn't have one."

Something unreadable flickered through Grady's eyes. "Then, you've reached your goal before a single vote has been cast."

They stood looking at each other, the conversation coming to a premature close. Was the ache in his heart as heavy as the one in hers? She'd wounded him deeply, if unintentionally. Could she ever make things right with him, even though a shared future wasn't to be? If only so many people weren't milling about, people with whom they were expected to get in a final word that might sway a vote. She had much she wanted to say to him. *Needed* to say.

"We have punch and cookies over here." Mayor Silas urged them forward.

"Coming," Grady acknowledged, but didn't move. Neither did Sunshine.

"Grady," she said, desperate to speak before the moment passed. "I'm so sorry that—"

"I think it's for the best that we not belabor the issue." Sadness filled his eyes—a sadness she'd put there. "I don't hold hard feelings against you. You were doing what you thought you needed to do to provide for Tessa. But we both need to accept that it is what it is and let it go."

But she didn't want to let it go.

"Sunshine! There you are." Local artist Maeve Malone approached, her arms wide to gather Sunshine into a hug. "No matter what happens at the polls, you've drawn attention to the issues surrounding those who don't make their living from the great outdoors. Thank you."

Maeve chatted for what seemed an eternity before disappearing into the crowd once more. When Sunshine turned back to Grady, he'd stepped away, his cell phone pressed to his ear and his expression intent.

"Right. Right. I'll see you shortly."

When he pocketed his phone, he glanced up, looking almost surprised to see her still standing there. Then he swiftly turned his attention to the crowd around them before she could pick up where they'd left off. "I have to leave. Dad's taking Mom to the regional hospital."

"What's wrong?"

"Dad thinks she's dehydrated. Electrolytes or whatever out of balance. Either that or an infection. She wouldn't let him take her earlier today, but now she's giving in."

"I'll be praying."

"Thanks. If you'll excuse me, I need to make a quick round through this crowd, then head to the hospital." He paused, his eyes searching hers. "And, Sunshine—?"

"Yes?" Would he say they needed to talk in private soon?

"Please don't say anything to anyone about Mom and the hospitalization. They'll probably stick an IV in her and she'll be back on her feet before you know it."

"If anyone asks, I'll say you had pressing Hunter's Hideaway business."

"Thanks." To her surprise, he reached for her hand and gave it a gentle squeeze, then immediately released it.

"Remember, Grady, I'm praying."

Did he recognize what she was saying? That not only was she praying for his mother, but for him, too? Praying God would heal the hurt she'd dealt him and he'd find it in his heart to forgive her even though he could no longer love her?

As he'd predicted, Mom was back home by Saturday afternoon. Prematurely, in his opinion, after seeing Dad help her from the car in what looked to him to still be a weakened state. How long was she going to insist on going through with this election? Were Uncle Doug and her other supporters putting too much pressure on her to hold out until after the first of the year?

As much as he didn't want to run for office, it was his concern for Mom that drove his doubts as to the wisdom of that plan. Was it really so important that a Hunter be on the council, an unbroken chain since the founding of the first one? If he refused to run in the special election—let his family and their friends down—would that provoke Mom into dropping out of the race or would she keep up the fight to remain in office?

He had a night of heavy-duty praying ahead of him.

"You're deep in thought."

He looked up from his desk to see Grandma Jo in his office doorway. "Busy times, Grandma."

"They are indeed." She approached and he rose to pull up a chair for her. "Your mother is resting comfortably now, glad to be home."

Grandma sat down, but he remained standing. "How long do you think she can keep pushing herself like this?"

"Elaine is a very strong-willed woman."

"At what price?" His words echoed those of his father as he found himself pacing the floor. "Who cares what that council does when she's fighting for her life?"

"I can't argue with you, Grady." Grandma sounded resigned. "But it's not my decision. You know your father wants her to step down, but he won't tell her what to do."

"Maybe he should."

"That's not how the two of them have operated for almost forty years. I imagine you'd like your new friend to drop out of the campaign, too. But are you telling Sunshine to do that?"

He halted his efforts to wear out the carpet. "What she does is none of my business."

"I thought from what I saw at the cookout a few weeks ago and from what your father said recently that there might be a relationship kindling."

"Not anymore."

"Care to talk about it?"

"Not really." But he might need Grandma Jo's help to piece together irrefutable documentation that Walter Royce had never owned so much as the foundation his cabin had been built on. Reluctantly, he moved to shut the door to the hallway, then sat down at his desk once again. "Your grandson's legendary ability to spot a woman taking advantage of him took another hit."

Concern darkened Grandma Jo's eyes, but she didn't say anything, so he continued.

"It's a long story, but almost unbelievably, Sunshine is Walter and Flora Royce's great-great-granddaughter. You know who I'm talking about, don't you?"

"Of course I do. How extraordinary."

"She came here to prove a story she'd heard from her grandmother—that Hunters cheated Royces out of the property that's now Hunter's Hideaway. She came here not only to prove it, but to cash in on it. And some of the information she gathered to help her she got straight from me. She played me, Grandma, just like Jasmine did."

"I'm sorry to hear this, Grady."

"No more sorry than I am."

"You were coming to care for her, weren't you?"

"Oh, yeah. And her daughter." The hopes and dreams he'd harbored for a too-short time filled his mind. "I can't believe this happened again. What is it about me that tells women I'm a sitting duck to be taken advantage of?"

"The problem isn't you, Grady. It's the women."

"I'd like to believe that, but evidence to the contrary is mounting."

"Sunshine confessed to you, then, that she intends to press the family for money if she can prove this family story?"

"She admitted that's why she moved here in the first place. Of course, she now denies that she'd have gone through with it."

"Do you think she's telling the truth? That perhaps meeting you—even falling in love with you—could have changed her plans?"

"You have no idea how much I'd like to believe that, but it's a little hard to swallow, don't you think?"

"Maybe not. You're a fine young man, Grady. One most women would find it difficult *not* to fall in love with."

Yeah, right.

"She admitted her original plans in coming here. That's a point in her favor."

"After I almost dragged it out of her."

"I imagine it wasn't something easy to admit. We all make mistakes, wrong decisions, but we don't always have to confess them to someone we want to think highly of us."

"You sound as if you believe her."

Grandma rose from her chair to look down at him. "I don't know whether to believe her or not. I just don't want you making a decision based on pride and misunderstanding."

But the decision had already been made.

And after he'd pushed Sunshine away that night, reeling from the blows both she and Jasmine had dealt him, he didn't deserve another chance even if he wanted one.

Chapter Nineteen

"Are you saying what I think you're saying, Grady?" A scowling Uncle Doug, standing among those crowded into Grandma Jo's living room after lunch on Sunday, sounded none too pleased. Undoubtedly he wouldn't be the only one who'd resent Grady's decision once word got out.

So be it.

"I think I've made myself clear," Grady concluded as he looked around the room where he'd gathered his extended family and a few of Mom's closest supporters. "I appreciate your confidence in me and that you believe I'd serve our community well if voted in during a special election. I understand, too, the honor it's been for our family to have had a long, unbroken tradition in Hunter Ridge leadership."

Uncle Doug folded his arms. "You understand that honor, yet you're letting us down."

He didn't want to argue with his uncle. He'd prayerfully made his decision, and nothing would dissuade him. "You can view it that way if you choose to. But I don't think anyone in this room will argue that in the past I've been willing to make sacrifices I've believed to be in the best interests of a family I love. This time, however, I'm being true to myself—and to the God I answer to."

Uncle Doug snorted, eyeing the room to look for those who might share his sentiments. "You're following your heart and sticking this town with the likes of Irvin Baydlin or Sunshine Carston?"

"As always—" Grady refused to sound defensive, knowing what he was about to say wouldn't set well with some "—our family and friends will make their own decisions. But I truly believe that Sunshine Carston will serve this community with fairness and integrity. I encourage you to vote for her. I will be."

As the old saying went, you could hear a pin drop.

With a meaningful glance at Grady's mother—looking fragile this morning, but nevertheless as if a weight had been lifted from her shoulders—Dad rose from where he'd been seated next to her on the sofa. He approached Grady and thrust out his hand.

"Thank you, son. You've made what your mother and I also wish to share that much easier."

What was he talking about?

Dad looked at Grady's mother with love in his eyes, then at those gathered around them. "I'm here to officially announce that Elaine will be resigning from the town council Monday morning—and withdrawing from the election, as well."

Several in the room gasped.

"See what you've done?" Uncle Doug took a step forward, angry eyes fixed on Grady.

"Now, Doug." Dad held up a halting hand to his younger brother. "Elaine and I made this decision last night, before Grady had come to any conclusions of his own. You can't hold him at fault. Blame me and Elaine if you want to blame someone. We decided if God wants her whole and healthy, we're going to do all in our power to keep her that way. And the town council just doesn't fit in the picture."

"I can't believe this." Uncle Doug turned incredulous eyes to Grandma Jo. "Mother? What do you have to say about this? You're just going to let Dave and Grady make this ill-advised decision for all of us?"

Everyone turned to a grim Grandma Jo rising to her feet, and Grady once again admired the regal, almost aristocratic bearing of his grandmother.

"I do have something to say, Doug."

Relief momentarily passed through Uncle

Doug's eyes before he shot Grady an I-told-you-so look.

Grandma Jo gave Grady's mother a tender smile, then fixed her gaze once again on her second son. "What I want, Doug, is to keep Elaine with us for as long as God grants us that privilege. If that means the Hunters relinquish the town council seat, then so be it."

"Now, Mother—"

She turned abruptly from Uncle Doug's appeal to look at Grady, her steady gaze filled with love. "Thank you for your courage, Grady. Courage to stand up for what you believe in despite opposition from those you love and admire most. You've not allowed yourself to be pushed down a road where God doesn't want you to go. I love you and I'm proud of you."

Her gaze continued to hold his as he returned her smile.

"Thank you, Grandma. I love you, too."

She'd won.

Still stunned at the news, Sunshine's smile remained frozen following her acceptance speech as supporters cheered and high-fived each other, hugged her and each other. The atmosphere in the restaurant's private room where her campaign team had awaited the election's outcome was euphoric, but standing in the middle of the celebrating crowd, it seemed nothing but surreal. And meaningless. She'd won by default, Elaine Hunter having abruptly withdrawn from the race on Monday morning.

"We did it!" Benton Mason's wife, Lizzie, gave her a hug. "Maybe things will start looking up for the artists in this town."

"I have no doubt," a smiling Benton chimed in, his even white teeth flashing in contrast to his dark beard, "that by next summer an art-in-the-park event will become a reality."

"Hear! Hear!" others around them shouted.

Numb, Sunshine cringed inwardly. She hoped that would be the case. But there were no guarantees. She'd be one voice among five others and Mayor Silas. Half a dozen who might not be pleased to have her in their midst for the next four years. Would people expect more of her than she could deliver? Be disappointed when she might not make a significant difference?

And what about the Hunters? Had the family gotten word of the election results? Were they disappointed that Irvin Baydlin had been beat out by a newcomer?

"Sunshine?"

She stiffened at the familiar voice behind her, then fixing a smile on her face she turned to Gideon Edlow who somewhat reluctantly thrust out his hand.

"I guess congratulations are in order."

"For all of us, Gideon. While I can't make guarantees as to what the next four years will bring, I give you my word that I'll represent the artists and other community members to the best of my ability."

He squinted one eye. "No hard feelings?"

The likelihood that he was done with challenging her and that she'd ever be able to trust him were slim, but bearing a grudge would serve no good purpose. "None."

To her relief, he was apparently satisfied, for he stepped aside to allow other well-wishers in to offer their congratulations.

The remainder of the evening sped by with the mayor and other council members stopping in to offer good wishes and welcome her to the team. Even Irvin came by to concede defeat with surprising graciousness, and Tori allowed Tessa to make a late-night phone call to her mother. Elaine Hunter didn't put in an appearance, but she did make a congratulatory call and explained that it had been a rough day health-wise, which was why she wasn't there in person.

There had been no mention of her son.

It was after midnight before Sunshine, restless and tense, could slip away from the noisy, crowded, too-warm room. In the quiet of the restroom she stared into the mirror at her reflection—into the face of an expressionless stranger. Where was the triumphant, glowing countenance of someone who'd just been elected?

Well, I won, Lord. Now what?

Although Elaine had pulled out at the last minute, her own win hadn't been *entirely* by default. A surprisingly healthy number of votes cast in her favor had by far trumped Irvin's, so at least that meant others outside the artists' community had backed her. Supported her. Clearly, a number of Elaine's supporters had switched loyalties when she'd bowed out, as well.

But although Sunshine hadn't expected to win, the victory felt hollow without Grady at her side. She clearly recognized now that searching for the truth of her grandmother's tale and running for office hadn't been about money or winning. It was about a need to belong. To have roots.

But it wasn't to Hunter Ridge that her soul truly longed to be connected. It was to her Lord. *I am the vine, you are the branches...for apart from Me you can do nothing.*

Reluctantly, she stepped into the dimly lit hallway, the chatter and laughter of those still celebrating coming from the main room. Maybe if she went outside, got a breath of fresh air, the tension that gripped her would ease?

Pushing open a glass door, she exited onto the shadowed porch, grateful for the stillness of this postmidnight hour. It was chilly, but the wind wasn't blowing, and her wool skirt and jacket provided an element of protection.

She moved to the edge of the porch to gaze up at the starry night. At this high elevation, the pinpoints of light glittered more sharply than in lower regions, a breathtaking sweep across the dark expanse above. A reminder of God the Creator, who was in control. A God who still had plans for her—good plans—even though that seemed far from her reality now.

Hey, girl, she chided herself as she rubbed her hands up and down her arms to warm them, *you won a seat on the Hunter Ridge Town Council.*

That had to be a God thing, didn't it?

But, ungratefully, it wasn't enough. If only she could go back in time and rearrange her life. Purify her motive for coming to Hunter Ridge and abandon the selfish pursuit to unearth the truth about the Hunters and her great-great-grandparents before she'd even gotten started.

Stop herself from hurting the man she loved.

"Sunshine?"

Startled, she spun toward Grady as he stepped up on the far side of the shadowed porch.

"I was hoping to see you. To offer my congratulations." His words came hesitantly. "But I wasn't sure if I'd be welcome."

"You'll always be welcomed, Grady." Always.

But how stupid to have said that. As if expecting him to casually brush off the deep wound she'd inflicted. "I'm more sorry than you'll ever know. I understand why it's difficult for you to believe it, but I never intended—"

He held up his hand to halt her. "I know that now."

A spark of hope flared as he moved closer, but she tamped it down. It would be too much to bear if he'd solely come here tonight to seek closure. To say a final goodbye.

He looked down the concrete porch and scuffed the toe of his boot against it. "We've both grown up with different versions of the same story, haven't we?"

"We have."

"You wouldn't think that something that happened a hundred years ago would trickle down through the generations to impact us now. Influence who we are. But I know for my part, I grew up with tales of how my ancestor generously supported a friend facing hard times and was taken advantage of. Then when Uncle Doug's wife divorced him and did him and the town dirty when I was a little boy, well, that was another layer of distrust and fear of betrayal that carved itself into who I am."

"And then Jasmine."

"Yes, and then Jasmine." He looked skyward

for a long moment, then back at her. "But you've been impacted by a story, as well. An often-told story shared with you by someone you loved and trusted—your grandmother. A tale that, as with me, seeped inside and planted itself in how you perceive the world. As betraying. Untrustworthy. And your ex-husband's abandonment reinforced that."

"It did."

"I guess what I'm trying to say here is that we both blindly walked into a relationship carrying a ton of personal baggage. Heavy baggage we weren't fully aware we were carrying until now. Some of it with century-old roots."

"Kind of crazy."

"Major crazy." He raked his hand through his hair. "I'm confident, Sunshine, that the evidence you've discovered can easily be explained. That it can be proved beyond a shadow of a doubt that your great-great-grandfather never owned Hunter's Hideaway. But I don't expect you to take my word on that. I'm willing to research it further with you and, if the Hunters did your family an injustice, we'll make it right."

"I don't want anything from the Hunters." Except Grady's trust, his heart. "Please believe that."

"I believe you'd come to a decision that you wouldn't press my family for financial gain. I've thought long and hard about what you said or, rather, what you were trying to say when I refused to listen. When I was being stubbornly sure you were no better than Jasmine. Than Aunt Char. Than your ancestors."

Despite his assurance that he believed her, she cringed inwardly at the string of past betrayals carving a path into his future. Was it any wonder he'd reacted the way he had?

"But God—and Grandma Jo—opened my eyes, Sunshine."

"Your grandmother?"

"That's a story to be told later." He reached for her hand, his gaze intense. "I had to ask myself if something that happened or didn't happen a hundred years ago to people long dead even matters. To us, I mean. Here. Now."

"Only if we choose to let it."

He swallowed, his hands tightening gently on hers. "Will you forgive me, Sunshine? For not believing in you? I can see now that my betrayal of you was every bit as harsh as the one I'd imagined inflicted on myself."

"Of course, Grady. But I owe you an apology as well, so please hear me out. My original motives for coming here were wrong. Very wrong. I was intent on being compensated for an injustice done to my family—an injustice I'd clung to so tightly, but now realize was a fabrication."

The lines of tension in his face eased.

"I now also realize," she hurried on, "that coming here and then running for a town council seat wasn't all about money or fighting for justice. Those things masked a search for the fulfillment of another deeper need. A need for roots, a sense of belonging. But this past week I've come to better understand that true belonging can only be found by not withholding pieces of my heart from God."

The stillness of the night pressing in around them, they stood facing each other in the dim light. Despite words of reconciliation and a desire to put the past in the past, he'd said nothing of wanting to see her again. To start over. Was it too late for that?

"Grady, I—"

"I have something I need to say first." And then, as her heart leaped into her throat, he dropped down on one knee to look up at her, his hands still holding hers. "I know this is coming out of the blue. That it might be premature. That you might think it's downright crazy. But I love you, Sunshine. Tessa, too. And I want to spend the rest of my life with both of you. Will you give me a second chance? Will you marry me?"

Heart pounding, she stood staring down at him, trying to absorb his unexpected declaration. *Grady loves me. He wants to marry me.*

"I understand," he said, almost stumbling over

his words, "if you can't give an answer right now. But would you be willing to think it over? To pray about it—as I've done?"

He thought she needed more time?

"I don't need to think about it any further. I've prayed about it, too."

Uncertainty flickered through his eyes. Then he swallowed, as though steeling himself for a turndown. Did he have no idea how she felt about him? How for weeks she'd dreamed of someday hearing him utter those words? How thrilled Tessa would be?

"I love you, Grady Hunter," she said softly, "and, yes, I will marry you."

He stared at her, uncomprehending. "You—?"

She laughed. "I love you. And Tessa loves you, too."

He blinked. Once. Twice. Absorbing her words. Then an uncontrollable grin surfaced and he rose swiftly to his feet to gaze down at her, still speechless.

"Cat got your tongue?" she coaxed playfully.

With a laugh, he slowly shook his head, his eyes filled with wonder. "You've made me the happiest man in the world, Sunshine."

"And you'll—hopefully soon—be married to the happiest woman in the world."

He gently cupped her face with his warm hands.

"I do love you, Sunshine, and I promise to make you a good husband. And Tessa a good father."

"I don't doubt that for a moment."

Grady chuckled. "I'm not sure how God managed this. We did our best to botch up His plans, didn't we?"

"We did."

"So I guess we need to show Him our appreciation and make up for lost time." With that declaration and a twinkle in his eyes, he leaned in to tenderly press his lips to hers.

Epilogue

"It's beautiful, Grady." Sunshine held out her hand to admire the glittering diamond ring, her breath coming as a frosty cloud on the crisp mid-November morning air. Returning from an exhilarating forest hike, they'd paused at the edge of Hunter's Hideaway property, where they'd soon join Tessa, Tori and Grady's family for an engagement celebration brunch.

How quickly her life had changed. Whoever would have imagined what God had in mind when she'd come to Hunter Ridge, determined to uncover the truth about her great-great-grandparents? She'd never have guessed what He had planned the day she'd brazenly marched up to Grady, demanding he call off the noisy workers next door. Whoever would have thought she'd win a council seat and her assistance would help Grady receive unanimous approval to pursue his dream of a wildlife-photography element at Hunter's Hideaway? Or almost unanimous. She didn't count his uncle Doug's dissenting vote.

"That ring isn't half as beautiful as you are." Grady leaned in for a lingering kiss, then gently tugged her leather glove back on. "If you keep taking that glove off, your fingers are going to turn into blocks of ice."

"I'm not worried." She slipped her arms around his scarf-wrapped neck. "Isn't it your job to keep me warm now?"

"You think so, huh?" His eyes twinkled as he pulled her close. Or as close as they could get with them both wearing down-filled jackets. "I believe I can handle that assignment."

She cuddled into him. "I'm glad we won't be waiting until next summer to get married. Valentine's Day is perfect."

"I wish it could be Christmas. Or Thanksgiving." He gently rested his forehead against hers. "But hopefully, if the chemo finally begins to work its wonders, Mom will feel up to enjoying the wedding by February."

"She still has long way to go, doesn't she?"

"More treatments. More meds. More physical therapy. But, God willing, next year she and Dad will celebrate their fortieth wedding anniversary together, and then each year thereafter for a long time to come."

"I think she's relieved not to be facing another four years on the town council."

"I get that impression, too—that pulling out of the campaign took a lot of pressure off her." His gloved finger touched the tip of her nose. "Thanks to you."

"Me?" She laughed. "Oh, right. I challenged her for the council seat and won by default. I'm sure it's going to take your folks a while to forgive me for that."

"They're grateful. Especially Dad. Mom never would have withdrawn if she didn't think you could beat Irvin. She'd have kept pushing herself, wearing herself out."

She tilted her head. "She thought I'd beat him?"

"Hands down. And look how it's turned out." He arched a brow. "The town council seat remains in the Hunter family. The tradition unbroken."

"Ah, but don't forget." She lifted her chin with mock defiance. "I'll be representing the artists in the community, too, you know. Not just Hunters."

"I know that, and I'm proud that you will be." He again captured her lips with his and, with a quick intake of breath and pounding heart, she returned the kiss, marveling that God had given her—and Tessa—a man like Grady Hunter.

"Hey, you two!" Guiltily jerking apart at the sound of a gruff voice, they looked across the clearing to where Pastor McCrae stood at the back patio door of the inn, motioning them forward. "There's plenty of time for that lovey-dovey stuff later. Get yourselves on in here. Time to eat."

"Spoilsport!" a grinning Grady taunted back at his cousin, then reached for Sunshine's gloved hand. "So are you ready to officially unveil that ring? The whole family will be in there by now, waiting to see it."

The *extended* Hunter family. Consisting of many who might not be thrilled that she'd won the election instead of Elaine. Who might be less than thrilled that she was marrying into the Hunter clan, claiming Grady as her own.

"Once they get to know you, they're going to love you." He'd guessed what was on her mind. "Just as I do."

Then, before she could protest, he leaned in to again move his warm lips gently on hers. She could barely keep her knees from buckling or from throwing herself into his arms.

"Hey!" Garrett called again, amusement evident in his tone. "What part of 'bacon and eggs getting cold' don't you two understand?"

Sunshine giggled and Grady drew back, shaking his head. "I never knew a preacher could be so annoying."

Gazing up into Grady's warm blue eyes, she linked her arm with his. "I guess we'd better not force him to come out here after us, huh?"

He sighed. "Guess not."

With her free hand, she reached up to touch her beloved's face, her words coming softly. "I love you, Grady."

"I love you, too, my very own Sunshine."

Smiling, they headed toward the inn—and a lifetime shared together.

* * * * *

Dear Reader,

Welcome back to Hunter Ridge! I loved writing Grady and Sunshine's story—the journey of two wounded hearts learning to trust God so He can enable them to overcome past betrayals and learn to love again.

It's a rocky road at times. Not only do they have their personal pasts to overcome, but their lives are uniquely entangled with others who have come before them—both in the recent and distant past.

Have you ever felt betrayed by someone you trusted? Did it impact your ability to trust others? Or perhaps made you so fearful of letting others down that you haven't always listened to and obeyed God's direction? Never forget that one of the beauties of a relationship with God is that He tells us "never will I leave you, never will I forsake you."

You can contact me via email at glynna@glynnakaye.com. Please visit my website at glynnakaye.com—and stop by loveinspiredauthors.com, seekerville.net and seekerville.blogspot.com!

Glynna Kaye

LARGER-PRINT BOOKS!

GET 2 FREE
LARGER-PRINT NOVELS
PLUS 2 FREE
MYSTERY GIFTS

Love Inspired®

Larger-print novels are now available...

YES! Please send me 2 FREE LARGER-PRINT Love Inspired® novels and my 2 FREE mystery gifts (gifts are worth about $10). After receiving them, if I don't wish to receive any more books, I can return the shipping statement marked "cancel." If I don't cancel, I will receive 6 brand-new novels every month and be billed just $5.49 per book in the U.S. or $5.99 per book in Canada. That's a savings of at least 19% off the cover price. It's quite a bargain! Shipping and handling is just 50¢ per book in the U.S. and 75¢ per book in Canada.* I understand that accepting the 2 free books and gifts places me under no obligation to buy anything. I can always return a shipment and cancel at any time. Even if I never buy another book, the two free books and gifts are mine to keep forever.

122/322 IDN GH6D

Name	(PLEASE PRINT)

Address	Apt. #

City	State/Prov.	Zip/Postal Code

Signature (if under 18, a parent or guardian must sign)

Mail to the **Reader Service:**
IN U.S.A.: P.O. Box 1867, Buffalo, NY 14240-1867
IN CANADA: P.O. Box 609, Fort Erie, Ontario L2A 5X3

**Are you a current subscriber to Love Inspired® books
and want to receive the larger-print edition?
Call 1-800-873-8635 or visit www.ReaderService.com.**

* Terms and prices subject to change without notice. Prices do not include applicable taxes. Sales tax applicable in N.Y. Canadian residents will be charged applicable taxes. Offer not valid in Quebec. This offer is limited to one order per household. Not valid to current subscribers to Love Inspired Larger-Print books. All orders subject to credit approval. Credit or debit balances in a customer's account(s) may be offset by any other outstanding balance owed by or to the customer. Please allow 4 to 6 weeks for delivery. Offer available while quantities last.

Your Privacy—The Reader Service is committed to protecting your privacy. Our Privacy Policy is available online at www.ReaderService.com or upon request from the Reader Service.

We make a portion of our mailing list available to reputable third parties that offer products we believe may interest you. If you prefer that we not exchange your name with third parties, or if you wish to clarify or modify your communication preferences, please visit us at www.ReaderService.com/consumerchoice or write to us at Reader Service Preference Service, P.O. Box 9062, Buffalo, NY 14240-9062. Include your complete name and address.

LARGER-PRINT BOOKS!

GET 2 FREE
LARGER-PRINT NOVELS
PLUS 2 FREE
MYSTERY GIFTS

Love Inspired®

SUSPENSE
RIVETING INSPIRATIONAL ROMANCE

Larger-print novels are now available...

YES! Please send me 2 FREE LARGER-PRINT Love Inspired® Suspense novels and my 2 FREE mystery gifts (gifts are worth about $10). After receiving them, if I don't wish to receive any more books, I can return the shipping statement marked "cancel." If I don't cancel, I will receive 4 brand-new novels every month and be billed just $5.49 per book in the U.S. or $5.99 per book in Canada. That's a savings of at least 19% off the cover price. It's quite a bargain! Shipping and handling is just 50¢ per book in the U.S. and 75¢ per book in Canada.* I understand that accepting the 2 free books and gifts places me under no obligation to buy anything. I can always return a shipment and cancel at any time. Even if I never buy another book, the two free books and gifts are mine to keep forever.

110/310 IDN GH6P

Name _____ (PLEASE PRINT) _____

Address _____ Apt. # _____

City _____ State/Prov. _____ Zip/Postal Code _____

Signature (if under 18, a parent or guardian must sign) _____

Mail to the **Reader Service:**
IN U.S.A.: P.O. Box 1867, Buffalo, NY 14240-1867
IN CANADA: P.O. Box 609, Fort Erie, Ontario L2A 5X3

**Are you a current subscriber to Love Inspired® Suspense books
and want to receive the larger-print edition?
Call 1-800-873-8635 or visit www.ReaderService.com.**

* Terms and prices subject to change without notice. Prices do not include applicable taxes. Sales tax applicable in N.Y. Canadian residents will be charged applicable taxes. Offer not valid in Quebec. This offer is limited to one order per household. Not valid for current subscribers to Love Inspired Suspense larger-print books. All orders subject to credit approval. Credit or debit balances in a customer's account(s) may be offset by any other outstanding balance owed by or to the customer. Please allow 4 to 6 weeks for delivery. Offer available while quantities last.

Your Privacy—The Reader Service is committed to protecting your privacy. Our Privacy Policy is available online at www.ReaderService.com or upon request from the Reader Service.

We make a portion of our mailing list available to reputable third parties that offer products we believe may interest you. If you prefer that we not exchange your name with third parties, or if you wish to clarify or modify your communication preferences, please visit us at www.ReaderService.com/consumerchoice or write to us at Reader Service Preference Service, P.O. Box 9062, Buffalo, NY 14240-9062. Include your complete name and address.

LISLP15

REQUEST YOUR FREE BOOKS!

2 FREE INSPIRATIONAL NOVELS
PLUS 2 *FREE* MYSTERY GIFTS

Love Inspired® **HISTORICAL**

YES! Please send me 2 FREE Love Inspired® Historical novels and my 2 FREE mystery gifts (gifts are worth about $10). After receiving them, if I don't wish to receive any more books, I can return the shipping statement marked "cancel." If I don't cancel, I will receive 4 brand-new novels every month and be billed just $4.99 per book in the U.S. or $5.49 per book in Canada. That's a saving of at least 17% off the cover price. It's quite a bargain! Shipping and handling is just 50¢ per book in the U.S. and 75¢ per book in Canada.* I understand that accepting the 2 free books and gifts places me under no obligation to buy anything. I can always return a shipment and cancel at any time. Even if I never buy another book, the two free books and gifts are mine to keep forever.

102/302 IDN GH6Z

Name	(PLEASE PRINT)

Address	Apt. #

City	State/Prov.	Zip/Postal Code

Signature (if under 18, a parent or guardian must sign)

Mail to the **Reader Service:**
IN U.S.A.: P.O. Box 1867, Buffalo, NY 14240-1867
IN CANADA: P.O. Box 609, Fort Erie, Ontario L2A 5X3

Want to try two free books from another series?
Call 1-800-873-8635 or visit www.ReaderService.com.

* Terms and prices subject to change without notice. Prices do not include applicable taxes. Sales tax applicable in N.Y. Canadian residents will be charged applicable taxes. Offer not valid in Quebec. This offer is limited to one order per household. Not valid for current subscribers to Love Inspired Historical books. All orders subject to credit approval. Credit or debit balances in a customer's account(s) may be offset by any other outstanding balance owed by or to the customer. Please allow 4 to 6 weeks for delivery. Offer available while quantities last.

Your Privacy—The Reader Service is committed to protecting your privacy. Our Privacy Policy is available online at www.ReaderService.com or upon request from the Reader Service.

We make a portion of our mailing list available to reputable third parties that offer products we believe may interest you. If you prefer that we not exchange your name with third parties, or if you wish to clarify or modify your communication preferences, please visit us at www.ReaderService.com/consumerschoice or write to us at Reader Service Preference Service, P.O. Box 9062, Buffalo, NY 14240-9062. Include your complete name and address.

LIH15

REQUEST YOUR FREE BOOKS!
2 FREE WHOLESOME ROMANCE NOVELS IN LARGER PRINT
PLUS 2 FREE MYSTERY GIFTS

HEARTWARMING™
Wholesome, tender romances

YES! Please send me 2 FREE Harlequin® Heartwarming Larger-Print novels and my 2 FREE mystery gifts (gifts worth about $10). After receiving them, if I don't wish to receive any more books, I can return the shipping statement marked "cancel." If I don't cancel, I will receive 4 brand-new larger-print novels every month and be billed just $5.24 per book in the U.S. or $5.99 per book in Canada. That's a savings of at least 19% off the cover price. It's quite a bargain! Shipping and handling is just 50¢ per book in the U.S. and 75¢ per book in Canada.* I understand that accepting the 2 free books and gifts places me under no obligation to buy anything. I can always return a shipment and cancel at any time. Even if I never buy another book, the two free books and gifts are mine to keep forever.

161/361 IDN GHX2

Name   (PLEASE PRINT)

Address   Apt. #

City   State/Prov.   Zip/Postal Code

Signature (if under 18, a parent or guardian must sign)

Mail to the **Reader Service:**
IN U.S.A.: P.O. Box 1867, Buffalo, NY 14240-1867
IN CANADA: P.O. Box 609, Fort Erie, Ontario L2A 5X3

* Terms and prices subject to change without notice. Prices do not include applicable taxes. Sales tax applicable in N.Y. Canadian residents will be charged applicable taxes. Offer not valid in Quebec. This offer is limited to one order per household. Not valid for current subscribers to Harlequin Heartwarming larger-print books. All orders subject to credit approval. Credit or debit balances in a customer's account(s) may be offset by any other outstanding balance owed by or to the customer. Please allow 4 to 6 weeks for delivery. Offer available while quantities last.

Your Privacy—The Reader Service is committed to protecting your privacy. Our Privacy Policy is available online at www.ReaderService.com or upon request from the Reader Service.

We make a portion of our mailing list available to reputable third parties that offer products we believe may interest you. If you prefer that we not exchange your name with third parties, or if you wish to clarify or modify your communication preferences, please visit us at www.ReaderService.com/consumerschoice or write to us at Reader Service Preference Service, P.O. Box 9062, Buffalo, NY 14240-9062. Include your complete name and address.

HW15

PRAISE FOR TOM CLANCY'S
WITHOUT REMORSE

"CLANCY'S WRITING IS SO STRONG THAT READERS FEEL THEY ARE THERE, IN THE MIDDLE OF THE ACTION . . . SATISFYING AND ENGROSSING."
—*Boston Sunday Herald*

"LIKE *PATRIOT GAMES*, *WITHOUT REMORSE* DEPENDS LESS ON TECHNOLOGY AND MORE ON PERSONAL VENDETTA . . . A PAGE-TURNER." —*Houston Chronicle*

"MAY BE CLANCY'S FINEST . . . *WITHOUT REMORSE* WILL CAPTURE THE IMAGINATIONS OF A LEGION OF NEW READERS . . . A VERY HUMAN STORY."
—*San Diego Union-Tribune*

"A CAPTIVATING, DOUBLE-EDGED THRILLER."
—*Virginian Pilot & Ledger-Star*

"AS A HERO CAUGHT IN THE WEB OF HIS OWN AND HIS NATION'S TRAGEDIES, KELLY IS A RIVETING FIGURE . . . AND AS A STORY, *WITHOUT REMORSE* IS AS QUICK, COMPELLING AND EXCITING AS ANYTHING MR. CLANCY HAS EVER DONE." —*Dallas Morning News*

"THIS IS CLANCY'S MOST HUMAN BOOK, YET IT'S STILL A THRILLER—AND A GOOD ONE."
—*Greensboro News & Record*

"RIP-ROARING ENTERTAINMENT . . . ANOTHER CLANCY SMASH." —*Tampa Tribune & Times*

Turn the page for reviews of
Tom Clancy's previous novels . . .

PRAISE FOR TOM CLANCY
and his bestselling novels . . .

"HE CONSTANTLY TAPS THE CURRENT WORLD SITUATION FOR ITS IMMINENT DANGERS AND SPINS THEM INTO AN ENGROSSING TALE."
—New York Times Book Review

"TOM CLANCY IS THE BEST THERE IS."
—San Francisco Chronicle

THE HUNT FOR RED OCTOBER
The smash bestseller that launched Tom Clancy's career—the incredible search for a Soviet defector and the nuclear submarine he commands . . .

"BREATHLESSLY EXCITING." *—Washington Post*

THE SUM OF ALL FEARS
The disappearance of an Israeli nuclear weapon threatens the balance of power in the Mideast—and the world . . .

"TOM CLANCY AT HIS BEST . . . NOT TO BE MISSED."
—Dallas Morning News

CLEAR AND PRESENT DANGER
The killing of three U.S. officials in Colombia ignites the American government's violent, and top secret, response . . .

"ROUSING ADVENTURE . . . A CRACKLING GOOD YARN." *—Washington Post*

THE CARDINAL OF THE KREMLIN
The superpowers race for the ultimate Star Wars missile defense system . . .

"*CARDINAL* EXCITES, ILLUMINATES . . . A REAL PAGE-TURNER." —*Los Angeles Daily News*

PATRIOT GAMES
CIA man Jack Ryan stops an assassination—and incurs the wrath of Irish terrorists . . .

"A HIGH PITCH OF EXCITEMENT." —*Wall Street Journal*

RED STORM RISING
The ultimate scenario for World War III—the final battle for global control . . .

"THE ULTIMATE WAR GAME . . . BRILLIANT." —*Newsweek*

And his fascinating nonfiction work . . .

SUBMARINE
A Guided Tour Inside a Nuclear Warship—Tom Clancy gives readers a rare glimpse inside the weapons, procedures, and people. Here are the facts behind the fiction, richly illustrated with diagrams and photographs . . .

"TAKES READERS DEEPER THAN THEY'VE EVER GONE INSIDE A NUCLEAR SUBMARINE . . . A FAST-PACED SILENT RUNNING THAT WILL PLEASE MANY OF THE AUTHOR'S FANS." —*Kirkus Reviews*

Berkley Books by Tom Clancy

THE HUNT FOR RED OCTOBER
RED STORM RISING
PATRIOT GAMES
THE CARDINAL OF THE KREMLIN
CLEAR AND PRESENT DANGER
THE SUM OF ALL FEARS
WITHOUT REMORSE

NONFICTION
SUBMARINE:
A Guided Tour Inside a Nuclear Warship

Tom Clancy

Without Remorse

B

BERKLEY BOOKS, NEW YORK

If you purchased this book without a cover, you should be aware that this book is stolen property. It was reported as "unsold and destroyed" to the publisher, and neither the author nor the publisher has received any payment for this "stripped book."

This Berkley book contains the complete text of
the original hardcover edition. It has been
completely reset in a typeface designed for
easy reading and was printed from new film.

This is a work of fiction. The events described here are imaginary:
the settings and characters are fictitious and not intended to represent
specific places or living persons.

WITHOUT REMORSE

A Berkley Book / published by arrangement with
Jack Ryan Limited Partnership

PRINTING HISTORY
G. P. Putnam's Sons edition / August 1993
Berkley edition / August 1994

All rights reserved.
Copyright © 1993 by Jack Ryan Limited Partnership.
Cover illustration by Rob Wood—Wood Ronsaville Harlin, Inc.
Author photo copyright © by John Earle.
This book may not be reproduced in whole or in part,
by mimeograph or any other means, without permission.
For information address: The Berkley Publishing Group,
200 Madison Avenue, New York, New York 10016.

ISBN: 0-425-14332-5

BERKLEY®
Berkley Books are published by The Berkley Publishing Group,
200 Madison Avenue, New York, New York 10016.
BERKLEY and the "B" design
are trademarks belonging to Berkley Publishing Corporation.

PRINTED IN THE UNITED STATES OF AMERICA

10 9 8 7 6 5 4 3 2 1

It never happens without help:
Bill, Darrell, and Pat, for "professional" advice;
C.J., Craig, Curt, Gerry, and Steve, for more of the same;
Russell for unexpected expertise

And for some *ex post facto* help of the highest magnitude:
G.R. and Wayne, for finding it;
Shelly, for doing the work;
Craig, Curt, Gerry, Steve P., Steve R.,
and Victor, for helping me to understand:

Think where man's glory most begins and ends.
And say my glory was I had such friends.
—William Butler Yeats

he is

in loving memory of Kyle Haydock,
July 5, 1983–August 1, 1991

Arma virumque cano
—*Publius Vergilius Maro*

Beware the fury of a patient man
—*John Dryden*

Without Remorse

Meeting Places

NOVEMBER

Camille had either been the world's most powerful hurricane or the largest tornado in history. Certainly it had done the job to this oil rig, Kelly thought, donning his tanks for his last dive into the Gulf. The superstructure was wrecked, and all four of the massive legs weakened—twisted like the ruined toy of a gigantic child. Everything that could safely be removed had already been torched off and lowered by crane onto the barge they were using as their dive base. What remained was a skeletal platform which would soon make a fine home for local game fish, he thought, entering the launch that would take him alongside. Two other divers would be working with him, but Kelly was in charge. They went over procedures on the way over while a safety boat circled nervously to keep the local fishermen away. It was foolish of them to be here—the fishing wouldn't be very good for the next few hours—but events like this attracted the curious. And it would be quite a show, Kelly thought with a grin as he rolled backwards off the dive boat.

It was eerie underneath. It always was, but comfortable, too. The sunlight wavered under the rippled surface, making variable curtains of light that trained across the legs of the platform. It also made for good visibility. The C4 charges were already in place, each one a block about six inches square and three inches deep, wired tight against the steel and fused to blow inward. Kelly took his time, checking each one, starting with the first rank ten feet above the bottom. He did it quickly because he didn't want to be down here that long, and neither did the others. The men behind him ran the prima-cord, wrapping it tight around the blocks. Both were local, experienced UDT men, trained almost as well as Kelly. He checked their work, and they checked his, for caution and thoroughness was the mark of such men. They finished the lower level in twenty minutes, and came up slowly to the upper rank, just ten feet below the surface, where the process was repeated, slowly and carefully. When you dealt with explosives, you didn't rush and you didn't take chances.

Colonel Robin Zacharias concentrated on the task at hand. There was an SA-2 site just over the next ridge. Already it had volleyed off three missiles, searching for the fighter-bombers he was here to protect. In the back seat of his F-105G Thunderchief was Jack Tait, his "bear," a lieutenant colonel and an expert in the field of defense-suppression. The two men had helped invent the doctrine which they were now implementing. He drove the Wild Weasel fighter, showing himself, trying to draw a shot, then ducking under it, closing in on the rocket site. It was a deadly, vicious game, not of hunter and prey, but of hunter and hunter—one small, swift, and delicate, and the other massive, fixed, and fortified. This site had given fits to the men of his wing. The commander was just too good with his radar, knowing when to switch it on and when to switch it off. Whoever the little bastard was, he'd killed two Weasels under Robin's command in the previous week, and so the colonel had drawn the mission for himself as soon as the frag order had gone up to hit this area again. It was his specialty: diagnosing, penetrating, and destroying air defenses—a vast, rapid, three-dimensional game in which the prize of winning was survival.

He was roaring low, never higher than five hundred feet, his fingers controlling the stick semiautomatically while Zacharias's eyes watched the karsk hilltops and his ears listened to the talk from the back seat.

"He's at our nine, Robin," Jack told him. "Still sweeping, but he doesn't have us. Spiraling in nicely."

We're not going to give him a Shrike, Zacharias thought. *They tried that the last time and he spoofed it somehow.* That error had cost him a major, a captain, and an aircraft . . . a fellow native of Salt Lake City, Al Wallace . . . friends for years . . . . damn it! He shook the thought off, not even reproving himself for the lower-case profanity.

"Giving him another taste," Zacharias said, pulling back on the stick. The Thud leaped upwards into the radar coverage of the site, hovering there, waiting. This site commander was probably Russian-trained. They weren't sure how many aircraft the man had killed—only that it had been more than enough—but he had to be a proud one because of it, and pride was deadly in this business.

"Launch . . . two, two valid launches, Robin," Tait warned from the back.

"Only two?" the pilot asked.

"Maybe he has to pay for them," Tait suggested cooly. "I have them at nine. Time to do some pilot magic, Rob."

"Like this?" Zacharias rolled left to keep them in view, pulling into them, and split-S-ing back down. He'd planned it well, ducking behind a ridge. He pulled out at a dangerous low altitude, but the SA-2 Guideline missiles went wild and dumb four thousand feet over his head.

"I think it's time," Tait said.

"I think you're right." Zacharias turned hard left, arming his cluster munitions. The F-105 skimmed over the ridge, dropping back down again while his eyes checked the next ridge, six miles and fifty seconds away.

"His radar is still up," Tait reported. "He knows we're coming."

"But he's only got one left." *Unless his reload crews are really hot today. Well, you can't allow for everything.*

"Some light flak at ten o'clock." It was too far to be a matter of concern, though it did tell him which way out not to take. "There's the plateau."

Maybe they could see him, maybe not. Possibly he was just one moving blip amid a screen full of clutter that some radar operator was striving to understand. The Thud moved faster at low level than anything ever made, and the camouflage motif on the upper surfaces was effective. They were probably looking up. There was a wall of jamming there now, part of the plan he'd laid out for the other Weasel bird, and normal American tactics were for a medium-altitude approach and steep dive. But they'd done that twice and failed, and so Zacharias decided to change the technique. Low level, he'd Rockeye the place, then the other Weasel would finish things off. His job was killing the command van and the commander within. He jinked the Thud left and right, up and down, to deny a good shooting track to anybody on the ground. You still had to worry about guns, too.

"Got the star!" Robin said. The SA-6 manual, written in Russian, called for six launchers around a central control point. With all the connective paths, the typical Guideline site looked just like a Star of David, which seemed rather blasphemous to the Colonel, but the thought only hovered at the edge of his mind as he centered the command van on his bombsight pipper.

"Selecting Rockeye," he said aloud, confirming the action to himself. For the last ten seconds, he held the aircraft rock steady. "Looking good . . . release . . . now!"

Four of the decidedly un-aerodynamic canisters fell free of the fighter's ejector racks, splitting open in midair, scattering thousands of submunitions over the area. He was well beyond the site before the bomblets landed. He didn't see people running for slit trenches, but he stayed low, reefing the Thud into a tight left turn, looking up to make sure he'd gotten the place once and for all. From three miles out his eyes caught an immense cloud of smoke in the center of the Star.

That's for Al, he allowed himself to think. No victory roll, just a thought, as he leveled out and picked a likely spot to egress the area. The strike force could come in now, and that SAM battery was out of business. Okay. He selected a notch in the ridge, racing for it just under Mach-1, straight and level now that the threat was behind him. *Home for Christmas.*

The red tracers that erupted from the small pass startled him. That wasn't supposed to be there. No deflection on them, just coming right in. He jinked up, as the gunner had thought he would, and the body of the aircraft passed right through the stream of fire. It shook violently and in the passage of a second good changed to evil.

"Robin!" a voice gasped over the intercom, but the main noise was from wailing alarms, and Zacharias knew in a fatal instant that his aircraft was doomed. It got worse almost before he could react. The engine died in flames, and then the Thud started a roll-yaw that told him the controls were gone. His reaction was automatic, a shout for ejection, but another gasp from the back made him turn just as he yanked the handles even though he knew the gesture was useless. His last sight of Jack Tait was blood that hung below the seat like a vapor trail, but by then his own back was wrenched with more pain than he'd ever known.

"Okay," Kelly said and fired off a flare. Another boat started tossing small explosive charges into the water to drive the fish away from the area. He watched and waited for five minutes, then looked at the safety man.

"Area's clear."

"Fire in the hole," Kelly said, repeating the mantra three times more. Then he twisted the handle on the detonator. The results were gratifying. The water around the legs turned to foam as the rig's legs were chopped off bottom and top. The fall was surprisingly slow. The entire structure slid off in one direction. There was an immense splash as the platform hit, and for one incongruous moment it appeared as though steel might float. But it couldn't. The see-through collection of light I-beams sank below sight, to rest right on the bottom, and another job was done.

Kelly disconnected the wires from the generator and tossed them over the side.

"Two weeks early. I guess you really wanted that bonus," the executive said. A former Navy fighter pilot, he admired a job well and quickly done. The oil wasn't going anywhere, after all. "Dutch was right about you."

"The Admiral is a good guy. He's done a lot for Tish and me."

"Well, we flew together for two years. Bad-ass fighter jock. Good to know those nice things he said were true." The executive liked working with people who'd had experiences like his own. He'd forgotten the terror of combat somehow. "What's with that? I've been meaning to ask." He pointed to the tattoo on Kelly's arm, a red seal, sitting up on his hind flippers and grinning impudently.

"Something we all did in my unit," Kelly explained as offhandedly as he could.

"What unit was that?"

"Can't say." Kelly added a grin to mute the refusal.

"I bet it's something to do with how Sonny got out—but okay." A former naval officer had to respect the rules. "Well, the check'll be in your account by the end of the business day, Mr. Kelly. I'll radio in so your wife can pick you up."

Tish Kelly was glowing her me-too look at the women in The Stork Shop. Not even three months yet, she could wear anything she wanted—well, almost. Too soon to shop for anything special, but she had the free time and wanted to see what the options were. She thanked the clerk, deciding that she'd bring John here in the evening and help him pick something out for her because he liked doing that. Now it was time to pick him up. The Plymouth wagon they'd driven down from Maryland was parked right outside, and she'd learned to navigate the streets of the coastal town. It was a nice break from the cold autumn rain of their home, to be here on the Gulf Coast where the summer was never really gone for more than a few days. She brought the wagon onto the street, heading south for the oil company's huge support yard. Even the traffic lights were in her favor. One changed to green in such a timely fashion that her foot didn't even have to touch the brakes.

The truck driver frowned as the light changed to amber. He was late, and running a little too fast, but the end of his six-hundred-mile run from Oklahoma was in sight. He stepped on the clutch and brake pedals with a sigh that abruptly changed to a gasp of surprise as both pedals went all the way to the floor at the same speed. The road ahead was clear, and he kept going straight, downshifting to cut speed, and frantically blowing his diesel horn. *Oh God, oh God, please don't—*

She never saw it coming. Her head never turned. The station wagon just jumped right through the intersection, and the driver's lingering memory would be of the young woman's profile disappearing under the hood of his diesel tractor, and then the awful lurch and shuddering surge upwards as the truck crushed the wagon under his front wheels.

The worst part of all was not feeling. Helen was her friend. Helen was dying, and Pam knew she should feel something, but she couldn't. The body was gagged, but that didn't stop all the sounds as Billy and Rick did what they were doing. Breath found its way out, and though her mouth couldn't move, the sounds were those of a woman soon to leave her life behind, but the trip had a price which had to be paid first, and Rick and Billy and Burt and Henry were doing the collecting. She tried to tell herself that she was really in another place, but the awful choking sounds kept bringing her eyes and her consciousness back to what reality had become. Helen was bad. Helen had tried to run away, and they couldn't have that. It had been explained to them all more than once, and was now being explained again in a way, Henry said, that they would be sure to remember. Pam felt where her ribs had once been broken, remembering her lesson. She knew there was nothing she could do as Helen's eyes fixed on her face. She tried to convey sympathy with her eyes. She didn't dare do more than that, and presently Helen stopped making noise, and it was over, for now. Now she could close her eyes and wonder when it would be her turn.

The crew thought it was pretty funny. They had the American pilot tied up right outside their sandbagged emplacement so he could see the guns that had shot him down. Less funny was what their prisoner had done, and they'd expressed their displeasure for it with fists and boots. They had the other body, too, and they set it right next to him, enjoying the look of sorrow and despair on his face as he looked at his fellow bandit. The intelligence officer from Hanoi was here now, checking the man's name against a list he'd brought along, bending down again to read off the name. It must have been something special, the gunners all thought, from the way he reacted to it, and the urgent phone call he'd made. After the prisoner passed out from his pain, the intelligence officer had swabbed some blood from the dead body and covered the live one's face with it. Then he'd snapped a few photos. That puzzled the gun crew. It was almost as though he wanted the live one to look as dead as the body next to him. How very odd.

It wasn't the first body he'd had to identify, but Kelly had thought that aspect of his life was a thing left far behind. Other people were there to support him, but not falling down wasn't the same thing as surviving, and there was no consolation at a moment such as this. He walked out of the emergency room, people's eyes on him, doctors and nurses. A priest had been called to perform his last duty, and had said a few things that he knew were unheard. A police officer explained that it hadn't been the driver's fault. The brakes had failed. Mechanical defect. Nobody's fault, really. Just one of those things. All the things he'd said before, on other such occasions, trying to explain to some innocent person why the main part of his world had just ended, as though it mattered. This Mr. Kelly was a tough one, the officer saw, and all the more vulnerable because of it. His wife and unborn child, whom he might have protected against any hazard, were dead by an accident. Nobody to blame. The trucker, a family man himself, was in the hospital, under sedation after having gone under his rig in the hope of finding her alive. People Kelly had been working with sat with him, and would help him make arrangements. There was nothing else to be done for a man who would have accepted hell rather than this; because he'd seen hell. But there was more than one hell, and he hadn't seen them all quite yet.

1
Enfant perdu

MAY

He'd never know why he stopped. Kelly pulled his Scout over to the shoulder without a conscious thought. She hadn't had her hand out soliciting a ride. She'd just been standing at the side of the road, watching the cars speed past in a spray of highway grit and a wake of fumes. Her posture was that of a hitchhiker, one knee locked, the other bent. Her clothes were clearly well used and a backpack was loosely slung over one shoulder. Her tawny, shoulder-length hair moved about in the rush of air from the traffic. Her face showed nothing, but Kelly didn't see that until he was already pressing his right foot on the brake pedal and angling onto the loose rock of the shoulder. He wondered if he should go back into the traffic, then decided that he was already committed, though to what he didn't know, exactly. The girl's eyes followed the car and, as he looked in his rearview mirror, she shrugged without any particular enthusiasm and walked towards him. The passenger window was down already, and in a few seconds she was there.

"Where you goin'?" she asked.

That surprised Kelly. He thought the first question—*Need*

10

a ride?—was supposed to be his. He hesitated for a second or two, looking at her. Twenty-one, perhaps, but old for her years. Her face wasn't dirty, but neither was it clean, perhaps from the wind and dust on the interstate. She wore a man's cotton shirt that hadn't been ironed in months, and her hair was knotted. But what surprised him most of all were her eyes. Fetchingly gray-green, they stared past Kelly into . . . what? He'd seen the look before often enough, but only on weary men. He'd had the look himself, Kelly remembered, but even then he'd never known what his eyes saw. It didn't occur to him that he wore a look not so different now.

"Back to my boat," he answered finally, not knowing what else to say. And that quickly, her eyes changed.

"You have a boat?" she asked. Her eyes lit up like a child's, a smile started there and radiated down the remainder of her face, as though he'd just answered an important question. She had a cute gap between her front teeth, Kelly noticed.

"Forty-footer—she's a diesel cruiser." He waved to the back of the Scout, whose cargo area was completely filled with cartons of groceries. "You want to come along?" he asked, also without thinking.

"Sure!" Without hesitation she yanked open the door and tossed her backpack on the floor in front of the passenger seat.

Pulling back into traffic was dangerous. Short of wheelbase and short of power, the Scout wasn't built for interstate-highway driving, and Kelly had to concentrate. The car wasn't fast enough to go in any other lane than the right, and with people coming on and off at every interchange, he had to pay attention because the Scout wasn't nimble enough to avoid all the idiots who were heading out to the ocean or wherever the hell people went on a three-day weekend.

You want to come along? he'd asked, and she'd said *Sure,* his mind reported to him. *What the hell?* Kelly frowned in frustration at the traffic because he didn't know the answer, but then there were a lot of questions to which he hadn't known the answers in the last six months. He told his mind to be quiet and watched the traffic, even though it kept up its inquiries in a nagging sort of background noise. One's mind, after all, rarely obeys its own commands.

Memorial Day weekend, he thought. The cars around him were filled with people rushing home from work, or those who'd already made that trip and picked up their families. The faces of children stared out of the rear-seat windows. One or two waved at him, but Kelly pretended not to notice. It was hard not having a soul, most especially when you could remember having had one.

Kelly ran a hand across his jaw, feeling the sandpaper texture. The hand itself was dirty. No wonder they'd acted that way at the grocery warehouse. *Letting yourself go, Kelly.*

Well, who the hell cares?

He turned to look at his guest and realized that he didn't know her name. He was taking her to his boat, and he didn't know her name. Amazing. She was staring forward, her face serene. It was a pretty face in profile. She was thin—perhaps willowy was the right word, her hair halfway between blonde and brown. Her jeans were worn and torn in a few places, and had begun life at one of those stores where they charged you extra to sell jeans that were pre-faded—or whatever they did with them. Kelly didn't know and cared less. One more thing not to care about.

Christ, how did you ever get this screwed up? his mind demanded of him. He knew the answer, but even that was not a full explanation. Different segments of the organism called John Terrence Kelly knew different parts of the whole story, but somehow they'd never all come together, leaving the separate fragments of what had once been a tough, smart, decisive man to blunder about in confusion—and despair? There was a happy thought.

He remembered what he'd once been. He remembered all the things that he had survived, amazed that he had done so. And perhaps the worst torment of all was that he didn't understand what had gone wrong. Sure, he knew what had *happened,* but those things had all been on the outside, and somehow his understanding had gotten lost, leaving him alive and confused and without purpose. He was on autopilot. He knew that, but not where fate was taking him.

She didn't try to talk, whoever she was, and that was just as well, Kelly told himself, though he sensed that there was something he ought to know. The realization came as a surprise. It was instinctual, and he'd always trusted his instincts, the warning chill on his neck and forearms. He looked around at the traffic and Kelly saw no particular danger other than cars with too much engine under the hood and not enough brains behind the wheel. His eyes scanned carefully and found nothing. But the warning didn't go away, and Kelly found himself checking the mirror for no good reason, while his left hand wandered down between his legs and found the checkered grips of the Colt automatic that hung hidden under the seat. His hand was stroking the weapon before he realized it.

Now what the hell did you do that for? Kelly pulled his hand back and shook his head with a grimace of frustration. But he did keep checking the mirror—just the normal watch on traffic, he lied to himself for the next twenty minutes.

The boatyard was a swarm of activity. The three-day weekend, of course. Cars were zipping about too fast for the small and badly paved parking lot, each driver trying to evade the Friday rush that each was, of course, helping to create. At least here the Scout came into its own. The high ground clearance and visibility gave Kelly an advantage as he maneuvered to *Springer*'s transom, and he looped around to back up to the slip he'd left six hours before. It was a relief, to crank up the windows and lock the car. His adventure on the highways was over, and the safety of the trackless water beckoned.

Springer was a diesel-powered motor yacht, forty-one feet long, custom built but similar in her lines and internal arrangements to a Pacemaker Coho. She was not especially pretty, but she had two sizable cabins, and the midships salon could be converted easily into a third. Her diesels were large but not supercharged, because Kelly preferred a large comfortable engine to a small straining one. He had a high-quality marine radar, every sort of communications gear that he could legally use, and navigation aids normally reserved for offshore fishermen. The fiberglass hull was immaculate, and there was not a speck of rust on the chromed rails, though he had deliberately done without the topside varnish that most yacht-owners cherished because it wasn't worth the maintenance time. *Springer* was a workboat, or was supposed to be.

Kelly and his guest alighted from the car. He opened the cargo door and started carrying the cartons aboard. The young lady, he saw, had the good sense to stay out of the way.

"Yo, Kelly!" a voice called from the flying bridge.

"Yeah, Ed, what was it?"

"Bad gauge. The generator brushes were a little worn, and I replaced them, but I think it was the gauge. Replaced that, too." Ed Murdock, the yard's chief mechanic, started down, and spotted the girl as he began to step off the ladder. Murdock tripped on the last step and nearly landed flat on his face in surprise. The mechanic's face evaluated the girl quickly and approvingly.

"Anything else?" Kelly asked pointedly.

"Topped off the tanks. The engines are warm," Murdock said, turning back to his customer. "It's all on your bill."

"Okay, thanks, Ed."

"Oh, Chip told me to tell you, somebody else made an offer in case you ever want to sell—"

Kelly cut him off. "No chance, Ed."

"She's a jewel, Kelly," Murdock said as he gathered his tools and walked away smiling, pleased with himself for the double entendre.

It took several seconds for Kelly to catch that one. It evoked a belated grunt of semi-amusement as he loaded the last of the groceries into the salon.

"What do I do?" the girl asked. She'd just been standing there, and Kelly had the impression that she was trembling a little and trying to hide it.

"Just take a seat topside," Kelly said, pointing to the flying bridge. "It'll take me a few minutes to get things started."

"Okay." She beamed a smile at him guaranteed to melt

ice, as though she knew exactly what one of his needs was.

Kelly walked aft to his cabin, pleased at least that he kept his boat tidy. The master-cabin head was also neat, and he found himself staring into the mirror and asking, "Okay, now what the fuck are you going to do?"

There was no immediate answer, but common decency told him to wash up. Two minutes later he entered the salon. He checked to see that the grocery cartons were secure, then went topside.

"I, uh, forgot to ask you something—" he began.

"Pam," she said, extending her hand. "What's yours?"

"Kelly," he replied, nonplussed yet again.

"Where we going, Mr. Kelly?"

"Just Kelly," he corrected her, keeping his distance for the moment. Pam just nodded and smiled again.

"Okay, Kelly, where to?"

"I own a little island about thirty—"

"You own an *island?*" Her eyes went wide.

"That's right." Actually, he just leased it, and that had been a fact long enough that Kelly didn't find it the least bit remarkable.

"Let's go!" she said with enthusiasm, looking back at the shore.

Kelly laughed out loud. "Okay, let's do that!"

He flipped on the bilge blowers. *Springer* had diesel engines, and he didn't really have to worry about fumes building up, but for all his recently acquired slovenliness, Kelly was a seaman, and his life on the water followed a strict routine, which meant observing all the safety rules that had been written in the blood of less careful men. After the prescribed two minutes, he punched the button to start the portside, then the starboard-side diesel. Both of the big Detroit Diesel engines caught at once, rumbling to impressive life as Kelly checked the gauges. Everything looked fine.

He left the flying bridge to slip his mooring lines, then came back and eased the throttles forward to take his boat out of the slip, checking tide and wind—there was not much of either at the moment—and looking for other boats.

Kelly advanced the port throttle a notch farther as he turned the wheel, allowing *Springer* to pivot all the more quickly in the narrow channel, and then he was pointed straight out. He advanced the starboard throttle next, bringing his cruiser to a mannerly five knots as he headed past the ranks of motor and sail yachts. Pam was looking around at the boats, too, mainly aft, and her eyes fixed on the parking lot for a long couple of seconds before she looked forward again, her body relaxing more as she did so.

"You know anything about boats?" Kelly asked.

"Not much," she admitted, and for the first time he noticed her accent.

"Where you from?"

"Texas. How about you?"

"Indianapolis, originally, but it's been a while."

"What's this?" she asked. Her hands reached out to touch the tattoo on his forearm.

"It's from one of the places I've been," he said. "Not a very nice place."

"Oh, over there." She understood.

"That's the place." Kelly nodded matter-of-factly. They were out of the yacht basin now, and he advanced the throttles yet again.

"What did you do there?"

"Nothing to talk to a lady about," Kelly replied, looking around from a half-standing position.

"What makes you think I'm a lady?" she asked.

It caught him short, but he was getting used to it by now. He'd also found that talking to a girl, no matter what the subject, was something that he needed to do. For the first time he answered her smile with one of his own.

"Well, it wouldn't be very nice of me if I assumed that you weren't."

"I wondered how long it would be before you smiled." *You have a very nice smile,* her tone told him.

How's six months grab you? he almost said. Instead he laughed, mainly at himself. That was something else he needed to do.

"I'm sorry. Guess I haven't been very good company." He turned to look at her again and saw understanding in her eyes. Just a quiet look, very human and feminine, but it shook Kelly. He could feel it happen, and ignored the part of his consciousness that told him that it was something he'd needed badly for months. That was something he didn't need to hear, especially from himself. Loneliness was bad enough without reflection on its misery. Her hand reached out yet again, ostensibly to stroke the tattoo, but that wasn't what it was all about. It was amazing how warm her touch was, even under a hot afternoon sun. Perhaps it was a measure of just how cold his life had become.

But he had a boat to navigate. There was a freighter about a thousand yards ahead. Kelly was now at full cruising power, and the trim tabs at the stern had automatically engaged, bringing the boat to an efficient planing angle as her speed came to eighteen knots. The ride was smooth until they got into the merchant ship's wake. Then *Springer* started pitching, up and down three or four feet at the bow as Kelly maneuvered left to get around the worst of it. The freighter grew before them like a cliff as they overtook her.

"Is there someplace I can change?"

"My cabin is aft. You can move in forward if you want."

"Oh, really?" She giggled. "Why would I do that?"

"Huh?" She'd done it to him again.

Pam went below, careful to hold on to the rails as she carried her backpack. She hadn't been wearing much. She reappeared in a few minutes wearing even less, short-shorts and a halter, no shoes, and perceptibly more relaxed. She had dancer's legs, Kelly noticed, slim and very feminine. Also very pale, which surprised him. The halter was loose on her, and frayed at the edges. Perhaps she'd recently lost weight, or maybe she'd deliberately bought it overlarge. Whatever the reason, it showed quite a bit of her chest. Kelly caught himself shifting his eyes, and chastised himself for ogling the girl. But Pam made it hard not to. Now she grasped his upper arm and sat up against him. Looking over, he could see right down the halter just as far as he wanted.

"You like them?" she asked.

Kelly's brain and mouth went into lock. He made a few embarrassed sounds, and before he could decide to say anything she was laughing. But not at him. She was waving at the crew of the freighter, who waved back. It was an Italian ship, and one of the half dozen or so men hanging over the rail at the stern blew Pam a kiss. She did the same in return.

It made Kelly jealous.

He turned the wheel to port again, taking his boat across the bow wave of the freighter, and as he passed the vessel's bridge he tooted his horn. It was the correct thing to do, though few small boaters ever bothered. By this time, a watch officer had his glasses on Kelly—actually Pam, of course. He turned and shouted something to the wheelhouse. A moment later the freighter's enormous "whistle" sounded its own bass note, nearly causing the girl to leap from her seat.

Kelly laughed, and so did she, and then she wrapped her arms tightly around his bicep. He could feel a finger tracing its way around the tattoo.

"It doesn't feel like—"

Kelly nodded. "I know. Most people expect it to feel like paint or something."

"Why did—"

"—I get it? Everybody in the outfit did. Even the officers. It was something to do, I guess. Pretty dumb, really."

"I think it's cute."

"Well, I think you're pretty cute."

"You say the nicest things." She moved slightly, rubbing her breast against his upper arm.

Kelly settled down to a steady cruising speed of eighteen knots as he worked his way out of Baltimore harbor. The Italian freighter was the only merchant ship in view, and the seas were flat, with one-foot ripples. He kept to the main shipping channel all the way out into the Chesapeake Bay.

"You thirsty?" she asked as they turned south.

"Yeah. There's a fridge in the kitchenette—it's in the—"

"I saw it. What do you want?"

"Get two of anything."

"Okay," she replied brightly. When she stood, the soft feeling worked its way straight up his arm, finally departing at the shoulder.

"What's that?" she asked on returning. Kelly turned and winced. He'd been so content with the girl on his arm that he'd neglected to pay attention to the weather. "That" was a thunderstorm, a towering mass of cumulonimbus clouds that reached eight or ten miles skyward.

"Looks like we're going to get some rain," he told her as he took the beer from her hand.

"When I was a little girl, that meant a tornado."

"Well, not here, it doesn't," Kelly replied, looking around the boat to make sure that there was no loose gear. Below, he knew, everything was in its proper place, because it always was, ennui or not. Then he switched on his marine radio. He caught a weather forecast at once, one that ended with the usual warning.

"Is this a small craft?" Pam asked.

"Technically it is, but you can relax. I know what I'm doing. I used to be a chief bosun's mate."

"What's that?"

"A sailor. In the Navy, that is. Besides, this is a pretty big boat. The ride might get a little bumpy, is all. If you're worried, there are life jackets under the seat you're on."

"Are you worried?" Pam asked. Kelly smiled and shook his head. "Okay." She resumed her previous position, her chest against his arm, her head on his shoulder, a dreamy expression in her eyes, as though anticipating something that was to be, storm or no storm.

Kelly wasn't worried—at least not about the storm—but he wasn't casual about things either. Passing Bodkin Point, he continued east across the shipping channel. He didn't turn south until he was in water he knew to be too shallow for anything large enough to run him down. Every few minutes he turned to keep an eye on the storm, which was charging right in at twenty knots or so. It had already blotted out the sun. A fast-moving storm most often meant a violent one, and his new southerly course meant that he wasn't outrunning it any longer. Kelly finished off his beer and decided against another. Visibility would drop fast. He pulled out a plastic-coated chart and fixed it in place on the table to the right of the instrument panel, marked his position with a grease pencil, and then checked to make sure that his course didn't take him into shallows—*Springer* drew four and a half feet of water, and for Kelly anything less than eight feet constituted shallow water. Satisfied, he set his compass course and relaxed again. His training was his buffer against both danger and complacency.

"Won't be long now," Pam observed, just a trace of unease in her voice as she held on to him.

"You can head below if you want," Kelly said. "It's gonna get rainy and windy. And bumpy."

"But not dangerous."

"No, unless I do something really dumb. I'll try not to," he promised.

"Can I stay here and see what it's like?" she asked, clearly unwilling to leave his side, though Kelly did not know why.

"It's going to get wet," he warned her again.

"That's okay." She smiled brightly, fixing even more tightly to his arm.

Kelly throttled back some, taking the boat down off plane. There was no reason to hurry. With the throttles eased back, there was no longer a need for two hands on the controls either. He wrapped his arm around the girl, her head came automatically down on his shoulder again, and despite the approaching storm everything was suddenly right with the world. Or that's what Kelly's emotions told him. His reason said something else, and the two views would not reconcile themselves. His reason reminded him that the girl at his side was—what? He didn't know. His emotions told him that it didn't matter a damn. She was what he needed. But Kelly was not a man ruled by emotions, and the conflict made him glower at the horizon.

"Something wrong?" Pam asked.

Kelly started to say something, then stopped, and reminded himself that he was alone on his yacht with a pretty girl. He let emotion win this round for a change.

"I'm a little confused, but, no, nothing is wrong that I know about."

"I can tell that you—"

Kelly shook his head. "Don't bother. Whatever it is, it can wait. Just relax and enjoy the ride."

The first gust of wind arrived a moment later, heeling the boat a few degrees to port. Kelly adjusted his rudder to compensate. The rain arrived quickly. The first few warning sprinkles were rapidly followed by solid sheets that marched like curtains across the surface of the Chesapeake Bay. Within a minute visibility was down to only a few hundred yards, and the sky was as dark as late twilight. Kelly made sure his running lights were on. The waves started kicking up in earnest, driven by what felt like thirty knots of wind. Weather and seas were directly on the beam. He decided that he could keep going, but he was in a good anchoring place now, and wouldn't be in another for five hours. Kelly took another look at the chart, then switched on his radar to verify his position. Ten feet of water, a sand bottom that the chart called HRD and was therefore good holding ground. He brought *Springer* into the wind and eased the throttles until the propellers were providing just enough thrust to overcome the driving force of the wind.

"Take the wheel," he told Pam.

"But I don't know what to do!"

"It's all right. Just hold her steady and steer the way I tell you to. I have to go forward to set the anchors. 'Kay?"

"You be careful!" she shouted over the gusting wind. The waves were about five feet now, and the bow of the boat was leaping up and down. Kelly gave her shoulder a squeeze and went forward.

He had to watch himself, of course, but his shoes had no-skid soles, and Kelly knew his business. He kept his hands on the grab rail all the way around the superstructure, and in a minute he was on the foredeck. Two anchors were clipped to the deck, a Danforth and a CQR plow-type, both slightly oversized. He tossed the Danforth over first, then signaled for Pam to ease the wheel to port. When the boat had moved perhaps fifty feet south, he dropped the CQR over the side as well. Both ropes were already set to the proper lengths, and after checking that all was secure, Kelly made his way back to the flying bridge.

Pam looked nervous until the moment that he sat back down on the vinyl bench—everything was covered with water now, and their clothes were soaked through. Kelly eased the throttles to idle, allowing the wind to push *Springer* back nearly a hundred feet. By that time both anchors had dug into the bottom. Kelly frowned at their placement. He ought to have set them farther apart. But only one anchor was really necessary. The second was just insurance. Satisfied, he switched off the diesels.

"I could fight the storm all the way down, but I'd prefer not to," he explained.

"So we park here for the night?"

"That's right. You can go down to your cabin and—"

"You want me to go away?"

"No—I mean, if you don't like it here—" Her hand came up to his face. He barely caught her words through the wind and rain.

"I like it here." Somehow it didn't seem like a contradiction at all.

A moment later Kelly asked himself why it had taken so long. All the signals had been there. There was another brief discussion between emotion and reason, and reason lost again. There was nothing to be afraid of here, just a person as lonely as he. It was so easy to forget. Loneliness didn't tell you what you had lost, only that something was missing. It took something like this to define that emptiness. Her skin was soft, dripping with rain, but warm. It was so different from the rented passion that he'd tried twice in the past month, each time coming away disgusted with himself.

But this was something else. This was real. Reason cried out one last time that it couldn't be, that he'd picked her up at the side of the road and had known her for only a brief span of hours. Emotion said that it didn't matter. As though observing the conflict in his mind, Pam pulled the halter over her head. Emotion won.

"They look just fine to me," Kelly said. His hand moved to them, touching delicately. They felt just fine, too. Pam hung the halter on the steering wheel and pressed her face against his, her hands pulling him forward, taking charge in a very feminine way. Somehow her passion wasn't animalistic. Something made it different. Kelly didn't know what it was, but didn't search for the reason, not now.

Both rose to their feet. Pam nearly slipped, but Kelly caught her, dropping to his knees to help remove her shorts. Then it was her turn to unbutton his shirt after placing his hands on her breasts. His shirt remained in place for a long moment because neither wanted his hands to move, but then it was done, one arm at a time, and his jeans went next. Kelly slipped out of his shoes as the rest came off. Both stood for the next embrace, weaving as the boat pitched and rocked beneath them, the rain and wind pelting them. Pam took his hand and led him just aft of the driver's console, guiding him down to a supine position on the deck. She mounted him at once. Kelly tried to sit up, but she didn't let him, instead leaning forward while her hips moved with gentle violence. Kelly was as unready for that as he'd been for everything else this afternoon, and his shout seemed to outscream the thunder. When his eyes opened, her face was inches from him, and the smile was like that on a stone angel in a church.

"I'm sorry, Pam, I—"

She stopped his apology with a giggle. "Are you always this good?"

Long minutes later, Kelly's arms were wrapped around her thin form, and so they stayed until the storm passed. Kelly was afraid to let go, afraid of the possibility that this was as unreal as it had to be. Then the wind acquired a chill, and they went below. Kelly got some towels and they dried each other off. He tried to smile at her, but the hurt was back, all the more powerful from the joy of the previous hour, and it was Pam's turn to be surprised. She sat beside him on the deck of the salon, and when she pulled his face down to her chest, he was the one who wept, until her chest was wet again. She didn't ask. She was smart enough for that. Instead she held him tightly until he was done and his breathing came back to normal.

"I'm sorry," he said after a while. Kelly tried to move but she wouldn't let him.

"You don't have to explain. But I'd like to help," she said, knowing that she already had. She'd seen it from almost the first moment in the car: a strong man, badly hurt. So different from the others she had known. When he finally spoke, she could feel his words on her breast.

"It's been nearly seven months. Down in Mississippi on a job. She was pregnant, we just found out. She went to the store, and—it was a truck, a big tractor-trailer rig. The linkage broke." He couldn't make himself say more, and he didn't have to.

"What was her name?"

"Tish—Patricia."

"How long were you—"

"Year and a half. Then she was just . . . gone. I never expected it. I mean, I put my time in, did some dangerous stuff, but that's all over, and that was me, not her. I never thought—" His voice cracked again. Pam looked down at him in the muted light of the salon, seeing the scars she'd missed before and wondering what their story was. It didn't matter. She brought her cheek down to the top of his head. *He should have been a father right about now. Should have been a lot of things.*

"You never let it out, did you?"

"No."

"And why now?"

"I don't know," he whispered.

"Thank you." Kelly looked up in surprise. "That's the nicest thing a man has ever done to me."

"I don't understand."

"Yes, you do," Pam replied. "And Tish understands, too. You let me take her place. Or maybe she did. She loved you, John. She must have loved you a lot. And she still does. Thank you for letting me help."

He started crying again, and Pam brought his head back down, cradling him like a small child. It lasted ten minutes, though neither looked at a clock. When he was done, he kissed her in gratitude that rapidly turned to renewed passion. Pam lay back, letting him take charge as he needed to do now that he was again a man in spirit. Her reward was in keeping with the magnitude of what she had done for him, and this time it was her cries that canceled out the thunder. Later, he fell asleep at her side, and she kissed his unshaven cheek. That was when her own tears began at the wonder of what the day had brought after the terror with which it had begun.

2

Encounters

Kelly awoke at his accustomed time, thirty minutes before sunrise, to the mewing of gulls and saw the first dull glow on the eastern horizon. At first he was confused to find a slender arm across his chest, but other feelings and memories explained things in a few seconds. He extricated himself from her side and moved the blanket to cover her from the morning chill. It was time for ship's business.

Kelly got the drip coffee machine going, then he pulled on a pair of swim trunks and headed topside. He hadn't forgotten to set the anchor light, he was gratified to see. The sky had cleared off, and the air was cool after the thunderstorms of the previous night. He went forward and was surprised to see that one of his anchors had dragged somewhat. Kelly reproached himself for that, even though nothing had actually gone wrong. The water was a flat, oily calm and the breeze gentle. The pink-orange glow of first light decorated the tree-spotted coastline to the east. All in all, it seemed as fine a morning as he could remember. Then he remembered that what had changed had nothing at all to do with the weather.

"Damn," he whispered to the dawn not yet broken. Kelly was stiff, and did some stretching exercises to get the kinks out, slow to realize how fine he felt without the usual hangover. Slower still to recall how long it had been. Nine hours of sleep? he wondered. That much? No wonder he felt so good. The next part of the morning routine was to get a squeegee to dispose of the water that had pooled on the fiberglass deck.

His head turned at the low, muted rumble of marine diesels. Kelly looked west to spot it, but there was a little mist that way, being pushed his way by the breeze, and he couldn't make anything out. He went to the control station on the flying bridge and got out his glasses, just in time to have a twelve-inch spotlight blaze through the marine 7 x 50s. Kelly was dazzled by the lights, which just as suddenly switched off, and a loud-hailer called across the water.

"Sorry, Kelly. Didn't know it was you." Two minutes later the familiar shape of a Coast Guard forty-one-foot patrol boat eased alongside *Springer*. Kelly scrambled along the portside to deploy his rubber fenders.

"You trying to kill me or something?" Kelly said in a conversational voice.

"Sorry." Quartermaster First Class Manuel "Portagee" Oreza stepped from one gun'l to the other with practiced ease. He gestured to the fenders. "Wanna hurt my feelings?"

"Bad sea manners, too," Kelly went on as he walked towards his visitor.

"I spoke to the young lad about that already," Oreza assured him. He held out his hand. "Morning, Kelly."

The outstretched hand had a Styrofoam cup filled with coffee. Kelly took it and laughed.

"Apology accepted, sir." Oreza was famous for his coffee.

"Long night. We're all tired, and it's a young crew," the coastguardsman explained wearily. Oreza was nearly twenty-eight himself, and by far the oldest man of his boat crew.

"Trouble?" Kelly asked.

Oreza nodded, looking around at the water. "Kinda. Some damned fool in a little day-sailer turned up missing after that little rainstorm we had last night, and we've been looking all over bejazzus for him."

"Forty knots of wind. Fair blow, Portagee," Kelly pointed out. "Came in right fast, too."

"Yeah, well, we rescued six boats already, just this one still missing. You see anything unusual last night?"

"No. Came outa Baltimore around . . . oh, sixteen hundred, I suppose. Two and a half hours to get here. Anchored right after the storm hit. Visibility was pretty bad, didn't see much of anything before we went below."

"We," Oreza observed, stretching. He walked over to the wheel, picked up the rain-soaked halter, and tossed it to Kelly. The look on his face was neutral, but there was interest behind the eyes. He hoped his friend had found someone. Life hadn't been especially fair to the man.

Kelly handed the cup back with a similarly neutral expression.

"There was one freighter coming out behind us," he went on. "Italian flag, container boat about half full, must have been knocking down fifteen knots. Anybody else clear the harbor?"

"Yeah." Oreza nodded and spoke with professional irritation. "I'm worried about that. Fuckin' merchies plowing out at full speed, not paying attention."

"Well, hell, you stand outside the wheelhouse, you might get wet. Besides, sea-and-anchor detail might violate some union rule, right? Maybe your guy got run down," Kelly noted darkly. It wouldn't have been the first time, even on a body of water as civilized as the Chesapeake.

"Maybe," Oreza said, surveying the horizon. He frowned, not believing the suggestion and too tired to hide it. "Anyway, you see a little day-sailer with an orange-and-white candystripe sail, you want to give me a call?"

"No problem."

Oreza looked forward and turned back. "Two anchors for that little puff o' wind we had? They're not far enough apart. Thought you knew better."

"Chief Bosun's Mate," Kelly reminded him. "Since when does a bookkeeper get that snotty with a real seaman?" It was only a joke. Kelly knew Portagee was the better man in a small boat. Though not by much of a margin, and both knew that, too.

Oreza grinned on his way back to the cutter. After jumping back aboard, he pointed to the halter in Kelly's hand. "Don't forget to put your shirt on, *Boats!* Looks like it oughta fit just fine." A laughing Oreza disappeared inside the wheelhouse before Kelly could come up with a rejoinder. There appeared to be someone inside who was not in uniform, which surprised Kelly. A moment later, the cutter's engines rumbled anew and the forty-one-boat moved northwest.

"Good mornin'." It was Pam. "What was that?"

Kelly turned. She wasn't wearing any more now than when he'd put the blanket on her, but Kelly instantly decided that the only time she'd surprise him again would be when she did something predictable. Her hair was a medusalike mass of tangles, and her eyes were unfocused, as though she'd not slept well at all.

"Coast Guard. They're looking for a missing boat. How'd you sleep?"

"Just fine." She came over to him. Her eyes had a soft, dreamlike quality that seemed strange so early in the morning, but could not have been more attractive to the wide-awake sailor.

"Good morning." A kiss. A hug. Pam held her arms aloft and executed something like a pirouette. Kelly grabbed her slender waist and hoisted her aloft.

"What do you want for breakfast?" he asked.

"I don't eat breakfast," Pam replied, reaching down for him.

"Oh." Kelly smiled. "Okay."

She changed her mind about an hour later. Kelly fixed eggs and bacon on the galley stove, and Pam wolfed it down so speedily that he fixed seconds despite her protests. On further inspection, the girl wasn't merely thin, some of her ribs were visible. She was undernourished, an observation that prompted yet another unasked question. But whatever the cause, he could remedy it. Once she'd consumed four eggs, eight slices of bacon, and five pieces of toast, roughly double Kelly's normal morning intake, it was time for the day to begin properly. He showed her how to work the galley appliances while he saw to recovering the anchors.

They got back under way just shy of a lazy eight o'clock. It promised to be a hot, sunny Saturday. Kelly donned his sunglasses and relaxed in his chair, keeping himself alert with the odd sip from his mug. He maneuvered west, tracing down the edge of the main ship channel to avoid the hundreds of fishing boats he fully expected to sortie from their various harbors today in pursuit of rockfish.

"What are those things?" Pam asked, pointing to the floats decorating the water to port.

"Floats for crab pots. They're really more like cages. Crabs get in and can't get out. You leave floats so you know where they are." Kelly handed Pam his glasses and pointed to a bay-build workboat about three miles to the east.

"They trap the poor things?" Kelly laughed.

"Pam, the bacon you had for breakfast? The hog didn't commit suicide, did he?"

She gave him an impish look. "Well, no."

"Don't get too excited. A crab is just a big aquatic spider, even though it tastes good."

Kelly altered course to starboard to clear a red nun-buoy.

"Seems kinda cruel, though."

"Life can be that way," Kelly said too quickly and then regretted it.

Pam's response was as heartfelt as Kelly's. "Yeah, I know."

Kelly didn't turn to look at her, only because he stopped himself. There'd been emotional content in her reply, something to remind him that she, too, had demons. The moment passed quickly, however. She leaned back into the capacious conning chair, leaning against him and making things right again. One last time Kelly's senses warned him that something was not right at all. But there were no demons out here, were there?

"You'd better go below."

"Why?"

"Sun's going to be hot today. There's some lotion in the medicine cabinet, main head."

"Head?"

"Bathroom!"

"Why is everything different on a boat?"

Kelly laughed. "That's so sailors can be the boss out here. Now, shoo! Go get that stuff and put a lot on or you'll look like a french fry before lunch."

Pam made a face. "I need a shower, too. Is that okay?"

"Good idea," Kelly answered without looking. "No sense scaring the fish away."

"You!" She swatted him on the arm and headed below.

"Vanished, just plain vanished," Oreza growled. He was hunched over a chart table at the Thomas Point Coast Guard Station.

"We shoulda got some air cover, helicopter or something," the civilian observed.

"Wouldn't have mattered, not last night. Hell, the gulls rode that blow out."

"But where'd he go?"

"Beats me, maybe the storm sank his ass." Oreza glowered at the chart. "You said he was northbound. We covered all these ports and Max took the western shore. You sure the description of the boat was correct?"

"Sure? Hell, we did everything but buy the goddamned boat for 'em!" The civilian was as short-tempered as twenty-eight hours of caffeine-induced wakefulness could explain, even worse for having been ill on the patrol boat, much to the amusement of the enlisted crew. His stomach felt like it was coated with steel wool. "Maybe it did sink," he concluded gruffly, not believing it for a moment.

"Wouldn't that solve your problem?" His attempt at levity earned him a growl, and Quartermaster First Class

Manuel Oreza caught a warning look from the Station commander, a gray-haired warrant officer named Paul English.

"You know," the man said in a state of exhaustion, "I don't think anything is going to solve this problem, but it's my job to try."

"Sir, we've all had a long night. My crew is racked out, and unless you have a really good reason to stay up, I suggest you find a bunk and get a few Zs, sir."

The civilian looked up with a tired smile to mute his earlier words. "Petty Officer Oreza, smart as you are, you ought to be an officer."

"If I'm so smart, how come we missed our friend last night?"

"That guy we saw around dawn?"

"Kelly? Ex–Navy chief, solid guy."

"Kinda young for a chief, isn't he?" English asked, looking at a not very good photo the spotlight had made possible. He was new at the station.

"It came along with a Navy Cross," Oreza explained.

The civilian looked up. "So, you wouldn't think—"

"Not a chance in hell."

The civilian shook his head. He paused for a moment, then headed off to the bunk room. They'd be going out again before sunset, and he'd need the sack time.

"So how was it?" English asked after the man left the room.

"That guy is shipping a lot of gear, Cap'n." As a station commander, English was entitled to the title, all the more so that he let Portagee run his boat his way. "Sure as hell he doesn't sleep much."

"He's going to be with us for a while, on and off, and I want you to handle it."

Oreza tapped the chart with a pencil. "I still say this would be a perfect place to keep watch from, and I know we can trust the guy."

"The man says no."

"The man ain't no seaman, Mr. English. I don't mind when the guy tells me what to do, but he don't know enough to tell me how to do it." Oreza circled the spot on the chart.

• • •

"I don't like this."

"You don't have to like it," the taller man said. He unfolded his pocket knife and slit the heavy paper to reveal a plastic container of white powder. "A few hours' work and we turn three hundred thousand. Something wrong with that, or am I missin' something?"

"And this is just the start," the third man said.

"What do we do with the boat?" asked the man with the scruples.

The tall one looked up from what he was doing. "You get rid of that sail?"

"Yeah."

"Well, we can stash the boat . . . but probably smarter to scuttle. Yeah, that's what we'll do."

"And Angelo?" All three looked over to where the man was lying, unconscious still, and bleeding.

"I guess we scuttle him, too," the tall one observed without much in the way of emotion. "Right here ought to be fine."

"Maybe two weeks, there won't be nothin' left. Lots of critters out there." The third one waved outside at the tidal wetlands.

"See how easy it is? No boat, no Angelo, no risk, and three hundred thousand bucks. I mean, how much more do you expect, Eddie?"

"His friends still ain't gonna like it." The comment came more from a contrarian disposition than moral conviction.

"What friends?" Tony asked without looking. "He ratted, didn't he? How many friends does a rat have?"

Eddie bent to the logic of the situation and walked over to Angelo's unconscious form. The blood was still pumping out of the many abrasions, and the chest was moving slowly as he tried to breathe. It was time to put an end to that. Eddie knew it; he'd merely been trying to delay the inevitable. He pulled a small .22 automatic from his pocket, placed it to the back of Angelo's skull, and fired once. The body spasmed, then went slack. Eddie set his gun aside and dragged the body outside, leaving Henry and his friend to do the important stuff. They'd brought some fish netting, which he wrapped around the body before dumping it in the water behind their small motorboat. A cautious man, Eddie looked around, but there wasn't much danger of intruders here. He motored off until he found a likely spot a few hundred yards off, then stopped and drifted while he lifted a few concrete blocks from the boat and tied them to the netting. Six were enough to sink Angelo about eight feet to the bottom. The water was pretty clear here, and that worried Eddie a little until he saw all the crabs. Angelo would be gone in less than two weeks. It was a great improvement over the way they usually did business, something to remember for the future. Disposing of the little sailboat would be harder. He'd have to find a deeper spot, but he had all day to think about it.

Kelly altered course to starboard to avoid a gaggle of sports craft. The island was visible now, about five miles ahead. Not much to look at, just a low bump on the horizon, not even a tree, but it was his and it was as private as a man could wish. About the only bad news was the miserable TV reception.

Battery Island had a long and undistinguished history. Its current name, more ironic than appropriate, had come in the early nineteenth century, when some enterprising militiaman had decided to place a small gun battery there to guard a narrow spot in the Chesapeake Bay against the British, who were sailing towards Washington, D.C., to punish the new nation that had been so ill-advised as to challenge the power of the world's foremost navy. One British squadron commander had taken note of a few harmless puffs of smoke on the island, and, probably with more amusement than malice, had taken one ship within gun range and let loose a few salvos from the long guns on his lower deck. The citizen soldiers manning the battery hadn't needed much encouragement to make a run for their rowboats and hustle to the mainland, and shortly thereafter a landing party of Jack Tars and a few Royal Marines had rowed ashore in a pinnace to drive nails into the touch holes, which was what "spiking guns" meant. After this brief diversion, the British had continued their leisurely sail up the Patuxent River, from which their army had walked to Washington and back, having forced Dolley Madison to evacuate the White House. The British campaign had next headed to Baltimore, where a somewhat different outcome resulted.

Battery Island, under reluctant federal ownership, became an embarrassing footnote to a singularly useless war. Without so much as a caretaker to look after the earthen emplacements, weeds overtook the island, and so things had remained for nearly a hundred years.

With 1917 came America's first real foreign war, and America's navy, suddenly faced with the U-boat menace, needed a sheltered place to test its guns. Battery Island seemed ideal, only a few steaming hours from Norfolk, and so for several months in the fall of that year, 12- and 14-inch battleship rifles had crashed and thundered, blasting nearly a third of the island below mean low water and greatly annoying the migratory birds, who'd long since realized that no hunters ever shot at them from the place. About the only new thing that happened was the scuttling of over a hundred World War I–built cargo ships a few miles to the south, and these, soon overgrown with weeds, rapidly took on the appearance of islands themselves.

A new war and new weapons had brought the sleepy island back to life. The nearby naval air station needed a place for pilots to test weapons. The happy coincidence of the location of Battery Island and the scuttled ships from World War I had made for an instant bombing range. As a result, three massive concrete observation bunkers were built, from which officers could observe TBFs and SB2C bombers practicing runs on targets that looked like ship-shaped islands—and pulverizing quite a few of them until one bomb hung on the rack just long enough to obliterate one of the bunkers, thankfully empty. The site of the destroyed bunker had been cleared in the name of tidiness, and the island converted to a rescue station, from which a crashboat might respond to an aircraft accident. *That* had required building a concrete quay and boathouse and refurbishment of the two remaining bunkers. All in all, the island had served the local economy, if not the federal budget, well, until the advent of helicopters made crashboats unnecessary, and the island had been declared surplus. And so the island remained unnoticed on a register of unwanted federal property until Kelly had managed to acquire a lease.

Pam leaned back on her blanket as they approached, basting in the warm sun beneath a thick coating of suntan lotion. She didn't have a swimsuit, and wore only a bra and panties. It didn't offend Kelly, but the impropriety of it was vaguely disturbing for no reason that stood up to logical analysis. In any case, his current job was driving his boat. Further contemplation of her body could wait, he told himself about every minute, when his eyes darted that way to make sure she was still there.

He eased the wheel farther to the right to pass well clear of a large fishing yacht. He gave Pam another look. She'd slipped the straps of her bra down off her shoulders for a more even tan. Kelly approved.

The sound startled both of them, rapid short blasts on the fishing boat's diesel horns. Kelly's head scanned all the way around, then centered on the boat that lay two hundred yards to port. It was the only thing close enough to be of concern, and also seemed to be the source of the noise. On the flying bridge a man was waving at him. Kelly turned to port to approach. He took his time bringing *Springer* alongside. Whoever this guy was, he wasn't much of a boat handler, and when he brought his craft to a halt, twenty feet away, he kept his hand on the throttles.

"What's the problem?" Kelly called over the loud-hailer.

"Lost our props!" a swarthy man hollered back. "What do we do?"

Row, Kelly almost replied, but that wasn't very neighborly. He brought his boat closer in to survey the situation. It was a medium-sized fishing cruiser, a fairly recent Hatteras. The man on the bridge was about five-eight, fiftyish, and bare-chested except for a mat of dark hair. A woman was also visible, also rather downcast.

"No screws at all?" Kelly asked when they were closer.

"I think we hit a sandbar," the man explained. "About half a mile that way." He pointed to a place Kelly kept clear of.

"Sure enough, there's one that way. I can give you a tow if you want. You have good enough line for it?"

"Yes!" the man replied immediately. He went forward to his rope locker. The woman aboard continued to look embarrassed.

Kelly maneuvered clear for a moment, observing the other "captain," a term his mind applied ironically. He couldn't read charts. He didn't know the proper way of attracting another boat's attention. He didn't even know how to call the Coast Guard. All he'd managed to do was buy a Hatteras yacht, and while that spoke well of his judgment, Kelly figured it had more likely come from a smart salesman. But then the man surprised Kelly. He handled his lines with skill and waved *Springer* in.

Kelly maneuvered his stern in close, then went aft to his well deck to take the towing line, which he secured to the big cleat on the transom. Pam was up and watching now. Kelly hustled back to the fly bridge and coaxed his throttle a crack.

"Get on your radio," he told the Hatteras owner. "Leave your rudder amidships till I tell you different. Okay?"

"Got it."

"Hope so," Kelly whispered to himself, pushing the throttle levers until the towing line came taut.

"What happened to him?" Pam asked.

"People forget there's a bottom under this water. You hit it hard enough and you break things." He paused. "You might want to put some more clothes on."

Pam giggled and went below. Kelly increased speed carefully to about four knots before starting the turn south. He'd done this all before, and grumbled that if he did it one more time he'd have special stationery printed up for the bills.

Kelly brought *Springer* alongside very slowly, mindful of the boat he was towing. He scurried off the bridge to drop his fenders, then jumped ashore to tie off a pair of spring lines before heading towards the Hatteras. The owner already had his mooring lines set up, and tossed them to Kelly on the quay while he set his fenders. Hauling the boat in a few feet was a good chance to show his muscles to Pam. It only took five minutes to get her snugged in, after which Kelly did the same with *Springer*.

"This is yours?"

"Sure enough," Kelly replied. "Welcome to my sandbar."

"Sam Rosen," the man said, holding his hand out. He'd pulled a shirt on, and while he had a strong grip, Kelly noted that his hands were so soft as to be dainty.

"John Kelly."

"My wife, Sarah."

Kelly laughed. "You must be the navigator."

Sarah was short, overweight, and her brown eyes wavered between amusement and embarrassment. "Somebody needs to thank you for your help," she observed in a New York accent.

"A law of the sea, ma'am. What went wrong?"

"The chart shows six feet where we struck. This boat only takes four! And low tide was five hours ago!" the lady snapped. She wasn't angry at Kelly, but he was the closest target, and her husband had already heard what she thought.

"Sandbar, it's been building there from the storms we had last winter, but my charts show less than that. Besides, it's a soft bottom."

Pam came up just then, wearing clothing that was nearly respectable, and Kelly realized he didn't know her last name.

"Hi, I'm Pam."

"Y'all want to freshen up? We have all day to look at the problem." There was general agreement on that point, and Kelly led them off to his home.

"What the hell is that?" Sam Rosen asked. "That" was one of the bunkers that had been built in 1943, two thousand square feet, with a roof fully three feet thick. The entire structure was reinforced concrete and was almost as sturdy as it looked. A second, smaller bunker lay beside it.

"This place used to belong to the Navy," Kelly explained, "but I lease it now."

"Nice dock they built for you," Rosen noted.

"Not bad at all," Kelly agreed. "Mind if I ask what you do?"

"Surgeon," Rosen replied.

"Oh, yeah?" That explained the hands.

"Professor of surgery," Sarah corrected. "But he can't drive a boat worth a damn!"

"The goddamned charts were off!" the professor grumbled as Kelly led them inside. "Didn't you hear?"

"People, that's history now, and lunch and a beer will allow us to consider it in comfort." Kelly surprised himself with his words. Just then his ears caught a sharp *crack* coming across the water from somewhere to the south. It was funny how sound carried across the water.

"What was that?" Sam Rosen had sharp ears, too.

"Probably some kid taking a muskrat with his .22," Kelly judged. "It's a pretty quiet neighborhood, except for that. In the fall it can get a little noisy around dawn—ducks and geese."

"I can see the blinds. You hunt?"

"Not anymore," Kelly replied.

Rosen looked at him with understanding, and Kelly decided to reevaluate him for a second time.

"How long?"

"Long enough. How'd you know?"

"Right after I finished residency, I made it to Iwo and Okinawa. Hospital ship."

"Hmm, kamikaze time?"

Rosen nodded. "Yeah, lots of fun. What were you on?"

"Usually my belly," Kelly answered with a grin.

"UDT? You look like a frogman," Rosen said. "I had to fix a few of those."

"Pretty much the same thing, but dumber." Kelly dialed the combination lock and pulled the heavy steel door open.

The inside of the bunker surprised the visitors. When Kelly had taken possession of the place, it had been divided into three large, bare rooms by stout concrete walls, but now it looked almost like a house, with painted drywall and rugs. Even the ceiling was covered. The narrow view-slits were the only reminder of what it had once been. The furniture and rugs showed the influence of Patricia, but the current state of semiarray was evidence that only a man lived here now. Everything was neatly arranged, but not as a woman would do things. The Rosens also noted that it was the man of the house who led them to the "galley" and got things out of the old-fashioned refrigerator box while Pam wandered around a little wide-eyed.

"Nice and cool," Sarah observed. "Damp in the winter, I bet."

"Not as bad as you think." Kelly pointed to the radiators around the perimeter of the room. "Steam heat. This place was built to government specifications. Everything works and everything cost too much."

"How do you get a place like this?" Sam asked.

"A friend helped me get the lease. Surplus government property."

"He must be some friend," Sarah said, admiring the built-in refrigerator.

"Yes, he is."

Vice Admiral Winslow Holland Maxwell, USN, had his office on the E-Ring of the Pentagon. It was an outside office, allowing him a fine view of Washington—and the demonstrators, he noted angrily to himself. *Baby Killers!* one placard read. There was even a North Vietnamese flag. The chanting, this Saturday morning, was distorted by the thick window glass. He could hear the cadence but not the words, and the former fighter pilot couldn't decide which was more enraging.

"That isn't good for you, Dutch."

"Don't I know it!" Maxwell grumbled.

"The freedom to do that is one of the things we defend," Rear Admiral Casimir Podulski pointed out, not quite making that leap of faith despite his words. It was just a little too much. His son had died over Haiphong in an A-4 strike-fighter. The event had made the papers because of the young aviator's parentage, and fully eleven anonymous telephone calls had come in the following week, some just laughing, some asking his tormented wife where the blotter was supposed to be shipped. "All those nice, peaceful, sensitive young people."

"So why are you in such a great mood, Cas?"

"This one goes in the wall safe, Dutch." Podulski handed over a heavy folder. Its edges were bordered in red-and-white-striped tape, and it bore the coded designator BOXWOOD GREEN.

"They're going to let us play with it?" *That* was a surprise.

"It took me till oh-three-thirty, but yes. Just a few of us, though. We have authorization for a complete feasibility study." Admiral Podulski settled into a deep leather chair and lit up a cigarette. His face was thinner since the death of his son, but the crystal-blue eyes burned as bright as ever.

"They're going to let *us* go ahead and do the planning?" Maxwell and Podulski had worked towards that end for several months, never in any real expectation that they'd be allowed to pursue it.

"Who'd ever suspect us?" the Polish-born Admiral asked with an ironic look. "They want us to keep it off the books."

"Jim Greer, too?" Dutch asked.

"Best intel guy I know, unless you're hiding one somewhere."

"He just started at CIA, I heard last week," Maxwell warned.

"Good. We need a good spy, and his suit's still blue, last time I checked."

"We're going to make enemies doing this, lots of 'em."

Podulski gestured at the window and the noise. He hadn't changed all that much since 1944 and USS *Essex*. "With all those a hundred feet away from us, what'll a few more matter?"

"How long have you had the boat?" Kelly asked about halfway through his second beer. Lunch was rudimentary, cold cuts and bread supplemented by bottled beer.

"We bought it last October, but we've only been running it two months," the doctor admitted. "But I took the Power Squadron courses, finished top in my class." He was the sort who finished number one in nearly everything, Kelly figured.

"You're a pretty good line-handler," he observed, mainly to make the man feel better.

"Surgeons are pretty good with knots, too."

"You a doc, too, ma'am?" Kelly asked Sarah.

"Pharmacologist. I also teach at Hopkins."

"How long have you and your wife lived here?" Sam asked, and the conversation ground to an awkward halt.

"Oh, we just met," Pam told them artlessly. Naturally enough it was Kelly who was the most embarrassed. The two physicians merely accepted the news as a matter of course, but Kelly worried that they'd see him as a man taking advantage of a young girl. The thoughts associated with his behavior seemed to race in circles around the inside of his skull until he realized that no one else seemed to care all that much.

"Let's take a look at that propeller." Kelly stood. "Come on."

Rosen followed him out the door. The heat was building outside, and it was best to get things done quickly. The secondary bunker on the island housed Kelly's workshop. He selected a couple of wrenches and wheeled a portable air compressor towards the door.

Two minutes later he had it sitting next to the doctor's Hatteras and buckled a pair of weight belts around his waist.

"Anything I have to do?" Rosen asked.

Kelly shook his head as he stripped off his shirt. "Not really. If the compressor quits, I'll know pretty quick, and I'll only be down five feet or so."

"I've never done that." Rosen turned his surgeon's eyes to Kelly's torso, spotting three separate scars that a really good surgeon might have been skillful enough to conceal. Then he remembered that a combat surgeon didn't always have the time for cosmetic work.

"I have, here and there," Kelly told him on the way to the ladder.

"I believe it," Rosen said quietly to himself.

Four minutes later, by Rosen's watch, Kelly was climbing back up the ladder.

"Found your problem." He set the remains of both props on the concrete dock.

"God! What did we hit?"

Kelly sat down for a moment to strip off the weights. It was all he could do not to laugh. "Water, doc, just water."

"What?"

"Did you have the boat surveyed before you bought it?"

"Sure, the insurance company made me do that. I got the best buy around, he charged me a hundred bucks."

"Oh, yeah? What deficiencies did he give you?" Kelly stood back up and switched the compressor off.

"Practically nothing. He said there was something wrong with the sinks, and I had a plumber check it, but they were fine. I guess he had to say something for his money, right?"

"Sinks?"

"That's what he told me over the phone. I have the written survey somewhere, but I took the information over the phone."

"Zincs," Kelly said, laughing. "Not sinks."

"What?" Rosen was angry at not getting the joke.

"What destroyed your props was electrolysis. Galvanic reaction. It's caused by having more than one kind of metal in saltwater, corrodes the metal. All the sandbar did was to scuff them off. They were already wrecked. Didn't the Power Squadron tell you about that?"

"Well, yes, but—"

"*But*—you just learned something, Doctor Rosen." Kelly held up the remains of the screw. The metal had the flaked consistency of a soda cracker. "This used to be bronze."

"Damn!" The surgeon took the wreckage in his hand and picked off a waferlike fragment.

"The surveyor meant for you to replace the zinc anodes on the strut. What they do is to absorb the galvanic energy. You replace them every couple of years, and that protects the screws and rudder by remote control, like. I don't know all the science of it, but I do know the effects, okay? Your rudder needs replacement, too, but it's not an emergency. Sure as hell, you need two new screws."

Rosen looked out at the water and swore. "Idiot."

Kelly allowed himself a sympathetic laugh. "Doc, if that's the biggest mistake you make this year, you're a lucky man."

"So what do I do now?"

"I make a phone call and order you a couple of props. I'll call a guy I know over in Solomons, and he'll have somebody run them down here, probably tomorrow." Kelly gestured. "It's not that big a deal, okay? I want to see your charts, too."

Sure enough, when he checked their dates, they were five years old. "You need new ones every year, doc."

"Damn!" Rosen said.

"Helpful hint?" Kelly asked with another smile. "Don't take it so seriously. Best kind of lesson. It hurts a little but not much. You learn and you get on with it."

The doctor relaxed, finally, allowing himself a smile. "I suppose you're right, but Sarah'll never let me forget it."

"Blame the charts," Kelly suggested.

"Will you back me up?"

Kelly grinned. "Men have to stick together at times like this."

"I think I'm going to like you, Mr. Kelly."

"So where the fuck is she?" Billy demanded.

"How the hell should I know?" Rick replied, equally angry—and fearful of what Henry would say when he got back. Both their eyes turned to the woman in the room.

"You're her friend," Billy said.

Doris was trembling already, wishing she could run from the room, but there was no safety in that. Her hands were shaking as Billy took the three steps to her, and she flinched but didn't evade the slap that landed her on the floor.

"*Bitch.* You better tell me what you know!"

"I don't know anything!" she screamed up at him, feeling the burning spot on her face where she'd been hit. She looked over to Rick for sympathy, but saw no emotion at all on his face.

"You know something—and you better tell me right now," Billy said. He reached down to unbutton her shorts, then removed the belt from his pants. "Get the rest in here," he told Rick.

Doris stood without waiting for the order, nude from the waist down, crying silently, her body shaking with sobs for the pain soon to come, afraid even to cower, knowing she couldn't run. There was no safety for her. The other girls came in slowly, not looking in her direction. She'd known that Pam was going to run, but that was all, and her only satisfaction as she heard the belt whistle through the air was that she would reveal nothing that could hurt her friend. As searing as the pain was, Pam had escaped.

3

Captivity

After replacing all the diving gear in the machine shop, Kelly took a two-wheel hand truck out onto the quay to handle the groceries. Rosen insisted on helping. His new screws would arrive by boat the next day, and the surgeon didn't seem in any hurry to take his boat back out.

"So," Kelly said, "you teach surgery?"

"Eight years now, yeah." Rosen evened up the boxes on the two-wheeler.

"You don't look like a surgeon."

Rosen took the compliment with grace. "We're not all violinists. My father was a bricklayer."

"Mine was a fireman." Kelly started wheeling the groceries towards the bunker.

"Speaking of surgeons . . . " Rosen pointed at Kelly's chest. "Some good ones worked on you. That one looks like it was nasty."

Kelly nearly stopped. "Yeah, I got real careless that time. Not as bad as it looks, though, just grazed the lung."

Rosen grunted. "So I see. Must have missed your heart by nearly two inches. No big deal."

Kelly moved the boxes into the pantry. "Nice to talk

46

to somebody who understands, doc," he noted, wincing inwardly at the thought, remembering the feel of the bullet when it had spun him around. "Like I said—careless."

"How long were you over there?"

"Total? Maybe eighteen months. Depends on if you count the hospital time."

"That's a Navy Cross you have hanging on the wall. Is that what it's for?"

Kelly shook his head. "That was something else. I had to go up north to retrieve somebody, A-6 pilot. I didn't get hurt, but I got sicker 'n' hell. I had some scratches—you know—from thorns and stuff. They got infected as hell from the river water, would you believe? Three weeks in the hospital from that. It was worse'n being shot."

"Not a very nice place is it?" Rosen asked as they came back for the last load.

"They say there's a hundred different kinds of snake there. Ninety-nine are poisonous."

"And the other one?"

Kelly handed a carton over to the doctor. "That one eats your ass whole." He laughed. "No, I didn't like it there much. But that was the job, and I got that pilot out, and the Admiral made me a chief and got me a medal. Come on, I'll show you my baby." Kelly waved Rosen aboard. The tour took five minutes, with the doctor taking note of all the differences. The amenities were there, but not glitzed up. This guy, he saw, was all business, and his charts were all brand new. Kelly fished out another beer from his cooler for the doctor and another for himself.

"What was Okinawa like?" Kelly asked with a smile, each man sizing up the other, each liking what he saw.

Rosen shrugged and grunted eloquently. "Tense. We had a lot of work, and the kamikazes seemed to think the red cross on the ship made a hell of a nice target."

"You were working while they were coming in at you?"

"Injured people can't wait, Kelly."

Kelly finished his beer. "I'd rather be shooting back. Let me get Pam's stuff and we can get back in the air conditioning." He headed aft and picked up her backpack. Rosen was already on the quay, and Kelly tossed the backpack across. Rosen looked too late, missed the catch, and the pack landed on the concrete. Some contents spilled out, and from twenty feet away, Kelly immediately saw what was wrong even before the doctor's head turned to look at him.

There was a large brown plastic prescription bottle, but without a label. The top had been loose, and from it had spilled a couple of capsules.

Some things are instantly clear. Kelly stepped slowly off the boat to the quay. Rosen picked up the container and placed the spilled capsules back in it before snapping down the white plastic top. Then he handed it to Kelly.

"I know they're not yours, John."

"What are they, Sam?"

His voice could not have been more dispassionate. "The trade name is Quaalude. Methaqualone. It's a barbiturate, a sedative. A sleeping pill. We use it to get people off into dreamland. Pretty powerful. A little too powerful, in fact. A lot of people think it ought to be taken off the market. No label. It's not a prescription."

Kelly suddenly felt tired and old. And betrayed somehow. "Yeah."

"You didn't know?"

"Sam, we only met—not even twenty-four hours ago. I don't know anything about her."

Rosen stretched and looked around the horizon for a moment. "Okay, now I'm going to start being a doctor, okay? Have you ever done drugs?"

"No! I *hate* the goddamned stuff. People die because of it!" Kelly's anger was immediate and vicious, but it wasn't aimed at Sam Rosen.

The professor took the outburst calmly. It was his turn to be businesslike. "Settle down. People get hooked on these things. How doesn't matter. Getting excited doesn't help. Take a deep breath, let it out slow."

Kelly did, and managed a smile at the incongruity of the moment. "You sound just like my dad."

"Firemen are smart." He paused. "Okay, your lady friend may have a problem. But she seems like a nice girl, and you seem like a *mensch*. So do we try and solve the problem or not?"

"I guess that's up to her," Kelly observed, bitterness creeping into his voice. He felt betrayed. He'd started giving his heart away again, and now he had to face the fact that he might have been giving it to drugs, or what drugs had made of what ought to have been a person. It might all have been a waste of time.

Rosen became a little stern. "That's right, it is up to her, but it might be up to you, too, a little, and if you act like an idiot, you won't help her very much."

Kelly was amazed by how rational the man sounded under the circumstances. "You must be a pretty good doc."

"I'm one hell of a good doc," Rosen announced. "This isn't my field, but Sarah is damned good. It may be you're both lucky. She's not a bad girl, John. Something's bothering her. She's nervous about something, in case you didn't notice."

"Well, yes, but—" And some part of Kelly's brain said, *See!*

"But you mainly noticed she's pretty. I was in my twenties once myself, John. Come on, we may have a little work ahead." He stopped and peered at Kelly. "I'm missing something here. What is it?"

"I lost a wife less than a year ago." Kelly explained on for a minute or two.

"And you thought that maybe she—"

"Yeah, I guess so. Stupid, isn't it?" Kelly wondered why he was opening up this way. Why not just let Pam do whatever she wanted? But that wasn't an answer. If he did that, he would just be using her for his selfish needs, discarding her when the bloom came off the rose. For all the reverses his life had taken in the past year, he knew that he couldn't do that, couldn't be one of those men. He caught Rosen looking fixedly at him.

Rosen shook his head judiciously. "We all have vulnerabilities. You have training and experience to deal with your problems. She doesn't. Come on, we have work to do." Rosen took the hand truck in his large, soft hands and wheeled it towards the bunker.

The cool air inside was a surprisingly harsh blast of reality. Pam was trying to entertain Sarah, but not succeeding. Perhaps Sarah had written it off to the awkward social situation, but physicians' minds are always at work, and she was starting to apply a professional eye to the person in front of her. When Sam entered the living room, Sarah turned and gave him a look that Kelly was able to understand.

"And so, well, I left home when I was sixteen," Pam was saying, rattling on in a monotonal voice that exposed more than she knew. Her eyes turned, too, and focused on the backpack Kelly held in his hands. Her voice had a surprisingly brittle character that he'd not noticed before.

"Oh, great. I need some of that stuff." She came over and took the pack from his hands, then headed towards the master bedroom. Kelly and Rosen watched her leave, then Sam handed his wife the plastic container. She needed only one look.

"I didn't know," Kelly said, feeling the need to defend himself. "I didn't see her take anything." He thought back, trying to remember times when she had not been in his sight, and concluded that she might have taken pills two or perhaps three times, then realizing what her dreamy eyes had really been after all.

"Sarah?" Sam asked.

"Three-hundred-milligram. It ought not to be a severe case, but she does need assistance."

Pam came back into the room a few seconds later, telling Kelly that she'd left something on the boat. Her hands weren't trembling, but only because she was holding them together to keep them still. It was so clear, once you knew what to look for. She was trying to control herself, and almost succeeding, but Pam wasn't an actress.

"Is this it?" Kelly asked. He held the bottle in his hands. His reward for the harsh question was like a well-earned knife in the heart.

Pam didn't reply for a few seconds. Her eyes fixed on the brown plastic container, and the first thing Kelly saw was a sudden, hungry expression as though her thoughts were already reaching for the bottle, already picking one

or more of the tablets out, already anticipating whatever
it was that she got from the damned things, not caring,
not even noting that there were others in the room. Then
the shame hit her, the realization that whatever image she
had tried to convey to the others was rapidly diminishing.
But worst of all, after her eyes swept over Sam and Sarah,
they settled on Kelly again, oscillating between his hand
and his face. At first hunger vied with shame, but shame
won, and when her eyes locked on his, the expression on
her face began as that of a child caught misbehaving, but
it and she matured into something else, as she saw that
something which might have grown into love was changing
over an interval of heartbeats into contempt and disgust.
Her breathing changed in a moment, becoming rapid, then
irregular as the sobs began, and she realized that the greatest disgust was within her own mind, for even a drug addict
must look inward, and doing so through the eyes of others
merely added a cruel edge.

"I'm s–s–s-orry, Kel–el–y. I di–didn't tel–el . . . " she
tried to say, her body collapsing into itself. Pam seemed
to shrink before their eyes as she saw what might have been
a chance evaporate, and beyond that dissipating cloud was
only despair. Pam turned away, sobbing, unable to face the
man she'd begun to love.

It was decision time for John Terrence Kelly. He could
feel betrayed, or he could show the same compassion to
her that she had shown to him less than twenty hours
before. More than anything else, what decided it was her
look to him, the shame so manifest on her face. He could
not just stand there. He had to do something, else his own
very proud image of himself would dissolve as surely and
rapidly as hers.

Kelly's eyes filled with tears as well. He went to her
and wrapped his arms around her to keep her from falling,
cradling her like a child, pulling her head back against his
chest, because it was now his time to be strong for her, to
set whatever thoughts he had aside for a while, and even
the dissonant part of his mind refused to cackle its *I told
you so* at this moment, because there was someone hurt
in his arms, and this wasn't the time for that. They stood

together for a few minutes while the others watched with a mixture of personal unease and professional detachment.

"I've been trying," she said presently, "I really have—but I was so scared."

"It's okay," Kelly told her, not quite catching what she had just said. "You were there for me, and now it's my turn to be here for you."

"But—" She started sobbing again, and it took a minute or so before she got it out. "I'm not what you think I am."

Kelly let a smile creep into his voice as he missed the second warning. "You don't know what I think, Pammy. It's okay. Really." He'd concentrated so hard on the girl in his arms that he hadn't noticed Sarah Rosen at his side.

"Pam, how about we take a little walk?" Pam nodded agreement, and Sarah led her outside, leaving Kelly to look at Sam.

"You are a *mensch,*" Rosen announced with satisfaction at his earlier diagnosis of the man's character. "Kelly, how close is the nearest town with a pharmacy?"

"Solomons, I guess. Shouldn't she be in a hospital?"

"I'll let Sarah make the call on that, but I suspect it's not necessary."

Kelly looked at the bottle still in his hand. "Well, I'm going to deep-six these damned things."

"No!" Rosen snapped. "I'll take them. They all carry lot numbers. The police can identify the shipment that was diverted. I'll lock them up on my boat."

"So what do we do now?"

"We wait a little while."

Sarah and Pam came back in twenty minutes later, holding hands like mother and daughter. Pam's head was up now, though her eyes were still watery.

"We got a winner here, folks," Sarah told them. "She's been trying for a month all by herself."

"She says it isn't hard," Pam said.

"We can make it a lot easier," Sarah assured her. She handed a list to her husband. "Find a drugstore. John, get your boat moving. Now."

"What happens?" Kelly asked thirty minutes and five miles later. Solomons was already a tan-green line on the northwestern horizon.

"The treatment regime is pretty simple, really. We support her with barbiturates and ease her off."

"You give her drugs to get her off drugs?"

"Yep." Rosen nodded. "That's how it's done. It takes time for the body to flush out all the residual material in her tissues. The body becomes dependent on the stuff, and if you try to wean them off too rapidly, you can get some adverse effects, convulsions, that sort of thing. Occasionally people die from it."

"What?" said Kelly, alarmed. "I don't know anything about this, Sam."

"Why should you? That's our job, Kelly. Sarah doesn't think that's a problem in this case. Relax, John. You give"—Rosen took the list from his pocket—"yeah, I thought so, phenobarb, you give that to attenuate the withdrawal symptoms. Look, you know how to drive a boat, right?"

"Yep," Kelly said, turning, knowing what came next.

"Let us do our job. Okay?"

The man didn't feel much like sleep, the coastguardsmen saw, much to their own displeasure. Before they'd had the chance to recover from the previous day's adventures, he was up again, drinking coffee in the operations room, looking over the charts yet again, using his hand to make circles, which he compared with the memorized course track of the forty-one-boat.

"How fast is a sailboat?" he asked an annoyed and irritable Quartermaster First Class Manuel Oreza.

"That one? Not very, with a fair breeze and calm seas, maybe five knots, a little more if the skipper is smart and experienced. Rule of thumb is, one point three times the square root waterline length is your hull speed, so for that one, five or six knots." And he hoped the civilian was duly impressed with that bit of nautical trivia.

"It was windy last night," the official noted crossly.

"A small boat doesn't go faster on choppy seas, it goes

slower. That's because it spends a lot of time going up and down instead of forward."

"So how did he get away from you?"

"He didn't get away from *me,* okay?" Oreza wasn't clear on who this guy was or how senior a position he actually held, but he wouldn't have taken this sort of abuse from a real officer—but a real officer would not have harassed him this way; a real officer would have listened and understood. The petty officer took a deep breath, wishing for once that there was an officer here to explain things. Civilians listened to officers, which said a lot about the intelligence of civilians. "Look, sir, you told me to lay back, didn't you? I *told* you that we'd lose him in the clutter from the storm, and we did. Those old radars we use aren't worth a damn in bad weather, least not for a dinky little target like a day-sailer."

"You already said that."

And I'll keep saying it until you figure it out, Oreza managed not to say, catching a warning look from Mr. English. Portagee took a deep breath and looked down at the chart.

"So where do you think he is?"

"Hell, the Bay ain't that wide, so's you have two coastlines to worry about. Most houses have their own little docks, you have all these creeks. If it was me, I'd head up a creek. Better place to hide than a dock, right?"

"You're telling me he's gone," the civilian observed darkly.

"Sure as hell," Oreza agreed.

"Three *months* of work went into that!"

"I can't help that, sir." The coastguardsman paused. "Look, he probably went east rather than west, okay? Better to run before the wind than tack into it. That's the good news. Problem is, a little boat like that you can haul it out, put it on a trailer. Hell, it could be in Massachusetts by now."

He looked up from the chart. "Oh, that's just what I wanted to hear!"

"Sir, you want me to lie to you?"

"Three months!"

He just couldn't let go, Oreza and English thought at the same time. You had to learn how to do that. Sometimes the sea took something, and you did your best looking and searching, and mostly you found it, but not always, and when you failed, the time came when you had to let the sea claim the prize. Neither man had ever grown to like it, but that was the way things were.

"Maybe you can whistle up some helicopter support. The Navy has a bunch of stuff at Pax River," Warrant Officer English pointed out. It would also get the guy out of his station, an objective worthy of considerable effort for all the disruption he was causing to English and his men.

"Trying to get rid of me?" the man asked with an odd smile.

"Excuse me, sir?" English responded innocently. A pity, the warrant officer thought, that the man wasn't a total fool.

Kelly tied back up at his quay after seven. He let Sam take the medications ashore while he snapped various covers over his instrument panels and settled his boat down for the night. It had been a quiet return trip from Solomons. Sam Rosen was a good man at explaining things, and Kelly a good questioner. What he'd needed to learn he'd picked up on the way out, and for most of the return trip he'd been alone with his thoughts, wondering what he would do, how he should act. Those were questions without easy answers, and attending to ship's business didn't help, much as he'd hoped that it would. He took even more time than was necessary checking the mooring lines, doing the same for the surgeon's boat as well before heading inside.

The Lockheed DC-130E Hercules cruised well above the low cloud deck, riding smoothly and solidly as it had done for 2,354 hours of logged flight time since leaving the Lockheed plant at Marietta, Georgia, several years earlier. Everything had the appearance of a pleasant flying day. In the roomy front office, the flight crew of four watched the clear air and various instruments, as their duties required. The four turboprop engines hummed along with their accustomed reliability, giving the aircraft a steady high-pitched vibration that transmitted itself through the comfortable high-backed seats and created standing circular ripples in their Styrofoam coffee cups. All in all, the atmosphere was one of total normality. But anyone seeing the exterior of the aircraft could tell different. This aircraft belonged to the 99th Strategic Reconnaissance Squadron.

Beyond the outer engines on each wing of the Hercules hung additional aircraft. Each of these was a Model-147SC drone. Originally designed to be high-speed targets with the designation Firebee-II, now they bore the informal name "Buffalo Hunter." In the rear cargo area of the DC-130E was a second crew which was now powering up both of the miniature aircraft, having already programmed them for a mission sufficiently secret that none of them actually knew what it was all about. They didn't have to. It was merely a matter of telling the drones what to do and when to do it. The chief technician, a thirty-year-old sergeant, was working a bird code-named Cody-193. His crew station allowed him to turn and look out a small porthole to inspect his bird visually, which he did even though there was no real reason to do so. The sergeant loved the things as a child will love a particularly entertaining toy. He'd worked with the drone program for ten years, and this particular one he had flown sixty-one times. That was a record for the area.

Cody-193 had a distinguished ancestry. Its manufacturers, Teledyne-Ryan of San Diego, California, had built Charles Lindbergh's *Spirit of St. Louis,* but the company had never quite managed to cash in on that bit of aviation history. Struggling from one small contract to another, it had finally achieved financial stability by making targets. Fighter aircraft had to practice shooting at something. The Firebee drone had begun life as just that, a miniature jet aircraft whose mission was to die gloriously at the hands of a fighter pilot—except that the sergeant had never quite seen things that way. He was a drone controller, and his job, he thought, was to teach those strutting eagles a lesson by flying "his" bird in such a way as to make their missiles hit nothing more substantial than air. In fact, fighter pilots had learned to curse his name, though Air Force etiquette also required them to buy him a bottle of booze for every miss. Then a few years earlier someone had noted that if a Firebee drone was hard for our people to hit, the same might be true of others who fired at aircraft for more serious purposes than the annual William Tell competition. It was also a hell of a lot easier on the crews of low-level reconnaissance aircraft.

Cody-193's engine was turning at full power, hanging from its pylon and actually giving the mother aircraft a few knots of free airspeed. The sergeant gave it a final look before turning back to his instruments. Sixty-one small parachute symbols were painted on the left side just forward of the wing, and with luck, in a few days he would paint a sixty-second. Though he was not clear on the precise nature of this mission, merely beating the competition was reason enough to take the utmost care in preparing his personal toy for the current game.

"Be careful, baby," the sergeant breathed as it dropped free. Cody-193 was on its own.

Sarah had a light dinner cooking. Kelly smelled it even before opening the door. Kelly came inside to see Rosen sitting in the living room.

"Where's Pam?"

"We gave her some medication," Sam answered. "She ought to be sleeping now."

"She is," Sarah confirmed, passing through the room on the way to the kitchen. "I just checked. Poor thing, she's exhausted, she's been doing without sleep for some time. It's catching up with her."

"But if she's been taking sleeping pills—"

"John, your body reacts strangely to the things," Sam explained. "It fights them off, or tries to, at the same time it becomes dependent on them. Sleep will be her big problem for a while."

"There's something else," Sarah reported. "She's very frightened of something, but she wouldn't say what it was." She paused, then decided that Kelly ought to know. "She's been abused, John. I didn't ask about it—one thing at a time—but somebody's given her a rough time."

"Oh?" Kelly looked up from the sofa. "What do you mean?"

"I mean she's been sexually assaulted," Sarah said in a calm, professional voice that belied her personal feelings.

"You mean raped?" Kelly asked in a low voice while the muscles of his arms tensed.

Sarah nodded, unable now to hide her distaste. "Almost certainly. Probably more than once. There is also evidence of physical abuse on her back and buttocks."

"I didn't notice."

"You're not a doctor," Sarah pointed out. "How did you meet?"

Kelly told her, remembering the look in Pam's eyes and knowing now what it must have been from. Why hadn't he noticed it? Why hadn't he noticed a lot of things? Kelly raged.

"So she was trying to escape . . . . I wonder if the same man got her on the barbiturates?" Sarah asked. "Nice guy, whoever it was."

"You mean that somebody's been working her over, and got her on drugs?" Kelly said. "But why?"

"Kelly, please don't take this wrong . . . but she might have been a prostitute. Pimps control girls that way." Sarah Rosen hated herself for saying that, but this was business and Kelly had to know. "She's young, pretty, a runaway from a dysfunctional family. The physical abuse, the undernourishment, it all fits the pattern."

Kelly was looking down at the floor. "But she's not like that. I don't understand." But in some ways he did, he told himself, thinking back. The ways in which she'd clung to him and drawn him to her. How much was simply skill, and how much real human feelings? It was a question he had no desire to face. What was the right thing to do? Follow your mind? Follow your heart? And where might they lead?

"She's fighting back, John. She's got guts." Sarah sat across from Kelly. "She's been on the road for over four years, doing God knows what, but something in her won't quit. But she can't do it alone. She needs you. Now I have a question." Sarah looked hard at him. "Will you be there to help her?"

Kelly looked up, his blue eyes the color of ice as he searched for what he really felt. "You guys are really worked up about this, aren't you?"

Sarah sipped from a drink she'd made for herself. She was rather a dumpy woman, short and overweight. Her black hair hadn't seen a stylist in months. All in all she looked like the sort of woman who, behind the wheel of a car, attracts the hatred of male drivers. But she spoke with focused passion, and her intelligence was already very clear to her host. "Do you have any idea how bad it's getting? Ten years ago, drug abuse was so rare that I hardly had to bother with it. Oh, sure, I *knew* about it, read the articles from Lexington, and every so often we'd get a heroin case. Not very many. Just a black problem, people thought. Nobody really gave much of a damn. We're paying for that mistake now. In case you didn't notice, that's all changed—and it happened practically overnight. Except for the project I'm working on, I'm nearly full-time on kids with drug problems. I wasn't *trained* for this. I'm a *scientist,* an expert on adverse interactions, chemical structures, how we can design new drugs to do special things—but now I have to spend nearly all of my time in clinical work, trying to keep children alive who should be just learning how to drink a beer but instead have their systems full of chemical *shit* that never should have made it outside a goddamned laboratory!"

"And it's going to get worse," Sam noted gloomily.

Sarah nodded. "Oh yeah, the next big one is cocaine. She needs you, John," Sarah said again, leaning forward. It was as though she had surrounded herself with her own storm cloud of electrical energy. "You'd damned well better be there for her, boy. You be there for her! Somebody dealt her a really shitty hand, but she's *fighting.* There's a *person* in there."

"Yes, ma'am," Kelly said humbly. He looked up and smiled, no longer confused. "In case you were worried, I decided that a while back."

"Good." Sarah nodded curtly.

"What do I do first?"

"More than anything else, she needs rest, she needs good food, and she needs time to flush the barbiturates out of her system. We'll support her with phenobarb, just in case we have withdrawal problems—I don't expect that. I examined her while you two were gone. Her physical problem is not so much addiction as exhaustion and undernourishment. She ought to be ten pounds heavier than she is. She ought to tolerate withdrawal rather well if we support her in other ways."

"Me, you mean?" Kelly asked.

"That's a lot of it." She looked over towards the open bedroom door and sighed, the tension going out of her. "Well, given her underlying condition, that phenobarb will probably have her out for the rest of the night. Tomorrow we start feeding her and exercising her. For now," Sarah announced, "we can feed ourselves."

Dinner talk focused deliberately on other subjects, and Kelly found himself delivering a lengthy discourse on the bottom contours of the Chesapeake Bay, segueing into what he knew about good fishing spots. It was soon decided that his visitors would stay until Monday evening. Time over the dinner table lengthened, and it was nearly ten before they rose. Kelly cleaned up, then quietly entered his bedroom to hear Pam's quiet breathing.

Only thirteen feet long, and a scant three thousand sixty-five pounds of mass—nearly half of that fuel—the Buffalo Hunter angled towards the ground as it accelerated to an initial cruising speed of over five hundred knots. Already its navigational computer, made by Lear-Siegler, was monitoring time and altitude in a very limited way. The drone was programmed to follow a specific flight path and altitude, all painstakingly predetermined for systems that were by later standards absurdly primitive. For all that, Cody-193 was a sporty-looking beast. Its profile was remarkably like that of a blue shark with a protruding nose and underslung air intake for a mouth—stateside it was often painted with aggressive rows of teeth. In this particular case, an experimental paint scheme—flat white beneath and mottled brown and green atop—was supposed to make it harder to spot from the ground—and the air. It was also stealthy—a term not yet invented. Blankets of RAM—radar-absorbing material—were integral with the wing surfaces, and the air intake was screened to attenuate the radar return off the whirling engine blades.

Cody-193 crossed the border between Laos and North Vietnam at 11:41:38 local time. Still descending, it leveled out for the first time at five hundred feet above ground level, turning northeast, somewhat slower now in the thicker air this close to the ground. The low altitude and small size of the speeding drone made it a difficult target, but by no means an impossible one, and outlying gun positions of the dense and sophisticated North Vietnamese air-defense network spotted it. The drone flew directly towards a recently sited 37mm twin gun mount whose alert crew got their mount slued around quickly enough to loose twenty quick rounds, three of which passed within feet of the diminutive shape but missed. Cody-193 took no note of this, and neither jinked nor evaded the fire. Without a brain, without eyes, it continued along on its flight path rather like a toy train around a Christmas tree while its new owner ate breakfast in the kitchen. In fact it was being watched. A distant EC-121 Warning Star tracked -193 by means of a coded radar transponder located atop the drone's vertical fin.

"Keep going, baby," a major whispered to himself, watching his scope. He knew of the mission, how important it was, and why nobody else could be allowed to know. Next to him was a small segment from a topographical map. The drone turned north at the right place, dropping down to three hundred feet as it found the right valley, following a small tributary river. At least the guys who programmed it knew their stuff, the major thought.

-193 had burned a third of its fuel by now and was consuming the remaining amount very rapidly at low level, flying below the crests of the unseen hills to the left and right. The programmers had done their best, but there was one chillingly close call when a puff of wind forced it to the right before the autopilot could correct, and -193 missed an unusually tall tree by a scant seventy feet. Two militiamen were on that crest and fired off their rifles at it, and again the rounds missed. One of them started down the hill towards a telephone, but his companion called for him to stop as -193 flew blindly on. By the time a call was made and received, the enemy aircraft would be long gone, and besides, they'd done their duty in shooting at it. He worried about where their bullets had landed, but it was too late for that.

Colonel Robin Zacharias, USAF, was walking across the dirt of what might in other times and circumstances be called a parade ground, but there were no parades here. A prisoner for over six months, he faced every day as a struggle, contemplating misery more deep and dark than anything he'd been able to imagine. Shot down on his eighty-ninth mission, within sight of rotation home, a completely successful mission brought to a bloody end by nothing more significant than bad luck. Worse, his "bear" was dead. And he was probably the lucky one, the Colonel thought as he was led across the compound by two small, unfriendly men with rifles. His arms were tied behind him, and his ankles were hobbled because they were afraid of him despite their guns, and even with all that he was also being watched by men in the guard towers. *I must really look scary to the little bastards,* the fighter pilot told himself.

Zacharias didn't feel very dangerous. His back was still injured from the ejection. He'd hit the ground severely crippled, and his effort to evade capture had been little more than a token gesture, a whole hundred yards of movement over a period of five minutes, right into the arms of the gun crew which had shredded his aircraft.

The abuse had begun there. Paraded through three separate villages, stoned and spat upon, he'd finally ended up here. Wherever here was. There were sea birds. Perhaps he was close to the sea, the Colonel speculated. But the memorial in Salt Lake City, several blocks from his boyhood home, reminded him that gulls were not merely creatures of the sea. In the preceding months he had been subjected to all sorts of physical abuse, but it had strangely slackened off in the past few weeks. Perhaps they'd become tired of hurting him, Zacharias told himself. And maybe there really was a Santa Claus, too, he thought, his head looking down at the dirt. There was little consolation to be had here. There were other prisoners, but his attempts at communicating with them had all failed. His cell had no windows. He'd seen two faces, neither of which he had recognized. On both occasions he'd started to call out a greeting only to be clubbed to the ground by one of his guards. Both men had seen him but made no sound. In both cases he'd seen a smile and a nod, the best that they could do. Both men were of his age, and, he supposed, about his rank, but that was all he knew. What was most frightening to a man who had much to be frightened about was that this was not what he had been briefed to expect. It wasn't the Hanoi Hilton, where all the POWs were supposed to have been congregated. Beyond that he knew virtually nothing, and the unknown can be the most frightening thing of all, especially to a man accustomed over a period of twenty years to being absolute master of his fate. His only consolation, he thought, was that things were as bad as they could be. On that, he was wrong.

"Good morning, Colonel Zacharias," a voice called across the compound. He looked up to see a man taller than himself, Caucasian, and wearing a uniform very different from that of his guards. He strode towards the prisoner with a smile. "Very different from Omaha, isn't it?"

That was when he heard a noise, a thin screeching whine, approaching from the southwest. He turned on instinct—an aviator must always look to see an aircraft, no matter where he might be. It appeared in an instant, before the guards had a chance to react.

Buffalo Hunter, Zacharias thought, standing erect, turning to watch it pass, staring at it, holding his head up, seeing the black rectangle of the camera window, whispering a prayer that the device was operating. When the guards realized what he was doing, a gun butt in the kidneys dropped the Colonel to the ground. Suppressing a curse, he tried to deal with the pain as a pair of boots came into his restricted field of vision.

"Do not get overly excited," the other man said. "It's heading to Haiphong to count the ships. Now, my friend, we need to become acquainted."

Cody-193 continued northeast, holding a nearly constant speed and altitude as it entered the dense air-defense belt surrounding North Vietnam's only major port. The cameras in the Buffalo Hunter recorded several triple-A batteries, observation points, and more than a few people with AK-47s, all of whom made at least a token shot at the drone. The only thing -193 had going for it was its small size. Otherwise it flew on a straight and level course while its cameras snapped away, recording the images on 2.25-inch film. About the only thing not shot at it were surface-to-air missiles: -193 was too low for that.

"Go, baby, go!" the Major said, two hundred miles away. Outside, the four piston engines of the Warning Star were straining to maintain the altitude necessary for him to watch the drone's progress. His eyes were locked on the flat glass screen, following the blinking blip of the radar transponder. Other controllers monitored the location of other American aircraft also visiting the enemy country, in constant communication with RED CROWN, the Navy ship that managed air operations from the seaward side. "Turn east, baby—now!"

Right on schedule, Cody-193 banked hard to the right, coming a touch lower and screaming over the Haiphong docks at 500 knots, a hundred tracer rounds in its wake. Longshoremen and sailors from various ships looked up in curiosity and irritation, and not a little fear for all the steel flying in the sky over their heads.

"Yes!" the Major shouted, loudly enough that the sergeant-controller to his left looked up in irritation. You were supposed to keep things quiet here. He keyed his mike to speak to RED CROWN. "Cody-one-niner-three is bingo."

"Roger, copy bingo on one-niner-three," the acknowledgment came back. It was a false use of the "bingo" code word, which ordinarily meant an aircraft with a low fuel state, but it was a term so commonly used that it made a more than adequate disguise. The Navy enlisted man on the other end of the circuit then told an orbiting helicopter crew to wake up.

The drone cleared the coast right on schedule, keeping low for a few more miles before going into its final climb, down to its last hundred pounds of fuel as it reached its pre-programmed point thirty miles offshore and began circling. Now another transponder came on, one tuned to the search radars of U.S. Navy picket ships. One of these, the destroyer *Henry B. Wilson*, took note of the expected target at the expected time and place. Her missile technicians used the opportunity to run a practice intercept problem, but had to switch off their illumination radars after a few seconds. It made the airedales nervous.

Circling at five thousand feet, Cody-193 finally ran out of fuel and became a glider. When the airspeed fell to the right number, explosive bolts blew a hatch cover off the top, deploying a parachute. The Navy helicopter was already on station, and the white 'chute made for a fine target. The drone's weight was a scant fifteen hundred pounds now, barely that of eight men. Wind and visibility cooperated this day. The 'chute was snagged on their first attempt, and the helicopter turned at once, heading for the carrier USS *Constellation*, where the drone was carefully lowered into a cradle, ending its sixty-second combat mission. Before the helicopter could find its own spot on the flight deck, a technician was already unfastening the cover plate on the photo compartment and yanking the heavy film cassette from its slot. He took it below at once, and handed it over to another technician in the ship's elaborate photo lab. Processing required a brief six minutes, and the still-damp film was wiped clean and handed over yet again to an intelligence officer. It was better than good. The film was run from one spool to another over a flat glass plate under which was a pair of fluorescent lights.

"Well, Lieutenant?" a captain asked tensely.

"Okay, sir, wait one . . . " Turning the spool, he pointed to the third image. "There's our first reference point . . .

there's number two, she was right on course . . . okay, here's the IP . . . down the valley, over the hill—there, sir! We have two, three frames! Good ones, the sun was just right, clear day—you know why they call these babies Buffalo Hunters? It's—"

"Let me see!" The Captain nearly shoved the junior officer out of the way. There was a man there, an American, with two guards, and a fourth man—but it was the American he wanted to see.

"Here, sir." The Lieutenant handed over a magnifying glass. "We might get a good face off of this, and we can play with the negative some more if you give us a little time. Like I said, the cameras can tell the difference between a male and a female—"

"Mmmmm." The face was black, meaning a white man on the negative. But— "Damn, I can't tell."

"Cap'n, that's our job, okay?" He was an intelligence officer. The Captain was not. "Let us do our job, sir."

"He's one of ours!"

"Sure as hell, sir, and this guy isn't. Let me take these back to the lab for positive prints and blowups. The air wing will want a look at the port shots, too."

"They can wait."

"No, sir, they can't," the Lieutenant pointed out. But he took a pair of scissors and removed the relevant shots. The remainder of the roll was handed to a chief petty officer, while the Lieutenant and the Captain went back to the photo lab. Fully two months of work had gone into the flight of Cody-193, and the Captain lusted for the information he knew to be on those three two-and-a-quarter-inch frames.

An hour later he had it. An hour after that, he boarded a flight to Danang. Another hour and he was on a flight to Cubi Point Naval Air Station in the Philippines, followed by a puddle-jumper to Clark Air Force Base, and a KC-135 that would fly directly to California. Despite the time and rigors of the next twenty hours of flying, the Captain slept briefly and fitfully, having solved a mystery whose answer just might change the policy of his government.

4
First Light

Kelly slept nearly eight hours, again arising at the sound of the gulls to find that Pam wasn't there. He went outside and saw her standing on the quay, looking out over the water, still weary, still robbed of the ability to get the rest she needed. The Bay had its usual morning calm, the glassy surface punctuated by the circular ripples of bluefish chasing after insects. Conditions like this seemed so fitting to the start of a day; a gentle westerly breeze in his face, and the odd silence that allowed one to hear the rumble of a boat's motor from so far away that the boat could not be seen. It was the sort of time that allowed you to be alone with nature, but he knew that Pam merely felt alone. Kelly walked out to her as quietly as he could and touched her waist with both his hands.

"Good morning." She didn't answer for a long time, and Kelly stood still, holding her lightly, just enough that she could feel his touch. She was wearing one of his shirts, and he didn't want his touch to be sexual, only protective. He was afraid to press himself on a woman who'd suffered that kind of abuse, and could not predict where the invisible line might be.

"So now you know," she said, just loudly enough to be heard over the silence, unable to turn and face him.

"Yes," Kelly answered, equally quiet.

"What do you think?" Her voice was a painful whisper.

"I'm not sure what you mean, Pam." Kelly felt the trembling start, and he had to resist the urge to hold her tighter.

"About me."

"About you?" He allowed himself to get a little closer, altering his hold until his arms wrapped around her waist, but not tightly. "I think you're beautiful. I think I'm real glad we met."

"I do drugs."

"The docs say you're trying to quit. That's good enough for me."

"It's worse than that, I've done things—" Kelly cut her off.

"I don't care about that, Pam. I've done things, too. And one thing you did, for me was very nice. You gave me something to care about, and I didn't ever expect that to happen." Kelly pulled her tighter. "The things you did before we met don't matter. You're not alone, Pam. I'm here to help if you want me to."

"When you find out . . . " she warned.

"I'll take my chances. I think I know the important parts already. I love you, Pam." Kelly surprised himself with those words. He'd been too afraid to voice the thought even to himself. It was too irrational, but again emotion won out over reason, and reason, for once, found itself approving.

"How can you say that?" Pam asked. Kelly gently turned her around and smiled.

"Damned if I know! Maybe it's your tangled hair—or your runny nose." He touched her chest through the shirt. "No, I think it's your heart. No matter what's behind you, your heart is just fine."

"You mean that, don't you?" she asked, looking at his chest. There was a long moment, then Pam smiled up at him, and that, too, was like a dawn. The orange-yellow glow of the rising sun lit up her face and highlighted her fair hair.

Kelly wiped the tears from her face, and the wet feel of her cheeks eliminated whatever doubts he might have had. "We're going to have to get you some clothes. This is no way for a lady to dress."

"Who says I'm a lady?"

"I do."

"I'm so scared!"

Kelly pulled her against his chest. "It's okay to be scared. I was scared all the time. The important part is to know that you're going to do it." His hands rubbed up and down her back. He hadn't intended to make this a sexual encounter, but he found himself becoming aroused until he realized that his hands were rubbing over scars made by men with whips or ropes or belts or other odious things. Then his eyes looked straight out over the water, and it was just as well that she couldn't see his face.

"You must be hungry," he said, stepping away from her, holding on to her hands.

She nodded. "Starving."

"That I can fix." Kelly led her by the hand back to the bunker. Already he loved her touch. They met Sam and Sarah coming from the other side of the island after a morning's walk and stretch.

"How are our two lovebirds?" Sarah asked with a beaming smile, because she'd already seen the answer, watching from two hundred yards away.

"Hungry!" Pam replied.

"And we're getting a couple of screws today," Kelly added with a wink.

"What?" Pam asked.

"Propellers," Kelly explained. "For Sam's boat."

"Screws?"

"Sailor talk, trust me." He grinned at her, and she wasn't sure if she could believe it or not.

"That took long enough," Tony observed, sipping coffee from a paper cup.

"Where's mine?" Eddie demanded, irritable from lack of sleep.

"You told me to put the fucking heater outside, remember? Get your own."

"You think I want all that smoke and shit in here? You can die from that monoxide shit," Eddie Morello said irritably.

Tony was tired as well. Too tired to argue with this loudmouth. "Okay, man, well, the coffeepot's outside. Cups are there too."

Eddie grumbled and went outside. Henry, the third man, was bagging the product and kept out of the argument. It had actually worked out a little better than he'd planned. They'd even bought his story about Angelo, thus eliminating one potential partner and problem. There was at least three hundred thousand dollars' worth of finished drugs now being weighed and sealed in plastic bags for sale to dealers. Things hadn't gone quite as planned. The expected "few hours" of work had lingered into an all-night marathon as the three had discovered that what they paid for others to do wasn't quite as easy as it looked. The three bottles of bourbon they'd brought along hadn't helped either. Still and all, over three hundred thousand dollars of profit from sixteen hours of work wasn't all that bad. And this was just the beginning. Tucker was just giving them a taste.

Eddie was still worried about the repercussions of Angelo's demise. But there was no turning back, not after the killing, and he'd been forced into backing Tony's play. He grimaced as he looked out of a vacant porthole towards an island north of what had once been a ship. Sunlight was reflecting off the windows of what was probably a nice, large power cruiser. Wouldn't it be nice to get one of those? Eddie Morello liked to fish, and maybe he could take his kids out sometime. It would be a good cover activity, wouldn't it?

Or maybe crab, he told himself. After all, he knew what crabs ate. The thought evoked a quiet bark of a laugh, followed by a brief shudder. Was he safe, linked up with these men? They—he—had just killed Angelo Vorano, not twenty-four hours earlier. But Angelo wasn't part of the outfit, and Tony Piaggi was. He was their legitimacy, their pipeline to the street, and that made him safe—for a while. As long as Eddie stayed smart and alert.

"What room do you suppose this was?" Tucker asked Piaggi, just to make conversation.

"What do you mean?"

"When this was a ship, looks like it was a cabin or something," he said, sealing the last envelope and placing it inside the beer cooler. "I never thought about that." Which was actually true.

"Captain's cabin, you think?" Tony wondered. It was something to pass the time, and he was thoroughly sick of what they'd done all night.

"Could be, I suppose. It's close to the bridge." The man stood, stretching, wondering why it was that he had to do all the hard work. The answer came easily enough. Tony was a "made" man. Eddie wanted to become one. He would never be, and neither would Angelo, Henry Tucker reflected, glad for it. He'd never trusted Angelo, and now he was no longer a problem. One thing about these people, they seemed to keep their word—and they would continue to, as long as he was their connection to the raw material, and not one minute longer. Tucker had no illusions about that. It had been good of Angelo to make his connection with Tony and Eddie, and Angelo's death had had exactly the effect on Henry that his own death would have on the other two: none. All men have their uses, Tucker told himself, closing the beer cooler. And the crabs had to eat too.

With luck that would be the last killing for a while. Tucker didn't shrink from it, but he disliked complications that often came from killing. A good business ran smoothly, without fuss, and made money for everyone, which kept everyone happy, even the customers at the far end of the process. Certainly this load would keep them happy. It was good Asian heroin, scientifically processed and moderately cut with nontoxic elements that would give the users a rocketship high and a calm, gentle descent back to whatever reality they were trying to escape. The sort of rush they would want to experience again, and so they'd return to their pushers, who could charge a little extra for this very good stuff. "Asian Sweet" was already the trade name.

There was danger, having a street name. It gave the police something to target, a name to chase after, specific questions to ask, but that was the risk in having a hot product, and for that reason he'd selected his associates for their experience, connections, and security. His processing site had also been selected with an eye to security. They had a good five miles of visibility, and a fast boat with which to make their escape. Yeah, there was danger, to be sure, but all life was danger, and you measured risk against reward. Henry Tucker's reward for less than a single day's work was one hundred thousand dollars in untaxed cash, and he was willing to risk a lot for that. He was willing to risk far more for what Piaggi's connections could do, and now he had them interested. Soon they'd become as ambitious as he was.

The boat from Solomons arrived a few minutes early, with the propellers. The doctors hadn't told Kelly to keep Pam busy, but it was a simple enough prescription for her problems. Kelly wheeled the portable compressor back onto the dock and started it up, telling her how to regulate the airflow by keeping an eye on a gauge. Next he got the wrenches he needed and set them on the dock also.

"One finger, this one, two fingers, that one, and three fingers, this one here, okay?"

"Right," Pam replied, impressed with Kelly's expertise. He was hamming things up a little, the rest of them knew, but that was okay with everyone.

Kelly climbed down the ladder into the water, and his first job was to check the threads on the prop shafts, which appeared to be in decent shape. He reached his hand out of the water with one finger up and was rewarded with the right wrench, which he used to remove the retaining nuts, then handed them up one at a time. The whole operation took only fifteen minutes, and the shiny new screws were fully attached, and new protective anodes set in place. He took his time giving the rudders a look, and decided that they'd be okay for the rest of the year, though Sam should keep an eye on them. It was a relief, as usual, to climb out of the water and breathe air that didn't taste like rubber.

"What do I owe you?" Rosen asked.

"For what?" Kelly took off his gear and switched off the compressor.

"I always pay a man for his work," the surgeon said somewhat self-righteously.

Kelly had to laugh. "Tell you what, if I ever need a back operation, you can make it a freebie. What is it you docs call this sort of thing?"

"Professional courtesy—but you're not a physician," Rosen objected.

"And you're not a diver. You're not a seaman yet, either, but we're going to fix that today, Sam."

"I was at the top of my power-squadron class!" Rosen boomed.

"Doc, when we got kids from training school, we used to say, 'That's fine, sonny, but this here's the fleet.' Let me get the gear stowed and we'll see how well you can really drive this thing."

"I bet I'm a better fisherman than you are," Rosen proclaimed.

"Next they're going to see who can pee the farthest," Sarah observed acidly to Pam.

"That, too." Kelly laughed on his way back inside. Ten minutes later he'd cleaned off and changed into a T-shirt and cutoffs.

He took a place on the flying bridge and watched Rosen prepare his boat for getting under way. The surgeon actually impressed Kelly, particularly with his line handling.

"Next time let your blowers work for a while before you light off the engines," Kelly said after Rosen started up.

"But it's a diesel."

"Number one, 'it' is a 'she,' okay? Number two, it's a good habit to get into. The next boat you drive might be gas. Safety, doc. You ever take a vacation and rent a boat?"

"Well, yes."

"In surgery you do the same thing the same way, every time?" Kelly asked. "Even when you don't really have to?"

Rosen nodded thoughtfully. "I hear you."

"Take her out." Kelly waved. This Rosen did, and rather smartly, the surgeon thought. Kelly didn't: "Less rudder, more screws. You won't always have a breeze helping you away from alongside. Propellers push water; rudders just direct it a little. You can always depend on your engines, especially at low speed. And steering breaks sometimes. Learn how to do without it."

"Yes, Captain," Rosen growled. It was like being an intern again, and Sam Rosen was used to having those people snap to his orders. Forty-eight, he thought, was a little old to be a student.

"You're the captain. I'm just the pilot. These are my waters, Sam." Kelly turned to look down at the well deck. "Don't laugh, ladies, it'll be your turn next. Pay attention!" Quietly: "You're being a good sport, Sam."

Fifteen minutes later they were drifting lazily on the tide, fishing lines out under a warm holiday sun. Kelly had little interest in fishing, and instead assigned himself lookout duty on the flying bridge while Sam taught Pam how to bait her line. Her enthusiasm surprised all of them. Sarah made sure that she was liberally covered with Coppertone to protect her pale skin, and Kelly wondered if a little tan would highlight her scars. Alone with his thoughts on the flying bridge, Kelly asked himself what sort of man would abuse a woman. He stared out through squinted eyes at a gently rolling surface dotted with boats. How many people like that were within his sight? Why was it that you couldn't tell from looking at them?

Packing the boat was simple enough. They'd stocked in a good supply of chemicals, which they would have to replenish periodically, but Eddie and Tony had access through a chemical-supply business whose owner had casual ties to their organization.

"I want to see," Tony said as they cast off. It wasn't as easy as he'd imagined, snaking their eighteen-footer through the tidal swamps, but Eddie remembered the spot well enough, and the water was still clear.

"Sweet Jesus!" Tony gasped.

"Gonna be a good year for crabs," Eddie noted, glad that Tony was shocked. A fitting kind of revenge, Eddie thought, but it was not a pleasant sight for any of them. Half a bushel's worth of crabs were already on the body. The face was fully covered, as was one arm, and they could see more of the creatures coming in, drawn by the smell of decay that drifted through the water as efficiently as through the air: nature's own form of advertising. On land, Eddie knew, it would be buzzards and crows.

"What do you figure? Two weeks, maybe three, and then no more Angelo."

"What if somebody—"

"Not much chance of that," Tucker said, not bothering to look. "Too shallow for a sailboat to risk coming in, and motorboats don't bother much. There's a nice wide channel half a mile south, fishing's better there, they say. I guess the crabbers don't like it here either."

Piaggi had trouble looking away, though his stomach had already turned over once. The Chesapeake Bay blue crabs, with their claws, were dismantling the body already softened by warm water and bacteria, one little pinch at a time, tearing with their claws, picking up the pieces with smaller pincers, feeding them into their strangely alien mouths. He'd wondered if there would still be a face there, eyes to stare up at a world left behind, but crabs covered it, and somehow it seemed likely that the eyes had been the first things to go. The frightening part, of course, was that if one man could die this way, so could another, and even though Angelo had already been dead, somehow Piaggi was sure that being disposed of this way was worse than mere death. He would have regretted Angelo's death, except that it was business, and . . . Angelo had deserved it. It was a shame, in a way, that his gruesome fate had to be kept a secret, but that was business, too. That was how you kept the cops from finding out. Hard to prove murder without a body, and here they had accidentally found a way to conceal a number of murders. The only problem was getting the bodies here—and not letting others know of the method of disposal, because people talk, Tony Piaggi told himself, as Angelo had talked. A good thing that Henry had found out about that.

"How 'bout crab cakes when we get back to town?" Eddie Morello asked with a laugh, just to see if he could make Tony puke.

"Let's get the fuck outa here," Piaggi replied quietly, settling into his seat. Tucker took the engine out of idle and picked his way out of the tidal marsh, back into the Bay.

Piaggi took a minute or two to get the sight out of his mind, hoping that he could forget the horror of it and remember only the efficiency of their disposal method. After all, they might be using it again. Maybe after a few hours he'd see humor in it, Tony thought, looking at the cooler. Under the fifteen or so cans of National Bohemian was a layer of ice, under which were twenty sealed bags of heroin. In the unlikely event that anyone stopped them, it was unlikely that they'd look farther than the beer, the real fuel for Bay boaters. Tucker drove the boat north, and the others laid out their fishing rods as though they were trying to find a good place to harvest a few rockfish from the Chesapeake.

"Fishing in reverse," Morello said after a moment, then he laughed loudly enough that Piaggi joined in.

"Toss me a beer!" Tony commanded between laughs. He was a "made man," after all, and deserved respect.

"Idiots," Kelly said quietly to himself. That eighteen-footer was going too fast, too close to other fishing boats. It could catch a few lines, and certainly would throw a wake sure to disturb other craft. That was bad sea manners, something Kelly was always careful to observe. It was just too easy to—hell, it wasn't even hard enough to be "easy." All you had to do was buy a boat and you had the right to sail her around. No tests, no nothing. Kelly found Rosen's 7 x 50 binoculars and focused them on the boat that was coming close aboard. Three assholes, one of them holding up a can of beer in mock salute.

"Bear off, dickhead," he whispered to himself. The jerks in a boat, drinking beer, probably half-potted already, not even eleven o'clock yet. He gave them a good look, and was vaguely grateful that they passed no closer than fifty yards. He caught the name: *Henry's Eighth*. If he saw that name again, Kelly told himself, he'd remember to keep clear.

"I got one!" Sarah called.

"Heads up, we got a big wake coming in from starboard!" It arrived a minute later, causing the big Hatteras to rock twenty degrees left and right of vertical.

"That," Kelly said, looking down at the other three, "is what I mean by bad sea manners!"

"Aye aye!" Sam called back.

"I've still got him," Sarah said. She worked the fish in, Kelly saw, with consummate skill. "Pretty big, too!"

Sam got the net and leaned over the side. A moment later he stood back up. The net contained a struggling rockfish, maybe twelve or fourteen pounds. He dumped the net in a water-filled box in which the fish could wait to die. It seemed cruel to Kelly, but it was only a fish, and he'd seen worse things than that.

Pam started squealing a moment later as her line went taut. Sarah put her rod in its holder and started coaching her. Kelly watched. The friendship between Pam and Sarah was as remarkable as that between himself and the girl. Perhaps Sarah was taking the place of the mother who had been lacking in affection, or whatever Pam's mother had lacked. Regardless, Pam was responding well to the advice and counsel of her new friend. Kelly watched with a smile that Sam caught and returned. Pam was new at this, tripping twice as she walked the fish around. Again Sam did the honors with the net, this time recovering an eight-pound blue.

"Toss it back," Kelly advised. "They don't taste worth a damn!"

Sarah looked up. "Throw back her first fish? What are you, a Nazi? You have any lemon at your place, John?"

"Yeah, why?"

"I'll show you what you can do with a bluefish, that's why." She whispered something to Pam that evoked a laugh. The blue went into the same tank, and Kelly wondered how it and the rock would get along.

Memorial Day, Dutch Maxwell thought, alighting from his official car at Arlington National Cemetery. To many just a time for a five-hundred-mile auto race in Indianapolis, or a day off, or the traditional start of the summer beach season, as testified to by the relative lack of auto traffic in Washington. But not to him, and not to his fellows. This was their day, a time to remember fallen comrades while others attended to other things both more and less personal. Admiral Podulski got out with him, and the two walked slowly and out of step, as admirals do. Casimir's son, Lieutenant (junior grade) Stanislas Podulski, was not here, and probably never would be. His A-4 had been blotted from the sky by a surface-to-air missile, the reports had told them, nearly a direct hit. The young pilot had been too distracted to notice until perhaps the last second, when his voice had spoken its last epithet of disgust over the "guard" channel. Perhaps one of the bombs he'd been carrying had gone off sympathetically. In any case, the small attack-bomber had dissolved into a greasy cloud of black and yellow, leaving little behind; and besides, the enemy wasn't all that fastidious about respecting the remains of fallen aviators. And so the son of a brave man had been denied his resting place with comrades. It wasn't something that Cas spoke about. Podulski kept such feelings inside.

Rear Admiral James Greer was at his place, as he'd been for the previous two years, about fifty yards from the paved driveway, setting flowers next to the flag at the headstone of his son.

"James?" Maxwell said. The younger man turned and saluted, wanting to smile in gratitude for their friendship on a day like this, but not quite doing so. All three wore their navy-blue uniforms because they carried with them a proper sort of solemnity. Their gold-braided sleeves glistened in the sun. Without a spoken word, all three men lined up to face the headstone of Robert White Greer, First Lieutenant, United States Marine Corps. They saluted smartly, each remembering a young man whom they had bounced on their knees, who had ridden his bike at Naval Station Norfolk and Naval Air Station Jacksonville with Cas's son, and Dutch's. Who had grown strong and proud, meeting his father's ships when they'd returned to port, and talked only about following in his father's footsteps, but not too closely, and whose luck had proven insufficient to the moment, fifty miles southwest of Danang. It was the curse of their profession, each knew but never said, that their sons were drawn to it also, partly from reverence for what their fathers were, partly from a love of country imparted by each to each, most of all from a love of their fellow man. As each of the men standing there had taken his chances, so had Bobby Greer and Stas Podulski taken theirs. It was just that luck had not smiled on two of the three sons.

Greer and Podulski told themselves at this moment that it *had* mattered, that freedom had a price, that some men must pay that price else there would be no flag, no Constitution, no holiday whose meaning people had the right to ignore. But in both cases, those unspoken words rang hollow. Greer's marriage had ended, largely from the grief of Bobby's death. Podulski's wife would never be the same. Though each man had other children, the void created by the loss of one was like a chasm never to be bridged, and as much as each might tell himself that, yes, it was worth the price, no man who could rationalize the death of a child could truly be called a man at all, and their real feelings were reinforced by the same humanity that compelled them to a life of sacrifice. This was all the more true because each had feelings about the war that the more polite called "doubts," and which they called something else, but only among themselves.

"Remember the time Bobby went into the pool to get Mike Goodwin's little girl—saved her life?" Podulski asked. "I just got a note from Mike. Little Amy had twins last week, two little girls. She married an engineer down in Houston, works for NASA."

"I didn't even know she was married. How old is she now?" James asked.

"Oh, she must be twenty . . . twenty-five? Remember her freckles, how the sun used to breed them down at Jax?"

"Little Amy," Greer said quietly. "How they grow." Maybe she wouldn't have drowned that hot July day, but it was one more thing to remember about his son. *One life saved, maybe three?* That was something, wasn't it? Greer asked himself.

The three men turned and left the grave without a word, heading slowly back to the driveway. They had to stop there. A funeral procession was coming up the hill, soldiers of the Third Infantry Regiment, "The Old Guard," doing their somber duty, laying another man to rest. The admirals lined up again, saluting the flag draped on the casket and the man within. The young Lieutenant commanding the detail did the same. He saw that one of the flag officers wore the pale blue ribbon denoting the Medal of Honor, and the severity of his gesture conveyed the depth of his respect.

"Well, there goes another one," Greer said with quiet bitterness after they had passed by. "Dear God, what are we burying these kids for?"

"'Pay any price, bear any burden, meet any hardship, support any friend, oppose any foe . . . '" Cas quoted. "Wasn't all that long ago, was it? But when it came time to put the chips on the table, where were the bastards?"

"We *are* the chips, Cas," Dutch Maxwell replied. "This *is* the table."

Normal men might have wept, but these were not normal men. Each surveyed the land dotted with white stones. This had been the front lawn of Robert E. Lee once—the house was still atop the hill—and the placement of the cemetery had been the cruel gesture of a government that had felt itself betrayed by the officer. And yet Lee had in the end given his ancestral home to the service of those men whom he had most loved. That was the kindest irony of this day, Maxwell reflected.

"How do things look up the river, James?"

"Could be better, Dutch. I have orders to clean house. I need a pretty big broom."

"Have you been briefed in on BOXWOOD GREEN?"

"No." Greer turned and cracked his first smile of the day. It wasn't much, but it was something, the others told themselves. "Do I want to be?"

"We'll probably need your help."

"Under the table?"

"You know what happened with KINGPIN," Casimir Podulski noted.

"They were damned lucky to get out," Greer agreed. "Keeping this one tight, eh?"

"You bet we are."

"Let me know what you need. You'll get everything I can find. You doing the 'three' work, Cas?"

"That's right." Any designator with a -3 at the end denoted the operations and planning department, and Podulski had a gift for that. His eyes glittered as brightly as his Wings of Gold in the morning sun.

"Good," Greer observed. "How's little Dutch doing?"

"Flying for Delta now. Copilot, he'll make captain in due course, and I'll be a grandfather in another month or so."

"Really? Congratulations, my friend."

"I don't blame him for getting out. I used to, but not now."

"What's the name of the SEAL who went in to get him?"

"Kelly. He's out, too," Maxwell said.

"You should have gotten the Medal for him, Dutch," Podulski said. "I read the citation. That was as hairy as they come."

"I made him a chief. I couldn't get the Medal for him." Maxwell shook his head. "Not for rescuing the son of an admiral, Cas. You know the politics."

"Yeah." Podulski looked up the hill. The funeral procession had stopped, and the casket was being moved off the gun carriage. A young widow was watching her husband's time on earth end. "Yeah, I know about politics."

• • •

Tucker eased the boat into the slip. The inboard-outboard drive made that easy. He cut the engine and grabbed the mooring lines, which he tied off quickly. Tony and Eddie lifted the beer cooler out while Tucker collected the loose gear and snapped a few covers into place before joining his companions on the parking lot.

"Well, that was pretty easy," Tony noted. The cooler was already in the back of his Ford Country Squire station wagon.

"Who do you suppose won the race today?" Eddie asked. They'd neglected to take a radio with them for the trip.

"I had a yard bet on Foyt, just to make it interesting."

"Not Andretti?" Tucker asked.

"He's a paisan, but he ain't lucky. Betting is business," Piaggi pointed out. Angelo was a thing of the past now, and the manner of his disposal was, after all, a little amusing, though the man might never eat crab cakes again.

"Well," Tucker said, "you know where to find me."

"You'll get your money," Eddie said, speaking out of place. "End of the week, the usual place." He paused. "What if demand goes up?"

"I can handle it," Tucker assured him. "I can get all you want."

"What the hell kind of pipeline do you have?" Eddie asked, pushing further.

"Angelo wanted to know that, too, remember? Gentlemen, if I told you that, you wouldn't need me, would you?"

Tony Piaggi smiled. "Don't trust us?"

"Sure." Tucker smiled. "I trust you to sell the stuff and share the money with me."

Piaggi nodded approval. "I like smart partners. Stay that way. It's good for all of us. You have a banker?"

"Not yet, haven't thought about it much," Tucker lied.

"Start thinking, Henry. We can help set you up, overseas bank. It's secure, numbered account, all that stuff. You can have somebody you know check it out. Remember, they can track money if you're not careful. Don't live it up too much. We've lost a lot of friends that way."

"I don't take chances, Tony."

Piaggi nodded. "Good way to think. You have to be careful in this business. The cops are getting smart."

"Not smart enough." Neither were his partners, when it came to that, but one thing at a time.

5

Commitments

The package arrived with a very jet-lagged Captain at the Navy's intelligence headquarters in Suitland, Maryland. On-staff photo-interpretation experts were supplemented by specialists from the Air Force's 1127th Field Activities Group at Fort Belvoir. It took twenty hours to go through the entire process, but the frames from the Buffalo Hunter were unusually good, and the American on the ground had done what he was supposed to do: look up and stare at the passing reconnaissance drone.

"Poor bastard paid the price for it," a Navy chief observed to his Air Force counterpart. Just behind him the photo caught an NVA soldier with his rifle up and reversed. "I'd like to meet you in a dark alley, you little fuck."

"What do you think?" The Air Force senior master sergeant slid an ID photo over.

"Close enough I'd bet money on it." Both intelligence specialists thought it odd that they had such a thin collection of files to compare with these photographs, but whoever had guessed had guessed well. They had a match. They didn't know that what they had was a series of photographs of a dead man.

• • •

Kelly let her sleep, glad that she was able to without any chemical help. He got himself dressed, went outside, and ran around his island twice—the circumference was about three quarters of a mile—to work up a sweat in the still morning air. Sam and Sarah, early risers also, bumped into him while he was cooling down on the dock.

"The change in you is remarkable, too," she observed. She paused for a moment. "How was Pam last night?"

The question jarred Kelly into a brief silence, followed by: *"What?"*

"Oh, shit, Sarah . . . " Sam looked away and nearly laughed. His wife flushed almost as crimson as the dawn.

"She persuaded me not to medicate her last night," Sarah explained. "She was a little nervous, but she wanted to try and I let her talk me out of it. That's what I meant, John. Sorry."

How to explain last night? First he'd been afraid to touch her, afraid to seem to be pressing himself on her, and then she'd taken that as a sign that he didn't like her anymore, and then . . . things had worked out.

"Mainly she has some damned-fool idea—" Kelly stopped himself. Pam could talk to her about this, but it wasn't proper for him to do so, was it? "She slept fine, Sarah. She really wore herself out yesterday."

"I don't know that I've ever had a more determined patient." She stabbed a hard finger into Kelly's chest. "You've helped a lot, young man."

Kelly looked away, not knowing what he was supposed to say. *The pleasure was all mine*? Part of him still believed that he was taking advantage of her. He'd stumbled upon a troubled girl and . . . exploited her? No, that wasn't true. He loved her. Amazing as that seemed. His life was changing into something recognizably normal—probably. He was healing her, but she was healing him as well.

"She's—she's worried that I won't—the stuff in her past, I mean. I really don't care much about that. You're right, she's a very strong girl. Hell, I have a somewhat checkered past, too, y'know? I ain't no priest, guys."

"Let her talk it out," Sam said. "She needs that. You have to let things in the open before you start dealing with them."

"You're sure it won't affect you? It might be some pretty ugly stuff," Sarah observed, watching his eyes.

"Uglier than war?" Kelly shook his head. Then he changed the subject. "What about the . . . medications?"

The question relieved everyone, and Sarah was talking work again. "She's been through the most crucial period. If there were going to be a serious withdrawal reaction, it would have happened already. She may still have periods of agitation, brought on by external stress, for example. In that case you have the phenobarb, and I've already written out instructions for you, but she's gutting it out. Her personality is far stronger than she appreciates. You're smart enough to see if she's having a bad time. If so, make her—*make her*—take one of the tablets."

The idea of forcing her to do anything bridled Kelly. "Look, doc, I can't—"

"Shut up, John. I don't mean jamming it down her throat. If you tell her that she really needs it, she's going to listen to you, okay?"

"How long?"

"For another week, maybe ten days," Sarah said after a moment's reflection.

"And then?"

"Then you can think about the future you two might have together," Sarah told him.

Sam felt uneasy getting this personal. "I want her fully checked out, Kelly. When's the next time you're due into Baltimore?"

"A couple of weeks, maybe sooner. Why?"

Sarah handled that: "I wasn't able to do a very thorough exam. She hasn't seen a physician in a long time, and I'll feel better if she has a CPX—complete history and physical. Who do you think, Sam?"

"You know Madge North?"

"She'll do," Sarah thought. "You know, Kelly, it wouldn't hurt for you to get checked out, too."

"Do I look sick?" Kelly held his arms out, allowing them to survey the magnificence of his body.

"Don't give me that crap," Sarah snapped back. "When she shows up, you show up. I want to make sure you're both completely healthy—period. Got it?"

"Yes, ma'am."

"One more thing, and I want you to hear me through," Sarah went on. "She needs to see a psychiatrist."

"Why?"

"John, life isn't a movie. People don't put their problems behind and ride into a sunset in real life, okay? She's been sexually abused. She's been on drugs. Her self-esteem isn't very high right now. People in her position blame *themselves* for being victims. The right kind of therapy can help to fix that. What you're doing is important, but she needs professional help, too. Okay?"

Kelly nodded. "Okay."

"Good," Sarah said, looking up at him. "I like you. You listen well."

"Do I have a choice, ma'am?" Kelly inquired with a twisted grin.

She laughed. "No, not really."

"She's always this pushy," Sam told Kelly. "She really ought to be a nurse. Docs are supposed to be more civilized. Nurses are the ones who push us around." Sarah kicked her husband playfully.

"Then I better never run into a nurse," Kelly said, leading them back off the dock.

Pam ended up sleeping just over ten hours, and without benefit of barbiturates, though she did awaken with a crushing headache which Kelly treated with aspirin.

"Get Tylenol," Sarah told him. "Easier on the stomach." The pharmacologist made a show of checking Pam again while Sam packed up their gear. On the whole she liked what she saw. "I want you to gain five pounds before I see you again."

"But—"

"And John's going to bring you in to see us so that we can get you completely checked out—two weeks, say?"

"Yes, ma'am." Kelly nodded surrender again.

"But—"

"Pam, they ganged up on me. I have to go in, too," Kelly reported in a remarkably docile voice.

"You have to leave so early?"

Sarah nodded. "We really should have left last night, but what the hell." She looked at Kelly. "If you don't show up like I said, I'll call you and scream."

"Sarah. Jesus, you're a pushy broad!"

"You should hear what Sam says."

Kelly walked her out to the dock, where Sam's boat was already rumbling with life. She and Pam hugged. Kelly tried just to shake hands, but had to submit to a kiss. Sam jumped down to shake their hands.

"New charts!" Kelly told the surgeon.

"Aye, Cap'n."

"I'll get the lines."

Rosen was anxious to show him what he'd learned. He backed out, drawing mainly on his starboard shaft and turning his Hatteras within her own length. The man didn't forget. A moment later Sam increased power on both engines and drove straight out, heading directly for water he knew to be deep. Pam just stood there, holding Kelly's hand, until the boat was a white speck on the horizon.

"I forgot to thank her," Pam said finally.

"No, you didn't. You just didn't say it, that's all. So how are you today?"

"My headache's gone." She looked up at him. Her hair needed washing, but her eyes were clear and there was a spring in her step. Kelly felt the need to kiss her, which he did. "So what do we do now?"

"We need to talk," Pam said quietly. "It's time."

"Wait here." Kelly went back into the shop and returned with a pair of folding lounge chairs. He gestured her into one. "Now tell me how terrible you are."

Pamela Starr Madden was three weeks shy of her twenty-first birthday, Kelly learned, finally discovering her surname as well. Born to a lower-working-class family in the Panhandle region of northern Texas, she'd grown up under the firm hand of a father who was the sort of man to make a Baptist minister despair. Donald Madden was a man who understood the form of religion, but not the substance, who was strict because he didn't know how to love, who drank from frustration with life—and was angry at himself for that, too—yet never managed to come to terms with it. When his children misbehaved, he beat them, usually with a belt or a switch of wood until his conscience kicked in, something which did not always happen sooner than fatigue. The final straw for Pam, never a happy child, had come on the day after her sixteenth birthday, when she'd stayed late at a church function and ended up going on what was almost a date with friends, feeling that she finally had the right to do so. There hadn't even been a kiss at the end of it from the boy whose household was almost as restrictive as her own. But that hadn't mattered to Donald Madden. Arriving home at ten-twenty on a Friday evening, Pam came into a house whose lights blazed with anger, there to face an enraged father and a thoroughly cowed mother.

"The things he said . . . " Pam was looking down at the grass as she spoke. "I didn't do any of that. I didn't even *think* of doing it, and Albert was so innocent . . . but so was I, then."

Kelly squeezed her hand. "You don't have to tell me any of this, Pam." But she did have to, and Kelly knew that, and so he continued to listen.

After sustaining the worst beating of her sixteen years, Pamela Madden had slipped out her first-floor bedroom window and walked the four miles to the center of the bleak, dusty town. She'd caught a Greyhound bus for Houston before dawn, only because it had been the first bus, and it hadn't occurred to her to get off anywhere in between. So far as she could determine, her parents had never even reported her as missing. A series of menial jobs and even worse housing in Houston had merely given emphasis to her misery, and in short order she'd decided to head elsewhere. With what little money she'd saved, she'd caught yet another bus—this one Continental Trailways—and stopped in New Orleans. Scared, thin, and young, Pam had never learned that there were men who preyed on young runaways. Spotted almost at once by a well-dressed and smooth-talking twenty-five-year-old named Pierre Lamarck, she'd taken his offer of shelter and assistance after he had sprung for dinner and sympathy. Three days later he had become her first lover. A week after that, a firm slap across the face had coerced the sixteen-year-old girl into her second sexual adventure, this one with a salesman from Springfield, Illinois, whom Pam had reminded of his own daughter—so much so that he'd engaged her for the entire evening, paying Lamarck two hundred fifty dollars for the experience. The day after that, Pam had emptied one of her pimp's pill containers down her throat, but only managed to make herself vomit, earning a savage beating for the defiance.

Kelly listened to the story with a serene lack of reaction, his eyes steady, his breathing regular. Inwardly it was another story entirely. The girls he'd had in Vietnam, the little childlike ones, and the few he'd taken since Tish's death. It had never occurred to him that those young women might not have enjoyed their life and work. He'd never even thought about it, accepting their feigned reactions as genuine human feelings—for wasn't he a decent, honorable man? But he had paid for the services of young women whose collective story might not have been the least bit different from Pam's, and the shame of it burned inside him like a torch.

By nineteen, she'd escaped Lamarck and three more pimps, always finding herself caught with another. One in Atlanta had enjoyed whipping his girls in front of his peers, usually using light cords. Another in Chicago had started Pam on heroin, the better to control a girl he deemed a little too independent, but she'd left him the next day, proving him right. She'd watched another girl die in front of her eyes from a hot-shot of uncut drugs, and that frightened her more than the threat of a beating. Unable to go home—she'd called once and had the phone slammed down by her mother even before she could beg for help—and not trusting the social services which might have helped her along a different path, she finally found herself in Washington, D.C., an experienced street prostitute with a drug habit that helped her to hide from what she thought of herself. But not enough. And that, Kelly thought, was probably what had saved her. Along the way she'd had two abortions, three cases of venereal disease, and four arrests, none of which had ever come to trial. Pam was crying now, and Kelly moved to sit beside her.

"You see what I really am?"

"Yes, Pam. What I see is one very courageous lady." He wrapped his arm tightly around her. "Honey, it's okay. Anybody can mess up. It takes guts to change, and it really takes guts to talk about it."

The final chapter had begun in Washington with someone named Roscoe Fleming. By this time Pam was hooked solidly on barbiturates, but still fresh and pretty-looking when someone took the time to make her so, enough to command a good price from those who liked young faces. One such man had come up with an idea, a sideline. This man, whose name was Henry, had wanted to broaden his drug business, and being a careful chap who was used to having others do his bidding, he'd set up a stable of girls to run drugs from his operation to his distributors. The girls he bought from established pimps in other cities, in each case a straight cash transaction, which each of the girls found ominous. This time Pam tried to run almost at once, but she'd been caught and beaten severely enough to break three ribs, only later to learn of her good fortune that the first lesson hadn't gone further. Henry had also used the opportunity to cram barbiturates into her, which both attenuated the pain and increased her dependence. He'd augmented the treatment by making her available to any of his associates who wanted her. In this, Henry had achieved what all the others had failed to do. He had finally cowed her spirit.

Over a period of five months, the combination of beatings, sexual abuse, and drugs had depressed her to a nearly catatonic state until she'd been jarred back to reality only four weeks earlier by tripping over the body of a twelve-year-old boy in a doorway, a needle still in his arm. Remaining outwardly docile, Pam had struggled to cut her drug use. Henry's other friends hadn't complained. She was a much better lay this way, they thought, and their male egos had attributed it to their prowess rather than her increased level of consciousness. She'd waited for her chance, waiting for a time when Henry was away somewhere, because the others got looser when he wasn't around. Only five days earlier she'd packed what little she had and bolted. Penniless—Henry had never let them have money—she'd hitched her way out of town.

"Tell me about Henry," Kelly said softly when she'd finished.

"Thirty, black, about your height."

"Did any other girls get away?"

Pam's voice went cold as ice. "I only know of one who tried. It was around November. He . . . killed her. He thought she was going to the cops, and"—she looked up—"he made us all watch. It was terrible."

Kelly said quietly, "So why did you try, Pam?"

"I'd rather die than do that again," she whispered, the thought now out in the open. "I wanted to die. That little boy. Do you know what happens? You just *stop*. Everything stops. And I was helping. I helped kill him."

"How did you get out?"

"Night before . . . I . . . fucked them all . . . so they'd like me, let me . . . let me out of their sight. You understand now?"

"You did what was necessary to escape," Kelly replied. It required every bit of his strength to keep his voice even. "Thank God."

"I wouldn't blame you if you took me back and sent me on my way. Maybe Daddy was right, what he said about me."

"Pam, do you remember going to church?"

"Yes."

"Do you remember the story that ends, 'Go forth and sin no more'? You think that I've never done something wrong? Never been ashamed? Never been scared? You're not alone, Pam. Do you have any idea how brave you've been to tell me all this?"

Her voice by now was entirely devoid of emotion. "You have a right to know."

"And now I do, and it doesn't change anything." He paused for a second. "Yes, it does. You're even gutsier than I thought you were, honey."

"Are you sure? What about later?"

"The only 'later' thing I'm worried about is those people you left behind," Kelly said.

"If they ever find me . . . " Emotion was coming back now. Fear. "Every time we go back to the city, they might see me."

"We'll be careful about that," Kelly said.

"I'll never be safe. Never."

"Yeah, well, there's two ways to handle that. You can just keep running and hiding. Or you can help put them away."

She shook her head emphatically. "The girl they killed. They knew. They knew she was going to the cops. That's why I can't trust the police. Besides, you don't know how scary these people are."

Sarah had been right about something else, Kelly saw. Pam was wearing her halter again, and the sun had given definition to the marks on her back. There were places which the sun didn't darken as it did the others. Echoes of the welts and bloody marks that others had made for their pleasure. It had all started with Pierre Lamarck, or more correctly, Donald Madden, small, cowardly men who managed their relations with women through force.

Men? Kelly asked himself.

No.

Kelly told her to stay in place for a minute and headed off into the machinery bunker. He returned with eight empty soda and beer cans, which he set on the ground perhaps thirty feet from their chairs.

"Put your fingers in your ears," Kelly told her.

"Why?"

"Please," he replied. When she did, Kelly's right hand moved in a blur, pulling a .45 Colt automatic from under his shirt. He brought it up into a two-hand hold, going left to right. One at a time, perhaps half a second apart, the cans alternatively fell over or flew a foot or two in the air to the crashing report of the pistol. Before the last was back on the ground from its brief flight, Kelly had ejected the spent magazine and was inserting another, and seven of the cans moved a little more. He checked to be sure the weapon was clear, dropped the hammer, and replaced it in his belt before sitting down next to her.

"It doesn't take all that much to be scary to a young girl without friends. It takes a little more to scare me. Pam, if anybody even *thinks* about hurting you, he has to talk to me first."

She looked over at the cans, then up at Kelly, who was pleased with himself and his marksmanship. The demonstration had been a useful release for him, and in the brief flurry of activity, he'd assigned a name or a face to each of the cans. But he could see she still was not convinced. It would take a little time.

"Anyway." He sat down with Pam again. "Okay, you told me your story, right?"

"Yes."

"Do you still think it makes a difference to me?"

"No. You say it doesn't. I guess I believe you."

"Pam, not all the men in the world are like that—not very many, as a matter of fact. You've been unlucky, that's all. There isn't anything wrong with you. Some people get hurt in accidents or get sick. Over in Vietnam I saw men get killed from bad luck. It almost happened to me. It wasn't because there was something wrong with them. It was just bad luck, being in the wrong place, turning left instead of right, looking the wrong way. Sarah wants you to meet some docs and talk it through. I think she's right. We're going to get you all fixed up."

"And then?" Pam Madden asked. He took a very deep breath, but it was too late to stop now.

"Will you . . . stay with me, Pam?"

She looked as though she'd been slapped. Kelly was stunned by her reaction. "You can't, you're just doing it because—"

Kelly stood and lifted her by the arms. "Listen to me, okay? You've been sick. You're getting better. You've taken everything that goddamned world could toss at you, and you didn't quit. I *believe* in you! It's going to take time. Everything does. But at the end of it, you will be one goddamned fine person." He set her down on her feet and stepped back. He was shaking with rage, not only at what had happened to her, but at himself for starting to impose his will on her. "I'm sorry. I shouldn't have done that. Please, Pam . . . just believe in yourself a little."

"It's hard. I've done terrible things."

Sarah was right. She did need professional help. He was angry at himself for not knowing exactly what to say.

The next few days settled into a surprisingly easy routine. Whatever her other qualities, Pam was a horrible cook, which failing made her cry twice with frustration, though Kelly managed to choke down everything she prepared with a smile and a kind word. But she learned quickly, too, and by Friday she'd figured out how to make hamburger into something tastier than a piece of charcoal. Through it all, Kelly was there, encouraging her, trying hard not to be overpowering and mainly succeeding. A quiet word, a gentle touch, and a smile were his tools. She was soon aping his habit of rising before dawn. He started getting her to exercise. This came very hard indeed. Though basically healthy, she hadn't run more than half a block in years, and so he made her walk around the island, starting with two laps, by the end of the week up to five. She spent her afternoons in the sun, and without much to wear she most often did so in her panties and bra. She acquired the beginnings of a tan, and never seemed to notice the thin, pale marks on her back that made Kelly's blood chill with anger. She began to pay more serious attention to her appearance, showering and washing her hair at least once per day, brushing it out to a silky gloss, and Kelly was always there to comment on it. Not once did she appear to need the phenobarbital Sarah had left behind. Perhaps she struggled once or twice, but by using exercise instead of chemicals, she worked herself onto a normal wake-sleep routine. Her smiles acquired more confidence, and twice he caught her looking into the mirror with something other than pain in her eyes.

"Pretty nice, isn't it?" he asked Saturday evening, just after her shower.

"Maybe," she allowed.

Kelly lifted a comb from the sink and started going through her wet hair. "The sun has really lightened it up for you."

"It took a while to get all the dirt out," she said, relaxing to his touch.

Kelly struggled with a tangle, careful not to pull too hard. "But it did come out, Pammy, didn't it?"

"Yeah, I guess so, maybe," she told the face in the mirror.

"How hard was that to say, honey?"

"Pretty hard." A smile, a real one with warmth and conviction.

Kelly set the comb down and kissed the base of her neck, letting her watch in the mirror. Kelly got the comb back and continued his work. It struck him as very unmanly, but he loved doing this. "There, all straight, no tangles."

"You really ought to buy a hair-dryer."

Kelly shrugged. "I've never needed one."

Pam turned around and took his hands. "You will, if you still want to."

He was quiet for perhaps ten seconds, and when he spoke, the words didn't quite come out as they should, for now the fear was his. "You sure?"

"Do you still—"

"Yes!" It was hard lifting her with wet hair, still nude and damp from the shower, but a man had to hold his woman at a time like this. She was changing. Her ribs were less pronounced. She'd gained weight on a regular, healthy diet. But it was the person inside who had changed the most. Kelly wondered what miracle had taken place, afraid to believe that he was part of it, but knowing that it was so. He set her down after a moment, looking at the mirth in her eyes, proud that he'd helped to put it there.

"I have my rough edges, too," Kelly warned her, unaware of the look in his eyes.

"I've seen most of them," she assured him. Her hands started rubbing over his chest, tanned and matted with dark hair, marked with scars from combat operations in a faraway place. Her scars were inside, but so were some of his, and together each would heal the other. Pam was sure of that now. She'd begun to look at the future as more than a dark place where she could hide and forget. It was now a place of hope.

6
Ambush

The rest was easy. They made a quick boat trip to Solomons, where Pam was able to buy a few simple things. A beauty shop trimmed her hair. By the end of her second week with Kelly, she'd started to run and had gained weight. Already she could wear a two-piece swimsuit without an overt display of her rib cage. Her leg muscles were toning up; what had been slack was now taut, as it ought to be on a girl her age. She still had her demons. Twice Kelly woke to find her trembling, sweating, and murmuring sounds that never quite turned into words but were easily understood. Both times his touch calmed her, but not him. Soon he was teaching her to run *Springer,* and whatever the defects in her schooling, she was smart enough. She quickly grasped how to do the things that most boaters never learned. He even took her swimming, surprised somehow that she'd learned the skill in the middle of Texas.

Mainly he loved her, the sight, the sound, the smell, and most of all the feel of Pam Madden. Kelly found himself slightly anxious if he failed to see her every few minutes, as though she might somehow disappear. But she was always there, catching his eye, smiling back playfully. Most of the time. Sometimes he'd catch her with a different expression, allowing herself to look back into the darkness of her past or forward into an alternate future different from that which he had already planned. He found himself wishing that he could reach into her mind and remove the bad parts, knowing that he would have to trust others to do that. At those times, and the others, for the most part, he'd find an excuse to head her way, and let his fingertips glide over her shoulder, just to be sure she knew that he was there.

Ten days after Sam and Sarah had left, they had a little ceremony. He let her take the boat out, tie the bottle of phenobarbital to a large rock, and dump it over the side. The splash it made seemed a fitting and final end to one of her problems. Kelly stood behind her, his strong arms about her waist, watching the other boats traveling the Bay, and he looked into a future bright with promise.

"You were right," she said, stroking his forearms.

"That happens sometimes," Kelly replied with a distant smile, only to be stunned by her next statement.

"There are others, John, other women Henry has . . . like Helen, the one he killed."

"What do you mean?"

"I have to go back. I have to help them . . . before Henry—before he kills more of them."

"There's danger involved, Pammy," Kelly said slowly.

"I know . . . but what about them?"

It was a symptom of her recovery, Kelly knew. She had become a normal person again, and normal people worried about others.

"I can't hide forever, can I?" Kelly could feel her fear, but her words defied it and he held her a little tighter.

"No, you can't, not really. That's the problem. It's too hard to hide."

"Are you sure you can trust your friend on the police?" she asked.

"Yes: he knows me. He's a lieutenant I did a job for a year ago. A gun got tossed, and I helped find it. So he owes me one. Besides, I ended up helping to train their divers, and I made some friends." Kelly paused. "You don't have to do it, Pam. If you just want to walk away from it, that's okay with me. I don't *have* to go back to Baltimore ever, except for the doctor stuff."

"All the things they did to me, they're doing to the others. If I don't do something, then it'll never really be gone, will it?"

Kelly thought about that, and his own demons. You simply could not run away from some things. He knew. He'd tried. Pam's collection was in its way more horrible than his own, and if their relationship were to go further, those demons had to find their resting place.

"Let me make a phone call."

"Lieutenant Allen," the man said into his phone in Western District. The air conditioning wasn't working well today, and his desk was piled with work as yet undone.

"Frank? John Kelly," the detective heard, bringing a smile.

"How's life in the middle of the Bay, fella?" *Wouldn't I like to be there.*

"Quiet and lazy. How about you?" the voice asked.

"I wish," Allen answered, leaning back in his swivel chair. A large man, and like most cops of his generation, a World War II veteran—in his case a Marine artilleryman—Allen had risen from foot patrol on East Monument Street to homicide. For all that, the work was not as demanding as most thought, though it did carry the burden associated with the untimely end of human life. Allen immediately noted the change in Kelly's voice. "What can I do for you?"

"I, uh, met somebody who might need to talk with you."

"How so?" the cop asked, fishing around in his shirt pocket for a cigarette and matches.

"It's business, Frank. Information regarding a killing."

The cop's eyes narrowed a bit, while his brain changed gears. "When and where?"

"I don't know yet, and I don't like doing this over a phone line."

"How serious?"

"Just between us for now?"

Allen nodded, staring out the window. "That's fine, okay."

"Drug people."

Allen's mind went *click*. Kelly had said his informant was "somebody," not a "man." That made the person a female, Allen figured. Kelly was smart, but not all that sophisticated in this line of work. Allen had heard the shadowy reports of a drug ring using women for something or other. Nothing more than that. It wasn't his case. It was being handled by Emmet Ryan and Tom Douglas downtown, and Allen wasn't even supposed to know that much.

"There's at least three drug organizations up and running now. None of them are very nice folks," Allen said evenly. "Tell me more."

"My friend doesn't want much involvement. Just some information for you, that's it, Frank. If it goes further, we can reevaluate then. We're talking some scary people if this story is true."

Allen considered that. He'd never dwelt upon Kelly's background, but he knew enough. Kelly was a trained diver, he knew, a bosun's mate who'd fought in the brown-water Navy in the Mekong Delta, supporting the 9th Infantry; a squid, but a very competent, careful squid whose services had come highly recommended to the force from somebody in the Pentagon and who'd done a nice job retraining the force's divers, and, by the way, earning a nice check for it, Allen reminded himself. The "person" had to be female. Kelly would never worry about guarding a man that tightly. Men just didn't think that way about other men. If nothing else, it sure sounded interesting.

"You're not screwing me around, are you?" he had to ask.

"That's not my way, man," Kelly assured him. "My rules: it's for information purposes only, and it's a quiet meet. Okay?"

"You know, anybody else, I'd probably say come right in here and that would be it, but I'll play along with you. You did break the Gooding case open for me. We got him, you know. Life plus thirty. I owe you for that. Okay, I'll play along for now. Fair enough?"

"Thanks. What's your schedule like?"

"Working late shift this week." It was just after four in the afternoon, and Allen had just come on duty. He didn't know that Kelly had called three times that day already without leaving a message. "I get off around midnight, one o'clock, like that. It depends on the night," he explained. "Some are busier than others."

"Tomorrow night. I'll pick you up at the front door. We can have a little supper together."

Allen frowned. This was like a James Bond movie, secret agent crap. But he did know Kelly to be a serious man, even if he didn't know squat about police work.

"See you then, sport."

"Thanks, Frank. 'Bye." The line clicked off and Allen went back to work, making a note on his desk calendar.

"Are you scared?" he asked.

"A little," she admitted.

He smiled. "That's normal. But you heard what I said. He doesn't know anything about you. You can always back out if you want. I'll be carrying a gun all the time. And it's just a talk. You can get in and get out. We'll do it in one day—one night, really. And I'll be with you all the time."

"Every minute?"

"Except when you're in the ladies' room, honey. There you have to look out for yourself." She smiled and relaxed.

"I have to fix dinner," she said, heading off to the kitchen.

Kelly went outside. Something in him called for more weapons practice, but he'd done that already. Instead he walked into the equipment bunker and took the .45 down from the rack. First he depressed the stud and action spring. Next he swiveled the bushing. That allowed the spring to go free. Kelly dismounted the slide assembly, removing the barrel, and now the pistol was field-stripped. He held the barrel up to a light, and, as expected, it was dirty from firing. He cleaned every surface, using rags, Hoppe's cleaning solvent, and a toothbrush until there was no trace of dirt on any metal surface. Next he lightly oiled the weapon. Not too much oil, for that would attract dirt and grit, which could foul and jam the pistol at an inconvenient moment. Finished cleaning, he reassembled the Colt quickly and expertly—it was something he could and did do with his eyes closed. It had a nice feel in his hand as he jacked the slide back a few times to make sure it was properly assembled. A final visual inspection confirmed it.

Kelly took two loaded magazines from a drawer, along with a single loose round. He inserted one loaded clip into the piece, working the slide to load the first round in the chamber. He carefully lowered the hammer before ejecting the magazine and sliding another round into place. With eight cartridges in the weapon, and a backup clip, he now had a total of fifteen rounds with which to face danger. Not nearly enough for a walk in the jungles of Vietnam, but he figured it was plenty for the dark environs of a city. He could hit a human head with a single aimed shot from ten yards, day or night. He'd never once rattled under fire, and he'd killed men before. Whatever the dangers might be, Kelly was ready for them. Besides, he wasn't going after the Vietcong. He was going in at night, and the night was his friend. There would be fewer people around for him to worry about, and unless the other side knew he was there—which they wouldn't—he didn't have to worry about an ambush. He just had to stay alert, which came easily to him.

Dinner was chicken, something Pam knew how to fix. Kelly almost got out a bottle of wine but thought better of it. Why tempt her with alcohol? Maybe he'd stop drinking himself. It would be no great loss, and the sacrifice would validate his commitment to her. Their conversation avoided serious matters. He'd already shut the dangers from his mind. There was no need to dwell on them. Too much imagination made things worse, not better.

"You really think we need new curtains?" he said.

"They don't match the furniture very well."

Kelly grunted. "For a boat?"

"It's kinda dull there, you know?"

"Dull," he observed, clearing the table. "Next thing, you'll say that men are all alike—" Kelly stopped dead in his tracks. It was the first time he'd slipped up that way. "Sorry . . . "

She gave him an impish smile. "Well, in some ways you are. And stop being so nervous about talking to me about things, okay?"

Kelly relaxed. "Okay." He grabbed her and pulled her close. "If that's the way you feel . . . well . . . "

"Mmm." She smiled and accepted his kiss. Kelly's hands wandered across her back, and there was no feel of a bra under the cotton blouse. She giggled at him. "I wondered how long it would take you to notice."

"The candles were in the way," he explained.

"The candles were nice, but smelly." And she was right. The bunker was not well ventilated. Something else to fix. Kelly looked forward into a very busy future as he moved his hands to a nicer place.

"Have I gained enough weight?"

"Is it my imagination, or . . . ?"

"Well, maybe just a little," Pam admitted, holding his hands on her.

"We need to get you some new clothes," he said, watching her face, the new confidence. He had her on the wheel, steering the proper compass course past Sharp's Island Light, well east of the shipping channel, which was busy today.

"Good idea," she agreed. "But I don't know any good places." She checked the compass like a good helmsman.

"They're easy to find. You just look at the parking lot."

"Huh?"

"Lincolns and Caddys, honey. Always means good clothes," Kelly noted. "Never fails."

She laughed as intended. Kelly marveled at how much more in control she seemed, though there was still a long ways to go.

"Where will we stay tonight?"

"On board," Kelly answered. "We'll be secure here." Pam merely nodded, but he explained anyway.

"You look different now, and they don't know me from Adam. They don't know my car or my boat. Frank Allen doesn't know your name or even that you're a girl. That's operational security. We ought to be safe."

"I'm sure you're right," Pam said, turning to smile at him. The confidence in her face warmed his blood and fed his already capacious ego.

"Going to rain tonight," Kelly noted, pointing at distant clouds. "That's good, too. Cuts down visibility. We used to do a lot of stuff in the rain. People just aren't alert when they're wet."

"You really know about this stuff, don't you?"

A manly smile. "I learned in a really tough school, honey."

They made port three hours later. Kelly made a great show of being alert, checking out the parking lot, noting that his Scout was in its accustomed place. He sent her below while he tied up, then left her there while he drove the car right to the dock. Pam, as instructed, walked straight from the boat to the Scout without looking left or right, and he drove off the property at once. It was still early in the day, and they drove immediately out of the city, finding a suburban shopping center in Timonium, where Pam over a period of two—to Kelly, interminable—hours selected three nice outfits, for which he paid cash. She dressed in the one he liked best, an understated skirt and blouse that went well with his jacket and no tie. For once Kelly was dressing in accordance with his own net worth, which was comfortable.

Dinner was eaten in the same area, an upscale restaurant with a dark corner booth. Kelly didn't say so, but he'd needed a good meal, and while Pam was okay with chicken, she still had a lot to learn about cooking.

"You look pretty good—relaxed, I mean," he said, sipping his after-dinner coffee.

"I never thought I'd feel this way. I mean, it's only been . . . not even three weeks?"

"That's right." Kelly set his coffee down. "Tomorrow we'll see Sarah and her friends. In a couple of months everything will be different, Pam." He took her left hand, hoping that it would someday bear a gold ring on the third finger.

"I believe that now. I really do."

"Good."

"What do we do now?" she asked. Dinner was over and there were hours until the clandestine meeting with Lieutenant Allen.

"Just drive around some?" Kelly left cash on the table and led her out to the car.

It was dark now. The sun was nearly set, and rain was starting to fall. Kelly headed south on York Road towards the city, well fed and relaxed himself, feeling confident and ready for the night's travail. Entering Towson, he saw the recently abandoned streetcar tracks that announced his proximity to the city and its supposed dangers. His senses perked up at once. Kelly's eyes darted left and right, scanning the streets and sidewalks, checking his three rearview mirrors every five seconds. On getting in the car, he'd put his .45 Colt automatic in its accustomed place, a holster just under the front seat that he could reach faster than one in his belt—and besides, it was a lot more comfortable that way.

"Pam?" he asked, watching traffic, making sure the doors were locked—a safety provision that seemed outrageously paranoid when he was so alert.

"Yes?"

"How much do you trust me?"

"I do trust you, John."

"Where did you—work, I mean?"

"What do you mean?"

"I mean, it's dark and rainy, and I'd like to see what it's like down there." Without looking, he could feel her body tense. "Look, I'll be careful. If you see anything that worries you, I'll make tracks like you won't believe."

"I'm scared of that," Pam said immediately, but then she stopped herself. She *was* confident in her man, wasn't she? He'd done so much for her. He'd saved her. She had to trust him—no, he had to know that she did. She had to show him that she did. And so she asked: "You promise you'll be careful?"

"Believe it, Pam," he assured her. "You see one single thing that worries you and we're gone."

"Okay, then."

It was amazing, Kelly thought, fifty minutes later. The things that are there but which you never see. How many times had he driven through this part of town, never stopping, never noticing? And for years his survival had depended on his noting everything, every bent branch, every sudden bird-call, every footprint in the dirt. But he'd driven through this area a hundred times and never noticed what was happening because it was a different sort of jungle filled with very different game. Part of him just shrugged and said, *Well, what did you expect?* Another part noted that there had always been danger here, and he'd failed to take note of it, but the warning was not as loud and clear as it should have been.

The environment was ideal. Dark, under a cloudy, moonless sky. The only illumination came from sparse streetlights that created lonely globes of light along sidewalks both deserted and active. Showers came and went, some fairly heavy, mostly moderate, enough to keep heads down and limit visibility, enough to reduce a person's normal curiosity. That suited Kelly fine, since he was circulating around and around the blocks, noting changes from the second to the third pass by a particular spot. He noted that not even all the streetlights were functioning. Was that just the sloth of city workers or creative maintenance on the part of the local "businessmen"? Perhaps a little of both, Kelly thought. The guys who changed the bulbs couldn't make all that much, and a twenty-dollar bill would probably persuade them to be a little slow, or maybe not screw the bulb in all the way. In any case, it set the mood. The streets were dark, and the dark had always been Kelly's trusted friend.

The neighborhoods were so . . . sad, he thought. Shabby storefronts of what had been mom-and-pop grocery stores, probably run out of business by supermarkets which had themselves been wrecked in the '68 rioting, opening a hole in the economic fabric of the area, but one not yet filled. The cracked cement of the sidewalks was littered with all manner of debris. Were there people who lived here? Who were they? What did they do? What were their dreams? Surely not all could be criminals. Did they hide at night? And if then, what about the daylight? Kelly had learned it in Asia: give the enemy one part of the day and he would secure it for himself, and then expand it, for the day had twenty-four hours, and he would want them all for himself and his activities. No, you couldn't give the other side anything, not a time, not a place, nothing that they could reliably use. That's how people lost a war, and there *was* a war going on here. And the winners were not the forces of good. That realization struck him hard. Kelly had already seen what he knew to be a losing war.

The dealers were a diverse group, Kelly saw as he cruised past their sales area. Their posture told him of their confidence. They owned the streets at this hour. There might be competition from one to the other, a nasty Darwinian process that determined who owned what segment of what sidewalk, who had territorial rights in front of this or that broken window, but as with all such competition, things would soon attain some sort of stability, and business would be conducted, because the purpose of the competition was business, after all.

He turned right onto a new street. The thought evoked a grunt and a thin, ironic smile. New street? No, these streets were old ones, so old that "good" people had left them years ago to move out of the city into greener places, allowing other people, deemed less valuable than themselves, to move in, and then they too had moved away, and the cycle had continued for another few generations until something had gone very badly wrong to create what he saw now in this place. It had taken an hour or so for him to grasp the fact that there were people here, not just trash-laden sidewalks and criminals. He saw a woman leading a child by the hand away from a bus stop. He wondered where they were returning from. A visit with an aunt? The public library? Some place whose attractions were worth the uncomfortable passage between the bus stop and home, past sights and sounds and people whose very existence could damage that little child.

Kelly's back got straighter and his eyes narrower. He'd seen that before. Even in Vietnam, a country at war since before his birth, there were still parents, and children, and, even in war, a desperate quest for something like normality. Children needed to play some of the time, to be held and loved, protected from the harsher aspects of reality for as long as the courage and talents of their parents could make that possible. And it was true here, too. Everywhere there were victims, all innocent to some greater or lesser degree, and the children the most innocent of all. He could see it there, fifty yards away, as the young mother led her child across the street, short of the corner where a dealer stood, making a transaction. Kelly slowed his car to allow her safe passage, hoping that the care and love she showed that night would make a difference to her child. Did the dealers notice her? Were the ordinary citizens worthy of note at all? Were they cover? Potential customers? Nuisances? Prey? And what of the child? Did they care at all? Probably not.

"Shit," he whispered quietly to himself, too detached to show his anger openly.

"What?" Pam asked. She was sitting quietly, leaning away from the window.

"Nothing. Sorry." Kelly shook his head and continued his observation. He was actually beginning to enjoy himself. It was like a reconnaissance mission. Reconnaissance was learning, and learning had always been a passion for Kelly. Here was something completely new. Sure, it was evil, destructive, ugly, but it was also different, which made it exciting. His hands tingled on the wheel.

The customers were diverse, too. Some were obviously local, you could tell from their color and shabby clothing. Some were more addicted than others, and Kelly wondered what that meant. Were the apparently functional ones the newly enslaved? Were the shambling ones the veterans of self-destruction, heading irrevocably towards their own deaths? How could a normal person look at them and not be frightened that it was possible to destroy yourself one dose at a time? What drove people to do this? Kelly nearly stopped the car with that thought. That was something beyond his experience.

Then there were the others, the ones with medium-expensive cars so clean that they had to come from the suburbs, where standards had to be observed. He pulled past one and gave the driver a quick look. *Even wears a tie!* Loose in the collar to allow for his nervousness in a neighborhood such as this one, using one hand to roll down the window while the other perched at the top of the wheel, his right foot doubtless resting lightly on the gas pedal, ready to jolt the car forward if danger should threaten. The driver's nerves must be on edge, Kelly thought, watching him in the mirror. He could not be comfortable here, but he had come anyway. Yes, there it was. Money was passed out the window, and something received for it, and the car moved off as quickly as the traffic-laden street would allow. On a whim, Kelly followed the Buick for a few blocks, turning right, then left onto a main artery, where the car got into the left lane and stayed there, driving as rapidly as was prudent to get the hell out of this dreary part of the city, but without drawing the unwanted attention of a police officer with a citation book.

Yeah, the police, Kelly thought as he gave up the pursuit. *Where the hell are they?* The law was being violated with all the apparent drama of a block party, but they were nowhere to be seen. He shook his head as he turned back into the trading area. The disconnect from his own neighborhood in Indianapolis, merely ten years before, was vast. How had things changed so rapidly? How had he missed it? His time in the Navy, his life on the island, had insulated him from everything. He was a rube, an innocent, a tourist in his own country.

He looked over at Pam. She seemed all right, though a little tense. Those people were dangerous, but not to the two of them. He'd been careful to remain invisible, to drive like everyone else, meandering around the few blocks of the "business" area in an irregular pattern. He was not blind to the dangers, Kelly told himself. In searching for patterns of activity, he hadn't made any of his own. If anyone had eyeballed him and his vehicle especially hard, he would have noticed. And besides, he still had his Colt .45 between his legs. However formidable these thugs might appear, they were nothing compared to the North Vietnamese and Vietcong he'd faced. They'd been good. He'd been better. There was danger on these streets, but far less than he had survived already.

Fifty yards away was a dealer dressed in a silk shirt that might have been brown or maroon. It was hard to tell the color in the poor illumination, but it had to be silk from the way it reflected light. Probably real silk, Kelly was willing to bet. There was a flashiness to these vermin. It wasn't enough for them merely to violate the law, was it? Oh, no, they had to let people know how bold and daring they were.

Dumb, Kelly thought. *Very dumb to draw attention to yourself that way. When you do dangerous things, you conceal your identity, conceal your very presence, and always leave yourself with at least one route of escape.*

"It's amazing they can get away with this," Kelly whispered to himself.

"Huh?" Pam's head turned.

"They're so stupid." Kelly waved at the dealer near the corner. "Even if the cops don't do anything, what if somebody decides to—I mean, he's holding a lot of money, right?"

"Probably a thousand, maybe two thousand," Pam replied.

"So what if somebody tries to rob him?"

"It happens, but he's carrying a gun, too, and if anyone tries—"

"Oh—the guy in the doorway?"

"He's the real dealer, Kelly. Didn't you know that? The guy in the shirt is his lieutenant. He's the guy who does the actual—what do you call it?"

"Transaction," Kelly replied dryly, reminding himself that he'd failed to spot something, knowing that he'd allowed his pride to overcome his caution. *Not a good habit,* he told himself.

Pam nodded. "That's right. Watch—watch him now."

Sure enough, Kelly saw what he now realized was the full transaction. Someone in a car—another visitor from the suburbs, Kelly thought—handed over his money (an assumption, since Kelly couldn't really see, but surely it wasn't a BankAmericard). The lieutenant reached inside the shirt and handed something back. As the car pulled off, the one in the flamboyant shirt moved across the sidewalk, and in shadows that Kelly's eyes could not quite penetrate there was another exchange.

"Oh, I get it. The lieutenant holds the drugs and makes the exchange, but he gives the money to his boss. The boss holds the earnings, but he also has a gun to make sure nothing goes wrong. They're not as dumb as I thought they were."

"They're smart enough."

Kelly nodded and made a mental note, chastising himself for having made at least two wrong assumptions. But that's why you did reconnaissance, after all.

Let's not get too comfortable, Kelly, he told himself. *Now you know that there's* two *bad guys up there, one armed and well concealed in that doorway.* He settled in his seat and locked his eyes on the potential threat, watching for patterns of activity. The one in the doorway would be the real target. The misnamed "lieutenant" was just a hireling, maybe an apprentice, undoubtedly expendable, living on crumbs or commission. The one he could just barely see was the real enemy. And that fit the time-honored pattern, didn't it? He smiled, remembering a regional political officer for the NVA. That job had even carried a code name. ERMINE COAT. Four days they'd stalked that bastard, *after* they'd positively identified him, just to make sure he was the one, then to learn his habits, and determine the best possible way to punch his ticket. Kelly would never forget the look on the man's face when the bullet entered his chest. Then their three-mile run to the LZ, while the NVA's reaction team headed in the wrong direction because of the misleading pyro-charge he'd set up.

What if that man in the shadows was his target? How would he do it? It was an interesting mental game. The feeling was surprisingly godlike. He felt like an eagle, watching, cataloging, but above it all, a predator at the top of the food chain, not hungry now, riding the thermals over them.

He smiled, ignoring the warnings that the combat-experienced part of his brain was beginning to generate.

Hmm. He hadn't seen that car before. It was a muscle car, a Plymouth Roadrunner, red as a candy apple, half a block away. There was something odd about the way it—

"Kelly . . . " Pam suddenly tensed in her seat.

"What is it?" His hand found the .45 and loosened it in the holster just a millimeter or so, taking comfort from the worn wooden grips. But the fact that he'd reached for it, and the fact that he'd felt a sudden need for that comfort, were a message that his mind could not ignore. The cautious part of his brain began to assert itself, his combat instincts began to speak more loudly. Even that brought a surge of reflective pride. *It's so nice,* he reflected in the blink of an eye, *that I still have it when I need it.*

"I know that car—it's—"

Kelly's voice was calm. "Okay, I'll get us out of here. You're right, it's time to leave." He increased speed, maneuvering left to get past the Roadrunner. He thought to tell Pam to get down, but that really wasn't necessary. In less than a minute he'd be gone, and—*damn!*

It was one of the gentry customers, someone in a black Karmann-Ghia convertible who'd just made his transaction, and, eager to have this area behind him, shot left from beyond the Roadrunner only to stop suddenly for yet another car doing much the same thing. Kelly stood on his brakes to avoid a collision, didn't want that to happen right now, did he? But the timing worked out badly, and he stopped almost right next to the Roadrunner, whose driver picked that moment to get out. Instead of going forward, he opted to walk around the back of the car, and in the course of turning, his eyes ended up not three feet from Pam's cringing face. Kelly was looking that way also, knowing that the man was a potential danger, and he saw the look in the man's eyes. He recognized Pam.

"Okay, I see it," his voice announced with an eerie calm, his combat voice. He turned the wheel farther to the left and stepped on the gas, bypassing the little sports car and its invisible driver. Kelly reached the corner a few seconds later, and after the briefest pause to check traffic, executed a hard left turn to evacuate the area.

"He saw me!" Her voice hovered on the edge of a scream.

"It's okay, Pam," Kelly replied, watching the road and his mirror. "We are leaving the area. You're with me and you're safe."

Idiot, his instincts swore at the rest of his consciousness. *You'd better hope they don't follow. That car has triple your horsepower and—*

"Okay." Bright, low-slung headlights made the same turn Kelly'd executed twenty seconds earlier. He saw them wiggle left and right. The car was accelerating hard and fishtailing on the wet asphalt. Double headlights. It wasn't the Karmann-Ghia.

You are now in danger, his instincts told him calmly. *We don't know how much yet, but it's time to wake up.*

Roger that.

Kelly put both hands on the wheel. The gun could wait. He started evaluating the situation, and not much of it was good. His Scout was not made for this sort of thing. It wasn't a sports car, wasn't a muscle car. He had four puny cylinders under the hood. The Plymouth Roadrunner had eight, each one of them bigger than what Kelly was now calling on. Even worse, the Roadrunner was made for low-end acceleration and cornering, while the Scout had been designed for plodding across unpaved ground at a hot fifteen miles per hour. This was not good.

Kelly's eyes divided their time equally between the windshield and the rearview mirror. There wasn't much of a gap, and the Roadrunner was closing it rapidly.

Assets, his brain started cataloging. *The car isn't completely useless, she's a rugged little bitch. You have big, mean bumpers, and that high ground-clearance means you can ram effectively. So what about the coachwork? That Plymouth might be a status symbol for jerks, but this little baby can be—is—a weapon, and you know how to use weapons.* The cobwebs fell completely from his mind.

"Pam," Kelly said as quietly as he could manage, "you want to get down on the floor, honey?"

"Are they—" She started to turn, the fear still manifest in her voice, but Kelly's right hand pushed her down towards the floor.

"Looks like they're following us, yes. Now, you let me handle this, okay?" The last unengaged part of his consciousness was proud of Kelly's calm and confidence. Yes, there was danger, but Kelly knew about danger, knew a hell of a lot more than the people in the Roadrunner. If they wanted a lesson in what danger really was, they'd come to the right fucking place.

Kelly's hands tingled on the wheel as he eased left, then braked and turned hard right. He couldn't corner as well as the Roadrunner, but these streets were wide—and being in front gave him the choice of path and timing. Losing them would be hard, but he knew where the police station was. It was just a matter of leading them there. They'd break contact at that point.

They might shoot, might find a way to disable the car, but if that happened, he had the .45, and a spare clip, and a box of ammo in the glove compartment. They might be armed, but they sure as hell weren't trained. He'd let them get close . . . how many? Two? Maybe three? He ought to have checked, Kelly told himself, remembering that there hadn't been time.

Kelly looked in the mirror. A moment later he was rewarded. The headlights of another, uninvolved car a block away shone straight through the Roadrunner. Three of them. He wondered what they might be armed with. Worst-case was a shotgun. The real worst-case was a rapid-fire rifle, but street hoods weren't soldiers, and that was unlikely.

Probably not, but let's not make any assumptions, his brain replied.

His .45 Colt, at close range, was as lethal as a rifle. He quietly blessed his weekly practice as he turned left. *If it comes to that, let them get close and go for a quick ambush.*

Kelly knew all there was to know about ambushes. Suck 'em in and blow 'em away.

The Roadrunner was ten yards behind now, and its driver was wondering what to do next.

That's the hard part, isn't it? Kelly thought for his pursuer. *You can get close as you want, but the other guy is still surrounded by a ton of metal. What are you going to do now? Ram me, maybe?*

No, the other driver wasn't a total fool. Sitting on the rear bumper was the trailer hitch, and ramming would have driven it right through the Roadrunner's radiator. Too bad.

The Roadrunner made a move to the right. Kelly saw its headlights rock backwards as the driver floored his big V-8, but being in front helped. Kelly snapped the wheel to the right to block. He immediately learned that the other driver didn't have the stomach to hurt his car. He heard tires squeal as the Roadrunner braked down to avoid a collision. *Don't want to scratch that red paint, do we? Good news for a change!* Then the Roadrunner snapped left, but Kelly covered that move also. It was like sailboats in a tacking duel, he realized.

"Kelly, what's happening?" Pam asked, her voice cracking on every word.

His reply was in the same calm voice he'd used for the past few minutes. "What's happening is that they're not very smart."

"That's Billy's car—he loves to race."

"Billy, eh? Well, Billy likes his car a little too much. If you want to hurt somebody, you ought to be willing to—" Just to surprise them, Kelly stomped on his brakes. The Scout nose-dived, giving Billy a really good look at the chromed trailer hitch. Then Kelly accelerated again, watching the Roadrunner's reaction. *Yeah, he wants to follow close, but I can intimidate him real easy, and he won't like that. He's probably a proud little fuck.*

There, that's how I do it.

Kelly decided to go for a soft kill. No sense getting things complicated. Still, he knew that he had to play this one very carefully and very smart. His brain started measuring angles and distances.

Kelly hit his accelerator too hard taking a corner. It almost made him spin out, but he'd planned for that and only botched the recovery enough to make his driving look sloppy to Billy, who was doubtless impressed with his own abilities. The Roadrunner used its cornering and wide tires to close the distance and hold formation on Kelly's starboard-quarter. A deliberate collision now could throw the Scout completely out of control. The Roadrunner held the better hand now, or so its driver thought.

Okay . . .

Kelly couldn't turn right now. Billy had blocked that. So he turned hard left, taking a street through a wide strip of vacant lots. Some highway would be built here. The houses had been cleared off, and the basements filled in with dirt, and the night's rain had turned that to mud.

Kelly turned to look at the Roadrunner. *Uh-oh.* The right-side passenger window was coming down. That meant a gun, sure as hell. *Cutting this a little close, Kelly . . .* But that, he realized instantly, could be made to help. He let them see his face, staring at the Roadrunner, mouth open now, fear clearly visible. He stood on the brakes and turned hard right. The Scout bounded over the half-destroyed curb, obviously a maneuver of panic. Pam screamed with the sudden jolt.

The Roadrunner had better power, its driver knew, better tires, and better brakes, and the driver had excellent reflexes, all of which Kelly had noted and was now counting on. His braking maneuver was covered and nearly matched by the Roadrunner, which then mimicked his turn, also bouncing over the crumbling cement of an eradicated neighborhood, following the Scout across what had recently been a block of homes, falling right into the trap Kelly had sprung. The Roadrunner made it about seventy feet.

Kelly had already downshifted. The mud was a good eight inches deep, and there was the off-chance that the Scout might get stuck momentarily, but the odds were heavily against that. He felt his car slow, felt the tires sink a few inches into the gooey surface, but then the big, coarsely treaded tires bit and started pulling again. *Yeah.* Only then did he turn around.

The headlights told the story. The Roadrunner, already low-slung for cornering paved city streets, yawed wildly to the left as its tires spun on the gelatinous surface, and when the vehicle slowed, their spinning merely dug wet holes. The headlights sank rapidly as the car's powerful engine merely excavated its own grave. Steam rose instantly when the hot engine block boiled off some standing water.

The race was over.

Three men got out of the car and just stood there, uncomfortable to have mud on their shiny punk shoes, looking at the way their once-clean car sat in the mud like a weary sow hog. Whatever nasty plans they'd had, had been done in by a little rain and dirt. *Nice to know I haven't lost it yet,* Kelly thought.

Then they looked up to where he was, thirty yards away.

"You dummies!" he called through the light rain. "See ya 'round, assholes!" He started moving again, careful, of course, to keep his eyes on them. That's what had won him the race, Kelly told himself. Caution, brains, experience. Guts, too, but Kelly dismissed that thought after allowing himself just the tiniest peek at it. Just a little one. He nursed the Scout back onto a strip of pavement, upshifted, and drove off, listening to the little clods of mud thrown by his tires into the wheel wells.

"You can get up now, Pam. We won't be seeing them for a while."

Pam did that, looking back to see Billy and his Roadrunner. The sight of him so close made her face go pale again. "What did you do?"

"I just let them chase me into a place that I selected," Kelly explained. "That's a nice car for running the street, but not so good for dirt."

Pam smiled for him, showing bravery she didn't feel at the moment, but completing the story just as Kelly would have told it to a friend. He checked his watch. Another hour or so until shift change at the police station. Billy and his friends would be stuck there for a long time. The smart move was to find a quiet place to wait. Besides, Pam looked like she needed a little calming down. He drove for a little while, then, finding an area with no major street activity, he parked.

"How are you feeling?" he asked.

"That was scary," she replied, looking down and shaking badly.

"Look, we can go right back to the boat and—"

"No! Billy raped me . . . and killed Helen. If I don't stop him, he'll just keep doing it to people I know." The words were as much to persuade herself as him, Kelly knew. He'd seen it before. It was courage, and it went part and parcel with fear. It was the thing that drove people to accomplish missions, and also the thing that selected those missions for them. She'd seen the darkness, and finding the light, she had to extend its glow to others.

"Okay, but after we tell Frank about it, we get you the hell out of Dodge City."

"I'm okay," Pam said, lying, knowing he saw the lie, and ashamed of it because she didn't grasp his intimate understanding for her feelings of the moment.

You really are, he wanted to tell her, but she hadn't learned about those things yet. And so he asked a question: "How many other girls?"

"Doris, Xantha, Paula, Maria, and Roberta . . . they're all like me, John. And Helen . . . when they killed her, they made us watch."

"Well, with a little luck you can do something about that, honey." He put his arm around her, and after a time the shaking stopped.

"I'm thirsty," she said.

"There's a cooler on the backseat."

Pam smiled. "That's right." She turned in the seat to reach for a Coke—and her body suddenly went rigid. She gasped, and Kelly's skin got that all-too-familiar unwelcome feeling, like an electric charge running along its surface. The danger feeling.

"Kelly!" Pam screamed. She was looking towards the car's left rear. Kelly was already reaching for his gun, turning his body as he did so, but it was too late, and part

of him already knew it. The outraged thought went through his mind that he'd erred badly, fatally, but he didn't know how, and there was no time to figure it out because before he could reach his gun, there was a flash of light and an impact on his head, followed by darkness.

7

Recovery

It was a routine police patrol that spotted the Scout. Officer Chuck Monroe, sixteen months on the force, just old enough to have his own solo radio car, made it a habit to patrol his part of the District after taking to the street. There wasn't much he could do about the dealers—that was the job of the Narcotics Division—but he could show the flag, a phrase he'd learned in the Marine Corps. Twenty-five, newly married, young enough to be dedicated and angry at what was happening in his city and his old neighborhood, the officer noted that the Scout was an unusual vehicle for this area. He decided to check it out, record its tag number, and then came the heart-stopping realization that the car's left side had taken at least two shotgun blasts. Officer Monroe stopped his car, flipped on his rotating lights, and made the first, preliminary call of possible trouble, please stand by. He stepped out of the car, switching his police baton into his left hand, leaving his right at the grip of his service revolver. Only then did he approach the car. A well-trained officer, Chuck Monroe moved in slowly and carefully, his eyes scanning everything in sight.

"Oh, shit!" The return to his radio car was rapid. First Monroe called for backup and then for an ambulance, and then he notified his District desk of the license number of the subject automobile. Then, grabbing his first-aid kit, he returned to the Scout. The door was locked, but the window was blown out, and he reached inside to unlock it. What he saw then froze him in his tracks.

The head rested on the steering wheel, along with the left hand, while the right rested in his lap. Blood had sprayed all over the inside. The man was still breathing, which surprised the officer. Clearly a shotgun blast, it had obliterated the metal and fiberglass of the Scout's body and hit the victim's head, neck, and upper back. There were several small holes in the exposed skin, and these were oozing blood. The wound looked as horrible as any he had seen on the street or in the Marine Corps, and yet the man was alive. That was sufficiently amazing that Monroe decided to leave his first-aid kit closed. There would be an ambulance here in minutes, and he decided that any action he took was as likely to make things worse as better. Monroe held the kit under his right hand like a book, looking at the victim with the frustration of a man of action to whom action was denied. At least the poor bastard was unconscious.

Who was he? Monroe looked at the slumped form and decided that he could extricate the wallet. The officer switched the first-aid kit to his left hand and reached in for the wallet pocket with his right. Unsurprisingly, it was empty, but his touch had elicited a reaction. The body moved a little, and that wasn't good. He moved his hand to steady it, but then the head moved, too, and he knew that the head had better stay still, and so his hand automatically and wrongly touched it. Something rubbed against something else, and a cry of pain echoed across the dark, wet street before the body went slack again.

"Shit!" Monroe looked at the blood on his fingertips and unconsciously rubbed it off on his blue uniform trousers. Just then he heard the banshee-wail of a Fire Department ambulance approaching from the east, and the officer whispered a quiet prayer of thanks that people who knew what they were doing would shortly relieve him of this problem.

The ambulance turned the corner a few seconds later. The large, boxy, red-and-white vehicle halted just past the radio car, and its two occupants came at once to the officer.

"What d'we got." Strangely, it didn't come out like a question. The senior fireman-paramedic hardly needed to ask in any case. In this part of town at this time of night, it wouldn't be a traffic accident. It would be "penetrating trauma," in the dry lexicon of his profession. "Jesus!"

The other crewman was already moving back to the ambulance when another police car arrived on the scene.

"What gives?" the watch supervisor asked.

"Shotgun, close range, and the guy's still alive!" Monroe reported.

"I don't like the neck hits," the first ambulance guy observed tersely.

"Collar?" the other paramedic called from an equipment bay.

"Yeah, if he moves his head . . . damn." The senior firefighter placed his hands on the victim's head to secure it in place.

"ID?" the sergeant asked.

"No wallet. I haven't had a chance to look around yet."

"Did you run the tags?"

Monroe nodded. "Called 'em in; it takes a little while."

The sergeant played his flashlight on the inside of the car to help the firemen. A lot of blood, otherwise empty. Some kind of cooler in the backseat. "What else?" he asked Monroe.

"The block was empty when I got here." Monroe checked his watch. "Eleven minutes ago." Both officers stood back to give the paramedics room to work.

"You ever seen him before?"

"No, Sarge."

"Check the sidewalks."

"Right." Monroe started quartering the area around the car.

"I wonder what this was all about," the sergeant asked nobody in particular. Looking at the body and all the blood, his next thought was that they might never find out. So many crimes committed in this area were never really solved. That was not something pleasing to the sergeant. He looked at the paramedics. "How is he, Mike?"

"Damned near bled out, Bert. Definite shotgun," the man answered, affixing the cervical collar. "A bunch of pellets in the neck, some near the spine. I don't like this at all."

"Where you taking him?" the police sergeant asked.

"University's full up," the junior paramedic advised. "Bus accident on the Beltway. We have to take him to Hopkins."

"That's an extra ten minutes." Mike swore. "You drive, Phil, tell them we have a major trauma and we need a neurosurgeon standing by."

"You got it." Both men lifted him onto the gurney. The body reacted to the movement, and the two police officers—three more radio cars had just arrived—helped hold him in place while the firefighters applied restraints.

"You're a real sick puppy, my friend, but we'll have you in the hospital real quick now," Phil told the body, which might or might not still be alive enough to hear the words. "Time to roll, Mike."

They loaded the body in the back of the ambulance. Mike Eaton, the senior paramedic, was already setting up an IV bottle of blood-expanders. Getting the intravenous line was difficult with the man facedown, but he managed it just as the ambulance started moving. The sixteen-minute trip to Johns Hopkins Hospital was occupied with taking vital signs—the blood pressure was perilously low—and doing some preliminary paperwork.

Who are you? Eaton asked silently. Good physical shape, he noted, twenty-six or -seven. Odd for a probable drug user. This guy would have looked pretty tough standing up, but not now. Now he was more like a large, sleeping child, mouth open, drawing oxygen from the clear plastic mask, breathing shallowly and too slowly for Eaton's comfort.

"Speed it up," he called to the driver, Phil Marconi.

"Roads are pretty wet, Mike, doing my best."

"Come on, Phil, you wops are supposed to drive crazy!"

"But we don't drink like you guys," came the laughing reply. "I just called ahead, they got a neck-cutter standing by. Quiet night at Hopkins, they're all ready for us."

"Good," Eaton responded quietly. He looked at his shooting victim. It often got lonely and a little spooky in the back of an ambulance, and that made him glad for the otherwise nerve-grating wail of the electronic siren. Blood dripped off the gurney down to the floor of the vehicle; the drops traveled around on the metal floor, as though they had a life entirely of their own. It was something you never got used to.

"Two minutes," Marconi said over his shoulder. Eaton moved to the back of the compartment, ready to open the door. Presently he felt the ambulance turn, stop, then back up quickly before stopping again. The rear doors were yanked open before Eaton could reach for them.

"Yeow!" the ER resident observed. "Okay, folks, we're taking him into Three." Two burly orderlies pulled the gurney out while Eaton disconnected the IV bottle from the overhead hook and carried it beside the moving cart.

"Trouble at University?" the resident asked.

"Bus accident," Marconi reported, arriving at his side.

"Better off here anyway. Jesus, what did he back into?" The doctor bent down to inspect the wound as they moved. "Must be a hundred pellets in there!"

"Wait till you see the neck," Eaton told him.

"Shit . . . " the resident breathed.

They wheeled him into the capacious emergency room, selecting a cubicle in the corner. The five men moved the victim from the gurney to a treatment table, and the medical team went to work. Another physician was standing by, along with a pair of nurses.

The resident, Cliff Severn, reached around delicately to remove the cervical collar after making sure the head was secured by sandbags. It took only one look.

"Possible spine," he announced at once. "But first we have to replace blood volume." He rattled off a series of orders. While the nurses got two more IVs started, Severn took the patient's shoes off and ran a sharp metal instrument across the sole of his left foot. The foot moved. Okay, there was no immediate nerve damage. Good news. A few more sticks on the legs also got reactions. Remarkable. While that was happening, a nurse took blood for the usual battery of tests. Severn scarcely had to look as his well-trained crew did their separate jobs. What appeared to be a flurry of activity was more like the movement of a football backfield, the end product of months of diligent practice.

"Where the hell's neuro?" Severn asked the ceiling.

"Right here!" a voice answered.

Severn looked up. "Oh—Professor Rosen."

The greeting stopped there. Sam Rosen was not in a good mood, as the resident saw at once. It had been a twenty-hour day for the professor already. What ought to have been a six-hour procedure had only begun a marathon effort to save the life of an elderly woman who'd fallen down a flight of stairs, an effort that had ended unsuccessfully less than an hour before. He ought to have saved her, Sam was telling himself, still not sure what had gone wrong. He was grateful rather than angry about this extension to a hellish day. Maybe he could win this one.

"Tell me what we have," the professor ordered curtly.

"Shotgun wound, several pellets very close to the cord, sir."

"Okay." Rosen bent down, his hands behind his back. "What's with the glass?"

"He was in a car," Eaton called from the other side of the cubicle.

"We need to get rid of that, need to shave the head, too," Rosen said, surveying the damage. "What's his pressure?"

"BP fifty over thirty," a nurse-practitioner reported. "Pulse is one-forty and thready."

"We're going to be busy," Rosen observed. "This guy is very shocky. Hmm." He paused. "Overall condition of the patient looks good, good muscle tone. Let's get that blood volume back up." Rosen saw two units being started even as he spoke. The ER nurses were especially good and he nodded approval at them.

"How's your son doing, Margaret?" he asked the senior one.

"Starting at Carnegie in September," she answered, adjusting the drip-rate on the blood bottle.

"Let's get the neck cleaned off next, Margaret. I need to take a look."

"Yes, doctor."

The nurse selected a pair of forceps, grabbed a large cotton ball, which she dipped in distilled water, then wiped across the patient's neck with care, clearing away the blood and exposing the actual wounds. It looked worse than it might really be, she saw at once. While she swabbed the patient off, Rosen looked for and got sterile garb. By the time he got back to the bedside, Margaret Wilson had a sterile kit in place and uncovered. Eaton and Marconi stayed in the corner, watching it all.

"Nice job, Margaret," Rosen said, putting his glasses on. "What's he going to major in?"

"Engineering."

"That's good." Rosen held his hand up. "Tweezers." Nurse Wilson set a pair in his hand. "Always room for a bright young engineer."

Rosen picked a small, round hole on the patient's shoulder, well away from anything really vital. With a delicacy that his large hands made almost comical to watch, he probed for and retrieved a single lead ball which he held up to the light. "Number seven shot, I believe. Somebody mistook this guy for a pigeon. That's good news," he told the paramedics. Now that he knew the shot size and probable penetration, he bent down low over the neck. "Hmm . . . what's the BP now?"

"Checking," another nurse said from the far side of the table. "Fifty-five over forty. Coming up."

"Thank you," Rosen said, still bent over the patient. "Who started the first IV?"

"I did," Eaton replied.

"Good work, fireman." Rosen looked up and winked. "Sometimes I think you people save more lives than we do. You saved this one, that's for damned sure."

"Thank you, doctor." Eaton didn't know Rosen well, but he made a note that the man's reputation was deserved. It wasn't every day that a fireman-paramedic got that sort of praise from a full professor. "How's he going to—I mean, the neck injury?"

Rosen was down again, examining it. "Responses, doctor?" he asked the senior resident.

"Positive. Good Babinski. No gross indications of peripheral impairment," Severn replied. This was like an exam, which always made the young resident nervous.

"This may not be as bad as it looks, but we're going to have to clean it up in a hurry before these pellets migrate. Two hours?" he asked Severn. Rosen knew the ER resident was better on trauma than he was.

"Maybe three."

"I'll get a nap out of it anyway." Rosen checked his watch. "I'll take him at, oh, six."

"You want to handle this one personally?"

"Why not? I'm here. This one is straightforward, just takes a little touch." Rosen figured he was entitled to an easy case, maybe once a month. As a full professor, he drew a lot of the hard ones.

"Fine with me, sir."

"Do we have an ID on the patient?"

"No, sir," Marconi replied. "The police ought to be here in a few."

"Good." Rosen stood and stretched. "You know, Margaret, people like us shouldn't work these kind of hours."

"I need the shift-differential," Nurse Wilson replied. Besides which, she was the nursing-team leader for this shift. "What's this, I wonder?" she said after a moment.

"Hmph?" Rosen walked around to her side of the table while the rest of the team did its work.

"A tattoo on his arm," she reported. Nurse Wilson was surprised by the reaction it drew from Professor Rosen.

The transition from sleep to wakefulness was usually easy for Kelly, but not this time. His first coherent thought was to be surprised, but he didn't know why. Next came pain, but not so much pain as the distant warning that there would be pain, and lots of it. When he realized that he could open his eyes, he did, only to find himself staring at a gray linoleum floor. A few scattered drops of liquid reflected the bright overhead fluorescents. He felt needles in his eyes, and only then did he realize that the real stabs were in his arms.

I'm alive.

Why does that surprise me?

He could hear the sound of people moving around, muted conversations, distant chimes. The sound of rushing air was explained by air-conditioning vents, one of which had to be nearby, since he could feel the moving chill on the skin of his back. Something told him that he ought to move, that being still made him vulnerable, but even after he managed a command to his limbs to do something, nothing happened. That's when the pain announced its presence. Like the ripple on a pond from the fall of an insect, it started somewhere on his shoulder and expanded. It took a moment to classify. The nearest approximation was a bad sunburn, because everything from the left side of his neck on down to his left elbow felt scorched. He knew he was forgetting something, probably something important.

Where the fuck am I?

Kelly thought he felt the distant vibration of—what? Ship's engines? No, that wasn't right somehow, and after a few more seconds he realized it was the faraway sound of a city bus pulling away from a stop. Not a ship. A city. Why am I in a city?

A shadow crossed his face. He opened his eyes to see the bottom half of a figure dressed all over in light-green cotton. The hands held a clipboard of some sort. Kelly couldn't even focus his eyes well enough to tell if the figure was male or female before it went away, and it didn't occur to him to say anything before he drifted back to sleep.

"The shoulder wound was extensive but superficial," Rosen told the neurosurgical resident, thirty feet away.

"Bloody enough. Four units," she noted.

"Shotgun wounds are like that. There was only one real threat to the spine. Took me a little while to figure how to remove it without endangering anything."

"Two hundred thirty-seven pellets, but"—she held the X ray up to the light—"looks like you got them all. This fellow just got a nice collection of freckles, though."

"Took long enough," Sam said tiredly, knowing that he ought to have let someone else handle it, but he'd volunteered, after all.

"You know this patient, don't you?" Sandy O'Toole said, arriving from the recovery room.

"Yeah."

"He's coming out, but it'll be a while." She handed over the chart which showed his current vitals. "Looking good, doctor."

Professor Rosen nodded and explained further to the resident, "Great physical shape. The firemen did a nice job holding up his BP. He did almost bleed out, but the wounds looked worse than they really were. Sandy?"

She turned back. "Yes, doctor?"

"This one is a friend of mine. Would you mind terribly if I asked you to take—"

"A special interest?"

"You're our best, Sandy."

"Anything I need to know?" she asked, appreciating the compliment.

"He's a good man, Sandy." Sam said it in a way that carried real meaning. "Sarah likes him, too."

"Then he must be all right." She headed back into recovery, wondering if the professor was playing match-maker again.

"What do I tell the police?"

"Four hours, minimum. I want to be there." Rosen looked over at the coffeepot and decided against it. Any more and his stomach might rupture from all the acid.

"So who is he?"

"I don't know all that much, but I ran into trouble on the Bay in my boat and he helped me out. We ended up staying at his place for the weekend." Sam didn't go any further. He didn't really know that much, but he had inferred a lot, and that scared him very much indeed. He'd done his part. While he hadn't saved Kelly's life—luck and the firemen had probably done that—he had performed an exceedingly skillful procedure, though he had also annoyed the resident, Dr. Ann Pretlow, by not allowing her to do much of anything except watch. "I need a little sleep. I don't have much scheduled for today. Can you do the follow-up on Mrs. Baker?"

"Certainly."

"Have someone wake me up in three hours," Rosen said on the way to his office, where a nice comfortable couch awaited.

"Nice tan," Billy observed with a smirk. "I wonder where she got it." There was general amusement. "What do we do with her?"

He thought about that. He'd just discovered a fine way to deal with bodies, much cleaner, in its way, and far safer than what they'd been doing. But it also involved a lengthy boat trip, and he just didn't have the time to be bothered. He also didn't want to have anyone else use that particular method. It was too good to share with anyone. He knew that one of them would talk. That was one of his problems.

"Find a spot," he said after a moment's consideration. "If she's found, it doesn't matter much." Then he looked around the room, cataloging the expressions he saw. The lesson had been learned. Nobody else would try this again, not anytime soon. He didn't even have to say anything.

"Tonight? Better at night."

"That's fine. No hurry." Everyone else could learn even more from looking at her for the rest of the day, lying there in the middle of the floor. He took only a little pleasure from it, and people had to learn their lessons, and even when it was too late for one of them, others could learn from that one's mistakes. Especially when the lessons were clear and hard. Even the drugs wouldn't block this one out.

"What about the guy?" he asked Billy.

Billy smirked again. It was his favorite expression. "Blew him away. Both barrels, ten feet. We won't be seeing him no more."

"Okay." He left. There was work to be done and money to collect. This little problem was behind him. It was a pity, he thought on the way to his car, that they couldn't all be solved this easily.

The body remained in place. Doris and the others sat in the same room, unable to look away from what had once been a friend, learning their lesson as Henry wished.

Kelly vaguely noted that he was being moved. The floor moved under him. He watched the lines between the floor tiles travel like movie credits until they backed him into another room, a small one. This time he tried to raise his head, and indeed it moved a few inches, enough to see the legs of a woman. The green surgical slacks ended above her ankles, and they were definitely a woman's. There was a whirring sound, and his horizon moved downwards. After a moment he realized that he was on a powered bed, hanging between two hoops of stainless steel. His body was attached to the bed somehow, and as the platform rotated he could feel the pressure of the restraints that held him in place, not uncomfortable, but there. Presently he saw a woman. His age, perhaps a year or two younger, with brown hair stuffed under a green cap and light eyes that sparkled in a friendly way.

"Hello," she said from behind her mask. "I'm your nurse."

"Where am I?" Kelly asked in a raspy voice.

"Johns Hopkins Hospital."

"What—"

"Somebody shot you." She reached out to touch his hand.

The softness of her hand ignited something in his drug-suppressed consciousness. For a minute or so, Kelly couldn't figure out what it was. Like a cloud of smoke, it shifted and revolved, forming a picture before his eyes. The missing pieces began to come together, and even though he understood it was horror that awaited him, his mind struggled to hurry them along. In the end it was the nurse who did it for him.

Sandy O'Toole had left her mask on for a reason. An attractive woman, like many nurses she felt that male patients responded well to the idea of someone like her taking a personal interest in them. Now that Patient Kelly, John, was more or less alert, she reached up and untied the mask to give him her beaming feminine smile, the first good thing of the day for him. Men liked Sandra O'Toole, from her tall, athletic frame to the gap between her front teeth. She had no idea why they considered the gap sexy—food got caught there, after all—but as long as it worked, it was one more tool for her business of helping to make sick people well. And so she smiled at him, just for business. The result was like no other she had encountered.

Her patient went ghostly pale, not the white of snow or fresh linen, but the mottled, sickly look and texture of Styrofoam. Her first thought was that something had gone gravely wrong, a massive internal bleed, perhaps, or even a clot-driven thrombosis. He might have screamed, but couldn't catch his breath, and his hands fell limp. His eyes never left her, and after a moment O'Toole realized that she had somehow caused whatever it was. O'Toole's first instinct was to take his hand and say that everything was all right, but she knew instantly that it wasn't true.

"Oh, God . . . oh, God . . . Pam." The look on what ought to have been a ruggedly handsome face was one of black despair.

"She was with me," Kelly told Rosen a few minutes later. "Do you know anything, doc?"

"The police will be here in a few minutes, John, but, no, I don't know anything. Maybe they took her to another hospital." He tried to hope. But Sam knew that it was a lie, and he hated himself for lying. He made a show of taking Kelly's vital signs, something Sandy could have done just as well, before examining his patient's back. "You're going to be okay. How's the shoulder?"

"Not real great, Sam," Kelly replied, still groggy. "How bad?"

"Shotgun—you took quite a bit, but—was the window on the car rolled up?"

"Yeah," Kelly said, remembering the rain.

"That's one of the things that saved you. The shoulder muscles are pretty beaten up, and you damned near bled to death, but there won't be any permanent damage except for some scarring. I did the job myself."

Kelly looked up. "Thanks, Sam. Pain isn't so bad . . . worse the last time I—"

"Quiet down, John," Rosen ordered gently, giving the neck a close look. He made a mental note to order a complete new set of X rays just to make sure there wasn't something he had missed, maybe close to the spine. "The pain medication will kick in pretty fast. Save the heroics. We don't award points for that here. 'Kay?"

"Aye aye. Please—check the other hospitals for Pam, okay?" Kelly asked, hope yet in his voice though he knew better, too.

Two uniformed officers had been waiting the whole time for Kelly to come out from under. Rosen brought in the older of the two a few minutes later. The questioning was brief, on doctor's orders. After confirming his identity, they asked about Pam; they already had a physical description from Rosen, but not a surname, which Kelly had to provide. The officers made note of his appointment with Lieutenant Allen and left after a few minutes as the victim started to fade out. The shock of the shooting and surgery, added to the pain medications, would diminish the value of what he said anyway, Rosen pointed out.

"So who's the girl?" the senior officer asked.

"I didn't even know her last name until a couple minutes ago," Rosen said, seated in his office. He was dopey from lack of sleep, and his commentary suffered as well. "She was addicted to barbiturates when we met them—she and Kelly were living together, I suppose. We helped her clean up."

"Who's 'we'?"

"My wife, Sarah. She's a pharmacologist here. You can talk to her if you want."

"We will," the officer assured him. "What about Mr. Kelly?"

"Ex-Navy, Vietnam vet."

"Do you have any reason to believe that he's a drug user, sir?"

"Not a chance," Rosen answered, a slight edge on his voice. "His physical condition is too good for that, and I saw his reaction when we found out that Pam was using pills. I had to calm him down. Definitely not an addict. I'm a physician, I would have noticed."

The policeman was not overly impressed, but accepted it at face value. The detectives would have a lot of fun with this one, he thought. What had appeared to be a simple robbery was now at least a kidnapping as well. Wonderful news. "So what was he doing in that part of town?"

"I don't know," Sam admitted. "Who's this Lieutenant Allen?"

"Homicide, Western District," the cop explained.

"I wonder why they had an appointment."

"That's something we'll get from the Lieutenant, sir."

"Was this a robbery?"

"Probably. It sure looks that way. We found his wallet a block away, no cash, no credit cards, just his driver's license. He also had a handgun in his car. Whoever robbed him must have missed that. That's against the law, by the way," the cop noted. Another officer came in.

"I checked the name again—I *knew* I heard it before. He did a job for Allen. Remember last year, the Gooding case?"

The senior man looked up from his notes. "Oh, yeah! He's the guy who found the gun?"

"Right, and he ended up training our divers."

"It still doesn't explain what the hell he was doing over there," the cop pointed out.

"True," his partner admitted. "But it makes it hard to believe he's a player."

The senior officer shook his head. "There was a girl with him. She's missing."

"Kidnapping, too? What do we have on her?"

"Just a name. Pamela Madden. Twenty, recovering doper, missing. We have Mr. Kelly, his car, his gun, and that's it. No shells from the shotgun. No witnesses at all. A missing girl, probably, but a description that could fit ten thousand local girls. Robbery-kidnapping." All in all, not that atypical a case. They often started off knowing damned little. In any case, the two uniformed officers had mainly determined that the detectives would take this one over almost immediately.

"She wasn't from around here. She had an accent, Texas, somewhere out there."

"What else?" the senior officer asked. "Come on, doc, anything you know, okay?"

Sam grimaced. "She had been the victim of sexual abuse. She might have been a hooker. My wife said—hell, I saw it, evidence of scars on her back. She'd been whipped, some permanent scarring from welts, that sort of thing. We didn't press, but she might have been a prostitute."

"Mr. Kelly has strange habits and acquaintances, doesn't he?" the officer observed while making notes.

"From what you just said, he helps cops, too, doesn't he?" Professor Rosen was getting angry. "Anything else? I have rounds to make."

"Doctor, what we have here is a definite attempted murder, probably as part of a robbery, and maybe a kidnapping also. Those are serious crimes. I have procedures to follow, just like you do. When will Kelly be up for a real interview?"

"Tomorrow, probably, but he's going to be very rocky for a couple of days."

"Is ten in the morning okay, sir?"

"Yes."

The cops rose. "Somebody will be back then, sir."

Rosen watched them leave. This, strangely enough, had been his first real experience with a major criminal investigation. His work more often dealt with traffic and industrial accidents. He found himself unable to believe that Kelly could be a criminal, yet that had seemed to be the thrust of their questions, wasn't it? That's when Dr. Pretlow came in.

"We finished the lab work on Kelly." She handed the data over. "Gonorrhea. He should be more careful. I recommend penicillin. Any known allergies?"

"No." Rosen closed his eyes and swore. What the hell else would happen today?

"Not that big a deal, sir. It looks like a very early case. When he's feeling better I'll have Social Services talk to him about—"

"No, you won't ," Rosen said in a low growl.

"But—"

"But the girl he got it from is probably dead, and we will *not* force him to remember her that way." It was the first time Sam had admitted the probable facts to himself, and that made it all the worse, declaring her dead. He had little to base it on, but his instincts told him it must be so.

"Doctor, the law requires—"

It was just too much. Rosen was on the point of exploding. "That's a good *man* in there. I watched him fall in love with a girl who's probably been murdered, and his last memory of her will *not* be that she gave him venereal disease. Is that clear, doctor? As far as the patient is concerned, the medication is for a post-op infection. Mark the chart accordingly."

"No, doctor, I will not do that."

Professor Rosen made the proper notations. "Done." He looked up. "Doctor Pretlow, you have the makings of an excellent technical surgeon. Try to remember that the patients upon whom we perform our procedures are human beings, with feelings, will you? If you do so, I think you will find that the job is somewhat easier in the long run. It will also make you a much better physician."

And what was he so worked up about? Pretlow asked herself on the way out.

8

Concealment

It was a combination of things. June 20 was a hot day, and a dull one. A photographer for the *Baltimore Sun* had a new camera, a Nikon to replace his venerable Honeywell Pentax, and while he mourned for his old one, the new camera, like a new love, had all sorts of new features to explore and enjoy. One of them was a whole collection of telephoto lenses that the distributor had thrown in. The Nikon was a new model, and the company had wanted it accepted within the news-photo community quickly, and so twenty photographers at various papers around the country had gotten free sets. Bob Preis had gotten his because of a Pulitzer Prize earned three years before. He was sitting in his car on Druid Lake Drive now, listening to his police radio, hoping for something interesting to happen, but nothing was. And so he was playing with his new camera, practicing his lens-switching skills. The Nikon was beautifully machined, and as an infantryman will learn to strip and clean his rifle in total darkness, Preis was changing from one lens to another by feel, forcing himself to scan the area just as a means of keeping his eyes off a procedure that had to become as natural and automatic as zipping his pants.

It was the crows that caught his attention. Located off-center in the irregularly shaped lake was a fountain. No example of architectural prowess, it was a plain concrete cylinder sticking six or eight feet up from the water's surface, and in it were a few jets that shot water more or less straight up, though today shifting winds were scattering the water haphazardly in all directions. Crows were circling the water, trying occasionally to get in, but defeated by the swirling sheets of clear white spray, which appeared to frighten them. What were the crows interested in? His hands searched the camera case for the 200mm lens, which he attached to the camera body, bringing it up to his eyes smoothly.

"Sweet Jesus!" Preis instantly shot ten rapid frames. Only then did he get on his car radio, telling his base office to notify the police at once. He switched lenses again, this time selecting a 300mm, his longest. After finishing one roll, he threaded another, this one 100-speed color. He steadied the camera on the windowsill of the tired old Chevy and fired off another roll. One crow, he saw, got through the water, settling on—

"Oh, God, no . . . " Because it was, after all, a human body there, a young woman, white as alabaster, and in the through-the-lens optics, he could see the crow right there, its clawed feet strutting around the body, its pitiless black eyes surveying what to the bird was nothing more than a large and diverse meal. Preis sat his camera down and shifted his car into gear. He violated two separate traffic laws getting as close to the fountain as he could, and in what was for him a rare case of humanity overcoming professionalism, slammed his hand down on the horn, hoping to startle the bird away. The bird looked up, but saw that whatever the noise came from, there was no immediate threat here, and it went back to selecting the first morsel for its iron-hard beak. It was then that Preis made a random but effective guess. He blinked his lights on and off, and to the bird that was unusual enough that it thought better of things and flew away. It might have been an owl, after all, and the meal wasn't going anywhere. The bird would just wait for the threat to go away before returning to eat.

"What gives?" a cop asked, pulling alongside.

"There's a body on the fountain. Look." He handed the camera over.

"God," the policeman breathed, handing it back after a long quiet moment. He made the radio call while Preis shot another roll. Police cars arrived, rather like the crows, one at a time, until eight were parked within sight of the fountain. A fire truck arrived in ten minutes, along with someone from the Department of Recreation and Parks, trailering a boat behind his pickup. This was quickly put into the water. Then came the forensics people with a lab truck, and it was time to go out to the fountain. Preis asked to go along—he was a better photographer than the one the cops used—but was rebuffed, and so he continued to record the event from the lake's edge. There wouldn't be another Pulitzer in this. There could have been, he thought. But the price of that would have involved immortalizing the instinctive act of a carrion bird, defiling the body of a girl in the midst of a major city. And that wasn't worth the nightmares. He had enough of those already.

A crowd had already gathered. The police officers congregated in small knots, trading quiet comments and barbed attempts at grim humor. A TV news truck arrived from its studio on Television Hill just north of the park, which held the city zoo. It was a place Bob Preis often took his young children, and they especially liked the lion, not so originally named Leo, and the polar bears, and all the other predators that were safely confined behind steel bars and stone walls. *Unlike some people,* he thought, watching them lift the body and place it in a rubber bag. At least her torment was over. Preis changed rolls one more time to record the process of loading the body into the coroner's station wagon. A *Sun* reporter was here now. He'd ask the questions while Preis determined how good his new camera really was back at his darkroom on Calvert Street.

"John, they found her," Rosen said.

"Dead?" Kelly couldn't look up. The tone of Sam's

voice had already told him the real news. It wasn't a surprise, but the end of hope never comes easily to anyone.

Sam nodded. "Yeah."

"How?"

"I don't know yet. The police called me a few minutes ago, and I came over as quick as I could."

"Thanks, pal." If a human voice could sound dead, Sam told himself, Kelly's did.

"I'm sorry, John. I—you know how I felt about her."

"Yes, sir, I do. It's not your fault, Sam."

"You're not eating." Rosen gestured to the food tray.

"I'm not real hungry."

"If you want to recover, you have to get your strength back."

"Why?" Kelly asked, staring at the floor.

Rosen came over and grasped Kelly's right hand. There wasn't much to say. The surgeon didn't have the stomach to look at Kelly's face. He'd pieced enough together to know that his friend was blaming himself, and he didn't know enough to talk to him about it, at least not yet. Death was a companion for Sam Rosen, M.D., F.A.C.S. Neurosurgeons dealt with major injuries to that most delicate part of the human anatomy, and the injuries to which they most often responded were frequently beyond anyone's power to repair. But the unexpected death of a person one knows can be too much for anyone.

"Is there anything I can do?" he asked after a minute or two.

"Not right now, Sam. Thanks."

"Maybe a priest?"

"No, not now."

"It wasn't your fault, John."

"Whose, then? She trusted me, Sam. I blew it."

"The police want to talk to you some more. I told them tomorrow morning."

He'd been through his second interview in the morning. Kelly had already told them much of what he knew. Her full name, her hometown, how they'd met. Yes, they had been intimate. Yes, she had been a prostitute, a runaway. Yes, her body had shown signs of abuse. But not everything. Somehow he'd been unable to volunteer information because to have done so would have entailed admitting to other men the dimensions of his failure. And so he had avoided some of their inquiries, claiming pain, which was quite real, but not real enough. He already sensed that the police didn't like him, but that was okay. He didn't much like himself at the moment.

"Okay."

"I can—I should do some things with your medications. I've tried to go easy, I don't like overdoing the things, but they'll help you relax, John."

"Dope me up more?" Kelly's head lifted, and the expression was not something that Rosen ever wanted to see again. "You think that's really going to make a difference, Sam?"

Rosen looked away, unable to meet his eyes now that it was possible to do so. "You're ready for a regular bed. I'll have you moved into one in a few minutes."

"Okay."

The surgeon wanted to say more, but couldn't find the right words. He left without any others.

It took Sandy O'Toole and two orderlies to move him, as carefully as they could, onto a standard hospital bed. She cranked up the head portion to relieve the pressure on his injured shoulder.

"I heard," she told him. It bothered her that his grief wasn't right. He was a tough man, but not a fool. Perhaps he was one of those men who did his weeping alone, but she was sure he hadn't done it yet. And that was necessary, she knew. Tears released poisons from inside, poisons which if not released could be as deadly as the real kind. The nurse sat beside his bed. "I'm a widow," she told him.

"Vietnam?"

"Yes, Tim was a captain in the First Cavalry."

"I'm sorry," Kelly said without turning his head. "They saved my butt once."

"It's hard. I know."

"Last November I lost Tish, and now—"

"Sarah told me. Mr. Kelly—"

"John," he said softly. He couldn't find it in himself to be gruff to her.

"Thank you, John. My name is Sandy. Bad luck does not make a bad person," she told him in a voice that meant what it said, though it didn't quite sound that way.

"It wasn't luck. She told me it was a dangerous place and I took her there anyway because I wanted to see for myself."

"You almost got yourself killed trying to protect her."

"I didn't protect her, Sandy. I killed her." Kelly's eyes were wide open now, looking at the ceiling. "I was careless and stupid and I killed her."

"Other people killed her, and other people tried to kill you. You're a victim."

"Not a victim. Just a fool."

We'll save that for later, Nurse O'Toole told herself. "What sort of girl was she, John?"

"Unlucky." Kelly made an effort to look at her face, but that just made it worse. He gave the nurse a brief synopsis of the life of Pamela Starr Madden, deceased.

"So after all the men who hurt her or used her, you gave her something that nobody else did." O'Toole paused, waiting for a reply and getting none. "You gave her love, didn't you?"

"Yes." Kelly's body shuddered for a moment. "Yes, I did love her."

"Let it out," the nurse told him. "You have to."

First he closed his eyes. Then he shook his head. "I can't."

This would be a difficult patient, she told herself. The cult of manhood was a mystery to her. She'd seen it in her husband, who had served a tour in Vietnam as a lieutenant, then rotated back again as a company commander. He hadn't relished it, hadn't looked forward to it, but he hadn't shrunk from it. It was part of the job, he'd told her on their wedding night, two months before he'd left. A stupid, wasteful job that had cost her a husband and, she feared, her life. Who really cared what happened in a place so far away? And yet it had been important to Tim. Whatever that force had been, its legacy to her was emptiness, and it had no more real meaning than the grim pain she saw on the face of her patient. O'Toole would have known more about that pain if she'd been able to take her thought one step further.

"That was really stupid."

"That's one way of looking at it," Tucker agreed. "But I can't have my girls leaving without permission, can I?"

"You ever hear of burying them?"

"Anybody can do that." The man smiled in the darkness, watching the movie. They were in the back row of a downtown theater, a 1930s film palace that was gradually falling to ruin, and had started running films at 9 A.M. just to keep up with the painting bill. It was still a good place for a covert meeting with a confidential informant, which was how this meeting would go on the officer's time sheet.

"Sloppy not killing the guy, too."

"Will he be a problem?" Tucker asked.

"No. He didn't see anything, did he?"

"You tell me, man."

"I can't get that close to the case, remember?" The man paused for a handful of popcorn and munched away his irritation. "He's known to the department. Ex-Navy guy, skin diver, lives over on the Eastern Shore somewhere, sort of a rich beach bum from what I gather. The first interview didn't develop anything at all. Ryan and Douglas are going to be working the case now, but it doesn't look like they have much of anything to work with."

"That's about what she said when we . . . 'talked' to her. He picked her up, and it looks like they had a mighty good time together, but her supply of pills ran out, she said, and she had him bring her in town to score some 'ludes. So, no harm done?"

"Probably not, but let's try to control loose ends, okay?"

"You want me to get him in the hospital?" Tucker asked lightly. "I can probably arrange that."

"No! You damned fool, this is going on the books as a robbery. If anything else happens, it just gets bigger.

We don't want that. Leave him be. He doesn't know anything."

"So he's not a problem?" Tucker wanted to be clear on that.

"No. But try to remember that you can't open a murder investigation without a body."

"I have to keep my people in line."

"From what I hear you did to her—"

"Just keeping them in line," Tucker reemphasized. "Making an example, like. You do that right and you don't have any more problems for a while. You're not a part of that. Why does it bother you?"

Another handful of popcorn helped him bend to the logic of the moment. "What do you have for me?"

Tucker smiled in the darkness. "Mr. Piaggi is starting to like doing business with me."

A grunt in the darkness. "I wouldn't trust him."

"It does get complicated, doesn't it?" Tucker paused. "But I need his connections. We're about to hit the big time."

"How long?"

"Soon," Tucker said judiciously. "Next step, I think, we start feeding stuff north. Tony is up there talking to some people today, matter of fact."

"What about now? I could use something juicy."

"Three guys with a ton of grass good enough?" Tucker asked.

"Do they know about you?"

"No, but I know about them." That was the point, after all—his organization was tight. Only a handful of people knew who he was, and those people knew what would happen if they got a little loose. You just had to have the stones to enforce discipline.

"Take it easy on him," Rosen said outside the private room. "He's recovering from a major injury and he's still on several medications. He's really not capable of talking to you with a full deck."

"I have my job, too, doctor." It was a new officer on the case now, a detective sergeant named Tom Douglas.

He was about forty, and looked every bit as tired as Kelly, Rosen thought, and every bit as angry.

"I understand that. But he's been badly hurt, plus the shock of what happened to his girlfriend."

"The quicker we get the information we need, the better our chances are to find the bastards. Your duty is to the living, sir. Mine is to the dead."

"If you want my medical opinion, he's not really capable of helping you right now. He's been through too much. He's clinically depressed, and that has implications for his physical recovery."

"Are you telling me that you want to sit in?" Douglas asked. *Just what I need—an amateur Sherlock to watch over us.* But that was a battle he couldn't win and wouldn't bother to fight.

"I'll feel better if I can keep an eye on things. Go easy on him," Sam repeated, opening the door.

"Mr. Kelly, we're sorry," the detective said after introducing himself. Douglas opened his notebook. The case had been booted up the ladder to his office because of its high profile. The first-page color photo on the *Evening Sun* had come as close to the pornographic as anything the media could publish, and the mayor had personally called for action on this one. Because of that, Douglas had taken the case, wondering how long the mayor's interest would last. *Not very,* the detective thought. The only thing that occupied a politician's mind for more than a week was getting and holding votes. This case had more spin on it than one of Mike Cuellar's screwballs, but it was his case, and what was always the worst part was about to take place. "Two nights ago you were in the company of a young lady named Pamela Madden?"

"Yes." Kelly's eyes were closed when Nurse O'Toole came in with his morning antibiotic dose. She was surprised to see the two other men there and stopped in the doorway, not knowing if she should interrupt or not.

"Mr. Kelly, yesterday afternoon we discovered the body of a young woman who fits the physical description of Miss Madden." Douglas reached into his coat pocket.

"No!" Rosen said, getting out of his chair.

"Is this she?" Douglas asked, holding the photo before Kelly's face, hoping that his proper grammar would somehow lessen the impact.

"God *damn* it!" The surgeon turned the cop around and pushed him against the wall. In the process the photo dropped on the patient's chest.

Kelly's eyes went wide in horror. His body sprang upwards, fighting the restraints. Then he collapsed, his skin pasty white. All in the room turned away but for the nurse, whose eyes were locked on her patient.

"Look, doc, I—" Douglas tried to say.

"Get the hell out of my hospital!" Rosen fairly screamed. "You can *kill* somebody with that kind of shock! Why didn't you tell me—"

"He has to identify—"

"*I* could have done that!"

O'Toole heard the noise as the two grown men scuffled like children in a playground, but John Kelly was her concern, the antibiotic medication still in her hand. She tried to remove the photograph from Kelly's view, but her own eyes were first drawn to the image and then repulsed by it as Kelly's hand seized the print and held it a scant twelve inches from his own wide-open eyes. It was his expression now that occupied her consciousness. Sandy recoiled briefly at what she saw there, but then Kelly's face composed itself and he spoke.

"It's okay, Sam. He has his job to do, too." Kelly looked down at the photo one last time. Then he closed his eyes and held it up for the nurse to take.

And things settled down for everyone except Nurse O'Toole. She watched Kelly swallow the oversized pill and left the room for the calm of the corridor.

Sandra O'Toole walked back to the nurses' station, remembering what she alone had seen. Kelly's face turning so pale that her first reaction to it was that he must be in shock, then the tumult behind her as she reached for her patient—but then what? It wasn't like the first time at all. Kelly's face had transformed itself. Only an instant, like opening a door into some other place, and she'd seen something she had never imagined. Something very old and feral and ugly. The eyes not wide, but focused on something she could not see. The pallor of his face not that of shock, but of rage. His hands balled briefly into fists of quivering stone. And then his face had changed again. There had been comprehension to replace the blind, killing rage, and what she'd seen next was the most dangerous sight she had ever beheld, though she knew not why. Then the door closed. Kelly's eyes shut, and when he opened them, his face was unnaturally serene. The complete sequence had not taken four seconds, she realized, all of it while Rosen and Douglas had been scuffling against the wall. He'd passed from horror to rage to understanding—then to concealment, but what had come in between comprehension and disguise was the most frightening thing of all.

What had she seen in the face of this man? It took her a moment to answer the question. Death was what she'd seen. Controlled. Planned. Disciplined.

But it was still Death, living in the mind of a man.

"I don't like doing this sort of thing, Mr. Kelly," Douglas said back in the room as he adjusted his coat. The detective and the surgeon traded a look of mutual embarrassment.

"John, are you all right?" Rosen looked him over and took his pulse quickly, surprised to find it nearly normal.

"Yeah." Kelly nodded. He looked at the detective. "That's her. That's Pam."

"I'm sorry. I really am," Douglas said with genuine sincerity, "but there's no easy way to do this. There never is. Whatever happened, it's over now, and now it's our job to try and identify the people who did it. We need your help to do that."

"Okay," Kelly said neutrally. "Where's Frank? How come he's not here?"

"He can't have a hand in this," Sergeant Douglas answered, with a look to the surgeon. "He knows you. Personal involvement in a criminal case isn't terribly professional." It wasn't entirely true—in fact, was hardly true at all—but it served the purpose. "Did you see the people who—"

Kelly shook his head, looking down at the bed, and he

spoke just above a whisper. "No. I was looking the wrong way. She said something, but I didn't get around. Pam saw them, I turned right, then started turning left. I never made it."

"What were you doing at the time?"

"Observing. Look, you talked to Lieutenant Allen, right?"

"That's correct." Douglas nodded.

"Pam witnessed a murder. I was bringing her in to talk to Frank about it."

"Go on."

"She was linked up with people who deal drugs. She saw them kill somebody, a girl. I told her she had to do something about it. I was curious about what it was like," Kelly said in a flat monotone, still bathing in his guilt while his mind replayed the image.

"Names?"

"None that I remember," Kelly answered.

"Come on," Douglas said, leaning forward. "She must have told you something!"

"I didn't ask much. I figured that was your job—Frank's job, I mean. We were supposed to meet with Frank that night. All I know is it's a bunch of people who deal drugs and who use women for something."

"That's all you know?"

Kelly looked him straight in the eyes. "Yes. Not very helpful, is it?"

Douglas waited a few seconds before going on. What might have been an important break in an important case was not going to happen, and so it was his turn to lie again, beginning with some truth to make it easier. "There's a pair of robbers working the west side of town. Two black males, medium size, and that's all we have for a description. Their MO is a sawed-off shotgun. They specialize in taking down people coming in for a drug buy, and they particularly like the gentry customers. Probably most of their robberies don't even get reported. We have them linked to two killings. This might be number three."

"That's all?" Rosen asked.

"Robbery and murder are major crimes, doctor."

"But that's just an accident!"

"That's one way of looking at it," Douglas agreed, turning back to his witness. "Mr. Kelly, you must have seen something. What the hell were you doing around there? Was Miss Madden trying to buy something—"

"No!"

"Look, it's over. She's dead. You can tell me. I have to know."

"Like I said, she was linked up with this bunch, and I—dumb as it sounds, I don't know shit about drugs." *I'll be finding out, though.*

Alone in his bed, alone with his mind, Kelly's eyes calmly surveyed the ceiling, scanning the white surface like a movie screen.

First, the police are wrong, Kelly told himself. He didn't know how he knew, but he did, and that was enough. *It wasn't robbers, it was* them, *the people Pam were afraid of.*

What had happened fit what Pam had told him. It was something they had done before. He had allowed himself to be spotted—twice. His guilt was still quite real, but that was history now and he couldn't change it. Whatever he had done wrong, it was done. Whoever had done this to Pam, they were still out there, and if they'd done this twice already, they would do it again. But that was not really what occupied his mind behind the blank staring mask.

Okay, he thought. *Okay. They've never met anyone like me before.*

I need to get back into shape, Chief Bosun's Mate John Terrence Kelly told himself.

The injuries were severe, but he'd survive them. He knew every step of the process. Recovery would be painful, but he'd do what they told him, he'd push the envelope a little bit, enough to make them proud of their patient. Then the really hard part would start. The running, the swimming, the weights. Then the weapons training. Then the mental preparation—but that was already underway, he realized . . .

Oh, no. Not in their wildest nightmares have they ever met anyone like me.

The name they had given him in Vietnam boiled up from the past.

Snake.

Kelly pushed the call button pinned to his pillow. Nurse O'Toole appeared within two minutes.

"I'm hungry," he told her.

"I hope I never have to do that again," Douglas told his lieutenant, not for the first time.

"How did it go?"

"Well, that professor might make a formal complaint. I think I calmed him down enough, but you never know with people like that."

"Does Kelly know anything?"

"Nothing we can use," Douglas replied. "He's still too messed up from being shot and all to be coherent, but he didn't see any faces, didn't—hell, if he had seen anything, he would probably have done something. I even showed him the picture, trying to shake him a little. I thought the poor bastard would have a heart attack. The doctor went crazy. I'm not real proud of that, Em. Nobody should have to see something like that."

"Including us, Tom, including us." Lieutenant Emmet Ryan looked up from a large collection of photos, half taken at the scene, half at the coroner's office. What he saw there sickened him despite all his years of police work, especially because this wasn't a crime of madness or passion. No, this event had been done for a purpose by coldly rational men. "I talked to Frank. This Kelly guy is a good scout, helped him clear the Gooding case. He's not linked up with anything. The doctors all say that he's clean, not a user."

"Anything on the girl?" Douglas didn't need to say that this could have been the break they'd needed. If only Kelly had called them instead of Allen, who didn't know about their investigation. But he hadn't, and their best potential source of information was dead.

"The prints came back. Pamela Madden. She was picked

up in Chicago, Atlanta, and New Orleans for prostitution. Never came to trial, never did any time. The judges just kept letting her go. Victimless crime, right?"

The sergeant suppressed a curse at the many idiots on the bench. "Sure, Em, no victims at all. So we're not any closer to these people than we were six months ago, are we? We need more manpower," Douglas said, stating the obvious.

"To chase down the murder of a street hooker?" the Lieutenant asked. "The mayor didn't like the picture, but they've already told him what she was, and after a week, things go back to normal. You think we'll break something loose in a week, Tom?"

"You could let him know—"

"No." Ryan shook his head. "He'd talk. Ever know a politician who didn't? They've got somebody inside this building, Tom. You want more manpower? Tell me, where do we get it, the kind we can trust?"

"I know, Em." Douglas conceded the point. "But we're not getting anywhere."

"Maybe Narcotics will shake something loose."

"Sure." Douglas snorted.

"Can Kelly help us?"

"No. Damned fool was just looking the wrong way."

"Then do the usual follow-up, just to make sure everything looks okay and leave it at that. Forensics isn't in yet. Maybe they'll turn something."

"Yes, sir," Douglas replied. As so often happened in police work, you played for breaks, for mistakes the other side made. These people didn't make many, but sooner or later they all did, both officers told themselves. It was just that they never seemed to come soon enough.

Lieutenant Ryan looked back down at the photos. "They sure had their fun with her. Just like the other one."

"Good to see you're eating."

Kelly looked up from a mostly empty plate. "The cop was right, Sam. It's over. I have to get better, have to focus on something, right?"

"What are you going to do?"

"I don't know. Hell, I could always go back in the Navy or something."

"You have to deal with your grief, John," Sam said, sitting down next to the bed.

"I know how. I've had to do that before, remember?" He looked up. "Oh—what did you tell the police about me?"

"How we met, that sort of thing. Why?"

"What I did over there. It's secret, Sam." Kelly managed to look embarrassed. "The unit I belonged to, it doesn't officially exist. The things we did, well, they never really happened, if you know what I mean."

"They didn't ask. Besides, you never really told me," the surgeon said, puzzled—even more so by the relief on his patient's face.

"I got recommended to them by a pal in the Navy, mainly to help train their divers. What they know is what I'm allowed to tell. It's not what I really did, exactly, but it sounds good."

"Okay."

"I haven't thanked you for taking such good care of me."

Rosen stood and walked to the door, but he stopped dead three feet short of it and turned.

"You think you can fool me?"

"I guess not, Sam," Kelly answered guardedly.

"John, I have spent my whole damned *life* using these hands to fix people. You have to stay aloof, you can't get too involved, because if you do you can lose it, lose the edge, lose the concentration. I've never hurt anyone in my life. You understand me?"

"Yes, sir, I do."

"What are you going to do?"

"You don't want to know, Sam."

"I want to help. I really do," Rosen said, genuine wonder in his voice. "I liked her, too, John."

"I know that."

"So what can I do?" the surgeon asked. He was afraid that Kelly might ask for something he was unfitted to do; more afraid still that he might agree.

"Get me better."

9

Labor

It was almost grim to watch, Sandy thought. The strange thing was that he was being a good patient. He didn't whine. He didn't bitch. He did just what they told him to do. There was a streak of the sadist in all physical therapists. There had to be, since the job meant pushing people a little further than they wanted to go—just as an athletic coach would do—and the ultimate aim was to help, after all. Even so, a good therapist had to push the patient, encourage the weak, and browbeat the strong; to cajole and to shame, all in the name of health; that meant taking satisfaction from the exertion and pain of others, and O'Toole could not have done that. But Kelly, she saw, would have none of it. He did what was expected, and when the therapist asked for more, more was delivered, and on, and on, until the therapist was pushed beyond the point of pride in the result of his efforts and began to worry.

"You can ease off now," he advised.

"Why?" Kelly asked somewhat breathlessly.

"Your heart rate is one-ninety-five." And had been there for five minutes.

"What's the record?"

154

"Zero," the therapist replied without a smile. That earned him a laugh, and a look, and Kelly slowed his pace on the stationary bike, easing himself down over a period of two minutes to a reluctant stop.

"I've come to take him back," O'Toole announced.

"Good, do that before he breaks something."

Kelly got off and toweled his face, glad to see that she hadn't brought a wheelchair or something similarly insulting. "To what do I owe this honor, ma'am?"

"I'm supposed to keep an eye on you," Sandy replied. "Trying to show us how tough you are?"

Kelly had been a touch lighthearted, but turned serious. "Mrs. O'Toole, I'm supposed to get my mind off my troubles, right? Exercise does that for me. I can't run with one arm tied up, I can't do push-ups, and I can't lift weights. I *can* ride a bike. Okay?"

"You have me there. Okay." She pointed to the door. Out in the bustling anonymity of the corridor, she said, "I'm very sorry about your friend."

"Thank you, ma'am." He turned his head, slightly dizzy from the exertion, as they walked along in the crowd. "We have rituals in uniform. The bugle, the flag, the guys with rifles. It works fairly well for the men. It helps you to believe that it all meant something. It still hurts, but it's a formal way to say goodbye. We learned to deal with it. But what happened to you is different, and what just happened to me is different. So what did you do? Get more involved in work?"

"I finished my masters. I'm a nurse-practitioner. I teach. I worry about patients." And that was her whole life now.

"Well, you don't have to worry about me, okay? I know my limits."

"Where are the limits?"

"A long way off," Kelly said with the beginnings of a smile that he quickly extinguished. "How am I doing?"

"Very well."

It hadn't gone all that smoothly, and both knew it. Donald Madden had flown to Baltimore to claim the body of his daughter from the coroner's office, leaving his wife home, never meeting with anyone despite pleas from Sarah

Rosen. He wasn't interested in talking to a fornicator, the man had said over the phone, a remark that Sandy knew about but which neither medic had passed on. The surgeon had filled her in on the background of the girl, and it was merely a final sad chapter to a brief and sad life, something the patient didn't need to know. Kelly had asked about funeral arrangements, and both had told him that he would be unable to leave the hospital in any case. Kelly had accepted that in silence, surprising the nurse.

His left shoulder was still immobilized, and there had to be pain, the nurse knew. She and others could see the occasional wince, especially close to the time for a new pain medication, but Kelly wasn't the type to complain. Even now, still breathing hard from a murderous thirty minutes on the bike, he was making quite a point of walking as rapidly as he could, cooling himself down like a trained athlete.

"Why the big show?" she asked.

"I don't know. Does there have to be a reason for everything? It's the way I am, Sandy."

"Well, your legs are longer than mine. Slow down, okay?"

"Sure." Kelly eased off his pace as they reached the elevator. "How many girls are there—like Pam I mean?"

"Too many." She didn't know the numbers. There were enough that they were noticed as a class of patient, enough that you knew they were there.

"Who helps them?"

The nurse pushed the elevator button. "Nobody. They're starting up programs for dealing with the drug habits, but the real problems, the abusive backgrounds and what comes from it—there's a new term now, 'behavioral disorder.' If you're a thief, there are programs. If you abuse kids, there's a program, but girls like that are outcasts. Nobody does much of anything. The only people who deal with that are church groups. If somebody said it was a disease, maybe people would pay attention."

"Is it a disease?"

"John, I'm not a doctor, just a nurse-practitioner, and it's outside my field anyway. I do post-op care for surgical patients. Okay, we talk over lunch, and I know a little. It's surprising how many of them show up dead. Drug overdoses, accidental or deliberate, who can say? Or they meet the wrong person or their pimp gets a little too rough, and they show up here, and their underlying medical problems don't help very much, and a lot of them just don't make it. Hepatitis from bad needles, pneumonia, add that to a major injury and it's a deadly combination. But is anybody going to do anything about it?" O'Toole looked down as the elevator arrived. "Young people aren't supposed to die that way."

"Yeah." Kelly gestured for her to get in the elevator first.

"You're the patient," she objected.

"You're the lady," he insisted. "Sorry, it's the way I was raised."

Who is this guy? Sandy asked herself. She was managing the care of more than one patient, of course, but the professor had ordered her—well, not exactly, she told herself, but a "suggestion" from Dr. Rosen carried a lot of weight, especially since she had great respect for him as a friend and counselor—to keep a special eye on him. It wasn't matchmaking, as she'd initially suspected. He was still too hurt—and so was she, though she would not admit it. Such a strange man. So like Tim in many ways, but much more guarded. A strange mixture of the gentle and the rough. She hadn't forgotten what she had seen the previous week, but it was gone now, and never a hint of it had returned. He treated her with respect and good humor, never once commenting on her figure, as many patients did (and to which she pretended to object). He was so unlucky and yet so purposeful. His furious effort in rehab. His outward toughness. How to reconcile that with his incongruous good manners?

"When will I get out?" Kelly asked in a voice that was light but not light enough.

"Another week," O'Toole replied, leading him off the elevator. "Tomorrow we unwrap your arm."

"Really? Sam didn't tell me. Then I can start using the arm again?"

"It's going to hurt when you do," the nurse warned.

"Hell, Sandy, it hurts already." Kelly grinned. "I might as well get some use out of the pain."

"Lie down," the nurse ordered. Before he could object, she had a thermometer in his mouth and was taking his pulse. Then she checked his blood pressure. The numbers she put on the chart were 98.4, 64, and 105/60. The last two were especially surprising, she thought. Whatever else she might say about the patient, he was rapidly getting himself back into shape. She wondered what the urgency was.

One more week, Kelly thought after she left. *Got to get this damned arm working.*

"So what have you found out for us?" Maxwell asked.

"Good news and bad news," Greer replied. "The good news is that the opposition has very little in the way of regular ground forces within response distance of the objective. We have ID'd three battalions. Two are training to go south. One just returned from Eye Corps. It's pretty beat-up, in the process of reconstituting. The usual TO and E. Not much in the way of heavy weapons. What mechanized formations they have are well away from here."

"And the bad news?" Admiral Podulski asked.

"Do I have to tell you? Enough triple-A along the coast to turn the sky black. SA-2 batteries here, here, and probably here, too. It's dangerous there for fast-movers, Cas. For helicopters? One or two rescue birds, sure, it's doable, but a large lift will be real dicey. We went all over this when we scoped out KINGPIN, remember?"

"It's only thirty miles from the beach."

"Fifteen or twenty minutes in a helo, flying in a straight line, which they will *not* be able to do, Cas. I went over the threat maps myself. The best route I can identify—it's your area, Cas, but I do know a little, okay?—is twenty-five minutes, and I wouldn't want to fly it in daylight."

"We can use -52s to blast a corridor through," Podulski suggested. He'd never been the most subtle man in the world.

"I thought you wanted to keep this small," Greer

observed. "Look, the real bad news is that there isn't much enthusiasm for this kind of mission anywhere. KINGPIN failed—"

"That wasn't our fault!" Podulski objected.

"I know that, Cas," Greer said patiently. Podulski had always been a passionate advocate.

"It ought to be doable," Cas growled.

All three men hovered over the reconnaisance photos. It was a good collection, two from satellites, two from SR-71 Blackbirds, and three very recent low-obliques from Buffalo Hunter drones. The camp was two hundred meters square, an exact square in fact, undoubtedly fitting exactly the diagram in some East Bloc manual for building secure facilities. Each corner had a guard tower, each of which was exactly ten meters in height. Each tower had a tin roof to keep the rain off the NVA-standard-issue RPD light machine gun, an obsolete Russian design. Inside the wire were three large buildings and two small ones. Inside one of the large buildings were, they believed, twenty American officers, all lieutenant-colonel/commander rank or higher, for this was a special camp.

It was the Buffalo Hunter photos that had first come to Greer's attention. One was good enough to have identified a face, Colonel Robin Zacharias, USAF. His F-105G Wild Weasel had been shot down eight months earlier; he and his weapons-systems operator had been reported killed by the North Vietnamese. Even a picture of his body had been published. This camp, whose code name, SENDER GREEN, was known to fewer than fifty men and women, was separate from the better-known Hanoi Hilton, which had been visited by American citizens and where, since the spectacular but unsuccessful Operation KINGPIN raid on the camp at Song Tay, nearly all American POWs had been concentrated. Out of the way, located in the most unlikely of places, not acknowledged in any way, SENDER GREEN was ominous. However the war would turn out, America wanted her pilots back. Here was a place whose very existence suggested that some would never be returned. A statistical study of losses had shown an ominous irregularity: flight officers of relatively high rank were reported killed at a higher rate than those of lower rank. It was known that the enemy had good intelligence sources, many of them within the American "peace" movement, that they had dossiers on senior American officers, who they were, what they knew, what other jobs they had held. It was possible that those officers were being held in a special place, that their knowledge was being used by North Vietnam as a bargaining chip for dealing with their Russian sponsors. The prisoners' knowledge in areas of special strategic interest was being traded—maybe—for continuing support from a sponsor nation that was losing interest in this lengthy war, with the new atmosphere of detente. So many games were going on.

"Gutsy," Maxwell breathed. The three blowups showed the man's face, each one staring straight at the camera. The last of the three caught one of his guards in the act of swinging a rifle butt into his back. The face was clear. It was Zacharias.

"This guy is Russian," Casimir Podulski said, tapping the drone photos. The uniform was unmistakable.

They knew what Cas was thinking. The son of Poland's one-time ambassador to Washington, by heredity a count and scion of a family that had once fought at the side of King John Sobieski, his family had been extinguished on one side of the demarcation line by the Nazis along with the rest of the Polish nobility and on the other by the Russians in Katyn Forest, where two brothers had been murdered after fighting a brief and futile two-front war. In 1941, the day after graduating Princeton University, Podulski had joined the U.S. Navy as an aviator, adopting a new country and a new profession, both of which he had served with pride and skill. And rage. That was now all the more intense because soon he would be forced to retire. Greer could see the reason. His surprisingly delicate hands were gnarled with arthritis. Try as he might to conceal it, his next physical would down-check him for good, and Cas would face retirement with memories of a dead son and a wife on antidepressant medications, after a career he would probably deem a failure despite his medals and personal flag.

"We've got to find a way," Podulski said. "If we don't, we'll never see these men again. You know who might be there, Dutch? Pete Francis, Hank Osborne."

"Pete worked for me when I had *Enterprise*," Maxwell acknowledged. Both men looked at Greer.

"I concur in the nature of the camp. I had my doubts. Zacharias, Francis, and Osborne are all names they'd be interested in." The Air Force officer had spent a tour at Omaha, part of the joint-targeting staff that selected the destinations for strategic weapons, and his knowledge of America's most secret war plans was encyclopedic. The two naval officers had similarly important information, and while each might be brave, and dedicated, and obstinately determined to deny, conceal, and disguise, they were merely men, and men had limits; and the enemy had time. "Look, if you want, I can try to sell the idea to some people, but I'm not very hopeful."

"If we don't, we're breaking faith with our people!" Podulski slammed his fist on the desk. But Cas had an agenda, too. Discovery of this camp, rescue of its prisoners, would make it explicitly clear that North Vietnam had publicly lied. That might poison the peace talks enough to force Nixon to adopt yet another optional plan being drawn up by a larger Pentagon working group: the invasion of the North. It would be that most American of military operations, a combined-arms assault, without precedent for its daring, scope, and potential dangers: an airborne drop directly into Hanoi, a division of marines hitting the beaches on both sides of Haiphong, air-mobile assaults in the middle, supported by everything America could bring to bear in one massive, crushing attempt to break the North by capture of its political leadership. That plan, whose cover name changed on a monthly basis—currently it was CERTAIN CORNET—was the Holy Grail of vengeance for all the professionals who had for six years watched their country blunder about in indecision and the profligate waste of America's children.

"Don't you think I know that? Osborne worked for me at Suitland. I went with the chaplain when he delivered the fucking telegram, okay? I'm on your side, remember?"

Unlike Cas and Dutch, Greer knew that CERTAIN CORNET would never be more than a staff study. It just couldn't happen, not without briefing Congress, and Congress had too many leaks. A possibility in 1966 or '67, maybe even as late as 1968, such an operation was unthinkable now. But SENDER GREEN was still there, and this mission was possible, just.

"Cool down, Cas," Maxwell suggested.

"Yes, sir."

Greer shifted his gaze to the relief map. "You know, you airedales kind of limit your thinking."

"What do you mean?" Maxwell asked.

Greer pointed to a red line that ran from a coastal town nearly to the camp's main gate. On the overhead photos it looked like a good road, blacktopped and all. "The reaction forces are here, here, and here. The road's here, follows the river most of the way up. There are flak batteries all over the place, the road supports them, but, you know, triple-A isn't dangerous to the right sort of equipment."

"That's an invasion," Podulski observed.

"And sending in two companies of air-mobile troops isn't?"

"I've always said you were smart, James," Maxwell said. "You know, this is right where my son was shot down. That SEAL went in and recovered him right about here," the Admiral said, tapping the map.

"Somebody who knows the area from ground level?" Greer asked. "That's a help. Where is he?"

"Hi, Sarah." Kelly waved her to the chair. She looked older, he thought.

"This is my third time, John. You were asleep the other two."

"I've been doing a lot of that. It's okay," he assured her. "Sam's in here a couple times a day." He was already uncomfortable. The hardest part was facing friends, Kelly told himself.

"Well, we've been busy in the lab." Sarah spoke rapidly. "John, I needed to tell you how sorry I am that I asked you to come into town. I could have sent you somewhere else. She didn't need to see Madge. There's a guy I know in Annapolis, perfectly good practitioner . . . " Her voice stumbled on.

So much guilt, Kelly thought. "None of this was your fault, Sarah," he said when she stopped talking. "You were a good friend to Pam. If her mom had been like you, maybe—"

It was almost as though she hadn't heard him. "I should have given you a later date. If the timing had been a little different—"

She was right on that part, Kelly thought. The variables. What if? What if he'd selected a different block to be parked on? What if Billy had never spotted him? *What if I hadn't moved at all and let the bastard just go on his way?* A different day, a different week? What if a lot of things. The past happened because a hundred little random things had to fall exactly into place in exactly the right way, in exactly the proper sequence, and while it was easy to accept the good results, one could only rage at the bad ones. What if he'd taken a different route from the food warehouse? What if he'd not spotted Pam at the side of the road and never picked her up? What if he'd never spotted the pills? What if he hadn't cared, or what if he'd been so outraged that he had abandoned her? Would she be alive now? If her father had been a little more understanding, and she'd never run away, they would never have met. Was that good or bad?

And if all that were true, then what *did* matter? Was *everything* a random accident? The problem was that you couldn't tell. Maybe if he were God looking down on everything from above, maybe then it would fit some pattern, but from the inside it merely *was,* Kelly thought, and you did the best you could, and tried to learn from your mistakes for when the next random event happened to you. But did that make sense? Hell, did anything really make sense? That was far too complex a question for a former Navy chief lying in a hospital bed.

"Sarah, none of this is your fault. You helped her in the best way you could. How could you change that?"

"Damn it, Kelly, we had her saved!"

"I know. And I brought her here, and I got careless, not you. Sarah, everyone tells me it's not my fault, and then you come in here and tell me it's yours." The grimace was almost a smile. "This can be very confusing, except for one thing."

"It wasn't an accident, was it?" Sarah noted.

"No, it wasn't."

"There he is," Oreza said quietly, keeping his binoculars on the distant speck. "Just like you said."

"Come to papa," the policeman breathed in the darkness.

It was just a happy coincidence, the officer told himself. The people in question owned a corn farm in Dorchester County, but between the cornrows were marijuana plants. Simple, as the saying went, but effective. With a farm came barns and outbuildings, and privacy. Being clever people, they didn't want to drive their product across the Bay Bridge in their pickup truck, where the summer traffic was unpredictably interrupted, and besides, a sharp-eyed toll taker had helped the State Police make a bust only a month before. They were careful enough to become a potential threat to his friend. That had to be stopped.

So they used a boat. This heaven-sent coincidence gave the Coast Guard the chance to participate in a bust and thus to raise his stature in their eyes. It couldn't hurt, after he'd used them as the stalking horse to help get Angelo Vorano killed, Lieutenant Charon thought, smiling in the wheelhouse.

"Take 'em now?" Oreza asked.

"Yes. The people they're delivering to are under our control. Don't tell anybody that," he added. "We don't want to compromise them."

"You got it." The quartermaster advanced his throttles and turned the wheel to starboard. "Let's wake up, people," he told his crew.

The forty-one-boat squatted at the stern with the increased power. The rumble of the diesels was intoxicating to the boat's commander. The small steel wheel vibrated in his hands as he steadied up on his new course. The funny part was that it would come as a surprise to them. Although the Coast Guard was the principal law-enforcement agency on the water, their main activity had always been search and rescue, and the word hadn't quite gotten out yet. Which, Oreza told himself, was just too goddamned bad. He'd found a few coastguardsmen smoking pot in the past couple of years, and his wrath was something still talked about by those who'd seen it.

The target was easily seen now, a thirty-foot Bay-built fishing boat of the sort that dotted the Chesapeake, probably with an old Chevy engine, and that meant she couldn't possibly outrun his cutter. It was a perfectly good thing to have a good disguise, Oreza thought with a smile, but not so clever to bet your life and your freedom on one card, however good it might be.

"Just let everything look normal," the policeman said quietly.

"Look around, sir," the quartermaster replied. The boat crew was alert but not obviously so, and their weapons were holstered. The boat's course was almost a direct one toward their Thomas Point station, and if the other boat even took note of them—and nobody was looking aft at the moment—they could easily assume that the forty-one-footer was just heading back to the barn. Five hundred yards now. Oreza jammed the throttles to the stops to get the extra knot or two of overtake speed.

"There's Mr. English," another crewman said. The other forty-one-boat from Thomas Point was on a reciprocal course, outbound from the station, holding steady on a straight line, roughly towards the lighthouse that the station also supported.

"Not real smart, are they?" Oreza asked.

"Well, if they were smart, why break the law?"

"Roger that, sir." Three hundred yards now, and a head turned aft to see the gleaming white shape of the small cutter. Three people aboard the target craft, and the one who had looked at them leaned forward to say something to the guy at the wheel. It was almost comical to watch. Oreza could imagine every word they were saying. *There's a Coast Guard boat back there. So just play it cool,* maybe they're just changing the duty boat or something, see the one there . . . Uh-oh, I don't like this . . . Just be cool, damn it! I really don't like this. Settle down, their lights aren't on and their station is right down there, for Christ's sake.

Just about time, Oreza smiled to himself, *just about time for: oh, shit!*

He grinned when it happened. The guy at the wheel turned, and his mouth opened and shut, having said just that. One of the younger crewmen read the man's lips and laughed.

"I think they just figured it out, skipper."

"Hit the lights!" the quartermaster ordered, and the cop lights atop the wheelhouse started blinking, somewhat to Oreza's displeasure.

"Aye aye!"

The Bay boat turned rapidly south, but the outbound cutter turned to cover the maneuver, and it was instantly clear that neither could outrun the twin-screw forty-one-boats.

"Should have used the money to buy something sportier, boys," Oreza said to himself, knowing that criminals learned from their mistakes, too, and buying something to outrun a forty-one-foot patrol boat was not exactly a taxing problem. This one was easy. Chasing another little sailboat would be easy, if this damned fool of a cop would let them do it right, but the easy ones wouldn't last forever.

The Bay boat cut power, trapped between two cutters. Warrant Officer English kept station a few hundred yards out while Oreza drove in close.

"Howdy," the quartermaster said over his loud-hailer. "This is the U.S. Coast Guard, and we are exercising our right to board and conduct a safety inspection. Let's everybody stay where we can see you, please."

It was remarkably like watching people who'd just lost a pro-football game. They knew they couldn't change anything no matter what they did. They knew that resistance was futile, and so they just stood there in dejection and acceptance of their fate. Oreza wondered how long that would last. How long before somebody would be dumb enough to fight it out?

Two of his sailors jumped aboard, covered by two more on the forty-one's fantail. Mr. English brought his boat in closer. A good boat-handler, Oreza saw, like a warrant was supposed to be, and he had his people out to offer cover, too, just in case the bad guys got a crazy idea. While the three men stood in plain view, mostly looking down at the deck and hoping that it might really be a safety inspection, Oreza's two men went into the forward cabin. Both came out in less than a minute. One tipped the bill of his cap, signaling all-clear, then patted his belly. Yes, there were drugs aboard. Five pats—a lot of drugs aboard.

"We have a bust, sir," Oreza observed calmly.

Lieutenant Mark Charon of the Narcotics Division, Baltimore City Police Department, leaned against the door-frame—hatch, whatever these sailors called the thing—and smiled. He was dressed in casual clothes, and might have easily been mistaken for a coastie with the required orange life jacket.

"You handle it, then. How does it go in the books?"

"Routine safety inspection, and, golly, they had drugs aboard," Oreza said in mock surprise.

"Exactly right, Mr. Oreza."

"Thank you, sir."

"My pleasure, Captain."

He'd already explained the procedure to Oreza and English. In order to protect his informants, credit for the arrest would go to the coasties, which didn't exactly displease the quartermaster or the warrant officer. Oreza would get to paint a victory symbol on his mast, or whatever they called the thing the radar was attached to, a representation of the five-leafed marijuana plant, and the crewmen would have something to brag about. They might even have the adventure of testifying before a federal district court—probably not, since these small-timers would undoubtedly cop to the smallest offense their attorney could negotiate. They would get word out that the people to whom they were making the delivery had probably informed on them. With luck those people might even disappear, and that would really make his task easy. There would be an opening in the drug ecostructure—another new buzzword

Charon had picked up on. At the very least, a potential rival in that ecostructure was now out of business for good. Lieutenant Charon would get a pat on the back from his captain, probably a flowery thank-you letter from the United States Coast Guard and the U.S. Attorney's office, not to mention congratulations for running such a quiet and effective operation that had not compromised his informants. One of our best men, his captain would affirm again. How do you get informants like that? Cap'n, you know how that works, I have to protect these people. Sure, Mark, I understand. You just keep up the good work.

I'll do my best, sir, Charon thought to himself, staring off at the setting sun. He didn't even watch the coasties cuffing the suspects, reading them their constitutional rights from the plastic-coated card, smiling as they did so, since for them this was a very entertaining game. But then, that's what it was for Charon, too.

Where were the damned helicopters? Kelly asked himself.

Everything about the damned mission had been wrong from the first moment. Pickett, his usual companion, had come down with violent dysentery, too bad for him to go out, and Kelly had gone out alone. Not a good thing, but the mission was too important, and they had to cover every little hamlet or *ville*. So he'd come in alone, very, very carefully moving up the stinking water of this—well, the map called it a river, but it wasn't quite large enough for Kelly to think of it that way.

And, of course, this is the *ville* they'd come to, the fuckers.

PLASTIC FLOWER, he thought, watching and listening. *Who the hell came up with* that *name?*

PLASTIC FLOWER was the code name for an NVA political-action team or whatever they called it. His team had several other names, none of them complimentary. Certainly they weren't the precinct workers he'd seen on election day in Indianapolis. Not these people, schooled in Hanoi on how to win hearts and minds.

The *ville*'s headman, chief, mayor, whatever the hell he was, was just a little too courageous to be called anything but a fool. He was paying for that foolishness before the distant eyes of Bosun's Mate 1/c J. T. Kelly. The team had arrived at oh-one-thirty, and in a very orderly and almost civilized way, entered every little hooch, awakening the whole population of farmers, bringing them into the common area to see the misguided hero, and his wife, and his three daughters, all waiting for them, sitting in the dirt, their arms cruelly tied behind their backs. The NVA major who led PLASTIC FLOWER invited them all to sit in a mannerly voice that reached Kelly's observation point, less than two hundred meters away. The *ville* needed a lesson in the foolishness of resistance to the people's liberation movement. It was not that they were bad people, just misguided, and he hoped that this simple lesson would make clear to them the error of their ways.

They started with the man's wife. That took twenty minutes.

I have to do something! he told himself.

There's eleven of them, idiot. And while the Major might be a sadistic motherfucker, the ten soldiers with him had not been selected exclusively for their political correctness. They would be reliable, experienced, and dedicated soldiers. How a man could be dedicated to such things as this, Kelly didn't have the imagination to understand. That they were was a fact that he could not afford to ignore.

Where was the fucking reaction team? He'd called in forty minutes earlier, and the support base was only twenty minutes off by chopper. They wanted this Major. His team might also be useful, but they wanted the Major alive. He knew the location of the local political leaders, those the Marines hadn't swept up in a superb raid six weeks earlier. This mission was probably a reaction to that, a deliberate response so close to the American base, to say that, no, you haven't gotten us all yet, and you never will.

And they were probably right, Kelly thought, but that question went far beyond the mission for tonight.

The oldest daughter was maybe fifteen. It was hard to tell with the small, deceptively delicate Vietnamese women. She'd lasted all of twenty-five minutes and was not yet dead. Her screams carried clearly across the flat, open ground to Kelly's watery post, and his hands squeezed the plastic of his CAR-15 so hard that had he thought or noticed, he might have worried about breaking something.

The ten soldiers with the Major were deployed as they should be. Two men were with the Major, and they rotated duty with the perimeter guards so that all of them could partake in the evening's festivities. One of them finished the girl with a knife. The next daughter was perhaps twelve.

Kelly's ears scanned the cloudy sky, praying to hear the distinctive mutter of a Huey's two-bladed rotor. There were other sounds. The rumble of 155s from the marine fire base to the east. Some jets screaming overhead. None were loud enough to mask the high-pitched screech of a child, but there were still eleven of them, and only one of him, and even if Pickett had been here, the odds would not have been remotely close enough to try a play. Kelly had his CAR-15 carbine, a thirty-round magazine securely fixed in its place, another taped, inverted, to the end of that one, and two more similar sets. He had four fragmentation grenades, two willie-petes, and two smokes. His deadliest appliance was his radio, but he'd already called out twice and gotten an acknowledgment both times, along with orders to sit tight.

Easy thing to say back at the base, wasn't it?

Twelve years old, maybe. Too young for this. There was no age for this, he told himself, but he'd never be able to change things alone, and there was no good for anyone in adding his death to those of this family.

How could they do it? Were they not men, soldiers, professional warriors like himself? Could anything be so important that they could cast aside their humanity? What he saw was impossible. It could not be. But it was. The rumbles of the distant artillery continued, dropping planned fire-missions on a suspected supply route. A continuous stream of aircraft overhead, maybe Marine intruders doing a Mini-Arc Light strike at something or other, probably empty woods, because most of those targets were just that. Not here, where the enemy was, but that wouldn't help anything, would it? These villagers had bet their lives and their families on something that wasn't working, and maybe that Major thought he was being merciful in just eliminating one family in the most graphic method possible instead of ending all their lives in a more efficient way. Besides, dead men told no tales, and this was a tale he would want repeated. Terror was something they could use, and use well.

Time crept on, slowly and rapidly, and presently the twelve-year-old stopped making noise and was cast aside. The third and final daughter was eight, he saw through his binoculars. The *arrogance* of the fuckers, building a large fire. They couldn't have anyone miss this, could they?

Eight years old, not even old enough, not a throat large enough for a proper scream. He watched the changing of the guard. Two more men moved from the perimeter into the center of the *ville*. R&R for the political-action group, who couldn't go to Taiwan as Kelly had. The man nearest to Kelly hadn't had his chance yet, probably wouldn't. The headman didn't have enough daughters, or maybe this one was on the Major's shit list. Whatever the real reason, he wasn't getting any, and it must have frustrated him. The soldier's eyes were looking in now, watching his squadmates partake in something that he would miss tonight. Maybe next time . . . but at least he could watch . . . and he did, Kelly saw, forgetting his duty for the first time tonight.

Kelly was halfway there before his mind remarked on the fact, crawling as rapidly as he could in silence, helped by the moist ground. A low crawl, his body as flat as he could manage, closer, closer, both driven and drawn by the whine that emanated from near the fire.

Should have done it sooner, Johnnie-boy.

It wasn't possible then.

Well, fuck, it isn't possible now!

It was then that fate intervened in the sound of a Huey, probably more than one, off to the southeast. Kelly heard it first, rising carefully behind the soldier, his knife drawn. They still hadn't heard it when he struck, driving his knife into the base of the man's skull, where the spinal cord meets the base of the brain—the medulla, someone had told him in a lecture. He twisted it, almost like a screw-driver, his other hand across the soldier's mouth, and, sure enough, it worked. The body went instantly limp, and he lowered it gently, not from any feelings of humanity, but to limit noise.

But there was noise. The choppers were too close now. The Major's head went up, turning southeast, recognizing the danger. He shouted an order for his men to assemble, then turned and shot the child in the head just as soon as one of his privates moved off of her and out of the way.

It only took a few seconds for the squad to assemble. The Major did a quick and automatic head count, coming up one short, and he looked in Kelly's direction, but his eyes and his vision had been long since compromised by the fire, and the only thing he did see was some spectral movement in the air.

"One, two, three," Kelly whispered to himself after pull-ing the cotter pin out of one of his frags. The boys in 3rd SOG cut their own fuses. You never knew what the little old lady in the factory might do. Theirs burned for exactly five seconds, and on "three," the grenade left his hand. It was just metallic enough to glint with the orange firelight. A nearly perfect toss, it landed in the exact center of the ring of soldiers. Kelly was already prone in the dirt when it landed. He heard the shout of alarm that was just a second too late to help anyone.

The grenade killed or wounded seven of the ten men. He stood with his carbine and dropped the first one with three rounds to the head. His eyes didn't even pause to see the flying red cloud, for this was his profession, and not a hobby. The Major was still alive, lying on the ground but trying to aim his pistol until his chest took five more. His death made the night a success. Now all Kelly had to do was survive. He had committed himself to a foolish act, and caution was his enemy.

Kelly ran to the right, his carbine held high. There were at least two NVA moving, armed and angry and confused enough that they weren't running away as they should. The first chopper overhead was an illum bird, dropping flares that Kelly cursed, because the darkness was his best friend right now. He spotted and hosed down one of the NVA, emptying his magazine into the running figure. Moving right still, he switched magazines, circling around, hoping to find the other one, but his eyes lingered on the center of the *ville.* People scurrying around, some of them probably hurt by his grenade, but he couldn't worry himself about that. His eyes froze on the victims—worse, they stayed too long on the fire, and when he turned away, the shape of it stayed in his eyes, alternating between orange and blue ghost images that wrecked his night vision. He could hear the roar of a Huey flared for landing close to the *ville,* and that was loud enough to mask even the screams of the villagers. Kelly hid behind the wall of a hooch, eyes looking outward, away from the fire as he tried to blink them clear. At least one more unhurt NVA was moving, and he wouldn't be running towards the sound of the chopper. Kelly kept heading right, more slowly now. There was a ten-meter gap from this hooch to the next, like a corridor of light in the glow of the fire. He looked around the corner before making the run, then took off fast, his head low for once. His eyes caught a moving shadow, and when he turned to look, he stumbled over something and went down.

Dust flew up around him, but he couldn't find the source of the noise quickly enough. Kelly rolled left to avoid the shots, but that took him towards the light. He half stood and pushed himself backwards, hitting the wall of a hooch, eyes scanning frantically for the muzzle flashes. There! He brought his CAR-15 to bear and fired just as two 7.62 rounds caught him in the chest. The impact spun him around, and two more hits destroyed the carbine in his hands. When next he looked up he was on his back, and it was quiet in the *ville.* His first attempt to move achieved nothing but pain. Then the muzzle of a rifle pressed to his chest.

"Over here, Lieutenant!" Followed by: "Medic!"

The world moved as they dragged him closer to the fire. Kelly's head hung limply to the left, watching the soldiers sweep through the *ville,* two of them disarming and examining the NVA.

"This fucker's alive," one of them said.

"Oh, yeah?" The other walked over from the body of the eight-year-old, touched his muzzle to the NVA's forehead, and fired once.

"Fuck, Harry!"

"Knock that shit off!" the Lieutenant screamed.

"Look at what they done, sir!" Harry screamed back, falling to his knees to vomit.

"What's your problem?" the medical corpsman asked Kelly, who was quite unable to reply. "Oh, shit," he observed further. "Ell-Tee, this must be the guy who called in!"

One more face appeared, probably the Lieutenant commanding the Blue Team, and the oversized patch on his shoulder was that of the 1st Cavalry Division.

"Lieutenant, looks all clear, sweeping the perimeter again now!" an older voice called.

"All dead?"

"That's affirm, sir!"

"Who the hell are you?" the Lieutenant said, looking back down. "Crazy fucking Marines!"

"Navy!" Kelly gasped, spraying a little blood on the medic.

"What?" Nurse O'Toole asked.

Kelly's eyes opened wide. His right arm moved rapidly across his chest as his head swiveled to survey the room. Sandy O'Toole was in the corner, reading a book under a single light.

"What are you doing here?"

"Listening to your nightmare," she answered. "Second time. You know, you really ought to—"

"Yeah, I know."

10
Pathology

"Your gun's in the back of the car," Sergeant Douglas told him. "Unloaded. Keep it that way from now on."

"What about Pam?" Kelly asked from his wheelchair.

"We've got some leads," Douglas replied, not troubling himself to conceal the lie.

And that said it all, Kelly thought. Someone had leaked it to the papers that Pam had an arrest record for prostitution, and with that revelation, the case had lost its immediacy.

Sam brought the Scout up to the Wolfe Street entrance himself. The bodywork was all fixed, and there was a new window on the driver's side. Kelly got out of the wheelchair and gave the Scout a long look. The doorframe and adjacent pillar had broken up the incoming shot column and saved his life. Bad aim on someone's part, really, after a careful and effective stalk—helped by the fact that he hadn't troubled himself to check his mirrors, Kelly told himself behind a blank expression. How had he managed to forget that? he asked himself for the thousandth time. Such a simple thing, something he'd stressed for every new arrival in 3rd SOG: always check your back, because there might be somebody hunting you. Simple thing to remember, wasn't it?

But that was history. And history could not be changed.

"Back to your island, John?" Rosen asked.

Kelly nodded. "Yeah. I have work waiting, and I have to get myself back into shape."

"I want to see you back here in, oh, two weeks, for a follow-up."

"Yes, sir. I'll be back," Kelly promised. He thanked Sandy O'Toole for her care, and was rewarded with a smile. She'd almost become a friend in the preceding eighteen days. Almost? Perhaps she already was, if only he would allow himself to think in such terms. Kelly got into his car and fixed the seat belt in place. Goodbyes had never been his strong suit. He nodded and smiled at them and drove off, turning right towards Mulberry Street, alone for the first time since his arrival at the hospital.

Finally. Next to him, on the passenger seat where he'd last seen Pam alive, was a manila envelope marked *Patient Records/Bills* in Sam Rosen's coarse handwriting.

"God," Kelly breathed, heading west. He wasn't just watching traffic now. The cityscape was forever transformed for John Kelly. The streets were a curious mixture of activity and vacancy, and his eyes swept around in a habit he'd allowed himself to forget, zeroing in on people whose inactivity seemed to display a purpose. It would take time, he told himself, to distinguish the sheep from the goats. The city traffic was light, and in any case, people didn't linger on these streets. Kelly looked left and right to see that the other drivers' eyes were locked forward, shutting out what lay around them, just as he had once done, stopping uneasily for red lights they couldn't comfortably run and hitting the gas hard when the lights changed. Hoping that they could leave it all behind, that the problems here would stay here and never move outward to where the good people lived. In that sense it was a reversal of Vietnam, wasn't it? There the bad things were out in the boonies, and you wanted to keep them from moving in. Kelly realized that he'd come home to see the same kind of lunacy and the same kind of failure in a very different kind of place. And he'd been as guilty and as foolish as everyone else.

The Scout turned left, heading south past another hospital, a large white one. Business district, banks and offices, courthouse, city hall, a good part of town where good people came in daylight, leaving quickly at night, all together because there was safety in their hurried numbers. Well-policed, because without these people and their commerce, the city would surely die. Or something like that. Maybe it wasn't a question of life or death at all, but merely of speed.

Only a mile and a half, Kelly wondered. *That much?* He'd have to check a map. A dangerously short distance in any case between these people and what they feared. Stopped at an intersection, he could see a long way, because city streets, like firebreaks, offered long and narrow views. The light changed and he moved on.

Springer was in her accustomed place, twenty minutes later. Kelly assembled his things and went aboard. Ten minutes after that, the diesels were chugging away, the air conditioning was on, and he was back in his little white bubble of civilization, ready to cast off. Off of pain medications and feeling the need for a beer and some relaxation—just the symbolic return to normality—he nevertheless left the alcohol alone. His left shoulder was distressingly stiff despite his having been able to use it, after a fashion, for almost a week. He walked around the main salon, swinging his arms in wide circles, and wincing from the pain on the left side, before heading topside to cast off. Murdock came out to watch, but said nothing from the door into his office. Kelly's experience had made the papers, though not the involvement with Pam, which somehow the reporters had failed to connect. The fuel tanks were topped off, and all the boat's systems appeared to be operating, but there was no bill for whatever the yard had done.

Kelly's line-handling was awkward as his left arm refused to do the things his mind commanded in the usual timely fashion. Finally, the lines were slipped, and *Springer* headed out. After clearing the yacht basin, Kelly settled into the salon control station, steering a straight course out to the

Bay in the comfort of the air conditioning and the security of
the enclosed cabin. Only after clearing the shipping channel
an hour later did he look away from the water. A soft drink
chased two Tylenol down his throat. That was the only drug
he'd allowed himself for the last three days. He leaned back
in the captain's chair and opened the envelope Sam had left
him, while the autopilot drove the boat south.

Only the photos had been left out. He'd seen one of
them, and that one had been enough. A handwritten cover
note—every page in the envelope was a photocopy, not an
original—showed that the professor of pathology had gotten the copies from his friend, the state medical examiner,
and could Sam please be careful how he handled this. Kelly
couldn't read the signature.

The "wrongful death" and "homicide" blocks on the
cover sheet were both checked. The cause of death, the
report said, was manual strangulation, with a deep, narrow set of ligature marks about the victim's neck. The
severity and depth of the ligature marks suggested that
brain death had occurred from oxygen deprivation even
before the crushed larynx terminated airflow to the lungs.
Striations on the skin suggested that the instrument used
was probably a shoestring, and from bruises that appeared
to come from the knuckles of a large-handed man about
the throat, that the killer had faced the supine victim while
performing the act. Beyond that, the report went on for
five single-spaced pages, the victim had been subjected
to violent and extensive traumatic insult prior to death,
all of which was cataloged at length in dry medical prose.
A separate form noted that she had been raped, further
that the genital area showed definite signs of bruising and
other abuse. An unusually large quantity of semen was
still evident in her vagina upon her discovery and autopsy,
indicating that the killer had not been alone in raping the
victim. ("Blood types O+, O– and AB–, per attached serol-
ogy report.") Extensive cuts and bruises about the hands
and forearms were termed "defensive-classical." Pam had
fought for her life. Her jaw had been broken, along with
three other bones, one of them a compound fracture of the
left ulna. Kelly had to set the report down, staring at the

horizon before reading on. His hands didn't shake, and he didn't utter a word, but he needed to look away from the cold medical terminology.

"As you can see from the photos, Sam," the handwritten page at the back said, "this was something from a couple of really sick folks. It was deliberate torture. It must have taken hours to do all this. One thing the report leaves out. Check Photo #6. Her hair was combed or brushed out, probably, almost certainly postmortem. The pathologist who handled the case missed it somehow. He's a youngster. (Alan was out of town when she came in, or I'm sure he would have handled it himself.) It seems a little odd, but it's clear from the photo. Funny how you can miss the obvious things. It was probably his first case like this, and probably he was too focused on listing the major insults to notice something so minor. I gather you knew the girl. I'm sorry, my friend. Brent," the page was signed, more legibly than the cover sheet. Kelly slid the package back into the envelope.

He opened a drawer in the console and removed a box of .45 ACP ammunition, loading the two magazines for his automatic, which went back into the drawer. There were few things more useless than an unloaded pistol. Next he went into the galley and found the largest can on the shelves. Sitting back down at the control station, he held the can in his left hand, and continued what he'd been doing for almost a week, working the can like a dumbbell, up and down, in and out, welcoming the pain, savoring it while his eyes swept the surface of the water.

"Never again, Johnnie-boy," he said aloud in a conversational tone. "We're not going to make any more mistakes. Not ever."

The C-141 landed at Pope Air Force Base, adjacent to Fort Bragg, North Carolina, soon after lunch, ending a routine flight that had originated over eight thousand miles away. The four-engine jet transport touched down rather hard. The crew was tired despite their rest stops along the way, and their passengers required no particular care. On flights such as this, there was rarely any live cargo. Troops returning from the theater of operations rode "Freedom Birds," almost invariably chartered commercial airliners whose stewardesses passed out smiles and free booze for the duration of the lengthy return trip to the real world. No such amenities were required on the flights into Pope. The flight crew ate USAF-standard box lunches, and for the most part flew without the usual banter of young airmen.

The roll-out slowed the aircraft, which turned at the end of the runway onto a taxiway, while the crew stretched at their seats. The pilot, a Captain, knew the routine by heart, but there was a brightly painted jeep in case he forgot, and he followed it to the receiving center. He and his crew had long since stopped dwelling on the nature of their mission. It was a job, a necessary one, and that was that, they all thought as they left the aircraft for their mandated crew-rest period, which meant, after a short debrief and notification of whatever shortcomings the aircraft had exhibited in the past thirty hours, heading off to the O-Club for drinks, followed by showers and sleep in the Q. None of them looked back at the aircraft. They'd see it again soon enough.

The routine nature of the mission was a contradiction. In most previous wars, Americans had lain close to where they fell, as testified to by American cemeteries in France and elsewhere. Not so for Vietnam. It was as though people understood that no American wanted to remain there, living or dead, and every recovered body came home, and having passed through one processing facility outside Saigon, each body would now be processed again prior to transshipment to whatever hometown had sent the mainly young men off to die in a distant place. The families would have had time by now to decide where burial would take place, and instructions for those arrangements waited for each body identified by name on the aircraft's manifest.

Awaiting the bodies in the receiving center were civilian morticians. That was one occupational specialty that the military did not carry in its multiplicity of training regimens. A uniformed officer was always present to verify identification, for that *was* a responsibility of the service, to make sure that the right body went off to the right family, even though the caskets that left this place were in almost all cases sealed. The physical insult of combat death, plus the ravages of often late recovery in a tropical climate, were not things families wanted or needed to see on the bodies of their loved ones. As a result, positive identification of remains wasn't really something that anyone could check, and for that very reason, it was something the military took as seriously as it could.

It was a large room where many bodies could be processed at once, though the room was not as busy as it had been in the past. The men who worked here were not above grim jokes, and some even watched weather reports from that part of the world to predict what the next week's work load would be like. The smell alone was enough to keep the casual observer away, and one rarely saw a senior officer here, much less a civilian Defense Department official, for whose equilibrium the sights here might be a little too much to bear. But one becomes accustomed to smells, and that of the preserving agents was much preferred over the other odors associated with death. One such body, that of Specialist Fourth Class Duane Kendall, bore numerous wounds to the torso. He'd made it as far as a field hospital, the mortician saw. Some of the scarring was clearly the desperate work of a combat surgeon—incisions that would have earned the wrath of a chief of service in a civilian hospital were far less graphic than the marks made by fragments from an explosive booby-trap device. The surgeon had spent maybe twenty minutes trying to save this one, the mortician thought, wondering why he had failed—probably the liver, he decided from the location and size of the incisions. You can't live without one of those no matter how good the doctor is. Of more interest to the man was a white tag located between the right arm and the chest which confirmed an apparently random mark on the card on the outside of the container in which the body had arrived.

"Good ID," the mortician said to the Captain who was making his rounds with a clipboard and a sergeant. The officer checked the required data against his own records and moved on with a nod, leaving the mortician to his work.

There was the usual number of tasks to be performed, and the mortician went about them with neither haste nor indolence, lifting his head to make sure the Captain was at the other end of the room. Then he pulled a thread from the stitches made by another mortician at the other end of the pipeline. The stitches came completely undone almost instantly, allowing him to reach into the body cavity and remove four clear-plastic envelopes of white powder, which he quickly put into his bag before reclosing the gaping hole in Duane Kendall's body. It was his third and last such recovery of the day. After spending half an hour on one more body, it was the end of his working day. The mortician walked off to his car, a Mercury Cougar, and drove off post. He stopped off at a Winn-Dixie supermarket to pick up a loaf of bread, and on the way out dropped some coins into a public phone.

"Yeah?" Henry Tucker said, picking it up on the first ring.

"Eight." The phone clicked off.

"Good," Tucker said, really to himself, putting the receiver down. Eight kilos from this one. Seven from his other man; neither man knew that the other was there, and the pickups from each were done on different days of the week. Things could pick up rapidly now that he was getting his distribution problems in hand.

The arithmetic was simple enough. Each kilo was one thousand grams. Each kilo would be diluted with nontoxic agents like milk sugar, which his friends obtained from a grocery-supply warehouse. After careful mixing to ensure uniformity throughout the entire batch, others would divide the bulk powder into smaller "hits" of the drugs that could be sold in smaller batches. The quality and burgeoning reputation of his product guaranteed a slightly higher than normal price which was anticipated by the wholesale cost he received from his white friends.

The problem would soon become one of scale. He'd started his operation small, since Tucker was a careful man, and size made for greed. That would soon become impossible. His supply of pure refined heroin was far more extensive than his partners knew. They were, for now, happy that its quality was so high, and he would gradually reveal to them the magnitude of his supply, while never giving them a hint of his method of shipment, for which he regularly congratulated himself. The sheer elegance of it was striking, even to him. The best government estimates—he kept track of such things—of heroin imports from Europe, the "French" or "Sicilian" connection, since they could never seem to get the terminology right, amounted to roughly one metric ton of pure drugs per year. That, Tucker judged, would have to grow, because drugs were the coming thing in American vice. If he could bring in a mere twenty kilos of drugs per week—and his shipment modality was capable of more than that—he had that number beaten, and he didn't have to worry about customs inspectors. Tucker had set up his organization with a careful eye on the security issue. For starters, none of the important people on his team touched drugs. To do so was death, a fact that he had made clear early on in the simplest and clearest possible way. The distant end of the operation required only six people. Two procured the drugs from local sources whose security was guaranteed by the usual means—large sums of cash paid to the right people. The four on-site morticians were also very well paid and had been selected for their businesslike stability. The United States Air Force handled transportation, reducing his costs and headaches for what was usually the most complicated and dangerous part of the import process. The two at the receiving station were similarly careful men. More than once, they'd reported, circumstances had compelled them to leave the heroin in the bodies, which had been duly buried. That was too bad, of course, but a good business was a careful business, and the street markup easily compensated for the loss. Besides, those two knew what would happen if they even thought about diverting a few kilos for their own enterprises.

From there it was merely a matter of transport by automobile to a convenient place, and that was handled by a trusted and well-paid man who never once exceeded a speed limit. Doing things on the Bay, Tucker thought, sipping on his beer and watching a baseball game, was his masterstroke. In addition to all the other advantages that the location gave him, he'd given his new partners reason to believe that the drugs were dropped off ships heading up the Chesapeake Bay to the Port of Baltimore—which they thought wonderfully clever—when in fact he transported them himself from a covert pickup point. Angelo Vorano had proven that by buying his dumb little sailboat and offering to make a pickup. Convincing Eddie and Tony that he'd burned them to the police had been so easy.

With a little luck he could take over the entire East Cost heroin market for as long as Americans continued to die in Vietnam. It was also time, he told himself, to plan for the peace that would probably break out someday. In the meantime he needed to think about finding a way to expand his distribution network. What he had, while it had worked, and while it had brought him to the attention of his new partners, was rapidly becoming outdated. It was too small for his ambitions, and soon it would have to be restructured. But one thing at a time.

"Okay, it's official." Douglas dropped the case file on the desk and looked at his boss.

"What's that?" Lieutenant Ryan asked.

"First, nobody saw anything. Second, nobody knew what pimp she worked for. Third, nobody even knows who she was. Her father hung up on me after he said he hasn't talked to his daughter in four years. That boyfriend didn't see shit before or after he was shot." The detective sat down.

"And the mayor's not interested anymore," Ryan finished the case summary.

"You know, Em, I don't mind running a covert investigation, but it is hurting my success rate. What if I don't get promoted next board?"

"Funny, Tom."

Douglas shook his head and stared out the window. "Hell, what if it really was the Dynamic Duo?" the sergeant asked in frustration. The pair of shotgun robbers had killed again two nights before, this time murdering an attorney from Essex. There had been a witness in a car fifty yards away, who had confirmed that there were two of them, which wasn't exactly news. There was also a generally held belief in police work that the murder of a lawyer ought not to be a crime at all, but neither man joked about this investigation.

"Let me know when you start believing that," Ryan said quietly. Both knew better, of course. These two were only robbers. They'd killed several times, and had twice driven their victim's car a few blocks, but in both cases it had been a sporty car, and probably they'd wanted no more than to have a brief fling with a nice set of wheels. The police knew size, color, and little else. But the Duo were businesslike crooks, and whoever had murdered Pamela Madden had wanted to make a very personal impression; or there was a new and very sick killer about, which possibility added merely one more complication to their already busy lives.

"We were close, weren't we?" Douglas asked. "This girl had names and faces, and she was an eyewitness."

"But we never knew she was there until after that bonehead lost her for us," Ryan said.

"Well, he's back to wherever the hell he goes to, and we're back to where we were before, too." Douglas picked up the file and walked back to his desk.

It was after dark when Kelly tied *Springer* up. He looked up to note that a helicopter was overhead, probably doing something or other from the nearby naval air station. In any case it didn't circle or linger. The outside air was heavy and moist and sultry. Inside the bunker was even worse, and it took an hour to get the air conditioning up to speed. The "house" seemed emptier than before, for the second time in a year, the rooms automatically larger without a second person to help occupy the space. Kelly wandered about for fifteen minutes or so. His movements were aimless until he found himself staring at Pam's clothes. Then his brain clicked in to tell him that he was looking for someone no longer there. He took the articles of clothing and set them in a neat pile on what had once been Tish's dresser, and might have become Pam's. Perhaps the saddest thing of all was that there was so little of it. The cutoffs, the halter, a few more intimate things, the flannel shirt she'd worn at night, her well-worn shoes on top of the pile. So little to remember her by.

Kelly sat on the edge of his bed, staring at them. How long had it all lasted? Three weeks? Was that all? It wasn't a matter of checking the days on a calendar, because time wasn't really measured in that way. Time was something that filled the empty spaces in your life, and his three weeks with Pam had been longer and deeper than all the time since Tish's death. But all that was now a long time ago. His hospital stay seemed like a mere blink of an eye, but it was as though it had become a wall between that most precious part of his life and where he was now. He could walk up to the wall and look over it at what had been, but he could never more reach out and touch it. Life could be so cruel and memory could be a curse, the taunting reminder of what had been and what might have developed from it if only he'd acted differently. Worst of all, the wall between where he was and where he might have gone was one of his own construction, just as he had moments earlier piled up Pam's clothes because they no longer had a use. He could close his eyes and see her. In the silence he could hear her, but the smells were gone, and her feel was gone.

Kelly reached over from the bed and touched the flannel shirt, remembering what it had once covered, remembering how his large strong hands had clumsily undone the buttons to find his love inside, but now it was merely a piece of cloth whose shape contained nothing but air, and little enough of that. It was then that Kelly began sobbing for the first time since he'd learned of her death. His body shook with the reality of it, and alone inside the walls of rebarred concrete he called out her name, hoping that somewhere she might hear, and somehow she might forgive him for killing her with his stupidity. Perhaps she was at rest now. Kelly prayed that God would understand that she'd never really had a chance, would recognize the goodness of her character and judge her with mercy, but that was one mystery whose solutions were well beyond his ability to solve. His eyes were limited by the confines of this room, and they kept returning to the pile of clothing.

The bastards hadn't even given her body the dignity of being covered from the elements and the searching eyes of men. They'd wanted everybody to know how they'd punished her and enjoyed her and tossed her aside like a piece of rubbish, something for a bird to pick at. Pam Madden had been of no consequence to them, except perhaps a convenience to be used in life, and even in death, as a demonstration of their prowess. As central as she had been to his life, that was how unimportant she had been to them. Just like the headman's family, Kelly realized. A demonstration: defy us and suffer. And if others found out, so much the better. Such was their pride.

Kelly lay back in the bed, exhausted by weeks of bed rest followed by a long day of exertion. He stared at the ceiling, the light still on, hoping to sleep, hoping more to find dreams of Pam, but his last conscious thought was something else entirely.

If his pride could kill, then so could theirs.

Dutch Maxwell arrived at his office at six-fifteen, as was his custom. Although as Assistant Chief of Naval Operations (Air) he was no longer part of any operational command hierarchy, he was still a Vice Admiral, and his current job required him to think of every single aircraft in the U.S. Navy as his own. And so the top item on his pile of daily paperwork was a summary of the previous day's air operations over Vietnam—actually it was today's, but had happened yesterday due to the vagaries of the International Dateline, something that had always seemed outrageous even though he'd fought one battle practically astride the invisible line on the Pacific Ocean.

He remembered it well: less than thirty years earlier, flying an F4F-4 Wildcat fighter off USS *Enterprise,* an ensign, with all his hair—cut very short—and a brand-new wife, all piss-and-vinegar and three hundred hours under his belt. On the fourth of June, 1942, in the early afternoon, he'd spotted three Japanese "Val" dive bombers that ought to have followed the rest of the Hiryu air group

to attack *Yorktown* but had gotten lost and headed towards
his carrier by mistake. He'd killed two of them on his first
surprise pass out of a cloud. The third had taken longer, but
he could remember every glint of the sun off his target's
wings and the tracers from the gunner's futile efforts to
drive him off. Landing on his carrier forty minutes later,
he'd claimed three kills before the incredulous eyes of
his squadron commander—then had all three confirmed
by gunsight cameras. Overnight, his "official" squadron
coffee mug had changed from "Winny"—a nickname he'd
despised—to "Dutch," engraved into the porcelain with
blood-red letters, a call sign he'd borne for the remainder
of his career.

Four more combat cruises had added twelve additional
kills to the side of his aircraft, and in due course he'd
commanded a fighter squadron, then a carrier air wing,
then a carrier, then a group, and then been Commander,
Air Forces, U.S. Pacific Fleet, before assuming his current
job. With luck a fleet command lay in his future, and that
was as far as he'd ever been able to see. Maxwell's office
was in keeping with his station and experience. On the
wall to the left of his large mahogany desk was the side
plate from the F6F Hellcat he'd flown at Philippine Sea
and off the coast of Japan. Fifteen rising-sun flags were
painted on the deep blue background lest anyone forget
that the Navy's elder statesman of aviators had really done
it once, and done it better than most. His old mug from the
old *Enterprise* sat on his desk as well, no longer used for
something so trivial as drinking coffee, and certainly not
for pencils.

This near-culmination of his career should have been a
matter of the utmost satisfaction to Maxwell, but instead
his eyes fell upon the daily loss report from Yankee Station. Two A-7A Corsair light-attack bombers had been lost,
and the notation said they were from the same ship and the
same squadron.

"What's the story on this?" Maxwell asked Rear Admiral Podulski.

"I checked," Casimir replied. "Probably a midair. Anders
was the element leader, his wingman, Robertson, was a new

kid. Something went wrong but nobody saw what it was. No SAM call, and they were too high for flak."

"'Chutes?"

"No." Podulski shook his head. "The division leader saw the fireball. Just bits and pieces came out."

"What were they in after?"

Cas's face said it all. "A suspected truck park. The rest of the strike went in, hit the target, good bomb patterns, but no secondaries."

"So the whole thing was a waste of time." Maxwell closed his eyes, wondering what had gone wrong with the two aircraft, with the mission assignment, with his career, with his Navy, with his whole country.

"Not at all, Dutch. *Somebody* thought it was an important target."

"Cas, it's too early in the morning for that, okay?"

"Yes, sir. The CAG is investigating the incident and will probably take some token action. If you want an explanation, it's probably that Robertson was a new kid, and he was nervous—second combat mission—and probably he thought he saw something, and probably he jinked too hard, but they were the trail element and nobody saw it. Hell, Dutch, we saw that sort of thing happen, too."

Maxwell nodded. "What else?"

"An A-6 got shredded north of Haiphong—SAM—but they got it back to the boat all right. Pilot and B/N both get DFCs for that," Podulski reported. "Otherwise a quiet day in the South China Sea. Nothing much in the Atlantic. Eastern Med, picking up some signs the Syrians are getting frisky with their new MiGs, but that's not our problem yet. We have that meeting with Grumman tomorrow, and then it's off to The Hill to talk with our worthy public servants about the F-14 program."

"How do you like the numbers on the new fighter?"

"Part of me wishes we were young enough to qualify, Dutch." Cas managed a smile. "But, Jesus, we used to build carriers for what one of these things is going to cost."

"Progress, Cas."

"Yeah, we have so much of that." Podulski grunted. "One other thing. Got a call from Pax River. Your friend may be back home. His boat's at the dock, anyway."

"You made me wait this long for it?"

"No sense rushing it. He's a civilian, right? Probably sleeps till nine or ten."

Maxwell grunted. "That must be nice. I'll have to try it sometime."

11
Fabrication

Five miles can be a long walk. It is always a long swim. It is a particularly long swim alone. It was an especially long swim alone and for the first time in weeks. That fact became clear to Kelly before the halfway point, but even though the water east of his island was shallow enough that he could stand in many places, he didn't stop, didn't allow himself to slacken off. He altered his stroke to punish his left side all the more, welcoming the pain as the messenger of progress. The water temperature was just about right, he told himself, cool enough that he didn't overheat, and warm enough that it didn't drain the energy from his body. Half a mile out from the island his pace began to slow, but he summoned the inner reservoir of whatever it was that a man drew on and gutted it out, building the pace up again until, when he touched the mud that marked the eastern side of Battery Island, he could barely move. Instantly his muscles began to tighten up, and Kelly had to force himself to stand and walk. It was then that he saw the helicopter. He'd heard one twice during his swim, but made no note of it. He had long experience with helicopters, and hearing them as natural as the buzz of an insect. But having one land on his sandbar was not all that common, and he walked over towards it until a voice called him back towards the bunkers.

"Over here, Chief!"

Kelly turned. The voice was familiar, and on rubbing his eyes he saw the undress whites of a very senior naval officer—that fact made clear by the golden shoulder boards that sparkled in the late-morning sun.

"Admiral Maxwell!" Kelly was glad for the company, especially this man, but his lower legs were covered in mud from the walk out of the water. "I wish you'd called ahead, sir."

"I tried, Kelly." Maxwell came up to him and took his hand. "We've been calling here for a couple of days. Where the hell were you? Out on a job?" The Admiral was surprised at the instant change in the boy's face.

"Not exactly."

"Why don't you go get washed off? I'll go looking for a soda." It was then that Maxwell saw the recent scars on Kelly's back and neck. *Jesus!*

Their first meeting had been aboard USS *Kitty Hawk,* three years earlier, he as AirPac, Kelly as a very sick Bosun's Mate First Class. It wasn't the sort of thing a man in Maxwell's position could forget. Kelly had gone in to rescue the flight crew of Nova One One, whose pilot had been Lieutenant, junior grade, Winslow Holland Maxwell III, USN. Two days of crawling about in an area that was just too hot for a rescue helicopter to go trolling, and he'd come out with Dutch 3rd, injured but alive, but Kelly had caught a vicious infection from the putrid water. And how, Maxwell still asked himself, how did you thank a man for saving your only son? So young he'd looked in the hospital bed, so much like his son, the same sort of defiant pride and shy intelligence. In a just world Kelly would have received the Medal of Honor for his solo mission up that brown river, but Maxwell hadn't even wasted the paper. Sorry, Dutch, CINCPAC would have said, I'd like to go to bat for you on this, but it's a waste of effort, just would look too, well, suspicious. And so he'd done what he could.

"Tell me about yourself."

"Kelly, sir, John T., bosun's mate first—"

"No." Maxwell had interrupted him with a shake of the head. "No, I think you look more like a *Chief* Bosun's Mate to me."

Maxwell had stayed on *Kitty Hawk* for three more days, ostensibly to conduct a personal inspection of flight operations, but really to keep an eye on his wounded son and the young SEAL who'd rescued him. He'd been with Kelly for the telegram announcing the death of his father, a firefighter who'd had a heart attack on the job. And now, he realized, he'd arrived just after something else.

Kelly returned from his shower in a T-shirt and shorts, dragging a little physically, but with something tough and strong in his eyes.

"How far was that swim, John?"

"Just under five miles, sir."

"Good workout," Maxwell observed, handing over a Coca-Cola for his host. "You better cool down some."

"Thank you, sir."

"What happened to you? That mess on your shoulder is new." Kelly told his story briefly, in the way of one warrior to another, for despite the difference in age and station they were of a kind, and for the second time Dutch Maxwell sat and listened like the surrogate father he had become.

"That's a hard hit, John," the Admiral observed quietly.

"Yes, sir." Kelly didn't know what else he was supposed to say, and looked down for a moment. "I never thanked you for the card . . . when Tish died. That was good of you, sir. How's your son doing?"

"Flying a 727 for Delta. I'm going to be a grandfather any day now," the Admiral said with satisfaction, then he realized how cruel the addition might have seemed to this young, lonely man.

"Great!" Kelly managed a smile, grateful to hear something good, that something he'd done had come to a successful conclusion. "So what brings you out here, sir?"

"I want to go over something with you." Maxwell opened his portfolio and unfolded the first of several maps on Kelly's coffee table.

The younger man grunted. "Oh, yeah, I remember this place." His eyes lingered on some symbols that were hand-sketched in. "Classified information here, sir."

"Chief, what we're going to talk about is very sensitive."

Kelly turned to look around. Admirals always traveled around with aides, usually a shiny young lieutenant who would carry the official briefcase, show his boss where the head was, fuss over where the car was parked, and generally do the things beneath the dignity of a hardworking chief petty officer. Suddenly he realized that although the helicopter had its flight crew, now wandering around outside, Vice Admiral Maxwell was otherwise alone, and that was most unusual.

"Why me, sir?"

"You're the only person in the country who's seen this area from ground level."

"And if we're smart, we'll keep it that way." Kelly's memories of the place were anything but pleasant. Looking at the two-dimensional map instantly brought bad three-dimensional recollections.

"How far did you go up the river, John?"

"About to here." Kelly's hand wandered across the map. "I missed your son on the first sweep so I doubled back and found him right about here."

And that wasn't bad, Maxwell thought, tantalizingly close to the objective. "This highway bridge is gone. Only took us sixteen missions, but it's *in* the river now."

"You know what that means, don't you? They build a ford, probably, or a couple underwater bridges. You want advice on taking those out?"

"Waste of time. The objective is here." Maxwell's finger tapped a spot marked with red pen.

"That's a long way to swim, sir. What is it?"

"Chief, when you retired you checked the box for being in the Fleet Reserve," Maxwell said benignly.

"Hold on, sir!"

"Relax, son, I'm not recalling you." *Yet,* Maxwell thought. "You had a top-secret clearance."

"Yeah, we all did, because of—"

"This stuff is higher than TS, John." And Maxwell explained why, pulling additional items from his portfolio.

"Those motherfuckers . . . " Kelly looked up from the recon photo. "You want to go in and get them out, like Song Tay?"

"What do you know about that?"

"Just what was in the open," Kelly explained. "We talked it around the group. It sounded like a pretty slick job. Those Special Forces guys can be real clever when they work at it. But—"

"Yeah, *but* there was nobody home. This guy"—Maxwell tapped the photo—"is positively ID'd as an Air Force colonel. Kelly, you can never repeat this."

"I understand that, sir. How do you plan to do it?"

"We're not sure yet. You know something about the area, and we want your information to help look at alternatives."

Kelly thought back. He'd spent fifty sleepless hours in the area. "It would be real hairy for a helo insertion. There's a lot of triple-A there. The nice thing about Song Tay, it wasn't close to anything, but this place is close enough to Haiphong, and you have these roads and stuff. This is a tough one, sir."

"Nobody ever said it was going to be easy."

"If you loop around here, you can use this ridgeline to mask your approach, but you have to hop the river somewhere . . . here, and you run into that flak trap . . . and that one's even worse, 'cording to these notations."

"Did SEALs plan air missions over there, Chief?" Maxwell asked, somewhat amused, only to be surprised at the reply.

"Sir, 3rd SOG was always short of officers. They kept getting shot up. I was the group operations officer for two months, and we *all* knew how to plan insertions. We had to, that was the most dangerous part of most missions. Don't take this wrong, sir, but even enlisted men know how to think."

Maxwell bristled a little. "I never said they didn't."

Kelly managed a grin. "Not all officers are as enlightened as you are, sir." He looked back down at the map.

"You plan this sort of thing backwards. You start with what do you need on the objective, then you backtrack to find out how you get it all there."

"Save that for later. Tell me about the river valley," Maxwell ordered.

Fifty hours, Kelly remembered, picked up from Danang by helo, deposited aboard the submarine USS *Skate,* which then had moved Kelly right into the surprisingly deep estuary of that damned stinking river, fighting his way up against the current behind an electrically powered sea-scooter, which was still there, probably, unless some fisherman had snagged a line on it, staying underwater until his air tanks gave out, and he remembered how frightening it was not to be able to hide under the rippled surface. When he couldn't do that, when it had been too dangerous to move, hiding under weeds on the bank, watching traffic move on the river road, hearing the ripping thunder of the flak batteries on the hilltops, wondering what some 37mm fire could do to him if some North Vietnamese boy scout stumbled across him and let his father know. And now this flag officer was asking him how to risk the lives of other men in the same place, trusting him, much as Pam had, to know what to do. That sudden thought chilled the retired chief bosun's mate.

"It's not a really nice place, sir. I mean, your son saw a lot of it, too."

"Not from your perspective," Maxwell pointed out.

And that was true, Kelly remembered. Little Dutch had bellied up in a nice thick place, using his radio only on alternate hours, waiting for Snake to come and fetch him while he nursed a broken leg in silent agony, and listened to the same triple-A batteries that had splashed his A-6 hammer the sky at other men trying to take out the same bridge that his own bombs had missed. *Fifty hours,* Kelly remembered, no rest, no sleep, just fear and the mission.

"How much time, sir?"

"We're not sure. Honestly, I'm not sure if we can get the mission green-lighted. When we have a plan, then we can present it. When it's approved, we can assemble assets, and train, and execute."

"Weather considerations?" Kelly asked.

"The mission has to go in the fall, this fall, or maybe it'll never go."

"You say these guys will never come back unless we get them?"

"No other reason for them to set this place up in the way they did," Maxwell replied.

"Admiral, I'm pretty good, but I'm just an enlisted guy, remember?"

"You're the only person who's been close to the place." The Admiral collected the photographs and the maps. He handed Kelly a fresh set of the latter. "You turned down OCS three times. I'd like to know why, John."

"You want the truth? It would have meant going back. I pushed my luck enough."

Maxwell accepted that at face value, silently wishing that his best source of local information had accumulated the rank to match his expertise, but Maxwell also remembered flying combat missions off the old *Enterprise* with enlisted pilots, at least one of whom had displayed enough savvy to be an air-group commander, and he knew that the best helicopter pilots around were probably the instant Warrant Officers the Army ran through Fort Rucker. This wasn't the time for a wardroom mentality.

"One mistake from Song Tay," Kelly said after a moment.

"What's that?"

"They probably overtrained. After a certain period of time, you're just dulling the edge. Pick the right people, and a couple of weeks, max, will handle it. Go further than that and you're just doing embroidery."

"You're not the first person to say that," Maxwell assured him.

"Will this be a SEAL job?"

"We're not sure yet. Kelly, I can give you two weeks while we work on other aspects of the mission."

"How do I get in touch, sir?"

Maxwell dropped a Pentagon pass on the table. "No phones, no mail, it's all face-to-face contact."

Kelly stood and walked him out to the helicopter. As soon as the Admiral came into view, the flight crew started lighting up the turbine engines on the SH-2 SeaSprite. He grabbed the Admiral's arm as the rotor started turning.

"Was the Song Tay job burned?"

That stopped Maxwell in his tracks. "Why do you ask?"

Kelly nodded. "You just answered my question, Admiral."

"We're not sure, Chief." Maxwell ducked his head under the rotor and got into the back of the helicopter. As it lifted off, he found himself wishing again that Kelly had taken the invitation to officer-candidate school. The lad was smarter than he'd realized, and the Admiral made a note to look up his former commander for a fuller evaluation. He also wondered what Kelly would do on his formal recall to active duty. It seemed a shame to betray the boy's trust—it might seem that way to him, Maxwell thought as the SeaSprite turned and headed northeast—but his mind and soul lingered with the twenty men believed to be SENDER GREEN, and his first loyalty had to be to them. Besides, maybe Kelly needed the distraction from his personal troubles. The Admiral consoled himself with that thought.

Kelly watched the helo disappear into the forenoon haze. Then he walked towards his machine shop. He'd expected that by this time today his body would be hurting and his mind relaxed. Strangely, the reverse was now true. The exercise at the hospital had paid off more handsomely than he'd dared to hope. There was still a problem with stamina, but his shoulder, after the usual start-up pain, had accepted the abuse with surprising good grace, and now having passed through the customary post-exercise agony, the secondary period of euphoria had set in. He'd feel good all day, Kelly expected, though he'd hit the bed early tonight in anticipation of yet another day's punishing exercise, and tomorrow he'd take a watch and start exercising in earnest by rating himself against the clock. The Admiral had given him two weeks. That was about the time he'd given to himself for his physical preparation.

Now it was time for another sort.

Naval stations, whatever their size and purpose, were all alike. There were some things they all had to have. One of these was a machine shop. For six years there had been crashboats stationed at Battery Island, and to support them, there had to be machine tools to repair and fabricate broken machine parts. Kelly's collection of tools was the rough equivalent of what would be found on a destroyer, and had probably been purchased that way, the Navy Standard Mark One Mod Zero machine shop selected straight out of some service catalog. Maybe even the Air Force had the same thing for all he knew. He switched on a South Bend milling machine and began checking its various parts and oil reservoirs to make sure it would do what he wanted.

Attendant to the machine were numerous hand tools and gauges and drawers full of various steel blanks, just roughly machined metal shapes intended for further manufacturing into whatever specific purpose a technician might need. Kelly sat in a stool to decide exactly what he needed, then decided that he needed something else first. He took down the .45 automatic from its place on the wall, unloaded and disassembled it before giving the slide and barrel a very careful look inside and out.

"You're going to need two of everything," Kelly said to himself. But first things first. He set the slide on a sturdy jig and used the milling machine first of all to drill two small holes in the top of the slide. The South Bend machine made an admirably efficient drill, not even a tenth of a turn on the four-handled wheel and the tiny cutting bit lanced through the ordnance steel of the automatic. Kelly repeated the exercise, making a second hole 1.25 inches from the first. Tapping the holes for threads was just as easy, and a screwdriver completed the exercise. That ended the easy part of the day's work and got him used to operating the machine, something he hadn't done in over a year. A final examination of the modified gun slide assured Kelly that he hadn't hurt anything. It was now time for the tricky part.

He didn't have the time or equipment to do a really proper job. He knew how to use a welding set well enough, but lacked the gear to fabricate the special parts needed for the sort of instrument he would have liked to have. To do that would mean going to a small foundry whose artisans might have guessed what he was up to, and that was something he could not risk. He consoled himself with the thought that good enough was good enough, while perfect was always a pain in the ass and often not worth the effort anyway.

First he got a sturdy steel blank, rather like a can, but narrower and with thicker walls. Again he drilled and tapped a hole, this time in the center of the bottom plate, axial with the body of the "can," as he already thought of it. The hole was .60 inches in diameter, something he had already checked with a pair of calipers. There were seven similar blanks, but of lesser outside diameter. These he cut off to a length of three quarters of an inch before drilling holes in their bottoms. These new holes were .24 inches, and the shapes he ended up with were like small cups with holes in the bottom, or maybe diminutive flowerpots with vertical sides, he thought with a smile. Each of these was a "baffle." He tried to slide the baffles into the "can," but they were too wide. That earned Kelly a grumble at himself. Each baffle had to go on his lathe. This he did, trimming down the outside of each to a shiny, uniform diameter exactly one millimeter less than that of the inside of the can, a lengthy operation that had him swearing at himself for the fifty minutes it required. Finished, finally, he rewarded himself with a cold Coke before sliding the baffles inside the can. Agreeably, they all fit snugly enough that they didn't rattle, but loosely enough that they slid out with only a shake or two. Good. He dumped them out and next machined a cover cap for the can, which had to be threaded as well. Finished with that task, he first screwed it into place with the baffles out, and then with the baffles in, congratulating himself for the tight fit of all the parts—before he realized that he hadn't cut a hole in the cover plate, which he had to do next, again with the milling machine. This hole was a scant .23 inches in diameter, but when he was done he could see straight through the entire assembly. At least he'd managed to drill everything straight.

Next came the important part. Kelly took his time setting up the machine, checking the arrangements no less than five times before doing the last tapping operation with one pull on the operating handle—that after a long breath. This was something he'd observed a few times but never actually done himself, and though he was pretty good with tools, he was a retired bosun, not a machinist's mate. Finished, he dismounted the barrel and reassembled the pistol, heading outside with a box of .22 Long Rifle ammunition.

Kelly had never been intimidated by the large, heavy Colt automatic, but the cost of .45 ACP was far higher than that of .22 rimfire cartridges, and so the previous year he'd purchased a conversion kit allowing the lighter rounds to be fired through the pistol. He tossed the Coke can about fifteen feet before loading three rounds in the magazine. He didn't bother with ear protection. He stood as he always did, relaxed, hands at his sides, then brought the gun up fast, dropping into a crouching two-hand stance. Kelly stopped cold, realizing that the can screwed onto the barrel blanked out his sights. That would be a problem. The gun went back down, then came up again, and Kelly squeezed off the first round without actually seeing the target. With the predictable results: when he looked, the can was untouched. That was the bad news. The good news was that the suppressor had functioned well. Often misrepresented by TV and movie sound editors into an almost musical *zing,* the noise radiated by a really good silencer is much like that made by swiping a metal brush along a piece of finished lumber. The expanding gas from the cartridge was trapped in the baffles as the bullet passed through the holes, largely plugging them and forcing the gas to expand in the enclosed spaces inside the can. With five internal baffles—the cover plate made for number six—the noise of the firing was muted to a whisper.

All of which was fine, Kelly thought, but if you missed the target, he would probably hear the even louder sound of the pistol's slide racking back and forth, and the mechanical sounds of a firearm were impossible to mistake for anything harmless. Missing a soda can at fifteen feet did not speak well of his marksmanship. The human head was bigger, of course, but his target area inside the human head was not. Kelly relaxed and tried again, bringing the gun up from his side in a smooth and quick arc. This time he started pulling the trigger just as the silencer can began to occult the target. It worked, after a fashion. The can went down with a .22-inch hole an inch from the bottom. Kelly's timing wasn't quite right. His next shot was roughly in the center of the can, however, evoking a smile. He ejected the magazine, loading five hollow-point rounds, and a minute later, the can was no longer usable as a target, with seven holes, six of them roughly grouped in the center.

"Still have the old touch, Johnnie-boy," Kelly said to himself, safing the pistol. But this was in daylight against a stationary piece of red metal, and Kelly knew that. He walked back to his shop and stripped the pistol down again. The suppressor had tolerated the use without any apparent damage, but he cleaned it anyway, lightly oiling the internal parts. One more thing, he thought. With a small brush and white enamel he painted a straight white line down the top of the slide. Now it was two in the afternoon. Kelly allowed himself a light lunch before starting his afternoon exercises.

"Wow, that much?"

"You complaining?" Tucker demanded. "What's the matter, can't you handle it?"

"Henry, I can handle whatever you deliver," Piaggi replied, more than a little miffed at first by the man's arrogance, then wondering what might come next.

"We're going to be here three days!" Eddie Morello whined for his part.

"Don't trust your old lady that long?" Tucker grinned at the man. Eddie would have to be next, he had already decided. Morello didn't have much sense of humor anyway. His face flushed red.

"Look, Henry—"

"Settle down, everybody." Piaggi looked at the eight kilos of material on the table before turning back to Tucker. "I'd love to know where you get this stuff."

"I'm sure you would, Tony, but we already talked about that. Can you handle it?"

"You gotta remember, once you start this sort of thing, it's kinda hard to stop it. People depend on you, kinda like what do you tell the bear when you're outa cookies, y'know?" Piaggi was already thinking. He had contacts in Philadelphia and New York, young men—like himself, tired of working for a mustache with old-fashioned rules. The money potential here was stunning. Henry had access to—what? he wondered. They had started only two months before, with two kilograms that had assayed out to a degree of purity that only the best Sicilian White matched, but at half the delivery price. And the problems associated with delivery were Henry's, not his, which made the deal doubly attractive. Finally, the physical security arrangements were what most impressed Piaggi. Henry was no dummy, not some upstart with big ideas and small brains. He was, in fact, a businessman, calm and professional, someone who might make a serious ally and associate, Piaggi thought now.

"My supply is pretty solid. Let me worry about that, paisan."

"Okay." Piaggi nodded. "There is one problem, Henry. It'll take me a while to get the cash together for something this big. You should have warned me, man."

Tucker allowed himself a laugh. "I didn't want to scare you off, Anthony."

"Trust me on the money?"

A nod and a look. "I know you're a serious guy." Which was the smart play. Piaggi wouldn't walk away from the chance to establish a regular supply to his associates. The long-term money was just too good. Angelo Vorano might not have grasped that, but he had served as the means to meet Piaggi, and that was enough. Besides, Angelo was now crab shit.

"This is pure stuff, same as before?" Morello asked, annoying both of the others.

"Eddie, the man isn't going to trust us on the cash and fuck us at the same time, is he?" Piaggi asked.

"Gentlemen, let me tell you what's happening here, okay? I got a big supply of good stuff. Where I get it, how I get it, that's my business. I even got a territory I don't want you fooling with, but we ain't bumped heads yet on the street and we'll keep it that way." Both of the Italians nodded, Tucker saw. Eddie dumbly, but Tony with understanding and respect. Piaggi spoke the same way:

"You need distribution. We can handle that. You have your own territory, and we can respect that, too."

It was time for the next play. "I didn't get this far by being stupid. After today, you guys are out of this part of the business."

"What do you mean?"

"I mean, no more boat rides. I mean you guys don't handle the material anymore."

Piaggi smiled. He'd done this four times now, and the novelty had already worn off. "You have no argument from me on that. If you want, I can have my people take deliveries whenever you want."

"We separate the stuff from the money. We handle it like a business," Tucker said. "Line of credit, like."

"The stuff comes over first."

"Fair enough, Tony. You pick good people, okay? The idea is we separate you and me from the drugs as much as possible."

"People get caught, they talk," Morello pointed out. He felt excluded from the conversation, but wasn't quite bright enough to grasp the significance of that.

"Mine don't," Tucker said evenly. "My people know better."

"That was you, wasn't it?" Piaggi asked, making the connection and getting a nod. "I like your style, Henry. Try to be more careful next time, okay?"

"I spent two years getting this all set up, cost me a lot of money. I want this operation to run for a long time, and I'm not taking any more chances than I have to anymore. Now, when can you pay me off for this load?"

"I brought an even hundred with me." Tony waved towards the duffel bag on the deck. This little operation had grown with surprising rapidity as it was, but the first three loads had sold off for fine prices, and Tucker, Piaggi thought, was a man you could trust, insofar as you could trust anyone in this line of work. But, he figured, a rip would have happened already if that was what Tucker wanted, and this much drugs was too much for a guy running that kind of setup. "It's yours to take, Henry. Looks like we're going to owe you another . . . five hundred? I'll need some time, like a week or so. Sorry, man, but you kinda sandbagged me this way. Takes time to front up that much cash, y'know?"

"Call it four, Tony. No sense squeezing your friends first time out. Let's generate a little goodwill at first, okay?"

"Special introductory offer?" Piaggi laughed at that and tossed Henry a beer. "You gotta have some Italian blood in you, boy. Okay! We'll do it like you say, man." *Just how good is that supply of yours, Henry?* Piaggi couldn't ask.

"And now there's work to do." Tucker slit open the first plastic bag and dumped it into a stainless-steel mixing bowl, glad that he wouldn't have to trouble himself with this mess again. The seventh step in his marketing plan was now complete. From now on he'd have others do this kitchen stuff, under his supervision at first, of course, but starting today Henry Tucker would start acting like the executive he had become. Mixing the inert material into the bowl, he congratulated himself on his intelligence. He'd started the business in exactly the right way, taking risks, but carefully considered ones, building his organization from the bottom up, doing things himself, getting his hands dirty. Perhaps Piaggi's antecedents had started the same way, Tucker thought. Probably Tony had forgotten that, and forgotten also its implications. But that wasn't Tucker's problem.

"Look, Colonel, I was just an aide, okay? How many times do I have to tell you that? I did the same thing your generals' aides do, all the littler dumb stuff."

"Then why take such a job?" It was sad, Colonel Nikolay Yevgeniyevich Grishanov thought, that a man had to go through this, but Colonel Zacharias wasn't a man. He was an enemy, the Russian reminded himself with some reluctance, and he wanted to get the man talking again.

"Isn't it the same in your air force? You get noticed by a general and you get promoted a lot faster." The

American paused for a moment. "I wrote speeches, too." That couldn't get him into any trouble, could it?

"That's the job of a political officer in my air force." Grishanov dismissed that frivolity with a wave.

It was their sixth session. Grishanov was the only Soviet officer allowed to interview these Americans, the Vietnamese were playing their cards so carefully. Twenty of them, all the same, all different. Zacharias was as much an intelligence officer as fighter pilot, his dossier said. He'd spent his twenty-odd-year career studying air-defense systems. A master's degree from the University of California, Berkeley, in electrical engineering. The dossier even included a recently acquired copy of his master's thesis, "Aspects of Microwave Propagation and Diffusion over Angular Terrain," photocopied from the university archives by some helpful soul, one of the unknown three who had contributed to his knowledge of the Colonel. The thesis ought to have been classified immediately upon its completion—as would have happened in the Soviet Union, Grishanov knew. It was a very clever examination of what happened to low-frequency search-radar energy—and how, incidentally, an aircraft could use mountains and hills to mask itself from it. Three years after that, following a tour of duty in a fighter squadron, he'd been assigned to a tour of duty at Offutt Air Force Base, just outside Omaha, Nebraska. Part of the Strategic Air Command's war-plans staff, he'd worked on flight profiles which might allow American B-52 bombers to penetrate Soviet air defenses, applying his theoretical knowledge of physics to the practical world of strategic-nuclear war.

Grishanov could not bring himself to hate this man. A fighter pilot himself, having just completed a regimental command in PVO-Strany, the Soviet air-defense command, and already selected for another, the Russian colonel was in a curious way Zacharias's exact counterpart. His job, in the event of war, was to stop those bombers from ravaging his country, and in peace to plan methods of making their penetration of Soviet air space as difficult as possible. That identity made his current job both difficult and necessary. Not a KGB officer, certainly not one of these little brown savages, he took no pleasure at all in hurting people—shooting them down was something else entirely—even Americans who plotted the destruction of his country. But those who knew how to extract information did not know how to analyze what he was looking for, nor even what questions to ask—and writing the questions down would be no help; you had to see the man's eyes when he spoke. A man clever enough to formulate such plans was also clever enough to lie with enough conviction and authority to fool almost anyone.

Grishanov didn't like what he saw now. This was a skillful man, and a courageous one, who had fought to establish missile-hunting specialists the Americans called Wild Weasels. It was a term a Russian might have used for the mission, named for vicious little predators who chased their prey into their very dens. This prisoner had flown eighty-nine such missions, if the Vietnamese had recovered the right pieces from the right aircraft—like Russians, Americans kept a record of their accomplishments on their aircraft—this was exactly the man he needed to talk to. Perhaps that was a lesson he would write about, Grishanov thought. Such pride told your enemies whom they had captured, and much of what he knew. But that was the way of fighter pilots, and Grishanov would himself have balked at the concealment of his deeds against his country's enemies. The Russian also tried to tell himself that he was sparing harm to the man across the table. Probably Zacharias had killed many Vietnamese—and not simple peasants, but skilled, Russian-trained missile technicians—and this country's government would want to punish him for that. But that was not his concern, and he didn't want to allow political feelings to get in the way of his professional obligations. His was one of the most scientific and certainly the most complex aspects of national defense. It was his duty to plan for an attack of hundreds of aircraft, each of which had a crew of highly trained specialists. The way they thought, their tactical doctrine, was as important as their plans. And as far as he was concerned, the Americans could kill all of the bastards they wanted. The nasty little fascists had as much to do with his country's political philosophy as cannibals did with gourmet cooking.

"Colonel, I do know better than that," Grishanov said patiently. He laid the most recently arrived document on the table. "I read this last night. It's excellent work."

The Russian's eyes never left Colonel Zacharias. The American's physical reaction was remarkable. Though something of an intelligence officer himself, he had never dreamed that someone in Vietnam could get word to Moscow, then have Americans under their control find something like this. His face proclaimed what he was thinking: *How could they know so much about me?* How could they have reached that far back into his past? Who possibly could have done it? Was anyone that good, that professional? The Vietnamese were such fools! Like many Russian officers, Grishanov was a serious and thorough student of military history. He'd read all manner of arcane documents while sitting in regimental ready rooms. From one he'd never forget, he learned how the Luftwaffe had interrogated captured airmen, and that lesson was one he would try to apply here. While physical abuse had only hardened this man's resolve, he had just been shaken to his soul by a mere sheaf of paper. Every man had strengths and every man had weaknesses. It took a person of intelligence to recognize the differences.

"How is it that this was never classified?" Grishanov asked, lighting a cigarette.

"It's just theoretical physics," Zacharias said, shrugging his thin shoulders, recovering enough that he tried to conceal his despair. "The telephone company was more interested than anybody else."

Grishanov tapped the thesis with his finger. "Well, I tell you, I learned several things from that last night. Predicting false echoes from topographical maps, modeling the blind spots mathematically! You can plan an approach route that way, plot maneuvers from one such point to another. Brilliant! Tell me, what sort of place is Berkeley?"

"Just a school, California style," Zacharias replied before catching himself. He was talking. He wasn't supposed to talk. He was trained not to talk. He was trained on what to expect, and what he could safely do, how to evade and disguise. But that training never quite anticipated this. And, dear God, was he tired, and scared, and sick of living up to a code of conduct that didn't count for beans to anyone else.

"I know little of your country—except professional matters, of course. Are there great regional differences? You come from Utah. What sort of place is it?"

"Zacharias, Robin G. Colonel—"

Grishanov raised his hands. "Please, Colonel. I know all that. I also know your place of birth in addition to the date. There is no base of your air force near Salt Lake City. All I know is from maps. I will probably never visit this part—any part of your country. In this Berkeley part of California, it is green, yes? I was told once they grow wine grapes there. But I know nothing of Utah. There is a large lake there, but it's called Salt Lake, yes? It's salty?"

"Yes, that's why—"

"How can it be salty? The ocean is a thousand kilometers away, with mountains in between, yes?" He didn't give the American time to reply. "I know the Caspian Sea quite well. I was stationed at a base there once. It isn't salty. But this place is? How strange." He stubbed out his cigarette.

The man's head jerked up a little. "Not sure, I'm not a geologist. Something left over from another time, I suppose."

"Perhaps so. There are mountains there, too, yes?"

"Wasatch Mountains," Zacharias confirmed somewhat drunkenly.

One clever thing about the Vietnamese, Grishanov thought, the way they fed their prisoners, food a hog would eat only from necessity. He wondered if it were a deliberate and thought-out diet or something fortuitously resulting from mere barbarity. Political prisoners in the Gulag ate better, but the diet of these Americans lowered their resistance to disease, debilitated them to the point that the act of escape would be doomed by inadequate stamina. Rather like what the *fascisti* did to Soviet prisoners, distasteful or not, it was useful to Grishanov. Resistance, physical and mental, required energy, and you could watch these men lose their strength during the hours of interrogation, watch their courage wane as their physical needs drew more and more upon their supply of psychological resolve. He was learning how to do this. It was time-consuming, but it was a diverting process, learning to pick apart the brains of men not unlike himself.

"The skiing, is it good?"

Zacharias's eyes blinked, as though the question took him away to a different time and place. "Yeah, it is."

"That is something one will never do here, Colonel. I like cross-country skiing for exercise, and to get away from things. I had wooden skis, but in my last regiment my maintenance officer made me steel skis from aircraft parts."

"Steel?"

"Stainless steel, heavier than aluminum but more flexible. I prefer it. From a wing panel on our new interceptor, project E-266."

"What's that?" Zacharias knew nothing of the new MiG-25.

"Your people now call it Foxbat. Very fast, designed to catch one of your B-70 bombers."

"But we stopped that project," Zacharias objected.

"Yes, I know that. But your project got me a wonderfully fast fighter to fly. When I return home, I will command the first regiment of them."

"Fighter planes made of steel? Why?"

"It resists aerodynamic heating much better than aluminum," Grishanov explained. "And you can make good skis from discarded parts." Zacharias was very confused now. "So how well do you think we would do with my steel fighters and your aluminum bombers?"

"I guess that depends on—" Zacharias started to say, then stopped himself cold. His eyes looked across the table, first with confusion at what he'd almost said, then with resolve.

Too soon, Grishanov told himself with disappointment. He'd pushed a little too soon. This one had courage. Enough to take his Wild Weasel "downtown," the phrase the Americans used, over eighty times. Enough to resist for a long time. But Grishanov had plenty of time.

12

Outfitters

63 VW, LOW MLGE, RAD, HTR. . . .

Kelly dropped a dime in the pay phone and called the number. It was a blazing hot Saturday, temperature and humidity in a neck-and-neck race for triple digits while Kelly fumed at his own stupidity. Some things were so blatantly obvious that you didn't see them until your nose split open and started bleeding.

"Hello? I'm calling about the ad for the car . . . that's right," Kelly said. "Right now if you want . . . Okay, say about fifteen minutes? Fine, thank you, ma'am. I'll be right there. 'Bye." He hung up. At least something had gone right. Kelly grimaced at the inside of the phone booth. *Springer* was tied up in a guest slip at one of the marinas on the Potomac. He had to buy a new car, but how did you get to where the new car was? If you drove there, then you could drive the new car back, but what about the one you took? It was funny enough that he started laughing at himself. Then fate intervened, and an empty cab went driving past the marina's entrance, allowing him to keep his promise to a little old lady.

"The 4500 block, Essex Avenue," he told the driver.

"Where's that, man?"

"Chevy Chase."

"Gonna cost extra, man," the driver pointed out, turning north.

Kelly handed a ten-dollar bill across. "Another one if you get me there in fifteen minutes."

"Cool." And the acceleration dropped Kelly back in his seat. The taxi avoided Wisconsin Avenue most of the way. At a red light the driver found Essex Avenue on his map, and he ended up collecting the extra ten with about twenty seconds to spare.

It was an upscale residential neighborhood, and the house was easy to spot. There it was, a VW Beetle, an awful peanut-butter color speckled with a little body rust. It could not have been much better. Kelly hopped up the four wooden front steps and knocked on the door.

"Hello?" It was a face to match the voice. She had to be eighty or so, small and frail, but with fey green eyes that hinted at what had been, enlarged by the thick glasses she wore. Her hair still had some yellow in the gray.

"Mrs. Boyd? I called a little while ago about the car."

"What's your name?"

"Bill Murphy, ma'am." Kelly smiled benignly. "Awful hot, isn't it?"

"T'rble," she said, meaning *terrible*. "Wait a minute." Gloria Boyd disappeared and then came back a moment later with the keys. She even came out to walk him to the car. Kelly took her arm to help her down the steps.

"Thank you, young man."

"My pleasure, ma'am," he replied gallantly.

"We got the car for my granddaughter. When she went to college, then Ken used it," she said, expecting Kelly to know who Ken was.

"Excuse me?"

"My husband," Gloria said without turning. "He died a month ago."

"I'm very sorry to hear that, ma'am."

"He was sick a long time," said the woman, not yet recovered from the shock of her loss but accepting the fact of it. She handed him the keys. "Here, take a look."

Kelly unlocked the door. It looked like the car used by a college student and then by an elderly man. The seats were well worn, and one had a long slash in it, probably by a packing box of clothes or books. He turned the key in the lock and the engine started immediately. There was even a full tank of gas. The ad hadn't lied about the mileage, only 52,000 miles on the odometer. He asked for and got permission to take it around the block. The car was mechanically sound, he decided, bringing it back to the waiting owner.

"Where did all the rust come from?" he asked her, giving the keys back.

"She went to school in Chicago, at Northwestern, all that terrible snow and salt."

"That's a good school. Let's get you back inside." Kelly took her arm and directed her back to the house. It smelled like an old person's house, the air heavy with dust that she was too tired to wipe, and stale food, for the meals she still fixed were for two, not one.

"Are you thirsty?"

"Yes, ma'am, thank you. Water will be just fine." Kelly looked around while she went to the kitchen. There was a photo on the wall, a man in a high-necked uniform and Sam Browne belt, holding the arm of a young woman in a very tight, almost cylindrical, white wedding dress. Other photos cataloged the married life of Kenneth and Gloria Boyd. Two daughters and a son, a trip to the ocean, an old car, grandchildren, all the things earned in a full and useful life.

"Here you go." She handed over a glass.

"Thank you. What did your husband do?"

"He worked for the Commerce Department for forty-two years. We were going to move to Florida, but then he got sick so now I'm going alone. My sister lives in Fort Pierce, she's a widow too, her husband was a policeman . . . " Her voice trailed off as the cat came in to examine the new visitor. That seemed to invigorate Mrs. Boyd. "I'm moving down there next week. The house is already sold, have to get out next Thursday. I sold it to a nice young doctor."

"I hope you like it down there, ma'am. How much do you want for the car?"

"I can't drive anymore because of my eyes, cataracts. People have to drive me everywhere I go. My grandson says it's worth one thousand five hundred dollars."

Your grandson must be a lawyer to be that greedy, Kelly thought. "How about twelve hundred? I can pay cash."

"Cash?" Her eyes became fey again.

"Yes, ma'am."

"Then you can have the car." She held out her hand and Kelly took it carefully.

"Do you have the paperwork?" It made Kelly feel guilty that she had to get up again, this time heading upstairs, slowly, holding on to the banister while Kelly took out his wallet and counted off twelve crisp bills.

It should have taken only another ten minutes, but instead it was thirty. Kelly had already checked up on how to do the mechanics of a title transfer, and besides, he wasn't going to do all of that. The auto-insurance policy was tucked into the same cardboard envelope as the title, in the name of Kenneth W. Boyd. Kelly promised to take care of that for her, and the tags, too, of course. But it turned out that all the cash made Mrs. Boyd nervous, and so Kelly helped her fill out a deposit ticket, and then drove her to her bank, where she could drop it into the night depository. Then he stopped off at the supermarket for milk and cat food before bringing her home and walking her to the door again.

"Thank you for the car, Mrs. Boyd," he said in parting.

"What are you going to use it for?"

"Business." Kelly smiled and left.

At quarter of nine that night, two cars pulled into the service area on Interstate 95. The one in front was a Dodge Dart and the one behind it a red Plymouth Roadrunner. Roughly fifty feet apart, they picked a half-full area north of Maryland House, a rest stop set in the median of the John F. Kennedy Highway, offering full restaurant services along with gas and oil—good coffee, but, understandably, no alcoholic beverages. The Dart took a few meandering turns in the parking lot, finally stopping three spaces from a white Oldsmobile with Pennsylvania tags and a brown vinyl top. The Roadrunner took a space in the next row. A woman got out and walked towards the brick restaurant, a path that took her past the Olds.

"Hey, baby," a man said. The woman stopped and took a few steps towards the vinyl-topped automobile. The man was Caucasian, with long but neatly combed black hair and an open-necked white shirt.

"Henry sent me," she said.

"I know." He reached out to stroke her face, a gesture which she did not resist. He looked around a little before moving his hand downwards. "You have what I want, baby?"

"Yes." She smiled. It was a forced, uneasy smile, frightened but not embarrassed. Doris was months beyond embarrassment.

"Nice tits," the man said with no emotional content at all in his voice. "Get the stuff."

Doris walked back to her car, as though she'd forgotten something. She returned with a large purse, almost a small duffel, really. As she walked past the Olds, the man's hand reached out and took it. Doris proceeded into the building, returning a minute later holding a can of soda, her eyes on the Roadrunner, hoping that she'd done everything right. The Olds had its motor running, and the driver blew her a kiss, to which she responded with a wan smile.

"That was easy enough," Henry Tucker said, fifty yards away, at the outdoor eating area on the other side of the building.

"Good stuff?" another man asked Tony Piaggi. The three of them sat at the same table, "enjoying" the sultry evening while the majority of the patrons were inside with the air conditioning.

"The best. Same as the sample we gave you two weeks ago. Same shipment and everything," Piaggi assured him.

"And if the mule gets burned?" the man from Philadelphia asked.

"She won't talk," Tucker assured him. "They've all seen what happens to bad girls." As they watched, a man got out of the Roadrunner and got into the Dart's driver's seat.

"Very good," Rick told Doris.

"Can we go now?" she asked him, shaking now that the job was over, sipping nervously at her soda.

"Sure, baby, I know what you want." Rick smiled and started the car. "Be nice, now. Show me something."

"There's people around," Doris said.

"So?"

Without another word, Doris unbuttoned her shirt—it was a man's shirt—leaving it tucked into her faded shorts. Rick reached in and smiled, turning the wheel with his left hand. *It could have been worse,* Doris told herself, closing her eyes, pretending that she was someone else in some other place, wondering how long before her life would end too, hoping it wouldn't be long.

"The money?" Piaggi asked.

"I need a cup of coffee." The other man got up and walked inside, leaving his briefcase, which Piaggi took in his hand. He and Tucker walked off to his car, a blue Cadillac, without waiting for the other man to come back.

"Not going to count it?" Tucker asked halfway across the parking lot.

"If he stiffs us, he knows what happens. This is business, Henry."

"That's right," Tucker agreed.

"Bill Murphy," Kelly said. "I understand you have some vacant apartments." He held up the Sunday paper.

"What are you looking for?"

"A one-bedroom would be fine. I really just need a place to hang my clothes," Kelly told the man. "I travel a lot."

"Salesman?" the manager asked.

"That's right. Machine tools. I'm new here—new territory, I mean."

It was an old garden-apartment complex, built soon after the Second World War for returning veterans, composed exclusively of three-story brick structures. The trees looked about right for that time period. They'd been planted then and grown well, tall enough now to support a good population of squirrels, wide enough to give shade to the parking areas. Kelly looked around approvingly as the manager took him to a first-floor furnished unit.

"This is just fine," Kelly announced. He looked around, testing the kitchen sink and other plumbing fixtures. The furniture was obviously used, but in decent shape. There were even air conditioners in the windows of every room.

"I have other ones—"

"This is just what I need. How much?"

"One seventy-five a month, one month security deposit."

"Utilities?"

"You can pay them yourself or we can bill it. Some of our renters prefer that. They'll average about forty-five dollars a month."

"Easier to pay one bill than two or three. Let's see. One seventy-five, plus forty-five . . ."

"Two-twenty," the manager said helpfully.

"Four-forty," Kelly corrected. "Two months, right? I can pay you with a check, but it's an out-of-town bank. I don't have a local account yet. Is cash okay?"

"Cash is always okay with me," the manager assured him.

"Fine." Kelly took out his wallet, handing over the bills. He stopped. "No, six-sixty, we'll make it three months, if that's okay. And I need a receipt." The helpful manager pulled a pad from his pocket and wrote one up on the spot. "How about a phone?" Kelly asked.

"I can have that done by Tuesday if you want. There's another deposit for that."

"Please take care of that, if you would." Kelly handed over some more money. "My stuff won't be here for a while. Where can I get sheets and stuff?"

"Nothing much open today. Tomorrow, lots of 'em."

Kelly looked through the bedroom door at the bare mattress. He could see the lumps from this distance. He shrugged. "Well, I've slept on worse."

"Veteran?"

"Marine," Kelly said.

"So was I once," the manager replied, surprising Kelly. "You don't do anything wild, do you?" He didn't expect so, but the owner insisted that he ask, even ex-Marines. The answer was a sheepish, reassuring grin.

"I snore pretty bad, they tell me."

Twenty minutes later Kelly was in a cab heading downtown. He got out at Penn Station and caught the next train to D.C., where another taxi delivered him to his boat. By nightfall, *Springer* was headed down the Potomac. It would have been so much easier, Kelly told himself, if there were just one person to help him. So much of his time was tied up with useless commuting. But was it really useless? Maybe not. He was getting a lot of thinking done, and that was as important as his physical preparations. Kelly arrived at his home just before midnight after six continuous hours of thinking and planning.

Despite a weekend of almost nonstop motion, there was no time to dawdle. Kelly packed clothing, most of it purchased in the suburbs of Washington. Linens he would buy in Baltimore. Food the same. His .45 automatic, plus the .22–.45 conversion kit, was packed in with old clothing, along with two boxes of ammunition. He shouldn't need more than that, Kelly thought, and ammo was heavy. While he fabricated one more silencer, this one for the Woodsman, he thought through his preparations. His physical condition was excellent, nearly as good as it had been in 3rd SOG, and he'd been shooting every day. His aim was probably better than it had ever been, he told himself, going through what were now almost mindless mechanical operations on the machine tools. By three in the morning the new suppressor was fitted to the Woodsman and tested. Thirty minutes after that he was back aboard *Springer,* headed north, looking forward to a few hours' sleep once he got past Annapolis.

It was a lonely night, with scattered clouds, and his mind drifted somewhat before he commanded himself to concentrate. He was not a lazy civilian anymore, but Kelly allowed himself his first beer in weeks while his mind churned over variables. What had he forgotten? The reassuring answer was that he could think of nothing. The less-than-satisfactory thought was that he still knew little. Billy with his red Plymouth muscle car. A black guy named Henry. He knew their area of operation. And that was all.

But.

But he'd fought armed and trained enemies with less knowledge than that, and though he would force himself to be just as careful now as he had been there, deep down he knew that he would accomplish this mission. Partly it was because he was more formidable than they, and far more highly motivated. The other part, Kelly realized with surprise, was because he didn't care about the consequences, only the results. He remembered something from his Catholic prep school, a passage from Virgil's *Aeneid* that had defined his mission almost two thousand years before: *Una salus victus nullam sperare salutem.* The one hope of the doomed is not to hope for safety. The very grimness of the thought made him smile as he sailed under the stars, light dispatched from distances so vast that it had begun its journey long before Kelly, or even Virgil, had been born.

The pills helped shut out reality, but not all the way. Doris didn't so much think the thought as listen to it, sense it, like recognizing something that she didn't wish to face but refused to go away. She was too dependent on the barbiturates now. Sleep came hard to her, and in the emptiness of the room she was unable to avoid herself. She would have taken more pills if she could, but they didn't allow her what she wanted, not that she wanted much. Just brief oblivion, a short-term liberation from her fear, that was all—and that was something they had no interest in granting her. She could see more than they knew or would have expected, she could peer into the future, but that was little consolation. Sooner or later she would be caught by the police. She'd been arrested before, but not for something of this magnitude, and she'd go away for a long time for this. The police would try to

get her to talk, promise her protection. She knew better.
Twice now she'd seen friends die. Friends? As close to
that as was possible, someone to talk to, someone who
shared her life, such as it was, and even in this captivity
there were little jokes, small victories against the forces
that ruled her existence, like distant lights in a gloomy
sky. Someone to cry with. But two of them were dead, and
she'd watched them die, sitting there, drugged but unable
to sleep and blot it out, the horror so vast that it became
numbing, watching their eyes, seeing and feeling the pain,
knowing that she could do nothing, knowing even that they
knew it as well. A nightmare was bad enough, but one of
those couldn't reach out and touch you. You could wake
up and flee from one of those. Not this. She could watch
herself from outside, as though she were a robot outside
her own command but not that of others. Her body would
not move unless others commanded it, and she even had
to conceal her thoughts, was even afraid to voice them
within her own mind lest they hear them or see them on
her face, but now, try as she might, she could not force
them away.

Rick lay next to her, breathing slowly in the darkness.
Part of her liked Rick. He was the gentlest of them, and
sometimes she allowed herself to think that he liked her,
maybe a little, because he didn't beat her badly. She had
to stay in line, of course, because his anger was every bit
as bad as Billy's, and so around Rick she tried very hard
to be good. Part of her knew that it was foolish, but her
reality was defined by other people now. And she'd seen
the results of real resistance. After one especially bad night
Pam had held her, and whispered her desires to escape.
Later, Doris had prayed that she had gotten away, that
there might be hope after all, only to see her dragged in
and to watch her die, sitting helplessly fifteen feet away
while they did everything to her that they could imagine.
Watching her life end, her body convulsing from lack of
oxygen with the man's face staring at her, laughing at her
from an inch away. Her only act of resistance, thankfully
unnoticed by the men, had been to brush out her friend's
hair, crying all the while, hoping somehow that Pam would

know there was someone who cared, even in death. But the gesture had seemed empty even as she'd done it, making her tears all the more bitter.

What had she done wrong? Doris wondered, how badly had she offended God that her life should be this way? How could anyone possibly deserve such a bleak and hopeless existence?

"I'm impressed, John," Rosen said, staring at his patient. Kelly sat on the examining table, his shirt off. "What have you been doing?"

"Five-mile swim for the shoulders. Better than weights, but a little of that, too, in the evening. A little running. About what I used to do back in the old days."

"I wish I had your blood pressure," the surgeon observed, removing the cuff. He'd done a major procedure that morning, but he made time for his friend.

"Exercise, Sam," Kelly advised.

"I don't have the time, John," the surgeon said—rather weakly, both thought.

"A doc should know better."

"True," Rosen conceded. "How are you otherwise?"

The reply was just a look, neither a smile nor a grimace, just a neutral expression that told Rosen all he needed to know. One more try: "There's an old saying: Before setting out on revenge, dig two graves."

"Only two?" Kelly asked lightly.

Rosen nodded. "I read the post report, too. I can't talk you out of it?"

"How's Sarah?"

Rosen accepted the deflection with good grace. "Deep into her project. She's excited enough that she's telling me about it. It's pretty interesting stuff."

Just then Sandy O'Toole came in. Kelly startled both of them by lifting his T-shirt and covering his chest. "Please!"

The nurse was so startled that she laughed, and so did Sam until he realized that Kelly was indeed ready for whatever he was planning. The conditioning, the looseness, the steady, serious eyes that changed to mirth when he wanted them to. *Like a surgeon,* Rosen thought, and what a strange thought that was, but the more he looked at this man, the more intelligence he saw.

"You're looking healthy for a guy who got shot a few weeks ago," O'Toole said with a friendly look.

"Clean living, ma'am. Only one beer in thirty-some days."

"Mrs. Lott is conscious now, Doctor Rosen," the nurse reported. "Nothing unusual, she appears to be doing fine. Her husband's been in to see her. I think he'll be okay, too. I had my doubts."

"Thanks, Sandy."

"Well, John, you're healthy, too. Put your shirt on before Sandy starts blushing," Rosen added with a chuckle.

"Where do you get lunch around here?" Kelly asked.

"I'd show you myself, but I have a conference in about ten minutes. Sandy?"

She checked her watch. "About time for mine. You want to risk hospital food or something outside?"

"You're the tour guide, ma'am."

She guided him to the cafeteria, where the food was hospital-bland, but you could add salt and other spices if you wanted. Kelly selected something that might be filling, even healthy, to compensate for the lack of taste.

"Have you been keeping busy?" he asked after they selected a table.

"Always," Sandy assured him.

"Where do you live?"

"Off Loch Raven Boulevard, just in the County." She hadn't changed, Kelly saw. Sandy O'Toole was functioning, quite well in fact, but the emptiness in her life wasn't qualitatively different from his. The real difference was that he could do something; she could not. She was reaching out, she had a capacity for good humor, but her grief overcame it at every turn. A powerful force, grief. There were advantages in having enemies you could seek out and eliminate. Fighting a shadow was far more difficult.

"Row house, like they have around here?"

"No, it's an old bungalow, whatever you call it, big square two-story house. Half an acre. That reminds me," she added. "I have to cut the grass this weekend." Then she remembered that Tim had liked cutting grass, had decided to leave the Army after his second Vietnam tour and get his law degree and live a normal kind of life, all of that taken away from her by little people in a distant place.

Kelly didn't know what she was thinking, exactly, but he didn't have to. The change in her expression, the way her voice trailed off, said it all. How to cheer her up? It was a strange question for him, considering his plans for the next few weeks.

"You were very kind to me while I was upstairs. Thanks."

"We try to take care of our patients," she said with a friendly and unaccustomed expression.

"A face as pretty as yours should do that more," Kelly told her.

"Do what?"

"Smile."

"It's hard," she said, serious again.

"I know, ma'am. But I did have you laughing before," Kelly told her.

"You surprised me."

"It's Tim, isn't it?" he asked, jolting her. People weren't supposed to talk about that, were they?

She stared into Kelly's eyes for perhaps five seconds. "I just don't understand."

"In some ways it's easy. In some ways it's hard. The hard part," Kelly said, thinking it through himself as he did so, "is understanding why people make it necessary, why people do things like that. What it comes down to is, there are bad people out there, and somebody has to deal with them, 'cuz if you don't, then someday they'll deal with you. You can try ignoring them, but that doesn't ever work, really. And sometimes you see things you just can't ignore." Kelly leaned back, searching for more words. "You see lots of bad things here, Sandy. I've seen worse. I've watched people doing things—"

"Your nightmare?"

Kelly nodded. "That's right. I almost got myself killed that night."

"What was—"

"You don't want to know, honest. I mean, I don't understand that part either, how people can do things like that. Maybe they believe in something so much that they stop remembering that it's important to be human. Maybe they want something so much that they don't care. Maybe there's just something wrong with them, how they think, how they feel. I don't know. But what they do is real. Somebody has to try and stop it." *Even when you know it's not going to work,* Kelly didn't have the heart to add. How could he tell her that her husband had died for a failure?

"My husband was a knight in shiny armor on a white horse? Is that what you're telling me?"

"You're the one wearing white, Sandy. You fight against one kind of enemy. There's other kinds. Somebody has to fight against them, too."

"I'll never understand why Tim had to die."

It really came down to that, Kelly thought. It wasn't about great political or social issues. Everyone had a life, which was supposed to have a natural end after an amount of time determined by God or Fate or something men weren't supposed to control. He'd seen young men die, and caused his share of deaths, each life something of value to its owner and others, and how did you explain to the others what it was all about? For that matter, how did you explain it to yourself? But that was from the outside. From the inside it was something else. Maybe that was the answer.

"You do some pretty hard work, right?"

"Yes," Sandy said, nodding a little.

"Why not do something easier? I mean, work a department where it's different, I don't know—the nursery, maybe? That's a happy place, right?"

"Pretty much," the nurse admitted.

"It's still important, too, right? Taking care of little babies, it's routine, yeah, but it still has to be done the right way, doesn't it?"

"Of course."

"But you don't do that. You work Neuro. You do the hard stuff."

"Somebody has to—" *Bingo!* Kelly thought, cutting her off.

"It's hard—hard to do the work, hard on you—it hurts you some, right?"

"Sometimes."

"But you do it anyway," Kelly pointed out.

"Yes," Sandy said, not as an admission, but something stronger.

"That's why Tim did what he did." He saw the understanding there, or perhaps the beginnings of it, just for a moment before her lingering grief pushed the argument aside.

"It still doesn't make sense."

"Maybe the *thing* doesn't make sense, but the *people* do," Kelly suggested. That was about as far as his mind stretched. "Sorry, I'm not a priest, just a broken-down Navy chief."

"Not too broken down," O'Toole said, finishing her lunch.

"And part of that is your doing, ma'am. Thank you." That earned him another smile.

"Not all our patients get better. We're kind of proud of those who do."

"Maybe we're all trying to save the world, Sandy, one little bit at a time," Kelly said. He rose and insisted on walking her back to the unit. It took the whole five minutes to say what he wanted to say.

"You know, I'd like to have dinner with you, maybe? Not now, but, well—"

"I'll think about it," she allowed, half dismissing the idea, half wondering about it, knowing as Kelly did that it was too soon for both of them, though probably not as much for her. What sort of man was this? she asked herself. What were the dangers of knowing him?

13

Agendas

It was his first-ever visit to the Pentagon. Kelly felt ill at ease, wondering if he should have worn his khaki chief's uniform, but his time for wearing that had passed. Instead he wore a blue lightweight suit, with a miniature of the Navy Cross ribbon on the lapel. Arriving in the bus and car tunnel, he walked up a ramp and searched for a map of the vast building, which he quickly scanned and memorized. Five minutes later he entered the proper office.

"Yes?" a petty officer asked.

"John Kelly, I have an appointment with Admiral Maxwell." He was invited to take a seat. On the coffee table was a copy of *Navy Times,* which he hadn't read since leaving the service. But Kelly was able to control his nostalgia. The bitches and gripes he read about hadn't changed very much.

"Mr. Kelly?" a voice called. He rose and walked through the open door. After it closed, a red do-not-disturb light blinked on to warn people off.

"How are you feeling, John?" Maxwell asked first of all.

"Fine, sir, thank you." Civilian now or not, Kelly could not help feeling uneasy in the presence of a flag officer.

That got worse at once when another door opened to admit two more men, one in civilian clothes, the other a rear admiral—another aviator, Kelly saw, with the medal of honor, which was even more intimidating. Maxwell did the introductions.

"I've heard a lot about you," Podulski said, shaking the younger man's hand.

"Thank you, sir." Kelly didn't know what else to say.

"Cas and I go back a ways," Maxwell observed, handling the introductions. "I got fifteen"—he pointed to the aircraft panel hanging on the wall—"Cas got eighteen."

"All on film, too," Podulski assured him.

"I didn't get any," Greer said, "but I didn't let the oxygen rot my brain either." In addition to wearing soft clothes, this admiral had the map case. He took one out, the same panel he had back at his home, but more marked up. Then came the photographs, and Kelly got another look at the face of Colonel Zacharias, this time enhanced somehow or other, and recognizably similar to the ID photo Greer put next to it.

"I was within three miles of the place," Kelly noted. "Nobody ever told me about—"

"It wasn't there yet. This place is new, less than two years old," Greer explained.

"Any more pictures, James?" Maxwell asked.

"Just some SR-71 overheads, high-obliques, nothing new in them. I have a guy checking every frame of this place, a good guy, ex–Air Force. He reports to me only."

"You're going to be a good spy," Podulski noted with a chuckle.

"They need me there," Greer replied in a lighthearted voice bordered with serious meaning. Kelly just looked at the other three. The banter wasn't unlike that in a chief's mess, but the language was cleaner. He looked over at Kelly again. "Tell me about the valley."

"A good place to stay away from—"

"First, tell me how you got little Dutch back. Every step of the way," Greer ordered.

Kelly needed fifteen minutes for that, from the time he left USS *Skate* to the moment the helicopter had lifted him and Lieutenant Maxwell from the river's estuary for the flight to *Kitty Hawk*. It was an easy story to tell. What surprised him were the looks the admirals passed back and forth.

Kelly wasn't equipped to understand the looks yet. He didn't really think of the admirals as old or even as totally human. They were *admirals,* godlike, ageless beings who made important decisions and looked as they should look, even the one out of uniform. Nor did Kelly think of himself as young. He'd seen combat, after which every man is forever changed. But their perspective was different. To Maxwell, Podulski, and Greer, this young man was not terribly unlike what they had been thirty years earlier. It was instantly clear that Kelly was a warrior, and in seeing him they saw themselves. The furtive looks they traded were not unlike those of a grandfather watching his grandson take his first tentative step on the living-room rug. But these were larger and more serious steps.

"That was some job," Greer said when Kelly finished. "So this area is densely populated?"

"Yes and no, sir. I mean, it's not a city or like that, but some farms and stuff. I heard and saw traffic on this road. Only a few trucks, but lots of bicycles, oxcarts, that sort of thing."

"Not much military traffic?" Podulski asked.

"Admiral, that stuff would be on this road here." Kelly tapped the map. He saw the notations for the NVA units. "How are you planning to get in here?"

"There's nothing easy, John. We've looked at a helicopter insertion, maybe even trying an amphibious assault and racing up this road."

Kelly shook his head. "Too far. That road is too easy to defend. Gentlemen, you have to understand, Vietnam is a real nation in arms, okay? Practically everybody there has been in uniform, and giving people guns makes them feel like part of the team. There are enough people with guns there to give you a real pain coming up this way. You'd never make it."

"The people really support the communist government?"

Podulski asked. It was just too much for him to believe. But not for Kelly.

"Jesus, Admiral, why do you think we've been fighting there so long? Why do you think nobody helps pilots who get shot down? They're not *like* us over there. That's something we've never understood. Anyway, if you put Marines on the beach, nobody's going to welcome them. Forget racing up this road, sir. I've been there. It ain't much of a road, not even as good as it looks on these pictures. Drop a few trees and it's closed." Kelly looked up. "Has to be choppers."

He could see the news was not welcome, and it wasn't hard to understand why. This part of the country was dotted with antiaircraft batteries. Getting a strike force in wasn't going to be easy. At least two of these men were pilots, and if a ground assault had looked promising to them, then the triple-A problem must have been worse than Kelly appreciated.

"We can suppress the flak," Maxwell thought.

"You're not talking about -52s again, are you?" Greer asked.

"*Newport News* goes back on the gunline in a few weeks. John, ever see her shoot?"

Kelly nodded. "Sure did. She supported us twice when we were working close to the coast. It's impressive what those eight-inchers can do. Sir, the problem is, how many things do you need to go right for the mission to succeed? The more complicated things get, the easier it is for things to go wrong, and even one thing can be real complicated." Kelly leaned back on the couch, and reminded himself that what he had just said wasn't only for the admirals to consider.

"Dutch, we have a meeting in five minutes," Podulski said reluctantly. This meeting had not been a successful one, he thought. Greer and Maxwell weren't so sure of that. They had learned a few things. That counted for something.

"Can I ask why you're keeping this so tight?" Kelly asked.

"You guessed it before." Maxwell looked over at the junior flag officer and nodded.

"The Song Tay job was compromised," Greer said. "We don't know how, but we found out later through one of our sources that they knew—at least suspected—something was coming. They expected it later, and we ended up hitting the place right after they evacuated the prisoners, but before they had their ambush set up. Good luck, bad luck. They didn't expect Operation KINGPIN for another month."

"Dear God," Kelly breathed. "Somebody over here deliberately betrayed them?"

"Welcome to the real world of intelligence operations, Chief," Greer said with a grim smile.

"But *why?*"

"If I ever meet the gentleman, I will be sure to ask." Greer looked at the others. "That's a good hook for us to use. Check the records of the operation, real low-key like?"

"Where are they?"

"Eglin Air Force base, where the KINGPIN people trained."

"Whom do we send?" Podulski asked.

Kelly could feel the eyes turn in his direction. "Gentlemen, I was just a chief, remember?"

"Mr. Kelly, where's your car parked?"

"In the city, sir. I took the bus over here."

"Come with me. There's a shuttle bus you can take back later."

They walked out of the building in silence. Greer's car, a Mercury, was parked in a visitor slot by the river entrance. He waved for Kelly to get in and headed towards the George Washington Parkway.

"Dutch pulled your package. I got to read it. I'm impressed, son." What Greer didn't say was that on his battery of enlistment tests, Kelly had scored an average of 147 on three separately formatted IQ tests. "Every commander you had sang your praises."

"I worked for some good ones, sir."

"So it appears, and three of them tried to get you into OCS, but Dutch asked you about that. I also want to know why you didn't take the college scholarship."

"I was tired of schools. And the scholarship was for swimming, Admiral."

"That's a big deal at Indiana, I know, but your marks were plenty good to get an academic scholarship. You attended a pretty nice prep school—"

"That was a scholarship, too." Kelly shrugged. "Nobody in my family ever went to college. Dad served a hitch in the Navy during the war. I guess it just seemed like something to do." That it had been a major disappointment to his father was something he'd never told anyone.

Greer pondered that. It still didn't answer things. "The last ship I commanded was a submarine, *Daniel Webster.* My chief of the boat, senior chief sonarman, the guy had a doctorate in physics. Good man, knew his job better than I knew mine, but not a leader, shied away from it some. You didn't, Kelly. You tried to, but you didn't."

"Look, sir, when you're out there and things happen, somebody has to get it done."

"Not everybody sees things that way. Kelly, there's two kinds of people in the world, the ones who need to be told and the ones who figure it out all by themselves," Greer pronounced.

The highway sign said something that Kelly didn't catch, but it wasn't anything about CIA. He didn't tumble to it until he saw the oversized guardhouse.

"Did you ever interact with Agency people while you were over there?"

Kelly nodded. "Some. We were—well, you know about it, Project PHOENIX, right? We were part of that, a small part."

"What did you think of them?"

"Two or three of them were pretty good. The rest—you want it straight?"

"That's exactly what I want," Greer assured him.

"The rest are probably real good mixing martinis, shaken not stirred," Kelly said evenly. That earned him a rueful laugh.

"Yeah, people here do like to watch the movies!" Greer found his parking place and popped his door open. "Come with me, Chief." The out-of-uniform admiral led Kelly in the front door and got him a special visitor's pass, the kind that required an escort.

For his part, Kelly felt like a tourist in a strange and foreign land. The very normality of the building gave it a sinister edge. Though an ordinary, and rather new, government office building, CIA headquarters had some sort of aura. It wasn't like the real world somehow. Greer caught the look and chuckled, leading Kelly to an elevator, then to his sixth-floor office. Only when they were behind the closed wooden door did he speak.

"How's your schedule for the next week?"

"Flexible. I don't have anything tying me down," Kelly answered cautiously.

James Greer nodded soberly. "Dutch told me about that, too. I'm very sorry, Chief, but my job right now concerns twenty good men who probably won't see their families again unless we do something." He reached into his desk drawer.

"Sir, I'm real confused right now."

"Well, we can do it hard or easy. The hard way is that Dutch makes a phone call and you get recalled to active duty," Greer said sternly. "The easy way is, you come to work for me as a civilian consultant. We pay you a per-diem that's a whole lot more than chief's pay."

"Doing what?"

"You fly down to Eglin Air Force Base, via New Orleans and Avis, I suppose. This"—Greer tossed a billfold-like ID in Kelly's lap—"gives you access to their records. I want you to go over the operations plans as a model for what we want to do." Kelly looked at the photo-ID. It even had his old Navy photograph, which showed only his head, as in a passport.

"Wait a minute, sir. I am not qualified—"

"As a matter of fact I think you are, but from the outside it will look like you're not. No, you're just a very junior consultant gathering information for a low-level report that nobody important will ever read. Half the money we spend in this damned agency goes out the door that way, in case nobody ever told you," Greer said, his irritation with the Agency giving flight to mild exaggeration. "That's how routine and pointless we want it to look."

"Are you really serious about this?"

"Chief, Dutch Maxwell is willing to sacrifice his career for those men. So am I. If there's a way to get them out—"

"What about the peace talks?"

How do I explain that to this kid? Greer asked himself. "Colonel Zacharias is officially dead. The other side said so, even published a photo of a body. Somebody went to visit his wife, along with the base chaplain and another Air Force wife to make things easier. Then they gave her a week to vacate the official quarters, just to make things official," Greer added. "He's *officially* dead. I've had some very careful talks with some people, and we"—this part came very hard—"our country will not screw up the peace talks over something like this. The photo we have, enhancement and all, isn't good enough for a court of law, and that's the standard that is being used. That's a standard of proof that we can't possibly meet, and the people who made the decision know it. They don't want the peace talks sidetracked, and if the lives of twenty more men are necessary to end the goddamned war, then that's what it takes. Those men are being written off."

It was almost too much for Kelly to believe. How many people did America write off every year? And not all were in uniform, were they? Some were right at home, in American cities.

"It's really that bad?"

The fatigue on Greer's face was unmistakable. "You know why I took this job? I was ready to retire. I've served my time, commanded my ships, done my work. I'm ready for a nice house and playing golf twice a week and doing a little consulting on the side, okay? Chief, too many people come to places like this, and reality to them is a memo. They focus in on 'process' and forget that there's a human being at the far end of the paper chain. That's why I stayed in. Somebody has to try and put a little reality back into the process. We're handling this as a 'black' project. Do you know what that means?"

"No, sir, I don't."

"It's a new term that's cropped up. That means it doesn't exist. It's crazy. It shouldn't be that way, but it is. Are you on the team or not?"

New Orleans . . . Kelly's eyes narrowed for a moment that lingered into fifteen seconds and a slow nod. "If you think I can help, sir, then I will. How much time do I have?"

Greer managed a smile and tossed a ticket folder into Kelly's lap. "Your ID is in the name of John Clark; should be easy to remember. You fly down tomorrow afternoon. The return ticket is open, but I want to see you next Friday. I expect good work out of you. My card and private line are in there. Get packed, son."

"Aye aye, sir."

Greer rose and walked Kelly to the door. "And get receipts for everything. When you work for Uncle Sam you have to make sure everyone gets paid off properly."

"I will do that, sir." Kelly smiled.

"You can catch the blue bus back to the Pentagon outside." Greer went back to work as Kelly left the office.

The blue shuttle bus arrived moments after he walked up to the covered pickup point. It was a curious ride. About half the people who boarded were uniformed, and the other half civilians. Nobody talked to anyone, as though merely exchanging a pleasantry or a comment on the Washington Senators' continuing residency at the bottom of the American League would violate security. He smiled and shook his head until he reflected on his own secrets and intentions. And yet—Greer had given him an opportunity that he'd not considered. Kelly leaned back in his seat and looked out the window while the other passengers on the bus stared fixedly forward.

"They're real happy," Piaggi said.

"I told you all along, man. It helps to have the best product on the street."

"Not everybody's happy. Some people are sitting on a couple hundred keys of French stuff, and we've knocked the price down with our special introductory offer."

Tucker allowed himself a good laugh. The "old guard" had been overcharging for years. That was monopoly pricing for you. Anyone would have taken the two of them for businessmen, or perhaps lawyers, since there were lots of both in this restaurant two blocks from the new Garmatz courthouse. Piaggi was somewhat better dressed, in Italian silk, and he made a mental note to introduce Henry to his tailor. At least the guy had learned how to groom himself. Next he had to learn not to dress too flashy. Respectable was the word. Just enough that people treated you with deference. The flashy ones, like the pimps, were playing a dangerous game that they were too dumb to understand.

"Next shipment, twice as much. Can your friends handle it?"

"Easy. The people in Philly are especially happy. Their main supplier had a little accident."

"Yeah, I saw the paper yesterday. Sloppy. Too many people in the crew, right?"

"Henry, you just keep getting smarter and smarter. Don't get too smart, okay? Good advice," Piaggi said with quiet emphasis.

"That's cool, Tony. What I'm saying is, let's not make that kind of mistake ourselves, okay?"

Piaggi relaxed, sipping his beer. "That's right, Henry. And I don't mind saying that it's nice to do business with somebody who knows how to organize. There's a lot of curiosity about where your stuff comes from. I'm covering that for you. Later on, though, if you need more financing . . . "

Tucker's eyes blazed briefly across the table. "No, Tony. No now, no forever."

"Okay for now. Something to think about for later."

Tucker nodded, apparently letting it go at that, but wondering what sort of move his "partner" might be planning. Trust, in this sort of enterprise, was a variable quantity. He trusted Tony to pay on time. He'd offered Piaggi favorable terms, which had been honored, and the eggs this goose laid were his real life insurance. He was already at the point that a missed payment wouldn't harm his operation, and as long as he had a steady supply of good heroin, they'd do business like a business, which was why he'd approached them in the first place. But there was no real loyalty here. Trust stopped at his usefulness. Henry had never expected any more than that, but if his associate ever started pressing on his pipeline . . .

Piaggi wondered if he'd pressed too far, wondering if Tucker knew the potential of what they were doing. To control distribution on the entire East Coast, and do so from within a careful and secure organization, that was like a dream come true. Surely he would soon need more capital, and his contacts were already asking how they might help. But he could see that Tucker did not recognize the innocence of the inquiry, and if he discussed it further, protesting his goodwill, that would only make things worse. And so Piaggi went back to his lunch and decided to leave things be for a while. It was too bad. Tucker was a very smart small-timer, but still a small-timer at heart. Perhaps he'd learn to grow. Henry could never be "made," but he could still become an important part of the organization.

"Next Friday okay?" Tucker asked.

"Fine. Keep it secure. Keep it smart."

"You got it, man."

It was an uneventful flight, a Piedmont 737 out of Friendship International Airport. Kelly rode coach, and the stewardess brought him a light lunch. Flying over America was so different from his other adventures aloft. It surprised him how many swimming pools there were. Everywhere you flew, lifting off from the airport, over the rolling hills of Tennessee, the overhead sun would sparkle off little square patches of chlorine-blue water surrounded by green grass. His country appeared to be so benign a place, so comfortable, until you got closer. But at least you didn't have to watch for tracer fire.

The Avis counter had a car waiting, along with a map. It turned out that he could have flown into Panama City, Florida, but New Orleans, he decided, would suit him just fine. Kelly tossed both his suitcases into the trunk and headed east. It was rather like driving his boat, though somewhat more hectic, dead time in which he could let his mind work, examining possibilities and procedures, his eyes sweeping the traffic while his mind saw something else entirely. That was when he started to smile, a thin, composed expression that he never thought about while his imagination took a careful and measured look at the next few weeks.

Four hours after landing, having passed through the lower ends of Mississippi and Alabama, he stopped his car at the main gate of Eglin AFB. A fitting place for the KINGPIN troopers to have trained, the heat and humidity were an exact match with the country they'd ultimately invaded, hot and moist. Kelly waited outside the guard post for a blue Air Force sedan to meet him. When it did, an officer got out.

"Mr. Clark?"

"Yes." He handed over his ID folder. The officer actually saluted him, which was a novel experience. Clearly someone was overly impressed with CIA. This young officer had probably never interacted with anybody from there. Of course, Kelly had actually bothered to wear a tie in the hope of looking as respectable as possible.

"If you'll follow me, please, sir." The officer, Captain Griffin, led him to a first-floor room at the Bachelor Officers' Quarters, which was somewhat like a medium-quality motel and agreeably close to the beach. After helping Kelly get unpacked, Griffin walked him to the Officers' Club, where, he said, Kelly had visitor's privileges. All he had to do was show his room key.

"I can't knock the hospitality, Captain." Kelly felt obligated to buy the first beer. "You know why I'm here?"

"I work intelligence," Griffin replied.

"KINGPIN?" As though in a movie, the officer looked around before replying.

"Yes, sir. We have all the documents you need ready for you. I hear you worked special ops over there, too."

"Correct."

"I have one question, sir," the Captain said.

"Shoot," Kelly invited between sips. He'd dried out on the drive from New Orleans.

"Do they know who burned the mission?"

"No," Kelly replied, and on a whim added, "Maybe I can pick up something on that."

"My big brother was in that camp, we think. He'd be home now except for whatever . . . "

"Motherfucker," Kelly said helpfully. The Captain actually blushed.

"If you identify him, then what?"

"Not my department," Kelly replied, regretting his earlier comment. "When do I start?"

"Supposed to be tomorrow morning, Mr. Clark, but the documents are all in my office."

"I need a quiet room, a pot of coffee, maybe some sandwiches."

"I think we can handle that, sir."

"Then let me get started."

Ten minutes later, Kelly got his wish. Captain Griffin had supplied him with a yellow legal pad and a battery of pencils. Kelly started off with the first set of reconnaissance photographs, these taken by an RF-101 Voodoo, and as with SENDER GREEN, the discovery of Song Tay had been a complete accident, the random discovery of an unexpected thing in a place expected to have been a minor military training installation. But in the yard of the camp had been letters stomped in the dirt, or arranged with stones or hanging laundry: "K" for "come and get us out of here," and other such marks that had been made under the eyes of the guards. The list of people who had become involved was a genuine who's who of the special operations community, names that he knew only by reputation.

The configuration of the camp was not terribly different from the one in which he was interested now, he saw, making appropriate notes. One document surprised him greatly. It was a memo from a three-star to a two-star, indicating that the Song Tay mission, though important in and of itself, was also a means to an end. The three-star had wanted to validate his ability to get special-ops teams into North Vietnam. That, he said, would open all sorts of possibilities, one of which was a certain dam with a generator room . . . oh, yeah, Kelly realized. The three-star wanted a hunting license, to insert several teams in-country and play the same games OSS had behind German lines in the Second World War. The memo concluded with a note that political factors made the latter aspect of POLAR CIRCLE—one of the first cover names for what became Operation KINGPIN—extremely sensitive. Some would see it as a widening of the war. Kelly looked up, finishing his second cup of coffee. What was it about politicians? he wondered. The enemy could do anything he wanted, but our side was always trembling at the possibility of being seen to widen the war. He'd even seen some of that at his level. The PHOENIX project, the deliberate targeting of the enemy's political infrastructure, was a matter of the greatest sensitivity. Hell, they wore uniforms, didn't they? A man in a combat zone wearing a uniform was fair game in anyone's book of rules, wasn't he? The other side took out local mayors and schoolteachers with savage abandon. There was a blatant double standard to the way the war had been conducted. It was a troubling thought, but Kelly set it aside as he turned back to the second pile of documents.

Assembling the team and planning the operation had taken half of forever. Good men all, however. Colonel Bull Simons, another man he knew only by his reputation as one of the toughest sharp-end combat commanders any Army had ever produced. Dick Meadows, a younger man in the same mold. Their only waking thought was to bring harm and distraction to the enemy, and they were skilled in doing so with small forces and minimum exposure. How they must have lusted for this mission, Kelly thought. But the oversight they'd had to deal with . . . Kelly counted ten separate documents to higher authority, promising success—as though a memo could make such a claim in the harsh world of combat operations—before he stopped bothering to count them. So many of them used the same language until he suspected that a form letter had been ginned up by some unit clerk. Probably someone who'd run out of fresh words for his colonel, and then expressed a sergeant's contempt for the interlocutors by giving them the same words every time, in the expectation that the repeats would never be noticed—and they hadn't been. Kelly spent three hours going through reams of paper between Eglin and CIA, concerns of deskbound bean-counters distracting the men in green suits, "helpful" suggestions from people who probably wore ties to bed, all of which had required answers from the operators who carried guns . . . and so KINGPIN had grown from a relatively minor and dramatic insertion mission to a Cecil B. De Mille epic which had more than once gone to the White House, there becoming known to the President's National Security Council staff—

And that's where Kelly stopped, at two-thirty in the morning, defeated by the next pile of paper. He locked everything up in the receptacles provided and jogged back to his room at the Q, leaving notice for a seven-o'clock wake-up call.

It was surprising how little sleep you needed when there was important work to be done. When the phone rang at seven, Kelly bounced from the bed, and fifteen minutes later was running along the beach barefoot, in a pair of shorts. He was not alone. He didn't know how many people were based at Eglin, but they were not terribly different from himself. Some had to be special operations types, doing things that he could only guess at. You could tell them from the somewhat wider shoulders. Running was only part of their fitness game. Eyes met and evaluated others, and expressions were exchanged as each man knew what the other was thinking—*How tough is* he, *really?*—as an automatic mental exercise, and Kelly smiled to himself that he was enough a part of the community that he merited that kind of competitive respect. A large breakfast and shower left him fully refreshed, enough to get him back to his clerk's work, and on the walk back to the office building, he asked himself, surprisingly, why he'd ever left this community of men. It was, after all, the only real home he'd known after leaving Indianapolis.

And so the days continued. He allowed himself two days of six-hours' sleep, but never more than twenty minutes for a meal, and not a single drink after that first beer, though his exercise periods grew to several hours per day, mainly, he told himself, to firm up. The real reason was one that he never quite admitted. He wanted to be the toughest man on that early-morning beach, not just an associate part of the small, elite community. Kelly was a SEAL again, more than that, a bullfrog, and more still, he was again becoming *Snake*. By the third or fourth morning, he could see the change. His face and form were now an expected part of the morning routine for the others. The anonymity only made it better, that and the scars of battle, and some would wonder what he'd done wrong, what mistakes he'd made. Then they would remind themselves that he was still in the business, scars and all, not knowing that he'd left it—*quit,* Kelly's mind corrected, with not a little guilt.

The paperwork was surprisingly stimulating. He'd never before tried to figure things out in quite this way, and he was surprised to find he had a talent for it. The operational planning, he saw, had been a thing of beauty flawed by time and repetition, like a beautiful girl kept too long in her house by a jealous father. Every day the mockup of the Song Tay camp had been erected by the players, and each day, sometimes more than once, taken down lest Soviet reconnaissance satellites take note of what was there. How debilitating that must have been to the soldiers. And it had all taken so long, the soldiers practicing while the higher-ups had dithered, pondering the intelligence information so long that . . . the prisoners had been moved.

"Damn," Kelly whispered to himself. It wasn't so much that the operation might have been betrayed. It had just taken too long . . . and that meant that *if* it had been betrayed, the leaker had probably been one of the last people to discover what was afoot. He set that thought aside with a penciled question.

The operation itself had been meticulously planned, everything done just right, a primary plan and a number of alternates, with each segment of the team so fully briefed and trained that every man could do every function in his sleep. *Crashing* a huge Sikorsky helicopter right in the camp itself so that the strike team would not have to wait to get to the objective. Using miniguns to take down the guard towers like chainsaws against saplings. No finesse, no pussyfooting, no movie-type bullshit, just brutally direct

force. The after-action debriefs showed that the camp guards
had been immolated in moments. How elated the troopers
must have felt as the first minute or two of the operation
had run more smoothly than their simulations, and then
the stunning, bitter frustration when the "negative Item"
calls had come again and again over their radio circuits.
"Item" was the simple code word for an American POW,
and none were home that night. The soldiers had assaulted
and liberated an empty camp. It wasn't hard to imagine
how quiet the choppers must have been for the ride back
to Thailand, the bleak emptiness of failure after having
done everything better than right.

There was, nonetheless, much to learn here. Kelly made
his notes, cramping fingers and wearing out numerous pencils. Whatever else it had been, KINGPIN was a supremely
valuable lesson. So much had gone right, he saw, and all
of that could be shamelessly copied. All that had gone
wrong, really, was the time factor. Troops of that quality
could have gone in much sooner. The quest for perfection
hadn't been demanded at the operational level, but higher,
from men who had grown older and lost contact with
the enthusiasm and intelligence of youth. And a consequence had been the failure of the mission, not because
of Bull Simons, or Dick Meadows, or the Green Berets
who'd gladly placed their lives at risk for men they'd
never met, but because of others too afraid to risk their
careers and their offices—matters of far greater importance, of course, than the blood of the guys at the sharp
end. Song Tay was the whole story of Vietnam, told in
the few minutes it had taken for a superbly-trained team
to fail, betrayed as much by process as by some misguided or traitorous person hidden in the federal bureaucracy.

SENDER GREEN would be different, Kelly told himself.
If for no other reason than that it was being run as a private
game. If the real hazard to the operation was oversight,
then why not eliminate the oversight?

"Captain, you've been very helpful," Kelly said.
"Find what you wanted, Mr. Clark?" Griffin asked.

"Yes, Mr. Griffin," he said, dropping unconsciously back into naval terminology for the young officer. "The analysis you did on the secondary camp was first-rate. In case nobody ever told you, that might have saved a few lives. Let me say something for myself: I wish we'd had an intel-weenie like you working for us when I was out in the weeds."

"I can't fly, sir. I have to do something useful," Griffin replied, embarrassed by the praise.

"You do." Kelly handed over his notes. Under his eyes they were placed in an envelope that was then sealed with red wax. "Courier the package to this address."

"Yes, sir. You're due some time off. Did you get any sleep at all?" Captain Griffin asked.

"Well, I think I'll depressurize in New Orleans before I fly back."

"Not a bad place for it, sir." Griffin walked Kelly to his car, already loaded.

One other bit of intelligence had been stunningly easy, Kelly thought, driving out. His room in the Q had contained a New Orleans telephone directory in which, to his amazement, had been the name he'd decided to look up while sitting in James Greer's office in CIA.

This was the shipment that would make his reputation, Tucker thought, watching Rick and Billy finish loading things up. Part of it would find its way to New York. Up until now he'd been an interloper, an outsider with ambition. He'd provided enough heroin to get people interested in himself and his partners—the fact that he had partners had attracted interest of its own, in addition to the access. But now was different. Now he was making his move to be part of the crew. He would be seen as a serious businessman because this shipment would handle all the needs of Baltimore and Philadelphia for . . . maybe a month, he estimated. Maybe less if their distribution network was as good as they said. The leftovers would start meeting the growing needs in the Big Apple, which needed the help after a major bust. After so long a time of making small steps, here was the giant one. Billy turned on a radio to get the sports news, and got a weather forecast instead.

"I'm glad we're going now. Storms coming in later."

Tucker looked outside. The sky was still clear and untroubled. "Nothing for us to worry about," he told them.

He loved New Orleans, a city in the European tradition, which mixed Old World charm with American zest. Rich in history, owned by Frenchmen and Spaniards in their turn, it had never lost its traditions, even to its maintenance of a legal code that was nearly incomprehensible to the other forty-nine states, and was often a matter of some befuddlement to federal authorities. So was the local patois, for many mixed French into their conversations, or what they called French. Pierre Lamarck's antecedents had been Acadians, and some of his more distant relatives were still residents in the local bayous. But customs that were eccentric and entertaining to tourists, and a comfortable life rich in tradition to others, had little interest to Lamarck except as a point of reference, a personal signature to distinguish him from his peers. That was hard enough to do, as his profession demanded a certain flash, a personal flair. He accentuated his uniqueness with a white linen suit complete with vest, a white, long-sleeved shirt, and a red, solid-color tie, which fitted his own image as a respectable, if ostentatious, local businessman. That went along well with his personal automobile, an eggshell-white Cadillac. He eschewed the ornamental excesses that some other pimps placed on their automobiles, nonfunctional exhaust pipes. One supposed Texan even had the horns of a longhorn steer on his Lincoln, but that one was really poor white trash from lower Alabama, and a boy who didn't know how to treat his ladies.

This latter quality was Lamarck's greatest talent, he told himself with great satisfaction, opening the door of his car for his newest acquisition, fifteen years old and recently broken in, possessed of an innocent look and demure movement that made her a noteworthy and enticing member of his eight-girl stable. She'd earned the pimp's unaccustomed courtesy with a special service of her own

earlier in the day. The luxury car started on the first turn
of the key, and at seven-thirty, Pierre Lamarck set off on
another night's work, for the nightlife in his city started
early and lasted late. There was a convention in town,
distributors for something or other. New Orleans attracted
a lot of conventions, and he could track the cash flow of
his business by their comings and goings. It promised to
be a warm and lucrative night.

It had to be him, Kelly thought, half a block away, behind
the wheel of his still-rented car. Who else would wear
a three-piece suit and be accompanied by a young girl
dressed in a tight mini? Certainly not an insurance agent.
The girl's jewelry looked cheap-showy even from this
distance. Kelly slipped the car into gear, following. He
was able to lie back. How many white Caddies could
there be? he wondered, crossing the river, three cars back,
eyes locked on his target while peripheral parts of his mind
dealt with the other traffic. Once he had to risk a ticket at
a traffic light, but otherwise the tracking was simple. The
Caddy stopped at the entrance to an upscale hotel, and
he saw the girl get out, and walk towards the door, her
stride a mixture of the businesslike and the resigned. He
didn't want to see her face all that closely, afraid of what
memories might result from it. This was not a night for
emotion. Emotion was what had given him the mission.
How he accomplished it had to come from something else.
That would be a constant struggle, Kelly told himself, but
one he would have to contend with successfully. That was,
after all, why he'd come to this place, on this night.

The Cadillac moved on a few more blocks, finding a
parking place by a seedy, flashy bar close enough to the
nice hotels and businesses that a person could walk there
quickly, yet never be far from the safety and comfort of
civilized safety. A fairly constant stream of taxicabs told
him that this aspect of local life had a firm, institutional
foundation. He identified the bar in question and found
himself a place to park three blocks away.

There was a dual purpose in parking so far from his
objective. The walk in along Decatur Street gave him both

a feel for the territory and a look at likely places for his action. Surely it would be a long night. Some short-skirted girls smiled at him as mechanically as the changing of the traffic lights, but he walked on, his eyes sweeping left and right while a distant voice reminded him of what he had once thought of such gestures. He silenced that voice with another, more current thought. His clothes were casual, what a moderately comfortable man might wear in this humid heat and heavy atmosphere, dark and anonymous, loose and baggy. They proclaimed money, but not too much, and his stride told people that he was not one to be trifled with. A man of understated substance having a discreet night on the wild side.

He walked into Chats Sauvages at eight-seventeen. His initial impression of the bar was smoke and noise. A small but enthusiastic rock band played at the far end. There was a dance floor, perhaps twenty-five feet square, where people his age and younger moved with the music; and there was Pierre Lamarck, sitting at a table in the corner with a few acquaintances, or so they seemed from their demeanor. Kelly walked to the men's room, both an immediate necessity and an opportunity to look the place over. There was another entrance on the side, but no closer to Lamarck's table than the one through which both he and Kelly had entered. The nearest path to the white Caddy led past Kelly's place at the bar, and that told him where his perch had to be. Kelly ordered a beer and turned conveniently to watch the band.

At nine-ten two young women came to Lamarck. One sat on his lap while the other nibbled at his ear. The other two men at the table watched with neutral interest while both women handed over something to him. Kelly couldn't tell what it was because he was looking towards the band, careful not to stare too often in Lamarck's direction. The pimp solved that problem immediately: it turned out, unsurprisingly, to be cash, and the man somewhat ostentatiously wrapped the bills around a roll removed from his pocket. Flash money, Kelly had troubled himself to learn, an important part of a pimp's public image. The first two women left, and Lamarck was soon joined by another, in what became an intermittent stream that didn't stop. His table mates enjoyed the same sort of traffic, Kelly saw, sipping their drinks, paying cash, joshing with and occasionally fondling the waitress who served them, then tipping her heavily by way of apology. Kelly moved from time to time. He removed his jacket, rolling up his sleeves, to present a different image to the bar's patrons, and limiting himself to two beers, which he nursed as carefully as he could. Tedious as it was, he disregarded the unpleasant nature of the evening, instead noticing things. Who went where. Who came and left. Who stayed. Who lingered in one place. Kelly soon started recognizing patterns and identifying individuals to whom he assigned names of his own creation. Most of all he observed everything there was to see about Lamarck. He never took off his suit jacket, kept his back to the wall. He talked amiably with his two companions, but their familiarity was not that of friends. Their joking was too affected. There was too much emphasis on their interactive gestures, not the casual comfort that you saw among people whose company was shared for some purpose other than money. Even pimps got lonely, Kelly thought, and though they sought out their own kind, theirs was not friendship but mere association. The philosophical observations he put aside. If Lamarck never took off his coat, he had to be carrying a weapon.

Just after midnight, Kelly put his coat back on and made yet another trip to the men's room. In the toilet stall he took the automatic he'd hidden inside his slacks and moved it to the waistband. Two beers in four hours, he thought. His liver ought to have eliminated the alcohol from his system, and even if it hadn't, two beers should not have had much effect on one as bulky as he. It was an important statement which, he hoped, wasn't a lie.

His timing was good. Washing his hands for the fifth time, Kelly saw the door open in the mirror. Only the back of the man's head, but under the dark hair was a white suit, and so Kelly waited, taking his time until he heard the urinal flush. A sanitary sort of fellow, the man turned, and their eyes met in the mirror.

"Excuse me," Pierre Lamarck said. Kelly stepped away from the sink, still drying his hands with a paper towel.

"I like the ladies," he said quietly.

"Hmph?" Lamarck had no less than six drinks in him, and his liver had not been up to the task, which didn't prevent his self-admiration in the dirty mirror.

"The ones that come up to you." Kelly lowered his voice. "They, uh, work for you, like?"

"You might say that, my man." Lamarck took out a black plastic comb to readjust his coiffeur. "Why do you ask?"

"I might need a few," Kelly said with embarrassment.

"A few? You sure you can handle that, my man?" Lamarck asked with a sly grin.

"Some friends in town with me. One's having a birthday, and—"

"A party," the pimp observed pleasantly.

"That's right." Kelly tried to be shy, but mainly came off as being awkward. The error worked in his favor.

"Well, why didn't you say so? How many ladies do you require, sir?"

"Three, maybe four. Talk about it outside? I could use some air."

"Sure thing. Just let me wash my hands, okay?"

"I'll be outside the front door."

The street was quiet. Busy city though New Orleans might be, it was still the middle of the week, and the sidewalks, while not empty, weren't crowded either. Kelly waited, looking away from the bar's entrance until he felt a friendly hand on his back.

"It's nothing to be embarrassed about. We all like to have a little fun, especially when we're away from home, right?"

"I'll pay top dollar," Kelly promised with an uneasy smile.

Lamarck grinned, like the man of the world he was, to put this chicken farmer at ease. "With my ladies, you have to. Anything else you might need?"

Kelly coughed and took a few steps, willing Lamarck to follow, which he did. "Maybe some, well, something to help us party, like?"

"I can handle that, too," Lamarck said as they approached an alley.

"I think I met you before, couple years back. I remember the girl, really, her name was . . . Pam? Yeah, Pam. Thin, tawny hair."

"Oh, yeah, she was fun. She's not with me anymore," Lamarck said lightly. "But I have lots more. I cater to the men who like 'em young and fresh."

"I'm sure you do," Kelly said, reaching behind his back. "They're all on—I mean they all use things that make it—"

"Happy stuff, man. So they're always in the mood to party. A lady has to have the proper attitude." Lamarck stopped at the entrance to the alley, looking outward, maybe worried about cops, which suited Kelly just fine. Behind him, he had not troubled to see, was a dark, scarcely lit corridor of blank brick walls, inhabited by nothing more than trash cans and stray cats, and open at the far end. "Let's see. Four girls, rest of the evening, shall we say, and something to help get the party started . . . five hundred should do it. My girls aren't cheap, but you will get your money's—"

"Both hands in the open," Kelly said, the Colt automatic leveled twelve inches from the man's chest.

Lamarck's first response was a disbelieving bluster: "My man, that is a very foolish—"

Kelly's voice was all business. "Arguing with a gun is even more foolish, my man. Turn, walk down the alley, and you might even make it back to the bar for a nightcap."

"You must need money real bad to try something this dumb," the pimp said, trying an implied threat.

"Your roll worth dying for?" Kelly asked reasonably. Lamarck measured the odds and turned, moving into the shadows.

"Stop," Kelly told him after fifty yards, still behind the blank wall of the bar, or perhaps another just like it. His left arm grabbed the man's neck and pushed him against the bricks. His eyes looked up and down the alley three times. His ears searched for sounds separate from traffic noise and distorted music. For the moment it was a safe and quiet place. "Hand me your gun—real careful."

"I don't—" The sound of a hammer being cocked sounded awfully loud, that close to his ear.

"Do I look stupid?"

"Okay, okay," Lamarck said, his voice losing its smooth edge now. "Let's be real cool. It's only money."

"That's smart," Kelly said approvingly. A small automatic appeared. Kelly put his right index finger into the trigger guard. There was no sense in putting fingerprints on the weapon. He was taking enough chances, and as careful as he'd been to this point, the dangers of his action were suddenly very real and very large. The pistol fit nicely into his coat pocket.

"Let's see the roll next."

"Right here, man." Lamarck was starting to lose it. That was both good and bad, Kelly thought. Good because it was pleasing to see. Bad because a panicked man might do something foolish. Instead of relaxing, Kelly actually became more tense.

"Thank you, Mr. Lamarck," Kelly said politely, to calm the man.

Just then he wavered, and his head turned a few inches or so, as his consciousness asserted itself through the six drinks he'd had this evening. "Wait a minute—you said you knew Pam."

"I did," Kelly said.

"But why—" He turned farther to see a face that was bathed in darkness, only eyes showing with light glistening off their moisture, and the rest of the face a shadow white.

"You're one of the guys who ruined her life."

Outrage: "Hey, man, she came to *me!*"

"And you got her on pills so she could party real good, right?" the disembodied voice asked. Lamarck could hardly remember what the man looked like now.

"That was *business,* so you met her, so she was a good fuck, right?"

"She certainly was."

"I shoulda trained her better an' you coulda had her again insteada—was, you say?"

"She's dead," Kelly told him, reaching in his pocket. "Somebody killed her."

"So? I didn't do it!" It seemed to Lamarck that he was facing a final exam, a test he didn't understand, based on rules he didn't know.

"Yes, I know that," Kelly said, screwing the silencer onto the pistol. Lamarck saw that somehow, his eyes making the adjustment to the darkness. His voice became a shrill rasp.

"Then what are you doing this for?" the man said, too puzzled even to scream, too paralyzed by the incongruity of the past few minutes, by the passage of his life from the normality of his hangout bar to its end only forty feet away in front of a windowless brick wall, and he had to have an answer. Somehow it was more important than the escape, whose attempt he knew to be futile.

Kelly thought about that for a second or two. He could have said many things, but it was only fair, he decided, to tell the man the truth as the gun came up quickly and finally.

"Practice."

14
Lessons Learned

The early flight back from New Orleans to Washington National was too short for a movie, and Kelly had already eaten breakfast. He settled on a glass of juice at his window seat and was thankful that the flight was only about a third full as, after every combat action of his life, he went over every detail. It was a habit that had begun in the SEALs. Following every training exercise there had been an event called various things by his various commanders. "Performance Critique" seemed most appropriate at the moment.

His first mistake had been the product of something desired and something forgotten. In wanting to see Lamarck die in the darkness, he'd stood too close, simultaneously forgetting that head wounds often bleed explosively. He'd jumped out of the way of the spouting blood like a child avoiding a wasp in his backyard, but had still not escaped it entirely. The good news was that he'd made only that one mistake; and his selection of dark clothing had mitigated the danger there. Lamarck's wounds had been immediately and definitively fatal. The pimp had fallen to the ground as limp as a rag doll. The two screws that Kelly had drilled in the top of his pistol held a small cloth bag he'd sewn himself, and the bag had caught the two ejected cartridge cases, leaving the police who'd investigate the scene without that valuable bit of evidence. His stalk had been effectively carried out, just one more anonymous face in a large and anonymous bar.

His hastily selected site for the elimination had also worked well enough. He remembered walking down the alley and blending back into the sidewalk traffic, walking the distance to his car and driving back to the motel. There, he'd changed clothes, bundling the blood-splattered slacks, shirt, and, just to be sure, the underwear as well, into a plastic cleaner bag, which he'd walked across the street and deposited in a supermarket Dumpster. If the clothing was discovered, it might well be taken as something soiled by a sloppy meatcutter. He hadn't met with Lamarck in the open. The only lighted place in which they'd spoken was the bar's men's room, and there fortune—and planning—had smiled on him. The sidewalk they'd walked on was too dark and too anonymous. Perhaps a casual observer who might have known Lamarck could give an investigator a rough idea of Kelly's size, but little else, and that was a reasonable gamble to have taken, Kelly judged, looking down at the wooded hills of northern Alabama. It had been an apparent robbery, the pimp's one thousand, four hundred seventy dollars of flash money tucked away in his bag. Cash was cash, after all, and not to have taken it would have shown the police that there had been a real motive in the elimination aside from something easily understandable and agreeably random. The physical side of the event—he could not think of it as a crime—was, he thought, as clean as he could have done it.

Psychological? Kelly asked himself. More than anything else Kelly had tested his nerve, the elimination of Pierre Lamarck having been a kind of field experiment, and in that he'd surprised himself. It had been some years since Kelly had entered combat, and he'd halfway expected a case of the shakes after the event. Such things had happened to him more than once before, but though his stride away from Lamarck's body had been slightly uneasy, he'd handled the escape with the sort of tense aplomb that had marked many of his operations in Vietnam. So much had come back to him. He could catalog the familiar sensations that had returned as though he'd been watching a training film of his own production: the increased sensory awareness, as though his skin had been sandblasted, exposing every nerve; hearing, sight, smell all amplified. *I was so fucking alive at that moment,* he thought. It was vaguely sad that such a thing had happened due to the ending of a human life, but Lamarck had long since forfeited his right to life. In any just universe, a person—Kelly simply could not think of him as a *man*—who exploited helpless girls simply did not deserve the privilege of breathing the same air used by other human beings. Perhaps he'd taken the wrong turn, been unloved by his mother or beaten by his father. Perhaps he'd been socially deprived, raised in poverty, or exposed to inadequate schooling. But those were matters for psychiatrists or social workers. Lamarck had acted normally enough to function as a person in his community, and the only question that mattered to Kelly was whether or not he had lived his life in accordance with his own free will. That had clearly been the case, and those who took improper actions, he had long since decided, ought to have considered the possible consequences of those actions. Every girl they exploited might have had a father or mother or sister or brother or lover to be outraged at her victimization. In knowing that and in taking the risk, Lamarck had knowingly gambled his life to some greater or lesser degree. *And gambling means that sometimes you lose,* Kelly told himself. If he hadn't weighed the hazards accurately enough, that was not Kelly's problem, was it?

No, he told the ground, thirty-seven thousand feet below.

And what did Kelly feel about it? He pondered that question for a while, leaning back and closing his eyes as though napping. A quiet voice, perhaps conscience, told him that he ought to feel *something,* and he searched for a genuine emotion. After several minutes of consideration, he could find none. There was no loss, no grief, no remorse. Lamarck had meant nothing to him and probably would be no loss to anyone else. Perhaps his girls—Kelly had counted five of them in the bar—would be without a pimp, but then maybe one of them would seize the opportunity to correct her life. Unlikely, perhaps, but possible. It was realism that told Kelly he couldn't fix all the problems of the world; it was idealism that told him his inability to do so did not preclude him from addressing individual imperfections.

But all that took him away from the initial question: What did he *feel* about the elimination of Pierre Lamarck? The only answer he could find was, Nothing. The professional elation of having done something difficult was different from satisfaction, from the nature of the task. In ending the life of Pierre Lamarck he had removed something harmful from the surface of the planet. It had enriched him not at all—taking the money had been a tactic, a camouflage measure, certainly not an objective. It had not avenged Pam's life. It had not changed very much. It had been like stepping on an offensive insect—you did it and moved on. He would not try to tell himself different, but neither would his conscience trouble him, and that was sufficient to the moment. His little experiment had been a success. After all the mental and physical preparation, he had proven himself worthy of the task before him. Kelly's mind focused behind closed eyes on the mission before him. Having killed many men better than Pierre Lamarck, he could now think with confidence about killing men worse than the New Orleans pimp.

This time they visited him, Greer saw with satisfaction. On the whole, CIA's hospitality was better. James Greer had arranged parking in the VIP Visitors' area—the equivalent at the Pentagon was always haphazard and difficult to use—and a secure conference room. Cas Podulski thoughtfully selected a seat at the far end, close to the air-conditioning vent, where his smoking wouldn't bother anyone.

"Dutch, you were right about this kid," Greer said, handing out typed copies of the handwritten notes which had arrived two days earlier.

"Somebody ought to have put a gun to his head and walked him into OCS. He would have been the kind of junior officer we used to be."

Podulski chuckled at his end of the table. "No wonder he got out," he said with lighthearted bitterness.

"I'd be careful putting a gun to his head," Greer observed with a chuckle of his own. "I spent a whole night last week going through his package. This guy's a wild one in the field."

"Wild?" Maxwell asked with a hint of disapproval in his voice. "Spirited, you mean, James?"

Perhaps a compromise, Greer thought: "A self-starter. He had three commanders and they backed him on every play he made except one."

"PLASTIC FLOWER? The political-action major he killed?"

"Correct. His lieutenant was furious about that, but if it's true about what he had to watch, the only thing you can fault was his judgment, rushing in the way he did."

"I read through that, James. I doubt I could have held back," Cas said, looking up from the notes. Once a fighter pilot, always a fighter pilot. "Look at this, even his grammar is good!" Despite his accent, Podulski had been assiduous in learning his adopted language.

"Jesuit high school," Greer pointed out. "I've gone over our in-house assessment of KINGPIN. Kelly's analysis tracks on every major point except where he calls a few spades."

"Who did the CIA assessment?" Maxwell asked.

"Robert Ritter. He's a European specialist they brought in. Good man, a little terse, knows how to work the field, though."

"Operations guy?" Maxwell asked.

"Right." Greer nodded. "Did some very nice work working Station Budapest."

"And why," Podulski asked, "did they bring in a guy from that side of the house to look over the KINGPIN operation?"

"I think you know the answer, Cas," Maxwell pointed out.

"If BOXWOOD GREEN goes, we need an Operations guy from this house. We have to have it. I don't have the juice to do everything. Are we agreed on that?" Greer looked around the table, seeing the reluctant nods. Podulski looked back down at his documents before saying what they all thought.

"Can we trust him?"

"He's not the one who burned KINGPIN. Cas, we have Jim Angleton looking at that. It was his idea to bring Ritter onboard. I'm new here, people. Ritter knows the bureaucracy here better than I do. He's an operator; I'm just an analyst-type. And his heart's in the right place. He damned near lost his job protecting a guy—he had an agent working inside GRU, and it was time to get him out. The decision-weenies upstairs didn't like the timing, with the arms talks going on, and they told him no. Ritter brought the guy out anyway. It turned out his man had something State needed, and that saved Ritter's career." It hadn't done much for the martini-mixer upstairs, Greer didn't add, but that was a person CIA was doing rather well without.

"Swashbuckler?" Maxwell asked.

"He was loyal to his agent. Sometimes people here forget about that," Greer said.

Admiral Podulski looked up the table. "Sounds like our kind of guy."

"Brief him in," Maxwell ordered. "But you tell him that if I ever find out some civilian in the building fucked up our chance to get these men out, I will *personally* drive down to Pax River, *personally* check out an A-4, and *personally* napalm his house."

"You should let me do that, Dutch," Cas added with a smile. "I've always had a better hand for dropping things. Besides, I have six hundred hours in the Scooter."

Greer wondered how much of that was humor.

"What about Kelly?" Maxwell asked.

"His CIA identity is 'Clark' now. If we want him in, we can utilize him better as a civilian. He'd never get over being a chief, but a civilian doesn't have to worry about rank."

"Make it so," Maxwell said. It was convenient, he thought, to have a naval officer seconded to CIA, wearing civilian clothes but still subject to military discipline.

"Aye aye, sir. If we get to training, where will it be done?"

"Quantico Marine Base," Maxwell replied. "General Young is a pal from the old days. Aviator. He understands."

"Marty and I went through test-pilot school together," Podulski explained. "From what Kelly says, we don't need that many troops. I always figured KINGPIN was overmanned. You know, if we bring this off, we have to get Kelly his Medal."

"One thing at a time, Cas." Maxwell set that aside, looking back to Greer as he stood. "You will let us know if Angleton finds out anything?"

"Depend on it," Greer promised. "If there's a bad guy inside, we'll get his ass. I've fished with the guy. He can pull a brook trout out of thin air." After they left he set an afternoon meeting with Robert Ritter. It meant putting Kelly off, but Ritter was more important now, and while there was a rush on the mission, it wasn't all that great a rush.

Airports were useful places, with their bustling anonymity and telephones. Kelly placed his call, as he waited for his baggage to appear—he hoped—in the proper place.

"Greer," the voice said.

"Clark," Kelly replied, smiling at himself. It seemed so James Bond to have a cover name. "I'm at the airport, sir. Do you still want me in this afternoon?"

"No. I'm tied up." Greer flipped through his daybook. "Tuesday . . . three-thirty. You can drive in. Give me your car type and license number."

Kelly did that, surprised that he'd been bumped. "You get my notes, sir?"

"Yes, and you did a fine job, Mr. Clark. We'll be going over them Tuesday. We are very pleased with your work."

"Thank you, sir," Kelly said into the phone.

"See you Tuesday." The line clicked off.

"And thanks for that, too," Kelly said after he hung up. Twenty minutes later he had his bags and was walking off to his car. About an hour after that he was in his Baltimore apartment. It was lunchtime, and he fixed a couple of sandwiches, chasing both down with Coca-Cola. He hadn't shaved today, and his heavy beard made a shadow on his face, he saw in the mirror. He'd leave it. Kelly headed into the bedroom for a lengthy nap.

The civilian contractors didn't really understand what they were up to, but they were being paid. That was all they really required, since they had families to feed and house payments to make. The buildings they had just erected were well to the right of spartan: bare concrete block, nothing in the way of utilities, built to odd proportions, not like American construction at all except for the building materials. It was as though their size and shape had been taken from some foreign construction manual. All the dimensions were metric, one worker noted, though the actual plans were noted in odd numbers of inches and feet, as American building plans had to be. The job itself had been simple enough, the site already cleared when they'd first arrived. A number of the construction workers were former servicemen, most ex-Army, but a few Marines as well, and they were at turns pleased and uncomfortable to be at this sprawling Marine base in the wooded hills of northern Virginia. On the drive into the construction site they could see the morning formations of officer candidates jogging along the roads. All those bright young kids with shaved heads, one former corporal of the 1st Marines had thought this very morning. How many would get their commissions? How many would deploy *there?* How many would come home early, shipped in steel boxes? It was nothing he could foresee or control, of course. He'd served his time in hell and returned unscratched, which was still remarkable to the former grunt who'd heard all too often the supersonic *crack* of rifle bullets. To have survived at all was amazing enough.

The roofs were finished. Soon it would be time to leave the site for good, after a mere three weeks of well-paid work. Seven-day weeks. Plenty of overtime on every working day he'd been here. Somebody had wanted this place built in a hurry. Some very odd things about it, too. The parking lot, for one. A hundred-slot blacktopped lot. Someone was even painting the lines. For buildings with no utilities? But strangest of all was the current job that he'd drawn because the site foreman liked him. Playground equipment. A large swing set. A huge jungle gym. A sandbox, complete with half a dump truck's load of sand. All the things that his two-year-old son would someday cavort on when he was old enough for kindergarten in the Fairfax County Schools. But it was structural work, and it required assembly, and the former Marine and two others fumbled through the plans like fathers in a backyard, figuring which bolts went where. Theirs was not to reason why, not as union construction workers on a government contract. Besides, he thought, there was no understanding the Green Machine. The Corps operated according to a plan that no man really figured out, and if they wanted to pay him overtime for this, then that was another monthly house payment earned for every three days he came here. Jobs like this might be crazy, but he sure liked the money. About the only thing he didn't like was the length of the commute. Maybe they'd have to do something equally crazy at Fort Belvoir, he hoped, finishing the last item on the jungle gym. He could drive from his house to that place in twenty minutes or so. But the Army was a little more rational than the Corps. It had to be.

"So what's new?" Peter Henderson asked. They were dining just off The Hill, two acquaintances from New England, one a Harvard graduate, the other from Brown, one a junior aide to a senator, the other a junior member of the White House staff.

"It never changes, Peter," Wally Hicks said resignedly. "The peace talks are going nowhere. We keep killing their people. They keep killing ours. I don't think there's ever going to be peace in our time, you know?"

"It has to, Wally," Henderson said, reaching for his second beer.

"If it doesn't—" Hicks started to say gloomily.

Both had been seniors at the Andover Academy in October 1962, close friends and roommates who had shared class notes and girlfriends. Their real political majority had come one Tuesday night, however, when they'd watched their country's president give a tense national address on the black-and-white television in the dormitory lounge. There were missiles in Cuba, they'd learned, something that had been hinted at in the papers for several days, but these were children of the TV generation, and contemporary reality came in horizontal lines on a glass tube. For both of them it had been a stunning if somewhat belated entrée into the real world for which their expensive boarding school ought to have prepared them more speedily. But theirs was the fat and lazy time for American youth, all the more so that their wealthy families had further insulated them from reality with the privilege that money could buy without imparting the wisdom required for its proper use.

The sudden and shocking thought had arrived in both minds at the same instant: it could all be *over*. Nervous chatter in the room told them more. They were *surrounded* by Targets. Boston to the southeast, Westover Air Force Base to the southwest, two other SAC bases, Pease and Loring, within a hundred-mile radius. Portsmouth Naval Base, which housed nuclear submarines. If the missiles flew, they would not survive; either the blast or the fallout would get them. And neither of them had even gotten *laid* yet. Other boys in the dorm had made their claims—some of them, perhaps, might even have been true—but Peter and Wally didn't lie to each other, and neither had scored, despite repeated and earnest efforts. How was it possible that the world didn't take their personal needs into account? Weren't they the elite? Didn't their lives *matter?*

It was a sleepless night, that Tuesday in October, Henderson and Hicks sitting up, whispering their conversation, trying to come to terms with a world that had transformed itself from comfort to danger without the proper warning. Clearly, they had to find a way to change things. After graduation, though each went a separate way, Brown and Harvard were separated by only a brief drive, and both their friendship and their mission in life continued and grew. Both majored in political science because that was the proper major for entering into the process which really mattered in the world. Both got master's degrees, and most important of all, both were noticed by people who mattered—their parents helped there, and in finding a form of government service that did not expose them to uniformed servitude. The time of their vulnerability to the draft was early enough that a quiet telephone call to the right bureaucrat was sufficient.

And so, now, both young men had achieved their own entry-level positions in sensitive posts, both as aides to important men. Their heady expectations of landing policymaking roles while still short of thirty had run hard into the blank wall of reality, but in fact they were closer to it than they fully appreciated. In screening information for their bosses and deciding what appeared on the master's desk in what order, they had a real effect on the decision process; and they also had access to data that was wide, diverse, and sensitive. As a result in many ways both knew more than their bosses did. And that, Hicks and Henderson thought, was fitting, because they often *understood* the important things better than their bosses did. It was all so clear. War was a *bad thing* and had to be avoided entirely, or when that wasn't possible, ended as rapidly as one could bring it about; because war ended lives, and that was a *very bad thing,* and with war out of the way, people could learn to solve their disagreements peacefully. It was so obvious both stood in wonder that so many people failed to grasp the simple clarity of the Truth that both men had discovered in high school.

There was only one difference between the two, really. As a White House staffer, Hicks worked inside the system. But he shared everything with his classmate, which was okay because both had Special Access security clearances—and besides, he needed the feedback of a trained mind he both understood and trusted.

Hicks didn't know that Henderson had taken one step beyond him. If he couldn't change government policy from the inside, Henderson had decided during the Days of Rage following the Cambodia incursion, he had to get help from the outside—some outside agency that could assist him in blocking government actions that endangered the world. There were others around the world who shared his aversion to war, people who saw that you couldn't force people to accept a form of government they really didn't want. The first contact had come at Harvard, a friend in the peace movement. Now he communicated with someone else. He ought to have shared this fact with his friend, Henderson told himself, but the timing just wasn't right. Wally might not understand yet.

"—it has to, and it will," Henderson said, waving to the waitress for another round. "The war will end. We will get out. Vietnam will have the government it wants. We will have lost a war, and that will be a good thing for our country. We'll learn from that. We'll learn the limits of our power. We'll learn to live and let live, and then we can give peace a chance."

Kelly arose after five. The events of the previous day had left him more fatigued than he had appreciated, and besides, traveling had always tired him out. But he was not tired now. A total of eleven hours' sleep in the last twenty-four had left him fully rested and alert. Looking in the mirror, he saw the heavy beard from almost two days' worth of growth. Good. Then he selected his clothing. Dark, baggy, and old. He'd taken the whole bundle down to the laundry room and washed everything with hot water and extra bleach to abuse the fabric and mute the colors, making already shabby clothing look all the more unsightly. Old white gym socks and sneakers completed the picture, though both were more serviceable than their appearance suggested. The shirt was too large for him, and long, which suited his purposes. A wig completed the picture he wanted, made of coarse black Asian hair, none too long. He held it under a hot-water faucet and soaked it, then brushed it out in a deliberately sloppy way. He'd have to find a way to make it smell, too, Kelly thought.

Nature again provided some additional cover. Evening storms were rolling in, bringing with them leaf-swirling wind and rain that covered him on the way to his Volkswagen. Ten minutes later he parked near a neighborhood liquor store, where he purchased a bottle of cheap yellow wine and a paper bag to semiconceal it. He took off the twist cap and poured about half of it into a gutter. Then it was time to go.

It all looked different now, Kelly thought. It was no longer an area he could pass through, seeing the dangers or not. Now it was a place of sought danger. He drove past the spot where he'd led Billy and his Roadrunner, turning to see if the tire marks were still there—they weren't. He shook his head. That was in the past, and the future occupied his thoughts.

In Vietnam there always seemed to be the treeline, a spot where you passed from the openness of a field or farmed area into the jungle, and in your mind that was the place where safety ended and danger began because Charlie lived in the woods. It was just a thing of the mind, a boundary imaginary rather than real, but in looking around this area he saw the same thing. Only this time he wasn't walking in with five or ten comrades in striped jungle fatigues. He was driving through the barrier in a rust-speckled car. He accelerated, and just like that, Kelly was in the jungle, and again at war.

He found a parking place among autos as decrepit as his own, and quickly got out, as he once would have run away from a helicopter LZ the enemy might see and approach, and headed into an alley dotted with trash and several discarded appliances. His senses were alert now. Kelly was already sweating, and that was good. He wanted to sweat and smell. He took a mouthful of the cheap wine and sloshed it around his mouth before letting it dribble out onto his face, neck, and clothing. Bending down briefly, he got a handful of dirt, which he rubbed onto his hands and forearms, and a little onto his face. An afterthought added some to the hair of his wig, and by the time Kelly had passed through the city-block-length of the alley, he was just one more wino, a street bum like those who dotted the area even more than the drug pushers. Kelly adjusted his gait, slowing down and becoming deliberately sloppy in his movements while his eyes searched for a good perch. It wasn't all that difficult. Several of the houses in the area were vacant, and it was just a matter of finding one with a good view. That required half an hour. He settled for a corner house with upstairs bay windows. Kelly entered it from the back door. He nearly jumped out of his skin when he saw two rats in the wreckage of what a few years before had been a kitchen. *Fuckin' rats!* It was foolish to fear them, but he loathed their small black eyes and leprous hair and naked tails.

"Shit!" he whispered to himself. Why hadn't he thought about that? Everybody got a creeping chill from something: spiders, snakes, or tall buildings. For Kelly, it was rats. He walked towards the doorway, careful to keep his distance. The rats merely looked at him, edging away but less afraid of him than he was of them. "Fuck!" they heard him whisper, leaving them to their meal.

What followed was anger. Kelly made his way up the unbanistered stairs and found the corner bedroom with the bay windows, furious with himself for allowing such a dumb and cowardly distraction. Didn't he have a perfectly good weapon for dealing with rats? What were they going to do, assemble into a battalion for a rat-wave attack? That thought finally caused an embarrassed smile in the darkness of the room. Kelly crouched at the windows, evaluating his field of view and his own visibility. The windows were dirty and cracked. Some glass panels were missing entirely, but each window had a comfortable sill on which he could sit, and the house's location at the corner of two streets gave him a long view along each of the four main points of the compass, since this part of the city streets was laid out along precisely surveyed north-south, east-west lines. There wasn't enough illumination on the streets for those below him to see into the house. With his dark, shabby clothing, in this unfit and derelict house, Kelly was invisible. He took out a small pair of binoculars and began his reconnaissance.

His first task was to learn the environment. The rain showers passed, leaving moisture in the air that made for little globes of light punctuated by the flying insects attracted to their eventual doom by streetlights. The air was still warm, perhaps mid-eighties, falling slowly, and Kelly was perspiring a little. His first analytical thought was that he should have brought water to drink. Well, he could correct that in the future, and he didn't really need a drink for some hours. He had thought to bring chewing gum, and that made things easier. The sounds of the streets were curious. In the jungle he'd heard the tittering of insects, the calls of birds, and the flapping of bats. Here it was automotive sounds near or distant, the occasional squeal of brakes, conversations loud or muted, barking dogs, and rattling trash cans, all of which he analyzed while watching through his binoculars and considering his actions for the evening.

Friday night, the start of the weekend, and people were making their purchases. It seemed this was a busy night for the gentry business. He identified one probable dealer a block and a half away. Early twenties. Twenty minutes of observation gave him a good physical picture of both the dealer and his assistant-"lieutenant." Both moved with the ease that came both with experience and security in their place, and Kelly wondered if they had fought either to take this place or to defend it. Perhaps both. They had a thriving trade, perhaps regular customers, he thought, watching both men approach an imported car, joshing with the driver and passenger before the exchange was made, shaking hands and waving afterwards. The two were of roughly the same height and build, and he assigned them the names Archie and Jughead.

Jesus, what an innocent I was, Kelly told himself, looking down another street. He remembered that one asshole they'd caught smoking grass in 3rd SOG—right before going out on a job. It had been Kelly's team, and Kelly's man, and though he was an FNK right from SEAL school, that was no excuse at all. Confronting the man, he'd explained reasonably but positively that going into the field in anything less than a hundred-percent-alert state could mean death for the entire team. "Hey, man, it's cool, I know what I'm doing" had not been a particularly intelligent response, and thirty seconds later another team member had found it necessary to pull Kelly off the instantly ex-member of the team, who was gone the next day, never to return.

And that had been the only instance of drug use in the entire unit as far as Kelly knew. Sure, off-duty they'd had their beer bashes, and when Kelly and two others had flown to Taiwan for R&R, their collective vacation had not been terribly unlike a mobile earthquake of drunken excesses. Kelly truly believed that was different, blind to the explicit double standard. But they didn't drink beer before heading into the boonies either. It was a matter of common sense. It had also been one of unit morale. Kelly knew of no really elite unit that had developed a drug problem. The problem—a very serious one indeed, he'd heard—was mainly in the REMFs and the draftee units composed of young men whose presence in Vietnam was even less willing than was his own, and whose officers hadn't been able to overcome the problem either because of their own failings or their not dissimilar feelings.

Whatever the cause, the fact that Kelly had hardly considered the problem of drug use was both logical and absurd. He set all of that aside. However late he had learned about it, it was here before his eyes.

Down another street was a solo dealer who didn't want, need, or have a lieutenant. He wore a striped shirt and had his own clientele. Kelly thought of him as Charlie Brown. Over the next five hours, he identified and classified three other operations within his field of view. Then the selection process began. Archie and Jughead seemed to be doing the most business, but they were in line of sight to two others. Charlie Brown seemed to have his block entirely to himself, but there was a bus stop only a few yards away. Dagwood was right across the street from the Wizard. Both had lieutenants, and that took care of that. Big Bob was even larger than Kelly, and his lieutenant was larger still. That was a challenge. Kelly wasn't really looking for challenges—yet.

I need to get a good map of the area and memorize it. Divide it into discrete areas, Kelly thought. *I need to plot bus lines, police stations. Learn police shift times. Patrol patterns. I have to learn this area, a ten-block radius ought to be enough. I can't ever park the car in the same place twice, no one parking place even visible from another.*

You can hunt a specific area only once. That means you have to be careful whom you select. No movement on the street except in darkness. Get a backup weapon . . . not a gun . . . a knife, a good one. A couple lengths of rope or wire. Gloves, rubber ones like women use to wash dishes. Another thing to wear, like a bush jacket, something with pockets—no, something with pockets on the inside. A water bottle. Something to eat, candy bars for energy. More chewing gum . . . maybe bubble gum? Kelly thought, allowing himself some levity. He checked his watch: three-twenty.

Things were slowing down out there. Wizard and his number-two walked away from their piece of sidewalk, disappearing around a corner. Dagwood soon did the same, getting right into his car while his lieutenant drove. Charlie was gone the next time he looked. That left Archie and Jughead to his south, and Big Bob to the west, both still making sporadic sales, many of them still to upscale clients. Kelly continued to watch for another hour, until Arch and Jug were the last to call it quits for the night . . . and they disappeared rather fast, Kelly thought, not sure how they'd done it. Something else to check. He was stiff when he rose, and made another note on that. He shouldn't sit still so much. His dark-accustomed eyes watched the stairs as he descended, as quietly as he could, for there was activity in the house next door. Fortunately, the rats were gone, too. Kelly looked out the back door, and finding the alley empty, walked away from the house, keeping his pace to that of a drunk. Ten minutes later his car was in sight. Fifty yards away, Kelly realized that he'd unthinkingly parked the car close to a streetlight. That was a mistake not to be repeated, he reproached himself, approaching slowly and drunkenly until he was within a car length. Then, first checking up and down the now-vacant street, he got in quickly, started the engine, and pulled away. He didn't flip on the headlights until he was two blocks away, turning left and reentering the wide vacant corridor, leaving the not-so-imaginary jungle and heading north towards his apartment.

In the renewed comfort and safety of his car he went over everything he'd seen in the past nine hours. The dealers were all smokers, igniting their cigarettes with what seemed to be Zippo lighters whose bright flames would injure their night vision. The longer the night got, the less business there was and the sloppier they seemed to become. They were human. They got tired. Some stayed out longer than others. Everything he'd seen was useful and important. In their operating characteristics, and especially in their differences, were their vulnerabilities.

It had been a fine night, Kelly thought, passing the city's baseball stadium and turning left onto Loch Raven Boulevard, relaxing finally. He even considered a sip of the wine, but this wasn't the time to indulge in any bad habits. He removed his wig, wiping away the sweat it had caused. Jesus, he was thirsty.

He addressed that need ten minutes later, having parked his car in the proper place and made his way quietly into the apartment. He looked longingly at the shower, needing the clean feeling after being surrounded by dust and squalor and . . . rats. That final thought made him shudder. *Fucking rats,* he thought, filling a large glass with ice, then adding tap water. He followed it with several more, using his free hand to strip off his clothing. The air conditioning felt wonderful, and he stood in front of the wall unit, letting the chilled air wash over his body. All this time, and he didn't need to urinate. Had to take water with him from now on. Kelly took a package of lunch meat from the refrigerator and made two thick sandwiches, chased down by another pint of ice water.

Need a shower bad, he told himself. But he couldn't allow himself one. He'd have to get used to the feeling of a sticky, plasticlike coating all over his body. He'd have to like it, cultivate it, for in that was a part of his personal safety. His grime and odor were part of his disguise. His looks and smell had to make people look away from him, to avoid coming too close. He couldn't be a person now. He had to be a street creature, shunned. Invisible. The beard was even darker now, he saw in the mirror before heading to the bedroom, and his last decision of the day was to sleep on the floor. He couldn't dirty up new sheets.

15

Lessons Applied

Hell began promptly at eleven that morning, though Colonel Zacharias had no way of knowing the time. The tropical sun seemed always to be overhead, beating mercilessly down. Even in his windowless cell there was no escaping it, any more than he could escape the insects that seemed to thrive on the heat. He wondered how anything could thrive here, but everything that did seemed to be something that hurt or offended him, and that was as concise a definition of hell as anything he'd learned in the temples of his youth. Zacharias had been trained for possible capture. He'd been through the survival, evasion, resistance, and escape course, called SERE School. It was something you had to do if you flew airplanes for a living, and it was purposefully the most hated thing in the military because it did things to otherwise pampered Air Force and Navy officers that Marine drill instructors would have quailed at—things which were, in any other context, deeds worthy of a general court-martial followed by a lengthy term at Leavenworth or Portsmouth. The experience for Zacharias, as for most others, had been one he would never willingly repeat. But his current situation was not of his own volition either, was it? And he *was* repeating SERE School.

He'd considered capture in a distant sort of way. It wasn't the sort of thing you could really ignore once you'd heard the awful, despairing electronic *rawwwww* of the emergency radios, and seen the 'chutes, and tried to organize a RESCAP, hoping the Jolly Green Giant helicopter could swoop in from its base in Laos or maybe a Navy "Big Mutha"—as the squids called the rescue birds—would race in from the sea. Zacharias had seen that work, but more often he'd seen it fail. He'd heard the panicked and tragically unmanly cries of airmen about to be captured: "Get me out of here," one major had screamed before another voice had come on the radio, speaking spiteful words none of them could understand, but which they had understood even so, with bitterness and killing rage. The Jolly crews and their Navy counterparts did their best, and though Zacharias was a Mormon and had never touched alcohol in his life, he had bought those chopper crews enough drinks to lay low a squad of Marines, in gratitude and awe at their bravery, for that was how you expressed your admiration within the community of warriors.

But like every other member of that community, he'd never really thought capture would happen to him. Death, that was the chance and the likelihood he'd thought about. Zacharias had been King Weasel. He'd helped invent that branch of his profession. With his intellect and superb flying skills he'd created the doctrine and validated it in the air. He'd driven his F-105 into the most concentrated antiair network anyone had yet built, actually seeking out the most dangerous weapons for his special attention, and using his training and intelligence to duel with them, matching tactic for tactic, skill for skill, teasing them, defying them, baiting them in what had become the most exhilarating contest any man had ever experienced, a chess game played in three dimensions over and under Mach-1, with him driving his two-seater Thud and with them manning Russian-built radars and missile launchers. Like mongoose and cobra, theirs was a very private vendetta played for keeps every day, and in his pride and his skill, he'd thought he would win, or, at worst, meet his end in the form of a yellow-black cloud that would mark a proper airman's death: immediate, dramatic, and ethereal.

He'd never thought himself a particularly brave man. He had his faith. Were he to meet death in the air, then he could look forward to staring God in the face, standing with humility at his lowly station and pride at the life he had lived, for Robin Zacharias was a righteous man, hardly ever straying from the path of virtue. He was a good friend to his comrades, a conscientious leader mindful of his men's needs; an upright family man with strong, bright, proud children; most of all, he was an Elder in his church who tithed his Air Force salary, as his station in the Church of Jesus Christ of Latter-Day Saints required. For all of those reasons he had never feared death. What lay beyond the grave was something whose reality he viewed with confidence. It was life that was uncertain, and his current life was the most uncertain of all, and faith even as strong as his had limits imposed by the body which contained it. That was a fact he either did not fully understand or somehow did not believe. His faith, the Colonel told himself, should be enough to sustain him through anything. Was. Should be. *Was,* he'd learned as a child from his teachers. But those lessons had been taught in comfortable classrooms in sight of the Wasatch Mountains, by teachers in clean white shirts and ties, holding their lesson books, speaking with confidence imparted by the history of their church and its members.

It's different here. Zacharias heard the little voice that said so, trying to ignore it, trying his best *not* to believe it, for believing it was a contradiction with his faith, and that contradiction was the single thing his mind could not allow. Joseph Smith had died for his faith, murdered in Illinois. Others had done the same. The history of Judaism and Christianity was replete with the names of martyrs—*heroes* to Robin Zacharias, because that was the word used by his professional community—who had sustained torture at Roman or other hands and had died with God's name on their lips.

But they didn't suffer as long as you, the voice pointed out. A few hours. The brief hellish minutes burning at the stake, a day or two, perhaps, nailed to the cross. That was one thing; you could see the end of it, and if you knew what lay beyond the end, then you could concentrate on that. But to see beyond the end, you had to know *where* the end was.

Robin Zacharias was alone. There were others here. He'd caught glimpses, but there was no communication. He'd tried the tap code, but no one ever answered. Wherever they were, they were too distant, or the building's arrangements didn't allow it, or perhaps his hearing was off. He could not share thoughts with anyone, and even prayers had limits to a mind as intelligent as his. He was afraid to pray for deliverance—a thought he was unable even to admit, for it would be an internal admission that his faith had somehow been shaken, and that was something he could not allow, but part of him knew that in *not* praying for deliverance, he was admitting something by omission; that if he prayed, and after a time deliverance didn't come, then his faith might start to die, and with that his soul. For Robin Zacharias, that was how despair began, not with a thought, but with the unwillingness to entreat his God for something that might not come.

He couldn't know the rest. His dietary deprivation, the isolation so especially painful to a man of his intelligence, and the gnawing fear of pain, for even faith could not take pain away, and all men know fear of that. Like carrying a heavy load, however strong a man might be, his strength was finite and gravity was not. Strength of body was easily understood, but in the pride and righteousness that came from his faith, he had failed to consider that the physical acted upon the psychological, just as surely as gravity but far more insidiously. He interpreted the crushing mental fatigue as a weakness assignable to something not supposed to break, and he faulted himself for nothing more than being human. Consultation with another Elder would have righted everything, but that wasn't possible, and in denying himself the escape hatch of merely admitting his human frailty, Zacharias forced himself further and further into a trap of his own creation, aided and abetted by people who wanted to destroy him, body and soul.

It was then that things became worse. The door to his cell opened. Two Vietnamese wearing khaki uniforms looked at him as though he were a stain on the air of their country. Zacharias knew what they were here for. He tried to meet them with courage. They took him, one man on each arm, and a third following behind with a rifle, to a larger room—but even before he passed through the doorway, the muzzle of the rifle stabbed hard into his back, right at the spot that still hurt, fully nine months after his painful ejection, and he gasped in pain. The Vietnamese didn't even show pleasure at his discomfort. They didn't ask questions. There wasn't even a plan to their abuse that he could recognize, just the physical attacks of five men operating all at once, and Zacharias knew that resistance was death, and while he wished for his captivity to end, to seek death in that way might actually be suicide, and he couldn't do that.

It didn't matter. In a brief span of seconds his ability to do anything at all was taken away, and he merely collapsed on the rough concrete floor, feeling the blows and kicks and pain add up like numbers on a ledger sheet, his muscles paralyzed by agony, unable to move any of his limbs more than an inch or two, wishing it would stop, knowing that it never would. Above it all he heard the cackling of their voices now, like jackals, devils tormenting him because he was one of the righteous and they'd gotten their hands on him anyway, and it went on, and on, and on—

A screaming voice blasted its way past his catatonia. One more desultory half-strength kick connected with his chest, and then he saw their boots draw back. His peripheral vision saw their faces cringe, all looking towards the door at the source of the noise. A final bellow and they hastily made their way out. The voice changed. It was a . . . *white* voice? How did he know that? Strong hands lifted him, sitting him up against the wall, and the face came into view. It was Grishanov.

"My God," the Russian said, his pale cheeks glowing red with anger. He turned and screamed something else in oddly accented Vietnamese. Instantly a canteen appeared, and he poured the contents over the American's face. Then he screamed something else and Zacharias heard the door close.

"Drink, Robin, drink this." He held a small metal flask to the American's lips, lifting it.

Zacharias took a swallow so quickly that the liquid was in his stomach before he noted the acidic taste of vodka. Shocked, he lifted his hand and tried to push it away.

"I can't," the American gasped, " . . . can't drink, can't . . . "

"Robin, it is medicine. This is not entertainment. Your religion has no rule against this. Please, my friend, you need this. It's the best I can do for you," Grishanov added in a voice that shuddered with frustration. "You must, Robin."

Maybe it is medicine, Zacharias thought. Some medicines used an alcohol base as a preservative, and the Church permitted that, didn't it? He couldn't remember, and in not knowing he took another swallow. Nor did he know that as the adrenaline that the beating had flooded into his system dissipated, the natural relaxation of his body would only be accentuated by the drink.

"Not too much, Robin." Grishanov removed the flask, then started tending to his injuries, straightening out his legs, using moistened cloth to clean up the man's face.

"Savages!" the Russian snarled. "Bloody stinking savages. I'll throttle Major Vinh for this, break his skinny little monkey neck." The Russian colonel sat down on the floor next to his American colleague and spoke from the heart. "Robin, we are enemies, but we are men also, and even war has rules. You serve your country. I serve mine. These . . . these people do not understand that without honor there is no true service, only barbarism." He held up the flask again. "Here. I cannot get anything else for the pain. I'm sorry, my friend, but I can't."

And Zacharias took another swallow, still numb, still disoriented, and even more confused than ever.

"Good man," Grishanov said. "I have never said this, but you are a courageous man, my friend, to resist these little animals as you have."

"Have to," Zacharias gasped.

"Of course you do," Grishanov said, wiping the man's face clean as tenderly as he might have done with one of his children. "I would, too." He paused. "God, to be flying again!"

"Yeah. Colonel, I wish—"

"Call me Kolya." Grishanov gestured. "You've known me long enough."

"Kolya?"

"My Christian name is Nikolay. Kolya is—nickname, you say?"

Zacharias let his head back against the wall, closing his eyes and remembering the sensations of flight. "Yes, Kolya, I would like to be flying again."

"Not too different, I imagine," Kolya said, sitting beside the man, wrapping a brotherly arm around his bruised and aching shoulders, knowing it was the first gesture of human warmth the man had experienced in almost a year. "My favorite is the MiG-17. Obsolete now, but, God, what a joy to fly. Just fingertips on the stick, and you—you just think it, just wish it in your mind, and the aircraft does what you want."

"The -86 was like that," Zacharias replied. "They're all gone, too."

The Russian chuckled. "Like your first love, yes? The first girl you saw as a child, the one who first made you think as a man thinks, yes? But the first airplane, that is better for one like us. Not so warm as a woman is, but much less confusing to handle." Robin tried to laugh, but choked. Grishanov offered him another swallow. "Easy, my friend. Tell me, what is your favorite?"

The American shrugged, feeling the warm glow in his belly. "I've flown nearly everything. I missed the F-94 and the -89, too. From what I hear, I didn't miss much there. The -104 was fun, like a sports car, but not much legs. No, the -86H is probably my favorite, just for handling."

"And the Thud?" Grishanov asked, using the nickname for the F-105 Thunderchief.

Robin coughed briefly. "You take the whole state of Utah to turn one in, darned if it isn't fast on the deck, though. I've had one a hundred twenty knots over the redline."

"Not really a fighter, they say. Really a bomb truck." Grishanov had assiduously studied American pilots' slang.

"That's all right. It will get you out of trouble in a hurry. You sure don't want to dogfight in one. The first pass better be a good one."

"But for bombing—one pilot to another, your bomb delivery in this wretched place is excellent."

"We try, Kolya, we surely do try," Zacharias said, his voice slurred. It amazed the Russian that the liquor had worked so quickly. The man had never had a drink in his life until twenty minutes earlier. How remarkable that a man would choose to live without drink.

"And the way you fight the rocket emplacements. You know, I've watched that. We are enemies, Robin," Kolya said again. "But we are also pilots. The courage and skill I have watched here, they are like nothing I have ever seen. You must be a professional gambler at home, yes?"

"Gamble?" Robin shook his head. "No, I can't do that."

"But what you did in your Thud . . . "

"Not gambling. Calculated risk. You plan, you know what you can do, and you stick to that, get a feel for what the other guy is thinking."

Grishanov made a mental note to refill his flask for the next one on his schedule. It had taken a few months, but he'd finally found something that worked. A pity that these little brown savages didn't have the wit to understand that in hurting a man you most often made his courage grow. For all their arrogance, which was considerable, they saw the world through a lens that was as diminutive as their stature and as narrow as their culture. They seemed unable to learn lessons. Grishanov sought out such lessons. Strangest of all, this one had been something learned from a fascist officer in the Luftwaffe. A pity also that the Vietnamese allowed only him and no others to perform these special interrogations. He'd soon write to Moscow about that. With the proper kind of pressure, they could make real use of this camp. How incongruously clever of the savages to establish this camp, and how disappointingly consistent that they'd failed to see its possibilities. How distasteful that he had to live in this hot, humid, insect-ridden country, surrounded by arrogant little people with arrogant little minds and the vicious dispositions of serpents. But the information he needed was here. As odious as his current work was, he'd discovered a phrase for it in a contemporary American novel of the type he read to polish up his already impressive language skills. A very American turn of phrase, too. What he was doing was "just business." That was a way of looking at the world he readily understood. A shame that the American next to him probably would not, Kolya thought, listening to every word of his rambling explanation of the life of a Weasel pilot.

The face in the mirror was becoming foreign, and that was good. It was strange how powerful habits were. He'd already filled the sink with hot water and had his hands lathered before his intellect kicked in and reminded him that he wasn't supposed to wash or shave. Kelly did brush his teeth. He couldn't stand the feel of film there, and for that part of the disguise he had his bottle of wine. *What foul stuff that was,* Kelly thought. *Sweet and heavy, strangely colored.* Kelly was not a wine connoisseur, but he did know that a decent table wine wasn't supposed to be the color of urine. He had to leave the bathroom. He couldn't stand to look in the mirror for long.

He fortified himself with a good meal, filling up with bland foods that would energize his body without making his stomach rumble. Then came the exercises. His ground-floor unit allowed him to run in place without the fear of disturbing a neighbor. It wasn't the same as real running, but it would suffice. Then came the push-ups. At long last his left shoulder was fully recovered, and the aches in his muscles were perfectly bilateral. Finally came the hand-to-hand exercises, which he practiced for general quickness in addition to the obvious utilitarian applications.

He'd left his apartment in daylight the day before, taking the risk of being seen in his disreputable state in order to visit a Goodwill store, where he'd found a bush jacket to go over his other clothing. It was so oversize and threadbare that they hadn't charged for it. Kelly had come to realize that disguising his size and physical conditioning was difficult, but that loose, shabby clothing did the trick. He'd also taken the opportunity to compare himself to the other patrons of the store. On inspection his disguise seemed to be effective enough. Though not the worst example of a street person, he certainly fit into the lower half, and the clerk who'd handed over the bush jacket for free had probably done so as much to get him out of the building as to express compassion for his state in life. And wasn't that an improvement? What would he have given in Vietnam to have been able to pass himself off as just another villager, and thus waited for the bad guys to come in?

He'd spent the previous night continuing his reconnaissance. No one had given him as much as a second look as he'd moved along the streets, just one more dirty, smelly drunk, not even worth mugging, which had ended his concerns about being spotted for what he really was. He'd spent another five hours in his perch, watching the streets from the second-story bay windows of the vacant house. Police patrols had turned out to be routine, and the bus noises far more regular than he'd initially appreciated.

Finished with his exercises, he disassembled his pistol and cleaned it, though it hadn't been used since his return flight from New Orleans. The same was done with the suppressor. He reassembled both, checking the match-up of the parts. He'd made one small change. Now there was a thin white painted line down the top of the silencer that served as a night-sight. Not good enough for distance shooting, but he wasn't planning any of that. Finished with the pistol, he loaded a round into the chamber and dropped the hammer carefully before slapping the clip into the bottom of the handgrip. He'd also acquired a Ka-Bar Marine combat knife in a surplus store, and while he'd watched the streets the night before, he'd worked the seven-inch Bowie-type blade across a whetstone. There was something that men feared about a knife even more than a bullet. That was foolish but useful. The pistol and knife went into his waistband side by side in the small of his back, well hidden by the loose bulk of the dark shirt and bush jacket. In one of the jacket pockets went a whiskey flask filled with tap water. Four Snickers went on the other side. Around his waist was a length of eight-gauge electrical wire. In his pants pocket was a pair of Playtex rubber gloves. These were yellow, not a good color for invisibility, but he'd been unable to find anything else. They did cover his hands without giving away much in feel and dexterity, and he decided to take them along. He already had a pair of cotton work gloves in the car that he wore when driving. After buying the car he'd cleaned it inside and out, wiping every glass, metal, and plastic surface, hoping that he'd removed every trace of fingerprints. Kelly blessed every police show and movie he'd ever seen, and prayed that he was being paranoid *enough* about his every tactic.

What else? he asked himself. He wasn't carrying any ID. He had a few dollars in cash in a wallet also obtained at Goodwill. Kelly had thought about carrying more, but there was no point in it. Water. Food. Weapons. Rope-wire. He'd leave his binoculars home tonight. Their utility wasn't worth the bulk. Maybe he'd get a set of compact ones—make a note. He was ready. Kelly switched on the TV and watched the news to get a weather forecast—cloudy, chance of showers, low around seventy-five. He made and drank two cups of instant coffee for the caffeine, waiting for night to fall, which it presently did.

Leaving the apartment complex was, oddly enough, one of the most difficult parts of the exercise. Kelly looked out the windows, his interior lights already off, making sure that there wasn't anyone out there, before venturing out himself. Out the door of the building he stopped again, looking and listening before he walked directly to the Volkswagen, which he unlocked and entered. At once he put on the work gloves, and only after that did he close the car's door and start the engine. Two minutes after that he passed the place where he parked the Scout, wondering how lonely the car was now. Kelly had selected a single radio station, playing contemporary music, soft rock and folk, just to have the company of familiar noise as he drove south into the city.

Part of him was surprised at how tense it was, driving in. As soon as he got there he settled down, but the drive in, like the insertion flight on a Huey, was the time in which you contemplated the unknown, and he had to tell himself to be cool, to keep his face in an impassive mien while his hands sweated a little inside the gloves. He carefully obeyed every traffic law, observed all lights, and ignored the cars that sped past him. Amazing, he thought, how long twenty minutes could seem. This time he used a slightly different insertion route. He'd scouted the parking place the night before, two blocks from the objective—in his mind, the current tactical environment translated one block to a kilometer in the real jungle, a complementarity that made him smile to himself, briefly, as he pulled his car in behind someone's black 1957 Chevy. As before, he left the car quickly, ducking into an alley for the cover of darkness and the assumption of his physical disguise. Inside of twenty yards he was just one more shambling drunk.

"Hey, dude!" a young voice called. There were three of them, mid-to-late teens, sitting on a fence and drinking beer. Kelly edged to the other side of the alley to maximize his distance, but that wasn't to be. One of them hopped down off the fence and came towards him.

"Whatcha lookin' for, bum?" the boy inquired with all the unfeeling arrogance of a young tough. "Jesus, you sure do stink, man! Dint your mama teach ya to wash?"

Kelly didn't even turn as he cringed and kept moving. This wasn't part of the plan. Head down, turned slightly away from the lad who walked alongside him, keeping pace in a way calculated to torment the old bum, who switched his wine bottle to his other hand.

"I needs a drink, man," the youth said, reaching for the bottle.

Kelly didn't surrender it, because a street wino didn't do that. The youngster tripped him, shoving him against the fence to his left, but it ended there. He walked back to his friend, laughing, as the bum rose and continued on his way.

"And don' ya come back neither, man!" Kelly heard as he got to the end of the block. He had no plans to do so. He passed two more such knots of young people in the next ten minutes, neither of which deemed him worthy of any action beyond laughter. The back door of his perch was still ajar, and tonight, thankfully, the rats weren't present. Kelly paused inside, listening, and, hearing nothing, he stood erect, allowing himself to relax.

"Snake to Chicago," he whispered to himself, remembering his old call signs. "Insertion successful. At the observation point." Kelly went up the same rickety stairs for the third and last time, finding his accustomed place in the southeast corner, sat down, and looked out.

Archie and Jughead were also in their accustomed place, a block away, he saw at once, talking to a motorist. It was ten-twelve at night. Kelly allowed himself a sip of water and a candy bar as he leaned back, watching them for any changes in their usual pattern of activity, but there was none he could see in half an hour of observation. Big Bob was in his place, too, as was his lieutenant, whom Kelly now called Little Bob. Charlie Brown was also in business tonight, as was Dagwood, the former still working alone and the latter still teamed up with a lieutenant Kelly had not bothered to name. But the Wizard wasn't visible tonight. It turned out that he arrived late, just after eleven, along with his associate, whose assigned name was Toto, for he tended to scurry around like a little dog that belonged in the basket on the back of the Wicked Witch's bicycle. "And your little dog, too . . . " Kelly whispered to himself in amusement.

As expected, Sunday night was slower than the two preceding nights, but Arch and Jug seemed busier than the others. Perhaps it was because they had a slightly more upscale client base. Though all served both local and outside customers, Arch and Jug seemed more often to draw the larger cars whose cleanliness and polish made Kelly think they didn't belong in this part of town. That might have been an unwarranted assumption, but it was not important to the mission. The really important thing was something he had scoped out the previous night on his walk into the area and confirmed tonight as well. Now it was just a matter of waiting.

Kelly made himself comfortable, feeling his body relax now that all the decisions had been made. He stared down at the street, still intensely alert, watching, listening, noting everything that came and went as the minutes passed. At twelve-forty, a police radio car traveled one of the cross streets, doing nothing more than showing the flag. It would return a few minutes after two, probably. The city buses made their whirring diesel noises, and Kelly recognized the one-ten, with the brakes that needed work. Their thin screech must have annoyed every person who tried to sleep along its route. Traffic slowed perceptibly just after two. The dealers were smoking more now, talking more. Big Bob crossed the street to say something to the Wizard, and their relations seemed cordial enough, which surprised Kelly. He hadn't seen that before. Maybe the man just needed change for a hundred. The police cruiser made its scheduled pass. Kelly finished his third Snickers bar of the evening, collecting the wrappers. He checked the area. He'd left nothing. No surface he had touched was likely to retain a fingerprint. There was just too much dust and grit, and he'd been very careful not to touch a windowpane.

Okay.

Kelly made his way down the stairs and out the back door. He crossed the street into the continuation of the alley that paralleled the street, still keeping to the shadows, still moving in a shambling but now exceeding quiet gait.

The mystery of the first night had turned out to be a boon. Archie and Jughead had vanished from his sight in a span of two or three seconds. He hadn't looked away from them any longer than that. They hadn't driven away, and they hadn't had time to walk to the end of the block. Kelly had figured it out the previous night. These overlong blocks of row houses had not been built by fools. Halfway down, many of the continuous blocks had an arched passageway so that people could get to the alley more easily. It also made a fine escape route for Arch and Jug, and when conducting business they never strayed more than twenty feet from it. But they never really appeared to watch it either.

Kelly made sure of that, leaning against an outbuilding that might have been big enough to contain a Model-T Ford. Finding a pair of beer cans, he connected them with a piece of string and set them across the cement walk that led to the passage, making sure that no one could approach him from behind without making noise. Then he moved in, walking very lightly on his feet and reaching into his waistband for his silenced pistol. It was only thirty-five feet to cover, but tunnels transmitted sound better than telephones, and Kelly's eyes scanned the surface for anything on which he might trip or make noise. He avoided some newspaper and a patch of broken glass, arriving close to the other end of the passageway.

They looked different close-up, human almost. Archie was leaning back against the brown bricks of a wall, smoking a cigarette. Jughead was also smoking, sitting on someone's car fender, looking down the street, and every ten seconds the flaring of their cigarettes attacked and degraded their vision. Kelly could see them, but even ten feet away they couldn't see him. It didn't get much better.

"Don't move," he whispered, just for Archie. The man's head turned, more in annoyance than alarm, until he saw the pistol with the large cylinder screwed onto the end. His eyes flickered to his lieutenant, who was still facing the wrong way, humming some song or other, waiting for a customer who would never come. Kelly handled the notification.

"Hey!" Still a whisper, but enough to carry over the diminishing street sounds. Jughead turned and saw the gun aimed at his employer's head. He froze without being bidden. Archie had the gun and the money and most of the drugs. He also saw Kelly's hand wave him in, and not knowing what else to do, he approached.

"Business good tonight?" Kelly asked.

"Fair 'nuf," Archie responded quietly. "What you want?"

"Now what do you suppose?" Kelly asked with a smile.

"You a cop?" Jughead asked, rather stupidly, the other two thought.

"No, I'm not here to arrest anybody." He motioned with his hand. "In the tunnel, facedown, quick." Kelly let them go in ten feet or so, just enough to be lost to outside view, not so far that he didn't have some exterior light to see by. First he searched them for weapons. Archie had a rusty .32 revolver that went into a pocket. Kelly next took the electrical wire from around his waist and wrapped it tightly around both sets of hands. Then he rolled them over.

"You boys have been very cooperative."

"You better never come back here, man," Archie informed him, hardly realizing that he hadn't been robbed at all. Jug nodded and muttered. The response puzzled both of them.

"Actually, I need your help."

"What with?" Archie asked.

"Looking for a guy, name of Billy, drives a red Roadrunner."

"What? You dickin' my ass?" Archie asked in rather a disgusted voice.

"Answer the question, please," Kelly said reasonably.

"You get you fuckin' ass outa here," Archie suggested spitefully.

Kelly turned the gun slightly and fired two rounds into Jug's head. The body spasmed violently, and blood flew, but not on Kelly this time. Instead it showered across Archie's face, and Kelly could see the pusher's eyes open wide in horror and surprise, like little lights in the darkness. Archie had not expected that. Jughead hadn't seemed much of a conversationalist anyway, and the operation's clock was ticking.

"I said please, didn't I?"

"Sweet Jesus, man!" the voice rasped, knowing that to make any more noise would be death.

"Billy. Red Plymouth Roadrunner, loves to show it off. He's a distributor. I want to know where he hangs out," Kelly said quietly.

"If I tell you that—"

"You get a new supplier. Me," Kelly said. "And if you tell Billy that I'm out here, you'll get to see your friend again," he added, gesturing to the body whose warm bulk pressed limply against Archie's side. He had to offer the man hope, after all. Maybe even a little left-handed truth, Kelly thought: "Do you understand? Billy and his friends have been screwing around with the wrong people, and it's my job to straighten things out. Sorry about your friend, but I had to show you that I'm serious, like."

Archie's voice tried to calm itself, but didn't quite make it, though he reached for the hope he'd been offered. "Look, man, I can't—"

"I can always ask somebody else." Kelly paused significantly. "Do you understand what I just said?"

Archie did, or thought he did, and he talked freely until the time came for him to rejoin Jughead.

A quick search of Archie's pockets turned up a nice wad of cash and a collection of small drug envelopes which also found their way into his jacket pockets. Kelly stepped carefully over both bodies and made his way to the alley, looking back to make sure that he hadn't stepped in any blood. He'd discard the shoes in any case. Kelly untied the string from the cans and replaced them where he'd found them, before renewing his drunken gait, taking a roundabout path back to his car, repeating his carefully considered routine every step of the way. Thank God, he thought, driving north again, he'd be able to shower and shave tonight. But what the hell would he do with the drugs? That was a question that fate would answer.

The cars started arriving just after six, not so incongruous an hour for activity on a military base. Fifteen of them, clunkers, none less than three years old, and all of them had been totaled in auto accidents and sold for scrap. The only thing unusual about them was that though they were no longer drivable, they almost looked as though they were. The work detail was composed of Marines, supervised by a gunnery sergeant who had no idea what this was all about. But he didn't have to. The cars were worked into place, haphazardly, not in neat military rows, but more the way real people parked. The job took ninety minutes, and the work detail left. At eight in the morning another such detail arrived, this one with mannequins. They came in several sizes, and they were dressed in old clothes. The child-size ones went on the swings and in the sandbox. The adult ones were stood up, using the metal stands that came with them. And the second work party left, to return twice a day for the indefinite future and move the mannequins around in a random way prescribed by a set of instructions thought up and written down by some damned fool of an officer who didn't have anything better to do.

Kelly's notes had commented on the fact that one of the most debilitating and time-consuming aspects of Operation KINGPIN had been the daily necessity of setting up and striking down the mockup of their objective. He hadn't been the first to note it. If any Soviet reconnaissance satellites took note of this place, they would see an odd collection of buildings serving no readily identifiable purpose. They would also see a child's playground, complete with children, parents, and parked cars, all of which elements would move every day. That bit of information would counter the more obvious observation—that this recreational facility was half a mile off any paved road and invisible to the rest of the installation.

16
Exercises

Ryan and Douglas stood back, letting the forensics people do their jobs. The discovery had happened just after five in the morning. On his routine patrol pattern, Officer Chuck Monroe had come down the street, and spotting an irregular shadow in this passage between houses, shone his car light down it. The dark shape might easily have been a drunk passed out and sleeping it off, but the white spotlight had reflected off the pool of red and bathed the arched bricks in a pink glow that looked wrong from the first instant. Monroe had parked his car and come in for a look, then made his call. The officer was leaning on the side of his car now, smoking a cigarette and going over the details of his discovery, which was to him less horrific and more routine than civilians understood. He hadn't even bothered to call an ambulance. These two men were clearly beyond any medical redemption.

"Bodies sure do bleed a lot," Douglas observed. It wasn't a statement of any significance, just words to fill the silence as the cameras flashed for one last roll of color film. It looked as if two full-size cans of red paint had been poured in one spot.

"Time of death?" Ryan asked the representative from the coroner's office.

"Not too long ago," the man said, lifting one hand. "No rigor yet. After midnight certainly, probably after two."

The cause of death didn't require a question. The holes in both men's foreheads answered that.

"Monroe?" Ryan called. The young officer came over. "What do you know about these two?"

"Both pushers. Older one on the right there is Maceo Donald, street name is Ju-Ju. The one on the left, I don't know, but he worked with Donald."

"Good eye spotting them, patrolman. Anything else?" Sergeant Douglas asked.

Monroe shook his head. "No, sir. Nothing at all. Pretty quiet night in the district, as a matter of fact. I came through this area maybe four times on my shift, and I didn't see anything out of the ordinary. The usual pushers doing the usual business." The implied criticism of the situation that everyone had to acknowledge as normal went unanswered. It was a Monday morning, after all, and that was bad enough for anyone.

"Finished," the senior photographer said. He and his partner, on the other side of the bodies, got out of the way.

Ryan was already looking around. There was a good deal of ambient light in the passageway, and the detective augmented that with a large flashlight, playing its beam over the edges of the walkway, his eyes looking for a coppery reflection.

"See any shell casing, Tom?" he asked Douglas, who was doing the same thing.

"Nope. They were shot from this direction, too, don't you think?"

"Bodies haven't been moved," the coroner said unnecessarily, adding, "Yes, definitely both shot from this side. Both were lying down when they were shot."

Douglas and Ryan took their time, examining every inch of the passageway three times, for thoroughness was their main professional weapon, and they had all the time in the world—or at least a few hours, which amounted to the same thing. A crime scene like this was one you prayed for. No grass to conceal evidence, no furniture, just a bare brick corridor not five feet wide, everything self-contained. That would be a time-saver.

"Nothing at all, Em," Douglas said, finishing his third sweep. "Probably a revolver, then." It was a logical observation. Light .22 shell casings, ejected from an automatic, could fly incredible distances, and were so small that finding them could drive one to distraction. Rare was the criminal who recovered his brass, and to have recovered four little .22s in the dark—no, that wasn't very likely.

"Some robber with a cheap one, want to bet?" Douglas asked.

"Could be." Both men approached the bodies and squatted down close to them for the first time.

"No obvious powder marks," the sergeant said in some surprise.

"Any of these houses occupied?" Ryan asked Monroe.

"Not either one of these, sir," Monroe said, indicating both of those bordering the passageway. "Most of the ones on the other side of the street are, though."

"Four shots, early in the morning, you figure somebody might have heard?" *The brick tunnel ought to have focused the sound like the lens of a telescope,* Ryan thought, and the .22 had a loud, sharp bark. But how often had there been cases just like this one in which no one had heard a thing? Besides, the way this neighborhood was going, people divided into two classes: those who didn't look because they didn't care, and those who knew that looking merely increased the chance of catching a stray round.

"There's two officers knocking on doors now, Lieutenant. Nothing yet."

"Not bad shooting, Em." Douglas had his pencil out, pointing to the holes in the forehead of the unidentified victim. They were scarcely half an inch apart, just above the bridge of the nose. "No powder marks. The killer must have been standing . . . call it three, four feet, max." Douglas stood back at the feet of the bodies and extended his arm. It was a natural shot, extending your arm and aiming down.

"I don't think so. Maybe there's powder marks we can't see, Tom. That's why we have medical examiners." He meant that both men had dark complexions, and the light wasn't all that good. But if there was powder tattooing around the small entrance wounds, neither detective could see it. Douglas squatted back down to give the entrance wounds another look.

"Nice to know somebody appreciates us," the coroner's representative said, ten feet away, scribbling his own notes.

"Either way, Em, our shooter has a real steady hand." The pencil moved to the head of Maceo Donald. The two holes in his forehead, maybe a little higher on the forehead than the other man, were even closer together. "That's unusual."

Ryan shrugged and began his search of the bodies. Though the senior of the two, he preferred to do this himself while Douglas took the notes. He found no weapon on either man, and though both had wallets and ID, from which they identified the unknown as Charles Barker, age twenty, the amount of cash discovered wasn't nearly what men in their business would customarily have on their persons. Nor were there any drugs—

"Wait, here's something—three small glassine bags of white powdery substance," Ryan said in the language of his profession. "Pocket change, a dollar seventy-five; cigarette lighter, Zippo, brushed steel, the cheap one. Pack of Pall Malls from the shirt pocket—and another small glassine bag of white powdery substance."

"A drug ripoff," Douglas said, diagnosing the incident. It wasn't terribly professional but it was pretty obvious. "Monroe?"

"Yes, sir?" The young officer would never stop being a Marine. Nearly everything he said, Douglas noted, had "sir" attached to it.

"Our friends Barker and Donald—experienced pushers?"

"Ju-Ju's been around since I've been in the district, sir. I never heard of anybody messin' with him."

"No signs of a fight on the hands," Ryan said after turning them over. "Hands are tied up with . . . electrical wire, copper wire, white insulation, trademark on it, can't read it yet. No obvious signs of a struggle."

"Somebody got Ju-Ju!" It was Mark Charon, who had just arrived. "I had a case running on that fuck, too."

"Two exit wounds, back of Mr. Donald's head," Ryan went on, annoyed at the interruption. "I expect we'll find the bullets somewhere at the bottom of this lake," he added sourly.

"Forget ballistics," Douglas grunted. That wasn't unusual with the .22. First of all, the bullet was made of soft lead, and was so easily deformed that the striations imparted by the rifling of the gun barrel were most often impossible to identify. Second, the little .22 had a lot of penetrating power, more even than a .45, and often ended up splattering itself on some object beyond the victim. In this case the cement of the walkway.

"Well, tell me about him," Ryan ordered.

"Major street pusher, big clientele. Drives a nice red Caddy," Charon added. "Pretty smart one, too."

"Not anymore. His brain got homogenized about six hours ago."

"Rip?" Charon asked.

Douglas answered. "Looks that way. No gun, no drugs or money to speak of. Whoever did it knew their business. Looks real professional, Em. This wasn't some junkie who got lucky."

"I'd have to say that's the morning line, Tom," Ryan replied, standing up. "Probably a revolver, but those groups are awfully tight for a Saturday-night special. Mark, any word on an experienced robber working the street?"

"The Duo," Charon said. "But they use a shotgun."

"This is almost like a mob hit. Look 'em straight in the eye—whack." Douglas thought about his words. No, that wasn't quite right either, was it? Mob hits were almost never this elegant. Criminals were not proficient marksmen, and they used cheap weapons for the most part. He and Ryan had investigated a handful of gang-related murders, and typically the victim had either been shot in the back of the head at contact range, with all the obvious forensic signs that attended such an event, or the damage was done so haphazardly that the victim was more likely to have a dozen widely scattered holes in his anatomy. These two had been taken out by someone who knew his business, and the collection of highly skilled Mafia soldiers was very slim indeed. But who had ever said that homicide investigation was an exact science? This crime scene was a mix of the routine and the unusual. A simple robbery in that the drugs and money of the victims were missing, but an unusually skillful killing in the fact that the shooter had been either very lucky—twice—or an expert shot. And a mob hit was usually not disguised as a robbery or anything else. A mob murder was most often a public statement.

"Mark, any noise on the street about a turf war?" Douglas asked.

"No, not really, nothing organized. A lot of stuff between pushers over street corners, but that isn't news."

"You might want to ask around," Lieutenant Ryan suggested.

"No problem, Em. I'll have my people check that out."

We're not going to solve this one fast—maybe never, Ryan thought. *Well,* he thought, *only on TV do you solve them in the first half hour—between commercials.*

"Can I have 'em now?"

"All yours," Ryan told the man from the medical examiner's office. His black station wagon was ready, and the day was warming up. Already flies were buzzing around, drawn to the smell of blood. He headed off to his own car, accompanied by Tom Douglas. Junior detectives would have the rest of the routine work.

"Somebody that knows how to shoot—better than me even," Douglas said as they drove back downtown. He'd tried out for the department's pistol team once.

"Well, lots of people with that skill are around now, Tom. Maybe some have found employment with our organized friends."

"Professional hit, then?"

"We'll call it skillful for now," Ryan suggested as an alternative. "We'll let Mark do some of the scutwork on the intelligence side."

"That makes me feel warm all over." Douglas snorted.

• • •

Kelly arose at ten-thirty, feeling clean for the first time in several days. He'd showered immediately on returning to his apartment, wondering if in doing so he'd left rings on the sewers. Now he could shave, even, and that compensated for the lack of sleep. Before breakfast—brunch—Kelly drove half a mile to a local park and ran for thirty minutes, then drove back home for another thoroughly wonderful shower and some food. Then there was work to do. All the clothing from the previous evening was in a brown paper grocery bag—slacks, shirt, underwear, socks, and shoes. It seemed a shame to part with the bush jacket, whose size and pockets had proven to be so useful. He'd have to get another, probably several. He felt certain that he hadn't been splattered with blood this time, but the dark colors made it difficult to be sure, and they probably *did* carry powder residue, and this was not the time to take any chances at all. Leftover food and coffee grounds went on top of the clothing, and found their way into the apartment complex's Dumpster. Kelly had considered taking them to a distant dumpsite, but that might cause more trouble than it solved. Someone might see him, and take note of what he did, and wonder why. Disposing of the four empty .22 cases was easy. He'd dumped them down a sewer while jogging. The noon news broadcast announced the discovery of two bodies, but no details. Maybe the newspaper would say more. There was one other thing.

"Hi, Sam."

"Hey, John. You in town?" Rosen asked from his office.

"Yeah. Do you mind if I come down for a few minutes? Say around two?"

"What can I do for you?" Rosen asked from behind his desk.

"Gloves," Kelly said, holding his hand up. "The kind you use, thin rubber. Do they cost much?"

Rosen almost asked what the gloves were for, but decided he didn't need to know. "Hell, they come in boxes of a hundred pair."

"I don't need that many."

The surgeon pulled open a drawer in his credenza and tossed over ten of the paper-and-plastic bags. "You look awfully respectable." And so Kelly did, dressed in a button-down white shirt and his blue CIA suit, as he'd taken to calling it. It was the first time Rosen had seen him in a tie.

"Don't knock it, doc." Kelly smiled. "Sometimes I have to be. I even have a new job, sort of."

"Doing what?"

"Sort of consulting." Kelly gestured. "I can't say about what, but it requires me to dress properly."

"Feeling okay?"

"Yes, sir, just fine. Jogging and everything. How are things with you?"

"The usual. More paperwork than surgery, but I have a whole department to supervise." Sam touched the pile of folders on his desk. The small talk was making him uneasy. It seemed that his friend was wearing a disguise, and though he knew Kelly was up to something, in *not* knowing exactly what it was, he managed to keep his conscience under control. "Can you do me a favor?"

"Sure, doc."

"Sandy's car broke down. I was going to run her home, but I've got a meeting that'll run till four. She gets off shift at three."

"You're letting her work regular hours now?" Kelly asked with a smile.

"Sometimes, when she's not teaching."

"If it's okay with her, it's okay with me."

It was only a twenty-minute wait that Kelly disposed of by going to the cafeteria for a light snack. Sandy O'Toole found him there, just after the three-o'clock change of shift.

"Like the food better now?" she asked him.

"Even hospitals can't hurt a salad very much." He hadn't figured out the institutional fascination with Jell-O, however. "I hear your car's broke."

She nodded, and Kelly saw why Rosen had her working a more regular schedule. Sandy looked very tired, her fair skin sallow, with puffy dark patches under both eyes.

"Something with the starter—wiring. It's in the shop."

Kelly stood. "Well, my lady's carriage awaits." His remark elicited a smile, but it was one of politeness rather than amusement.

"I've never seen you so dressed up," she said on the way to the parking garage.

"Well, don't get too worked up about it. I can still roll in the mud with the best of 'em." And his jesting failed again.

"I didn't mean—"

"Relax, ma'am. You've had a long day at the office, and your driver has a crummy sense of humor."

Nurse O'Toole stopped and turned. "It's not your fault. Bad week. We had a child, auto accident. Doctor Rosen tried, but the damage was too great, and she faded out on my shift, day before yesterday. Sometimes I hate this work," Sandy concluded.

"I understand," Kelly said, holding the door open for her. "Look, you want the short version? It's never the right person. It's never the right time. It never makes any sense."

"That's a nice way of looking at things. Weren't you trying to cheer me up?" And that, perversely, made her smile, but it wasn't the kind of smile that Kelly wanted to see.

"We all try to fix the broken parts as best we can, Sandy. You fight your dragons. I fight mine," Kelly said without thinking.

"And how many dragons have you slain?"

"One or two," Kelly said distantly, trying to control his words. It surprised him how difficult that had become. Sandy was too easy to talk with.

"And what did it make better, John?"

"My father was a fireman. He died while I was over there. House fire, he went inside and found two kids, they were down from smoke. Dad got them out okay, but then he had a heart attack on the spot. They say he was dead before he hit the ground. That counted for something," Kelly said, remembering what Admiral Maxwell had said, in the sick bay of USS *Kitty Hawk,* that death should mean something, that his father's death had.

"You've killed people, haven't you?" Sandy asked.

"That's what happens in a war," Kelly agreed.

"What did that mean? What did it do?"

"If you want the big answer, I don't have it. But the ones I took out didn't ever hurt anybody else." PLASTIC FLOWER sure as hell didn't, he told himself. No more village chiefs and their families. Maybe someone else had taken the work over, but maybe not, too.

Sandy watched the traffic as he headed north on Broadway. "And the ones who killed Tim, did they think the same thing?"

"Maybe they did, but there's a difference." Kelly almost said that he'd never seen one of his people murder anyone, but he couldn't say *that* anymore, could he?

"But if everybody believes that, then where are we? It's not like diseases. You fight against things that hurt everybody. No politics and lying. We're not killing people. That's why I do this work, John."

"Sandy, thirty years ago there was a guy named Hitler who got his rocks off killing people like Sam and Sarah just because of what their goddamned names were. He had to be killed, and he was, too damned late, but he was." Wasn't that a simple enough lesson?

"We have problems enough right here," she pointed out. That was obvious from the sidewalks they passed, for Johns Hopkins was not in a comfortable neighborhood.

"I know that, remember?"

That statement deflated her. "I'm sorry, John."

"So am I." Kelly paused, searching for words. "There is a difference, Sandy. There are good people. I suppose most people are decent. But there are bad people, too. You can't wish them away, and you can't wish them to be good, because most won't change, and somebody has to protect the one bunch from the other. That's what I did."

"But how do you keep from turning into one of them?"

Kelly took his time considering that, regretting the fact that she was here at all. He didn't need to hear this, didn't want to have to examine his own conscience. Everything had been so clear the past couple of days. Once you decided that there was an enemy, then acting on that information was simply a matter of applying your training and experience. It wasn't something you had to *think* about. Looking at your conscience was hard, wasn't it?

"I've never had that problem," he said, finally, evading the issue. That was when he saw the difference. Sandy and her community fought against a *thing,* and fought bravely, risking their sanity in resisting the actions of forces whose root causes they could not directly address. Kelly and his fought against *people,* leaving the actions of their enemies to others, but able to seek them out and fight directly against their foe, even eliminating them if they were lucky. One side had absolute purity of purpose but lacked satisfaction. The other could attain the satisfaction of destroying the enemy, but only at the cost of becoming too much like what they struggled against. Warrior and healer, parallel wars, similarity of purpose, but so different in their actions. Diseases of the body, and diseases of humanity itself. Wasn't that an interesting way to look at it?

"Maybe it's like this: it's not what you fight against. It's what you fight for."

"What are we fighting for in Vietnam?" Sandy asked Kelly again, having asked herself that question no less than ten times per day since she'd received the unwelcome telegram. "My husband died there and I don't still understand why."

Kelly started to say something but stopped himself. Really there was no answer. Bad luck, bad decisions, bad timing at more than one level of activity created the random events that caused soldiers to die on a distant battlefield, and even if you were there, it didn't always make sense. Besides, she'd probably heard every justification more than once from the man whose life she mourned. Maybe looking for that kind of meaning was nothing more than an exercise in futility. Maybe it wasn't supposed to make sense. Even if that were true, how could you live without the pretense that it did, somehow? He was still pondering that one when he turned onto her street.

"Your house needs some paint," Kelly told her, glad that it did.

"I know. I can't afford painters and I don't have the time to do it myself."

"Sandy—a suggestion?"

"What's that?"

"Let yourself live. I'm sorry Tim's gone, but he is gone. I lost friends over there, too. You have to go on."

The fatigue in her face was painful to see. Her eyes examined him in a professional sort of way, revealing nothing of what she thought or what she felt inside, but the fact that she troubled herself to conceal herself from him told Kelly something.

Something's changed in you. I wonder what it is. I wonder why, Sandy thought. Something had resolved itself. He'd always been polite, almost funny in his overpowering gentility, but the sadness she'd seen, that had almost matched her own undying grief, was gone now, replaced with something she couldn't quite fathom. It was strange, because he had never troubled to hide himself from her, and she thought herself able to penetrate whatever disguises he might erect. On that she was wrong, or perhaps she didn't know the rules. She watched him get out, walk around the car, and open her door.

"Ma'am?" He gestured toward the house.

"Why are you so nice? Did Doctor Rosen . . . ?"

"He just said you needed a ride, Sandy, honest. Besides, you look awful tired." Kelly walked her to the door.

"I don't know why I like talking to you," she said, reaching the porch steps.

"I wasn't sure that you did. You do?"

"I think so," O'Toole replied, with an almost-smile. The smile died after a second. "John, it's too soon for me."

"Sandy, it's too soon for me, too. Is it too soon to be friends?"

She thought about that. "No, not too soon for that."

"Dinner sometime? I asked once, remember?"

"How often are you in town?"

"More now. I have a job—well, something I have to do in Washington."

"Doing what?"

"Nothing important." And Sandy caught the scent of a lie, but it probably wasn't one aimed at hurting her.

"Next week maybe?"

"I'll give you a call. I don't know any good places around here."

"I do."

"Get some rest," Kelly told her. He didn't attempt to kiss her, or even take her hand. Just a friendly, caring smile before he walked away. Sandy watched him drive off, still wondering what there was about the man that was different. She'd never forget the look on his face, there on the hospital bed, but whatever that had been, it wasn't something she needed to fear.

Kelly was swearing quietly at himself as he drove away, wearing the cotton work gloves now, and rubbing them across every surface in the car that he could reach. He couldn't risk many conversations like this one. What was it all about? How the hell was he supposed to know? It was easy in the field. You identified the enemy, or more often somebody told you what was going on and who he was and where he was—frequently the information was wrong, but at least it gave you a starting place. But mission briefs never told you, really, how it was going to change the world or bring the war to an end. That was stuff you read in the paper, information repeated by reporters who didn't care, taken down from briefers who didn't know or politicians who'd never troubled themselves to find out. "Infrastructure" and "cadre" were favorite words, but he'd hunted people, not infrastructure, whatever the hell that was supposed to be. Infrastructure was a *thing,* like what Sandy fought against. It wasn't a person who did evil things and could be hunted down like an offensive big-game animal. And how did that apply to what he was doing now? Kelly told himself that he had to control his thinking, stay to the easy stuff, just remember that he was hunting *people,* just as he had before. He wasn't going to change the whole world, just clean up one little corner.

"Does it still hurt, my friend?" Grishanov asked.

"I think I have some broken ribs."

Zacharias sat down in the chair, breathing slowly and in obvious pain. That worried the Russian. Such an injury could lead to pneumonia, and pneumonia could kill a man in this physical condition. The guards had been a little too enthusiastic in their assault on the man, and though it had been done at Grishanov's request, he hadn't wanted to do more than to inflict some pain. A dead prisoner would not tell him what he needed to know.

"I've spoken to Major Vinh. The little savage says he has no medicines to spare." Grishanov shrugged. "It might even be true. The pain, it is bad?"

"Every time I breathe," Zacharias replied, and he was clearly speaking the truth. His skin was even paler than usual.

"I have only one thing for pain, Robin," Kolya said apologetically, holding out his flask.

The American colonel shook his head, and even that appeared to hurt him. "I can't."

Grishanov spoke with the frustration of a man trying to reason with a friend. "Then you are a fool, Robin. Pain serves no one, not you, not me, not your God. Please, let me help you a little. Please?"

Can't do it, Zacharias told himself. To do so was to break his covenant. His body was a temple, and he had to keep it pure of such things as this. But the temple was broken. He feared internal bleeding most of all. Would his body be able to heal itself? It should, and under anything approaching normal circumstances, it would do so easily, but he knew that his physical condition was dreadful, his back still injured, and now his ribs. Pain was a companion now, and pain would make it harder for him to resist questions, and so he had to measure his religion against his duty to resist. Things were less clear now. Easing the pain might make it easier to heal, and easier to stick to his duty. So what was the right thing? What ought to have been an easy question was clouded, and his eyes looked at the metal container. There was relief there. Not much, but some, and some relief was what he needed if he were to control himself.

Grishanov unscrewed the cap. "Do you ski, Robin?"

Zacharias was surprised by the question. "Yes, I learned when I was a kid."

"Cross-country?"

The American shook his head. "No, downhill."

"The snow in the Wasatch Mountains, it is good for skiing?"

Robin smiled, remembering. "Very good, Kolya. It's dry snow. Powdery, almost like very fine sand."

"Ah, the best kind of all. Here." He handed the flask over.

Just this once, Zacharias thought. *Just for the pain.* He took a swallow. *Push the pain back a few steps, just so I can keep myself together.*

Grishanov watched him do it, saw his eyes water, hoping the man wouldn't cough and hurt himself more. It was good vodka, obtained from the embassy's storeroom in Hanoi, the one thing his country always had in good supply, and the one thing the embassy always had enough of. The best quality of paper vodka, Kolya's personal favorite, actually flavored with old paper, something this American was unlikely to note—and something he himself missed after the third or fourth drink, if the truth be known.

"You are a good skier, Robin?"

Zacharias felt the warmth in his belly as it spread out and allowed his body to relax. In that relaxation his pain lessened, and he felt a little stronger, and if this Russian wanted to talk skiing, well, that couldn't hurt much, could it?

"I ski the expert slopes," Robin said with satisfaction. "I started when I was a kid. I think I was five when Dad took me the first time."

"Your father—also a pilot?"

The American shook his head. "No, a lawyer."

"My father is a professor of history at Moscow State University. We have a dacha, and in the winter when I was little, I could ski in the woods. I love the silence. All you can hear is the—how you say, swish? Swish of the skis in the snow. Nothing else. Like a blanket on the earth, no noise, just silence."

"If you go up early, the mountains can be like that. You pick a day right after the snow ends, not much wind."

Kolya smiled. "Like flying, isn't it? Flying in a single-seat aircraft, a fair day with a few white clouds." He leaned forward with a crafty look. "Tell me, do you ever turn your radio off for a few minutes, just to be alone?"

"They let you do that?" Zacharias asked.

Grishanov chuckled, shaking his head. "No, but I do it anyway."

"Good for you," Robin said with a smile of his own, remembering what it was like. He thought of one particular afternoon, flying out of Mountain Home Air Force Base one February day in 1964.

"It is how God must feel, yes? All alone. You can ignore the noise of the engine. For me it just goes away after a few minutes. Is it the same for you?"

"Yeah, if your helmet fits right."

"That is the real reason I fly," Grishanov lied. "All the other rubbish, the paperwork, and the mechanical things, and the lectures, they are the price. To be up there, all alone, just like when I was a boy skiing in the woods—but better. You can see so far on a clear winter day." He handed Zacharias the flask again. "Do you suppose these little savages understand that?"

"Probably not." He wavered for a moment. Well, he'd already had one. Another couldn't hurt, could it? Zacharias took another swallow.

"What I do, Robin, I hold the stick just in my fingertips, like this." He demonstrated with the top of the flask. "I close my eyes for a moment, and when I open them, the world is different. Then I am not part of the world anymore. I am something else—an angel, perhaps," he said with good humor. "Then I possess the sky as I would like to possess a woman, but it is never quite the same. The best feelings are supposed to be alone, I think."

This guy really understands, doesn't he? He really understands *flying.* "You a poet or something?"

"I love poetry. I do not have the talent to make it, but that does not prevent me from reading it, and memorizing it, feeling what the poet tells me to feel," Grishanov said quietly, actually meaning what he said as he watched the American's eyes lose focus, becoming dreamy. "We are much alike, my friend."

"What's the story on Ju-Ju?" Tucker asked.

"Looks like a ripoff. He got careless. One of yours, eh?" Charon said.

"Yeah, he moved a lot for us."

"Who did it?" They were in the Main Branch of the Enoch Pratt Free Library, hidden in some rows, an ideal place, really. Hard to approach without being spotted, and impossible to bug. Even though a quiet place, there were just too many of the little alcoves.

"No telling, Henry. Ryan and Douglas were there, and it didn't look to me like they had much. Hey, you going to get that worked up over one pusher?"

"You know better than that, but it puts a little dent in things. Never had one of mine wasted before."

"You know better than *that,* Henry." Charon flipped through some pages. "It's a high-risk business. Somebody wanted a little cash, maybe some drugs, too, maybe break into the business quick? Look for a new pusher selling your stuff, maybe. Hell, as good as they were on the hit, maybe you could reach an understanding with 'em."

"I have enough dealers. And making peace like that is bad for business. How they do 'em?"

"Very professional. Two in the head each. Douglas was talking like it was a mob hit."

Tucker turned his head. "Oh?"

Charon spoke calmly, his back to the man. "Henry, this wasn't the outfit. Tony isn't going to do anything like that, is he?"

"Probably not." *But Eddie might.*

"I need something," Charon said next.

"What?"

"A dealer. What did you expect, a tip on the second at Pimlico?"

"Too many of 'em are mine now, remember?" It had been all right—better than that, really—to use Charon to eliminate the major competition, but as Tucker had consolidated his control on the local trade, he was able to target fewer and fewer independent operators for judicial elimination. That was particularly true of the majors. He had systematically picked out people with whom he had no interest in working, and the few who were left might be useful allies rather than rivals, if he could only find a way to negotiate with them.

"If you want me to be able to protect you, Henry, then I have to be able to control investigations. For me to control the investigations, I have to land some big fish from time to time." Charon put the book back on the shelf. Why did he have to explain things like this to the man?

"When?"

"Beginning of the week, something tasty. I want to take down something that looks nice."

"I'll get back to you." Tucker replaced his book and walked away. Charon spent another few minutes, searching for the right book. He found it, along with the envelope that sat next to it. The police lieutenant didn't bother counting. He knew that the amount would be right.

Greer handled the introductions.

"Mr. Clark, this is General Martin Young, and this is Robert Ritter."

Kelly shook hands with both. The Marine was an aviator, like Maxwell and Podulski, both of whom were absent from this meeting. He hadn't a clue who Ritter was, but he was the one who spoke first.

"Nice analysis. Your language wasn't exactly bureaucratic, but you hit all the high points."

"Sir, it's not really all that hard to figure out. The ground assault ought to be fairly easy. You don't have first-line troops in a place like this, and those you have are looking in, not out. Figure two guys in each tower. The MGs are going to be set to point in, right? It takes a few seconds to move them. You can use the treeline to get close enough for M-79 range." Kelly moved his hands around the diagram. "Here's the barracks, only two doors, and I bet there's not forty guys in there."

"Come in here?" General Young tapped the southwest corner on the compound.

"Yes, sir." For an airedale, the Marine caught on pretty fast. "The trick's getting the initial strike team in close. You'll use weather for that, and this time of the year that shouldn't be real hard. Two gunships, just regular rockets and miniguns to hose these two buildings. Land the evac choppers here. It's all over in under five minutes from when the shooting starts. That's the land phase. I'll leave the rest to the fliers."

"So you say the real key is to get the assault element in close on the ground—"

"No, sir. If you want to do another Song Tay, you can duplicate the whole plan, crash the chopper in the compound, the whole nine yards—but I keep hearing you want it done small."

"Correct," Ritter said. "Has to be small. There's no way we can sell this as a major operation."

"Fewer assets, sir, and you have to use different tactics. The good news is that it's a small objective, not all that many people to get out, not many bad guys to get in the way."

"But no safety factor," General Young said, frowning.

"Not much of one," Kelly agreed. "Twenty-five people. Land them in this valley, they hump over this hill, get into place, do the towers, blow this gate. Then the gunships come in and hose these two buildings while the assault element hits this building here. The snakes orbit while the slicks do the pickup, and we all boogie the hell down the valley."

"Mr. Clark, you're an optimist," Greer observed, reminding Kelly of his cover name at the same time. If General Young found out that Kelly had been a mere chief, they'd never get his support, and Young had already stretched a long way for them, using up his whole year's construction budget to build the mockup in the woods of Quantico.

"It's all stuff I've done before, Admiral."

"Who's going to get the personnel?" Ritter asked.

"That's being taken care of," James Greer assured him.

Ritter sat back, looking at the photos and diagrams. He was putting his career on the line, as was Greer and everyone else. But the alternative to doing something was doing nothing. Doing nothing meant that at least one good man, and perhaps twenty more, would never come home again. That wasn't the real reason, though, Ritter admitted to himself. The real reason was that others had decided that the lives of those men didn't matter, and those others might make the same decision again. That kind of thinking would someday destroy his Agency. You couldn't recruit agents if the word got out that America didn't protect those who worked for her. Keeping faith was more than the right thing. It was also good business.

"Better to get things going before we break the story," he said. "It'll be easier to get a 'go-mission' if we've already got it ready to go. Make it look like a unique opportunity. That's the other big mistake they made with KINGPIN. It was too obviously aimed at getting a hunting license, and that was never in the cards. What we have here is a one-time rescue mission. I can take that to my friends in the NSC. That'll fly, probably, but we have to be ready to go when I do that."

"Bob, does that mean you're on our side?" Greer asked.

Ritter took a long moment before answering. "Yes, it does."

"We need an additional safety factor," Young said, looking at the large-scale map, figuring how the helicopters would get in.

"Yes, sir," Kelly said. "Somebody has to go in early and eyeball things." They still had both photos of Robin Zacharias out, one of an Air Force colonel, standing upright, holding his cap under his arm, chest decorated with silver wings and ribbons, smiling confidently into the camera with his family arrayed around him; and the other of a bowed, bedraggled man, about to be butt-stroked from behind. *Hell,* he thought, *why not one more crusade?*

"I guess that's me."

17

Complications

Archie hadn't known much, but it turned out to be enough for Kelly's purposes. All he really needed now was a little more sleep.

Tracking someone in a car, he found, was harder than it appeared on TV, and harder than it had been in New Orleans the one time he'd attempted it. If you followed too closely you ran the risk of being spotted. If you held too far back, you might lose the guy. Traffic complicated everything. Trucks could obstruct your vision. Watching one car half a block away necessarily caused you to ignore cars closer to you, and those, he found, could do the damnedest things. For all that, he blessed Billy's red Roadrunner. It was easy to spot, with its bright color, and even though the driver liked to lay rubber on the street and corner, he still couldn't break all that many traffic laws without attracting the attention of the police, something he didn't want to do any more than Kelly did.

Kelly had sighted the car just after seven in the evening, close to the bar which Archie had identified. Whatever he was like, Kelly thought, he didn't know much about being covert, but the car told him that. The mud was gone, he saw at once. The car looked freshly washed and waxed, and from their previous encounter, he knew Billy to be a man who treasured the thing. It offered a few interesting possibilities which Kelly considered while he trailed him, never closer than half a block, getting a feel for how he moved. It was soon apparent that he stayed clear of the major thoroughfares as much as possible and knew the side streets as a weasel knew his den. That placed Kelly at a disadvantage. Balancing it was the fact that Kelly was driving a car nobody noticed. There were just too many used Beetles on the street for one more to attract notice.

After forty minutes the pattern became clear. The Roadrunner turned right quickly and came to a stop at the end of the block. Kelly weighed his options and kept going, slowly. As he approached he saw a girl get out, carrying a purse. She walked up to an old friend, the Wizard, several blocks from his usual hangout. Kelly didn't see a transfer of any kind—the two walked into a building and remained hidden for a minute or two until the girl came out—but he didn't have to. The event fitted what Pam had told him. Better yet, it identified the Wizard, Kelly told himself, turning left and approaching a red light. Now he knew two things he hadn't known before. In his rearview mirror he saw the Roadrunner cross the street. The girl headed the same way, disappearing from his view as the light changed. Kelly turned right and right again, spotting the Plymouth as it proceeded south with three people inside. He hadn't noticed the man—probably a man—before, crouching in back.

Darkness was falling rapidly, the good time of the day for John Kelly. He continued to follow the Roadrunner, leaving his lights off as long as he dared, and was rewarded by seeing it stop at a brownstone corner house, where all three occupants got out, having made their deliveries for the night to four pushers. He gave them a few minutes, parking his car a few blocks away and coming back on foot to observe, again disguised as a street drunk. The local architecture made it easier. All of the houses on the other side of the street had marble front steps, large, rectangular blocks of stone that made for good cover and concealment.

It was just a matter of sitting on the sidewalk and leaning back against them, and he could not be seen from behind. Picking the right set of steps, close but not too close to a working street light, gave him a nice shadow in which to conceal himself, and besides, who paid any attention to a street bum anyway? Kelly adopted the same sort of drunken huddle he'd seen in others, occasionally lifting his bag-covered bottle for a simulated sip while he watched the corner brownstone for several hours.

Blood types O+, O–, and AB–, he remembered from the pathology report. The semen left inside Pam had been matched to those blood types, and he wondered what blood type Billy's was, as he sat there, fifty yards away from the house. The traffic moved on the street. People walked back and forth. Perhaps three people had given him a look, but nothing more than that as he feigned sleep, watching the house from the corner of his eye and listening to every sound for possible danger as the hours passed. A pusher was working the sidewalk perhaps twenty yards or so behind him, and he listened to the man's voice, for the first time hearing how he described his product and negotiated the price, listening also to the different voices of the customers. Kelly had always possessed unusually good hearing—it had saved his life more than once—and this, too, was valuable intelligence information for his mind to catalog and analyze as the hours passed. A stray dog came up to him, sniffing in a curious, friendly way, and Kelly didn't shoo it away. That would have been out of character—had it been a rat things might have been different, he thought—and maintaining his disguise was important.

What sort of neighborhood had this been? Kelly wondered. On his side the dwellings were fairly ordinary brick row-houses. The other side was a little different, the more substantial brownstones perhaps fifty percent wider. Maybe this street had been the border between ordinary working people and the more substantial members of the turn-of-the-century middle class. Maybe that brownstone had been the upscale home of a merchant or a sea captain. Maybe it had resonated to the sound of a piano on the weekends, from a daughter who'd studied at the Peabody

Conservatory. But they'd all moved on to places where there was grass, and this house, too, was now vacant, a brown, three-story ghost of a different time. He was surprised at how wide the streets were, perhaps because when they'd been laid out the principal mode of transport had been horse-powered wagons. Kelly shook the thought off. It was not relevant, and his mind had to concentrate on what was.

Four hours, finally, had passed when the three came out again, the men in the lead, the girl following. Shorter than Pam, stockier. Kelly risked himself slightly by lifting his head to watch. He needed to get a good look at Billy, who he assumed to be the driver. Not a very impressive figure, really, perhaps five-nine, slim at one-fifty or so, something shiny at his wrist, a watch or bracelet; he moved with brisk economy—and arrogance. The other was taller and more substantial, but a subordinate, Kelly thought, from the way he moved and the way he followed. The girl, he saw, followed more docilely still, her head down. Her blouse, if that's what it was, wasn't fully buttoned, and she got into the car without raising her head to look around or do anything else that might proclaim interest in the world around her. The girl's movements were slow and uneven, probably from drugs, but that wasn't all of it. There was something else, something Kelly didn't quite catch about her that was disturbing nonetheless . . . a slackness, perhaps. Not laziness in her movement but something else. Kelly blinked hard when he remembered where he'd seen it before. At the *ville,* during PLASTIC FLOWER, the way the villagers had moved to assemble when they'd been summoned. Resigned, automatic motion, like living robots under the control of that major and his troops. They would have moved the same way to their deaths. And so she moved. And so would she.

So it was all true, then, Kelly thought. *They really did use girls as couriers . . . among other things.* The car started as he watched, and Billy's manner with the car matched the name to the driver. The car jerked a few feet to the corner, then turned left, accelerating with the squeal of tires across the intersection and out of Kelly's sight. *Billy,*

five-nine, slim, watch or bracelet, arrogant. The positive
identification was set in Kelly's brain, along with the face
and the hair. He wouldn't forget it. The other male form
was recorded as well, the one without a name—just a
destiny far more immediate than its owner knew.

Kelly checked the watch in his pocket. One-forty. What
had they been doing in there? Then he remembered other
things that Pam had said. A little party, probably. That girl,
whoever she was, probably also had O+, O–, or AB– fluid in
her. But Kelly couldn't save the whole world, and the best
way to save her had nothing at all to do with freeing her
directly. He relaxed himself, just a little, waiting, because
he didn't want his movement to appear to be linked with
anything in case someone might have seen him, even be
watching him now. There were lights in some of these
houses, and so he lingered in his spot for another thirty
minutes, enduring his thirst and some minor cramps before
rising and shambling off to the corner. He'd been very
careful tonight, very careful and very effective, and it was
time for the second phase of the night's work. Time to
continue his efforts at making a diversion.

Mainly he stuck to alleys, moving slowly, allowing his
gait to wander left and right for several blocks in the
undulating path of a snake—he smiled—before he went
back to the streets, only pausing briefly to put on the pair
of rubber surgical gloves. He passed a number of pushers
and their lieutenants as time passed, looking for the right
one. His path was what is called a quartering search, a
series of ninety-degree turns centered actually on where his
Volkswagen was parked. He had to be careful, as always,
but he was the unknown hunter, and the prey animals had
no idea what they were, deeming themselves to be predators themselves. They were entitled to their illusions.

It was almost three when Kelly selected him. A loner, as
Kelly had taken to calling them. This one had no lieutenant,
perhaps was a new one in this business, just learning the
ropes. He wasn't that old, or didn't appear so from forty
yards away, as he counted through his roll after the night's
enterprise. There was a lump at his right hip, undoubtedly
a handgun, but his head was down. He was somewhat alert.

On hearing Kelly's approach the head came up and turned, giving him a quick once-over, but the head went back to its task, dismissing the approaching shape and counting the money as the distance closed.

Kelly had troubled himself to go to his boat earlier in the day, using the Scout because he didn't want anyone at the yard to know that he had a different car, and retrieving something. As he approached Junior—everyone had to have an assigned name, however briefly—Kelly shifted the wine bottle from his right hand to his left. The right hand then pulled the cotter pin from the tip of the bang stick that was inside his new bush jacket, held in cloth loops on the left side on the now unbuttoned garment. It was a simple metal rod, eighteen inches long, with a screw-on cylinder at the tip, and the cotter pin dangled from a short length of light chain. Kelly's right hand removed it from the loops, still holding it in place as he closed on Junior.

The pusher's head turned again in annoyance. Probably he had trouble counting, and now he was arranging the bills by denomination. Maybe Kelly's approach had disturbed his concentration, or maybe he was just dumb, which seemed the more likely explanation.

Kelly stumbled, falling to the sidewalk, his head lowered, making himself look all the more harmless. His eyes looked backwards as he rose. He saw no other pedestrians within more than a hundred yards, and the only automobile lights he noted were red, not white, all pointed or heading away. As his head came up, there was no one at all in his view except for Junior, who was finishing up the night's work, ready to go wherever home was for a nightcap or something else.

Ten feet now, and the pusher was ignoring him as he might ignore a stray dog, and Kelly knew the exhilaration that came the moment before it happened, that last moment of excited satisfaction when you just knew it was going to work, the enemy in the kill zone, unsuspecting that his time had come. The moment in which you could feel the blood in your veins, when you alone knew the silence was about to be violated, the wonderful satisfaction of knowing. Kelly's right hand came out a little as he took another step, still not headed all that close to the target, clearly walking past him, not towards him, and the criminal's eyes looked up again, just for a moment to make sure, no fear in his eyes, hardly even annoyance; not moving, of course, because people walked around *him*, not the reverse. Kelly was just an object to him, one of the things that occupied the street, of no more interest than an oil stain on the blacktop.

The Navy called it CPA, Closest Point of Approach, the nearest distance that a straight course took you to another ship or point of land. CPA here was three feet. When he was half a step away, Kelly's right hand pulled the bang stick from under his jacket. Then he pivoted on his left foot and drove off the right while his right arm extended almost as though to deliver a punch, all one hundred ninety-five pounds of his body mass behind the maneuver. The swollen tip of the bang stick struck the pusher just under the sternum, aimed sharply upward. When it did, the combined push of Kelly's arm and the inertial mass of the body pushed the chamber backwards, jamming the primer on the fixed firing pin, and the shotgun shell went off, its crimped green-plastic face actually in contact with Junior's shirt.

The sound was like that of dropping a cardboard box on a wooden floor. *Whump.* Nothing more than that, certainly not like a shot at all, because all the expanding gas from the powder followed the shot column into Junior's body. The light trap load—a low-brass shell with #8 birdshot, like that used for competition shooting, or perhaps an early-season dove hunt—would have only injured a man at more than fifteen yards, but in contact with his chest, it might as easily have been an elephant gun. The brutal power of the shot drove the air from his lungs in a surprisingly loud *whoosh*, forcing Junior's mouth open in a way that surprise might have done. And truly he was surprised. His eyes looked into Kelly's, and Junior was still alive, though his heart was already as destroyed as a toy balloon, and the bottom of his lungs torn to bits. Gratifyingly, there was no exit wound. The upward angle of the strike left all of the energy and shot inside the chest, and the power of the explosion served to keep his body erect for a second—no more than that, but for Junior and Kelly it seemed a moment that lasted for hours. Then the body just fell, straight down, like a collapsing building. There was an odd, deep sigh, from air and gun-gases forced out of the entrance wound by the fall, a foul odor of acrid smoke and blood and other things that stained the air, not unlike the ended life it represented. Junior's eyes were still open, still looking at Kelly, still focusing on his face and trying to say something, his mouth open and quivering until all movement stopped with the question un-asked and -answered. Kelly took the roll from Junior's still-firm hand and kept moving up the street, his eyes and ears searching for danger, and finding none. At the corner he angled to the gutter and swished the tip of the bang stick in some water to remove whatever blood might be there. Then he turned, heading west to his car, still moving slowly and unevenly. Forty minutes later he was home, richer by eight hundred forty dollars and poorer by one shotgun shell.

"And who's this one?" Ryan asked.

"Would you believe, Bandanna?" the uniformed officer answered. He was an experienced patrol officer, white, thirty-two years old. "Deals smack. Well, not anymore."

The eyes were still open, which was not terribly common in murder victims, but this one's death had been a surprise, and a very traumatic one at that, despite which the body was amazingly tidy. There was a three-quarter-inch entrance wound with a jet-black ring around it like a donut, perhaps an eighth of an inch in thickness. That was from powder, and the diameter of the hole was unmistakably that of a 12-gauge shotgun. Beyond the skin was just a hole, like into an empty box. All of the internal organs had either been immolated or simply pulled down by gravity. It was the first time in his life that Emmet Ryan had ever looked *into* a dead body this way, as though it were not a body at all, but a mannequin.

"Cause of death," the coroner observed with early-morning irony, "is the total vaporization of his heart. The only way we'll even be able to identify heart tissue is under a microscope. Steak tartare," the man added, shaking his head.

"An obvious contact wound. The guy must have jammed the muzzle right into him, then triggered it off."

"Jesus, he didn't even cough up any blood," Douglas said. The lack of an exit wound left no blood at all on the sidewalk, and from a distance Bandanna actually looked as though he were asleep—except for the wide and lifeless eyes.

"No diaphragm," the ME explained, pointing to the entrance *hole.* "That's between here and the heart. We'll probably find that the whole respiratory system is wiped out, too. You know, I've never seen anything this clean in my life." And the man had been working this job for sixteen years. "We need *lots* of pictures. This one will find its way into a textbook."

"How experienced was he?" Ryan asked the uniformed officer.

"Long enough to know better."

The detective lieutenant bent down, feeling around the left hip. "Still has a gun here."

"Somebody he knew?" Douglas wondered. "Somebody he let get real close, that's for damned sure."

"A shotgun's kinda hard to conceal. Hell, even a sawed-off is bulky. No warning at all?" Ryan stepped back for the ME to do his work.

"Hands are clean, no signs of a struggle. Whoever did this got real close without alarming our friend at all." Douglas paused. "Goddamn it, a shotgun's *noisy.* Nobody heard anything?"

"Time of death, call it two or three for now," the medical examiner estimated, for again there was no rigor.

"Streets are quiet then," Douglas went on. "And a shotgun makes a shitload of noise."

Ryan looked at the pants pockets. No bulge of a money roll, again. He looked around. There were perhaps fifteen people watching from behind the police line. Street entertainment was where you found it, and the interest on their faces was no less clinical and no more involved than that of the medical examiner.

"The Duo maybe?" Ryan asked nobody in particular.

"No, it wasn't," the ME said at once. "This was a single-barrel weapon. A double would have made a mark left or right of the entrance wound, and the powder distribution would have been different. Shotgun, this close, you only need one. Anyway, a single-barrel weapon."

"Amen," Douglas agreed. "Someone is doing the Lord's work. Three pushers down in a couple of days. Might put Mark Charon out of business if this keeps up."

"Tom," Ryan said, "not today." *One more folder,* he thought. *Another drug-pusher ripoff, done very efficiently—but not the same guy who'd taken Ju-Ju down. Different MO.*

Another shower, another shave, another jog in Chinquapin Park during which he could think. Now he had a place and a face to go along with the car. The mission was on profile, Kelly thought, turning right on Belvedere Avenue to cross the stream before jogging back the other way and completing his third lap. It was a pleasant park. Not much in the way of playground equipment, but that allowed kids to run and play free-form, which a number of them were doing, some under the semiwatchful eyes of a few neighborhood mothers, many with books to go along with the sleeping infants who would soon grow to enjoy the grass and open spaces. There was an undermanned pickup game of baseball. The ball evaded the glove of a nine-year-old and came close to his jogging path. Kelly bent down without breaking stride and tossed the ball to the kid, who caught it this time and yelled a thank-you. A younger child was playing with a Frisbee, not too well, and wandered in Kelly's way, causing a quick avoidance maneuver that occasioned an embarrassed look from her mother, to which Kelly responded with a friendly wave and smile.

This is how it's supposed to be, he told himself. Not very different from his own youth in Indianapolis. Dad's at work. Mom's with the kids because it was hard to be a good mom and have a job, especially when they were little; or at least, those mothers who had to work or chose to work could leave the kids with a trusted friend, sure that the little ones would be safe to play and enjoy their summer vacation in a green and open place, learning to play ball. And yet society had learned to accept the fact that it wasn't this way for many. This area was so different from his area of operations, and the privileges these kids enjoyed ought not to be privileges at all, for how could a child grow to proper adulthood without an environment like this?

Those were dangerous thoughts, Kelly told himself. The logical conclusion was to try to change the whole world, and that was beyond his capacity, he thought, finishing his three-mile run with the usual sweaty and good-tired feel, walking it off to cool down before he drove back to the apartment. The sounds drifted over of laughing children, the squeals, the angry shouts of *cheater!* for some perceived violation of rules not fully understood by either player, and disagreements over who was out or who was "it" in some other game. He got into his car, leaving the sounds and thought behind, because he was cheating, too, wasn't he? He was breaking the rules, important rules that he *did* fully understand, but doing so in pursuit of justice, or what he called justice in his own mind.

Vengeance? Kelly asked himself, crossing a street. *Vigilante* was the next word that came unbidden into his mind. That was a better word, Kelly thought. It came from *vigiles*, a Roman term for those who kept the watch, the *vigilia* during the night in the city streets, mainly watchmen for fire, if he remembered correctly from the Latin classes at St. Ignatius High School, but being Romans they'd probably carried swords, too. He wondered if the streets of Rome had been safe, safer than the streets of this city. Perhaps so—probably so. Roman justice had been . . . stern. Crucifixion would not have been a pleasant way to die, and for some crimes, like the murder of one's father, the penalty prescribed by law was to be bound in a cloth sack along with a dog and a rooster, and some other animal, then to be tossed in the Tiber—not to drown, but to be torn apart while drowning by animals crazed to get out of the sack. Perhaps he was the linear descendant of such times, of a *vigile,* Kelly told himself, keeping watch at night. It made him feel better than to believe that he was breaking the law. And "vigilantes" in American history books were very different from those portrayed in the press. Before the organization of real police departments, private citizens had patrolled the streets and kept the peace in a rough-and-ready way. As he was doing?

Well, no, not really, Kelly admitted to himself, parking the car. So what if it was vengeance? Ten minutes later another garbage bag filled with another set of discarded clothes found its way to the Dumpster, and Kelly enjoyed another shower before making a telephone call.

"Nurses' station, O'Toole."

"Sandy? It's John. Still getting out at three?"

"You do have good timing," she said, allowing herself a private smile at her stand-up desk. "The damn car is broke again." And taxicabs cost too much.

"Want me to look at it?" Kelly asked.

"I wish somebody could fix it."

"I make no promises," she heard him say. "But I come cheap."

"How cheap?" Sandy asked, knowing what the reply would be.

"Permit me to buy you dinner? You can pick the place, even."

"Yes, okay . . . but . . ."

"But it's still too soon for both of us. Yes, ma'am, I know that. Your virtue is not endangered—honest."

She had to laugh. It was just so incongruous that this big man could be so self-effacing. And yet she knew that she could trust him, and she was weary of cooking dinner for one, and being alone and alone and alone. Too soon or not, she needed company sometimes.

"Three-fifteen," she told him, "at the main entrance."

"I'll even wear my patient bracelet."

"Okay." Another laugh, surprising another nurse who passed by the station with a trayful of medications. "Okay, I said yes, didn't I?"

• • •

"Yes, ma'am. See you then," Kelly said with a chuckle, hanging up.

Some human contact would be nice, he told himself, heading out the door. First Kelly headed to a shoe store, where he purchased a pair of black high-tops, size eleven. Then he found four more shoe stores, where he did the same, trying not to get the same brand, but he ended up with one duplicate pair even so. The same problem attended the purchase of bush jackets. He could find only two brand names for that type of garment, and ended up getting a pair of duplicates, then to discover that they were exactly the same, different only in the name tag inside the neck. Planned diversity in disguise, he found, was harder than he'd expected it to be, but that didn't lessen the necessity of sticking to his plan. On getting back to his apartment—he was, perversely, thinking of it as "home" though he knew better—he stripped everything of tags and headed for the laundry room, where all the clothes went into the machine on a hot-hot cycle with plenty of Clorox bleach, along with the remaining dark-color clothes he'd picked up at yard sales. He was down to three clothing sets now, and realized he'd have to shop for more.

The thought evoked a frown. More yard sales, which he found tedious, especially now that he'd developed an operational routine. Like most men Kelly hated shopping, now all the more since his adventures were of necessity repetitive. His routine was also tiring him out, both from lack of sleep and the unremitting tension of his activity. None of it was routine, really. Everything was dangerous. Even though he was becoming accustomed to his mission, he would not become inured to the dangers, and the stress was there. That was partly good news in that he wasn't taking anything lightly, but stress could also wear at any man in little, hard-to-perceive ways such as the increased heart rate and blood pressure that resulted in fatigue. He was controlling it with exercise, Kelly thought, though sleep was becoming a problem. All in all it was not unlike working the weeds in 3rd SOG, but he was older now, and the lack of backup, the absence of companions to share the stress and ease the strain in the off-hours, was taking its toll. *Sleep,* he told himself, checking his watch. Kelly switched on the TV set in the bedroom, catching a noon news show.

"Another drug dealer was found dead in west Baltimore today," the reporter announced.

"I know," Kelly said back, fading out for his nap.

"Here's the story," a Marine colonel said at Camp Lejeune, North Carolina, while another was doing much the same thing at exactly the same time at Camp Pendleton, California. "We have a special job. We're selecting volunteers exclusively from Force Recon. We need fifteen people. It's dangerous. It's important. It's something you'll be proud of doing after it's over. The job will last two to three months. That's all I can say."

At Lejeune a collection of perhaps seventy-five men, all combat veterans, all members of The Corps' most exclusive unit, sat in their hard-backed chairs. Recon Marines, they'd all volunteered to become Marines first—there were no draftees here—then done so again to join the elite within the elite. There was a slightly disproportionate representation of minorities, but that was only a matter of interest to sociologists. These men were *Marines* first, last, always, as alike as their green suits could make them. Many bore scars on their bodies, because their job was more dangerous and demanding than that of ordinary infantrymen. They specialized in going out in small groups, to look and learn, or to kill with a very high degree of selectivity. Many of them were qualified snipers, able to place an aimed shot in a particular head at four hundred yards, or a chest at over a thousand, if the target had the good manners to stand still for the second or two needed for the bullet to cover the longer distance. They were the hunters. Few had nightmares from their duties, and none would ever fall victim to delayed-stress syndrome, because they deemed themselves to be predators, not prey, and lions know no such feelings.

But they were also men. More than half had wives and/or children who expected Daddy to come home from time to time; the rest had sweethearts and looked forward to settling down in the indeterminate future. All had served one thirteen-month tour of duty. Many had served two; a handful had actually served three, and none of this last group would volunteer. Some of them might have, perhaps most, had they only known the nature of the mission, because the call of duty was unusually strong in them, but duty takes many forms, and these men judged that they had served as much as any man should for one war. Now their job was to train their juniors, passing along the lessons that had enabled them to return home when others almost as good as they were had not; that was their institutional duty to The Corps, they all thought, as they sat quietly in their chairs and looked at the Colonel on the stage, wondering what *it* was, intensely curious but not curious enough to place their lives at risk again after having done so too often already. A few of them looked furtively left and right, reading the faces of the younger men, knowing from the expressions which ones would linger in the room and place their names in the hat. Many would regret not staying behind, knowing even now that not knowing what it was all about, and probably never finding out, would forever leave a blank spot on their consciences—but against that they weighed the faces of their wives and children and decided no, not this time.

After a few moments the men rose and filed out. Perhaps twenty-five or thirty stayed behind to register their names as volunteers. Their personnel jackets would be collected quickly and evaluated, and fifteen of their number would be selected in a process that appeared random but was not. Some special slots had to be filled with special skills, and in the nature of volunteering, some of the men rejected would actually be better and more proficient warriors than some of those accepted because their personal skills had been made redundant by another volunteer. Such was life in uniform, and the men all accepted it, each with feelings of regret and relief as they returned to their normal duties. By the end of the day, the men who were going were assembled and briefed on departure times and nothing more. A bus would be taking them, they noted. They couldn't be going very far. At least not yet.

Kelly awoke at two and got himself cleaned up. This afternoon's mission demanded that he look civilized, and so he wore a shirt and a tie and a jacket. His hair, still growing back from being shaved, needed a trim, but it was a little late for that. He selected a blue tie for his blue blazer and white shirt and walked out to where the Scout was parked, looking like the executive salesman he'd pretended to be, waving at the apartment manager on the way.

Luck smiled on Kelly. There was an opening on the traffic loop at the hospital's main entrance, and he walked in to see a large statue of Christ in the lobby, perhaps fifteen or twenty feet high, staring down at him with a benign expression more fitting to a hospital than to what Kelly had been doing only twelve hours earlier. He walked around it, his back to the statue's back because he didn't need that sort of question on his conscience—not now.

Sandy O'Toole appeared at three-twelve, and when he saw her come through the oak doors Kelly smiled until he saw the look on her face. A moment later he understood why. A surgeon was right behind her, a short, swarthy man in greens, walking as rapidly as his short legs permitted and talking loudly at her. Kelly hesitated, looking on with curiosity as Sandy stopped and turned, perhaps tired of running away or merely bending to the necessity of the moment. The doctor was of her height, perhaps a little less, speaking so rapidly that Kelly didn't catch all the words while Sandy looked in his eyes with a blank expression.

"The incident report is filed, doctor," she said during a brief pause in his tirade.

"You have no right to do that!" The eyes blazed angrily in his dark, pudgy face, causing Kelly to draw a little closer.

"Yes, I do, doctor. Your medication order was incorrect. I am the team leader, and I am *required* to report medication errors."

"I am *ordering* you to withdraw that report! Nurses do not give orders to doctors!" What followed was language that Kelly didn't like, especially in the presence of God's image. As he watched, the doctor's dark face grew darker, and he leaned into the nurse's space, his voice growing louder. For her part, Sandy didn't flinch, refusing to allow herself to be intimidated, which goaded the doctor further.

"Excuse me." Kelly intruded on the dispute, not too close, just to let everyone know that someone was here, and momentarily drawing an angry look from Sandra O'Toole. "I don't know what you two are arguing about, but if you're a doctor and the lady here is a nurse, maybe you two can disagree in a more professional way," he suggested in a quiet voice.

It was as though the physician hadn't heard a thing. Not since he was sixteen years old had anyone ignored Kelly so blatantly. He drew back, wanting Sandy to handle this herself, but the doctor's voice merely grew louder, switching now to a language he didn't understand, mixing English vituperation with Farsi. Through it all Sandy stood her ground, and Kelly was proud of her, though her face was growing wooden and her impassive mien had to be masking some real fear now. Her impassive resistance only goaded the doctor into raising his hand and then his voice even more. It was when he called her a "fucking cunt," doubtless something learned from a local citizen, that he stopped. The fist that he'd been waving an inch from Sandy's nose had disappeared, encased, he saw with surprise, in the hairy forepaw of a very large man.

"Excuse me," Kelly said in his gentlest voice. "Is there somebody upstairs who knows how to fix a broken hand?" Kelly had wrapped his fingers around the surgeon's smaller, more delicate hand, and was pressing the fingers inward, just a little.

A security guard came through the door just then, drawn by the noise of the argument. The doctor's eyes went that way at once.

"He won't get here fast enough to help you, doctor. How many bones in the human hand, sir?" Kelly asked.

"Twenty-eight," the doctor replied automatically.

"Want to go for fifty-six?" Kelly tightened his pressure.

The doctor's eyes closed on Kelly's, and the smaller man saw a face whose expression was neither angry nor pleased, merely there, looking at him as though he were an object, whose polite voice was a mocking expression of superiority. Most of all, he knew that the man would do it.

"Apologize to the lady," Kelly said next.

"I do not abase myself before women!" the doctor hissed. A little more pressure on the hand caused his face to change. Only a little additional force, he knew, and things would begin to separate.

"You have very bad manners, sir. You only have a little time to learn better ones." Kelly smiled. "Now," he commanded. "Please."

"I'm sorry, Nurse O'Toole," the man said, without really meaning it, but the humiliation was still a bleeding gash on his character. Kelly released the hand. Then he lifted the doctor's name tag, and read it before staring again into his eyes.

"Doesn't that feel better, Doctor Khofan? Now, you won't ever yell at her again, at least not when she's right and you're wrong, will you? And you won't *ever* threaten her with bodily harm, will you?" Kelly didn't have to explain why that was a bad idea. The doctor was flexing his fingers to work off the pain. "We don't like that here, okay?"

"Yes, okay," the man said, wanting to run away.

Kelly took his hand again, shaking it with a smile, just enough pressure for a reminder. "I'm glad you understand, sir. I think you can go now."

And Dr. Khofan left, walking past the security guard without so much as a look. The guard did give one to Kelly, but let it go at that.

"Did you have to do that?" Sandy asked.

"What do you mean?" Kelly replied, turning his head around.

"I was handling it," she said, now moving to the door.

"Yes, you were. What's the story, anyway?" Kelly asked in a reasonable voice.

"He prescribed the wrong medication, elderly man with a neck problem, he's allergic to the med, and it's on the chart," she said, the words spilling out rapidly as Sandy's stress started bleeding off. "It could have really hurt Mr. Johnston. Not the first time with him, either. Doctor Rosen might get rid of him this time, and he wants to stay here. He likes pushing nurses around, too. We don't like that. But I was handling it!"

"Next time I'll let him break your nose, then." Kelly waved to the door. There wouldn't be a next time; he'd seen that in the little bastard's eyes.

"And then what?" Sandy asked.

"Then he'll stop being a surgeon for a while. Sandy, I don't like seeing people do things like that, okay? I don't like bullies, and I really don't like seeing them push women around."

"You really hurt people like that?"

Kelly opened the door for her. "No, not very often. Mainly they listen to my warnings. Look at it this way, if he hits you, you get hurt and he gets hurt. This way nobody gets hurt except for a few bent feelings, maybe, and nobody ever died from that."

Sandy didn't press the issue. Partly she was annoyed, feeling that she'd stood up well to the doctor, who wasn't all that good a surgeon and was far too careless on his post-op technique. He only did charity patients, and only those with simple problems, but that, she knew, was beside the point. Charity patients were *people,* and *people* merited the best care the profession could provide. He had frightened her. Sandy had been glad of the protection, but somehow felt cheated that she hadn't faced Khofan down herself. Her incident report would probably sink him once and for all, and the nurses on the unit would trade chuckles about it. Nurses in hospitals, like NCOs in any military unit, really ran things, after all, and it was a foolish doctor who crossed them.

But she'd learned something about Kelly this day. The look she'd seen and been unable to forget had not been an illusion. Holding Khofan's right hand, the look on John's face had been—well, no expression at all, not even amusement at his humiliation of the little worm, and that was vaguely frightening to her.

"So what's wrong with your car?" Kelly asked, pulling onto Broadway and heading north.

"If I knew that, it wouldn't be broke."

"Yeah, I guess that makes sense," Kelly allowed with a smile.

He's a changeling, Sandy told herself. He turns things on and off. With Khofan he was like a gangster or something. First he tried to calm things down with a reasonable word, but then he acted like he was going to inflict a permanent injury. Just like that. No emotion at all. Like squashing a bug. But if that's true, what *is* he? Was it temper? No, she told herself, probably not. He's too in control for that. A psychopath? That was a scary thought—but no, that wasn't possible either. Sam and Sarah wouldn't have a friend like that, and they're two very smart people.

What, then?

"Well, I brought my toolbox. I'm pretty good on diesels. Aside from our little friend, how was work?"

"A good day," Sandy said, glad again for the distraction. "We discharged one we were really worried about. Little black girl, three, fell out of her crib. Doctor Rosen did a wonderful job on her. In a month or two you'll never know she was hurt at all."

"Sam's a good troop," Kelly observed. "Not just a good doc—he's got class, too."

"So's Sarah." *Good troop, that's what Tim would have said.*

"Great lady." Kelly nodded, turning left onto North Avenue. "She did a lot for Pam," he said, this time reporting facts without the time for reflection. Then Sandy saw his face change again, freezing in place as though he'd heard the words from another's voice.

The pain won't ever go away, will it? Kelly asked himself. Again he saw her in his mind, and for a brief, cruel second, he told himself—lied, knowing it even as it happened—that she was beside him, sitting there on the right seat. But it wasn't Pam, never would be again. His hands tightened on the plastic of the steering wheel, the knuckles suddenly white as he commanded himself to set it aside. Such thoughts were like minefields. You wandered into them, innocent, expecting nothing, then found out too late that there was danger. *It would be better not to remember,* Kelly thought. *I'd really be better off that way.* But if without memories, good and bad, what was life, and if you forgot those who mattered to you, then what did you become? And if you didn't act on those memories, what value did life have?

Sandy saw it all on his face. A changeling, perhaps, but not always guarded. *You're not a psychopath. You feel pain and they don't—at least not from the death of a friend. What are you, then?*

18
Interference

"Do it again," he told her.

Thunk.

"Okay, I know what it is," Kelly said. He leaned over her Plymouth Satellite, jacket and tie off, sleeves rolled up. His hands were already dirty from half an hour's probing.

"Just like that?" Sandy got out of her car, taking the keys with her, which seemed odd, on reflection, since the damned car wouldn't start. *Why not leave them in and let some car thief go nuts?* she wondered.

"I got it down to one thing. It's the solenoid switch."

"What's that?" she asked, standing next to Kelly and looking at the oily-blue mystery that was an automobile engine.

"The little switch you put the key in isn't big enough for all the juice you need to turn the starter, so that switch controls a bigger one here." Kelly pointed with a wrench. "It activates an electromagnet that closes a bigger switch, and that one lets the electricity go to the starter motor. Follow me so far?"

"I think so." Which was almost true. "They told me I needed a new battery."

"I suppose somebody told you that mechanics love to—"

"Jerk women around 'cuz we're so dumb with cars?" Sandy noted with a grimace.

"Something like that. You're going to have to pay me something, though," Kelly told her, rummaging in his toolbox.

"What's that?"

"I'm going to be too dirty to take you out to dinner. We have to eat here," he said, disappearing under the car, white shirt, worsted slacks and all. A minute later he was back out, his hands dirty. "Try it now."

Sandy got back in and turned the key. The battery was down a little but the engine caught almost at once.

"Leave it on to charge things up."

"What was it?"

"Loose wire. All I did was tighten it up some." Kelly looked at his clothes and grimaced. So did Sandy. "You need to take it into the shop and have a lock washer put on the nut. Then it shouldn't get loose again."

"You didn't have to—"

"You have to get to work tomorrow, right?" Kelly asked reasonably. "Where can I wash up?"

Sandy led him into the house and pointed him towards a bathroom. Kelly got the grime off his hands before rejoining her in the living room.

"Where'd you learn to fix cars?" she asked, handing him a glass of wine.

"My dad was a shade-tree mechanic. He was a fireman, remember? He had to learn all that stuff, and he liked it. I learned from him. Thanks." Kelly toasted her with the glass. He wasn't a wine drinker, but it wasn't bad.

"Was?"

"He died while I was in Vietnam, heart attack on the job. Mom's gone, too. Liver cancer, when I was in grade school," Kelly explained as evenly as he could. The pain was distant now. "That was tough. Dad and I were pretty close. He was a smoker, that's probably what killed him. I was sick myself at the time, infection from a job I did. I couldn't get home or anything. So I just stayed over there when I got better."

"I wondered why nobody came to visit you, but I didn't ask," Sandy said, realizing how alone John Kelly was.

"I have a couple uncles and some cousins, but we don't see each other much."

It was a little clearer now, Sandy thought. Losing his mother at a young age, and in a particularly cruel and lingering way. He'd probably always been a big kid, tough and proud, but helpless to change things. Every woman in his life had been taken away by force of one kind or another: his mother, his wife, and his lover. *How much rage he must feel,* she told herself. It explained so much. When he'd seen Khofan threatening her, it was something he could protect her from. She still thought she could have handled it herself, but now she understood a little better. It defused her lingering anger, as did his manner. He didn't get too close to her, didn't undress her with his eyes—Sandy particularly hated that, though, strangely, she allowed patients to do it because she felt that it helped to perk them up. He acted like a *friend,* she realized, as one of Tim's fellow officers might have done, mixing familiarity with respect for her identity, seeing her as a person first, a woman after that. Sandra Manning O'Toole found herself liking it. As big and tough as he was, there was nothing to fear from this man. It seemed an odd observation with which to begin a relationship, if that was the thing happening.

Another *thunk* announced the arrival of the evening paper. Kelly got it and scanned the front page before dropping it on the coffee table. A front-page story on this slow summer news day was the discovery of another dead drug pusher. She saw Kelly looking at it, scanning the first couple of paragraphs.

Henry's increasing control of the local drug traffic virtually ensured that the newly dead dealer had been one of his distant minions. He'd known the dead man by his street name and only learned the real one, Lionel Hall, from the news article. They'd never actually met, but Bandanna had been mentioned to him as a clever chap, one worth keeping his eye on. Not clever enough, Tucker thought. The ladder to success in his business was steep, with slippery rungs, the selection process brutally Darwinian, and somehow Lionel Hall had not been equal to the demands of his new profession. A pity, but not a matter of great import. Henry rose from his chair and stretched. He'd slept late, having taken delivery two days earlier of fully fifteen kilograms of "material," as he was starting to call it. The boat trip to and from the packaging point had taken its toll—it was becoming a pain in the ass, Tucker thought, maintaining that elaborate cover. Those thoughts were dangerous, however, and he knew it. This time he'd merely watched his people do the work. And now two more knew more than they'd known before, but he was tired of doing such menial work himself. He had minions for that, little people who knew that they were little and knew they would prosper only so long as they followed orders exactly.

Women were better at that than men. Men had egos that they had to nurture within their own fertile minds, and the smaller the mind the greater the ego. Sooner or later one of his people would rebel, get a little too uppity. The hookers he used were so much more easily cowed, and then there was the fringe benefit of having them around. Tucker smiled.

Doris awoke about five, her head pounding with a barbiturate-induced hangover made worse still by the double shot of whiskey that someone had decided to give her. The pain told her that she would have to live another day, that the mixture of drugs and alcohol hadn't done the job she'd dared to hope for when she'd looked at the glass, hesitated, then gunned it down before the party. What had followed the whiskey and the drugs was only half remembered, and it blended into so many other such nights that she had trouble separating the new from the old.

They were more careful now. Pam had taught them that. She sat up, looking at the handcuff on her ankle, its other end locked in a chain that was in turn fastened to a fitting screwed into the wall. Had she thought about it, she might have tried ripping it out, which a healthy young woman might have accomplished with a few hours of determined effort. But escape was death, a particularly hard and lengthy death, and as much as she desired the escape from a life grown horrid beyond any nightmare, pain still frightened her. She stood, causing the chain to rattle. After a moment or two Rick came in.

"Hey, baby," the young man said with a smile that conveyed amusement rather than affection. He bent down, unlocked the cuffs, and pointed to the bathroom. "Shower. You need it."

"Where did you learn to cook Chinese?" Kelly asked.

"A nurse I worked with last year. Nancy Wu. She's teaching at the University of Virginia now. You like it?"

"You kidding me?" If the shortest distance to any man's heart is his stomach, then one of the better compliments a man can give a woman is to ask for seconds. He held himself to one glass of wine, but attacked the food as quickly as decent table manners allowed.

"It's not that good," Sandy said, blatantly fishing for a compliment.

"It's much better than what I fix for myself, but if you're thinking about writing a cookbook, you need somebody with better taste." He looked up. "I visited Taipei for a week once, and this is almost that good."

"What did you do there?"

"R and R, sort of a vacation from getting shot at." Kelly stopped it there. Not everything he and his friends had done was proper information to convey to a lady. Then he saw that he'd gone too far already.

"That's what Tim and—I already had it planned for us to meet in Hawaii, but—" Her voice stopped again.

Kelly wanted to reach out to her, take her hand across the table, just to comfort her, but he feared it might seem to be an advance.

"I know, Sandy. So what else did you learn to cook?"

"Quite a lot. Nancy stayed with me for a few months and made me do all the cooking. She's a wonderful teacher."

"I believe it." Kelly cleaned his plate. "What's your schedule like?"

"I usually get up quarter after five, leave here just after six. I like to be on the unit half an hour before shift change so I can check the status of the patients and get ready for the new arrivals from the OR. It's a busy unit. What about you?"

"Well, it depends on the job. When I'm shooting—"

"Shooting?" Sandy asked, surprised.

"Explosives. It's my specialty. You spend a lot of time planning it and setting it up. Usually there's a few engineers around to fuss and worry and tell me what not to do. They keep forgetting that it's a hell of a lot easier to blow something up than it is to build it. I do have one trademark, though."

"What's that?"

"On my underwater work, I shoot some blasting caps a few minutes before I do the real shoot." Kelly chuckled. "To scare the fish away."

She was puzzled for a second. "Oh—so they won't get hurt?"

"Right. It's a personal quirk."

It was just one more thing. He'd killed people in war, threatened a surgeon with permanent injury right in front of her and a security guard, but he went out of his way to protect *fish?*

"You're a strange one."

He had the good grace to nod. "I don't kill for the fun of it. I used to hunt, and I gave that up. I fish a little, but not with dynamite. Anyway, I set the caps a good ways from the real job—that's so it won't have any effect on the important part. The noise scares most of them away. Why waste a perfectly good game fish?" Kelly asked.

It was automatic. Doris was somewhat nearsighted, and the marks looked like dirt when her eyes were clouded by the falling water, but they weren't dirt and they didn't wash off. They never disappeared, merely migrating to different places at the vagaries of the men who inflicted them. She rubbed her hands over them, and the pain told her what they were, reminders of the more recent parties, and then the effort to wash herself became futile. She knew she'd never be clean again. The shower was only good for the smell, wasn't it? Even Rick had made that clear enough, and he was the nicest of them, Doris told herself, finding a fading brown mark that he had placed on her, not one so painful as the bruises that Billy seemed to like.

She stepped out to dry off. The shower was the only part of the room that was even vaguely tidy. Nobody ever bothered to clean the sink or toilet, and the mirror was cracked.

"Much better," Rick said, watching. His hand extended to give her a pill.

"Thanks." And so began another day, with a barbiturate to put distance between herself and reality, to make life, if not comfortable, not tolerable, then endurable. Barely. With a little help from her friends, who saw to it that she did endure the reality they made. Doris swallowed the pill with a handful of water, hoping that the effects would come fast. It made things easier, smoothing the sharp edges, putting a distance between herself and her self. It had once been a distance too great to see across, but no longer. She looked at Rick's smiling face as it swept over her.

"You know I love ya, baby," he said, reaching to fondle her.

A wan smile as she felt his hands. "Yes."

"Special party tonight, Dor. Henry's coming over."

Click. Kelly could almost hear the sound as he got out of the Volkswagen, four blocks from the corner brownstone, as he switched trains of thought. Entering the "treeline" was becoming routine. He'd established a comfort level that tonight's dinner had enhanced, his first with another human being in . . . five weeks, six? He returned to the matter at hand.

He settled into a spot on the other side of the cross street, again finding marble steps which generated a shadow, and waited for the Roadrunner to arrive. Every few minutes he'd lift the wine bottle—he had a new one now, with a red street wine instead of the white—for a simulated drink, while his eyes continuously swept left and right, even up and down to check second- and third-floor windows.

Some of the other cars were more familiar now. He spotted the black Karmann-Ghia which had played its part in Pam's death. The driver, he saw, was someone of his age, with a mustache, prowling the street looking for his connection. He wondered what the man's problem was that to assuage it he had to come from wherever his home might be to this place, risking his physical safety so that he might shorten his life with drugs. He was also leaving corruption and destruction in his wake with the money from the illicit traffic. Didn't he care about that? Didn't he see what drug money did to these neighborhoods?

But that was something Kelly was working very hard to ignore as well. There were still real people trying to eke out their lives here. Whether on welfare or subsisting on menial employment, real people lived here, in constant danger, perhaps hoping to escape to someplace where a real life was possible. They ignored the traffickers as best they could, and in their petty righteousness they ignored the street bums like Kelly, but he could not find it in himself to dislike them for that. In such an environment they, like he, had to concentrate on personal survival. Social conscience was a luxury that most people here could scarcely afford. You needed some rudimentary personal security of your own before you could take from its surplus and apply it to those more needy than yourself—and besides, how many were more needy than they were?

There were times when it was just a pleasure to be a man, Henry thought in the bathroom. Doris had her charms. Maria, the spindly, dumb one from Florida. Xantha, the one most drug-dependent, a cause for minor concern, and Roberta, and Paula. None were much beyond twenty, two still in their teens. All the same and all different. He patted some after-shave onto his face. He ought to have a real main-lady of his own, someone glamorous for other men to see and envy. But that was dangerous. To do that invited notice. No, this was just fine. He walked out of the room, refreshed and relaxed. Doris was still there, semiconscious now from the experience and the two-pill reward, looking at him with a smile that he decided was respectful enough. She'd made the proper noises at the proper times, done the things that he'd wanted done without being asked. He could mix his own drinks, after all, and the silence of solitude was one thing, while the silence of a dumb bitch in the house was something else, something tedious. Just to be pleasant he bent down, offering a finger to her lips, which she duly kissed, her eyes unfocused.

"Let her sleep it off," Henry told Billy on the way out.

"Right. I have a pickup tonight anyway," Billy reminded him.

"Oh?" Tucker had forgotten in the heat of the moment. Even Tucker was human.

"Little Man was short a thousand last night. I let it slide. It's the first time, and he said he just goofed on his count. The vig is an extra five yards. His idea."

Tucker nodded. It was the first time ever that Little Man had made that kind of mistake, and he had always shown proper respect, running a nice trade on his piece of sidewalk. "Make sure he knows that one mistake's the house limit."

"Yes, sir." Billy bobbed his head, showing proper respect himself.

"Don't let that word get out, either."

That was the problem. Actually several problems, Tucker thought. First, the street dealers were such small-timers, stupidly greedy, unable to see that a regular approach to their business made for stability, and stability was in everyone's interest. But street pushers were street pushers—criminals, after all—and he'd never change that. Every so often one would die from a rip or a turf fight. Some were even dumb enough to use their own stuff—Henry was as careful as he could be to avoid them, and had been mainly successful. Occasionally one would try to press the limits, claiming to be cash-short just to chisel a few hundred bucks when he had a street trade many times that. Such cases had a single remedy, and Henry had enforced that rule with sufficient frequency and brutality that it hadn't been necessary to repeat it for a long time. Little Man had probably spoken the truth. His willingness to pay the large penalty made it likely, also evidence of the fact that he valued his steady supply, which had grown in recent months as his trade increased. Still, for months to come he would have to be watched carefully.

What most annoyed Tucker was that he had to trouble himself with such trivialities as Little Man's accounting mistake. He knew it was just a case of growing pains, the natural transition process from small-time local supplier to major distributor. He'd have to learn to delegate his authority, letting Billy, for example, handle a higher level of responsibility. Was he ready? Good question, Henry told himself, leaving the building. He handed a ten to the youth who'd watched over his car, still considering the question. Billy had a good instinct for keeping the girls in line. A clever white boy from Kentucky's coal country, no criminal record. Ambitious. Team player. Maybe he was ready for a step up.

Finally, Kelly thought to himself. It was quarter after two when the Roadrunner appeared, after at least an hour's worrying that it might not appear at all. He settled back in the shadows, becoming a little more erect, and turned his head to give the man a good look. Billy and his sidekick. Laughing about something. The other one stumbled on the steps, maybe having had a drink too many or something. More to the point, when he fell there was a flutter of light little twirling rectangles that had to be banknotes.

That's where they count their money? Kelly wondered. *How interesting.* Both men bent down quickly to recover the cash, and Billy cuffed the other man on the shoulder, half playfully, saying something that Kelly couldn't make out from fifty yards off.

The buses passed every forty-five minutes at this time of night, and their route was several blocks away. The police patrol was highly predictable. The neighborhood routine was predictable as well. By eight the regular traffic was gone, and by nine-thirty the local citizens abandoned the streets entirely, barricading themselves behind triple-locked doors, thanking Providence that they had survived another day, already dreading the dangers of the next, and leaving the streets mainly to the illicit traffic. That traffic lingered until about two, Kelly had long since established, and on careful consideration he decided that he knew all that he needed to know. There were still random elements to be considered. There always were, but you could not predict the random, only prepare for it. Alternate evasion routes, constant vigilance, and weapons were the defense against it. Something was always left to chance, and however uncomfortable *that* was, Kelly had to accept it as a part of normal life—not that anything about his mission was normal.

He rose, tiredly, crossing the street and heading to the brownstone with his accustomed drunken gait. The door, he confirmed, wasn't locked. The brass plate behind the knob was askew, he saw as he took a single long look while he passed by. The image fixed itself in his mind, and as he moved he began planning his mission for the following night. He heard Billy's voice again, a laugh filtering through the upstairs windows, an oddly accented sound, decidedly unmusical. A voice he already loathed, and for which he had special plans. For the first time he was close to one of the men who had murdered Pam. Probably two of them. It didn't have the physical effect one might have expected. His body relaxed. He'd do this one right.

Be seeing you, guys, he promised in the silence of his thoughts. This was the next really big step forward, and he couldn't risk blowing it. Kelly headed up the block, his eyes fixed on the two Bobs, a quarter mile away, clearly visible due to their size and the perfectly straight, wide city street.

This was another test—he had to be sure of himself. He headed north, without crossing the street, because if he followed a straight path all the way to them, they might notice and be at least curious about it, if not really alert. His approach had to be invisible, and by changing his angle relative to his targets instead of holding constant, he allowed his stooped body to blend into the background of housefronts and parked cars. Just a head, a small dark shape, nothing dangerous. At one block's distance he crossed the street, taking the opportunity again to scan all four compass points. Turning left, he headed up the sidewalk. It was fully twelve or fifteen feet wide, punctuated by the marble steps, giving useful maneuvering room for his uneven, meandering walk. Kelly stopped, lifting the bag-wrapped bottle to his lips before moving on. Better yet, he thought, another demonstration of his harmless nature. He stopped again to urinate in the gutter.

"Shit!" a voice said, Big or Little, he didn't bother to check. The disgust in the word was enough, the sort of thing that made a man turn away from what he beheld. Besides, Kelly thought, he'd needed the relief.

Both men were larger than he. Big Bob, the dealer, was six-three. Little Bob, the lieutenant, was fully six-five, muscular, but already developing a pot from beer or starchy food. Both were quite formidable enough, Kelly decided, making a quick reevaluation of his tactics. Better to pass by and leave them be?

No.

But he did pass by first. Little Bob was looking across the street. Big Bob was leaning back against the building. Kelly drew an imaginary line between the two and counted three steps before turning left slowly so as not to alert them. He moved his right hand under the new-old bush jacket as he did so. As the right came out, the left covered it, wrapping around the handle of the Colt automatic in a two-hand grip and boxing posture later to be called the Weaver stance. His eyes went down, acquiring the white-painted line on the top of the suppressor as the gun came up. His arms extended full-length without locking the elbows, and the physical maneuver brought the sights in alignment with the first target, quickly but smoothly. The human eye is drawn to motion, particularly at night. Big Bob saw the move, knowing that something untoward was happening, but not sure what. His street-smart instincts made the correct analysis and screamed for action. Too late. *Gun,* he saw, starting to move his hand to a weapon of his own instead of dodging, which might have delayed his death.

Kelly's fingertip depressed the trigger twice, the first as the suppressor covered the target, the second right behind it, as soon as his wrist compensated for the .22's light recoil. Without shifting his feet he swiveled right, a mechanical turn that took the gun in an exact horizontal plane towards Little Bob, who had reacted already, seeing his boss starting to fall and reaching for his own weapon at his hip. Moving, but not fast enough. Kelly's first shot was not a good one, hitting low and doing little damage. But the second entered the temple, caroming off the thicker portions of the skull and racing around inside like a hamster in a cage. Little Bob fell on his face. Kelly lingered only long enough to be sure that both were dead, then turned and moved on.

Six, he thought, heading for the corner, his heart settling down from the rush of adrenaline, putting the gun back in its place next to the knife. It was two fifty-six as Kelly began his evasion drill.

Things hadn't started off well, the Recon Marine thought. The chartered bus had broken down once, and the "shortcut" the driver had selected to make up lost time had come to a halt behind a traffic tieup. The bus pulled into Quantico Marine Base just after three, following a jeep to its final destination. The Marines found an isolated barracks building already half occupied by snoring men and picked bunks for themselves so they could get some sleep. Whatever the interesting, exciting, dangerous mission was to be, the startup was just one more day in the Green Machine.

Her name was Virginia Charles, and her night wasn't going well either. A nurse's aide at St. Agnes Hospital, only a few miles out from her neighborhood, her shift had been extended by the late arrival of her relief worker and her own unwillingness to leave her part of the floor unattended. Though she'd worked the same shift at the hospital for eight years, she hadn't known that the bus schedule changed soon after her normal departure time, and having just missed one bus, she'd had to wait what seemed to be forever for the next. Now she was getting off, two hours past her normal bedtime, and having missed

"The Tonight Show," which she watched religiously on weekdays. Forty, divorced from a man who had given her two children—one a soldier, thankfully in Germany not Vietnam, and the other still in high school—and little else. On her union job, which was somewhere between menial and professional, she'd managed to do well for both of her sons, ever worrying as mothers do about their companions and their chances.

She was tired when she got off the bus, asking herself again why she hadn't used some of the money she'd saved over the years to get herself a car. But a car demanded insurance, and she had a young son at home who would both increase the cost of driving and give her something else to worry about. Maybe in a few years when that one, too, entered the service, which was his only hope for the college education she wished for him but would never be able to afford on her own.

She walked quickly and alertly, a tense stiffness in her weary legs. How the neighborhood had changed. She'd lived within a three-block radius all her life, and she could remember a lively and *safe* street life with friendly neighbors. She could even remember being able to walk to the New Zion A.M.E. Church without a worry on a rare Wednesday night off, which she had missed again due to her job. But she consoled herself with two hours of overtime which she could bank, and watched the streets for danger. It was only three blocks, she told herself. She walked fast, smoking a cigarette to stay alert, telling herself to be calm. She'd been mugged—the local term was actually "yoked"—twice in the previous year, both times by drug addicts needing money to support whatever habits they had, and the only good thing to come from that was the object lesson it had given to her sons. Nor had it cost her much in monetary terms. Virginia Charles never carried much more money than carfare and other change to get dinner at the hospital cafeteria. It was the assault on her dignity that hurt, but not quite as badly as her memories of better times in a neighborhood peopled by mostly law-abiding citizens. One more block to go, she told herself, turning a corner.

"Hey, mama, spare a dollar?" a voice said, already behind her. She'd seen the shadow and kept walking past it, not turning, not noticing, ignoring it in the hope that the same courtesy would be extended to her, but that sort of courtesy was becoming rare. She kept moving, lowering her head, telling herself to keep moving, that not too many street toughs would attack a woman from behind. A hand on her shoulder gave the lie to that assumption.

"Give me money, bitch," the voice said next, not even with anger, just a matter-of-fact command in an even tone that defined what the new rules of the street were.

"Ain't got enough to interest you, boy," Virginia Charles said, twisting her shoulders so that she could keep moving, still not looking back, for there was safety in movement. Then she heard a *click*.

"I'll cut you," the voice said, still calm, explaining the hard facts of life to the dumb bitch.

That sound frightened her. She stopped, whispering a quiet prayer, and opened her small purse. She turned slowly, still more angry than frightened. She might have screamed, and only a few years earlier it would have made a difference. Men would have heard it and looked, perhaps come out to chase the assailant away. She could see him now, just a boy, seventeen or eighteen, and his eyes had the lifeless amplification of some sort of drug, that plus the arrogant inhumanity of power. Okay, she thought, pay him off and go home. She reached into the purse and extracted a five-dollar bill.

"Five whole dollar?" The youth smirked. "I need more'n that, bitch. Come on, or I'll cut you."

It was the look in the eyes that really scared her, causing her to lose her composure for the first time, insisting, "It's all I have!"

"More, or you bleed."

Kelly turned the corner, only half a block from his car, just starting to relax. He hadn't heard anything until he made the turn, but there were two people, not twenty feet from the rusting Volkswagen, and a flare of reflected light told him that one was holding a knife.

His first thought was *Shit!* He'd already decided about this sort of thing. He couldn't save the whole world, and he wasn't going to try. Stopping one street crime might be fine for a TV show, but he was after bigger game. What he had not considered was an incident right next to his car.

He stopped cold, looking, and his brain started grinding as quickly as the renewed flood of adrenaline allowed. If anything serious happened here, the police would come right to this place, might be here for hours, and he'd left a couple of dead bodies less than a quarter mile behind him—not even that far, because it wasn't a straight line. This was not good, and he didn't have much time to make a decision. The boy had the woman by the arm, brandishing a knife, with his back to him. Twenty feet was an easy shot even in the dark, but not with a .22 that penetrated too much, and not with someone innocent or at least nonthreatening behind him. She was wearing some sort of uniform, older, maybe forty, Kelly saw, starting to move that way. That's when things changed again. The boy cut the woman's upper arm, the red clear in the glow of the streetlights.

Virginia Charles gasped when the knife sliced her arm, and yanked away, or tried to, dropping the five-dollar bill. The boy's other hand grabbed her throat to control her, and she could see in his eyes that he was deciding the next place for the knife to go. Then she saw movement, a man perhaps fifteen feet away, and in her pain and panic she tried to call for help. It wasn't much of a sound, but enough for the mugger to notice. Her eyes were fixed on something—what?

The youth turned to see a street wino ten feet away. What had been an instant and automatic alarm changed to a lazy smile.

Shit. This was not going well at all. Kelly's head was lowered, his eyes up and looking at the boy, sensing that the event was not really in his control.

"Maybe you got some money, too, pop?" he asked, intoxicated with power, and on a whim he took a step towards the man who had to have more money than this nursey bitch.

Kelly hadn't expected it, and it threw his timing off. He reached for his gun, but the silencer caught on his waistband, and the incoming mugger instinctively took his movement for the threatening act it had to be. He took another step, more quickly, extending his knife hand. There was no time now to bring the gun out. Kelly stopped, backing off a half step and coming up to an erect stance.

For all his aggressiveness, the mugger wasn't very skillful. His first lunge with the knife was clumsy, and he was surprised at how easily the wino batted it aside, then stepped inside its arc. A stiff, straight right to the solar plexus deflated his lungs, winding him but not stopping his movements entirely. The knife hand came back wildly as the mugger started folding up. Kelly grabbed the hand, twisting and extending the arm, then stepping over the body already headed to the pavement. An extended ripping/cracking sound announced the dislocation of the youth's shoulder, and Kelly continued the move, rendering the arm useless.

"Why don't you go home, ma'am," he told Virginia Charles quietly, turning his face away and hoping she hadn't seen it very well. She ought not to have done so, Kelly told himself; he'd moved with lightning speed.

The nurse's aide stooped down to recover the five-dollar bill from the sidewalk and left without a word. Kelly watched sideways, seeing her hold her right hand on the bleeding left arm as she tried not to stagger, probably in shock. He was grateful that she didn't need any help. She would call someone, sure as hell, at least an ambulance, and he really ought to have helped her deal with her wound, but the risks were piling up faster than his ability to deal with them. The would-be mugger was starting to moan now, the pain from his destroyed shoulder penetrating the protective fog of narcotics. And this one had definitely seen his face, close up.

Shit, Kelly told himself. Well, he'd attempted to hurt a woman, and he'd attacked Kelly with a knife, both of them, arguably, failed attempts at murder. Surely this wasn't his first such attempt. He'd picked the wrong game and, tonight, the wrong playground, and mistakes like that had a price. Kelly took the knife from his limp hand and shoved it hard into the base of his skull, leaving it there. Within a minute his Volkswagen was half a block away.

Seven, he told himself, turning east.

Shit.

19
Quantity of Mercy

It was becoming more routine than the morning coffee and Danish at his desk, Lieutenant Ryan told himself. Two pushers down, both with a pair of .22s in the head, but *not* robbed this time. No loose cartridge cases around, no evident sign of a struggle. One with his hand on his pistol grip, but the gun hadn't cleared his hip pocket. For all that, it was unusual. He'd at least seen danger and reacted to it, however ineffectively. Then had come the call from only a few blocks away, and he and Douglas had rolled to that one, leaving junior detectives to deal with this crime scene. The call had identified the new one as interesting.

"Whoa," Douglas said, getting out first. One did not often see a knife sticking in the back of a head, up in the air like a fence post. "They weren't kidding."

The average murder in this part of the city, or any part of any city for that matter, was some sort of domestic argument. People killed other family members, or close friends, over the most trivial disputes. The previous Thanksgiving a father had killed his son over a turkey leg. Ryan's personal "favorite" was a homicide over a crab cake—not so much a matter of amusement as hyperbole. In all such cases the contributing factors were usually alcohol and a bleak life that transformed ordinarily petty disputes into matters of great import. *I didn't mean it* was the phrase most often heard afterwards, followed by some variation of *why didn't he just back off a little?* The sadness of such events was like a slow-acting acid on Ryan's soul. The sameness of those murders was the worst part of all. Human life ought not to end like variations of a single theme. It was too precious for that, a lesson learned in the bocage country of Normandy and the snowy forests around Bastogne when he'd been a young paratrooper in the 101st Airborne. The typical murderer claimed not to have meant it, and frequently copped to the crime immediately, as remorseful as he or she could be over the loss of a friend or loved one by his or her own hand, and so two lives were often destroyed by the crime. Those were crimes of passion and poor judgment, and that's what murder was, for the most part. But not this one.

"What the hell's the matter with the arm?" he asked the medical examiner. Aside from the needle tracks the arm was twisted around so much that he realized he was looking at the wrong side of it.

"The victim's shoulder appears to be dislocated. Make that wrecked," the ME added after a second's consideration. "We have bruising around the wrist from the force of the grip. Somebody held the arm with two hands and damned near tore the arm off, like taking a branch off a tree."

"Karate move?" Douglas asked.

"Something like that. That sure slowed him down some. You can see the cause of death."

"Lieutenant, over here," a uniformed sergeant called. "This is Virginia Charles, she lives a block over. She reported the crime."

"Are you okay, Miss Charles?" Ryan asked. A fireman-paramedic was checking the bandage she'd placed on her own arm, and her son, a senior at Dunbar High School, stood by her side, looking down at the murder victim without a trace of sympathy. Within four minutes Ryan had a goodly quantity of information.

"A bum, you say?"

"Wino—that's the bottle he dropped." She pointed. Douglas picked it up with the greatest care.

"Can you describe him?" Lieutenant Ryan asked.

The routine was so exactingly normal that they might have been at any Marine base from Lejeune to Okinawa. The daily-dozen exercises followed by a run, everyone in step, the senior NCO calling cadence. They took particular pleasure in passing formations of new second lieutenants in the Basic Officers Course, or even more wimpy examples of officer-wannabes doing their summer school at Quantico. Five miles, passing the five-hundred-yard KD range and various other teaching facilities, all of them named for dead Marines, approaching the FBI Academy, but turning back off the main road then, into the woods towards their training site. The morning routine merely reminded them that they were Marines, and the length of the run made them Recon Marines, for whom Olympic-class fitness was the norm. They were surprised to see a general officer waiting for them. Not to mention a sandbox and a swing set.

"Welcome to Quantico, Marines," Marty Young told them after they'd had a chance to cool down and been told to stand at ease. Off to the side, they saw two naval officers in sparkling undress whites, and a pair of civilians, watching and listening. Eyes narrowed collectively, and the mission was suddenly very interesting indeed.

"Just like looking at the photos," Cas observed quietly, looking around the training site; they knew what the lecture was about. "Why the playground stuff?"

"My idea," Greer said. "Ivan has satellites. The overhead schedules for the next six weeks are posted inside Building A. We don't know how good the cameras are, and so I'm going to assume that they're as good as ours, okay? You show the other guy what he wants to see or you make it easy for him to figure out. Any really harmless place has a parking lot." The drill was already determined. Every day the new arrivals would move the cars around randomly. Around ten every day they would take the mannequins from the cars and distribute them around the playground equipment. At two or three the cars would be moved again and the mannequins rearranged. They suspected correctly that the ritual would acquire a great deal of institutional humor.

"And after it's all over, it becomes a real playground?" Ritter asked, then answered his own question. "Hell, why not? Nice job, James."

"Thank you, Bob."

"It looks small this way," Admiral Maxwell said.

"The dimensions are accurate to within three inches. We cheated," Ritter said. "We have the Soviet manual for building places like this. Your General Young did a nice job."

"No glass in the windows on Building C," Casimir noted.

"Check the photos, Cas," Greer suggested. "There's a shortage of window glass over there. That building just has shutters, here and there. The callback"—he pointed to Building B—"has the bars. Just wood so that they can be removed later. We've just guessed at the inside arrangements, but we've had a few people released from the other side and we've modeled this place on the debriefs. It's not totally made up from thin air."

The Marines were already looking around, having learned a little of the mission. Much of the plan they already knew, and they were thinking about how to apply their lessons of real combat operations to this perverted playground, complete with child mannequins who would watch them train with blue doll eyes. M-79 grenades to blast the guard towers. Willie-pete through the barracks windows. Gunships to hose things down after that . . . the "wives" and "kids" would watch the rehearsal and tell no one.

The site had been carefully selected for its similarity with another place—the Marines hadn't needed to be told that; it had to be so—and a few eyes lingered on a hill half a mile from the site. You could see everything from there. After the welcoming speech, the men divided into predetermined units to draw their weapons. Instead of M16A1 rifles, they had the shorter CAR-15 carbines, shorter, handier, preferred for close work. Grenadiers had standard M-79 grenade launchers, whose sights had been painted with radioactive tritium to glow in the dark, and their bandoleers were heavy with practice rounds because weapons training would start immediately. They'd start in daylight for feel and proficiency, but almost immediately their training would switch exclusively to night work, which the General had left out. It was obvious in any case. This sort of job only happened at night. The men marched to the nearest weapons-firing range to familiarize themselves. Already set up were window frames, six of them. The grenadiers exchanged looks and fired off their first volley. One, to his shame, missed. The other five razzed him at once, after making sure that the white puffs from their training rounds had appeared behind the frames.

"All right, all right, I just have to warm up," the corporal said defensively, then placed five shots through the target in forty seconds. He was slow—it had been a mainly sleepless night.

"How strong do you have to be to do that, I wonder?" Ryan asked.

"Sure as hell isn't Wally Cox," the ME observed. "The knife severed the spinal cord just where it enters the medulla. Death was instantaneous."

"He already had the guy crippled. The shoulder as bad as it looks?" Douglas asked, stepping aside for the photographer to finish up.

"Worse, probably. We'll look at it, but I'll bet you the whole structure is destroyed. You don't repair an injury like this, not all the way. His pitching career was over even before the knife."

White, forty or older, long black hair, short, dirty. Ryan looked at his notes. "Go home, ma'am," he'd told Virginia Charles.

Ma'am.

"Our victim was still alive when she walked away." Douglas came over to his lieutenant. "Then he must have taken his knife away and gave it back. Em, in the past week we've seen four very expert murders and six very dead victims."

"Four different MOs. Two guys tied up, robbed, and executed, .22 revolver, no sign of a struggle. One guy with a shotgun in the guts, also robbed, no chance to defend himself. Two last night just shot, probably a .22 again, but not robbed, not tied up, and they were alerted before they were shot. Those were all pushers. But this guy's just a street hood. Not good enough, Tom." But the Lieutenant had started thinking about it. "Have we ID'd this one yet?"

The uniformed sergeant answered. "Junkie. He's got a rap sheet, six arrests for robbery, God knows what else."

"It doesn't fit," Ryan said. "It doesn't fit anything, and if you're talking about a really clever guy, why let somebody see him, why let her leave, why talk to her—hell, why take this guy out at all? What pattern does that fit?" There was no pattern. Sure, the two pairs of drug dealers had been taken down with a .22, but the small-bore was the most commonly used weapon on the street, and while one pair had been robbed, the other had not; nor had the second pair been shot with the same deadly precision, though each *did* have two head wounds. The other murdered and robbed dealer had been done by a shotgun. "Look, we have the murder weapon, and we have the wine bottle, and from one or both we'll get prints. Whoever this guy was, he sure as hell wasn't real careful."

"A wino with a sense of justice, Em?" Douglas prodded. "Whoever took this punk down—"

"Yeah, yeah, I know. He wasn't Wally Cox." *But who and* what *the hell was he?*

Thank God for gloves, Kelly thought, looking at the bruises on his right hand. He'd let his anger get the better of him, and that wasn't smart! Looking back, reliving the incident, he realized that he'd been faced with a difficult situation. If he'd let the woman get killed or seriously injured, and just gotten into his car and driven off, first, he'd never really have been able to forgive himself, and second, if anyone had seen the car, he'd be a murder suspect. That extended thought evoked a snort of disgust. He *was* a murder suspect now. Well, somebody would be. On coming home, he'd looked in the mirror, wig and all. Whatever that woman had seen, it had not been John Kelly, not with a face shadowed by his heavy beard, smeared with dirt, under a long and filthy wig. His hunched-over posture made him appear several inches shorter than he was. And the light on the street had not been good. And she'd been even more interested in getting away than anything else. Even so. He'd somehow left his wine bottle behind. He remembered dropping it to parry the knife thrust, and then in the heat of the moment he'd not recovered it. *Dumb!* Kelly raged at himself.

What would the police know? The physical description would not be a good one. He'd worn a pair of surgical gloves, and though they allowed him to bruise his hands, they hadn't torn and he hadn't bled. Most important of all, he had never touched the wine bottle with ungloved hands. Of that he was certain because he'd decided from the beginning to be careful about it. The police would know a street bum had killed that punk, but there were lots of street bums, and he only needed one more night. It meant that he'd have to alter his operational pattern even so, and that tonight's mission was more dangerous than it ought to be, but his information on Billy was too good to pass up on, and the little bastard might be smart enough to change his own patterns. What if he used different houses to count his cash or only used one for a few nights? If that was true, any wait beyond a day or two might invalidate his whole reconnaissance effort, forcing him to start again with a new disguise—*if* he could select something equally effective, which was not immediately likely. Kelly told himself that he'd killed six people to get this far—the seventh was a mistake and didn't count . . . except maybe to that lady, whoever she was. He took a deep breath. If he'd watched her get hurt worse, or killed, how would he be able to look in a mirror? He had to tell himself that he'd made the best of a bad situation. Shit happens. It ran the risks up, but the only concern there was failure in the mission, not in danger to himself. It was time to set his thoughts aside. There were other responsibilities as well. Kelly lifted his phone and dialed.

"Greer."

"Clark," Kelly responded. At least that was still amusing.

"You're late," the Admiral told him. The call was supposed to have been before lunch, and Kelly's stomach churned a little at the rebuke. "No harm done, I just got back. We're going to need you soon. It's started."

That's fast, Kelly thought. *Damn.* "Okay, sir."

"I hope you're in shape. Dutch says you are," James Greer said more kindly.

"I think I can hold up, sir."

"Ever been to Quantico?"

"No, Admiral."

"Bring your boat. There's a marina there and it'll give us a place to chat. Sunday morning. Ten sharp. We'll be waiting, Mr. Clark."

"Aye aye." Kelly heard the phone click off.

Sunday morning. He hadn't expected that. It was going too fast, and it made his other mission all the more urgent. Since when had the government ever moved that quickly? Whatever the reason, it affected Kelly directly.

"I hate it, but it's the way we work," Grishanov said.

"You really are that tied to your ground radar?"

"Robin, there is even talk of having the missile firing done by the intercept-control officer from his booth on the ground." The disgust in his voice was manifest.

"But then you're just a driver!" Zacharias announced. "You have to trust your pilots."

I really should have this man speak to the general staff, Grishanov told himself with no small degree of disgust. *They won't listen to me. Perhaps they would listen to him.* His countrymen had vast respect for the ideas and practices of Americans, even as they planned to fight and defeat them.

"It is a combination of factors. The new fighter regiments will be deployed along the Chinese border, you see—"

"What do you mean?"

"You didn't know? We've fought the Chinese three times this year, at the Amur River and farther west."

"Oh, come on!" This was too incredible for the American to believe. "You're allies!"

Grishanov snorted. "Allies? Friends? From the outside, yes, perhaps it looks as though all socialists are the same. My friend, we have battled with the Chinese for centuries. Don't you read history? We supported Chiang over Mao for a long time—we trained his army for him. Mao hates us. We foolishly gave him nuclear reactors, and now they have nuclear arms, and do you suppose their missiles can reach my country or yours? They have Tu-16 bombers—Badgers you call them, yes? Can they reach America?"

Zacharias knew that answer. "No, of course not."

"They can reach Moscow, I promise you, and they carry half-megaton nuclear bombs, and for that reason the MiG-25 regiments are on the Chinese border. Along that axis we have no strategic depth. Robin, we've had real battles with these yellow bastards, division-size engagements! Last winter we crushed their attempt to take an island that belongs to us. They struck first, they killed a battalion of border guards and mutilated the dead—why do that, Robin, because of their red hair or because of their freckles?" Grishanov asked bitterly, quoting verbatim a wrathful article in *Red Star*. This was a very strange turn of events for the Russian. He was speaking the literal truth, and it was harder to convince Zacharias of this than any one of a number of clever lies he might have used. "We are not allies. We've even stopped shipping weapons to this country by train—the Chinese steal the consignments right off the rail carriages!"

"To use against you?"

"Against whom, then, the Indians? Tibet? Robin, these people are *different* from you and me. They don't see the world as we do. They're like the Hitlerites my father fought, they think they are better than other men—how you say?"

"Master race?" the American suggested helpfully.

"That is the word, yes. They believe it. We're animals to them, useful animals, yes, but they hate us, and they want what we have. They want our oil and our timber and our land."

"How come I've never been briefed on this?" Zacharias demanded.

"Shit," the Russian answered. "Is it any different in your country? When France pulled out of NATO, when they told your people to take your bases out, do you think any of us were told about it beforehand? I had a staff job then in Germany, and nobody troubled himself to tell me that anything was happening. Robin, the way you look to us is the same as how we look to you, a great colossus, but the internal politics in your country are as much a mystery to me as mine are to you. It can all be very confusing, but I tell you this, my friend, my new MiG regiment will be based between China and Moscow. I can bring a map and show you."

Zacharias leaned back against the wall, wincing again with the recurring pain from his back. It was just too much to believe.

"It hurts still, Robin?"

"Yeah."

"Here, my friend." Grishanov handed over his flask, and this time it was accepted without resistance. He watched Zacharias take a long pull before handing it back.

"So just how good is this new one?"

"The MiG-25? It's a *rocket*," Grishanov told him enthusiastically. "It probably turns even worse than your Thud, but for straight-line speed, you have no fighter close to it. Four missiles, no gun. The radar is the most powerful ever made for a fighter, and it cannot be jammed."

"Short range?" Zacharias asked.

"About forty kilometers." The Russian nodded. "We give away range for reliability. We tried to get both but failed."

"Hard for us, too," the American acknowledged with a grunt.

"You know, I do not expect a war between my country and yours. Truly I do not. We have little that you might wish to take away. What we have—resources, space, land—all these things you have. But the Chinese," he said, "they need these things, and they share a border with us. And we gave them the weapons that they will use against us, and there are so *many* of them! Little, evil people, like these here, but so many more."

"So what are you going to do about it?"

Grishanov shrugged. "I will command my regiment. I will plan to defend the Motherland against a nuclear attack from China. I just haven't decided how yet."

"It's not easy. It helps if you have space and time to play with, and the right people to play against."

"We have bomber people, but nothing like yours. You know, even without resistance, I doubt we could place as many as twenty bombers over your country. They're all based two thousand kilometers from where I will be. You know what that means? Nobody even to train against."

"You mean a red team?"

"We would call it a blue team, Robin. I hope you understand." Grishanov chuckled, then turned serious again. "But, yes. It will all be theoretical, or some fighters will pretend to be bombers, but their endurance is too short for a proper exercise."

"This is all on the level?"

"Robin, I will not ask you to trust me. That is too much. You know that and so do I. Ask yourself, do you really think your country will ever make war on my country?"

"Probably not," Zacharias admitted.

"Have I asked you about your war plans? Yes, certainly, they are most interesting theoretical exercises and I would probably find them fascinating war games, but have I asked about them?" His voice was that of a patient teacher.

"No, you haven't, Kolya, that's true."

"Robin, I am not worried about B-52s. I am worried about Chinese bombers. That is the war my country is preparing for." He looked down at the concrete floor, puffing on a cigarette and going on softly. "I remember when I was eleven. The Germans were within a hundred kilometers of Moscow. My father joined his transport regiment—they made it up from university teachers. Half of them never came back. My mother and I evacuated the city, east to some little village whose name I can't remember—it was so confusing then, so dark all the time—worrying about my father, a professor of history, driving a truck. We lost twenty million citizens to the Germans, Robin. Twenty million. People I knew. The fathers of friends—my wife's father died in the war. Two of my uncles died. When I went through the snow with my mother, I promised myself that someday I would defend my country, too, and so I am a fighter pilot. I do not invade. I do not attack. I defend. Do you understand this thing I tell you, Robin? My job is to protect my country so that other little boys will not have to run away from home in the middle of winter. Some of my classmates died, it was so cold. That is why I defend my country. The Germans wanted what we had, and now the Chinese want it, too." He waved towards the door of the cell. "People like . . . like *that.*"

Even before Zacharias spoke, Kolya knew he had him. Months of work for this moment, Grishanov thought, like seducing a virgin, but much sadder. This man would never see his home again. The Vietnamese had every intention of killing these men when their utility ended. It was such a colossal waste of talent, and his antipathy to his supposed allies was every bit as real as he feigned it to be—it was no longer pretense. From the first moment he'd arrived in Hanoi, he'd seen first-hand their arrogant superiority, and their incredible cruelty—and their stupidity. He had just achieved more with kind words and not even a liter of vodka than what they and their torturers had failed to do with years of mindless venom. Instead of inflicting pain, he had shared it. Instead of abusing the man beside him, he had given kindness, respecting his virtues, assuaging his injuries as best he could, protecting him from more, and bitterly regretting that he'd necessarily been the agent of the most recent of them.

There was a downside, however. To achieve this break-through, he'd opened his soul, told true stories, dredged up his own childhood nightmares, reexamined his true reason for joining the profession he loved. Only possible, only thinkable, because he'd known that the man sitting next to him was doomed to a lonely, unknown death—already dead to his family and his country—and an unattended grave. This man was no fascist Hitlerite. He was an enemy, but a straightforward one who had probably done his utmost to spare harm to noncombatants because he, too, had a family. There was in him no illusion of racial superiority—not even hatred for the North Vietnamese, and that was the most remarkable thing of all, for he, Grishanov, was learning to hate them. Zacharias didn't deserve to die, Grishanov told himself, recognizing the greatest irony of all.

Kolya Grishanov and Robin Zacharias were now friends.

"How does this grab you?" Douglas asked, setting it on Ryan's desk. The wine bottle was in a clear plastic bag, and the smooth, clear surface was uniformly coated with a fine yellow dust.

"No prints?" Emmet looked it over in considerable surprise.

"Not even a smudge, Em. Zilch." The knife came down next. It was a simple switchblade, also dusted and bagged.

"Smudges here."

"One partial thumbprint, matched with the victim. Nothing else we can use, but smudges, uniform smudges, the prints department says. Either he stabbed himself in the back of the neck or our suspect was wearing gloves."

It was awfully warm this time of the year to wear gloves. Emmet Ryan leaned back, staring at the evidence items on his desk, then at Tom Douglas, sitting beside them. "Okay, Tom, go on."

"We've had four murder scenes, a total of six victims. No evidence left behind. Five of the victims—three incidents—are pushers, two different MOs. But in every case, no witnesses, roughly the same time of day, all within a five-block radius."

"Craftsmanship." Lieutenant Ryan nodded. He closed his eyes, first mentally viewing the different crime scenes, then correlating the data. Rob, not rob, change MO. But the last one did have a witness. *Go home, ma'am.* Why was he polite? Ryan shook his head. "Real life isn't Agatha Christie, Tom."

"Our young lad, today, Em. Tell me about the method our friend used to dispatch him?"

"Knife there . . . I haven't seen anything like that in a long time. Strong son of a bitch. I did see one . . . back in '58 or '59." Ryan paused, collecting his thoughts. "A plumber, I think, big, tough guy, found his wife in bed with somebody. He let the man leave, then he took a chisel, held her head up—"

"You have to be really pissed off to do it the hard way. Anger, right? Why do it that way?" Douglas asked. "You can cut a throat a lot easier, and the victim is just as dead."

"A lot messier, too. Noisy . . . " Ryan's voice trailed off as he thought it through. It was not appreciated that people with their throats cut made a great deal of noise. If you opened the windpipe there could be the most awful gurgling sound, and if not, people screamed their way to death. Then there was the blood, so much of it, flying like water from a cut hose, getting on your hands and clothes.

On the other hand, if you wanted to kill someone in a hurry, like turning off a light switch, and if you were strong and had him crippled already, the base of the skull, where the spinal cord joined the brain, was just the perfect spot: quick, quiet, and relatively clean.

"The two pushers were a couple blocks away, time of death almost identical. Our friend does them, walks over this way, turns a corner, and sees Mrs. Charles being hassled."

Lieutenant Ryan shook his head. "Why not just keep going? Cross the street, that's the smart move. Why get involved? A killer with morals?" Ryan asked. That was where the theory broke down. "And if the same guy is wasting pushers, what's the motive? Except for the two last night, it looks like robbery. Maybe with those two something spooked him off before he could collect the money and the drugs. A car going down the street, some noise? If we're dealing with a robber, then it doesn't connect with Mrs. Charles and her friend. Tom, it's just speculation."

"Four separate incidents, no physical evidence, a guy wearing gloves—a street wino wearing gloves!"

"Not enough, Tom."

"I'm going to have Western District start shaking them down anyway."

Ryan nodded. That was fair enough.

It was midnight when he left his apartment. The area was so agreeably quiet on a weekday night. The old apartment complex was peopled with residents who minded their own business. Kelly had not so much as shaken a hand since the manager's. A few friendly nods, that was all. There were no children in the complex, just middle-aged people, almost all married couples sprinkled with a few widowed singles. Mainly white-collar workers, a surprising number of whom rode the bus to work downtown, watched TV at night, heading to bed around ten or eleven. Kelly moved out quietly, driving the VW down Loch Raven Boulevard, past churches and other apartment complexes, past the city's sports stadium as the neighborhoods evolved downward from middle- to working-class, and from working-class to subsistence, passing darkened office buildings downtown in his continuing routine. But tonight there was a difference.

Tonight would be his first major payoff. That meant risk, but it always did, Kelly told himself, flexing his hands on the plastic steering wheel. He didn't like the surgical gloves. The rubber held heat in, and though the sweat didn't affect his grip, the discomfort was annoying. The alternative was not acceptable, however, and he remembered not liking a lot of the things he'd done in Vietnam, like the leeches, a thought that generated a few chills. They were even worse than rats. At least rats didn't suck your blood.

Kelly took his time, driving around his objective almost randomly while he sized things up. It paid off. He saw a pair of police officers talking to a street bum, one of them close, the other two steps back, seemingly casual, but the distance between the two cops told him what he needed to know. One was covering the other. They saw the wino as someone potentially threatening.

Looking for you, Johnnie-boy, he told himself, turning the wheel and changing streets.

But the cops wouldn't change their whole operating routine, would they? Looking at and talking to winos would be an additional duty for the next few nights. There were other things that had higher priority: answering calls for holdup alarms in liquor stores, responding to family disputes, even traffic violations. No, hassling drunks would just be one more burden on men already overworked. It would be something with which to spice up their normal patrol patterns, and Kelly had troubled himself to learn what those patterns were. The additional danger was therefore somewhat predictable, and Kelly reasoned that he'd had his supply of bad luck for this mission. Just one more time and he'd switch patterns. To what he didn't know, but if things went right, what he should soon learn would provide the necessary information.

Thank you, he said to destiny, a block away from the corner brownstone. The Roadrunner was right there, and it was early still, a collection night; the girl wouldn't be there. He drove past it, continuing up the next block before turning right, then another block, and right again. He saw a police cruiser and checked the clock on the car. It was within five minutes of its normal schedule, and this one was a solo car. There wouldn't be another pass for about two hours, Kelly told himself, making a final right turn and heading towards the brownstone. He parked as close to it as he dared, then got out and walked away from the target house, heading back to the next block before dropping into his disguise.

There were two pushers on this block, both lone operators. They looked a little tense. Perhaps the word was getting out, Kelly thought with a suppressed smile. Some of their brethren were disappearing, and that had to be cause for concern. He kept well clear of both as he covered the block, inwardly amused that neither knew how close Death had passed them. How tenuous their lives were, and yet they didn't know. But that was a distraction, he told himself, turning yet again and heading to the objective. He paused at the corner, looking around. It was after one in the morning now, and things were settling down into the accustomed boredom that comes at the end of any working day, even the illegal kind. Activity on the street was diminishing, just as expected from all the reconnaissance he had done. There was nothing untoward on this street, and Kelly headed south past the rows of brownstones on one side of the street and brick row-houses on the other. It required all of his concentration to maintain his uneven, harmless gait. One of those who had hurt Pam was now within a hundred yards. Probably two of them. Kelly allowed his mind to see her face again, to hear her voice, to feel the curves of her body. He allowed his face to become a frozen mask of stone and his hands to ball into tight fists as his legs shambled down the wide sidewalk, but only for a few seconds. Then he cleared his mind and took five deep, slow breaths.

"Tactical," he murmured to himself, slowing his pace and watching the corner house, now only thirty yards away. Kelly took in a mouthful of wine and let it dribble down on his shirt again. *Snake to Chicago, objective in sight. Moving in now.*

The sentry, if that's what he was, betrayed himself. The streetlights revealed puffs of cigarette smoke coming out the door, telling Kelly exactly where the first target was. He switched the wine bottle to his left hand and flexed his right one, turning his wrist around to make sure his muscles were loose and ready. Approaching the wide steps, he slumped against them, coughing. Then he walked up towards the door, which he knew to be ajar, and fell against it. Kelly tumbled to the floor, finding himself at the feet of the man whom he'd seen accompany Billy. Along the way, the wine bottle broke, and Kelly ignored the man, whimpering over the broken glass and spreading stain of cheap California red.

"That's tough luck, partner," a voice said. It was surprisingly gentle. "You best move along now."

Kelly just continued his whimpering, down on all fours, weaving on them. He coughed a little more, turning his head to see the sentry's legs and shoes, confirming his identification.

"Come on, pop." Strong hands reached down. Both hands, lifting him. Kelly allowed his own arms to dangle, one going behind as the man started to turn him towards the door. He staggered, turning yet more, and now the sentry was supporting him almost fully. Weeks of training and preparation and careful reconnaissance came together in a single instant.

Kelly's left hand slapped against his face. The right drove the Ka-Bar through the ribs, and so alert were his senses that his fingertips could feel the heart, trying to beat, but only destroying itself on the razor-sharp, double-edged blade of the fighting knife. Kelly twisted the blade, leaving it in as the body shuddered. The dark eyes were wide and shocked, and the knees already buckling. Kelly let him down slowly, quietly, still holding the knife, but he had to allow himself a bit of satisfaction this time. He'd worked too hard for this moment to turn his emotions off completely.

"Remember Pam?" he whispered to the dying body in his hands, and for the question he received his satisfaction. There was recognition through the pain before the eyes rolled back.

Snake.

Kelly waited, counting to sixty before he withdrew the knife, which he wiped off on the victim's shirt. It was a good knife, and it didn't deserve to be stained with that kind of blood.

Kelly rested himself for a moment, breathing deeply. He'd gotten the right target, the subordinate. The principal objective was upstairs. Everything was going according to plan. He allowed himself exactly one minute to calm down and collect himself.

The stairs were creaky. Kelly attenuated that by keeping close to the wall, minimizing the displacement of the wooden treads, moving very slowly, eyes locked upwards because there was nothing below to concern him now. He had already replaced the knife in its scabbard. His .45/.22 was in his right hand now, suppressor screwed on, held low in his right hand as the left traced the cracked plaster wall.

Halfway up he started hearing sounds other than that of the blood coursing through his arteries. A slap, a whimper, a whine. Distant, animal sounds, followed by a cruel chuckle, barely audible even as he reached the landing and turned left towards their source. Breathing next, heavy, rapid and low.

Oh . . . shit! But he couldn't stop now.

"Please . . . " A despairing whisper that caused Kelly's knuckles to turn white around the pistol grip. He moved along the upstairs corridor slowly, again rubbing up against the wall. There was light coming from the master bedroom, only the illumination from streetlights through dirty windows, but with his eyes adjusted to darkness, he could see shadows on one wall.

"What's the matter, Dor?" a male voice asked as Kelly reached the doorframe. Very slowly he moved his head around the vertical barrier of painted wood.

There was a mattress in the room, and on the mattress a woman, kneeling, head down while a hand roughly squeezed her breast, then shook it. Kelly watched her mouth open in silent pain, remembering the photo that the detective had shown him. *You did that to Pam, too, didn't you . . . you little fuck!* Liquid dripped from the girl's face, and the face staring down at her was smiling when Kelly took a step into the room.

His voice was light, relaxed, almost comical. "This looks like fun. Can I play, too?"

Billy turned, looking at the shadow that had just spoken, and saw an extended arm with a big automatic. The face turned back to a pile of clothing and a carry bag of some sort. The rest of him was naked, and his left hand held a tool of some sort, but not a knife or a gun. Those tools were elsewhere, ten feet away, and his eyes could not bring them closer.

"Don't even think it, Billy," Kelly said in a conversational tone.

"Who the fuck—"

"On your face, spread-eagle, or I'll shoot that little dick of yours right off." Kelly altered his aim. It was amazing how much importance men placed on that organ, how easily a threat to it intimidated. Not even a serious threat, what with its size. The brain was much larger and easier to hit. "Down! Now!"

Billy did what he was told. Kelly pushed the girl back on the mattress and reached in his belt for the electrical wire. In a few seconds the hands were securely wrapped and knotted. The left hand still held a pair of pliers, which Kelly took and used to tighten the wire yet more, drawing a gasp from Billy.

Pliers?

Jesus.

The girl was staring at his face, eyes wide, breath heavy, but her movements were slow and her head was tilted. She was drugged to some extent. And she had seen his face, was looking at it now, memorizing it.

Why do you have to be here? This is out of the pattern. You're a complication. I ought to . . . ought to . . .

If you do that, John, then what the fuck are you?

Oh, shit!

Kelly's hands started shaking then. This was real danger. If he let her live, then someone would know who he was—a description, enough to start a proper manhunt, and that would—might—prevent him from accomplishing his goal. But the greater danger was to his soul. If he killed her, that was lost forever. Of that he was certain. Kelly closed his eyes and shook his head. Everything was supposed to have gone so smoothly.

Shit happens, Johnnie-boy.

"Get dressed," he told her, tossing some stuff in her direction. "Do it now, be quiet, and stay there."

"Who are you?" Billy asked, giving Kelly an outlet for his rage. The distributor felt something cold and round at the back of his head.

"You even breathe loud, and your brains go on this floor, got it?" The head nodded by way of an answer.

Now what the hell do I do? Kelly demanded of himself. He looked over at the girl, struggling to put panties on. The light caught her breasts and Kelly's stomach revolted at the marks he saw there. "Hurry up," he told her.

Damn damn damn. Kelly checked the wire on Billy's wrists and decided to do another loop at the elbows, hurting him badly, straining the shoulders, but ensuring that he wouldn't be doing any resisting. To make things worse, he lifted Billy by the arms to a standing position, which evoked a scream.

"Hurt a little, does it?" Kelly asked. Then he applied a gag and turned him to the door. "Walk." To the girl: "You, too."

Kelly conducted them down the steps. There was some broken glass, and Billy's feet danced around it, sustaining cuts. What surprised Kelly was the girl's reaction to the body at the bottom.

"Rick!" she gasped, then stooped down to touch the body.

It had a name, Kelly thought, lifting the girl. "Out the back."

He stopped them at the kitchen, leaving them alone for an instant and looking out the back door. He could see his car, and there was no activity in his view. There was danger in what came next, but danger had again become his companion. Kelly led them out. The girl was looking at Billy, and he at her, motioning with his eyes. Kelly was dumbfounded to see that she was reacting to his silent entreaties. He took her arm and moved her aside.

"Don't worry about him, miss." He pointed her to the car, maneuvering Billy by the upper arm.

A distant voice told him that if she tried to help Billy, then he would have an excuse to—

No, goddamn it!

Kelly unlocked the car, forcing Billy in, then the girl into the front seat, before moving fast to the left-side door. Before starting the car he leaned over the seat and wired up Billy's ankles and knees.

"Who are you?" the girl asked as the car started moving.

"A friend," Kelly said calmly. "I am not going to hurt you. If I wanted to do that, I could have left you with Rick, okay?"

Her reply was slow and uneven, but for all that, still amazing to Kelly. "Why did you have to kill him? He was nice to me."

What the hell? Kelly thought, looking over at her. Her face was scraped, her hair a mess. He turned his eyes back to the street. A police cruiser went past on a reciprocal heading, and despite a brief moment of panic on Kelly's part, it just kept going, disappearing as he turned north.

Think fast, boy.

Kelly could have done many things, but only one alternative was realistic. *Realistic?* he asked himself. *Oh, sure.*

One does not expect to hear doorbells at a quarter to three in the morning. Sandy first thought she had dreamed it, but her eyes had opened, and in the way of the mind, the sound played back to her as though she had actually awakened a second earlier. Even so, she must have dreamed it, the nurse told herself, shaking her head. She'd just started to close her eyes again when it repeated. Sandy rose, slipped on a robe, and went downstairs, too disoriented to be frightened. There was a shape on the porch. She turned on the lights as she opened the door.

"Turn that fucking light off!" A rasping voice that was nonetheless familiar. The command it carried caused her to flip the switch without so much as a thought.

"What are you doing here?" There was a girl at his side, looking thoroughly horrible.

"Call in sick. You're not going to work today. You're going to take care of her. Her name is Doris," Kelly said, speaking in the low commanding tone of a surgeon in the middle of a complex procedure.

"Wait a minute!" Sandy stood erect and her mind started racing. Kelly was wearing a woman's wig—well, too dirty for that. He was unshaven, had on awful clothes, but his eyes were burning with something. Rage was part of it, a fury at something, and the man's strong hands were shaking at his side.

"Remember about Pam?" he asked urgently.

"Well, yes, but—"

"This girl's in the same spot. I can't help her. Not now. I have to do something else."

"What are you doing, John?" Sandy asked, a different sort of urgency in her voice. And then, somehow, it was very clear. The TV news reports she'd been watching over dinner on the black-and-white set in the kitchen, the look she'd seen in his eyes in the hospital; the look she saw now, so close to the other, but different, the desperate compassion and the trust it demanded of her.

"Somebody's been beating the shit out of her, Sandy. She needs help."

"John," she whispered. "John . . . you're putting your life in my hands . . . "

Kelly actually laughed, after a fashion, a bleak snort that went beyond irony. "Yeah, well, you did okay the first time, didn't you?" He pushed Doris in the door and walked away, off to a car, without looking back.

"I'm going to be sick," the girl, Doris, said. Sandy hustled her to the first-floor bathroom and got her to the toilet in time. The young woman knelt there for a minute or two, emptying her belly into the white porcelain bowl. After another minute or so, she looked up. In the glare of incandescent lights off the white-tile walls, Sandra O'Toole saw the face of hell.

20

Depressurization

It was after four when Kelly pulled into the marina. He backed the Scout to the transom of his boat and got out to open the cargo hatch after checking the darkness for spectators, of which, thankfully, there were none.

"Hop," he told Billy, and that he did. Kelly pushed him aboard, then directed him into the main salon. Once there, Kelly got some shackles, regular marine hardware, and fastened Billy's wrists to a deck fitting. Ten minutes more and he had cast off, heading out to the Bay, and finally Kelly allowed himself to relax. With the boat on autopilot, he loosed the wires on Billy's arms and legs.

Kelly was tired. Moving Billy from the back of the VW into the Scout had been harder than he'd expected, and at that he'd been lucky to miss the newspaper distributor, dumping his bundles on street corners for the paper boy to unwrap and deliver before six. He settled back into the control chair, drinking some coffee and stretching by way of reward to his body for its efforts.

Kelly had the lights turned way down so that he could navigate without being blinded by the internal glow of the salon. Off to port were a half-dozen cargo ships tied up at

Dundalk Marine Terminal, but very little in his sight was moving. There was always something relaxing about the water at a time like this, the winds were calm, and the surface a gently undulating mirror that danced with lights on the shore. Red and green lights from buoys blinked on and off while telling ships to stay out of dangerous shallows. *Springer* passed by Fort Carroll, a low octagon of gray stone, built by First Lieutenant Robert E. Lee, U.S. Army Corps of Engineers; it had held twelve-inch rifles as recently as sixty years before. The orange fires of the Bethlehem Steel Sparrow's Point Works glowed to the north. Tugboats were starting to move out of their basins to help various ships out of their berths, or to help bring new ones alongside, and their diesels growled across the flat surface in a distant, friendly way. Somehow that noise only emphasized the pre-dawn peace. The quiet was overwhelmingly comforting, just as things should be in preparation for the start of a new day.

"Who the fuck are you?" Billy asked, relieved of his gag and unable to bear the silence. His arms were still behind him, but his legs were free, and he sat up on the deck of the salon.

Kelly sipped his coffee, allowing his tired arms to relax and ignoring the noise behind him.

"I said, who the fuck are you!" Billy called more loudly.

It was going to be a warm one. The sky was clear. There were plenty of stars visible, with not even a hint of gathering clouds. No "Red Sky at Morning" to cause Kelly concern, but the outside temperature had dipped only to seventy-seven, and that boded ill for the coming day, with the hot August sun to beat down on things.

"Look, asshole, I want to know who the fuck you are!"

Kelly shifted a little in the wide control chair, taking another sip of his coffee. His compass course was one-two-one, keeping to the southern edge of the shipping channel, as was his custom. A brightly lit tug was coming in, probably from Norfolk, towing a pair of barges, but it was too dark to see what sort of cargo they bore. Kelly checked the lights and saw that they were properly displayed. That would please the Coast Guard, which wasn't always happy with the way the local tugs operated. Kelly wondered what sort of life it was, moving barges up and down the Bay. Had to be awfully dull doing the same thing, day in and day out, back and forth, north and south, at a steady six knots, seeing the same things all the time. It paid well, of course. A master and a mate, and an engineer, and a cook—they had to have a cook. Maybe a deckhand or two. Kelly wasn't sure about that. All taking down union wages, which were pretty decent.

"Hey, okay. I don't know what the problem is, but we can talk about it, okay?"

The maneuvering in close was probably pretty tricky, though. Especially in any kind of wind, the barges had to be unhandy things to bring alongside. But not today. Today it wouldn't be windy. Just hotter than hell. Kelly started his turn south as he passed Bodkin Point, and he could see the red lights blinking on the towers of the Bay Bridge at Annapolis. The first glow of dawn was decorating the eastern horizon. It was kind of sad, really. The last two hours before sunrise were the best time of the day, but something that few ever bothered to appreciate. Just one more case of people who never knew what was going on around them. Kelly thought he saw something, but the glass windshield interfered with visibility, and so he left the control station and went topside. There he lifted his marine 7 x 50s, and then the microphone of his radio.

"Motor Yacht *Springer* calling Coast Guard forty-one-boat, over."

"This is Coast Guard, *Springer*. Portagee here. What are you doing up so early, Kelly? Over."

"Carrying out my commerce on the sea, Oreza. What's your excuse? Over."

"Looking out for feather merchants like you to rescue, getting some training done, what do you think? Over."

"Glad to hear that, Coast Guard. You push those lever-things towards the front of the boat—that's the pointy part, usually—and she goes faster. And the pointy part goes the same way you turn the wheel—you know, left to go left, right to go right. Over."

Kelly could hear the laughter over the FM circuit. "Roger, copy that, *Springer,* I will pass that along to my crew. Thank you, sir, for the advice. Over."

The crew on the forty-one-foot boat was howling after a long eight hours of patrol, and doing very little. Oreza was letting a young seaman handle the wheel, leaning on the wheelhouse bulkhead and sipping his own coffee as he played with the radio mike.

"You know, *Springer,* I don't take that sort of guff off many guys. Over."

"A good sailor respects his betters, Coast Guard. Hey, is it true your boats have wheels on the bottom? Over."

"Ooooooo," observed a new apprentice.

"Ah, that's a negative, *Springer.* We take the training wheels off after the Navy pukes leave the shipyard. We don't like it when you ladies get seasick just from looking at them. Over!"

Kelly chuckled and altered course to port to stay well clear of the small cutter. "Nice to know that our country's waterways are in such capable hands, Coast Guard, 'specially with a weekend coming up."

"Careful, *Springer,* or I'll hit you for a safety inspection!"

"My federal tax money at work?"

"I hate to see it wasted."

"Well, Coast Guard, just wanted to make sure y'all were awake."

"Roger and thank you very much, sir. We were dozing a little. Nice to know we have real pros like you out here to keep us on our toes."

"Fair winds, Portagee."

"And to you, Kelly. Out." The radio frequency returned to the usual static.

And that took care of that, Kelly thought. It wouldn't do to have him come alongside for a chat. Not just now. Kelly secured the radio and went below. The eastern horizon was pink-orange now, another ten minutes or so until the sun made its appearance.

"What was that all about?" Billy asked.

Kelly poured himself another cup of coffee and checked the autopilot. It was warm enough now that he removed his shirt. The scars on his back from the shotgun blast could hardly have been more clear, even in the dim light of a breaking dawn. There was a remarkable long silence, punctuated by a deep intake of breath.

"You're . . . "

This time Kelly turned, looking down at the naked man chained to the deck. "That's right."

"I killed you," Billy objected. He'd never gotten the word. Henry hadn't passed it along, deeming it to be irrelevant to his operation.

"Think so?" Kelly asked, looking forward again. One of the diesels was running a little warmer than the other, and he made a note to check the cooling system after his other business was done. Otherwise the boat was behaving as docilely as ever, rocking gently on the almost invisible swells, moving along at a steady twenty knots, the bow pitched up at about fifteen degrees on an efficient planing angle. On the step, as Kelly called it. He stretched again, flexing muscles, letting Billy see the scars and what lay under them.

"So that's what it's about . . . she told us all about you before we snuffed her."

Kelly scanned the instrument panel, then checked the chart as he approached the Bay Bridge. Soon he'd cross over to the eastern side of the channel. He was now checking the boat's clock—he thought of it as a chronometer—at least once a minute.

"Pam was a great little fuck. Right up to the end," Billy said, taunting his captor, filling the silence with his own malignant words, finding a sort of courage there. "Not real smart, though. Not real smart."

Just past the Bay Bridge, Kelly disengaged the autopilot and turned the wheel ten degrees to port. There was no morning traffic to speak of, but he looked carefully anyway before initiating the maneuver. A pair of running lights just on the horizon announced the approach of a merchant ship, probably twelve thousand yards off. Kelly could have flipped on the radar to check, but in these weather conditions it just would have been a waste of electricity.

"Did she tell you about the passion marks?" Billy sneered. He didn't see Kelly's hands tighten on the wheel.

The marks about the breasts appear to have been made with an ordinary set of pliers, the pathology report had said. Kelly had it all memorized, every single word of the dry medical phraseology, as though engraved with a diamond stylus on a plate of steel. He wondered if the medics had felt the same way he did. Probably so. Their anger had probably manifested itself in the increased detachment of their dictated notes. Professionals were like that.

"She talked, you know, she told us everything. How you picked her up, how you partied. We taught her that, mister. You owe us for that! Before she ran, I bet she didn't tell you, she fucked us all, three, four times each. I guess she thought that was pretty smart, eh? I guess she never figured that we'd all get to fuck her some more."

O+, O–, AB–, Kelly thought. Blood type O was by far the most common of all, and so that meant there could well have been more than three of them. *And what blood type are you, Billy?*

"Just a whore. A pretty one, but just a fucking little whore. That's how she died, did you know? She died while she was fucking a guy. We strangled her, and her cute little ass was pumping hard, right up till the time her face turned purple. Funny to watch," Billy assured him with a leer that Kelly didn't have to see. "I had my fun with her—three times, man! I hurt her, I hurt her bad, you hear me?"

Kelly opened his mouth wide, breathing slowly and regularly, not allowing his muscles to tense up now. The morning wind had picked up some, letting the boat rock perhaps five degrees left and right of the vertical, and he allowed his body to ride with the rolls, commanding himself to accept the soothing motion of the sea.

"I don't know what the big deal is, I mean, she's just a dead whore. We should be able to cut a deal, like. You know how dumb you are? There was seventy grand back in the house, you dumb son of a bitch. Seventy grand!" Billy stopped, seeing it wasn't working. Still, an angry man made mistakes, and he'd rattled the guy before. He was sure of that, and so he continued.

"You know, the real shame, I guess, is she needed drugs. You know, if she just knew another place to score, we never woulda seen y'all. Then you fucked up, too, remember."

Yes, I remember.

"I mean, you really were dumb. Didn't you know about phones? Jesus, man. After our car got stuck, we called Burt and got his car, and just went cruisin', like, and there you were, easy as hell to spot in that jeep. You must've really been under her spell, man."

Phones? It was something that simple that had killed Pam? Kelly thought. His muscles went taut. *You fucking idiot, Kelly.* Then his shoulders went slack, just for a second, with the realization of how thoroughly he had failed her, and part of him recognized the emptiness of his efforts at revenge. But empty or not, it was something he would have. He sat up straighter in the control chair.

"I mean, shit, car easy to spot like that, how fuckin' dumb can a guy be?" Billy asked, having just seen real feedback from his taunts. Now perhaps he could start real negotiations. "I'm kinda surprised you're alive—hey, I mean, it wasn't anything personal. Maybe you didn't know the work she did for us. We couldn't let her loose with what she knew, right? I can make it up to you. Let's make a deal, okay?"

Kelly checked the autopilot and the surface. *Springer* was moving on a safe and steady course, and nothing in sight was on a converging path. He rose from his chair and moved to another, a few feet from Billy.

"She told you that we were in town to score some drugs? She told you that?" Kelly asked, his eyes level with Billy's.

"Yeah, that's right." Billy was relaxing. He was puzzled when Kelly started weeping in front of him. Perhaps here was a chance to get out of his predicament. "Geez, I'm sorry, man," Billy said in the wrong sort of voice. "I mean, it's just bad luck for you."

Bad luck for me? He closed his eyes, just a few inches from Billy's face. *Dear God, she was protecting me. Even after I failed her. She didn't even know if I was alive or not, but she lied to protect me.* It was more than he could bear, and Kelly simply lost control of himself for several minutes. But even that had a purpose. His eyes dried up after a time, and as he wiped his face, he also removed any human feelings he might have had for his guest.

Kelly stood and walked back to the control chair. He didn't want to look the little bastard in the face any longer. He might really lose control, and he couldn't risk that.

"Tom, I think you may be right after all," Ryan said.

According to his driver's license—already checked out: no arrest record, but a lengthy list of traffic violations—Richard Oliver Farmer was twenty-four and would grow no older. He had expired from a single knife thrust into the chest, through the pericardium, fully transiting the heart. The size of the knife wound—ordinarily such traumatic insults closed up until they became difficult for the layman to see—indicated that the assailant had twisted the blade as much as the space between the ribs allowed. It was a large wound, indicating a blade roughly two inches in width. More important, there was additional confirmation.

"Not real smart," the ME announced. Ryan and Douglas both nodding, looking. Mr. Farmer had been wearing a white cotton, button-down-collar shirt. There was a suit jacket, too, hanging on a doorknob. Whoever had killed him had wiped the knife on the shirt. Three wipes, it appeared, and one of them had left a permanent impression of the knife, marked in the blood of the victim, who had a revolver in his belt but hadn't had a chance to use it. Another victim of skill and surprise, but, in this case, less circumspection. The junior of the pair pointed to one of the stains with his pencil.

"You know what it is?" Douglas asked. It was rhetorical; he answered his own question immediately. "It's a Ka-Bar, standard-issue Marine combat knife. I own one myself."

"Nice edge on it, too," the ME told them. "Very clean cut, almost surgical in the way it went through the skin. He must have sliced the heart just about in half. A very accurate thrust, gentlemen, the knife came in perfectly horizontal so it didn't jam on the ribs. Most people think the heart's on the left. Our friend knew better. Only one penetration. He knew exactly what he was doing."

"One more, Em. Armed criminal. Our friend got in close and did him so fast—"

"Yeah, Tom, I believe you now." Ryan nodded and went upstairs to join the other detective team. In the front bedroom was a pile of men's clothes, a cloth satchel with a ton of cash in it, a gun, and a knife. A mattress with semen stains, some still moist. Also a lady's purse. So much evidence for the younger men to catalog. Blood types from the semen stains. Complete ID on all three—they assumed three—people who had been here. Even a car outside to run down. Finally something like a normal murder case. Latent Prints would be all over the place. The photographers had already shot a dozen rolls of film. But for Ryan and Douglas the matter was already settled in its curious way.

"You know that guy Farber over at Hopkins?"

"Yeah, Em, he worked the Gooding case with Frank Allen. I set the date up. He's real smart," Douglas allowed. "A little peculiar, but smart. I have to be in court this afternoon, remember?"

"Okay, I think I can handle it. I owe you a beer, Tom. You figured this one faster than I did."

"Well, thanks, maybe I can be a lieutenant, too, someday."

Ryan laughed, fishing out a cigarette as he walked down the stairs.

"You going to resist?" Kelly asked with a smile. He'd just come back into the salon after tying up to the quay.

"Why should I help you with anything?" Billy asked with what he thought to be defiance.

"Okay." Kelly drew the Ka-Bar and held it next to a particularly sensitive place. "We can start right now if you want."

The whole body shriveled, but one part more than the others. "Okay, okay!"

"Good. I want you to learn a little from this. I don't want you ever to hurt another girl again." Kelly loosed the shackles from the deck fitting, but his arms were still together, bolted in tight, as he stood Billy up.

"Fuck you, man! You're gonna kill me! And I ain't gonna tell you shit."

Kelly twisted him around to stare in his eyes. "I'm not going to kill you, Billy. You'll leave this island alive. I promise."

The confusion on his face was sufficiently amusing that Kelly actually smiled for a second. Then he shook his head. He told himself that he was treading a very narrow and hazardous path between two equally dangerous slopes, and to both extremes lay madness, of two different types but equally destructive. He had to detach himself from the reality of the moment, yet hold on to it. Kelly helped him down from the boat and walked him towards the machinery bunker.

"Thirsty?"

"I need to take a piss, too."

Kelly guided him onto some grass. "Go right ahead." Kelly waited. Billy didn't like being naked, not in front of another man, not in a subordinate position. Foolishly, he wasn't trying to talk to Kelly now, at least not in the right way. Coward that he was, he'd tried to build up his manhood earlier, trying to talk not so much to Kelly as to himself as he'd recounted his part in ending Pam's life, creating for himself an illusion of power, when silence might—well, would probably not have saved him. It might have created doubts, though, especially if he'd been clever enough to spin a good yarn, but cowardice and stupidity were not strangers to each other, were they? Kelly let him stand untended while he dialed the combination lock. Turning on the interior lights, he pushed Billy inside.

It looked like—was in fact a steel cylinder, seventeen inches in diameter, sitting on its own legs with large caster-wheels at the bottom, just where he'd left it. The steel cover on the end was not in place, hanging down on its hinge.

"You going to get in that," Kelly told him.

"Fuck you, man!" Defiance again. Kelly used the butt end of the Ka-Bar to club him on the back of the neck. Billy fell to his knees.

"One way or another, you're getting in—bleeding or not bleeding, I really don't care." Which was a lie, but an effective one. Kelly lifted him by the neck and forced his head and shoulders into the opening. "Don't move."

It was so much easier than he'd expected. Kelly pulled a key off its place on the wall and unbolted the shackles on Billy's hands. He could feel his prisoner tense, thinking that he might have a chance, but Kelly was fast on the wrench—he only had to remove one bolt to free both hands, and a prod from the knife in the right place encouraged Billy not to back up, which was the necessary precursor to any kind of effective resistance. Billy was just too cowardly to accept pain as the price for a chance at escape. He trembled but didn't resist at all, for all his lavish and desperate thoughts.

"Inside!" A push helped, and when his feet were inside the rim, Kelly lifted the hatch and bolted it into place. Then he walked out, flipping the lights off. He needed something to eat and a nap. Billy could wait. The waiting would just make things easier.

"Hello?" Her voice sounded very worried.

"Hi, Sandy, it's John."

"John! What's going on?"

"How is she?"

"Doris, you mean? She's sleeping now," Sandy told him. "John, who—I mean, what's happened to her?"

Kelly squeezed the phone receiver in his hand. "Sandy, I want you to listen to me very carefully, okay? This is really important."

"Okay, go ahead." Sandy was in her kitchen, looking at a pot of coffee. Outside she could see neighborhood children playing a game of ball on a vacant field whose comforting normality now seemed to be very distant indeed.

"Number one, don't tell anybody that she's there. Sure as hell you don't tell the police."

"John, she's badly injured, she's hooked on pills, she probably has severe medical problems on top of that. I have to—"

"Sam and Sarah, then. Nobody else. Sandy, you got that? *Nobody else.* Sandy . . . " Kelly hesitated. It was too hard a thing to say, but he had to make it clear. "Sandy, I have placed you in danger. The people who worked Doris over are the same ones—"

"I know, John. I kinda figured that one out." The nurse's expression was neutral, but she too had seen the photo of Pamela Starr Madden's body. "John, she told me that you—killed somebody."

"Yes, Sandy, I did."

Sandra O'Toole wasn't surprised. She'd made the right guesses a few hours before, but hearing it from him—it was the way he'd just said it. Calm, matter-of-fact. *Yes, Sandy, I did.* Did you take the garbage out? Yes, Sandy, I did.

"Sandy, these are some very dangerous people. I could have left Doris behind—but I couldn't, could I? Jesus, Sandy, did you see what they—"

"Yes." It had been a long time since she'd worked the ER, and she'd almost forgotten the dreadful things that people did to one another.

"Sandy, I'm sorry that I—"

"John, it's done. I'll handle it, okay?"

Kelly stopped talking for a moment, taking strength from her voice. Perhaps that was the difference between them. His instinct was to lash out, to identify the people who did the evil things and to deal with them. *Seek out and destroy.* Her instinct was to protect in a different way, and it struck the former SEAL that her strength might well be the greater.

"I'll have to get her proper medical attention." Sandy thought about the young woman upstairs in the back bedroom. She'd helped her get cleaned off and been horrified at the marks on her body, the vicious physical abuse. But worst of all were her eyes, dead, absent of the defiant spark that she saw in patients even as they lost their fight for life. Despite years of work in the care of critically ill patients, she'd never realized that a person could be destroyed on purpose, through deliberate, sadistic malice. Now she might come to the attention of such people herself, Sandy knew, but greater than her fear for them was her loathing.

For Kelly those feelings were precisely inverted. "Okay, Sandy, but please be careful. Promise me."

"I will. I'm going to call Doctor Rosen." She paused for a moment. "John?"

"Yes, Sandy?"

"What you're doing . . . it's *wrong,* John." She hated herself for saying that.

"I know," Kelly told her.

Sandy closed her eyes, still seeing the kids chasing a baseball outside, then seeing John, wherever he was, knowing the expression that had to be on his face. She knew she had to say the next part, too, and she took a deep breath: "But I don't care about that, not anymore. I understand, John."

"Thank you," Kelly whispered. "Are you okay?"

"I'll do fine."

"I'll be back as soon as I can. I don't know what we can do with her—"

"Let me worry about that. We'll take care of her. We'll come up with something."

"Okay, Sandy . . . Sandy?"

"What, John?"

"Thanks." The line clicked off.

You're welcome, she thought, hanging up. What a strange man. He was killing people, ending the lives of fellow human beings, doing it with an utter ruthlessness that she hadn't seen—had no desire to see—but which his voice proclaimed in its emotionless speech. But he'd taken the time and endangered himself to rescue Doris. She still didn't understand, Sandy told herself, dialing the phone again.

Dr. Sidney Farber looked exactly as Emmet Ryan expected: forty or so, small, bearded, Jewish, pipe-smoker. He didn't rise as the detective came in, but merely motioned his guest to a chair with a wave of the hand. Ryan had messengered extracts from the case files to the psychiatrist before lunch, and clearly the doctor had them. All of them were laid open on the desk, arrayed in two rows.

"I know your partner, Tom Douglas," Farber said, puffing on his pipe.

"Yes, sir. He said your work on the Gooding case was very helpful."

"A very sick man, Mr. Gooding. I hope he'll get the treatment he needs."

"How sick is this one?" Lieutenant Ryan asked.

Farber looked up. "He's as healthy as we are—rather healthier, physically speaking. But that's not the important part. What you just said. 'This one.' You're assuming one murderer for all these incidents. Tell me why." The psychiatrist leaned back in his chair.

"I didn't think so at first. Tom saw it before I did. It's the craftsmanship."

"Correct."

"Are we dealing with a psychopath?"

Farber shook his head. "No. The true psychopath is a person unable to deal with life. He sees reality in a very individual and eccentric way, generally a way that is very different from the rest of us. In nearly all cases the disorder is manifested in very open and easily recognized ways."

"But Gooding—"

"Mr. Gooding is what we—there's a new term, 'organized psychopath.'"

"Okay, fine, but he wasn't obvious to his neighbors."

"That's true, but Mr. Gooding's disorder manifested itself in the gruesome way he killed his victims. But with these killings, there's no ritual aspect to them. No mutilation. No sexual drive to them—that's usually indicated by cuts on the neck, as you know. No." Farber shook his head again. "This fellow is all business. He's not getting any emotional release at all. He's just killing people and he's doing it for a reason that is probably rational, at least to him."

"Why, then?"

"Obviously it's not robbery. It's something else. He's a very angry man, but I've met people like this before."

"Where?" Ryan asked. Farber pointed to the opposite wall. In an oaken frame was a piece of red velvet on which were pinned a combat infantryman's badge, jump wings, and a RANGER flash. The detective was surprised enough to let it show.

"Pretty stupid, really," Farber explained with a deprecating gesture. "Little Jewish boy wants to show how tough he is. Well"—Farber smiled—"I guess I did."

"I didn't like Europe all that much myself, but I didn't see the nice parts."

"What outfit?"

"Easy Company, Second of the Five-Oh-Sixth."

"Airborne. One-Oh-One, right?"

"All the way, doc," the detective said, confirming that he too had once been young and foolish, and remembering how skinny he'd been, leaping out the cargo doors of C-47s. "I jumped into Normandy and Eindhoven."

"And Bastogne?"

Ryan nodded. "That really wasn't fun, but at least we went in by truck."

"Well, that's what you're up against, Lieutenant Ryan."

"Explain?"

"Here's the key to it." Farber held up the transcribed interview with Mrs. Charles. "The disguise. Has to be a disguise. It takes a strong arm to slam a knife into the back of the skull. That wasn't any alcoholic. They have all sorts of physical problems."

"But that one doesn't fit the pattern at all," Ryan objected.

"I think it does, but it's not obvious. Turn the clock back. You're in the Army, you're an elite member of an elite unit. You take the time to recon your objective, right?"

"Always," the detective confirmed.

"Apply that to a city. How do you do that? You camouflage yourself. So our friend decides to disguise himself as a wino. How many of those people on the street? Dirty, smelly, but pretty harmless except to one another. They're invisible and you just filter them out. Everyone does."

"You still didn't—"

"But how does he get in and out? You think he takes a bus—a taxi?"

"Car."

"A disguise is something you put on and take off." Farber held up the photo of the Charles murder scene. "He makes his double-kill two blocks away, he clears the area, and comes here—why do you suppose?" And there it was, right on the photo, a gap between two parked cars.

"Holy shit!" The humiliation Ryan felt was noteworthy. "What else did I miss, Doctor Farber?"

"Call me Sid. Not much else. This individual is very clever, changing his methods, and this is the only case where he displayed his anger. That's it, do you see? This is the only crime with rage in it—except maybe for the one this morning, but we'll set that aside for the moment. Here we see rage. First he cripples the victim, then he kills him in a particularly difficult way. Why?" Farber paused for a few contemplative puffs. "He was angry, but *why* was he angry? It had to have been an unplanned act. He wouldn't have planned something with Mrs. Charles there. For some reason he had to do something that he hadn't expected to do, and that made him angry. Also, he let her go—*knowing* that she saw him."

"You still haven't told me—"

"He's a combat veteran. He's very, very fit. That means he's younger than we are, and highly trained. Ranger, Green Beret, somebody like that."

"Why is he out there?"

"I don't know. You're going to have to ask him. But what you have is somebody who takes his time. He's watching his victims. He's picking the same time of day—when they're tired, when street traffic is low, to reduce the chance of being spotted. He's not robbing them. He may take the money, but that's not the same thing. Now tell me about this morning's kill," Farber commanded in a gentle but explicit way.

"You have the photo. There was a whole lot of cash in a bag upstairs. We haven't counted it yet, but at least fifty thousand dollars."

"Drug money?"

"We think so."

"There were other people there? He kidnapped them?"

"Two, we think. A man definitely, and probably a woman, too."

Farber nodded and puffed away for a few seconds. "One of two things. Either that's the person he was after all along, or he's just one more step towards something else."

"So all the pushers he killed were just camouflage."

"The first two, the ones he wired up—"

"Interrogated them." Ryan grimaced. "We should have figured this out. They were the only ones who weren't killed in the open. He did it that way to have more time."

"Hindsight is always easy," Farber pointed out. "Don't feel too bad. That one really did look like a robbery, and you had nothing else to go on. By the time you came here, there was a lot more information to look at." The psychiatrist leaned back and smiled at the ceiling. He loved playing detective. "Until this one"—he tapped the photos from the newest scene with his pipe—"you didn't really have much. This is the one that makes everything else clear. Your suspect knows weapons. He knows tactics. He's very patient. He stalks his victims like a hunter after a deer. He's changing his methodology to throw you off, but today he made a mistake. He showed a little rage this time, too, because he used a knife deliberately, and he showed the kind of training he had by cleaning the weapon right away."

"But he's not crazy, you say."

"No, I doubt he's disturbed in a clinical sense at all, but sure as hell he's motivated by something. People like this are highly disciplined, just like you and I were. Discipline shows in how he operates—but his anger also shows in *why* he operates. Something made this man start to do this."

"'Ma'am.'"

That one caught Farber short. "Exactly! Very good. Why didn't he eliminate her? That's the only witness we know about. He was polite to her. He let her go . . . interesting . . . but not enough to go on, really."

"Except to say that he's not killing for fun."

"Correct." Farber nodded. "Everything he does will have a purpose, and he has a lot of specialized training that he can apply to this mission. It is a *mission*. You have one really dangerous cat prowling the street."

"He's after drug people. That's pretty clear," Ryan said. "The one—maybe two—he kidnapped . . . "

"If one is a woman, she'll survive. The man will not. From the condition of his body we'll be able to tell if he was the target."

"Rage?"

"That will be obvious. One other thing—if you have police looking for this guy, remember that he's better with weapons than almost anybody. He'll look harmless. He'll avoid a confrontation. He doesn't want to kill the wrong people, or he would have killed this Mrs. Charles."

"But if we corner him—"

"You don't want to do that."

"All comfy?" Kelly asked.

The recompression chamber was one of several hundred produced for a Navy contract requirement by the Dykstra Foundry and Tool Company, Inc., of Houston, Texas, or so the name plate said. Made of high-quality steel, it was designed to reproduce the pressure that came along with scuba diving. At one end was a triple-paned four-inch-square Plexiglas window. There was even a small air lock so that items could be passed in, like food or drink, and inside the chamber was a twenty-watt reading light in a protected fixture. Under the chamber itself was a powerful, gasoline-powered air compressor, which could be controlled from a fold-down seat, adjacent to which were two pressure gauges. One was labeled in concentric circles of millimeters and inches of mercury, pounds-per-square-inch, kilograms-per-square-centimeter, and "bar" or multiples of normal atmospheric pressure, which was 14.7 PSI. The other gauge showed equivalent water depth both in feet and meters. Each thirty-three feet of simulated depth raised the atmospheric pressure by 14.7 PSI, or one bar.

"Look, whatever you want to know, okay . . . " Kelly heard over the intercom.

"I thought you'd see things my way." He yanked the rope on the motor, starting the compressor. Kelly made sure that the simple spigot valve next to the pressure gauges was tightly shut. Then he opened the pressurization valve, venting air from the compressor to the chamber, and watched the needles rotate slowly clockwise.

"You know how to swim?" Kelly asked, watching his face.

Billy's head jerked with alarm. "What—look, please, don't drown me, okay?"

"That's not going to happen. So, can you swim?"

"Yeah, sure."

"Ever do any skin diving?" Kelly asked next.

"No, no, I haven't," replied a very confused drug distributor.

"Okay, well, you're going to learn what it's like. You should yawn and work your ears, like, to get used to the pressure," Kelly told him, watching the "depth" gauge pass thirty feet.

"Look, why don't you just ask your fucking questions, okay?"

Kelly switched the intercom off. There was just too much fear in the voice. Kelly didn't really like hurting people all that much, and he was worried about developing sympathy for Billy. He steadied the gauge at one hundred feet, closing off the pressurization valve but leaving the motor running. While Billy adjusted to the pressure, Kelly found a hose which he attached to the motor's exhaust pipe. This he extended outside to dump the carbon monoxide into the atmosphere. It would be a time-consuming process, just waiting for things to happen. Kelly was going on memory, and that was worrisome. There was a useful but rather rough instruction table on the side of the chamber, the bottom line of which commanded reference to a certain diving manual which Kelly did not have. He'd done very little deep diving of late, and the only one that had really concerned him had been a team effort, the oil rig down in the Gulf. Kelly spent an hour tidying things up around the machine shop, cultivating his memories and his rage before coming back to his fold-down seat.

"How are you feeling?"

"Look, okay, all right?" Rather a nervous voice, actually.

"Ready to answer some questions?"

"Anything, okay? Just let me outa here!"

"Okay, good." Kelly lifted a clipboard. "Have you ever been arrested, Billy?"

"No." A little pride in that one, Kelly noted. Good.

"Been in the service?"

"No." Such a stupid question.

"So you've never been in jail, never been fingerprinted, nothing like that?"

"Never." The head shook inside the window.

"How do I know you're telling the truth?"

"I am, man! I am!"

"Yeah, you probably are, but I have to make sure, okay?" Kelly reached with his left hand and twisted the spigot valve. Air hissed loudly out of the chamber while he watched the pressure gauges.

Billy didn't know what to expect, and it all came as a disagreeable surprise. In the preceding hour, he had been surrounded by four times the normal amount of air for the space he was in. His body had adapted to that. The air taken in through his lungs, also pressurized, had found its way into his bloodstream, and now his entire body was at 58.8 pounds per square inch of ambient pressure. Various gas bubbles, mainly nitrogen, were dissolved into his bloodstream, and when Kelly bled the air out of the chamber, those bubbles started to expand. Tissues around the bubbles resisted the force, but not well, and almost at once cell walls started first to stretch, and then, in some cases, to rupture. The pain started in his extremities, first as a dull but widespread ache and rapidly evolving into the most intense and unpleasant sensation Billy had ever experienced. It came in waves, timed exactly with the now-rapid beating of his heart. Kelly listened to the moan that turned into a scream, and the air pressure was only that of sixty feet. He twisted the release valve shut and re-engaged the pressurization one. In another two minutes the pressure was back to that of four bar. The restored pressure eased the pain almost completely, leaving behind the sort of ache associated with strenuous exercise. That was not something to which Billy was accustomed, and for him the pain was not the welcome sort that athletes know. More to the point, the wide and terrified eyes told Kelly that his guest was thoroughly cowed. They didn't look like human eyes now, and that was good.

Kelly switched on the intercom. "That's the penalty for a lie. I thought you should know. Now. Ever been arrested, Billy?"

"Jesus, man, no!"

"Never been in jail, fingerprinted—"

"No, man, like speeding tickets, I ain't never been busted."

"In the service?"

"No, I told you that!"

"Good, thank you." Kelly checked off the first group of questions. "Now let's talk about Henry and his organization." There was one other thing happening that Billy did not expect. Beginning at about three bar, the nitrogen gas that constitutes the majority of what humans call air has a narcotic effect not unlike that of alcohol or barbiturates. As afraid as Billy was, there was also a whiplash feeling of euphoria, along with which came impaired judgment. It was just one more bonus effect from the interrogation technique that Kelly had selected mainly for the magnitude of the injury it could inflict.

"Left the money?" Tucker asked.

"More than fifty thousand. They were still counting when I left," Mark Charon said. They were back in the theater, the only two people in the balcony. But this time Henry wasn't eating any popcorn, the detective saw. It wasn't often that he saw Tucker agitated.

"I need to know what's going on. Tell me what you know."

"We've had a few pushers whacked in the past week or ten days—"

"Ju-Ju, Bandanna, two others I don't know. Yeah, I know that. You think they're connected?"

"It's all we got, Henry. Was it Billy who disappeared?"

"Yeah. Rick's dead. Knife?"

"Somebody cut his fuckin' heart out," Charon exaggerated. "One of your girls there, too?"

"Doris," Henry confirmed with a nod. "Left the money . . . why?"

"It could have been a robbery that went wrong somehow, but I don't know what would have screwed that up. Ju-Ju and Bandanna were both robbed—hell, maybe those cases are unrelated. Maybe what happened last night was, well, something else."

"Like what?"

"Like maybe a direct attack on your organization, Henry," Charon answered patiently. "Who do you know who would want to do that? You don't have to be a cop to understand motive, right?" Part of him—a large part, in fact—enjoyed having the upper hand on Tucker, however briefly. "How much does Billy know?"

"A lot—shit, I just started taking him to—" Tucker stopped.

"That's okay. I don't need to know and I don't want to know. But somebody else does, and you'd better think about that." A little late, Mark Charon was beginning to appreciate how closely his well-being was associated with that of Henry Tucker.

"Why not at least make it *look* like a robbery?" Tucker demanded, eyes locked unseeingly on the screen.

"Somebody's sending you a message, Henry. Not taking the money is a sign of contempt. Who do you know who doesn't need money?"

The screams were getting louder. Billy had just taken another excursion to sixty feet, staying there for a couple of minutes. It was useful to be able to watch his face. Kelly saw him claw at his ears when both tympanic membranes ruptured, not a second apart. Then his eyes and sinuses had been affected. It would be attacking his teeth, too, if he had any cavities—which he probably did, Kelly thought, but he didn't want to hurt him too much, not yet.

"Billy," he said, after restoring the pressure and eliminating most of the pain, "I'm not sure I believe that one."

"You motherfucker!" the person inside the chamber screamed at the microphone. "I fixed her, you know? I watched your little babydoll die with Henry's dick in her, slinging her cunt for him, and I seen you cry like a fucking baby about it, you fucking pussy!"

Kelly made sure his face was at the window when his hand opened the release valve again, bringing Billy back to eighty feet, just enough for a good taste. There would be bleeding in the major joints now, because the nitrogen bubbles tended to collect there for one reason or another, and the instinctive reaction of decompression sickness was to curl up in a ball, from which had come the original name for the malady, "the bends." But Billy couldn't fold up inside the chamber, much as he tried to. His central nervous system was being affected now, too, the gossamer fibers being squeezed, and the pain was multifaceted now, crushing aches in the joints and extremities, and searing, fiery threads throughout his body. Nerve spasms started as the tiny electrical fibers rebelled against what was happening to them, and his body jerked randomly as though being stung with electric shocks. The neurological involvement was a little disquieting this early on. That was enough for now. Kelly restored the pressure, watching the spasms slow down.

"Now, Billy, do you know how it was for Pam?" he asked, just to remind himself, really.

"Hurts." He was crying now. He'd gotten his arms up, and his hands were over his face, but for all that he couldn't conceal his agony.

"Billy," Kelly said patiently. "You see how it works? If I think you're lying, it hurts. If I don't like what you say, it hurts. You want me to hurt you some more?"

"Jesus—no, please!" The hands came away, and their eyes weren't so much as eighteen inches apart.

"Let's try to be a little bit more polite, okay?"

" . . . sorry . . . "

"I'm sorry, too, Billy, but you have to do what I tell you, okay?" He got a nod. Kelly reached for a glass of water. He checked the interlocks on the pass-through system before opening the door and setting the glass inside. "Okay, if you open the door next to your head, you can have something to drink."

Billy did as he was told and was soon sipping water through a straw.

"Now let's get back to business, okay? Tell me more about Henry. Where does he live?"

"I don't know," he gasped.

"Wrong answer!" Kelly snarled.

"Please, no! I don't know, we meet at a place off Route 40, he doesn't let us know where—"

"You have to do better than that or the elevator goes back to the sixth floor. Ready?"

"*NOOOOOO!*" The scream was so loud that it came right through the inch-thick steel. "*Please, no! I don't know—I really don't.*"

"Billy, I don't have much reason to be nice to you," Kelly reminded him. "You killed Pam, remember? You tortured her to death. You got your rocks off using pliers on her. How many hours, Billy, how long did you and your friends work on her? Ten? Twelve? Hell, Billy, we've only been talking for seven hours. You're telling me you've worked for this guy for almost two years and you don't even know where he lives? I have trouble believing that. Going up," Kelly announced in a mechanical voice, reaching for the valve. All he had to do was crack it. The first hiss of pressurized air bore with it such terror that Billy was screaming before any real pain had a chance to start.

"*I DON'T FUCKING KNOOOOOOOOOWWW!*"

Damn! What if he doesn't?

Well, Kelly thought, *it doesn't hurt to be sure.* He brought him up just a little, just to eighty-five feet, enough to renew old pains without spreading the effects any further. Fear of pain was now as bad as the real thing, Kelly thought, and if he went too far, pain could become its own narcotic. No, this man was a coward who had often enjoyed inflicting pain and terror on others, and if he discovered that pain, however dreadful, could be survived, then he might actually find courage in himself. That was a risk Kelly was unwilling to run, however remote it might be. He closed the release valve again and brought the pressure back up, this time to one hundred ten feet, the better to attenuate the pain and increase the narcosis.

"My God," Sarah breathed. She hadn't seen the post-mortem photos of Pam, and her only question on the matter had been discouraged by her husband, a warning which she'd heeded.

Doris was nude, and disturbingly passive. The best thing that could be said for her was that Sandy had helped her bathe. Sam had his bag open, passing over his stethoscope. Her heart rate was over ninety, strong enough but too rapid for a girl her age. Blood pressure was also elevated. Temperature was normal. Sandy moved in, drawing four 5-cc test tubes of blood which would be analyzed at the hospital lab.

"Who does this sort of thing?" Sarah whispered to herself. There were numerous marks on her breasts, a fading bruise to her right cheek, and other, more recent edemas on her abdomen and legs. Sam checked her eyes for pupillary response, which was positive—except for the total absence of reaction.

"The same people who killed Pam," the surgeon replied quietly.

"Pam?" Doris asked.

"You knew her? How?"

"The man who brought you here," Sandy said. "He's the one—"

"The one Billy killed?"

"Yes," Sam answered, then realized how foolish it might sound to an outside listener.

"I just know the phone number," Billy said, drunkenly now from the high partial-pressure of nitrogen gas, and his release from pain was helping him to be much more compliant.

"Give it to me," Kelly ordered. Billy did as he was told and Kelly wrote it down. He had two full pages of penciled notes now. Names, addresses, a few phone numbers. Seemingly very little, but far more than he'd had only twenty-four hours before.

"How do the drugs come in?"

Billy's head turned away from the window. "Don't know . . . "

"We have to do better than that." *Hissssssssssssss . . .*

Again Billy screamed, and this time Kelly let it happen, watching the depth-gauge needle rotate to seventy-five feet. Billy started gagging. His lung function was impaired now, and the choking coughs merely amplified the pain that now filled every cubic inch of his racked body. His whole body felt like a balloon, or more properly a collection of them, large and small, all trying to explode, all pressing on others, and he could feel that some were stronger and some weaker than others, and the weaker ones were those at the most important places inside him. His eyes were hurting now, seeming to expand beyond their sockets, and the way in which his paranasal sinuses were also expanding only made it worse, as though his face would detach from the rest of his skull; his hands flew there, desperately trying to hold it in place. The pain was beyond anything he had ever felt and beyond anything he had ever inflicted. His legs were bent as much as the steel cylinder allowed, and his kneecaps seemed to dig grooves into the steel, so hard they pressed against it. He was able to move his arms, and those twisted and turned about his chest, seeking relief, but only generating more pain as he struggled to hold his eyes in the sockets. He was unable even to scream now. Time stopped for Billy and became eternity. There was no light, no darkness, no sound or silence. All of reality was pain.

" . . . please . . . please . . . " the whisper carried over the speaker next to Kelly. He brought the pressure back up slowly, stopping this time at one hundred ten feet.

Billy's face was mottled now, like the rash from some horrible allergy. Some blood vessels had let go just below the surface of the skin, and a big one had ruptured on the surface of the left eye. Soon half of the "white" was red, closer to purple, really, making him look even more like the frightened, vicious animal he was.

"The last question was about how the drugs come in."

"I don't know," he whined.

Kelly spoke quietly into the microphone. "Billy, there's something you have to understand. Up until now what's happened to you, well, it hurts pretty bad, but I haven't really hurt you yet. I mean, not *really* hurt you."

Billy's eyes went wide. Had he been able to consider things in a dispassionate way, he would have remarked to himself that surely horror must stop *somewhere,* an observation that would have been both right and wrong.

"Everything that's happened so far, it's all things that doctors can fix, okay?" It wasn't much of a lie on Kelly's part, and what followed was no lie at all. "The next time we let the air out, Billy, then things will happen that nobody can fix. Blood vessels inside your eyeballs will break open, and you'll be blind. Other vessels inside your brain will let go, okay? They can't fix either one. You'll be blind and you'll be crazy. But the pain will never go away. The rest of your life, Billy, blind, crazy, and hurt. You're what? Twenty-five? You have lots more time to live. Forty years, maybe, blind, crazy, crippled. So it's a good idea to not lie to me, okay?

"Now—how do the drugs come in?"

No pity, Kelly told himself. He would have killed a dog or a cat or a deer in the condition he'd inflicted on this . . . object. But Billy wasn't a dog or a cat or a deer. He was a human being, after a fashion. Worse than the pimp, worse than the pushers. Had the situation been reversed, Billy would not have felt what he was feeling. He was a person whose universe was very small indeed. It held only one person, himself, surrounded by *things* whose sole function was to be manipulated for his amusement or profit. Billy was one who enjoyed the infliction of pain, who enjoyed establishing dominance over *things* whose feelings were nothing of importance, even if they truly existed at all. Somehow he'd never learned that there were other human beings in his universe, *people* whose right to

life and happiness was equal to his own; because of that he
had run the unrecognized risk of offending another person
whose very existence he had never really acknowledged.
He was learning different now, perhaps, though it was a
little late. Now he was learning that his future was indeed a
lonely universe which he would share not with people, but
with pain. Smart enough to see that future, Billy broke. It
was obvious on his face. He started talking in a choked and
uneven voice, but one which, finally, was completely truthful. It was only about ten years too late, Kelly estimated,
looking up from his notes at the relief valve. That ought to
have been a pity, and truly it was for many of those who
had shared Billy's rather eccentric universe. Perhaps he'd
just never figured it out, Kelly thought, that someone else
might treat him the same way in which he treated so many
others, smaller and weaker than himself. But that also was
too late in coming. Too late for Billy, too late for Pam,
and, in a way, too late for Kelly. The world was full of
inequities and not replete with justice. It was that simple,
wasn't it? Billy didn't know that justice might be out there
waiting, and there simply hadn't been enough of it to warn
him. And so he had gambled. And so he had lost. And so
Kelly would save his pity for others.

"I don't know . . . I don't—"

"I warned you, didn't I?" Kelly opened the valve,
bringing him all the way to fifty feet. The retinal blood
vessels must have ruptured early. Kelly thought he saw
a little red in the pupils, wide as their owner screamed
even after his lungs were devoid of air. Knees and feet
and elbows drummed against the steel. Kelly let it happen,
waiting before he reapplied the air pressure.

"Tell me what you know, Billy, or it just gets worse.
Talk fast."

His voice was that of confession now. The information
was somewhat remarkable, but it had to be true. No person
like this had the imagination to make it up. The final part
of the interrogation lasted for three hours, only once letting
the valve *hiss,* and then only for a second or two. Kelly
left and revisited questions to see if the answers changed,
but they didn't. In fact, the renewed question developed

yet more information that connected some bits of data to others, formulating an overall picture that became clearer still, and by midnight he was sure that he'd emptied Billy's mind of all the useful data that it contained.

Kelly was almost captured by humanity when he set his pencils down. If Billy had shown Pam any mercy at all, perhaps he might have acted differently, for his own wounds were, just as Billy had said, only a business matter—more correctly, had been occasioned by his own stupidity, and he could not in good conscience harm a man for taking advantage of his own errors. But Billy had not stopped there. He had tortured a young woman whom Kelly had loved, and for that reason Billy was not a *man* at all, and did not merit Kelly's solicitude.

It didn't matter in any case. The damage had been done, and it progressed at its own speed as tissues torn loose by the barometric trauma wandered about blood vessels, closing them off one at a time. The worst manifestation of this was in Billy's brain. Soon his sightless eyes proclaimed the madness that they held, and though the final depressurization was a slow and gentle one, what came out of the chamber was not a man—but then, it never had been.

Kelly loosed the retaining bolts on the hatch. He was greeted with a foul stench that he ought to have expected but didn't. The buildup and release of pressure in Billy's intestinal tract and bladder had produced predictable effects. He'd have to hose it out later, Kelly thought, pulling Billy out and laying him on the concrete floor. He wondered if he had to chain him to something, but the body at his feet was useless to its owner now, the major joints nearly destroyed, the central nervous system good only to transmit pain. But Billy was still breathing, and that was just fine, Kelly thought, heading off to bed, glad it was over. With luck he would not have to do something like this again. With luck and good medical care, Billy would live for several weeks. If you could call it that.

21
Possibilities

Kelly was actually disturbed by how well he slept. It wasn't fitting, he worried, that he should have gotten ten hours of uninterrupted sleep after what he'd done to Billy. This was an odd time for his conscience to manifest itself, Kelly said to the face in the mirror as he shaved; also a little late. If a person went around injuring women and dealing drugs, then he should have considered the possible consequences. Kelly wiped his face off. He felt no elation at the pain he'd inflicted—he was sure of that. It had been a matter of gathering necessary information while meting out justice in a particularly fitting and appropriate way. Being able to classify his actions in familiar terms went a long way towards keeping his conscience under control.

He also had to go someplace. After dressing, Kelly got a plastic drop cloth. This went to the after well-deck of his cruiser. He was already packed, and his things went into the main salon.

It would be a trip of several hours, most of it boring and more than half in darkness. Heading south for Point Lookout, Kelly took the time to scan the collection of derelict "ships" near Bloodsworth Island. Built for the First

World War, they were an exceedingly motley collection. Some made of timber, others of concrete—which seemed very odd indeed—all of them had survived the world's first organized submarine campaign, but had not been commercially viable even in the 1920s, when merchant sailors had come a lot cheaper than the tugboat crews who routinely plied the Chesapeake Bay. Kelly went to the flying bridge and while the autopilot handled his southerly course, he examined them through binoculars, because one of them probably held interest. He could discern no movement, however, and saw no boats in the morass that their final resting place had become. That was to be expected, he thought. It wouldn't be an ongoing industrial enterprise, though it was a clever hiding place for the activity in which Billy had so recently played a part. He altered course to the west. This matter would have to wait. Kelly made a conscious effort to change his thinking. He would soon be a team player, associated again with men like himself. A welcome change, he thought, during which he would have time to consider his tactics for the next phase of his operation.

The officers had merely been briefed on the incident with Mrs. Charles, but their alert level had been raised by follow-up information on the method by which her assailant had met his end. No additional cautionary words were needed. Two-man patrol cars handled most of them, though some solo cars driven by experienced—or overly confident—officers performed the same function in a way that would have grated on Ryan and Douglas had they seen it. One officer would approach while the other stood back, his hand resting casually on his service revolver. The lead officer would stand the wino up and frisk him, checking for weapons, and often finding knives, but no firearms—anyone in possession of one pawned it for money with which to buy alcohol or, in some cases, drugs. In the first night eleven such people were rousted and identified, with two arrests being made for what the officers deemed an improper attitude. But at the end of the shift, nothing of value had been turned up.

• • •

"Okay—I found something out," Charon said. His car sat in the parking lot outside a supermarket, next to a Cadillac.

"What's that?"

"They're looking for a guy disguised as a bum."

"You kidding me?" Tucker asked with some disgust.

"That's the word, Henry," the detective assured him. "They have orders to approach with caution."

"Shit," the distributor snorted.

"White, not too tall, forties. He's pretty strong, and he moves real good when he has to. They're going soft on the information that's out, but about the same time he interfered with a yoking, two more pushers turned up dead. I'm betting it's the same guy who's been taking pushers out."

Tucker shook his head. "Rick and Billy, too? It doesn't make any sense."

"Henry, whether it makes sense or not, that's what the word is, okay? Now, you take this seriously. Whoever this guy is, he's a pro. You got that? A pro."

"Tony and Eddie," Tucker said quietly.

"That's my best guess, Henry, but it's only a guess." Charon pulled out of his parking place.

But none of it made any real sense, Tucker told himself, driving out onto Edmondson Avenue. Why would Tony and Eddie try to do—what? What the hell was going on? They didn't know much about his operation, merely that it existed, and that he wanted it and his territory left alone while he evolved into their principal supplier. For them to harm his business without first suborning his method of importing the product was not logical. Suborning . . . he'd used the wrong word . . . but—

Suborned. What if Billy were still alive? What if Billy had cut a deal and Rick hadn't gone along with it—a possibility; Rick had been weaker but more reliable than Billy.

Billy kills Rick, takes Doris out and dumps her somewhere—Billy knows how to do that, doesn't he?—why? Billy has made contact with—who? Ambitious little bastard, Billy, Tucker thought. *Not all that smart, but ambitious and tough when he has to be.*

Possibilities. Billy makes contact with somebody. Who? What does Billy know? He knows where the product is processed, but not how it comes in . . . maybe the smell, the formaldehyde smell on the plastic bags. Henry had been careful about that before; when Tony and Eddie had helped him package the product in the start-up phase, Tucker had taken the trouble to rebag everything, just to be on the safe side. But not the last two shipments . . . *damn.* That was a mistake, wasn't it? Billy knew roughly where the processing was done, but could he find it on his own? Henry didn't think so. He didn't know much about boats and didn't even like them all that much, and navigating wasn't an easily acquired art.

Eddie and Tony know about boats, you idiot, Tucker reminded himself.

But *why* would they cross him now, just when things were blooming?

Whom else had he offended? Well, there was the New York crew, but he'd never even had direct contact with them. He'd invaded their market, though, taking advantage of a supply shortfall to establish an entry position. Might they be upset about that?

What about the Philadelphia crew? They had become the interface between himself and New York, and perhaps they were greedy. Perhaps they had found out about Billy.

Perhaps Eddie was making his move, betraying Tony and Henry at the same time.

Perhaps a lot of things. Whatever was happening, Henry still controlled the import pipeline. More to the point, he had to stand and defend what he had, his own territory, and his connections. Things were just starting to pay off big. Years of effort had been required to get to where he was now, Henry told himself, turning right towards his home. Starting over would entail dangers that, once run, were not easily repeated. A new city, setting up a new network. And Vietnam would be cooling off soon. The body count upon which he depended was declining. A problem now could wreck everything. If he could maintain his operation, his worst-case scenario was banking over ten million dollars—closer to twenty if he played the cards right—and leaving the business for good. That was not an unattractive option. Two years of high payoff to reach that spot. It might not be possible to start over from scratch. He had to stand and fight.

Stand and fight, boy. A plan began to form. He'd put the word out: he wanted Billy and he wanted him alive. He'd talk to Tony and sound him out on the chance that Eddie was playing a game of some sort, that Eddie was connected with rivals to the north. That was his starting point to gather information. Then he would act on it.

There's a likely spot, Kelly told himself. *Springer* was just crawling along, quietly. The trick was to find a place that was populated but not alert. Nothing unusual about that mission requirement, he smiled to himself. Toss in a bend in the river, and here was one. He checked the shoreline out carefully. It looked like a school, probably a boarding school, and there were no lights in the buildings. There was a town behind it, a small, sleepy one, just a few lights there, a car every couple of minutes, but those followed the main road, and nobody there could possibly see him. He let the boat proceed around a bend—better yet, a farm, probably tobacco from the look of it, an old one with a substantial house maybe six hundred yards off, the owners inside and enjoying their air conditioning, the glare from their lights and TV preventing them from seeing outside. He'd risk it here.

Kelly idled his motors and went forward to drop his lunch-hook, a small anchor. He moved quickly and quietly, lowering his small dinghy into the water and pulling it aft. Lifting Billy over the rail was easy enough, but putting the body in the dinghy defeated him. Kelly hurried into the after stateroom and returned with a life jacket which he put on Billy before tossing him over the side. It was easier this way. He tied the jacket off to the stern. Then he rowed as quickly as he could to the shore. It only took three or four minutes before the dinghy's bow touched the muddy banks. It was a school, Kelly saw. It probably had a summer program, and almost certainly had a maintenance staff which would show up in the morning. He stepped out of the dinghy and hauled Billy onto the bank before removing the life jacket.

"You stay here, now."

" . . . stay . . ."

"That's right." Kelly pushed the dinghy back into the river. As he began rowing back, his aft-facing position forced him to look at Billy. He'd left him naked. No identification. He bore no distinguishing marks that Kelly had not created. Billy had said more than once that he'd never been fingerprinted. If true, then there was no way for police to identify him easily, probably not at all. And he couldn't live too long the way he was. The brain damage was more profound than Kelly had intended, and that indicated that other internal organs had to be severely damaged as well. But Kelly had shown some mercy after all. The crows probably wouldn't have a chance to pick at him. Just doctors. Soon Kelly had *Springer* moving back up the Potomac.

Two more hours and Kelly saw the marina at Quantico Marine Base. Tired, he made a careful approach, selecting a guest berth at the end of one of the piers.

"Who might you be?" a voice asked in the dark.

"The name's Clark," Kelly replied. "You should be expecting me."

"Oh, yeah. Nice boat," the man said, heading back to the small dock house. Within minutes a car came down the hill from officer-quarters.

"You're early," Marty Young said.

"Might as well get started, sir. Come aboard?"

"Thanks, Mr. Clark." He looked around the salon. "How did you get this baby? I suffer along with a little day-sailer."

"I don't know that I really should say, sir," Kelly replied. "Sorry." General Young accepted that with good grace.

"Dutch says you're going to be part of the op."

"Yes, sir."

"Sure you can hack it?" Young noticed the tattoo on Kelly's forearm and wondered what it denoted.

"I worked PHOENIX for over a year, sir. What sort of people have signed on?"

"They're all Force Recon. We're training them pretty hard."

"Kick 'em loose around five-thirty?" Kelly asked.

"That's right. I'll have somebody pick you up." Young smiled. "We need to get you nice and fit, too."

Kelly just smiled. "Fair enough, General."

"So what's so damned important?" Piaggi asked, annoyed to be bothered at short notice on a weekend night.

"I think somebody's making a move on me. I want to know who."

"Oh?" And *that* made the meeting important, if poorly timed, Tony thought. "Tell me what's happened."

"Somebody's been taking pushers down on the west side," Tucker said.

"I read the papers," Piaggi assured him. He poured some wine into his guest's glass. It was important at times like these to make a show of normality. Tucker would never be part of the family to which Piaggi belonged, but for all that he was a valuable associate. "Why is that important, Henry?"

"The same guy took down two of my people. Rick and Billy."

"The same ones who—"

"That's right. One of my girls is missing, too." He lifted his glass and sipped, watching Piaggi's eyes.

"Rip?"

"Billy had about seventy thousand, cash. The cops found it, right there." Tucker filled in a few more details. "The police say it looks real professional, like."

"You have any other enemies on the street?" Tony inquired. It wasn't a terribly bright question—anyone in the business had enemies—but the skill factor was the important one.

"I've made sure the cops know about my major competitors."

Piaggi nodded. That was within normal business practice, but somewhat risky. He shrugged it off. Henry could be a real cowboy, a source of occasional worry to Tony and his colleagues. Henry was also very careful when he had to be, and the man seemed to understand how to mix the two traits.

"Somebody getting even?"

"None of them would walk away from that kind of cash."

"True," Piaggi conceded. "I got news for you, Henry. *I* don't leave that sort of bundle laying around."

Oh, really? Tucker wondered behind impassive eyes. "Tony, either the guy fucked up or he's trying to tell me something. He's killed like seven or eight people, real smart. He took Rick down with a knife. I don't think he fucked up, y'dig?" The odd thing was that both men thought that a knifing was something the other would do. Henry had the impression that knives were the weapon of Italians. Piaggi thought it the trademark of a black.

"What I hear, somebody is doing pushers with a pistol—a little one."

"One was a shotgun, right in the guts. The cops are rousting street bums, doing it real careful."

"I didn't hear that," Piaggi admitted. This man had some great sources, but then he lived closer to that part of town, and it was to be expected that his intelligence network would be speedier than Piaggi's.

"It sounds like a pro doing this," Tucker concluded. "Somebody really good, y'know?"

Piaggi nodded understanding while his mind was in a quandary. The existence of highly skilled Mafia assassins was for the most part a fiction created by TV and movies. The average organized-crime murder was not a skilled act, but rather something carried out by a man who mainly did other, real, money-generating activities. There was no special class of killers who waited patiently for telephone calls, made hits, then returned to their posh homes to await the next call. There *were* made members who were unusually good or experienced at killing, but that wasn't the same thing. One simply got a reputation as a person whom killing didn't affect—and that meant that the elimination would be done with a minimum of fuss, not a maximum of artistry. True sociopaths were rare, even in the Mafia, and bungled killings were the rule rather than the exception. And so "professional" to Henry meant something that existed only as a fiction, the TV image of a Mafia button man. But how the hell did Tony explain *that?*

"It isn't one of mine, Henry," he said after a moment's contemplation. That he didn't have *any* was another issue entirely, Piaggi told himself, watching the effect of his words on his associate. Henry had always assumed that Piaggi knew a good deal about killing. Piaggi *knew* that Tucker had more experience with that end of business than he ever wished to have, but that was just one more thing he would have to explain, and this clearly was not the time. For now, he watched Tucker's face, trying to read his thoughts as he finished his glass of Chianti.

How do I know he's telling the truth? The thought didn't require any special perception to read.

"You need some help, Henry?" Piaggi said, to break a very awkward silence.

"I don't think you're doing it. I think you're too smart," Tucker said, finishing his own glass.

"Glad to hear that." Tony smiled and refilled both glasses.

"What about Eddie?"

"What do you mean?"

"Is he ever going to get 'made'?" Tucker looked down, swirling the wine around the glass. One thing about Tony, he always set the right kind of atmosphere for a business discussion. It was one of the reasons they'd been drawn together. Tony was quiet, thoughtful, always polite, even when you asked a sensitive question.

"That's kind of touchy, Henry, and I really shouldn't talk that over with you. You can never be 'made.' You know that."

"No equal-opportunity in the outfit, eh? Well, that's okay. I know I'd never fit in real good. Just so's we can do business, Anthony." Tucker took the occasion to grin, breaking the tension somewhat and, he hoped, making it easier for Tony to answer the question. He got his wish.

"No," Piaggi said after a moment's contemplation.

"Nobody thinks Eddie's got what it takes."

"Maybe he's lookin' for a way to prove differ'nt."

Piaggi shook his head. "I don't think so. Eddie's going to make a good living off this. He knows that."

"Who, then?" Tucker asked. "Who else knows enough? Who else would do a bunch of killings to cover up a move like this? Who else would make it look like a pro job?"

Eddie's not smart enough. Piaggi knew that, or thought he did.

"Henry, taking Eddie out would cause major problems." He paused. "But I'll check around."

"Thank you," Tucker said. He stood and left Tony alone with his wine.

Piaggi stayed at his table. Why did things have to be so complicated? Was Henry being truthful? Probably, he thought. He was Henry's only connection to the outfit, and severing that tie would be very bad for everyone. Tucker could become highly important but would never be an insider. On the other hand he was smart and he delivered. The outfit had lots of such people, inside-outsiders, associate members, whatever you might call them, whose value and status were proportional to their utility. Many of them actually wielded more power than some "made" members, but there was always a difference. In a real dispute, being made counted for much—in most cases, counted for *everything*.

That could explain matters. Was Eddie jealous of Henry's status? Did he crave becoming a real member so much that he might be willing to forfeit the benefits of the current business arrangement? It didn't make sense, Piaggi told himself. But what did?

"Ahoy the *Springer!*" a voice called. The Marine corporal was surprised to see the cabin door open immediately. He'd expected having to jolt this . . . civilian . . . from his cushy bed. Instead he saw a man come out in jungle boots and bush fatigues. They weren't Marine "utilities," but close enough to show the man was serious. He could see where some badges had been removed, where a name and something else would have gone, and that somehow made Mr. Clark look more serious still.

"This way, sir." The corporal gestured. Kelly followed without a word.

Sir didn't mean anything, Kelly knew. When in doubt, a Marine would call a lightpole "Sir." He followed the youngster to a car and they drove off, crossing the railroad tracks and climbing uphill while he wished for another few hours of sleep.

"You the General's driver?"

"Yes, sir." And that was the extent of their conversation.

There were about twenty-five of them, standing in the morning mist, stretching and chatting among themselves as the squad NCOs walked up and down the line, looking for bleary eyes or slack expressions. Heads turned when the General's car stopped and a man got out. They saw he wore the wrong sort of fatigues and wondered who the hell he was, especially since he had no rank insignia at all. He walked right up to the senior NCO.

"You Gunny Irvin?" Kelly asked.

Master Gunnery Sergeant Paul Irvin nodded politely as he sized the visitor up. "Correct, sir. Are you Mr. Clark?"

Kelly nodded. "Well, I'm trying to be, this early."

Both men traded a look. Paul Irvin was dark and serious-looking. Not as overtly threatening as Kelly had expected, he had the eyes of a careful, thoughtful man, which was to be expected for someone of his age and experience.

"What kinda shape you in?" Irvin asked.

"Only one way to find that out," "Clark" answered.

Irvin smiled broadly. "Good. I'll let you lead the run, sir. Our captain's away somewhere jerking off."

Oh, shit!

"Now let's get loosened up." Irvin walked back to the formation, calling it to attention. Kelly took a place on the right side of the second rank.

"Good morning, Marines!"

"Recon!" they bellowed back.

The daily dozen wasn't exactly fun, but Kelly didn't have to show off. He did watch Irvin, who was becoming more serious by the minute, doing his exercises like some sort of robot. Half an hour later they were indeed all loosened up, and Irvin brought them back to attention in preparation for the run.

"Gentlemen, I want to introduce a new member of our team. This is Mr. Clark. He'll be leading the run with me."

Kelly took his place, whispering, "I don't know where the hell we're going."

Irvin smiled in a nasty way. "No problem, sir. You can follow us in after you fall out."

"Lead off, jarhead," Kelly replied, one pro to another.

Forty minutes later, Kelly was still in the lead. Being there allowed him to set the pace, and that was the only good news. Not staggering was his other main concern, and that was becoming difficult, since when the body tires the fine-tuning controls go first.

"Left," Irvin said, pointing. Kelly couldn't know that he'd needed ten seconds to assemble the surplus air to speak. He'd also had the burden of singing the cadence, however. The new path, just a dirt trail, took them into the piney woods.

Buildings, oh Jesus, I hope that's the stopping place. Even his thoughts were gasps now. The path wound around a little, but there were cars there, and that had to be—what? He almost stopped in surprise, and on his own called, "Quick-time, march!" to slow the formation down.

Mannequins?

"Detail," Irvin called out, *"halt!* Stand at ease," he added.

Kelly coughed a few times, bending down slightly, blessing his runs in the park and around his island for allowing him to survive this morning.

"Slow," was all Irvin had to say at the moment.

"Good morning, Mr. Clark." It turned out that one of the cars was real, Kelly saw. James Greer and Marty Young waved him over.

"Good morning. I hope y'all slept well," Kelly told them.

"You volunteered, John," Greer pointed out.

"They're four minutes slow this morning," Young observed. "Not bad for a spook, though."

Kelly turned away in semidisgust. It took a minute or so for him to realize what this place was.

"Damn!"

"There's your hill." Young pointed.

"Trees are taller here," Kelly said, evaluating the distance.

"So's the hill. It's a wash."

"Tonight?" Kelly asked. It wasn't hard to catch the meaning of the General's words.

"Think you're up to it?"

"I suppose we need to know that. When's the mission going to go?"

Greer took that one. "You don't need to know that yet."

"How much warning will I have?"

The CIA official weighed that one before answering. "Three days before we move out. We'll be going over mission parameters in a few hours. For now, watch how these men are setting up." Greer and Young headed off to their car.

"Aye aye," Kelly replied to their backs. The Marines had coffee going. He got a cup and started blending in with the assault team.

"Not bad," Irvin said.

"Thanks. I always figured it's one of the most important things you need to know in this business."

"What's that?" Irvin asked.

"How to run away as far and fast as you can."

Irvin laughed and then came the first work detail of the day, something that let the men cool down and have a laugh of their own. They started moving the mannequins around. It had become a ritual, which woman went with which kids. They'd discovered that the models could be posed, and the Marines made great fun of that. Two had brought new outfits, both rather skimpy bikinis, which they ostentatiously put on two lounging lady-figures. Kelly watched with incredulous amazement, then realized that the swimsuit models had had their bodies—painted, in the interests of realism. *Jesus,* he thought, *and they say sailors are screwy!*

USS *Ogden* was a new ship, or nearly so, having emerged from the New York Naval Shipyard's building ways in 1964. Rather a strange-looking ship, she was 570 feet long, and her forward half had a fairly normal superstructure and eight guns to annoy attacking aircraft. The odd part was the after half, which was flat on top and hollow underneath. The flat part was good for landing helicopters, and directly under that was a well deck designed to be filled with water from which landing craft could operate. She and her eleven sister ships had been designed to support landing operations, to put Marines on the beach for the amphibious-assault missions that The Corps had invented in the 1920s and perfected in the 1940s. But the Pacific Fleet amphibious ships were without a mission now—the Marines *were* on the beach, generally brought in by chartered jetliners to conventional airports—and so some of the 'phibs were being outfitted for other missions. As *Ogden* was.

Cranes were lifting a series of trailer vans onto the flight deck. When secured in place, deck parties erected various radio antennas. Other such objects were being bolted into place on the superstructure. The activity was being done in the open—there is no convenient way of hiding a 17,000-ton warship—and it was clear that *Ogden,* like two more sister ships, was transforming herself into a platform for the gathering of electronic intelligence—ELINT. She sailed out of the San Diego Naval Base just as the sun began to set, without an escort and without the Marine battalion she was built to carry. Her Navy crew of thirty officers and four hundred ninety enlisted men settled into their routine watch bill, conducting training exercises and generally doing what most had chosen to do by enlisting in the Navy instead of risking a slot in the draft. By sunset she was well under the horizon, and her new mission had been communicated to various interested parties, not all of whom were friendly to the flag which she flew. With all those trailers aboard and a score of antennas looking like a forest of burnt trees to clutter up her flight deck—and no Marines embarked—she wouldn't be doing anyone direct harm. That was obvious to all who had seen her.

Twelve hours later, and two hundred miles at sea, bosun's mates assembled parties from the deck division and told some rather confused young men to unbolt all but one of the trailers—which were empty—and to strike down all of the antennas on the flight deck. Those on the superstructure would remain in place. The antennas went below first, into the capacious equipment-storage spaces. The empty trailers were wheeled after them, clearing the flight deck entirely.

At Subic Bay Naval Base, the commanding officer of USS *Newport News,* along with his executive officer and gunnery officer, looked over their missions for the coming month. His command was one of the last true cruisers in the world, with eight-inch guns like few others. They were semiautomatic, and loaded their powder charges not in loose bags but in brass cartridge cases different only in scale from the kind any deer hunter might jack into his Winchester .30-30. Able to reach almost twenty miles, *Newport News* could deliver a stunning volume of fire, as an NVA battalion had learned only two weeks earlier, much to its misfortune. Fifty rounds per gun tube per minute. The center gun of the number-two turret was damaged, and so the cruiser could be counted on to put only four *hundred* rounds per minute on target, but that was the equivalent of one hundred thousand-pound bombs. The cruiser's task for the next deployment, the Captain learned, was to go after selected triple-A batteries on the Vietnamese coast. That was fine with him, though the mission he really lusted for was to enter Haiphong harbor one night.

"Your lad seems to know his business—till now, anyway," General Young observed about quarter of two.

"It's a lot to ask him to do something like this the first night, Marty," Dutch Maxwell countered.

"Well, hell, Dutch, if he wants to play with my Marines . . . " That's how Young was. They were all "his" Marines. He'd flown with Foss off Guadalcanal, covered Chesty Puller's regiment in Korea, and was one of the men who'd perfected close-air support into the art form it now was.

They stood on the hilltop overlooking the site Young had recently erected. Fifteen of the Recon Marines were on the slopes, and their job was to detect and eliminate Clark as he climbed to his notional perch. Even General Young thought it an overly harsh test on Clark's first day with the team, but Jim Greer had made a very big deal of telling them how impressive the lad was, and spooks needed to be put in their place. Even Dutch Maxwell had agreed with that.

"What a crummy way to earn a living," said the admiral with seventeen hundred carrier landings under his belt.

"Lions and tigers and bears." Young chuckled. "Oh, my! I don't really expect him to make it here the first time. We have some fine people in this team, don't we, Irvin?"

"Yes, sir," the master gunnery sergeant agreed at once.

"So what do you think of Clark?" Young asked next.

"Seems like he knows a thing or two," Irvin allowed. "Pretty decent shape for a civilian—and I like his eyes."

"Oh?"

"You notice, sir? He's got cold eyes. He's been around the block." They spoke in low murmurs. Kelly was supposed to get here, but they didn't want their voices to make it too easy for him, nor to add any extraneous noise that might mask the sounds of the woods. "But not tonight. I told the people what would happen if this guy gets through the line on his first try."

"Don't you Marines know how to play fair?" Maxwell objected with an unseen smile. Irvin handled the answer.

"Sir, 'fair' means all my Marines get back home alive. Fuck the others, beg your pardon, sir."

"Funny thing, Sergeant, that's always been my definition of 'fair,' too." *This guy would have made one hell of a command master chief,* Maxwell thought to himself.

"Been following baseball, Marty?" The men relaxed. No way Clark would make it.

"I think the Orioles look pretty tough."

"Gentlemen, we're losing our concentration, like," Irvin suggested diplomatically.

"Quite right. Please excuse us," General Young replied. The two flag officers settled back into stillness, watching the illuminated hands of their watches turn to three o'clock, the operation's agreed stop-time. They didn't hear Irvin speak, or even breathe, for all that time. That took an hour. It was a comfortable one for the Marine general, but the Admiral just didn't like being in the woods, with all the bloodsucking bugs, and probably snakes, and all manner of unpleasant things not ordinarily found in the cockpit of a fighter aircraft. They listened to the whispering breezes in the pines, heard the flapping of bats and owls and perhaps some other night fliers, and little else. Finally it was 02:55. Marty Young stood and stretched, fishing in his pocket for a cigarette.

"Anybody got a smoke? I'm out, and I could sure use one," a voice murmured.

"Here you go, Marine," Young said, the gracious general. He held one out to the shadow and flicked his trusty Zippo. Then he jumped back a step. "Shit!"

"Personally, General, I think Pittsburgh looks pretty tough this year. The Orioles are a little weak in the pitching department." Kelly took one puff, without inhaling, and dropped it to the ground.

"How long have you been here?" Maxwell demanded.

"'Lions and tigers and bears, oh, my!'" Kelly mimicked. 'I 'killed' you around one-thirty, sir."

"You son of a bitch!" Irvin said. "You killed *me.*"

"And you were very polite about being quiet, too."

Maxwell turned on his flashlight. Mr. Clark—the Admiral had consciously decided to change the boy's name in his own mind—just stood there, a rubber knife in his hand, his face painted with green and black shadows, and for the first time since the Battle of Midway, his body shuddered with fear. The young face split into a grin as he pocketed his "knife."

"How the hell did you do that?" Dutch Maxwell demanded.

"Pretty well, I think, Admiral." Kelly chuckled, reaching down for Marty Young's canteen. "Sir, if I told, then everybody'd be able to, right?"

Irvin stood up from his place of repose and walked next to the civilian.

"Mr. Clark, sir, I think you'll do."

22
Titles

Grishanov was in the embassy. Hanoi was a strange city, a mixture of French-Imperial architecture, little yellow people and bomb craters. Traveling about a country at war was an unusual exercise, all the more so in an automobile daubed with camouflage paint. A passing American fighter-bomber coming back from a mission with an extra bomb or some unexpended 20-millimeter cannon rounds could easily use the car for practice, though they never seemed to do so. The luck of the draw made this a cloudy, stormy day, and air activity was at a minimum, allowing him to relax, but not to enjoy the ride. Too many bridges were down, too many roads cratered, and the trip lasted three times what ought to have been the norm. A helicopter trip would have been much faster, but would also have been madness. The Americans seemed to live under the fiction that an automobile might be civilian-owned—this in a country where a bicycle was a status symbol! Grishanov marveled—but a helicopter was an aircraft, and killing one was a *kill*. Now in Hanoi, he got the chance to sit in a concrete building where the electricity was a sometime thing—off at the moment—and air conditioning an absurd fantasy. The open windows and poorly fitting screens allowed insects freer reign than the people who worked and sweated here. For all that, it was worth the trip to be here in his country's embassy, where he could speak his native tongue and for a precious few hours stop being a semidiplomat.

"So?" his general asked.

"It goes well, but I must have more people. This is too much for one man to do alone."

"That is not possible." The General poured his guest a glass of mineral water. The principal mineral present was salt. The Russians drank a lot of that here. "Nikolay Yevgeniyevich, they're being difficult again."

"Comrade General, I know that I am only a fighter pilot and not a political theorist. I know that our fraternal socialist allies are on the front line of the conflict between Marxism-Leninism and the reactionary Capitalist West. I know that this war of national liberation is a vital part of our struggle to liberate the world from oppression—"

"Yes, Kolya"—the General smiled slyly, allowing the man who was *not* a political theorist to dispense with further ideological incantations—"we know that all of this is true. Do go on. I have a busy day planned."

The Colonel nodded his appreciation. "These arrogant little bastards are not helping us. They are using us, they are using me, they are using *my* prisoners to blackmail us. And if this is Marxism-Leninism, then I'm a Trotskyite." It was a joke that few would have been able to make lightly, but Grishanov's father was a Central Committee member with impeccable political credentials.

"What are you learning, Comrade Colonel?" the General said, just to keep things on track.

"Colonel Zacharias is everything that we were told, and more. We are now planning how to defend the *Rodina* against the Chinese. He is the 'blue team' leader."

"What?" The General blinked. "Explain?"

"This man is a fighter pilot, but also an expert on defeating air defenses. Can you believe it, he's only flown bombers as a guest, but he's actually planned SAC missions and helped to write SAC doctrine for defense-avoidance and -suppression. So now he's doing that for me."

"Notes?"

Grishanov's face darkened. "Back at the camp. Our fraternal socialist comrades are 'studying' them. Comrade General, do you know how important this data is?"

The General was by profession a tank officer, not an aviator, but he was also one of the brighter stars rising in the Soviet firmament, here in Vietnam to study everything the Americans were doing. It was one of the premier jobs in his country's uniformed service.

"I would imagine that it's highly valuable."

Kolya leaned forward. "In another two months, perhaps six weeks, I will be able to reverse-plan SAC. I'll be able to think as they think. I will know not only what their current plans are, but I will also be able to duplicate their thinking into the future. Excuse me, I do not mean to inflate my importance," he said sincerely. "This American is giving me a graduate course in American doctrine and philosophy. I've *seen* the intelligence estimates we get from KGB and GRU. At least half of it is wrong. That's only one man. Another one has told me about their carrier doctrine. Another about NATO war plans. It goes on, Comrade General."

"How do you do this, Nikolay Yevgeniyevich?" The General was new at this post, and had met Grishanov only once before, though his service reputation was better than excellent.

Kolya leaned back in his chair. "Kindness and sympathy."

"To our enemies?" the General asked sharply.

"Is it our mission to inflict pain on these men?" He gestured outside. "That's what *they* do, and what do they get for it? Mainly lies that sound good. My section in Moscow discounted nearly everything these little monkeys sent. I was told to come here to *get information*. That is what I am doing. I will take all the criticism I must in order to get information such as this, Comrade."

The General nodded. "So why are you here?"

"I need more people! It's too much for one man. What if I am killed—what if I get malaria or food poisoning—who will do my work? I can't interrogate all of these prisoners myself. Especially now that they are beginning to talk, I take more and more time with each, and I lose energy. I lose continuity. There are not enough hours in the day."

The General sighed. "I've tried. They offer you their best—"

Grishanov almost snarled in frustration. "Their best *what?* Best barbarians? That would destroy my work. I need *Russians*. Men, *kulturny* men! Pilots, experienced officers. I'm not interrogating private soldiers. These are real professional warriors. They are valuable to us because of what they know. They know much because they are intelligent, and because they are intelligent they will not respond well to crude methods. You know what I really need to support me? A good psychiatrist. And one more thing," he added, inwardly trembling at his boldness.

"Psychiatrist? That is not serious. And I doubt that we'll be able to get other men into the camp. Moscow is delaying shipments of antiaircraft rockets for 'technical reasons.' Our local allies are being difficult again, as I said, and the disagreement escalates." The General leaned back and wiped sweat from his brow. "What is this other thing?"

"Hope, Comrade General. I need hope." Colonel Nikolay Yevgeniyevich Grishanov gathered himself.

"Explain."

"Some of these men know their situation. Probably all suspect it. They are well briefed on what happens to prisoners here, and they know that their status is unusual. Comrade General, the knowledge these men have is encyclopedic. Years of useful information."

"You're building up to something."

"We can't let them die," Grishanov said, immediately qualifying himself to lessen the impact of what he was saying. "Not all of them. Some we must have. Some will serve us, but I must have something to offer to them."

"Bring them back?"

"After the hell they've lived here—"

"They're *enemies,* Colonel! They all trained to kill *us!* Save your sympathy for your own countrymen!" growled a man who'd fought in the snows outside Moscow.

Grishanov stood his ground, as the General had once done. "They are men, not unlike us, Comrade General. They have knowledge that is useful, if only we have the intelligence to extract it. It is that simple. Is it too much to ask that we treat them with kindness, that we give something in return for learning how to save our country from possible destruction? We could torture them, as our 'fraternal socialist allies' have done, and get *nothing!* Does that serve our country?" It came down to that, and the General knew it. He looked at the Colonel of Air Defense and his first expressed thought was the obvious one.

"You wish to risk my career along with yours? My father is not a Central Committeeman." *I could have used this man in my battalion. . . .*

"Your father was a soldier," Grishanov pointed out. "And like you, a good one." It was a skillful play and both knew it, but what really mattered was the logic and significance of what Grishanov was proposing, an intelligence coup that would stagger the professional spies of KGB and GRU. There was only one possible reaction from a real soldier with a real sense of mission.

General-Lieutenant Yuri Konstantinovich Rokossovskiy pulled a bottle of vodka from his desk. It was the Starka label, dark, not clear, the best and most expensive. He poured two small glasses.

"I can't get you more men. Certainly I cannot get you a physician, not even one in uniform, Kolya. But, yes, I will try to get you some hope."

The third convulsion since her arrival at Sandy's house was a minor one, but still troubling. Sarah had gotten her quieted down with as mild a shot of barbiturate as she dared. The blood work was back, and Doris was a veritable collection of problems. Two kinds of venereal disease, evidence of another systemic infection, and possibly a borderline diabetic. She was already attacking the first three problems with a strong dose of antibiotics. The fourth would be handled with diet and reevaluated later. For Sarah the signs of physical abuse were like something from a nightmare about another continent and another generation, and it was the mental aftermath of that that was the most disquieting of all, even as Doris Brown closed her eyes and lapsed into sleep.

"Doctor, I—"

"Sandy, will you *please* call me Sarah? We're in your house, remember?"

Nurse O'Toole managed an embarrassed smile. "Okay, Sarah. I'm worried."

"So am I. I'm worried about her physical condition, I'm worried about her psychological condition. I'm worried about her 'friends'—"

"I'm worried about John," Sandy said discordantly. Doris was under control. She could see that. Sarah Rosen was a gifted clinician, but something of a worrier, as many good physicians were.

Sarah headed out of the room. There was coffee downstairs. She could smell it and was heading for it. Sandy came with her. "Yes, that, too. What a strange and interesting man."

"I don't throw my newspapers away. Every week, same time, I bundle them together for the garbage collection—and I've been checking the back issues."

Sarah poured two cups. She had very delicate movements, Sandy thought. "I know what I think. Tell me what you think," the pharmacologist said.

"I think he's killing people." It caused her physical pain to say that.

"I think you're right." Sarah Rosen sat down and rubbed her eyes. "You never met Pam. Prettier than Doris, willowy, sort of, probably from an inadequate diet. It was much easier to wean her off the drugs. Not as badly abused, physically anyway, but just as much emotional hurt. We never got the whole story. Sam says that John did. But that's not the important part." Sarah looked up, and the pain O'Toole saw there was real and deep. "We had her *saved,* Sandy, and then something happened, and then something—something changed in John."

Sandy turned to look out the window. It was quarter of seven in the morning. She could see people coming out in pajamas and bathrobes to get their morning papers and collect half-gallon bottles of milk. The early crowd was leaving for their cars, a process that in her neighborhood lasted until eight-thirty or so. She turned back. "No, nothing changed. It was always there. Something—I don't know, released it, let it out? Like opening the door of a cage. What sort of man—part of him's like Tim, but another part I just don't understand."

"What about his family?"

"He doesn't have any. His mother and father are dead, no siblings. He was married—"

"Yes, I know about that, and then Pam." Sarah shook her head. "So lonely."

"Part of me says he's a good man, but the other part . . . " Sandy's voice trailed off.

"My maiden name was Rabinowicz," Sarah said, sipping her coffee. "My family comes from Poland. Papa left when I was too young to remember; mother died when I was nine, peritonitis. I was eighteen when the war started," she went on. For her generation "the war" could mean only one thing. "We had lots of relatives in Poland. I remember writing to them. Then they all just disappeared. All gone—even now it's hard to believe it really happened."

"I'm sorry, Sarah, I didn't know."

"It's not the sort of thing you talk a lot about." Dr. Rosen shrugged. "People took something from me, though, and I couldn't do anything about it. My cousin Reva was a good pen pal. I suppose they killed her one way or another, but I never found out who or where. Back then I was too young to understand. I suppose I was more puzzled than anything else. Later, I got angry—but against whom? I didn't do anything. I couldn't. And there's this empty space where Reva was. I still have her picture, black-and-white of a girl with pigtails, twelve years old, I guess. She wanted to be a ballet dancer." Sarah looked up. "Kelly's got an empty place, too."

"But revenge—"

"Yeah, revenge." The doctor's expression was bleak. "I know. We're supposed to think he's a bad person, aren't we? Call the police, even, turn him in for doing that."

"I can't—I mean, yes, but I just—"

"Neither will I. Sandy, if he were a bad person, why did he bring Doris up here? He's risking his life two different ways."

"But there's something very scary about him."

"He could have just walked away from her," Sarah went on, not really hearing. "Maybe he's just the sort of person who thinks he has to fix everything himself. But now we have to help."

That turned Sandy around, giving her a respite from her real thoughts. "What are we going to do with her?"

"We're going to get her well, as far as we can, and after that it'll be up to her. What else can we do?" Sarah asked, watching Sandy's face change again, returning to her real dilemma.

"But what about John?"

Sarah looked up. "I have never seen him do anything illegal. Have you?"

It was a weapons-training day. A solid cloud cover meant that no reconnaissance satellites, American or Soviet, could see what was happening here. Cardboard targets were set up around the compound, and the lifeless eyes of mannequins watched from the sandbox and swing set as the Marines emerged from the woods, passing through the simulated gate, firing low-powered rounds from their carbines. The targets were shredded in seconds. Two M-60 machine guns poured fire into the open door of the "barracks"—which would already have been wrecked by the two Huey Cobra gunships—while the snatch team raced into the "prison block." There, twenty-five more mannequins were in individual rooms. Each was weighted to about one hundred fifty pounds—nobody thought that the Americans at SENDER GREEN would weigh even that much—and every one was dragged out while the fire-support element covered the evacuation.

Kelly stood next to Captain Pete Albie, who, it had been assumed for the purpose of the exercise, was dead. He was the only officer on the team, an aberration that was compensated for by the presence of so many senior NCOs. As they watched, the mannequins were dragged to the simulated fuselages of the rescue helicopters. These were mounted on semitrailers, and had come in at dawn. Kelly clicked his stopwatch when the last man was aboard.

"Five seconds under nominal, Captain." Kelly held up the watch. "These boys are pretty good."

"Except we're not doing it in daylight, are we, Mr. Clark?" Albie, like Kelly, knew the nature of the mission. The Marines as yet did not—at least not officially—though by now they had to have a fairly good idea. He turned and smiled. "Okay, it's only the third run-through."

Both men went into the compound. The simulated targets were in feathery pieces, and their number was exactly double the worst-case estimate for the SENDER GREEN guard force. They replayed the assault in their minds, checking angles of fire. There were advantages and disadvantages to how the camp was set up. Following the rules in some nameless East Bloc manual, it didn't fit the local terrain. Most conveniently indeed, the best avenue of approach coincided with the main gate. In adhering to a standard that allowed for maximum security against a possible escape attempt of the prisoners, it also facilitated an assault from without—but they didn't expect that, did they?

Kelly ran over the assault plan in his mind. The insertion would put the Recon Marines on the ground one ridge away from SENDER GREEN. Thirty minutes for the Marines to approach the camp. M-79 grenades to eliminate the guard towers. Two Huey Cobra gunships—known with lethal elegance as "snakes" to the troops, and that appealed to him—would hose the barracks and provide heavy fire support—but the grenadiers on the team, he was sure, could take out the towers in a matter of five seconds, then pour willie-pete into the barracks and burn the guard force alive with deadly fountains of white flame, doing without the snakes entirely if they had to. Small and lean as this operation was, the size of the objective and the quality of the team made for unplanned safety factors. He thought of it as overkill, a term that didn't just apply to nuclear weapons. In combat operations, safety lay in not giving the other guy a chance, to be ready to kill him two, three, a dozen times over in as little time as possible. Combat wasn't supposed to be fair. To Kelly, things were looking very good indeed.

"What if they have mines?" Albie worried.

"On their own turf?" Kelly asked. "No sign of it from the photographs. The ground isn't disturbed. No warning signs to keep their people away."

"Their people would know, wouldn't they?"

"On one of the photos there's some goats grazing just outside the wire, remember?"

Albie nodded with some embarrassment. "Yeah, you're right. I remember that."

"Let's not borrow trouble," Kelly told him. He fell silent for a moment, realizing that he had been a mere E-7 chief petty officer, and now he was talking as an equal—more accurately as a superior—to an O-3 captain of Recon Marines. That ought to have been—what? Wrong? If so, then why was he doing so well at it, and why was the captain accepting his words? Why was he *Mr. Clark* to this experienced combat officer? "We're going to do it."

"I think you're right, Mr. Clark. And how do you get out?"

"As soon as the choppers come in, I break the Olympic record coming down that hill to the LZ. I call it a two-minute run."

"In the dark?" Albie asked.

Kelly laughed. "I run especially fast in the dark, Captain."

"Do you know how many Ka-Bar knives there are?"

From the tone of Douglas's question, Lieutenant Ryan knew the news had to be bad. "No, but I suppose I'm about to find out."

"Sunny's Surplus just took delivery of a thousand of the goddamn things a month ago. The Marines must have enough and so now the Boy Scouts can buy them for four ninety-five. Other places, too. I didn't know how many of the things were out there."

"Me, neither," Ryan admitted. The Ka-Bar was a very large and bulky weapon. Hoods carried smaller knives, especially switchblades, though guns were becoming increasingly common on the streets.

What neither man wanted to admit openly was that they were stymied again, despite what had appeared to be a wealth of physical evidence in the brownstone. Ryan looked down at the open file and about twenty forensic photographs. There had *almost* certainly been a woman there. The murder victim—probably a hood himself, but still officially a victim—had been identified immediately from the cards in his wallet, but the address on his driver's license had turned out to be a vacant building. His collection of traffic violations had been paid on time, with cash. Richard Farmer had brushed with the police, but nothing serious enough to have merited a detailed inquiry. Tracking his family down had turned up precisely nothing. His mother—the father was long dead—had thought him a salesman of some sort. But somebody had nearly carved his heart out with a fighting knife, so quickly and decisively that the gun on the body hadn't been touched. A full set of fingerprints from Farmer merely generated a new card. The central FBI register did not have a match. Neither did the local police, and though Farmer's prints would be compared with a wide selection of unknowns, Ryan and Douglas didn't expect much. The bedroom had provided three complete sets of Farmer's, all on window glass, and semen stains had matched his blood type—O. Another set of stains had been typed as AB, which could mean the killer or the supposed (not quite certain) missing owner of the Roadrunner. For all they knew the killer might have taken the time to have a quickie with the suspected female—unless homosexuality was involved, in which case the suspected female might not exist at all.

There were also a selection of partial prints, one of a girl (supposition, from their size), and one of a man (also supposition), but they were so partial that he didn't expect much in the way of results. Worst of all, by the time the latent-prints team had gotten to check out the car parked outside, the blazing August sun had heated the car up so much that what might have been something to match prints with the registered owner of the car, one William Peter Grayson, had merely been a collection of heat-distorted blobs. It wasn't widely appreciated that matching partial prints with less than ten points of identification was difficult at best.

A check of the FBI's new National Crime Information Computer had turned up nothing on Grayson or Farmer. Finally, Mark Charon's narcotics team had nothing on the names Farmer or Grayson. It wasn't so much a matter of being back to square one. It was just that square seventeen didn't lead them anywhere. But that was often the way of things in homicide investigation. Detective work was a combination of the ordinary and the remarkable, but more of the former than the latter. Forensic sciences could tell you much. They did have the imprint of a common-brand sneaker from tracks in the brownstone—brand new, a help. They did know the approximate stride of the killer, from which they had generated a height range of from five-ten to six-three, which, unfortunately, was taller than Virginia Charles had estimated—something they, however, discounted. They knew he was Caucasian. They knew he had to be strong. They knew that he was either very, very lucky or highly skilled with all manner of weapons. They knew that he probably had at least rudimentary skills in hand-to-hand combat—or, Ryan sighed to himself, had been lucky; after all, there had been only one such encounter, and that with an addict with heroin in his bloodstream. They knew he was disguising himself as a bum.

All of which amounted to not very much. More than half of male humanity fell into the estimated height range. Considerably more than half of the men in the Baltimore metropolitan area were white. There were millions of combat veterans in America, many from elite military units—and the fact of the matter was that infantry skills were infantry skills, and you didn't have to be a combat vet to know them, and his country had had a draft for over thirty years, Ryan told himself. There were perhaps as many as thirty thousand men within a twenty-mile radius who fit the description and skill-inventory of his unknown suspect. Was he in the drug business himself? Was he a robber? Was he, as Farber had suggested, a man on some sort of mission? Ryan leaned heavily to the latter model, but he could not afford to discount the other two. Psychiatrists, and detectives, had been wrong before. The most elegant theories could be shattered by a single inconvenient fact. *Damn.* No, he told himself, this one was exactly what Farber said he was. This wasn't a *criminal.* This was a *killer,* something else entirely.

"We just need the one thing," Douglas said quietly, knowing the look on his lieutenant's face.

"The one thing," Ryan repeated. It was a private bit of shorthand. *The one thing* to break a case could be a name, an address, the description or tag number of a car, a person who knew something. Always the same, though frequently different, it was for the detective the crucial piece in the jigsaw puzzle that made the picture clear, and for the suspect the brick which, taken from the wall, caused everything to fall apart. And it was out there. Ryan was sure of it. It had to be there, because this killer was a clever one, much too clever for his own good. A suspect like this who eliminated a single target could well go forever undetected, but this one was not satisfied with killing one person, was he? Motivated neither by passion nor by financial gain, he was committed to a *process,* every step of which involved complex dangers. That was what would do him in. The detective was sure of it. Clever as he was, those complexities would continue to mount one upon the other until something important fell loose from the pile. It might even have happened already, Ryan thought, correctly.

"Two weeks," Maxwell said.

"That fast?" James Greer leaned forward, resting his elbows on his knees. "Dutch, that's really fast."

"You think we should fiddle around?" Podulski asked.

"Damn it, Cas, I said it was fast. I didn't say it was wrong. Two weeks' more training, one week of travel and setup?" Greer asked, getting a nod. "What about weather?"

"The one thing we can't control," Maxwell admitted. "But weather works both ways. It makes flying difficult. It also messes up radar and gunnery."

"How in hell did you get all the pieces moving this early?" Greer asked with a mixture of disbelief and admiration.

"There are ways, James. Hell, we're admirals, aren't we? We give orders, and guess what? Ships actually move."

"So the window opens in twenty-one days?"

"Correct. Cas flies out tomorrow to *Constellation.* We start briefing the air-support guys. *Newport News* is already clued in—well, partway. They think they're going to sweep the coast for triple-A batteries. Our command ship is plodding across the big pond right now. They don't know anything either except to rendezvous with TF-77."

"I have a lot of briefing to do," Cas confirmed with a grin.

"Helicopter crews?"

"They've been training at Coronado. They come into Quantico tonight. Pretty standard stuff, really. The tactics are straightforward. What does your man 'Clark' say?"

"He's my man now?" Greer asked. "He tells me he's comfortable with how things are going. Did you enjoy being killed?"

"He told you?" Maxwell chuckled. "James, I knew the boy was good from what he did with Sonny, but it's different when you're there to see it—hell, to *not* see or hear it. He shut Marty Young up, and that's no small feat. Embarrassed a lot of Marines, too."

"Give me a timeline on getting mission approval," Greer said. It was serious now. He'd always thought the operation had merit, and watching it develop had been a lesson in many things that he'd need to know at CIA. Now he believed it possible. BOXWOOD GREEN might well succeed if allowed to go.

"You're sure Mr. Ritter won't waffle on us?"

"I don't think he will. He's one of us, really."

"Not until all the pieces are in place," Podulski said.

"He'll want to see a rehearsal," Greer warned. "Before you ask a guy to stick it on the line, he has to have confidence in the job."

"That's fair. We have a full-up live-fire rehearsal tomorrow night."

"We'll be there, Dutch," Greer promised.

The team was in an old barracks designed for at least sixty men, and there was plenty of room for everyone, enough that no one had a top bunk. Kelly had a private room set aside, one of those designed into the standard barracks for squad sergeants to sleep in. He'd decided not to live on his boat. One could not be part of the team and yet be totally separate from it.

They were enjoying their first night off since arriving at Quantico, and some kind soul had arranged for three cases of beer. That made for exactly three bottles each, since one of their number only drank Dr Pepper, and Master Gunnery Sergeant Irvin made sure that none of their number exceeded the limit.

"Mr. Clark," one of the grenadiers asked, "what's this all about?"

It wasn't fair, Kelly thought, to make them train without letting them know. They prepared for danger without knowing why, without knowing what purpose occasioned the risk of their lives and their future. It wasn't fair at all, but it wasn't unusual either. He looked straight in the man's eyes.

"I can't tell you, Corp. All I can say is, it's something you'll be mighty proud of. You have my word on that, Marine."

The corporal, at twenty-one the youngest and most junior man of the group, hadn't expected an answer, but he'd had to ask. He accepted the reply with a raise-can salute.

"I know that tattoo," a more senior man said.

Kelly smiled, finishing his second. "Oh, I got drunk one night, and I guess I got mistook for somebody else."

"All SEALs are good for is balancing a ball on their nose," a buck sergeant said, following it with a belch.

"Want me to demonstrate with one of yours?" Kelly asked quickly.

"Good one!" The sergeant tossed Kelly another beer.

"Mr. Clark?" Irvin gestured to the door. It was just as sticky-hot out there as inside, with a gentle breeze coming through the long-needled pines and the flapping of bats, invisibly chasing insects.

"What is it?" Kelly asked, taking a long pull.

"That's my question, Mr. Clark, sir," Irvin said lightly. Then his voice changed. "I know you."

"Oh?"

"Third Special Operations Group. My team backed you guys up on ERMINE COAT. You've come far for an E-6," Irvin observed.

"Don't spread it around, but I made chief before I left. Does anybody else know?"

Irvin chuckled. "No, I expect Captain Albie would sure as hell get his nose outa joint if he found out, and General Young might have a conniption. We'll just keep it 'tween us, Mr. Clark," Irvin said, establishing his position in oblique but uncertain terms.

"This wasn't my idea—being here, I mean. Admirals are easy to impress, I suppose."

"I'm not, Mr. Clark. You almost gave me a fucking heart attack with that rubber knife of yours. I don't remember your name, your real one, I mean, but you're the guy they called Snake, aren't you? You're the guy did PLASTIC FLOWER."

"That wasn't the smartest thing I ever did," Kelly pointed out.

"We were your backup on that, too. The goddamned chopper died—engine quit ten feet off the ground—*thump*. That's why we didn't make it. Nearest alternate was from First Cav. That's why it took so long."

Kelly turned. Irvin's face was as black as the night. "I didn't know."

The master gunnery sergeant shrugged in the darkness. "I seen the pictures of what happened. The skipper told us that you were a fool to break the rules like that. But that was our fault. We should have been there twenty minutes after your call. If'n we got there on time, maybe one or two of those little girls might have made it. Anyway, reason we didn't was a bad seal on the engine, just a little goddamn piece of rubber that cracked."

Kelly grunted. On such events the fates of nations turned. "Could have been worse—it could have let go at altitude and you woulda really been in the shitter."

"True. Miserable fuckin' reason for a child to die, isn't it?" Irvin paused, gazing into the darkness of the piney woods as men of his profession did, always looking and listening. "I understand why you did it. I wanted you to know. Probably woulda done the same myself. Maybe not as good as you, but sure as hell, I would have tried, and I wouldn't have let that motherfucker live, orders or no orders."

"Thanks, Guns," Kelly said quietly, dropping back into Navyspeak.

"It's Song Tay, isn't it?" Irvin observed next, knowing that he'd get his answer now.

"Something close to that, yes. They should be telling you soon."

"You have to tell me more, Mr. Clark. I have Marines to worry about."

"The site is set up just right, perfect match. Hey, I'm going in, too, remember?"

"Keep talking," Irvin ordered gently.

"I helped plan the insertion. With the right people, we can do it. Those are good boys you have in there. I won't say it's easy or any dumb shit like that, but it's not all that hard. I've done harder. So have you. The training is going right. It looks pretty good to me, really."

"You sure it's worth it?"

That was a question with meaning so deep that few would have understood it. Irvin had done two combat tours, and though Kelly hadn't seen his official "salad bar" of decorations, he was clearly a man who had circled the block many times. Now Irvin was watching what might well be the destruction of his Marine Corps. Men were dying for hills that were given back as soon as they were taken and the casualties cleared, then to return in six months to repeat the exercise. There was just something in the professional soldier that hated repetition. Although training was just that—they had "assaulted" the site numerous times—the reality of war was supposed to be one battle for one place. In that way a man could tell what progress was. Before looking forward to a new objective, you could look back to see how far you had come and measure your chance for success by what you had learned before. But the third time you watched men die for the same piece of ground, then you knew. You just knew how things were going to end. Their country was still sending men to that place, asking them to risk their lives for dirt already watered in American blood. The truth was that Irvin would not have voluntarily gone back for a third combat tour. It wasn't a question of courage or dedication or love of country. It was that he knew his life was too valuable to be risked for nothing. Sworn to defend his country, he had a right to ask for something in return—a real mission to fight for, not an abstraction, something *real*. And yet Irvin felt guilt, felt that he had broken faith, had betrayed the motto of The Corps, *Semper Fidelis:* Always Faithful. The guilt had compelled him to volunteer for one last mission despite his doubts and questions. Like a man whose beloved wife has slept with another man, Irvin could not stop loving, could not stop caring, and he would accept to himself the guilt unacknowledged by those who had earned it.

"Guns, I can't tell you this, but I will anyway. The place we're hitting, it's a prison camp, like you think, okay?"

Irvin nodded. "More to it. There has to be."

"It's not a regular camp. The men there, they're all dead, Guns." Kelly crushed the beer can. "I've seen the photos. One guy we identified for sure, Air Force colonel, the NVA said he was killed, and so we think these guys, they'll never come home unless we go get 'em. I don't want to go back either, man. I'm scared, okay? Oh, yeah, I'm good, I'm real good at this stuff. Good training, maybe I have a knack for it." Kelly shrugged, not wanting to say the next part.

"Yeah. But you can only do it so long." Irvin handed over another beer.

"I thought three was the limit."

"I'm a Methodist, not supposed to drink at all." Irvin chuckled. "People like us, Mr. Clark."

"Dumb sunzabitches, aren't we? There's Russians in the camp, probably interrogating our people. They're all high-rank, and we think they're all officially dead. They're probably being grilled real hard for what they know, because of who they are. We know they're there, and if we don't do anything . . . what's that make us?" Kelly stopped himself, suddenly needing to go further, to *tell* what else he was doing, because he had found someone who might truly understand, and for all his obsession with avenging Pam his soul was becoming heavy with its burden.

"Thank you, Mr. Clark. That's a fuckin' mission," Master Gunnery Sergeant Paul Irvin told the pine trees and the bats. "So you're first in and last out?"

"I've worked alone before."

23

Altruism

"Where am I?" Doris Brown asked in a barely understandable voice.

"Well, you're in my house," Sandy answered. She sat in the corner of the guest bedroom, switching off the reading light and setting down the paperback she'd been reading for the past few hours.

"How did I get here?"

"A friend brought you here. I'm a nurse. The doctor is downstairs fixing breakfast. How are you feeling?"

"Terrible." Her eyes closed. "My head . . . "

"That's normal, but I know it's bad." Sandy stood and came over, touching the girl's forehead. No fever, which was good news. Next she felt for a pulse. Strong, regular, though still a touch fast. From the way her eyes were screwed shut, Sandy guessed that the extended barbiturate hangover must have been awful, but that too was normal. The girl smelled from sweating and vomiting. They'd tried to keep her clean, but that had been a losing battle, if a not terribly important one compared to the rest. Until now, perhaps. Doris's skin was sallow and slack, as though the person inside had shrunk. She must have lost ten or fifteen

437

pounds since arriving, and while that wasn't an entirely bad thing, she was so weak that she'd not yet noticed the restraints holding her hands, feet, and waist in place.

"How long?"

"Almost a week." Sandy took a sponge and wiped her face. "You gave us quite a scare." Which was an understatement. No less than seven convulsions, the second of which had almost panicked both nurse and physician, but number seven—a mild one—was eighteen hours behind them now, and the patient's vital signs were stabilized. With luck that phase of her recovery was behind them. Sandy let Doris have some water.

"Thank you," Doris said in a very small voice. "Where's Billy and Rick?"

"I don't know who they are," Sandy replied. It was technically correct. She'd read the articles in the local papers, always stopping short of reading any names. Nurse O'Toole was telling herself that she didn't really know anything. It was a useful internal defense against feelings so mixed that even had she taken the time to figure things out, she knew she would have only confused herself all the more. It was not a time for bare facts. Sarah had convinced her of that. It was a time for riding with the shape of events, not the substance. "Are they the ones who hurt you?"

Doris was nude except for the restraints and the oversized diapers used on patients unable to manage their bodily functions. It was easier to treat her that way. The horrid marks on her breasts and torso were fading now. What had been ugly, discrete marks of blue and black and purple and red were fading to poorly defined areas of yellow-brown as her body struggled to heal itself. She was young, Sandy told herself, and while not yet healthy, she could become so. Enough to heal, perhaps, inside and outside. Already her systemic infections were responding to the massive doses of antibiotics. The fever was gone, and her body could now turn to the more mundane repair tasks.

Doris turned her head and opened her eyes. "Why are you doing this for me?"

That answer was an easy one: "I'm a nurse, Miss Brown. It's my job to take care of sick people."

"Billy and Rick," she said next, remembering again. Memory for Doris was a variable and spotty thing, mainly the recollection of pain.

"They're not here," O'Toole assured her. She paused before going on, and to her surprise found satisfaction in the words: "I don't think they'll be bothering you again." There was almost comprehension in the patient's eyes, Sandy thought. Almost. And that was encouraging.

"I have to go. Please—" She started to move and then noticed the restraints.

"Okay, wait a minute." Sandy removed the straps. "You think you can stand today?"

" . . . try," she groaned. Doris rose perhaps thirty degrees before her body betrayed her. Sandy got her sitting up, but the girl couldn't quite make her head sit straight on her neck. Standing her up was even harder, but it wasn't that far to the bathroom, and the dignity of making it there was worth the pain and the effort for her patient. Sandy sat her down there, holding her hand. She took the time to dampen a washcloth and do her face.

"That's a step forward," Sarah Rosen observed from the door. Sandy turned and smiled by way of communicating the patient's condition. They put a robe on her before bringing her back to the bedroom. Sandy changed the linen first, while Sarah got a cup of tea into the patient.

"You're looking much better today, Doris," the physician said, watching her drink.

"I feel awful."

"That's okay, Doris. You have to feel awful before you can start to feel better. Yesterday you weren't feeling much of anything. Think you can try some toast?"

"So hungry."

"Another good sign," Sandy noted. The look in her eyes was so bad that both doctor and nurse could *feel* the skull-rending headache which today would be treated only with an ice pack. They'd spent a week leaching the drugs from her system, and this wasn't the time for adding new ones. "Lean your head back."

Doris did that, resting her head on the back of the overstuffed chair Sandy had once bought at a garage sale.

Her eyes were closed and her limbs so weak that her arms merely rested on the fabric while Sarah handled the individual slices of dry toast. The nurse took a brush and started working on her patient's hair. It was filthy and needed washing, but just getting it straightened out would help, she thought. Medical patients put an amazing amount of stock in their physical appearance, and however odd or illogical it might seem to be, it was real, and therefore something which Sandy recognized as important. She was a little surprised by Doris's shudder a minute or so after she started.

"Am I alive?" The alarm in the question was startling.

"Very much so," Sarah answered, almost smiling at the exaggeration. She checked her blood pressure. "One twenty-two over seventy-eight."

"Excellent!" Sandy noted. It was the best reading all week.

"Pam . . . "

"What's that?" Sarah asked.

It took Doris a moment to go on, still wondering if this were life or death, and if the latter, what part of eternity she had found. "Hair . . . when she was dead . . . brushed her hair."

Dear God, Sarah thought. Sam had related that one part of the postmortem report to her, morosely sipping a highball at their home in Green Spring Valley. He hadn't gone further than that. It hadn't been necessary. The photo on the front page of the paper had been quite sufficient. Dr. Rosen touched her patient's face as gently as she could.

"Doris, who killed Pam?" She thought that she could ask this without increasing the patient's pain. She was wrong.

"Rick and Billy and Burt and Henry . . . killed her . . . watching . . . " The girl started crying, and the racking sobs only magnified the shuddering waves of pain in her head. Sarah held back on the toast. Nausea might soon follow.

"They made you watch?"

"Yes . . . " Doris's voice was like one from the grave.

"Let's not think about that now." Sarah's body shuddered with the kind of chill she associated with death itself as she stroked the girl's cheek.

"There!" Sandy said brightly, hoping to distract her. "That's much better."

"Tired."

"Okay, let's get you back to bed, dear." Both women helped her up. Sandy left the robe on her, setting an ice bag on her forehead. Doris faded off into sleep almost at once.

"Breakfast is on," Sarah told the nurse. "Leave the restraints off for now."

"Brushed her hair? What?" Sandy asked, heading down the stairs.

"I didn't read the report—"

"I saw the photo, Sarah—what they did to her—Pam, her name was, right?" Sandy was almost too tired to remember things herself.

"Yes. She was my patient, too," Dr. Rosen confirmed. "Sam said it was pretty bad. The odd thing, somebody brushed her hair out after she was dead, he told me that. I guess it was Doris who did it."

"Oh." Sandy opened the refrigerator and got milk for the morning coffee. "I see."

"I don't," Dr. Rosen said angrily. "I don't *see* how people can do that. Another few months and Doris would have died. As it was, any closer—"

"I'm surprised you didn't admit her under a Jane Doe," Sandy observed.

"After what happened to Pam, taking a chance like that—and it would have meant—"

O'Toole nodded. "Yes, it would have meant endangering John. That's what I understand."

"Hmph?"

"They killed her friend and made her watch . . . the things they did to her . . . To them *she* was just a *thing!* . . . Billy and Rick," Sandy said aloud, not quite realizing it.

"Burt and Henry," Sarah corrected. "I don't think the other two will be hurting anybody anymore." The two women shared a look, their eyes meeting across the breakfast table, their thoughts identical, though both were distantly shocked at the very idea of holding them, much less understanding them.

"Good."

• • •

"Well, we've shaken down every bum west of Charles Street," Douglas told his lieutenant. "We've had one cop cut—not seriously, but the wino is in for a long drying-out period at Jessup. A bunch have been puked on," he added with a smirk, "but we still don't know crap. He's not out there, Em. Nothing new in a week."

And it was true. The word had gotten out to the street, surprisingly slow but inevitable. Street pushers were being careful to the point of paranoia. That might or might not explain the fact that not a single one had lost his life in over a week.

"He's still out there, Tom."

"Maybe so, but he's not doing anything."

"In which case everything he did was to get Farmer and Grayson," Ryan noted with a look at the sergeant.

"You don't believe that."

"No, I don't, and don't ask me why, because I don't know why."

"Well, it would help if Charon could tell us something. He's been pretty good taking people down. Remember that bust he did with the Coast Guard?"

Ryan nodded. "That was a good one, but he's slowed down lately."

"So have we, Em," Sergeant Douglas pointed out. "The only thing we really know about this guy is that he's strong, he wears new sneaks, and he's white. We don't know age, weight, size, motive, what kind of car he drives."

"Motive. We know he's pissed about something. We know he's very good at killing. We know he's ruthless enough to kill people just to cover his own activities . . . and he's patient." Ryan leaned back. "Patient enough to take time off?"

Tom Douglas had a more troubling idea. "Smart enough to change tactics."

That was a disturbing thought. Ryan considered it. What if he'd seen the shakedowns? What if he'd decided that you could only do one thing so long, and then you had to do something else? What if he'd developed information from William Grayson, and that information was now taking him in other directions—out of town, even? What if they'd never know, never close these cases? That would be a professional insult to Ryan, who hated leaving cases open, but he had to consider it. Despite dozens of field interviews, they had not turned up so much as a single witness except for Virginia Charles, and she'd been sufficiently traumatized that her information was scarcely believable—and contradicted the one really useful piece of forensic evidence they had. The suspect had to be taller than she had said, had to be younger, and sure as hell was as strong as an NFL linebacker. He wasn't a wino, but had chosen to camouflage himself as one. You just didn't *see* people like that. How did you describe a stray dog?

"The Invisible Man," Ryan said quietly, finally giving the case a name. "He should have killed Mrs. Charles. You know what we've got here?"

Douglas snorted. "Somebody I don't want to meet alone."

"Three groups to take Moscow out?"

"Sure, why not?" Zacharias replied. "It's your political leadership, isn't it? It's a huge communications center, and even if you get the Politburo out, they'll still get most of your military and political command and control—"

"We have ways to get our important people out," Grishanov objected out of professional and national pride.

"Sure." Robin almost laughed, Grishanov saw. Part of him was insulted, but on reflection he was pleased with himself that the American colonel felt that much at ease now. "Kolya, we have things like that, too. We have a real ritzy shelter set up in West Virginia for Congress and all that. The 1st Helicopter Squadron is at Andrews, and their mission is to get VIPs the heck out of Dodge—but guess what? The durned helicopters can't hop all the way to the shelter and back without refueling on the return leg. Nobody thought about that when they selected the shelter, because *that* was a political decision. Guess what else? We've never tested the evacuation system. Have you tested yours?"

Grishanov sat down next to Zacharias, on the floor, his back against the dirty concrete wall. Nikolay Yevgeniyevich just looked down and shook his head, having learned yet more from the American. "You see? You see why I say we'll never fight a war? We're *alike!* No, Robin, we've never tested it, we've never tried to evacuate Moscow since I was a child in the snow. Our big shelter is at Zhiguli. It's a big stone—not a mountain, like a big—bubble? I don't know the word, a huge circle of stone from the center of the earth."

"Monolith? Like Stone Mountain in Georgia?"

Grishanov nodded. There was no harm in giving secrets to this man, was there? "The geologists say it is immensely strong, and we tunneled into it back in the late 1950s. I've been there twice. I helped supervise the air-defense office when they were building it. We expect—this is the truth, Robin—we expect to get our people there by *train.*"

"It won't matter. We know about it. If you know where it is, you can take it out, just a matter of how many bombs you put there." The American had a hundred grams of vodka in him. "Probably the Chinese do, too. But they'll go for Moscow anyway, especially if it's a surprise attack."

"Three groups?"

"That's how I'd do it." Robin's feet straddled an air-navigation chart of the southeastern Soviet Union. "Three vectors, from these three bases, three aircraft each, two to carry the bombs, one a protective jammer. Jammer takes the lead. Bring in all three groups on line, like, spaced wide like this." He traced likely courses on the map. "Start your penetration descent here, take 'em right into these valleys, and by the time they hit the plains—"

"Steppes," Kolya corrected.

"They're through your first line of defense, okay? They're smoking in low, like three hundred feet. Maybe they don't even jam at first. Maybe you have one special group, even. The guys you really train."

"What do you mean, Robin?"

"You have night flights into Moscow, airliners, I mean?"

"Of course."

"Well, what say you take a Badger, and you leave the strobes on, okay, and maybe you have little glow lights down the fuselage that you can turn on and off—you know, like windows? Hey, I'm an airliner."

"You mean?"

"It's something we looked at once. There's a squadron with the light kits still at . . . Pease, I think. That used to be the job—the B-47s based in England. If we ever decided like you guys were going to go after us, from intelligence or something, okay? You gotta have a plan for everything. That was one of ours. We called it JUMPSHOT. Probably in the dead files now, that was one of LeMay's specials. Moscow, Leningrad, Kiev—and Zhiguli. Three birds targeted there, two weapons each. Decap your whole political and military command structure. Hey look, I'm an airliner!"

It would work, Grishanov thought with an eerie chill. The right time of year, the right time of day . . . the bomber comes in on a regularly scheduled airliner route. Even in a crisis, the very illusion of something normal would be like a touchstone while people looked for the unusual. Maybe an air-defense squadron would put an aircraft up, a young pilot standing night alert while the senior men slept. He'd close to a thousand meters or so, but at night . . . at night your mind saw what the brain told it to see. Lights on the fuselage, well, of course it's an airliner. What bomber would be lit up? That was one op-plan the KGB had never tumbled to. How many more gifts would Zacharias give him?

"Anyway, if I was John Chinaman, that's one option. If they don't have much imagination, and go with a straight attack, over this terrain, yeah, they can do that. Probably one group is diversionary. They have a real target, too, but short of Moscow. They fly in high, off vector. About this far out"—he swept a hand across the map—"they make a radical turn and hit something, you can decide what's important, lots of good targets there. Chances are your fighters keep after them, right?"

"Da." They'd think the inbound bombers were turning away for a secondary target.

"The other two groups loop around from another direction, and they smoke in low. One of 'em's gonna make it, too. We've played it out a million times, Kolya. We know your radars, we know your bases, we know your airplanes, we know how you train. You're not that hard to beat. And the Chinese, they studied with you, right? You taught them. They know your doctrine and everything."

It was how he said it. No guile at all. And this was a man who had penetrated the North Vietnamese air defenses over eighty times. Eighty times.

"So how do I—"

"Defend against it?" Robin shrugged, bending down to examine the chart again. "I need better maps, but first thing, you examine the passes one at a time. You remember that a bomber isn't a fighter. He can't maneuver all that great, especially low. Most of what he's doing is keeping the airplane from crunching into the ground, right? I don't know about you, but that makes me nervous. He's going to pick a valley he can maneuver in. Especially at night. You put your fighters there. You put ground radars there. You don't need big sexy ones. That's just a bell-ringer. Then you plan to catch him when he comes out."

"Move the defenses back? I can't do that!"

"You put your defenses where they can work, Kolya, not to follow a dotted line on a piece of paper. Or do you like eating Chinese all that much? That's always been a weakness with you people. By the way, it also shortens your lines, right? You save money and assets. Next thing, you remember that the other guy, he knows how pilots think, too—a kill is a kill, right? Maybe there's decoy groups designed to draw your people out, okay? We have scads of radar lures we plan to use. You have to allow for that. You *control* your people. They stay in their sectors unless you have a really good reason to move them. . . ."

Colonel Grishanov had studied his profession for more than twenty years, had studied Luftwaffe documents not merely related to prisoner interrogation, but also classified studies of how the Kammhuber Line had been set up. This was incredible, almost enough to make him take a drink himself. But not quite, he told himself. This wasn't a briefing document in the making, wasn't a learned White Paper for delivery at the Voroshilov Academy. This was a learned book, highly classified, but a *book*: *Origin and Evolution of American Bomber Doctrine*. From such a book he could go on to marshal's stars, all because of his American friend.

"Let's all stay back here," Marty Young said. "They're shooting all live stuff."

"Makes sense to me," Dutch said. "I'm used to having things go off a couple hundred yards behind me."

"And four hundred knots of delta-V," Greer added for him.

"A lot safer that way, James," Maxwell pointed out.

They stood behind an earthen berm, the official military term for a pile of dirt, two hundred yards from the camp. It made watching difficult, but two of the five had aviator's eyes, and they knew where to look.

"How long have they been moving in?"

"About an hour. Any time now," Young breathed.

"I can't hear a thing," Admiral Maxwell whispered.

It was hard enough to see the site. The buildings were visible only because of their straight lines, something which nature abhors for one reason or another. Further concentration revealed the dark rectangles of windows. The guard towers, erected only that day, were hard to spot as well.

"There's a few tricks we play," Marty Young noted. "Everybody gets vitamin-A supplements for night vision. Maybe a few percentage points of improvement in night vision. You play every card in the deck, right?"

All they heard was the wind whispering through the treetops. There was a surreal element to being in the woods like this. Maxwell and Young were accustomed to the hum of an aircraft engine and the faint glow of instrument lights that their eyes scanned automatically between outward sweeps for hostile aircraft, and the gentle floating sensation of an aircraft moving through the night sky. Being rooted to the land gave the feeling of motion that didn't exist as they waited to see something they had never experienced.

"There!"

"Bad news if you saw him move," Maxwell observed.

"Sir, SENDER GREEN doesn't have a parking lot with white cars on it," the voice pointed out. The fleeting shadow had been silhouetted against it, and only Kelly had seen it in any case.

"I guess that's right, Mr. Clark."

The radio sitting on the berm had been transmitting only the noise of static. That changed now, with four long dashes. They were answered at intervals by one, then two, then three, then four dots.

"Teams in place," Kelly whispered. "Hold your ears. The senior grenadier takes the first shot when he's ready, and that's the kickoff."

"Shit," Greer sneered. He soon regretted it.

The first thing they heard was a distant mutter of twin-bladed helicopter rotors. Designed to make heads turn, and even though every man at the berm knew the plan in intimate detail, it still worked, which pleased Kelly no end. He'd drawn up much of the plan, after all. All heads turned but his.

Kelly thought he might have caught a glimpse of the tritium-painted M-79 sights of one grenadier, but it might as easily have been the blink of a lonely lightning bug. He saw the muted flash of a single launch, and not a second later the blinding white-red-black flash of a fragmentation grenade against the floor of one of the towers. The sudden, sharp bark made the men at his side jump, but Kelly wasn't paying attention to that. The tower where men and guns would have been disintegrated. The echo had not yet dispersed through the theater of pines when the other three were similarly destroyed. Five seconds later the gunships came skimming in over the treetops, not fifty feet separating their rotors as miniguns ripped into the barracks building, two long neon fingers reaching in. The grenadiers were already pumping white-phosphorus rounds into the windows, and any semblance of night vision was lost in an instant.

"Jesus!" The way that the spreading fountains of burning phosphorus were concealed inside the building made the spectacle only more horrid, while the miniguns concentrated on the exits.

"Yeah," Kelly said, loudly to make himself heard. "Anybody inside is a crispy critter. The smart ones who try to run come right into the mini fire. Slick."

The fire element of the Marine assault force continued to pour fire into the barracks and admin buildings while the snatch team raced to the prison block. Now the rescue choppers came in, behind the AH-1 Huey Cobras, landing noisily close to the main gate. The fire element split, with half deploying around the choppers while the other half continued to hose the barracks. One of the gunships began circling the area now, like an anxious sheepdog on the prowl for wolves.

The first Marines appeared, dragging the simulated prisoners in relays. Kelly could see Irvin checking and doing a count at the gate. There were shouts now, men calling off numbers and names, and the roar of the big Sikorsky choppers almost covered it all. The last Marines in were the fire-support teams, and then the rescue choppers increased power and lifted off into the darkness.

"That was fast," Ritter breathed as the sound faded. A moment later two fire engines appeared to extinguish the blazes left behind by the various explosive devices.

"That was fifteen seconds under nominal," Kelly said, holding up his watch.

"What if something goes wrong, Mr. Clark?" Ritter asked.

Kelly's face lit up in a wicked grin. "Some things did, sir. Four of the team were 'killed' coming in. I assume maybe a broke leg or two—"

"Wait a minute, you mean there's a chance—"

"Let me explain, sir?" Kelly said. "From the photos there is no reason to believe there are any people between the LZ and the objective. No farming on those hills, okay? For tonight's exercise, I eliminated four people at random. Call all of them broken legs. The people had to be carried into the objective and carried out, in case you didn't notice. Backups on everything. Sir, I *expect* a clean mission, but I messed it up some tonight just to check."

Ritter nodded, impressed. "I expected everything to be run by the book for this rehearsal."

"In combat things go wrong, sir. I allowed for that. Every man is cross-trained for at least one alternate job." Kelly rubbed his nose. He'd been nervous, too. "What you just saw was a successful simulated mission despite greater-than-expected complications. This one's going to work, sir."

"Mr. Clark, you sold me." The CIA field officer turned to the others. "What about medical support, that sort of thing?"

"When *Ogden* forms up with Task Force 77, we cross-deck medical personnel over to her," Maxwell said. "Cas is on his way there now to brief the people in. CTF-77 is one of my people, and he'll play ball. *Ogden*'s a pretty large boat. We'll have everything we need to care for them, medics, intel guys to debrief, the works. She sails them right to Subic Bay. We hop them out of Clark ASAP. From the time the rescue choppers get off, we'll have them in California in . . . four and a half days."

"Okay, this part of the mission looks fine. What about the rest?"

Maxwell handled the answer: "*Constellation*'s whole air group will be in support. *Enterprise* will be farther up north working the Haiphong area. That should get the attention of their air-defense net and their high command. *Newport News* will be trolling the coast shooting up triple-A sites for the next few weeks. It's to be done randomly, and this area will be the fifth. She lays ten miles out and lobs in heavy fire. The big antiaircraft belt is within the range of her guns. Between the cruiser and the air group, we can blast a corridor for the helos to get in and out. Essentially we'll be doing so much that they oughtn't to notice this mission until it's already over."

Ritter nodded. He'd read through the plan, and had only wished to hear it from Maxwell—more to the point, to hear how he expressed himself. The Admiral was calm and confident, more so than Ritter had expected.

"It's still very risky," he said after a moment.

"It is that," Marty Young agreed.

"What's the risk to our country if the people in that camp tell everything they know?" Maxwell asked.

Kelly wanted to step back from this part of the discussion. Danger to country was something beyond his purview. His reality was at the small-unit level—or, more recently, even lower than that—and though his country's health and welfare started at that lowest common denominator, the big stuff required a perspective he didn't have. But there was no gracious way for him to withdraw, and so he stayed and listened and learned.

"You want an honest answer?" Ritter asked. "I'll give you one—none."

Maxwell took it with surprising calm that concealed outrage. "Son, you want to explain that?"

"Admiral, it's a matter of perspective. The Russians want to know a lot about us, and we want to know a lot about them. Okay, so this Zachary guy can tell them about SAC War Plans, and the other notional people there can tell them other things. So—we change our plans. It's the strategic stuff you're worried about, right? First, those plans change on a monthly basis. Second, do you ever think we'll implement them?"

"We might have to someday."

Ritter fished out a cigarette. "Admiral, do you *want* us to implement those plans?"

Maxwell stood a little straighter. "Mr. Ritter, I flew my F6F over Nagasaki just after the war ended. I've seen what those things do, and that was just a little one." Which was all the answer anyone needed.

"And they feel the same way. How does that grab you, Admiral?" Ritter just shook his head. "They're not crazy either. They're even more afraid of us than we are of them. What they learn from those prisoners might scare them enough to sober them up, even. It works that way, believe it or not."

"Then why are you supporting—*are* you supporting us?"

"Of course I am." *What a stupid question,* his tone said, enraging Marty Young.

"But why then?" Maxwell asked.

"Those are our people. We sent them. We have to get them back. Isn't that reason enough? But don't tell me about vital national-security interests. You can sell that to the White House staff, even on The Hill, but not to me. Either you keep faith with your people or you don't," said the field spook who had risked his career to rescue a foreigner whom he hadn't even liked very much. "If you don't, if you fall into that habit, then you're not worth saving or protecting, and then people stop helping you, and *then* you're in real trouble."

"I'm not sure I approve of you, Mr. Ritter," General Young said.

"An operation like this one will have the effect of saving our people. The Russians will respect that. It shows them we're serious about things. That will make my job easier, running agents behind the curtain. That means we'll be able to recruit more agents and get more information. That way I gather information that you want, okay? The game goes on until someday we find a new game." That was all the agenda he needed. Ritter turned to Greer. "When do you want me to brief the White House?"

"I'll let you know. Bob, this is important—you are backing us?"

"Yes, sir," replied the Texan. For reasons that the others didn't understand, didn't trust, but had to accept.

"So? What's the beef?"

"Look, Eddie," Tony said patiently. "Our friend's got a problem. Somebody took down two of his people."

"Who?" Morello asked. He was not in a particularly good mood. He'd just learned, again, that he was not a candidate to be accepted as a full member of the outfit. After all he'd done. Morello felt betrayed. Incredibly, Tony was siding with a black man instead of blood—they were distant cousins after all—and now the bastard was coming to him for help, of course.

"We don't know. His contacts, my contacts, we got nothin'."

"Well, ain't that just too fuckin' bad?" Eddie segued into his own agenda. "Tony, he came to *me,* remember?

Through Angelo, and maybe Angelo tried to set us up, and we took care of that, remember? You wouldn't have this setup except for me, so now what's happening? I get shut out and he gets closer in—so what gives, Tony, you gonna get *him* made?"

"Back off, Eddie."

"How come you didn't stand up for me?" Morello demanded.

"I can't make it happen, Eddie. I'm sorry, but I can't." Piaggi hadn't expected this conversation to go well, but neither had he expected it to go this badly, this quickly. Sure, Eddie was disappointed. Sure, he had expected to be taken in. But the dumb fuck was getting a good living out of it, and what was it about? Being inside or making a living? Henry could see that. Why couldn't Eddie? Then Eddie took it one step further.

"I set this deal up for you. Now, you got a little-bitty problem, and who you come to—me! You *owe* me, Tony." The implications of the words were clear for Piaggi. It was quite simple from Eddie's point of view. Tony's position in the outfit was growing in importance. With Henry as a potential—a very real—major supplier, Tony would have more than a position. He would have influence. He'd still have to show respect and obeisance to those over him, but the command structure of the outfit was admirably flexible, and Henry's double-blind methods meant that whoever was his pipeline into the outfit had real security. Security of place in his organization was a rare and treasured thing. Piaggi's mistake was in not taking the thought one step further. He looked inward instead of outward. All he saw was that Eddie could replace him, become the intermediary, and then become a made man, adding status to his comfortable living. All Piaggi had to do was die, obligingly, at the right time. Henry was a businessman. He'd make the accommodation. Piaggi knew that. So did Eddie.

"Don't you see what he's doing? He's using you, man." The odd part was that while Morello was beginning to understand that Tucker was manipulating both of them, Piaggi, the target of that manipulation, did not. As a result,

Eddie's correct observation was singularly ill-timed.

"I've thought about that," Piaggi lied. "What's in it for him? A linkup with Philadelphia, New York?"

"Maybe. Maybe he thinks he can do it. Those people are getting awful big for their pants, man."

"We'll sweat that one out later, and I don't see him doing that. What we want to know is, who's taking his people down? You catch anything about somebody from out of town?" *Put him on the spot,* Piaggi thought. *Make him commit.* Tony's eyes bored in across the table at a man too angry to notice or care what the other man was thinking.

"I haven't heard shit about that."

"Put feelers out," Tony ordered, and it was an order. Morello had to follow it, had to check around.

"What if he was taking out some people from inside, reliability problems, like? You think he's loyal to anybody?"

"No. But I don't think he's offing his own people, either." Tony rose with a final order. "Check around."

"Sure," Eddie snorted, left alone at his table.

24
Hellos

"People, that went very well," Captain Albie announced, finishing his critique of the exercise. There had been various minor deficiencies on the approach march, but nothing serious, and even his sharp eye had failed to notice anything of consequence on the simulated assault phase. Marksmanship especially had been almost inhumanly accurate, and his men had sufficient confidence in one another that they were now running within mere feet of fire streams in order to get to their assigned places. The Cobra crews were in the back of the room, going over their own performance. The pilots and gunners were treated with great respect by the men they supported, as were the Navy flight crews of the rescue birds. The normal us-them antipathy found among disparate units was down to the level of friendly joshing, so closely had the men trained and dedicated themselves. That antipathy was about to disappear entirely.

"Gentlemen," Albie concluded, "you're about to learn what this little picnic outing is all about."

"Ten-*hut!*" Irvin called.

Vice Admiral Winslow Holland Maxwell walked up the center of the room, accompanied by Major General Martin

Young. Both flag officers were in their best undress uniforms. Maxwell's whites positively glistened in the incandescent lights of the building, and Young's Marine khakis were starched so stiff that they might well have been made of plywood. A Marine lieutenant carried a briefing board that nearly dragged on the floor. This he set on an easel as Maxwell took his place behind the lectern. From his place on the corner of the stage, Master Gunnery Sergeant Irvin watched the young faces in the audience, reminding himself that he had to pretend surprise at the announcement.

"Take your seats, Marines," Maxwell began pleasantly, waiting for them to do so. "First of all, I want to tell you for myself how proud I am to be associated with you. We've watched your training closely. You came here without knowing why, and you've worked as hard as any people I have ever seen. Here's what it's all about." The Lieutenant flipped the cover off the briefing board, exposing an aerial photograph.

"Gentlemen, this mission is called BOXWOOD GREEN. Your objective is to rescue twenty men, fellow Americans who are now in the hands of the enemy."

John Kelly was standing next to Irvin, and he, too, was watching faces instead of the Admiral. Most were younger than his, but not by much. Their eyes were locked on the reconnaissance photographs—an exotic dancer would not have drawn the sort of focus that was aimed at the blowups from the Buffalo Hunter drone. The faces were initially devoid of emotion. They were like young, fit, handsome statues, scarcely breathing, sitting at attention while the Admiral spoke to them.

"This man here is Colonel Robin Zacharias, U.S. Air Force," Maxwell went on, using a yard-long wooden pointer. "You can see what the Vietnamese did to him just for looking at the asset that snapped the picture." The pointer traced over to the camp guard about to strike the American from behind. "Just for looking up."

Eyes narrowed at that, all of them, Kelly saw. It was a quiet, determined kind of anger, highly disciplined, but that was the deadliest kind of all, Kelly thought, suppressing a smile that only he would have understood. And so it was

for the young Marines in the audience. It wasn't a time
for smiles. Each of the people in the room knew about
the dangers. Each had survived a minimum of thirteen
months of combat operations. Each had seen friends die
in the most terrible and noisy way that the blackest of
nightmares could create. But there was more to life than
fear. Perhaps it was a quest. A sense of duty that few
could articulate but which all of them felt. A vision of
the world that men shared without actually seeing. Every
man in the room had seen death in all its dreadful majesty,
knowing that all life came to an end. But all knew there
was more to life than the avoidance of death. Life had to
have a purpose, and one such purpose was the service of
others. While no man in the room would willingly give his
life away, every one of them would run the risk, trusting
to God or luck or fate in the knowledge that each of the
others would do the same. The men in these pictures were
unknown to the Marines, but they were comrades—more
than friends—to whom loyalty was owed. And so they
would risk their lives for them.

"I don't have to tell you how dangerous the mission is,"
the Admiral concluded. "The fact of the matter is, you
know those dangers better than I do, but these people are
Americans, and they have the right to expect us to come
for them."

"Fuckin' A, *sir!*" a voice called from the floor, surprising the rest of the Marines.

Maxwell almost lost it then. *It's all true,* he told himself.
*It really does matter. Mistakes and all, we're still what
we are.*

"Thank you, Dutch," Marty Young said, walking to center stage. "Okay, Marines, now you know. You volunteered
to be here. You have to volunteer again to deploy. Some
of you have families, sweethearts. We won't make you go.
Some of you might have second thoughts," he went on,
examining the faces, and seeing the insult he had caused
them, not by accident. "You have today to think it over.
Dismissed."

The Marines got to their feet, to the accompaniment
of the grating sound of chairs scraping on the tile floor,

and when all were at attention, their voices boomed as one:

"RECON!"

It was clear to those who saw the faces. They could no more shrink from this mission than they could deny their manhood. There were smiles now. Most of the Marines traded remarks with their friends, and it wasn't glory they saw before their eyes. It was purpose, and perhaps the look to be seen in the eyes of the men whose lives they would redeem. *We're Americans and we're here to take you home.*

"Well, Mr. Clark, your admiral makes a pretty good speech. I wish we recorded it."

"You're old enough to know better, Guns. It's going to be a dicey one."

Irvin smiled in a surprisingly playful way. "Yeah, I know. But if you think it's a crock, why the hell are you going in alone?"

"Somebody asked me to." Kelly shook his head and went off to join the Admiral with a request of his own.

She made it all the way down the steps, holding on to the banister, her head still hurting, but not so badly this morning, following the smell of the coffee to the sound of conversation.

Sandy's face broke into a smile. "Well, good morning!"

"Hi," Doris said, still pale and weak, but she smiled back as she walked through the doorway, still holding on. "I'm real hungry."

"I hope you like eggs." Sandy helped her to a chair and got her a glass of orange juice.

"I'll eat the shells," Doris replied, showing her first sign of humor.

"You can start with these, and don't worry about the shells," Sarah Rosen told her, shoveling the beginnings of a normal breakfast from the frying pan onto a plate.

She had turned the corner. Doris's movements were painfully slow, and her coordination was that of a small child, but the improvement from only twenty-four hours before was miraculous. Blood drawn the day before showed still more favorable signs. The massive doses of antibiotics had obliterated her infections, and the lingering signs of barbiturates were almost completely gone—the remnants were from the palliative doses Sarah had prescribed and injected, which would not be repeated. But the most encouraging sign of all was how she ate. Awkwardness and all, she unfolded her napkin and sat it in the lap of the terrycloth robe. She didn't shovel the food in. Instead she consumed her first real breakfast in months in as dignified a manner as her condition and hunger allowed. Doris was turning back into a person.

But they still didn't know anything about her except her name—Doris Brown. Sandy got a cup of coffee for herself and sat down at the table.

"Where are you from?" she asked in as innocent a voice as she could manage.

"Pittsburgh." A place as distant to her house guest as the back end of the moon.

"Family?"

"Just my father. Mom died in '65, breast cancer," Doris said slowly, then unconsciously felt inside her robe. For the first time she could remember, her breasts didn't hurt from Billy's attention. Sandy saw the movement and guessed what it meant.

"Nobody else?" the nurse asked evenly.

"My brother . . . Vietnam."

"I'm sorry, Doris."

"It's okay—"

"Sandy's my name, remember?"

"I'm Sarah," Dr. Rosen added, replacing the empty plate with a full one.

"Thank you, Sarah." This smile was somewhat wan, but Doris Brown was reacting to the world around her now, an event far more important than the casual observer might have guessed. *Small steps,* Sarah told herself. *They don't have to be big steps. They just have to head in the right direction.* Doctor and nurse shared a look.

There was nothing like it. It was too hard to explain to someone who hadn't been there and done it. She and

Sandy had reached into the grave and pulled this girl back from grasping earth. Three more months, Sarah had estimated, maybe not that long, and her body would have been so weakened that the most trivial outside influence would have ended her life in a matter of hours. But not now. Now this girl would live, and the two medics shared without words the feeling that God must have known when He had breathed life into Adam. They had defeated Death, redeeming the gift that only God could give. For this reason both had entered their shared profession, and moments like this one pushed back the rage and sorrow and grief for those patients whom they couldn't save.

"Don't eat too fast, Doris. When you don't eat for a while, your stomach actually shrinks down some," Sarah told her, returning to form as a medical doctor. There was no sense in warning her about problems and pain sure to develop in her gastrointestinal tract. Nothing would stop it, and getting nourishment into her superseded other considerations at the moment.

"Okay. I'm getting a little full."

"Then relax a little. Tell us about your father."

"I ran away," Doris replied at once. "Right after David . . . after the telegram, and Daddy . . . he had some trouble, and he blamed me."

Raymond Brown was a foreman in the Number Three Basic Oxygen Furnace Shed of the Jones and Laughlin Steel Company, and that was all he was, now. His house was on Dunleavy Street, halfway up one of the steep hills of his city, one of many detached frame dwellings built around the turn of the century, with wood clapboard siding that he had to paint every two or three years, depending on the severity of the winter winds that swept down the Monongahela Valley. He worked the night shift because his house was especially empty at night. Nevermore to hear the sounds of his wife, nevermore to take his son to Little League or play catch in the sloped sanctity of his tiny backyard, nevermore to worry about his daughter's dates on weekends.

He'd tried, done everything a man could do, after it was

too late, which was so often the way of things. It had just been too much. His wife, discovering a lump, still a pretty young woman in her thirty-seventh year, his best and closest friend. He'd supported her as best he could after the surgery, but then came another lump, another surgery, medical treatment, and the downhill slide, always having to be strong for her until the end. It would have been a crushing burden for any man, and then followed by another. His only son, David, drafted, sent to Vietnam, and killed two weeks later in some nameless valley. The support of his fellow workers, the way they had come to Davey's funeral, hadn't stopped him from crawling inside a bottle, desperately trying to cling to what he had left, but too tightly. Doris had borne her own grief, something Raymond hadn't fully understood or appreciated, and when she'd come home late, her clothing not quite right, the cruel and hateful things he'd said. He could remember every word, the hollow sound as the front door had slammed.

Only a day later he'd come to his senses, driving with tears in his eyes to the police station, abasing himself before men whose understanding and sympathy he never quite recognized, desperate again to get his little girl back, to beg from her the forgiveness that he could never give himself. But Doris had vanished. The police had done what they could, and that wasn't much. And so for two years he'd lived inside a bottle, until two fellow workers had taken him aside and talked as friends do once they have gathered the courage to invade the privacy of another man's life. His minister was a regular guest in the lonely house now. He was drying out—Raymond Brown still drank, but no longer to excess, and he was working to cut it down to zero. Man that he was, he had to face his loneliness that way, had to deal with it as best he could. He knew that solitary dignity was of little value. It was an empty thing to cling to, but it was all he had. Prayer also helped, some, and in the repeated words he often found sleep, though not the dreams of the family which had once shared the house with him. He was tossing and turning in his bed, sweating from the heat, when the phone rang.

"Hello?"

"Hello, is this Raymond Brown?"

"Yeah, who's this?" he asked with closed eyes.

"My name is Sarah Rosen. I'm a doctor in Baltimore, I work at Johns Hopkins Hospital."

"Yes?" The tone of her voice opened his eyes. He stared at the ceiling, the blank white place that so closely matched the emptiness of his life. And there was sudden fear. Why would a doctor from Baltimore call him? His mind was spinning off towards a named dread when the voice went on quickly.

"I have somebody here who wants to talk to you, Mr. Brown."

"Huh?" He next heard muffled noises that might have been static from a bad line, but was not.

"I can't."

"You have nothing to lose, dear," Sarah said, handing over the phone. "He's your father. Trust him."

Doris took it, holding it in both hands close to her face, and her voice was a whisper.

"Daddy?"

From hundreds of miles away, the whispered word came through as clearly as a church bell. He had to breathe three times before answering, and that came out as a sob.

"Dor?"

"Yes—Daddy, I'm sorry."

"Are you okay, baby?"

"Yes, Daddy, I'm fine." And incongruous as the statement was, it was not a lie.

"Where are you?"

"Wait a minute." Then the voice changed. "Mr. Brown, this is Doctor Rosen again."

"She's there?"

"Yes, Mr. Brown, she is. We've been treating her for a week. She's a sick girl, but she's going to be okay. Do you understand? She's going to be okay."

He was grasping his chest. Brown's heart was a steel fist, and his breathing came in painful gasps that a doctor might have taken for something they were not.

"She's okay?" he asked anxiously.

"She's going to be fine," Sarah assured him. "There's no doubt of that, Mr. Brown. Please believe me, okay?"

"Oh, sweet Jesus! Where, where are you?"

"Mr. Brown, you can't see her just yet. We will bring her to you just as soon as she's fully recovered. I worried about calling you before we could get you together, but—but we just couldn't *not* call you. I hope you understand."

Sarah had to wait two minutes before she heard anything she could understand, but the sounds that came over the line touched her heart. In reaching into one grave, she had extracted two lives.

"She's really okay?"

"She's had a bad time, Mr. Brown, but I promise you she will recover fully. I'm a good doc, okay? I wouldn't say that unless it were true."

"Please, please let me talk to her again. Please!"

Sarah handed the phone over, and soon four people were weeping. Nurse and physician were the luckiest, sharing a hug and savoring their victory over the cruelties of the world.

Bob Ritter pulled his car into a slot in West Executive Drive, the closed-off former street that lay between the White House and the Executive Office Building. He walked towards the latter, perhaps the ugliest building in Washington—no mean accomplishment—which had once held much of the executive branch of government, the State, War, and Navy departments. It also held the Indian Treaty Room, designed for the purpose of overawing primitive visitors with the splendor of Victorian gingerbread architecture and the majesty of the government which had constructed this giant tipi. The wide corridors rang with the sound of his footsteps on marble as he searched for the right room. He found it on the second floor, the room of Roger MacKenzie, Special Assistant to the President for National Security Affairs. "Special," perversely, made him a second-line official. The National Security *Advisor* had a corner office in the West Wing of the White House. Those who reported to him had offices elsewhere, and though distance from the Seat of Power defined influence, it didn't define arrogance of position. MacKenzie had to have a staff of his own in order to remind himself of his importance, real or illusory. Not really a bad man, and actually a fairly bright one, Ritter thought, MacKenzie was nonetheless jealous of his position, and in another age he would have been the clerk who advised the chancellor who advised the King. Except today the clerk had to have an executive secretary.

"Hi, Bob. How are things at Langley?" MacKenzie asked in front of his secretarial staff, just to be sure they would know that he was meeting with an up-and-coming CIA official, and was therefore still very important indeed to have such guests calling on him.

"The usual." Ritter smiled back. *Let's get on with it.*

"Trouble with traffic?" he asked, letting Ritter know that he was almost, if not quite, late for the appointment.

"There's a little problem on the GW." Ritter gestured with his head towards MacKenzie's private office. His host nodded.

"Wally, we need someone to take notes."

"Coming, sir." His executive assistant rose from his desk in the secretarial area and brought a pad.

"Bob Ritter, this is Wally Hicks. I don't think you've met."

"How do you do, sir?" Hicks extended his hand. Ritter took it, seeing yet one more eager White House aide. New England accent, bright-looking, polite, which was about all he was entitled to expect of such people. A minute later they were sitting in MacKenzie's office, the inner and outer doors closed in the cast-iron frames that gave the Executive Office Building the structural integrity of a warship. Hicks hurried himself about to get coffee for everyone, like a page at some medieval court, which was the way of things in the world's most powerful democracy.

"So what brings you in, Bob?" MacKenzie asked from behind his desk. Hicks flipped open his note pad and began his struggle to take down every word.

"Roger, a rather unique opportunity has presented itself over in Vietnam." Eyes opened wider and ears perked up.

"What might that be?"

"We've identified a special prison camp southwest of Haiphong," Ritter began, quickly outlining what they knew and what they suspected.

MacKenzie listened intently. Pompous though he might have been, the recently arrived investment banker was also a former aviator himself. He'd flown B-24s in the Second World War, including the dramatic but failed mission to Ploesti. A patriot with flaws, Ritter told himself. He would try to make use of the former while ignoring the latter.

"Let me see your imagery," he said after a few minutes, using the proper buzzword instead of the more pedestrian "pictures."

Ritter took the photo folder from his briefcase and set it on the desk. MacKenzie opened it and took a magnifying glass from a drawer. "We know who this guy is?"

"There's a better photo in the back," Ritter answered helpfully.

MacKenzie compared the official family photo with the one from the camp, then with the enhanced blowup.

"Very close. Not definitive but close. Who is he?"

"Colonel Robin Zacharias. Air Force. He spent quite some time at Offutt Air Force Base, SAC War Plans. He knows everything, Roger."

MacKenzie looked up and whistled, which, he thought, was what he was supposed to do in such circumstances. "And this guy's no Vietnamese . . . "

"He's a colonel in the Soviet Air Force, name unknown, but it isn't hard to figure what he's there for. Here's the real punchline." Ritter handed over a copy of the wire-service report on Zacharias's death.

"Damn."

"Yeah, all of a sudden it gets real clear, doesn't it?"

"This sort of thing could wreck the peace talks," MacKenzie thought aloud.

Walter Hicks couldn't say anything. It wasn't his place to speak in such circumstances. He was like a necessary appliance—an animated tape machine—and the only real reason he was in the room at all was so his boss would have a record of the conversation. <u>Wreck the peace talks</u> he scribbled down, taking the time to underline it, and though nobody else noticed, his fingers went white around the pencil.

"Roger, the men we believe to be in this camp know an awful lot, enough to seriously compromise our national security. I mean *seriously,*" Ritter said calmly. "Zacharias knows our nuclear war plans, he helped write SIOP. This is very serious business." Merely in speaking *sy-op,* merely by invoking the unholy name of the "Single Integrated Operations Plan," Ritter had knowingly raised the stakes of the conversation. The CIA field officer amazed himself at the skillful delivery of the lie. The White House pukes might not grasp the idea of getting people out because they were *people.* But they had their hot issues, and nuclear war-plans were the unholy of unholies in this and many other temples of government power.

"You have my attention, Bob."

"Mr. Hicks, right?" Ritter asked, turning his head.

"Yes, sir."

"Could you please excuse us?"

The junior assistant looked to his boss, his neutral face imploring MacKenzie to let him stay in the room, but that was not to be.

"Wally, I think we'll carry on for the moment in executive session," the special assistant to the President said, easing the impact of the dismissal with a friendly smile—and a wave towards the door.

"Yes, sir." Hicks stood and walked out the door, closing it quietly.

Fuck, he raged to himself, sitting back down at his desk. How could he advise his boss if he didn't hear what came next? Robert Ritter, Hicks thought. The guy who'd nearly destroyed sensitive negotiations at a particularly sensitive moment by violating orders and bringing some goddamned *spy* out of Budapest. The information he'd brought *had* somehow changed the U.S. negotiating position, and *that* had set the treaty back three months because America had decided to chisel something else out of the Soviets, who had been reasonable *as hell* to concede the matters already agreed to. That fact had saved Ritter's career—and probably encouraged him in that idiotically romantic view that individual people were more important than world peace, when peace itself was the only thing that mattered.

And Ritter knew how to jerk Roger around, didn't he? All that war-plans stuff was pure horseshit. Roger had his office walls covered with photos from The Old Days, when he'd flown his goddamned airplane all over hell and gone, pretending that he was personally winning the war against Hitler, just one more fucking war that good diplomacy would have prevented if only people had focused on the real issues as he and Peter hoped someday to do. This thing wasn't about war plans or SIOP or any of the other uniformed bullshit that people in this section of the White House Staff played with every goddamned day. It was about *people,* for Christ's sake. Uniformed people. Dumbass soldiers, people with big shoulders and little minds who did nothing more useful than kill, as though that made anything in the world better. And besides, Hicks fumed, they took their chances, didn't they? If they wanted to drop bombs on a peaceful and friendly people like the Vietnamese, well, they should have thought ahead of time that those people might not like it very much. Most important of all, if they were dumb enough to gamble their *lives,* then they implicitly accepted the possibility of losing them, and so why then should people like Wally Hicks give a flying fuck about them when the dice came up wrong? They probably loved the action. It undoubtedly attracted the sort of women who thought that big dicks came along with small brains, who liked "men" who dragged their knuckles on the ground like well-dressed apes.

This could wreck the peace talks. Even MacKenzie thought that.

All those kids from his generation, dead. And now they might risk not ending the war because of *fifteen* or *twenty* professional *killers* who probably liked what they did. It just made no sense. *What if they gave a war and nobody came?* was one of his generation's favored aphorisms, though he knew it to be a fantasy. Because people like that *one* guy—Zacharias—would always seduce people into following them because little people who lacked Hicks's understanding and perspective wouldn't be able to see that it was just all a waste of energy. That was the most amazing part of all. Wasn't it *clear* that war was just plain *awful?* How smart did you have to be to understand *that?*

Hicks saw the door open. MacKenzie and Ritter came out.

"Wally, we're going across the street for a few minutes. Could you tell my eleven o'clock that I'll be back as soon as I can?"

"Yes, sir."

Wasn't that typical? Ritter's seduction was complete. He had MacKenzie sold enough that Roger would make the pitch to the National Security Advisor. And they would probably raise pure fucking hell at the peace table, and maybe set things back three months or more, unless somebody saw through the ruse. Hicks lifted his phone and dialed a number.

"Senator Donaldson's office."

"Hi, I was trying to get Peter Henderson."

"I'm sorry, he and the Senator are in Europe right now. They'll get back next week."

"Oh, that's right. Thanks." Hicks hung up. *Damn.* He was so upset that he'd forgotten.

Some things have to be done very carefully. Peter Henderson didn't even know that his code name was CASSIUS. It had been assigned to him by an analyst in the U.S.-Canada Institute whose love of Shakespeare's plays was as genuine as that of any Oxford don. The photo in the file, along with the one-page profile of the agent, had made him think of the self-serving "patriot" in *The Tragedy of Julius Caesar.* Brutus would not have been right. Henderson, the analyst had judged, did not have sufficient quality of character.

His senator was in Europe on a "fact-finding" tour, mainly having to do with NATO, though they would stop in on the peace talks at Paris just to get some TV tape that might be shown on Connecticut TV stations in the fall. In fact, the "tour" was mainly a shopping trip punctuated by a brief every other day. Henderson, enjoying his first such trip as the Senator's expert on national-security issues, had to be there for the briefs, but the rest of the time was his, and he had made his own arrangements. At the moment he was touring the White Tower, the famous centerpiece of Her Majesty's Tower of London, now approaching its nine hundredth year of guardianship on the River Thames.

"Warm day for London," another tourist said.

"I wonder if they get thunderstorms here," the American replied casually, examining Henry VIII's immense suit of armor.

"They do," the man replied, "but not as severe as those in Washington."

Henderson looked for an exit and headed towards it. A moment later he was strolling around Tower Green with his new companion.

"Your English is excellent."

"Thank you, Peter. I am George."

"Hi, George." Henderson smiled without looking at his new friend. It really was like James Bond, and doing it here—not just in London, but in the historical seat of Britain's royal family—well, that was just delicious.

George was his real name—actually Georgiy, which was the Russian equivalent—and he rarely went into the field anymore. Though he'd been a highly effective field officer for KGB, his analytical ability was such that he'd been called back to Moscow five years earlier, promoted to lieutenant colonel and placed in charge of a whole section. Now a full colonel, George looked forward to general's stars. The reason he'd come to London, via Helsinki and Brussels, was that he'd wanted to eyeball CASSIUS himself—and get a little shopping done for his own family. Only three men of his age in KGB shared his rank, and his young and pretty wife liked to wear Western clothes. Where else to shop for them but London? George didn't speak French or Italian.

"This is the only time we will meet, Peter."

"Should I be honored?"

"If you wish." George was unusually good-natured for a Russian, though that was part of his cover. He smiled at the American. "Your senator has access to many things."

"Yes, he does," Henderson agreed, enjoying the courtship ritual. He didn't have to add, *and so do I.*

"Such information is useful to us. Your government, especially with your new president—honestly, he frightens us."

"He frightens me," Henderson admitted.

"But at the same time there is hope," George went on, speaking in a reasonable and judicious voice. "He is also a realist. His proposal for *détente* is seen by my government as a sign that we can reach a broad international understanding. Because of that we wish to examine the possibility that his proposal for discussions is genuine. Unfortunately we have problems of our own."

"Such as?"

"Your president, perhaps he means well. I say that sincerely, Peter," George added. "But he is highly . . . competitive. If he knows too much about us, he will press us too hard in some areas, and that might prevent us from reaching the accommodation that we all desire. You have adverse political elements in your government. So do we—leftovers from the Stalin era. The key to negotiations such as those which may soon begin is that both sides must be reasonable. We need your help to control the unreasonable elements on our side."

Henderson was surprised by that. The Russians could be so open, like Americans. "How can I do that?"

"Some things we cannot allow to be leaked. If they are, it will poison our chances for *détente.* If we know too much about you, or you know too much about us, well, the game becomes skewed. One side or the other seeks too much advantage, and then there can be no understanding, only domination, which neither side will accept. Do you see?"

"Yes, that makes sense."

"What I am asking, Peter, is that you let us know from time to time certain special things that you have learned about us. I won't even tell you what, exactly. I think you are intelligent enough to see for yourself. We will trust you on that. The time for war is behind us. The coming peace, if it does come, will depend on people like you and me. There must be trust between our nations. That trust begins between two people. There is no other way. I wish there were, but that is how peace must begin."

"Peace—that would be nice," Henderson allowed. "First we have to get our damned war ended."

"We are working towards that end, as you know. We're—well, not pressuring, but we are *encouraging* our friends to take a more moderate line. Enough young men have died. It is time to put an end to it, an end that both sides will find acceptable."

"That's good to hear, George."

"So can you help us?"

They'd walked all around Tower Green, now facing the chapel. There was a chopping block there. Henderson didn't know if it had actually been used or not. Around it was a low chain fence, and standing on it at the moment was a raven, one of those kept on Tower grounds for the mixed reasons of tradition and superstition. Off to their right a Yeoman Warder was conducting a bunch of tourists around.

"I've been helping you, George." Which was true. Henderson had been nibbling at the hook for nearly two years. What the KGB colonel had to do now was to sweeten the bait, then see if Henderson would swallow the hook down.

"Yes, Peter, I know that, but now we are asking for a little more, some very sensitive information. The decision is yours, my friend. It is easy to wage war. Waging peace can be far more dangerous. No one will ever know the part you played. The important people of ministerial rank will reach their agreements and shake hands across the table. Cameras will record the events for history, and people like you and me, our names will never find their way into the history books. But it will matter, my friend. People like us will set the stage for the ministers. I cannot force you in this, Peter. You must decide if you wish to help us on your own account. You will also decide what it is that we need to know. You're a bright young man, and your generation in America has learned the lessons that must be learned. If you wish, I will let you decide over time—"

Henderson turned, making his decision. "No. You're right. Somebody has to help make the peace, and dithering around won't change that. I'll help you, George."

"There is danger involved. You know that," George warned. It was a struggle not to react, but now that Henderson was indeed swallowing the hook, he had to set it firmly.

"I'll take my chances. It's worth it."

Ahhh.

"People like you need to be protected. You will be contacted when you get home." George paused. "Peter, I am a father. I have a daughter who is six and a son who is two. Because of your work, and mine, they will grow up in a much better world—a peaceful world. For them, Peter, I thank you. I must go now."

"See you, George," Henderson said. It caused George to turn and smile one last time.

"No, Peter, you will not." George walked down the stone steps towards Traitor's Gate. It required all of his considerable self-control not to laugh aloud at the mixture of what he had just accomplished and the thundering irony of the portcullised stone arch before his eyes. Five minutes later he stepped into a black London taxi and directed the driver to head towards Harrods Department Store in Knightsbridge.

Cassius, he thought. No, that wasn't right. Casca, perhaps. But it was too late to change it now, and besides, who would have seen the humor in it? Glazov reached in his pocket for his shopping list.

25
Departures

One demonstration, however perfect, wasn't enough, of course. For each of the next four nights, they did it all again, and twice more in daylight, just so that positioning was clear to everyone. The snatch team would be racing into the prison block only ten feet away from the stream of fire from an M-60 machine gun—the physical layout of the camp demanded it, much to everyone's discomfort—and that was the most dangerous technical issue of the actual assault. But by the end of the week, the BOXWOOD GREEN team was as perfectly trained as men could be. They knew it, and the flag officers knew it. Training didn't exactly slack off, but it did stabilize, lest the men become over-trained and dulled by the routine. What followed was the final phase of the preparation. While training, men would stop the action and make small suggestions to one another. Good ideas were bumped immediately to a senior NCO or to Captain Albie and more often than not incorporated in the plan. This was the intellectual part of it, and it was important that every member of the team felt as though he had a chance to affect things to some greater or lesser degree. From that came confidence, not the bravado so often associated with elite troops, but the deeper and far more significant professional judgment that considered and adjusted and readjusted until things were just right—and then *stopped*.

Remarkably, their off-duty hours were more relaxed now. They knew about the mission, and the high-spirited horseplay common to young men was muted. They watched TV in the open bay, read books or magazines, waiting for the word in the knowledge that halfway across the world other men were waiting, too, and in the quiet of twenty-five individual human minds, questions were being asked. Would things go right or wrong? If the former, what elation would they feel? If the latter—well, they all had long since decided that win or lose, this wasn't the sort of thing you walked away from. There were husbands to be restored to their wives, fathers to their children, men to their country. Each knew that if death was to be risked, then this was the time and the purpose for it.

At Sergeant Irvin's behest, chaplains came to the group. Consciences were cleared. A few wills were drafted—just in case, the embarrassed Marines told the visiting officers—and all the while the Marines focused more and more on the mission, their minds casting aside extraneous concerns and concentrating on something identified only by a code name selected at random from separate lists of words. Every man walked over to the training site, checking placement and angles, usually with his most immediate teammate, practicing their run-in approach or the paths they'd take once the shooting started. Every one began his own personal exercise regime, running a mile or two on his own in addition to the regular morning and afternoon efforts, both to work off tension and to be just a little bit more certain that he'd be ready for it. A trained observer could see it from their look: serious but not tense, focused but not obsessive, confident but not cocky. Other Marines at Quantico kept their distance when they saw the team, wondering why the special place and the odd schedule, why the Cobras on the flight line, why the Navy rescue pilots in the Q, but one look at the team in the piney woods was all the warning they needed to mute the questions and keep their distance. Something special was happening.

"Thanks, Roger," Bob Ritter said in the sanctity of his office in Langley. He switched buttons on his phone and dialed another in-house number. "James? Bob. It's a go. Start pushing buttons."

"Thank you, James." Dutch Maxwell turned in his swivel chair and looked at the side panel affixed to his wall, blue aluminum from his F6F Hellcat fighter, with its even rows of red-and-white painted flags, each denoting a victim of his skill. It was his personal touchstone to his profession. "Yeoman Grafton," he called.

"Yes, sir?" a petty officer appeared in his doorway.

"Make signal to Admiral Podulski on *Constellation:* 'Olive Green.'"

"Aye aye, sir."

"Have my car come around, then call Anacostia. I need a helo in about fifteen minutes."

"Yes, Admiral."

Vice Admiral Winslow Holland Maxwell, USN, rose from his desk and headed out the side door into the E-Ring corridor. His first stop was at the office in the Air Force's section of the building.

"Gary, we're going to need that transport we talked about."

"You got it, Dutch," the General replied, asking no questions.

"Let my office know the details. I'm heading out now, but I'll be calling in every hour."

"Yes, sir."

Maxwell's car was waiting at the River entrance, a master chief aviation bosun's mate at the wheel. "Where to, sir?"

"Anacostia, Master Chief, the helo pad."

"Aye." The senior chief dropped the car into gear and headed for the river. He didn't know what it was all about, but he knew it was about something. The Old Man had a spring in his step like the chief's daughter heading out for a date.

• • •

Kelly was working on his woodcraft, again, as he'd been doing for several weeks. He'd picked his weapons load-out in the fervent hope that he would not need to fire a single shot. The primary weapon was a CAR-15 carbine version of the M-16 assault rifle. A silenced 9mm automatic went into a shoulder holster, but his real weapon was a radio, and he would be carrying two of those, just to be sure, plus food and water and a map—and extra batteries. It came out to a twenty-three-pound load, not counting his special gear for the insertion. The weight wasn't excessive, and he found that he could move through the trees and over the hills without noticing it. Kelly moved quickly for a man of his size, and silently. The latter was a matter of where he walked more than anything else, where he placed his feet, how he twisted and turned to pass between trees and bushes, watching both his path and the area around him with equal urgency.

Overtraining, he told himself. *You should take it easier now.* He stood erect and headed down the hill, surrendering to his instincts. He found the Marines training in small groups, miming the use of their weapons while Captain Albie consulted with the four helicopter crews. Kelly was just approaching the site's LZ when a blue Navy helo landed and Admiral Maxwell emerged. Kelly, by chance, was the first one there. He knew the purpose and the message of the visit before anyone had a chance to speak.

"We're going?"

"Tonight," Maxwell confirmed with a nod.

Despite the expectation and enthusiasm, Kelly felt the usual chill. It wasn't practice anymore. His life was on the line again. The lives of others would depend on him. He would have to get the job done. *Well,* he told himself, *I know how to do that.* Kelly waited by the chopper while Maxwell went over to Captain Albie. General Young's staff car pulled up so that he could deliver the news as well. Salutes were exchanged as Kelly watched. Albie got the word, and his back went a little straighter. The Recon Marines gathered around, and their reaction was surprisingly sober and matter-of-fact. Looks were exchanged, rather dubious ones, but they soon changed to simple, determined nods. The mission was GO. The message delivered, Maxwell came back to the helicopter.

"I guess you want that quick liberty."

"You said you'd do it, sir."

The Admiral clapped the younger man on the shoulder and pointed to the helo. Inside, they put on headsets while the flight crew spooled up the engine.

"How soon, sir?"

"You be back here by midnight." The pilot looked back at them from the right seat. Maxwell motioned for him to stay on the ground.

"Aye aye, sir." Kelly removed the headset and jumped out of the helicopter, going to join General Young.

"Dutch told me," Young said, the disapproval clear in his voice. You just didn't do things this way: "What do you need?"

"Back to the boat to change, then run me up to Baltimore, okay? I'll drive back myself."

"Look, Clark—"

"General, I helped plan this mission. I'm first in and I'm last out." Young wanted to swear but didn't. Instead he pointed to his driver, then to Kelly.

Fifteen minutes later, Kelly was in another life. Since leaving *Springer* tied up at the guest slip, the world had stopped, and he'd moved backwards in time. Now he was in forward motion for a brief period. A quick look determined that the dockmaster was keeping an eye on things. He raced through a shower and changed into civilian clothes, heading back to the General's staff car.

"Baltimore, Corporal. Matter of fact, I'll make it easy on you. Just drop me off at the airport. I'll catch a cab the rest of the way."

"You got it, sir," the driver told a man already fading into sleep.

"So what's the story, Mr. MacKenzie?" Hicks asked.

"They approved it," the special assistant replied, signing a few papers and initialing a few others for various official archives where future historians would record his name as a minor player in the great events of his time.

"Can you say what?"

What the hell, MacKenzie thought. Hicks had a clearance, and it was a chance to display something of his importance to the lad. In two minutes he covered the high points of BOXWOOD GREEN.

"Sir, that's an invasion," Hicks pointed out as evenly as he could manage, despite the chill on his skin and the sudden knot in his stomach.

"I suppose they might think so, but I don't. They've invaded three sovereign countries, as I recall."

More urgently: "But the peace talks—you said yourself."

"Oh, screw the peace talks! Damn it, Wally, we have *people* over there, and what they know is vital to our national security. Besides"—he smiled—"I helped sell it to Henry." *And if this one comes off . . .*

"But—"

MacKenzie looked up. Didn't this kid get it? "But *what,* Wally?"

"It's dangerous."

"War is that way, in case nobody ever told you."

"Sir, I'm supposed to be able to talk here, right?" Hicks asked pointedly.

"Of course you are, Wally. So talk."

"The peace talks are at a delicate stage now—"

"Peace talks are always delicate, aren't they? Go on," MacKenzie ordered, rather enjoying his pedagogic discourse. Maybe this kid would learn something for a change.

"Sir, we've lost too many people already. We've killed a *million* of them. And for what? What have we gained? What has anybody gained?" His voice was almost a plea.

That wasn't exactly new, and MacKenzie was tired of responding to it. "If you're asking me to defend how we got stuck with this mess, Wally, you're wasting your time. It's been a mess since the beginning, but that wasn't the work of *this* Administration, was it? We got elected with the mandate to get us the hell out of there."

"Yes, sir," Hicks agreed, as he had to. "That's exactly my point. Doing this might harm our chances to bring it to an end. I think it's a mistake, sir."

"Okay." MacKenzie relaxed, giving a tolerant eye to his aide. "That point of view may—I'll be generous, *does* have merit. What about the people, Wally?"

"They took their chances. They lost," Hicks answered with the coldness of youth.

"You know, that sort of detachment may have its use, but one difference between us is that I've been there and you haven't. You've never been in uniform, Wally. That's a shame. You might have learned something from it."

Hicks was genuinely taken aback by the irrelevancy. "I don't know what that might be, sir. It would only have interfered with my studies."

"Life isn't a book, son," MacKenzie said, using a word that he'd intended to be warm, but which merely sounded patronizing to his aide. "Real people bleed. Real people have feelings. Real people have dreams, and families. They have real lives. What you would have learned, Wally, is that they may not be *like* you, but they're still real people, and if you work in this government of the people, you must take note of that."

"Yes, sir." What else could he say? There was no way he'd win this argument. Damn, he really needed someone to talk to about this.

"John!" Not a word in two weeks. She'd feared that something had happened to him, but now she had to face the contradictory thought that he was indeed alive, and perhaps doing things best considered in the abstract.

"Hello, Sandy." Kelly smiled, dressed decently again, in a tie and blue blazer. It was so obviously a disguise, and so different from the way she'd last seen the man, that even his appearance was disturbing.

"Where have you been?" Sandy asked, waving him in, not wanting the neighbors to know.

"Off doing something," Kelly dodged.

"Doing what?" The immediacy of her tone demanded a substantive response.

"Nothing illegal, I promise," was the best he could do.

"You're sure?" A very awkward moment developed out of thin air. Kelly just stood there, right inside the door, suddenly oscillating between anger and guilt, wondering why he'd come here, why he'd asked Admiral Maxwell for a very special favor, and not really knowing the answer now.

"John!" Sarah called down the stairs, saving both from their thoughts.

"Hey, doc," Kelly called, and both were glad for the distraction.

"Have we got a surprise for you!"

"What?"

Dr. Rosen came down the stairs, looking as frumpy as ever despite her smile. "You look different."

"I've been exercising pretty regularly," Kelly explained.

"What brings you here?" Sarah asked.

"I'm going to be going somewhere, and I wanted to stop over before I left."

"Where to?"

"I can't say." The answer chilled the room.

"John," Sandy said. "We know."

"Okay." Kelly nodded. "I figured you would. How is she?"

"She's doing fine, thanks to you," Sarah answered.

"John, we need to talk, okay?" Sandy insisted. Dr. Rosen bent to her wishes and went back upstairs while nurse and former patient drifted into the kitchen.

"John, what exactly have you been doing?"

"Lately? I can't say, Sandy. I'm sorry, but I can't."

"I mean—I mean everything. What have you been up to?"

"You're better off not knowing, Sandy."

"Billy and Rick?" Nurse O'Toole said, putting it on the table.

Kelly motioned his head to the second floor. "You've seen what they did to her? They won't be doing that anymore."

"John, you can't do things like that! The police—"

"—are infiltrated," Kelly told her. "The organization has compromised somebody, probably someone very high up.

Because of that I can't trust the police, and neither can you, Sandy," he concluded as reasonably as he could.

"But there are others, John. There are others who—" His statement finally penetrated. "How do you know that?"

"I asked Billy some questions." Kelly paused, and her face gave him yet more guilt. "Sandy, do you really think somebody is going to go out of his way to investigate the death of a prostitute? That's what it is to them. Do you think anybody really cares about them? I asked you before, remember? You said that nobody even has a program to help them. You care. That's why I brought her here. But do the cops? No. Maybe I could scratch up information to burn the drug ring. I'm not sure, it's not what I've been trained for, but that's what I've been doing. If you want to turn me in, well, I can't stop you. I won't hurt you—"

"I know that!" Sandy almost screamed. "John, you can't do this," she added more calmly.

"Why not?" Kelly asked. "They kill people. They do horrible things, and nobody's doing anything about it. What about the victims, Sandy? Who speaks for them?"

"The law does!"

"And when the law doesn't work, then what? Do we just let them die? Die like that? Remember the picture of Pam?"

"Yes," Sandy replied, losing the argument, knowing it, wishing it were otherwise.

"They took hours on her, Sandy. Your—house-guest—watched. They *made her watch.*"

"She told me. She's told us everything. She and Pam were friends. After—after Pam died, she's the one who brushed Pam's hair out, John."

The reaction surprised her. It was immediately clear that Kelly's pain was behind a door, and some words could bring it out in the open with a sudden speed that punished him badly. He turned away for a moment and took a deep breath before turning back. "She's okay?"

"We're going to take her home in a few days. Sarah and I will drive her there."

"Thanks for telling me that. Thank you for taking care of her."

It was the dichotomy that unsettled her so badly. He could talk about inflicting death on people so calmly, like Sam Rosen in a discussion of a tricky surgical procedure—and like the surgeon, Kelly cared about the people he—saved? Avenged? Was that the same thing? He thought so.

"Sandy, it's like this: They killed Pam. They raped and tortured and killed her—as an *example,* so they could use other girls the same way. I'm going to get every one of them, and if I die in the process, that's the chance I'm going to take. I'm sorry if you don't like me for that."

She took a deep breath. There was nothing more to be said.

"You said you're going away."

"Yes. If things work out I should be back in about two weeks."

"Will it be dangerous?"

"Not if I do it right." Kelly knew she would see through that one.

"Doing what?"

"A rescue mission. That's as far as I can go, and please don't repeat that to anyone. I'm leaving tonight. I've been off training for it, down at a military base."

It was Sandy's turn to look away, back towards the kitchen door. He wasn't giving her a chance. There were too many contradictions. He'd saved a girl who would otherwise have certainly died, but he'd killed to do it. He loved a girl who was dead. He was willing to kill others because of that love, to risk everything for it. He'd trusted her and Sarah and Sam. Was he a bad man or a good one? The mixture of facts and ideas was impossible to reconcile. Seeing what had happened to Doris, working so hard now to get her well, hearing her voice—and her father's—it had all made sense to her at the time. It was always easy to consider things dispassionately, when they were at a distance. But not now, faced with the man who had done it all, who explained himself calmly and directly, not lying, not concealing, just telling the truth, and trusting her, again, to understand.

"Vietnam?" she asked after a few moments, temporizing, trying to add more substance to a very muddled collection of thoughts.

"That's right." Kelly paused. He had to explain it, just a little, to help her understand. "There are some people over there who won't get back unless we do something, and I am part of it."

"But why do *you* have to go?"

"Why me? It has to be somebody, and I'm the one they asked. Why do *you* do the things you do, Sandy? I asked that before, remember?"

"Damn you, John! I've started to *care* about you," she blurted out.

The pain returned to his face one more time. "Don't. You might get hurt again, and I wouldn't want that." Which was exactly the wrong thing for him to say. "People who get attached to me get hurt, Sandy."

Sarah came in just then, leading Doris into the kitchen, for the moment saving both of them from themselves. The girl was transformed. Her eyes were animated now. Sandy had trimmed her hair and found decent clothes for her. She was still weak, but moving under her own power now. Her soft brown eyes fixed on Kelly.

"You're him," she said quietly.

"I guess I am. How are you?"

She smiled. "I'm going home soon. Daddy—Daddy wants me back."

"I'm sure he does, ma'am," Kelly said. She was so different from the victim he'd seen only a few weeks before. Maybe it did all mean something.

The same thought came into Sandy's mind just then. Doris was the innocent one, the real victim of forces that had descended on her, and but for Kelly, she would be dead. Nothing else could have saved her. Other deaths had been necessary, but—but *what?*

"So maybe it was Eddie," Piaggi said. "I told him to sniff around and he says he doesn't have anything."

"And nothing's happened since you talked to him. Everything's back to normal, like," Henry replied, telling

Anthony Piaggi what he already knew and following with a conclusion that he had also considered. "What if he was just trying to shake things up a little? What if he just wanted to be more important, Tony?"

"Possible."

Which led to the next question: "How much you want to bet that if Eddie takes a little trip, nothing else happens?"

"You think he's making a move?"

"You got anything else that makes sense?"

"Anything happens to Eddie, there could be trouble. I don't think I can—"

"Let me handle it? I have a way that'll work just fine."

"Tell me about it," Piaggi said. Two minutes later he nodded approval.

"Why did you come here?" Sandy asked while she and Kelly cleaned up the dinner table. Sarah took Doris back upstairs for more rest.

"I wanted to see how she was doing." But that was a lie, and not an especially good one.

"It's lonely, isn't it?" Kelly took a long time to answer.

"Yeah." She'd forced him to face something. Being alone was not the sort of life he wanted to have, but fate and his own nature had forced it on him. Every time he'd reached out, something terrible had happened. Vengeance against those who had made his life into what it now was did make for a purpose, but it wasn't enough to fill the void they'd created. And now it was clear that what he was doing, all of it, was merely distancing him from someone else. How did life get so complicated as this?

"I can't say it's okay, John. I wish I could. Saving Doris was a fine thing, but not through killing people. There is supposed to be another way—"

"—and if there isn't, then what?"

"Let me finish?" Sandy asked quietly.

"Sorry."

She touched his hand. "Please be careful."

"I usually am, Sandy. Honest."

"What you're doing, what you're going off to, it's not—"

He smiled. "No, it's a real job. Official stuff and everything."

"Two weeks?"

"If it goes according to plan, yes."

"Will it?"

"Sometimes it actually does."

Her hand squeezed his. "John, please, think it over. Please? Try to find another way. Let it go. Let it stop. You saved Doris. That's a wonderful thing. Maybe with what you've learned you can save the others without—without any more killing?"

"I'll try." He couldn't say no to that, not with the warmth of her hand on his, and Kelly's trap was that his word, once given, could not be taken back. "Anyway, I have other things to worry about now." Which was true.

"How will I know, John—I mean—"

"About me?" He was surprised she would even want to know.

"John, you can't just leave me not knowing."

Kelly thought for a moment, pulled a pen from his coat, and wrote down a phone number. "This goes to a guy—an admiral named James Greer. He'll know, Sandy."

"Please be careful." Her grip and her eyes were desperate now.

"I will. I promise. I'm good at this, okay?"

So was Tim. She didn't have to say it. Her eyes did, and Kelly understood how cruel it could be to leave anyone behind.

"I have to go now, Sandy."

"Just make sure you come back."

"I will. Promise." But the words sounded empty, even to him. Kelly wanted to kiss her but couldn't. He moved away from the table, feeling her hand still on his. She was a tall woman, and very strong and brave, but she'd been hurt badly before, and it frightened Kelly that he might bring yet more pain to her life. "See you in a couple weeks. Say goodbye to Sarah and Doris for me, okay?"

"Yes." She followed him towards the front door. "John, when you get back, let it stop."

"I'll think about it," he said without turning, because he was afraid to look at her again. "I will."

Kelly opened the door. It was dark outside now, and he'd have to hustle to get to Quantico on time. He could hear her behind him, hear her breathing. Two women in his life, one taken by an accident, one by murder, and now perhaps a third whom he was driving away all by himself.

"John?" She hadn't let go of his hand, and he had to turn back despite his fear.

"Yes, Sandy?"

"Come back."

He touched her face again, and kissed her hand, and drew away. She watched him walk to the Volkswagen and drive off.

Even now, she thought. *Even now he's trying to protect me.*

Is it enough? Can I stop now? But what was "enough"?

"Think it through," he said aloud. "What do you know that others can use?"

It was quite a lot, really. Billy had told him much, perhaps a sufficient amount. The drugs were processed on one of those wrecked ships. He had Henry's name, and Burt's. He knew a senior narcotics officer was in Henry's employ. Could the police take that and spin it into a case firm enough to put them all behind bars for drug trafficking and murder? Might Henry get a death sentence? And if the answer to every question was yes, was that good enough?

As much as Sandy's misgivings, his association with the Marines had brought the same questions to the front of his mind. What would they think if they knew that they were associating with a murderer? Would they see it that way or would they be sympathetic to his point of view?

"The bags stink," Billy had said. "Like dead bodies, like the stuff they use."

What the hell did that mean? Kelly wondered, going through town one last time. He saw police cars operating. They couldn't all be driven by corrupt cops, could they?

"Shit," Kelly snarled at the traffic. "Clear your mind, sailor. There's a job waiting, a real job."

But that had said it all. BOXWOOD GREEN was a *real* job, and the realization came as clear and bright as the headlights of approaching cars. If someone like Sandy didn't understand—it was one thing to do it alone, just with your own thoughts and rage and loneliness, but when others saw and knew, even people who liked you, and knew exactly what it was all about. . . . When even they asked you to stop. . . .

Where was right? Where was wrong? Where was the line between them? It was easy on the highway. Some crew painted the lines, and you had to stay in the proper lane, but in real life it wasn't so clear.

Forty minutes later he was on I-495, the Washington Beltway. What was more important, killing Henry or getting those other women out of there?

Another forty and he was across the river into Virginia. Seeing Doris—what a dumb name—alive, after the first time when she'd been almost as dead as Rick. The more he thought about it, the better that seemed.

BOXWOOD GREEN wasn't about killing the enemy. It was about rescuing people.

He turned south on Interstate 95, and a final forty-five or so delivered him to Quantico. It was eleven-thirty when he drove into the training site.

"Glad you made it," Marty Young observed sourly. He was dressed in utilities for once instead of his khaki shirt.

Kelly looked hard into the General's eyes. "Sir, I've had a bad enough night. Be a pal and stow it, all right?"

Young took it like the man he was. "Mr. Clark, you sound like you're ready."

"That isn't what it's about, sir. Those guys in SENDER GREEN are ready."

"Fair enough, tough guy."

"Can I leave the car here?"

"With all these clunkers?"

Kelly paused, but the decision came quickly enough. "I think it's served its purpose. Junk it with the rest of 'em."

"Come on, the bus is down the hill a ways."

Kelly collected his personal gear and carried them to the staff car. The same corporal was driving as he sat in the back with the Marine aviator who wouldn't be going.

"What do you think, Clark?"

"Sir, I think we have a really good chance."

"You know, I wish just once, just one goddamned time, we could say, yeah, this one's going to work."

"Was it ever that way for you?" Kelly asked.

"No," Young admitted. "But you don't stop wishing."

"How was England, Peter?"

"Pretty nice. It rained in Paris, though. Brussels was pretty decent, my first time there," Henderson said.

Their apartments were only two blocks apart, comfortable places in Georgetown built during the late thirties to accommodate the influx of bureaucrats serving a growing government. Built of solid cinder-arch construction, they were more structurally sound than more recent buildings. Hicks had a two-bedroom unit, which compensated for the smallish living-dining room.

"So what's happening that you wanted to tell me about?" the Senate aide asked, still recovering from jet lag.

"We're invading the North again," the White House aide answered.

"What? Hey, I was at the peace talks, okay? I observed some of the chitchat. Things are moving along. The other side just caved in on a big one."

"Well, you can kiss that goodbye for a while," Hicks said morosely. On the coffee table was a plastic bag of marijuana, and he started putting a smoke together.

"You should lay off that shit, Wally."

"Doesn't give me a hangover like beer does. Shit, Peter, what's the difference?"

"The difference is your fucking security clearance!" Henderson said pointedly.

"Like that matters? Peter, they don't listen. You talk and talk and talk to them, and they just don't listen." Hicks lit up and took a long pull. "I'm going to leave soon anyway.

Dad wants me to come and join the family business. Maybe after I make a few mill', maybe then somebody'll listen once in a while."

"You shouldn't let it get to you, Wally. It takes time. Everything takes time. You think we can fix things overnight?"

"I don't think we can fix things at all! You know what this all is? It's like Sophocles. We have our fatal flaw, and they have their fatal flaw, and when the fucking *deus* comes *ex* the fucking *machina,* the *deus* is going to be a cloud of ICBMs, and it's all going to be over, Peter. Just like we thought a few years ago up in New Hampshire." It wasn't Hicks's first smoke of the evening, Henderson realized. Intoxication always made his friend morose.

"Wally, tell me what the problem is."

"There's supposedly this camp . . . " Hicks began, his eyes down, not looking at his friend at all now as he related what he knew.

"That is bad news."

"They *think* there's a bunch of people there, but it's just supposition. We only know about one. What if we're fucking over the peace talks for *one guy,* Peter?"

"Put that damned thing out," Henderson said, sipping his beer. He just didn't like the smell of the stuff.

"No." Wally took another big hit.

"When is it going?"

"Not sure. Roger didn't say exactly."

"Wally, you have to stay with it. We need people like you in the system. Sometimes they will listen."

Hicks looked up. "When will that be, do you think?"

"What if this mission fails? What if it turns out that you're right? Roger will listen to you then, and Henry listens to Roger, doesn't he?"

"Well, yeah, sometimes."

What a remarkable chance this was, Henderson thought.

The chartered bus drove to Andrews Air Force Base, duplicating, Kelly saw, more than half of his drive. There was a new C-141 on the ramp, painted white on the top and gray on the bottom, its strobe lights already rotating. The

Marines got out of the bus, finding Maxwell and Greer waiting for them.

"Good luck," Greer said to each man.

"Good hunting," was what Dutch Maxwell told them.

Built to hold more than double their number, the Lockheed Starlifter was outfitted for litter patients, with a total of eighty beds bolted to the side of the aircraft and room for twenty or so attendants. That gave every Marine a place to lie down and sleep, plus room for all the prisoners they expected to rescue. The time of night made it easy for everyone, and the Starlifter started turning engines as soon as the cargo hatch was shut.

"Jesus, I hope this works," Maxwell said, watching the aircraft taxi into the darkness.

"You've trained them well, Admiral," Bob Ritter observed. "When do we go out?"

"Three days, Bob," James Greer answered. "Got your calendar clear?"

"For this? You bet."

26
Transit

A new aircraft, the Starlifter was also a disappointingly slow one. Its cruising speed was a mere 478 miles per hour, and their first stop was Elmendorf Air Force base in Alaska, 3,350 miles and eight hours away. It never ceased to amaze Kelly that the shortest distance to any place on Earth was a curve, but that was because he was used to flat maps, and the world was a sphere. The great-circle route from Washington to Danang would actually have taken them over Siberia, and that, the navigator said, just wouldn't do. By the time of their arrival at Elmendorf, the Marines were up and rested. They departed the aircraft to look at snow on not-so-distant mountains, having only a few hours before left a place where heat and humidity were in a daily race for 100. But here in Alaska they found mosquitoes sufficiently large that a few might have carried one of their number off. Most took the opportunity to jog a couple of miles, to the amusement of the Air Force personnel, who typically had little contact with Marines. Servicing the C-141 took a programmed time of two and a quarter hours. After refueling and one minor instrument replacement, the Marines were just as happy to reboard the aircraft for the second leg of the journey, for Yokota, in Japan. Three hours after that, Kelly walked onto the flight deck, growing bored with the noise and confinement.

"What's that over there?" he asked. In the distant haze was a brown-green line that denoted somebody's coast.

"Russia. They have us on radar right now."

"Oh, that's nice," Kelly observed.

"It's a small world, sir, and they own a big hunk of it."

"You talk to them—air-traffic control, like?"

"No." The navigator laughed. "They're not real neighborly. We talk on HF to Tokyo for this leg, and after Yokota, we're controlled through Manila. Is the ride smooth enough?"

"No beefs so far. Gets long, though."

"It does that," the navigator acknowledged, turning back to his instruments.

Kelly walked back into the cargo area. The C-141 was noisy, a constant high-frequency whine from the engines and the air through which they were passing. The Air Force didn't waste any money, as airlines did, on sound insulation. Every Marine was wearing earplugs, which made conversation difficult, and after a time didn't really block the noise anyway. The worst part of air travel was the boredom, Kelly thought, made worse by the sound-induced isolation. You could only sleep so much. Some of the men were honing knives which they would never really use, but it gave you something to do, and a warrior had to have a knife for some reason. Others were doing push-ups on the metal cargo deck of the aircraft. The Air Force crewmen watched impassively, not wanting to laugh, wondering what this obviously select group of Marines was up to, but unable to ask. It was for them just one more mystery as their aircraft slid down the Siberian coast. They were used to it, but to a man they wished the Marines well on whatever their job was.

The problem was the first thing on his mind when his eyes opened. *What do I do about this?* Henderson asked himself crossly.

It wasn't what he wanted to do, but what he would be able to do. He'd delivered information before. At first unknowingly, through contacts in the peace movement, he'd—well, not so much given over information as had joined in rambling discussions which over time had become more and more pointed until finally one of his friends had asked something just a little too directed to be a random inquiry. A friendly question she'd asked, and at a very friendly moment, but the look in her eyes was a little too interested in the reply and not enough interested in him, a situation which had immediately reversed when he'd answered the question. A spoonful of sugar, he'd told himself later, rather vexed with himself that he'd fallen prey to such an obvious and old-fashioned—well, not an error, really. He liked her, believed as she did in the way the world should be, and if anything he was annoyed that she'd felt it necessary to manipulate his body in order to get something that reason and intellect would have elicited quite readily from his mind . . . well, probably.

She was gone now, gone somewhere. Henderson didn't know where, though he was sure that he'd never see her again. Which was sad, really. She'd been a great lay. One thing had led to another in a seemingly gradual and natural series of steps ending with his brief conversation at H.M. Tower of London, and now—now he had something the other side really needed. It was just that he didn't have anyone to tell it to. Did the Russians really know what they had there at that damned-fool camp southwest of Haiphong? It was information which, if used properly, would make them feel far more comfortable about *détente,* would allow them to back off a little, in turn allowing America to back off a little. That was how it had to start. It was a shame Wally didn't grasp that it had to start as little things, that you couldn't change the world all at once. Peter knew that he had to get that message across. He couldn't have Wally leave government service now, to become just one more goddamned financial puke, as though the world didn't have enough of them already. He was valuable where he was. Wally just liked to talk too much. It went along with his emotional instability. And his drug use, Henderson thought, looking in the mirror as he shaved.

Breakfast was accompanied by a morning paper. There it was again, on the first page as it was almost every day. Some medium-sized battle for some hill that had been exchanged a dozen or more times, X number of Americans and Y number of Vietnamese, all dead. The implications for the peace talks of some air raid or other, another boring and predictable editorial. Plans for a demonstration. *One, Two, Three, Four. We don't want your fucking war.* As though something so puerile as that really meant anything. In a way, he knew, it did. It did put pressure on political figures, did catch media attention. There was a mass of politicians who wanted the war to end, as Henderson did, but not yet a critical mass. His own senator, Robert Donaldson, was still on the fence. He was called a reasonable and thoughtful man, but Henderson merely found him indecisive, always considering everything about an issue and then most often going with the crowd as though he hadn't thought anything at all on his own. There had to be a better way, and Henderson was working on that, advising his senator carefully, shading things just a little bit, taking his time to become trusted so that he could learn things that Donaldson wasn't supposed to tell anyone—but that was the problem with secrets. You just *had to* let others know, he thought on the way out the door.

Henderson rode the bus to work. Parking on The Hill was such a pain in the rump, and the bus went nearly from door to door. He found a seat in the back where he could finish reading the paper. Two blocks later he felt the bus stop, and immediately thereafter a man sat down next to him.

"How was London?" the man asked in a conversational voice, barely over the noise of the bus's diesel. Henderson looked over briefly. It wasn't someone he'd met before. Were they *that* efficient?

"I met someone there," Peter said cautiously.

"I have a friend in London. His name is George." Not a trace of an accent, and now that contact was established, the man was reading the sports page of the *Washington*

Post. "I don't think the Senators will make it this year. Do you?"

"George said he had a . . . friend in town."

The man smiled at the box score. "My name is Marvin; you can call me that."

"How do we . . . how do I . . . ?"

"What are you doing for dinner tonight?" Marvin asked.

"Nothing much. Want to come over—"

"No, Peter, that is not smart. Do you know a place called Alberto's?"

"Wisconsin Avenue, yeah."

"Seven-thirty," Marvin said. He rose and got off at the next stop.

The final leg started at Yokota Air Base. After another programmed two-and-a-quarter-hour service wait, the Starlifter rotated off the runway, clawing its way back into the sky. That was when things started to get real for everyone. The Marines made a concerted effort to sleep now. It was the only way to deal with the tension that grew in inverse proportion to the distance from their final destination. Things were different now. It wasn't just a training exercise, and their demeanor was adapting itself to a new reality. On a different sort of flight, a commercial airliner, perhaps, where conversation might have been possible, they'd trade jokes, stories of amorous conquests, talk about home and family and plans for the future, but the noise of the C-141 denied them that, and so they traded brave smiles that hung under guarded eyes, each man alone with his thoughts and fears, needing to share them and deflect them, but unable to in the noisy cargo compartment of the Starlifter. That was why many of them exercised, just to work off the stress, to tire themselves enough for the oblivion of sleep. Kelly watched it, having seen and done it himself, alone with his own thoughts even more complex than theirs.

It's about rescue, Kelly told himself. What had started the whole adventure was saving Pam, and the fact of her death was his fault. Then he had killed, to get even, telling himself it was for her memory and for his love, but was that really true? What good things came from death? He'd *tortured* a man, and now he had to admit to himself that he'd taken satisfaction in Billy's pain. If Sandy had learned that, then what? What would she think of him? It was suddenly important to consider what she thought about him. She who worked so hard to save that girl, who nurtured and protected, following through on his more simple act of rescue, what would she think of someone who'd torn Billy's body apart one cell at a time? He could not, after all, stop all the evil in the world. He could not win the war to which he was now returning, and as skilled as this team of Recon Marines was, they would not win the war either. They were going for something else. Their purpose was rescue, for while there could be little real satisfaction in the taking of life, saving life was ever something to recall with the deepest pride. That was his mission now, and must be his mission on returning. There were four other girls in the control of the ring. He'd get them clear, somehow . . . and maybe he could somehow let the cops know what Henry was up to, and then they could deal with him. Somehow. How exactly he wasn't sure. But at least then he could do something that memory would not try to wash away.

And all he had to do was survive this mission. Kelly grunted to himself. No big deal, right?

Tough guy, he told himself with bravado that rang false even within the confines of his own skull. *I can do this. I've done it before.* Strange, he thought, how the mind doesn't always remember the scary parts until it was too late. Maybe it was proximity. Maybe it was easier to consider dangers that were half a world away, but then when you started getting closer, things changed. . . .

"Toughest part, Mr. Clark," Irvin said loudly, sitting down beside him after doing his hundred push-ups.

"Ain't it the truth?" Kelly half-shouted back.

"Something you oughta remember, squid—you got inside and took me out that night, right?" Irvin grinned. "And I'm pretty damned good."

"They ought not to be all that alert, their home turf an' all," Kelly observed after a moment.

"Probably not, anyway, not as alert as we were that night. Hell, we knew you were coming in. You kinda expect home troops, like, go home to the ol' lady every night, thinking about havin' a piece after dinner. Not like us, man."

"Not many like us," Kelly agreed. He grinned. "Not many dumb as we are."

Irvin slapped him on the shoulder. "You got that right, Clark." The master gunnery sergeant moved off to encourage the next man, which was his way of dealing with it.

Thanks, Guns, Kelly thought, leaning back and forcing himself back into sleep.

Alberto's was a place waiting to be fully discovered. A small and rather typical mom-and-pop Italian place where the veal was especially good. In fact, everything was good, and the couple who ran it waited patiently for the *Post*'s food critic to wander in, bringing prosperity with him. Until then they subsisted on the college crowd from nearby Georgetown University and a healthy local trade of neighborhood diners without which no restaurant could really survive. The only disappointing note was the music, schmaltzy tapes of Italian opera that oozed out of substandard speakers. The mom and pop in question would have to work on that, he thought.

Henderson found a booth in the back. The waiter, probably an illegal Mexican who comically tried to mask his accent as Italian, lit the candle on the table with a match and went off for the gin-and-tonic the new customer wanted.

Marvin arrived a few minutes later, dressed casually and carrying the evening paper, which he sat on the table. He was of Henderson's age, totally nondescript, not tall or short, portly or thin, his hair a neutral brown and of medium length, wearing glasses that might or might not have held prescription lenses. He wore a blue short-sleeve shirt without a tie, and looked like just another local resident who didn't feel like doing his own dinner tonight.

"The Senators lost again," he said when the waiter arrived with Henderson's drink. "The house red for me," Marvin told the Mexican.

"*Sí,*" the waiter said and moved off.

Marvin had to be an illegal, Peter thought, appraising the man. As a staffer for a member of the Select Committee on Intelligence, Henderson had been briefed in by serious members of the FBI's Intelligence Division. "Legal" KGB officers had diplomatic covers, and if caught could only be PNG'd—declared persona non grata—and sent home. So they were secure from serious mishandling on the part of the American government, which was the good news; the bad news was that they were also more easily tracked, since their residences and automobiles were known. Illegals were just that, Soviet intelligence officers who came into the country with false papers and who if caught would end up in federal prison until the next exchange, which could take years. Those facts explained Marvin's superb English. Any mistake he made would have serious consequences. That made his relaxed demeanor all the more remarkable.

"Baseball fan, eh?"

"I learned the game long ago. I was a pretty good shortstop, but I never learned to hit a curve ball." The man grinned. Henderson smiled back. He'd seen satellite imagery of the very place where Marvin had learned his trade, that interesting little city northwest of Moscow.

"How will it work?"

"I like that. Good. Let's get down to business. We won't be doing this very often. You know why."

Another smile. "Yeah, they say that winters at Leavenworth are a motherfucker."

"Not a laughing matter, Peter," the KGB officer said. "This is a very serious business." *Please, not another bloody cowboy,* Marvin thought to himself.

"I know. Sorry," Henderson apologized. "I'm new to this."

"First of all, we need to set up a way of contacting me. Your apartment has curtains on the front windows. When they are all the way open, or all the way closed, there is nothing to concern us. When there is, leave them halfway closed. I will check your windows twice a week, on Tuesday and Friday mornings, about nine. Is that acceptable?"

"Yes, Marvin."

"For starters, Peter, we'll use a simple transfer method. I will park my car on a street close to your home. It's a dark-blue Plymouth Satellite with license number HVR-309. Repeat that back to me. Don't ever write it down."

"HVR-309."

"Put your messages in this." He passed something under the table. It was small and metallic. "Don't get it too close to your watch. There's a powerful magnet in it. When you walk past my car, you can bend down to pick up a piece of litter, or rest your foot on the bumper and tie your shoe. Just stick the container on the inside surface of the bumper. The magnet will hold it in place."

It seemed very sophisticated to Henderson, though everything he'd just heard was kindergarten-level spycraft. This was good for the summer. Winter weather would require something else. The dinner menu arrived, and both men selected veal.

"I have something now if you're interested," Henderson told the KGB officer. *Might as well let them know how important I am.*

Marvin, whose real name was Ivan Alekseyevich Yegorov, had a real job, and everything that went along with it. Employed by the Aetna Casualty and Surety Company as a loss-control representative, he'd been through company training on Farmington Avenue in Hartford, Connecticut, before returning to the Washington regional office, and his job was to identify safety hazards at the many clients of the company, known in the trade as "risks." Selected mainly for its mobility—the post even came with a company car—the job carried with it the unexpected bonus of visiting the offices of various government contractors whose employees were not always as careful covering up the papers on their desks as they ought to have been. His immediate boss was delighted with Marvin's performance. His new man was highly observant and downright superb at documenting his business affairs. He'd already turned down promotion and transfer to Detroit—*sorry, boss, but I just like the Washington area too much*—which didn't bother his supervisor at all. A guy with his skills, holding a fairly low-paying job, just made his part of the office look all the better. For Marvin, the job meant being out of the office four days out of five, which allowed him to meet people whenever and wherever he wished, along with a free car—Aetna even paid gas and maintenance—and a life so comfortable that had he believed in God he might have thought himself dead and in heaven. A genuine love for baseball took him to RFK Stadium, where the anonymity of the crowd was as perfect a place for brush-passes and other meets as the *KGB Field Operations Manual* dared to hope for. All in all, Captain Yegorov was a man on the way up, comfortable with his cover and his surroundings, doing his duty for his country. He'd even managed to arrive in America just in time to catch the sexual revolution. All he really missed was the vodka, something Americans did poorly.

Isn't this interesting? Marvin asked himself in his Chevy Chase apartment. It was downright hilarious that he had learned about a high-level Russian intelligence operation from an American, and here was a chance to hurt his country's Main Enemy through surrogates—if they could get things moving in time. He would also be able to inform his control officers of something the Soviet Air Force cretins had running that had significant implications for the Soviet Union's defense. They'd probably try to take that operation over. You couldn't trust pilots—it had to be a PVO Strany officer doing the questioning, he was sure—with something as important as national defense. He made his notes, photographed them, and rewound the film into the tiny cassette. His first appointment tomorrow was an early call at a local contractor. From there he would stop off to have breakfast at a Howard Johnson's, where he'd make his transfer. The cassette would be in Moscow in two days, maybe three, by diplomatic pouch.

Captain Yegorov ended his work for the evening just in time to catch the end of the Senators game—despite a ninth-inning homer by Frank Howard they fell short again, losing to Cleveland 5–3. Wasn't this something, he thought, sipping at his beer. Henderson was a plum all by himself, and nobody had bothered to tell him—probably hadn't known—that he had his own source within the White House Office of National Security Affairs. Wasn't that a kick in the ass?

Mission stress and all, it was a relief when the C-141 thumped down at Danang. They'd been in transit for a total of twenty-three noisy and mind-numbing hours, and that was quite long enough, they all thought, until reality struck them hard and fast. Scarcely had the cargo hatch opened when the smell hit them. It was what all veterans of this place came to think of as the Smell of Vietnam. The contents of various latrines were dumped into barrels and burned with diesel fuel.

"Smell o' home!" one Marine joked, badly, evoking isolated barks of semiamusement.

"Saddle up!" Irvin shouted as the engine noise died. It took a little time. Reactions were slowed by fatigue and stiffness. Many shook their heads to clear off the dizziness induced by the earplugs, along with yawns and stretches which psychologists would have called typical nonverbal expressions of unease.

The flight crew came aft just as the Marines left. Captain Albie went to them, thanking them for the ride, which had been smooth, if long. The Air Force crew looked forward to several days of enforced crew-rest after the marathon stint, not yet knowing that they would hold in this area until the team was ready to fly home, perhaps catching a few cargo hops back and forth to Clark. Then Albie led his men off the aircraft. Two trucks were waiting, and they drove to a different part of the air base, where two aircraft waited. These were Navy C-2A Greyhounds. With a few desultory moans, the Marines selected seats for the next part of their journey, a one-hour hop to USS *Constellation.* Once there, they boarded a pair of CH-46 Sea Knight helicopters for a transfer to USS *Ogden,* where, disoriented and exhausted by travel, they were led to capacious and empty troop quarters—and bunks. Kelly watched them file off, wondering what came next for him.

"How was the trip?" He turned to see Admiral Podulski, dressed in wrinkled khakis and far too cheerful for the moment.

"Aviators gotta be crazy," Kelly bitched.

"Does get kinda long. Follow me," the Admiral ordered, leading him into the superstructure. Kelly looked around first. *Constellation* was on the eastern horizon, and he could see aircraft flying off one end while others circled to land on the other. Two cruisers were in close attendance, and destroyers ringed the formation. It was part of the Navy which Kelly had rarely seen, the Big Blue Team at work, commanding the ocean. "What's that?" he asked, pointing.

"Russian fishing trawler, AGI." Podulski waved Kelly through a watertight door.

"Oh, that's just great!"

"Don't worry. We can deal with that," the Admiral assured him.

Inside the superstructure, the two men headed up a series of ladders, finding flag quarters, or what passed for them at the moment. Admiral Podulski had taken over the Captain's in-port cabin for the duration of the mission, relegating *Ogden*'s CO to his smaller accommodations nearer the bridge. There was a comfortable sitting room, and the ship's captain was there.

"Welcome aboard!" Captain Ted Franks said in greeting. "You're Clark?"

"Yes, sir."

Franks was a fifty-year-old pro who'd been in amphibious ships since 1944. *Ogden* was his fifth and would be his last command. Short, pudgy, and losing his hair, he still had the look of a warrior on a face that was by turns good-natured and deadly serious. At the moment, it was the former. He waved Kelly to a chair next to a table in the center of which was a bottle of Jack Daniel's.

"That ain't legal," Kelly observed at once.

"Not for me," Captain Franks agreed. "Aviator rations."

"I arranged for them," Casimir Podulski explained. "Brought 'em over from *Connie*. You need something to steady down after all that time with the Air Scouts."

"Sir, I never argue with admirals." Kelly dropped two ice cubes into a tumbler and covered them with alcohol.

"My XO is talking with Captain Albie and his people. They're all getting entertained, too," Franks added, meaning that every man had two miniatures on his assigned bunk. "Mr. Clark, our ship is yours. Anything we have, you got it."

"Well, Cap'n, you surely know how to say hello." Kelly sipped at his drink, and the first touch of the booze made his body remember how wrung-out he was. "So when do we start?"

"Four days. You need two to recover from the trip," the Admiral said. "The submarine will be with us two days after that. The Marines go in Friday morning, depending on weather."

"Okay." There was nothing else he could say.

"Only the XO and I know anything yet. Try not to spread things around. We've got a pretty good crew. The intel team is aboard and working. The medical team gets here tomorrow."

"Recon?"

Podulski handled that one. "We'll have photos of the camp later today, from a Vigilante working off *Connie*. Then another set twelve hours before you move out. We have Buffalo Hunter shots, five days old. The camp is still there, still guarded, same as before."

"Items?" Kelly asked, using the code word for prisoners.

"We've only got three shots of Americans in the compound." Podulski shrugged. "They don't make a camera yet that can see through a tile roof."

"Right." Kelly's face said it all.

"I'm worried about that, too," Cas admitted.

Kelly turned. "Captain, you have an exercise place, something like that?"

"Weight room, aft of the crew's mess. Like I said, it's yours if you want it."

He finished off his drink. "Well, I think I need to get some rack time."

"You'll mess with the Marines. You'll like the food

here," Captain Franks promised.

"Fair enough."

"I saw two men not wearing their hard-hats," Marvin Wilson said to the boss.

"I'll talk to them."

"Aside from that, thanks a lot for your cooperation." He'd made a total of eleven safety recommendations, and the owner of the cement company had adopted every one, hoping for a reduction in his insurance rates. Marvin took off his white hard-hat and wiped the sweat from his brow. It was going to be a hot one. The summer climate was not all that much unlike Moscow, but more humid. At least the winters were milder.

"You know, if they made these things with little holes in them for ventilation, they'd be a lot more comfortable to wear."

"I've said that myself," Captain Yegorov agreed, heading off to his car. Fifteen minutes later he pulled into a Howard Johnson's. The blue Plymouth took a spot along the west side of the building, and as he got out, a patron inside finished off his coffee and left his spot at the counter, along with a quarter tip to thrill the waitress. The restaurant had a double set of doors to save on the air-conditioning bill, and when the two men met there, just the two of them, moving, with the glass of the doors interfering with anyone who might be observing them, the film was passed. Yegorov/Wilson continued inside, and a "legal" KGB major named Ishchenko went his way. Relieved of his burden for the day, Marvin Wilson sat at the counter and ordered orange juice to start. There were so many good things to eat in America.

"I'm eating too much." It was probably true, but it didn't stop Doris from attacking the pile of hotcakes.

Sarah didn't understand the Americans' love for emaciation. "You lost plenty in the last two weeks. It won't hurt you to put a little back," Sarah Rosen told her graduating patient.

Sarah's Buick was parked outside, and today would see

them in Pittsburgh. Sandy had worked on Doris's hair a little more, and made one more trip to get clothes that befitted the day, a beige silk blouse and a burgundy skirt that ended just above the knee. The prodigal son could return home in rags, but the daughter had to arrive with some pride.

"I don't know what to say," Doris Brown told them, standing to collect the dishes.

"You just keep getting better," Sarah replied. They went out to the car, and Doris got in the back. If nothing else, Kelly had taught them caution. Dr. Sarah Rosen headed out quickly, turning north on Loch Raven, getting on the Baltimore Beltway and heading west to Interstate 70. The posted limit on the new highway was seventy miles per hour, and Sarah exceeded it, pushing her heavy Buick northwest toward the Catoctin Mountains, every mile between them and the city an additional safety factor, and by the time they passed Hagerstown she relaxed and started enjoying the ride. What were the chances, after all, of being spotted in a moving car?

It was a surprisingly quiet ride. They'd talked themselves out in the previous few days as Doris had returned to a condition approximating normality. She still needed drug counseling, and seriously needed psychiatric help, but Sarah had already taken care of that with a colleague at the University of Pittsburgh's excellent medical school, a sixtyish woman who knew not to report things to the local police, assured that that part of the matter was already in hand. In the silence of the car Sandy and Sarah could feel the tension build. It was something they'd talked about. Doris was returning to a home and a father she'd left for a life that had nearly become a death. For many months the principal component of her new life would be guilt, part earned, part not. On the whole she was a very lucky young lady, something Doris had yet to grasp. She was, first of all, alive. With her confidence and self-esteem restored she might in two or three years be able to continue her life on a course so normal that no one would ever suspect her past or notice the fading scars. Restored health would change this girl, returning her not only to her father but also to the world of real people.

Perhaps she might even become stronger, Sarah hoped, if the psychiatrist brought her along slowly and carefully. Dr. Michelle Bryant had a stellar reputation, a correct one, she hoped. For Dr. Rosen, still racing west slightly over the legal limit, this was one of the hard parts of medicine. She had to let the patient go with the job not yet complete. Her clinical work with drug abusers had prepared her for it, but those jobs, like this one, were never really finished. It was just that there came a time when you had to let go, hoping and trusting that the patient could do the rest. Perhaps sending your daughter off to be married was like this, Sarah thought. It could have been so much worse in so many ways. Over the phone her father seemed a decent man, and Sarah Rosen didn't need a specialization in psychiatry to know that more than anything else, Doris needed a relationship with an honorable and loving man so that she could, one day, develop another such relationship that would last her lifetime. That was now the job of others, but it didn't stop Sarah from worrying about her patient. Every doctor can be a Jewish mother, and in her case it was difficult to avoid.

The hills were steep in Pittsburgh. Doris directed them along the Monongahela River and up the right street, suddenly tense while Sandy checked the numbers on the houses. And there it was. Sarah pulled the red Buick into a parking place and everyone took a deep breath.

"You okay?" she asked Doris, getting a frightened nod in response.

"He's your father, honey. He loves you."

There was nothing remarkable about Raymond Brown, Sarah saw a moment later. He must have been waiting at the door for hours, and he, too, was nervous, coming down the cracked concrete steps, holding the rail as he did so with a trembling hand. He opened the car door, helping Sandy out with awkward gallantry. Then he reached inside, and though he was trying to be brave and impassive, when his fingers touched Doris's, the man burst into tears. Doris tripped coming out of the car, and her father kept her from falling, and clutched her to his chest.

"Oh, Daddy!"

Sandy O'Toole turned away, not put off by the emotion of the moment, but wanting them to have it alone, and the look she gave Dr. Rosen was its own culminating moment for people of their profession. Both medics bit their lips and examined the other's moist eyes.

"Let's get you inside, baby," Ray Brown said, taking his little girl up the steps, needing to have her in his house and under his protection. The other two women followed without being bidden.

The living room was surprisingly dark. A day-sleeper, Mr. Brown had added dark shades to his home and had forgotten to raise them this day. It was a cluttered room of braided rugs and overstuffed '40s furniture, small mahogany tables with lacelike doilies. There were framed photos everywhere. A dead wife. A dead son. And a lost daughter—four of those. In the dark security of the house, father clutched daughter again.

"Honey," he said, recounting words that he'd been practicing for days. "The things I said, I was wrong, I was so damned wrong!"

"It's okay, Daddy. Thank you for . . . for letting me—"

"Dor, you're my little girl." Nothing more had to be said. That hug lasted over a minute, and then she had to draw back with a giggle.

"I have to go."

"The bathroom's in the same place," her father said, wiping his own eyes. Doris moved off, finding the stairs and going up. Raymond Brown turned his attention to his guests.

"I, uh, I have lunch ready." He paused awkwardly. This wasn't a time for good manners or considered words. "I don't know what I'm supposed to say."

"That's okay." Sarah smiled her benign doctor's smile, the sort that told him that everything was all right, even though it wasn't, really. "But we need to talk. This is Sandy O'Toole, by the way. Sandy's a nurse, and she's more responsible for your daughter's recovery than I am."

"Hi," Sandy said, and handshakes were exchanged all around.

"Doris still needs a lot of help, Mr. Brown," Dr. Rosen said. "She's been through a really terrible time. Can we talk a little bit?"

"Yes, ma'am. Please, sit down. Can I get you anything?" he asked urgently.

"I've set your daughter up with a doctor at Pitt. Her name's Michelle Bryant. She's a psychiatrist—"

"You mean Doris is . . . sick?"

Sarah shook her head. "No, not really. But she's been through a very bad time, and good medical attention will help her recover a lot faster. Do you understand?"

"Doc, I will do *anything* you tell me, okay? I've got all the medical insurance I need through the company."

"Don't worry about that. Michelle will handle this as a matter of professional courtesy. You have to go there with Doris. Now, it is very important that you understand, she's been through a really horrible experience. Terrible things. She's going to get better—she's going to recover fully, but you have to do your part. Michelle can explain all that better than I can. What I'm telling you, Mr. Brown, is this: no matter what awful things you learn, please—"

"Doc," he interrupted softly, "that's my little girl. She's all I have, and I'm not going to . . . foul up and lose her again. I'd rather die."

"Mr. Brown, that is exactly what we needed to hear."

Kelly awoke at one in the morning, local time. The big slug of whiskey he'd downed along the way had blessedly not resulted in a hangover. In fact, he felt unusually rested. The gentle rocking of the ship had soothed his body during the day/night, and lying in the darkness of his officers' accommodations he heard the gentle creaks of steel compressing and expanding as USS *Ogden* turned to port. He made his way to the shower, using cold water to wake himself up. In ten minutes he was dressed and presentable. It was time to explore the ship.

Warships never sleep. Though most work details were synchronized to daylight hours, the unbending watch cycle of the Navy meant that men were always moving about. No less than a hundred of the ship's crew were always at their duty stations, and many others were circulating about the dimly lit passageways on their way to minor maintenance tasks. Others were lounging in the mess spaces, catching up on reading or letter-writing.

He was dressed in striped fatigues. There was a name tag that said *Clark,* but no badges of rank. In the eyes of the crew that made "Mr. Clark" a civilian, and already they were whispering that he was a CIA guy—to the natural accompaniment of James Bond jokes that evaporated on the sight of him. The sailors stood aside in the passageways as he wandered around, greeting him with respectful nods that he acknowledged, bemused to have officer status. Though only the Captain and Executive Officer knew what this mission was all about, the sailors weren't dumb. You didn't send a ship all the way from 'Dago just to support a short platoon of Marines unless there was one hell of a good reason, and the bad-ass bunch that had come aboard looked like the sort to make John Wayne take a respectful step back.

Kelly found the flight deck. Three sailors were walking there, too. *Connie* was still on the horizon, still operating aircraft whose strobes blinked away against the stars. In a few minutes his eyes adapted to the darkness. There were destroyers present, a few thousand yards out. Aloft on *Ogden,* radar antennas turned to the hum of electric motors, but the dominating sound was the continuous broomlike swish of steel hull parting water.

"Jesus, it's pretty," he said, mainly to himself.

Kelly headed back into the superstructure and wandered forward and upwards until he found the Combat Information Center. Captain Franks was there, sleepless, as many captains tended to be.

"Feeling better?" the CO asked.

"Yes, sir." Kelly looked down at the plot, counting the ships in this formation, designated TF-77.1. Lots of radars were up and running, because North Vietnam had an air force and might someday try to do something really dumb.

"Which one's the AGI?"

"This is our Russian friend." Franks tapped the main display. "Doing the same thing we are. The Elint guys we have embarked are having a fine old time," the Captain went on. "Normally they go out on little ships. We're like the *Queen Mary* for them."

"Pretty big," Kelly agreed. "Seems real empty, too."

"Yep. Well, no scuffles to worry about, 'tween my kids and the Marine kids, I mean. You need to look at some charts? I have the whole package under lock in my cabin."

"Sounds like a good idea, Cap'n. Maybe some coffee, too?"

Franks's at-sea cabin was comfortable enough. A steward brought coffee and breakfast. Kelly unfolded the chart, again examining the river he'd be taking up.

"Nice and deep," Franks observed.

"As far as I need it to be," Kelly agreed, munching on some toast. "The objective's right here."

"Better you than me, my friend." Franks pulled a pair of dividers out of his pocket and walked off the distance. "How long you been in this business?"

"Gator navy?" Franks laughed. "Well, they kicked my ass out of Annapolis in two and a half years. I wanted destroyers, so they gave me a first-flight LST. XO as a jaygee, would you believe? First landing was Pelileu. I had my own command for Okinawa. Then Inchon, Wonsan, Lebanon. I've scraped off a lot of paint on a lot of beaches. You think . . . ?" he asked, looking up.

"We're not here to fail, Captain." Kelly had every twist of the river committed to memory, yet he continued to look at the chart, an exact copy of the one he'd studied at Quantico, looking for something new, finding nothing. He continued to stare at it anyway.

"You're going in alone? Long swim, Mr. Clark," Franks observed.

"I'll have some help, and I don't have to swim back, do I?"

"I suppose not. Sure will be nice to get those guys out."

"Yes, sir."

27

Insertion

Phase One of Operation BOXWOOD GREEN began just before dawn. The carrier USS *Constellation* reversed her southerly course at the transmission of a single code word. Two cruisers and six destroyers matched her turn to port, and the handles on nine different sets of engine-room enunciators were pushed down to the FULL setting. All of the various ships' boilers were fully on line already, and as the warships heeled to starboard, they also started accelerating. The maneuver caught the Russian AGI crew by surprise. They'd expected *Connie* to turn the other way, into the wind to commence flight operations, but unknown to them the carrier was standing down this morning and racing northeast. The intelligence-gathering trawler also altered course, increasing power on her own in the vain hope of soon catching up with the carrier task force. That left *Ogden* with two Adams-class missile-destroyer escorts, a sensible precaution after what had so recently happened to USS *Pueblo* off the Korean coast.

Captain Franks watched the Russian ship disappear an hour later. Two more hours passed, just to be sure. At eight that morning a pair of AH-1 Huey Cobras completed their lonely overwater flight from the Marine air base at Danang, landing on *Ogden*'s ample flight deck. The Russians might have wondered about the presence of two attack helicopters on the ship which, their intelligence reports confidently told them, was on an electronic-intelligence mission not unlike their own. Maintenance men already aboard immediately wheeled the "snakes" to a sheltered spot and began a complete maintenance check which would verify the condition of every component. Members of *Ogden*'s crew lit up their own machine shop, and skilled chief machinist's mates offered everything they had to the new arrivals. They were still not briefed on the mission, but it was clear now that something most unusual indeed was under way. The time for questioning was over. Whatever the hell it was, every resource of their ship was made available even before officers troubled themselves to relay that order to their various divisions. Cobra gunships meant action, and every man aboard knew they were a hell of a lot closer to North Vietnam than South. Speculation was running wild, but not that wild. They had a spook team aboard, then Marines, now gunships, and more helicopters would land this afternoon. The Navy medical corpsmen aboard were told to open up the ship's hospital spaces for new arrivals.

"We're going to raid the fuckers," a bosun's mate third observed to his chief.

"Don't spread that one around," the twenty-eight-year veteran growled back.

"Who the fuck am I gonna tell, Boats? Hey, man, I'm for it, okay?"

What is my Navy coming to? the veteran of Leyte Gulf asked himself.

"You, you, you," the junior man called, pointing to some new seamen. "Let's do a FOD walkdown." That started a detailed examination of the flight deck, searching for any object that might get sucked into an engine intake. He turned back to the bosun. "With your permission, Boats."

"Carry on." *College boys,* the senior chief thought, *avoiding the draft.*

"And if I see anybody smoking out here, I'll tear him a

new asshole!" the salty third-class told the new kids.

But the real action was in officers' country.

"A lot of routine stuff," the intelligence officer told his visitors.

"We've been working on their phone systems lately," Podulski explained. "It makes them use radios more."

"Clever," Kelly noted. "Traffic from the objective?"

"Some, and one last night was in Russian."

"That's the indicator we want!" the Admiral said at once. There was only one reason for a Russian to be at SENDER GREEN. "I hope we get that son of a bitch!"

"Sir," Albie promised with a smile, "if he's there, he's got."

Demeanors had changed again. Rested now, and close to the objective, thoughts turned away from abstract dread and back into focus on the hard facts of the matter. Confidence had returned—leavened with caution and concern, but they *had* trained for this. They were now thinking of the things that would go right.

The latest set of photos had come aboard, taken by an RA-5 Vigilante that had screamed low over no less than three SAM sites to cover its interest in a minor and secret place. Kelly lifted the blowups.

"Still people in the towers."

"Guarding something," Albie agreed.

"No changes I see," Kelly went on. "Only one car. No trucks . . . nothing much in the immediate area. Gentlemen, it looks pretty normal to me."

"*Connie* will hold position forty miles off seaward. The medics cross-deck today. The command team arrives tomorrow, and the next day—" Franks looked across the table.

"I go swimming," Kelly said.

The film cassette sat, undeveloped, in a safe in the office of a section chief of the KGB's Washington Station, in turn part of the Soviet Embassy, just a few blocks up 16th Street from the White House. Once the palatial home of George Mortimer Pullman—it had been purchased by the government of Nikolay II—it contained both the second-oldest elevator and the largest espionage operation in the city. The volume of material generated by over a hundred trained field officers meant that not all the information that came in through the door was processed locally, and Captain Yegorov was sufficiently junior that his section chief didn't deem his information worthy of inspection. The cassette finally went into a small manila envelope which was sealed with wax, then found its way into the awkward canvas bag of a diplomatic courier who boarded a flight to Paris, flying first class courtesy of Air France. At Orly, eight hours later, the courier walked to catch an Aeroflot jet to Moscow, which developed into three and a half hours of pleasant conversation with a KGB security officer who was his official escort for this part of the journey. In addition to his official duties, the courier did quite well for himself by purchasing various consumer goods on his regular trips west. The current item of choice was pantyhose, two pairs of which went to the KGB escort.

Upon arriving in Moscow and walking past customs control, the waiting car took him into the city, where the first stop was not the Foreign Ministry, but KGB Headquarters at #2 Dzerzhinskiy Square. More than half the contents of the diplomatic pouch were handed over there, which included most of the flat pantyhose packages. Two more hours allowed the courier to find his family flat, a bottle of vodka, and some needed sleep.

The cassette landed on the desk of a KGB major. The identification chit told him which of his field force had originated it, and the desk officer filled out a form of his own, then called a subordinate to convey it to the photo lab for development. The lab, while large, was also quite busy today, and he'd have to wait a day, perhaps two, his lieutenant told him on returning. The Major nodded. Yegorov was a new though promising field officer, and was starting to develop an agent with interesting legislative connections, but it was expected that it would be a while before CASSIUS turned over anything of great importance.

Raymond Brown left the University of Pittsburgh Medical School struggling not to quiver with anger after their first visit to Dr. Bryant. It had actually gone quite well. Doris had explained many of the events of the preceding three years with a forthright if brittle voice, and throughout he'd held her hand to lend support, both physical and moral. Raymond Brown actually blamed himself for everything that had happened to his daughter. If only he'd controlled his temper that Friday night so long before—but he hadn't. It was done. He couldn't change things. He'd been a different person then. Now he was older and wiser, and so he controlled his rage on the walk to the car. This process was about the future, not the past. The psychiatrist had been very clear about that. He was determined to follow her guidance on everything.

Father and daughter had dinner at a quiet family restaurant—he'd never learned to cook well—and talked about the neighborhood, which of Doris's childhood friends were doing what, in a gentle exercise at catching up on things. Raymond kept his voice low, telling himself to smile a lot and let Doris do most of the talking. Every so often her voice would slow, and the hurt look would reappear. That was his cue to change the subject, to say something nice about her appearance, maybe relate a story from the shop. Most of all he had to be strong and steady for her. Over the ninety minutes of their first session with the doctor, he'd learned that the things he'd feared for three years had indeed come to pass, and somehow he knew that other things as yet unspoken were even worse. He would have to tap on undiscovered resources to keep his anger in, but his little girl needed him to be a—a *rock,* he told himself. A great big rock that she could hold on to, as solid as the hills on which his city was built. She needed other things, too. She needed to rediscover God. The doctor had agreed with him about it, and Ray Brown was going to take care of it, with the help of his pastor, he promised himself, staring into his little girl's eyes.

It was good to be back at work. Sandy was running her floor again, her two-week absence written off by Sam Rosen as a special-duty assignment, which his status as a department chairman guaranteed would pass without question. The post-op patients were the usual collection of major and minor cases. Sandy's team organized and managed their care. Two of her fellow nurses asked a few questions about her absence. She answered merely by saying she'd done a special research project for Dr. Rosen, and that was enough, especially with a full and busy patient load. The other members of the nursing team saw that she was somewhat distracted. There was a distant look in her eyes from time to time, her thoughts elsewhere, dwelling on something. They didn't know what. Perhaps a man, they all hoped, glad to have the team leader back. Sandy was better at handling the surgeons than anyone else on the service, and with Professor Rosen backing her up, it made for a comfortable routine.

"So, you replace Billy and Rick yet?" Morello asked.

"That'll take a while, Eddie," Henry replied. "This is going to mess up our deliveries."

"Aw, crap! You got that too complicated anyway."

"Back off, Eddie," Tony Piaggi said. "Henry has a good routine set up. It's safe and it works—"

"And it's too complicated. Who's gonna take care of Philadelphia now?" Morello demanded.

"We're working on that," Tony answered.

"All you're doing is dropping the stuff off and collecting the money, for Crissake! They're not going to rip anybody off, we're dealing with *business* people, remember?" *Not street niggers,* he had the good sense not to add. That part of the message got across anyway. *No offense, Henry.*

Piaggi refilled the wineglasses. It was a gesture Morello found both patronizing and irritating.

"Look," Morello said, leaning forward. "I helped set up this deal, remember? You might not even be starting with Philly yet if it wasn't for me."

"What are you saying, Eddie?"

"I'll make your damn delivery while Henry gets his shit back together. How hard is it? Shit, you got broads doing it for you!" *Show a little panache,* Morello thought, *show them I have what it takes.* Hell, at least he'd show the guys in Philly, and maybe they could do for him what Tony wouldn't do. Yeah.

"Sure you want to take the chance, Eddie?" Henry asked with an inward smile. This wop was so easy to predict.

"Fuck, yeah."

"Okay," Tony said with a display of being impressed. "You make the call and set it up." Henry was right, Piaggi told himself. It had been Eddie all along, making his own move. How foolish. How easily dealt with.

"Still nothing," Emmet Ryan said, summarizing the Invisible Man Case. "All this evidence—and nothing."

"Only thing that makes sense, Em, is somebody was making a move." Murders didn't just start and stop. There had to be a reason. The reason might be hard, even impossible to discover in many cases, but an organized and careful series of murders was a different story. It came down to two possibilities. One was that someone had launched a series of killings to cover the real target. That target had to be William Grayson, who had dropped from the face of the earth, probably never to return alive, and whose body might someday be discovered—or not. Somebody very angry about something, very careful, and very skilled, and that somebody—the Invisible Man—had taken it to that point and stopped there.

How likely was that? Ryan asked himself. The answer was impossible to evaluate, but somehow the start-stop sequence seemed far too arbitrary. Far too much build-up for a single, seemingly inconsequential target. Whatever Grayson had been, he hadn't been the boss of anyone's organization, and if the murders had been a planned sequence, his death simply was not a logical stopping place. At least, Ryan frowned, that was what his instincts told him. He'd learned to trust those undefined inner feelings, as all cops do. And yet the killings *had* stopped. Three more pushers had died in the last few weeks; he and Douglas had visited every crime scene only to find that they'd been two quite ordinary robberies gone bad, with the third a turf fight that one had lost and another won. The Invisible Man was gone, or at least inactive, and that fact blew away the theory which had to him seemed the most sensible explanation for the killings, leaving only something far less satisfying.

The other possibility did make more sense, after a fashion. Someone had made a move on a drug ring as yet undiscovered by Mark Charon and his squad, eliminating pushers, doubtless encouraging them to switch allegiance to a new supplier. Under that construction, William Grayson had been somewhat more important in the great scheme of things—and perhaps there was another murder or two, as yet undiscovered, which had eliminated the command leadership of this notional ring. One more leap of imagination told Ryan that the ring taken down by the Invisible Man was the same he and Douglas had been chasing after, lo these many months. It all tied together in a very neat theoretical bundle.

But murders rarely did that. Real murder wasn't like a TV cop show. You never figured it all out. When you knew who, you might never really learn why, at least not in a way that really satisfied, and the problem with applying elegant theories to the real-life fact of death was that people didn't fit theories terribly well. Moreover, even if that model for the events of the past month were correct, it had to mean that a highly organized, ruthless, and deadly-efficient individual was now operating a criminal enterprise in Ryan's city, which wasn't exactly good news.

"Tom, I just don't buy it."

"Well, if he's your commando, why did he stop?" Douglas asked.

"Do I remember right? Aren't you the guy who came up with that idea?"

"Yeah, so?"

"So you're not helping your lieutenant very much, Sergeant."

"We have a nice weekend to think about it. Personally, I'm going to cut the grass and catch the double-header on Sunday, and pretend I'm just a regular citizen. Our friend is gone, Em. I don't know where, but he might as well be on the other side of the world. Best guess, somebody from out of town who came here on a job, and he did the job, and now he's gone."

"Wait a minute!" That was a new theory entirely, a contract assassin right out of the movies, and those people simply did not exist. But Douglas just headed out of the office, ending the chance for a discussion that might have demonstrated that each of the detectives was half wrong and half right.

Weapons practice started under the watchful eyes of the command team, plus whatever sailors could find an excuse to come aft. The Marines told themselves that the two newly arrived admirals and the new CIA puke had to be as jet-lagged as they'd been upon arrival, not knowing that Maxwell, Greer, and Ritter had flown a VIP transport most of the way, taking the Pacific in easier hops, with drinks and comfortable seats.

Trash was tossed over the side, with the ship moving at a stately five knots. The Marines perforated the various blocks of wood and paper sacks in an exercise that was more a matter of entertainment for the crew than real training value. Kelly took his turn, controlling his CAR-15 with two- and three-round bursts, and hitting the target. When it was over the men safed their weapons and headed back to their quarters. A chief stopped Kelly as he was reentering the superstructure.

"You're the guy going in alone?"

"You're not supposed to know that."

The chief machinist's mate just chuckled. "Follow me, sir." They headed forward, diverting from the Marine detail and finding themselves in *Ogden*'s impressive machine shop. It had to be impressive, as it was designed not merely to service the ship herself, but also the needs of whatever mobile equipment might be embarked. On one of the worktables, Kelly saw the sea sled he'd be using to head up the river.

"We've had this aboard since San Diego, sir. Our chief electrician and I been playing with it. We've stripped it down, cleaned everything, checked the batteries—they're good ones, by the way. It's got new seals, so it oughta keep the water out. We even tested it in the well deck. The guarantee says five hours. Deacon and I worked on it. It's good for seven," the chief said with quiet pride. "I figured that might come in handy."

"It will, Chief. Thank you."

"Now let's see this gun." Kelly handed it over after a moment's hesitation, and the chief started taking it apart. In fifteen seconds it was field-stripped, but the chief didn't stop there.

"Hold on!" Kelly snapped as the front-sight assembly came off.

"It's too noisy, sir. You *are* going in alone, right?"

"Yes, I am."

The machinist didn't even look up. "You want me to quiet this baby down or do you like to advertise?"

"You can't do that with a rifle."

"Says who? How far you figure you have to shoot?"

"Not more than a hundred yards, probably not that much. Hell, I don't even want to have to use it—"

"'Cuz it's noisy, right?" The chief smiled. "You want to watch me, sir? You're gonna learn something."

The chief walked the barrel over to a drill press. The proper bit was already in place, and under the watchful eyes of Kelly and two petty officers he drilled a series of holes in the forward six inches of the hollow steel rod.

"Now, you can't silence a supersonic bullet all the way, but what you can do is trap all the gas, and that'll surely help."

"Even for a high-power cartridge?"

"Gonzo, you all set up?"

"Yeah, Chief," a second-class named Gonzales replied. The rifle barrel went onto a lathe, which cut a shallow but lengthy series of threads.

"I already got this made up." The chief held up a can-type suppressor, fully three inches in diameter and fourteen inches long. It screwed nicely onto the end of the barrel. A gap in the can allowed reattachment of the front sights, which also locked the suppressor fully in place.

"How long did you work on this?"

"Three days, sir. When I looked over the arms we embarked, it wasn't hard to figure what you might need, and I had the spare time. So I played around some."

"But how the hell did you know I was going—"

"We're exchanging signals with a sub. How hard is all that to figure out?"

"How did you know that?" Kelly demanded, knowing the answer even so.

"Ever know a ship that had secrets? Captain's got a yeoman. Yeomen talk," the machinist explained, completing the reassembly process. "It makes the weapon about six inches longer, I hope you don't mind."

Kelly shouldered the carbine. The balance was actually improved somewhat. He preferred a muzzle-heavy weapon since it made for better control.

"Very nice." He had to try it out, of course. Kelly and the chief headed aft. Along the way the machinist got a discarded wooden box. On the fantail, Kelly slapped a full magazine into the carbine. The chief tossed the wood into the water and stepped back. Kelly shouldered the weapon and squeezed off his first round.

Pop. A moment later came the sound of the bullet hitting the wood, actually somewhat louder than the report of the cartridge. He'd also distinctly heard the working of the bolt mechanism. This chief machinist's mate had done for a high-powered rifle what Kelly himself had done for a .22 pistol. The master craftsman smiled benignly.

"The only hard part's making sure there's enough gas to work the bolt. Try it full auto, sir."

Kelly did that, rippling off six rounds. It still sounded like gunfire, but the actual noise generated was reduced by at least ninety-five percent, and that meant that no one could hear it beyond a couple hundred yards—as opposed to over a thousand for a normal rifle.

"*Good* job, Chief."

"Whatever you're up to, sir, you be careful, hear?" the chief suggested, walking off without another word.

"You bet," Kelly told the water. He hefted the weapon a little more, and emptied the magazine at the wood before it grew too far off. The bullets converted the wooden box into splinters to the accompaniment of small white fountains of seawater.

You're ready, John.

• • •

So was the weather, he learned a few minutes later. Perhaps the world's most sophisticated weather-prediction service operated to support air operations over Vietnam—not that the pilots really appreciated or acknowledged it. The senior meteorologist had come across from *Constellation* with the admirals. He moved his hands across a chart of isobars and the latest satellite photo.

"The showers start tomorrow, and we can expect rain on and off for the next four days. Some heavy stuff. It'll go on until this slow-moving low-pressure area slides up north into China," the chief petty officer told them.

All of the officers were there. The four flight crews assigned to the mission evaluated this news soberly. Flying a helicopter in heavy weather wasn't exactly fun, and no aviator liked the idea of reduced visibility. But falling rain would also muffle the noise of the aircraft, and reduced visibility worked both ways. The main hazard that concerned them was light antiaircraft guns. Those were optically aimed, and anything that hindered the ability of the crews to hear and see their aircraft made for safety.

"Max winds?" a Cobra pilot asked.

"At worst, gusts to thirty-five or forty knots. It will be a little bumpy aloft, sir."

"Our main search radar is pretty good for weather surveillance. We can steer you around the worst of it," Captain Franks offered. The pilots nodded.

"Mr. Clark?" Admiral Greer asked.

"Rain sounds good to me. The only way they can spot me on the inbound leg is the bubbles I leave on the surface of the river. Rain'll break that up. It means I can move in daylight if I have to." Kelly paused, knowing that to go on would merely make the final commitment. "*Skate* ready for me?"

"Whenever we say so," Maxwell answered.

"Then it's 'go-mission' on my end, sir." Kelly could feel his skin go cold. It seemed to contract around his entire body, making him seem smaller somehow. But he'd said it anyway.

Eyes turned to Captain Albie, USMC. A vice admiral, two rear admirals, and an up-and-coming CIA field officer now depended on this young Marine to make the final decision. He would take the main force in. His was the ultimate operational responsibility. It seemed very strange indeed to the young captain that seven stars needed him to say "go," but twenty-five Marines and perhaps twenty others had their lives riding on his judgment. It was his mission to lead, and it had to be exactly right the first time. He looked over at Kelly and smiled.

"Mr. Clark, sir, you be real careful. I think it's time for your swim. This mission is 'go.'"

There was no exultation. In fact, every man around the chart table looked down at the maps, trying to convert the two-dimensional ink on paper into three-dimensional reality. Then the eyes came up, almost simultaneously, and each pair read all the others. Maxwell spoke first to one of the helicopter crews.

"I guess you'd better get your helo warmed up." Maxwell turned. "Captain Franks, would you signal *Skate?*" Two crisp *aye aye, sir*s answered him, and the men stood erect, stepping back from the chart and their decision.

It was a little late for the sober pause, Kelly told himself. He put his fear aside as best he could and started focusing his mind on twenty men. It seemed so strange to risk his life for people he hadn't met, but then, risk of life wasn't supposed to be rational. His father had spent a lifetime doing it, and had lost his life in the successful rescue of two children. *If I can take pride in my dad,* he told himself, *then I can honor him best in this way.*

You can do it, man. You know how. He could feel the determination begin to take over. All the decisions were made. He was committed to action now. Kelly's face took a hard set. Dangers were no longer things to be feared, but to be dealt with. To be overcome.

Maxwell saw it. He'd seen the same thing in ready rooms on carriers, fellow pilots going through the mental preparations necessary before you tossed the dice, and the Admiral remembered how it had been for him, the way the muscles tense, how your eyesight suddenly becomes very sharp. First in, last out, just as his mission had often been, flying his F6F Hellcat to eliminate fighters and then cover the attack aircraft all the way home. *My second son,* was what Dutch suddenly told himself, *as brave as Sonny and just as smart.* But he'd never sent Sonny into danger personally, and Dutch was far older than he'd been at Okinawa. Somehow danger assigned to others was larger and more horrid than that which you assumed for yourself. But it had to be this way, and Maxwell knew that Kelly trusted him, as he in his time had trusted Pete Mitscher. That burden was a heavy one, all the more because he had to see the face he was sending into enemy territory, alone. Kelly caught the look from Maxwell, and his face changed into a knowing grin.

"Don't sweat it, sir." He walked out of the compartment to pack up his gear.

"You know, Dutch"—Admiral Podulski lit up a cigarette—"we could have used that lad, back a few years. I think he would have fit in just fine." It was far more than a "few" years, but Maxwell knew the truth of the statement. They'd been young warriors once, and now was the time of the new generation.

"Cas, I just hope he's careful."

"He will be. Just like we were."

The sea sled was wheeled out to the flight deck by the men who had prepared it. The helicopter was up and running now, its five-bladed rotor turning in the pre-dawn darkness as Kelly walked through the watertight door. He took a deep breath before striding out. He'd never had an audience like this before. Irvin was there, along with three of the other senior Marine NCOs, and Albie, and the flag officers, and the Ritter guy, seeing him off like he was goddamned Miss America or something. But it was the two Navy chiefs who came up to him.

"Batteries are fully charged. Your gear's in the container. It's watertight, so no problems there, sir. The rifle is loaded and chambered in case you need it in a hurry, safety on. New batteries for all the radios, and two sets of spares. If there's anything else to do, I don't know what it is," the chief machinist's mate shouted over the sound of the helicopter engines.

"Sounds good to me!" Kelly shouted back.

"Kick ass, Mr. Clark!"

"See you in a few—and thanks!" Kelly shook hands with the two chiefs, then went to see Captain Franks. For comic effect he stood at attention and saluted. "Permission to leave the ship, sir."

Captain Franks returned it. "Permission granted, sir."

Then Kelly looked at all the rest. *First in, last out.* A half smile and a nod were sufficient gestures for the moment, and at this moment they took their courage from him.

The big Sikorsky rescue chopper lifted off a few feet. A crewman attached the sled to the bottom of the helo, and then it headed aft, out of the burble turbulence of *Ogden's* superstructure, flying off into the darkness without strobes and disappearing in a matter of seconds.

USS *Skate* was an old-fashioned submarine, modified and developed from the first nuclear boat, USS *Nautilus.* Her hull was shaped almost like that of a real ship rather than a whale, which made her relatively slow underwater, but her twin screws made for greater maneuverability, especially in shallow water. For years *Skate* had drawn the duty of inshore intelligence ship, creeping close to the Vietnamese coast and raising whip antennas to snoop on radar and other electronic emissions. She'd also put more than one swimmer on the beach. That included Kelly, several years before, though there was not a single member of that crew still aboard to remember his face. He saw her on the surface, a black shape darker than the water that glistened with the waning quarter moon soon to be hidden by clouds. The helicopter pilot first of all set the sled on *Skate's* foredeck, where the sub's crew secured it in place. Then Kelly and his personal gear were lowered by hoist. A minute later he was in the sub's control room.

"Welcome aboard," Commander Silvio Esteves said, anticipating his first swimmer mission. He was not yet through his first year in command.

"Thank you, sir. How long to the beach?"

"Six hours, more until we scope things out for you. Coffee? Food?"

"How about a bed, sir?"

"Spare bunk in the XO's cabin. We'll see you're not disturbed." Which was a better deal than that accorded the technicians aboard from the National Security Agency.

Kelly headed forward to the last real rest he'd have for the next three days—if things went according to plan. He was asleep before the submarine dived back under the waters of the South China Sea.

"This is interesting," the Major said. He dropped the translation on the desk of his immediate superior, another major, but this one was on the Lieutenant Colonel's list.

"I've heard about this place. GRU is running the operation—trying to, I mean. Our fraternal socialist allies are not cooperating very well. So the Americans know about it at last, eh?"

"Keep reading, Yuriy Petravich," the junior man suggested.

"Indeed!" He looked up. "Who exactly is this CASSIUS fellow?" Yuriy had seen the name before, attached to a large quantity of minor information that had come through various sources within the American left.

"Glazov did the final recruitment only a short time ago." The Major explained on for a minute or so.

"Well, I'll take it to him, then. I'm surprised Georgiy Borissovich isn't running the case personally."

"I think he will now, Yuriy."

They knew something bad was about to happen. North Vietnam had a multitude of search radars arrayed along its coast. Their main purpose was to provide raid warning for incoming strikes from the aircraft carriers the Americans had sailing on what they called Yankee Station, and the North Vietnamese called something else. Frequently the search radars were jammed, but not this badly. This time the jammer was so powerful as to turn the Russian-made screen into a circular mass of pure white. The operators leaned in more closely, looking for particularly bright dots that might denote real targets amid the jamming noise.

"Ship!" a voice called into the operations center. "Ship on the horizon." It was yet another case where the human eye outperformed radar.

If they were dumb enough to put their radars and guns on hilltops, that wasn't his lookout. The master chief firecontrolman was in "Spot 1," the forward fire-director tower that made the most graceful part of his ship's profile. His eyes were glued to the eyepieces of the long-base rangefinders, designed in the late 1930s and still as fine a piece of optical gear as America had ever produced. His hand turned a small wheel, which operated not unlike the focusing mechanism of a camera, bringing a split-image together. His focus was on the radar antenna, whose metal framework, not protected now with camouflage netting, made a nearly perfect aiming reference.

"Mark!"

The firecontrolman 2/c next to him keyed the microphone, reading the numbers off the dial. "Range One-Five-Two-Five-Zero."

In central fire-control, a hundred feet below Spot 1, mechanical computers accepted the data, telling the cruiser's eight guns how much to elevate. What happened next was simple enough. Already loaded, the guns rotated with their turrets, coming up to the proper angle of elevation calculated a generation earlier by scores of young women—now grandmothers—on mechanical calculators. On the computer, the cruiser's speed and course were already set, and since they were firing at a stationary target, it was assigned an identical but reversed velocity vector. In this way the guns would automatically remain locked on target.

"Commence firing," the gunnery officer commanded. A young sailor closed the firing keys, and USS *Newport News* shook with the first salvo of the day.

"Okay, on azimuth, we're short by . . . three hundred . . . " the master chief said quietly, watching the fountains of dirt in the twenty-power rangefinders.

"Up three hundred!" the talker relayed, and the next salvo thundered off fifteen seconds later. He didn't know that the first salvo had inadvertently immolated the command bunker for the radar complex. The second salvo arced through the air. "This one does it," the master chief whispered.

It did. Three of the eight rounds landed within fifty yards of the radar antenna and shredded it.

"On target," he said over his own microphone, waiting for the dust to clear. "Target destroyed."

"Beats an airplane any day," the Captain said, observing from the bridge. He'd been a young gunnery officer on USS *Mississippi* twenty-five years earlier, and had learned shore-bombardment against live targets in the Western Pacific, as had his treasured master chief in Spot 1. This was sure to be the last hurrah for the Navy's real gunships, and the Captain was determined that it would be a loud one.

A moment later some splashes appeared a thousand yards off. These would be from 130mm long guns the NVA used to annoy the Navy. He would engage them before concentrating on triple-A sites.

"Counterbattery!" the skipper called to central fire-control.

"Aye, sir, we're on it." A minute later *Newport News* shifted fire, her rapid-fire guns searching for and finding the six 130s that really should have known better.

It was a diversion, the Captain knew. It had to be. Something was happening somewhere else. He didn't know what, but it had to be something good to allow him and his cruiser on the gunline north of the DMZ. Not that he minded, the CO said to himself, feeling his ship shudder yet again. Thirty seconds later a rapidly expanding orange cloud announced the demise of that gun battery.

"I got secondaries," the CO announced. The bridge crew hooted briefly, then settled back down to work.

"There you are." Captain Mason stepped back from the periscope.

"Pretty close." Kelly needed only one look to see that

Esteves was a cowboy. *Skate* was scraping off barnacles. The periscope was barely above water, the water lapping at the lower half of the lens. "I suppose that'll do."

"Good rainstorm topside," Esteves said.

"'Good' is right." Kelly finished off his coffee, the real Navy sort with salt thrown in. "I'm going to use it."

"Right now?"

"Yes, sir." Kelly nodded curtly. "Unless you plan to go in closer," he added with a challenging grin.

"Unfortunately, we don't have any wheels on the bottom or I might just try." Esteves gestured him forward. "What's this one about? I usually know."

"Sir, I can't say. Tell you this, though: if it works, you'll find out." That would have to do, and Esteves understood.

"Then you better get ready."

As warm as the waters were, Kelly still had to worry about the cold. Eight hours in water with only a small temperature differential could sap the energy from his body like a short-circuited battery. He worked his way into a green-and-black neoprene wet suit, adding double the normal amount of weight belts. Alone in the executive officer's stateroom, he had his last sober pause, beseeching God to help not himself, but the men whom he was trying to rescue. It seemed a strange thing to pray, Kelly thought, after what he'd done so recently yet so far away, and he took the time to ask forgiveness for anything wrong he might have done, still wondering if he had transgressed or not. It was a time for that sort of reflection, but only briefly. He had to look forward now. Maybe God would help him to rescue Colonel Zacharias, but he had to do his part, too. Kelly's last thought before leaving the stateroom was of the photo of a lonely American about to be clubbed from behind by some little NVA fuck. It was time to put an end to that, he told himself, opening the door.

"Escape trunk's this way," Esteves said.

Kelly climbed up the ladder, watched by Esteves and perhaps six or seven other men of *Skate*.

"Make sure we find out," the Captain said, levering the hatch shut himself.

"I'll sure as hell try," Kelly replied, just as the metal fitting locked into place. There was an aqualung waiting for him. The gauge read full, Kelly saw, checking it again himself. He lifted the waterproof phone.

"Clark here. In the trunk, ready to go."

"Sonar reports nothing except heavy rain on the surface. Visual search is negative. *Vaya con dios,* Señor Clark."

"*Gracias,*" Kelly chuckled his reply. He replaced the phone and opened the flooding valve. Water entered the bottom of the compartment, the air pressure changing suddenly in the cramped space.

Kelly checked his watch. It was eight-sixteen when he cracked the hatch and pulled himself to the submerged foredeck of USS *Skate*. He used a light to illuminate the sea sled. It was tied down at four points, but before loosing it he clipped a safety line to his belt. It wouldn't do to have the thing motor off without him. The depth gauge read forty-nine feet. The submarine *was* in dangerously shallow water, and the sooner he got away the sooner her crew would be safe again. Unclipping the sled, he flipped the power switch, and two shrouded propellers started turning slowly. Good. Kelly pulled the knife from his belt and banged it twice on the deck, then adjusted the flippers on the sled and headed off, on a compass course of three-zero-eight.

There was now no turning back, Kelly told himself. But for him there rarely was.

28
First In

It was just as well that he couldn't smell the water. At least not at first. Few things can be as unnerving or disorienting as swimming underwater at night. Fortunately the people who'd designed the sled were divers themselves, and knew that. The sled was slightly longer than Kelly was tall. It was, in fact, a modified torpedo with attachments allowing a man to steer it and control its speed, essentially making it a minisubmarine, though in appearance it was more like an aircraft drawn by a child. The "wings"—actually referred to as flippers—were controlled by hand. There was a depth gauge and an up/down-angle indicator, along with a battery-strength gauge and the vital magnetic compass. The electric motor and batteries had originally been designed to drive the shape through the water at high speed for over ten thousand yards. At lower speeds it could go much farther. In this case, it had five-to-six-hour endurance at five knots—more if the craftsmen aboard *Ogden* were right.

It was strangely like flying over in the C-141. The whirring of the twin props couldn't be heard any great distance, but Kelly was a mere six feet from them; the steady high-speed whine was already making him grimace inside his diving mask. Part of that was all the coffee he'd drunk. He had to stay nervously alert, and he had enough caffeine in him to enliven a corpse. So many things to worry about. There was boat traffic on the river. Whether it was ferrying triple-A ammo from one bank of the river to another or perhaps the Vietnamese version of a teenybopper crossing to see his girlfriend, there were small boats here. Running into one could be lethal in one of several ways, differing only in immediacy, not the final outcome. Perversely, visibility was almost nil, and so Kelly had to assume that he'd have no more than two or three seconds to avoid something. He held to the middle of the channel as best he could. Every thirty minutes he'd slow down and ease his head above the surface for a position fix. There was no activity at all he could see. This country didn't have much in the way of electrical power stations anymore, and without lights by which to read or perhaps power radios, life for the ordinary people was as primitive as it was brutish for their enemies. It was all vaguely sad. Kelly didn't think that the Vietnamese people were any more innately warlike than any other, but there·was a war here, and their behavior, as he had seen, fell short of exemplary. He took his fix and headed down again, careful not to go deeper than ten feet. He'd heard of a case of a diver who'd died while making an overly rapid ascent after being pressurized for a few hours at *fifteen* feet, and he had no desire at all to relive it himself.

Time crept by. Every so often the overhead clouds would thin out, and the light of the quarter moon would give definition to the raindrops on the surface of the river, fragile black circles expanding and disappearing on the ghostly blue screen ten feet above his head. Then the clouds would thicken again, and all he'd see was a dark gray roof, and the sound of the falling drops would compete with the infernal whirring of the props. Another danger was hallucination. Kelly had an active mind, and he was now in an environment devoid of input. Worse, his body was being lulled. He was in a nearly weightless state, rather like it must have been in the womb, and the sheer comfort of the experience was dangerous. His mind might react by dreaming, and he couldn't have that. Kelly developed a routine, sweeping his eyes over the rudimentary instruments, playing little games, like trying to hold his craft exactly level without using the angle indicator—but that proved impossible. What pilots called vertigo happened even more quickly here than in the air, and he found that he couldn't manage it for more than fifteen or twenty seconds before he started to tilt and go deeper. Every so often he'd do a complete roll, just for the difference of it, but mainly he cycled his eyes to the water and back to the instruments, repeating the process again and again, until that also became dangerously monotonous. Only two hours into the passage, Kelly had to tell himself to concentrate—but he couldn't concentrate on just one thing, or even two. Comfortable as he was, every human being within a five-mile radius would wish nothing better than to end his life. Those people lived here, knew the land and the river, knew the sounds and the sights. And theirs was a country at war, where the unusual meant the dangerous, and the enemy. Kelly didn't know if the government paid bounty for dead or live Americans, but something like that must have been operating. People worked harder for a reward, especially one that coincided with patriotism. Kelly wondered how it had all happened. Not that it mattered. These people were enemies. Nothing would soon change that. Certainly not in the next three days, which was as far as the future went for Kelly. If there were to be anything beyond it, he had to pretend that there was not.

His next programmed halt was at a meandering horseshoe bend. Kelly slowed the sled and lifted his head carefully. Noise on the north bank, perhaps three hundred yards. It carried across the water. Male voices speaking in the language whose lilts had somehow always sounded poetic to him—but quickly turned ugly when the content was anger. Like the people, he supposed, listening for perhaps ten seconds. He took the sled back down, watching the course change on the compass as he followed the sweeping bend. What a strange intimacy that had been, if only for a few seconds. What were they talking about?

Politics? Boring subject in a Communist country. Farming, perhaps? Talk of the war? Perhaps, for the voices were subdued. America was killing enough of this country's young men that they had reason to hate us, Kelly thought, and the loss of a son could be little different here than at home. They might talk to others about their pride for the little boy gone off to be a soldier—fried in napalm, dismembered by a machine gun, or turned to vapor by a bomb; the stories had to come back one way or another, even as lies, which amounted to the same thing—but in every case it must have been a child who'd taken a first step and said "daddy" in his native tongue. But some of the same children had grown up to follow PLASTIC FLOWER, and he did not regret killing them. The talk he'd heard sounded human enough, even if he couldn't understand it, and then came the casual question, What made them different?

They are *different, asshole! Let the politicians worry about why.* Asking those kinds of questions distracted him from the fact that there were twenty people like Kelly up the river. He swore in his mind and concentrated again on driving the sled.

Few things distracted Pastor Charles Meyer from the preparation of his weekly sermons. It was perhaps the most important part of his ministry, telling people what they needed to hear in a clear, concise manner, because his flock saw him only once a week unless something went wrong—and when something went badly wrong they needed the foundation of faith already in place if his special attention and counsel were to be truly effective. Meyer had been a minister for thirty years, all of his adult life, and the natural eloquence that was one of his true gifts had been polished by years of practice to the point where he could choose a Scripture passage and develop it into a finely focused lesson in morality. The Reverend Meyer was not a stern man. His message of faith was that of mercy and love. He was quick to smile and to joke, and though his sermons were of necessity a serious business, for salvation was the most serious of human goals, it was his task, he thought, to emphasize God's true nature. Love. Mercy. Charity. Redemption. His entire life, Meyer thought, was dedicated to helping people return after a bout of forgetfulness, to embrace despite rejection. A task as important as that was worth a diversion of his time.

"Welcome back, Doris," Meyer said as he entered Ray Brown's house. A man of medium height, his thick head of gray hair gave him a stately and learned appearance. He took both her hands in his, smiling warmly. "Our prayers are answered."

For all his pleasant and supportive demeanor, this would be an awkward meeting for all three participants. Doris had erred, probably rather badly, he thought. Meyer recognized that, trying not to dwell on it in a punitive way. The really important thing was that the prodigal had returned, and if Jesus had spent His time on earth for any reason, that parable contained it all in just a few verses. All of Christianity in a single story. No matter how grave one's misdeeds might be, there would always be a welcome for those with the courage to return.

Father and daughter sat together on the old blue sofa, with Meyer to their left in an armchair. Three cups of tea were on the low table. Tea was the proper drink for a moment like this.

"I'm surprised how good you look, Doris." He smiled, concealing his desperate desire to put the girl at ease.

"Thank you, Pastor."

"It's been hard, hasn't it?"

Her voice became brittle. "Yes."

"Doris, we all make mistakes. God made us imperfect. You have to accept that, and you have to try to do better all the time. We don't always succeed—but you *did* succeed. You're back now. The bad things are behind you, and with a little work you can leave them behind you forever."

"I will," she said with determination. "I really will. I've seen . . . and done . . . such awful things. . . ."

Meyer was a difficult man to shock. Clergymen were in the profession of listening to stories about the reality of hell, because sinners could not accept forgiveness until they were able to forgive themselves, a task which always required a sympathetic ear and a calm voice of love and reason. But what he heard now did shock him. He tried to freeze his body into place. Above all he tried to remember that what he heard was indeed *behind* his afflicted parishioner as over the course of twenty minutes he learned of things that even he had never dreamed of, things from another time, since his service as a young Army chaplain in Europe. There was a devil in creation, something for which his Faith had prepared him, but the face of Lucifer was not for unprotected eyes of men—certainly not for the eyes of a young girl whom an angry father had mistakenly driven away at a young and vulnerable age.

It only got worse. Prostitution was frightening enough. What damage it did to young women could last a lifetime, and he was grateful to learn that Doris was seeing Dr. Bryant, a wonderfully gifted physician to whom he'd referred two of his flock. For several minutes he shared Doris's pain and shame while her father bravely held her hand, fighting back his own tears.

Then it turned to drugs, first the use of them, then the transfer of them to other, evil men. She was honest through it all, trembling, with tears dripping from her eyes, facing a past to make the strongest of hearts quail. Next came the recounting of sexual abuse, and, finally, the worst part of all.

It became very real to Pastor Meyer. Doris seemed to remember it all—as well she might. It would take all of Dr. Bryant's skills to drive this horror into the past. She told the story in the manner of a motion picture, seemingly leaving nothing out. That was a healthy thing, to put it all in the open in this way. Healthy for Doris. Even healthy for her father. But Charles Meyer necessarily became the recipient of the horror that others were attempting to cast away. Lives had been lost. Innocent lives—victims' lives, two girls not unlike the one before him, murdered in a way worthy of . . . damnation, the pastor told himself in a voice of sadness mixed with rage.

"The kindness you showed to Pam, my dear, that is one of the most courageous things I've ever heard," the pastor said quietly, after it was all over, moved nearly to tears himself. "That was God, Doris. That was God acting through your hands and showing you the goodness of your character."

"You think so?" she asked, bursting then into uncontrolled tears.

He had to move then, and he did, kneeling in front of father and daughter, taking their hands in his. "God visited you, and saved you, Doris. Your father and I prayed for this moment. You've come back, and you won't ever do things like that again." Pastor Meyer couldn't know what he hadn't been told, the things that Doris had deliberately left out. He knew that a Baltimore physician and nurse had restored his parishioner to physical health. He didn't know how Doris had come to that point, and Meyer assumed that she'd escaped, as the girl Pam had almost done. Nor did he know that Dr. Bryant had been warned to keep all of this information close. That might not have mattered in any case. There were other girls still in the control of this Billy person and his friend Rick. As he had dedicated his life to denying souls to Lucifer, so also he had a duty to deny their bodies to him. He had to be careful. A conversation like this one was privileged in the ultimate sense. He would counsel Doris to speak with the police, though he could never force her to do so. But as a citizen, as a man of God, he had to do *something* to help those other girls. Exactly what, he wasn't sure. He'd ask his son about that, a young sergeant with the Pittsburgh city police force.

There. Kelly's head was above the water only enough to expose his eyes. He reached up with his hands to pull the rubber hood off his head, allowing his ears better access to the sounds of the area. There was all manner of noise. Insects, the flapping of bats, and loudest of all the rain that was sprinkling lightly at the moment. To his north was darkness that his acclimated eyes began to break into shapes. There was "his" hilltop, a mile away past another, lower hill. He knew from the aerial photographs that there were no habitations between where he was and where he had to go. There was a road only a hundred yards away, and at the moment it was totally vacant. So quiet it was that any mechanical sound would surely have reached him. There was none. It was time.

Kelly steered the sled close to the bank. He selected a place with overhanging trees for the additional concealment. His first physical contact with the soil of North Vietnam had an electric feel to it. That soon passed. Kelly stripped off the wet suit, stuffing it in the waterproof container on the now surfaced sled. He quickly donned his camouflage fatigues. The jungle boots had soles copied from the NVA's in case anyone spotted tracks that looked out of the ordinary. Next he did his camouflage makeup, dark green on forehead and cheekbones and jaw, with lighter colors under his eyes and in the hollow of his cheeks. Shouldering his gear, he flipped the power switch on the sled. It motored off towards the middle of the river, its flotation chambers vented now, sinking it to the bottom. Kelly made an effort not to watch it hum away. It was bad luck, he remembered, to watch the helicopter fly away from the LZ. It showed lack of purpose. Kelly turned to the land, listening again for traffic on the road. Hearing none, he climbed the bank and crossed the gravel path immediately, disappearing at once into the thick foliage, moving slowly and deliberately up the first hill.

People cut wood here for cooking fires. That was disturbing—might people be out cutting tomorrow?—but helpful, too, as it allowed him to make his way more quickly and more quietly. He walked in a tense crouch, careful where he placed his feet, his eyes and ears sweeping around constantly as he moved. His carbine was in his hands. His thumb felt the selector switch, in the "safe" position. A round was chambered. He'd already checked that. The Navy chief had prepared the weapon properly and would understand that Kelly had needed to verify it visually, but if there was any one thing Kelly did not wish to do, it was to fire a single round from his CAR-15.

Climbing the first hill took half an hour. Kelly stopped there, finding a clear spot from which to look and listen. It was approaching three in the morning, local time. The only people awake were those who had to be, and they wouldn't like it very much. The human body was linked to a day/night cycle, and at this time of the morning bodily functions ebbed.

Nothing.

Kelly moved on, going down the hill. At the bottom was a small stream that fed into the river. He took the opportunity to fill one of his canteens, dropping in a purification tablet as he did so. Again he listened, since sound followed nicely down valleys and over streams. Still nothing. He looked up at "his" hill, a gray mass under the cloudy sky. The rain was picking up as Kelly started his climb. Fewer trees had been cut here, which made sense, as the road didn't come all that close. This area was a little steep for proper farming, and with good bottomland so close by, he felt he could depend on a minimum of visitors. Probably that's why SENDER GREEN had been placed here, he told himself. There was nothing around to attract serious attention. That would cut both ways.

Halfway up, his eyes got their first look at the prison camp. It was an open space amidst forest. He didn't know if the area had started off as a meadow or if the trees had been cut for one reason or another. A branch of the river road came straight in from the other side of "his" hill. Kelly saw a flare of light from one of the guard towers—someone with a cigarette, no doubt. Didn't people ever learn? It could take hours to get your night vision really working, and just that much could ruin it. Kelly looked away, concentrating on the remainder of his climb, moving around bushes, seeking open spots where his uniform wouldn't rub against branches and leaves, making deadly noise. It almost came as a surprise when he reached the top.

He sat down for a moment, making himself totally still, looking and listening some more before he began his examination of the camp. He found a very good spot, perhaps twenty feet below the crest. The far side of the hill was steep, and a casual climber would make noise. In this place he wouldn't be skylined to an observer below. His place was within the shroud of bushes to break up whatever outline he might present. This was his place on his hill. He reached in his vest and pulled out one of his radios.

"SNAKE calling CRICKET, over."

"SNAKE, this is CRICKET, reading you five by five," one of the communicators replied inside the commo van parked on *Ogden*'s deck.

"In place, beginning surveillance. Over."

"Copy that. Out." He looked up at Admiral Maxwell. Phase Two of BOXWOOD GREEN was now complete.

Phase Three began at once. Kelly took the marine 7 x 50 binoculars from their case and began examining the camp. There were guards in all four towers, two of them smoking. That had to mean their officer was asleep. The NVA had adamantine discipline and punished transgressions harshly—death was not an uncommon price for even a minor offense. There was a single automobile present, parked as expected near the building which had to house the officers at this compound. There were no lights at all, and no sounds. Kelly rubbed the rain from his eyes and checked the focus on both eyepieces before he commenced his survey. In a strange way it was like being back at Quantico Marine Base. The similarity of angle and perspective was uncanny. There seemed to be some minor differences in the buildings, but it could be the dark causing that, or perhaps a slight change in color. No, he realized. It was the courtyard, parade ground—whatever he was supposed to call it. There was no grass there. The surface was flat and bare, just the red clay of this region. The different color and lack of texture gave the buildings a subtly different setting. Different roofing materials, but the same slope. It *was* like being at Quantico, and with luck the battle would be as successful as the drills. Kelly settled in, allowing himself a sip of water. It had the distilled tastelessness of what they made on the submarine, clean and foreign, as he was in this alien place.

At quarter to four he saw some lights in the barracks, flickering yellow, like candles. Guard change, perhaps. The two soldiers in the tower nearest him were stretching, chatting to each other casually. Kelly could barely make out the murmur of conversation but not the words or cadence. They were bored. This would be that sort of duty. They might grouse about it, but not that badly.

The alternative would be a stroll down the Ho Chi Minh Trail through Laos, and, patriotic though they might have been, only a fool would relish that thought. Here they kept watch on twenty or so men, locked in individual cells, perhaps chained to walls or otherwise hobbled, with as much chance of escaping the camp as Kelly had of walking on water—and even if they succeeded in that most impossible of feats, what would they be? Six-foot-tall white men in a land of small yellow people, none of whom would lift a hand on their behalf. Alcatraz Federal Prison could be no more secure than this. So the guards had three squares a day and quiet boring duty that would dull their senses.

Good news, Kelly told himself. *Stay bored, guys.*

The barracks doors opened. Eight men came out. No NCO in charge of the detail. That was interesting, surprisingly casual for the NVA. They broke into pairs, each heading for a tower. In each case the relief crew climbed up before the duty crew came down, which was to be expected. A few remarks were exchanged, and the soldiers going off duty climbed down. Two lit up before heading back in the barracks, speaking to each other at the entrance. It was all in all a comfortable and grossly normal routine conducted by men who'd been doing the same thing for months.

Wait. Two of them limped, Kelly realized. *Veterans.* That was good news and bad news. People with combat experience were simply different. The time would come for action, and they'd react well, probably. Even without recent training, instincts would kick in, and they'd try to fight back effectively even without leadership—but as veterans they'd also be softer, disdainful of their duty, however cushy it might be, lacking the awkward eagerness of fresh young troops. As with all swords, that one cut in two directions. In either case, the plan of attack allowed for it. Kill people without warning, and their training was a moot point, which made it a hell of a lot safer.

Anyway, that was one wrong assumption. Troops on POW-guard duty were usually second-raters. These at least were combat troops, even if they had sustained wounds that relegated them to backup service. Any other mistakes?

Kelly wondered. He couldn't see any yet.

His first substantive radio message was a single code group which he tapped out using Morse Code.

"EASY SPOT, sir." The communications technicians tapped out an acknowledgment.

"Good news?" Captain Franks asked.

"It means everything is as expected, no major news," Admiral Podulski replied. Maxwell was catching a nap. Cas wouldn't sleep until the mission was concluded. "Our friend Clark even delivered it exactly on time."

Colonel Glazov didn't like working on weekends any more than his Western counterparts, even less so when it was because his administrative assistant had made a mistake and set this report on the wrong pile. At least the boy had admitted it, and called his boss at home to report his error. He couldn't very well do much more than chide the oversight, at the same time he had to praise the lad's honesty and sense of duty. He drove his personal car into Moscow from his dacha, found a parking place in the rear of the building, and submitted himself to the tiresome security-clearance procedures before taking the elevator up. Then came the necessity of unlocking his office and sending for the right documents from Central Files, which also took longer than usual on this weekend day. All in all, just getting to the point at which he could examine the damned thing required two hours from the unwelcome phone call that had started the process. The Colonel signed for the documents and watched the file clerk depart.

"Bloody hell," the Colonel said in English, finally alone in his fourth-floor office. CASSIUS had a friend in the White House National Security Office? No wonder some of his information had been so good—good enough to force Georgiy Borissovich to fly to London to consummate the recruitment. The senior KGB officer now had to chide himself. CASSIUS had kept that bit of information up his sleeve, perhaps in the knowledge that he'd rattle his ultimate control officer. The case officer, Captain Yegorov, had taken it in stride—as well he might—and described the first-contact meeting in exquisite detail.

"BOXWOOD GREEN," Glazov said. Just a code name for the operation, selected for no particular reason, as the Americans did. The next question was whether or not to forward the data to the Vietnamese. That would be a political decision, and one to be made quickly. The Colonel lifted the phone and dialed his most immediate superior, who was also at home and instantly in a foul humor.

Sunrise was an equivocal thing. The color of the clouds changed from the gray of slate to the gray of smoke as somewhere aloft the sun made its presence known, though that would not be the case here until the low-pressure area had passed north into China—or so the weather briefing had declared. Kelly checked his watch, making his mental notes at every point. The guard force was forty-four men, plus four officers—and maybe a cook or two. All except the eight on tower duty formed up just after dawn for calisthenics. Many had trouble doing their morning exercises, and one of the officers, a senior lieutenant from his shoulder boards, hobbled around with a cane—probably a bad arm, too, from the way he used it. *What got you?* Kelly wondered. A crippled and foul-tempered NCO walked the lines of soldiers, swearing at them in a way that showed long months of practice. Through his binoculars Kelly watched the expressions that trailed behind the little bastard's back. It gave the NVA guards a human quality that he didn't welcome.

Morning exercise lasted half an hour. When it ended, the soldiers headed off for morning chow, falling out in a decidedly casual and unmilitary way. The tower guards spent most of their time looking in, as expected, most often leaning on their elbows. Their weapons were probably not chambered, a sensible safety precaution that would count against them either this night or the next, depending on weather. Kelly made another check of his surroundings. It would not do for him to fix too closely on the objective. He wouldn't move about now, not even in the gray daylight that had come with the morning, but he could turn his head to look and listen. Catching the patterns of bird calls, getting used to it so that a change would register at once. He had a green cloth across the muzzle of his weapon, a floppy hat to break up the outline of his head within and behind the bush, and facial camouflage paint, all of which conspired to make him invisible, part of this warm, humid environment that—*I mean, why do people fight for the damned place?* he wondered. Already he could feel bugs on his skin. The worst of them were put off by the unscented repellent he'd spread around. But not all, and the feel of things crawling on him combined with the knowledge that he couldn't make any rapid moves. There were no small risks in a place like this. He'd forgotten so much. Training was good and valuable, but it never quite made it all the way to full preparation. There was no substitute for the actual dangers involved, the slightly increased heart rate that could tire you out even when you lay still. You never quite forgot it, but you never really remembered it all, either.

Food, nourishment, strength. He reached into a pocket, moving his hand slowly and withdrawing a pair of food bars. Nothing he'd eat by choice in any other place, but it was vital now. He tore off the plastic wrappers with his teeth and chewed the bars up slowly. The strength they imparted to his body was probably as much psychological as real, but both factors had their uses, as his body had to deal with both fatigue and stress.

At eight, the guard cycle changed again. Those relieved from the towers went in for chow. Two men took posts at the gate, bored before they got there, looking out at the road for traffic that would probably never come to this backwater camp. Some work details formed, and the jobs they performed were as clearly useless to Kelly as to those who carried them out in a stoic, unhurried way.

Colonel Grishanov arose just after eight. He'd been up late the night before, and though he'd planned to arise earlier, he'd just learned to his displeasure that his mechanical alarm clock had finally given up the ghost, corroded to death by the miserable climate. Eight-ten, he saw, looking at his aviator's watch. *Damn.* No morning run. It would soon be too hot for that, and besides, it looked like it would be raining all day. He brewed his own pot of tea over a small army-type cook stove. No morning paper to read—again. No news of the football scores. No review of a new ballet production. Nothing at all in this miserable place to distract him. Important as his duty was, he needed distraction as much as any man did. Not even decent plumbing. He was used to all of that, but it didn't help. God, to be able to go home, to hear people speaking his native language again, to be in a cultured place where there was something to talk about. Grishanov frowned in the shaving mirror. Months more to go, and he was grumbling like a private soldier, a damned recruit. He was supposed to know better.

His uniform needed pressing. The humidity here attacked the cotton fibers, making his usually crisp blouse look like pajamas, and he was already on his third set of shoes, Grishanov thought, sipping now at his tea and going over notes from the previous night's interrogations. All work and no play . . . and he was already late. He tried to light a cigarette, but the humidity had also rendered his matches useless. Well, he had the cookstove for that. Where had he left his lighter . . . ?

There were compensations, if you could call them that. The Vietnamese soldiers treated him with respect, almost awe—except for the camp commander, Major Vinh, worthless bastard that he was. Courtesy to a fellow socialist ally demanded that Grishanov be given an orderly, in this case a small, ignorant peasant boy with only one eye who was able to make the bed and carry out the slops bowl every morning. The Colonel was able to walk out in the knowledge that his room would be somewhat tidy when he returned. And he had his work. Important, professionally stimulating. But he would have killed for his morning *Sovietskiy Sport*.

"Good morning, Ivan," Kelly whispered to himself. He didn't even need the binoculars for that. The size was so different—the man was over six feet—and the uniform far neater than that worn by the NVA. The glasses showed

Kelly the man's face, pale with a narrowed-eye expression to contemplate the day. He made a gesture to a small private who'd been waiting outside the door of the officers' quarters. *Orderly,* Kelly thought. A visiting Russian colonel would like his comforts, wouldn't he? Definitely a pilot from the wings over the blouse pocket, plenty of ribbons. *Only one?* Kelly wondered. *Only one Russian officer to help torture the prisoners? Odd when you think about it.* But that meant only one extraneous person to have to kill, and for all his lack of political sophistication, Kelly knew that killing Russians wouldn't do anyone much good. He watched the Russian walk across the parade ground. Then the senior visible Vietnamese officer, a major, went towards him. Another limper, Kelly saw. The little Major saluted the tall Colonel.

"Good morning, Comrade Colonel."

"Good morning, Major Vinh." *Little bastard can't even learn to salute properly. Perhaps he simply cannot make a proper gesture to his betters.* "The rations for the prisoners?"

"They will have to be satisfied with what they have," the smaller man replied in badly accented and phrased Russian.

"Major, it is important that you understand me," Grishanov said, stepping closer so that he could look more sharply down at the Vietnamese. "I need the information they have. I cannot get it if they are too sick to speak."

"Tovarich, we have problems enough feeding our own people. You ask us to waste good food on murderers?" The Vietnamese soldier responded quietly, using a tone that both conveyed his contempt for the foreigner and at the same time seemed respectful to his soldiers, who would not have understood exactly what this was all about. After all, they thought that the Russians were fast allies.

"Your people do not have what my country needs, Major. And if *my* country gets what she needs, then *your* country might get more of what *it* needs."

"I have my orders. If you are experiencing difficulty in questioning the Americans, then I am prepared to help." *Arrogant dog.* It was a suffix that didn't need to be spoken, and Vinh knew how to stick his needle into a sensitive place.

"Thank you, Major. That will not be necessary." Grishanov made a salute himself, even sloppier than that given him by this annoying little man. It would be good to watch him die, the Russian thought, walking off to the prison block. His first "appointment" with the day was with an American naval aviator who was just about ready to crack.

Casual enough, Kelly thought from several hundred yards away. *Those two must get along fairly well.* His scrutiny of the camp was relaxed now. His greatest fear was that the guard force might send out security patrols, as a line unit in hostile country would surely have done. But they were not in hostile territory, and this was not really a line unit. His next radio message to *Ogden* confirmed that everything was within acceptable risk limits.

Sergeant Peter Meyer smoked. His father didn't approve, but accepted his son's weakness so long as he did it outside, as they were now, on the back porch of the parsonage after Sunday evening dinner.

"It's Doris Brown, right?" Peter asked. At twenty-six he was one of his department's youngest sergeants, and like most of the current class of police officers a Vietnam veteran. He was within six credit hours of completing his night-school degree and was considering making an application to the FBI Academy. Word that the wayward girl had returned was now circulating through the neighborhood. "I remember her. She had a reputation as a hot number a few years back."

"Peter, you know I can't say. This is a pastoral matter. I will counsel the person to speak to you when the time is right, but—"

"Pop, I understand the law on that, okay? You have to understand, we're talking two homicides here. Two dead people, plus the drug business." He flipped the butt of his Salem into the grass. "That's pretty heavy stuff, Pop."

"Even worse than that," his father reported more quietly still. "They don't just kill the girls. Torture, sexual abuse. It's pretty horrible. The person is seeing a doctor about it. I know I have to do something, but I can't—"

"Yeah, I know you can't. Okay, I can call the people in Baltimore and fill them in on what you've told me. I really ought to hold off until we can give them something they can really use, but, well, like you say, we have to do something. I'll call down first thing tomorrow morning."

"Will it put her—the person—in danger?" the Reverend Meyer asked, vexed with himself for the slip.

"Shouldn't," Peter judged. "If she's gotten herself away—I mean, they ought not to know where she is, and if they did, they might have got her already."

"How can people do things like that?"

Peter lit up another. His father was just too good a man to understand. Not that he did either. "Pop, I see it all the time, and I have trouble believing it, too. The important part's getting the bastards."

"Yes, I suppose it is."

The KGB *rezident* in Hanoi had General-Major rank, and his job was mainly that of spying on his country's putative allies. What were their real objectives? Was their supposed estrangement with China real or a sham? Would they cooperate with the Soviet Union when and if the war came to a successful conclusion? Might they allow the Soviet Navy use of a base after the Americans left? Was their political determination really as solid as they said it was? Those were all questions whose answers he thought he had, but orders from Moscow and his own skepticism about everyone and everything compelled him to keep asking. He employed agents within the CPVN, the country's Foreign Ministry, and elsewhere, Vietnamese whose willingness to give information to an ally would probably have meant death—though to be politic about it, the deaths would be disguised "suicides" or "accidents" because it was in neither country's interest to have a formal breach. Lip-service was even more important in a socialist country than a capitalist one, the General knew, because symbols were far easier to produce than reality.

The enciphered dispatch on his desk was interesting, all the more so since it did not give him direct guidance on what to do about it. How like the Moscow bureaucrats! Always quick to meddle in matters that he was able to handle himself, now they didn't know what to do—but they were afraid to do nothing. So they stuck him with it.

He knew about the camp, of course. Though he ran a military-intelligence operation, he had people in the office of the attaché who reported to him as well. The KGB watched everyone, after all; that was their job. Colonel Grishanov was using irregular methods, but he was reporting good results, better than the General's own office got from these little savages. Now the Colonel had come up with the boldest idea of all. Instead of letting the Vietnamese kill the prisoners in due course, bring them home to Mother Russia. It was brilliant in its way, and the KGB general was trying to decide if he'd endorse the idea to Moscow, where this decision would surely be kicked up to ministerial, or perhaps even Politburo level. On the whole, he thought that the idea had real merit . . . and that decided matters.

As entertaining as it might be for the Americans to rescue their people with this BOXWOOD GREEN operation, as much as it might show the Vietnamese again that they should cooperate more closely with the Soviet Union, that they really were a *client* state, it would also mean that the knowledge locked in those American minds would be lost to his country, and it was knowledge they must have.

How long, he wondered, could he let this one wait? The Americans moved quickly, but not that quickly. The mission had been approved at White House level only a week or so earlier. All bureaucracies were alike, after all. In Moscow it would take forever. Operation KINGPIN had gone on forever, else it would have succeeded. Only the good luck of a low-level agent in the Southern United States had allowed them to warn Hanoi, and then almost too late—but now they had real forewarning.

Politics. You just couldn't separate that from intelligence operations. Before, they'd all but accused him of delaying matters—he shouldn't give them that excuse again. Even client states need to be treated as comrades. The General lifted his phone to make a luncheon date. He'd bring his contact over to the embassy, just to be sure that he had some decent food to eat.

29
Last Out

There was a vicarious exhilaration in watching them. The twenty-five Marines worked out, finishing with a single-file run that looped around the helicopters parked on the deck. Sailors looked on quietly. The word was out now. The sea sled had been seen by too many, and like professional intelligence officers, sailors at their mess tables assembled the few facts and garnished them with speculation. The Marines were going into the North. After what, nobody knew, but everyone wondered. Maybe to trash a missile site and bring back some important piece of hardware. Maybe to take down a bridge, but most likely the target was human. The Vietnamese party bosses, perhaps.

"Prisoners," a bosun's mate third-class said, finishing his hamburger, called a "slider" in the Navy. "It's gotta be," he added, motioning his head to the newly arrived medical corpsmen who ate at their own isolated table. "Six corpsmen, four doctors, awful lot of talent, guys. What d'ya suppose they're here for?"

"Jesus," another sailor observed, sipping at his milk. "You're right, man."

"Feather in our cap if it comes off," noted another.

"Dirty weather tonight," a quartermaster put in. "The fleet-weather chief was smiling about it—and I seen him puke his guts out last night. I guess he can't handle anything smaller'n a carrier." USS *Ogden* did have an odd ride, which resulted from her configuration, and running broadside to the gusting westerly winds had only worsened it. It was always entertaining to see a chief petty officer lose his lunch—dinner in this case—and a man was unlikely to be *happy* about weather conditions that made him ill. There had to be a reason for it. The conclusion was obvious, and the sort of thing to make a security officer despair.

"Jesus, I hope they make it."

"Let's get the flight deck fodded again," the junior bosun suggested. Heads nodded at once. A work gang was quickly assembled. Within an hour there would be not so much as a matchstick on the black no-skid surface.

"Good bunch of kids, Captain," Dutch Maxwell observed, watching the walkdown from the starboard wing of the bridge. Every so often a man would bend down and pick up something, a "foreign object" that might destroy an engine, a result called *FOD,* for "foreign-object damage." Whatever might go wrong tonight, the men were promising with their actions, it wouldn't be the fault of their ship.

"Lots of college kids," Franks replied, proudly watching his men. "Sometimes I think the deck division's as smart as my wardroom." Which was an entirely forgivable hyperbole. He wanted to say something else, the same thing that everyone was thinking: *What do you suppose the chances are?* He didn't voice the thought. It would be the worst kind of bad luck. Even thinking it loudly might harm the mission, but hard as he tried he couldn't stop his mind from forming the words.

In their quarters, the Marines were assembled around a sand-table model of the objective. They'd already gone over the mission once and were doing so again. The process would be repeated once more before lunch, and many times after it, as a whole group and as individual teams.

Each man could see everything with his eyes closed, thinking back to the training site at Quantico, reliving the live-fire exercises.

"Captain Albie, sir?" A yeoman came into the compartment. He handed over a clipboard. "Message from Mr. Snake."

The Captain of Marines grinned. "Thanks, sailor. You read it?"

The yeoman actually blushed. "Beg pardon, sir. Yes, I did. Everything's cool." He hesitated for the moment before adding a dispatch of his own. "Sir, my department says good luck. Kick some ass, sir."

"You know, skipper," Sergeant Irvin said as the yeoman left the space, "I may never be able to punch out a swabbie again."

Albie read the dispatch. "People, our friend is in place. He counts forty-four guards, four officers, one Russian. Normal duty routine, nothing unusual is happening there." The young captain looked up. "That's it, Marines. We're going in tonight."

One of the younger Marines reached in his pocket and pulled out a large rubber band. He broke it, marked two eyes on it with his pen, and dropped it atop what they now called Snake Hill. "That dude," he said to his teammates, "is one cool motherfucker."

"Y'all remember now," Irvin warned loudly. "You fire-support guys remember, he's gonna be pounding down that hill soon as we show up. It wouldn't do to shoot his ass."

"No prob', Gunny," the fire-team leader said.

"Marines, let's get some chow. I want you people to rest up this afternoon. Eat your veggies. We want our eyes to work in the dark. Weapons stripped and cleaned for inspection at seventeen-hun'rd," Albie told them. "Y'all know what this is all about. Let's stay real cool and we'll get it done." It was his time to meet again with the chopper crews for a final look at the insertion and extraction plans.

"Aye aye, sir," Irvin said for the men.

"Hello, Robin."

"Hi, Kolya," Zacharias said weakly.

"I'm still working on better food."

"Would be nice," the American acknowledged.

"Try this." Grishanov handed over some black bread his wife had sent him. The climate had already started to put mold on it, which Kolya had trimmed off with a knife. The American wolfed it down anyway. A sip from the Russian's flask helped.

"I'll turn you into a Russian," the Soviet Air Force colonel said with an unguarded chuckle. "Vodka and good bread go together. I would like to show you my country." Just to plant the seed of the idea, in a friendly way, as one man talks to another.

"I have a family, Kolya. God willing—"

"Yes, Robin, God willing." Or North Vietnam willing, or the Soviet Union willing. Or someone. Somehow he'd save this man, and the others. So many were friends now. He knew so much about them, their marriages, good and bad, their children, their hopes and dreams. These Americans were so strange, so open. "Also, God willing, if the Chinese decide to bomb Moscow, I have a plan now to stop them." He unfolded the map and set it on the floor. It was the result of all his talks with his American colleague, everything he had learned and analyzed formulated on a single sheet of paper. Grishanov was quite proud of it, not the least because it was the clear presentation of a highly sophisticated operational concept.

Zacharias ran his fingers over it, reading the notations in English, which looked incongruous on a map whose legend was in Cyrillic. He smiled his approval. A bright guy, Kolya, a good student in his way. The way he layered his assets, the way he had his aircraft patrolling back rather than forward. He understood defense in depth now. SAM traps at the ends of the most likely mountain passes, positioned for maximum surprise. Kolya was thinking like a bomber pilot now instead of a fighter jock. That was the first step in understanding how it was done. If every Russian PVO commander understood how to do this, then SAC would have one miserable time . . .

Dear God.

Robin's hands stopped moving.

This wasn't about the ChiComs at all.

Zacharias looked up, and his face revealed his thought even before he found the strength to speak.

"How many Badgers do the Chinese have?"

"Now? Twenty-five. They are trying to build more."

"You can expand on everything I've told you."

"We'll have to, as they build up their force, Robin. I've told you that," Grishanov said quickly and quietly, but it was too late, he saw, at least in one respect.

"I've told you everything," the American said, looking down at the map. Then his eyes closed and his shoulders shook. Grishanov embraced him to ease the pain he saw.

"Robin, you've told me how to protect the children of my country. I have not lied to you. My father *did* leave his university to fight the Germans. I *did* have to evacuate Moscow as a child. I *did* lose friends that winter in the snow—little boys and little girls, Robin, children who froze to death. It *did* happen. I *did* see it."

"And I did betray my country," Zacharias whispered. The realization had come with the speed and violence of a falling bomb. How could he have been so blind, so stupid? Robin leaned back, feeling a sudden pain in his chest, and in that moment he prayed it was a heart attack, for the first time in his life wishing for death. But it wasn't. It was just a contraction of his stomach and the release of a large quantity of acid, just the perfect thing, really, to eat away at his stomach as his mind ate away the defenses of his soul. He'd broken faith with his country and his God. He was damned.

"My friend—"

"You *used* me!" Robin hissed, trying to pull away.

"Robin, you must listen to me." Grishanov wouldn't let go. "I love my country, Robin, as you love yours. I have sworn an oath to defend her. I have never lied to you about that, and now it is time for you to learn other things." Robin had to understand. Kolya had to make it clear to Zacharias, as Robin had made so many things clear to Kolya.

"Like what?"

"Robin, you are a dead man. The Vietnamese have reported you dead to your country. You will never be allowed to return home. That is why you are not in the prison—Hoa Lo, the Hilton, your people call it, yes?" It seared Kolya's soul when Robin looked at him, the accusation there was almost more than he could bear. When he spoke again, his voice was the one doing the pleading.

"What you are thinking is wrong. I have *begged* my superiors to let me save your life. I swear this on the lives of my children: *I will not let you die.* You cannot go back to America. I will make for you a new home. You will be able to *fly* again, Robin! You will have a new life. I can do no more than that. If I could restore you to your Ellen and your children, I would do it. I am not a monster, Robin, I am a man, like you. I have a country, like you. I have a family, like you. In the name of your God, man, put yourself in my place. What would you have done in my place? What would you feel in my place?" There was no reply beyond a sob of shame and despair.

"Would you have me let them torture you? I can do that. Six men in this camp have died, did you know that? Six men died before I came here. *I put a stop to it!* Only one has died since my arrival—only one, and I wept for him, Robin, did you know that! I would gladly kill Major Vinh, the little fascist. *I have saved you!* I've done everything in my power, and I have begged for more. I give you my own food, Robin, things that my Marina sends to me!"

"And I've told you how to kill American pilots—"

"Only if they attack my country can I hurt them. Only if they try to kill my people, Robin! Only then! Do you wish them to kill my family?"

"It's not like that!"

"Yes, it is. Don't you see? This is not a game, Robin. We are in the business of death, you and I, and to save lives one must also take them."

Perhaps he'd see it in time, Grishanov hoped. He was a bright man, a rational man. Once he had time to examine the facts, he would see that life was better than death, and perhaps they could again be friends. For the moment, Kolya told himself, I have saved the man's life. *Even if the American curses me for that, he will have to breathe air to speak his curse.* Colonel Grishanov would bear that burden with pride. He'd gotten his information and saved a life in the process, as was entirely proper for an air-defense pilot of PVO Strany who'd sworn his life's real oath as a frightened and disoriented boy on his way from Moscow to Gorkiy.

The Russian came out of the prison block in time for dinner, Kelly saw. He had a notebook in his hands, doubtless full of the information he'd sweated out of the prisoners.

"We're going to get your sorry red ass," Kelly whispered to himself. "They're gonna put three willie-petes through that window, pal, and cook you up for dinner—along with all your fucking notes. Yeah."

He could feel it now. It was, again, the private pleasure of knowing what would be, the godlike satisfaction of seeing the future. He took a sip from his canteen. He couldn't afford to dehydrate. Patience came hard now. Within his sight was a building with twenty lonely, frightened, and badly hurt Americans, and though he'd never met any of them, and though he only knew one by name, his was a worthy quest. For the rest, he tried to find the Latin from his high school: *Morituri non cognant,* perhaps. Those who are about to die—just don't know. Which was just fine with Kelly.

"Homicide."

"Hi, I'm trying to get Lieutenant Frank Allen."

"You got him," Allen replied. He'd been at his desk just five minutes this Monday morning. "Who's this?"

"Sergeant Pete Meyer, Pittsburgh," the voice replied. "Captain Dooley referred me to you, sir."

"I haven't talked to Mike in a while. Is he still a Pirates fan?"

"Every night, Lieutenant. I try to catch some of the games myself."

"You want a line on the Series, Sarge?" Allen asked with a grin. Cop fellowship.

"Bucs in five. Roberto's real tough this year." Clemente was having a career year.

"Oh, yeah? Well, so are Brooks and Frank." The Robinsons weren't doing so badly either. "What can I do for you?"

"Lieutenant, I have some information for you. Two homicides, both victims female, in their late teens, early twenties."

"Back up, please." Allen got a clean sheet of paper. "Who's your source?"

"I can't reveal that yet. It's privileged. I'm working on changing that, but it might take a while. Can I go on?"

"Very well. Names of victims?"

"The recent one was named Pamela Madden—very recent, only a few weeks ago."

Lieutenant Allen's eyes went wide. "Jesus—the fountain murder. And the other one?"

"Her name was Helen, sometime last fall. Both murders were ugly, Lieutenant, torture and sexual abuse."

Allen hunched forward with the phone very close to his ear. "You telling me you have a witness to both killings?"

"That is correct, sir, I believe we do. I got two likely perps for you, too. Two white males, one named Billy and the other named Rick. No descriptions, but I can work on that, too."

"Okay, they're not my cases. It's being handled downtown—Lieutenant Ryan and Sergeant Douglas. I know both names—both victims, I mean. These are high-profile cases, Sarge. How solid is your information?"

"I believe it to be very solid. I have one possible indicator for you. Victim number two, Pamela Madden—her hair was brushed out after she was killed."

In every major criminal case, several important pieces of evidence were always left out of press accounts in order to screen out the usual collection of nuts who called in to confess to something—anything that struck their twisted fancies. This thing with the hair was sufficiently protected that even Lieutenant Allen didn't know about it.

"What else do you have?"

"The murders were drug-related. Both girls were mules."

"Bingo!" Allan exclaimed quietly. "Is your source in jail or what?"

"I'm pushing the edge here, but—okay, I'll level with you. My dad's a preacher. He's counseling the girl. Lieutenant, this is really off-the-record stuff, okay?"

"I understand. What do you want me to do?"

"Could you please forward the info to the investigating officers? They can contact me through the station." Sergeant Meyer gave over his number. "I'm a watch supervisor here, and I have to roll out now to deliver a lecture at the academy. I'll be back about four."

"Very well, Sergeant. I'll pass that along. Thanks a lot for the input. You'll be hearing from Em and Tom. Depend on it." *Jesus, we'll give Pittsburgh the fuckin' Series to bag these bastards.* Allen switched buttons on his phone.

"Hey, Frank," Lieutenant Ryan said. When he set his coffee cup down, it appeared like slow-motion. That stopped when he picked up a pen. "Keep talking. I'm writing this down."

Sergeant Douglas was late this morning because of an accident on I-83. He came in with his usual coffee and danish to see his boss scribbling furiously.

"Brushed out the hair? He said that?" Ryan asked. Douglas leaned across the desk, and the look in Ryan's eyes was like that of a hunter who just heard the first rustle in the leaves. "Okay, what names did he—" The detective's hand balled into a fist. A long breath. "Okay, Frank, where is this guy? Thanks. 'Bye."

"Break?"

"Pittsburgh," Ryan said.

"Huh?"

"Call from a police sergeant in Pittsburgh, a possible witness in the murders of Pamela Madden and Helen Waters."

"No shit?"

"This is the one who brushed her hair, Tom. And guess what other names came along with it?"

"Richard Farmer and William Grayson?"

"Rick and Billy. Close enough? Possible mule for a drug ring. Wait . . . " Ryan leaned back, staring at the yellowed ceiling. "There was a girl there when Farmer was killed—we think there was," he corrected himself. "It's the connection, Tom. Pamela Madden, Helen Waters, Farmer, Grayson, they're all related . . . and that means—"

"The pushers, too. All connected somehow. What connects them, Em? We know they were all—probably all—in the drug business."

"Two different MOs, Tom. The girls were slaughtered like—no, you don't even do that to cattle. All the rest, though, all of them were taken down by the Invisible Man. Man on a mission! That's what Farber said, a man on a mission."

"Revenge," Douglas said, pacing Ryan's analysis on his own. "If one of those girls was close to me—Jesus, Em, who could blame him?"

There was only one person connected with either murder who'd been close with a victim, and he was known to the police department, wasn't he? Ryan grabbed his phone and called back to Lieutenant Allen.

"Frank, what was the name of that guy who worked the Gooding case, the Navy guy?"

"Kelly, John Kelly, he found the gun off Fort McHenry, then downtown contracted him to train our divers, remember? Oh! Pamela Madden! Jesus!" Allen exclaimed when the connection became clear.

"Tell me about him, Frank."

"Hell of a nice guy. Quiet, kinda sad—lost his wife, auto accident or something."

"Veteran, right?"

"Frogman, underwater demolitions. That's how he earns his living, blowing things up. Underwater stuff, like."

"Keep going."

"Physically he's pretty tough, takes care of himself." Allen paused. "I saw him dive, there's some marks on him, scars, I mean. He's seen combat and caught some fire. I got his address and all if you want."

"I have it in my case file, Frank. Thanks, buddy." Ryan hung up. "He's our guy. He's the Invisible Man."

"Kelly?"

"I have to be in court this morning—damn it!" Ryan swore.

"Nice to see you again," Dr. Farber said. Monday was an easy day for him. He'd seen his last patient of the day and was heading out for after-lunch tennis with his sons. The cops had barely caught him heading out of his office.

"What do you know about UDT guys?" Ryan asked, walking out into the corridor with him.

"Frogmen, you mean? Navy?"

"That's right. Tough, are they?"

Farber grinned around his pipe. "They're the first guys on the beach, ahead of the Marines. What do you think?" He paused. Something clicked in his mind. "There's something even better now."

"What do you mean?" the detective lieutenant asked.

"Well, I still do a little work for the Pentagon. Hopkins does a lot of things for the government. Applied Physics Lab, lots of special things. You know my background." He paused. "Sometimes I do psychological testing, consulting—what combat does to people. This is classified material, right? There's a new special-operations group. It's a spin-off of UDT. They call them SEALs now, for Sea Air Land—they're commandos, real serious folks, and their existence is not widely known. Not just tough. Smart. They're trained to think, to plan ahead. Not just muscle. Brains, too."

"Tattoo," Douglas said, remembering. "He has a tattoo of a seal on his arm."

"Doc, what if one of these SEAL guys had a girl who was brutally murdered?" It was the most obvious of questions, but he had to ask it.

"That's the mission you were looking for," Farber said, heading out the door, unwilling to reveal anything else, even for a murder investigation.

"That's our boy. Except for one thing," Ryan said quietly to the closed door.

"Yeah. No evidence. Just one hell of a motive."

• • •

Nightfall. It had been a dreary day for everyone at SENDER GREEN except for Kelly. The parade ground was mush, with fetid puddles, large and small. The soldiers had spent most of the day trying to keep dry. Those in the towers had adjusted their position to the shifting winds. Weather like this did things to people. Most humans didn't like being wet. It made them irritable and dull of mind, all the more so if their duty was also boring, as it was here. In North Vietnam, weather like this meant fewer air attacks, yet another reason for the men down below to relax. The increasing heat of the day had energized the clouds, adding moisture to them which the clouds just as quickly gave back to the ground.

What a shitty day, all the guards would be saying to one another over their dinner. All would nod and concentrate on their meals, looking down, not up, looking inward, not outward. The woods would be damp. It was far quieter to walk on wet leaves than dry ones. No dry twigs to snap. The humid air would muffle sound, not transmit it. It was, in a word, perfect.

Kelly took the opportunity of the darkness to move around some, stiff from the inactivity. He sat up under his bush, brushing off his skin and eating more of his ration concentrates. He drained down a full canteen, then stretched his arms and legs. He could see the LZ, and had already selected his path to it, hoping the Marines wouldn't be trigger-happy when he ran down towards them. At twenty-one hundred he made his final radio transmission.

Light Green, the technician wrote on his pad. *Activity Normal.*

"That's it. That's the last thing we need." Maxwell looked at the others. Everyone nodded.

"Operation BOXWOOD GREEN, Phase Four, commences at twenty-two hundred. Captain Franks, make signal to *Newport News.*"

"Aye aye, sir."

On *Ogden,* flight crews dressed in their fire-protective suits, then walked aft to preflight their aircraft. They found sailors wiping all the windows. In the troop spaces, the Marines were donning their striped utilities. Weapons were clean. Magazines were full with fresh ammo just taken from airtight containers. The individual grunts paired off, each man applying camouflage paint to his counterpart. No smiles or joking now. They were as serious as actors on opening night, and the delicacy of the makeup work gave a strange counterpoint to the nature of the evening's performance. Except for one of their number.

"Easy on the eye shadow, sir," Irvin told a somewhat jumpy Captain Albie, who had the usual commander's jitters and needed a sergeant to steady him down.

In the squadron ready room aboard USS *Constellation,* a diminutive and young squadron commander named Joshua Painter led the briefing. He had eight F-4 Phantoms loaded for bear.

"We're covering a special operation tonight. Our targets are SAM sites south of Haiphong," he went on, not knowing what it was all about, hoping that it was worth the risk to the fifteen officers who would fly with him tonight, and that was just his squadron. Ten A-6 Intruders were also flying Iron Hand, and most of the rest of *Connie's* air wing would trail their coats up the coast, throwing as much electronic noise into the air as they could. He hoped it was all as important as Admiral Podulski had said. Playing games with SAM sites wasn't exactly fun.

Newport News was twenty-five miles off the coast now, approaching a point that would put her exactly between *Ogden* and the beach. Her radars were off, and the shore stations probably didn't know quite where she was. After the last few days the NVA were getting a little more circumspect about using their coastal surveillance systems. The Captain was sitting in his bridge chair. He checked his watch and opened a sealed manila envelope, reading quickly through the action orders he'd had in his safe for two weeks.

"Hmm," he said to himself. Then: "Mr. Shoeman, have engineering bring boilers one and four fully on line. I want full power available as soon as possible. We're doing some more surfing tonight. My compliments to the XO, gunnery officer, and his chiefs. I want them in my at-sea cabin at once."

"Aye, sir." The officer of the deck made the necessary notifications. With all four of her boilers on line, *Newport News* could make thirty-four knots, the quicker to close the beach, and the quicker to depart from it.

"Surf City, here we come!" the petty officer at the wheel sang out loud as soon as the Captain was off the bridge. It was the official ship's joke—because the Captain liked it—actually made up several months before by a seaman first-class. It meant going inshore, right into the surf, for some shooting. "Goin' to Surf City, where it's two-to-one!"

"Mark your head, Baker," the OOD called to end the chorus.

"Steady on one-eight-five, Mr. Shoeman." His body moved to the beat. *Surf City, here we come!*

"Gentlemen, in case you're wondering what we've done to deserve the fun of the past few days, this is it," the Captain said in his cabin just off the bridge. He explained on for several minutes. On his desk was a map of the coastal area, with every triple-A battery marked from data on aerial and satellite photographs. His gunnery department looked things over. There were plenty of hilltops for good radar references.

"Oh, yeah!" the master chief firecontrolman breathed. "Sir, everything? Five-inchers, too?"

The skipper nodded. "Chief Skelley, if we bring any ammo back to Subic, I'm going to be very disappointed with you."

"Sir, I propose we use number-three five-inch mount for star shell and shoot visually as much as we can."

It was an exercise in geometry, really. The gunnery experts—that included the commanding officer—leaned across the map and decided quickly how it would be done. They were already briefed on the mission; the only change was that they had expected to do it in daylight.

"There won't be anybody left alive to fire on those helos, sir."

The growler phone on the CO's desk rang. He grabbed it. "Captain speaking."

"All four boilers are now on line, sir. Full-speed bell is thirty, flank is thirty-three."

"Nice to know the ChEng is all awake. Very well. Sound General Quarters." He hung up the phone as the ship's gong started sounding. "Gentlemen, we have some Marines to protect," he said confidently. His cruiser's gunnery department was as fine as *Mississippi*'s had ever been. Two minutes later he was back on the bridge.

"Mr. Shoeman, I have the conn."

"Captain has the conn," the OOD agreed.

"Right-standard rudder, come to new course two-six-five."

"Right-standard rudder, aye, come to new course two-six-five, aye." Petty Officer Sam Baker rotated the wheel. "Sir, my rudder is right-standard."

"Very well," the Captain acknowledged, adding, "Surf City, here we come!"

"Aye aye, sir!" the helmsman hooted back. The skipper was really with it for an old fart.

It was the time for nerves now. *What could go wrong?* Kelly asked himself atop his hill. Lots of things. The helicopters might collide in midair. They might come right over an unknown flak site and be blotted from the sky. Some little widget or seal could let go, crashing them to the ground. What if the local National Guard was having a training exercise tonight? Something was always left to chance. He'd seen missions go wrong for any number of dumb and unpredictable reasons. But not tonight, he promised himself. Not with all this preparation. The helo crews had trained intensively for three weeks, as had the Marines. The birds had been lovingly maintained. The sailors on *Ogden* had invented helpful things to do. You could never eliminate risk, but preparation and training could attenuate it. Kelly made sure his weapon was in proper shape and stayed in a tight sitting position. This wasn't sitting in a corner house in west Baltimore. This was real. This would enable him to put it all behind. His attempt to save Pam had ended in failure due to his error, but perhaps it had had a purpose after all. He'd made no mistakes for this mission. Nobody had. He wasn't rescuing one person. He was rescuing twenty. He checked the illuminated dial of his watch. The sweep hand was moving so slowly now. Kelly closed his eyes, hoping that when he opened them it would move more quickly. It didn't. He knew better. The former Chief of SEALs commanded himself to take a deep breath and continue the mission. For him that meant laying the carbine across his lap and concentrating on his binoculars. His reconnaissance had to continue right to the moment the first M-79 grenades were fired at the guard towers. The Marines were counting on him.

Well, maybe this would show the guys from Philly how important he was. Henry's operation breaks down and I handle things. *Eddie Morello is important,* he thought, stoking the fires of his own ego as he drove up Route 40 towards Aberdeen.

Idiot can't run his own operation, can't get dependable people. I told Tony he was too smart for his own good, too clever, not really a serious businessman—Oh, no, he's serious. He's more serious than you are, Eddie. Henry is going be the first nigger to get "made." You watch. Tony is going to do it. Can't do it for you. Your own cousin can't do it for you, after you connected him with Henry. Goddamned deal wouldn't be made except for me. I made the deal but I can't get made.

"Fuck!" he snarled at a red light. *Somebody starts taking Henry's operation apart and they ask* me *to check it out. Like Henry can't figure things out himself. Probably can't, not as smart as he thinks he is. So then what—he gets between me and Tony.*

That was it, wasn't it? Eddie thought. *Henry* wanted *to separate me from* Piaggi—*just like he got them to take Angelo out. Angelo was his first connection. Angelo introduced him to me . . . I introduced him to Tony . . . Tony and I handle the connection with Philly and New York . . . Angelo and me were a pair of connections . . . Angelo was the weak one . . . and Angelo gets whacked . . .*

Tony and I are another pair of connections . . .

He only needs one, doesn't he? Just one connection to the rest of the outfit.

Separating me from Tony . . .

Fuck.

Morello fished in his pocket for a cigarette and punched the lighter on his Cadillac convertible. The top was down. Eddie liked the sun and the wind. It was almost like being out on his fishing boat. It also gave him fine visibility. That it made him somewhat easier to spot and trail hadn't occurred to him. Next to him, on the floor, was a leather attaché case. Inside that were six kilos of pure stuff. Philadelphia, they'd told him, was real short, and would handle the cutting themselves. Big cash deal. The identical case that was now southbound would be filled with nothing smaller than twenties. Two guys. Nothing to worry about. They were pros, and this was a long-term business relationship. He didn't have to worry about a rip, but he had his snubby anyway, concealed under his loose shirt, just at his belt buckle, the most useful, most uncomfortable place.

He had to think this one through, Morello told himself urgently. He might just have it all figured out. Henry was manipulating them. *Henry* was *manipulating* the outfit. A jig was trying to outthink them.

And succeeding. Probably he whacked his own people. The fuck liked to shit all over women—especially white ones. That figured, Morello thought. They were all like that. Thought he was pretty smart, probably. Well, he *was* pretty smart. But not smart enough. Not anymore. It wouldn't be hard to explain all of this to Tony. Eddie was sure of that. Make the transfer and drive back. Dinner with Tony. Be calm and reasonable. Tony likes that. Like he went to Harvard or something. Like a damned lawyer. Then we work on Henry, and we take over his operation. It was business. His people would play. They weren't in it because they loved him. They were in it for the money. Everybody was. And then he and Tony could take the operation over, and *then* Eddie Morello would be a made man.

Yeah. He had it all figured out now. Morello checked the time. He was right on as he pulled into the half-empty parking lot of a diner. The old-fashioned kind, made from a railroad car—the Pennsylvania Railroad was close by. He remembered his first meal out of the house with his father, in a place just like this, watching the trains go past. The memory made him smile as he finished the cigarette and flipped it onto the blacktop.

The other car pulled in. It was a blue Oldsmobile, as he'd been led to expect. The two guys got out. One carried an attaché case and walked towards him. Eddie didn't know him, but he was well-dressed, respectable, like a businessman should be, in a nice tan suit. Like a lawyer. Morello smiled to himself, not looking too obviously in his direction while the backup man stayed at the car, watching, just to be on the safe side. Yeah, serious people. And soon they'd know that Eddie Morello was a serious man, too, he thought, with his hand in his lap, six inches from his hidden revolver.

"Got the stuff?"

"Got the money?" Morello asked in return.

"You made a mistake, Eddie," the man said without warning as he opened the briefcase.

"What do you mean?" Morello asked, suddenly alert, about ten seconds and a lifetime too late.

"I mean, it's goodbye, Eddie," he added quietly.

The look in the eyes said it all. Morello immediately went for his weapon, but it only helped the other man.

"Police, freeze!" the man shouted just before the first round burst through the opened top of the case.

Eddie got his gun out, just, and managed to fire one round into the floor of his car, but the cop was only three feet away and couldn't possibly miss. The backup officer was already running in, surprised that Lieutenant Charon hadn't been able to get the drop on the guy. As he watched, the attaché case fell aside and the detective extended his arm, nearly placing his service revolver on the man's chest and firing straight into his heart.

It was all so clear to Morello now, but only for a second or two. Henry had done it all. He'd made himself, that was it. And Morello knew that his only purpose in life had been to get Henry and Tony together. It didn't seem like much, not now.

"Backup!" Charon screamed over the dying man. He reached down to seize Eddie's revolver. Within a minute two State Police cars screeched into the parking lot.

"Damned fool," Charon told his partner five minutes later, shaking as he did so, as men do after killing. "He just went for the gun—like I didn't have the drop on him."

"I saw it all," the junior detective said, thinking that he had.

"Well, it's just what you said, sir," the State Police sergeant said. He opened the case from the floor of the Olds. It was filled with bags of heroin. "Some bust."

"Yeah," Charon growled. "Except dead the dumb fuck can't tell anybody anything." Which was exactly true. Remarkable, he thought, succeeding in his struggle not to smile at the mad humor of the moment. He'd just committed the perfect murder, under the eyes of other police officers. Now Henry's organization was safe.

Almost time now. The guard had changed. *Last time for that.* The rain continued to fall steadily. *Good.* The soldiers in the towers were huddling to stay dry. The dreary day had bored them even more than normal, and bored men were less alert. All the lights were out now. Not even candles in the barracks. Kelly made a slow, careful sweep with his binoculars. There was a human shape in the window of the officers' quarters, a man looking out at the weather—the Russian, wasn't it? *Oh, so that's your bedroom? Great: The first shot from grenadier number three—Corporal Mendez, wasn't it?—is programmed for that opening. Fried Russian.*

Let's get this one on. I need a shower. God, you suppose they have any more of that Jack Daniel's left? Regs were regs, but some things were special.

The tension was building. It wasn't the danger factor. Kelly deemed himself to be in no danger at all. The scary part had been the insertion. Now it was up to the airedales, then the Marines. His part was almost done, Kelly thought.

"Commence firing," the Captain ordered.

Newport News had switched her radars on only a few moments earlier. The navigator was in central fire-control, helping the gunnery department to plot the cruiser's exact position by radar fixes on known landmarks. That was being overly careful, but tonight's mission called for it. Now navigation and fire-control radars were helping everyone compute their position to a whisker.

The first rounds off were from the portside five-inch mount. The sharp bark of noise from the twin 5″/38s was very hard on the ears, but along with it came something oddly beautiful. With each shot the guns generated a ring of yellow fire. It was some empirical peculiarity of the weapon that did it. Like a yellow snake chasing its tail, undulating for its few milliseconds of life. Then it vanished. Six thousand yards downrange, the first pair of star shells ignited, and it was the same metallic yellow that had a few seconds earlier decorated the gun mount. The wet, green landscape of North Vietnam turned orange under the light.

"Looks like a fifty-seven-mike-mike mount. I can see the crew, even." The rangefinder in Spot-1 was already trained into the proper bearing. The light just made it easier. Master Chief Skelley dialed in the range with remarkable delicacy. It was transmitted at once to "central." Ten seconds after that, eight guns thundered. Another fifteen, and the triple-A site vanished in a cloud of dust and fire.

"On target with the first salvo. Target Alfa is destroyed." The master chief took his command from below to shift bearings to the next. Like the Captain he would soon retire. Maybe they could open a gun store.

It was like distant thunder, but not right somehow. The surprising part was the absence of reaction below. Through the binoculars he could see heads turn. Maybe some remarks were exchanged. Nothing more than that. It was a country at war, after all, and unpleasant noises were normal here, especially the kind that sounded like distant thunder. Clearly too far away to be a matter of concern. You couldn't even see any flashes through the weather. Kelly had expected an officer or two to come out and look around. He would have done that in their place—probably. But they didn't.

Ninety minutes and counting.

The Marines were lightly loaded as they filed aft. Quite a few sailors were there to watch them. Albie and Irvin counted them off as they headed out onto the flight deck, directing them to their choppers.

The last sailors in line were Maxwell and Podulski. Both were wearing their oldest and most disreputable khakis, shirts and pants they'd worn in command at sea, things associated with good memories and good luck. Even admirals were superstitious. For the first time the Marines saw that the pale Admiral—that's how they thought of him—had the Medal of Honor. The ribbon caught many glances, and quite a few nods of respect that his tense face acknowledged.

"All ready, Captain?" Maxwell asked.

"Yes, sir," Albie replied calmly over his nervousness. Showtime. "See you in about three hours."

"Good hunting." Maxwell stood ramrod-straight and saluted the younger man.

"They look pretty impressive," Ritter said. He, too, was wearing khakis, just to fit in with the ship's wardroom. "Oh, Jesus, I hope this works."

"Yeah," James Greer breathed as the ship turned to align herself with the wind. Deck crewmen with lighted wands went to both troop carriers to guide their takeoffs, and then, one by one, the big Sikorskys lifted off, steadying themselves in the burble and turning west towards land and the mission. "It's in their hands now."

"Good kids, James," Podulski said.

"That Clark guy is pretty impressive, too. Smart," Ritter observed. "What's he do in real life?"

"I gather he's sort of at odds at the moment. Why?"

"We always have room for a guy who can think on his feet. The boy's smart," Ritter repeated as all headed back to CIC. On the flight deck, the Cobra crews were doing their final preflight checks. They'd get off in forty-five minutes.

"Snake, this is Cricket. Time check is nominal. Acknowledge."

"Yes!" Kelly said aloud—but not too loud. He tapped three long dashes on his radio, getting two back. *Ogden* had just announced that the mission was now running and copied his acknowledgment. "Two hours to freedom, guys," he told the prisoners in the camp below. That the event would be less liberating for the other people in the camp was not a matter of grave concern.

Kelly ate his last ration bar, sliding all the wrappers and trash into the thigh pockets of his fatigues. He moved from his hiding place. It was dark now, and he could afford to. Reaching back in, he tried to erase the marks of his presence. A mission like this might be tried again, after all, and why let the other side know anything about how it had happened? The tension finally reached the point that he had to urinate. It was almost funny, and made him feel like a little kid, though he'd drunk half a gallon of water that day.

Thirty minutes' flying time to the first LZ, thirty more for the approach. When they crest the far hill, I go into live contact with them to control the final approach.

Let's get it on.

"Shifting fire right. Target Hotel in sight," Skelley reported. "Range . . . nine-two-five-zero." The guns thundered once more. One of the hundred-millimeter gun mounts was actually firing at them, now. The crew had watched *Newport News* immolate the rest of their antiaircraft battalion and, unable to desert their guns, they were trying, at least, to fire back and wound the monster that was hovering off their coastline.

"There's the helos," the XO said at his post in CIC. The blips on the main radar display crossed the coast right over where Targets Alfa and Bravo had been. He lifted the phone.

"Captain here."

"XO here, sir. The helos are feet-dry, going right up the corridor we made them."

"Very well. Prepare to stand-down the fire mission. We'll be HIFR-ing those helos in thirty minutes. Keep a very sharp eye on that radar, X."

"Aye, sir."

"Jesus," a radar operator observed. "What's going on here?"

"First we shoot their ass," his neighbor opined, "then we invade their ass."

Only minutes now until the Marines were on the ground. The rain remained steady though the wind had died down.

Kelly was in the open now. It was safe. He wasn't skylined. There was ample flora behind him. All of his clothing and exposed skin was colored to blend in. His eyes were sweeping everywhere, searching for danger, for something unusual, finding nothing. It was muddy as hell. The wet and the red clay of these miserable hills was part of him now, through the fabric of his uniform, into every pore.

Ten minutes out from the LZ. The distant thunder from the coast continued sporadically, and its very continuance made it less of a danger. It sounded even more like thunder now, and only Kelly knew that it was the eight-inch guns of a ship of war. He sat back, resting his elbows on his knees, sweeping the glasses over the camp. Still no lights. Still no movement. Death was racing towards them and they didn't know. He was concentrating so much with his eyes that he almost neglected his ears.

It was hard to pick it out through the rain: a distant rumble, low and tenuous, but it didn't fade. It grew in intensity. Kelly lifted his head from the eyepieces, turning, his mouth open, trying to figure it out.

Motors.

Truck motors. Well, okay, there was a road not too far away—no, the main road is too far . . . other direction.

A supply truck maybe. Delivering food and mail.

More than one.

Kelly moved to the top of the hill, leaning against a tree, looking down to where this spur of a dirt road reached out to the one that traced the north bank of the river. Movement. He put the glasses on it.

Truck . . . two . . . three . . . four . . . oh, my God . . .

They had lights on—just slits, the headlights taped over. That meant military trucks. The lights of the second gave some illumination to the first. People in the back, lined on both sides.

Soldiers.

Wait, Johnnie-boy, don't panic. Take your time . . . maybe . . .

They turned around the base of Snake Hill. A guard in one of the towers shouted something. The call was relayed. Lights came on in the officers' quarters. Somebody came out, probably the Major, not dressed, shouting a question.

The first truck stopped at the gate. A man got out and roared for somebody to open it. The other truck stopped behind it. Soldiers dismounted. Kelly counted . . . ten . . . twenty . . . thirty . . . more . . . but it wasn't the number. It was what they started to do.

He had to look away. What more would fate take away from him? Why not just take his life and be done with it? But it wasn't just his life that fate was interested in. It never was. He was responsible, as always, for more than that. Kelly reached for his radio and flipped it on.

"CRICKET, this is SNAKE, over."

Nothing.

"CRICKET, this is SNAKE, over."

"What gives?" Podulski asked.

Maxwell took the microphone. "SNAKE, this is CRICKET ACTUAL, what is your message, over?"

"Abort abort abort—acknowledge," was what they all heard.

"Say again SNAKE. Say again."

"Abort the mission," Kelly said, too loudly for his own safety. "Abort abort abort. Acknowledge immediately."

It took a few seconds. "We copy your order to abort. Acknowledged. Mission aborted. Stand by."

"Roger, standing by."

"What is it?" Major Vinh asked.

"We have information that the Americans may try to raid your camp," the Captain replied, looking back at his men. They were deploying skillfully, half heading for trees, the other half taking positions inside the perimeter, digging in as soon as they picked their places. "Comrade Major, I am ordered to take charge of the defense until more units arrive. You are ordered to take your Russian guest to Hanoi for safety."

"But—"

"The orders come from General Giap himself, Comrade Major." Which settled matters very quickly indeed. Vinh went back to his quarters to dress. His camp sergeant went to awaken his driver.

Kelly could do nothing more than watch. Forty-five, maybe more. It was hard to count them as they moved. Teams digging machine gun pits. Patrol elements in the woods. That was an immediate danger to him, but he waited even so. He had to be sure that he'd done the right thing, that he hadn't panicked, hadn't been a sudden coward.

Twenty-five against fifty, with surprise and a plan, not hard. Twenty-five against a hundred, without surprise . . . hopeless. He'd done the right thing. There was no reason to add twenty-five more bodies to the ledger sheet that they kept in Washington. His conscience didn't have room for that kind of mistake or for those kinds of lives.

"Helos coming back, sir, same way they went in," the radar operator told the XO.

"Too fast," the XO said.

"Goddamn it, Dutch! Now what—"

"The mission's aborted, Cas," Maxwell said, staring down at the chart table.

"But *why?*"

"Because Mr. Clark said so," Ritter answered. "He's the eyes. He makes the call. You don't need anybody to tell you that, Admiral. We still have a man in there, gentlemen. Let's not forget that."

"We have *twenty* men in there."

"That's true, sir, but only one of them is coming out tonight." *And then only if we're lucky.*

Maxwell looked up to Captain Franks. "Let's move in towards the beach, fast as you can."

"Yes, sir."

"Hanoi? Why?"

"Because we have orders." Vinh was looking over the dispatch the Captain had delivered. "Well, the Americans wanted to come here, eh? I hope they do. This will be no Song Tay for them!"

The idea of an infantry action didn't exactly thrill Colonel Grishanov, and a trip to Hanoi, even an unannounced one, also meant a trip to the embassy. "Let me pack, Major."

"Be quick about it!" the little man snapped back, wondering if his trip to Hanoi was for some manner of transgression.

It could be worse. Grishanov now had all his notes together and slid them into a backpack. All of his work, now that Vinh had so kindly released it back to him. He'd drop it off with General Rokossovskiy, and with that in official hands, he could make his case for keeping these Americans alive. It was an ill wind, he thought, remembering the English aphorism.

He could hear them coming. Far off, moving without a great deal of skill, probably tired, but coming.

"CRICKET, this is SNAKE, over."

"We read you, SNAKE."

"I'm moving. There are people on my hill, coming my way. I will head west. Can you send a helo for me?"

"Affirmative. Be careful, son." It was Maxwell's voice, still concerned.

"Moving now. Out." Kelly pocketed the radio and headed to the crest. He took a moment to look, comparing what he saw now with what he'd seen before.

I run especially fast in the dark, he'd told the Marines. Time now to prove it. With one last listen to the approaching NVA, Kelly picked a thin spot in the foliage and headed down the hill.

30

Travel Agents

It was obvious to everyone that things were wrong. The two rescue helos touched down on *Ogden* not an hour after they'd left. One was wheeled aside at once. The other, flown by the senior pilot, was refueled. Captain Albie was out almost the second it landed, sprinting to the superstructure, where the command team was waiting for him. He could feel that *Ogden* and her escorts were racing into the beach. His dejected Marines trailed out as well, silent, looking down at the flight deck as they cleared their weapons.

"What happened?" Albie asked.

"Clark waved it off. All we know is that he's moved off his hill; he said other people were there. We're going to try to get him out. Where do you think he'll go?" Maxwell asked.

"He'll look for a place the helo can get him. Let's see the map."

Had he had the time to reflect, Kelly might have considered how quickly things could go from good to bad. But he didn't. Survival was an all-encompassing game, and at the moment it was also the only game in town. Certainly it wasn't a boring one, and with luck not overly demanding. There weren't all that many troops for the purpose of securing the camp against an assault, not enough—yet—to conduct real defensive patrols. If they were worried about another Song Tay–type mission, they'd keep their firepower in close. They'd put observation teams on hilltops, probably nothing more than that at least for the moment. The top of Snake Hill was now five hundred meters in his wake. Kelly slowed his descent, catching his breath—he was more winded from fear than effort, though the two traded off heavily against each other. He found a secondary crest and rested on the far side of it. Standing still now, he could hear talk behind him—talk, not movement. Okay, good, he'd guessed right on the tactical situation. Probably more troops would be arriving in due course, but he'd be long gone by then.

If they can get that helo in.

Pleasant thought.

I've been in tighter spots than this, Defiance proclaimed.

When? Pessimism inquired delicately.

The only thing that made sense at the moment was to put as much distance as possible between himself and the NVA. Next came the necessity of finding something approximating an LZ so that he could get the hell out of this place. It wasn't a time to panic, but he couldn't dally either. Come daylight there would be more troops here, and if their commander was a competent one, he'd want to know if there might be an enemy reconnaissance element on his turf. Failure to get out before dawn would materially degrade Kelly's chances of ever escaping this country. Move. Find a good spot. Call the helo. Get the hell out of here. He had four hours until dawn. The helo was about thirty minutes away. Make it two or three hours to find a spot and make the call. That didn't seem overly difficult. He knew the area around SENDER GREEN from the recon photos. Kelly took a few minutes to look around, orienting himself. The quickest way to a clear spot was that way, across a twist in the road. It was a gamble but a good one. He rearranged his load, moving his spare magazines within easier reach. More than anything else, Kelly feared capture, to be at the mercy of men like PLASTIC FLOWER, to be unable to fight back, to lose control of his life. A quiet little voice in the back of his mind told him that death was preferred to that. Fighting back, even against impossible odds, wasn't suicide. Okay. That was decided. He started moving.

"Call him?" Maxwell asked.

"No, not now." Captain Albie shook his head. "He'll call us. Mr. Clark is busy right now. We leave him be." Irvin came into the Combat Information Center.

"Clark?" the master gunnery sergeant asked.

"On the run," Albie told him.

"Want me and some people on Rescue One, riding shotgun?" That they would try to get Clark out was not a question. Marines have an institutional loathing of leaving people behind.

"My job, Irvin," Albie said.

"Better you run the rescue, sir," Irvin said reasonably. "Anybody can shoot a rifle."

Maxwell, Podulski, and Greer stayed out of the conversation, watching and listening to two professionals who knew what they were about. The Marine commander bent to the wisdom of his most senior NCO.

"Take what you need." Albie turned to Maxwell. "Sir, I want Rescue One up now."

The Assistant Chief of Naval Operations (Air) handed over the headset to a Marine officer only twenty-eight years old; with it came tactical command of the busted mission. With it went the end of Dutch Maxwell's career.

It was less fearful to be moving. Movement gave Kelly the feeling that he had control of his life. It was an illusion, and intellectually he knew it, but his body took the message that way, which made things better. He got to the bottom of the hill, into thicker growth. There. Right across the road was an open space, a meadow or something, maybe a floodplain area from the river. That would do just fine. Nothing fancy. He grabbed his radio.

"SNAKE to CRICKET, over."

"This is CRICKET. We read you, and we are standing by."

The message came in gasps, spoken one short breath at a time: "West of my hill, past the road, about two miles west of objective, open field. I'm close. Send the helo. I can mark with strobe."

Albie looked at the map, then the aerial photos. Okay, that looked easy enough. He stabbed a finger on the map, and the air-control petty officer relayed the information at once. Albie waited for the confirmation before transmitting back to Clark.

"Roger, copy. Rescue One is moving in now, two-zero minutes away."

"Copy that." Albie could hear the relief in Clark's voice through the static. "I'll be ready. Out."

Thank you, God.

Kelly took his time now, moving slowly and quietly towards the road. His second sojourn into North Vietnam wouldn't end up being as long as the first. He didn't have to swim out this time, and with all the shots he'd gotten before coming in, maybe this time he wouldn't be getting sick from the water in that goddamned river. He didn't so much relax as lose some of his tension. As though on cue, the rain picked up, dampening noise and reducing visibility. More good news. Maybe God or fate or the Great Pumpkin hadn't decided to curse him after all. He stopped again, ten meters short of the road, and looked around. Nothing. He gave himself a few minutes to relax and let the stress bleed off. There was no sense in hurrying across just to be in open ground. Open ground was dangerous for a man alone in enemy territory. His hands were tight on his carbine, the infantryman's teddy bear, as he forced himself to breathe deeply and slowly in order to bring his heart rate down. When he felt approximately normal again, he allowed himself to approach the road.

Miserable roads, Grishanov thought, *even worse than those in Russia.* The car was something French, oddly enough.

More remarkably, it ran fairly well, or would have done so, except for the driver. Major Vinh ought to have driven it himself. As an officer he probably knew how, but status-conscious fool that he was, he had to let his orderly do it, and this little lump of a peasant probably didn't know how to drive anything more complicated than an ox. The car was swerving in the mud. The driver was having trouble seeing in the rain as well. Grishanov closed his eyes in the rear seat, clutching his backpack. No sense watching. It might just scare him to watch. It was like flying in bad weather, he thought, something no pilot relished—even less so when someone else was in control.

He waited, looking before crossing, listening for the sound of a truck's engine, which was the greatest danger to him. Nothing. Okay, about five minutes on the helo now. Kelly stood erect, reaching back with his left hand for the marker-strobe. As he crossed the road, he kept looking to his left, the route that additional troop trucks would take to approach the now entirely secure prison camp. *Damn!*

Rarely had concentration ever worked against John Kelly, but it did this time. The sound of the approaching car, swishing through the muddy surface of the road, was a little too close to the environmental noises, and by the time he recognized the difference it was too late. When the car came around the bend, he was right in the middle of the road, standing there like a deer in the headlights, and surely the driver must see him. What followed was automatic.

Kelly brought his carbine up and fired a short burst into the driver's area. The car didn't swerve for a moment, and he laid a second burst into the front-passenger seat. The car changed directions then, slamming directly into a tree. The entire sequence could not have taken three seconds, and Kelly's heart started beating again after a dreadfully long hiatus. He ran to the car. Whom had he killed?

The driver had come through the windshield, two rounds in his brain. Kelly wrenched open the passenger door. The person there was—the Major! Also hit in the head. The shots weren't quite centered, and though the man's skull was opened on the right side, his body was still quivering. Kelly yanked him out of the vehicle and had knelt down to search him before he heard a groan from the inside. He lunged inside, finding another man—Russian!—on the floor in the rear. Kelly pulled him out, too. The man had a backpack clutched in his hands.

The routine came as automatically as the shot. Kelly clubbed the Russian to full unconsciousness with his buttstock, then quickly turned back to rifle the Major's uniform for intelligence material. He stuffed all documents and papers into his pockets. The Vietnamese was looking at him, one of his eyes still functioning.

"Life's a bitch, ain't it?" Kelly said coldly as the eyes lost their animation.

"What the hell do I do with you?" Kelly asked, turning to the Russian body. "You're the guy who's been hassling our guys, aren't you?" He knelt there, opening the backpack and finding whole sheaves of paper, which answered his question for him—something the Soviet colonel was singularly unable to do.

Think fast, John—the helo isn't very far out now.

"I got the strobe!" the copilot said.

"Coming in hot." The pilot was driving his Sikorsky as hard as the engines would allow. Two hundred yards short of the clearing he pulled back sharply on the cyclic, and the forty-five-degree nose-up attitude stopped forward motion quickly—perfectly in fact, as he leveled out within feet of the blinking infrared strobe light. The rescue helicopter came to a steady hover two feet over the deck, buffeted by the winds. The Navy commander was fighting all manner of forces to hold his aircraft steady, and was slow to respond to something his eyes had told him. He had seen the rotor wash knock his intended survivor down, but—

"Did I see *two* people out there?" he asked over the intercom.

"Go go go!" another voice said over the IC circuit. "Pax aboard now, go!"

"Getting the hell outa Dodge City, now!" The pilot pulled collective for altitude, kicked rudder pedal, and dropped his nose, heading back to the river as the helicopter accelerated. *Wasn't there just supposed to be one person?* He set it aside. He had to fly now, and it was thirty twisty miles to the water and safety.

"Who the fuck is this?" Irvin asked.

"Hitchhiker," Kelly answered over the din of the engines. He shook his head. Explanations would be lengthy and would have to wait. Irvin understood, offering him a canteen. Kelly drained it. That's when the shaking started. In front of the helicopter crew and five Marines, Kelly shivered like a man in the Arctic, huddling and clutching himself, holding his weapon close until Irvin took it away and cleared it. It had been fired, the master gunnery sergeant saw. Later he'd find out why and at what. The door gunners scanned the river valley while their aircraft screamed out, barely a hundred feet over the meandering surface. The ride proved uneventful, far different from what they had expected, as was the case with this whole night. What had gone wrong? they all wanted to know. The answer was in the man they'd just picked up. But who the hell was the other one, and wasn't that a Russian uniform? Two Marines sat over him. One of them tied his hands up. A third secured the pack's flap in place with the straps.

"Rescue One, feet-wet. We have SNAKE aboard, over."

"Rescue One, this is CRICKET, roger, copy that. Standing by. Out." Albie looked up. "Well, that's it."

Podulski took it the hardest of all. BOXWOOD GREEN had been his idea from the start. Had it been successful, it might have changed everything. It might have opened the door for CERTAIN CORNET, might have changed the course of the war—and his son's death would not have been for nothing. He looked up at the others. He almost asked if they might still try it again, but he knew better. Washout. It was a bitter concept and an even more bitter reality for one who had served his adopted country for nearly thirty years.

"Tough day?" Frank Allen asked.

Lieutenant Mark Charon was surprisingly chipper for a

man who'd been through a fatal shooting and the almost-as-rigorous interrogation that had followed it.

"The damned fool. Didn't have to happen that way," Charon said. "I guess he didn't like the idea of life on Falls Road," the narcotics-division lieutenant added, referring to the Maryland State Penitentiary. Located in downtown Baltimore, the building was so grim that its inmates referred to it as Frankenstein's Castle.

Allen didn't have to tell him much. The procedures for the incident were straightforward. Charon would go on administrative leave for ten working days while the Department made sure that the shooting had not been contrary to official policy guidelines for the use of "deadly force." It was essentially a two-week vacation with pay, except that Charon might have to face additional interviews. Not likely in this case, as several police officers had observed the whole thing, one from a mere twenty feet away.

"I've got the case, Mark," Allen told him. "I've been over the preliminaries. Looks like you'll come out okay on this. Anything you might have done to spook him?"

Charon shook his head. "No, I didn't shout or anything until he went for his piece. I tried to ease him into it, y'know, calm him down, like? But he just jumped the wrong way. Eddie Morello died of the dumbs," the Lieutenant observed, impassively enjoying the fact that he was telling the exact truth.

"Well, I'm not gonna cry over the death of a doper. Good day all around, Mark."

"How's that, Frank?" Charon sat down and stole a cigarette.

"Got a call from Pittsburgh today. Seems there may be a witness for the Fountain Murder that Em and Tom are handling."

"No shit? That's good news. What do we have?"

"Somebody, probably a girl from how the guy was talking, who saw Madden and Waters get it. Sounds like she's talking to her minister about it and he's trying to coax her into opening up."

"Great," Charon observed, concealing his inward chill as well as he'd hid his elation at his first contract murder.

One more thing to clean up. With luck that would be the end of it.

The helicopter flared and made a soft landing on USS *Ogden*. As soon as it was down, people came back out on the flight deck. Deck crewmen secured the aircraft in place with chains while they approached. The Marines came out first, relieved to be safe, but also bitterly disappointed at the way the night had turned out. The timing was nearly perfect, they knew. This was their programmed time to return to the ship, with their rescued comrades, and they'd looked forward to this moment as a sports team might anticipate the joys of a winning locker room. But not now. They'd lost and they still didn't know why.

Irvin and another Marine climbed out, holding a body, which really surprised the assembled flag officers as Kelly alighted next. The helicopter pilot's eyes grew wide as he watched. There had been two bodies in the meadow. But mainly he was relieved at achieving another semisuccessful rescue mission into North Vietnam.

"What the hell?" Maxwell asked as the ship commenced a turn to the east.

"Uh, guys, let's get this guy inside and isolated right now!" Ritter said.

"He's unconscious, sir."

"Then get a medic, too," Ritter ordered.

They picked one of *Ogden*'s many empty troop-berthing spaces for the debrief. Kelly was allowed to wash his face, but nothing else. A medical corpsman checked out the Russian, pronouncing him dazed but healthy, both pupils equal and reactive, no concussion. A pair of Marines stood guard over him.

"Four trucks," Kelly said. "They just drove right in. A reinforced platoon—weapons platoon, probably, they showed up while the assault team was inbound, started digging in right away—about fifty of 'em. I had to blow it off."

Greer and Ritter traded a look. *No coincidence.*

Kelly looked at Maxwell. "God, I'm sorry, sir." He paused. "It would not have been possible to execute the mission. I had to leave the hill because they were putting listening posts out. I mean, even if we were able to deal with that—"

"We had gunships, remember?" Podulski growled.

"Back off, Cas," James Greer warned.

Kelly looked long at the Admiral before responding to the accusation. "Admiral, the chances of success were exactly zero. You guys gave me the job of eyeballing the objective so that we could do it on the cheap, right? With more assets, maybe we could have done it—the Song Tay team could have done it. It would have been messy, but they had enough firepower to bring it off, coming right into the objective like they did." He shook his head again. "Not this way."

"You're sure?" Maxwell asked.

Kelly nodded. "Yes, sir. Sure as hell."

"Thank you, Mr. Clark," Captain Albie said quietly, knowing the truth of what he'd just heard. Kelly just sat there, still tensed from the night's events.

"Okay," Ritter said after a moment. "What about our guest, Mr. Clark?"

"I fucked up," Kelly admitted, explaining how the car had gotten so close. He reached into his pockets. "I killed the driver and the camp commander—I think that's what he was. He had all this on him." Kelly reached into his pockets and handed over the documents. "Lots of papers on the Russian. I figured it wasn't smart to leave him there. I figured—I thought maybe he might be useful to us."

"These papers are in Russian," Irvin announced.

"Give me some," Ritter ordered. "My Russian's pretty good."

"We need somebody who can read Vietnamese, too."

"I have one of those," Albie said. "Irvin, get Sergeant Chalmers in here."

"Aye aye, sir."

Ritter and Greer moved to a corner table "Lord," the field officer observed, flipping through the written notes. "This guy's gotten a lot . . . Rokossovskiy? He's in Hanoi? Here's a summary sheet."

Staff Sergeant Chalmers, an intelligence specialist,

started reading through the papers taken from Major Vinh. Everyone else waited for the spooks to get through the papers.

"Where am I?" Grishanov asked in Russian. He tried to reach for his blindfold, but his hands couldn't move.

"How are you feeling?" a voice answered in the same language.

"Car smashed into something." The voice stopped. "Where am I?"

"You're aboard USS *Ogden*, Colonel," Ritter told him in English.

The body strapped in the bunk went rigid, and the prisoner immediately said, in Russian, that he didn't speak English.

"Then why are some of your notes in English?" Ritter asked reasonably.

"I am a Soviet officer. You have no right—"

"We have as much right as you had to interrogate American prisoners of war, and to conspire to kill them, Comrade Colonel."

"What do you mean?"

"Your friend Major Vinh is dead, but we have his dispatches. I guess you were finished talking to our people, right? And the NVA were trying to figure the most convenient way to eliminate them. Are you telling me you didn't know that?"

The oath Ritter heard was a particularly vile one, but the voice held genuine surprise that was interesting. This man was too injured to dissimulate well. He looked up at Greer.

"I've got some more reading to do. You want to keep this guy company?"

The one good thing that happened to Kelly that night was that Captain Franks hadn't tossed the aviator rations over the side after all. Finished with his debrief, he found his cabin and downed three stiff ones. With the release from the tension of the night, physical exhaustion assaulted the young man. The three drinks knocked him out, and he collapsed into his bunk without so much as a cleansing shower.

It was decided that *Ogden* would continue as planned, steaming at twenty knots back towards Subic Bay. The big amphibious ship became a quiet place. The crew, pumped up for an important and dramatic mission, became subdued with its failure. Watches were changed, the ship continued to function as before, but the mess rooms' only noise was that of the metal trays and utensils. No jokes, no stories. The additional medical personnel took it the hardest of all. With no one to treat and nothing to do, they just wandered about. Before noon the helicopters departed, the Cobras for Danang and the rescue birds back to their carrier. The signal-intelligence people switched over to more regular duties, searching the airways for radio messages, finding a new mission to replace the old.

Kelly didn't awaken until 1800 hours. After showering, he headed below to find the Marines. He owed them an explanation, he thought. Somebody did. They were in the same space. The sand-table model was still there as well.

"I was right up here," he said, finding the rubber band with two eyes on it.

"How many bad guys?"

"Four trucks, they came in this road, stopped here," Kelly explained. "They were digging in crew-served weapons here and here. They sent people up my hill. I saw another team heading this way right before I moved."

"Jesus," a squad leader noted. "Right on our approach route."

"Yeah," Kelly confirmed. "Anyway, that's why."

"How'd they know to send in the reinforcements?" a corporal asked.

"Not my department."

"Thanks, Snake," the squad leader said, looking from the model that would soon be tossed over the side. "Tough call, wasn't it?"

Kelly nodded. "I'm sorry, pal. Jesus God, I'm sorry."

"Mr. Clark, I got a baby due in two months. 'Cept for you, well . . ." The Marine extended his hand across the model.

"Thank you, sir." Kelly took it.

"Mr. Clark, sir?" A sailor stuck his head into the compartment. "The admirals are looking for you. Up in officer country, sir."

"Doctor Rosen," Sam said, lifting the phone.

"Hi, doctor. This is Sergeant Douglas."

"What can I do for you?"

"We're trying to track down your friend Kelly. He isn't answering his phone. Do you have any idea where he is?"

"I haven't seen him in a long time," the surgeon said guardedly.

"You know anybody who has?"

"I'll check around. What's the story?" Sam added, asking what he knew might be a highly inconvenient question, wondering what sort of answer he might get.

"I, uh, can't say, sir. I hope you understand."

"Ummhmm. Yeah, okay, I'll ask."

"Feeling better?" Ritter asked first.

"Some," Kelly allowed. "What's the story on the Russian?"

"Clark, you just might have done something useful." Ritter gestured to a table with no fewer than ten piles of documents on them.

"They're planning to kill the prisoners," Greer said.

"Who? The Russians?" Kelly asked.

"The Vietnamese. The Russians want them alive. This guy you picked up is trying to take them home," Ritter said, lifting a sheet of paper. "Here's his draft of the letter justifying it."

"Is that good or bad?"

The outside noises were different, Zacharias thought. More of them, too. Shouts with purpose to them, though he didn't know what purpose. For the first day in a month, Grishanov hadn't visited him, even for a few minutes. The loneliness he felt became even more acute, and his only company was the realization that he'd given to the Soviet Union a graduate-level course in continental air-defense. He hadn't meant to do it. He hadn't even known what he was doing. That was no consolation, however. The Russian had played him for a fool, and Colonel Robin Zacharias, USAF, had just given it all up, outsmarted by some kindness and fellowship from an atheist . . . and drink. Stupidity and sin, such a likely combination of human weaknesses, and he'd done it all.

He didn't even have tears for his shame. He was beyond that, sitting on the floor of his cell, staring at the rough, dirty concrete between his bare feet. He'd broken faith with his God and his country, Zacharias told himself, as his evening meal was pushed through the slot at the bottom of his door. Thin, bodiless pumpkin soup and maggoty rice. He made no move towards it.

Grishanov knew he was a dead man. They wouldn't give him back. They couldn't even admit that they had him. He'd disappear, as other Russians in Vietnam had disappeared, some at SAM sites, some doing other things for those ungrateful little bastards. Why were they feeding him so well? It had to be a large ship, but it was also his first time at sea. Even the decent food was hard to get down, but he swore not to disgrace himself by succumbing to motion sickness mixed with fear. He was a fighter pilot, a good one who had faced death before, mainly at the controls of a malfunctioning aircraft. He remembered wondering at the time what they'd tell his Marina. He wondered now. A letter? What? Would his family be looked after by his fellow officers in PVO Strany? Would the pension be sufficient?

"Are you kidding me?"

"Mr. Clark, the world can be a very complicated place. Why did you think the Russians like them?"

"They give them weapons and training, don't they?"

Ritter stubbed out his Winston. "We give those things to people all over the world. They're not all nice folks, but we have to work with them. It's the same for the Russians, maybe less so, but still pretty much the same. Anyway, this

Grishanov guy was going to a considerable effort to keep our people alive." Ritter held up another sheet. "Here's a request for better food—for a *doctor,* even."

"So what do we do with him?" Admiral Podulski asked.

"That, gentlemen, is our department," Ritter said, looking at Greer, who nodded.

"Wait a minute," Kelly objected. "He was pumping them for information."

"So?" Ritter asked. "That was his job."

"We're getting away from the real issue here," Maxwell said.

James Greer poured some coffee for himself. "I know. We have to move fast."

"And finally . . . " Ritter tapped a translation of the Vietnamese message. "We know that somebody burned the mission. We're going to track that bastard down."

Kelly was still too drugged from sleep to follow it all, much less see far enough into the future to realize how he had assumed his place in the center of the affair.

"Where's John?"

Sandy O'Toole looked up from her paperwork. It was close to the end of her shift, and Professor Rosen's question brought to the fore a worry that she'd managed to suppress for over a week.

"Out of the country. Why?"

"I got a call today from the police. They're looking for him."

Oh, God. "Why?"

"He didn't say." Rosen looked around. They were alone at the nurses' station. "Sandy, I know he's been doing things—I mean, I think I know, but I haven't—"

"I haven't heard from him, either. What are we supposed to do?"

Rosen grimaced and looked away before replying. "As good citizens, we're supposed to cooperate with the police—but we're not doing that, are we? No idea where he is?"

"He told me, but I'm not supposed to—he's doing something with the government . . . over in . . . " She couldn't finish, couldn't bring herself to say the word. "He gave a number I can call. I haven't used it."

"I would," Sam told her, and left.

It wasn't right. He was off doing something scary and important, only to come back to a police investigation. It seemed to Nurse O'Toole that the unfairness of life had gotten as bad as it could. She was wrong.

"Pittsburgh?"

"That's what he said," Henry confirmed.

"It's cute, by the way, having him as your man on the inside. Very professional," Piaggi said with respect.

"He said we need to take care of it quick, like. She hasn't said much yet."

"She saw it all?" Piaggi didn't have to add that he didn't think that very professional at all. "Henry, keeping people in line is one thing. Making them into witnesses is another."

"Tony, I'm going to take care of that, but we need to handle this problem right quick, y'dig?" It seemed to Henry Tucker that he was in the stretch run, and over the finish line were both safety and prosperity. That five more people had to die to get him across that line was a small matter after the race he'd already run.

"Go on."

"The family name is Brown. Her name is Doris. Her father's name is Raymond."

"You sure of this?"

"The girls talk to each other. I got the street name and everything. You got connections. I need you to use 'em fast."

Piaggi copied down the information. "Okay. Our Philly connections can handle it. It's not going to be cheap, Henry."

"I didn't expect it would be."

The flight deck looked very empty. All four of the aircraft briefly assigned to *Ogden* were gone now, and the deck reassumed its former status as the ship's unofficial town square. The stars were the same as before, now that the ship was again under clear skies, and a sliver of a waning moon was high in the sky in these early hours. No sailors were out now, however. Those awake at this hour were on duty, but for Kelly and the Marines the day/night cycle was askew, and the gray steel walls of their spaces were too confining for the thoughts they had. The ship's wake was a curious luminescent green from the photoplankton stirred up by the ship's screws, and left a long trail showing where she'd been. Half a dozen men stood well aft, staring at it without words.

"It could have been a hell of a lot worse, you know." Kelly turned. It was Irvin. It had to be.

"Could have been a hell of a lot better, too, Guns."

"Wasn't no accident, them showing up like that, was it?"

"I don't think I'm supposed to say. Is that a good enough answer?"

"Yes, sir. And Lord Jesus said, 'Father, forgive them, for they know not what they do.'"

"And what if they do know?"

Irvin grunted. "I think you know what my vote is. Whoever it was, they could have killed all of us."

"You know, Guns, just once, *just one time,* I'd like to finish something the right way," Kelly said.

"Yeah." Irvin took a second before going on, and going back. "Why the hell would anybody do something like that?"

A shape loomed close. It was *Newport News,* a lovely silhouette only two thousand yards off, and visible in a spectral way despite the absence of lights. She, too, was heading back, the last of the Navy's big-gun cruisers, creature of a bygone age, returning home after the same failure that Kelly and Irvin knew.

"Seven-one-three-one," the female voice said.

"Hello, I'm trying to get Admiral James Greer," Sandy told the secretary.

"He's not in."

"Can you tell me when he'll be back?"

"Sorry, no, I don't know."

"But it's important."

"Could you tell me who's calling, please?"

"What is this place?"

"This is Admiral Greer's office."

"No, I mean, is it the Pentagon?"

"Don't you know?"

Sandy didn't know, and that question led her off in a direction she didn't understand. "Please, I need your help."

"Who's calling, please?"

"Please, I need to know where you are!"

"I can't tell you that," the secretary responded, feeling herself to be one of the fortress walls that protected U.S. National Security.

"Is this the Pentagon?"

Well, she could tell her that. "No, it isn't."

What then? Sandy wondered. She took a deep breath. "A friend of mine gave me this number to call. He's with Admiral Greer. He said I could call here to find out if he's okay."

"I don't understand."

"Look, I *know* he went to Vietnam!"

"Miss, I cannot discuss where Admiral Greer is." *Who violated security!* She'd have to make a report on this.

"It's not about him, it's about John!" *Calm down. You're not helping anyone this way.*

"John who?" the secretary asked.

Deep breath. Swallow. "Please get a message to Admiral Greer. This is Sandy. It's about John. He will understand. Okay? He will understand. This is most important." She gave her home and work numbers.

"Thank you. I will do what I can." The line went dead.

Sandy wanted to scream, and nearly did so. So the Admiral had gone, too. Okay, he'd be close to where John is. The secretary would get the message through. She would have to. People like that, if you said *most important,* didn't have the imagination not to do it. Settle down. Anyway, where he was, the police couldn't get him either. But for the rest of the day, and into the next, the second hand on her watch seemed to stand still.

• • •

USS *Ogden* pulled into Subic Bay Naval Station in the early afternoon. Coming alongside seemed to take forever in the moist tropical heat. Finally lines were tossed and a brow advanced to the ship's side. A civilian sprinted up first even before it was properly secured. Soon thereafter the Marines filed off to a bus which would take them to Cubi Point. The deck division watched them walk off. A few hands were shaken as everyone tried to leave at least one good memory from the experience, but "good try" just didn't make it, and "good luck" seemed blasphemous. Their C-141 was waiting there for the flight stateside. Mr. Clark, they saw, wasn't with them.

"John, it seems you have a lady friend who's worried about you," Greer said, handing the message over. It was the friendliest of the dispatches that the junior CIA officer had brought up from Manila. Kelly scanned it while three admirals reviewed the others.

"Do I have time to call her, sir? She's worried about me."

"You left her my office number?" Greer was slightly vexed.

"Her husband was killed with the First Cav, sir. She worries," Kelly explained.

"Okay." Greer put his own troubles aside for the moment. "I'll have Barbara tell her you're safe."

The rest of the messages were less welcome. Admirals Maxwell and Podulski were being summoned back to Washington soonest to report on the failure of BOXWOOD GREEN. Ritter and Greer had similar orders, though they also had an ace in the hole. Their KC-135 was waiting at Clark Air Force Base. A puddle jumper would hop over the mountains. The best news at the moment was their disrupted sleep cycle. The flight back to the American East Coast would bring them back in just the right way.

Colonel Grishanov came into the sunlight along with the admirals. He was wearing clothing borrowed from Captain Franks—they were of approximately the same size—and escorted by Maxwell and Podulski. Kolya was under no illusions of his chance to escape anywhere, not on an American naval base located on the soil of an American ally. Ritter was talking to him quietly, in Russian, as all six men walked down to the waiting cars. Ten minutes later, they climbed into an Air Force C-12 twin-prop Beechcraft. Half an hour later that aircraft taxied right alongside the larger Boeing jet, which got off less than an hour after they'd left *Ogden*. Kelly found himself a nice wide seat and strapped himself in, asleep before the windowless transport started rolling. The next stop, they'd told him, was Hickam in Hawaii, and he didn't plan to be awake for any of that.

31
Home Is the Hunter

The flight wasn't as restful for the others. Greer had managed to get a couple of messages taken care of before the takeoff, but he and Ritter were the busiest. Their aircraft—the Air Force had lent it to them for the mission, no questions asked—was a semi-VIP bird belonging to Andrews Air Force Base, and was often used for Congressional junkets. That meant an ample supply of liquor, and while they drank straight coffee, their Russian guest's cups were laced with brandy, a little at first, then in increasing doses that his decaffeinated brew didn't begin to attenuate.

Ritter handled most of the interrogation. His first task was to explain to Grishanov that they had no plans to kill him. Yes, they were CIA. Yes, Ritter was a field officer—a spy, if you like—with ample experience behind the Iron Curtain—excuse me, working as a slinking spy in the peace-loving Socialist East Bloc—but that was his job, as Kolya—do you mind if I call you Kolya?—had *his* job. Now, please, Colonel, can you give us the names of our men? (That was already listed in Grishanov's voluminous notes.) Your friends, you say? Yes, we are very grateful indeed for your efforts to keep them alive. They all have families, you know, just like you do. More coffee, Colonel? Yes, it is good coffee, isn't it? Of *course* you'll go home to your family. What do you think we are, barbarians? Grishanov had the good manners not to answer that one

Damn, Greer thought, *but Bob is good at this sort of thing.* It wasn't about courage or patriotism. It was about humanity. Grishanov was a tough hombre, probably a hell of a good airplane-driver—what a shame they couldn't let Maxwell or especially Podulski in on this!—but he was at bottom a man, and the quality of his character worked against him. He didn't want the American prisoners to die. That plus the stress of capture, plus the whiplash surprise of the cordial treatment, plus a lot of good brandy, all conspired to loosen his tongue. It helped a lot more that Ritter didn't even approach matters of grave concern to the Soviet state. *Hell, Colonel, I know you're not going to give up any secrets—so why ask?*

"Your man killed Vinh, did he?" the Russian asked halfway across the Pacific.

"Yes, he did. It was an accident and—" The Russian cut Ritter off with a wave.

"Good. He was *nekulturny,* a vicious little fascist bastard. He wants to kill those men, murder them," Kolya added with the aid of six brandies.

"Well, Colonel, we're hoping to find a way to prevent that."

"Neurosurgery West," the nurse said.

"Trying to get Sandra O'Toole."

"Hold on, please. Sandy?" The nurse on desk duty held the phone up. The nursing-team leader took it.

"This is O'Toole."

"Miss O'Toole, this is Barbara—we spoke earlier. Admiral Greer's office?"

"Yes!"

"Admiral Greer told me to let you know—John is okay and he's now on his way home."

Sandy's head spun around, to look in a direction where there were no eyes to see the sudden tears of relief. A mixed blessing perhaps, but a blessing still. "Can you tell me when?"

"Sometime tomorrow, that's all I know."

"Thank you."

"Surely." The line went immediately dead.

Well, that's something—maybe a lot. She wondered what would happen when he got here, but at least he was coming back alive. More than Tim had managed to do.

The hard landing at Hickam—the pilot was tired—startled Kelly into wakefulness. An Air Force sergeant gave him a friendly shake to make sure as the aircraft taxied to a remote part of the base for refueling and servicing. Kelly took the time to get out and walk around. The climate was warm here, but not the oppressive heat of Vietnam. It was American soil, and things were different here. . . .

Sure they are.

Just once, just one time . . . he remembered saying. *Yes, I'm going to get those other girls out just like I got Doris out. It shouldn't be all that hard. I'll get Burt next and we'll talk. I'll even let the bastard go when I'm done, probably. I can't save the whole world, but . . . by Jesus, I'll save some of it!*

He found a phone in the Distinguished Visitors lounge and placed a call.

"Hello?" the groggy voice said, five thousand miles away.

"Hi, Sandy. It's John!" he said with a smile. Even if those aviators weren't coming home just yet—well, he was, and he was grateful for that.

"John! Where are you?"

"Would you believe Hawaii?"

"You're okay?"

"A little tired, but, yes. No holes or anything," he reported with a smile. Just the sound of her voice had brightened his day. But not for long.

"John, there's a problem."

The sergeant at the reception desk saw the DV's face change. Then he turned back into the phone booth and became less interesting.

"Okay. It must be Doris," Kelly said. "I mean, only you and the docs know about me, and—"

"It wasn't us," Sandy assured him.

"Okay. Please call Doris and . . . be careful, but—"

"Warn her off?"

"Can you do that?"

"Yes!"

Kelly tried to relax a little, almost succeeding. "I'll be back in about . . . oh, nine or ten hours. Will you be at work?"

"I have the day off."

"Okay, Sandy. See you soon. 'Bye."

"John!" she called urgently.

"What?"

"I want . . . I mean . . . " her voice stopped.

Kelly smiled again. "We can talk about that when I get there, honey." Maybe he wasn't just going home. Maybe he was going home *to* something. Kelly made a quick inventory of everything he'd done. He still had his converted pistol and other weapons on the boat, but everything he'd worn on every job: shoes, socks, outer clothing, even underwear, were now in whatever trash dump. He'd left behind no evidence that he knew of. The police might be interested in talking to him, fine. He did *not* have to talk to them. That was one of the nice things about the Constitution, Kelly thought as he walked back to the aircraft and trotted up the stairs.

One flight crew found the beds just aft of the flight deck while the relief crew started engines. Kelly sat with the CIA officers. The Russian, he saw, was snoring loudly and blissfully.

Ritter chuckled. "He's going to have one hell of a hangover."

"What'd you get into him?"

"Started off with good brandy. Ended up with California stuff. Brandy really messes me up the next day," Ritter said tiredly as the KC-135 started rolling. He was drinking a martini now that his prisoner was no longer able to answer questions.

"So what's the story?" Kelly asked.

Ritter explained what he knew. The camp had indeed been established as a bargaining chip for use with the Russians, but it seemed that the Vietnamese had used that particular chip in a rather inefficient way and were now thinking about eliminating it along with the prisoners.

"You mean because of the raid?" *Oh, God!*

"Correct. But settle down, Clark. We got us a Russian, and that's a bargaining chip too. Mr. Clark," Ritter said with a tight smile, "I like your style."

"What do you mean?"

"Bringing that Russian in, you showed commendable initiative. And the way you blew the mission off, that showed good judgment."

"Look, I didn't—I mean, I couldn't—"

"You didn't screw up. Somebody else might have. You made a quick decision, and it was the right decision. Interested in serving your country?" Ritter asked with an alcohol-aided smile of his own.

Sandy awoke at six-thirty, which was late for her. She got her morning paper, started the coffee, and decided to stick to toast for breakfast, watching the kitchen-wall clock and wondering how early she might call Pittsburgh.

The lead story on the front page was the drug shooting. A police officer had gotten himself in a gunfight with a drug dealer. Well, good, she thought. Six kilograms of "pure" heroin, the news piece said—that was a lot. She wondered if this was the same bunch that . . . no, the leader of that group was black, at least Doris had said so. Anyway, another druggie had left the face of the planet. Another look at the clock. Still too early for a civilized call. She went into the living room to switch on the TV. It was already a hot, lazy day. She'd been up late the night before and had difficulty getting back to sleep after John's call. She tried to watch the "Today Show" and didn't quite notice that her eyes were growing heavy. . . .

It was after ten when her eyes opened back up. Angry with herself, she shook her head clear and went back to the kitchen. Doris's number was pinned next to the phone. She called, and heard the phone ring . . . four—six—ten times, without an answer. Damn. Out shopping? Off to see Dr. Bryant? She'd try again in an hour. In the meantime she'd try to figure out exactly what she would say. Might this be a crime? Was she obstructing justice? How deeply was she involved in this business? The thought came as an unpleasant surprise. But she was involved. She'd helped rescue this girl from a dangerous life, and she couldn't stop now. She'd just tell Doris not to hurt the people who had helped her, to be very, very careful. Please.

Reverend Meyer came late. He'd been held up by a phone call at the parsonage and was in a profession where one couldn't say that he had to leave for an appointment. As he parked, he noticed a flower-delivery truck heading up the hill. It turned right, disappearing from view as he took the parking place it had occupied a few doors up from the Brown house. He was a little worried as he locked his car. He had to persuade Doris to speak with his son. Peter had assured him that they'd be extremely careful. Yes, Pop, we can protect her. Now all he had to do was to get that message across to a frightened young woman and a father whose love had survived the most rigorous of tests. Well, he'd handled more delicate problems than this, the minister told himself. Like shortstopping a few divorces. Negotiating treaties between nations could not be harder than saving a rocky marriage.

Even so, the way up to the front porch seemed awfully steep, Meyer thought, holding the rail as he climbed up the chipped and worn concrete steps. There were a few buckets of paint on the porch. Perhaps Raymond was going to do his house now that it contained a family again. A good sign, Pastor Meyer thought as he pushed the button. He could hear the doorbell's two-tone chime. Raymond's white Ford was parked right here. He knew they were home . . . but no one came to the door. Well, maybe someone was dressing or in the bathroom, as often happened to everyone's embarrassment. He waited another minute or so, frowning as he pushed the button again. He was slow to note that the door wasn't quite closed all the way. *You are a minister,* he told himself, *not a burglar.*

With a small degree of uneasiness, he pushed it open and stuck his head inside.

"Hello? Raymond? . . . Doris?" he called, loudly enough to be heard anywhere in the house. The TV was on, some mindless game show playing on the living-room set. "Hellooooo!"

This was odd. He stepped inside, somewhat embarrassed with himself for doing so, wondering what the problem was. There was a cigarette burning in an ashtray here, almost down to the filter, and the vertical trail of smoke was a clear warning that something was amiss. An ordinary citizen possessed of his intelligence would have withdrawn then, but Reverend Meyer was not ordinary. He saw a box of flowers on the rug, opened, long-stem roses inside. Roses were not made to lie on the floor. He remembered his military service just then, how unpleasant it had been, but how uplifting to attend the needs of men in the face of death—he wondered why that thought had sprung so clearly into his mind; its sudden relevance started his heart racing. Meyer walked through the living room, quiet now, listening. He found the kitchen empty too, a pot of water coming to boil on the stove, cups and tea bags on the kitchen table. The basement door was open as well, the light on. He couldn't stop now. He opened the door all the way and started down. He was halfway to the bottom when he saw their legs.

Father and daughter were facedown on the bare concrete floor, and the blood from their head wounds had pooled together on the uneven surface. The horror was immediate and overwhelming. His mouth dropped open with a sudden intake of breath as he looked down at two parishioners whose funeral he would officiate in two days' time. They were holding hands, he saw, father and daughter. They'd died together, but the consolation that this tragically afflicted family was now united with their God could not stop a scream of fury at those who had been in this home only ten minutes earlier. Meyer recovered after a few seconds, continued down the stairs and knelt, reaching down to touch the intertwined hands and entreating God to have mercy on their souls. Of that he had confidence. Perhaps she'd lost her life, but not her soul, Meyer would say over the bodies, and her father had reclaimed his daughter's love. He'd let his parishioners know that both had been saved, Meyer promised himself. Then it was time to call his son.

The stolen flower truck was left in a supermarket parking lot. Two men got out and walked into the store, just to be careful, and out the back door, where their car was parked. They drove southeast onto the Pennsylvania Turnpike for the three-hour trip back to Philadelphia. Maybe longer, the driver thought. They didn't want a state cop to stop them. Both men were ten thousand dollars richer. They didn't know the story. They had no need to know.

"Hello?"

"Mr. Brown?"

"No. Who's this?"

"This is Sandy. Is Mr. Brown there?"

"How do you know the Brown family?"

"Who is this?" Sandy asked, looking out her kitchen window with alarm.

"This is Sergeant Peter Meyer, Pittsburgh Police Department. Now, who are you?"

"I'm the one who drove Doris back—what's the matter?"

"Your name, please?"

"Are they okay?"

"They appear to have been murdered," Meyer replied in a harshly patient way. "Now, I need to know your name and—"

Sandy brought her finger down on the switch, cutting the circuit before she could hear more. To hear more might force her to answer questions. Her legs were shaking, but there was a chair close by. Her eyes were wide. It wasn't possible, she told herself. How could anyone know where she was? Surely she hadn't called the people who—no, not possible, the nurse thought.

"Why?" she whispered the question aloud. "Why, why, why?" *She couldn't hurt anyone—yes, she could . . . but how did they find out?*

They have the police infiltrated. She remembered the words from John's mouth. He was right, wasn't he?

But that was a side issue.

"Damn it, we saved her!" Sandy told the kitchen. Sandy could remember every minute of that nearly sleepless first week, and then the progress, the elation, the purest and best kind of professional satisfaction for a job well done, the joy of seeing the look in her dad's face. Gone. A waste of her time.

No.

Not a waste of time. That was her task in life, to make sick people well. She'd done that. She was proud of that. It was not wasted time. It was stolen time. Stolen time, two stolen lives. She started crying and had to go to the downstairs bathroom, grabbing tissue to wipe her eyes. Then she looked in the mirror, seeing eyes that she'd never beheld before. And seeing that, she truly understood.

Disease was a dragon that she fought forty hours or more per week. A skilled nurse and teacher who worked well with the surgeons on her unit, Sandra O'Toole fought those dragons in her way, with professionalism and kindness and intelligence, more often winning than losing. And every year things got better. Progress was never fast enough, but it was real and could be measured, and perhaps she'd live long enough to see the last dragon on her unit die once and for all.

But there was more than one kind of dragon, wasn't there? Some couldn't be killed with kindness and medications and skilled nursing care. She'd defeated one, but another had killed Doris anyway. *That* dragon needed the sword, in the hands of a warrior. The sword was a tool, wasn't it? A necessary tool, if you wanted to slay that particular dragon. Perhaps it was one she could never use herself, but necessary nonetheless. Someone had to hold that sword. John wasn't a bad man at all, just realistic.

She fought her dragons. He fought his. *It was the same fight.* She'd been wrong to judge him. Now she understood, seeing in her eyes the same emotion that she'd beheld months earlier in his, as her rage passed, but not very far, and the determination set in.

"Well, everybody lucked out," Hicks said, handing over a beer.

"How so, Wally?" Peter Henderson asked.

"The mission was a washout. It aborted just in time. Didn't even get anyone hurt in the process, thank God. Everyone's flying home right now."

"Good news, Wally!" Henderson said, meaning it. He didn't want to kill anybody either. He just wanted the damned war to end, the same as Wally did. It was a shame about the men in that camp, but some things couldn't be helped. "What happened exactly?"

"Nobody knows yet. You want me to find out?"

Peter nodded. "Carefully. It's something the Intelligence Committee ought to know about, when the Agency fucks up like that. I can get the information to them. But you have to be careful."

"No problem. I'm learning how to stroke Roger." Hicks lit up his first joint of the evening, annoying his guest.

"You could lose your clearance that way, you know?"

"Well, gee, then I'll have to join Dad and make a few mill' on The Street, eh?"

"Wally, do you want to change the system or do you want to let other people keep it the same?"

Hicks nodded. "Yeah, I suppose."

The following winds had allowed the KC-135 to make the hop in from Hawaii without a refueling stop, and the landing was a gentle one. Remarkably, Kelly's sleep cycle was about right now. It was five in the afternoon, and in another six or seven hours he'd be ready for more sleep.

"Can I get a day or two off?"

"We'll want you back to Quantico for an extended debrief," Ritter told him, stiff and sore from the extended flight.

"Fine, just so I'm not in custody or anything. I could use a lift up to Baltimore."

"I'll see what I can do," Greer said as the plane came to a halt.

Two security officers from the Agency were the first up the mobile stairs, even before the oversized cargo hatch swung up. Ritter woke the Russian up.

"Welcome to Washington."

"Take me to my embassy?" he asked hopefully. Ritter almost laughed.

"Not quite yet. We'll find you a nice, comfortable place, though."

Grishanov was too groggy to object, rubbing his head and needing something for the pain. He went with the security officers, down the steps to their waiting car. It left at once for a safe house near Winchester, Virginia.

"Thanks for the try, John," Admiral Maxwell said, taking the younger man's hand.

"I'm sorry for what I said before," Cas said, doing the same. "You were right." They, too, had a car waiting. Kelly watched them enter it from the hatch.

"So what happens to them?" he asked Greer.

James shrugged, leading Kelly out and down the stairs. Noise from other aircraft made his voice hard to hear. "Dutch was in line for a fleet, and maybe the CNO's job. I don't suppose that'll happen now. The operation—well, it was his baby, and it didn't get born. That'll finish him."

"That's not fair," Kelly said loudly. Greer turned.

"No, it isn't, but that's the way things are." Greer, too, had a ride waiting. He directed his driver to head to the wing-headquarters building, where he arranged a car to take Kelly to Baltimore. "Get some rest and call me when you're ready. Bob was serious about what he said. Think it over."

"Yes, sir," Kelly replied, heading to the blue Air Force sedan.

It was amazing, Kelly thought, the way life was. Within five minutes the sergeant drove onto an interstate highway. Scarcely twenty-four hours earlier he'd been on a ship approaching Subic Bay. Thirty-six hours prior to that he'd been on the soil of an enemy country—and now here he was in the backseat of a government Chevy, and the only dangers to which he was exposed came from other drivers. At least for a little while. All the familiar things, the highway exit signs painted that pleasant shade of green, traveling in the last half of the local rush hour. Everything about him proclaimed the normality of life, when three days earlier everything had been alien and hostile. Most amazing of all, he'd adjusted to it.

The driver didn't speak a word except to inquire about directions, though he must have wondered who the man was that had arrived on a special flight. Perhaps he had many such jobs, Kelly mused as the car pulled off Loch Raven Boulevard, enough that he'd stopped wondering about things he'd never be told.

"Thanks for the lift," Kelly told him.

"Yes, sir, you're welcome." The car pulled away and Kelly walked to his apartment, amused that he'd taken his keys all the way to Vietnam and back. Did the keys know how far they had come? Five minutes later he was in the shower, the quintessentially American experience, changing from one reality into another. Another five and he was dressed in slacks and a short-sleeve shirt, and headed out the door to his Scout, parked a block away. Another ten and he'd parked the car within sight of Sandy's bungalow. The walk from his Scout to her door was yet another transition. He'd come home to something, Kelly told himself. For the first time.

"John!" He hadn't expected the hug. Even less so the tears in her eyes.

"It's okay, Sandy. I'm fine. No holes or scratches or anything." He was slow to grasp the desperation of her hold on him, pleasant as it was. But then the face against his chest started sobbing, and he knew that this event was not for him at all. "What's wrong?"

"They killed Doris."

Time stopped again. It seemed to split into many pieces. Kelly closed his eyes, in pain at first, and in that instant he was back on his hilltop overlooking SENDER GREEN, watching the NVA troops arrive; he was in his hospital bed looking at a photograph; he was outside some nameless village listening to the screams of children. He'd come home, all right, but to the same thing he'd left. No, he realized, to the thing that he had never left, which followed him everywhere he went. He'd never get away from it because he'd never really finished it, not even once. *Not even once.*

And yet there was a new element as well, this woman holding him and feeling the same blazing pain that sliced through his chest.

"What happened, Sandy?"

"We got her well, John. We took her home, and then I called today like you told me to, and a policeman answered. Doris and her father, too, both murdered."

"Okay." He moved her to the sofa. He wanted at first to let her calm down, not to hold her too close, but that didn't work. She clung to him, letting out the feelings that she'd closeted off, along with worry for his safety, and he held Sandy's head to his shoulder for several minutes. "Sam and Sarah?"

"I haven't told them yet." Her face came up, and she looked across the room, her gaze unfocused. Then the nurse in her came out, as it had to. "How are you?"

"A little frazzled from all the traveling," he said, just to put words after her question. Then he had to tell the truth. "It was a washout. The mission didn't work. They're still there."

"I don't understand."

"We were trying to get some people out of North Vietnam, prisoners—but something went wrong. Failed again," he added quietly.

"Was it dangerous?"

Kelly managed a grunt. "Yeah, Sandy, you might say that, but I came out okay."

Sandy set that one aside. "Doris said there were others, other girls, they still have 'em."

"Yeah. Billy said the same thing. I'm going to try and get them out." Kelly noticed she didn't react to his mention of Billy's name.

"It won't matter—getting them out, unless . . . "

"I know." The thing that kept following him around, Kelly thought. There was only one way to make it stop.

Running couldn't distance him from it. He had to turn and face it.

"Well, Henry, that little job was taken care of this morning," Piaggi told him. "Nice and clean."

"They didn't leave—"

"Henry, they were two pros, okay? They did the job and now they're back home, couple hundred miles away. They didn't leave anything behind except for the two bodies." The phone report had been very clear on that. It had been an easy job, since neither target had expected anything.

"Then that's that," Tucker observed with satisfaction. He reached into his pocket and pulled out a fat envelope. He handed it to Piaggi, who had fronted the money himself, good partner that he was.

"With Eddie out of the way, and with that leak plugged, things ought to go back to normal." *Best twenty grand I ever spent,* Henry thought.

"Henry, the other girls?" Piaggi pointed out. "You've got a real business now. People inside like them are dangerous. Take care of it, okay?" He pocketed the envelope and left the table.

"Twenty-two's, back of the head, both of 'em," the Pittsburgh detective reported over the phone. "We've dusted the whole house—nothing. The flower box—nothing. The truck—nothing. The truck was stolen sometime last night—this morning, whatever. The florist has eight of them. Hell, we recovered it before the all-points was on the air. It was wise guys, had to be. Too smooth, too clean for local talent. No word on the street. They're probably out of town already. Two people saw the truck. One woman saw two guys walking to the door. She figured it was a flower delivery, and besides she was across the street half a block away. No description, nothing. She doesn't even remember what color they were."

Ryan and Douglas were listening on the same line, and their eyes met every few seconds. They knew it all from the tone of the man's voice. The sort of case that policemen hate and fear. No immediately apparent motive, no witnesses, no usable evidence. Nowhere to start and nowhere to go. The routine was as predictable as it was futile. They'd pump the neighbors for information, but it was a working-class neighborhood, and few had been at home at the time. People noticed mainly the unusual, and a flower truck wasn't unusual enough to attract the inquiring look that developed into a physical description. Committing the perfect murder wasn't really all that demanding, a secret known within the fraternity of detectives and belied by a whole body of literature that made them into superhuman beings they never claimed to be, even among themselves in a cop bar. Someday the case might be broken. One of the killers might be caught for something else and cop to this one in order to get a deal. Less likely, someone would talk about it, bragging in front of an informant who'd pass it along to someone else, but in either case it would take time and the trail, cold as it already was, would grow colder still. It was the most frustrating part of the business of police work. Truly innocent people had died, and there was no one to speak for them, to avenge their deaths, and other cases would come up, and the cops would set this one aside for something fresher, and from time to time someone would reopen the file and look things over, then put it back in the *Unsolved* drawer, where it would grow thicker only because of the forms that announced that there was still nothing new on the case.

It was even worse for Ryan and Douglas. Yet again there had been a possible link that might open up two of their *Unsolved* files. Everyone would care about Raymond and Doris Brown. They'd had friends and neighbors, evidently a good minister. They'd be missed, and people would think *what a shame it was* . . . But the files on Ryan's desk were for people about whom no one but police officers cared, and somehow that only made it worse because someone should mourn for the dead, not just cops who were paid to do so. Worse still, it was yet another MO in a string of homicides that were somehow linked, but not in a way that made any sense. This was not their Invisible Man. Yes, the weapon had been a .22, but he'd had a chance to kill the innocent twice. He'd spared Virginia Charles, and he had somehow gone dangerously far out of his way to spare Doris Brown. He had saved her from Farmer and Grayson, probably, and someone else. . . .

"Detective," Ryan asked, "what was the condition of Doris's body?"

"What do you mean?"

It seemed an absurd question even as his mind formed it, but the man on the other end of the line would understand. "What was her physical condition?"

"The autopsy is tomorrow, Lieutenant. She was neatly dressed, all cleaned up, hair was nice, she looked pretty decent." *Except for the two holes in the back of her head,* the man didn't have to add.

Douglas read his lieutenant's mind and nodded. *Somebody took the time to get her well.* That was a starting place.

"I'd appreciate it if you could send me anything that might be useful. It'll work both ways," Ryan assured him.

"Some guy went way out of his way to murder them. We don't see many like this. I don't like it very much," the detective added. It was a puerile conclusion, but Ryan fully understood. How else did you say it, after all?

It was called a safe house, and it was indeed safe. Located on a hundred rolling acres in the Virginia hills, there was on the estate a stately house and a twelve-stall stable half-occupied with hunter-jumpers. The title for the house showed a name, but that person owned another place nearby and leased this one to the Central Intelligence Agency—actually to a shadow corporation that existed only as a piece of paper and a post-office box—because he'd served his time in OSS, and besides, the money was right. Nothing unusual from the outside, but a more careful inspection might show that the doors and doorframes were steel, the windows unusually thick and strong, and sealed. It was as secure from outside assault and from an internal attempt at escape as a maximum-security prison, just a lot more pleasant to behold.

Grishanov found clothing to wear, and shaving things that worked but with which he couldn't harm himself. The bathroom mirror was steel, and the cup in the holder was paper. The couple that managed the house spoke passable Russian and were just as pleasant as they could be, already briefed on the nature of their new guest—they were more accustomed to defectors, though all their visitors were "protected" by a team of four security guards inside who came when they had "company," and two more who lived full-time in the caretaker's house close to the stables.

Not unusually, their guest was out of synch with local time, and his disorientation and unease made him talkative. They were surprised that their orders were to limit their conversations to the mundane. The lady of the house fixed breakfast, always the best meal for the jet-lagged, while her husband launched a discussion of Pushkin, delighted to find that like many Russians, Grishanov was a serious devotee of poetry. The security guard leaned against the doorframe, just to keep an eye on things.

"The things I have to do, Sandy—"

"John, I understand," she told him quietly. Both were surprised at how strong her voice was, how determined. "I didn't before, but I do now."

"When I was over there"—was it only three days before?—"I thought about you. I need to thank you," he told her.

"What for?"

Kelly looked down at the kitchen table. "Hard to explain. It's scary, the things I do. It helps when you have somebody to think about. Excuse me—I don't mean—" Kelly stopped. He did, actually, mean that. The mind wanders when alone, and his had wandered.

Sandy took his hand and smiled in a gentle way. "I used to be afraid of you."

"Why?" he asked with considerable surprise.

"Because of the things you do."

"I'd never hurt you," he said without looking up, yet more miserable now that she had felt the need to fear him.

"I know that now."

Despite her words, Kelly felt a need to explain himself. He wanted her to understand, not realizing that she already did. How to do it? Yes, he killed people, but only for a reason. How had he come to be what he was? Training was part of it, the rigorous months spent at Coronado, the time and effort spent to inculcate automatic responses, more deadly still, to learn patience. Along with that had somehow come a new way of seeing things—and then, actually seeing them and seeing the reasons why killing sometimes had to be. Along with the reasons had come a code, a modification, really, of what he'd learned from his father. His actions had to have a purpose, usually assigned by others, but his mind was agile enough to make its own decisions, to fit his code into a different context, to apply it with care—but to apply it. A product of many things, he sometimes surprised himself with what he was. Someone had to try, and he most often was best suited to—

"You love too much, John," she said. "You're like me."

Those words brought his head up.

"We lose patients on my floor, we lose them all the time—and I *hate* it! I hate being there when life goes away. I *hate* watching the family cry and knowing that we couldn't stop it from happening. We all do our best. Professor Rosen is a wonderful surgeon, but we don't always win, and I hate it when we lose. And with Doris—we won that one, John, and somebody took her away anyway. And that wasn't disease or some damned auto accident. Somebody meant to do it. She was one of *mine,* and somebody killed her and her father. So I do understand, okay? I really do."

Jesus, she really does . . . better than me.

"Everybody connected with Pam and Doris, you're all in danger now."

Sandy nodded. "You're probably right. She told us things about Henry. I know what kind of person he is. I'll tell you everything she told us."

"You do understand what I'm going to do with that information?"

"Yes, John, I do. Please be careful." She paused and told him why he had to be. "I want you back."

32
Home Is the Prey

The one bit of usable information to come out of Pittsburgh was a name. *Sandy*. Sandy had driven Doris Brown back home to her father. Just one word, not even a proper name, but cases routinely broke on less than that. It was like pulling on a string. Sometimes all you got was a broken piece of thread, sometimes you got something that just didn't stop until everything unraveled into a tangled mess in your hands. Somebody named Sandy, a female voice, young. She'd hung up before saying anything, though it hardly seemed likely that she'd had anything at all to do with the murders. One might return to the scene of the crime—it really did happen—but not via telephone.

How did it fit in? Ryan leaned back in his chair, staring at the ceiling while his trained mind examined everything he knew.

The most likely supposition was that Doris Brown, deceased, had been directly connected with the same criminal enterprise that had killed Pamela Madden and Helen Waters, and that had also included as active members Richard Farmer and William Grayson. John Terrence Kelly, former UDT sailor, and perhaps a former Navy

SEAL, had somehow happened upon and rescued Pamela Madden. He'd called Frank Allen about it several weeks later, telling him not very much. Something had gone badly wrong—short version, he'd been an ass—and Pamela Madden had died as a result. The photos of the body were something Ryan would never fully put from his mind. Kelly had been badly shot. A former commando whose girlfriend had been brutally murdered, Ryan reminded himself. Five pushers eliminated as though James Bond had appeared on the streets of Baltimore. One extraneous killing in which the murderer had intervened in a street robbery for reasons unknown. Richard Farmer—"Rick"?—eliminated with a knife, the second possible show of rage (and the first one didn't count, Ryan reminded himself). William Grayson, probably kidnapped and killed. Doris Brown, probably rescued at the same time, cleaned up over a period of weeks and returned to her home. That meant some sort of medical care, didn't it? Probably. *Maybe,* he corrected himself. The Invisible Man . . . could he have done that himself? Doris was the girl who'd brushed out Pamela Madden's hair. There was a connection.

Back up.

Kelly had rescued the Madden girl, but he'd had help getting her straightened out. Professor Sam Rosen and his wife, another physician. So Kelly finds Doris Brown—whom would he take her to? *That* was a starting place! Ryan lifted his phone.

"Hello."

"Doc, it's Lieutenant Ryan."

"I didn't know I gave you my direct line," Farber said. "What's up?"

"Do you know Sam Rosen?"

"Professor Rosen? Sure. He runs a department, hell of a good cutter, world-class. I don't see him very often, but if you ever need a head worked on, he's the man."

"And his wife?" Ryan could hear the man sucking on his pipe.

"I know her quite well. Sarah. She's a pharmacologist, research fellow across the street, also works with our drug-abuse unit. I help out with that group, too, and we—"

"Thank you." Ryan cut him off. "One more name. Sandy."

"Sandy who?"

"That's all I have," Lieutenant Ryan admitted. He could imagine Farber now, leaning away from his desk in the high-backed leather chair with his contemplative look.

"Let me make sure I understand things, okay? Are you asking me to check up on two colleagues as part of a criminal investigation?"

Ryan weighed the merits of lying. This guy was a psychiatrist. His job was looking around in people's minds. He was good at it.

"Yes, doctor, I am," the detective admitted after a pause long enough for the psychiatrist to make an accurate guess as to its cause.

"You're going to have to explain yourself," Farber announced evenly. "Sam and I aren't exactly close, but he is not a person who would *ever* hurt another human being. And Sarah is a damned angel with these messed-up kids we see in here. She's setting aside some important research work to do that, stuff she could make a big reputation with." Then Farber realized that she'd been away an awful lot in the past couple of weeks.

"Doctor, I'm just trying to develop some information, okay? I have no reason whatever to believe that either one of them is implicated in any illegal act." His words were too formal, and he knew it. Perhaps another tack. It was even honest, maybe. "If my speculation is correct, there may be some danger to them that they don't know about."

"Give me a few minutes." Farber broke the connection.

"Not bad, Em," Douglas said.

It was bottom-fishing, Ryan thought, but, hell, he'd tried just about everything else. It seemed an awfully long five minutes before the phone rang again.

"Ryan."

"Farber. No docs on neuro by that name. One nurse, though, Sandra O'Toole. She's a team leader on the service. I don't know her myself. Sam thinks highly of her, or so I just found out from his secretary. She was working

something special for him, recently. He had to fiddle the
pay records." Farber had already made his own connection.
Sarah had been absent from her clinical work at the same
time. He'd let the police develop that themselves. He'd
gone far enough—too far. These were colleagues, after all,
and this wasn't a game.

"When was that?" Ryan asked casually.

"Two or three weeks ago, lasted ten working days."

"Thank you, doctor. I'll be back to you."

"Connection," Douglas observed after the circuit was
broken. "How much you want to bet that she knows Kelly,
too?"

The question was more hopeful than substantive, of
course. Sandra was a common-enough name. Still, they'd
been on this case, this endless series of deaths, for more
than six months, and after all that time spent with no
evidence and no connections at all, it looked like the
morning star. The problem was that it was evening now,
and time to go home for dinner with his wife and children.
Jack would be returning to Boston College in another week
or so, Ryan thought, and he missed time with his son.

There was no easy way to get things organized. Sandy had
to drive him to Quantico. It was her first time on a Marine
base, but only briefly, as Kelly guided her to the marina.
Already, he thought. You get home for once with your
body in tune with the local day/night cycle, and already
he had to break it. Sandy was not yet back on I-95 when
he pulled away from the dock, heading out for the middle
of the river, advancing his throttles to max-cruise as soon
as he could.

The lady had brains to go with her guts, Kelly told
himself, sipping his first beer in a very long time. He
supposed it was normal that a clinical nurse would have
a good memory. Henry, it seemed, had been a talker at
certain moments, one of them being when he had a girl
under his direct control. A boastful man, Kelly thought,
the best sort. He still didn't have an address to go along
with the phone number, but he had a new name, Tony
P-something—Peegee, something like that. White, Italian,

drove a blue Lincoln, along with a decent physical description. Mafia, probably, either in it or a wannabe. Somebody else named Eddie—but Sandy had matched that name with a guy who had been killed by a police officer; it had made the front page of the local paper. Kelly took it one step further: what if that cop was the man Henry had inside? It struck him as odd that a senior officer like a lieutenant would be involved in a shooting. Speculation, he told himself, but worth checking out—he wasn't sure yet exactly how. He had all night for it, and a smooth body of water to reflect his thoughts as it did the stars. Soon he passed the spot where he'd left Billy. At least someone had collected the body.

The ground was settling over the grave in a place that some still called Potter's Field, a tradition dating back to someone named Judas. The doctors at the community hospital that had treated the man were still going over the pathology report from the Medical College of Virginia. Baro-Trauma. There were fewer than ten severe cases of this condition in the whole country in a year, and all of those in coastal regions. It was no disgrace that they hadn't made the diagnosis—and, the report went on, there was no difference it could have made. The precise cause of death had been a fragment of *bone marrow* that had somehow found its way into a cerebral artery, occluding it and causing a massive, fatal stroke. Damage to other organs had been so extensive that it would only have been a matter of a few more weeks in any case. The bone-marrow blockage was evidence of a very large pressurization imbalance, 3-bar, probably more. Even now police were inquiring about divers in the Potomac, which could be very deep in some places. There was still hope that someone would eventually claim the body, whose location was recorded in the county administrator's office. But not much.

"What do you mean, you don't know?" General Rokossovskiy demanded. "He's my man! Did you misplace him?"

"Comrade General," Giap replied sharply, "I have told you everything I know!"

"And you say an American did it?"

"You have seen the intelligence information as well as I have."

"That man has information that the Soviet Union requires. I find it hard to believe that the Americans planned a raid whose only result was the abduction of the one Soviet officer in the area. I would suggest, Comrade General, that you make a more serious effort."

"We are at war!"

"Yes, I am aware of that," Rokossovskiy observed dryly. "Why do you think I am here?"

Giap could have sworn at the taller man who stood before his desk. He was the commander of his country's armed forces, after all, and a general of no mean abilities himself. The Vietnamese general swallowed his pride with difficulty. He also needed the weapons that only the Russians could provide, and so he had to abase himself before him for the sake of his country. Of one thing he was certain. The camp wasn't worth the trouble it had caused him.

The strange part was that the routine had become relatively benign. Kolya wasn't here. That was certain. Zacharias was sufficiently disoriented that he had difficulty determining the passage of days, but for four sleeps now he hadn't heard the Russian's voice even outside the door. By the same token, no one had come in to abuse him. He'd eaten and sat and thought in solitude. To his surprise it had made things better instead of worse. His time with Kolya had become an addiction more dangerous than his dalliance with alcohol, Robin saw now. It was loneliness that was his real enemy, not pain, not fear. From a family and a religious community that fostered fellowship, he'd entered a profession that lived on the same, and being denied it his mind had fed on itself. Then add a little pain and fear, and what did you have? It was something far more easily seen from without than from within. Doubtless it had been apparent to Kolya. *Like you,* he'd said so often, *like you.* So, Zacharias told himself, that's how he did his job. Cleverly, too, the Colonel admitted to himself.

Though not a man accustomed to failure and mistakes, he was not immune to them. He'd almost killed himself with a youthful error at Luke Air Force Base while learning to fly fighters, and five years later, the time he'd wondered what the inside of a thunderstorm was really like and nearly ended up hitting the ground in the manner of a thunderbolt. And now he'd made another.

Zacharias didn't know the reason for his respite from the interrogations. Perhaps Kolya was off reporting on what he'd learned. Whatever the reason, he had been granted the chance to reflect. *You've sinned,* Robin told himself. *You've been very foolish. But you won't do that again.* The determination was weak, and Zacharias knew he'd have to work to strengthen it. Fortunately, he now had the time for reflection. If it was not a real deliverance, it was something. Suddenly he was shocked into full concentration, as if he were flying a combat mission. *My God,* he thought, *that word. I was afraid to pray for deliverance ... and yet ...* His guards would have been surprised to see the wistful smile on his face, especially had they known that he was starting to pray again. Prayer, they'd all been taught, was a farce. But that was their misfortune, Robin thought, and might yet be his salvation.

He couldn't make the call from his office. It just wouldn't do. Nor did he wish to do so from his home. The call would cross a river and a state line, and he knew that for security reasons there were special provisions for telephone calls made in the D.C. area. They were all recorded on computer tape, the only place in America where that was true. Even so, there was a procedure for what he had to do. You were supposed to have official sanction for it. You had to discuss it with your section head, then with the chief of the directorate, and it could well go all the way to the "front office" on the seventh floor. Ritter didn't want to wait that long, not with lives at stake. He took the day off, not unreasonably claiming that he needed the time to recover from all the travel. So he decided to drive into town, and picked the Smithsonian's Museum of Natural History. He walked past the elephant in the lobby and consulted the YOU ARE HERE plate on the wall to find the public telephones, into one of which he dropped a dime and called 347-1347. It was almost an institutional joke. That number connected him to a telephone that rang on the desk of the KGB *rezident,* the chief of station for Washington, D.C. They knew, and knew that people interested knew they knew. The espionage business could be so baroque, Ritter told himself.

"Yes?" a voice said. It was the first time Ritter had done this, a whole new collection of sensations—his own nervousness, the evenness of the voice at the other end, the excitement of the moment. What he had to say, however, was programmed in such a way that outsiders could not interfere with official business:

"This is Charles. There is a matter of concern to you. I propose a brief meeting and discussion. I'll be at the National Zoo in an hour, at the enclosure for the white tigers."

"How will I know you?" the voice asked.

"I'll be carrying a copy of *Newsweek* in my left hand."

"One hour," the voice grumbled. He probably had an important meeting this morning, Ritter thought. Wasn't that too bad? The CIA field officer left the museum for his car. On the right seat was a copy of *Newsweek* he'd purchased at a drugstore on the way into town.

Tactics, Kelly thought, turning to port, finally rounding Point Lookout. There was a wide selection. He still had his safe house in Baltimore with a false name on everything. The police might be interested in talking to him, but they hadn't made contact with him yet. He'd try to keep it that way. The enemy didn't know who he was. That was his starting place. The fundamental issue was the three-way balance among what he knew, what he didn't know, and how he might use the first to affect the second. The third element, the *how,* was tactics. He could prepare for what he did not yet know. He could not yet act upon it, but he actually knew what he would do. Getting to that point simply required a strategic approach to the problem. It was frustrating, though. Four young women awaited his action.

An as yet undetermined number of people awaited death.

They were driven by fear, Kelly knew. They'd been afraid of Pam, and afraid of Doris. Afraid enough to kill. He wondered if the death of Edward Morello had been a further manifestation. Certainly they had killed for their safety, and now they probably did feel safe. That was good; if fear was their driving force, then they had more of it now that they felt it a thing of their past.

The worrisome part was the time element. There was a clock on this. The police were sniffing at him. While he thought there was nothing they could possibly have to use against him, he still couldn't feel good about it. The other worry was the safety—he snorted—of those four young women. There was no such thing as a good *long* operation. Well, he'd have to be patient on one thing, and with luck, just the one.

He hadn't been to the zoo in years. Ritter thought he'd have to bring his kids here again now that they were old enough to appreciate things a little more. He took the time to look at the bear pit—there was just something interesting about bears. Kids thought of them as large, animated versions of the stuffed toys they clutched at night. Not Ritter. They were the image of the enemy, large and strong, far less clumsy and far more intelligent than they appeared. A good thing to remember, he told himself, heading over to the tiger cage. He rolled the *Newsweek* in his left hand, watching the large cats and waiting. He didn't bother checking his watch.

"Hello, Charles," a voice said beside him.

"Hello, Sergey."

"I do not know you," the *rezident* observed.

"This conversation is unofficial," Ritter explained.

"Aren't they all?" Sergey noted. He started walking. Any single place could be bugged, but not a whole zoo. For that matter, his contact could be wearing a wire, though that would not have been in accordance with the rules, such as they were. He and Ritter walked down the gentle paved slope to the next animal exhibit, with the *rezident*'s security guard in close attendance.

"I just returned from Vietnam," the CIA officer said.

"Warmer there than here."

"Not at sea. It's rather pleasant out there."

"The purpose of your cruise?" the *rezident* asked.

"A visit, an unplanned one."

"I believe it failed," the Russian said, not tauntingly, just letting "Charles" know that he knew what was going on.

"Not completely. We brought someone home with us."

"Who might that be?"

"His name is Nikolay." Ritter handed over Grishanov's paybook. "It would be an embarrassment to your government if it were to be revealed that a Soviet officer was interrogating American POWs."

"Not a great embarrassment," Sergey replied, flipping briefly through the paybook before pocketing it.

"Well, actually it would be. You see, the people he's been interrogating have been reported as being dead by your little friends."

"I don't understand." He was telling the truth, and Ritter had to explain for a few minutes. "I did not know any of that," Sergey said after hearing the facts of the matter.

"It's true, I assure you. You will be able to verify it through your own means." And he would, of course. Ritter knew that, and Sergey knew that he knew.

"And where is our colonel?"

"In a safe place. He's enjoying better hospitality than our people are."

"Colonel Grishanov hasn't dropped bombs on anyone," the Russian pointed out.

"That is true, but he did take part in a process that will end with the death of American prisoners, and we have hard evidence that they are alive. As I said earlier, a potential embarrassment for your government."

Sergey Voloshin was a highly astute political observer and didn't need this young CIA officer to tell him that. He could also see where this discussion was headed.

"What do you propose?"

"It would be helpful if your government could persuade Hanoi to restore these men to life, as it were. That is, to take them to the same prison where the other prisoners are, and make the proper notifications so that their families will know they are alive after all. In return for that, Colonel Grishanov will be returned unharmed, and uninterrogated."

"I will forward that proposal to Moscow." With a favorable endorsement, his tone said clearly.

"Please be quick. We have reason to believe that the Vietnamese may be contemplating something drastic to relieve themselves of the potential embarrassment. That would be a very serious complication," Ritter warned.

"Yes, I suppose it would be." He paused. "Your assurance that Colonel Grishanov is alive and well?"

"I can have you to him in . . . oh, about forty minutes if you wish. Do you think I would lie about something as important as this?"

"No, I do not. But some questions must be asked."

"Yes, Sergey Ivan'ch, I know that. We have no wish to harm your colonel. He seems to have behaved rather honorably in his treatment of our people. He was also a very effective interrogator. I have his notes." Ritter added, "The offer to meet with him is open if you wish to make use of it."

Voloshin thought about it, seeing the trap. Such an offer, if taken, would have to be reciprocated, because that was the way things were. To call Ritter's hand on this would commit his own government to something, and Voloshin didn't want to do that without guidance. Besides, it would be madness for CIA to lie in a case like this. Those prisoners could always be made to disappear. Only the goodwill of the Soviet Union could save them, and only the continuance of that goodwill would keep them healthy.

"I will take you at your word, Mister—"

"Ritter, Bob Ritter."

"Ah! Budapest."

Ritter grinned rather sheepishly. Well, after all he'd done to get his agent out, it was clear that he'd never go back into the field again, at least not in any place that mattered—which for Ritter started at the River Elbe. The Russian poked him in the chest.

"You did well getting your man out. I commend you on your loyalty to your agent." Most of all Voloshin respected him for the risk he'd taken, something not possible in the KGB.

"Thank you, General. And thank you for responding to my proposal. When can I call you?"

"I'll need two days . . . shall I call you?"

"Forty-eight hours from now. I'll make the call."

"Very well. Good day." They shook hands like the professionals they were. Voloshin walked back to his driver/bodyguard and headed back to the car. Their walk had ended up at the enclosure for the Kodiak bear, large, brown, and powerful. Had that been an accident? Ritter wondered.

On the walk back to his car he realized that the whole thing had been an accident of sorts. On the strength of this play, Ritter would become a section chief. Failed rescue mission or not, he'd just negotiated an important concession with the Russians, and it had all happened because of the presence of mind of a man younger than himself, scared and on the run, who'd taken the time to think. He wanted people like that in the Agency, and now he had the clout to bring him in. Kelly had demurred and temporized on the flight back from Hawaii. Okay, so he'd need a little convincing. He'd have to work with Jim Greer on that, but Ritter decided on the spot that his next mission was to bring Kelly in from the cold, or the heat, or whatever you called it.

"How well do you know Mrs. O'Toole?" Ryan asked.

"Her husband's dead," the neighbor said. "He went to Vietnam right after they bought the house, and then he was killed. Such a nice young man, too. She's not in any trouble, is she?"

The detective shook his head. "No, not at all. I've only heard good things about her."

"It's been awful busy over there," the elderly lady went on. She was the perfect person to talk to, about sixty-five, a widow with nothing to do who compensated for the empty space in her life by keeping track of everyone else's. With a little reassurance that she wasn't hurting anyone, she'd relate everything she knew.

"What do you mean?"

"I think she had a houseguest a while back. She sure was shopping a lot more than usual. She's such a nice, pretty girl. It's so sad about her husband. She really ought to start dating again. I'd like to tell her, but I don't want her to think I'm nosy. Anyway, she was shopping a lot, and somebody else came almost every day, stayed overnight a lot, even."

"Who was that?" Ryan asked, sipping his iced tea.

"A woman, short like me, but heavier, messy hair. She drove a big car, a red Buick, I think, and it had a sticker-thing on the windshield. Oh! That's right!"

"What's that?" Ryan asked.

"I was out with my roses when the girl came out, that's when I saw the sticker-thing."

"Girl?" Ryan asked innocently.

"That's who she was shopping for!" the elderly lady said, pleased with herself for the sudden discovery. "She bought clothes for her, I bet. I remember the Hecht Company bags."

"Can you tell me what the girl looked like?"

"Young, like nineteen or twenty, dark hair. Kinda pale, like she was sick. They drove away, when was that . . . ? Oh, I remember. It's the day my new roses came from the nursery. The eleventh. The truck came very early because I don't like the heat, and I was out there working when they came out. I waved at Sandy. She's such a nice girl. I don't talk to her very much, but when I do she always has a kind word. She's a nurse, you know, she works at Johns Hopkins, and—"

Ryan finished off his tea without letting his satisfaction show. Doris Brown had returned home to Pittsburgh on the afternoon of the eleventh. Sarah Rosen drove a Buick, and it undoubtedly had a parking sticker in the window. Sam Rosen, Sarah Rosen, Sandra O'Toole. They had treated Miss Brown. Two of them had also treated Miss Madden. They had also treated Mr. Kelly. After months of frustration, Lieutenant Emmet Ryan had a case.

"There she is now," the lady said, startling him out of his private thoughts. Ryan turned and looked to see an attractive young lady, on the tall side, carrying a bag of groceries.

"I wonder who that man was?"

"What man?"

"He was there last night. Maybe she has a boyfriend after all. Tall, like you, dark hair—big."

"How do you mean?"

"Like a football player, you know, big. He must be nice, though. I saw her hug him. That was just last night."

Thank God, Ryan thought, *for people who don't watch TV.*

For his long gun, Kelly had selected a bolt-action .22, a Savage Model 54, the lightweight version of that company's Anschutz match weapon. It was expensive enough at a hundred fifty dollars with tax. Almost as costly were the Leupold scope and mounts. The rifle was almost too good for its purpose, which was the hunting of small game, and had a particularly fine walnut stock. It was a shame that he'd have to scar it up. It would have been more of a shame to waste the lesson from that chief machinist's mate, however.

The one bad thing about the demise of Eddie Morello was that sweetening the deal had required the loss of a large quantity of pure, uncut heroin, a six-kilogram donation to the police evidence locker. That had to be made up. Philadelphia was hungry for more, and his New York connections were showing increasing interest now that they'd had their first taste. He'd do one last batch on the ship. Now he could change over again. Tony was setting up a secure lab that was easier to reach, more in keeping with the burgeoning success he was enjoying, but until that was ready, one more time the old way. He wouldn't make the trip himself.

"How soon?" Burt asked.

"Tonight."

"Fair enough, boss. Who goes with me?"

"Phil and Mike." The two new ones were from Tony's organization, young, bright, ambitious. They didn't know

Henry yet, and would not be part of his local distribution network, but they could handle out-of-town deliveries and were willing to do the menial work that was part of this business, mixing and packaging. They saw it, not inaccurately, as a rite of passage, a starting place from which their status and responsibility would grow. Tony guaranteed their reliability. Henry accepted that. He and Tony were bound now, bound in business, bound in blood. He'd accept Tony's counsel now that he trusted him. He'd rebuild his distribution network, removing the need for his female couriers, and with the removal of the need for them, so would end the reason for their lives. It was too bad, but with three defections, it was plain that they were becoming dangerous. A useful part of his operation in the growth phase, perhaps, but now a liability.

But one thing at a time.

"How much?" Burt asked.

"Enough to keep you busy for a while." Henry waved to the beer coolers. There wasn't room for much beer in them now, but that was as it should be. Burt carried them out to his car, not casual, but not tense. Businesslike, the way things should be. Perhaps Burt would become his principal lieutenant. He was loyal, respectful, tough when he had to be, far more dependable than Billy or Rick, and a brother. It was funny, really. Billy and Rick had been necessary at the beginning since the major distributors were always white, and he'd taken them on as tokens. Well, fate had settled that. Now the white boys were coming to him, weren't they?

"Take Xantha with you."

"Boss, we're going to be busy," Burt objected.

"You can leave her there when you're done." Perhaps one at a time was the best way to do it.

Patience never came easy. It was a virtue he'd learned, after a fashion, but only from necessity. Activity helped. He set the gun barrel in the vise, damaging the finish even before he started to do anything substantive. Setting the milling machine on high-speed, rotating the control wheel, he started drilling a series of holes at regular intervals in the outermost six inches of the barrel. An hour later he had a steel can–body affixed over it, and the telescopic sight attached. The rifle, as modified, proved to be quite accurate, Kelly thought.

"Tough one, Dad?"

"Eleven months' worth, Jack," Emmet admitted over dinner. He was home on time for once, to his wife's pleasure—almost.

"That awful one?" his wife asked.

"Not over dinner, honey, okay?" he replied, answering the question. Emmet did his best to keep that part of his life out of the house. He looked over at his son and decided to comment on a decision his son recently made. "Marines, eh?"

"Well, Dad, it pays for the last two years of school, doesn't it?" It was like his son to worry about things like that, about the cost of education for his sister, still in high school and away at camp for the moment. And like his father, Jack craved a little adventure before settling down to whatever place life would find for him.

"My son, a jarhead," Emmet grumbled good-naturedly. He also worried. Vietnam wasn't over, might not be over when his son graduated, and like most fathers of his generation, he wondered why the hell he'd had to risk his life fighting Germans—so that his son might have to do the same, fighting people he'd never even heard about at his son's age.

"What falls out of the sky, pop?" Jack asked with a college-boy grin, repeating something Marines like to say.

Such talk worried Catherine Burke Ryan, who remembered seeing Emmet off, remembered praying all day in St. Elizabeth Church on June 6, 1944, and many days thereafter despite the regular letters and assurances. She remembered the waiting. She knew this kind of talk worried Emmet too, though not quite in the same way.

What falls out of the sky? Trouble! the detective almost told his son, for the Airborne, too, were a proud group, but the thought stopped before it got to his lips.

Kelly. We tried calling him. We had the Coast Guard look at that island he lives on. The boat wasn't there. The boat wasn't anywhere. Where was he? He was back now, though, if the little old lady was right. What if he was away? But now he's back. The killings just plain stopped after the Farmer–Grayson–Brown incident. The marina had remembered seeing the boat about that time, but he'd left in the middle of the night—*that night*—and just vanished. Connection. Where had the boat been? Where was it now? What falls out of the sky? Trouble. That's exactly what had happened before. It just dropped out of the sky. Started and stopped.

His wife and son saw it again. Chewing on his food, his eyes focused on infinity, unable to turn his mind off as it churned his information over and over. Kelly's not really all that different from what I used to be, Ryan thought. One-Oh-One, the Screaming Eagles of the 101st Infantry Division (Airborne), who still swaggered in their baggy pants. Emmet had started off as a buck private, ended up with a late-war battlefield commission to the rank he still held, lieutenant. He remembered the pride of being something very special, the sense of invincibility that strangely came arm in arm with the terror of jumping out of an aircraft, being the first on enemy territory, in the dark, carrying light weapons only. The hardest men with the hardest mission. Mission. He'd been like that once. But no one had ever killed his lady . . . what might have happened, back in 1946, perhaps, if someone had done that to Catherine?

Nothing good.

He'd saved Doris Brown. He'd given her over to people he trusted. He'd seen one of them last night. He knows she's dead. He saved Pamela Madden, she died, and he was in the hospital, and a few weeks after he got out people started dying in a very expert way. A few weeks . . . to get in shape. Then the killings just stopped and Kelly was nowhere to be found.

What if he's just been away?

He's back now.

Something's going to happen.

It wasn't a thing he could take to court. The only physical evidence they had was the imprint of a shoe sole—a common brand of sneaker, of course, hundreds sold every day. Zilch. They had motive. But how many murders happened every year, and how many people followed up on it? They had opportunity. Could he account for his time in front of a jury? No one could. How, the detective thought, do you explain this to a judge—no, some judges would understand, but no jury would, not after a brand-new law-school graduate had explained a few things to them.

The case was solved, Ryan thought. He *knew*. But he had nothing for it but the knowledge that something was going to happen.

"Who's that, you suppose?" Mike asked.

"Some fisherman, looks like," Burt observed from the driver's seat. He kept *Henry's Eighth* well clear of the white cabin cruiser. Sunset was close. They were almost too late to navigate the tangled waters into their laboratory, which looked very different at night. Burt gave the white boat a look. The guy with the fishing rod waved, a gesture he returned as he turned to port—left, as he thought of it. There was a big night ahead. Xantha wouldn't be much help. Well, maybe a little, when they broke for meals. A shame, really. Not really a bad girl, just dumb, badly spaced out. Maybe that's how they'd do it, just give her a nice taste of real good stuff before they broke out the netting and the cement blocks. They were sitting right in the open, right in the boat, and she didn't have a clue what they were for. Well, that wasn't his lookout.

Burt shook his head. There were more important things to consider. How would Mike and Phil feel about working under him? He'd have to be polite about it, of course. They'd understand. With the money involved, they ought to. He relaxed in his chair, sipping his beer and looking for the red marker buoy.

"Lookee, lookee," Kelly breathed. It wasn't hard, really. Billy had told him all he needed to know. They had a place in there. They came in the Bay side, by boat, usually at night, and usually left the following morning. Turned in at the red lighted buoy. Hard as hell to find, almost impossible in the dark. Well, probably was if you didn't know the water. Kelly did. He reeled in the unbaited hook and lifted his binoculars. Size and color were right. *Henry's Eighth* was the name. Check. He settled back, watching it move south, then turn east at the red buoy. Kelly marked his chart. Twelve hours at least. That should be plenty of time. The problem with so secure a place was that it depended absolutely on secrecy which, once blown, became a fatal liability. People never learned. One way in, one way out. Another clever way to commit suicide. He'd wait for sunset. While waiting, Kelly got out a can of spray paint and put green stripes on his dinghy. The inside he painted black.

33

Poisoned Charm

It usually took all night, Billy had told him. That gave Kelly time to eat, relax, and prepare. He moved *Springer* in close to the cluttered ground he would be hunting tonight and set his anchors. The meal he prepared was only sandwiches, but it was better than he'd had atop "his" hill less than a week before. *God, a week ago I was on* Ogden, *getting ready,* he thought with a rueful shake of the head. How could life be so mad as this?

His small dinghy, now camouflaged, went into the water after midnight. He'd attached a small electric trolling motor to the transom, and hoped he had enough battery power to get in and out. It couldn't be too far. The chart showed that the area was not a large one, and the place they used had to be in the middle for maximum isolation. With darkened face and hands he moved into the maze of derelicts, steering the dinghy with his left hand while his eyes and ears searched for something that didn't belong. The sky helped. There was no moon, and the starlight was just enough to show him the grass and reeds that had grown in this tidal wetland that had been created when the hulks had been left there, silting up this part of the Bay and making a place that birds loved in the fall season.

It was like before. The low hum of the trolling motor was so much like that of the sled he'd used, moving him along at perhaps two knots, conserving power, guided this time by stars. The marsh grass grew to perhaps six or seven feet above the water, and it wasn't hard to see why they didn't navigate their way in by night. It truly was a maze if you didn't know how. But Kelly did. He watched the stars, knowing which to follow and which to ignore as their position rotated in the arching sky. It was a matter of comfort, really. They were from the city, were not seamen as he was, and as secure as they felt in their chosen place to prepare their illicit product, they weren't at ease here in this place of wild things and uncertain paths. *Won't you come into my parlor,* Kelly told himself. He was more listening than looking now. A gentle breeze rustled through the tall grass, following the widest channel here among the silted bars; twisty as it was, it had to be the one they'd followed. The fifty-year-old hulks around him looked like ghosts of another age, as indeed they were, relics of a war that had been won, cast-offs of a much simpler time, some of them sitting at odd angles, forgotten toys of the huge child their country had been, a child now grown into a troubled adult.

A voice. Kelly stopped his motor, drifting for a few seconds, pivoting his head around to get a fix on it. He'd guessed right on the channel. It looped around to the right just ahead there, and the noise had come from the right as well. Carefully now, slowly, he came around the bend. There were three of the derelicts. Perhaps they'd been towed in together. The tugboat skippers had probably tried to leave them in a perfect line as a personal conceit. The westernmost one was sitting at a slight angle, and listed seven or eight degrees to port, resting on a shifting bottom. The profile was an old one, with a low superstructure whose tall steel funnel had long since rusted away. But there was a light where the bridge ought to be. Music, he thought, some contemporary rock from a station that tried to keep truckers awake at night.

Kelly waited a few minutes, letting his eyes gather a fuller picture in the darkness, selecting his route of approach. He'd come in fine on the bow so that the body of the ship would screen him from view. He could hear more than one voice now. A sudden rolling laugh from a joke, perhaps. He paused again, searching the ship's outline for a bump, something that didn't belong, a sentry. Nothing.

They'd been clever selecting this place. It was as unlikely a spot as one might imagine, ignored even by local fishermen, but you had to have a lookout because no place was ever quite that secure . . . there was the boat. Okay. Kelly crept up at half a knot now, sticking close to the side of the old ship until he got to their boat. He tied his painter off to the nearest cleat. A rope ladder led up to the derelict's weather deck. Kelly took a deep breath and started climbing.

The work was every bit as menial and boring as Burt had told them it would be, Phil thought. Mixing the milk sugar in was the easy part, sifting it into large stainless-steel bowls like flour for a cake, making sure it was all evenly distributed. He remembered helping his mother with baking when he'd been a small child, watching her and learning things that a kid forgot as soon as he discovered baseball. They came back now, the rattling sound of the sifter, the way the powders came together. It was actually rather a pleasant excursion back to a time when he hadn't even had to wake up and go to school. But that was the easy part. Then came the tedious job of doling out precisely measured portions into the little plastic envelopes which had to be stapled shut, and piled, and counted, and bagged. He shared an exasperated look with Mike, who felt the same way he did. Burt probably felt the same way, but didn't let it show, and he had been nice enough to bring entertainment along. They had a radio playing, and for breaks they had this Xantha girl, half-blasted on pills, but . . . compliant, they'd all found out at their midnight break. They'd gotten her nice and tired, anyway. She was sleeping in the corner. There would be another break at four, allowing each of them enough time to recover. It was hard staying awake, and Phil was worried about all this powder, some of it dust in the air. Was he breathing it in? Might he get high on the stuff? If he had to do this again, he promised himself some sort of mask. He might like the idea of making money off selling the shit, but he had no desire at all to use it. Well, Tony and Henry were setting up a proper lab. Travel wouldn't be such a pain in the ass. That was something.

Another batch done. Phil was a little faster than the others, wanting to get it done. He walked over to the cooler and lifted the next one-kilo bag. He smelled it, as he had the others. Foul, chemical smell, like the chemicals used in the biology lab at his high school, formaldehyde, something like that. He slit open the bag with a penknife, dumping the contents into the first mixing bowl at arm's length, then adding a premeasured quantity of sugar and stirring with a spoon by the light of one of the Coleman lamps.

"Hello."

There had been no warning at all. Suddenly there was someone else there at the door, holding a pistol. He was dressed in military clothes, striped fatigues, and his face was painted green and black.

There wasn't any need for silence. His prey had seen to that. Kelly had reconverted his Colt back to .45 caliber, and he knew that the hole in the front of the automatic would seem large enough to park a car to the others in the room. He pointed with his left hand. "That way. On the deck, facedown, hands at the back of the neck, one at a time, you first," he said to the one at the mixing bowl.

"Who the hell are you?" the black one asked.

"You must be Burt. Don't do anything dumb."

"How you know my name?" Burt demanded as Phil took his place on the deck.

Kelly pointed at the other white one, directing him next to his friend.

"I know lots of things," Kelly said, moving towards Burt now. Then he saw the sleeping girl in the corner. "Who's she?"

"Look, asshole!" The .45 went level with his face, an arm's length away.

"What was that?" Kelly asked in a conversational voice. "Down on the deck, now." Burt complied at once. The girl, he saw, was sleeping. He'd let that continue for the moment. His first task was to search them for weapons. Two had small handguns. One had a useless little knife.

"Hey, who are you? Maybe we can talk," Burt suggested.

"We're going to do that. Tell me about the drugs," Kelly started off.

It was ten in the morning in Moscow when Voloshin's dispatch emerged from the decoding department. A senior member of the KGB's First Chief Directorate, he had a pipeline into any number of senior officers, one of whom was an academician in Service I, an American specialist who was advising the senior KGB leadership and the Foreign Ministry on this new development that the American media called *détente*. This man, who didn't hold a paramilitary rank within the KGB hierarchy, was probably the best person to get fast action, though an information copy of the dispatch had also gone to the Deputy Chairman with oversight duties for Voloshin's Directorate. Typically, the message was short and to the point. The Academician was appalled. The reduction of tension between the two superpowers, in the midst of a shooting war for one of them, was little short of miraculous, and coming as it did in parallel with the American approach to China, it could well signal a new era in relations. So he had said to the Politburo in a lengthy briefing only two weeks earlier. The public revelation that a Soviet officer had been involved in something like this—it was madness. What cretin at GRU had thought this one up? Assuming it really was true, which was something he had to check. For that he called the Deputy Chairman.

"Yevgeniy Leonidovich? I have an urgent dispatch from Washington."

"As do I, Vanya. Your recommendations?"

"If the American claims are true, I urge immediate action. Public knowledge of such idiocy could be ruinous. Could you confirm that this is indeed under way?"

"Da. And then . . . Foreign Ministry?"

"I agree. The military would take too long. Will they listen?"

"Our fraternal socialist allies? They'll listen to a shipment of rockets. They've been screaming for them for weeks," the Deputy Chairman replied.

How typical, the Academician thought, *in order to save American lives we will send weapons to take more of them, and the Americans will understand.* Such madness. If there was ever an illustration as to why *détente* was necessary, this was it. How could two great countries manage their affairs when both were involved, directly or not, in the affairs of minor countries? Such a worthless distraction from important matters.

"I urge speed, Yevgeniy Leonidovich," the Academician repeated. Though far outranked by the Deputy Chairman, they'd been classmates, years earlier, and their careers had crossed many times.

"I agree completely, Vanya. I'll be back to you this afternoon."

It was a miracle, Zacharias thought, looking around. He hadn't seen the outside of his cell in months, and just to smell the air, warm and humid as it was, seemed a gift from God, but that wasn't it. He counted the others, eighteen other men in the single line, men like himself, all within the same five-year age bracket, and in the fading light of dusk he saw faces. There was the one he'd seen so long before, a Navy guy by the look of him. They exchanged a look and thin smiles as all the men did what Robin was doing. If only the guards would let them talk, but the first attempt had earned one of their number a slap. Even so, for the moment just seeing their faces was enough. To *not* be alone any longer, to know that there were others here, just that was enough. Such a small thing. Such a large one. Robin stood as tall as his injured back allowed, squaring his shoulders while that little officer was saying something to his people, who were also lined up. He hadn't picked up enough Vietnamese to understand the rapid speech.

"This is the enemy," the Captain was telling his men. He'd be taking his unit south soon, and after all the lectures and battle practice, here was an unexpected opportunity for them to get a real look. They weren't so tough, these Americans, he told them. See, they're not so tall and forbidding, are they? They bend and break and bleed—very easily, too! And these are the elite of them, the ones who drop bombs on our country and kill our people. These are the men you'll be fighting. Do you fear them now? And if the Americans are foolish enough to try to rescue these dogs, we'll get early practice in the art of killing them. With those rousing words, he dismissed his troops, sending them off to their night guard posts.

He could do this, the Captain thought. It wouldn't matter soon. He'd heard a rumor through his regimental commander that as soon as the political leadership got their thumbs out, this camp would be closed down in a very final way, and his men would indeed get a little practice before they had to walk down Uncle Ho's trail, where they would have the chance to kill *armed* Americans next. Until then he had them as trophies to show his men, to lessen their dread of the great unknown of combat, and to focus their rage, for these *were* the men who'd bombed their beautiful country into a wasteland. He'd select recruits who had trained especially hard and well . . . nineteen of them, so as to give them a taste of killing. They'd need it. The captain of infantry wondered how many of them he'd be bringing home.

Kelly stopped off for fuel at the Cambridge town dock before heading back north. He had it all now—well, he had enough now, Kelly told himself. Full bunkers, and a mind full of useful data, and for the first time he'd hurt the bastards. Two weeks, maybe three weeks of their product. That would shake things loose. He might have collected it himself and perhaps used it as bait, but no, he couldn't do that. He wouldn't have it around him, especially now that he suspected he knew how it might come in. Somewhere on the East Coast, was all that Burt actually knew. Whoever this Henry Tucker was, he was on the clever side of paranoid, and compartmentalized his operation in a way that Kelly might have admired under other circumstances. But it was Asian heroin, and the bags it arrived in smelled of death, and they came in on the East Coast. How many things from Asia that smelled of death came to the Eastern United States? Kelly could think of only one, and the fact that he'd known men whose bodies had been processed at Pope Air Force Base only fueled his anger and his determination to see this one thing through. He brought *Springer* north, past the brick tower of Sharp's Island Light, heading back into a city that held danger from more than one direction.

One last time.

There were few places in Eastern America as sleepy as Somerset County. An area of large and widely separated farms, the whole county had but one high school. There was a single major highway, allowing people to transit the area quickly and without stopping. Traffic to Ocean City, the state's beach resort, bypassed the area, and the nearest interstate was on the far side of the Bay. It was also an area with a crime rate so low as to be nearly invisible except for those who took note of a single-digit increase in one category of misbehavior or another. One lone murder could be headline news for weeks in the local papers, and rarely was burglary a problem in an area where a homeowner was likely to greet a nocturnal intruder with a 12-gauge and a question. About the only problem was the way people drove, and for that they had the State Police, cruising the roads in their off-yellow cars. To compensate for boredom the cars on the Eastern Shore of Maryland had unusually large engines with which to chase down speeders who all too often visited the local liquor stores beforehand in their effort to make a dull if comfortable area somewhat more lively.

Trooper First Class Ben Freeland was on his regular patrol routine. Every so often something real would happen, and he figured it was his job to know the area, every inch of it, every farm and crossroads, so that if he ever did get a really major call he'd know the quickest way to it.

Four years out of the Academy at Pikesville, the Somerset native was thinking about advancement to corporal when he spotted a pedestrian on Postbox Road near a hamlet with the unlikely name of Dames Quarter. That was unusual. Everybody rode down here. Even kids started using bikes from an early age, often starting to drive well under age, which was another of the graver violations he dealt with on a monthly basis. He spotted her from a mile away—the land was very flat—and took no special note until he'd cut that distance by three quarters. She—definitely a female now—was walking unevenly. Another hundred yards of approach told him that she wasn't dressed like a local. That was odd. You didn't get here except by car. She was also walking in zigzags, even the length of her stride changing from one step to another, and that meant possible public intoxication—a *huge* local infraction, the trooper grinned to himself—and *that* meant he ought to pull over and give her a look. He eased the big Ford over to the gravel, bringing it to a smooth and safe stop fifty feet from her, and got out as he'd been taught, putting his uniform Stetson on and adjusting his pistol belt.

"Hello," he said pleasantly. "Where you heading, ma'am?"

She stopped after a moment, looking at him with eyes that belonged on another planet. "Who're you?"

The trooper leaned in close. There was no alcohol on her breath. Drugs were not much of a problem here yet, Freeland knew. That might have just changed.

"What's your name?" he asked in a more commanding tone.

"Xantha, with a ex," she answered, smiling.

"Where are you from, Xantha?"

"Aroun'."

"Around where?"

"'Lanta."

"You're a long way from Atlanta."

"I *know* that!" Then she laughed. "He dint know I had more." Which, she thought, was quite a joke, and a secret worth confiding. "Keeps them in my brassiere."

"What's that now?"

"My pills. Keep them in my brassiere, and he dint know."

"Can I see them?" Freeland asked, wondering a lot of things and knowing that he had a real arrest to make this day.

She laughed as she reached in. "You step back, now."

Freeland did so. There was no sense alerting her to anything, though his right hand was now on his gunbelt just in front of his service revolver. As he watched, Xantha reached inside her mostly unbuttoned blouse and came out with a handful of red capsules. So that was that. He opened the trunk of his car and reached inside the evidence kit he carried to get an envelope.

"Why don't you put them in here so you don't lose any?"

"Okay!" What a helpful fellow this policeman was.

"Can I offer you a ride, ma'am?"

"Sure. Tired a' walkin'."

"Well, why don't you just come right along?" Policy required that he handcuff such a person, and as he helped her into the back of the car, he did. She didn't seem to mind a bit.

"Where we goin'?"

"Well, Xantha, I think you need a place to lie down and get some rest. So I think I'll find you one, okay?" He already had a dead-bang case of drug possession, Freeland knew, as he pulled back onto the road.

"Burt and the other two restin', too, 'cept they ain't gonna wake up."

"What's that, Xantha?"

"He killed their ass, bang bang bang." She mimed with her hand. Freeland saw it in the mirror, nearly going off the road as he did so.

"Who's that?"

"He a white boy, dint get his name, dint see his face neither, but he killed their ass, bang bang bang."

Holy shit.

"Where?"

"On the boat." Didn't everybody know that?

"What boat?"

"The one out on the water, fool!" That was pretty funny, too.

"You shittin' me, girl?"

"An' you know the funny thing, he left all the drugs right there, too, the white boy did. 'Cept'n he was *green.*"

Freeland didn't have much idea what this was all about, but he intended to find out just as fast as he could. For starters he lit up his rotating lights and pushed the car just as fast as the big 427 V-8 would allow, heading for the State Police Barracks "V" in Westover. He ought to have radioed ahead, but it wouldn't really have accomplished much except to convince his captain that he was the one on drugs.

"Yacht *Springer,* take a look to your port quarter."

Kelly lifted his mike. "Anybody I know?" he asked without looking.

"Where the H have you been, Kelly?" Oreza asked.

"Business trip. What do you care?"

"Missed ya," was the answer. "Slow down some."

"Is it important? I have to get someplace, Portagee."

"Hey, Kelly, one seaman to another, back down, okay?"

Had he not known the man . . . no, he had to play along regardless of who it was. Kelly cut his throttles, allowing the cutter to pull alongside in a few minutes. Next he'd be asked to stop for a boarding, which Oreza had every legal right to do, and trying to evade would solve nothing. Without being so bidden, Kelly idled his engines and was soon laying to. Without asking permission, the cutter eased alongside and Oreza hopped aboard.

"Hey, Chief," the man said by way of a greeting.

"What gives?"

"I was down your sandbar twice in the last couple of weeks looking to share a beer with you, but you weren't home."

"Well, I wouldn't want to make you unfit for duty."

"Kinda lonely out here with nobody to harass." Suddenly it was clear that both men were uneasy, but neither one knew why the other was. "Where the hell were you?"

"I had to go out of the country. Business," Kelly answered. It was clear that he'd go no further than that.

"Fair enough. Be around for a while?"

"I plan to be, yeah."

"Okay, maybe I'll stop by next week and you can tell me some lies about being a Navy chief."

"Navy chiefs don't have to lie. You need some pointers on seamanship?"

"In a pig's ass! Maybe I ought to give you a safety inspection right now!"

"I thought this was a friendly visit," Kelly observed, and both men became even more uncomfortable. Oreza tried to cover it with a smile.

"Okay, I'll go easy on you." But that didn't work. "Catch you next week, Chief."

They shook hands, but something had changed. Oreza waved for the forty-one-footer to come back in, and he jumped aboard like the pro he was. The cutter pulled away without a further word.

Well, that makes sense. Kelly advanced his throttles anyway.

Oreza watched *Springer* continue north, wondering what the hell was going on. *Out of the country,* he'd said. For sure his boat hadn't been anywhere on the Chesapeake—but where, then? Why were the cops so interested in the guy? Kelly a killer? Well, he'd gotten that Navy Cross for something. UDT guy, that much Oreza knew. Beyond that, just a good guy to have a beer with, and a serious seaman in his way. It sure got complicated when you stopped doing search-and-rescue and started doing all that other cop stuff, the quartermaster told himself, heading southwest for Thomas Point. He had a phone call to make.

"So what happened?"

"Roger, they knew we were coming," Ritter answered with a steady look.

"How, Bob?" MacKenzie asked.

"We don't know yet."

"Leak?"

Ritter reached into his pocket and extracted a photocopy of a document and handed it across. The original was written in Vietnamese. Under the text of the photocopy was the handwritten translation. In the printed English were the words "green bush."

"They knew the name?"

"That's a security breakdown on their side, Roger, but, yes, it appears that they did. I suppose they planned to use that information for any of the Marines they might have captured. That sort of thing is good for breaking people down in a hurry. But we got lucky."

"I know. Nobody got hurt."

Ritter nodded. "We put a guy on the ground in early. Navy SEAL, very good at what he does. Anyway, he was watching things when the NVA reinforcements came in. He's the guy who blew the mission off. Then he just walked off the hill." It was always far more dramatic to understate things, especially for someone who'd smelled gunsmoke in his time.

That, MacKenzie thought, was worth a whistle. "Must be rather a cool customer."

"Better than that," Ritter said quietly. "On the way out he bagged the Russian who was talking to our people, and the camp commander. We have them in Winchester. Alive," Ritter added with a smile.

"That's how you got the dispatch? I figured SigInt," MacKenzie said, meaning signals intelligence. "How'd he manage that?"

"As you said, a cool customer." Ritter smiled. "That's the good news."

"I'm not sure I want to hear the bad news."

"We have an indicator that the other side might want to eliminate the camp and everyone in it."

"Jesus . . . Henry is over in Paris right now," MacKenzie said.

"Wrong approach. If he brings this up, even in one of the informal sessions, they'll just deny, and it might spook them so much that they'll try to make sure they can deny it." It was well known that the real work at such conferences was done during the breaks, not when people had to address the issues formally over the conference table, the very shape of which had taken so much time.

"True. What then?"

"We're working through the Russians. We have a pipeline for that. I initiated the contact myself."

"Let me know how it turns out?"

"You bet."

"Thanks for letting me talk to you," Lieutenant Ryan said.

"What's this all about?" Sam Rosen asked. They were in his office—not a large one, and the room was crowded with four people in it. Sarah and Sandy were there, too.

"It's about your former patient—John Kelly." That news didn't come as much of a surprise, Ryan saw. "I need to talk to him."

"What's stopping you?" Sam asked.

"I don't know where he is. I was kind of hoping you folks might."

"About what?" Sarah asked.

"About a series of killings," Ryan answered at once, in the hope of shocking them.

"Killing who?" This question came from the nurse.

"Doris Brown, for one, and several others."

"John didn't hurt her—" Sandy said before Sarah Rosen was able to touch her hand.

"Then you know who Doris Brown is," the detective observed, just a little too quickly.

"John and I have become . . . friends," Sandy said. "He's been out of the country for the past couple of weeks. He couldn't have killed anybody."

Ouch, Ryan thought. That was both good and bad news. He'd overplayed his hand on Doris Brown, though the nurse's reaction to the accusation had resulted in a little too much emotional response. He'd also just had a speculation confirmed as fact, however. "Out of the country? Where? How do you know?"

"I don't think I'm supposed to say where. I'm not supposed to know that."

"What do you mean by that?" the cop asked in surprise.

"I don't think I'm supposed to say, sorry." The way she answered the question showed sincerity rather than evasion.

What the hell did that *mean?* There was no answering that one, and Ryan decided to go on. "Someone named Sandy called the Brown house in Pittsburgh. It was you, wasn't it?"

"Officer," Sarah said, "I'm not sure I understand why you're asking all these questions."

"I'm trying to develop some information, and I want you to tell your friend that he needs to talk with me."

"This is a criminal investigation?"

"Yes, it is."

"And you're asking us questions," Sarah observed. "My brother is a lawyer. Should I ask him to come here? You seem to be asking us what we know about some murders. You're making me nervous. I have a question—are any of us under suspicion of anything?"

"No, but your friend is." If there was anything Ryan didn't need now, it was to have an attorney present.

"Wait a minute," Sam said. "If you think John might have done something wrong, and you want us to find him for you, you're saying that you think we know where he is, right? Doesn't that make us possible . . . helpers, accessories is the word, isn't it?"

Are you? Ryan would have liked to ask. He decided on, "Did I say that?"

"I've never had questions like this before, and they make me nervous," the surgeon told his wife. "Call your brother."

"Look, I have no reason to believe that any of you has done anything wrong. I *do* have reason to believe that your friend has. What I'm telling you is this: you'll be doing him a favor by telling him to call me."

"Who's he supposed to have killed?" Sam pressed.

"Some people who deal drugs."

"You know what I do?" Sarah asked sharply. "What I spend most of my time on here, you know what it is?"

"Yes, ma'am, I do. You work a lot with addicts."

"If John's really doing that, maybe I ought to buy him a gun!"

"Hurts when you lose one, doesn't it?" Ryan asked quietly, setting her up.

"You bet it does. We're not in this business to lose patients."

"How did it feel to lose Doris Brown?" She didn't reply, but only because her intelligence stopped her mouth from reacting as it wanted to. "He brought her to you for help, didn't he? And you and Mrs. O'Toole here worked very hard to clean her up. You think I'm condemning you for that? But before he dropped her off with you, he killed two people. I *know* it. They were probably two of the people who murdered Pamela Madden, and those were his real targets. Your friend Kelly is a very tough guy, but he's not as smart as he thinks he is. If he comes in now, it's one thing. If he makes us catch him, it's something else. You tell him that. You'll be doing him a favor, okay? You'll be doing yourselves a favor, too. I don't think you've broken the law to this point. Do anything for him now except what I've told you, and you might be. I don't usually warn people this way," Ryan told them sternly. "You people aren't criminals. I know that. The thing you did for the Brown girl was admirable, and I'm sorry it worked out the way it did. But Kelly is out there killing people, and that's *wrong,* okay? I'm telling you that just in case you might have forgotten something along the way. I don't like druggies either. Pamela Madden, the girl on the fountain, that's *my* case. I *want* those people in a cage; I want to watch them walk into the gas chamber. That's *my* job, to see that justice happens. Not his, mine. Do you understand?"

"Yes, I think we do," Sam Rosen answered, thinking about the surgical gloves he'd given Kelly. It was different now. Back then he'd been distant from things—emotionally close to the terrible parts, yet far away from what his friend was doing, approving it as though reading a news article on a ballgame. It was different now, but he was involved. "Tell me, how close are you to getting the people who killed Pam?"

"We know a few things," Ryan answered without realizing that with his answer, he'd blown it after coming so close.

Oreza was back at his desk, the part of his work that he hated, and one reason he worried about striking for chief, which would entail having his own office, and becoming part of "management" instead of just being a boat-driver. Mr. English was on leave, and his second-in-command, a chief, was off seeing to something or other, leaving him as senior man present—but it was his job anyway. The petty officer searched on his desk for the card and dialed the number.

"Homicide."

"Lieutenant Ryan, please."

"He's not here."

"Sergeant Douglas?"

"He's in court today."

"Okay, I'll call back." Oreza hung up. He looked at the clock. Pushing four in the afternoon—he'd been at the station since midnight. He pulled open a drawer and started filling out the forms accounting for the fuel he'd burned up today, making the Chesapeake Bay safe for drunks who owned boats. Then he planned to get home, get dinner, and get some sleep.

The problem was making sense out of what she said. A physician was called in from his office across the street, and diagnosed her problem as barbiturate intoxication, which wasn't exactly news, and then went on to say that they'd just have to wait for the stuff to work its way out of her system, for which two opinions he charged the county twenty dollars. Talking to her for several hours had only made her at turns amused and annoyed, but her story hadn't changed, either. Three people dead, *bang bang bang*. It was less funny to her now. She'd started remembering what Burt was like, and that talk was quite foul.

"If this girl was any higher she'd be up on the moon with the astronauts," the Captain thought.

"Three dead people on a boat somewhere," Trooper Freeland repeated. "Names and everything."

"You believe it?"

"Story stays the same, doesn't it?"

"Yeah." The Captain looked up. "You like to fish out there. What's it sound like to you, Ben?"

"Like around Bloodsworth Island."

"We'll hold her overnight on public drunkenness . . . we have her dead-bang on possession, right?"

"Cap'n, all I had to do was ask. She *handed* the stuff to me."

"Okay, process her all the way through."

"And then, sir?"

"Like helicopter rides?"

He picked a different marina this time. It turned out to be pretty easy, with so many boats always out fishing or partying, and this one had plenty of guest slips for transient boats which in the summer season plied up and down the coast, stopping off on the way for food and fuel and rest much as motorists did. The dockmaster watched him move in expertly to his third-largest guest slip, which didn't always happen with the owners of the larger cruisers. He was more surprised to see the youth of the owner.

"How long you plan to be here?" the man asked, helping with the lines.

"Couple of days. Is that okay?"

"Sure."

"Mind if I pay cash?"

"We honor cash," the dockmaster assured him.

Kelly peeled off the bills and announced that he'd be sleeping aboard this night. He didn't say what would be happening the next day.

34
Stalking

"We missed something, Em," Douglas announced at eighten in the morning.

"What was it this time?" Ryan asked. Missing something wasn't exactly a new happening in their business.

"How they knew she was in Pittsburgh. I called that Sergeant Meyer, had 'em check the long-distance charges on the house phone. None, not a single outgoing call for the last month."

The detective lieutenant stubbed out his cigarette. "You have to assume that our friend Henry knew where she was from. He had two girls get loose from him, he probably took the time to ask where they were from. You're right," Ryan said after a second's thought. "He probably assumed she was dead."

"Who knew she was there?"

"The people who took her there. They sure as hell didn't tell anyone."

"Kelly?"

"Found out yesterday over at Hopkins, he was out of the country."

"Oh, really? Where?"

"The nurse, O'Toole, she says she knows but she isn't allowed to say, whatever the hell that means." He paused. "Back to Pittsburgh."

"The story is, Sergeant Meyer's dad is a preacher. He was counseling the girl and told his son a little of what he knew. Okay. The sergeant goes up the chain to his captain. The Captain knows Frank Allen, and the sarge calls him for advice on who's running the case. Frank refers him to us. Meyer didn't talk to anybody else." Douglas lit up one of his own. "So how did the info get to our friends?"

This was entirely normal, but not particularly comfortable. Now both men thought that they had a breaking case. This was happening, it *was* breaking open. Not unusually, things were now happening too fast for the analytical process that was necessary to make sense of it all.

"As we've thought all along, they have somebody inside."

"Frank?" Douglas asked. "He's never been connected with any of the cases. He doesn't even have access to the information that our friends would need." Which was true. The Helen Waters case had started in the Western District with one of Allen's junior detectives, but the Chief had turned it over to Ryan and Douglas almost immediately because of the degree of violence involved. "I suppose you could call this progress, Em. Now we're sure. There has to be a leak inside the Department."

"What other good news do we have?"

The State Police only had three helicopters, all Bell Jet Rangers, and were still learning how to make use of them. Getting one was not the most trivial of exercises, but the Captain running Barracks "V" was a senior man who ran a quiet county—this was less a matter of his competence than of the nature of his area, but police hierarchies tend to place stock in results, however obtained. The helicopter arrived on the barracks helicopter pad at a quarter to nine. Captain Ernest Joy and Trooper 1/c Freeland were waiting. Neither had taken a helicopter ride before, and both were a little nervous when they saw how small the aircraft was. They always look smaller close up, and smaller still on the inside. Mainly used for Medevac missions, the aircraft had a pilot and a paramedic, both of whom were gun-toting State Police officers in sporty flight suits that went well, they thought, with their shoulder holsters and aviator shades. The standard safety lecture took a total of ninety seconds, delivered so quickly as to be incomprehensible. The ground-pounders strapped in, and the helicopter spooled up. The pilot decided against jazzing up the ride. The senior man was a captain, after all, and cleaning vomit out of the back was a drag.

"Where to?" he asked over the intercom.

"Bloodsworth Island," Captain Joy told him.

"Roger that," the pilot replied as he thought an aviator ought, turning southeast and lowering the nose. It didn't take long.

The world looks different from above, and the first time people go up in helicopters the reaction is always the same. The takeoff, rather like jerking aloft in an amusement-park cable-car ride, is initially startling, but then the fascination begins. The world transformed itself before the eyes of both officers, and it was as though it all suddenly made sense. They could see the roads and the farms all laid out like a map. Freeland grasped it first. Knowing his territory as he did, he instantly saw that his mental picture of it was flawed; his idea of how things really were was not quite right. He was only a thousand feet above it, a linear distance his car traversed in seconds, but this perspective was new, and he immediately started learning from it.

"That's where I found her," he told the Captain over the intercom.

"Long way from where we're going. You think she walked that far?"

"No, sir." But it wasn't that far from the water, was it? Perhaps two miles away, they saw the old dock of a farm up for sale, and that was less than five miles from where they were heading, scarcely two minutes' flying time. The Chesapeake Bay was a wide blue band now, under the morning haze. To the northwest was the large expanse of Patuxent River Naval Air Test Center, and they could both see aircraft flying there—a matter of concern to the pilot, who kept a wary eye out for low-flying aircraft. The Navy jocks liked to smoke in low.

"Straight ahead," he said. The paramedic pointed so that the passengers would know where straight-ahead was. "Sure looks different from up here," Freeland said, a boy's wonder in his voice. "I fish around there. From the surface it just looks like marshes."

But it didn't now. From a thousand feet it looked like islands at first, connected by silt and grass, but islands for all that. As they got closer, the islands took on regular shapes, lozengelike at first, and then with the fine lines of ships, grown over, surrounded by grass and reeds.

"Jeez, there's a bunch of 'em," the pilot observed. He'd rarely flown down here, and then mostly at night with accident cases.

"World War One," the Captain said. "My father said they're leftovers from the war, the ones the Germans didn't get."

"What exactly are we looking for?"

"Not sure, maybe a boat. We picked up a druggie yesterday," the Captain explained. "Said there was a lab in there, and three dead people."

"No shit? A drug lab in *there?*"

"That's what the lady said," Freeland confirmed, learning something else. As forbidding as it looked from the surface, there *were* channels in here. Probably a hell of a good place to go crabbing. From the deck of his fishing boat, it looked like one massive island, but not from up here. Wasn't that interesting?

"Got a flash down this way." The paramedic pointed the pilot over to the right. "Off glass or something."

"Let's check it out." The stick went right and down a little as he brought the Jet Ranger down. "Yeah, I got a boat by those three."

"Check it out," the paramedic ordered with a grin.

"You got it." It would be a chance to do some real flying. A former Huey driver from the 1st Air Cav, he loved being able to play with his aircraft. Anyone could fly straight and level, after all. He circled the place first, checking winds, then lowered his collective a little, easing the chopper down to about two hundred feet.

"Call it an eighteen-footer," Freeland said, and they could see the white nylon line that held it fast to the remains of the ship.

"Lower," the Captain commanded. In a few seconds they were fifty feet over the deck of the derelict. The boat was empty. There was a beer cooler, and some other stuff piled up in the back, but nothing else. The aircraft jerked as a couple of birds flew out of the ruined superstructure of the ship. The pilot instinctively maneuvered to avoid them. One crow sucked into his engine intake could make them a permanent part of this man-made swamp.

"Whoever owns that boat sure isn't real interested in us," he said over the intercom. In the back, Freeland mimed three shots with his hand. The Captain nodded.

"I think you may be right, Ben." To the pilot: "Can you mark the exact position on a map?"

"Right." He considered the possibility of going into a low hover and dropping them off on the deck. Simple enough if they had been back in the Cav, it looked too dangerous for this situation. The paramedic pulled out a chart and made the appropriate notations. "Seen what you need?"

"Yeah, head back."

Twenty minutes later, Captain Joy was on the phone.

"Coast Guard, Thomas Point."

"This is Captain Joy, State Police. We need a little help." He explained on for a few minutes.

"Take about ninety minutes," Warrant Officer English told him.

"That'd be fine."

Kelly called a Yellow Cab, which picked him up at the marina entrance. His first stop of the day was a rather disreputable business establishment called Kolonel Klunker, where he rented a 1959 Volkswagen, prepaying it for a month, with no mileage charge.

"Thank you, Mr. Aiello," the man said to a smiling Kelly, who was using the ID from a man who no longer needed it. He drove the car back to the marina and started unloading the things he needed. Nobody paid much attention, and in fifteen minutes the Beetle was gone.

Kelly took the opportunity to drive through the area he'd be hunting, checking traffic patterns. It was agreeably vacant, a part of the city he'd never visited before, off a bleak industrial thoroughfare called O'Donnell Street, a place where nobody lived and few would want to. The air was laden with the smells of various chemicals, few of them pleasant. Not as busy as it once had been, many of the buildings in the district looked unused. More to the point, there was much open ground here, many buildings separated from one another by flat areas of bare dirt which trucks used for a convenient place to reverse direction. No kids playing sandlot ball, not a single house in sight, and because of that, not a single police car to be seen. Rather a clever ploy on the part of his enemies, Kelly thought, at least from one perspective. The place he was interested in was a single freestanding building with a half-destroyed sign over the entrance. The back of it was just a blank wall. There were only three doors, and though they were on two different walls, all could be observed from a single point, and to Kelly's rear was another vacant building, a tall concrete structure with plenty of broken windows. His initial reconnaissance complete, Kelly headed north.

Oreza was heading south. He'd already been partway there, conducting a routine patrol and wondering why the hell the Coast Guard didn't start up a ministation farther down on the Eastern Shore, or maybe by Cove Point Light, where there was an existing station for the guys who spent their waking hours, if any, making sure the light bulb at the top of the tower worked. That wasn't especially demanding duty to Oreza's mind, though it was probably all right for the kid who ran the place. His wife had just delivered twins, after all, and the Coast Guard was a family-oriented branch of the military.

He was letting one of his junior seamen do the driving, enjoying the morning, standing outside the cramped wheelhouse, drinking some of his home-brewed coffee.

"Radio," one of the crewmen said.

Oreza went inside and took the microphone. "Four-One Alfa here."

"Four-One Alfa, this is English at Thomas Base. Your pickup is at a dock at Dame's Choice. You'll see cop cars there. Got an ETA?"

"Call it twenty or twenty-five, Mr. E."

"Roger that. Out."

"Come left," Oreza said, looking at his chart. The water looked plenty deep. "One-six-five."

"One-six-five, aye."

Xantha was more or less sober, though weak. Her dark skin had a gray pallor to it, and she complained of a splitting headache that analgesics had scarcely touched. She was aware that she was under arrest now, and that her rap sheet had arrived on teletype. She was also canny enough to have requested the presence of a lawyer. Strangely, this had not bothered the police very much.

"My client," the attorney said, "is willing to cooperate." The agreement had taken all of ten minutes to strike. If she was telling the truth, and if she was not involved in a major felony, the possession charge against her would be dropped, subject to her enrollment in a treatment program. It was as good a deal as anyone had offered Xantha Matthews in some years. It was immediately apparent why this was true.

"They was gonna kill me!" she said, remembering it all now that she was outside the influence of the barbiturates, and now that her attorney gave her permission to speak.

"Who's 'they'?" Captain Joy asked.

"They dead. He killed 'em, the white boy, shot 'em dead. An' he left the drugs, whole shitload of 'em."

"Tell us about the white man," Joy asked, with a look to Freeland that ought to have been disbelieving but was not.

"Big dude, like him"—she pointed to Freeland—"but he face all green like a leaf. He blindfold me af'er he took me down, then he put me on that pier an' tol' me to catch a bus or somethin'."

"How do you know he was white?"

"Wrists was white. Hands was green, but not up here, like," she said, indicating on her own arms. "He wear green clothes with stripes on 'em, like a soldier, carry a big .45. I was asleep when he shoot, that wake me up, see? Make me get dress, take me away, drop me off, he boat just go away."

"What kind of boat?"

"Big white one, tall, like, big, like thirty feet lon'."

"Xantha, how do you know they were going to kill you?"

"White boy say so, he show me the things in the boat, the little one."

"What do you mean?"

"Fishnet shit, like, and cement blocks. He say they tell him they do it before."

The lawyer decided it was his turn to speak. "Gentlemen, my client has information about what may be a major criminal operation. She may require protection, and in return for her assistance, we would like to have state funding for her treatment."

"Counselor," Joy replied quietly, "if this is what it sounds like, I'll fund it out of my own budget. May I suggest, sir, that we keep her in our lockup for the time being? For her own safety, the need for which seems quite apparent, sir." The State Police captain had been negotiating with lawyers for years, and had started sounding like one, Freeland thought.

"The food here is fo' shit!" Xantha said, her eyes closed in pain.

"We'll take care of that, too," Joy promised her.

"I think she needs some medical help," the lawyer noted. "How can she get it here?"

"Doctor Paige will be here right after lunch to see her. Counselor, your client is in no condition to look after herself now. All charges against her are dropped pending verification of her story. You'll get everything you want, in return for her cooperation. I can't do any more than that."

"My client agrees to your conditions and suggestions," the lawyer said without consulting her. The county would even pay his fee. Besides, he felt as though he might be doing the world a good deed. It was quite a change from getting drunk drivers off.

"There's a shower that way. Why not get her cleaned up? You may also wish to get her some decent things to wear. Give us the bill."

"A pleasure doing business with you, Captain Joy," he said as the barracks commander left for Freeland's car.

"Ben, you really fell into something. You handled her real nice. I won't forget. Now show me how fast this beast goes."

"You got it, Cap'n." Freeland engaged the lights before passing seventy. They made it to the dock just as the Coast Guard turned out of the main channel.

The man wore lieutenant's bars—though he called himself a captain—and Oreza saluted him as he came aboard. Both police officers were given life jackets to wear because Coast Guard regulations required them on small boats, and then Joy showed him the chart.

"Think you can get in there?"

"No, but our launch can. What gives?"

"A possible triple homicide, possible drug involvement. We overflew the area this morning. There's a fishing boat right here."

Oreza nodded as impassively as possible and took the wheel himself, pushing the throttles to the stops. It was a bare five miles to the graveyard—that was how Oreza thought of it—and he plotted his approach as carefully as possible.

"No closer? The tide's in," Freeland said.

"That's the problem. Place like this, you go it at low water so's in case you beach you can float off. From here on we use the launch." Wheels were turning in his mind while his crewmen got the fourteen-foot launch deployed. Months earlier, that stormy night with Lieutenant Charon from Baltimore, a possible drug deal that he'd expected to take place somewhere on the Bay. *Some real serious guys,* he'd told Portagee. Oreza already wondered if there might be a connection.

They motored in, powered by a ten-horse outboard. The quartermaster took note of the tidal flow, following what appeared to be a channel that meandered generally in the direction indicated by their marked-up chart. It was quiet in here, and Oreza remembered his tour of duty for Operation MARKET TIME, the Coast Guard's effort to assist the Navy in Vietnam. He'd spent time with the brown-water guys, running Swift boats manufactured right in Annapolis by the Trumpy Yard. It was so similar, the tall grass that could, and often did, conceal people with guns. He wondered if they might be facing something similar soon. The cops were fingering their revolvers, and Oreza asked himself, too late, why he hadn't brought a Colt with him. Not that he knew how to use it. His next thought was that this would have been a good place to have Kelly with him. He wasn't quite sure what the story was on Kelly, but he suspected the man was one of the SEALs, with whom he'd worked briefly in the Mekong Delta. Sure as hell he'd gotten that Navy Cross for something, and the tattoo on his arm wasn't there by accident.

"Well, damn," Oreza breathed. "Looks like a Starcraft sixteen . . . no, more like eighteen." He lifted his portable radio. "Four-One Alpha, this is Oreza."

"Reading you, Portagee."

"We got the boat, right where they said. Stand by."

"Roger."

Suddenly things got very tense indeed. The two cops exchanged a look, wondering why they hadn't brought more people out. Oreza eased his launch right up to the Starcraft. The cops got aboard gingerly.

Freeland pointed to the back. Joy nodded. There were six cement blocks and a rolled-up section of nylon netting. Xantha hadn't lied about that. There was also a rope ladder going up. Joy went first, his revolver in his right hand. Oreza just watched as Freeland followed. Once they got to the deck, the men wrapped both hands around their handguns and headed for the superstructure, disappearing from view for what seemed like an hour, but in reality was only four minutes. Some birds scattered aloft. When Joy came back, his revolver wasn't visible.

"We have three bodies up here, and a hell of a large quantity of what looks like heroin. Call your boat, have them tell my barracks that we need crime lab. Sailor, you just started running a ferry service."

"Sir, fish-and-game has better boats for this. Want me to call them to support you?"

"Good idea. You might want to circle around this area some. The water looks pretty clear, and she told us that they've dumped some bodies hereabouts. See the stuff in the fishing boat?" Oreza looked, noticing the fishnet and blocks for the first time.

Jesus. "That's how you do it. Okay, I'll motor around." Which he did, after making his radio call.

"Hi, Sandy."

"John! Where are you?"

"My place in town."

"There was a policeman in to see us yesterday. They're looking for you."

"Oh?" Kelly's eyes narrowed as he chewed on his sandwich.

"He said you should come in and talk to him, that it's better if you do it right away."

"That's nice of him," Kelly observed with a chuckle.

"What are you going to do?"

"You don't want to know, Sandy."

"You sure?"

"Yes, I'm sure."

"Please, John, please think it through."

"I have, Sandy. Honest. It'll be okay. Thanks for the information."

"Something wrong?" another nurse asked after she hung up.

"No," Sandy replied, and her friend knew it was a lie.

Hmm. Kelly finished off his Coke. That confirmed his suspicion about Oreza's little visit. So things were getting complicated now, but they'd been pretty complicated the week before, too. He headed off to the bedroom, almost there when there came a knock at the door. That startled him rather badly, but he had to answer it. He'd opened windows to air the apartment out, and it was plain that someone was here. He took a deep breath and opened the door.

"Wondered where you were, Mr. Murphy," the manager said, much to Kelly's relief.

"Well, two weeks of work in the Midwest and a week's vacation down in Florida," he lied with a relaxed smile.

"You didn't get much of a tan."

An embarrassed grin. "Spent a lot of my time inside." The manager thought that was pretty good.

"Good for you, well, just wanted to see if everything was okay."

"No problems here," Kelly assured the man, closing the door before he could ask anything else. He needed a nap. It seemed that all of his work was at night. It was like being on the other side of the world, Kelly told himself, lying down on his lumpy bed.

It was a hot day at the zoo. Better to have met in the panda enclosure. It was crowded with people who wanted to gawk at this wonderful goodwill gift from the People's Republic of China—Chinese Communists to Ritter. The place was air conditioned and comfortable, but intelligence officers usually were uncomfortable in places like that, and so today he was strolling by the remarkably large area that contained the Galapagos tortoises, or turtles—Ritter didn't know the difference, if there was one. Why they needed so large an area, he didn't know either. Certainly it seemed expansive for a creature that moved at roughly the speed of a glacier.

"Hello, Bob." "Charles" was now an unnecessary subterfuge, though Voloshin had initiated the call—right to Ritter's desk, to show how clever he was. It worked both ways in the intelligence business. In the case of a call initiated by the Russians, the code name was "Bill."

"Hello, Sergey." Ritter pointed to the reptiles. "Kind of reminds you of the way our governments work, doesn't it?"

"Not my part of it." The Russian sipped at his soft drink. "Nor yours."

"Okay, what's the word from Moscow?"

"You forgot to tell me something."

"What's that?"

"That you have a Vietnamese officer also."

"Why should that concern you?" Ritter asked lightly, clearly concealing his annoyance that Voloshin knew this, as his interlocutor could see.

"It is a complication. Moscow doesn't know yet."

"Then don't tell them," Ritter suggested. "It is, as you say, a complication. I assure you that your allies don't know."

"How can that be?" the Russian demanded.

"Sergey, do you reveal methods?" Ritter replied, ending that phase of the discussion. This part of the game had to be played very carefully indeed, and for more than one reason. "Look, General, you don't like the little bastards any more than we do, right?"

"They are our fraternal socialist allies."

"Yes, and we have bulwarks of democracy all over Latin America, too. Did you come here for a quick course in political philosophy?"

"The nice thing about enemies is that you know where they stand. This is not always true of friends," Voloshin admitted. That also explained the comfort level of his government with the current American president. A bastard, perhaps, but a known bastard. And, no, Voloshin admitted—to himself—he had little use for the Vietnamese. The real action was in Europe. Always had been. Always would be. That was where the course of history had been set for centuries, and nothing was going to change that.

"Call it an unconfirmed report, check up on it, maybe? Delay? Please, General, the stakes here are too high for that. If anything happens to those men, I promise you, we *will* produce your officer. The Pentagon knows, Sergey, and they want those men back, and they don't care a rat-fuck about *détente*." The profanity showed what Ritter really thought.

"Do you? Does your Directorate?"

"It sure will make life a lot more predictable. Where were you in '62, Sergey?" Ritter asked—knowing and wondering what he'd say.

"In Bonn, as you know, watching your forces go on alert because Nikita Sergeyevich decided to play his foolish game." Which had been contrary to KGB and Foreign Ministry advice, as both men knew.

"We're never going to be friends, but even enemies can agree to rules for the game. Isn't that what this is about?"

A judicious man, Voloshin thought, which pleased him. It made for predictable behavior, and that above all things was what the Russians wanted of the Americans. "You are persuasive, Bob. You assure me that our allies do not know their man is missing?"

"Positive. My offer for you to meet your man is still open," he added.

"Without reciprocal rights?" Voloshin tried.

"For that I need permission from upstairs. I can try if you ask me to, but that also would be something of a complication." He dumped his empty drink cup in a bin.

"I ask." Voloshin wanted that made clear.

"Very well. I'll call you. And in return?"

"In return I will consider your request." Voloshin walked off without another word.

Gotcha! Ritter thought, heading towards where his car was parked. He'd played a careful but inventive game. There were three possible leaks on BOXWOOD GREEN. He'd visited each of them. To one he'd said that they actually had gotten a prisoner out, who had died of wounds. To another, that the Russian was badly wounded and might not survive. But Ritter had saved his best piece of bait for the most likely leak. Now he knew. That narrowed it to four suspects. Roger MacKenzie, that prep-school-reject aide, and two secretaries. This was really an FBI job, but he didn't want any additional complications, and an espionage investigation of the Office of the President of the United States was about as complicated as things could be. Back in his car, he decided to meet with a friend in the Directorate of Science and Technology. Ritter had a great deal of respect for Voloshin. A clever man, a very careful, methodical man, he'd run agents all over Western Europe before being assigned to the Washington *rezidentura.* He'd keep his word, and to make sure he didn't get into any trouble about it, he'd play everything strictly by the exacting rules of his parent agency. Ritter was gambling big on that. Pull this one off in addition to the other coup in the works, and how much higher might he rise? Better yet, he'd be earning his way up, not some fair-haired political payoff, but the son of a Texas Ranger who'd waited tables to get his degree at Baylor. Something Sergey would have appreciated, in good Marxist-Leninist fashion, Ritter told himself, pulling onto Connecticut Avenue. Working-class kid makes good.

It was an unusual way to gather information, something he'd never done before, and pleasant enough that he might even get used to it. He sat at a corner booth in Mama Maria's, working slowly through his second course—thank you, no wine, I'm driving. Dressed in his CIA suit, well-groomed and sporting a new businesslike haircut, he enjoyed the looks of a few unattached women, and a waitress who positively doted on him, especially with his good manners. The excellence of the food explained the crowded room, and the crowding explained why it was a convenient place for Tony Piaggi and Henry Tucker to meet here. Mike Aiello had been very forthcoming about that. Mama Maria's was, in fact, owned by the Piaggi family, now in its third generation of providing food and other, less legal, services to the local community, dating back to Prohibition. The owner was a bon vivant, greeting favored customers, guiding them to their places with Old World hospitality. Snappy dresser, too, Kelly saw, recording his face and build, gestures and mannerisms, as he ate through his calamari. A black man came in, dressed in a nicely cut suit. He looked like he knew the place, smiling at the hostess and waiting a few seconds for his reward, and Kelly's.

Piaggi looked up and headed to the front, stopping only briefly to shake hands with someone on the way. He did the same with the black man, then led him back past Kelly's table, and up the back stairs to where the private rooms were. No particular notice was taken. There were other black couples in the restaurant, treated the same as everyone else. But those others did honest work, Kelly was sure. He turned his thoughts away from the distraction. *So that's Henry Tucker. That's the one who killed Pam.* He didn't look like a monster. Monsters rarely did. To Kelly he looked like a target, and his particulars went into Kelly's memory, alongside Tony Piaggi's. He was surprised when he looked down and saw that the fork in his hands was bent.

"What's the problem?" Piaggi asked upstairs. He poured each of them a glass of Chianti, good host that he was, but as soon as the door had closed, Henry's face started telling him something.

"They haven't come back."

"Phil, Mike, and Burt?"

"Yes!" Henry snarled, meaning, *no.*

"Okay, settle down. How much stuff did they have?"

"Twenty kees of pure, man. This was supposed to take care of me and Philly, and New York for a while."

"Lot of stuff, Henry." Tony nodded. "Maybe it just took them a while, okay?"

"Shoulda been back by now."

"Look, Phil and Mike are new, probably clumsy, like Eddie and me were our first time—hell, Henry, that was only five kees, remember?"

"I allowed for that," he said, wondering if he'd really be right about that or not.

"Henry," Tony said, sipping his wine and trying to appear calm and reasonable, "look, okay? Why are you getting excited? We've taken care of all the problems, right?"

"Something's wrong, man."

"What?"

"I don't know."

"Want to get a boat and go down there to see?"

Tucker shook his head. "Takes too long."

"The meet with the other guys isn't for three days. Be cool. They're probably on their way here now."

Piaggi thought he understood Tucker's sudden case of the shakes. Now it was big-time. Twenty kilograms of pure translated into a huge quantity of street drugs, and selling it already diluted and packaged made for sufficient convenience to their customers that they were for the first time paying top dollar. This was the really big score that Tucker had been working towards for several years. Just assembling all the cash to pay for it was a major undertaking. It was an understandable case of nerves.

"Tony, what if it wasn't Eddie at all?"

Exasperation: "You're the one who said it had to be, remember?"

Tucker couldn't pursue that. He'd merely wanted an excuse to eliminate the man as an unnecessary complication. His anxiety was partly what Tony thought it was, but something else, too. The things that had happened earlier in the summer, the things that had just started for no reason, then stopped with no reason—he had told himself that they were Eddie Morello's doing. He'd managed to convince himself of that, but only because he had wanted to believe it. Somewhere else the little voice that had brought him this far had told him otherwise, and now the voice was back, and there was no Eddie to be the focus for his anxiety and anger. A streetwise man who'd gotten this far through the complex equation of brain and guts and instinct, he trusted that last quality most. Now it was telling him things that he didn't understand, couldn't reason out. Tony was right. It could just be a matter of clumsiness in the processing. That was one reason they were setting their lab up in east Baltimore. They could afford that now, with experience behind them and a viable front business setting up in the coming week. So he drank his wine and settled down, the rich, red alcohol soothing his abraded instincts.

"Give 'em until tomorrow."

"So how was it?" the man at the wheel asked. An hour north of Bloodsworth Island, he figured he'd waited long enough to ask the silent petty officer who stood beside him. After all, they just stood by and waited.

"They fed a guy to the fuckin' crabs!" Oreza told them. "They took like two square yards of net and weighted it down with blocks, and just sunk his ass—practically nothing left but the damned bones!" The police lab people were still discussing how to recover the body, for all he knew. Oreza was certain it was a sight he'd take years to forget, the skull just lying there, the bones still dressed, moving because of the water currents . . . or maybe some crabs inside. He hadn't cared to look that closely.

"Heavy shit, man," the helmsman agreed.

"You know who it is?"

"What d'ya mean, Portagee?"

"Back in May, when we had that Charon guy aboard—the day-sailer with the candystripe main, that's who it was, I'll bet ya."

"Oh, yeah. You could be right on that one, boss."

They'd let him see it all, just as a courtesy that in retrospect he would as soon have done without, but which at the time had been impossible to avoid. He could not have chickened out in front of cops, since he, too, was a cop of sorts. And so he'd climbed up the ladder after reporting on the body he'd found only fifty yards from the derelict, and seen three more, all lying facedown on the deck of what had probably been the freighter's wardroom, all dead, all shot in the back of the neck, the wounds having been picked at by birds. He'd almost lost control of himself at that realization. The birds had been sensible enough not to pick at the drugs, however.

"I'm talking twenty kilograms—forty-some pounds of the shit—that's what the cops said, anyway. Like, millions of bucks," Oreza related.

"Always said I was in the wrong business."

"Jesus, the cops look like they all had hard-ons, 'specially that captain. They'll probably be there all night, way it sounded."

"Hey, Wally?"

The tape was disappointingly scratchy. That was due to the old phone lines, the technician explained. Nothing he could do about that. The switch box in the building dated back to when Alexander Graham Bell was doing hearing aids.

"Yeah, what is it?" the somewhat uneven voice replied.

"The deal with the Vietnamese officer they got. You sure about that?"

"That's what Roger told me." *Bingo!* Ritter thought.

"Where they have him?"

"I guess out at Winchester with the Russian."

"You're sure?"

"Damned right. It surprised me, too."

"I wanted to check up on that before—well, you know."

"Sure thing, man." With that the line went dead.

"Who is he?" Greer asked.

"Walter Hicks. All the best schools, James—Andover and Brown. Father's a big-time investment banker who pulled a few well-tuned political strings, and look where little Wally ends up." Ritter tightened his hand into a fist. "You want to know why those people are still in SENDER GREEN? That's it, my friend."

"So what are you going to do about it?"

"I don't know." *But it won't be legal.* The tape wasn't. The tap had been set up without a court order.

"Think it over carefully, Bob," Greer warned. "I was there, too, remember?"

"What if Sergey can't get it done fast enough? Then this little *fuck* gets away with ending the lives of twenty men!"

"I don't like that very much either."

"I don't like it at all!"

"Treason is still a capital crime, Bob."

Ritter looked up. "It's supposed to be."

Another long day. Oreza found himself envying the first-class who was tending Cove Point Light. At least he had his family with him all the time. Here Oreza was with the brightest little girl in kindergarten and he hardly ever saw her. Maybe he'd take that teaching job at New London after all, Portagee thought, just so that he could have a family life for a year or two. It meant hanging out with children who would someday be officers, but at least they'd learn seamanship the right way.

Mainly he was lonely with his thoughts. His crew was bedding down now in the bunkroom that he should have gone to, but the images haunted him. The crabman, and the three bird-feeders would deny him sleep for hours unless he got it off his conscience . . . and he had an excuse, didn't he? Oreza rummaged around his desk, finding the card.

"Hello?"

"Lieutenant Charon? This is Quartermaster First Class Oreza, down at Thomas Point."

"It's kinda late, you know," Charon pointed out. He'd been caught on his way to bed.

"Remember back in May, looking for that sailboat?"

"Yeah, why?"

"I think maybe we found your man, sir." Oreza thought he could hear eyeballs click.

"Tell me about it?"

Portagee did, leaving nothing out, and he could feel the horror leaving him, almost as though he were transmitting it over the phone wire. He didn't know that was precisely what he was doing.

"Who's the captain running the case for the troopers?"

"Name's Joy, sir. Somerset County. Know him?"

"No, I don't."

"Oh, yeah, something else," Oreza remembered.

"Yeah?" Charon was taking lots of notes.

"You know a Lieutenant Ryan?"

"Yeah, he works downtown, too."

"He wanted me to check up a guy for him, fellow named Kelly. Oh, yeah! You've seen him, remember?"

"What do you mean?"

"The night we were out after the day-sailer, the guy in the cruiser we saw just before dawn. Lives on an island, not far from Bloodsworth. Anyway, this Ryan guy wanted me to find him for him, okay? He's back, sir, probably up in Baltimore right now. I tried calling, sir, but he was out, and I've been running my ass off all day. Could you pass that one along, please?"

"Sure," Charon replied, and his brain was working very quickly indeed now.

35
Rite of Passage

Mark Charon found himself in rather a difficult position. That he was a corrupted cop did not make him a stupid one. In fact, his was a careful and thoroughly analytical mind, and while he made mistakes, he was not blind to them. That was precisely the case as he lay alone in bed, hanging up the phone after his conversation with the Coast Guard. The first order of business was that Henry would not be pleased to learn that his lab was gone, and three of his people with it. Worse still, it sounded as though a vast quantity of drugs had been lost, and even Henry's supply was finite. Worst of all, the person or persons who had accomplished that feat was unknown, at large, and doing—what?

He knew who Kelly was. He'd even reconstructed matters to the rather stunning coincidence that Kelly had been the one who'd picked Pam Madden off the street quite by accident the day Angelo Vorano had been eliminated, and that she'd actually been aboard his boat, not twenty feet from the Coast Guard cutter after that stormy and vomitous night. Now Em Ryan and Tom Douglas wanted to know about him, and had taken the extraordinary step of having

673

the Coast Guard check up on him. Why? A follow-up interview with an out-of-town witness was something for the telephone more often than not. Em and Tom were working the Fountain Case, along with all the other ones that had started a few weeks later. "Rich beach bum" was what he'd told Henry, but the department's number-one homicide team was interested in him, and he'd been directly involved with one of the defectors from Henry's organization, and he had a boat, and he lived not too far from the processing lab that Henry was still foolish enough to use. That was a singularly long and unlikely string of coincidences made all the more troubling by the realization that Charon was no longer a policeman investigating a crime, but rather a criminal himself who was *part* of the crimes being checked out.

That realization struck surprisingly hard at the Lieutenant lying in his bed. Somehow he didn't think of himself in those terms. Charon actually had believed himself above it all, watching, taking an occasional part, but not *being* part of what unfolded below him. After all, he had the longest string of successes in the history of the narcotics unit, capped off with his personal elimination of Eddie Morello, perhaps the most artful action of his professional life—doubly so in that he had eliminated a genuine dealer by premeditated murder in front of no less than six other officers, then had it pronounced a clean shooting on the spot, which had given him a paid vacation in addition to what Henry had paid him for the event. Somehow it had seemed like a particularly entertaining game, and one not too far distanced from the job the citizens of his city paid him to do. Men live by their illusions, and Charon was no different from the rest. It wasn't so much that he'd told himself what he'd been doing was all right as that he'd simply allowed himself to concentrate on the breaks that Henry had been feeding him, thus taking off the street every supplier who'd threatened the man's market standing. Able to control which of his detectives investigated what, he'd actually been able to give the entire local market to the one supplier about whom he had no real information in his files. That had enabled Henry to expand his own operation, attracting the attention of Tony Piaggi and his own East Coast connections. Soon, and he'd told Henry this, he would be forced to allow his people to nibble at the edges of the operation. Henry had understood, doubtless after counseling from Piaggi, who was sophisticated enough to grasp the finer points of the game.

But someone had tossed a match into this highly volatile mixture. The information he had led only in one direction, but not far enough. So he had to get more, didn't he? Charon thought for a moment and lifted his phone. He needed three calls to get the right number.

"State Police."

"Trying to get Captain Joy. This is Lieutenant Charon, Baltimore City Police."

"You're in luck, sir. He just got back in. Please hold." The next voice that came on was a tired one.

"Captain Joy."

"Hello, this is Lieutenant Charon, Mark Charon, City Police. I work narcotics. I hear you just took down something big."

"You might say that." Charon could hear the man settling into his chair with a combination of satisfaction and fatigue.

"Could you give me a quick sketch? I may have some information on this one myself."

"Who told you about this anyway?"

"That Coast Guard sailor who drove you around—Oreza. I've worked with him on a couple cases. Remember the big marijuana bust, the Talbot County farm?"

"Was that you? I thought the Coasties took credit for that."

"I had to let them, to protect my informant. Look, you can call them if you want to confirm that. I'll give you the phone number, the boss of the station is Paul English."

"Okay, Charon, you sold me."

"Back in May I spent a day and a night out with them looking for a guy who just disappeared on us. We never found him, never found his boat. Oreza says—"

"The crabman," Joy breathed. "Somebody got dumped

in the water, looks like he's been there a while. Anything you can tell me about him?"

"His name is probably Angelo Vorano. Lived here in town, small-time dealer who was looking to make it into the bigs." Charon gave a description.

"Height's about right. We'll have to check dental records for a positive ID, though. Okay, that ought to help, Lieutenant. What do you need from me?"

"What can you tell me?" Charon took several minutes of notes. "What are you doing with Xantha?"

"Holding her as a material witness, with her lawyer's approval by the way. We want to take care of this girl. Looks like we're dealing with some pretty nasty folks here."

"I believe it," Charon replied. "Okay, let me see what I can shake loose for you at this end."

"Thanks for the assist."

"Jesus," Charon said after hanging up. *White boy . . . big white boat.* Burt and the two people Tony had evidently seconded to the operation, back of the head, .45s. Execution-style killings were not yet the vogue in the drug business, and the sheer coldness of it gave Charon a chill. But it wasn't so much coldness as efficiency, was it? Like the pushers. Like the case Tom and Em were working, and they wanted to see about this Kelly guy, and he was a white guy with a big white boat who lived not far from the lab. That was too much of a coincidence.

About the only good news was that he could call Henry in safety. He knew every drug-related wiretap in the area, and not one was targeted on Tucker's operation.

"Yeah?"

"Burt and his friends are dead," Charon announced.

"What's that?" said a voice that was fully waking up.

"You heard me. The State Police in Somerset have them bagged. Angelo, too, what's left of him. The lab is gone, Henry. The drugs are gone, and they have Xantha in custody." There was actually some satisfaction in this. Charon was still enough of a cop that the demise of a criminal operation was not yet a matter of grief for him.

"What the fuck is going on?" a shrill voice inquired.

"I think I can tell you that, too. We need to meet."

• • •

Kelly took another look at his perch, just driving by in his rented Beetle, before heading back to his apartment. He was tired, though sated from the fine dinner. His afternoon nap had been enough to keep him going after a long day, but mainly the reason was to work off the anger, which driving often did for him. He'd seen the man now. The one who had finished the process of killing Pamela, with a shoestring. It would have been so easy to take care of him there. Kelly had never killed anyone barehanded, but he knew how. A lot of skilled people had spent a lot of time at Coronado, California, teaching him the finer points until whenever he looked at any person his mind applied something like a sheet of graph paper, this place for this move, that place for that one—and seeing he'd known that, yes, it was all worth it. It was worth the danger, and it was worth the consequences . . . but that didn't mean that he had to embrace them, as risk of life didn't mean throwing it away. That was the other side of it.

But he could see the end now, and he had to start planning beyond the end. He had to be even more careful. Okay, so the cops knew who he was, but he was certain that they had nothing. Even if the girl, Xantha, someday decided to talk to the cops, she'd never seen his face—the camouflage paint took care of that. About the only danger was that she'd seen the registration number on his boat as he'd backed away from that dock, but that didn't seem to be much of a worry. Without physical evidence they had nothing they could use in front of a court of law. So they knew he disliked some people—fine. So they might even know what his training was—fine. The game he played was in accordance with one set of rules. The game they played had another. On balance, the rules worked in his favor, not theirs.

He looked out the car window, measuring angle and distance, making a preliminary plan and working in several variations. They'd picked a spot where there were few police patrols and lots of open ground. No one could approach them easily without being seen . . . probably so that they could destroy whatever they had in there if it became necessary. It was a logical approach to their tactical problem, except for one thing. They hadn't considered a different set of tactical rules.

Not my problem, Kelly thought, heading back to his apartment.

"God almighty . . . " Roger MacKenzie was pale and suddenly nauseated. They were standing on the breakfast porch of his house in northwest Washington. His wife and daughter were shopping in New York for the fall season. Ritter had arrived unannounced at six-fifteen, fully dressed and grim, a discordant note for the cool, pleasant morning breezes. "I've known his father for thirty years."

Ritter sipped his orange juice, though the acid in it didn't exactly do his stomach any good either. This was treason of the worst sort. Hicks had *known* what he did would hurt fellow citizens, one of whom he knew by name. Ritter had already made his mind up on the matter, but Roger had to have his time to rattle on.

"We went through Randolph together, we were in the same Bomb Group," MacKenzie was saying. Ritter decided to let him get it all out, even though it would take a little time. "We've done deals together . . . " the man finished, looking down at his untouched breakfast.

"I can't fault you for taking him into your office, Roger, but the boy's guilty of espionage."

"What do you want to do?"

"It's a criminal offense, Roger," Ritter pointed out.

"I'm going to be leaving soon. They want me on the reelection team, running the whole Northeast."

"This early?"

"Jeff Hicks will be running the campaign in Massachusetts, Bob. I'll be working directly with him." MacKenzie looked across the table, speaking in barely connected bursts. "Bob, an espionage investigation in our office—it could ruin things. If what we did—if your operation became public—I mean, the way it happened and what went wrong—"

"I'm sorry about that, Roger, but this little bastard betrayed his country."

"I could pull his security clearance, kick him out—"

"Not good enough," Ritter said coldly. "People may die because of him. He is *not* going to walk away from it."

"We could order you to—"

"To obstruct justice, Roger?" Ritter observed. "Because that's what it is. That's a felony."

"Your tap was illegal."

"National-security investigation—there's a war going on, remember?—slightly different rules, and besides, all that has to happen is let him hear it and he'll split open." Ritter was sure of that.

"And run the risk of bringing down the President? Now? At this time? Do you think that'll do the country any good? What about our relations with the Russians? This is a *crucial* time, Bob." *But then, it always is, isn't it?* Ritter wanted to add, but didn't.

"Well, I'm coming to you for guidance," Ritter said, and then he got it, after a fashion.

"We can't afford an investigation that leads to a public trial. That is politically unacceptable." MacKenzie hoped that would be enough.

Ritter nodded and stood. The drive back to his office at Langley was not all that comfortable. Though it was satisfying to have a free hand, Ritter was now faced with something that, however desirable, he did not want to become a habit. The first order of business was to pull the wiretap. In one big hurry.

After everything that had happened, it was the newspaper that broke things loose. The four-column head, below the fold, announced a drug-related triple murder in sleepy Somerset County. Ryan devoured the story, never getting to the sports page that usually occupied fifteen minutes of his morning routine.

It's got to be him, the Lieutenant thought. *Who else would leave "a large quantity" of drugs behind, along with three bodies?* He left the house forty minutes early that morning, surprising his wife.

"Mrs. O'Toole?" Sandy had just finished her first set of morning rounds, and was checking off some forms when the phone rang.

"Yes?"

"This is James Greer. You've spoken to my secretary, Barbara, I believe."

"Yes, I have. Can I help you?"

"I hate to bother you, but we're trying to track John down. He's not at home."

"Yes, I think he's in town, but I don't know where exactly."

"If you hear from him, could you please ask him to call me? He has my number. Please forgive me for asking this," the man said politely.

"I'll be glad to." *And what's that about?* she wondered.

It was getting to her. The police were after John, and she'd told him, and he hadn't seemed to care. Now somebody else was trying to get hold of him. Why? Then she saw a copy of the morning paper sitting on the table in the lounge area. The brother of one of her patients was reading something or other, but right there on the lower-right side of the front page was the headline: DRUG MURDER IN SOMERSET.

"Everybody's interested in that guy," Frank Allen observed.

"What do you mean?" Charon had come into Western District on the pretense of checking up on the administrative investigation of the Morello shooting. He'd talked Allen into allowing him to review the statements of the other officers and three civilian witnesses. Since he'd graciously waived his right to counsel, and since the shooting looked squeaky clean, Allen hadn't seen any harm in the matter, so long as it was done in front of him.

"I mean, right after the call from Pittsburgh, that Brown girl who got whacked, Em called here about him. Now you. How come?"

"His name came up. We're not sure why, and it's just a quick check. What can you tell me about him?"

"Hey, Mark, you're on vacation, remember?" Allen pointed out.

"You're telling me I won't be back to work soon? I'm

supposed to turn my brain off, Frank? Did I miss the article in the paper that says the crooks are taking a few weeks off?"

Allen had to concede the point. "All this attention, now I'm starting to think there might be something wrong with the guy. I suppose I have some information on him—yeah, that's right, I forgot. Wait a minute." Allen walked away from his desk toward the file room, and Charon pretended to read the statements for several minutes until he came back. A thin manila folder landed in his lap. "Here."

It was part of Kelly's service record, but not very much, Charon saw as he paged through it. It included his dive-qualification records, his instructor's rating, and a photograph, along with some other gingerbread stuff. Charon looked up. "Lives on an island? That's what I heard."

"Yeah, I asked him about that. Funny story. Anyway, why are you interested?"

"Just a name that came up, probably nothing, but I wanted to check it out. I keep hearing rumbles of a bunch that works out on the water."

"I really ought to send that down to Em and Tom. I forgot I had it."

Better yet. "I'm heading that way. Want me to drop it off?"

"Would you?"

"Sure." Charon tucked it under his arm. His first stop was a branch of the Pratt Library, where he made photocopies of the documents for ten cents each. Then he hit a photo shop. His badge enabled him to have five blowups of the small ID photo made in less than ten minutes. Those he left in the car when he parked at headquarters, but he only went inside long enough to have an officer run the file up to homicide. He could have just kept the information to himself, but on reflection it seemed the more intelligent choice to act like a normal cop doing a normal task.

"So what happened?" Greer asked behind the closed door of his office.

"Roger says an investigation would have adverse political consequences," Ritter answered.

"Well, isn't that just too goddamned bad?"

"Then he said to handle it," Ritter added. *Not in so many words, but that's what he meant.* There was no sense in confusing the issue.

"Meaning what?"

"What do you think, James?"

"Where did this come from?" Ryan asked when the file landed on his desk.

"Detective handed it to me downstairs, sir," the young officer answered. "I don't know the guy, but he said it was for your desk."

"Okay." Ryan waved him off and flipped it open, for the first time seeing a photograph of John Terrence Kelly. He'd joined the Navy two weeks after his eighteenth birthday, and stayed in . . . six years, honorably discharged as a chief petty officer. It was immediately apparent that the file had been heavily edited. That was to be expected, as the Department had mainly been interested in his qualifications as a diver. There was his graduation date from UDT School, and his later qualification as an instructor that the Department had been interested in. The three rating sheets in the folder were all 4.0, the highest Navy grade, and there was a flowery letter of recommendation from a three-star admiral which the Department had taken at face value. The Admiral had thoughtfully tucked in a list of his decorations, the more to impress the Baltimore City Police: Navy Cross, Silver Star, Bronze Star with Combat "V" and two clusters in lieu of repeat awards of the same decoration. Purple Heart with two clusters in lieu of—

Jesus, this guy's everything I thought, isn't he?

Ryan set the folder down, seeing that it was part of the Gooding Murder file. That meant Frank Allen—again. He called him.

"Thanks for the info on Kelly. What brought it up?"

"Mark Charon was over," Allen told him. "I'm doing the follow-up on his shoot, and he brought the name up, says it came up in one of his cases. Sorry, pal, I forgot I had this. He said he'd drop it off. He's not the sort of guy I'd figure for being drugged up, y'know, but ... " His voice went on past the point of Ryan's current interest.

This is going too fast now, too damned fast.

Charon. He keeps appearing, doesn't he?

"Frank, I got a tough one for you. When that Sergeant Meyer called in from Pittsburgh, anybody else you mention that to?"

"What do you mean, Em?" Allen asked, annoyance beginning to form in his mind at the suggestion.

"I'm not saying you called the papers, Frank."

"That was the day Charon popped the dealer, wasn't it?" Allen thought back. "I might have said something to him ... only other person I talked with that day, come to think of it."

"Okay, thanks, Frank." Ryan looked up the number of Barracks "V" of the State Police.

"Captain Joy," said a very weary voice. The barracks commander would have taken a bed in his own jail if he'd had to, but by tradition a State Police barracks was just that, and he'd found a comfortable bed for his four and a half hours of sleep. Joy was already wishing that Somerset County would go back to normal, though he well might make major's rank from this episode.

"Lieutenant Ryan, City Police homicide."

"You big-city boys sure are interested in us now," Joy commented wryly. "What do you want to know?"

"What do you mean?"

"I mean I was on my way to bed last night when another one of your people called down here, Lieutenant Chair—something like that, I didn't write it down. Said he could ID one of the bodies ... I *did* write that down somewhere. Sorry, I'm turning into a zombie."

"Could you fill me in? I'll take the short version." It turned out that the short version was plenty. "The woman is in custody?"

"You bet she is."

"Captain, you keep her that way until I say different, okay? Excuse me, *please* keep her that way. She may be a material witness in a multiple homicide."

"Yeah, I know that, remember?"

"I mean up here, too, sir. Two bad ones, I have nine months invested in this."

"She isn't going anywhere for a while," Joy promised. "We have a lot of talking to do with her ourselves, and her lawyer's playing ball."

"Nothing more on the shooter?"

"Just what I said: male Caucasian, six foot or so, and he painted himself green, the girl says." Joy hadn't included that in his initial recounting.

"What?"

"She said his face and hands were green, like camouflage stuff, I suppose. There is one more thing," Joy added. "He's a right good shot. The three people he whacked, one shot each, all in the X-ring—like, perfect."

Ryan flipped the folder back open. At the bottom of Kelly's list of awards: Distinguished Rifleman, Master Pistol.

"I'll be back to you, Captain. Sounds like you've handled this one awfully well for a guy who doesn't get many homicides."

"I'd just as soon stick to speeders," Joy confirmed, hanging up.

"You're in early," Douglas observed, coming in late. "See the paper?"

"Our friend's back, and he got on the scoreboard again." Ryan handed the photo across.

"He looks older now," the sergeant said.

"Three Purple Hearts'll do that." Ryan filled Douglas in. "Want to drive down to Somerset and interview this girl?"

"You think . . . ?"

"Yes, I think we have our witness. I think we have our leaker, too." Ryan explained that one quietly.

He had just called to hear the sound of her voice. So close to his goal, he was allowing himself to look beyond it. It wasn't terribly professional, but for all his professionalism, Kelly remained human.

"John, where are you?" The urgency in her voice was even greater than the day before.

"I have a place," was all he was willing to say.

"I have a message for you. James Greer, he said you should call him."

"Okay." Kelly grimaced—he was supposed to have done that the day before.

"Was that you in the paper?"

"What do you mean?"

"I mean," she whispered, "three dead people on the Eastern Shore!"

"I'll get back to you," he said almost as fast as the chill hit him.

Kelly didn't have the paper delivered to his apartment for the obvious reason, but now he needed one. There was a dispenser at the corner, he remembered. He only needed one look.

What does she know about me?

It was too late for recrimination. He'd faced the same problem with her as with Doris. She'd been asleep when he'd done the job, and the pistol shots had awakened her. He'd blindfolded her, dumped her, explained to her that Burt had planned to kill her, given her enough cash to catch a Greyhound to somewhere. Even with the drugs, she'd been shocked and scared. But the cops had her already. How the hell had that happened?

Screw the how, son, they have her.

Just that fast the world had changed for him.

Okay, so now what do you do? It was that thought which occupied his mind for the walk back to his apartment.

For starters, he had to get rid of the .45, but he'd already decided to do that. Even if he had left no evidence at all behind, it was a link. When this mission was over, it was *over*. But now he needed help, and where else to get it but from the people for whom he had killed?

"Admiral Greer, please? This is Mr. Clark."

"Hold, please," Kelly heard, then: "You were supposed to call in yesterday, remember?"

"I can be there in two hours, sir."

"I'll be waiting."

• • •

"Where's Cas?" Maxwell asked, annoyed enough to use his nickname. The chief who ran his office understood.

"I already called his home, sir. No answer."

"That's funny." Which it wasn't, but the chief understood that, too.

"Want me to have somebody at Bolling check it out, Admiral?"

"Good idea." Maxwell nodded and returned to his office.

Ten minutes later a sergeant of the Air Force's Security Police drove from his guard shack to the collection of semidetached dwellings used by senior officers on Pentagon duty. The sign on the yard said Rear Admiral C. P. Podulski, USN, and showed a pair of aviator wings. The sergeant was only twenty-three and didn't interact with flag officers any more than he had to, but he had orders to see if there was any trouble here. The morning paper was sitting on the step. There were two automobiles in the carport, one of which had a Pentagon pass on the windshield, and he knew that the Admiral and his wife lived alone. Summoning his courage, the sergeant knocked on the door, firmly but not too noisily. No luck. Next he tried the bell. No luck. *Now what?* the young NCO wondered. The whole base *was* government property, and he had the right under regulations to enter any house on the post, and he had orders, and his lieutenant would probably back him up. He opened the door. There was no sound. He looked around the first floor, finding nothing that hadn't been there since the previous evening. He called a few times with no result, and then decided that he had to go upstairs. This he did, with one hand on his white leather holster . . .

Admiral Maxwell was there twenty minutes later.

"Heart attack," the Air Force doctor said. "Probably in his sleep."

That wasn't true of his wife, who lay next to him. She had been such a pretty woman, Dutch Maxwell remembered, and devastated by the loss of their son. The half-filled glass of water sat on a handkerchief so as not to harm the wooden night table. She'd even replaced the top of the pill container before she'd lain back down beside her husband. Dutch looked over to the wooden valet. His undress white shirt was there, ready for another day's service to his adopted country, the Wings of Gold over the collection of ribbons, the topmost of which was pale blue, with five white stars. They'd had a meeting planned to talk about retirement. Somehow Dutch wasn't surprised.

"God have mercy," Dutch said, seeing the only friendly casualties of Operation BOXWOOD GREEN.

What do I say? Kelly asked himself, driving through the gate. The guard eyeballed him pretty hard despite his pass, perhaps wondering how badly the Agency paid its field personnel. He did get to park his wreck in the visitors' lot, better placement than people on the payroll, which seemed slightly odd. Walking into the lobby, Kelly was met by a security officer and led upstairs. It seemed more ominous now, walking the drab and ordinary corridors peopled with anonymous people, but only because this building was about to become a confessional of sorts for a soul who had not quite decided if he were a sinner or not. He hadn't visited Ritter's office before. It was on the fourth floor and surprisingly small. Kelly had thought the man important—and though he actually was, his office as yet was not.

"Hello, John," Admiral Greer said, still reeling from the news he'd received a half hour before from Dutch Maxwell. Greer pointed him to a seat, and the door was closed. Ritter was smoking, to Kelly's annoyance.

"Glad to be back home, Mr. Clark?" the field officer asked. There was a copy of the *Washington Post* on his desk, and Kelly was surprised to see that the Somerset County story had made the first page there, too.

"Yes, sir, I guess you can say that." Both of the older men caught the ambivalence. "Why did you want me to come in?"

"I told you on the airplane. It may turn out that your action bringing that Russian out might save our people yet. We need people who can think on their feet. You can. I'm offering you a job in my part of the house."

"Doing what?"

"Whatever we tell you to do," Ritter answered. He already had something in mind.

"I don't even have a college degree."

Ritter pulled a thick folder from his desk. "I had this brought in from St. Louis." Kelly recognized the forms. It was his complete Navy personnel-records package. "You really should have taken the college scholarship. Your intelligence scores are even higher than I thought, and it shows you have language skills that are better than mine. James and I can waive the degree requirements."

"A Navy Cross goes a long way, John," Greer explained. "What you did, helping to plan BOXWOOD GREEN and then later in the field, that sort of thing goes a long way, too."

Kelly's instinct battled against his reason. The problem was, he wasn't sure which part of him was in favor of what. Then he decided that he had to tell the truth to somebody. "There's a problem, gentlemen."

"What's that?" Ritter asked.

Kelly reached across the desk and tapped the article on the front page of the paper. "You might want to read that."

"I did. So? Somebody did the world a favor," the officer said lightly. Then he caught the look in Kelly's eyes, and his voice became instantly wary. "Keep talking, Mr. Clark."

"That's me, sir."

"What are you talking about, John?" Greer asked.

"The file's out, sir," the records clerk said over the phone.

"What do you mean?" Ryan objected. "I have some copies from it right here."

"Could you hold for a moment? I'll put my supervisor on." The phone went on hold, something that the detective cordially hated.

Ryan looked out his window with a grimace. He'd called the military's central records–storage facility, located in St. Louis. Every piece of paper relating to every man or woman who had ever served in uniform was there, in a secure and carefully guarded complex, the nature of which was a curiosity, but a useful one, to the detective, who'd more than once gotten data from the facility.

"This is Irma Rohrerbach," a voice said after some electronic chirping. The detective had the instant mental image of an overweight Caucasian female sitting at a desk cluttered with work that could have been done a week earlier.

"I'm Lieutenant Emmet Ryan, Baltimore City Police. I need information from a personnel file you have—"

"Sir, it's not here. My clerk just showed me the notes."

"What do you mean? You're not allowed to check files out that way. I know."

"Sir, that is not true. There *are* certain cases. This is one of them. The file was taken out and will be returned, but I do not know when."

"Who has it?"

"I'm not allowed to say, sir." The tone of the bureaucrat's voice showed her intensity of interest, too. The file was gone, and until it came back it was no longer part of the known universe as far as she was concerned.

"I can get a court order, you know." That usually worked on people, few of whom enjoyed the attention of a note from somebody's bench.

"Yes, you can. Is there any other way I can help you, sir?" She was also used to being blustered at. The call was from Baltimore, after all, and a letter from some judge eight hundred miles away seemed a distant and trivial thing. "Do you have our mailing address, sir?"

Actually, he couldn't. He still didn't quite have enough to take to a judge. Matters like this were handled more as a matter of courtesy than as actual orders.

"Thank you, I'll get back."

"Have a good day." The well-wish was in fact the bland dismissal of one more forgettable irrelevance in the day of a file clerk.

Out of the country. Why? For whom? What the hell's so different about this case? Ryan knew that it had many differences. He wondered if he'd ever have them all figured out.

• • •

"That's what they did to her," Kelly told them. It was the first time he'd actually said it all out loud, and in recounting the details of the pathology report it was as though he were listening to the voice of another person. "Because of her background the cops never really assigned much of a priority to the case. I got two more girls out. One they killed. The other one, well . . . " He waved at the newspaper.

"Why did you just turn her loose?"

"Was I supposed to murder her, Mr. Ritter? That's what they were planning to do," Kelly said, still looking down. "She was more or less sober when I let her go. I didn't have the time to do anything else. I miscalculated."

"How many?"

"Twelve, sir," he answered, knowing that Ritter wanted the total number of kills.

"Good Lord," Ritter observed. He actually wanted to smile. There was talk, actually, of getting CIA involved in antidrug operations. He opposed that policy—it wasn't important enough to divert the time of people who should be protecting their country against genuine national-security threats. But he couldn't smile. This was far too serious for that. "The article says twenty kilograms of the stuff. Is that true?"

"Probably." Kelly shrugged. "I didn't weigh it. There's one other thing. I think I know how the drugs come in. The bags smell like—embalming fluid. It's Asian heroin."

"Yes?" Ritter asked.

"Don't you see? Asian stuff. Embalming fluid. Comes in somewhere on the East Coast. Isn't it obvious? They're using the bodies of our KIAs to bring the fucking stuff in."

All this, and analytical ability too?

Ritter's phone rang. It was the intercom line.

"I said no calls," the field spook growled.

"It's 'Bill,' sir. He says it's important."

The timing was just perfect, the Captain thought. The prisoners were brought out in the darkness. There was no electricity, again, and the only illumination came from battery-powered flashlights and a few torches that his senior sergeant had cobbled together. Every prisoner had his feet hobbled; in each case the hands and elbows were bound behind their backs. They all walked slightly bent forward. It wasn't just to control them. Humiliation was important, too, and every man had in close attendance a conscript to chivvy him along, right to the center of the compound. His men were entitled to this, the Captain thought. They'd trained hard, were about to begin their long march south to complete the business of liberating and reuniting their country. The Americans were disoriented, clearly frightened at this break in their daily routine. Things had gone easy for them in the past week. Perhaps his earlier assembly of the group had been a mistake. It might have fostered some semblance of solidarity among them, but the object lesson to his troops was more than worth that. His men would soon be killing Americans in larger groups than this, the Captain was sure, but they had to start somewhere. He shouted a command.

As one man, the twenty selected soldiers took their rifles and butt-stroked their individual charges in the abdomen. One American managed to remain standing after the first blow, but not after the second.

Zacharias was surprised. It was the first direct attack on his person since Kolya had stopped that one, months before. The impact drove the air from him. His back already hurt from the lingering effect of his ejection and the deliberately awkward way they'd made him walk, and the impact of the steel buttplate of the AK-47 had taken control of his weakened and abused body away from him at once. He fell to his side, his body touching that of another prisoner, trying to draw his legs in and cover up. Then the kicks started. He couldn't even protect his face with his arms bound painfully behind him, and his eyes saw the face of the enemy. Just a boy, maybe seventeen, almost girlish in appearance, and the look on his face was that of a doll, the same empty eyes, the same absence of expression. No fury, not even baring his teeth, just kicking him as a child might kick at a ball, because it was something to do. He couldn't hate the boy, but he could despise him for his cruelty, and even after the first kick broke his nose he kept watching. Robin Zacharias had seen the depths of despair, had faced the fact that he'd broken on the inside and given up things that he knew. But he'd also had the time to understand it. He wasn't a coward any more than he was a hero, Robin told himself through the pain, just a man. He'd bear the pain as the physical penalty for his earlier mistake, and he would continue to ask his God for strength. Colonel Zacharias kept his now-blackened eyes on the face of the child tormenting him. *I will survive this. I've survived worse, and even if I die I'm still a better man than you will ever be,* his face told the diminutive soldier. *I've survived loneliness, and that's worse than this, kid.* He didn't pray for deliverance now. It had come from within, after all, and if death came, then he could face it as he had faced his weakness and his failings.

Another shouted command from their officer and they backed off. In Robin's case there was one last, final kick. He was bleeding, one eye almost shut, and his chest was racked with pain and coughs, but he was still alive, still an American, and he had survived one more trial. He looked over at the Captain commanding the detail. There was fury in his face, unlike that of the soldier who'd taken a few steps back. Robin wondered why.

"Stand them up!" the Captain screamed. Two of the Americans were unconscious, it turned out, and required two men each to lift them. It was the best he could do for his men. Better to kill them, but the order in his pocket prohibited that, and his army didn't tolerate the violation of orders.

Robin was now looking in the eyes of the boy who'd attacked him. Close, not six inches away. There was no emotion there, but he kept staring, and there was no emotion in his own eyes either. It was a small and very private test of wills. Not a word was spoken, though both men were breathing irregularly, one from exertion, the other from pain.

Care to try it again someday? Man to man. Think you can hack that, sonny? Do you feel shame for what you did? Was it worth it? Are you more of a man now, kid? I don't think so, and you might cover it up as best you can, but we both know who won this round, don't we? The soldier stepped to Robin's side, his eyes having revealed nothing, but the grip on the American's arm was very tight, the better to keep him under control, and Robin took that as his victory. The kid was still afraid of him, despite everything. He was one of those who roamed the sky—hated, perhaps, but feared too. Abuse was the weapon of the coward, after all, and those who applied it knew the fact as well as those who had to accept it.

Zacharias almost stumbled. His posture made it hard to look up, and he didn't see the truck until he was only a few feet away. It was a beat-up Russian vehicle, with fence wire over the top, both to prevent escape and to let people see the cargo. They were going somewhere. Robin had no real idea where he was and could hardly speculate on where he might go. Nothing could be worse than this place had been—and yet he'd survived it somehow, Robin told himself as the truck rumbled away. The camp faded into the darkness, and with it the worst trial of his life. The Colonel bowed his head and whispered a prayer of thanksgiving, and then, for the first time in months, a prayer for deliverance, whatever form it might take.

"That was your doing, Mr. Clark," Ritter said after a long, deliberate look at the phone he'd just replaced.

"I didn't exactly plan it that way, sir."

"No, you didn't, but instead of killing that Russian officer you brought him back." Ritter looked over at Admiral Greer. Kelly didn't see the nod that announced the change in his life.

"I wish Cas could have known."

"So what do they know?"

"They have Xantha, alive, in Somerset County jail. How much does she know?" Charon asked. Tony Piaggi was here, too. It was the first time the two had met. They were using the about-to-be-activated lab in east Baltimore. It would be safe for Charon to come here just one time, the narcotics officer thought.

"This is trouble," Piaggi observed. It seemed facile to the others until he went on. "But we can handle it. First order of business, though, is to worry about making our delivery to my friends."

"We've lost *twenty kees,* man," Tucker pointed out bleakly. He knew fear now. It was clear that there was something out there worthy of his fear.

"You have more?"

"Yeah, I have ten at my place."

"You keep it at home?" Piaggi asked. "Jesus, Henry!"

"The bitch doesn't know where I live."

"She knows your name, Henry. We can do a lot with just a name," Charon told him. "Why the hell do you think I've kept my people away from your people?"

"We've got to rebuild the whole organization," Piaggi said calmly. "We can do that, okay? We have to move, but moving's easy. Henry, your stuff comes in somewhere else, right? You move it in to here, and we move it out of here. So moving your operation is not a big deal."

"I lose my local—"

"Fuck local, Henry! I'm going to take over distribution for the whole East Coast. Will you think, for Christ's sake? You lose maybe twenty-five percent of what you figured you were going to take in. We can make that up in two weeks. Stop thinking small-time."

"Then it's a matter of covering your tracks," Charon went on, interested by Piaggi's vision of the future. "Xantha is just one person, an addict. When they picked her up she was wasted on pills. Not much of a witness unless they have something else to use, and if you move to another area, you ought to be okay."

"The other ones have to go. Fast," Piaggi urged.

"With Burt gone, I'm out of muscle. I can get some people I know—"

"No way, Henry! You want to bring new people in now? Let me call Philly. We have two people on retainer, remember?" Piaggi got a nod, settling that issue. "Next, we have to keep my friends happy. We need twenty kees' worth of stuff, processed and ready to go, and we need it right fast."

"I only have ten," Tucker noted.

"I know where there's some more, and so do you. Isn't hat right, Lieutenant Charon?" That question shook the op badly enough that he forgot to tell them something lse that concerned him.

36
Dangerous Drugs

It was a time for introspection. He'd never done anything like this before at the behest of others, except for
Vietnam, which was a different set of circumstances altogether. It had required a trip back to Baltimore, which
was now as dangerous a thing as any he'd ever done.
He had a new set of ID, but they were for a man known
to be dead, if anyone took the time to check them out.
He remembered almost fondly the time when the city
had been divided into two zones—one relatively small
and dangerous, and the other far larger and safe. That
was changed. Now it was all dangerous. The police had
his name. They might soon have his face, which would
mean that every police car—there seemed an awful lot
of them now—would have people in it who might spot
him, just like that. Worse still, he couldn't defend himself
against them, he could not allow himself to kill a police
officer.

And now this . . . Things had become very confused
today. Not even twenty-four hours earlier he'd seen his
ultimate target, but now he wondered if it would ever be
finished.

Maybe it would have been better if he had never begun, ist accepted Pam's death and gone on, waiting patiently or the police to break the case. But no, they would never ave broken it, would never have devoted the time and manpower to the death of a whore. Kelly's hands squeezed ne wheel. And her murder would never have been truly venged.

Could I have lived the rest of my life with that?

He remembered high school English classes, as he rove south, now on the Baltimore-Washington Parkway. Aristotle's rules of tragedy. The hero had to have a tragic law, had to drive himself to his fate. Kelly's flaw . . . he oved too much, cared too much, invested too much in the nings and the people who touched his life. He could not urn away. Though it might save his life, to turn away would nevitably poison it. And so he had to take his chances and ee things through.

He hoped Ritter understood it, understood why he was oing what he had been asked to do. He simply could not urn away. Not from Pam. Not from the men of BOXWOOD GREEN. He shook his head. But he wished they'd asked omeone else.

The parkway became a city street, New York Avenue. The sun was long since down. Fall was approaching, the hange of seasons from the moist heat of mid-Atlantic ummer. Football season would soon begin, and baseball nd, and the turning of the years went on.

Peter was right, Hicks thought. He had to stay in. His ather was taking his own step into the system, after a ashion, becoming the most important of political crea- ures, a fund-raiser and campaign coordinator. The Presi- dent would be reelected and Hicks would accumulate his own power. Then he could *really* influence events. Blow- ng the whistle on that raid was the best thing he had ever done. Yeah, yeah, it was all coming together, he hought, lighting up his third joint of the night. He heard he phone ring.

"How's it going?" It was Peter.

"Okay, man. How's with you?"

"Got a few minutes? I want to go over something with you." Henderson nearly swore to himself—he could tell Wally was stoned again.

"Half an hour?"

"See you then."

Not a minute later, there was a knock on the door. Hicks stubbed out his smoke and went to answer it. Too soon for Peter. Could it be a cop? Fortunately, it wasn't.

"You're Walter Hicks?"

"Yeah, who are you?" The man was about his age, if somewhat less polished-looking.

"John Clark." He looked nervously up and down the corridor. "I need to talk to you for a few minutes, if that's okay."

"What about?"

"BOXWOOD GREEN."

"What do you mean?"

"There's some things you need to know," Clark told him. He was working for the Agency now, so Clark was his name. It made it easier, somehow.

"Come on in. I only have a few minutes, though."

"That's all I need. I don't want to stay too long."

Clark accepted the waved invitation to enter and immediately smelled the acrid odor of burning rope. Hicks waved him to a chair opposite his.

"Can I get you anything?"

"No, thanks, I'm fine," he answered, careful where he put his hands. "I was there."

"What do you mean?"

"I was at SENDER GREEN, just last week."

"You were on the team?" Hicks asked, intensely curious and not seeing the danger that had walked into his apartment.

"That's right. I'm the guy who brought the Russian out," his visitor said calmly.

"You *kidnapped* a Soviet *citizen?* Why the fuck did you do that?"

"Why I did it is not important now, Mr. Hicks. One of the documents I took off his body is. It was an order to make preparations to kill all of our POWs."

"That's too bad," Hicks said with a perfunctory shake of the head. *Oh—your dog died? That's too bad.*

"Doesn't that mean anything to you?" Clark asked.

"Yes, it does, but people take chances. Wait a minute." Hicks's eyes went blank for a moment, and Kelly could see that he was trying to identify something he'd missed. "I thought we had the camp commander, too, didn't we?"

"No, I killed him myself. That bit of information was given to your boss so that we could identify the name of the guy who leaked the mission." Clark leaned forward. "That was you, Mr. Hicks. I was there. We had it wired. Those prisoners ought to be with their families right now—all twenty of them."

Hicks brushed it aside. "I didn't *want* them to die. Look, like I said, people take chances. Don't you understand, it just wasn't worth it. So what are you going to do, arrest me? For what? You think I'm dumb? That was a black operation. You can't reveal it or *you* run the risk of fucking up the talks, and the White House will never let you do that."

"That's correct. I'm here to kill you."

"What?" Hicks almost laughed.

"You betrayed your country. You betrayed twenty men."

"Look, that was a matter of conscience."

"So's this, Mr. Hicks." Clark reached into his pocket and pulled out a plastic bag. In it were drugs he'd taken off the body of his old friend Archie, and a spoon, and a glass hypodermic needle. He tossed the bag into his lap.

"I won't do it."

"Fair enough." From behind his back came his Ka-Bar knife. "I've done people this way, too. There are twenty men over there who ought to be home. You've stolen their life from them. Your choice, Mr. Hicks."

His face was very pale now, his eyes wide.

"Come on, you wouldn't really—"

"The camp commander was an enemy of my country. So are you. You got one minute."

Hicks looked at the knife that Clark was turning in his hand, and knew that he had no chance at all. He'd never seen eyes like those across the coffee table from him, but he knew what they held.

Kelly thought about the previous week as he sat there, remembering sitting in the mud generated by falling rain, only a few hundred yards from twenty men who ought now to be free. It became slightly easier for him, though he hoped never to have to obey such orders again.

Hicks looked around the room, hoping to see something that might change the moment. The clock on the mantel seemed to freeze as he considered what was happening. He'd faced the prospect of death in a theoretical way at Andover in 1962, and subsequently lived his life in accordance with the same theoretical picture. The world had been an equation for Walter Hicks, something to be managed and adjusted. He saw now, knowing it was too late, that he was merely one more variable in it, not the guy with the chalk looking at the blackboard. He considered jumping from the chair, but his visitor was already leaning forward, extending the knife a few inches, and his eyes fixed on the thin silvery line on the parkerized blade. It looked so sharp that he had trouble drawing breath. He looked at the clock again. The second hand had moved, after all.

Peter Henderson took his time. It was a weekday night, and Washington went to bed early. All the bureaucrats and aides and special-assistants-to rose early and had to have their rest so that they'd be alert in the management of their country's affairs. It made for empty sidewalks in Georgetown, where the roots of trees heaved up the concrete slabs of sidewalk. He saw two elderly folk walking their little dog, but only one other, on Wally's block. Just a man about his age, fifty yards away, getting into a car whose lawnmower sound marked it as a Beetle, probably an older one. Damned ugly things lasted forever if you wanted them to. A few seconds later he knocked on Wally's door. It wasn't fully closed. Wally was sloppy about some things. He'd never make it as a spy. Henderson pushed the door open, ready to reprove his friend, until he saw him there, sitting in the chair.

Hicks had his left sleeve rolled up. His right hand had caught on his collar, as though to help himself breathe, but the real reason was on the inside of his left elbow. Peter didn't approach the body. For a moment, he didn't do anything. Then he knew he had to get out of here.

He removed a handkerchief and wiped the doorknob, closed the door, and walked away, trying to keep his stomach under control.

Damn you, Wally! Henderson raged. *I needed you. And to die like this—from a drug overdose.* The finality of death was as clear to him as it was unexpected. But there remained his beliefs, Henderson thought as he walked home. At least those hadn't died. He would see to that.

The trip took all night. Every time the truck hit a bump, bones and muscles screamed their protest. Three of the men were hurt worse than he was, two of them unconscious on the floor, and there wasn't a thing he could do for them with his hands and legs bound up. Yet there was satisfaction of a sort. Every destroyed bridge they had to drive around was a victory for them. Someone was fighting back; someone was hurting these bastards. A few men whispered things that the guard at the back of the truck didn't hear over the engine noise. Robin wondered where they were going. The cloudy sky denied him the reference of stars, but with dawn came an indication of where east was, and it was plain that they were heading northwest. Their true destination was too much to hope for, Robin told himself, but then he decided that hope really was something without limit.

Kelly was relieved it was over. There was no satisfaction in the death of Walter Hicks. He'd been a traitor and coward, but there ought to have been a better way. He was glad that Hicks had decided to take his own life, for he wasn't at all sure that he could have killed him with a knife—or any other way. But Hicks had deserved his fate, of that one thing he had no doubts. *But don't we all,* Kelly thought.

Kelly packed his clothing into the suitcase, which was large enough to contain it all, and carried it out to the rented car, and with that his residence in the apartment ended. It was after midnight when he drove south again, into the center of the danger zone, ready to act one last time.

Things had settled down for Chuck Monroe. He still responded to break-ins and all manner of other crimes, but the slaughter of pushers in his district had ended. Part of him thought it was too bad, and he admitted as much to other patrolmen over lunch—in his case, the mercifully unnamed three-in-the-morning meal.

Monroe drove his radio car in his almost-regular patrol pattern, still looking for things out of the ordinary. He noted that two new people had taken Ju-Ju's place. He'd have to learn their street names, maybe have an informant check them out. Maybe the narcs from downtown could start making a few things happen out here. Someone had, however briefly, Monroe admitted, heading west towards the edge of his patrol area. Whoever the hell it was. A street bum. That made him smile in the darkness. The informal name applied to the case seemed so appropriate. The Invisible Man. Amazing that the papers hadn't picked that one up. A dull night made for such thoughts. He was thankful for it. People had stayed up late to watch the Orioles sock it to the Yankees. He had learned that you could often track street crime by sports teams and their activities. The O's were in a pennant race and were looking to go all the way on the strength of Frank Robinson's bat and Brooks Robinson's glove. Even hoods liked baseball, Monroe thought, perplexed by the incongruity but accepting it for the fact it was. It made for a boring night, and he didn't mind. It gave him a chance to cruise and observe and learn, and to think. He knew all the regulars on the street now, and was now learning to spot what was different, to eyeball it as a seasoned cop could, to decide what to check out and what to let slide. In learning that he would come to prevent some crimes, not merely respond to them. It was a skill that could not come too quickly, Monroe thought to himself.

The very western border of his area was a north-south street. One side was his, the other that of another officer.

He was about to turn onto it when he saw another street bum. Somehow the person looked familiar, though he was not one Monroe had shaken down several weeks earlier. Tired of sitting in his car, and bored with not having had anything more than a single traffic citation tonight, he pulled over.

"Yo, hold up there, sport." The figure kept moving, slowly, unevenly. Maybe a public-drunkenness arrest in the making, more likely a street person whose brain was permanently impaired by long nights of guzzling the cheap stuff. Monroe slid his baton into the ring holder and walked quickly to catch up. It was only a fifty-foot walk, but it was like the poor old bastard was deaf or something, he didn't even hear the click of his leather heels on the sidewalk. His hand came down on the bum's shoulder. "I said hold up, now."

Physical contact changed everything. This shoulder was firm and strong—and tense. Monroe simply wasn't ready for it, too tired, too bored, too comfortable, too sure of what he'd seen, and though his brain immediately shouted *The Invisible Man*, his body was not ready for action. That wasn't true of the bum. Almost before his hand came down, he saw the world rotate wildly from low-right to high-left, showing him a sky and then the sidewalk and then the sky again, but this time his view of the stars was interrupted by a pistol.

"Why couldn't you have just stayed in your fuckin' car?" the man asked angrily.

"Who—"

"Quiet!" The pistol against his forehead ensured that, almost. It was the surgical gloves that gave him away and forced the officer to speak.

"Jesus." It was a respectful whisper. "You're him."

"Yes, I am. Now, what the hell do I do about you?" Kelly asked.

"I ain't gonna beg." The man's name was Monroe, Kelly saw from the name tag. He didn't seem like the sort for begging.

"You don't have to. Roll over—now!" The policeman did so, with a little help. Kelly pulled the cuffs off his belt and secured them to both wrists. "Relax, Officer Monroe."

"What do you mean?" The man kept his voice even, earning his captor's admiration.

"I mean I'm not going to kill any cops." Kelly stood him up and started walking him back to the car.

"This doesn't change anything, sport," Monroe told him, careful to keep his voice low.

"Tell me about it. Where do you keep your keys?"

"Right side pocket."

"Thank you." Kelly took them as he put the officer in the backseat of the car. There was a screen there to keep arrested passengers from annoying the driver. He quickly started the patrol car and parked it in an alley. "Your hands okay, not too tight on the cuffs?"

"Yeah, I'm just fuckin' fine back here." The cop was shaking now, mainly rage, Kelly figured. That was understandable.

"Settle down. I don't want you to get hurt. I'll lock the car. Keys'll be in a sewer somewhere."

"Am I supposed to thank you or something?" Monroe said.

"I didn't ask for that, did I?" Kelly had an overwhelming urge to apologize for embarrassing the man. "You made it easy for me. Next time be more careful, Officer Monroe."

His own release of tension almost evoked a laugh as he walked away quickly to the rear. *Thank God,* he thought, heading west again, but not for everything. They're still rousting drunks. He'd hoped that they'd gotten bored with it in the past month. One more complication. Kelly kept to the shadows and alleys as much as possible.

It was a storefront, just as Billy had told him and Burt had confirmed, an out-of-business store with vacant houses to the left and right. Such talkative people, under the proper circumstances. Kelly looked at it from across the street. Despite the vacant ground level, there was a light on upstairs. The front door, he could see, was secured with a large brass lock. The back one, too, probably. Well, he could do this one the hard way ... or the other hard way. There was a clock ticking. Those cops had to have a regular reporting system. Even if not, sooner or later Monroe would be sent a call to get somebody's kitten out of a tree, and real quick his sergeant would start wondering where the hell he was, and then the cops would be all over the place, looking for a missing man. They'd look carefully and hard. That was a possibility Kelly didn't want to contemplate, and one which waiting would not improve.

He crossed the street briskly, for the first time breaking his cover in public, such as it was, weighing risks and finding the balance evenly set on madness. But then, the whole enterprise had been mad from the start, hadn't it? First he did his best to check out the street level for people. Finding none, Kelly took the Ka-Bar from his sheath and started attacking the caulking around the full-length glass pane in the old wooden door. Perhaps burglars just weren't patient, he thought, or maybe just dumb—or smarter than he was being at the moment, Kelly told himself, using both hands to strip the caulking away. It took six endless minutes, all of it under a streetlight not ten feet away, before he was able to lower the glass, cutting himself twice in the process. Kelly swore quietly, looking at the deep cut on his left hand. Then he stepped sideways through the opening and headed for the back of the building. Some mom-and-pop store, he thought, abandoned or something, probably because the neighborhood itself was dying. Well, it could have been worse. The floor was dusty but uncluttered. There were stairs in the back. Kelly could hear noise upstairs, and he went up, his .45 leading the way.

"It's been a nice party, honey, but it's over now," a male voice said. Kelly heard the rough humor in it, followed by a female whimper.

"Please . . . you don't mean you're . . . "

"Sorry, honey, but that's just the way things are," another voice said. "I'll do the front."

Kelly eased down the corridor. Again the floor was unobstructed, just dirty. The wooden floor was old, but had been recent—

—It creaked—

"What's that?"

Kelly froze for the briefest moment, but there was neither time nor a place to hide, and he darted the last fifteen feet, then dived in low and rolled to unmask his
pistol.

There were two men, both in their twenties, just shapes,
really, as his mind filtered out the irrelevancies and concentrated on what mattered now: size, distance, movement.
One was reaching for a gun as Kelly rolled, and even
got his gun out of his belt and coming around before
two rounds entered his chest and another his head. Kelly
brought his weapon around even before the body fell.

"Jesus Christ! Okay! Okay!" A small chrome revolver
dropped to the floor. There was a loud scream from the
front of the building, which Kelly ignored as he got back to
his feet, his automatic locked on the second man as though
connected by a steel rod.

"They're gonna kill us." It was a surprisingly mousy
voice, frightened but slow from whatever she was using.

"How many?" Kelly snapped at her.

"Just these two, they're going to—"

"I don't think so," Kelly told her, standing. "Which one
are you?"

"Paula." He was covering his target.

"Where are Maria and Roberta?"

"They're in the front room," Paula told him, still too
disoriented to wonder how he knew the names. The other
man spoke for her.

"Passed out, pal, okay?" *Let's talk,* the man's eyes tried
to say.

"Who are you?" There was just something about a .45
that made people talk, Kelly thought, not knowing what
his eyes looked like behind the sights.

"Frank Molinari." An accent, and the realization that
Kelly wasn't a policeman.

"Where from, Frank?—You stay put!" Kelly told Paula
with a pointed left hand. He kept the gun level, eyes
sweeping around, ears searching for a danger sound.

"Philly. Hey, man, we can talk, okay?" He was shaking,
eyes flickering down to the gun he'd just dropped, wondering what the hell was happening.

Why was somebody from Philadelphia doing Henry's dirty work? Kelly's mind raced. Two of the men at the lab had sounded the same way. Tony Piaggi. Sure, the mob connection, and Philadelphia. . . .

"Ever been to Pittsburgh, Frank?" Somehow the question just popped out.

Molinari took his best guess. It was not a good one. "How did you know that? Who you working for?"

"Killed Doris and her father, right?"

"It was a job, man, ever do a job?"

Kelly gave him the only possible answer, and there was another scream from the front as he brought the gun back in close to his chest. Time to think. The clock was still ticking. Kelly walked over and yanked Paula to her feet.

"That hurts!"

"Come on, let's get your friends."

Maria was wearing only panties and was too stoned to do any looking. Roberta was conscious and afraid. He didn't want to look at them, not now. He didn't have time. Kelly got them together and forced them down the stairs, then outside. None had shoes, and the combination of drugs and the grit and glass on the sidewalk made them walk in a crippled fashion, whimpering and crying on their way east. Kelly pushed at them, growled at them, making them move faster, fearing nothing more grave than a passing car, because that was enough to wreck everything he'd done. Speed was vital, and it took ten minutes as endless as his race down the hill from SENDER GREEN, but the police car was still there where he'd left it. Kelly unlocked the front and told the women to get in. He'd lied about the keys.

"What the fuck!" Monroe objected. Kelly handed the keys to Paula, who seemed the best able to drive. At least she was able to hold her head up. The other two huddled on the right side, careful to keep their legs away from the radio.

"Officer Monroe, these ladies will be driving you to your station. I have instructions for you. You ready to listen?"

"I got a choice, asshole?"

"You want to play power games or do you want some good information?" Kelly asked as reasonably as he could.

Two pairs of sober eyes lingered in a long moment of contact. Monroe swallowed hard on his pride and nodded.

"Go ahead."

"Sergeant Tom Douglas is the man you want to talk to—nobody else, just him. These ladies are in some really deep shit. They can help you break some major cases. Nobody but him—that's important, okay?" *You fuck that up and we'll meet again,* Kelly's eyes told him.

Monroe caught all the messages and nodded his head. "Yeah."

"Paula, you drive, don't stop for anything, no matter what he says, you got that?" The girl nodded. She'd seen him kill two men. "Get moving!"

She really was too intoxicated to drive, but it was the best he could do. The police car crept away, scraping a telephone pole halfway down the alley. Then it turned the corner and was gone. Kelly took a deep breath, turning back to where his own auto was. He hadn't saved Pam. He hadn't saved Doris. But he had saved these three, and Xantha, at a peril to his life that had at turns been both unintentional and necessary. It was almost enough.

But not quite.

The two-truck convoy had to take a route even more circuitous than planned, and they didn't arrive at the destination until after noon. That was Hoa Lo Prison. The name meant "place of cooking fires," and its reputation was well known to the Americans. When the trucks had pulled into the courtyard and the gates were secure, the men were let down. Again, each man was given an individual guard who took him inside. They were allowed a drink of water and nothing more before assignment to individual cells that were scattered around, and presently Robin Zacharias found his. It wasn't much of a change, really. He found a nice piece of floor and sat down, tired from the journey, resting his head against the wall. It took several minutes before he heard the tapping.

Shave and a haircut, six-bits.
Shave and a haircut, six-bits.

His eyes opened. He had to think. The POWs used a

communications code as simple as it was old, a graphic alphabet.

A	B	C	D	E
F	G	H	I	J
L	M	N	O	P
Q	R	S	T	U
V	W	X	Y	Z

tap-tap-tap-tap-tap pause tap-tap

5/2, Robin thought, the novelty of the moment fighting through fatigue. *Letter W. Okay, I can do this.*

2/3, 3/4, 4/2, 4/5

tap-tap-tap-tap-tap-tap . . . Robin broke that off for his reply.

4/2, 3/4, 1/2, 2/4, 3/3, 5/5, 1/1, 1/3

tap-tap-tap-tap-tap-tap

1/1, 3/1, 5/2, 1/1, 3/1, 3/1

Al Wallace? Al? He's alive?

tap-tap-tap-tap-tap-tap

HOW U? he asked his friend of fifteen years.

MAKIN IT came the reply, then an addition for his fellow Utahan.

1/3, 3/4, 3/2, 1/5, 1/3, 3/4, 3/2, 1/5, 5/4 1/5

Come, come, ye saints . . .

Robin gasped, not hearing the taps, hearing the Choir, hearing the music, hearing what it meant.

tap-tap-tap-tap-tap-tap

1/1, 3/1, 3/1 2/4, 4/3, 5/2, 1/5, 3/1, 3/1, 1/1, 3/1, 3/1 2/4, 4/3, 5/2, 1/5, 3/1, 3/1

Robin Zacharias closed his eyes and gave thanks to his God for the second time in a day and the second time in over a year. He'd been foolish, after all, to think that deliverance might not come. This seemed a strange place for it, and stranger circumstances, but there was a fellow Mormon in the next cell, and his body shuddered as his mind heard that most beloved of hymns, whose final line was not a lie at all, but an affirmation.

All is well, all is well.

• • •

Monroe didn't know why this girl, Paula, didn't listen to him. He tried reason, he tried a bellowed order, but she kept driving, albeit following his directions, creeping along the early-morning streets at all of ten miles per hour, and, at that, staying in her lane only rarely and with difficulty. It took forty minutes. She lost her way twice, mistaking right for left, and once stopped the car entirely when another of the women vomited out the window. Slowly Monroe came to realize what was happening. It was a combination of things that did it, but mainly that he had the time to dope it out.

"What did he do?" Maria asked.

"Th–th–they were going to kill us, just like the others, but he shot *them!*"

Jesus, Monroe thought. That cinched it.

"Paula?"

"Yes?"

"Did you ever know somebody named Pamela Madden?"

Her head went up and down slowly as she concentrated on the road once more. The station was in sight now.

"Dear God," the policeman breathed. "Paula, turn right into the parking lot, okay? Pull around the back . . . that's a good girl . . . you can stop right here, okay." The car jerked to a halt and Paula started crying piteously. There was nothing for him to do but wait a minute or two until she got over the worst of it, and Monroe's fear was now for *them,* not himself. "Okay, now, I want you to let me out."

She opened her door and then the rear one. The cop needed help getting to his feet, and she did it for him on instinct.

"The car keys, there's a handcuff key on it, can you unlock me, miss?" It took her three tries before his hands were free. "Thank you."

"This better be good!" Tom Douglas growled. The phone cord came across his wife's face, waking her up, too.

"Sergeant, this is Chuck Monroe, Western District. I have three witnesses to the Fountain Murder." He paused.

'I think I have two more bodies for the Invisible Man, too. He told me I should only talk to you."

"Huh?" The detective's face twisted in the darkness. "Who did?"

"The Invisible Man. You want to come down here, sir? It's a long one," Monroe said.

"Don't talk to anybody else. Not anybody, you got that?"

"He told me that, too, sir."

"What is it, honey?" Beverly Douglas asked, as awake as her detective husband now.

It was eight months now since the death of a sad, petite girl named Helen Waters. Then Pamela Madden. Then Doris Brown. He was going to get the bastards now, Douglas told himself, incorrectly.

"What are you doing here?" Sandy asked the figure standing next to her car, the one he had fixed.

"Saying goodbye for a while," Kelly told her quietly.

"What do you mean?"

"I'm going to have to go away. I don't know for how long."

"Where to?"

"I can't really say."

"Vietnam again?"

"Maybe. I'm not sure. Honest."

It just wasn't the time for this, as though it ever was, Sandy thought. It was early, and she had to be at work at six-thirty, and though she wasn't running late, there simply weren't the minutes she needed for what had to be said.

"Will you be back?"

"If you want, yes."

"I do, John."

"Thank you. Sandy . . . I got four out," he told her.

"Four?"

"Four girls, like Pam and Doris. One's over on the Eastern Shore, the other three are here in town at a police station. Make sure somebody takes care of them, okay?"

"Yes."

"No matter what you hear, I'll be back. Please believe that."

"John!"

"No time, Sandy. I'll be back," he promised her, walking away.

Neither Ryan nor Douglas wore a tie. Both sipped at coffee from paper cups while the lab boys did their job again.

"Two in the body," one of them was saying, "one in the head—always leaves the target dead. *This* is a professional job."

"The real kind," Ryan breathed to his partner. It was a .45. It had to be. Nothing else made that kind of mess—and besides, there were six brass cartridge cases on the hardwood floor, each circled in chalk for the photographers.

The three women were in a cell in Western District, with a uniformed officer in constant attendance. He and Douglas had spoken to them briefly, long enough to know that they had their witnesses against one Henry Tucker, murderer. Name, physical description, nothing else, but infinitely more than they'd had only hours before. They'd first check their own files for the name, then the FBI's national register of felons, then the street. They'd check motor-vehicle records for a license in that name. The procedure was entirely straightforward, and with a name they'd get him, maybe soon, maybe not. But then there was this other little matter before them.

"Both of them from out of town?" Ryan asked.

"Philadelphia. Francis Molinari and Albert d'Andino," Douglas confirmed, reading the names off their driver's licenses. "How much you want to bet . . . ?"

"No bet, Tom." He turned, holding up a photograph. "Monroe, this face look familiar?"

The patrol officer took the small ID photo from Ryan's hand and looked at it in the poor light of the upstairs apartment. He shook his head. "Not really, sir."

"What do you mean? You were face-to-face with the guy."

"Longer hair, smudges on his face, mainly when we

vere up close I saw the front end of a Colt. Too fast, oo dark."

t was tricky and dangerous, which wasn't unusual. There vere four automobiles parked out front, and he couldn't fford to make any noise—but it was the safest course f action as well, with those four cars parked in front. Ie was standing on the marginal space provided by a sill f a bricked-up window, reaching for the telephone cable. Kelly hoped nobody was using the phone as he clipped nto the wires, quickly attaching leads of his own. With that lone, he dropped down and started walking north along the back of the building, trailing out his own supply of commo vire, just letting it lie on the ground. He turned the corner, etting the spool dangle from his left hand like a lunch pail, crossing the little-used street, moving casually like a person who belonged here. Another hundred yards and he turned again, entering the deserted building and climbing to his perch. Once there he returned to his rented car and got out he rest of what he needed, including his trusty whiskey flask, filled with tap water, and a supply of Snickers bars. Ready, he settled down to his task.

The rifle wasn't properly sighted in. Mad as it seemed, the most sensible course of action was to use the building as his target. He shouldered the weapon in a sitting position and searched the wall for a likely spot. There, an off-color brick. Kelly controlled his breathing, with the scope dialed to its highest magnification, and squeezed gently.

It was strange firing this rifle. The .22 rimfire is a small, inherently quiet round, and with the elaborate suppressor he'd constructed on it, for the first time in his life he heard the music-note *pingggggggg* of the striker hitting the firing pin, along with the muted *pop* of the discharge. The novelty of it almost distracted Kelly from hearing the far louder *swat* of the impact of the round on the target. The bullet created a puff of dust, two inches left and one inch high of his point of aim. Kelly clicked in the adjustment on the Leupold scope and fired again. Perfect. Kelly worked the bolt and then fed three rounds into the magazine, dialing the scope back to low power.

• • •

"Did you hear something?" Piaggi asked tiredly.

"What's that?" Tucker looked up from his task. More than twelve hours now, doing the scut-work that he'd thought to be behind him forever. Not even halfway done despite the two "soldiers" that were down from Philadelphia. Tony didn't like it either.

"Like something falling," Tony said, shaking his head and getting back to it. The only good thing that could be said about this was that it would earn him respect when he related the tale to his associates up and down the coast. A serious man, Anthony Piaggi. When everything went to shit, he'd done the work himself. He makes his deliveries and meets his obligations. You can depend on Tony. It was a rep worth earning, even if this was the price. It was a resolute thought that persisted for perhaps thirty seconds.

Tony slit open another bag, noting the evil, chemical smell on it, not quite recognizing it for what it was. The fine white powder went into the bowl. Next he dumped in the milk sugar. He mixed the two elements with spoons, stirring it slowly. He was sure there must be a machine for this operation, but it was probably too large, like what they used at commercial bakeries. Mainly his mind was protesting that this was work for little people, hirelings. Still, he had to make that delivery, and there was no one else to help out.

"What'd you say?" Henry asked tiredly.

"Forget it." Piaggi concentrated on his task. Where the hell were Albert and Frank? They were supposed to be here a couple hours ago. Thought they were special because they whacked people, like that stuff really mattered.

"Hey, Lieutenant." The sergeant who ran the central evidence storage room was a former traffic officer whose three-wheel bike had run afoul of a careless driver. That had cost him one leg and relegated him to administrative duty, which suited the sergeant, who had his desk and his donuts and his paper in addition to clerkish duties that absorbed maybe three hours of real work per eight-hour shift. It was called retirement-in-place.

"How's the family, Harry?"

"Fine, thanks. What can I do for you?"

"I need to check the numbers on the drugs I brought in last week," Charon told him. "I think there might be a mixup on the tags. Anyway"—he shrugged—"I have to check it out."

"Okay, just give me a minute and I'll—"

"Read your paper, Harry. I know where to go," Charon told him with a pat on the shoulder. Official policy was that nobody wandered around in this room without an official escort, but Charon was a lieutenant, and Harry was short one leg, and his prosthesis was giving him trouble, as it usually did.

"That was a nice shoot, Mark," the sergeant told his back. *What the hell,* he thought, *Mark whacked the guy who'd been carrying the stuff.*

Charon looked and listened for any other person who might be here, but there was none. They'd pay him big-time for this. Talk about moving their operation, eh? Leave him out in the cold, back to chasing pushers . . . well, not entirely a bad thing. He had a lot of money banked away, enough to keep his former wife happy and educate the three kids he'd given her, plus a little for him. He'd probably even get a promotion soon because of the work he'd done, taking down several drug distributors . . . there.

The ten kilos he had taken from Eddie Morello's car were in a labeled cardboard box, sitting on the third shelf, right where they were supposed to be. He took the box down and looked to be sure. Each of the ten one-kilo bags had to be opened, tested, and resealed. The lab technician who'd done it had just initialed the tags, and his initials were easy to fake. Charon reached into his shirt and pants, pulling out plastic bags of Four-X sugar, which was of the same color and consistency as the heroin. Only his office would ever touch this evidence, and he could control that. In a month he'd send a memo recommending destruction of the evidence, since the case on it was closed. His captain would approve. He'd dump it down the drain with several other people watching, and the plastic bags would be burned, and nobody would ever know. It certainly seemed simple enough. Within three minutes he was walking away from the evidence racks.

"Numbers check out?"

"Yeah, Harry, thanks," Charon said, waving on the way out.

"Somebody get the fuckin' phone," Piaggi growled. Who the hell would be calling here, anyway? It was one of the Philly guys who walked over, taking the time to light a cigarette.

"Yeah?" The man turned. "Henry, it's for you."

"What the hell?" Tucker walked over.

"Hi, Henry," Kelly said. He'd wired a field phone into the building's telephone line, cutting it off from the outside world. He sat there, next to the canvas-covered instrument, having rung the other end just by turning the crank. It seemed rather primitive, but it was something familiar and comfortable to him, and it worked.

"Who's this?"

"The name's Kelly, John Kelly," he told him.

"So who's John Kelly?"

"Four of you killed Pam. You're the only one left, Henry," the voice said. "I got the rest. Now it's your turn." Tucker turned and looked around the room as though he expected to find the voice there. Was this some kind of sick joke that they were playing on him?

"How—how'd you get this number? Where are you?"

"Close enough, Henry," Kelly told him. "You nice and comfy in there with your friends?"

"Look, I don't know who you are—"

"I told you who I am. You're in there with Tony Piaggi. I saw you at his restaurant the other night. How was your dinner, by the way? Mine was just great," the voice taunted.

Tucker stood straight up, his hand tight on the phone. "So what the fuck are you gonna do, boy?"

"I ain't gonna kiss you on both cheeks, *boy.* I got Rick,

and I got Billy, and I got Burt, and now I'm going to get you. Do me a favor, put Mr. Piaggi on the line," the voice suggested.

"Tony, you better come here," Tucker said.

"What is it, Henry?" Piaggi tripped on his chair getting up. *So damned tired from all this. Those bastards in Philly better have the cash all ready.* Henry handed him the phone.

"Who's this?"

"Those two guys on the boat, the ones you gave to Henry? I got 'em. I got the other two this morning, too."

"What the fuck is this?"

"You figure it out." The line went dead. Piaggi looked over at his partner, and since he couldn't get an answer from the phone, he'd get one from Tucker.

"Henry, what the hell is this?"

Okay, let's see what that stirred up. Kelly allowed himself a sip of water and a Snickers. He was on the third story of the building. Some sort of warehouse, he thought, massively constructed of reinforced concrete, a good place to be when The Bomb went off. The tactical problem was an interesting one. He couldn't just burst inside. Even if he'd had a machine gun—he didn't—four against one was long odds, especially when you didn't know what was inside the door, especially when stealth was something you couldn't count on as an ally, and so he'd try another approach. He'd never done anything like this before, but from his perch he could cover every door of the building. The windows in the back were bricked up. The only ways out were under his sight, and at just over a hundred yards, he hoped that they'd try it. Kelly shouldered the rifle, but kept his head up, sweeping left and right in an even, patient way.

"It's him," Henry said quietly so the others couldn't hear.

"Who?"

"The guy who did all those pushers, the guy who got Billy and the rest, the guy who did the ship. It's *him.*"

"Well, who the fuck is *him,* Henry?"

"I don't know, goddamn it!" The voice was higher now,

and the other two heads looked up. Tucker got more control of himself. "He says he wants us to come out."

"Oh, that's just great—what are we up against? Wait a minute." Piaggi lifted the phone but got no dial tone. "What the hell?"

Kelly heard the buzz and lifted his handset. "Yeah, what is it?"

"Who the fuck are you?"

"It's Tony, right? Why did you have to kill Doris, Tony? She wasn't any danger to you. Now I have to do you, too."

"*I* didn't—"

"You know what I mean, but thanks for bringing those two down here. I wanted to tie that loose end up, but I didn't expect to have the chance. They're in the morgue by now, I suppose."

"Trying to scare me?" the man demanded over the scratchy phone line.

"No, just trying to kill you," Kelly told him.

"Fuck!" Piaggi slammed the phone down.

"He says he saw us at the restaurant, man. He says he was right there." It was clear to the other two that something was amiss. They were looking up now, mainly curious, but wary as they saw their two superiors in an agitated state. What the hell was this all about?

"How could he know—oh," Piaggi said, his voice trailing off to a quieter tone. "Yeah, they knew me, didn't they . . . ? Jesus."

There was only one window with clear glass. The others had glass bricks, the four-inch-square blocks favored for letting light in without being easily broken by vandals. They also prevented anyone from seeing out. The one window with clear glass had a crank, allowing the panes to open upward at an angle. This office had probably been set up by some asshole of a manager who didn't want his secretaries looking out the windows. Well, the bastard had gotten his wish. Piaggi cranked the window open—tried to, the three moving panes had only gone forty degrees before the mechanism froze.

Kelly saw it move and wondered if he should announce his presence in a more direct way. Better not to, he thought, better to be patient. *Waiting grows hard on those who don't know what's happening.*

The remarkable thing was that it was ten o'clock in the morning now, a clean, sunny late-summer day. There was truck traffic on O'Donnell Street, only half a block away, and some private autos as well, driving past, going about their business. Perhaps their drivers saw the tall abandoned building Kelly was in, wondering, as he was, what it had been constructed for; seeing the four automobiles parked at the former trucking building, wondering if that business was starting up again; but if they did, it wasn't worth anything more than a passing thought for people who had work to do. The drama was being played in plain sight, and only the players knew.

"I don't see shit," Piaggi said, squatting down to look out the windows. "There's nobody around."

This is the guy who did the pushers, Tucker was telling himself as he stood away from the window. *Five or six of 'em. Killed Rick with a fuckin' knife* . . .

Tony had picked the building. It was to be an ostensible part of a small interstate trucking concern whose owners were connected and very careful players. Just perfect, he'd thought, so close to major highways, quiet part of town, little police activity, just an anonymous building doing anonymous work. Perfect, Henry had thought on seeing it.

Oh, yeah, just perfect . . .

"Let me look." It wasn't time to back off. Henry Tucker didn't think of himself as a coward. He'd fought and killed, himself, and not just women. He'd spent years establishing himself, and the first part of the process hadn't been without bloodshed. Besides, he couldn't appear to be weak now, not in front of Tony and two "soldiers." "Nothin'," he agreed.

"Let's try something." Piaggi walked to the phone and lifted it. There wasn't a dial tone, just a buzz. . . .

Kelly looked at the field phone, listening to the noise it made. He'd let it be for the moment, let them do the waiting now. Though the tactical situation was of his design, still his options were limited. Talk, don't talk. Shoot, don't shoot. Move, don't move. With only three basic choices to be made, he had to select his actions carefully to achieve the desired effect. This battle was not a physical one. Like most battles, it was a thing of the mind.

It was getting warm. The last hot days before the leaves started turning. Already eighty degrees, maybe going past ninety, one last time. He wiped perspiration from his face, watching the building, listening to the buzz, letting them sweat from something other than the heat of the day.

"Shit," Piaggi snarled, slamming the phone down. "You two!"

"Yeah?" It was the taller one, Bobby.

"Take a walk around the building—"

"No!" Henry said, thinking. "What if he's right outside? You can't see shit out that window. He could be standing right next to the door. You want to risk that?"

"What do you mean?" Piaggi asked.

Tucker was pacing now, breathing a little faster than usual, commanding himself to think. *How would I do it?* "I mean, the bastard cuts the phone line, makes his call, spooks us, and then he just waits for us right outside, like."

"What do you know about this guy?"

"I know he killed five pushers, and four of my people—"

"And four of mine if he ain't lyin'—"

"So we gotta outthink him, okay? How would you handle it?"

Piaggi thought that one over. He'd never killed. It had just never worked out that way. He was more the brains side of the business. He had roughed people up in his time, however, had delivered some fearful beatings, and that was close enough, wasn't it? *How would I do this?* Henry's idea made sense. You just stay out of sight, like around a corner, in an alley, in the shadows, and then you let them look the other way. The nearest door, the one they'd used, swung to the left, and you could tell that from the outside from where the hinges were. It also had the virtue of being closest to the cars, and since that was their only means of escape, that's the one he'd expect them to use.

Yeah.

Piaggi looked over to his partner. Henry was looking up. The acoustical panels had been removed from the drop ceiling. Right there, in the flat roof, was an access door. It was locked shut with a simple manual latch to keep burglars out. It would open easily, maybe even quietly, to the flat tar-and-gravel roof, and a guy could get up there, and walk to the edge, and look down, and whack whoever was waiting there next to the front door.

Yeah.

"Bobby, Fred, come here," Piaggi ordered. He filled them in on the tactical situation. By this time they'd guessed that something was gravely wrong, but it wasn't cops—that was the worst thing that could go wrong, they thought, and the assurance that it wasn't cops actually relieved both of them. Both had handguns. Both were smart, and Fred had killed once, taking care of a small family problem in riverside Philadelphia. The two of them slid a desk under the access door. Fred was eager to show that he was a serious guy, and so gain favor with Tony, who also looked like a serious guy. He stood on the desk. It wasn't quite enough. They put a chair atop the desk, which allowed him to open the door and look out on the roof.

Aha! Kelly saw the man standing there—actually only his head and chest were visible. The rifle came up, and the crosshairs found the face. He almost took the shot. What stopped him was the way the man had his hands on the door coaming, the way he was looking around, scanning the flat roof before he moved farther. He wanted to get up there. *Well, I guess I'll let him,* Kelly thought as a tractor-trailer rumbled past, fifty yards away. The man lifted himself up on the roof. Through his telescopic sight, Kelly could see a revolver in his hand. The man stood erect, looking all the way around, and then moved very slowly towards the front of the building. It wasn't bad tactics, really. Always a good thing to do your reconnaissance first . . . *oh, that's what they're thinking,* he thought. Too bad.

Fred had removed his shoes. The small pea-size gravel hurt his feet, and so did the heat radiating from the sticky black tar under the stones, but he had to be quiet—and besides, he was a tough customer, as someone had once learned on the bank of the Delaware River. His hands flexed familiarly on the grip of his short-barreled Smith. If the bastard was there, he'd shoot straight down. Tony and Henry would pull the body in, and they'd pour water to wash the blood away, and get back to business, because this was an important delivery. Halfway there. Fred was very concentrated now. He approached the parapeted edge with his feet in the lead, his body leaning back until his stockinged toes got all the way to the low wall of bricks that extended above the roofline. Then, quickly, he leaned forward, gun aimed downwards at—nothing. Fred looked up and down the front of the building.

"Shit!" He turned, and called, "There's nobody here!"

"What?" Bobby's head came up in the opening to look, but Fred was now checking the cars out for someone crouching there.

Kelly told himself that patience was almost always rewarded. That thought had enabled him to fight off the buck fever that always came when you had a target in your sights. As soon as his peripheral vision caught movement at the opening, he brought the gun left. A face, white, twenties, dark eyes, looking at the other one, a pistol in his right hand. Just a target now. *Take him first.* Kelly centered the crosshairs in the bridge of the nose and squeezed gently.

Smack. Fred's head turned when he heard a sound that was both wet and hard, but when he did, there was nothing there. He'd heard nothing else but that wet, sharp sound, but now there was also a clatter, as though Bobby's chair had slipped off the desk and he'd fallen to the floor. Nothing else, but for no apparent reason the skin at the back of his neck turned to ice. He backed away from the edge of the roof, looking all around at the flat, rectangular horizon just as fast as his head could turn. Nothing.

The gun was new, and the bolt still a little stiff as he drove the second round home. Kelly brought it back to the right. Two for the price of one. The head was turning rapidly now. He could see the fear there. He knew there was danger but not where or what kind. Then the man started moving back to the opening. He couldn't allow that. Kelly applied about six inches of lead and squeezed again. *Pinggggg.*

Smack. The sound of the impact was far louder than the muted *pop* of the shot. Kelly ejected the spent cartridge and slammed in another as a car approached on O'Donnell Street.

Tucker was still looking at Bobby's face when his head jerked upwards, hearing the thud of what had to be another body, rattling the steel-bar joists of the roof. "Oh, my God . . ."

37
Trial by Ordeal

"You're looking much better than the last time, Colonel," Ritter said pleasantly in Russian. The security officer rose and walked out of the living room, giving the two men privacy. Ritter was carrying an attaché case, which he set on the coffee table. "Feeding you well?"

"I have no complaints," Grishanov said warily. "When can I go home?"

"This evening, probably. We're waiting for something." Ritter opened the case. This made Kolya uneasy, but he didn't allow it to show. For all he knew there might be a pistol in there. Comfortable as his imprisonment had been, friendly as his conversations with the residents in this place were, he was on enemy soil, under the control of enemies. It made him think of another man in a distant place under very different circumstances. The differences ate at his conscience and shamed him for his fear.

"What is that?"

"Confirmation that our people are in Hoa Lo Prison."

The Russian lowered his head and whispered something Ritter didn't catch. Grishanov looked up. "I am glad to hear that."

"You know, I believe you. Your letters back and forth to Rokossovskiy make that clear." Ritter poured himself some tea from the pot on the table, filling up Kolya's cup also.

"You have treated me correctly." Grishanov didn't know what else to say, and the silence was heavy in him.

"We have a lot of experience being friendly to Soviet guests," Ritter assured him. "You're not the first to stay here. Do you ride?"

"No, I've never been on a horse."

"Ummhmm." The attaché case was quite full with papers, Kolya saw, wondering what they were. Ritter took out two large cards and an ink pad. "Could I have your hands, please?"

"I don't understand."

"Nothing to worry about." Ritter took his left hand and inked the fingertips, rolling them one at a time in the appropriate boxes on one card, then the other. The procedure was duplicated with the right hand. "There, that didn't hurt, did it? You can wash your hands now, better to do it before the ink dries." Ritter slid one of the cards into the file, substituting it for the one removed. The other just went on top. He closed the case, then carried the old card to the fireplace, where he ignited it with his cigarette lighter. It burned fast, joining the ash pile from the fires that the custodians liked to have every other night. Grishanov came back with clean hands.

"I still don't understand."

"It's really nothing that need concern you. You just helped me out on something, that's all. What say we have lunch? Then we can meet with a countryman of yours. Please be at ease, Comrade Colonel," Ritter said as reassuringly as he could. "If your side sticks to the bargain, you'll be on your way home in about eight hours. Fair enough?"

Mark Charon was uncomfortable coming here again, safe though the location might be this early into its use. Well, this wouldn't take long. He pulled his unmarked Ford to the front of the building, got out, and walked to the front door. It was locked. He had to knock. Tony Piaggi yanked it open, a gun in his hand.

"What's this?" Charon demanded in alarm.

"What's this?" Kelly asked himself quietly. He hadn't expected the car to come right up to the building, and had been loading two more rounds into the clip when the man pulled in and got out. The rifle was so stiff that he had trouble getting the clip back in, and by the time he had it up, the figure was moving too rapidly for a shot. Damn. Of course, he didn't know who it was. He twisted the scope to max-power and examined the car. Cheap body . . . an extra radio antenna . . . police car? Reflected light prevented him from seeing the interior. Damn. He'd made a small mistake. He'd expected a down-time after dropping the two on the roof. *Never take anything for granted, dummy!* The slight error made him grimace.

"What the hell is going on?" Charon snapped at them. Then he saw the body on the floor, a small hole slightly above and to the left of the open right eye.

"It's him! He's out there!" Tucker said.

"Who?"

"The one who got Billy and Rick and Burt—"

"Kelly!" Charon exclaimed, turning around to look at the closed door.

"You know his name?" Tucker asked.

"Ryan and Douglas are after him—they want him for a string of killings."

Piaggi grunted. "The string is longer by two. Bobby here, and Fred on the roof." He stooped by the window again. *He's got to be right across the road there . . .*

Charon had his gun out now, for no apparent reason. Somehow the bags of heroin seemed unusually heavy now, and he set his service revolver down and unloaded them from his clothing onto the table with the rest of them, along with the mixing bowl, and the envelopes, and the stapler. That activity ended his current ability to do anything but look at the other two. That was when the phone rang. Tucker got it.

"Having fun, you cocksucker?"

• • •

"Did you have fun with Pam?" Kelly asked coldly. "So," he asked more pleasantly, "who's your friend? Is that the cop you have on the payroll?"

"You think you know it all, don't you?"

"No, not all. I don't know why a man would get his rocks off killing girls, Henry. You want to tell me that?" Kelly asked.

"Fuck you, man!"

"You want to come on out and try? You swing that way too, sweetie-pie?" Kelly hoped Tucker didn't break the phone, the way he slammed it down. He just didn't understand the game, and that was good. If you didn't know the rules, you couldn't fight back effectively. There was an edge of fatigue on his voice, and Tony's also. The one on the roof hadn't had his shirt buttoned; it was rumpled, Kelly saw, examining the body through his sight. The trousers had creases inside the knees, as though the man had been sitting up all night. Had he merely been a slob? That didn't seem likely. The shoes he'd left by the opening were quite shiny. Probably up all night, Kelly judged after a few seconds' reflection. *They're tired, and they're scared, and they don't know the game. Fine.* He had his water and his candy bars, and all day.

"If you knew that bastard's name, how come you—god-damn it!" Tucker swore. "You told me he's just a rich beach bum, I *said* I could take him out in the hospital, remember, but *no!* . . . you said leave him fuckin' be!"

"Settle down, Henry," Piaggi said as calmly as he could manage. *This is one very serious boy we have out there. He's done six of my people. Six! Jesus. This is not the time to panic.*

"We have to think this one through, okay?" Tony rubbed the heavy stubble on his face, collecting himself, thinking it through. "He's got a rifle and he's in that big white building across the street."

"You wanna just walk over there and get him, Tony?" Tucker pointed to Bobby's head. "Look what he did here!"

"Ever hear of nightfall, Henry? There's one light out there, right over the door." Piaggi walked over to the fuse box, checked the label inside the door, and unscrewed the proper fuse. "There, the light don't work anymore. We can wait for night and make our move. He can't get us all. If we move fast enough, he might not get any."

"What about the stuff?"

"We can leave one guy here to guard it. We get muscle in here to go after that bastard, and we finish business, okay?" It was a viable plan, Piaggi thought. The other guy didn't hold all the cards. He couldn't shoot through the walls. They had water, coffee, and time on their side.

The three stories were as close to word-for-word identical as anything he might have hoped for under the circumstances. They'd interviewed them separately, as soon as they'd recovered enough from their pills to speak, and their agitated state only made things better. Names, the place it had happened, how this Tucker bastard was dealing his heroin out-of-town now, something Billy had said about the way the bags stank—confirmed by the "lab" busted on the Eastern Shore. They now had a driver's license number and possible address on Tucker. The address might be bogus—not an unlikely situation—but they also had a car make, from which they'd gotten a tag number. He had it all, or at least was close enough that he could treat the investigation as something with an end to it. It was a time for him to stand back and let things happen. The all-points was just now going on the air. At the next series of squad-room briefings, the name Henry Tucker, and his car, and his tag number would be made known to the patrol officers who were the real eyes of the police force. They could get very lucky, very fast, bring him in, arraign him, indict him, try him, and put his ass away forever even if the Supreme Court had the bad grace to deny him the end his life had earned. Ryan was going to bag that inhuman bastard.

And yet.

And yet Ryan knew he was one step behind someone else. The Invisible Man was using a .45 now—not his silencer; he had changed tactics, was going for quick, sure kills . . . didn't care about noise anymore . . . and he'd talked to others before killing them, and probably knew even more than he did. That dangerous cat Farber had described to him was out on the street, hunting in the light now, probably, and Ryan didn't know where.

John T. Kelly, Chief Boatswain's Mate, U.S. Navy SEALs. Where the hell are you? If I were you . . . where would I be? Where would I go?

"Still there?" Kelly asked when Piaggi lifted the phone.

"Yeah, man, we're having a late lunch. Wanna come over and join us?"

"I had calamari at your place the other night. Not bad. Your mother cook it up?" Kelly inquired softly, wondering about the reply he'd get.

"That's right," Tony replied pleasantly. "Old family recipe, my great-grandmother brought it over from the Old Country, y'know?"

"You know, you surprise me."

"How's that, Mr. Kelly?" the man asked politely, his voice more relaxed now. He was wondering what effect it would have on the other end of the phone line.

"I expected you to try and cut a deal. Your people did, but I wasn't buying," Kelly told him, allowing irritation to show in his voice.

"Like I said, come on over and we can talk over lunch." The line clicked off.

Excellent.

"There, that ought to give the fucker something to think about." Piaggi poured himself another cup of coffee. The brew was old and thick and rancid now, but it was so heavily laced with caffeine that his hands remained still only with concerted effort. But he was fully awake and alert, Piaggi told himself. He looked at the other two, smiling and nodding confidently.

"Sad about Cas," the Superintendent observed to his friend.

Maxwell nodded. "What can I say, Will? He wasn't exactly a good candidate for retirement, was he? Family gone, here and there both. This was his life, and it was coming to an end one way or another." Neither man wanted to discuss what his wife had done. Perhaps after a year or so they might see the poetic symmetry in the loss of two friends, but not now.

"I hear you put your papers in, too, Dutch." The Superintendent of the United States Naval Academy didn't quite understand it. Talk was about that Dutch was a sure thing for a fleet command in the spring. The talk had died only days before, and he didn't know why.

"That's right." Maxwell couldn't say why. The orders—couched as a "suggestion"—had come from the White House, through the CNO. "Long enough, Will. Time for some new blood. Us World War Two guys . . . well, time to make room, I guess."

"Sonny doing okay?"

"I'm a grandfather."

"Good for them!" At least there was some good news in the room when Admiral Greer entered it, wearing his uniform for once.

"James!"

"Nice principal's office," Greer observed. "Hiya, Dutch."

"So, to what do I owe all this high-level attention?"

"Will, we're going to steal one of your sailboats. You have something nice and comfortable that two admirals can handle?"

"Wide selection. You want one of the twenty-sixes?"

"That's about right."

"Well, I'll call the Seamanship Department and have them chop one loose for you." It made sense, the Admiral thought. They'd both been close with Cas, and when you said goodbye to a sailor, you did it at sea. He placed his call, and they took their leave.

"Run outa ideas?" Piaggi asked. His voice showed defiant confidence now. The momentum had passed across the street, the man thought. Why not reinforce that?

"I don't see that you have any to speak of. You bastards afraid of the sunlight? I'll give you some!" Kelly snarled. "Watch."

He set the phone down and lifted the rifle, taking aim at the window.

Pop.

Crash.

"You dumb fuck!" Tony said into the phone, even though he knew it to be disconnected. "You see? He knows he can't get us. He knows time's on our side."

Two panes were shattered, then the shooting stopped again. The phone rang. Tony let it ring a while before he answered.

"Missed, you jerk!"

"I don't see you going anywhere, asshole!" The shout was loud enough that Tucker and Charon heard the buzz from ten feet away.

"I think it's time for you to start runnin', Mr. Kelly. Who knows, maybe we won't catch you. Maybe the cops will. They're after you too, I hear."

"You're still the ones in the trap, remember."

"You say so, man." Piaggi hung up on him again, showing who had the upper hand.

"And how are you, Colonel?" Voloshin asked.

"It has been an interesting trip." Ritter and Grishanov were sitting on the steps of the Lincoln Memorial, just two tourists tired after a hot day, joined by a third friend, under the watchful eyes of a security guard ten yards away.

"And your Vietnamese friend?"

"What?" Kolya asked in some surprise. "What friend?"

Ritter grinned. "That was just a little ploy on my part. We had to identify the leak, you see."

"I thought that was your doing," the KGB general observed sourly. It was such an obvious trap and he'd fallen right into it. Almost. Fortune had smiled on him, and probably Ritter didn't know that.

"The game goes on, Sergey. Will you weep for a traitor?"

"For a traitor, no. For a believer in the cause of a peaceful world, yes. You are very clever, Bob. You have done well." *Perhaps not,* Voloshin thought, *perhaps not as far into the trap as you believe, my young American friend. You moved too fast. You managed to kill this Hicks boy, but not CASSIUS. Impetuous, my young friend. You miscalculated and you really don't know it, do you?*

Time for business. "What about our people?"

"As agreed, they are with the others. Rokossovskiy confirms. Do you accept my word, Mr. Ritter?"

"Yes, I will. Very well, there's a PanAm flight from Dulles to Paris tonight at eight-fifteen. I'll deliver him there if you wish to see him off. You can have him met at Orly."

"Agreed." Voloshin walked away.

"Why did he leave me?" Grishanov asked, more surprised than alarmed.

"Colonel, that's because he believes my word, just like I believe his." Ritter stood. "We have a few hours to kill—"

"Kill?"

"Excuse me, that's an idiom. We have a few hours of private time. Would you like to walk around Washington? There's a moon rock in the Smithsonian. People love to touch it for some reason."

Five-thirty. The sun was in his eyes now. Kelly had to wipe his face more often. Watching the partly broken window, he saw nothing except an occasional shadow. He wondered if they were resting. That wouldn't do. He lifted the field phone and turned the crank. They made him wait again.

"Who's calling?" Tony asked. He was the formidable one, Kelly thought, almost as formidable as he thought he was. It was a shame, really.

"Your restaurant do carry-out?"

"Getting hungry, are we?" Pause. "Maybe you want to make a deal with us."

"Come on outside and we can talk about it," Kelly replied. The reply was a *click*.

Just about right, Kelly thought, watching the shadows move across the floor. He drank the last of his water and ate his last candy bar, looking around the area again for any changes. He'd long since decided what to do. In a way, they'd decided that for him. There was again a clock running, ticking down to a zero-time that was flexible but finite. He could walk away from this if he had to, but—no, he really couldn't. He checked his watch. It was going to be dangerous, and the passage of time would not change it any more than it already had. They'd been awake for twenty-four hours, probably longer. He'd given them fear and let them get comfortable with it. They thought they held a good playing hand now, just as he'd dared to hope they would.

Kelly slid backwards on the cement floor, leaving his gear behind. He'd need it no longer no matter how this turned out. Standing, he brushed off his clothes and checked his Colt automatic. One in the chamber, seven in the magazine. He stretched a little, and then he knew that he could delay no longer. He headed down the stairs, pulling out the keys to the VW. It started despite his sudden fear that it might not. He let the engine warm up while watching traffic on the north-south street in front of him. He darted across, incurring the noisy wrath of a southbound driver, but fitting neatly into the rush-hour traffic.

"See anything?"

Charon had been the one to suggest that the angles precluded Kelly from seeing all the way into their building. He might try to come across after all, they thought, but two of them could each cover one side of the white building. And they knew he was still there. They were getting to him. He hadn't thought it all the way through, Tony pronounced. He was pretty smart, but not that smart, and when it was dark, and when there were shadows, they'd make their move. It would work. A dinky little .22 wouldn't penetrate a car body if they could make it that far, and if they surprised him, they could—

"Just traffic on the other side."

"Don't get too close to the window, man."

"Fuckin' A," Henry said. "What about the delivery?"

"We got a saying in the family, man, better late than never, y'dig?"

Charon was the most uncomfortable of the three. Perhaps it was just the proximity to the drugs. Evil stuff. *A little late to think about that.* Could there be a way out of this?

The money for his delivery was right there, next to the desk. He had a gun.

To die like a criminal? He watched them there, left and right of the window. They were the criminals. He hadn't done anything to offend this Kelly. Well, nothing that he knew about. It was Henry who'd killed the girl, and Tony who'd set the other one up. Charon was just a crooked cop. This was a *personal* matter for Kelly. Not a hard thing to understand. Killing Pam that way had been brutal and foolish. He'd told Henry that. He could come out of this a hero, couldn't he? Got a tip, walked right into it. Crazy shoot-out. He could even help Kelly. And he'd never, ever get mixed up with anything like this again. Bank the money, get the promotion, and take down Henry's organization from what he knew. They'd never bust him back after that, would they? All he had to do was to get on the phone and *reason* with the man. Except for one little thing.

Kelly turned left, proceeded west one block, then left again, heading south towards O'Donnell Street. His hands were sweating now. There were three of them, and he'd have to be very, very good. But he *was* good, and he had to finish the job, even if the job might finish him. He stopped the car a block away, getting out, locking it, and walking the rest of the way to the building. The other businesses here were closed down now—he'd counted three, up and operating throughout the day, totally unaware of what was happening . . . in one case just across the street.

Well, you planned that one right, didn't you?

Yeah, Johnnie-boy, but that was the easy part.

Thanks. He stood right there at the corner of the building, looking in all directions. Better from the other side . . . he walked to the corner with the phone and electrical service, using the same half-windowsill he'd used before, reaching for the parapet and doing his best to avoid the electrical wires.

Okay, now you just have to walk across the roof without making any noise.

On tar and gravel?

There was one alternative he hadn't considered. Kelly stood on the parapet. It was at least eight inches wide, he told himself. It was also quiet as he walked the flat brick tightrope towards the opening in the roof, wondering if they might be using the phone.

Charon had to make his move soon. He stood, looking at the others, and stretched rather theatrically before heading in their direction. His coat was off, his tie loose, and his five-shot Smith was at his right hip. Just shoot the bastards and then talk to this Kelly character on the phone. Why not? They were *hoods,* weren't they? Why should he die for what they did?

"What are you doing, Mark?" Henry asked, not seeing the danger, too focused on the window. *Good.*

"Tired of sittin'." Charon pulled the handkerchief from his right hip pocket and wiped his face with it as he measured angles and distance, then back to the phone, where his only safety lay. He was sure of that. It was his only chance to get out of this.

Piaggi just didn't like the look in his eyes. "Why not just sit back down and relax, okay? It's going to get busy soon."

Why is he looking at the phone? Why is he looking at us?

"Back off, Tony, okay?" Charon said in a challenging voice, reaching back to replace the handkerchief. He didn't know that his eyes had given him away. His hand had barely touched the revolver when Tony aimed and fired one shot into his chest.

"Real smart guy, huh?" Tony said to the dying man. Then he noticed that the oblong rectangle of light from the roof door had a shadow in it. Piaggi was still looking at the shadow when it disappeared, replaced by a blur barely caught by his peripheral vision. Henry was looking at Charon's body.

• • •

The shot startled him—the obvious thought was that it had been aimed at himself—but he was committed, and jumped into the square hole. It was like a parachute jump, *keep your feet together, knees bent, back straight, roll when you hit.*

He hit hard. It was a tile-over-concrete floor, but his legs took the worst of it. Kelly rolled at once, straightening his arm. The nearest one was Piaggi. Kelly brought the gun up, leveling the sights with his chest and firing twice, changing aim then and hitting the man under the chin.

Shift targets.

Kelly rolled again, trained to do so by some NVA he'd met. There he was. Time stopped in that moment. Henry had his own gun out and aimed, and their eyes met and for what seemed the longest time they simply looked, hunter and hunter, hunter and prey. Then Kelly remembered, first, what the sight picture was for. His finger depressed the trigger, delivering a finely aimed shot into Tucker's chest. The Colt jumped in his hand, and his brain was running so fast now that he saw the slide dash backwards, ejecting the empty brass case, then dashing forward to feed another just as the tension in his wrist brought the gun back down, and that round, too, went into the man's chest. Tucker was off-balance from turning. Either he slipped on the floor or the impact of the two slugs destroyed his balance, dropping him to the floor.

Mission accomplished, Kelly told himself. At least he'd gotten one job done after all the failures of this bleak summer. He got to his feet and walked to Henry Tucker, kicking the gun from his hand. He wanted to say something to the face that was still alive, but Kelly was out of words. Maybe Pam would rest easier now, but probably not. It didn't work that way, did it? The dead were gone and didn't know or care what they'd left behind. Probably. Kelly didn't know how that worked, though he'd wondered about it often enough. If the dead still lived on the surface of this earth, then it was in the minds of those who remembered them, and for that memory he'd killed Henry Tucker and all the others. Perhaps Pam would not rest any more easily. But he would. Kelly saw that Tucker had departed this life while he'd been thinking, examining his thoughts and his conscience. No, there was no remorse for this man, none for the others. Kelly safed his pistol and looked around the room. Three dead men, and the best thing that could be said was that he wasn't one of them. He walked to the door, and out of it. His car was a block away, and he still had an appointment to keep, and one more life to end.

Mission accomplished.

The boat was where he'd left it. Kelly parked his car, an hour later, taking out the suitcase. He locked the car with the keys inside, for that too was something he'd never need again. The drive through town and into the marina had been blissfully empty of thought, mechanical action only, maneuvering the car, stopping for some lights, proceeding through others, heading for the sea, or the Bay, one of the few places where he felt he belonged. He hefted the suitcase, walked out the dock to *Springer,* and hopped aboard. Everything looked okay, and in ten minutes he'd be away from everything he'd come to associate with the city. Kelly slid open the door to the main salon and stopped dead when he first smelled smoke, then heard a voice.

"John Kelly, right?"

"Who might you be?"

"Emmet Ryan? You've met my partner, Tom Douglas."

"What can I do for you?" Kelly set his suitcase down on the deck, remembering the Colt automatic at the small of his back, inside the unbuttoned bush jacket.

"You can tell me why you've killed so many people," Ryan suggested.

"If you think I've done it, then you know why."

"True. I'm looking for Henry Tucker at the moment."

"He's not here, is he?"

"Maybe you could help me, then?"

"Corner of O'Donnell and Mermen might be a good place to look. He's not going anywhere," Kelly told the detective.

"What am I supposed to do about you?"

"The three girls this morning, are they—"

"They're safe. We'll look after them. You and your friends did nicely with Pam Madden and Doris Brown. Not your fault it didn't work out. Well, maybe a little." The officer paused. "I have to take you in, you know."

"What for?"

"For murder, Mr. Kelly."

"No." Kelly shook his head. "It's only murder when innocent people die."

Ryan's eyes narrowed. He saw only the outline of the man, really, with the yellowing sky behind him. But he'd heard what he said, and part of him wanted to agree with it.

"The law doesn't say that."

"I'm not asking you to forgive me. I won't be any more trouble to you, and I'm not going to any jail."

"I can't let you go." But his weapon wasn't out, Kelly saw. What did that mean?

"I gave you that Officer Monroe back."

"Thank you for that," Ryan acknowledged.

"I don't just kill people. I've been trained to do it, but there has to be a reason somewhere. I had a good enough reason."

"Maybe. Just what do you think you accomplished?" Ryan asked. "This drug problem isn't going away."

"Henry Tucker won't kill any more girls. I accomplished that. I never expected to do any more, but I took that drug operation down." Kelly paused. There was something else this man needed to know. "There's a cop at that building. I think he was dirty. Tucker and Piaggi shot him. Maybe he can come out of this a hero. There's a load of stuff there. It won't look too bad for your department that way." *And thank God I didn't have to kill a cop—even a bad one.* "I'll give you one more. I know how Tucker was getting his stuff in." Kelly elaborated briefly.

"I can't just let you go," the detective said again, though part of him wished it were otherwise. But that couldn't be, and he would not have made it so, for his life had rules, too.

"Can you give me an hour? I know you'll keep looking. One hour. It'll make things better for everybody."

The request caught Ryan by surprise. It was against everything he stood for—but then, so were the monsters the man had killed. *We owe him something . . . would I have cleared those cases without him? Who would have spoken for the dead . . . and besides, what could the guy do—where could he go? . . . Ryan, have you gone nuts?* Yes, maybe he had . . .

"You've got your hour. After that I can recommend you to a good lawyer. Who knows, a good one might just get you off."

Ryan rose and headed for the side door without looking back. He stopped at the door just for a second.

"You spared when you could have killed, Mr. Kelly. That's why. Your hour starts now."

Kelly didn't watch him leave. He hit his engine controls, warming up the diesels. One hour should just about do it. He scrambled out on the deck, slipping his lines, leaving them attached to the dock piles, and by the time he got back inside the salon, the diesels were ready for turning. They caught at once, and he pivoted the boat, heading out into the harbor. As soon as he was out of the yacht basin he firewalled both throttles, bringing *Springer* to her top speed of twenty-two knots. With the channel empty, Kelly set his autopilot and rushed to make the necessary preparations. He cut the corner at Bodkin Point. He had to. He knew who they'd send after him.

"Coast Guard, Thomas Point."

"This is the Baltimore City Police."

Ensign Tomlinson took the call. A new graduate of the Coast Guard Academy at New London, he was here for seasoning, and though he ranked the Chief Warrant Officer who ran the station, both the boy and the man understood what this was all about. Only twenty-two, young enough that his gold officer's bars still had the original shine, it was time to turn him loose on a mission, Paul English thought, but only because Portagee would really be running things. Forty-One-Bravo, the second of the station's big patrol craft, was warmed up and ready. The young ensign sprinted out, as though they might leave without him, much to the amusement of CWO English. Five seconds after the lad had snapped on his life vest, Forty-One-Bravo rumbled away from the dock, turning north short of the Thomas Point Light.

The man sure didn't give me any slack, Kelly thought, seeing the cutter closing from starboard. Well, he'd asked for an hour, and an hour he'd received. Kelly almost flipped on his radio for a parting salute, but that wouldn't have been right, and more was the pity. One of his diesels was running hot, and that was also a pity, though it wouldn't be running hot much longer.

It was a kind of race now, and there was a complication, a large French freighter standing out to sea, right where Kelly needed to be, and he would soon be caught between her and the Coast Guard.

"Well, here we are," Ritter said, dismissing the security guard who'd followed them like a shadow all afternoon. He pulled a ticket from his pocket. "First class. The booze is free, Colonel." They'd been able to skip passport control on the strength of an earlier phone call.

"Thank you for your hospitality."

Ritter chuckled. "Yeah, the U.S. government's flown you three quarters of the way around the world. I guess Aeroflot can handle the rest." Ritter paused and went on formally. "Your behavior to our prisoners was as correct as circumstances allowed. Thank you for that."

"It is my wish that they get home safely. They are not bad men."

"Neither are you." Ritter led him to the gate, where a large transfer vehicle waited to take him out to a brand-new Boeing 747. "Come back sometime. I'll show you more of Washington." Ritter watched him board and turned to Voloshin.

"A good man, Sergey. Will this injure his career?"

"With what he has in his head? I think not."

"Fine with me," Ritter said, walking away.

• • •

They were too closely matched. The other boat had a slight advantage, since it was in the lead, and able to choose, while the cutter needed her half-knot speed advantage to draw closer so painfully slowly. It was a question of skill, really, and that, too, was down to whiskers of difference from one to the other. Oreza watched the other man slide his boat across the wake of the freighter, surfing it, really, sliding her onto the front of the ship-generated wave and riding it to port, gaining perhaps half a knot's momentary advantage. Oreza had to admire it. He couldn't do anything else. The man really was sailing his boat downhill as though in a joke against the laws of wind and wave. But there was nothing funny about this, was there? Not with his men standing around the wheelhouse carrying loaded guns. Not with what he had to do to a friend.

"For Christ's sake," Oreza snarled, easing the wheel to starboard a little. "Be careful with those goddamned guns!" The other crewmen in the wheelhouse snapped the covers down on their holsters and ceased fingering their weapons.

"He's a dangerous man," the man behind Oreza said.

"No, he isn't, not to us!"

"What about all the people he—"

"Maybe the bastards had it comin'!" A little more throttle and Oreza slid back to port. He was at the point of scanning the waves for smooth spots, moving the forty-one-foot patrol boat a few feet left and right to make use of the surface chop and so gain a few precious yards in his pursuit, just as the other was doing. No America's Cup race off of Newport had ever been as exciting as this, and inwardly Oreza raged at the other man that the purpose of the race should be so perverse.

"Maybe you should let—"

Oreza didn't turn his head. "Mr. Tomlinson, you think anybody else can conn the boat better'n me?"

"No, Petty Officer Oreza," the Ensign said formally. Oreza snorted at the windowglass. "Maybe call a helicopter from the Navy?" Tomlinson asked lamely.

"What for, sir? Where you think he's goin', Cuba, maybe? I have double his bunkerage and half a knot more speed, and he's only three hundred yards ahead. Do the math, sir. We're alongside in twenty minutes any way you cut it, no matter how good he is." *Treat the man with respect,* Oreza didn't say.

"But he's dangerous," Ensign Tomlinson repeated.

"I'll take my chances. There . . . " Oreza started his slide to port now, riding through the freighter's wake, using the energy generated by the ship to gain speed. *Interesting, this is how a dolphin does it . . . that got me a whole knot's worth and my hull's better at this than his is . . .* Contrary to everything he should have felt, Manuel Oreza smiled. He'd just learned something new about boat-handling, courtesy of a friend he was trying to arrest for murder. For murdering people who needed killing, he reminded himself, wondering what the lawyers would do about that.

No, he had to treat him with respect, let him run his race as best he could, take his shot at freedom, doomed though he might be. To do less would demean the man, and, Oreza admitted, demean himself. When all else failed there was still honor. It was perhaps the last law of the sea, and Oreza, like his quarry, was a man of the sea.

It was devilishly close. Portagee was just too damned good at driving his boat, and for that reason all the harder to risk what he'd planned. Kelly did everything he knew how. Planing *Springer* diagonally across the ship's wake was the cleverest thing he'd ever done afloat, but that damned Coastie matched it, deep hull and all. Both his engines were redlined now, and both were running hot, and this damned freighter was going just a little too fast for things. *Why couldn't Ryan have waited another ten friggin' minutes?* Kelly wondered. The control for the pyro charge was next to him. Five seconds after he hit that, the fuel tanks would blow, but that wasn't worth a damn with a Coast Guard cutter two hundred goddamned yards back.

Now what?

• • •

"We just gained twenty yards," Oreza noted with both satisfaction and sorrow.

He wasn't even looking back, the petty officer saw. He knew. He had to know. *God, you're good,* the Quartermaster First Class tried to say with his mind, regretting all the needling he'd inflicted upon the man, but he had to know that it had only been banter, one seaman to another. And in running the race this way he, too, was doing honor to Oreza. He'd have weapons there, and he could have turned and fired to distract and annoy his pursuers. But he didn't, and Portagee Oreza knew why. It would have violated the rules of a race such as this. He'd run the race as best he could, and when the time came he'd accept defeat, and there would be both pride and sadness for both men to share, but each would still have the respect of the other.

"Going to be dark soon," Tomlinson said, ruining the petty officer's reverie. The boy just didn't understand, but he was only a brand-new ensign. Perhaps he'd learn someday. They mostly did, and Oreza hoped that Tomlinson would learn from today's lesson.

"Not soon enough, sir."

Oreza scanned the rest of the horizon briefly. The French-flagged freighter occupied perhaps a third of what he could see of the water's surface. It was a towering hull, riding high on the surface and gleaming from a recent painting. Her crew knew nothing of what was going on. A new ship, the petty officer's brain noted, and her bulbous bow made for a nice set of bow waves that the other boat was using to surf along.

The quickest and simplest solution was to pull the cutter up behind him on the starboard side of the freighter, then duck across the bow, and *then* blow the boat up . . . but . . . there was another way, a better way . . .

"Now!" Oreza turned the wheel perhaps ten degrees, sliding to port and gaining fully fifty yards seemingly in an instant. Then he reversed his rudder, leaped over another five-foot roller, and prepared to repeat the maneuver. One of the younger seamen hooted in sudden exhilaration.

"You see, Mr. Tomlinson? We have a better hull form for this sort of thing than he does. He can beat us by a whisker in flat seas, but not in chop. This is what we're made for." Two minutes had halved the distance between the boats.

"You sure you want this race to end, Oreza?" Ensign Tomlinson asked.

Not so dumb after all, is he? Well, he was an officer, and they were supposed to be smart once in a while.

"All races end, sir. There's always a winner and always a loser," Oreza pointed out, hoping that his friend would understand that, too. Portagee reached in his shirt pocket for a cigarette and lit it with his left hand while his right—just the fingertips, really—worked the wheel, making tiny adjustments as demanded by the part of his brain that read and reacted to every ripple on the surface. He'd told Tomlinson twenty minutes. He'd been pessimistic. Sooner than that, he was sure.

Oreza scanned the surface again. A lot of boats out, mostly heading in, not one of them recognizing the race for what it was. The cutter didn't have her police lights blinking. Oreza didn't like the things: they were an insult to his profession. When a cutter of the United States Coast Guard pulled alongside, you shouldn't need police lights, he thought. Besides, this race was a private thing, seen and understood only by professionals, the way things ought to be, because spectators always degraded things, distracted the players from the game.

He was amidships on the freighter now, and Portagee had swallowed the bait . . . as he had to, Kelly thought. Damn but that guy was good. Another mile and he'd be alongside, reducing Kelly's options to precisely zero, but he did have his plan now, seeing the ship's bulbous bow, partly exposed. A crewman was looking down from the bridge, as on that first day with Pam, and his stomach became hollow for a moment, remembering. So long ago, so many things in between. Had he done right or wrong?

Who would judge? Kelly shook his head. He'd let God do that. Kelly looked back for the first time in this race, measuring distance, and it was damnably close.

The forty-one boat was squatting back on her stern, pitched up perhaps fifteen degrees, her deep-displacement hull cutting through the choppy wake. She rocked left and right through a twenty-degree arc, her big down-rated marine diesels roaring in their special feline way. And it was all in Oreza's hands, throttles and wheels at his skilled fingertips while his eyes scanned and measured. His prey was doing exactly the same, milking every single turn from his own engines, using his skill and experience. But his assets added up short of Portagee's, and while that was too bad, that's how things were.

Just then Oreza saw the man's face, looking back for the first time.

It's time, my friend. Come on, now, let's end this honorably. Maybe you'll get lucky and you'll get out after a while and we can be friends again.

"Come on, cut power and turn to starboard," Oreza said, hardly knowing he spoke, and each man of his crew was thinking exactly the same thing, glad to know that they and their skipper were reading things the same way. It had been only a half-hour race, but it was the sort of sea story they would remember for their whole careers.

The man's head turned again. Oreza was barely half a ship-length back now. He could easily read the name on the transom, and there was no sense stringing it out to the last foot. That would spoil the race. It would show a meanness of spirit that didn't belong on the sea. That was something done by yachtsmen, not professionals.

Then Kelly did something unexpected. Oreza saw it first, and his eyes measured the distance once, then twice, and a third time, and in every case the answer came up wrong, and he reached for his radio quickly.

"Don't try it!" the petty officer shouted onto the "guard" frequency.

"What?" Tomlinson asked quickly.

Don't do it! Oreza's mind shouted, suddenly alone in a tiny world, reading the other's mind and revolting at the thought it held. This was no way for things to end. There was no honor in this.

Kelly eased his rudder right to catch the bow wave, his eyes watching the foaming forefoot of the freighter. When the moment was right, he put the rudder over. The radio squawked. It was Portagee's voice, and Kelly smiled hearing it. What a good guy he was. Life would be so lonely without men such as he.

Springer lurched to starboard from the force of the radical turn, then even more from the small hill of water raised by the freighter's bow. Kelly held on to the wheel with his left hand and reached with his right for the air tank around which he'd strung six weight belts. *Jesus,* he thought instantly as *Springer* went over ninety degrees, *I didn't check the depth. What if the water's not deep enough—oh, God . . . oh, Pam. . . .*

The boat turned sharply to port. Oreza watched from only a hundred yards away, but the distance might as well have been a thousand miles for all the good it did, and his mind saw it before reality caught up: already heeling hard to the right from the turn, the cruiser rode up high on the curling bow-wave of the freighter and, crosswise to it, rolled completely over, her white hull instantly disappearing in the foaming forefoot of the cargo ship . . .

It was no way for a seaman to die.

Forty-One-Bravo backed down hard, rocking violently with the passage of the ship's wake as she came to a stop. The freighter stopped at once, too, but it took fully two miles, and by that time Oreza and his cutter were poking through the wreckage. Searchlights came on in the gathering darkness, and the eyes of the coastguardsmen were grim.

"Coast Guard Forty-One, Coast Guard Forty-One, this is U.S. Navy sailboat on your port beam, can we render assistance, over?"

"We could use some extra eyes, Navy. Who's aboard?"

"Couple of admirals, the one talking's an aviator, if that helps."

"Join in, sir."

He was still alive. It was as much a surprise to Kelly as it would have been to Oreza. The water here was deep enough that he and the air tank had plummeted seventy feet to the bottom. He fought to strap the tank to his chest in the violent turbulence of the passing ship overhead. Then he fought to swim clear of the descending engines and heavy gear from what had seconds earlier been an expensive cruiser. Only after two or three minutes did he accept the fact that he'd survived this trial by ordeal. Looking back, he wondered just how crazy he'd been to risk this, but for once he'd felt the need to entrust his life to judgment superior to his own, prepared to take the consequences either way. And the judgment had spared him. Kelly could see the Coast Guard hull over to the east . . . and to the west the deeper shape of a sailboat, pray God the right one. Kelly disengaged four of the weight belts from the tank and swam towards it, awkwardly because he had it on backwards.

His head broke the surface behind the sailboat as it lay to, close enough to read the name. He went down again. It took another minute to come up on the west side of the twenty-six-footer.

"Hello?"

"Jesus—is that you?" Maxwell called.

"I think so." *Well, not exactly.* His hand reached up.

The doyen of naval aviation reached over the side, hauled the bruised and sore body aboard, and directed him below.

"Forty-One, this is Navy to your west now . . . this doesn't look real good, fella."

"I'm afraid you're right, Navy. You can break off if you want. I think we'll stay a while," Oreza said. It had been good of them to quarter the surface for three hours, a good assist from a couple of flag officers. They even handled their sailboat halfway decent. At another time he'd have taken the thought further and made a joke about Navy seamanship.

But not now. Oreza and Forty-One-Bravo would continue their search all night, finding only wreckage.

It made the papers in a big way, but not in any way that made sense. Detective Lieutenant Mark Charon, following up a lead on his own time—on administrative leave following a shooting, no less—had stumbled into a drug lab and in the ensuing gun battle had lost his life in the line of duty while ending those of two major traffickers. The coincidental escape of three young women resulted in the identification of one of the deceased traffickers as a particularly brutal murderer, which perhaps explained Charon's heroic zeal, and closed a number of cases in a fashion that the police reporters found overly convenient. On page six was a squib story about a boating accident.

Three days later, a file clerk from St. Louis called Lieutenant Ryan to say that the Kelly file was back but she couldn't say from where. Ryan thanked her for her effort. He'd closed that case along with the rest, and didn't even try the FBI records center for Kelly's card, and thus made unnecessary Bob Ritter's substitution of the prints of someone unlikely ever to visit America again.

The only loose end, which troubled Ritter greatly, was a single telephone call. But even criminals got one phone call, and Ritter didn't want to cross Clark on something like that. Five months later, Sandra O'Toole resigned her position at Johns Hopkins and moved to the Virginia tidewater, where she took over a whole floor of the area's teaching hospital on the strength of a glowing recommendation from Professor Samuel Rosen.

February 12,1973

"We are honored to have the opportunity to serve our country under difficult circumstances," Captain Jeremiah Denton said, ending a thirty-four-word statement that rang across the ramp at Clark Air Base with "God bless America."

"How about that," the commentator said, sharing the experience as he was paid to do. "Right there behind Captain Denton is Colonel Robin Zacharias, of the Air Force. He's one of the fifty-three prisoners about whom we had no information until very recently, along with . . . "

John Clark didn't listen to the rest. He looked at the TV that sat on his wife's dresser in the bedroom, at the face of a man half a world away, to whom he'd been much closer in body, closer still in spirit not so long before. He saw the man embrace his wife after what had to be five years of separation. He saw a woman who'd grown old with worry, but now was young with love for the husband she'd thought dead. Kelly wept with them, seeing the man's face for the first time as a thing of animation, seeing the joy that really could replace pain, no matter how vast. He squeezed Sandy's hand so hard that he almost hurt it until she rested his on her belly to feel the movement of their soon-to-be firstborn. The phone rang then, and Kelly was angry for the invasion of the moment until he heard the voice.

"I hope you're proud of yourself, John," Dutch Maxwell said. "We're getting all twenty back. I wanted to make sure you knew that. It wouldn't have happened without you."

"Thank you, sir." Clark hung up. There was nothing else to be said.

"Who was that?" Sandy asked, holding his hand in place.

"A friend," Clark said, wiping his eyes as he turned to kiss his wife. "From another life."

HE'S BACK!

Tom Clancy Debt of Honor

On the Pacific island of Saipan, a wealthy Japanese businessman regards his new-bought land with satisfaction. In the back streets of Tokyo, a young American woman is found murdered. Two seemingly unrelated incidents—but both are just the first links in a chain of events that will stun the world.

Called out of retirement to serve as the new president's National Security Advisor, Jack Ryan is faced with the complex problems of war and peace. Together with CIA officers John Clark and Domingo Chavez, Ryan plunges into nonstop high adventure when new enemies plot to strike at American territory and undermine the economy. Here is a riveting story that may become all too true.

Coming soon in hardcover to bookstores everywhere.

G. P. PUTNAM'S SONS
A member of
The Putnam Berkley Group, Inc.

From the **New York Times**
bestselling author of <u>Submarine</u>

Tom Clancy

ARMORED CAV

**A penetrating, in-depth look at the
technology, strategies, and people that
make up an armored cavalry regiment**

- *EXCLUSIVE PHOTOGRAPHS, ILLUSTRATIONS,
  AND DIAGRAMS* of the M1A2 Main Battle
  Tank, the AH-64A Apache Helicopter, and more

- An interview with General Frederick Franks,
  commanding officer of the U.S. Army's
  Training and Doctrine Command (TRADOC)

- A guided tour of the 3rd Armored Cavalry
  Regiment: the history, organization, and
  contributions of America's last heavily armored
  regiment

- From West Point cadet to Desert Storm
  commander–an interview with Captain H.R.
  McMaster, Jr., a combat cavalry officer

- *PLUS: THREE POSSIBLE FUTURE
  OPERATIONS AND THE ROLE THE
  ARMORED CAVALRY WOULD PLAY*

*A New Berkley Nonfiction Trade Paperback
Available November 1994*

#1 NEW YORK TIMES *BESTSELLING AUTHOR*

"Takes readers deeper than they've ever gone inside a nuclear submarine...a fast-paced silent running that will please the author's fans."
            –The Kirkus Reviews

Tom Clancy
SUBMARINE

"A masterful job... It's clear Clancy did his homework."–The Houston Post

The author of <u>The Hunt for Red October</u> takes you on a guided tour through a Los Angeles Class (SSN-688) Nuclear Submarine. Enter this top secret world and experience the drama and excitement of this stunning technological achievement...the weapons, the procedures, the startling facts behind the techno-fiction that made Tom Clancy a #1 bestseller.

* Exclusive photographs, illustrations, and diagrams
* Mock war scenarios and weapons' launch procedures
* An inside look at life on board, from captain to crew, from training exercises to operations
* The fascinating history and evaluation of submarines

__ 0-425-13873-9/$14.95

Payable in U.S. funds. No cash orders accepted. Postage & handling: $1.75 for one book, 75¢ for each additional. Maximum postage $5.50. Prices, postage and handling charges may change without notice. Visa, Amex, MasterCard call 1-800-788-6262, ext. 1, refer to ad # 477

Or, check above books and send this order form to: The Berkley Publishing Group 390 Murray Hill Pkwy., Dept. B East Rutherford, NJ 07073 Please allow 6 weeks for delivery.	Bill my: ☐ Visa ☐ MasterCard ☐ Amex _____ (expires) Card#_____ ($15 minimum) Signature_____ Or enclosed is my: ☐ check ☐ money order
Name_____	Book Total $____
Address_____	Postage & Handling $____
City_____	Applicable Sales Tax $____ (NY, NJ, PA, CA, GST Can.)
State/ZIP_____	Total Amount Due $____

#1 *NEW YORK TIMES* BESTSELLING AUTHOR

Tom Clancy

__WITHOUT REMORSE__   0-425-14332-5/$6.99

"A confident stride through corridors of power, an honest-to-God global war game, and...a pyrotechnic finish."
    –The Washington Post

__THE SUM OF ALL FEARS__   0-425-13354-0/$6.99

"Vivid...engrossing...a whiz-bang page-turner!"
    –The New York Times Book Review

__CLEAR AND PRESENT DANGER__   0-425-12212-3/$6.99

"The reader can't turn the pages fast enough to keep up with the action."*–Publishers Weekly*

__PATRIOT GAMES__   0-425-13435-0/$5.99

"Marvelously tense... He is a master of the genre he seems to have created."*–Publishers Weekly*

__THE HUNT FOR RED OCTOBER__   0-425-13351-6/$6.99

"Flawless authenticity, frighteningly genuine."
    –The Wall Street Journal

__THE CARDINAL OF THE KREMLIN__   0-425-11684-0/$6.99

"Fast paced and fascinating."*–The Chicago Tribune*

__RED STORM RISING__   0-425-10107-X/$6.99

"Brilliant... Staccato suspense."*–Newsweek*

Payable in U.S. funds. No cash orders accepted. Postage & handling: $1.75 for one book, 75¢ for each additional. Maximum postage $5.50. Prices, postage and handling charges may change without notice. Visa, Amex, MasterCard call 1-800-788-6262, ext. 1, refer to ad # 190a

Or, check above books **Bill my:** ☐ Visa ☐ MasterCard ☐ Amex		_____
and send this order form to:		(expires)
The Berkley Publishing Group	Card#_____	
390 Murray Hill Pkwy., Dept. B		($15 minimum)
East Rutherford, NJ 07073	Signature_____	
Please allow 6 weeks for delivery.	**Or enclosed is my:** ☐ check ☐ money order	
Name_____	Book Total	$_____
Address_____	Postage & Handling	$_____
City_____	Applicable Sales Tax	$_____
	(NY, NJ, PA, CA, GST Can.)	
State/ZIP_____	Total Amount Due	$_____

P9-CSW-891

New York Times and *USA Today* **bestseller**
A *Publishers Weekly* **Best Book of the Year**

THE *Heir*

"Luminous and graceful…a refreshing and captivating love story."

—*Publishers Weekly*, Starred Review

"A witty, sensual Regency romance featuring complex characters who ring true to the time period, leaving readers saying huzzah!"

—*Booklist*, Starred Review

"The heroine of Grace Burrowes's erotically charged romance is a woman of such mystery that both the hero and the reader become obsessed with her."

—*USA Today*

"Tons of intrigue, searing seduction, and wonderful humor…a must-read for fans of Georgette Heyer and Regency romances."

—*Night Owl Reviews*, Top Pick

"An irresistible love story… Ms. Burrowes's writing engages all the senses [and] makes the love scenes spellbinding, the danger a heart-pounding experience, and the caring, protective love for loved ones awe-inspiring."

—*The Long and Short of It*

"A sweet, sexy, tender romance between two characters so vibrant they seem to leap off the page. Burrowes's fresh, gorgeous writing held me riveted from start to finish."

—Meredith Duran, *USA Today* bestselling author

"A scorching, romantic novel; it is both hot and sweet, and it is sure to touch readers' hearts."

—*Romance Reviews Today*

"Highly passionate and fiery, and utterly enthralling... Grace Burrowes is a writer to be reckoned with."

—Romance Fiction on Suite101

Also by Grace Burrowes

The Duke's Disaster

The Windhams
The Heir
The Soldier
The Virtuoso
Lady Sophie's Christmas
Wish
Lady Maggie's Secret
Scandal
Lady Louisa's Christmas
Knight
Lady Eve's Indiscretion
Lady Jenny's Christmas
Portrait
The Courtship (novella)
The Duke and His Duchess
(novella)
Morgan and Archer
(novella)
Jonathan and Amy
(novella)

The MacGregors
The Bridegroom Wore Plaid
Once Upon a Tartan
The MacGregor's Lady
What a Lady Needs
for Christmas
Mary Fran and Matthew
(novella)

The Lonely Lords
Darius
Nicholas
Ethan
Beckman
Gabriel
Gareth
Andrew
Douglas
David

Captive Hearts
The Captive
The Traitor
The Laird

Sweetest Kisses
A Kiss for Luck (novella)
A Single Kiss
The First Kiss
Kiss Me Hello

True Gentlemen
Tremaine's True Love
Daniel's True Desire
Will's True Wish

THE Heir

GRACE BURROWES

sourcebooks
casablanca

Copyright © 2010, 2019 by Grace Burrowes
Cover and internal design © 2019 by Sourcebooks, Inc.
Cover design by Ann Cain
Cover images © Alenkasm/Dreamstime.com; Avava/Dreamstime.com

Sourcebooks and the colophon are registered trademarks of
Sourcebooks, Inc.

All rights reserved. No part of this book may be reproduced in
any form or by any electronic or mechanical means including
information storage and retrieval systems—except in the case of
brief quotations embodied in critical articles or reviews—without
permission in writing from its publisher, Sourcebooks, Inc.

The characters and events portrayed in this book are fictitious or
are used fictitiously. Any similarity to real persons, living or dead,
is purely coincidental and not intended by the author.

Published by Sourcebooks Casablanca, an imprint of Sourcebooks,
Inc.

P.O. Box 4410, Naperville, Illinois 60567–4410
(630) 961–3900
Fax: (630) 961–2168
sourcebooks.com

Printed and bound in Canada.
MBP 10 9 8 7 6 5 4 3 2 1

Dedicated to
The late Norman H. Lampman, the first person
Who honestly helped me with my writing,
And to loving families everywhere, of any description,
Most especially to the family who loves me.

One

GAYLE WINDHAM, EARL OF WESTHAVEN, WAS ENJOY-
ing a leisurely measure of those things that pleased him
most: solitude, peace, and quiet.

The best plans were the simplest, he reflected as
he poured himself a single finger of brandy, and his
brother's suggestion that Westhaven hide in plain
sight had proven brilliant. The unmarried heir to a
dukedom had a nigh impossible task if he wanted to
elude the predatory mamas and determined debutantes
of polite society. He was in demand everywhere, and
for form's sake, he had to be seen everywhere.

But not this summer. He smiled with relish. This
summer, this stinking, infernally hot summer, he was
going to remain right where he was, in the blessedly
empty confines of London itself. Not for him the
endless round of house parties and boating parties and
social gatherings in the country.

His father had too free a hand in those environs,
and Westhaven knew better than to give the duke any
unnecessary advantage.

The Duke of Moreland was a devious, determined,

unscrupulous old rogue. His goal in life was to see to it his heir married and produced sons, and Westhaven had made it a matter of pride to outwit the old man. There had already been one forced engagement, which the lady's family had thwarted at the last minute. One was more than enough. Westhaven was a dutiful son, conscientious in his responsibilities, a brother who could be relied upon, an heir more than willing to tend to the properties and investments as his father's power of attorney. He would not, however, be forced to marry some simpering little puppet to breed sons on her like a rutting hound.

And already, the pleasure of days and nights uncluttered by meaningless entertainments was bringing a certain cheer to Westhaven's normally reserved demeanor. He found himself noticing things, like the way his townhouse bore the fragrance of roses and honeysuckle, or how an empty grate was graced with a bouquet of flowers just for the pleasure of his eye. His solitary meals tasted more appealing; he slept better on his lavender-scented sheets. He heard his neighbor playing the piano late at night, and he caught the sound of laughter drifting up from his kitchen early in the morning.

I would have made an exemplary monk, he thought as he regarded the bowl of roses on the cold andirons. But then, monks had little solitude, and no recreational access to the fairer sex.

A modest exponent thereof silently entered the library, bobbed her little curtsy, and went about refilling the water in the several vases of flowers gracing the room. He watched her as she moved around without a sound, and wondered when she'd joined his household. She was a pretty little thing, with graceful ways and a sense of competence about her.

The chambermaid paused to water the flowers in the hearth, reaching over the fireplace screen to carefully top up the wide bowl of roses sitting on the empty grate. *Who would think to put flowers in a cold fireplace?* Westhaven wondered idly, but then he realized the chambermaid was taking rather too long to complete her task.

"Is something amiss?" he asked, not meaning to sound irritated but concluding he must have, for the girl flinched and cowered. She didn't, however, straighten up, make another curtsy, and leave him to his brandy.

"Is something amiss?" He spoke more slowly, knowing menials were not always of great understanding. The girl whimpered, an odd sound, not speech but an indication of distress. And she remained right where she was, bent over the hearth screen, her pitcher of water in her hand.

Westhaven set down his brandy and rose from his wing chair, the better to investigate the problem. The girl was making that odd sound continuously, which pleased him not at all. It wasn't as if he'd *ever* trifled with the help, for God's sake.

When he came near the hearth, the chambermaid positively cringed away from him, another irritant, but her movement allowed Westhaven to see the difficulty: The buttons on the front of her bodice were caught in the mesh of the hearth screen. She wasn't tall enough to set down her pitcher, leaving her only one hand with which to free herself. That hand, however, she needed for balance.

"Hush," Westhaven said more gently. He did have five sisters, after all, and a mother; he understood females were prone to dramatics. "I'll have you free in no time, if you'll just hold still and turn loose of this pitcher."

He had to pry the girl's fingers from the handle of the pitcher, so overset was she, but still she said nothing, just warbled her distress like a trapped animal.

"No need to take on so," he soothed as he reached around her so he could slide his fingers along the screen. "We'll have you free in a moment, and next time you'll know to move the screen before you try to water the flowers." It took an infernally long time, but he had one button forced back through the screen and was working on the other when the girl's whimpering escalated to a moan.

"Hush," he murmured again. "I won't hurt you, and I almost have your buttons free. Just hold still—"

The first blow landed across his shoulders, a searing flash of pain that left his fine linen shirt and his skin torn. The second followed rapidly, as he tightened his arms protectively around the maid, and at the third, which landed smartly on the back of his head, everything went black.

❦

Westhaven moaned, causing both women to startle then stare at him.

"St. Peter in a whorehouse," Westhaven muttered, bracing himself on his forearms and shaking his head.

Slowly, he levered up to all fours then sat back on his heels, giving his head another shake.

He raised a ferocious scowl to survey the room, caught sight of the chambermaid, and then the other woman. His mind stumbled around for the proper associations. She worked for him but was entirely too young for her post. Mrs.… Every housekeeper was a Mrs.…

Sidwell? He glared at her in concentration. Sommers…no. Seaton.

"Come here," he rasped at her. She was a sturdy thing, on the tall side, and always moving through the house at forced march. Cautiously, she approached him.

"Mrs. Seaton." He scowled at her thunderously. "I require your assistance."

She nodded, for once not looking quite so much like a general on campaign, and knelt beside him. He slid an arm around her shoulders, paused to let the pain of that simple movement ricochet around in his body, and slowly rose.

"My chambers," he growled, leaning on her heavily while his head cleared. She made no attempts at conversation, thank the gods, but paused to open the door to his room, and then again to carefully lower him to the settee flanking the hearth in his sitting room.

She turned to the chambermaid, who had followed them up the stairs. "Morgan, fetch the medical supplies, some hot water, and clean linens, and hurry."

Morgan nodded and disappeared, leaving the door slightly ajar.

"Silly twit," the earl muttered. "Does she think I'm in any condition to cause you mischief?"

"She does not, but there is no need to forego the proprieties."

"My privacy necessitates it," the earl bit out. "Moreover..." He paused, closed his eyes, and let out a slow breath. "As you tried to kill me, I don't think you're in a position to make demands, madam."

"I did not try to kill you," his housekeeper corrected him. "I attempted to protect your employee from what I thought were improper advances on the part of a guest."

He shot her a sardonic, incredulous look, but she was standing firm, arms crossed over her chest, eyes flashing with conviction.

"I sent word I would be returning from Morelands today," he said. "And the knocker isn't up. You misjudged."

"The post has not arrived for the past two days, your lordship. The heat seems to have disrupted a number of normal functions, and as to that, your brother does not observe the niceties when he is of a mind to see you."

"You thought *my brother* would bother a chambermaid?"

"He is friendly, my lord." Mrs. Seaton's bosom heaved with her point. "And Morgan is easily taken advantage of." Morgan reappeared, bobbing another curtsy at the earl then depositing the requested medical supplies on the low table before the settee.

"Thank you, Morgan." Mrs. Seaton looked right at the maid when she spoke, and her words were formed deliberately. "A tea tray, now, and maybe a muffin or some cookies to go with it."

A *muffin*? Westhaven felt his lips wanting to quirk. She was going to treat a bashed skull with tea and crumpets?

"If you would sit on the table, my lord?" Mrs. Seaton wasn't facing *him* as she spoke. "I can tend to your back and your…scalp."

Damn it all to hell, he needed her help just to rise, shift his weight, and sit on the coffee table. Each movement sent white-hot pain lancing through his skull and across his shoulders. For all that, he barely felt it as Mrs. Seaton deftly unbuttoned his shirt, tugged it free of his waistband, and eased it away.

"This is ruined, I'm afraid."

"Shirts can be replaced," the earl said. "My father rather has plans for me, however, so let's get me patched up."

"You were coshed with a fireplace poker," Mrs. Seaton said, bending over him to sift through the hair above his nape. "These wounds will require careful cleaning."

She wadded up his shirt and folded it to hold against the scalp wound.

"Passive voice," the earl said through clenched teeth, "will not protect you, Mrs. Seaton, since you did the coshing. Jesus and the apostles, that hurts." Her hand came up to hold his forehead even as she continued to press the linen of his ruined shirt against the bleeding wound.

"The bleeding is slowing down," she said, "and the wounds on your back are not as messy."

"Happily for me," her patient muttered. Her hand bracing his forehead had eased the pain considerably, and there was something else, too. A scent, flowery but also fresh, a hint of mint and rosemary that sent a cool remembrance of summer pleasures through his awareness.

A soft hand settled on his bare shoulder, but then she was tormenting him again, this time with disinfectant that brought the fires of hell raging across his back.

"Almost done," she said quietly some moments later, but Westhaven barely heard her through the roaring in his ears. When his mind cleared, he realized he was leaning into her, his face pressed against the soft curve of her waist, his shoulders hunched against the length of her thigh.

"That's the worst of it," she said, her hand again resting on his shoulder. "I am sorry, you know." She sounded genuinely contrite now—now that he was suffering mortal agonies and the loss of his dignity, as well.

"I'll mend."

"Would you like some laudanum?" Mrs. Seaton lowered herself to kneel before him, her expression concerned. "It's not encouraged for head injuries."

"I have been uncomfortable before. I'll manage," the earl said. "But you will have to get me into a dressing gown and fetch my correspondence from the library."

"A dressing gown?" Her finely arched sable eyebrows flew up. "I'll fetch a footman, perhaps, or Mr. Stenson."

"Can't." Westhaven tried to maneuver himself back onto the settee. "Stenson stayed at Morelands, as His Grace's man had some time off, and no footmen or butler either, as it's the men's half-day." Faced with that logic, Mrs. Seaton wrapped her arm around the earl's waist and assisted him to change his seat.

"A dressing gown it is, then." She capitulated easily, leaving him staring at her retreating figure as she went to fetch his garment.

~

How hard could it be to drape a dressing gown over a set of bare, masculine shoulders? Except seeing the earl, Anna had to refine on her question: a set of unbelievably well-muscled, broad, bare shoulders, God help her.

Anna had, of course, noticed her employer on occasion in the weeks she'd been in his household. He was a handsome man, several inches over six feet, green-eyed, with dark chestnut hair and features that bore the patrician stamp of aristocratic breeding. She put his age at just past thirty but had formed no opinion of him as a person. He came and went at all hours, seldom invading the lowest floor, closeting himself for long periods in his library with his man of business or other gentlemen.

He liked order, privacy, and regular meals. He ate prodigious amounts of food but never drank to excess. He went to his club on Wednesdays and Fridays, his mistress on Tuesday and Thursday afternoons. He had volumes of Byron and Blake in his library, and read them late at night. He had a sweet tooth and a fondness for his horse. He was tired more often than not, as his father had put the ducal finances in severe disarray before tossing his heir the reins, and righting that situation took much of the earl's time.

Westhaven appeared to have an exasperated sort of affection for his lone surviving brother, Valentine, and grieved still for the two brothers who had died.

He had no friends but knew everybody.

And he was being pressured to take a wife, hence this stubborn unwillingness to leave Town in the worst heat wave in memory.

These thoughts flitted through Anna's mind in the few moments it took her to rummage in the earl's wardrobe and find a silk dressing gown of dark blue. She'd bandaged his back, but if the scalp wound should reopen and start bleeding, the color of the fabric would hide any stain.

"Will this do, my lord?" She held up the dressing gown when she returned to his sitting room, and frowned at him. "You are pale, methinks. Can you stand?"

"Boots off first, *methinks*," he replied, hefting one large foot onto the coffee table. Anna's lips pressed together in displeasure, but she deposited the dressing gown on the settee and pushed the coffee table over at an angle. She tugged at his boots, surprised to find they weren't painted onto him, as most gentlemen's riding boots were.

"Better." He wiggled his bare toes when she'd peeled off his socks. "If you would assist me?" He held out an arm, indicating his desire to rise. Anna braced him and slowly levered him up. When he was on his feet, they stood linked like that for a long moment before Anna reached over and retrieved the dressing gown. She worked awkwardly, sliding it up one arm, then the other, before getting it draped across his shoulders.

"Can you stand unassisted?" she asked, still not liking his pallor.

"I can." But she saw him swallow against the pain. "My breeches, Mrs. Seaton."

She wasn't inclined to quibble when he looked ready to keel over at any minute, but as she deftly unfastened the fall of his trousers, she realized he intended for her to *undress* him. Did a man ask a woman he was going to charge with attempted murder to help him out of his clothes?

"Sometime before I reach my eternal reward, if it wouldn't be too great an imposition."

In his expression, Anna perceived he wasn't bothered by their enforced proximity anywhere near as much as she was, and so she unceremoniously shoved his waistband down over his hips.

Dear God, *the man wasn't wearing any smalls.* Blushing furiously, she wasn't prepared for him to thrust an arm across her shoulders and balance on her as he carefully lifted first one foot then the other free of his clothing. Again, he lost momentum as pain caught up with him, and for the space of two slow, deep breaths, he leaned on her heavily, his dressing gown gaping open over his nudity, his labored breathing soughing against her cheek.

"Steady," she murmured, reaching for the ends of the belt looping at his waist. She tucked his dressing gown closed and knotted it securely, but not before she'd seen...

She would never, *ever* stop blushing. Not ever, if she lived to be as old as Granny Fran, who sat in the kitchen telling stories that went back to old German George.

"To bed, I think," the earl said, his voice sounding strained.

She nodded, anchored her arm around his middle, and in small steps, walked him into the next room and up to the steps surrounding his great, canopied bed.

"Rest a minute," he bit out, leaning on her mightily. She left him propped against the foot of the bed and folded down his covers.

"On your stomach will likely be less uncomfortable, my lord." He nodded, his gaze fixed on the bed with grim determination. Anna took up her position at his side, and by careful steps, soon had him standing at the head of the bed. She turned so their backs were to the bed and sat with him on the mattress.

He paused again, his arm around her shoulders, catching his breath.

"My correspondence," he reminded her.

She gave him a dubious scowl but nodded. "Don't move, your lordship. You don't want to fall and hit your head again."

⁕

She took her leave at the stirring pace Westhaven associated with her, leaving him to admire the view again and consider her advice—were he to die, his brother Valentine would not forgive him. Carefully, he toed the chamber pot from under the bed, made use of it, replaced the lid as quietly as he could by hooking the handle with his toes, then pushed it back out of sight.

God, he thought as he gave his cock a little shake, his housekeeper had seen the ducal family jewels.

He should have been wroth with indignation, to be

subjected to her perusal, but all he felt was amusement and a vague gratitude she would provide him the care he needed. She could have sent for a physician, of course, but Westhaven hated doctors, and his housekeeper must have known it.

Reaching across the bed carefully, he rearranged pillows so he could rest on his side. That movement so pained his back, that when his housekeeper returned, he was still sitting on the bed.

He arched an eyebrow. "Tea?"

"It can't hurt," she replied, "and I brought iced lemonade, as well, as the warehouse just stocked your icehouse this morning."

"Lemonade, then."

His rooms were at the back of the house, heavily shaded and high-ceilinged. They remained particularly comfortable, probably because the clerestory windows had been left open, the better to draw the heat up and out.

Mrs. Seaton handed him a tall, sweating glass, which he sipped cautiously. She'd sugared it generously, so he took a larger sip.

"You aren't having any?" he asked, watching as she moved around the room.

"You are my employer." She went to the night table and retrieved a pitcher, giving the little bouquet in the window a drink. "Your roses are thirsty."

"So is it you who has turned my house into a flower shop?" Westhaven asked as he finished his drink.

"I have. You have a very pretty house, my lord. Flowers show it to advantage."

"You will waken me if I fall asleep for more than an

hour or so?" he asked, unable to reach the nightstand to place his glass on the tray. She took the glass from his hand and met his eyes.

"I will check on you each hour until daybreak, my lord, but as you had neither tea nor supper, I think you had best try a little food before you lie down."

He eyed the tray whereupon Mrs. Seaton had set a plate sporting a big, sugary muffin that looked to be full of berries.

"Half of that." He nodded warily. "And sit if you please." He thumped the mattress. "I cannot abide a fluttering female."

"You sound like your father sometimes, you know," she said as she sliced the muffin in half and took her place beside him. "Imperious."

"Ridiculous, you mean," he said as he glanced skeptically again at the muffin then tried a bite.

"He is not ridiculous, but some of his machinations are."

"My housekeeper is a diplomat"—the earl sent her a sardonic smile—"who makes passably edible muffins. Might as well eat the whole thing rather than waste half."

"Would you like some butter on this half?"

"A touch. How is it you know of my father's machinations?"

"There is always gossip belowstairs." She shrugged, but then must have realized she was perilously close to overstepping. She paused as she slathered butter on his muffin. "It is said he spies on you at your regular appointments."

"What is ridiculous," the earl retorted, "is to think

the old rascal is tricking the young ladies who waylay me at every social function, Mrs. Seaton. Those lambs go willingly to slaughter in hopes of becoming my duchess. I won't have it." And as for spies in his mistress's house, Westhaven thought darkly… Ye gods. "Despite my father's scheming, I will choose my own duchess, thank you very much. Did you bring up only one of these things?" He waved his last bite of muffin at her.

"On the off chance that they were passably edible, I brought up two. A touch more butter?" She withdrew the second muffin from the linen lining a little basket at the side of the tray.

He caught her eye, saw the humor in it, and found his own lips quirking.

"Just a touch. And perhaps a spot more lemonade."

"You aren't going to have me brought up on charges, are you?" She posed the question casually then frowned, as if it had come out of her mouth all unintended.

"Oh, that's a splendid notion," the earl said as he accepted the second muffin. "Tell the whole world the Moreland heir was subdued by his housekeeper who thought he was trying to molest a chambermaid in his own home."

"Well, you were. And it wasn't well done of you, my lord."

"Mrs. Seaton." He glared down his nose at her. "I do not accost women under my protection. Her buttons were caught in the mesh of the screen, and she could not free herself. Nothing more."

"Her buttons…?" Her hand went to her mouth,

and in her expression, Westhaven could see his explanation put a very different light on her conclusions. "My lord, I beg your pardon."

"I'll mend, Mrs. Seaton." He almost smiled at her distress. "Next time, a simple 'My lord, what are you about?' might spare us both a great lot of indignity." He handed her his glass. "I will have my revenge, though."

"You will?"

"I will. I make a terrible patient."

৵৽

Anna was dozing off after dark when she heard the earl call her from the other room.

"My lord?"

"In here, and I will not shout in my own home for the attention of my own staff."

Oh, he was going to make a perfectly insufferable duke, she fumed as she got to her feet and crossed to his bedroom. "What can I do for you?" she asked as pleasantly as she could.

"I am loathe to attempt the use of pen and ink while recumbent," he said, peering at her over wire-rimmed spectacles. "If you'd please fetch the lap desk and attend me?"

"Of course." Anna disappeared into the sitting room to retrieve the lap desk, but returned to the bed only to realize there was no chair for her to sit upon.

"The end of the bed will do." The earl gestured impatiently. Anna permitted herself to toss him a peevish look—a very peevish look, given the impropriety—but scuffed out of her slippers and climbed on the bed to sit cross-legged, her back against a bedpost.

"You are literate?" the earl asked, inspecting her again over his glasses.

"In French, English, and Latin, with a smattering of German, Gaelic, Welsh, and Italian."

His eyebrows rose momentarily at her tart reply, but he gave her a minute to get settled then began to slowly recite a memorandum to one of his land stewards, commending the man for progress made toward a sizeable crop of hay and suggesting irrigation ditches become a priority while the corn was maturing.

Another letter dealt with port sent to Morelands at the duke's request.

Yet another went to the widow of a man who'd held the living at one of the estate villages, expressing sorrow for her loss. And so it went, until a sizeable stack of correspondence was completed and the hour approaching midnight.

"Are you tired, Mrs. Seaton?" the earl asked as Anna paused to trim the pen.

"Serving as amanuensis is not that taxing, my lord," she said, and it hadn't been. His voice was beautiful, a mellifluous baritone that lost its habitual hauteur when he was concentrating on communication, leaving crisp consonants and round, plummy vowels redolent of education and good, prosperous breeding.

"Would that my man of business were so gracious," the earl said. "If you are not fatigued, then perhaps I can trouble you to fetch some libation from the kitchen. Speaking at such length tires the voice, or I wouldn't ask it."

"Is there anything else I could get you from the kitchen?" she asked, setting the desk on the night table.

"Perhaps one of those muffins," he allowed. "My digestion is tentative, but the last one stayed down easily enough."

"The last two," she said over her shoulder.

❧

He let her have the last word—or two—and also let himself enjoy the sight of her retreating backside again. He'd put her age well below thirty. The Corsican's years of mischief had left a record crop of widows in many lands, perhaps including his housekeeper.

And more than just young, he was seeing for the first time that she was pretty. Oh, she didn't emphasize it, no sane woman in service would. But to the earl's discerning eye, her drab gowns hid a marvelous figure, one enforced proximity had made all too apparent to him. Her hair was a lustrous shade of dark brown, shot with red and gold highlights, and her eyes a soft, luminous gray. The cast of her features was slightly exotic—Eastern, Mediterranean, or even Gypsy. She was the antithesis of his mistress, a petite, blond, blue-eyed woman who circulated easily on the fringes of polite society.

He wondered on a frown why he'd chosen a diminutive woman for his intimate attentions, as tall women fit him better. But then, finding a mistress of any description was no easy feat. Given his station, the earl was unwilling to frequent brothels. He was equally loathe to take his chances on the willing widows, knowing they would trap him in marriage just as quickly as their younger counterparts would.

So that left him with Elise, at least when she was in Town.

Still frowning, he picked up an epistle from his brother, who was standing guard at Morelands while the duke and duchess enjoyed a two-week holiday there. Valentine was happiest in the country, playing his piano at all hours and riding the countryside.

The man was no fribble, though, and he'd appended a little postscript to his report: "The land you rent on Tambray is being ploughed, if not planted, by Renfrew in your absence. One wonders to whom the harvest will fall."

Elise's rented house was on Tambray Street, and Baron Renfrew was one of those fun-loving, randy young lords the ladies doted on. Well, let Elise have her fun, the earl mused, as his arrangement with her was practical. When they were both in Town, he expected her to be available to him by appointment; otherwise, she was free to disport where she pleased, as was he.

If he had the time—and the inclination—which, lately anyway, he did not.

"Your drink, my lord." Mrs. Seaton placed a tray on the foot of the bed and held a glass out for him.

He glanced at the tray then regarded her thoughtfully. "I believe it might be more comfortable on the balcony, Mrs. Seaton."

"As you wish, my lord." She set the glass back on the tray, opened the French doors, and shifted to stand beside his bed. Carefully, he levered himself over to the side of the bed and waited for her to sit beside him and slip an arm around his waist.

"What is that scent?" he asked, pausing when she would have risen.

"I make my own," she said, glancing over at him. "Mostly lavender, with a few other notes. It turned out particularly well this year, I think."

He leaned in and sniffed at her, assessing.

"Lavender and something sweet," he decided, ignoring the presumptuousness of his gesture. "Lilies?"

"Perhaps." Mrs. Seaton was blushing, her gaze on her lap. "The details will shift, depending on one's sense of smell, and also with the ambient scents."

"You mean with what I'm wearing? Hadn't thought of that. Hmm."

He gave her another little sniff then squared his shoulders to rise. To his unending disgust, he had to steady himself momentarily on his housekeeper's shoulder. "Proceed," he said when his head had stopped swimming. They were soon out in the silky summer darkness of his balcony.

"Honeysuckle," he said, apropos of nothing but the night air.

"There is some of that," Mrs. Seaton said as they closed in on a padded wicker chaise. His balcony overlooked the back gardens, and a soft breeze was stirring the scents from the flowers below.

"Sit with me," the earl said as he settled onto the chaise. Mrs. Seaton paused in her retreat, and something in her posture alerted him to his overuse of the imperative. "Please," he added, unable to keep a hint of amusement from his tone.

"You were not born to service," the earl surmised as his housekeeper took a seat on a wicker rocking chair.

"Minor gentry," she concurred. "Very minor."

"Brothers and sisters?"

"A younger sister and an older brother. Your lemonade, my lord?"

"Please," he replied, recalling he'd sent her down two flights in the dark of night to fetch it.

But it was a moonless night and dark as pitch on the balcony, so when Mrs. Seaton retrieved the drink, she reached for his fingers with her free hand and wrapped his grip around the glass.

"You are warm," she said, a frown in her voice. She reached out again, no doubt expecting to put the back of her hand against his forehead but instead connecting with his cheek. "I beg your pardon." She snatched back her hand. "Do you think you are becoming fevered?"

"I am not," he replied tersely, setting down his drink. He reached for her hand and brought it to his forehead. "No warmer than the circumstances dictate."

He felt—or thought he felt—her fingers smooth back his hair before she resumed her seat. The gesture was no doubt intended as maternal, and it was likely Elise's protracted absence that had him experiencing it as something much less innocent.

"How is your head, my lord?"

"Hurts like blue blazes. My back is on fire, and I won't be wrestling my chestnut geldings any time soon, either. You pack quite a wallop, considering the worst I could have done in broad daylight was perhaps grope the girl."

This recitation inspired his housekeeper to a very quiet yawn.

"Is my company that tiresome, Mrs. Seaton?" He wasn't offended, but neither had he intended his tone to come out sounding so wistful.

"My day is long in your service, my lord. We do a big market on Wednesday, and Cook and I spend much of the day laying it in, as the men aren't underfoot to bother us."

"So you are tired," he concluded. "Go rest, Mrs. Seaton. The settee in my sitting room will do, and I'll call when I need your assistance." She rose but hesitated, as if filling her sails for a lecture about propriety and decency and other virtues known mostly to domestics.

"Go, Mrs. Seaton," he urged. "I treasure my solitude, and I have much to think about. I will not fall asleep out here, and you need to at least nap. Were you anybody but my housekeeper, you'd know the Earl of Westhaven has no need to bother his help."

That must have appeased her or spiked her guns, for she departed, leaving Westhaven to sip his tea and enjoy his thoughts.

Her scent, he reflected, blended beautifully with the summer night air. It made a man want to nibble on her, to see if she tasted of lavender, roses, and honeysuckle. He cast back, trying to recall when he'd hired the pretty, younger-than-she-should-be, more-protective-than-she-needed-to-be, Mrs. Seaton. Early spring, perhaps, when he'd made the decision to leave the ducal townhouse, lest he strangle his dear papa and the endless parade of shirttail cousins his mama trooped past him for consideration as his broodmare.

The whole business was demeaning. He understood

his parents, having lost two sons, were desperate for progeny from their two remaining legitimate sons. He understood Val affected a preference for men—at least he claimed it was an affectation—rather than suffer the duke's importuning. He understood Devlin would be years recovering from Waterloo and the Peninsular War.

He did not understand though, how—given that the ducal responsibilities took every spare hour and minute—he was going to find the time to locate a woman he could tolerate not just in his bed but as the mother of his children and his companion at the breakfast table.

"Westhaven!" Elise flew across her sitting room, arms outstretched to envelope him in an enthusiastic hug. "Did you miss me?" She squeezed him to her ample bosom and kissed his cheek. "I have expired for lack of you, Westhaven." She kept her hands wrapped around his arm, pressing her breast to his bicep as she did. "A month is too long, isn't it? I'm sure you were very naughty in my absence, but I'm here now, and you needn't go baying at the moon for lack of me."

She was tugging at his clothing, her mouth chattering on, and Westhaven knew a moment's impatience. Desire was a bodily craving, like fatigue or hunger or physical restlessness. He tended to it, usually twice a week, sometimes more, and lately less. It had been mildly alarming to find Elise's departure for a month-long house party had inconvenienced him not one bit.

But she was back, and it had been a month, and his clothes were rapidly accumulating in a pile on the floor.

"Elise," he said, stilling her hands, "you know I don't like to be untidy."

"But you do like to be naked," Elise quipped, bending to scoop up his shirt, waistcoat, and cravat. She dumped them over the back of a chair and pushed him onto her fainting couch, the better to extricate him from his boots. "And I like to get you naked." Like a small, blond fury, Elise finished peeling him out of his clothes, showing an enthusiasm he didn't usually find in her.

"You've added flesh," she observed when she'd thrown his breeches onto the chair, as well. "You aren't as skinny, Westhaven. Oh, and look, you are glad to see me."

His cock was glad to see her, anyway. Glad enough that when she pushed him onto his back on her silly red bed, he could concede a month of celibacy had been enough.

"Let me taste you." Elise was still in her dressing gown, but she climbed onto the bed and knelt at his hip.

Now this was something new. Elise liked having him for a protector, liked thinking the heir to a dukedom had chosen her for his pleasures. She did not, however, particularly like him or like sex. These factors bothered him a little, but no more than they bothered her. In many ways, it was easier if she wasn't personally attached to him, nor he to her.

Her tongue lapped at his cock, the sensations tantalizing and more arousing than the rest of Elise's

repertoire of foreplay put together. Elise, however, had
been reluctant to indulge him thus previously, so with
her, he usually contented himself with more pedestrian
sexual play. The lapse of time since they'd last been
together, and the enthusiastic efforts of her mouth,
combined to undermine his usual self-discipline.

"I'll come in your mouth, Elise," he warned her
several minutes later. "When you suck on my cock, it
tempts me—"

"You'll do no such thing." Elise glanced up at him
sharply, alarm flitting across her face. She opened her
dressing gown and lay down on the mattress beside
him. "You can't have all the fun, Westhaven."

She obligingly spread her legs, so he rolled and
settled himself over her.

"I take care of you, Elise," he said, nuzzling at her
neck. She wasn't much of one for kissing on the mouth,
but she tolerated attention to her breasts fairly well.

"You do," she agreed, arching up against him.
"Though you take your damned time about it." The
words were teasing, but something in her tone was
petulant, ungracious, so he dispensed with further
preliminaries and found the entrance to her body with
his cock.

"I will assume"—he began to rock his way to a
fuller penetration—"you have simply missed your
pleasures, Elise."

"I have," she said, wrapping her legs around his
flanks and locking her ankles at the small of his back.
"Now fuck my feeble brains out and cease jabbering."

His cock liked that idea just fine, but in the part
of him that always watched, always considered,

something about Elise felt just the slightest degree *off*. Her enthusiasm didn't seemed feigned, exactly, but neither was it…warm.

"Harder," she urged, flexing her hips to meet his thrusts. "I want it rough today, Westhaven."

Rough? Where in the hell did that come from? He obligingly thrust harder and felt his own arousal ratchet up. Elise's heels dug into his spine, though, and the distraction allowed him to hold back his orgasm as he listened for hers to approach.

"Oh, God…" Elise was flailing her hips at him desperately, her passion a welcome and uncharacteristic display. "God damn you, Westhaven…"

She bucked against him harder, until he felt his own climax bearing down on him. He held off until he was sure Elise had found her pleasure in full then arched his back to withdraw.

Elise held him all the more tightly, her legs vised around his waist.

With a sudden wrench, he broke her scissor hold and lunged back.

"What in God's name are you doing?" he roared. He sat back on his heels, panting with frustrated lust, while Elise stared up at him, eyes dazed with passion and anger.

"Why?" she yelled back. "Why for once couldn't you just come like most men and not be so goddamned careful? You can't just fuck, Westhaven. You have to be a damned duke even in this!"

"What on earth are you going on about?" He speared her with an incredulous look. "You know my terms, Elise, and…"

He watched her face, and realization dawned.

"Oh, Elise." He climbed to the side of the bed and sat with his back to her, lungs heaving. "You let Renfrew plant his bastard in your belly and hoped to pass it off as mine." He didn't need to see her eyes to know he'd come across yet another ducal ploy to trap him into marriage. Renfrew was tall, green-eyed, brown-haired, and randy as a goat.

"His Grace promised…" Elise wailed quietly. "His man said if I conceived, the duke would see us wed."

Westhaven shook his head in exasperation, "Elise, the duke would not have seen us wed when I told him the child was Renfrew's."

"And how would he have known that?"

"I am not stupid, Elise, and I have never spent my seed inside you. My father would believe me in that much, at least," he said as he rose.

"Where are you going?" She sat up, closing the dressing gown around her as if he might peek at her nakedness.

"I am going to take a cold bath, I suppose." He began to sort through his clothes. "Would you prefer diamonds, emeralds, or rubies?"

"All of the above," she replied, crossing her arms over her chest. "You were a damned lot of work, Westhaven."

"Was I really?" He was momentarily nonplussed by the thought but then resumed dressing. "How so?"

"This is just sex." Elise waved her hand at the bedroom in general. "But still, it's sex with another *person*."

"You don't think I know you are a person? I didn't see to your pleasure?" he asked, more curious than he wanted to let on.

"You." She glared at him with reluctant affection.

"You probably had a list in your pocket as you set out today: Replace right hind shoe on gelding; draft terms for running the universe; visit Elise; meet cronies at the club. Except you don't have cronies. And when you get here," she ranted on, "kiss her cheek, and carefully disrobe. After folding each article of clothing precisely *so*, twiddle her bubbies, twiddle her couche, insert cock, and stir briskly for five minutes. Oh"—she threw up her hands—"just forget I opened my mouth."

"Twiddle, Elise?" Westhaven said, sitting next to her on the bed. "I perceive you are disappointed in me, but twiddle is a bit harsh. And given your sentiments, perhaps it's best you aren't going to be my duchess, hmm?"

"Yes." She nodded. "I would likely have killed you, Westhaven, though you aren't a bad fellow underneath it all."

"A ringing endorsement." He rose then turned and studied her. "What will you do, Elise? Renfrew is pockets to let, for all that he's a good time."

"I don't know, but I'd appreciate it if you'd give me some time to figure it out."

"Take all the time you need." He hugged her, a simple, affectionate gesture that seemed somehow appropriate. "I believe I'll swear off mistresses for the nonce, and the lease here is paid up through the year, so you might as well put the place to use."

"Most generous. Now be gone with you." Elise shoved him away from her. "I'm swearing off titles. I'll find myself a rich, climbing cit and get the blighter to marry me, bastard and all."

"Seriously, Elise." He paused to force her to meet his eyes. "I'll provide if there's a child. You will allow it." He put every ounce of ducal authority into his expression, and she visibly shrank from his gaze.

"I will." She nodded, swallowing.

"Then goodbye." He bowed, as if they'd just shared a waltz, and kissed her cheek.

Westhaven left his mistress's pretty little house, thinking he should have been angry with Elise and most especially with his father. The duke, though, had simply covered a logical base: If Westhaven were already swiving a woman, it made sense that woman was the most likely to conceive his child.

But Elise, as a mother? Good God… His Grace must be getting senile.

Mentally, Westhaven found himself adding to his list of tasks to complete: Send parting gift to Elise, diamonds, emeralds, and rubies, if possible; replace Elise; draft epistle to His Grace, decrying his suborning of bastardy.

And had Val not sent him an alert, would Westhaven have seen through Elise's ploy?

He should just damned marry, he thought as he gained the steps to his townhouse. But if finding a mistress had been difficult, finding a woman worthy to be his duchess *and his wife* was going be almost impossible.

"The prodigal returns," a voice sang out in his front hallway.

"Valentine?" Westhaven found himself smiling at his younger brother, who lounged in the doorway to the library. "You left our sire unsupervised? Our sisters unprotected?"

"I'm up only for the weekend." Val shoved away from the door and extended a hand. "I got to fretting about you, and His Grace is under the supervision of Her Grace, which should be adequate for a few days."

"Fretting about me?"

"I overheard Renfrew bragging." Val turned to lead his brother into the library. "Then it occurred to me my note was perhaps not clear enough."

"Elise and I have come to an amicable if somewhat costly parting. I will call upon Renfrew in the near future to suggest, quite discreetly, that should he see fit to precede me into holy matrimony, a token of my good wishes would be forthcoming."

Val whistled. "Elise was playing a desperate game. The girl has cheek."

"She and Renfrew would understand each other," Westhaven said, "and I've been looking for a way to unload Monk's Crossing. It takes two weeks each year just to put in an appearance there, and it isn't as if we're lacking for properties."

"Why not sell what isn't entailed? You wear yourself out, Gayle, trying to keep track of it all and staying on top of His Grace's queer starts."

"I have sold several properties that were only marginally producing, and I should be doing a better job of keeping you informed of such developments, as you are, dear Brother, the spare of record."

"Yes," Val said, holding up a hand, "as in, 'spare me.' I'll pay attention if you insist, but please do not intimate to His Grace I give a hearty goddamn for any of it."

"Ah." Westhaven smiled, going to the sideboard to

pour them each a finger of brandy. "Except you do. How are the manufactories coming?"

"I don't think of them as manufactories, but we're managing."

"Business is good?" Westhaven asked, hoping he wasn't offending his brother.

"Business in the years immediately following decades of war is going to be unpredictable," Val said, accepting his drink. "People want pleasure and beauty and relief from their cares, and music provides that. But there is also a widespread lack of coin."

"In some strata," Westhaven agreed. "But organizations, like schools and churches and village assemblies are not quite as susceptible to that lack of coin, and they all buy pianos."

"So they do." Val saluted his brother with his glass. "I hadn't thought of that, because I myself have never performed in such venues, but you are right. This confirms, of course, my bone-deep conviction you are better suited to the dukedom than I."

"Because I have one minimally useful idea?" Westhaven asked, going to the bellpull.

"Because you think about things, endlessly, and in depth. I used to think you were slow."

"I am slow, compared to the rest of the family, but I have my uses."

"You don't honestly believe that. You are not as outgoing as our siblings, perhaps, but we lack your ability to concentrate on a problem until the damned thing lies in tiny pieces at our mental feet."

Westhaven set aside his drink. "Perhaps, but we needn't stand here throwing flowers at each other, when we could be stuffing ourselves with muffins and lemonade."

"Traveling does give one a thirst, and it is hotter than blazes, even at Morelands. Speaking of flowers, though, your establishment has benefited from the warmer weather." He nodded at the flowers around the room.

"My housekeeper," Westhaven said, going to the door to order tea. "Mrs. Seaton is…"

"Yes?" Westhaven saw Val was watching him closely, as only a sibling alert to the subtleties might.

"One can keep a house tidy," Westhaven said, "and one can make it…homey. She does both."

He'd noticed it, after his mishap with the fireplace poker earlier in the week. If he looked closely, the details were evident: The windows weren't just clean, they sparkled. The woodwork gleamed and smelled of lemon oil and beeswax; the carpets all looked freshly sanded and beaten; the whole house was free of dust and clutter. And more subtly, air moved through the rooms on softly fragrant currents.

"She must be feeding you properly, as well," Val noted. "You've lost some of that perpetually lean and hungry look."

"That is a function of simply having my own home for the past few months. His Grace wears on one, and our sisters, while dear, destroy a man's peace regularly."

"His Grace sets a very childish example." Val put his empty glass back on the sideboard. "I think you do well being both brother and earl, and you did better getting the damned power of attorney from him and corralling his ridiculous impulses where they can do little harm. That was particularly well done of you, Westhaven."

"At too high a price."

"But you didn't end up marrying the lady," Val pointed out, "so all's well."

"All will not be well until I have presented His Grace with several legitimate grandsons, and even then, he'll probably still want more." He went to the French doors overlooking his terrace as he spoke.

"He'll die eventually," Val said. "Almost did last winter, in fact."

"He was brought down more by the quacks who bled him incessantly than by lung fever itself." Westhaven glanced over his shoulder at his brother and scowled. "If I am ever seriously ill, Valentine, you must promise to keep the damned quacks and butchers away from me. A comely nurse and the occasional medicinal tot, but otherwise, leave it in the hands of the Almighty." He swiveled his gaze back to the terrace and watched as Mrs. Seaton appeared, baskets and shears in hand while she marched to the cutting garden along one low stone wall.

"You put me on the spot." Val smiled. "Do you honestly think I wouldn't do everything in my power to keep you alive, despite your wishes to the contrary?"

"Then pray for my continued good health." Mrs. Seaton was bareheaded today, her dark mane pulled back into a thick knot at her nape. By firelight, he knew, there were red highlights in that hair.

Lemonade arrived, complete with fat muffins, fresh bread with butter, sliced meats and cheese, sliced fruit, and a petite bouquet of violets on the tray. Nestled in a little folded square of linen were four pieces of marzipan, glazed to resemble fruit.

"This is tea at your house of late?" Val arched an eyebrow. "No wonder you look a bit more the thing. I will move in directly, provided you promise to tune the piano."

"You should, you know," Westhaven said. He was putting together a plate, but his words had come out far less casually than he'd planned. "I know you don't like staying at the ducal manse, and I have more than enough room here."

"Wouldn't want to impose," Val said, reaching for his own share of the bounty, "but that's generous of you."

"Not generous. The truth is...I could use the company. I miss your music, in fact. There's a neighbor, or somebody, who plays late at night, but it isn't you, for all that I enjoy it. I thought I'd have a harder time keeping track of His Grace were I to set up my own place, but I've been surprised at how little effort he makes to elude my scrutiny."

The door opened without the obligatory knock, and Mrs. Seaton marched into the room.

"I beg your pardon, your lordship, Lord Valentine." She stopped, her basket of flowers bouncing against her skirts. "My lord, I thought you'd be at your appointment until this evening."

Twiddling my mistress's bubbies, Westhaven thought with a lift of an eyebrow.

"Mrs. Seaton." Val rose, smiling as if he knew he was viewing the source of his brother's happier household and healthier appearance. "My compliments on the offerings to be had here for tea, and the house itself looks marvelous."

"Mrs. Seaton." The earl rose more slowly, the display of manners hardly necessary for a housekeeper.

"My lords." She curtsied but came up frowning at Westhaven. "Forgive me if I note you rise slowly. Are you well?"

The earl glanced at his brother repressively.

"My brother is not in good health?" Val asked, grinning. "Do tell."

"I merely suffered a little bump on the head," the earl said, "and Mrs. Seaton spared me the attentions of the physicians."

Mrs. Seaton was still frowning, but the earl went on, forestalling her reply. "You may tend to your flowers, Mrs. Seaton, and I echo my brother's compliments: Tea is most pleasant."

"I'll dice you for the marzipan," Val said to the earl.

"No need," Mrs. Seaton offered over her shoulder. "We keep a goodly supply in the kitchen, as his lordship favors it. There are cream cakes and chocolates, as well, but those are usually served with the evening meal." She busied herself with substituting fresh flowers for the wilted specimens as the fragrance of roses, lavender, and honeysuckle wafted around the room.

Val eyed his brother. "Perhaps I will avail myself of your hospitality after all, Westhaven."

"I would be honored," Westhaven said absently, though he noted the speculation in his brother's eyes. Mrs. Seaton was humming a little Handel; Westhaven was almost sure it was from the *Messiah*. She turned to go but flashed them a smile and a little curtsy on her way.

"Oh, Mrs. Seaton?" The earl stopped her two steps shy of the door.

"My lord?"

"You may tell the kitchen my brother and I will be dining in tonight, informally, and will continue to do so until further notice."

"Lord Valentine will be visiting?"

"He will; the blue bedroom will do." Westhaven turned back to the tray, still counting four pieces of marzipan.

"Might I suggest the green bedroom?" Mrs. Seaton rejoined. "It has higher ceilings and is at the back of the house, which would be both cooler and quieter. Then too, it has a balcony."

The earl considered castigating her for contradicting him, but she'd been polite enough about it, and the back bedrooms were worlds more comfortable, though smaller.

"As you suggest." The earl waved her on her way.

"That is a very different sort of housekeeper you have there," Val said, when the library door had closed behind her.

"I know." Westhaven made a sandwich and checked again to make sure his brother hadn't pilfered the marzipan. "She's a little cheeky, to be honest, but does her job with particular enthusiasm. She puts me in mind of Her Grace."

"How so?" Val asked, making a sandwich, as well.

"Has an indomitable quality about her," Westhaven said between bites. "She bashed me with a poker when she thought I was a caller molesting a housemaid. Put out my lights, thank you very much."

"Heavens." Val paused in his chewing. "You didn't summon the watch?"

"The appearances were deceiving, and she doesn't know I'd never trifle with a housemaid."

"And if you were of a mind to before," Val said, eyeing the marzipan, "you'd sure as hell think twice about it now."

"And what of you?" Westhaven paused to regard his brother. Val shared the Windham height and green eyes, but his eyes were a darker green, while Westhaven's shade was closer to jade, and Val's hair was sable, nearly black.

"What of me?" Val buttered a fat muffin.

"Are you bothering any housemaids, lately?"

"Doing an errand for Viscount Fairly earlier in the season, I met an interesting woman out in Little Weldon," Val said, "but no, I am more concerned with misleading His Grace than in having my ashes hauled."

"Don't mislead him too well," Westhaven cautioned. "There are those who are not tolerant of left-handed preferences."

"Well, of course there are," Val said, "and they're just the ones wondering what it would be like to be a little adventurous themselves. But fear not, Westhaven. I mince and lisp and titter and flirt, but my breeches stay buttoned."

"It appears," Westhaven said, frowning as he reached for the marzipan, "mine will be staying buttoned, as well."

He bit into a plump, soft confection shaped like a ripe melon and stifled a snort of incredulity. His breeches would be staying buttoned, and the only thing he'd be twiddling would be his...thumbs.

Two

THREE RULES, ANNA REMINDED HERSELF WHEN SHE reached the privacy of her own little sitting room. There were three rules to succeeding with any deception, and old Mr. Glickmann had drilled them into her:

Dress the part.

Believe your own lies.

Have more than you show—including an alternative plan.

Today, she was remiss on all three counts, God help her. A housekeeper wore caps, for pity's sake. Great homely caps, and gloves out of doors, and there she went, sailing into the library, bareheaded, barehanded, for the earl and his brother to see.

Believe your own lies—that meant living the deception as if it were real, never breaking role, and with the earl she'd broken role badly ever since she'd brained him with a poker. He had to have seen her, arms around Morgan, even as he lay bleeding on the floor. And then, curse her arrogant mouth, she'd as good as informed him she was raised as a bluestocking—fluent in three languages, Mother of God! Housekeepers read mostly their Bible, and that only slowly.

Have more than you show, including second and even third plans. On that count, she was an unmitigated disaster. She had a small stash of funds, thanks to her wages here, and Mr. Glickmann's final generosity, but funds were not a plan. Funds did not guarantee a new identity nor safe passage to foreign soil, if that's what it took.

"So what has you in such a dither?" Nanny Fran toddled into the kitchen, her button eyes alight with curiosity.

"We're to have company," Anna replied, forcing herself to sit down and meet Nanny Fran's eyes. "His lordship's brother will be staying with us, and as it's the first company since I've started here, I'm a little flustered."

"Right." Nanny Fran smiled at her knowingly. "Lord Val's a good sort, more easygoing than Westhaven. But these two"—she shook her head— "they weren't the ones who gave me trouble. Lord Bart was a rascal and spoiled, for all he wasn't mean; Lord Vic was just as bad, and didn't he get up to mischief, and nobody but Westhaven the wiser?"

"No carrying tales, Nanny." Anna rose, unwilling to start Nanny gossiping. "I'm off to warn Cook we'll have company, and their lordships will be dining informally at home for the foreseeable future. Have you seen Morgan?"

"She's in the stillroom," Nanny supplied, coming to her feet in careful increments. "Smells like lemons today, and limes."

Anna did find Morgan in what had become the

stillroom, a portion of the large laundry that took up part of the house's understory. The girl was humming tunelessly and grinding something to powder with her mortar and pestle.

"Morgan?" Anna touched Morgan's shoulder, pleased to find she hadn't startled her. "What are you making? Nanny said it smelled like lemon and lime."

Morgan held out a large ceramic bowl with dried flowers crushed into a colorful mixture. Anna dipped her face to inhale the scent, closing her eyes and smiling.

"That is lovely. What's in it?"

Morgan lined up a number of bottles, pointing to each in turn, then took a pencil and scrap of paper from her apron pocket, and wrote, "Needs something. Too bland."

Anna cocked her head and considered the pronouncement. Morgan's nose was sophisticated but unconventional.

"Whose room is it for?"

Morgan made a supercilious face and arched a haughty eyebrow.

"The earl's," Anna concluded. "It does need something, something subtly exotic and even decadent." Morgan grinned and nodded. She reached for a small vial and held it up for Anna's consideration.

"*Mouget du bois*?" Anna raised her own eyebrow. "That's feminine, Morgan."

Morgan shook her head, confident in her decision. She added a few drops, stirred the bowl's contents gently with one finger, then covered them with a fitted ceramic lid.

"I'm glad you're done here for now," Anna said.

"His lordship's brother will be staying with us for a time and will have need of the guest bedroom at the back of the house. Can you prepare it for him?"

Morgan nodded and tapped the left side of her collarbone, where a lady's watch pin might hang.

"You have time, because the gentlemen will be dining here this evening. Give him plenty of scented wash water and a crock of ice to start with tonight. He'll need flowers too, of course, and the sheets should be turned, as the ones on the bed have likely lost all their fragrance. Air the room, as well, and I'd leave the top windows open, the better to catch a zephyr."

Morgan smiled again and breezed past Anna, who followed her out but paused in the kitchen to talk to Cook.

"You'll be cooking for two gentlemen tonight," Anna said with a smile.

"His lordship's having company?" Cook asked, looking up from the bread dough she was turning on a floured board.

"Lord Valentine, his brother. He's a year or two younger than Westhaven but looks to be every bit as fit and busy as the earl."

"Good appetites, then." Cook nodded, pleased. "The earl's interest in his tucker has picked up here in recent months, I can tell you. Shall we do it a bit fancy tonight?"

"Not fancy, I don't think." Anna frowned in thought. "It's too hot for anything heavy, and the dining room can be stuffy. Why not a meal for the back terrace, something a little closer to a picnic but substantial enough for men?"

"Cold fare, maybe." Cook frowned as she put the dough in a bowl and covered it with a clean towel. "Chicken, with that basil you planted, and we've early tomatoes coming in. I can slice up some fruit and put it on ice..." Cook trailed off, her imagination putting together what was needed with what was on hand.

Anna's next stop was the head footman, whose job it would be to set up the terrace for dining. Anna set out scented torches, candles, linen, and cutlery suited to an al fresco meal, then quickly put together a little bouquet for a low centerpiece.

"Mrs. Seaton?" A male voice in the small confines of the butler's pantry gave her a start.

"Lord Valentine?" She turned to find him standing immediately behind her.

"My apologies." He smiled down at her, a perfectly charming expression. "I called, but the din in the kitchen probably drowned me out. Would it be possible at some point this evening to request a bath?"

"Of course. Your brother bathes before retiring most nights, unless he's going to be from home until late. There is time before dinner, but your room is only now being readied. We can send a bath up to the front guest room, if you'd like."

"That would be marvelous." He remained in the oversized closet with her, his smile fading. "You take good care of him, Mrs. Seaton, and it shows, though it must have been quite some blow to his hard head if it slowed him down even marginally."

Anna frowned at his retreating back and realized

Westhaven had discussed the week's earlier mishap with Lord Val. Well, damn the man anyway.

And that reminded her, his lordship had sneaked out that morning without letting her tend him. He would scar at this rate and prolong his convalescence. Grabbing her medical supplies, Anna went in search of her quarry, hoping to find him where he usually was at this pleasant hour of the early evening, out on his balcony.

He lounged on his wicker chaise in lordly splendor, his waistcoat slung over the back of the chair, cravat folded tidily over that, his shirt open at the throat, and his cuffs rolled back.

"Your lordship?" Anna waited for his permission to step from his bedroom, feeling absurd for doing it and abruptly self-conscious.

"Mrs. Seaton," he drawled, glancing up at her. "You've come to poke at my injured self. Does nothing deter you from the conscientious prosecution of your duties?"

"Craven evasion," she replied, stepping out onto the balcony. "As when my patient disappears at first light, not to be seen until tea time, and then only in the company of his protective little brother."

"Val is protective of me?" Westhaven scowled as he eased forward to the end of the chaise, then dragged his shirt over his head and turned his back to her. "I suppose he is at that, though he knows I'd bite his head off were he to imply I need protection. Jesus Christ, that still stings."

"We all need protection from time to time," she said, dabbing gently at his back with arnica. "Your bruises are truly magnificent, my lord. They will heal more quickly if you don't duck out of a morning—and skip your breakfast."

"It's too hot to ride later in the day, at least at the pace I prefer." He winced again as she went at the second large laceration.

"You shouldn't be out riding hell-bent, your lordship. Your injuries do not need the abuse, and I can see where you've pulled this cut open along this edge." She drew a chiding finger along the bottom seam of a laceration. "What if you were unseated, and no one else about in the dawn's early light?"

"So you would come along to protect me?" he challenged lazily. She began to redress his back.

"Somebody should," she muttered, focused on the purple, green, and mottled brown skin surrounding the two mean gashes on his back.

The earl frowned in thought. "In truth, I am in need of somebody to protect. I fired my mistress today."

"My lord!" She was abruptly scowling at him nineteen to the dozen, as much disapproval as she dared show, short of jeopardizing her position outright.

"There is always gossip," he quoted her sardonically, "belowstairs."

She pursed her lips. "Gossip and blatant disclosure are not the same thing. Though in this heat, why anyone would…"

She broke off, mortified at what had been about to come out of her mouth.

"Oh, none of that, Mrs. Seaton." The earl's smile became devilish. "In this heat?"

"Never mind, my lord." She wetted her cloth with arnica again and gently tucked his head against her waist. "This one is looking surprisingly tidy. Hold still."

"I have a thick skull," he said from her waist. And now that she was done with his back, came the part he always tolerated almost docilely. She sifted her fingers carefully through his hair and braced him this way, his crown snug against her body, the better to tend his scalp.

And if his hair was the silkiest thing she'd ever had the pleasure to drift her fingers over, well, that was hardly the earl's fault, was it?

❧

He should have brought himself off when he didn't complete matters at Elise's. Why else would he be baiting his housekeeper, a virtuous and supremely competent woman? She was done with her arnica and back to exploring the area around the scalp wound with careful fingers.

"I don't understand why you haven't more swelling here." She feathered his hair away from the scalp wound. "Head wounds are notoriously difficult, but you seem to be coming along wonderfully."

"So we can dispense with this nonsense?" He reluctantly sat back and waved his hand at her linen and tincture.

"Another two days, I think." She put the cap back on the bottle. "Why is it so difficult for you to submit to basic care, my lord? Do you relish being stiff and scarred?"

"I do not particularly care what the appearance of

my back is, Mrs. Seaton. Ever since my brother took several years to die of consumption, I have had an abiding disgust of all things medical."

"I'm sorry." She looked instantly appalled. "I had no idea, my lord."

"Most people don't," Westhaven said. "If you've never seen anyone go that way, you don't fully comprehend the horror of it. And all the while, there were medical vultures circling, bleeding, poking at him, prescribing useless nostrums. He tolerated it, because it created a fiction of hope that comforted my parents even as it tortured him."

He fell silent then stood and went to the railing to stare out at the lush evening sunlight falling over his back gardens.

"And then late this winter, my stubborn father had to go riding to hounds in a weeklong downpour, only to come home with a raging lung fever. The leeches went at him, his personal physicians doing nothing more than drinking his brandy and letting his blood. When he was too weak to argue with me, those idiots were thrown out, but they came damned close to costing me my father."

"I'm sorry," she said again, turning to stand beside him, laying a hand on his back. He heard her sharp intake of breath as she realized her error—his shirt was still off. He didn't move off, though, but waited to see how she'd manage. Her hand was comforting, and without him willing it, his own slid along her waist and drew her against his side.

She remained facing the gardens, her expression impassive, her breath moving in a measured rhythm, her hand resting on his back as if it had arrived there despite her complete indifference to him as a person. Slowly, he relaxed, sensing her innate decency had, for just a few moments, trumped her notions of propriety, class distinction, and personal rectitude.

She offered comfort, he decided. Just comfort, for him, upon his recounting some very dark moments and his frustration and helplessness in those moments.

But what about for her?

He turned her to face him, brought her slowly against his body, and rested his cheek against her temple.

Just that, but it changed the tenor of the moment from gestures of comfort to the embrace of a man and a woman. His arms draped over her shoulders while hers looped at his naked waist, even as he told himself to end this folly *immediately*, or she'd have grounds for believing he trifled with the help after all.

She didn't end it. She stood in the loose circle of his arms, letting him positively wallow in the clean summery scent of her, the soft curves fitting him in all the right places. He urged her with patient strokes of his hands on her back to rest more fully against him, to give him her weight. He wasn't even aroused, he realized, he was just…consoled.

When he finally did step back, he placed a single finger softly against her lips to stop her from the admonitory and apologetic stammers no doubt damming up behind her conscience.

"None of that." He shook his head, his expression solemn. "This wasn't on my list either, Anna Seaton."

She didn't tarry to find out if he would say more, but shook her head in dismay, no curtsy, no

resounding whack to his cheek, no offer of resignation. She left him, heir to the dukedom, standing half
dressed, bruised, and alone on his private balcony.

⤸

"His lordship begs the favor of yer comp'ny, mum,"
John Footman informed the housekeeper. Except,
Anna knew, the man's name really was John, and his
father and grandfather before him had also both, for a
time, been footmen in the ducal household.

"He's in the library?" Anna asked, putting her
mending aside with a sigh.

"He is," John replied, "and in a proper taking
over summat."

"Best I step lively." Anna smiled at the young man,
who looked worried for her. She squared her mental
shoulders and adopted a businesslike—but certainly
not anxious—gait. It had been a week since she'd
clobbered the earl with a poker, a few days since
that awkward scene on his balcony. She'd tended his
bruises for the last time this morning, and he'd been
nothing more than his usual acerbic, imperious self.

She knocked with a sense of trepidation nonetheless.

"Come." The word was barked.

"Mrs. Seaton." He waved her over to his desk.
"Take a chair; I need your skills."

She took a seat and reluctantly agreed with the
footman. His lordship was in a taking, or a snit, or
an upset over something. The faint frown that often
marked his features was a scowl, and his manner
peremptory to the point of rudeness.

"My man of business is unable to attend me, and

the correspondence will not wait. There's paper, pen, and ink." He nodded at the edge of the desk. "Here, take my seat, and I'll dictate. The first letter goes to Messrs. Meechum and Holly, as follows…"

Good morning to you, too, Anna thought, dipping her pen. An hour and a half and six lengthy letters later, Anna's hand was cramping.

"The next letter, which can be a memorandum, is to go to Morelands. A messenger will be up from Morelands either later today or tomorrow, but the matter is not urgent." The earl let out a breath, and Anna took the opportunity to stand.

"My lord," she interrupted, getting a personal rendition of the earl's scowl for her cheek. "My hand needs a rest, and you could probably use some lemonade for your voice. Shall we take a break?"

He glanced at the clock, ready to argue, but the time must have surprised him.

"A short break," he allowed.

"I'll see about your drink," Anna said. When she got to the hallway, she shook her poor hand vigorously. It wasn't so much that the earl expected her to take lightning-fast dictation, it was more the case that he never, ever needed a pause himself. He gave her time to carefully record his every word, and not one tick of the clock more.

Sighing, she made her way to the kitchen, loaded up a tray, then added a second glass of lemonade for herself and returned to the library. She had been away from her post for twelve minutes but returned to find the earl reading a handwritten note and looking more thoughtful than angry.

"One more note, Mrs. Seaton," he said, rummaging in the desk drawers, "and then I will have something to drink."

He retrieved a scrap of paper from the back of a drawer, glaring at it in triumph when his fingers closed over it. "I knew it was in here." As he was back in his rightful place behind the desk, Anna repositioned the blotter, paper, pen, and ink on her side of the desk and sat down.

"To Drs. Hamilton, Pugh, and Garner, You will attend Miss Sue-Sue Tolliver at your earliest convenience, on the invitation of her father, Marion Tolliver. Bills for services rendered will be sent to the undersigned. Westhaven, etc."

Puzzled, Anna dutifully recorded the earl's words, sanded the little epistle, and set it aside to dry.

"I see you have modified your interpretation of the rules of decorum in deference to the heat," the earl noted, helping himself to a glass of lemonade. "Good God!" He held the glass away from him after a single sip. "It isn't sweetened."

"You helped yourself to my glass," Anna said, suppressing a smile. She passed him the second glass, from which he took a cautious swallow. She was left to drink from the same glass he'd first appropriated or go back to the kitchen to fetch herself a clean glass.

Looking up, she saw the earl watching her with a kind of bemused curiosity, as if he understood her dilemma. She took a hefty swallow of lemonade—and it did have sugar in it, though just a dash—and set her glass on the blotter.

"Tolliver is your man of business, isn't he?" she asked, the association just occurring to her.

"He is. He sent word around he was unavoidably detained and would not attend me this morning, which is unusual for him. I put one of the footmen on it and just received Tolliver's explanation: his youngest is coming down with the chicken pox."

"And you sent not one but three physicians for a case of chicken pox?" Anna marveled.

"Those three," the earl replied in all seriousness, "were recommended by an acquaintance who is himself a physician. Garner and Pugh were instrumental in saving His Grace's life this winter."

"So you trust them."

"As much as I trust any physician," the earl countered, "which is to say no farther than I could throw them, even with my shoulders injured."

"So if we ever need a physician for you, we should consult Garner, Pugh, or Hamilton?"

"My first choice would be David Worthington, Viscount Fairly, who recommended the other three, but you had better hope I die of whatever ails me, as I will take any quackery quite amiss, Mrs. Seaton." The earl speared her with a particularly ferocious glare in support of his point.

"May I ask an unrelated question, my lord?" Anna sipped her drink rather than glare right back at him. He was in a mood this morning to try the patience of a saint.

"You may." He put his empty glass on the tray and sat back in his chair.

"Is this how you work with Mr. Tolliver?" she asked. "Dictating correspondence word-for-word?"

"Sometimes," the earl replied, frowning. "He's been with me several years, though, and more often than not, I simply scratch a few notes, and he drafts the final missive for my signature."

"Can we try that approach? It sounds like my grandfather's way of doing business, and so far, your correspondence has been perfectly mundane."

"We can try it, but I am reminded of another matter I wanted to raise with you, and I will warn you in advance I won't have you sniffing your indignation at me for it."

"Sniffing my indignation?"

The earl nodded once, decisively. "Just so. I told you the other night I have parted company with my current *chere amie*. I inform you of this, Mrs. Seaton, not because I want to offend your sensibilities, but because I suspect the duke will next turn his sights on my own household."

"What does His Grace have to do with your... personal associations?"

"Precisely my question," the earl agreed, but he went on to explain in terse, blunt language how his father had manipulated his mistress, and how Elise had altered the plan in its significant details. "My father will likely try to find a spy on my own staff to inform him of when and with whom I contract another liaison. You will foil his efforts, should you learn of them."

"My lord, if you wanted to elude your father's scrutiny, then why would you hire half your footmen from his household and give him exclusive access to your valet for weeks on end?"

The earl looked nonplussed as he considered the logic of her observation.

"I made those arrangements before I comprehended the lengths to which my father is prepared to go. And I did so without knowing he already had spies in Elise's household, as well."

Anna said nothing and resumed her seat across the desk from the earl. He shuffled the stack, put two or three missives aside, then passed pen and paper to Anna.

"To Barstow," he began, "a polite expression of noninterest at this time, perhaps in future, et cetera. To Williams and Williams, a stern reminder that payment is due on the first, per our arrangements, and sword-rattling to the effect that contractual remedies will be invoked." He passed over the first two and went on in that vein until Anna had her orders for the next dozen or so letters.

"And while you obligingly tend to spinning that straw into gold"—the earl smiled without warning—"I will fire off the next salvo to His Grace."

For the next hour, they worked in companionable silence, with Anna finding it surprisingly easy to address the tasks set before her. She'd spent many, many hours in this role with her grandfather and had enjoyed the sense of partnership and trust such a position evoked.

"Well, what have we here?" Lord Valentine strode into the library, smiling broadly at its occupants. "Have I interrupted a lofty session of planning menus?"

"Hardly." The earl smiled at his brother. "Tolliver's absence has necessitated I prevail on Mrs. Seaton's good offices. What has you up so early?"

"It's eleven of the clock," Val replied. "Hardly early when one expects to practice at least four hours at his pianoforte." He stopped and grimaced. "If, that is, you won't mind. I can always go back to the Pleasure House if you do."

"Valentine." The earl glanced warningly at Mrs. Seaton. "I've already told your housekeeper I am possessed of a healthy affection for pianos of easy virtue." Val turned his smile on Anna. "She was shocked insensible, of course."

"I was no such thing, your lordship."

"A man can take poetic license," Val said, putting a pair of Westhaven's glasses on his nose. "If you will excuse me, I will be off to labor in the vineyard to which I am best suited."

A little silence followed his departure, with the earl frowning pensively at the library door. Anna went back to the last of her assigned letters, and a few minutes later, heard the sound of scales tinkling through the lower floors of the house.

"Will he really play for four hours?" she asked.

"He will play forever," the earl said, "but he will practice for at least four hours each day. He spent more time at the keyboard by the age of twenty-five than a master at any craft will spend at his trade in his lifetime."

"He is besotted," Anna said, smiling. "You really don't mind the noise?"

"It is the sound of my only living little brother being happy," the earl said, tossing down his pen and going to stand in the open French doors. "It could never be noise." The earl frowned at her over his shoulder. "What? I can see you want to ask me something. I've worked you hard enough you deserve a shot or two."

"What makes you happy?" she asked, stacking the completed replies neatly, not meeting his eyes.

"An heir to a dukedom need not be happy. He need only be dutiful and in adequate reproductive health."

"So you are dutiful, but that evades the question. Your father manages to be both duke and happy, at least much of the time. So what, future Duke of Moreland, makes you happy?"

"A good night's sleep," the earl said, surprising them both. "Little pieces of marzipan showing up at unlikely spots in my day. A pile of correspondence that has been completed before luncheon, thank ye gods."

"You still need to read my efforts," Anna reminded him, pleased at his backhanded compliment, but troubled, somehow, that a good night's sleep was the pinnacle of his concept of pleasure.

The earl waggled his fingers at her. "So pass them over, and I will find at least three misspellings, lest you get airs above your station."

"You will find no misspellings, nor errors of punctuation or grammar." Anna passed the stack to him. "With your leave, I will go see about luncheon. Would you like to be served on the terrace, my lord, and will Lord Valentine be joining you?"

"I would like to eat on the terrace," the earl said, "and I doubt my brother will tear himself away from the piano, when he just sat down to his finger exercises. Send in a tray to him when you hear him shift from drills to etudes and repertoire."

"Yes, my lord." Anna bobbed a curtsy, but his lordship was already nose down into the correspondence, his brow knit in his characteristic frown.

"Oh, Mrs. Seaton?" The earl did not look up.

"My lord?"

"What does a child suffering chicken pox need for her comfort and recuperation?"

"Ice," Anna said, going on to name a litany of comfort nursing accoutrements.

"You can see to that?" he asked, looking up and eyeing his gardens. "The ice and so forth? Have it sent 'round to Tolliver's?"

"I can," Anna replied, cocking her head to consider her employer. "Regularly, until the child recovers."

"How long will that take?"

"The first few days are the worst, but by the fifth day, the fever has often abated. The itching can take longer, though. In this heat, I do not envy the child or her parents."

"A miserable thought," the earl agreed, "in comparison to which, dealing with my paltry letters is hardly any hardship at all, hmm? There will be more marzipan at lunch?"

"If your brother hasn't plundered our stores," Anna said, taking her leave.

She didn't see the earl smile at the door nor see that the smile didn't fade until he forced himself to resume perusing her drafts of correspondence. She wrote well, he thought, putting his ideas into words with far more graciousness and subtlety than old Tolliver could command. And so the chore of tending to correspondence, which had threatened to consume his entire day, was already behind him, leaving him free to…wonder what gave him pleasure.

∽

"I'd put John to setting the table," Cook said, "but he went off to get us some more ice from the warehouse, and Morgan has gone to fetch the eggs, since his lordship didn't take his ride this morning, and McCutcheon hasn't seen to the hens yet."

So I, Anna thought, will spend the next half hour setting up a table where his lordship will likely sit for all of twenty minutes, dining in solitary splendor on food he doesn't even taste, because he must finish reading *The Times* while at table.

His crabby mood had rubbed off on her, she thought as she spread a linen cloth over a wrought-iron table. Well, that wouldn't do. Mentally, she began making her list of things to send over to Tolliver's for the little girl, Sue-Sue.

"You look utterly lost in thought," the earl pronounced, causing Anna to jump and almost drop the basket of cutlery she was holding.

"I was," she said, blushing for no earthly reason. "I have yet to see to your request to send some supplies around to Tolliver and was considering the particulars."

"How is it you know how to care for a case of chicken pox?" The earl grabbed the opposite ends of the tablecloth and drew them exactly straight.

"It's a common childhood illness," Anna said, setting the basket of cutlery on the table. "I came down with it myself when I was six." The earl reached into the basket and fished out the makings of a place setting. Anna watched in consternation as he arranged his cutlery on the table, setting each piece of silverware precisely one inch from the edge of the table.

"Don't you want a linen for your place setting?" Anna asked, unfolding one from the basket and passing it to him.

"Well, of course. Food always tastes better when eaten off a plate that sits on both a linen and a tablecloth."

"No need to be snippy, my lord." Anna quirked an eyebrow at him. "We can feed you off a wooden trencher if that's your preference."

"My apologies." The earl shot her a fulminating look as he collected the silverware and waited for Anna to spread the underlinen. "I am out of sorts today for having missed my morning ride."

He was once again arranging his silverware a precise distance from the edge of the table while Anna watched. He would have made an excellent footman, she concluded. He was careful, conscientious, and incapable of smiling.

"In this heat, I did not want to tax my horse," the earl said, rummaging in the basket for salt and the pepper. He found them and eyed the table speculatively.

"Here." Anna set a small bowl of daisies and violets on the table. "Maybe that will give you some ideas."

"A table for one can so easily become asymmetric."

"Dreadful effect on the palate." Anna rolled her eyes. "And where, I ask you, will we hide his lordship's marzipan?"

"Careful, Mrs. Seaton. If he should come out here and overhear your disrespect, I wouldn't give two pence for your position."

"If he is so humorless and intolerant as all that," Anna said, "then he can find somebody else to feed him sweets on the terrace of a summer's day."

The earl's gaze cooled at that retort, and Anna wondered at her recent penchant for overstepping. He'd been annoying her all morning, though, from the moment she'd been dragooned into the library. It was no mystery to her why Tolliver would rather be dealing with a sick child than his lordship.

"Am I really so bad as all that?" the earl asked, his expression distracted. He set aside the pepper but hefted the salt in one hand.

"You are..." Anna glanced up from folding the linen napkin she'd retrieved from her basket.

The earl met her gaze and waited.

"Troubled, I think," she said finally. "It comes out as imperiousness."

"Troubled," the earl said with a snort. "Well, that covers a world of possibilities." He reached into the basket and withdrew a large glazed plate, positioning it exactly in the center of his place setting. "I tried to compose a letter to my father this morning, while you beavered away on my *mundane* business, and somehow, Mrs. Seaton, I could not come up with words to adequately convey to my father the extent to which I want him to just *leave me the hell alone*."

He finished that statement through clenched teeth, alarming Anna with the animosity in his tone, but he wasn't finished.

"I have come to the point," the earl went on, "where I comprehend why my older brothers would consider the Peninsular War preferable to the daily idiocy that comes with being Percival Windham's heir. I honestly believe that could he but figure a way to pull it off, my father would lock me naked in a room with the woman of his choice, there to remain until I got her pregnant with twin boys. And I am not just frustrated"—the earl's tone took on a sharper edge—"I am ready to do him an injury, because I don't think anything less will make an impression. Two unwilling people are going to wed and have a child because my father got up to tricks."

"Your father did not force those two people into one another's company all unawares and blameless, my lord, but why not appeal to your mother? By reputation, she is the one who can control him."

The earl shook his head. "Her Grace is much diminished by the loss of my brother Victor. I do not want to importune her, and she will believe His Grace only meant well."

Anna smiled ruefully. "And she wants grandchildren, too, of course."

"Why, of course." The earl gestured impatiently. "She had eight children and still has six. There will be grandchildren, and if for some reason the six of us are completely remiss, I have two half siblings, whose children she will graciously spoil, as well."

"Good heavens," Anna murmured. "So your father has sired ten children, and yet he plagues you?"

"He does. Except for the one daughter of Victor's, none of us have seen fit to reproduce. There was a rumor Bart had left us something to remember him by, but he likely started the rumor himself just to aggravate my father."

"So find a wife," Anna suggested. "Or at least a fiancée, and back your dear papa off. The right lady will cry off when you ask it of her, particularly if you are honest with your scheme from the start."

"See?" The earl raised his voice, though just a bit. "Honest with my *scheme*? Do you know how like my father that makes me sound?"

"And is this all that plagues you, my lord? Your father has no doubt been a nuisance for as long as you've been his heir, if not longer."

The earl glanced sharply at his housekeeper, then his lips quirked, turned back down, and then slowly curved back up.

"Why are you smiling?" she asked, his smiles being as rare as hen's teeth.

"I found your little parlor maid in the hay loft," the earl said, setting out his water glass and wine glass precisely one inch from the plate. "She discovered our mouser's new litter, and she was enthralled with the cat's purr. She could feel it, I think, and understood it meant the cat was happy."

"She would," Anna said, wondering how this topic was related to providing the duke his heirs. "She loves animals, but here in Town, she has little truck with them."

"You know Morgan that well?" the earl asked, his tone casual.

"We are related," she replied, telling herself it was a version of the truth. A prevaricating version.

"So you took pity on her," the earl surmised, "and hired her into my household. Has she always been deaf?"

"I do not know the particulars of her malady, my

lord," she said, lifting the basket to her hip. "All I care for is her willingness to do an honest day's work for an honest day's pay. Shall we serve you tea or lemonade with your luncheon?"

"Lemonade," Westhaven said. "But for God's sake don't forget to sugar it."

She bobbed a curtsy so low as to be mocking. "Any excuse to sweeten your disposition, my lord."

He watched her go, finding another smile on his face, albeit a little one. His housekeeper liked having the last word, which was fine with him—usually. But as their conversation had turned to the question of her *relation*, she had dodged him and begun to dissemble. It was evident in her eyes and in the slight defensiveness of her posture.

A person, even one in service to an earl, was entitled to privacy. But a person with secrets could be exploited by, say, an unscrupulous duke. And for that reason—for *that* reason—the earl would be keeping a very close eye on Anna Seaton.

Three

"Beg pardon, mum." John Footman bobbed a bow. "His lordship's asking fer ya, and I'd step lively."

"He's in the library?" Anna asked with a sigh. She'd spent three of the last four mornings in the library with his lordship, but not, thank the gods, today.

"In his chambers, mum." John was blushing now, even as he stared holes in the molding. Anna grimaced, knowing she'd sent a bath up to the earl's chambers directly after luncheon, which was unusual enough.

"Best see what he wants." Anna rose from the kitchen table, got a commiserating look from Cook, and made her way up two flights of stairs.

"My lord?" She knocked twice, heard some sort of lordly growl from the other side, and entered the earl's sitting room.

The earl was dressed, she noted with relief, but barely. His shirt was unbuttoned, as were his cuffs, he was barefoot, and the garters were not yet closed on his knee breeches.

He did not glance up when she entered the room but was fishing around on a bureau among brushes and combs. "My hair touches my collar, at the back." He waved two fingers impatiently behind his right ear. "As my valet continues to attend His Grace, you will please address the situation."

"You want me to trim your hair?" Anna asked, torn between indignation and amusement.

"If you please," he said, locating a pair of grooming scissors and handing them to her handles first. He obligingly turned his back, which left Anna circling him to address his face.

"It will be easier, my lord, if you will sit, as even your collar is above my eye level."

"Very well." He dragged a stool to the center of the room and sat his lordly arse upon it.

"And since you don't want to have stray hairs on that lovely white linen," Anna went on, "I would dispense with the shirt, were I you."

"Always happy to *dispense* with clothing at the request of a woman." The earl whipped his shirt over his head.

"Do you want your hair cut, my lord?" Anna tested the sharpness of the scissor blades against her thumb. "Or perhaps not?"

"Cut," his lordship replied, giving her a slow perusal. "I gather from your vexed expression there is something for which I must apologize. I confess to a mood both distracted and resentful."

"When somebody does you a decent turn," she said as she began to comb out his damp hair, "you do not respond with sarcasm and innuendo, my lord." She took particular care at the back of his head, where she knew he was yet healing from the drubbing she'd given him.

"You have a deft touch. Much more considerate than my valet."

"Your valet is a self-important little toady," Anna said, working around to the side of his head, "and that is not an apology."

"Well, I am sorry," the earl said, grabbing her hand by the wrist to still the comb. "I have an appointment at Carlton House this afternoon, and I most petulantly and assuredly do not want to go."

"Carlton House?" Anna lowered her hand, but the earl did not release her. "What an important fellow you are, to have business with the Regent himself."

He turned her hand over and studied the lines of her palm for a moment.

He smoothed his thumb over her palm. "Prinny will likely stick his head in the door briefly, tell us how much he appreciates our contributions to this great land, and then resume his afternoon's entertainments."

"But you cannot refuse to go," Anna said, taking a guess, "for it is a great honor, and so on."

"It is a tiresome damned pain in my arse," the earl groused. "You have no wedding ring, Mrs. Seaton, nor does your finger look to have ever been graced by one."

"Since I have no husband at present," Anna said, retrieving her hand, "a ring is understandably absent also."

"Who was this grandfather," the earl asked, "the one who taught you how to do Tolliver's job while smelling a great deal better than Tolliver?"

"My paternal grandfather raised me, more or less from childhood on," Anna said, knowing the truth would serve up to a point. "He was a florist and a perfumer and a very good man."

"Hence the flowers throughout my humble abode. Don't take off too much," he directed. "I prefer not to look newly shorn."

"You have no time for this," Anna said, hazarding another guess as she snipped carefully to trim up the curling hair at his nape. She'd snip, snip then brush the trimmings from his bare shoulders. It went like that, snip, snip, brush until she leaned up and blew gently on his nape instead, then resumed snipping.

When she leaned in again, she caught the scent of his woodsy, spicy cologne. The fragrance and putting her mouth just a few inches from his exposed nape left her insides with an odd, fluttery disconcerted feeling. She lingered behind him, hoping her blush was subsiding as she finished her task. "There." This time she brushed her fingers over his neck several more times. "I believe you are presentable, or your hair is."

"The rest of me is yet underdressed." He held out his hand for the scissors. "Now where is my damned shirt?"

She handed him his damned shirt and would have turned to go, except his cravat had also sprouted wings and flown off to an obscure location on the door of his wardrobe, followed by his cuff links, and stickpin, and so forth. When he started muttering that neckcloths were altogether inane in the blistering heat, she gently pushed his fingers aside and put both hands on his shoulders.

"Steady on." She looked him right in the eye. "It's only a silly committee, and you need only leave a bank draft then be about your day. How elegant do you want to look?"

"I want to look as plain as I can without being a Quaker," the earl said. "My father loves this sort of thing, back-slapping, trading stories, and haggling politics."

Anna finished a simple, elegant knot and took the stickpin from the earl's hand. "Once again, you find yourself doing that which you do not enjoy, because it is your duty. Quizzing glass?"

"No. I do put a pair of spectacles on a fob."

"How many fobs, and do you carry a watch?" Anna found a pair of spectacles on the escritoire and waited while the earl sorted through his collection of fobs. He presented her with one simple gold chain.

"I do not carry a time piece to Carlton House," he explained, "for it serves only to reinforce how many hours I am wasting on the Regent's business." Anna bent to thread the chain through the buttonhole of his waistcoat and tucked the glasses into his watch pocket, giving the earl's tummy a little pat when the chain was hanging just so across his middle.

"Will I do?" the earl asked, smiling at her proprietary gesture.

"Not without a coat, you won't, though in this heat, no one would censor you for simply carrying it until you arrived at your destination."

"Coat." The earl scowled, looking perplexed.

"On the clothespress," Anna said, shaking her head in amusement.

"So it is." The earl nodded, but his eyes were on Anna. "It appears you've put me to rights, Anna Seaton, my thanks."

He bent and kissed her cheek, a gesture so startling in its spontaneity and simple affection, she could only stand speechless as the earl whisked his coat across his arm and strode from his room. The door slammed shut behind him as he yelled for Lord Valentine to meet him in the mews immediately or suffer a walk in the afternoon's heat.

Dumbstruck, Anna sat on the stool the earl had used for his trimming. He had a backward sort of charm to him, Anna thought, her fingers drifting over her cheek. After four days of barking orders, hurling thunderbolts, and scribbling lists at her in Tolliver's absence, he thanked her with a lovely little kiss.

She should have chided him—might have, if he'd held still long enough—but he'd caught her unawares, just as when he'd frowned at her hand and seen she had no wedding ring.

Her pleasure at the earl's kiss evaporating, Anna looked at her left hand. Why hadn't she thought of this detail, for pity's sake? Dress the part, she reminded herself.

She hung up some discarded ensembles of court-worthy attire, straightened up both the escritoire and the earl's bureau, which looked as if a strong wind had blown all into disarray. When she opened his wardrobe, she unashamedly leaned in and took a big whiff of the expensive, masculine scent of him while running her hand along the sleeve of a finely tailored dark green riding jacket.

He was a handsome man, but he was also a very astute man, one who would continue to spot details and put together facts, until he began to see through her to the lies and deceptions. Before then, of course, she would be gone.

❧

When he finally returned to his townhouse that evening, the earl handed his hat, gloves, and cane to a footman then made his way through the dark house to the kitchens, wanting nothing so much as a tall, cold glass of sweetened lemonade. He could summon a servant to fetch it but was too restless and keyed up to wait.

"My lord?" Mrs. Seaton sat at the long wooden table in the kitchen, shelling peas into a wooden bowl, but stood as he entered the room.

"Don't get up. I'm only here to filch myself some cold lemonade."

"Lord Valentine sent word you'd both be missing dinner." She went to the dry sink and retrieved the pitcher. The earl rummaged in the cupboards and found two glasses, which he set down on the table. Anna glanced at him curiously but filled both, then brought the sugar bowl to the table.

Westhaven watched her as she stirred sugar into his glass, his eyebrows rising in consternation.

"I take that much sugar?"

Anna put the lid back on the sugar bowl. "Either that, or you curse and make odd faces and scowl thunderously at all and sundry." She pushed his glass over to him, and took a sip out of hers.

"You don't put any in yours?" he asked, taking a satisfying swallow of his own. God above, he'd been craving this exact cold, sweet, bracing libation.

"I've learned not to use much," Anna said, sipping again. "Sugar is dear."

"Here." He held up his glass. "If you enjoy it, then you should have it."

Anna leaned back against the sink and eyed him. "And where is that sentiment in application to yourself?"

He blinked and cocked his head. "It's too late in the day for philosophical digressions."

"Have you even eaten, my lord?"

"It appears I have not."

"Well, that much of the world's injustices I can remedy," she said as she rinsed their glasses. "If you'd like to go change out of those clothes, I can bring you up a tray in a few minutes."

"If you would just get me out of this damned cravat?" He went to stand near her at the sink, waiting while she dried her hands on a towel then nudged his chin up.

"The cravat is still spotless," she informed him, wiggling at the clasp on the stickpin, "though your beautiful shirt is a trifle dusty and wilted. Hold *still*." She wiggled a little more but still couldn't undo the tiny mechanism. "Let's sit you back down at the table, my lord."

He obligingly sat on the long bench at the table, chin up.

"That's it," she said, freeing the stickpin and peering at it. "You should have a jeweler look at this." She set it on the table as her fingers went to the knot of his neckcloth. "There." She loosened the knot until the ends were trailing around his neck, and a load of weariness abruptly intensified low down, in his gut, where sheer exhaustion could weight a man into immobility. He leaned in, his temple against her waist in a gesture reminiscent of when she tended his scalp wound.

"Lord Westhaven?" Her hand came down to rest on his nape, then withdrew, then settled on him again. He knew he should move but didn't until she stroked a hand over the back of his head. God in heaven, what was he about? And with his housekeeper, no less. He pushed to his feet and met her eyes.

"Apologies, Mrs. Seaton. A tray would be appreciated."

Anna watched him go, thinking she'd never seen him looking quite so worn and drawn. His day had been trying, it seemed, but it struck her that more than the challenge of a single meeting at Carlton House, what likely bothered him was the prospect of years of such meetings.

When she knocked on his door, there was no immediate response, so she knocked again and heard a muffled command of some sort. She balanced the tray and pushed open the door, only to find the earl was not in his sitting room.

"In here," the earl called from the bedroom. He was in a silk dressing gown and some kind of loose pajama pants, standing at the French doors to his balcony.

"Shall I put it outside?"

"Please." He opened the door and took half a step back, allowing Anna just enough room to pass before him. "Will you join me?" He followed her out and closed the door behind him.

"I can sit for a few minutes," Anna replied, eyeing the closed door meaningfully.

If he picked up on her displeasure, he ignored it.

Anna suspected he was too preoccupied with the thought of sustenance to understand her concern, though, so she tried to dismiss it, as well.

He was just in want of company at the end of a trying day.

He took the tray and set it on a low table then dragged the chaise next to it. "How is it you always know exactly what to put on a tray and how to arrange it, so a man finds his appetite perfectly satisfied?"

"When you are raised by a man who loves flowers," Anna said, "you develop an eye for what is pleasing and for how to please him."

"Was he an old martinet, your grandfather?" the earl asked, fashioning himself a sandwich.

"Absolutely not," Anna said, taking the other wicker seat. "He was the most gracious, loving, happy man it will ever be my pleasure to know."

"Somehow, I cannot see anyone describing me as gracious, loving, and happy." He frowned at his sandwich as if in puzzlement.

"You are loving," Anna replied staunchly, though she hadn't exactly planned for those words to leave her mouth.

"Now that is beyond surprising." The earl eyed her in the deepening shadows. "How do you conclude such a thing, Mrs. Seaton?"

"You have endless patience with your family, my lord," she began. "You escort your sisters everywhere; you dance attendance on them and their hordes of friends at every proper function; you harry and hound the duke so his wild starts are not the ruination of his duchy. You force yourself to tend to mountains of business which you do not enjoy, so your family may be safe and secure all their days."

"That is business," the earl said, looking nonplussed that his first sandwich had disappeared, until Anna handed him a second. "The head of the family tends to business."

"Did your sainted brother Bart ever tend to business?" Anna asked, stirring the sugar up from the bottom of the earl's drink.

"My sainted brother Bart, as you call him, did not live to be more than nine-and-twenty," the earl pointed out, "and at that age, the heir to a duke is expected to carouse, gamble, race his bloodstock, and enjoy life."

"And what age are you, your lordship?"

He sat back and took a sip of his drink. "Were you a man, I could tell you to go to hell, you know."

"Were I a man," Anna said, "I would have already told you the same thing."

"Oh?" He smiled, not exactly sweetly. "At which particular moment?"

"When you fail to offer a civil greeting upon seeing a person first thing in the day. When you can't be bothered to look a person in the eye when you offer your rare word of thanks or encouragement. When you take out your moods and frustrations on others around you, like a child with no sense of how to go on."

"Ye gods." The earl held up a staying hand. "Pax! You make me sound like the incarnation of my father."

"If the dainty little glass slipper fits, my lord..." Anna shot back, glad for the gathering shadows.

"You are fearless," the earl said, his tone almost humorous.

"I don't mean to scold you"—Anna shook her head, courage faltering—"because you are a truly decent man, but lately, my lord…"

"Lately?"

"You are out of sorts. I have mentioned this before."

"And how do you know, Anna Seaton, I am not always a bear with a sore paw? Some people are given to unpleasant demeanors, and it is just their nature."

Anna shook her head. "Not you. You are serious but not grim; you are proud but not arrogant; you care a great deal for the people you love but have only limited means of expressing it."

"You have made a study of me," the earl said, sounding as if he were relieved her conclusions were so flattering—if not quite accurate. "And where in my litany of virtues do you put my unwillingness to marry?"

Anna shrugged. "Perhaps you are simply not yet ready to limit your attentions to one woman."

"You think fidelity a hallmark of titled marriages, Mrs. Seaton?" The earl snorted and took a sip of his drink.

So I'm back to Mrs. Seaton, Anna thought, knowing the topic had gotten sensitive.

"You want what your parents have, my lord," Anna said, rising.

"Children who refuse to marry—assuming they remain extant?" the earl shot back.

"Your parents love each other," Anna said, taking in the back gardens below as moonlight cast them in silvery beauty. "They love each other as friends and lovers and partners and parents." She turned, finding him on his feet directly behind her. "That is why you will not settle for some little widgeon picked out by your well-meaning papa."

The earl took a step closer to her. "And what if I am in need, Anna Seaton, not of this great love you surmise between my parents but simply of some uncomplicated, lusty passion between two willing adults?"

He took the last step between them, and Anna's middle simply vanished. Where her vital organs used to reside, there was a great, gaping vacuum, a fluttery nothingness that grew larger and more dumbstruck as the earl's hands settled with breathtaking gentleness on her shoulders. He slid his palms down her arms, grasping her hands, and easing her toward him.

"Passion between two willing adults?" Anna repeated, her voice coming out whispery, not the incredulous retort she'd meant it to be.

The earl responded by taking her hands and wrapping them around his waist then enfolding Anna against his body.

She had been here before, she thought distractedly, held in his arms, the night breezes playing in the branches above them, the scent of flowers intoxicatingly sweet in the darkness. And as before, he caressed her back in slow, soothing circles that urged her more fully against him.

"I cannot allow this." Anna breathed in his scent and rested her cheek against the cool silk of his dressing gown. He shifted, easing the material aside, and her face touched his bare chest. She did not even try to resist the pleasure of his clean, male skin beneath her cheek.

"You cannot," he whispered, but it didn't sound like he was agreeing with her. "You should not," he clarified, "but perhaps, Anna Seaton, you can allow just a kiss, stolen on a soft summer evening."

Oh dear lord, she thought, wanting to hide her face against the warmth of his chest. He thought to kiss her. *He was kissing her*, delicate little nibbles that stole a march along her temple then her jaw. Oh, he knew what he was about, too, for his lips were soft and warm and coaxing, urging her to turn her head just so and tip her chin thus...

He settled his mouth over hers with a sigh, the joining of their lips making Anna more aware of every aspect of the moment—the crickets singing, the distant clop of hooves one street over, the soughing of the scented breeze, and the thumping of her heart like a kettledrum against her chest.

"Just a kiss, Anna..." he reminded her, her name on his lips a caress Anna felt to her soul. Her sturdy country-girl's bones melted, leaving her weight resting against him in shameless wonder. When his tongue slipped along the seam of her lips, her knees turned weak, and a whimper of pleasure welled. Soft, sweet, lemony tart and seductive, he stole into her mouth, giving her time to absorb each lush caress of lips and breath and tongue.

And then, as if his mouth weren't enough of a sin, his hands slid down her back in a slow, warm press that ended with him cupping her derriere, pulling her into his greater height and into the hard ridge of male flesh that rose between them. She didn't flinch back. She went up on her toes and pressed herself more fully against him, her hands finding their way inside his dressing gown to knead the muscles of his back.

She wrapped herself around him, clinging in complete abandon as her tongue gradually learned from his, and her conscience gave up, along with her common sense. She tasted him, learned the contours of his mouth and lips, then tentatively brushed a slow, curious hand over his chest.

Ye gods...

"Easy." He eased his mouth away but held her against his body, his chin on her temple. Anna forced her hands to go still as well, but she could not make herself step back.

"I'll tender my resignation first thing tomorrow," she said dully, her face pressed to his sternum.

"I won't accept it," the earl replied, stroking her back in slow sweeps.

"I'll leave anyway." She knew he could feel the blush on her face.

"I'll find you," the earl assured her, pressing one last kiss to her hair.

"This is intolerable."

"Anna," he chided, "it is just a kiss and entirely my fault. I am not myself of late, as you've noted. You must forgive me and accept my assurances I would never force an unwilling female."

She stayed in his arms, trying to puzzle out what he was going on about. Ah, God, it felt too good to be held, to be touched with such consideration and deliberation. She was wicked, shameless, lost and getting more lost still.

"Say you will forgive me," the earl rumbled, his

hands going quiet. "Men require frequent forgiveness, Anna. This is known to all."

"You don't sound sorry," she muttered, still against his chest.

"A besetting sin of my gender," and Anna could tell he was teasing—mostly.

"You aren't truly sorry." She found the strength to shove away from him but turned out to regard the night rather than face him. "But you have regret over this."

"I regret," he said directly above and behind her ear, "that I may have offended you. I regret just as much that we are not now tossing back my lavender-scented sheets in preparation for that passion between consenting adults I mentioned earlier."

"There will be no more of that," Anna said, inhaling sharply. "No more mentioning, no more kissing, no more talk of sheets and whatnot."

"As you wish," he said, still standing far too close behind her. He was careful not to touch her, but Anna could tell he was inhaling her scent, because she was doing the same with his.

"What I wish is of no moment," she said, "like the happiness of a future duke. No moment whatsoever."

He did step back at that, to her relief. Mostly, her relief.

"You have accepted my apology?" he asked, his voice cooling.

"I have."

"And you won't be resigning or disappearing without notice?"

"I will not."

"Your word, Anna?" he pressed, reverting to tones of authority.

"My word, *your lordship*."

He flinched at that, which was a minor gratification.

A silence, unhappy for her, God knew what for him, stretched between them.

"Were you to disappear, I would worry about you, you know," he said softly. He trailed his fingers down over her wrist to lace with hers and squeeze briefly.

She nodded, as there was nothing to say to such folly. Not one thing.

In the moonlight, he saw her face in profile, eyes closed, head back. His last comment seemed to strike her with the same brutal intensity as her use of his title had hit him, for she stiffened as if she'd taken an arrow in the back before dropping his hand and fleeing.

When he was sure she'd left his rooms, the earl went inside and locked his bedroom door then returned to the darkness of the balcony. He shucked his trousers, unfolded the napkin from the dinner tray, and lay back on the chaise. As his eyes fell closed, his dressing gown fell open, and he let memories of Anna Seaton fill his imagination.

In the soft, sweet darkness, he drew out his own pleasure, recalling each instant of that kiss, each *pleasure*. The clean, brisk scent of her, the softness of her lips, the way she startled minutely when his hands had settled on her shoulders. When he finally did allow himself satisfaction, the sensations were more gratifying and intense than anything he'd experienced with Elise.

It was enough, he assured himself. He was content

for one night to have kissed her and pleasured himself resoundingly. If she truly insisted he keep his distance, he would respect that, but he would make damned sure her decision was based on as much persuasive information as he could put before her.

As the night settled peacefully into his bones, he closed his eyes and started making a list.

৵ও

Anna was up early enough the next morning to see to her errand, one she executed faithfully on the first of each month—rain, shine, snow, or heat. She sat down with pen, plain paper, and ink, and printed, in the most nondescript hand she could muster, the same three words she had been writing each month for almost two years: All is well. She sanded that page and let it dry while she wrote the address of an obscure Yorkshire posting inn on an envelope. Just as she was tucking her missive into its envelope, booted footsteps warned her she would soon not have the kitchen to herself.

"Up early, aren't you, Mrs. Seaton?" the earl greeted her.

"As are you, my lord," she replied casually, sliding the letter into her reticule.

"I am off to let Pericles stretch his legs, but I find myself in need of sustenance."

"Would you like a muffin, my lord? I can fix you something more substantial, or you can take the muffin with you."

"A muffin will do nicely, or perhaps two." He narrowed his eyes at her. "You aren't going to be shy with me, are you, Mrs. Seaton?"

"Shy?" And just like that, she blushed, damn him. "Why ever would I…? Oh, shy. Of course not. A small, insignificant, forgivable indiscretion on the part of one's employer is hardly cause to become discomposed."

"Glad you aren't the type to take on, but I would not accost you where someone might come upon us," the earl said, pouring himself a measure of lemonade.

"My lord," she shot back, "you will not accost me *anywhere*."

"If you insist. Some lemonade before you go out?"

"You are attempting to be charming," Anna accused. "Part of your remorse over your misbehavior last evening."

"That must be it." He nodded. "Have some lemonade anyway. You will go marching about in the heat and find yourself parched in no time."

"It isn't that hot yet," Anna countered, accepting a glass of lemonade, "And a lady doesn't march."

"Here's to ladies who don't march." The earl saluted with his drink. "Now, about those muffins? Pericles is waiting."

"Mustn't inconvenience dear Pericles," Anna muttered loudly enough for the earl to hear her, but his high-handedness did not inspire blushes, so it was an improvement of sorts. She opened the bread box—where anybody would have known to look for the muffins—and selected the two largest. The earl was sitting on the wooden table and let Anna walk up to him to hand over the goodies.

"There's my girl." He smiled at her. "See? I don't bite, though I've been known to nibble. So what is in this batch?"

"Cinnamon and a little nutmeg, with a caramel sort of glaze throughout," Anna said. "You must have slept fairly well."

Now that she was close enough to scrutinize him, Anna saw that the earl's energy seemed to have been restored to him. He was in much better shape than he had been the previous evening, and—oh dear—the man was actually smiling, and at her.

"I did sleep well." The earl bit into a muffin. "And he is dear, you know. Pericles, that is. And this"—he looked her right in the eye—"is a superb muffin."

"Thank you, my lord." She couldn't help but smile at him when he was making such a concerted effort not to annoy her.

"Perhaps you'd like a bite?" He tore off a piece and held it out to her, and abruptly, he was being very annoying indeed.

"I'll just have one of my own."

"They are that good, aren't they?" the earl said, popping the bite into his maw. "Where do you go this early in the morning, Mrs. Seaton?"

"I have some errands," she said, pulling a crocheted summer glove over her left hand.

"Ah." The earl nodded sagely. "I have a mother and five sisters, plus scads of female cousins. I have heard of these errands. They are the province of women and seem to involve getting a dizzying amount done in a short time or spending hours on one simple task."

"They can," she allowed, watching two sizeable muffins meet their end in mere minutes. The earl rose and gave her another lordly smile.

"I'll leave you to your errands. I am fortified

sufficiently for mine to last at least until breakfast. Good day to you, Mrs. Seaton."

"Good day, my lord." Anna retrieved her reticule from the table and made for the hallway, relieved to have put her first encounter of the day with his lordship behind her.

"Mrs. Seaton?" His lordship was frowning at the table, but when he looked up at her, his expression became perfectly blank—but for the mischief in his eyes.

"My lord?" Anna cocked her head and wanted to stomp her foot. The earl in a playful mood was more bothersome than the earl in a grouchy mood, but at least he wasn't kissing her.

He held up her right glove, twirling it by a finger, and he wasn't going to give it back, she knew, unless she *marched* up to him and retrieved it.

"Thank you," she said, teeth not quite clenched. She walked over to him, and held out her hand, but wasn't at all prepared for him to take her hand in his, bring it to his lips, then slap the glove down lightly into her palm.

"You are welcome." He snagged a third muffin from the bread box and went out the back door, whistling some complicated theme by Herr Mozart that Lord Valentine had been practicing for hours earlier in the week.

Leaving Anna staring at the glove—the gauntlet?— the earl had just tossed down into her hand.

❧

"Good morning, Brother!"

Westhaven turned in the saddle to see Valentine drawing his horse alongside Pericles.

"Dare I hope that you, like I, are coming home after a night on the town?" Val asked.

"Hardly." The earl smiled at his brother as they turned up the alley toward the mews. "I've been exercising this fine lad and taking the morning air. I also ran into Dev, who seems to be thriving."

"He is becoming a much healthier creature, our brother," Val said, grinning. "He has this great, strapping 'cook/housekeeper' living with him. Keeps his appetites appeased, or so he says. But before we reach the confines of your domicile, you should be warned old Quimbey was at the Pleasure House last night, and he said His Grace is going to be calling on you to discuss the fact that your equipage was seen in the vicinity of Fairly's brother yesterday."

"So you might ply his piano the whole night through," Westhaven said, frowning mightily at his brother. Val grinned back at him and shook his head, and Westhaven felt some of his pleasure in the day evaporating in the hot morning air. "Then what is our story?"

"You have parted from Elise, as is known to all, so we hardly need concoct a story, do we?"

"Valentine." Westhaven frowned. "You know what His Grace will conclude."

"Yes, he will," Val said as he dismounted. "And the louder I protest to the contrary, the more firmly he'd believe it."

Westhaven swung down and patted Pericles's neck. "Next time, you're walking to any assignation you have with any piece of furniture housed in a brothel."

They remained silent until they were in the kitchen,

having used the back terrace to enter the house. Val went immediately to the bread box and fished out a muffin. "You want one?"

"I've already had three. Some lemonade, or tea?"

"Mix them," Val said, getting butter from the larder. "Half of each. There's cold tea in the dry sink."

"My little brother, ever the eccentric. Will you join me for breakfast?" Westhaven prepared his brother's drink as directed then poured a measure of lemonade for himself.

"Too tired." Val shook his head. "I kept an eye on things at the Pleasure House until the wee hours then found myself fascinated with a theme that closely resembles the opening to Mozart's symphony in G minor. When His Grace comes to call, I will be abed, sleeping off my night of sin with Herr Mozart. You will please inform Papa of this, and with a straight face."

His Grace presented himself in due course, with appropriate pomp and circumstance, while Val slept on in ignorant bliss above stairs. The footman minding the door, cousin to John, knew enough to announce such an important personage, and did so, interrupting the earl and Mr. Tolliver as they were wrapping up a productive morning.

"Show His Grace in," the earl said, excusing Tolliver and deciding not to deal with his father in a parlor, when the library was likely cooler and had no windows facing the street. Volume seemed to work as well as brilliance when negotiating with his father, but sheer ruthlessness worked best of all.

"Your Grace." The earl rose and bowed deferentially.

"A pleasure as always, though unexpected. I hope you fare well?"

"Unexpected." His Grace snorted, but he was in a good mood, his blue eyes gleeful. "I'll tell you what's unexpected is finding you at a bordello. Bit beneath you, don't you think? And at two of the clock on a broiling afternoon! Ah, youth."

"And how is Her Grace?" the earl asked, going to the sideboard. "Brandy, whiskey?"

"Don't mind if I have a tot," the duke said. "Damned hot out, and that's a fact. Your mother thrives as always in my excellent and devoted care. Your dear sisters are off to Morelands with her, and I was hoping to find your brother here so I might dispatch him there, as well."

The earl handed the duke his drink, declining to drink spirits himself at such an early hour.

The duke sipped regally at his liquor. "I suppose if Valentine were about, I'd be hearing his infernal racket. Not bad." He lifted his glass. "Not half bad, after all."

Mrs. Seaton's words returned to the earl as he watched his father sipping casually at some of the best whiskey ever distilled: You fail to offer a civil greeting upon seeing a person first thing in the day... You can't be bothered to look a person in the eye when you offer your rare word of thanks or encouragement...

And it hit him like a blow to the chest that as much as he didn't want to be the next Duke of Moreland, he very especially did not want to turn into another version of *this* Duke of Moreland.

"If I see Val," Westhaven said, "I will tell him the ladies are seeking his company at Morelands."

"Hah." The duke set aside his empty glass. "His mother and sisters, you mean. They're about the only ladies he has truck with these days."

"Not so," the earl said. "He is much in demand as an escort and considered very good company by many."

The duke heaved a martyr's sigh. "Your brother is a mincing fop, but word is you at least had him in hand at Fairly's whorehouse. Have to ask, how you'd do it?"

Now that was rare, for the duke to ask a question to which he sought an answer. Westhaven considered his reply carefully.

"I had heard Fairly has an excellent new Broadwood on the premises, which, in fact, he does." A truth, as far as it went.

"So all I have to do," the duke said with sudden inspiration, "is find some well-bred filly of a musical nature, and we can get him leg-shackled?"

"It might be worth considering, but I'd be subtle about it, ask him to escort Her Grace to musicales, for example. He won't come to the bridle if he sees your hand in things."

"Damned stubborn," His Grace pronounced. "Just like his mama. A bit more to wet the whistle, if you please." Westhaven brought the decanter to where his father sat on the leather couch, and poured half a measure into the glass. On closer inspection, the heat was taking a toll on His Grace. His ruddy complexion looked more florid than usual, and his breathing seemed a trifle labored.

"Speaking of stubbornness," the earl said when he'd put the decanter back on the sideboard, "I no longer have an association with the fair Elise."

"What?" His Grace frowned. "You've lost your taste for the little blonde?"

"I wouldn't say I've lost my taste for the little blonde, so much as I've never had a taste for my privacy being invaded nor fancied the Moreland title going to somebody who lacks a drop of Windham blood."

"What are you blathering on about, Westhaven? I rather liked your Elise. Seemed a practical woman, if you know what I mean."

"Meaning she took your bribe, or your dare," the earl concluded. "Then she turned around and offered her favors elsewhere, to at least one other tall, green-eyed lordling that I know of, and perhaps several others, as well."

"She's a bit of a strumpet, Westhaven, though passably discreet. What would you expect?" The duke finished his drink with a satisfied smack of his lips.

"She's Renfrew's intended, if your baiting inspired her to get with child, Your Grace," the earl replied. "You put her up to trying to get a child, and the only way she could do that was to pass somebody else's off as mine."

"Good God, Westhaven." The duke rose, looking pained. "You aren't telling me you can't bed a damned woman, are you?"

"Were that the case, I would not tell you, as such matters are *supposed* to be private. What I am telling you is if you attempt to manipulate one more woman into my bed, I will not marry. Back off, Your Grace, or you will wish you had."

"Are you threatening your own father, Westhaven?" The duke thumped his glass down, hard.

"I am assuring him," the earl replied softly, "if he attempts even once more to violate my privacy, I will make him regret it for all of his remaining days."

"Violate your…? Oh, for the love of God, boy." The duke turned to go, hand on the door latch. "I did not come here to argue with you, for once. I came to tell you it was well done, getting your brother to Fairly's, reminding him what… Never mind. I came with only good intentions, and here you are threatening me. What would your dear mama think of such disrespect? Of course I am concerned; you are past thirty, and you have neither bride nor heir nor promise thereof. You think you can live forever, but you and your brother are proof that even when a man has decades to raise up his sons, sometimes the task is yet incomplete and badly done. You aren't without sense, Westhaven, and you at least show some regard for the Moreland consequence. All I want is to see the succession secured before I die, and to see your mother has some grandchildren to spoil and love. Good day."

He made a grand, door-slamming exit and left his son eyeing the decanter longingly. When a soft knock came a few minutes later, the earl was still so lost in thought, he barely heard it.

"Come in."

"My lord?" Mrs. Seaton, looking prim, cool, and tidy, strode into the room and gave him her signature brisk curtsy. "The luncheon hour approaches. Shall we serve you on the terrace, in the dining parlor, or would you like a tray in here?"

"I seem to have lost my appetite, Mrs. Seaton." The

earl rose from his desk and walked around to sit on the front of it. "His Grace came to call, and our visit degenerated into its usual haranguing and shouting."

"One could hear this," Mrs. Seaton said, her expression sympathetic. "At least on His Grace's part."

"I was congratulated on dragging my little brother to a brothel, for God's sake. The old man would have fit in wonderfully in days of yore, when bride and groom were expected to bed each other before cheering onlookers."

"My lord, His Grace means well."

"He will tell you he does," the earl agreed. "Just being a conscientious steward of the Moreland succession. But in truth, it's his own consequence he wants to protect. If I fail to reproduce to his satisfaction, then he will be embarrassed, plain and simple. It's not enough that he sired five sons, three of whom still live, but he must see a dynasty at his feet before he departs this earth."

Mrs. Seaton remained quiet, and the earl recalled he'd sung this lament in her hearing before.

"Is my brother asleep?"

"He is, but he asked to be awakened not later than two of the clock. He wants to put in his four hours before repairing again to Viscount Fairly's establishment."

"I do believe my brother is studying to become a madam."

Again, his housekeeper did not see fit to make any reply.

"I'll take a tray out back," the earl said, "but you needn't go to all the usual bother...setting the table, arranging the flowers, and so forth. A tray will do, as long as there's plenty of sweetened lemonade to go with the meal."

"Of course, my lord." She bobbed her curtsy, but he snaked out a hand to encircle her wrist before she could go.

"Are you unhappy with me?" he asked, eyeing her closely. "Bad enough His Grace finds fault with me at every turn, Mrs. Seaton. I am trying very hard not to annoy my staff as much as my father annoys me."

"I do not think on your worst day you could be half so annoying to us as that man is to you. Your patience with him is admired."

"By whom?"

"Your staff," she replied. "And your housekeeper."

"The admiration of my housekeeper," the earl said, "is a consummation devoutly to be wished."

He brought her wrist to his lips and kissed the soft skin below the base of her thumb, lingering long enough that he felt the steady beat of her pulse.

She scowled at him, whirled, and left without a curtsy.

So much, the earl thought as he watched her retreat, for the admiration of his housekeeper.

Four

"I NEVER DID ASK IF YOU SUCCESSFULLY COMPLETED your errands this morning." Westhaven put aside his copy of *The Times* as Anna set his lunch tray before him.

"I did. Will there be anything else, my lord?"

He regarded her standing with her hands folded, her expression neutral amid the flowers and walks of his back garden.

"Anna," he began, but he saw his use of her name made her bristle. "Please sit, and I do mean will you please."

She sat, perched like an errant schoolgirl on the very edge of her chair, back straight, eyes front.

"You are scolding me without saying a word," the earl said on a sigh. "It was just a kiss, Anna, and I had the impression you rather enjoyed it, too."

She looked down, while a blush crept up the side of her neck.

"That's the problem, isn't it?" he said with sudden, happy insight. "You could accept my apology and treat me with cheerful condescension, but you *enjoyed* our kiss."

"My lord," she said, addressing the hands she fisted in her lap, "can you not accept that were I to encourage your…mischief, I would be courting my own ruin?"

"Ruin?" He said with a snort. "Elise will be enjoying an entire estate for the rest of her days as a token of ruin at my hands—among others—if ruin you believe it to be. I did not take her virginity, either, *Mrs. Seaton*, and I am not a man who casually discards others."

She was silent then raised her eyes, a mulish expression on her face.

"I will not seek another position as a function of what has gone between us so far, but you must stop."

"Stop what, Anna?"

"You should not use my name, my lord," she said, rising. "I have not given you leave to do so."

He rose, as well, as if she were a lady deserving of his manners. "May I ask your permission to use your given name, at least when we are private?"

He'd shocked her, he saw with some satisfaction. She'd thought him too autocratic to ask, and he was again reminded of his father's ways. But she was looking at him now, really looking, and he pressed his advantage.

"I find it impossible to think of you as Mrs. Seaton. In this house, there is no other who treats me as you do, *Anna*. You are kind but honest, and sympathetic without being patronizing. You are the closest thing I have here to an ally, and I would ask this small boon of you."

He watched as she closed her eyes and waged some internal struggle, but in the anguish on her face, he suspected victory in this skirmish was to be his. She'd grant him his request, precisely because he had made it a request, putting a small measure of power exclusively into her hands.

She nodded assent but looked miserable over it.

"And you," he said, letting concern—not guilt, surely—show in his gaze, "you must consider me an ally, as well, Anna."

She speared him with a stormy look. "An ally who would compromise my reputation, knowing without it I am but a pauper or worse."

"I do not seek to bring you ruin," he corrected her. "And I would never force my will on you."

Anna stood, and he thought her eyes were suspiciously bright. "Perhaps, my lord, you just did."

He stared after her for long moments, wrestling with her final accusation but coming to no tidy answers. He could offer Anna Seaton an option, a choice other than decades of stepping and fetching and serving. He desired her and enjoyed her company out of bed, a peculiar realization though not unwelcome. But his seduction would be complicated by her reticence, her infernal notions of decency.

For now, he could steal some delectable kisses—and perhaps more than kisses—while she found the resolve to refuse him altogether and send him packing.

He was lingering over his lemonade when Val wandered out looking sleepy and rumpled, shirt open at the throat and cuffs turned back.

"Ye gods, it is too hot to sleep." He reached over and drained the last of his brother's drink. "You do like it sweet."

"Helps with my disposition. And as I did indeed have to deal with His Grace this morning, I feel entitled."

"How bad was he?" Val asked as he sat and crossed his long legs at the ankle.

"Bad enough. Wanted to chat about the scene at Fairly's but left yelling about grandchildren and disrespect."

"Sounds about like your usual with him," Val said as John Footman brought out a second tray, this one bearing something closer to breakfast.

"Mrs. S said to tell you this one is sweetened, my lord." John set one glass before the earl. "And this one, less so," he said as he placed the other before Val.

"I think she puts mint in it," Val said after a long swallow.

"Mrs. Seaton?" the earl asked, sipping at his own drink. "Probably. She delights in all matters domestic."

"And she did not appear to be delighting in you, when she was out here earlier."

"Valentine." The earl stared hard at his brother. "Were you spying on me?"

Val pointed straight up, to where the balcony of his bedroom overlooked the terrace. "I sleep on that balcony most nights," he explained, "and you were not whispering. I, however, was sleeping and caught the tail end of an interesting exchange."

The earl had the grace to study his drink at some silent length.

"Well?" He met his younger brother's eyes, awaiting castigation.

"She is a decent woman, Westhaven, and if you trifle with her, she won't be decent any longer, ever again. What is a fleeting pleasure for you changes her life irrevocably, and you can never, ever change it back. I am not sure you want that on your appallingly overactive conscience, as much as I applaud your improvement in taste."

The earl swirled his drink and realized with a sinking feeling Val had gotten his graceful, talented hands on a truth.

"Maybe," Val went on, "you should just marry the woman, hmm? You get on with her, you respect her, and if you marry her, she becomes a duchess. She could do worse, and it would appease Their Graces."

"She would not like the duchess part."

"You could make it worth her while," Val said, his tone full of studied nonchalance.

"Listen to you. You would encourage me into the arms of a pox-ridden gin whore if it would result in His Grace getting a few grandsons."

"No, I would not, or you wouldn't have gotten that little postscript from me regarding Elise's summer recreation, would you?"

The earl rose and regarded his brother. "You are a pestilential irritant of biblical proportions. If I do not turn out to be an exact replica of His Grace, it will be in part due to your aggravating influence."

Val was grinning around a mouthful of muffin, but he nonetheless managed to reply intelligibly to his brother's retreating back. "Love you, too."

❧

Anna wasn't fooled. Since their confrontation over the lunch table earlier in the week, the earl had kept a distance, but it was a thoughtful distance. She'd caught him eyeing her as she watered the bouquets in his library, or rising to his feet when she entered a room. It was unnerving, like being stalked by a hungry tiger.

And as the week wore on, the heat became worse, with violent displays of lightning and thunder at night but no cooling rains to bring relief. The entire household was drinking cold tea, lemonade, and cold cider by the gallon, and livery was worn only at the front door. Everybody's cuffs were turned back, collars were loosened, and petticoats were discarded.

Anna heard the front door slam and knew the earl had returned after a long afternoon in the City, transacting business of some sort. She assembled a tray and waited to hear which door above would slam next. She had to cock her head, because Valentine was playing his pianoforte. The music wasn't loud, but rather dense with feeling, and not happy feeling at that.

"He misses our brothers," the earl said from the kitchen doorway. "More than I realized, as, perhaps, do I."

The music shifted and became dark, despairing, all the more convincingly so for being quiet. This wasn't the passionate, bewildered grief of first loss; it was the grinding, desolate ache that followed. Anna's own losses and grief rose up and threatened to swamp her, even as the earl moved into the kitchen and eyed the tray on the counter.

His eyes shifted back up just in time for Anna to be caught wiping a tear from the corner of her eye.

"Come." He took her hand and led her to the table, sitting her down, passing her his handkerchief, fetching the tray, then taking the place beside her, hip to hip.

They listened for long moments, the cool of the kitchen cocooning them both in the beauty and pain of the music, and then Val's playing shifted again, still sad but with a piercingly sweet lift of acceptance and peace to it. Death, his music seemed to say, was not the end, not when there was love.

"Your brother is a genius."

The earl leaned back to rest his shoulder blades along the wall behind them. "A genius who likely only plays like this late at night among whores and strangers. He's still a little lost with it." He slipped his fingers through Anna's and gently closed his hand. "As, I suppose, am I."

"It has been less than a year?"

"It has. Victor asked that we observe only six months of full mourning, but my mother is still grieving deeply. I should have offered Valentine a bunk months ago."

"He probably would not have come," Anna said, turning their hands over to study his brown knuckles. "I think your brother needs a certain amount of solitude."

"In that, he and I and Devlin are all alike."

"Devlin is your half brother?" Ducal bastards were apparently an accepted reality, at least in the Windham family.

"He is." Westhaven nodded, giving her back her hand. "Tea or cider or lemonade?"

"Any will do," Anna said, noting that Val's music was lighter now, still tender but sweetly wistful, the grief nowhere evident.

"Lemonade, then." The earl sugared his, added a spoonful to Anna's, and set it down before her. "You might as well drink it here with me, and I'll tell you of my illustrious family." He sat again, but more than their hips touched this time, as his whole side lay along hers, and Anna felt heat and weariness in his long frame. One by one, the earl described his siblings, both deceased and extant, legitimate and not.

"You speak of each of them with such affection," Anna said. "It isn't always so with siblings."

"If I credit my parents with one thing," the earl said, running his finger around the rim of his glass, "it is with making our family a real family. They didn't send us boys off to school until we were fourteen or so, and then just so we could meet our form before we went to university. We were frightfully well educated, too, so there was no feeling inadequate before our peers. We did things all together, though it took a parade of coaches to move us hither and thither, but Dev and Maggie often went with us, particularly in the summer."

"They are received, then?"

"Everywhere. Her Grace made it obvious that a virile young lord's premarital indiscretions were not to be censored, and the die was cast. It helps that Devlin is charming, handsome, and independently wealthy, and Maggie is as pretty and well mannered as her sisters."

"That would tend to encourage a few doors to open."

"And what of you, Anna Seaton?" The earl cocked his head to regard her. "You have a brother and a sister, and you had a grandpapa. Did you all get along?"

"We did not," Anna said, rising and taking her glass to the sink. "My parents died when I was young. My brother grew up with a lack of parental supervision, though my grandfather tried to provide guidance. My parents, I'm told, loved each other sincerely. Grandpapa took us into his home immediately when they died, but as my brother is ten years my senior, he was considerably less malleable. There was a lot of shouting."

"As there is between my father and me." The earl smiled at her when she sat back down across from him.

"Your mother doesn't shout at him, does she?"

"No." The earl looked intrigued with that observation. "She just gets this pained, disappointed look and calls him Percival or Your Grace instead of Percy."

"My grandfather had that look polished to a shine." Anna grimaced. "It crushed me the few times I merited it."

"So you were a good girl, Anna Seaton?" The earl was smiling at her with a particular light in his eyes, one Anna didn't understand, though it wasn't especially threatening.

"Headstrong, but yes, I was a good girl." She rose again, and this time took his glass with her. "And I am."

"Are you busy Tuesday next?" he asked, rising to lean against the wall, arms crossed over his chest as he watched her rinse out their glasses.

"Not especially," Anna replied. "We do our big market on Wednesday, which is also half-day for the men."

"Then can I requisition your time, if it's decent weather?"

"For?" She eyed him warily, unable to sense his mood.

"I have recently committed into another's keeping a Windham property known as Monk's Crossing," he explained. "My father and I agree each of my sisters ought to be dowered with some modestly profitable, pleasant property, preferably close to London. Having transferred ownership of one, I am looking at procuring another. The girls socialized little this year, due to Victor's death, but at least two of them have possibilities that might come to something in the next year. I'd like to have their dower properties in presentable condition."

"So what are we doing, Tuesday next?" Anna asked, folding her arms across her chest.

"I am going to inspect a potential dower property out in Surrey, a couple hours from Town, and for sale at a suspiciously reasonable price. I would like you to accompany me to assess its appeal to feminine sensibilities."

"Whatever does that mean?"

The earl pushed off the wall and waved a hand. "There are things about a house I just don't take in, being male. You women understand subtleties, like where windows will give effective ventilation, what rooms will be cold in winter, or which fireplaces are unfortunately situated. You can assess the functionality of a kitchen at a glance, whereas I can barely find the bread box."

He moved to stand before her, looking down at her. "I can assess if a property is priced properly in relation to its size, location, and appointments, but you can assess if a house can be made into a home."

"I will go then." Anna nodded. It was a task to which she was suited, and probably only a morning's work. "But you must consider which sister will end up with this property and think about her, so you can tell me her likes and dislikes."

"Fair enough. We can discuss those particulars on the way there."

He left, moving in the direction of the music room, where Val was once again between pieces, or moods. Anna watched him go, unable to help but appreciate the lean play of muscle along his flanks.

One had to wonder how the ladies of polite society had ever managed, when all the Windham brothers had assembled in one place, particularly in evening finery or riding attire or shirt sleeves…

Five

"THE ESTATE IS CALLED WILLOW BEND," THE EARL began as they tooled out of the mews in the gray predawn light. "We should be there in less than two hours, even giving Pericles a few chances to rest."

"Have you seen it before?" Anna asked, enjoying the breeze on her face as the horse gained the street and broke to the trot.

"I have seen only sketches, hence the necessity for this trip. I should warn you I am inclined to buy it based on proximity alone. There is only so much land for sale around London, and the city grows outward each year."

The miles fell away as they talked, occasionally challenging each other, more often just sharing viewpoints and observations. When they were well out of town, the earl pulled up his gig to let the horse rest.

"Shall we walk? Pericles will stand there until Domesday or he eats every blade of grass at his feet." The earl handed her down then released the checkrein so the horse could graze for a few minutes.

"He takes his victuals seriously," Anna said.

"To any Windham male, victuals are of significant import."

"Good thing I brought a very full hamper, then, isn't it?" The earl offered her his arm, and she took it, realizing they had never in the months she'd worked for him simply walked side by side like this.

"It's a lovely morning," Anna said, taking refuge in the weather. "After all the noise and wind, I was expecting we would get at least some rain last night."

"A few drops. Val sleeps on his balcony these days and said that's all he felt."

"And where was he off to this morning?"

"To see our little niece, Rose," the earl replied, pausing before a wooden stile. "Had I been able, I'd have moved this appointment to join him, but there are several people interested in Willow Bend."

"Or so the land agent told you."

"Repeatedly and emphatically. Had I coordinated more closely with Val, though, he could have at least escorted us for much of the distance. Welbourne is not far from Willow Bend."

"Do you like children?" The stile was level at the top, so Anna settled on it, the better to watch his smile disappear at the question when he took a seat beside her.

"Babies rather intimidate me, as one can drop them, and they break, but yes, I like children. I am not particularly charming, as Val is, but children don't mind that. They want honest regard, much like a good horse does."

"But Rose was not much taken with you?"

"More to the point, Rose's mother, to whom His

Grace would have seen me wed, was not much taken with me, and in the way of children, Rose comprehended that as clearly as I did."

They fell silent, sitting side by side, until Anna felt the earl's hand steal over hers to rest there.

"Today, I am going to call you Anna, and you are going to permit me to do so, please? We will be congenial with each other and forget I am the earl and you are my housekeeper. We will enjoy a pleasant morning in the country, Anna, with none of your frowning and scolding. This is agreeable to you?"

"We will share a lovely morning in the country," Anna agreed, wanting nothing so much as to start that morning by letting her head rest against his shoulder. It was a wicked impulse and would give him all the wrong ideas.

"And seal our agreement"—the earl shifted to stand before her—"with a kiss."

He gave her time to wiggle off the hook, to hop down off the stile and dash past him, to deliver a little lecture even, but she sat, still as a mouse, while he framed her face with his bare hands and brought his lips to hers. He propped one booted foot on the stile and leaned over her as his mouth settled fully over hers.

While Anna's common sense tried to riot, the earl was in no hurry, exploring the fullness of her lips with his own, then easing away to run his nose along her hairline, then cruising back over her mouth on the way to kissing the side of her neck.

Her common sense gave a last, despairing whimper and went silent, because Anna liked that, that business of him nuzzling and kissing at her neck, at the soft flesh below her ear, at the place where her neck met her shoulder. He must have liked it, too, as he spent long minutes learning the various flavors of her nape and throat, the spots that were ticklish and the spots he could soothe with his tongue and lips.

She swayed into him, wrapping a hand around the back of his neck for support, wishing she'd thought—as he had—to take off her gloves. Oh, she knew nothing of the details of being wicked, nothing at all except that with him, she liked it. She liked the way she felt more alive wherever he touched, liked the way her insides melted at the scent and taste of him. Liked the feel of his long, muscular body so close to hers.

Anna felt a hairpin plink against her cheek and made herself draw back.

"Oh dear." She stared up at him, dumbstruck by the heat in his green eyes. "Dear, dear, dear."

The earl looked down and traced a finger along the slope of her breast to pluck the hairpin from her dress. He held it out to her, smiling as if he were presenting her with a flower.

"I may be feeling winded," he said, offering her his arm, "but by now Pericles should be well rested."

Anna took his arm, glancing over at him cautiously. The sensation of his finger sliding down her breast had been enough to make her heart kick against her ribs. God in heaven, he knew how to touch a woman, but it didn't seem to wind him at all, contrary to his words.

"You are quiet, Anna," he remarked as they climbed aboard and gained the road.

"I am overwhelmed," she said. "I think I must be a very wicked woman, my... What do I call you?"

The earl urged Pericles to the trot. "Today, you call me whatever pleases you, but why do you say you are wicked?"

"I should be remonstrating you, making you behave, chiding you for your lapses," Anna informed him, warming to her topic. "Our lapses. But my self-restraint has departed for the Orient, I suppose, and all I want..."

"All you want?" The earl kept his eyes on the empty road.

"Is to forget every pretense of common sense." Anna completed the thought, and now—now that he was all cool composure beside her—she was uncomfortable with herself. "To share more lapses with you."

"I would like that, Anna," he replied simply. "If it would please you to lapse with me, then I would enjoy it, too."

"It can't lead to anything," Anna said miserably, "except more and worse mischief."

The earl glanced over at her but had to keep some focus on the road. "Why not just enjoy these hours as we choose to spend them? I will not take liberties you deny me, Anna, not today, not ever. But for today, I will enjoy your company to the fullest extent you allow, and I will do so without regard to whether today leads to something or merely rests in memory as a pleasurable few hours spent in your company."

Anna fell silent, considering his words. If Westhaven's brother Victor could have had such a morning, able to breathe without coughing, would he have fretted over a few kisses leading to nothing, or would he have seized the hours as a gift? Knowing he could well have been riding to his death in the next battle, would Lord Bartholomew have demurred, or would he have stashed a bottle of wine in the hamper?

"And now," Anna said after a time, "you are quiet."

"It is a pretty morning." He smiled at her, including her in that prettiness. "I am in good company, and we are about a pleasant errand. Just to be away from Town, away from Tolliver's infernal correspondence, and away from Stenson's grasping fingers is reason to rejoice."

"I could not abide the touch of someone I did not like," Anna said, grimacing.

"So I do my best to stay out of his reach and to bellow like the duke when he transgresses," Westhaven said. "He is getting better, but tell me, Anna, did you just indirectly admit to liking me?"

She drew in a swift breath and saw from his expression that while he was teasing, he was also…fishing.

"Of course I like you. I like you entirely too well, and it is badly done of you to make me admit it."

"Well, let's go from bad to worse, then, and you can tell me precisely why you like me."

"You are serious?"

"I am. If you want, I will return the favor, though we have only several hours, and my list might take much longer than that."

He is flirting with me, Anna thought, incredulous. In his high-handed, serious way, the Earl of Westhaven had just paid her a flirtatious compliment. A lightness spread out from her middle, something of warmth and humor and guilty pleasure in it.

"All right." Anna nodded briskly. "I like that you are shy and honorable in the ways that count. I like that you are kind to Morgan, and to your animals, and old Nanny Fran. You are as patient with His Grace as a human can be, and you adore your brother. You are fierce, too, though, and can be decisive when needs must. You are also, I think, a romantic, and this is no mean feat for a man who spends half his days with commercial documents. Mostly, I like that you are *good*; you look after those who depend on you, you have gratitude for your blessings, and you don't think enough of yourself."

Beside her, the earl was again silent.

"Shall I go on?" Anna asked, feeling a sudden awkwardness.

"You could not possibly pay me any greater series of compliments than you just have," he said. "The man you describe is a paragon, a fellow I'd very much like to meet."

"See?" Anna nudged him with her shoulder. "You do not think enough of yourself. But I can also tell you the parts of you that irritate me—if that will make you feel better?"

"I irritate you?" The earl's eyebrows rose. "This should be interesting. You gave me the good news first, fortifying me for more burdensome truths, so let fly."

"You are proud," Anna began, her tone thoughtful. "You don't think your papa can manage anything correctly, and you won't ask your brothers nor mother nor sisters even, for help with things directly affecting them. I wonder, in fact, if you have anybody you would call a friend."

"Ouch. A very definite ouch, Anna. Go on."

"You have forgotten how to play," Anna said, "how to frolic, though I cannot fault you for a lack of appreciation for what's around you. You appreciate; you just don't seem to…indulge yourself."

"I see. And in what should I indulge myself?"

"That is for you to determine," she replied. "Marzipan has gone over well, I think, and sweets in general. You have indulged your love of music by having Val underfoot. As to what else brings you pleasure, you would be the best judge of that."

The earl turned down a shady lane lined with towering oaks and an understory of rhododendrons in vigorous bloom.

"It was you," he said. "Before Val moved in, I thought it was a neighbor playing the piano late in the evenings, but it was you. Were you playing *for me?*"

Anna glanced off to the park beyond the trees and nodded.

"It seemed somebody should. Nanny Fran said you have a marvelous singing voice, and you play well yourself, but you'd stopped playing or singing when Bart died."

"Life did not change for the better for anyone when Bart died."

They pulled up to a pretty Tudor manor house, complete with fresh thatch on the roof and gleaming mullioned windows. Pericles blew out a horsy breath that sounded suspiciously like a sigh, but the earl did not climb down.

"Before Bart left," the earl said, fiddling with the reins, "he told me he wouldn't go if I forbade it. That was the word he used…forbid. He asked my permission, and knowing his temper and his penchant for dramatics, I had misgivings about his joining up, but I did not stop him. I could see that battling the duke day after day was killing them both. Bart was getting wilder, angrier, and the duke was becoming so bewildered by his cherished heir it was painful to watch."

"If you had to do it again, would you still give your permission?"

"I would." The earl nodded after a moment. "But first I would have told my brother I loved him, and then, just maybe, he would not have had to go."

"He knew," Anna said. "Just as you know he loved you, but he was coping as well as he could in a situation where every option came with significant costs."

A considering silence stretched between them, while Anna marveled that the man beside her was so given to introspection and so adept at hiding even that.

"Let's put away this difficult topic," the earl suggested, "and look over the property, shall we?" Because the place was uninhabited, it fell to them to lead Pericles to a roomy stall in the carriage house cum stable and see him tucked in with hay and water.

They made their way to the back terrace of the house, where the earl set down the wicker hamper he'd carried from the gig, and bent to loosen a particular brick from the back stoop. He produced a key from under the brick, opened the back door, and gestured for Anna to precede him.

"I like what I see," Anna said, folding her shawl on the kitchen counter. She turned to put her gloves on

top of the shawl, only to find the earl had been standing immediately behind her.

"As do I," he said, looking directly down at her.
His eyes were steady, even searching. Looking into
those eyes, Anna admitted she'd been deceiving
herself. She was a good girl, but at least part of her
was here to be wicked with him—maybe just a little
wicked by his standards but more wicked than Anna
had ever wanted to be before.

He made no move to touch her, though, and so she
frowned until insight struck: he was waiting for her to
touch him, to do as she pleased.

He merely stood there, hands at his sides, watching
her, until she closed the distance between them, slid
both hands around his waist, and rested her forehead
against his collarbone.

"Is this all you want, Anna?" He brought his arms
around her and urged her to lean into him. "Merely
an embrace? I'll understand it, if you do."

"It isn't merely an embrace," she replied, loving
the feel of his lean muscles and long bones against
her body. "It is *your* embrace, and your scent, and the
cadence of your breathing, and the warmth of your
hands. To me, there is nothing mere about it. "

She remained in his arms, feeling the way his hands
learned the planes and angles of her back, feeling his
mind absorb and consider her words.

"Let's explore the house," he suggested, "then
poke around the grounds and outbuildings before it
gets too hot."

She nodded, feeling a hint of wariness.

"Anna." He smiled faintly as he stepped back. "I am

not going to maul you, ever. And I did bring you out here for the purpose of evaluating this property, not becoming my next mistress."

"Your next…?"

"Badly put." The earl took her hand. "Forget I said it."

She let him tow her along out of the kitchen and through the various pantries, cellars, laundries, and servants' quarters on the ground floor. Not until he led her up the stairs to the main floor and she was standing beside him in the library did Anna find the words she needed.

"This was the former owner's pride and joy," the earl said, "and I must admit, for a country library, it is a magnificent room." The ceilings were twelve feet at least, with windows that ran the entire height of the room on two walls. Two massive fieldstone fireplaces sat one on each outside wall, both with raised hearths and richly carved chestnut mantels.

"It's such a pretty wood," the earl remarked, stroking a hand across one mantel. "Warmer to the eye than oak, and lighter in weight, but almost as strong." Anna watched that hand caressing the grain of the carved surface and felt an internal shiver.

"I would never be a man's mistress, you know." She sat on the hearth and regarded him. Somewhere in their travels through the house, he had taken off his jacket and waistcoat, and turned back his cuffs. He had dispensed with a neckcloth altogether in deference to the heat, but the informality of his attire only made him handsome in a different way.

"Why not?" The earl didn't seem surprised nor

offended, he just sat himself beside her on the cool, hard stones and shot her a sidewise glance.

"It isn't my precious virtue, if that's what you're thinking." Anna wrapped her arms around her knees.

"The thought had crossed my mind you might set store by a chaste reputation."

"Of course I do." She laid her cheek on her knees and regarded him with a frown. "Though only up to a point. Being a mistress has no appeal, though, because of the money."

"You eschew good coin?" the earl said, and though his tone was casual, Anna detected a hint of pique in it.

"I most assuredly do not, but how can a man accept intimacies from a woman who is paid to pretend she cares for his attentions? It seems to me an insupportable farce and as degrading to the man as the woman."

"Degrading how?" He was amused now, or at least diverted.

"If a woman will allow you liberties only if you pay her," Anna explained, "then it's your coin she treasures, not your kisses or caresses or whatnot."

He was trying not to smile now. "Most men care only for the whatnot, Anna. They trouble themselves little about what they parted with or put up with to procure it."

"Then most men are easily manipulated and to be pitied. One begins to suspect holy matrimony was devised for the protection of men, and not the fairer sex after all."

"So you have no more regard for being a wife than you do being a mistress?"

"It depends entirely on whose wife we're talking about." Anna rose and went to look out the windows. "This room is so pretty and light and inviting. I could particularly see curling up on one of these window seats with Sir Walter Scott or some John Donne."

"Let's assess some more of the house," the earl said, lacing his fingers with hers. As they wended their way from room to room, Anna noted that the earl, away from his townhouse at least, was a toucher. She'd seen the same tendency when he was with his brother. He laid a hand on Val's sleeve, straightened Val's collar, patted his back, and otherwise treated his brother with affection. It was the same with Nanny Fran, whom he kissed on the cheek, hugged, and allowed to treat him with similar familiarity.

With Anna, he took her hand, offered his arm, put his hand on the small of her back, brushed aside her hair, and otherwise kept up a steady campaign of casual touches.

Casual to him, Anna thought, knowing she was being sillier than any woman of five and twenty had a right to be. To her, these little gestures were sweet and attractive, that is, they fascinated her and made her want to stand too close to him.

Outside, he assisted her over stiles and fences, picked her a daisy and positioned it behind her ear, stole a little kiss under the rose arbor, and tucked her against his side while they explored the garden walks.

"Were you like this with Elise?" Anna asked when they'd found a wooden bench in some shade near the roses.

"Good God, Anna." The earl looked over at her in consternation. "A man does not discuss his mistress with decent women."

"I am not asking about Elise. I am asking about you."

"When I saw Elise in social settings," the earl replied, eyes on the house across the gardens, "we were cordial. I occasionally danced with her, but she did not enjoy my partnering, as I am too tall."

"You are too...?" Anna scowled at that. "You are not too tall."

"Perhaps you can prove that point by dancing with me sometime?"

She cocked her head at him and decided he was teasing. "So when you met socially, you behaved as acquaintances. What about when you were simply whiling away a morning?"

"When I did not run into Elise at an evening gathering of polite society, I saw her by appointment, in the afternoon," the earl said, resting an arm along the back of the bench with a sigh.

"By *appointment, only*?" Anna's surprise seemed to perplex him.

"You know my week included visits to her," the earl replied mildly. "Regular visits allowed her to schedule the rest of her affairs, so to speak."

"The rest of her affairs? And is this all you wanted? An hour of her attention twice a week, scheduled in advance so as to only minimally inconvenience her?"

"Well, more or less," the earl admitted, clearly puzzled by Anna's indignation.

"And *that* is how you go about *passion*? I suppose you

left her free to pursue any other pair of broad shoulders she pleased when you were not bothering her?"

"In retrospect, one can admit there were a few subtle indicators the situation was not ideal, but we are not discussing this further, Anna Seaton. And for your information, that is not how I prefer to go about passion." He folded her hand between both of his and fell silent. Topic closed.

"You deserve more than to be tolerated for a few hours a week in exchange for parting with your coin. Any good man does."

"Your sentiments are appreciated," the earl said, amusement back in his tone. "Shall we see what we can find in that hamper you brought? The thing weighed a ton, which is good, as my appetite is making itself known."

Topic closed, subject *changed*.

"We'll need the blanket from the gig, I think," Anna said, willing to drop the discussion of his former mistress. "I saw no dining table nor much in the way of chairs inside."

"I gather the matched sets and so forth were auctioned this spring," the earl said, tugging Anna to her feet. "What do you think of the place so far?"

"It's pretty, peaceful, and not too far from Town. So far I love it, but who are your neighbors?"

"Now that is not something I would have considered, except that you raise it, and to a widow, such a thing would matter. I will make inquiries, though I know my niece dwells less than three miles farther up the road we came in on."

"Her aunt would like that, I'm sure, being close

to Rose," Anna said as they walked back into the kitchen.

"Rose wouldn't mind, either. She gets on with everybody, even His Grace."

"You see him only as a father. As a grandpapa, he may be different."

They retrieved the blankets—two of them—and strolled through the lawns toward the spot for which the property was named, a grassy little knoll overlooking a wide, slow stream. Weeping willows grew on both banks, their branches trailing into the slow-moving water and giving the little space a private, magical quality.

"Perfect for wading," Anna said. "Will you be scandalized?"

"Not if you don't mind my disrobing to swim," the earl replied evenly.

"Naughty man. I bet you and your brothers did your share of that, growing up at Morelands."

"We did." The earl unfolded a blanket and flapped it out onto a shady patch of ground. "Morelands has grown, generation by generation, to the point where it's tens of thousands of acres, complete with ponds, streams, and even a waterfall. I learned to hunt, fish, swim, ride, and more just rambling around with my brothers."

"It sounds idyllic."

"So where did you grow up, Anna?" The earl sat down on the blanket. "You aren't going to loom over me, are you?"

Anna folded to the blanket beside him, realizing how vague her notion of the day had been. A few kisses, a tour of the property, and back to the realities of their lives at the townhouse. She hadn't considered they would talk and talk and talk, nor that she would enjoy that as much as the kissing.

"Hand me the hamper," she ordered. "I will make us up plates. There is lemonade and wine, both."

"Heaven forefend! Wine on a weekday before noon, Mrs. Seaton?"

"I love a good cold white," Anna admitted, "and a hearty red."

"I hope you put some of what you love in that hamper. This is a long way to come for bannocks."

"Not burned bannocks, please," she said, pawing carefully through the hamper. When she finished, Westhaven was presented with sliced strawberries, cheese, buttered slices of bread, cold chicken, and two pieces of marzipan.

"And what have we here?" The earl peered into the hamper and extracted a tall bottle. "Champagne?"

"What?" Anna looked up. "I didn't put that in there."

"I detect the subtle hand of Nanny Fran. A glass, if you please."

Anna obligingly held the glass while the earl popped the cork. She shamelessly sipped the fizzy overflow and held the glass out to him. He drank without taking the glass into his own hand and smiled at her.

"That will do," he declared. "For a hot summer day, it will do splendidly."

"Then you can pour me a glass, as well."

"As you wish," he replied, accommodating her order and filling a glass for himself, too. To Anna's surprise, before either drinking or diving into his meal, the earl paused to wrench off his boots and stockings.

"I have it on good authority extreme heat is dangerous and one shouldn't wear clothes unnecessarily, or so my footmen tell me when I catch them only half liveried." He sipped at his wine, hiding what had to be a smile.

"I did not precisely tell them that, though it's probably good advice."

"So are you wearing drawers and petticoats?" the earl asked, waggling his eyebrows.

"No more champagne for you, if only two sips make you lost to all propriety."

"You're not wearing them," he concluded, making himself a sandwich. "Sensible of you, as it seems even more oppressively hot today than yesterday."

"It is warming up. It also looks to be clouding up."

"More false hope." He glanced at the sky. "I can't recall a summer quite so brutal and early as this one. Seems we hardly had a real spring."

"It's better in the North. You get beastly winters there, but also a real spring, a tolerable summer, and a truly wonderful autumn."

"So you were raised in the North."

"I was. Right now, I miss it."

"I miss Scotland right now, or Stockholm. But this food is superb and the company even better. More champagne?"

"I shouldn't." Her eyes strayed to the bottle, sweating in its linen napkin. "It is such a pleasant drink."

The earl topped off both of their glasses. "This is a day for pleasant, not a day for shoulds and should nots, though I am thinking I should buy the place."

"It is lovely. The only thing that gives me pause

are the oaks along the lane. They will carpet the place with leaves come fall."

"And the gardeners will rake them." The earl shrugged. "Then the children can jump in the piles of leaves and scatter them all about again."

"A sound plan. Are you going to eat those strawberries?"

The earl paused, considered his plate, and picked up a perfect red, juicy berry.

"I'll share." He held it out to her but withdrew it when Anna extended her hand. Sensing his intent, she sat back but held still as he brought it to her mouth. She bit down, then found as the sweet fruit flavor burst across her tongue that her champagne glass was pressed to her lips, as well.

"I really did not pack that champagne," she said when she'd savored the wine.

"I did," the earl confessed. "Nanny Fran is sworn to secrecy as my accomplice."

"She adores you." Anna smiled. "She has more stories about 'her boys' than you would recognize."

"I know." The earl lounged back, resting on his elbows. "When Bart died and she'd launch into a reminiscence, I used to have to leave the room, so angry was I at her. Now I look for the chance to get her going."

"Grief changes. I recall as a child sitting for hours in my mother's wardrobe after she died; that was where I could still smell her."

"I recall you lost both parents quite young."

"I was raised by my father's father. He loved us as much as any parent could, probably more, because he'd lost his only son."

"I am sorry, Anna. I've talked about losing two

brothers, both during my adulthood, and I never considered that you have losses of your own." He did not raise the issue of the departed Mr. Seaton, for which Anna was profoundly grateful.

"It was a long time ago," Anna said. "My parents did not suffer. Their carriage careened down a muddy embankment, and their necks were broken. The poor horse, by contrast, had to wait hours to be shot."

"Dear God." The earl shuddered. "Were you in that carriage, as well?"

"I was not, though I often used to wish I had been."

"Anna…" His tone was concerned, and she found it needful in that moment to study her empty wine glass.

"I have become maudlin by virtue of imbibing."

"Hush," Westhaven chided, crawling across the blanket. He wrapped her in his arms then wrestled her down to lie beside him, her head on his shoulder. She cuddled into him, feeling abruptly cold except where his body lay along hers.

"Val had a bout of the weeps the other day." The earl sighed. "I forget he is so sensitive, because he hides with that great black beast of his and tries so hard not to trouble others. When Bart died, Val went for days without leaving the piano, and only Her Grace's insistence that he be indulged preserved him from the wrath of the duke."

"Your family has not had an easy time of it. One would think rank and riches would assure happiness, but by the Windham example, they do not."

"Nor do they condemn one to misery," the earl pointed out, his hand making circles on her back. "I, for one, do not relish the thought of being poor."

"There is poor, and there is poor. In some ways, I have more freedom than you do, and freedom is a form of great wealth."

"It is," Westhaven agreed, "but I don't see where you have it in such abundance."

"Oh, but I do." Anna sat up and put her chin on her drawn-up knees. "I can leave your employ tomorrow and hare off to Bath, there to keep house for any beldame who will have me. I can answer an advertisement to be a bride for an American tobacco farmer or go live with the natives in the American west. I can join a Scottish convent or journey to darkest Africa as a missionary to the heathen."

"And I, poor fellow"—the earl smiled up at her—"have none of those options."

"You do not," Anna agreed, grinning at him over her shoulder. "You are stuck with Tolliver and Stenson and His Grace, and barely recalling what pleasure is when your housekeeper remembers to sweeten your lemonade."

The earl folded his hands behind his head. "There is a pleasure you could allow me, Anna." He kept using her name, she thought, using it like a caress, a reminder that he knew the taste of her.

"There are many pleasures I could allow you," she said, caution in her tone, "few that I will."

"So I'm to earn your favors?" He merely smiled. "Then, allow me this: The heat and our rambling are threatening the integrity of your coiffure. Let me brush your hair."

"Brush my...?" Anna blinked and gave him a puzzled look.

"I used to brush Her Grace's hair when I was small, then my sisters'. I've taken a turn or two with Rose, but she demands a certain dispatch only her step-papa and mama seem to have perfected."

"You want to brush my hair," Anna said, as if to herself. "That is an unusual request."

"But not too unusual. It requires no removal of clothing nor touching of the hands nor lascivious glances."

"All right," Anna said, more perplexed than alarmed, but then, she was in the company of a man who scheduled his passions. She fished inside the hamper and withdrew her reticule, producing a small bone-handled brush.

"Pretty little thing," the earl remarked, thumbing the bristles. "Now"—he sat up—"sit you here." He thumped the blanket beside him, and Anna scooted, only to find that the earl had shifted so she sat between his bent knees.

"Is this decent?" she murmured.

"Have another glass of wine," the earl suggested. "It will feel frustratingly decent."

They fell silent, and Anna felt the earl's fingers easing through her hair to find her hairpins. He slid them free carefully and began piling them to one side. When the bun at the nape of Anna's neck was loosened, he let her thick plait tumble down her back.

"I like this part," he said. "When you free up a braid, and a single shiny rope becomes skeins and curls and riots of silky, soft hair. How do you keep it so fragrant?"

She felt him lean in for a sniff, and her heart nearly skipped a beat.

"I make a shampoo scented with roses." And ye gods, it had been a struggle to utter that single coherent sentence. His hands were lacing through her unbound hair to massage her scalp and the back of her neck. His touch was perfect—deliberate, knowing, and competent without using too much strength. He trailed her hair down her back, leaving little trickles of pleasure to skitter along her spine, and then she felt him gathering the mass of it, to move it to one side.

"It's beautiful," he murmured, his words breathed near her ear. "I'm going to forbid you to wear those hideous caps of yours when we return to Town."

His thumb brushed along her nape, and then something softer, followed by a puff of breath.

God, yes, Anna thought, letting her chin drop forward. Westhaven scooted closer, the better to kiss her neck, and Anna tilted her head, the better to allow it.

"Ah, Anna," he whispered before pressing his lips to her cheek and letting them drift to her throat. His mouth was open on her skin, as if he'd consume her or sink his teeth into her flesh. Then he paused and scooped her against his chest, dropping one knee and angling her legs across his thigh.

Anna blinked up at him, her back supported by his one upraised knee.

"None of that," he scolded. "I can see you preparing to think, Anna Seaton, and this is not a moment for thinking."

Before she could blink again, his mouth came down on hers in a voluptuously ravenous kiss. His tongue was in her mouth, plundering and demanding and promising. Oh, God, the things his kiss was promising.

His hand slipped down her arm to close around her fingers where they lay limp in her lap. He brought up her hand and put it around his neck, giving her a place to hold on as he gathered her more closely against him. His scent was all around her, and Anna felt heat, not the sweltering summer's heat but something clean and fiery and new singing through her veins. With it came desire—desire for him and desire for closeness with him. She clung and kissed him back, imitating the thrust and drag of his tongue with her own.

And then his lips were gone, leaving his forehead pressed to hers, his breath fanning against her cheek.

"God, Anna." He took a slow inhale then breathed out. "Almighty, everlasting God."

"What?" She felt suddenly unsure, wondering if she'd done something wrong.

"Lie back," he said, easing her to her back and stretching out on his side beside her. He laced his fingers through hers and squeezed. "I just need to catch my breath."

But he didn't catch his breath, instead he frowned down at her, as if trying to puzzle out some frustrating mystery.

"Anna." His frown deepened. "I want to make love with you."

"Isn't that what that was, lovemaking?"

"Let me be blunt: I want to fornicate with you. Urgently."

"Urgently," Anna repeated, still perplexed.

"Here." He took her hand in his and rolled to his

back, putting her palm over his very evident erection. "I want you."

She didn't pull away as she should have but gently shaped him along his length.

"This does not feel very comfortable," she said, knowing exactly what was beneath her fingers. She should be repulsed, but with him, she was fascinated.

"If you keep that up," the earl cautioned, "the urgency will only become greater."

She did keep it up but rolled to her side to peer at his face.

"And then what?" Anna asked, wanting badly to undo his breeches, knowing she could never manage it.

"I am not a rapist," the earl said, closing his eyes. "But I will want badly to spend. Very badly." Anna passed a long, thoughtful moment, stroking at him lazily. His hips began to undulate minutely as she mentally rooted around and tried to find the reasons why she should get up and walk straight into the nice, cold stream.

"What does that mean?" Anna said, using her nails to scratch along the rigid length of him through the fabric.

"Oh, for God's sake." He closed his eyes then pushed her hands away. She thought he was going plunge into the stream, or at least get up and stomp away, but instead, he undid the fall of his breeches and shoved them down over his hips then hiked up his shirt to his ribs.

"Please, love." He took her hand and wrapped it around his erection. "Just bring me off and have done with it."

To her shock, his hand was moving hers, stroking it along this very odd part of him, while Anna watched, shamelessly inspecting something she hadn't seen by the light of day at this range ever before. His skin was soft, smooth, and slightly pink, particularly around the head of his penis. The actual length of him, though, was surprisingly thick, rigid, and hot.

"Like that," he rasped. "Jesus, *yes*, just like that."

His hips moved in counterpoint to the way she was stroking him, and his fingers closed more tightly around hers. This had to be hurting him, she thought distractedly, as his back was arched, his jaw clenched, and the muscles of his neck taut.

"God, Anna, don't stop," he warned just when she would have said something. "That feels too good... Jesus Christ." His breath soughed out on a long, groaning sigh as a milky liquid spurted rhythmically over their fingers and onto the bare flesh of his stomach.

His hand went still over hers, but he kept their fingers laced.

"Dear, sweet, merciful God." He sighed, opening his eyes. "I did not plan for this to happen, Anna. Have we a napkin to hand?"

Dumbly, she handed him one, her eyes fixed on his softening penis.

"Can I let go now?"

"You may," he replied, frowning at her. He swiped at himself with the napkin and then tossed it aside.

"Does it hurt?" Anna nodded at him, and he regarded her carefully.

"You haven't done this before."

"I didn't know one *could*," she said, not taking her

eyes off his groin. "Or two could. It looked uncomfortable for you."

"Arousal has an element of discomfort to it, until satisfied, and then it is pleasurable beyond description." He did not move to tuck himself up, and she did not stop looking.

"One would not necessarily reach that conclusion, watching you," Anna said. "But you are not... aroused now?"

"No." His smile was sweet, pleased. "If you keep looking at me like that, I will be again soon."

"May I touch you?"

"Just be gentle, but indulge your curiosity however you please."

Anna didn't want to ask any more questions, feeling she'd revealed quite enough ignorance to a man who was utterly blasé about something so odd she could barely comprehend it.

So she let her fingers ask the questions, traveling along the softening length of him, lifting him this way and that, manipulating his foreskin and exploring his testicles, all with a frown of deepest puzzlement on her face, while he obligingly kept his eyes closed and gave every appearance of a man dozing off.

"You are..."—she waved a hand over his genitals—"becoming unrelaxed again."

He opened his eyes and smiled. "You are a treasure. Let me hold you."

When Anna hesitated, he tugged her down to his side, tucking her under his arm, her head on his shoulder. He lifted his hips to tug up his breeches but left the falls open and himself half exposed.

"If I touched you again," Anna asked, "would you do that a second time?"

"With you? At least three times, eventually. A man does need some time to recover, though. Anna…?"

"Hmm?" Her hand was resting over his cock, but just that, not moving him nor attempting any further exploration.

"Thank you." The earl's eyes drifted shut. "There's a great deal more to be said, of course, and soon, but for now, thank you."

Anna didn't know what to say to that, for she felt like thanking him, too. She had shared something with him, something wicked and dear and dangerous, and yet it was as he'd said. Her clothes were on and her physical virtue uncompromised. He had given her knowledge, of his body and of him, but he had not demanded comparable knowledge of her.

Maybe he would, Anna thought. Maybe that was the "great deal more" yet to be discussed. She hoped not, because as much as she might want to, she could not afford to allow him those liberties, not if she valued her freedom.

Six

"Come." The earl held out a hand and grabbed the hamper, putting the blankets on top. "We need to talk, and the library will be less gloomy than the kitchen."

They'd had to sprint for the kitchen when a summer squall had caught them napping on their blankets, and the rapid shift from pleasantly dozing to a dead run still had Anna disoriented. She put her hand in his but found she dreaded this talking he wanted. Words could land with the force of a blow, and she was going to hurt herself with what must be said, and very likely anger him, as well.

When they arrived at the library, he pulled the cushions from the window seats and fashioned a nest on the floor with those and the blankets. Retrieving the champagne bottle from the hamper and cracking one window, he settled cross-legged on the blanket and watched her as Anna moved restlessly around the room.

"Have some." He held up the bottle. "We can swill from the bottle like heathens if it won't offend you." She joined him and took a pull from the bottle.

"You are sworn to secrecy," she warned him. "Mrs. Seaton does not tipple."

"Neither does Westhaven." He followed her example. "Heir to a bloody duke, you know."

In that moment, she lost a piece of her heart to him. His hair was curling damply against his neck, his clothing was in disarray, and he was sitting cross-legged on the floor of an empty room, swilling champagne. In that posture, in his dishevelment, with grave humor dancing in his green eyes, the Earl of Westhaven was impossibly dear to her.

"I like that look in your eye, Anna," he said. "It bodes well for a man housebound with little to do."

"You are lusty," she said, not a little surprised.

"Not particularly," the earl said, passing her the bottle. "Or not any more than others of my age and station. But I am lusty as hell with you, dear lady."

His expression softened, the humor shifting to a tenderness she hadn't seen in him before.

She put aside the bottle. "That look does not bode well for a mere housekeeper who wants to preserve her paltry little reputation."

He reached into the hamper to retrieve her hairbrush, untying a hair ribbon from its handle. "We traveled in an open carriage, Anna, and when this rain blows over, I'll have you directly back to Town. You never even let me get a hand on your delicate ankles."

"That isn't the magnitude of the problem, and you know it."

"I can see we are going to have a substantial discussion. At least let me put your hair to rights so you can't glare at me while we do."

"I do not reproach you for what happened outside," Anna said, scooting around to present him her back.

"Good." The earl kissed her neck. "I want to reproach myself, but at present, I just feel too damned pleased with life, you know? Perhaps in a day or two I will get around to being ashamed, but, Anna, I would not bet on it."

She could hear the uncharacteristic smile in his voice, and thought: I put that smile there, just by sharing with him a few minutes of self-indulgence.

"I am not ashamed, either." Anna tried on the lie. "Well, only a little, but this direction could easily become shameful, and I would not want that. For you or for me, as we are not shameful people."

"You will not be my mistress," Westhaven said, sifting his hands through her hair in long, gentle sweeps. "And you did not sound too keen on being a wife."

Anna closed her eyes. "I said it depended on whose wife, but no, in the general case, taking a husband does not appeal."

"Why not?" He started with the brush in the same slow, steady movements. "Taking a husband has some advantages, you know."

"Name one."

"He brings you pleasure," the earl said, his voice dropping. "Or he damned well should. He provides for your comfort, gives you babies. He grows old with you, providing companionship and friendship; he shares your burdens and lightens your sorrows. Good sort of fellow to have around, a husband."

"Hah." Anna wanted to peer over her shoulder at him, but his hold on her hair prevented it.

"He *owns* you and the produce of your body," she retorted. "He has the right to demand intimate access to you at any time or place of his choosing, and strike you and injure you should you refuse him, or simply because he considers you in need of a beating. He can virtually sell your children, and you have nothing to say to it. He need not be loyal or faithful, and still you must admit him to your body, regardless of his bodily or moral appeal, or lack thereof. A very dangerous and unpleasant thing, a husband."

The earl was silent behind her, winding her hair into a long braid.

"Were your parents happy?" he asked at length.

"I believe they were, and my grandparents were."

"As are mine, as were mine," the earl said, fishing her hair ribbon out of his pocket and tying off her braid. "Can you not trust yourself, Anna, to choose the kind of husband I describe rather than that nightmare you recount?"

"The choice of a woman's husband is often not hers, and the way a man presents himself when courting is not how he will necessarily behave when his wife is fat with his third child a few years later."

"A housekeeper sees things from a curious and unpleasant perspective." He hunched forward to wrap his arms around her shoulders. "But, Anna, what about the example of our parents? The duke and duchess when they open an evening with the waltz still command every eye. They dance well, so well they move as one, and they function that way in life, too. My father adores my mother, and she sees only the best in him."

"They are happy," Anna said, "but what is your point? They are also very lucky, as you and I both know."

"You will not be my mistress," the earl said again, "and you are very leery of becoming a wife, but what, Anna, would you think of becoming a duchess?"

He said the words close to her ear, the heat and scent of him surrounding her, and she couldn't stop the shudder that passed through her at his question.

"Most women," she said as evenly as she could, "would not object to becoming a duchess, but look at your parents' example. Had I to become your father's duchess, I would likely do the man an injury."

"And what if you were to become my duchess?" the earl whispered, settling his lips on the juncture of her shoulder and neck. "Would that be such a dangerous and unpleasant thing?"

She absorbed the question and understood that he was asking a hypothetical question, not offering a proposal. In that moment, her heart broke. It flew into a thousand hurting pieces, right there in her chest. Her breath wouldn't come, her lungs felt heavy with pain, and an ache radiated out from her middle as if old age were overcoming her in the space of an instant.

And even if it had been a proposal, she was in no position to accept.

"Anna, love?" He nuzzled at her. "Do you think I would be such a loathsome, overbearing lout?"

"You would not," she said, swallowing around the lump in her throat. "Whomever you took to wife would be very, very blessed."

"So you will have me?" He drew her back against him, resting an arm across her collarbones.

"Have *you*?" Anna sat up and slewed around. "You are proposing to *me*?"

"I am proposing to you," he said. "If you'll have me as your husband, I would like you to be my duchess."

"Oh, God help us," Anna said under her breath, rising abruptly, and going to a long window.

He rose slowly. "That is not an expression of acceptance."

"You do me great honor," Anna said mechanically, "but I cannot accept your generous offer, my lord."

"No my lording," he chided. "Not after the way we've been behaving, Anna."

"It will have to be my lording, and Mrs. Seatoning, as well, until I can find another post."

"I never took you for a coward, Anna," he said, but there was more disappointment than anger in his voice.

"Were I free to accept you," she said, turning to face him, "I would still be hesitant." She left the *my lord* off, not wishing to anger him needlessly, but it was there in her tone, and he no doubt heard it.

"What would cause your hesitation?"

"I'm not duchess material, and we hardly know each other."

"You are as much duchess material as I am duke material," he countered, "and few titled couples know each other as well as we already do, Anna Seaton. You know I like marzipan and music and my horse. I know you like flowers, beauty, cleanliness, and pretty scents."

"You know you like kissing me, and I…"

"Yes?"

"I like kissing you, as well," she admitted on a brittle smile.

"Give me some time, Anna," he said, the aristocrat stooping to bargain, not the importuning suitor. "You think you'd not make a suitable duchess, and you think we don't know each other well. Give me the opportunity to convince you of your errors."

"You want me for a mistress," she said, "but I will not take your coin."

"I am *asking*," he said with great patience, "the opportunity to gain a place in your affections, Anna. Nothing more."

Was he asking for an affair? She should refuse him even that, but it was all too tempting.

"I will think about it, though I believe it best if I pursue another position. And no matter what, you mustn't be seen to embarrass me with your attentions."

"I will draft you a glowing character," the earl said, his eyes hooded, "but you must agree to give me at least the summer to change your mind."

"Write the character." Anna nodded, heart shattering all over again. "Give it to Lord Valentine for safekeeping, and I will promise not to seek other employment this summer, unless you give me cause."

"I would not disrespect you, and I would never get a bastard on any woman, Anna." The earl leveled a look of such frustration at her that Anna cringed.

"Were you to get a bastard on me, we would be forced to wed. I cannot see either of us inviting such circumstances."

His expression changed, becoming thoughtful.

"So if I were to get you pregnant, you would marry me?"

Anna realized too late the trap she had set for herself

and sat on the window seat with a sigh. "I would," she admitted, "which only indicates how unwilling I will be to permit the occasion to arise."

He sat down beside her and took her hand, and she sensed his mind beginning to sift and sort through the information she'd disclosed and the information she'd withheld.

He drew a pattern over her knuckles. "I am not your enemy, and I never will be."

She nodded, not arguing. He slipped an arm around her shoulders and hugged her to his side.

"You are not my enemy," Anna said, letting him tuck her against him. "And you cannot be my husband nor my keeper."

"I will be your very discreet suitor for the summer, and then we will see where we are. We are agreed on this." He voice was purposeful, as if he'd finished exploring the challenge before him and was ready to vanquish it.

"We are agreed," Anna said, knowing his best efforts would in a few weeks time put them no closer to his goals than they were in that moment. But she needed those weeks, needed them to plan and organize and regroup.

And in the alternative, she needed the time to grieve and to hoard up for herself the bittersweet procession of moments like this, when he held her and comforted her and reminded her of all she could not have.

They stayed like that, sitting side by side for a long time, the only sound the rain pelting against the windows. After a time, Westhaven got up and looked around the room.

"I will go check on Pericles. I am thinking I should also lay a fire in here, as the rain does not appear to be moving off."

"Lay a fire? We have hours of light yet," Anna said, though in truth they'd had more than a nap outside by the stream, and the afternoon was well advanced. "We could make it back to Town were we to leave in the next couple of hours."

He pursed his lips, obviously unwilling to argue. Anna let him go, knowing it would ruin his gig were they to try to get it back to Town in this downpour. He came back soaked to the skin but reporting the horse was contentedly munching hay and watching the rain from his stall.

They spent the next hour retrieving more blankets and the medical bag kept in the gig, then, as the rain had not let up, filling up the wood boxes in the library. The earl split logs from a supply on the back porch, and Anna toted them into the house. They continued in that fashion, until the wood boxes built beside the library hearths were full and the earl had left a tidy pile of logs split for the next time somebody needed a fire.

He returned to the library, where Anna had laid a fire but not lit it.

"I should not be chilled," he mused. "I've just hefted an ax for the first time in several years, but I find I am a trifle cold."

Unusual, Anna thought, as she herself was not cold, and she hadn't split wood, but then, the earl had gotten wet tending to his horse and Anna was quite dry. She'd found flint and steel in the wood box, thank heavens, or the earl would have had to get another soaking just as his clothing was drying.

"I'll light your fire," Anna said, missing entirely the smile her comment engendered on the earl's face.

"And I will forage for a piece of marzipan."

"There should be plenty," Anna said from the hearth, "and some lemonade, though it isn't likely very cold."

He found the marzipan, taking two pieces, and then the lemonade.

"So where should we sleep?" he asked, glancing around the room as he chomped on his candy.

"At home, I hope."

The earl gave her a quelling look. "I did not plan this weather."

"No, you did not, but if we stay here alone overnight, my reputation will be in tatters."

"And you still would not marry me?"

"England is a big place. A tattered reputation in London can easily be mended in Manchester."

"You would flee?"

"I would have to."

"I would not allow that, Anna." The earl frowned at her as he spoke. "If you come to harm as a result of this situation, you will permit me to provide for you."

"As you did for Elise?" Anna said, sitting on a stone hearth. "I think not."

"I'm going to check on the horse again," he said, "and bring in the last of the supplies from the gig, just in case the rain doesn't stop soon." Anna let him go, knowing his retreat was in part an effort to cool the irritation he must be feeling with her and the situation.

Westhaven did check on the horse and stepped out under the stables' overhang to relieve himself, undoing his breeches and taking his cock in hand. His throat was scratchy from all their talking, and hefting the ax had set up an ache in his muscles that was equally unwelcome. Anna was getting twitchy about being stranded with him, and his temper was growing short. Not his best moment.

But then he looked down at himself and smiled, recalling the day's earlier pleasures. Anna Seaton had a wanton streak that was going to win the day for them both. He shook himself off, gave himself a few affectionate strokes, then buttoned up. He was going to convince his housekeeper to trade her silly caps for a tiara, and he was going to use her passions against her shamelessly if he had to.

He tossed Pericles a small mountain of hay, topped off the water bucket from the cistern, and retrieved the provisions from the gig. On the way back to the house, he began to plan the seduction of his future wife, pausing to pluck her a single rose just as the sky opened up with a renewed downpour.

They dined on leftovers from the hamper, shared the lemonade, and talked by the fire as the light began to wane. He rubbed her back, held her hand, and avoided discussing the need to spend the night in the deserted house.

Anna rose from the cushions and stretched. "I suppose it's time to admit we'll be sleeping here tonight—the question is where specifically?"

Thank you, God, the earl thought. His Anna was being practical, though she wasn't pleased with their situation.

"The master bedroom comes to mind," the earl suggested. "The bed there was probably built where it stands and conveys with the house. The room was clean enough, but it will be cold without a fire."

"We can haul enough wood up there to get the room warmed up," Anna said. "Since the other option is this floor. With only a few blankets between us, we're probably better off sharing that bed."

"We are," he agreed, finding that for all they were before a fire, he still just couldn't quite banish a sense of chill in his bones. "And as splitting wood seems to have left me a little stiff, the bed appeals."

"To bed then," Anna said resignedly as she began to gather an armload of logs from the wood box. It took several trips to move wood, blankets, and provisions to the bedroom. By the time they were finished, the entire house was growing gloomy with the approaching night.

Westhaven left the room to fetch a bucket of wash water from the kitchen, while Anna scouted the bed drawers for the linens sewn to fit the bed.

"Your water," the earl said when he returned moments later. "I see your treasure hunt was successful."

"The bed is made up." Anna smiled at him. "We have soap and towels, though only our two blankets."

"That should suffice." The earl yawned as he knelt by the open drawer. "How about if you take the nightshirt, and I take the dressing gown?"

"As you wish, but a few minutes privacy would be appreciated, and…"

"And?" He was just pulling off his boots again, but

in the dim firelight, at the end of the day, it struck him as a particularly intimate thing for her to watch.

"You will not touch me tonight? You will not expect me to touch you?"

"Touch as in, your knee bumps my shin, or touch as in what happened this afternoon?" the earl asked, peering into his boot.

"What happened this afternoon. I'll try not to kick at you, either."

"I will not make demands of you," the earl said, leveling a look at her, "but I will want to." He set aside his boots and rose, leaving her the privacy she requested to wash, change into the nightshirt, and dive beneath the chilly sheets of the bed.

When Westhaven returned, he looked over at the bed and saw Anna was feigning sleep. He had every intention of keeping his word to her, of behaving himself once he climbed into that bed. He was more tired than he had a right to be, considering he'd done little more than tool along in the gig, stroll around the property, and talk with Anna.

But he was exhausted, and he'd taken some sort of chill in the rain, and he could barely keep his eyes open. Still, he wasn't going to waste an opportunity to torment his intended duchess, so he stripped out of his shirt, his breeches, stockings, and smalls, and took the bucket to the hearth, the better to illuminate him for Anna's peeping eyes.

Truth to tell, it felt good to be naked and in the same room with her. He found a towel and the soap on the hearth, where Anna had left them, and slowly began to wash himself from toes to fingertips. When he'd made a thorough job of it, he blew out their two candles, tossed the dressing gown to the foot of the bed, and climbed in beside Anna.

※

In the darkness hours later, Anna awoke to feel his hand on her flesh, making a slow journey over her hip to her buttock and back again. The creaking and shifting of the old bed suggested he was moving more than his hand, and his breathing—slow, but audible—supported the theory.

He's pleasuring himself again. Were all men so afflicted with lust? she wondered, even as that single, repetitive stroke of his hand left a trail of warmth across her flesh. If she rolled over, began kissing him or simply let him hold her, what other means would he find to torment her?

His breathing hitched, sighed, and hitched again, and then his hand went still. Anna felt him moving around and then subsiding down under the covers. That same hand curled around her middle, and her back was enveloped in the heat of his chest. He kissed her cheek then fitted himself behind her, leaving her bewildered but oddly pleased, as well.

She could not permit him the liberties he so clearly wanted, but this cuddling and drowsing together, it was more of a gift than he could ever know. While the storm pelted down from the heavens, Anna slept a dreamless, contented sleep in the arms of the man she could not marry.

※

Had Westhaven kept his dressing gown on, Anna might have been much slower to diagnose his ailment. As it was, they slept late, the day making a desultory arrival amid a steady rain that left the sky gray and the house gloomy. Anna's first sensation was of heat, too much heat. Of course it was summer, but with the change in weather, the house itself was downright chilly.

Westhaven, she realized, was still spooned around her, and the heat was radiating from his body. She shifted away, and he rolled to his back.

He reached for the water glass. "I feel like I came off Pericles at the first jump, and the whole flight rode over me. And it is deucedly hot in this bed." He rose, wrestling the blankets aside, and sat for a moment on the edge of the mattress as if finding his equilibrium.

"No," he went on. "I feel worse than that, no reflection on present company, of course." Without thinking, Anna rolled over to respond and saw him rise, naked as the day he was born, and make for the chamber pot.

"Good morning to you, too," she muttered, flouncing back to her side, unwilling to be as casual as he about his nudity. He came back to the bed, took a sip of his water, and frowned.

"I am inclined to purchase this property," he reflected, "but this bed will have to go. I have never risen feeling less rested."

Anna rolled to her other side, a retort on her lips regarding earls who did not keep their hands to themselves, but she stopped and fell silent. Westhaven was sitting up, leaning against the pillows, his water glass cradled in his lap.

"Oh, my Lord," Anna whispered, pushing her braid over her shoulder.

"No my lording," Westhaven groused. "I am quite simply not in the mood for it."

"No," Anna said, scrambling to her knees. "My Lord, as in Lord above." She reached out and ran a hand over his torso, causing him to look down at his own body.

"You were peeking last night," he said. "It isn't as if you haven't seen me unclothed, Anna Seaton."

"It isn't that," Anna said, drawing her hand back then brushing it over his stomach. "Oh, Lord."

"Oh, Lord, what?"

"You." She sat back, her head moving from side to side in disbelief. "You're coming down with the chicken pox." A stunned beat of silence followed, then the earl's snort of displeasure.

"I most certainly am not," he informed her. "Only children get the chicken pox, and I am not a child."

"You never had them as a child," Anna said, meeting his eyes, "or you wouldn't have them now."

The earl glared at his torso, which was sprinkled with small red dots. Not that many, but enough that they both knew they weren't there the night before. He inspected his arms, which sported a few more.

"This is Tolliver's fault," he declared. "I'll see him transported for this, and Sue-Sue with him."

"We need to get you home," Anna said, slogging her way to the edge of the bed. "In children, chicken pox are uncomfortable but usually not serious. In an adult, they can be much more difficult."

"You are going to make a sick man travel for hours in this damned rain?" The earl speared her with a look then glared at his stomach again. "Bloody hell."

"We have few medicinals here, and you will feel worse before you get better, possibly much worse. Best we get you home now."

"And if the damned gig should slide down a muddy embankment, Anna?" he retorted. "It wouldn't matter if the chicken pox got me, or a broken neck."

She turned her back on him for that and went to the window, assessing the weather. He had a point, though he'd made it as meanly as possible. The rain was pelting down in torrents, as it had been for much of the night.

"I'm sorry," the earl said, pushing himself to the edge of the bed. "Being ill unnerves me."

"Our situation is unnerving. Is there a village nearby large enough to sport a physician or apothecary?"

The earl grabbed the dressing gown and shrugged into it, even those movements looking painful. "*Nearby* is a relative term. About a mile the other side of Welbourne there is something large enough to boast a church, but not in the direction of London."

"Welbourne is where your niece lives."

"Anna, no." He rose off the mattress stiffly and paused, grimacing. "I am not imposing on Amery and his wife. You will recall the lady and I were briefly and miserably betrothed. They are the last people I want to see me unwell."

"I would rather they see you unwell, Westhaven, then see you laid out for burial."

"Are you implying I am too arrogant to accept assistance?"

"Stubborn." Anna crossed her arms. "And afraid to admit you are truly ill."

"Perhaps it is you who are anxious, Anna. Surely the chicken pox aren't so serious as all that?" He sat back down on the bed but held her eyes.

Her chin came up a half inch. "Who just said he's never risen feeling so uncomfortable?"

"Unrefreshed," the earl corrected her, considering his bodily state. He felt like pure, utter hell. His worst hangover at university did not compare with this, the flu did not, the broken arm he'd suffered at thirteen did not. He felt as if every muscle in his body had been pulled, every bone broken, every organ traumatized, and he had to piss again with a sort of hot, whiney insistence that suggested illness even to him.

"Welbourne it is," he said on a sigh. "Just to borrow a proper coach and a sturdy team. I won't have Amery gloating over this, nor his viscountess."

Getting even the three miles to Welbourne was an ordeal for them both and for the horse. In the hour it had taken them to dress, load, and hitch the gig, Westhaven's condition worsened. He sat beside Anna, half leaning on her, using what little strength he still claimed just to remain upright on the seat.

They didn't speak, the earl preoccupied with remaining conscious, Anna doing her best to help the horse pick his way along at a shuffling walk. When she saw the gateposts for Welbourne, Anna nearly cried, so great was her relief. Even through the layers of damp clothing between them, she could feel the earl's fever rising and sense the effort the journey was costing him.

The stables were closed up tight, but Anna didn't even turn into the yard. She steered Pericles up to the manor house and pulled him to a halt.

"Westhaven." She jostled him stoutly. "We're here. Sit up until I can get down and help you to alight."

He complied silently and nearly fell on Anna as she tried to assist him from the gig. Getting up the front steps saw them almost overbalancing twice, and Anna was panting with exertion by the time they gained the front porch.

The front door opened before Anna could knock. "For the love of God, get him in here."

Anna's burden was relieved as Westhaven's free arm was looped across a pair of broad shoulders belonging to a blond man dressed only to his waistcoat and shirt-sleeves. The man was fortunately as tall as Westhaven and far more equal to the task than Anna.

"You," the fellow barked at a footman. "Have Pericles put up and see he's offered a warm mash. You." He fixed fierce blue eyes on Anna. "Sit down before you fall down."

Taken aback, Anna could only follow as Westhaven was half-carried to a parlor and there deposited on a settee.

"He is coming down with chicken pox," Anna said, finding her voice at last. "He thought to come here only to borrow a closed vehicle that he might return to Town."

"Douglas Allen." The man offered her a bow. "Viscount Amery, at your service." He jerked the bellpull and surveyed the man dripping on his couch. "Westhaven?"

"Amery?"

The earl's voice was a croak, but one that conveyed a spark of pride.

"If you insist on attempting to travel on in your

condition," Amery said, "I will send a note forthwith to His Grace, and *tattle* on you. I will also hold you up to Rose as a *bad example*, and worse, my viscountess will *worry*. As she is the sole sustenance of my heir, I am loathe to worry her, do I make myself clear?"

"Ye gods..." Westhaven muttered, peering at his host. "You are serious."

Amery quirked an eyebrow. "As serious as the chicken pox, complicated by a lung fever, and further compounded by Windham pride and arrogance."

"Douglas?" A tall woman with dark auburn hair entered the parlor, her pretty features showing curiosity and then concern.

"Guinevere." The man slid a shameless arm around the lady's waist. "Look you, on yonder couch, 'tis your former betrothed, come to give us all the chicken pox."

"Oh, Westhaven." The woman stepped forward, but Anna had the presence of mind to rise from her seat and step between Lady Amery and the earl.

"My lady." Anna bobbed a curtsy. "His lordship informed me you have an infant in the house, so had best not be coming too close to the earl."

"She's right." Amery frowned. "I know I've had the chicken pox."

"As have I," Guinevere said, but she returned to her husband's side. "And so has Rose. Douglas, you can't let him travel like this."

"Using the third person," the earl rasped from the couch, "when a man is present and conscious, is rude and irritating."

"But fun," Amery said, coming to peruse his visitor. He put the back of his hand to the earl's forehead and knelt to consider him at closer range. Though both men were of an age, the viscount's gestures were curiously paternal. "You are burning up, which I needn't tell you. I know you hold physicians in no esteem whatsoever, but will you let me send for Fairly?"

"You will not notify the duke?" Westhaven met his host's eyes.

"Not yet, if you stay here like a good boy and get better before my Christian charity is outstripped by my honesty," Amery said, sending his wife a glance.

"Send for Fairly," the earl replied, "but only him, and not those damned quacks who think they attend His Grace."

"I would not so insult Fairly," the viscount said, rising. "Not even to aggravate you."

While the viscount wrested permission to summon the doctor from the earl, Lady Amery conferred with the footman then turned to Anna.

"I'm sorry," Lady Amery said, smiling. "You have me at a loss, Miss...?"

"Mrs. Seaton," Anna replied, curtsying again. "Mrs. Anna Seaton. I keep house for his lordship in Town and accompanied him to Willow Bend, a property three miles east of here, which he thinks to purchase."

"Pretty place," Amery murmured, "but first things first."

"The back bedroom will serve as a sick room and is being made up now," Guinevere said. "You and the earl could both probably use hot baths and some sustenance, and I'm sure we can find you something dry to change into, as you and I appear to be of a height."

"Come, Westhaven." The viscount tugged the

earl to his feet. "We'll ply you with foul potions and mutter incantations by your bedside until you are recovered for the sake of your sanity. You should probably see Rose now, or she will just sneak into your room when you are feeling even worse and read her stories to you."

It should have made him shudder, Westhaven thought as Amery tugged and carried and insulted him up to the bedroom. To be here with the man who had stopped his wedding to Gwen, and to be so ill and virtually helpless before him and Gwen. It should have been among his worst nightmares.

But as Douglas got him out of his wet clothes and shoved him into a steaming, scented bath, then fussed him into swilling some god-awful tea, Westhaven realized that what he felt was safe.

❧

"He'll want to notify his brother," Anna said, sipping her hot tea with profound gratitude.

"We'll send him a message with the one going to Fairly," Gwen replied, handing Anna a plate with a hot buttered scone on it.

"Send it in code."

"I beg your pardon?" Gwen set down her cup and waited for an explanation.

"It's the duke," Anna said. "His Grace has spies everywhere, and if you leave a note to the effect that Westhaven is seriously ill, where somebody can read it, the duke will be on your doorstep, wreaking havoc and giving orders in no time."

"He most assuredly will not." Douglas spoke from

the door of the parlor, and there was something like amusement in his expression. "This is one household where His Grace's mischief gets him nowhere. May I have a spot of tea, my love?" He lowered his long frame beside his wife, draping an arm across the back of the couch.

"How is Westhaven?" Gwen asked, fixing her husband a cup of tea.

"Sleeping, but uncomfortable. I thought you must be mistaken, Mrs. Seaton, as he has no evidence of chicken pox on his face, but your diagnosis is borne out by inspection of the rest of him."

"I had a rather severe case as a child," Anna said. "I'm available for nursing duty."

"I can assist," the viscount said, "and I will do so gleefully. But you, my love, should likely avoid the sickroom."

"I will," Gwen said, "for the sake of the baby, and because having you see him in distress is likely enough penance even for Westhaven. He doesn't need me gloating, too."

Anna sipped her tea, watching the smiles and glances and casual touches passing between these two.

"Westhaven said it was a miserable betrothal."

"For all three of us," Gwen said. "But quickly ended. You did the right thing, bringing him here. He is family, and we don't really hold the betrothal against him, any more than we delight in his illness."

"His sickness is serious," Anna said, "in adults, anyway. And he is…fretful about illness generally. I honestly would not let the doctors near him if it's avoidable."

"The man is too proud by half," Douglas remarked,

topping off his own tea cup. His wife watched, amused, but said nothing.

"It isn't pride, my lord," Anna said. "He is afraid."

"Afraid." Douglas pursed him lips thoughtfully. "Because of his brother Victor?"

"Not precisely." Anna tried to organize her thoughts—her feelings—into coherent order. "He is the spare, and dying would be a dereliction of his duty. For all he does not enjoy his obligations, he would not visit them on Lord Valentine, nor the grief on his remaining family. Then, too, he has seen more incompetent doctoring than most, both with his brother, and early this spring, with His Grace."

"Hadn't thought of that," Douglas said, flicking another glance at his wife. "Guinevere?"

"Send for David," Gwen said. "He'll know how to handle the earl and how to treat the chicken pox, too."

"We speak of the Viscount Fairly," Douglas explained. "A family connection of Gwen's, and friend of mine. He is a skilled physician, and we trust him, as, apparently, does Westhaven."

"He does," Anna said. "And in Fairly's absence, he would tolerate the attendance of…"—she struggled to recall the names—"Pugh, Hamilton, and there was a third name, but it escapes me."

"Fairly will know," Douglas assured her. "But how is it, Mrs. Seaton, you and the earl come to be on our doorstep at this hour? Surely Westhaven was not fool enough to venture from Town in this downpour?"

Gwen abruptly looked fascinated with her tea cup, while Anna felt like a butterfly, pinned to a specimen board by the viscount's steady blue eyes.

"We traveled out to Willow Bend yesterday," Anna said, knowing this man would not tolerate untruths. "And then the rain caught us unawares. I convinced the earl to come here this morning only when he realized he had fallen ill."

"Nonsense," Amery replied, crossing his legs at the knee. It should have been a fussy gesture on a man. On him it was...elegant. "Westhaven, being a man of sense and discretion, had you on our doorstep well before dark last evening, didn't he, Guinevere?"

"He did." Gwen nodded, swirling her tea placidly. "He was particularly quiet at dinner, though Rose was in transports to see him."

The viscount sent Anna an indecipherable look. "The child has no sense with those she loves. None at all. Takes after her dear mama. More tea, Mrs. Seaton?"

He poured for her, his wife smiling tolerantly as he did, and Anna felt the love between them almost as strongly as she felt her own gratitude toward them. Someday, she thought, I want to love a man so thoroughly that even when he pours tea for my guests, it is merely one more reason to be pleased with him and with my life because he is in it.

⌀

"Fairly can't attend you." Douglas waved a missive at Westhaven. "He doesn't know if he's had the chicken pox or not."

"Christ. How can you not know if you've turned as spotted as a leopard and felt like something a leopard killed last week?"

"He was raised by his mother in Scotland until he

was six and cannot consult with that lady regarding his early health. He has no recollection of having had the illness, either, so he is being cautious." Douglas sat on the end of the bed and surveyed the patient.

"Why are you staring?" Westhaven asked irritably. "Is my face breaking out?"

"No, though I might enjoy seeing that. Fairly writes in some detail we are to provide you comfort nursing and to particularly manage any tendency you have to fevers and discourage you strongly from being bled. And you are not to scratch."

"I don't itch," the earl said, "I *ache*." And he wondered, when she wasn't with him, how the viscount and his wife were treating Anna. Douglas was a stickler, at least with regard to manners and decorum, for all he'd been willing to break some rules to prevent Gwen's marriage to the earl—a lot of rules, come to that.

"Shall I beat you at cribbage?" Douglas offered. "Or perhaps you'd like me to send in Rose?"

"She was here earlier. She lent him to me." He held up a little brown stuffed bear.

"Mr. Bear." Douglas nodded. "He presided over my own sickroom when I ended up with the flu down in Sussex. Good fellow, Mr. Bear. Not much of one for handing out useful advice, however."

"We have Rose for that." Westhaven almost smiled. "She told me to obey her mother, and I would get better."

"Disobeying Guinevere would be rather like trying to disobey a force of nature. One does so at one's mortal peril. She is a formidable woman."

"She would have made a formidable duchess,"

Westhaven said then realized what had come out of his mouth. "Sorry."

"She would"—Douglas merely nodded—"but her taste in husbands is impeccable, and it is my ring she wears."

"Does it bother you?" Westhaven held up the bear and stared into his button eyes. "My being here?"

"Don't flatter yourself, Westhaven." Douglas rose and crossed the room to an escritoire, extracting a deck of cards and a cribbage board. "Gwen has explained to me you offered for her only because you assumed she was free to refuse you. She has since said you would have tried very hard to make the marriage happy, and I believe her. Cut for the deal." Douglas slapped the board and the deck down on the bed.

"That's it, then?" Westhaven turned up a two, and Douglas pitched his draw down in disgust. "I would have made her happy, no harm done?"

"If Guinevere sees no reason to dwell in the past, then why should I, as my future with Rose, little John, and Guinevere is an embarrassment of happiness?"

"My crib," Westhaven intoned, pondering Douglas's words. What was it like to face a future that could be described with a straight face as an embarrassment of happiness?

Douglas trounced him, going about the game with the same seriousness of purpose that he brought to every endeavor. By the time the board was put away, Westhaven's eyes were growing heavy, and Douglas was angling in the direction of a strategic retreat. A knock on the door heralded Anna's turn at the earl's bedside and allowed Douglas to leave in search of his wife.

"I see you have a friend." Anna nodded at the bear.

"A guardian bear, Rose claims." The earl again brought the bear up to face him and frowned thoughtfully. "He seems a solid sort, if a bit reserved."

"Rather like the viscount."

"Douglas?" The earl smiled at her characterization. "Don't underestimate him, as my father and I did. He appears to be a proper little Puritan, tending his acres and adoring his wife, but Heathgate, Greymoor, and Fairly all listen when Douglas deigns to address a topic."

"He does seem to adore his viscountess, but I believe he is just a protective sort of man in general."

"Protective?" The earl considered the word, but his brain was becoming as creaky as the rest of him. "Perhaps. He certainly dotes on Rose and would cheerfully strangle any who sought to do her harm."

"He has a problem with his memory, though," Anna said, opening a bottle of lotion and sniffing at it. "His wife is similarly afflicted."

"They are? That's news to me, as both of them exhibit frightening mental acuity."

Anna put the lid back on the bottle. "If anybody asks them, they will recall we joined them for an early dinner last night, and you were somewhat subdued, but Rose was quite glad to see you."

Westhaven's eyebrows shot up then crashed down.

"Gwen told you this?" he asked, surprise warring with gratitude.

"No," Anna said, her voice echoing with disbelief. "It was Amery's idea."

"Perhaps she married the better man after all."

Seven

"My, my, my." Douglas frowned as he closed the door to the sick room. "Is this the state Mrs. Seaton left you in, susceptible to any draft and breeze?"

"It is not." The earl sighed, trying to recall where he'd last put the chamber pot. "I was hot, and that nightshirt of yours itches like the very devil."

"Behind the screen," the viscount suggested. "A close stool and a chamber pot. I'll leave if you like, or assist."

"Neither." Westhaven made his way across the room, Douglas watching impassively.

"I thought you'd gained some flesh," Douglas remarked. "A closer inspection suggests I was right. You were getting too thin."

"I was." The earl yawned behind the privacy screen. "But, Anna...Mrs. Seaton has taken me in hand and seen to my meals. Part of the problem was an uninspired cook."

"And your housekeeper inspired her?"

"Anna...Mrs. Seaton interviewed the duchess's cook, who takes pride in knowing the preferences of each member of the family. The menus became interesting." The earl emerged from behind the screen, eyed the bed, and gathered his energy. "And she fussed at me did I not eat, told me I was offending my kitchen staff."

"Up you go." Douglas took him unceremoniously by one spotted arm and boosted him up the step to the bed. "Hold still." He dropped the nightshirt over the earl and peered at him. "You are ill," Douglas concluded on a sigh. "Best get back in bed, and behave yourself. Tonight will likely be the worst, and tomorrow night, but after that, you should be on the mend."

"Douglas?" Westhaven sat on the edge of the bed, and to his surprise, Amery sat beside him.

"Hmm?"

"When you were courting Gwen," Westhaven said, finding the bear among his pillows, "did you...?"

"Did I what?" Douglas prompted. "Mrs. Seaton will be returning with your next infusion, and hopefully some food, so you'd best spit it out, as she's guarding you rather carefully."

"She is?"

"She left your side to eat, but otherwise, unless I'm here, she is," Douglas replied. "You had a question?"

"When you were courting Gwen," the earl tried again. "Was there an almost constant...? I mean, did you find your thoughts turning always to...?"

"I swived her every chance I got," Douglas interjected. "And if I couldn't be inside her, I held her or held her hand or just looked at her like a starving man looks at a banquet he can't eat. The situation was particularly disturbing, because I had come to a point in my life where any kind of passion was beyond me, including the carnal."

"Why do you tell me this? It cannot be easy to part with such a confidence; not for you, and not to me."

"I am meddling," Douglas confessed, his blue eyes warming with humor. "I have my wife's permission, so it isn't quite as difficult as if I were acting without her knowledge."

"Meddling?"

"Encouraging your situation with Mrs. Seaton," Douglas clarified. "I believe you would suit."

"As do I. She is not of like mind."

"Then you must change her mind. If that means a very slow recovery, then so be it. You are the Moreland heir, after all, and no chances must be taken with your health."

The earl smiled crookedly. "A slow recovery...by God. I never stood a chance against you, did I?"

"One hoped not." Douglas rose. "Though you assuredly scared the hell out of me and put rather a wrench in my plans with Guinevere. You were never my enemy, nor hers. Rather, the duke was the common nuisance."

Douglas left the bedroom to admit Anna bearing a tray. She stayed with the patient when the viscount departed, and the next hour was spent nagging Westhaven to eat, making him as comfortable as she could, and letting him drift off to sleep until he woke in the small hours of the morning.

"Anna?" His voice was a croak.

"Here." She rose from the chair and sat on the bed at his hip.

"Feel like hell."

"Your fever is high," Anna said, the back of her hand on his forehead. "Now that you are awake, I can sponge you off, if you'd like. It will cool you down and probably soothe your skin, as well."

He nodded, and Anna brought bath sheets, a basin, and sponge to the bed. She got him arranged on top of the covers, his lower half covered by a blanket, the rest of him exposed and resting on layers of toweling.

"Fairly had a groom deliver this. It's witch hazel and some herbal infusions to help your skin heal." The cool sponge touched his skin, and Westhaven sighed. She brought it again and again down the length of his back, his arms, his shoulders, and sides, then shifted the blanket to bathe his legs and feet. She started the whole process over again and again, until he was nearly resting comfortably, his fever abating. By morning, Westhaven could honestly say he was at least no worse.

There was a discreet tap on the door, and then the viscount was with them, looking refreshed and ready for his day.

"Good morning, Mrs. Seaton, or might I call you Anna?" he asked. "And good morning, Westhaven." He laid his hand on the earl's forehead and frowned. "Better than I thought you might be."

He shooed off Anna to Gwen's company, leaving the men alone.

"How is it," Douglas asked his patient, "your fever responds only to her touch, hmm?"

"Shut up," the earl replied tiredly. "She put something in the water, if you must know. I think it helps."

By the time Douglas had clean sheets on the bed

and Westhaven extracted from his morning bath, the patient was once again growing drowsy. Douglas forced more willow bark tea down the hapless earl's gullet, tucked him in, and left him dozing peacefully beside his borrowed guardian bear.

∽

The next day was a mosaic of little activities and naps. Val sent out a note saying he'd visit shortly, Westhaven penned a note to His Grace, explaining that he was making a visit to Rose at Welbourne. Rose did visit her uncle, but Westhaven invariably found that fifteen minutes into any task or visit, he needed to either use the chamber pot or to nap or both.

The evening passed just as slowly, with Anna first beating him at cribbage then reading to him from a translation of Caesar's Gallic letters. He dozed in that twilight between sleeping and waking, aware of her voice but not the sense of her words. He did rise to wakefulness when she fell silent, but only to open his eyes and see Anna had paused, her own eyes closed, the book facedown on her lap. Sensing she was tired, he did not disturb her but let himself slip back into sleep.

The night was difficult for them both, with the earl again dozing between bouts of higher fever and Anna tending him as best she could. Sponge baths helped, but not as much as either of them wished.

"I think you would be more comfortable if we doused you in cool water from head to toe," Anna said as the clock struck two.

"That would involve moving, and right now, Anna, it hurts to breathe."

"But if we can get your fever down it won't hurt as much."

"If you insist." The earl made the monumental effort to push himself to the edge of the bed, but he needed Anna's assistance to climb into the tub and lower himself to the water. In less than ten minutes, his teeth were chattering, though to the touch, the water was almost warm. Anna got him out of the tub and wrapped him in bath sheets to sit by the fire while she toweled his hair dry.

"So tomorrow night should be easier?"

"It should," Anna said. "In adults, this sickness can be much more severe than in children."

"Do you have children?" the earl asked from the depths of the towel around his head.

Her hands went still, but her voice was steady when she answered. "I do not. Do you?"

"None. But marry me, Anna, and you can have all the children you can carry." In fact, he would enjoy having children with her, he thought, feeling—in the midst of his other discomforts—his cock stir.

"I will not marry you," she said, going to stand behind him. He felt the first gentle tug of the brush through his hair. "But you should have children. You will be a very good father, and children will be good for you."

"How so?" He closed his eyes, the better to enjoy the feel of the brush stroking gently across his scalp. "My father has hardly given me an example I want to emulate."

"That's just bluster." Anna waved a hand. "You paint him as a pompous, self-important, old-fashioned aristocrat, but he apparently went to tremendous lengths to attempt to secure access to his granddaughter."

"Ridiculous lengths," Westhaven said. "I would regale you with the details, but I hardly have the strength to keep my eyes open." He rose under his own power when Anna put down the brush, but grabbed her hand when he sat on the bed and brought it to his forehead. "I must trust you and Amery when you tell me I am following the predictable course for this illness, but I don't feel myself improving, particularly."

"Nor are you worsening, particularly."

"True." He closed his eyes and inhaled the rosy fragrance of her skin. "If I should worsen, you must promise me not to let His Grace inflict his cronies on me."

Anna leaned in and kissed his forehead.

"I will not let your father bother you. It has occurred to me that were you in need of someone to guard you from his mischief, Lord Amery and his wife are probably better equipped to do that than the Queen's own."

"Come to think of it, you are right. I will sleep better for the realization."

She tucked in the covers around him, laid a hand on his forehead, then smoothed back his hair. When his breathing evened out into sleep, she blew out the candles, banked the fire, and drew the extra blanket around her shoulders. As she curled down to rest her cheek against the bed, she felt the earl's hand stroking her hair in a slow, repetitive caress. The tenderness of the gesture soothed them both, and Anna soon followed him into slumber.

Eight

"YOUR GRACE WILL NOT DISTURB A GUEST UNDER my roof."

Douglas's voice, raised but not quite shouting, came from the corridor as Anna blinked herself awake. Dear God, the duke was going to find her in here, sprawled beside...

She hopped off the bed, shaking the earl's shoulder firmly.

"My lord," she hissed, "wake up." He groaned and rolled, the covers slipping down his naked, spotted torso. "My *lord*!" He curled to his side, frowning.

"Gayle Tristan Montmorency Windham, *wake up*!"

"I am awake," he said, automatically shoving the blankets aside, "and feeling like hell. Make way, lest I embarrass myself."

"Your father is here," Anna informed him, thrusting his dressing gown at him.

"Stand aside, Amery." The duke's voice rang with authority and disdain. "You will not keep a man from his son's sick bed, or the magistrate will know the reason why."

"Hurry." The earl shoved his arms into his dressing gown, his father's voice galvanizing him. "Find the book," he ordered, and in a feat of desperate strength, shoved the tub across the room behind the privacy screen. Anna tossed the covers back over the bed, opened the drapes, and pulled two chairs up to the hearth.

"Your son is not an infant," Douglas said with equal disdain. "He does not need his papa checking up on him. You will please wait in the parlor like any civilized caller, even at this uncivilized hour."

"You insult your betters, Amery," the duke stormed, "and you would not know a father's affection if it landed on the back of your horse. *I will see my son.*" The door crashed open, causing Anna to look up from where she was tending the hearth. She rose slowly but kept hold of the poker.

"Westhaven." The duke marched up to his son, who was reading Caesar by the hearth. "What are you doing rusticating here, when you should be in the care of our personal physicians?"

"Do I look ill?" Westhaven stood and raised a lordly eyebrow at his father, who did not quite match his son in height. "Or any more ill than I usually appear, as fatigue is a constant companion when one has as much to see to as I do."

Douglas stifled a snort at that but quickly frowned as two rotund gentlemen pushed past him into the room, having obviously escaped the barrier of footmen at the foot of the stairs.

"We can examine him immediately, Your Grace," the shorter of the two said, opening a black satchel. "If the young lady would please leave us?"

"Out, girl," the duke barked at Anna.

"I don't answer to you, my lord," Anna barked right back. "If your son were sick, his health would be best served by allowing him rest, *Your Grace*. I suggest you take your minions and wait in the parlor, lest Lord Amery be the one to summon the magistrate to eject trespassers."

The duke glared at his host. "Amery, your help is insufferable."

"No, *Your Grace*," Westhaven bit out with the same disdain Anna had shown. "You are insufferable. I am here to visit my niece, and there is no call whatsoever for you to interfere. You have, as usual, caused a great deal of drama at the expense of others, for your own entertainment. Your absence would be appreciated."

"And how about mine?" Valentine Windham strolled into the room. "Westhaven, my apologies. I have no idea how His Grace has managed to track you here. Shall I engage in a physical display of disrespect toward our parent?"

"This I must see," said another masculine voice from the corridor.

A tall, dark-haired man with icy blue eyes sauntered in behind Lord Valentine.

"Greymoor." Douglas nodded, his eyes glinting with humor.

"Amery." The latest player on the stage nodded in return.

"What is he doing here?" the duke thundered, glaring at Greymoor. "And I suppose your rakehell brother is bringing up the rear?"

Greymoor offered a slight bow. "The marquis may join us shortly, but was up most of the night with a colicky infant, which this fellow," Greymoor cocked an eyebrow at the earl, "is most assuredly not."

"I insist that I be assured of his health, and immediately," the duke snapped. "Woman, you will leave this room, or I will physically see to it myself."

"Lay a hand on her," the earl interjected softly, "and you will see just how robust I can be, Papa." Unbidden, Douglas, Valentine, and Greymoor shifted to flank Anna and the earl by the hearth.

"I will not have this," the duke shouted. "A man has the right to be assured of the health of his heir!"

"*Grandpapa!*" Rose trumpeted from the doorway. "Shame on you! There is a no-shouting-in-the-house rule, just as there is a no-running-in-the-barn rule."

And clearly, her tone said, a grandpapa was expected to know and obey the rules.

"Rose," the duke said, his volume substantially decreased, "if you will excuse us, poppet, your uncles and I were just having a small disagreement."

Rose crossed her arms over her skinny chest. "You were the one yelling, Grandpapa, and you didn't apologize."

To the amazement of all, the duke nodded at his older son and at Lord Amery. "Gentlemen, my apologies for raising my voice to a level that disturbed my granddaughter."

"Apology accepted," Westhaven ground out.

"Now, poppet," the duke said with exaggerated patience, "will you excuse us?"

"Papa?" Rose turned to her step-father, who held out a hand to her.

"No need to go just yet, Rose," he said. She bounded over to him and was soon perched on his hip. The duke, looking frustrated beyond bearing, stomped out of the room, snapping his fingers to indicate his lackeys were to follow.

Greymoor closed the door and locked it. Val went to assist his brother into a chair, and Douglas tossed Rose onto the bed.

"Grandpapa was in a temper," Rose said, bouncing on the mattress. "His neck was red, and I think his physicians ought to examine him."

"Apoplexy isn't something I would wish on even him," Douglas said. "Rose, don't bounce so high, you'll hit the canopy." This inspired Rose to reach up and try to touch the canopy on every leap, while Val scowled at his brother.

"You really do not look well, Westhaven," he concluded. "How in the hell did His Grace get word you were ill in the first place?"

"I know not," the earl replied wearily.

"Spies," Greymoor said. "Might I have an introduction to the other lovely lady in the room before we get to that?"

"My apologies," Douglas said. "Mrs. Anna Seaton, may I make known to you Andrew Alexander, Lord Greymoor. Mrs. Seaton is visiting with us while Westhaven recuperates."

"What about me?" Rose flopped down on the bed. "You didn't bow to me, Cousin Andrew."

"You get off that bed and make a proper curtsy," Lord Andrew said, "and I will make you a proper bow." He scooped up Rose as she made an elaborate curtsy. "Magic misses you," Lord Andrew whispered. "He's telling George just how much right now."

"Oh, can I go visit Sir Magic before you leave?"

Rose squealed, perfectly content to remain cuddled against her mother's cousin.

"Of course, but I think there are weighty matters to discuss first." He sat on the bed with Rose and tossed an expectant look at the earl. "Westhaven, what's wrong with you?"

"He has the chicken pox," Rose volunteered. "You know, where you get all spotty and itchy and cranky?"

"I noticed the cranky part." Greymoor nodded. "You must have a serious case, Westhaven, the symptoms have been in evidence for some time. I don't see the spots, though."

In reply, the earl hiked the sleeve of his dressing gown, exposing a spotty, hairy, muscular forearm.

"Poor blighter," Lord Andrew murmured. "Had 'em myself when I was seven."

"Seems we've all had them," Lord Valentine commented, "except for Fairly."

Westhaven sat down wearily. "I am told I'm recuperating despite the absence of a quack, but it seems we should send somebody downstairs to keep His Grace from further mischief."

"I'll go with you, Douglas," Greymoor said, "and referee your entertainment of the duke. Val, can you valet your brother?"

"Of course." Val rose and extended a hand to Anna. "Mrs. Seaton, as my brother appears to be recovering, you have my thanks." He drew her to her feet, smiling a particularly warm smile.

"Anna?" Westhaven caught her eye, and she turned a curious gaze on him. "My thanks, as well." She nodded and silently took her leave.

"Come, Rose." Greymoor snatched up his small cousin. "We have an assignation in the stable with two handsome knights."

Val closed the door behind the entourage and met his brother's eyes.

"I will raid Amery's wardrobe," Val said, "and then we will talk, brother."

The instant his brother was gone, Westhaven stepped behind the privacy screen, making the best use of the rare moment of solitude. God, how had his brother Victor survived the years of being an invalid, with no privacy, no hope, no possibility of recovery?

Looking as healthy as he possibly could, flanked by his brother, his host, and Lord Greymoor, Westhaven spent the next hour balancing the need to control his father with the respect due one's ducal sire. It was a long, largely unpleasant hour, made bearable only by Greymoor's willingness to occasionally distract the duke with insolent humor, and then, before His Grace got truly bilious, with talk of horses.

When the others had drifted off, leaving the duke alone with his heir and his spare, His Grace speared his son with a hard look.

"You two." The duke shook his head. "Don't think I am not appreciative of the interest you take in our Rose, but I know you're up to something, and I won't rest until I know what it is."

"Tell me," Westhaven asked, his tone bored, "does Her Grace know you've gone haring off in this downpour to bother Amery with your odd starts?"

"Your mother should not be needlessly worried."

"And wasn't it just such weather that precipitated your near fatal bout of lung fever, Your Grace?"

"Hush, boy," the duke hissed. "Don't be making your mother to fret, I say. I'll never hear the end of it."

"Behave yourself, and we won't have to tattle on you, Your Grace. Don't behave yourself, and you will leave us no choice."

"Behave myself." The duke scowled. "Behave myself; this from a grown man who has no mistress, no wife, no fiancée... Behave myself. You behave yourself, Westhaven, and see to the succession."

He swept out with perfect ducal hauteur, leaving Val and his brother to roll their eyes behind His Grace's back. The silence, in the wake of the duke's ranting and posturing, was profoundly comforting.

"Sit," Val said. "Or would you prefer to return to your room?"

"I should go back upstairs," the earl replied. "But, Val? I think he's getting worse. More heedless, to come out here and invade Amery's home... Gwen and Douglas would have been within their rights to have him barred from their property."

"He is Rose's grandfather," Val said as they gained Westhaven's room. "But I agree. Since Victor died, and since his own illness, I think our papa has become almost obsessed with the need for heirs."

"I nominate you."

"And I nominate you," Val responded. "Shall we sit?"

"We shall. I find my energy greatly depleted; though rest is helpful, the effect is temporary. When I lie down, I go out like the proverbial candle."

"I'll get your boots." Val pushed him into a wing

chair, hauled off his brother's boots, and ordered them up some breakfast.

"So you spent three nights with Mrs. Seaton," Val said, apropos of nothing.

"I did," the earl admitted, closing his eyes. "I behaved, Valentine." Barely, but he did. "She is a decent woman, and I would not force my attentions on any female."

"Your attentions?" Val's eyebrows rose. "His Grace will be marching you both down the aisle posthaste if he learns of your folly."

"She won't be marched, and neither will I. He did that to me once before, Val, and I won't let it happen again."

"He did it to you, and he did it to Gwen, who had one hell of a lot more family at her back than Mrs. Seaton does. If he can outflank Heathgate, Amery, Greymoor, and Fairly, what chance would one little housekeeper stand against him?"

"You raise a disturbing point, Valentine"—the earl frowned—"though His Grace manipulated Gwen into accepting my proposal largely by threatening her family. If Mrs. Seaton has no family, then she is less vulnerable to His Grace's machinations."

"Talk to her, Westhaven." Val rose and went to answer a tap on the door. "Make her understand what risks she's dealing with, and just what a desperate duke will do to see his heir wed." He opened the door, admitting a footman pushing a breakfast trolley.

As the earl joined his brother for tea, toast, and a few slices of orange, he considered that Val was right: If Anna Seaton had weaknesses or vulnerabilities, it was best she disclose them to the earl, for sooner or later, if the duke learned of them, he would be exploiting them.

And as much as Westhaven sensed they could make a good job of marriage to one another, the earl would not under any circumstances accept Anna Seaton served up as his wife, bound and gagged by the duke's infernal mischief.

Westhaven healed, albeit slowly, and had to agree with Douglas that what was needed was mostly sleep. On the third day, the rain stopped, on the fourth, the earl slept through the night. On the fifth, he began to grouse about returning home and was marshaling his arguments in the solitude of his room when Rose cajoled him into a visit to the stables. He managed to groom his horse and entertain Rose with a few stories of her father.

But the outing, tame as it was, had been taxing and left him overdue for a stint in bed, much to his disgust. He parted company from Rose, sending her off to draw pictures of the stories he'd told her, and sank down on his bed.

He had a feeling something was off, not right somehow in a nagging way. He peeled out of his clothes and stretched out on the mattress, but still, the sense of something missing wouldn't leave him.

Anna, he realized as he slipped between the freshly laundered sheets. He'd gone all of two or three hours without seeing her, and her absence was tolling in the back of his mind. All the more reason, he thought, closing his eyes, to get back to Town where his routine would prevent prolonged periods of proximity such as they'd had at Welbourne.

Wanting to bed the woman—even offering to wed her—wasn't the same as wanting to live in her pocket, after all. A man would have to be besotted to allow feelings like that.

Nine

A WEEK SPENT AT LORD AMERY'S HAD CREATED DEFI-
nite changes in the way Westhaven went on with the
object of his unbesottedness. By necessity, while in
Surrey he'd kept his hands to himself, and the enforced
discipline had yielded some odd rewards.

Anna, for example, had touched him, and in ways a
housekeeper would never have touched her employer.
She'd bathed him, shaved him, brushed his hair,
dressed and undressed him, and even dozed beside him
on the big bed. As soon as his fever had abated, she'd
left his most personal care to others, but the damage
had been done.

Or, Westhaven thought as he tugged on his boot,
the ground had been gained.

He had also had a chance to observe her over
longer periods of time and watch more carefully
how she interacted with others. The more he saw,
however, the more puzzled he became. The little
clues added up…and not to the conclusion that she
was a mere housekeeper.

"What on earth has put that frown on your face?"

Devlin St. Just came strolling into the earl's townhouse bedchamber, dressed to ride and sporting a characteristic charming grin.

"I am considering a lady," the earl replied, scrounging under his bed for the second boot.

"And frowning. What seek you under the bed, Westhaven? The lady?"

"My damned boot," Westhaven said, extracting the missing footwear. "I sent Stenson off to Brighton with Val, to assure myself some privacy, but the result is I must look after my own effects." He pulled on the boot, sat back, and smiled. "To what do I owe the pleasure of a visit?"

"Val commissioned me to keep an eye on you," Dev said, plopping down on the end of the bed. "Said he was decoying Stenson, so the state of your health would not become common knowledge in the ducal household."

"I am still very obviously recovering from the chicken pox," the earl admitted. "At least, it's very obvious when I am unclothed; hence, Stenson was sent elsewhere."

"His Grace came by to interrogate me." Dev leaned back on his elbows. "Knowing nothing, I could, as usual, divulge nothing. He looked particularly choleric to me, Westhaven. Are you and he at outs?"

"I don't think he tolerates the heat well," Westhaven said, glancing around the room for his cravat. He'd ring for his housekeeper, who seemed to know where his clothing got off to better than he did, but with Dev on the bed, that wasn't an option.

"He'd tolerate the heat better if he unbent a little in

his attire," Dev said. "He was in full regalia at two in the afternoon on a sweltering day. I'm surprised Her Grace lets him go about like that."

"She chooses her battles," Westhaven said, spying a clean pair of cravats in his wardrobe. "Do me up, would you? Nothing fancy." He held up the linen, and Dev rose from the bed.

"So where are you off to? Chinny up." He whipped the linen into a simple, elegant, and perfectly symmetric knot in moments.

"The wharves, unfortunately," Westhaven said, now seeking his waistcoat.

"Why unfortunately?" Dev asked, watching his brother root around in the wardrobe.

"The stench in this heat is nigh unbearable," Westhaven replied, extracting a lightweight green and gold paisley waistcoat from the wardrobe.

"Hadn't thought of that. And here I thought being the heir was largely a matter of dancing with all the wallflowers and bellowing His Grace into submission every other Tuesday."

"Don't suppose you'd like to join me?" Westhaven asked, his goal now to locate a suitable pin for his cravat.

"I have lived these thirty and more years," Dev said, plucking a gold pin from the vanity, "without experiencing the olfactory pleasure of the wharves on an unbearably hot day. We must remedy my ignorance. Hold still."

He deftly dealt with the cravat and stood back to survey the results.

"You'll do." He nodded. "If you attempt to wear your coat before we arrive, I will disown you for lunacy."

"You can't disown me. You've been formally recognized."

"Then I'll tattle to Her Grace," Dev said, grabbing his own coat, "and tell her you've been ill."

"For God's sake, Dev." Westhaven stopped and glared. "Don't even joke about such a thing. Fairly reports that a serious bout of chicken pox in an adult male has been blamed for a loss of reproductive function in rare cases. His Grace will have me stripped and studied within an inch of my most private life."

"No, he will not. You'll not allow it, neither will I, neither will Val."

"I do not put the use of force past him," Westhaven said as they traversed the house. "You think he appears choleric, Val, and I think he's become less constrained by appearances."

"He's afraid of dying," Dev suggested, "and he wants his legacy assured. And, possibly, he wants to please Her Grace."

"Possibly," Westhaven allowed as they reached the stables. "But enough of that depressing topic. How fares your dear Bridget?"

"Alas." Dev rolled his eyes. "She has taken me into disfavor or taken another into greater favor."

"Well, which is it? One wants the dirty details."

"Unbeknownst to me"—Devlin rolled his sleeve down then right back up—"my Bridget had a potential Mr. Bridget waiting for her in Windsor. One cannot in good conscience thwart the course of true love. She lacked only for a modest dowry."

"You dowered your doxy, thus proving you are a Windham," Westhaven said. "Though you do not bear the name, you yet have His Grace's inability to deal badly with a woman you care for."

"Perhaps his only redeeming feature," Dev said. "Hullo, sweetheart." Morgan was walking out of the stables, a kitten in her hand. She offered them a perfunctory curtsy but went on her way, keeping her customary silence.

"Is she simple?"

"Not in the least." Westhaven mounted Pericles and waited while Dev used the mounting block in his turn. "She does not speak, or not clearly, and can hear only a little, or so Val says. But she works hard and is a favorite of the older staff. She arrived with my housekeeper several months ago."

"The one with you at Amery's?" Dev asked with studied nonchalance.

"The very one." Westhaven shot him a look that said he wasn't fooled by Dev's tone. "What exactly do you want to know that you weren't able to get out of Val?"

"Where did you find her? I am in the market for same."

"I lured her to my employ with my endless buckets of charm," Westhaven said dryly.

"You are charming," Dev said when they were trotting along. "You just can't afford to be flirtatious, as well."

Westhaven aimed a smile at his brother, grateful for the simple understanding and support. His was grateful, as well, for his brother's continued company throughout the rest of the afternoon, as Dev was well versed in the mechanics of bringing a cargo to or from Ireland, which was the particular focus of Westhaven's errand.

"I am beyond glad to have that particular situation resolved," Westhaven said as they trotted into his mews. "I didn't know you exported your stock to France."

"Now that the Corsican is properly half a world away, there is a raging demand for horses on the Continent. The French cavalry that galloped off to Moscow in '12 boasted something like forty thousand horses. As best we can calculate, within a year, there were less than two thousand suitable mounts. If it has four hooves and will take a bridle, I can find a buyer on the Continent."

"Enterprising of you. What are you doing for dinner?" Westhaven asked as they swung down from their saddles. "In fact, as you are without a housekeeper, what are you doing for the next little while?"

Devlin's expression closed, but not before the earl saw the shadows clouding his eyes. Dev had been to war and come home, thankfully, but as a veteran of every major battle on the Peninsula, the Hundred Days, and Waterloo itself, Dev had also left pieces of his soul all over the Continent.

"If you're thinking of a sortie to the Pleasure House," Devlin said, "I will decline."

"Not my cup of tea." Westhaven shook his head. "From what Val tells me, the place has lost a little of its brilliance. I wasn't suggesting we go carousing, in any case, but rather that you move in with me and Val."

"Generous of you," Dev said, pursing his lips in thought. "I have at least three horses needing stabling and regular work if they're to be sold next spring as finished mounts."

"We've room," Westhaven said. "I'll confess to

curiosity. Are your beasts so sought after you can live on the proceeds of those sales?"

"Not just those sales," Dev replied, though it was as personal a question as they'd ever exchanged. "But I'd appreciate having you look over my whole operation sometime, if you've a mind to. I am sure, with your more extensive commercial connections, you'll see efficiencies I've overlooked."

Westhaven glanced over, but Dev was accomplished at keeping his emotions to himself. There was nothing to suggest the idea was anything other than a casual fancy.

"I'd be happy to do that."

"You might make the same offer to Val, you know," Dev said as they dismounted. "He imports instruments from all over the Continent and has two different manufactories producing pianos, but he hasn't wanted to impose on you regarding some of the business questions."

"Val hasn't wanted to *impose on me*? And you, Dev? Have you also not wanted to impose on me?"

Dev met his eye squarely and nodded.

"We do not envy you your burdens. We would not add to them."

"I see," Westhaven muttered, scowling. "And is that all you have to offer me? Burdens? Were you not more knowledgeable than I regarding the harbor at Rosslare? The packet schedule to Calais?"

"Westhaven, we think to spare you, not add to your load."

"My lord?" Anna Seaton stood to one side, her silly cap covering her glorious hair, her demeanor tentative, and it was a measure of the earl's consternation with his brothers he hadn't noticed her on the terrace.

"Mrs. Seaton." Westhaven smiled at her. "May I make known to you my dear brother, Devlin St. Just. St. Just, my housekeeper, florist, and occasional nurse, Mrs. Anna Seaton."

"My lord." Anna bobbed a curtsy while St. Just bowed and offered a slight, not quite warm smile.

"I am hardly a lord, Mrs. Seaton, being born on the wrong side of the ducal blanket, but I am acknowledged, thanks to Her Grace."

"And I have offered him a place in my household," Westhaven said, meeting his brother's eye, "if he will have it."

A beat of silence went by, rife with undercurrents.

"He will have it," Dev said on a grin, "until you toss me out."

"Val's playing might take some getting used to," Westhaven cautioned, "but Mrs. Seaton takes the best of care of us, even in this god-awful heat."

"Speaking of Lord Valentine?" Anna chimed in.

"Yes?" Westhaven handed off Pericles to the groom and cocked an eyebrow. The cap was more atrocious than silly, he saw, and Anna seemed tense.

"He writes he will be back from Brighton tomorrow," Anna said, "and warns you might need to have some other task arranged for Mr. Stenson."

"I'll take over Stenson," Dev said. "My former housekeeper had no skill with a needle, so Mr. Stenson can be set to looking after my wardrobe for at least the next few days."

"That will help. Was there something further, Anna?"

"I assume dinner will be for two, my lord, and on the terrace?"

"That will do, and some lemonade while we wait for our victuals, I think. Which bedroom shall we put my brother in?"

"There is only the one remaining at the back of the house, my lord. We have time to ready it before this evening."

He nodded, dismissing her but unable to take his eyes off her retreating figure until she was back through the garden gate. When he turned back to his brother, Westhaven found Dev eying him curiously.

"What?"

"Marry her," Dev said flatly. "She's too pretty to be a housekeeper and too well spoken to be a doxy. She won't be cowed by His Grace, and she'll keep you in fresh linens and good food all your days."

"Dev?" Westhaven cocked his head. "Are you serious?"

"I am. You have to marry, Westhaven. I would spare you that if I could, but there it is. This one will do admirably, and she's better bred than the average housekeeper, I can tell you that."

"How can you tell me that?"

"Her height for one thing," Dev said as they made for the house. "The peasantry are rarely tall, and they never have such good teeth. Her diction is flawless, not simply adequate. Her skin is that of lady, as are her manners. And look at her hands, man. It remains true you can tell a lady by her hands, and those are the hands of a lady."

Westhaven frowned, saying nothing. Those were the very observations he had made of Anna while they rusticated at Amery's. She was a lady, for all her wielding of dusters and wearing of caps.

"And yet she says her grandfather was in trade," Westhaven noted when they arrived to the kitchen. "He raised flowers commercially, and she bouquets the house with a vengeance. We're also boasting a very well-stocked pantry and a supply of marzipan for me. The sweet of your choice will be stocked, as well, as I won't take kindly to your pinching mine."

"Heaven forefend," Dev muttered as Westhaven procured a fistful of cookies.

"We are permitted to spoil our dinner, as well," Westhaven said. "Grab the pitcher, the sugar bowl, and two glasses."

Dev did as bid and followed his brother back onto the shady back terrace. Westhaven poured them both a tall glass of lemonade, adding liberal amounts of sugar to his own.

"I haven't had lemonade since I was a lad," Dev remarked when he'd chugged half of his. "It refreshes."

"Tastes better with extra sugar. Val adds cold tea to his. Try mine."

"As I have had the chicken pox," Dev said, sipping from Westhaven's glass. "Give me that sugar bowl."

They passed an amiable evening, chatting over dinner about the marriage prospects for their sisters, the house party at Morelands, and the state of British government in general.

When the earl was alone in the library at the end of the evening, he found himself wondering why he hadn't offered his brothers the use of the townhouse earlier. It would have allowed them both to be near their sisters without residing at the ducal mansion, and it would have provided some company.

Anna had been company out at Welbourne, but in the week since their return, she'd faded back into the role of invisible housekeeper. When he walked into a room, she left. When he sat down to a meal, she was nowhere to be found. When he retired to his rooms, she'd been through earlier, cleaning and tidying then disappearing.

The door clicked softly, and as if he'd conjured her with his thoughts, Anna padded in on bare feet, clad only in her night rail and wrapper.

❧

"Anna." He rose, and she watched as he took in her dishabille.

"My lord," she said and earned a thunderous scowl from him as he stalked over to her.

"What have I done, Anna, to earn your use of my title?"

"I cannot be sure we are private," she said then blinked at her tactical error. "And I do not believe such familiarity wise."

"Ah." He backed away, leaning on the desk, arms crossed. "Shall we discuss this change of heart on your part? You've been avoiding me since we got back to Town, and don't think to tell me otherwise."

"You are no longer ill," she said, raising her chin. "And you are capable of dressing yourself."

"Barely," he said with a snort. "So tell me, how am I to court you if you won't stay in the same room with me? How am I to persuade you to marry me if you maneuver always to have others present when I am about? You aren't playing fair, Anna."

She watched him warily, trying to formulate an answer that wouldn't aggravate him further. If she'd known he was in here, lurking in the solitude and darkness, she would have run in the opposite direction—she hoped.

"Come here." He gentled his tone and held out a hand.

"You will take liberties," Anna said, crossing her arms. "And you know I do not encourage your courting. I warned you your efforts would be for naught."

The difficulty, Anna silently admitted, was that she had made no efforts of her own, efforts to secure yet another position, another identity, another escape route. Like one of her grandfather's fat, wooly sheep, she'd just gone about her tasks, cutting flowers, airing sheets, and telling herself *soon* she would press his lordship for that character, *soon* she would explain the situation to Morgan, *soon* she would make inquiries at some different agencies.

A week had gone by, and she'd accomplished nothing, except another seven days of longing for a man she had no business desiring.

"You will make me work for it, won't you?" Westhaven said with a faint smile. He pushed away from the desk and approached her silently. "That's as it should be."

His arms closed around her, and Anna just bowed her head, knowing even more than his kisses and his wicked caresses, the comfort of his embrace had the power to paralyze her. He was warm, vital, and strong, and while it wasn't his aim to protect her, the illusion that he could was irresistible.

"Let me hold you," he whispered, "or I'll have a relapse of the chicken pox to inspire you to closer attendance of me."

"You can't have a relapse."

"Actually, I can," he murmured, his hands easing over her back, "but Fairly says it's quite rare. Relax, Anna, I just want to feel you in my arms, hmm?"

She couldn't remain tense, not with his big hands stroking so knowingly over her muscles and bones. He touched her the way he might touch a horse, listening with his hands for what her body would tell him without her mind's consent.

"You need to eat more," he said. "You've put weight on me but neglected yourself."

"You lost weight, being ill," Anna corrected him, her voice sleepier than she'd intended it. "And you have to stop this."

"Why is that?" She felt his lips against her temple, and leaned into him a little more heavily.

"Because, I like it too well, and then you'll be kissing me and your hands will be wandering and I will want to let them wander."

"Good," the earl said, humor in his voice and something else. Something not quite as relaxed as his hands might have suggested. "I do want to kiss you. Have for days, but you've been dodgy as a feral cat." His lips brushed her cheek, and Anna felt her meager defenses crumbling.

"You must not," she said, cuddling into his chest as if he could protect her from his own wayward intentions.

"I rather think I must," he argued softly. "I have never met a lady so in want of kissing." Those lips were moving along her jaw now, then teasing at her neck. Oh, the wretched, wretched man... Anna let her head fall to the side, vowing she would do better next time. She wouldn't let him get past the first embrace. But for now...

She was wicked. Her brother had told her she was headstrong, unnatural, and ungrateful, and all that added up to wickedness. She should not be misleading the earl like this, should not be giving him ideas, should not be *enjoying* giving him ideas. But he touched her, and all the loneliness and worry and fear went away, taking her honor and common sense with them, leaving her melting and trusting and entirely too willing.

"That's it," he coaxed, his teeth scraping gently at her skin. "Don't think, just let me bring you pleasure, bring us both pleasure."

"Westhaven..." she whispered, trying still to end this, to put him firmly in his place. He'd told her he would never force her; that he would stop if she asked it of him.

She could not ask it of *herself*, Anna thought despairingly as the earl's lips settled softly over hers.

She tried to hold back, to keep herself aloof from his caresses and his kisses, but she had no experience with sexual self-restraint. Her hands crept up to caress his neck and jaw, her body pressed into his with shameless disregard for anything save the need to be *closer*, and her mouth parted on a sigh.

"Oh, not this..." She broke the kiss when he began

to rock his hips against her but stayed in his arms, her forehead resting on his sternum. "You are interested, and soon you will be indecent with me again."

"I would love to be indecent with you, Anna."

"I cannot allow it," she wailed. "You do not understand all of my circumstances, Westhaven. This is nothing but folly. We must stop."

"Soon," he assured her. "Your virtue is not at risk, Anna. Not tonight. Just let me pleasure you."

"You want to be indecent," she accused again, gripping his waist tightly.

"Unless you ask it of me, I will not remove my clothing," he replied, his voice steadier than hers.

"Do you promise? You won't even unfasten your trousers?" She lifted her face to regard him by the light of the fire.

"I will not unfasten my trousers," he replied, his gaze rock steady with maybe a touch of humor in his green eyes. "Let me hold you and kiss you and bring you pleasure."

If he kept his pants up, Anna reasoned, she wouldn't be so tempted to wantonness, wouldn't be tempted to touch him, to explore his intriguingly hard and yet delicately smooth male member with her fingers... and lips and tongue. If he kept his pants up, she could manage to keep her own wits about her.

She leaned up and kissed him, only to find herself lifted in his arms, turned, and deposited on the corner of his huge desk.

"Here." He dragged over a chair and a hassock, the better to support her dangling feet. "If you need to hold on to something, hold on to me."

Hold on, she did, as his lips settled over hers with unmistakable purpose. His tongue was in her mouth, thrusting in the same lazy rhythm as his hips were pushing against her sex. He wedged himself more tightly between her legs, and Anna felt something hot and needy wake up below the pit of her stomach. One of his arms stayed anchored around her back, but his free hand was wandering, stealing around her waist, leaving heat and wanting in its wake.

"Touch me, Anna." Westhaven's voice was a rough whisper, insistent and seductive. "Touch me however it pleases you."

It pleased her to slide her hands over his chest, but the fine linen of his shirt wasn't the goal she sought. Without taking her mouth from his, Anna tugged his shirttails free and slid a hand along his ribs, the feel of his warm skin bringing her some unnameable sense of relief.

"Don't stop," he urged, as she lifted his shirt free, all the way around his waist, and further gratified herself with the smooth, muscular planes of his back beneath her other hand. To touch him like this, skin to skin, at once soothed and aroused. She needed to touch him and couldn't get enough of his skin beneath her hands.

"Jesus," Westhaven hissed when Anna found his nipple. She paused, and he nipped at her neck, "Jesus, that feels good." He shifted the angle of his hips, and Anna gasped, the sensation resulting from his rigid flesh against her sex sending a bolt of pure, hot desire skittering through her vitals.

"I like it, too," he murmured, repeating the move but making no effort to open his falls. "Spread your legs, love. I'll make it feel even better."

When she grasped the meaning of his words, she complied, her own hands greedily learning the contour and sensitivities of his chest and neck and abdomen. She wanted to put her mouth on him, but his damned shirt…

"Shirt off," she got out before drawing his tongue strongly into her mouth. She was growing frantic, but for what, she could not have said. *For more*, she thought. Please, almighty God, for *more*. They broke apart for a mere instant while Westhaven whipped the shirt over his head then plunged himself tongue-deep back into their kiss.

His hands shifted from her back to bunch the soft billows of her night rail and wrapper up in her lap.

Good, Anna thought, wanting only to be closer to him. And when Westhaven wedged himself between her legs again, she could only pull him closer, hoping he would again find that spot, that one place where the weight and thrust of his rigid length brought her such startling pleasure.

"Use me," he growled. "Let yourself come." Anna could not puzzle out the sense of his words but rocked her hips against him, seeking the same fit they'd found earlier.

"I can't find…" she panted, trying to form words as Westhaven's hand slipped lower and lower.

"I can," he whispered, his fingers slipping over her intimate folds. His touch was infernally knowing, light, and teasing, *maddening*. Then he shifted the angle of his hand, so his thumb was pressing, *right there*, and he gave her a hint of relief with the tip of his finger inside her body.

"Westhaven," she panted, "…dear God, what are you…?"

But his free hand had parted her night clothes enough to find a nipple and apply a gentle, pulsing pressure to it. That was all it took, just the start of attention to a breast, a bit of his finger, some pressure from his thumb, and her body seized in great, clutching spasms of pleasure.

She came silently, her body bucking against him for long fraught moments in complete abandon. When it was over, she hung limp and winded against him, shuddering as aftershocks wracked her, her cheek pressed over his heart.

∾

Westhaven wanted nothing more than to plunge his raging erection into her wet heat and thrust like a mad bull, but his instincts suggested the moment wasn't right. There had been too much ignorance in Anna's responses, too little ability to anticipate and manage her own reactions.

Too much *innocence*.

So he held her to his chest and stroked her hair, and tried to pay attention to her and not to the indignant clamoring of his impatient cock.

"I cannot fathom what just passed between us," she whispered.

"Has no one seen to your pleasure?" Westhaven kissed her temple, unable to stifle the smile in his voice. She might not be a virgin fresh from the schoolroom, but it pleased him to think he was the first to bring this to her. A husband exercised his rights, but a lover pleasured.

"Pleasure," she echoed his thought, sounding inebriated. "Profound pleasure."

"I hope so," the earl rumbled. "It's been a while, hasn't it?" He brushed her hair back over her ear, and regarded her carefully. The disorientation on her face, coupled with the trusting, boneless weight of her in his arms caused a spike of profound *affection* for her to spread out from the center of his chest.

"I would like a little of the same for myself," he whispered, arms going more tightly around her. "You will oblige me?"

"Oblige?" Anna's brain had clearly slipped its leash, and Westhaven was hard put not to gloat.

"Let me come against you," the earl urged, his voice intimate with anticipated pleasure. "The couch will do." Hearing no objection, he hoisted her from the desk and laid her down on the long sofa.

"Lovely," he whispered, coming down on top of her.

On top of her, thank Christ, he was at long last on top of her.

He blanketed her there on the couch, for the first time laying his half-naked body over hers, though he was careful with his weight. His lips found hers, his hand strayed to her breast, and he thought he heard her sigh "lovely" as she lifted up her hips, trying to stroke herself against him again.

"Easy," he murmured, nipping at her earlobe. "I promised not to remove my own clothing unless at your request; you will have to oblige."

Or, he reasoned, he could come in his knickers like the schoolboy he'd once been. But Anna was tugging at his falls and gently extracting his cock from his clothing.

"Much better," he breathed, feeling himself grow more aroused now that he was free of his clothing.

He took his time, though it had been a long, frustrating week, apparently for them both. There was a hint of revenge in the languor with which he went about this loving. He kept his kisses slow and sweet, and he only gradually let her have the full weight of his hips, snugging his cock low against her belly. But Anna took a little revenge of her own, as her hands were free to roam his back, his chest, into his hair, over his features. He groaned quietly when she found his nipples then less quietly when she fastened her mouth on one and her fingers on the other.

"Oh, love, I can't…Jesus, Anna…"

She eased off but didn't desist completely, and then he felt her tilt her hips, the better to trap him against her. Her arms urged him to rest on her more fully.

"I like it," she whispered, kissing his cheek. "I like your weight on me, like you being around me, above me."

Encouraged by the rasp in her voice as much as her words, he began to thrust with more purpose, firmly putting aside the temptation to shift his hips and hilt himself in the wet heat of her. Her tongue found his nipple again, but this time he arched his back to make the angle easier for her.

"Your mouth, Anna," he rasped, "please… *God in heaven*."

She wrapped her legs around his waist, suckled at him, and clamped her hand tightly on his buttocks as he thrust hard against her. When the warmth of his seed coursed onto her stomach, she held him all the more closely, until he levered up on his elbows and stared down at her in the firelight.

He lasted only a moment, suspended above her, before she slipped a hand around his nape and urged him back down against her. He capitulated to her silent request and was soon breathing in counterpoint with her, as naturally as if they'd made love every night for years. She traced patterns on his back, sifted her hands through his hair, and took his earlobe in her mouth for the occasional nip.

"One of us," the earl said, "is going to have to get up. I nominate you."

"Happy to serve," Anna murmured drowsily. "But can't fit it onto the schedule just at the moment."

"Suppose that leaves me." The earl sighed and heaved up, first onto straight arms then to his feet. He stood above her, brooding down at her half-naked, utterly relaxed sprawl so long she self-consciously moved to close her legs.

"Don't," he said, but it was a request, for all he didn't state it as such. "Please. You are lovely." But he moved away, sensing her defenses were weak, and she needed a moment. When he turned back to her, he'd pulled up his breeches but not buttoned them. To his shamelessly primitive delight, she'd not covered herself, not sat up, nor in any way disturbed the wanton pose in which he'd left her.

"Let me." The earl sat down at her hip and began to dab gently at her with his dampened handkerchief. He made a sensual game out of it, stroking the cool cloth over her stomach, up under her breasts, and down to her sex. When she shifted her dressing gown, likely thinking to afford herself some small modesty, he applied a gentle pressure to the inside of her thigh.

"Let me," he repeated. He held the cloth against her, and Anna closed her eyes, her blush evident even by firelight.

"Anna Seaton." He leaned down and brushed his lips over her heart. "The pleasures you and I could share…" He said no more, feeling strangely off balance by their encounter. He set aside the cloth, pushed the halves of her clothing even farther to the side, and climbed over her again.

He wasn't ready to bounce up and take himself upstairs to bed, wasn't ready to dive back into the last few pieces of correspondence, wasn't ready to pour himself a brandy and take it up to his balcony. Completely out of character for him, all he wanted to do was stay here with Anna, holding her and being held by her.

The feeling was mutual, he guessed, as Anna's arms went around his shoulders. She kissed his cheek, and with her hands, urged his head down to her shoulder. Westhaven obliged, keeping himself awake by force of will.

This situation with Anna was proving more complicated than he wanted it to be. With Elise, he would have been out the door by now. She had accommodated him, but in hindsight, Westhaven saw it was barely even that. Elise had never let her fingers drift over his scalp like this, making delicious circles on his skin. She would never have clutched at his buttocks, the better to hold him to her. Elise would never—probably not even if he'd asked it of her—put her mouth to his nipple.

And he would most assuredly not have asked it of her, not in a million years.

You shouldn't have had to ask. He could hear Anna's tart tones in his head, even as he knew the thought was also his own.

Anna was different, he conceded. Just how different, he hadn't accurately seen when he'd initially proposed. She held him at arm's length, or tried to, then capitulated with sweet abandon, leaving him disoriented, so great had been his pleasure.

"Love?" He raised up on his forearms and brushed her hair off her forehead. "How are you? You're too quiet, and you leave a fellow to fret."

"I am…beyond words." Anna smiled up at him. And he knew what thoughts were stirring in her busy brain: She should be vexed by this turn of events, troubled, dismayed, and she would be—soon. But not just yet, not with her body still languorous and pleased with itself, pleased with him.

He kissed her forehead. "I hope you're beyond words in a positive sense."

"I am." She sighed and stretched, bringing her pelvis up against his.

"None of that." He smiled and nuzzled at her neck, then slipped lower, going up on his knees to take a nipple into his mouth. Anna merely cradled his head against her and sighed again.

"Next time," he murmured, resting against her sternum, "I will know where to start. You have sensitive breasts, my dear. Inspiringly so."

"None of that."

"None of what?" He raised his face to regard her in puzzlement.

"None of that next-time talk," Anna clarified. "This was a lapse."

Westhaven hung above her, considering, even as he ignored the considering being done by his cock. "We need to discuss this, and for that, you will have to be decently covered."

"I will?"

His took his weight and warmth away from her and fortified himself with the disappointment in her voice.

"You will." He sat at her hip and began to straighten her clothing, but paused to brush his thumb over her pubic curls. "When this next time comes around, that we are not going talk about, I will put my mouth on you here." He closed his fingers over her sex. "You will enjoy it, but not half so much as I."

She looked surprised then intrigued as he closed her buttons and bows, and the earl concluded she was a virgin to oral sex as well as orgasms. Mr. Seaton, God rest his lazy, inconsiderate, bumbling, unimaginative, selfish soul, had much to answer for.

"Up you go." He tugged Anna to a sitting position then settled down beside her and wrapped an arm around her shoulders. Her head rested against his chest, and her hand stole onto his bare stomach.

He yawned sleepily. "I should put on a shirt if we're to have a meaningful discussion."

"You needn't," Anna assured him. "It won't take long at all to tell you this sort of thing has to stop."

"Going back on your word, Anna?" Westhaven

leaned over to kiss her temple and to again inhale the fragrance of her hair.

"I agreed not to seek another position until the end of summer," she reminded him. The glow in Westhaven's body faded a tad with each clipped syllable. "I did not agree to become your light-skirt."

"Were you a virgin, you would still be considered chaste."

"But I wouldn't be for much longer if this keeps up."

Westhaven knew some genuine puzzlement. "I will not force you, Anna."

"You won't have to," she bit back. "I will spread my legs for you just as eagerly as I did tonight."

"With results just as pleasurable, one hopes, but we're talking past each other, Anna. Why won't you let yourself enjoy my advances? That's the real issue. If you have a reason of any substance—a husband somewhere, a mortal fear of intercourse, something besides your silly conviction earls don't marry housekeepers—then I will consider desisting." He punctuated his comment with a soft kiss to her neck.

"Keep your lips off me, please." Anna straightened away from him but didn't move off the couch. "I cannot think. I do not even know right from wrong when you start with your kisses and your wandering hands. You don't mean to do it, but you leave me helpless and lost and... You have no clue what I mean, do you?"

"In truth," the earl said, urging her head back down to his shoulder, "I do. You would be astonished, Anna, at how surprised I am at the way matters have progressed between us, and I am not often surprised."

"Well, then," Anna huffed, "all the more reason to give up this courting you seem so bent on."

"Can't say I agree with you." His lips grazed her temple again, completely without conscious thought on his part. "And you have yet to name me a single reason why you could not wed me. Have you taken holy orders?"

"I have not."

"Have you a mortal fear of copulating with me?"

She buried her nose against his shoulder and mumbled something.

"I will take that for a no. Are you married?"

"I am not." And because he heard what he wanted to hear and insisted on hearing, the earl missed the slight hesitance in her answer.

"So why, Anna?" He bit her earlobe gently. "Those were my teeth, not my lips, mind you. We've gone only so far as lovers, and already you must know we would bring each other pleasure upon pleasure. So why do you play this game?"

"It isn't a game. There are matters I hold in confidence, matters I will not discuss with you or anyone, that prevent me from committing to you as a wife should commit."

"Ah." The earl was listening now and heard the resolution with which she spoke. "I will not pry a confidence from you, but I will make every effort to convince you to confide in me, Anna. When a man marries, his wife's goods become his, but so too, should her burdens."

"I've given you my reason." She lifted her head to regard him closely. "You will leave me in peace now? You will give up this notion of courting me?"

"Knowing you are burdened with confidences only makes me that much more convinced we should be wed. I'd take on your troubles, you know."

"You are a good man," Anna said, touching his cheek, her expression both solemn and sad, "but you cannot be my husband, and I cannot be your wife."

"I will content myself with being your suitor, as we agreed, though now, Anna Seaton, I will also be encouraging your trust, as well." He kissed her palm to emphasize his words. "One last question, Anna." The earl kept hold of her hand. "If you were free of these obligations that you hold in confidence, would you consider my suit then?"

He was encouraged she couldn't give him an immediate no, encouraged she'd offered him the smallest crumb of a confidence, encouraged they'd been more intimate with each other than ever before—encouraged, but also…concerned.

"I'd consider it," she allowed. "That is not the same as accepting it."

"I understand." He smiled at her. "Even a duke mustn't take his duchess for granted."

Anna fell asleep in the secure circle of his arms, her weight resting against him, his lips at her temple. As he carried her to her bedroom, the earl reflected that for a woman who insisted there be no next time, Anna had certainly been reluctant to bring an end to things this time.

It boded well, he thought, kissing her forehead as he tucked her in. All he needed to do now was gain her confidence and meet these obligations she was so determined to carry alone. She was a housekeeper, for pity's sake, how complicated could her obligations be?

❦

Anna awoke the next morning with a lingering sense of sweetness, of stolen pleasures not quite regretted, and—most incongruous of all—of hope. Hope that somehow, she might find a way to extricate herself from the situation with Westhaven that didn't leave them enemies. Westhaven was doing exactly as he said he would: He was giving her pleasure, pleasure beyond her wildest imaginings, pleasure she could keep for herself in memory long after her dealings with him were over, and she would give a great deal to see that those memories were not tainted with a bitter parting.

And under that hope there beat against the cage of reason and duty the wings of another hope, one she didn't even acknowledge: The hope that somehow, she might not have to leave him, not at the end of the summer, not any time soon. She could not marry him, she accepted that, but to leave him might prove equally impossible, and what options did that give her?

Anna was practical by nature, so she forced herself to leave those questions for another time, got out of bed, dressed, and went about her day. Memories of the night preoccupied her, though, and she forgot to don one of her homely lace caps.

She also forgot to chide Morgan for the wisps of hay sticking to her skirts, and she almost forgot to put extra sugar in the earl's first glass of lemonade. She wasn't looking forward to seeing him again, and yet she yearned for the sight of him.

The man and his ideas about courting were botheration personified.

"Post for ye, Missus." John Footman handed her a slim, worn missive posted from a remote inn on the Yorkshire dales, and Anna felt all the joy and potential in the day collapse into a single, hard lump of dread.

"Thank you, John." Anna nodded, her expression calm as she made her way to her private sitting room. She rarely closed the door, feeling the space was one of few places the servants could congregate with privacy, particularly as Mr. Stenson would never set a sanctimonious toe on her carpet.

But she closed the door before reading her missive. Closed it and locked it then sat down on the sofa and stared into the cold grate, trying to collect her courage.

Finding the exercise pointless, she carefully slit the seal on the envelope and read the brief contents:

Beware, as your location may be known.

Just that one cautionary sentence, thank God. Anna read it several times then tore both letter and envelope into tiny pieces, wrapped them into a sheet of foolscap, and put them onto the hearth grate to burn later that evening.

Beware as your location may be known.

A warning, but understandably vague. Her location may be known; it may not be. Her location— Southern England? London? Mayfair? Westhaven's household?—may be known. She pondered the possibilities and decided to assume that her location meant she'd been traced to London, at least, which meant her adoption of the profession of housekeeper might also be known and that Morgan was in service with her, as well.

All in all, it amounted to looming disaster and

ended, utterly, any foolish fantasies about dallying with the earl for the rest of the summer. Unlocking the door, Anna assembled her writing supplies and penned three inquiries to the employment agencies she'd noted when she and Morgan had passed through Manchester. Bath was worth a try, she decided, and maybe Bristol, as well. A port town had possibilities inland locations did not.

Without volition, her mind had shifted into the calculating, rational, unsentimental habits of a woman covering her tracks. If it hurt her to leave Nanny Fran, to uproot Morgan again, to part from the earl, well, she told herself, the fate trying to find her would hurt more and for a much longer time.

She assessed the room, mentally inventorying the things she'd brought with her, the few things she'd acquired while in London. Nothing could be left behind that might give her away, but little could be taken with them when they left.

She'd done this twice before—prepared, packed, and executed an escape, for that's how she had to think of it. Morgan would have to be warned, and she wasn't going to like this turn of events one bit. Anna didn't blame her, for here, in the earl's house, Morgan wasn't treated like a mute beast. The other servants were protective of her, and Anna had a sneaking suspicion Lord Valentine felt the same way.

It was no way to live, but Anna had cudgeled her brain, and there seemed to be no alternative. When they ran out of hiding places in England, then the Americas were a possibility, but Anna hated to think of going so far from home.

"Beg pardon, Missus?" John Footman was at her door, smiling, which told her it wasn't a summons from the earl, thank God. "Lunch be served, unless you'd like a tray?"

"I'll be along, John." Anna smiled up at him. "Just give me a minute."

She completed her correspondence and tucked it into her reticule. It wouldn't do for the rest of the household to know she was corresponding with employment agencies, much less in what cities. It wouldn't do for them to know she was upset, wouldn't do for them to know she'd soon be leaving, with or without the character Westhaven had promised her.

She got through lunch, feeling frozen inside and frantic at the same time. In the few months she'd held her position, she'd come to treasure the house itself, taking pride in its care and appearance. She treasured the staff, as well—with the exception of Stenson, but even he was dedicated to faithful execution of his duties. They were good people, their lives lived without substantial duplicity or deception. Such a one as she wasn't destined to fit in with them for long.

"Morgan?" Anna murmured as they rose from lunch, "will you join me for a moment?"

Morgan nodded. Anna slipped her arm through Morgan's and led her out to the back gardens, the only place where privacy might be assured. When they were out on the shaded terrace, Anna turned to face Morgan directly.

"I've had a letter from Grandmama," Anna said slowly but distinctly. "She warns us we may have been traced to London. We need to move on, Morgan, and soon."

Morgan's expression, at first joyous to think they'd heard from their grandmother, then wary, knowing it could be bad news, finally became thunderous. She scowled mightily and shook her head.

"I don't want to leave either," Anna said, holding the younger woman's eyes. "I truly would not if there were any choice, but there is no choice, and you know it."

Morgan glared at her and shook a fist.

"Fight," she mouthed. "Tell the truth."

"Fight with what?" Anna shot back. "Tell the truth to whom? The courts? The courts are run by old men, Morgan, and the law gives us no protection. And stuck out on the dales, we wouldn't be able to get to the courts, and well you know it."

"Not yet," Morgan mouthed, still glaring daggers. "Not so soon again."

"It's been months," Anna said on a sigh, "and of course we can't go immediately. I need a character from his lordship, and I have to find positions for us elsewhere."

"Go without me."

"I will not go without you," Anna said, shaking her head. "That would be foolish in the extreme."

"Split up," Morgan persisted. "They need only one of us."

Anna stared at Morgan in shock. The last sentence had been not just lipped but almost whispered, so close was it to audible speech.

"I won't let that one be you," Anna said, hugging her and deciding against making a fuss over Morgan's use of words. "And we'll fight if we have to."

"Tell Lord Val," Morgan suggested, less audibly. "Tell the earl."

"Lord Val and the earl cannot be trusted. They are men, too"—Anna shook her head—"in case you hadn't noticed."

"I noticed." Morgan's glare was temporarily leavened by a slight smile. "Handsome men."

"Morgan Elizabeth James"—Anna smiled back—"shame on you. They might be handsome men, but they can't change the laws, nor can we ask them to break the law."

"Hate this," Morgan said, laying her head on Anna's shoulder. She raised her face long enough for her sister to see the next words. "I miss Grandmother."

"I do, too." Anna hugged her close. "We will see her again, I promise."

Morgan just shook her head and stepped back, her expression resigned. This whole mad scheme had been undertaken more than two years ago, "just until we can think of something else." Well, it was two years, three positions, and many miles later, and nothing else was being thought of. In those years when a gently bred young girl—even one who appeared unable to hear or speak—should be thinking of beaus and ball gowns, Morgan was sweeping grates, lugging buckets of coal, and changing bed linens.

Anna watched her go, her heart heavy with Morgan's disappointment but also with her own. Two years was a long time never to see home or hearth, always to look over your shoulder for those meaning you harm. It was never supposed to go on this long, but as Anna contemplated her remaining years on earth, all she could see was more running and hiding and leaving behind the things—and people—that really mattered.

Ten

"YOUR HOUSEKEEPER IS KEEPING SECRETS."

Dev threw himself down on the library's sofa, yanked off his boots, and stretched out to his considerable length with a sigh. "And she's a damned pretty housekeeper to have served as your nurse."

"Nurses must be ugly?" Westhaven tossed down his pen. Dev was a different sort of housemate than Val. Dev didn't disappear into the music room for hours at a time, letting the entire household know where he was without being bothersome about it. Dev wandered at will, as apt to be in the library with a book or in the kitchen flirting with Cook and Nanny Fran. He'd seen to moving his riding horses into the mews but still had plenty of time for poking his nose into his brother's business.

"Nurses must be ugly." Dev closed his eyes. "Mistresses must be pretty. Housekeepers are not supposed to be pretty, but then we have your Mrs. Seaton."

"Hands off."

"My hands off?" Dev raised his head and eyed Westhaven. "My hands off your housekeeper?"

"Yes, Dev. Hands off, and this is not a request."

"Getting into the ducal spirit, are you?" Dev closed his eyes again and folded his hands on his chest. "Well, no need to issue a decree. I'll behave, as she is a female employed by a Windham household."

"Devlin St. Just." Westhaven's boots hit the floor with a thump. "Weren't you swiving your house-keeper *while* she was engaged to some clueless simian in Windsor?"

"Very likely." Dev nodded peacefully, eyes closed. "And I put away that toy when honor required it."

"What sort of honor is this? I comprehend what is expected of a gentleman, generally, but must have missed the part about how we go on when swiving housekeepers."

"You were going on quite enthusiastically," Dev said, opening one eye, "when I came down here last night to find a book."

"I see."

"On the sofa," Dev added, "if that pinpoints my interruption of your orgy."

"It wasn't an orgy."

"You were what?" Dev frowned. "Trying to keep her warm? Counting her teeth with your tongue? Teaching her how to sit the trot riding astride? Looked to me for all the world like you were rogering the daylights out of dear Mrs. Seaton."

"I wasn't," Westhaven spat, getting up and pacing to the hearth. "The next thing to it, but not quite the act itself."

"I believe you," Dev said, "and that makes it all better. Even though it looked like rogering and sounded like rogering and probably tasted like it, too."

"Dev…"

"Gayle…" Dev got up and put a hand on his brother's shoulder. "I am the last person to begrudge you your pleasures, but if I can walk in on you, and I've only been underfoot a day, then anybody else can, too."

Westhaven nodded, conceding the point.

"I don't care that you and Mrs. Seaton are providing each other some slap-and-tickle, but if you're so far gone you forget to lock the door, then I am concerned."

"I didn't…" Westhaven scrubbed a hand over his face. "I did forget to lock the door, and we haven't made a habit out of what you saw. I don't intend to make a habit of it, but if I do, I will lock the door."

"Good plan." Dev nodded, grinning. "I have to approve of the woman on general principles, you know, if she has you spouting such inanities and dropping your pants for all the world to see."

"I thought in my own library at nigh midnight I could have privacy," Westhaven groused.

Dev's expression became serious. "You cannot assume you have privacy anywhere. The duke owns half your staff and can buy the other half, for one thing. For another, you are considered a most eligible bachelor. If I were you, I would assume I had no privacy whatsoever, not even in your own home."

"You're right." Westhaven blew out a breath. "I know you're right, but I don't like it. We will be careful."

"*You* be careful," Dev admonished. "Earlier today, I was minding my own business up on the balcony that opens off my bedroom, and I saw your housekeeper in earnest discussion with the deaf maid. Mrs. Seaton was warning the maid you and Val are men who can't be trusted nor asked to break the law. I thought you should know."

"I appreciate your telling me, but I am loathe to react out of hand to words taken out of context. In some villages, there are laws against waving one's cane in public, and laws against drinking spirits on the Sabbath."

"Are you sure the maid can't speak?" Dev pressed. "Do you really know what became of Mr. Seaton and where the banns were cried? Just who were Mrs. Seaton's references?"

"You raise valid questions, but you cannot question that Mrs. Seaton does a splendid job of keeping this house."

"Absolutely splendid," Dev agreed, "and she trysts with you in the library."

"Are you telling me I shouldn't marry her now?" Westhaven tried for humor but found the question was partly serious.

"You might well end up having to marry her, if last night is any indication," Dev shot back. "Just make damned sure you know exactly who it is you're trysting with before the duke gets wind of same."

Knowing he wouldn't get any more work done after that discussion, Westhaven left the library in search of his housekeeper. He couldn't be precisely sure she was avoiding him—again—but he'd yet to see her that day. He found her in her private sitting room and closed the door behind him before she even rose to offer him a curtsy.

"I wish you wouldn't do that," he said, wrapping his arms around her. She stiffened immediately.

"I wish you wouldn't do *that*," she retorted, turning away her face when he tried to kiss her.

"You don't want me holding you?" he asked, kissing her cheek anyway.

"I don't want you closing the door, taking liberties, and *bothering* me," she said through clenched teeth. He dropped his arms and eyed her curiously.

"What is it?"

"What is what?" She crossed her arms over her chest.

"You were willing enough to be bothered last night, Anna Seaton, and it is perfectly acceptable that your employer might want to have a word or two with you privately. Dev said he saw you and Morgan in heated discussion after lunch. Is something troubling you? Those confidences you referred to last night, perhaps?"

"I should not have trusted you with even that much of a disclosure," Anna said, uncrossing her arms. "You know I intend to seek another position, my lord. I wonder if you've written out that character you promised me?"

"I have. Because Val has yet to return, it remains in my desk. You gave me your word we would have the rest of the summer, Anna. Are you dishonoring that promise so soon?"

She turned away from him, which was answer enough for Westhaven.

"I am still here."

"Anna…" He stole up behind her and wrapped his arms around her waist. "I am not your enemy."

She nodded once, then turned in his arms and buried her face against his throat.

"I'm just…upset."

"A lady's prerogative," he murmured, stroking her back. "The heat has everyone out of sorts, and while I was allowed to sit on my lordly backside for a week, claiming illness, you were expected to be up at all hours."

She didn't contradict him, but she did take a deep breath and step back.

"I did not intend to upset you." The earl offered her a smile, and she returned it just as the door swung open.

"I beg your pardon, my lord." Stenson drew himself up to his unimpressive height, shot a disdainful glance at Anna, and pulled the door shut again.

"Oh, God." Anna dropped down onto her sofa. "It needed only that."

The earl frowned at her in puzzlement. "I wasn't even touching you. There was a good two feet between us, and Stenson was the one in the wrong. He should have knocked."

"He never does," Anna sighed, "and we were not touching, but we looked at one another as something other than housekeeper and employer."

"Because I *smiled* at you?"

"And I smiled back. It was not a housekeeper's smile for her employer."

"Don't suppose it was, but it was still just a smile."

"You need a butler, Westhaven." Anna rose and advanced on him.

"Any footman can answer the damned door. Why do I need another mouth to feed?"

"Because, a butler will outrank that toadying little buffoon, will be loyal to you rather than the duke's coin, and will keep the rest of the male servants toeing the line, as well."

"You have a point."

"Or you could just get rid of Stenson," she went on, "or have your brother perpetually travel around the countryside with Stenson in tow."

"I suppose if Stenson is back, then Val can't be far behind," Westhaven observed.

"I have missed him," Anna said. She looked a trifle disconcerted to have made the admission but let it stand.

"I have, too." Westhaven nodded. "I miss his music, his irreverence, his humor... How is Dev settling in?"

Anna crossed the room and opened the door before answering his question.

"Well enough, I suppose," she replied, busying her hands with an arrangement of daylilies. "He doesn't sleep much, though, and doesn't seem to have much of a routine."

"He'll settle in," the earl said. "You will let me know when Lord Valentine returns?"

"No need for that." Val stepped into the room. "I am back and glad to be back. It is too damned hot to travel, and Stenson was unwilling to travel at night. Not a very servile servant, if you ask me, though he does a wicked job with a muddy boot."

"You." Westhaven pulled his brother into a hug. "No more haring off for you, sir. Nobody knows how to go on without your music in the house or your deviltry to keep up morale."

"I will wander no more," Val said, stepping back, "at least until the heat breaks. I came, though, in search of Miss Morgan."

"She might be in the kitchen," Anna said. "More likely she's reading in the barn. With dinner pushed back these days, she has some free time early in the evening."

"Val?" The earl stayed his brother's departure with a hand on his arm. "You should know, in your absence, I've asked Dev to bunk in with us. He was without his domestic help, and we have the room."

"Devlin, here?" Val's grin was spontaneous. "Oh ye gods and little fishes, that was a splendid idea, Westhaven. If we're to be stuck in Town with this heat, at least let us have good company and Mrs. Seaton's conscientious care while we're here."

He sailed out of the room, leaving Anna and the earl smiling in his wake.

"Good to have him back safe and sound," Westhaven said.

"Three for dinner on the terrace, then?" she asked, every inch a housekeeper.

"Three, and I wanted to speak with you about a practical matter."

"Dinner is very practical."

"Dinner is…yes, well." He glanced at the door. "I have commissioned a fair amount of furniture for Willow Bend, but the place needs drapes, carpets, and so forth. I'd like you to see to it."

"You want me to order those things? Shouldn't your mother or perhaps one of your sisters take that on?"

"Her Grace is bouncing between Town and Morelands and preparing for the summer's house parties. My sisters have not the expertise, nor do I have the patience for working with them on a project of this nature."

"But, my lord, one of them will eventually be living there. My tastes cannot possibly coincide with those of a woman I've never met."

"Not possibly." The earl smiled. "As yours will be better."

"You should not say such things." Anna's frown became a scowl. "It isn't gentlemanly."

"It's brotherly and the truth. Even I know salmon and purple don't go together, but that's the kind of scheme my sisters would consider 'daring,' or some such. And they would pester me endlessly, while you, as I know from firsthand experience, can turn a house into a home with very little guidance from its owner."

"I will take this on," Anna said, chin going up. "Be it on your head if the place turns out looking like one of Prinny's bad starts. What sort of furniture have you commissioned?"

"Why don't we finish this discussion in the library?" the earl asked. "I can make you lists, draw you some sketches, and argue with you without every single servant and both brothers hearing me."

"Give me a few minutes to talk with Cook, and I will join you."

"Twenty minutes, then." The earl took his leave, going up to his bedroom, where he'd no doubt Stenson was attempting to address more than a week's worth of others making shift with his responsibilities.

"Mr. Stenson?" The earl strode into the room without knocking—and why would he?—and caught the fellow actually sniffing the cravat discarded over the edge of the vanity mirror. "Whatever are you doing in my quarters?"

"I am your valet, my lord." Stenson bowed low. "Of course I must needs be in your quarters."

"You will stay out of here and busy yourself with Lord Val and Colonel St. Just instead."

"*Mr. St. Just?*" Stenson might as well have said: *That bastard?!* But Dev would have great good fun putting Stenson in his place, so Westhaven added a few more cautions about the bad form exhibited by the lower orders when they couldn't be bothered to knock on closed doors, and took his leave.

When he returned to the library, he did not immediately begin to list the furniture he'd ordered for Willow Bend. He instead wrote out an order to have all the interior locks above stairs changed and only two sets of keys made—one for him and his brothers, one for his housekeeper.

Sniffing his cravat, for God's sake. What on earth could Stenson have been about?

The question faded as Westhaven spent two hours arguing good-naturedly with his housekeeper over matters pertaining to Willow Bend. That was followed by an equally enjoyable dinner with both of his brothers, during which he realized he hadn't dined with them together since Victor had died months before.

"Will you two help me with my horses?" Dev pressed when they were down to their chocolates and brandy.

"If you insist." Val held his snifter under his nose. "Though coming up from Brighton has left me honestly saddle sore."

"I'll be happy to pitch in, as Pericles can use light duty in this heat, but if I'm to be up early"—Westhaven rose—"then I'd best seek my bed. You gentlemen have my thanks for keeping Mr. Stenson busy, though I don't think he was exactly pleased with the reassignment."

"My shirts will be pleased," Dev said. "It's mighty awkward having to always wear one's jacket and waistcoat because one's seams are all in jeopardy."

"And I found every mud puddle between here and Brighton just to make sure Mr. Stenson was gainfully occupied."

"I am blessed in my brothers," Westhaven said, leaving them with a smile.

"So tell me the truth," Dev said, pushing the decanter at his youngest brother. "You are willing to ride with us because you think it would be good for Westhaven. Just like his housekeeper has been good for him."

Val smiled and turned his glass around on the linen tablecloth. "It will be good for all of us, being together, living here, even if it's only for a little while. I find, though, that I've sat too long here in the evening breezes." He got to his feet and quirked an eyebrow at his oldest brother. "Shall we stroll in the moonlight?"

"Brother"—Dev grinned—"I have heard rumors about you."

"No doubt," Val said easily as they moved off. "They are nothing compared to what one hears about you."

"And that gossip is usually true," Dev said with no modesty whatsoever as they neared the mews. "Now why are we out here stumbling around in the night?"

Val turned and regarded his brother in the moonlight. "So I can remind you not to make disparaging remarks about Mrs. Seaton or her situation with Westhaven where anybody could overhear you. You know what the duke tried to do with the last mistress?"

"I'd heard about Elise. Then you are aware of a situation between Westhaven and Mrs. Seaton?"

"He's considering marrying her," Val said. "Or I think he is. They're certainly interested in each other."

"They're a bit more than interested," Dev said, rubbing his chin. "They were all but working on the succession when I came upon them in the library last night."

"Ye gods. I came upon them in her sitting room this afternoon, door open, all hands in view, but the way they look at each other…puts one in mind of besotted sheep."

"His Grace will be in alt," Dev said on a sigh.

"His Grace," Val retorted, "had best not get wind of it, unless you want Westhaven to immediately lose all interest."

"Gayle wouldn't be that stupid, but he would be that stubborn." Dev tossed a companionable arm around Val's shoulders. "This will be entertaining as hell, don't you think? I'm not sure Westhaven's wooing is entirely well received, and he has to go about it in stealth, winning the lady without alerting the duke. And we have front-row seats."

"Lucky us," Val rejoined. "Doesn't working on the succession comport with welcoming a man's suit?"

Dev's grin became devilish. "That, my boy, is a common misunderstanding among the besotted male sheep of this world. And the female sheep? They like us befuddled, you know…"

❦

"It's a speaking tube," Val explained. Morgan quirked an eyebrow at him, and he smiled reassuringly. "A lot of invalids take the sea air in Brighton," he went on, "so the medical community is much in evidence there. I discussed your loss of hearing with a physician or two, and I've brought it up with Fairly, as well. He'd like to examine you, though he isn't a specialist in the field of deafness."

Morgan tried to keep her emotions from her eyes, but it was difficult, when her eyes were so used to conveying what words could not. She was more than a little infatuated with this man, with his kindness and generosity of spirit, his acceptance of her disability, his care for his brothers and sisters. He was what a brother should be—decent, selfless, thoughtful, and good-humored.

"Will you let me try it?" he asked, holding up the tube. It was shaped like an old-style drinking horn, conical and twisted. He gently turned her by the shoulders and pushed her hair aside. Morgan felt the small end of the tube being anchored at her ear.

"Hello, Morgan. Can you hear me?"

She whirled on him, jaw gaping.

"I can hear you," she whispered, incredulous. "I can hear your words. Say more." She turned and waited for him to position the speaking tube again.

"Let's try this with the piano," Val suggested, and she heard his words, or much more of them than she'd heard before. She couldn't see his mouth when he used the speaking tube, so she must be hearing him. It felt like a tickling in her ear and like so much more.

"I remember this."

"You remember how to speak," Val said into the tube. "I thought you might. But come, let me play for you."

He grabbed her by the hand, and she followed, Sir Walter Scott forgotten in the hay as they ran to the house. He led her straight to the music room, shut the door, and sat her down on what she'd come to think of as her stool. It was higher, like the stools in the ale houses, and let her lay her head directly on the piano's closed case. Val took the tube and put it wide end down on the piano. He leaned down as if to put his ear to the narrow end of the tube.

"Try it like that."

Morgan perched on the stool and carefully positioned the tube at her ear. Val moved to the piano bench and began a soft, lyrical Beethoven slow movement, meeting Morgan's eyes several measures into the piece.

"Can you hear?"

She nodded, eyes shining.

"Then hear this," he said, launching into a rollicking, joyous final movement by the same composer. Morgan laughed, a rusty, rough sound of mirth and pleasure and joy, causing Val to play with greater enthusiasm. She settled in on the stool, horn to her ear, eyes closed, and prepared to be swept away.

She'd been wrong. She wasn't infatuated with Val Windham; she was in awe of him. He'd brought her music and the all-but-forgotten sensation of a human voice sounding in her ear. All it had taken was a simple metal tube and a kind thought.

"Good God almighty." Dev glanced across the library at Westhaven. "What's gotten into the prodigy?"

Westhaven looked up from his correspondence and focused on the chords crashing and thundering through the house.

"He's happy," Westhaven said, smiling. "He's happier than I've heard him since Victor died. Maybe happier than I've ever heard him… He tends to stay away from Herr Beethoven, but if I'm not mistaken, that's who it is. My God…"

He put down his letters and just listened. Val could improvise melodies so tender and lilting they brought tears. He could be the consummate chamber musician, his keyboard evoking grace, humor, and elegance. He knew every drinking song and Christmas carol, all the hymns, and folk tunes. This, however, was heady repertoire, full of emotion and substance.

And he plays the hell out of it, Westhaven thought, amazed. He knew his brother was talented and dedicated, but in those moments, he realized the man was *brilliant*. More gifted than any Windham had ever been at anything, transcendently gifted.

"Jesus Christ, he's good," Dev said. "Better than good. My God…"

"If His Grace could hear this," Westhaven said, "he'd never say another disparaging thing about our youngest brother."

"Hush." Dev's brow knit. "Let's just listen."

And they did, as Val played on and on, one piece following another in a recital of exuberant joy. In the kitchen, dinner preparations stopped. In the garden, the weeding took a hiatus. In the stables, grooms paused to lean on their pitchforks and marvel. Gradually, the music shifted to quieter beauty and more tender joy. As the evening sun slanted across the back gardens, the piano at last fell silent, but the whole household had been blasted with Val's joy.

In the music room, watching Morgan smile up at him, Val had a queer feeling in his chest. He wondered if it was something like what doctors experienced when they could save a life or safely bring one into the world, a joy and a humility so vast they could not be contained in one human body.

"Thank you," Morgan whispered, smile radiant. "Thank you, thank you."

She threw her arms around him and hugged him tight, and he hugged her back. There were some moments when words were superfluous, and holding her slight frame against him, Val could only thank God for the whim that had made him pick up the tube. He let her go and saw she was holding out the tube to him.

"You keep it," he said, but she shook her head.

"I cannot," she said clearly.

"Then let's leave it in here," Val suggested. "You can at least use it when we speak or when you want to hear me play." He put it on top of the piano, puzzled and not a little hurt by her unwillingness to keep the thing. He'd first thought to get her one when he'd seen a pair of old beldames strolling in Brighton, their speaking tubes on chains around their necks like lorgnettes.

Morgan nodded solemnly but put the tube inside the piano bench, out of sight.

"You don't want anyone to know?" Val guessed.

"Not yet," she replied, staring at the closed lid of the bench. "I heard once before," she said, her voice dropping back to a whisper so he had to lean in close to hear her. "We crossed the Penines, and something changed, in here." She pointed to her left ear. "But the next morning, I woke up, and it had changed back. Can we try the tube again tomorrow?"

"We can." Val smiled, comprehension dawning. "Your ear opened up because of the altitude. When you descended, it closed up again."

Morgan looked puzzled and turned her face away.

"Even if I can't hear tomorrow"—she hunched her shoulders against that terrible possibility—"thank you, Lord Valentine, for today. I will never forget your kindness."

"It was most assuredly my pleasure." He beamed at her. "Will you let Lord Fairly take a peek at you?"

"Look only," she said, her shoulders hunching more tightly still. "No treatments. And you will come with me?"

"I will. Westhaven trusts the man, and that should tell you worlds."

"It has to be soon," Morgan said, biting her lip.

"I'll track him down in the next few days. He's almost always at home these days, and I run tame around his pianos."

Morgan nodded and took her leave of him, her joy in the day colored by her recall of Anna's plans. It had been almost a week since Anna had gotten Grandmama's letter, and a perfectly pleasant if hot week, too. Morgan knew the earl had something to

do with Anna's lighter moods. Oh, Anna still fretted—
Anna was born to fret—but she also occasionally
hummed, and she hugged Morgan when no one was
about, and she smiled—when she wasn't staring off
into space, looking worried.

Good Lord. Morgan stopped in her tracks. What
was she going to tell Anna? When was she going
to tell Anna? Not for a day or two, Morgan knew,
as improvement could be deceptive. Her hearing
sometimes got better during really bad storms, only to
disappear when the weather moved. Worse than the
loss of hearing, though, was the loss of speech.

She'd never realized how the two were related
until she couldn't hear. She lost her ability to gauge
the volume of her voice and found she was whispering—or worse, shouting—when she thought her
tone was conversational. Eventually, she'd just given
up, until she was afraid to attempt speech again, the
patterns not even feeling familiar to her lips, teeth, and
tongue anymore.

But that could all change, she thought. If the speaking tube still worked tomorrow, it could all change.

༄

The week had gone so well, Anna thought as she rose
from her bed. It was another beautiful—if sweltering—
summer day, and she'd enjoyed her efforts to complete
the Willow Bend interiors. The earl had chosen
surprisingly pretty and comfortable furniture, suited to
a country home, and to a country home that wouldn't
be simply a gentleman's retreat from the city.

He'd had few suggestions regarding the decorative

schemes, predictably. "Avoid purple, if you please," or "no flights of Egyptian fancy. My sisters are imaginative enough as it is." He liked simple, cheerful, comfortable arrangements, which suited Anna just fine. They were easy to assemble, clean, and maintain, and better still, easy to live in.

And if she felt a pang of envy that some other woman, one dear to Westhaven, was going to be doing the living at Willow Bend, she smothered it. She smothered her anxieties regarding her grandmother's warning and set to bargaining with herself fiercely instead: I'll work on the Willow Bend interiors until the letters arrive from the agencies. I'll enjoy the earl's attentions until I have to leave. I'll leave Morgan in peace until I know for certain when and where we're going…

Her life, it seemed, had degenerated into a series of unenforceable bargains made with herself, while the business of the household moved along heedlessly.

The Windham males had taken to hacking in the park early in the morning, with Pericles sometimes escorting two of the younger stock or taking a day to enjoy his stall and hay. The men came back hungry and usually in high spirits.

When Devlin St. Just had moved in, he'd brought an ability to tease with him, and it was infectious. With only the earl and Lord Val in residence, it was as if their shared grief had pushed out all but the driest humor. With Dev underfoot, bad puns, jokes, ribbing, and sly innuendo cropped up among all three brothers. To Anna, the irreverent humor was the conversational equivalent of the occasional bouquet in the house.

It pleased the eye and brought visual warmth and pleasure to the odd corner or bare table.

Nonetheless, Colonel St. Just watched her with a calculating gleam foreign to either the earl or Lord Val. St. Just was a bastard and half Irish. Either burden would have been a strike against him, but his papa was a duke, and so he was received.

Received, Anna thought, but not welcomed. That difference put a harder edge on St. Just than on either of his brothers. In his own way, he was an outsider, and so Anna wanted to feel some sympathy for him. But his green eyes held such a measure of distance when they looked at her, all she felt was…wary.

Still, he was supportive of the earl, proud of Val's music, and well liked by the staff. He always cleaned his plate, flirted shamelessly with Nanny Fran, and occasionally sang to Cook in a lilting, lyrical baritone. He was, in a word, charming, even to Morgan, who usually left the room as quickly as she could when he started his blather.

"Hullo, my dear." The earl strolled into Anna's sitting room and glanced back at the door as if he wanted to close it.

"Good morning." Anna rose, smiling despite herself, because here was the handsomest of the Windham brothers, the heir, and he wanted to marry *her*. "What brings you to my sitting room on this lovely day?"

"We have household matters to discuss." His smile dimmed. "May I sit?"

"Shall I fetch the tea tray?" Anna frowned and realized he wanted to settle in, which would not do, for many reasons.

"No, thank you." The earl took the middle of the settee, extended an arm across the back, and crossed one ankle over the other knee. "How are you coming with the Willow Bend project?"

"I've ordered a great deal in the way of draperies, rugs, mirrors, smaller items of furniture, such as night tables, footstools, and so forth," Anna replied, grateful for a simple topic. "It is going to cost you a pretty penny, I'm warning you, but the results should be very pleasing."

"Pleasing is good. When will it be ready?"

"Much has already been delivered. The rest should arrive in the next few days. I understood there was some urgency about this project."

"There is. I want it done before fall, when I'm likely to be dragooned into the shires by my dear papa for some hunting."

"If you don't want to go hunting, you'd best arrange something with your brothers, so when Papa issues his summons, you are otherwise occupied."

"I'll get right on it."

"And have you gotten right on finding us a butler? Stenson is more in need of stern guidance than ever."

The earl burst out laughing at that image and shook his head as he rose.

"Send me some candidates," he said. "Their most important qualification must be their ability to withstand the duke's inveigling. I should be on hand Monday and Wednesday next week, though I have appointments back-to-back on Tuesday. I'll expect you to accompany me to Willow Bend on Thursday."

"Me?" Anna rose, as well, memories assaulting her:

The earl drinking champagne from the bottle on the library floor, his hand slipping over her bare buttocks in the dark of night, the single rose he'd brought her...

"I don't believe that's wise."

"Of course it's wise," the earl said. "How else am I to know which table goes in what room, and which drapes to hang where?"

"I can write it out," Anna suggested, "or go when you're not there."

"I am the owner, Anna." He peered down at her in consternation. "What if I take issue with your decisions? Are we to trundle out there on alternate days until all our quibbling is resolved?"

She admitted the silliness of that, but not out loud.

"You aren't afraid, are you?" He cocked his head, frowning. "It isn't likely we'll be stuck in a second monsoon, but we can take the coach if you'd feel better about it."

"Let's see what the weather portends." Anna did want to see the place put to rights. "Who will be doing all of the stepping and fetching?"

"The property is now swarming with locals ready to do the earl's bidding for a bit of the earl's coin. Much of the work should be done before we arrive, but I want your eye on the finished product."

"Very well, then. Thursday."

"And I've been meaning to ask you why you always fall silent when St. Just is in the room." He sidled a little closer and waited for her reply.

"The colonel doesn't particularly care for me. It's merely his tacitly stated and perfectly legitimate opinion."

"He likes you." The earl dipped his head and kissed

her cheek. "It might be he doesn't trust you. More likely, he simply envies me, because I saw you first."

Anna's eyebrows shot up in astonishment, but the earl was gone in an instant, no doubt drawn into the breakfast parlor by the scent of bacon, scones, omelets, and—more especially—by the sound of his brothers' laughter.

Eleven

"GOOD MORNING, YOUR GRACE."

Anna swept the deep, deferential curtsy required in the presence of a lady of high rank. "Would you like to wait in the formal parlor, the breakfast parlor, the family parlor, or the library?"

"It's such a pleasant morning," the duchess said. "Why not in the gardens?" Anna found herself returning her smile, as the gardens were the better choice. After several days of increasingly miserable weather, the humidity had dropped in the night, making the morning air delightful.

"Can I bring you some iced lemonade?" Anna asked when she'd seen the earl's mother ensconced on a shady bench. "The earl and his brothers usually return from their morning ride about this time and go directly in to breakfast."

"His brothers?" The duchess paused in the arrangements of her skirts and blinked once. "Can you spare a few minutes to sit with me, Mrs. Seaton?"

"Of course." Anna assumed a seat on the same bench as the duchess. There was a subtle, pleasant scent to the woman, a gracious but simple hint of rose with a note of spice. It didn't fit with what Anna thought a duchess should smell like; it was much less formal, prettier, more sweet and loving.

"Westhaven's brothers join him regularly for breakfast? I was aware Lord Valentine was a guest here, but you include St. Just in this breakfast club?"

"I do," Anna said, feeling cornered. Would the earl want his mother knowing St. Just lived here?

"Is St. Just another guest in the earl's home?" the duchess asked, frowning slightly at the roses. She was a pretty woman, even when she frowned: willowy, hair going from golden to flax, and green eyes slightly canted in a face graced with elegant bones.

"I would be more comfortable, Your Grace, did you put that question to your sons," Anna said. A small, surprised silence followed her comment, and the duchess's frown became a smile.

"You are protective of him," she observed. "Or of them. That is admirable and a trait we share. Can you tell me, Mrs. Seaton, how Westhaven is going on?"

Anna considered the question and decided she could answer it, honestly if somewhat vaguely.

"He is a very, very busy man," Anna said. "The business of the duchy is complicated and demands much of his time, but for the most part, I think he enjoys getting matters under control."

"His Grace did not always see to the details as conscientiously as he should. Westhaven does much better in this regard." As understatements went, that one was worthy of a duchess, Anna thought, and the duchess was loyal to her duke, which was no surprise.

"And how is Westhaven's health?"

"He enjoys good health," Anna said, thinking that was honest at least in the present tense. "He has an active man's appetite, much to Cook's delight."

"And is he treating you well, Mrs. Seaton?" The duchess turned guileless eyes on Anna, but the question was sincere.

"He is a very good employer," Anna said, feeling an abrupt, inconvenient, and wholly out-of-character wish that she had someone to talk to. The duchess was as pretty and gracious as an older woman could be, but she struck Anna as first, last, and always, a woman who had borne eight children, taken in two of her husband's by-blows, and buried two of her sons. She was a mother, a *mama*, and Anna sorely, sorely missed her mother. It had taken this conversation to remind her of it, and the realization brought an unwelcome lump to her throat.

The duchess patted Anna's hand. "A good employer can still be a selfish, inconsiderate, clueless *man*, Mrs. Seaton. I love my sons, but they will wear their muddy boots in the public rooms, flirt with the maids, and argue with their father in view of the servants. They are, in short, human, and sometimes trying as a result."

"It is no trial to work for Lord Westhaven," Anna said. "He pays honest coin for an honest day's wage and is both reasonable and kind."

"Your Grace?" Westhaven smiled as he strolled from the mews. "What a pleasure to see you." He bent to kiss his mother's cheek and used the gesture to wink at Anna surreptitiously. "Have you been haranguing Mrs. Seaton about how to fold the linens?"

"I've been trying without success to grill her about

whether you finish your pudding these days." The duchess stood and took her son's proffered arm. The earl smiled at Anna and winged his other elbow at her. "Mrs. Seaton?" Anna accepted the gallantry rather than make a fuss.

"I can see you are indeed faring well, Westhaven. You dropped too much weight this spring; gauntness did not become you."

"My staff is taking good care of me. You will be pleased to know both Dev and Val are enjoying my hospitality, as well. They'll be along shortly, but were arguing about a horse when I left the stables."

"I heard no shouting," the duchess remarked. "It cannot be a very serious argument."

"Dev wants Val to take on some work with one of his horses. Val is demurring," the earl explained. "Or letting Dev work for it. How are His Grace and my dear sisters?"

"The girls are glad to be at Morelands, with the heat being so oppressive. They might come back for Fairly's ball, however."

"About which you can regale us at breakfast," Westhaven said. "You will join us. I won't hear otherwise."

"I would be delighted." The duchess smiled at her son, a smile of such warmth and loving regard Anna had to look away. Westhaven's expression mirrored his mother's, and Anna knew the earl had no greater ally than Her Grace, at least in all matters that did not pit him against the duke.

"My lord, Your Grace." Anna slipped her arm from the earl's. "If you'll excuse me, I'll notify the kitchen we have a guest."

"Please don't put them to any bother, Mrs. Seaton," the duchess said. "The company of my sons is treat enough on any day." The earl offered Anna a slight bow, and Anna knew the gesture wasn't lost on his mother.

"She dotes on you," the duchess commented when Anna had retreated.

"She dotes on all three of us. We have all the comforts a conscientious housekeeper can imagine for us, and then some. Do you know, she keeps marzipan in the pantry for me, chocolates for Val, and candied violets for Dev? We have flowers in every room, the linens are all scented with lavender or rosemary, the house stays cool even in this heat, and I cannot comprehend how she accomplishes this."

Her Grace paused on the back steps. "She did all this before you'd brought your brothers to stay with you, didn't she?"

"She did. I just notice it more now."

"Grief can turn us inward," the duchess said quietly. "I was concerned for you, Westhaven. I know His Grace left the finances in a muddle, but it seems as if cleaning up after your father was all you made time for this spring."

"The finances are still not untangled, Your Grace. We were not faring very well when I was given the reins."

"Are we in difficulties?" the duchess asked carefully.

"No, but we nearly would have been. In some ways, Victor's mourning period saved us some very timely entertaining expenses. A house party at Morelands is nothing compared to one of your balls, Mother."

"You call me Mother when you scold me,

Westhaven, but this ball will be underwritten by Fairly and his in-laws, so you needn't frown at me."

"My apologies." They turned at the sound of his brothers' voices coming up the garden paths.

"What ho!" Dev called, grinning. "What light through yonder rose bush shines? Good morning, Your Grace." He bowed low over her hand then stepped back as Val sidled in to kiss the duchess's cheek.

"Mother." Val smiled down at her. "You will join us for breakfast so these two mind their manners around their baby brother?"

"I will join you for breakfast to feast my eyes on the greatest display of young male pulchritude to be had in all of London."

"She flatters," Westhaven said, "before interrogating, no doubt."

The duchess floated into the house, one hand tucked by Westhaven's side, the other wrapped on Val's arm. Dev watched them go, smiling at the tableau before turning back to the rose bushes along the far wall, where Anna was clipping a bouquet.

He propped a booted foot against the low stone wall bordering the bed. "How badly did she interrogate you?"

"Good morning, Colonel St. Just." Anna bobbed a curtsy and put her shears into the wicker basket sitting on the wall. "The duchess was all that was gracious." *Unlike present company.* "If you'll excuse me?"

"I will not," St. Just replied. He emphasized his response by putting a hand on Anna's arm. She met his eyes, looked pointedly down at his hand, and back up at his face, arching a brow in question.

"You need not like me," Anna said, "but you will respect me."

"Or what, Anna Seaton?" He leaned in, giving Anna a hint of his aftershave, a minty scent with a blend of meadow flowers. Anna went still, knowing if she made a fuss, the earl would appear, likely with his mother at his side.

"You are not a bully, Colonel, whatever else may trouble you."

He stepped back, frowning.

"You aggravate me, Mrs. Seaton," he said at length. "I want to assure myself you are a scheming, selfish, vapid little tramp with airs above your station, but the assurance just won't ring true."

Anna flashed him a look of consternation. "Why on earth would you attempt to make such a nasty prejudgment? You yourself have no doubt been subject to just the same sort of close mindedness."

"Now, see?" St. Just almost smiled. "That's what I mean. You don't bother to deny the labels, you just hand them back to me in a neat, tidy little package of subtle castigation. Perhaps I'm only wishing you were venal, so I might poach on my brother's preserves with moral impunity."

"You would not poach on your brother's preserves," Anna said, beginning to see how much of the man was a particularly well-aimed type of bluster. "You are not as wicked as you want the world to think, sir."

"Happens"—he did smile—"I am not, but it also happens you are not just the simple, devoted house-keeper you would have the world think you are, either."

"My past is my own business. Now have you

business with me, Colonel, or are you being gratu-
itously unpleasant?"

"Business," he said shortly. "You have rightly
surmised I brood and paw and snort at times for show,
Mrs. Seaton. It keeps His Grace from getting ideas, for
one thing. But make no mistake on this point: I will
defend my brother's interests without exception or
scruple. If I find you are playing him false in any sense
or trifling with him, I will become your worst enemy."

Anna smiled at him thinly. "Do you think he'd
appreciate these threats you make to his housekeeper?"

"He might understand them," St. Just said. "For the
other message I have to convey to you is that to the
extent you matter to my brother, you matter to me.
If he decides he values you in his life, then I will also
defend *you* without exception or scruple."

"What is it you are saying?"

"You are a woman with troubles, Anna Seaton.
You have no past anyone in this household knows of,
you have no people you'll admit to, you have the airs
and graces of a well-born lady, but you labor for your
bread instead. I've seen you conferring with Morgan,
and I know you have something to hide."

Anna raised her chin and speared him with a look.
"Everybody has something to hide."

"You have a choice, Anna," St. Just said, her given
name falling from his lips with surprising gentleness.
"You either trust the earl to resolve your troubles, or
you leave him in peace. He's too good a man to be
exploited by somebody under his own roof. He's had
that at the hands of his own father, and I won't stand
for it from you."

Anna hefted her basket and flashed St. Just a cold smile. "Like the duke, you'll wade in, bully and intimidate, and jump to conclusions regarding Westhaven's life, telling yourself all the while you do it because you love him, when in fact, you haven't the first notion how to really go about caring for the man. Very impressive—if one wants proof of your patrimony."

She bobbed him a curtsy with fine irony and walked off, her skirts twitching with her irritation.

As he pasted the requisite smile on his face and went in to breakfast, St. Just reflected he hadn't been wrong: Anna Seaton had secrets; she'd all but acknowledged it.

But his approach had been wrong. A woman who attached Westhaven's interest was going to have backbone to spare. He should not have threatened; he should not have, to use her word, bullied. Well, that could be remedied just as soon as he got through breakfast with Her Grace.

❧

"You are quiet," the earl remarked as they tooled along toward Willow Bend.

"If I am quiet enough, I can fool myself into thinking I am still abed, dreaming on my nice cool sheets." Dreaming of him, most nights.

"Am I working you too hard?" the earl asked, glancing over.

"You are not. The heat can disturb one's rest."

"Are my brothers behaving? Dev is tidy, but Val can be a slob."

"Lord Val's only crime is that he commandeers Morgan for a couple of hours each afternoon and lets her join him in the music room while he works on his repertoire."

"You can trust Val to be a gentleman with her."

"And can I trust you to be a gentleman?"

"You can trust me," the earl replied, "to stop when you tell me to, to never intentionally hurt you, to listen before I judge, and to tell you the truth as far as I know it. Will that do?" It was all he was going to give her, but Anna reflected on how much more he offered than other men in her life were willing to.

"It will do." It would have to.

He turned the conversation to the practicalities of the situation at Willow Bend. There was a temporary crew of day laborers on hand from the local village, and they'd been busily moving furniture, hanging drapes, unpacking the crates of linens and flatware. The scene was very different from their previous visit to the place, with wagons, people, and noise everywhere.

A young boy emerged from the stables to take Pericles, and the earl escorted Anna to the front door.

"I want you to see it the way my sister might," he said, "not as the servants and tradesmen do. So…" He opened the front door, and led her through. "Welcome to Willow Bend, Mrs. Seaton."

She appreciated the public nature of the greeting and appreciated even more that there was a public on hand to witness it. Carpenters, glaziers, laborers, and apprentices were bustling to and fro; hammers banged, the occasional yell sounded above stairs, and boys were scurrying everywhere with tools and supplies.

"Yer lordship!" A stocky man of medium height made his way to their side.

"Mr. Albertson, our pleasure. Mrs. Seaton, my foreman here, Allen Albertson. Mr. Albertson, Mrs. Seaton is the lady in charge of putting the finishing touches on all your work."

"Ma'am." Albertson smiled and tugged his forelock. "You been finishing the daylights out of this place, if I do say so. Where shall we start, milord?"

"Ma'am?" The earl turned to her, his deference bringing an inconvenient blush to her cheeks.

"The kitchen," Anna said. "It's the first room you'll want functional and a very important room to people both upstairs and below."

"To the kitchen, Mr. Albertson." Westhaven waved a hand and offered Anna his arm.

Room by room, floor by floor, they toured the house. Shelves that had been bare now held neat rows of cups and glasses, or stacks of dishes, toweling, table linen, and candles. Anna asked that the spice rack be moved closer to the work table and suggested a bench be added along the inside kitchen wall. She had a bench put into the back hallway, as well, and a pegged board nailed to the wall for jackets, capes, and coats.

"You need a boot scrape, too," she pointed out, "since this is the entrance closest to the stables and gardens."

"You will make a note, Mr. Albertson?" the earl prompted.

"Aye." Albertson nodded, rolling his eyes good-naturedly to show what he thought of feminine notions.

They went on through the house as the morning got under way, finding a set of drapes needing to be switched, some tables that had ended up in the wrong parlors, and a pair of carpets that should have gone in opposite bedrooms. In the music room, she had the harp covered and the piano's lid closed.

"You may leave us now, Mr. Albertson," Westhaven said as they approached the last bedroom. "I take it the men will soon break for their nooning?"

"They will. It be getting too hot to do the heavy work, but we'll be back when it cools. Ma'am." He bowed and took his leave, bellowing for the water dipper before he'd gained the stairs.

"He may lack a certain subtlety," the earl said, "but he's honest, and he's getting the job done."

"And a lovely job it is," Anna said. "The place is looking wonderful."

"I wanted to save this for last," the earl said, opening the door to the final bedroom. It was the room where they'd passed the night, and Anna felt her heart stutter as the earl ushered her over the threshold.

"The Earl of Westhaven Memorial Chicken Pox Ward," Anna quipped, trying desperately for a light tone.

"Among other things. How do you like it?"

She'd intended this to be a masculine room, decorating it in subdued greens with blue accents and choosing more substantial incidental furniture with fewer frills and fripperies. The canopy on the bed had been replaced with dark green velvet, the bedspread dyed to match. The drapes were a lighter version of the same shade, and all of it complemented the dark wood of the bed frame and the colorful Persian carpets scattered on the hardwood floors.

"You are quiet," Westhaven said. "I hoped you would be pleased with the differences."

"I'm pleased." Anna smiled at him. "This is not a room for the lady of the house."

"It is not, of course," the earl agreed. "We saw those rooms earlier. I wanted this to be a room worthy of the memories I hold of it."

"Westhaven…" Anna sighed. "You were being so good."

"I was, and I'm glad you appreciate the effort, but I've left you in peace for days now, Anna, and you didn't come here without expecting me to make some advances."

"I came here," Anna said, sitting down in an upholstered rocker, "to comply with your request to see the house set to rights. I've done that, so we can return to Town now."

"And make Pericles travel in the worst heat of the day."

She glared at him and rose. "Do not put the welfare of your horse above my reputation, *yet again*. Dear Pericles can walk us back to Town for all I care, but our work here is finished."

"Our work, perhaps." The earl regarded her levelly. "Not our dealings. Come." He took her hand and led her to window seat. She didn't resist when he pulled her down beside him and kept her hand trapped in his.

"Talk to me, Anna," he said, wrapping his second hand around the back of hers. "You've become inscrutable, and I have enough sisters to know this is not a good thing."

"You would leave me no privacy." But when the earl stretched out his legs, his thigh casually resting against hers, she did not move away.

"You have more privacy than anyone else in my household," the earl chided. "You answer only to me, have the run of the property, and have the only private sitting room on four floors besides my own. And"—he kissed her knuckles—"you are stalling."

She laid her head on his shoulder, closed her eyes, and felt him nuzzling at her temple.

"Sweetheart," he murmured, "tell me what's troubling you. Dev says you've shadows in your eyes, and I have to agree."

"Him." Anna's head came off his shoulder.

"Has he offended? Pinched Nanny Fran one too many times? Offended Cook?"

"He has offended me," Anna said on a sigh. "Or he would, if I could stay mad at him, but he's just protective of you."

"The duke used that same excuse to nearly unravel my niece's entire family. He was protecting me when he bribed Elise, and he was protecting someone every time he crossed the lines his duchess would not approve of."

"I pointed out the parallel to St. Just when he warned me not to trifle with you."

"And here I've been pleasuring myself nigh cross-eyed because you won't trifle with me," the earl said. Anna smiled at his rejoinder despite herself. When she glanced over, he obligingly crossed his eyes.

"What else did St. Just have to say?" the earl prompted when the moment of levity had passed.

"If you value me, he will, as well. I don't know what that meant, Westhaven. He is a difficult man to read."

"He was welcoming you to the family, and all without a word to me."

"If that is his welcome, one shudders to consider his threats."

"He says you are a lady with secrets. I could not gainsay him."

"I was a lady once," Anna said, not meeting his eyes. "I am in service now."

"And you choose to remain in service rather than accept my suit. It is very lowering to think my kisses, my wealth, I myself, am less appealing to you than bouquets needing water or silver in need of polish."

"You mustn't think that!" Anna lifted her eyes to his, horrified at the honest self-doubt she'd heard in his voice. "You must believe me when I say the failing is mine; any woman would be pleased to have your attentions."

"Any woman?" The earl's smile was self-deprecating. "Guinevere Allen was none too flattered."

"She was enamored of her viscount, and he of her," Anna argued, coming to her feet. "I cannot allow you to think like this. You can have your pick of the last three years' batch of debutantes, and you know it."

"Oh, lucky me." The earl rose, as well. "I can mince about with some child on my arm, one who fears her wedding night and dreads the thought of my attentions. And all the while, she will be hamstrung by my father's machinations, to say nothing of the parents who staked her out in the ballroom like some sacrificial lamb. No man worth his salt wants a wife on those terms. What?" He returned to her side. "I cannot tell if you are horrified, stupefied, or maybe, just perhaps, impressed."

"You understand," Anna said, peering up at him. "You understand what it's like to be that sacrificial lamb."

"I do." He nodded. "I also understand, Anna Seaton, if I cannot have more of you, this instant, I will not answer for the consequences." He brushed his lips over hers. "The workmen are gone, and they won't be back until the heat of the day has cooled. We have this time, Anna, and I would like to use it."

"I will not lie with you." Anna shook her head. "It would be…dishonest."

"I will not lie with you then, either." He kissed her again, more lingeringly. "But I would pleasure us both. Don't for the love of God argue with me, Anna." His arms slipped around her waist. "You need pleasuring almost as badly as I do, and there's nothing to stop us."

"There's me to stop us," she said, but she was kissing him back between her protests.

"Stop me later, then," the earl suggested, shrugging out of his waistcoat while his lips cruised her neck. "Preferably much later." He kissed her more deeply, but to her eternal consternation she was less committed to her protests than he was to his seduction.

For days she'd told herself physical pleasures were fleeting and an undesirable entanglement in her circumstances. She'd told herself she couldn't miss something she'd shared with the earl on only a handful of occasions—a few kisses, some caresses, unimaginable pleasure and intimacy.

But she'd missed *him* like the land misses spring and the flowers miss the sun. She'd missed him like a soldier misses home on the night before battle and the night after. She'd missed him so…

"That's it," the earl coaxed when Anna's arms went around his waist. "No more words, Anna. Unless it's to tell me how to please you."

He kissed her long and deeply, stilling her protests, stealing her will and making it his. She *did* want to share these pleasures with him, with him and no one else, ever. She did *not* want to leave him, and yet leave him she would.

She rose up to press her body more closely to his, and he gathered her more tightly in his arms. All of her reserve and self-control went flying out the window, and in their place was *need*. Need for him, for closeness with him.

"Your clothes," Anna breathed, arching against him.

"Yours," he whispered back. Deftly, he began to undo the buttons down the back of her dress, even as she continued to drink in his kisses. He pushed the cap sleeves of her dress off her shoulders and bent his head to worship her neck with his lips.

"I love that," she said. "The way you touch me there."

"And here," he murmured, shifting lower, "you taste like sunshine, and sweetness, and female."

She was trying to get his shirt out of his waistband but couldn't kiss him and make her hands work at the same time. Gasping, she stepped back.

She eyed him in frustration. "This isn't working. Please take your clothes off. Now, Westhaven."

He smiled an *I thought you would never ask* smile and pulled his shirt over his head, letting her watch. He arched an eyebrow, his hand going to the fall of his trousers, and Anna nodded, holding his gaze the whole time. With deliberate movements, he got out of his boots, stockings, and breeches, standing before her naked, aroused, and unselfconscious.

"Oh, dear…" Anna's eyes went wide as she surveyed him. "You are *very* interested."

He stalked toward her, his erection curving up against his taut belly. "While you are very overdressed. Clothes off, Anna. All of them."

She nodded, knowing it would represent new territory for them. She had never been naked before him, not in the broad light of day.

"Lock the door," she said, swallowing. His smile became feral as he complied with her command. He'd *told* her to strip for him; she deliberately used the imperative on him, as well.

"Quit dithering, love." His tone was gentler, amused but only so patient. Slowly, Anna let the bodice of her dress fall forward then shoved it below her hips. She stepped out of the dress and stood in the middle of its billows, like Venus rising. While Westhaven watched from just a few feet away, she bent to undo her boots and stockings then let her chemise join the dress on the floor.

"Better," he said, holding out a hand to her. "Much, much better."

She took a step toward him then hesitated. He closed the remaining distance and caught her against him, letting her press her face to his throat.

"Shy?" he asked, amusement back in his voice.

"We are…very undressed," Anna said as a blush rose up her chest and suffused her face. "This is new."

The earl bent his head to kiss her, then slid his hand down to cup her derriere. Before she could react with even another blush, he lifted her and tossed her onto the middle of the bed.

"Stay right there, shyness be damned," he said to her as she rose up to brace her elbows behind her. "You look adorably dazed, thoroughly kissed, and much in need of my company, as you, my dear, need to be relieved of a certain ignorance. Not your innocence, as no man can divest you of that, but your ignorance. I fault Mr. Seaton for not seeing to this."

"My ignorance?" she said, watching him climb onto the bed. "Westhaven…"

"That's talking, Anna," he chided. "You are only to talk if it's to tell me what pleases you."

"It pleases me not at all," she said sternly, "to be handled like a…oof!" He straddled her and gently pushed her onto her back. "What are you about?"

"Hush, sweetheart." He nuzzled her neck, crouching over her. "It's too hot for lecturing. We must conserve our strength."

The bed, Anna realized, took some of the urgency from him. When he could loom over her this way, passively rest his erection against her stomach and know she wasn't going to squirm away, he was easier to deal with. The pace of his kisses slowed, and the quiet of the house settled around them.

"Someday," he said, grazing his nose down her sternum, "you will want it fast and almost rough. You'll want me to shut up, and you won't care if we tear our clothes or leave the door unlocked or make a racket."

"Can you promise me such a day?" Anna arched her back, trying to get closer to him.

"I can promise you as many of those days as you want." He flicked his tongue over her nipple and rested his cheek on the swell of her breast. "I can promise you nights when we get no sleep but rise with more energy than had we slept soundly. I can promise you long afternoons spent in sensual abandon, when we both have places we must be, things we must do, but we let them all go hang." He turned his face and took her nipple into his mouth, and the pleasure he brought her was almost unbearable.

"Yes," Anna breathed, not sure if she'd spoken aloud or simply felt the word in every part of her body. The earl drew more strongly on her and used his fingers to tease the other nipple. He paused and raised himself enough to meet her gaze.

"Take your time, Anna. We have hours if you want them, and my appetite for you is without limit."

"I don't know what you mean," she said, letting her hands stroke through his hair. "Take my time?"

"Our time," he said, closing his eyes. He bent his head to her breasts again and spent long minutes using his mouth to arouse and please her. Her breasts were wonderfully sensitive, and she unabashedly reveled in the nudity that allowed him unfettered access to them.

"Westhaven…" Anna arched restlessly some minutes later. "It's too much."

"It's not enough," he said, easing a hand down over her stomach. He kept his movements deliberate, as if reminding her tacitly they had all the time in the world. Slowly, he caressed her midriff, occasionally letting his fingers tease at her nipples or drift down to tease at the curls above her sex.

"You are losing flesh," he said, leaning over to kiss her breast. "You will please stop this, as I require you to be sturdy."

"I always drop some weight in the summer," Anna said, realizing he was in a different mood entirely from when he tossed her onto the bed. "You are over your chicken pox." She ran a hand over his abdomen, marveling at how perfectly his skin had healed.

"I had good care"—the earl smiled up at her—"and I've been conserving my strength." His hand dipped lower, into her curls, and Anna felt her frustration spike. Well, turnabout was fair play, so she sent her own hand drifting down to explore his erection.

"How long can you stay like this?" She circled him with her fingers and sleeved his length.

"Many men are in a state of near perpetual arousal for much of their adolescence," he said, closing his eyes. "Myself included. It got better at university, when I could actually do something besides pleasure myself several times a day. Hold me tighter, love. Like that." He sighed, gave up, and rolled to his back.

Anna smiled, pleased with herself for getting the better of him. She pushed up and sat cross-legged at his hip then resumed her exploration.

"Are all men as well-endowed as you?" she asked, her free hand slipping up to brush over his nipples.

"I am the most well-endowed man on earth," he said, eyes still closed. "You are to be envied among all women; you'll be bowlegged when we become lovers in fact."

"Be serious," she chided, tugging at him gently.

"Serious…" he breathed. "God, that feels good…

It's hard to say really who is well-endowed and who isn't, as one seldom sees another fellow aroused. We peek, certainly, but I've seen very few cocks other than my own ready to do the deed."

"You've seen other men in this state?"

"Most men wake up in this state," he informed her. "Slow down, sweetheart, or I won't be able to maintain it much longer." She slowed her hand, fractionally, but leaned over and swirled her tongue over his nipple.

"Anna." His hand came up to cradle the back of her head and to contradict the warning in his tone.

"Hmm?" She began to suckle him, and he groaned, his hips moving to complement the stroke of her hand.

"I will get even."

"Shall I stop?" She stilled her hand and brushed his hair back from his forehead. His eyes opened, and she was relieved to see humor in his expression.

"I'm going to use my mouth on you, Anna, and you will scream for me and forget your own name, so much will you like it."

She frowned at that. He'd been very explicit about this threat before. Thinking about it had kept her awake more than one night.

She met his gaze soberly. "What if I want to use my mouth on you?"

"Come here." He wrestled her down to his side, wrapped his arms around her, and tucked her close. "When you are with me like this, there is nothing you can ask of me, nothing you can want or do or think that will earn my censure. I would love to feel your mouth on my cock; I would love to take you in any position you can think of. If you wanted to tie me up, blindfold me, paint my cock blue, I would not deny you."

"Why?"

"I trust you," he said, and his words left her stunned.

"You shouldn't," she replied, her voice small. She felt the impact of her honesty go through him and wondered if she'd destroyed his regard for her in those two little words.

"Why shouldn't I?" His question came slowly, in the same tempo as his hand moving over her body.

"Because I will disappoint you, and then you will feel ashamed and angry, and so will I," she said against his neck. She shifted to straddle him and felt his arms go around her when she curled down onto his chest.

"You will disappoint me in bed?" he asked, his tone tentative.

"Probably there, too," she replied, pressing her nose to his sternum.

"You still think you're leaving me," the earl concluded, his hands stroking along her spine.

"I know I am," she said more firmly, teething his nipple for emphasis. There, she'd said it; she'd been as honest as she could be.

"Because you will not marry me, and so you must take your virtuous self off when you've endured the requisite dose of my importuning."

Anna rose up and surveyed him balefully. "I did not say I enjoyed an entirely consistent position, nor one that makes sense in all circumstances, but I can't marry you."

"Cannot or will not?" the earl asked, catching her eye and holding it.

"Cannot. Absolutely cannot. Ever."

But she also could not stop toying with his nipples.

"If you could choose, Anna"—he reached down and tugged gently on one of her nipples in retaliation—"what would you choose? This duty that confidentially holds you, or the alternative?"

"You." She leaned up and kissed him. "Were I free to do so, I'd choose *you*."

Not marriage, not freedom, not the title, not security. She would choose him. Her kiss, when she brushed her lips over his again, was different, sweet, wistful, but also the kiss of a woman who felt deeply about the man with her.

She would choose him. She could tell him that—give him that.

Anna peered up at him. "Earlier, you said—"

"I say a lot of things." He smiled at her, and to Anna, the expression was tender, a little like the way he looked at Her Grace.

"You said…" She looked abruptly away, flummoxed to find she was still capable of shyness when she was naked, straddling his rigid cock. "You said you would love to feel my mouth on your…on you."

"I did." His hands went still. "I would."

"How does one do this?" she asked, a blush rising over her for him to see. But to her relief he didn't tease, he didn't remark on it, he just waited until she was facing him again.

"However you please," he said levelly, "and only if you please."

"Show me. I want to do this with you."

"Get comfortable," he said, shifting over to one side

of the bed. "And stop whenever you aren't comfortable. Take your time, and do what pleases you."

"What if I hurt you?" Anna shifted to rest her cheek low on his abdomen and took him in her hand.

"You can't, short of biting me and drawing blood, but even that can have a certain erotic appeal."

His hand settled on her hair, and she took a moment to inhale the scents of clean sheets, clean man, and anticipation. She licked delicately at his erection, as if she were trying to decide what flavor he was. When his hand sifted through her hair to caress her nape, she relaxed and put her focus on the task. Tentatively, she licked him all over, little teasing swipes of her tongue, like a mama cat patiently grooming a kitten. Inside her own body, she lit fires with that tongue, his permission to indulge her curiosity as incendiary as the naked length of him in the bed.

And then she slipped her mouth over him, and brush fires instantly converged into a wildfire. She experimented, taking him deep into her mouth then more shallowly. Without a word, his hips began to move, slowly, as if he didn't want to startle her. She was content to spend long minutes learning how to coordinate her movements with his, to let the fires rage and warm places in her gone cold longer than she'd realized. When her fingers wrapped around his wet length, he expelled a soft, pleased groan, as if passion was as much a relief to him as it was to her.

"Not much more, Anna," he cautioned hoarsely. "I'll spend…"

Well, that was the point, wasn't it? When he was thrusting smoothly through her hand into her mouth, and his breathing was coming in short, deep breaths, she closed her lips around him and drew firmly.

"Oh, God… Anna… No…" His thrusts grew stronger, despite his words. His hand cradled the back of her head, holding her close; his cock actually pulsed in her mouth, and Anna wasn't about to show him mercy.

"No…" he whispered again, even while his body shouted to the contrary for long, ecstatic moments. "Jesus…" He hissed, eyes closed, head thrown back, hips moving in convulsive shudders of pleasure. "Jesus, God… Anna…"

He went quiet but not quite still, his hand moving slowly over her scalp.

"And you say," he whispered, "I should not trust you." She let him slip from her mouth, and felt tears welling. He should not trust her, but he just had, profoundly. Even in her inexperience, she could divine that much.

"Come here." He leaned up and tugged her to lie along his side. "I can't believe you did that. I can't believe I did that. A man doesn't spend in a woman's mouth. It isn't gentlemanly."

"But it is gentlemanly to spend on her stomach?" Anna asked in puzzlement. "Or to spend in her body, getting a bastard on her?"

"What was it the great philosopher once said?" He kissed her nose. "The position is not entirely consistent, nor does it make sense under all circumstances?"

Anna continued to frown. "Do you mean you yourself do not spend in a woman's mouth, or that it's like pissing in a well, a civil wrong?"

"Good heavens, you did have a brother, didn't you?

It isn't quite like that. It's like eating the dessert set aside for company, or stealing the crown jewels and seeing another blamed. It's just…it's too good," he said. "Too selfish."

"Of me?" Anna asked, still confused. "I'm sorry, but I didn't want to stop, and you said I should stop only when I pleased."

"Love," he sighed, "you could not have pleased me more profoundly if you'd told me Val had sired legitimate twin boys. I have never experienced such generosity, never, and as soon as I recover my wits, I am going to get very, very even indeed."

That was enough to settle her down and put a period to her questions. She closed her eyes and drowsed on his shoulder while he drifted into sleep, his hand still tangled possessively in her hair.

∽

When Anna awoke, she felt replete with the same sense of sweetness she'd had after her encounter with Westhaven in the library. He was wrapped around her, her back spooned to his chest, a sweet breeze wafting in from the open window.

His hand closed gently around her breast, though his breathing did not change. Anna closed her eyes and let the pleasure of that single, soft caress drift through her body. He did it again, and she sighed audibly. A few moments later, his thumb brushed over her nipple, then again.

Take your time, he'd said.

As the earl's hands began to wander—up and down her back, over her buttocks, back to her breasts—she thought over their last encounter in this very bed. She'd lain still, feigning sleep then, too.

What a waste of a night, she thought on a sigh.

"You are awake," the earl murmured, his lips closing over her earlobe.

"I am," Anna said as Westhaven's mouth sent slow ripples of awareness through her body. "But without motivation to get up and seize the remainder of the day."

"There will be no getting up," he remonstrated, his hand sliding between her legs. "And the only thing you'll be seizing is me or the pleasure I owe you."

Anna tried to peer over her shoulder at him.

"You owe me nothing."

"Ah, but I do," he said, nudging her onto her stomach. "And a gentleman always pays his debts."

Anna didn't typically sleep on her stomach and found the position mildly disconcerting. She couldn't see him, could feel only his hand stroking down her back, over her buttocks, back up again.

"Relax, Anna." He kissed her nape. "This will take a while. Let your legs fall open, and just enjoy."

She closed her eyes and felt the caress of his hand dancing over her like the breeze, but better. He knew where to touch, how much pressure to use, when to tease, and when to gratify. His fingers explored her sex from behind then drifted away to trace the long muscles on either side of her spine. He caressed her buttocks with slow, almost pensive attention to the tension in the muscles there then pressed another series of kisses to her nape and shoulders.

She shouldn't let him, she thought... Whole after-noons, but not for them. This was their afternoon, their only afternoon, and then she'd be gone, betraying all the trust he showed her, taking his respect for her and tossing it back in his face.

"On to your back, sweetheart," Westhaven whispered in her ear. When she lazily complied, he started all over again, the same stroking and studying and teasing, but this time his attention wandered from her breasts to her face, to her sex, to her neck and shoulders, and back her breasts.

"Spread your legs for me," he coaxed, but when Anna did, he remained content to tease at her breasts with his fingers. Only gradually did he let his hand drift down in slow, smooth sweeps, then to rest over her sex. He turned his body, and though she didn't open her eyes, Anna felt him crouching over her, his mouth settling contentedly over a nipple.

He was tormenting her, she thought sluggishly, creating such a blend of languor and arousal she couldn't fight either. Why would she want to? His mouth drew on her, and she sifted her fingers through his hair, emotion tangling with the erotic lassitude he created. Precious, she thought. These moments, this man, these sensations…all precious.

He paused and moved lower, resting his face against her abdomen before levering up and reaching for a spare pillow.

"Hips up," he directed, tucking the pillow under her. "You'll see why soon enough." And then he was nuzzling at her belly, nipping at the underside of her breast, and stroking the insides of her thighs.

"Your job," he said, moving yet lower still, "is simply to enjoy. You can tell me to stop, but I might have trouble hearing you, as I intend to be enjoying myself, as well." His words floated into Anna's awareness and floated right back out again. She was nearly asleep, so relaxed had she become.

But not quite asleep, as the earl's caresses had also created a low, buzzing arousal throughout her body. Her breasts wanted his mouth and his fingers, her buttocks wanted that same hand, and her sex wanted all of him. If he'd asked, she'd have consented to join with him, so finely drawn was she between arousal, regret, and lassitude.

He moved to kiss her spread thighs, and Anna knew a fleeting self-consciousness. He was going to *look at her*, to see in the broad light of day the parts of her she hadn't seen herself.

"You are beautiful," he said, as if reading her mind, "and luscious."

The next sensation, as his mouth settled over her, was indescribable. It took the sweet, tender, languorous arousal of all his previous caresses and let it congeal where he drew on her. He was gentle at first, just hinting at what pleasures he could bring her. He'd suckle at her for a moment then use his tongue to lap at her folds, to paint her sex with pleasure.

But then he was back, applying just a little more pressure, and a soft groan escaped Anna's throat.

"Move if you want to," he urged, wrapping an arm around her thigh to anchor her. "Move against me, and you'll feel better."

Tentatively, she rocked her hips, a long, slow roll of her body that eased her ache and made it worse. She moved again, setting up a rhythm, working with him to craft her pleasure. It went on like that, minute after minute of bliss edged with longing, then longing coalescing into need.

"Westhaven?" If a man didn't come in a woman's mouth, was a woman permitted to find her pleasure with a man's mouth? She wanted to ask him, but her mind was too far gone with pleasure.

"Touch your breasts, sweetheart," he murmured. "You'll feel better. Like this." He reached up one long arm and gently pinched at her nipple. He fished for her hand, closed it around her own nipple, and used his fingers to close her grasp on herself.

It wasn't the same as his caresses, but he kept his hand resting over hers, and so there was part of him in the sensations she evoked. When her own hand went still, the better for her to focus on his busy mouth, he closed his fingers again in gentle reminder.

"Westhaven," Anna rasped. *Stop*, she wanted to say, but the word would not come to her lips. The feelings he aroused, the physical sensations…they were building, an inexorable welling of pleasure was advancing toward her, but—God help her—not fast enough.

"This will help," he said, and Anna felt him ease a finger shallowly into her body. He was careful, tentative, unwilling to advance beyond a certain point, but it helped focus her frustration. She clamped her muscles around that finger and felt him pause.

"You lovely, naughty girl," he whispered, adding a second finger—but not deep enough. He shifted the angle of his shoulders and took her in his mouth again.

"Please, Westhaven, please…"

She rocked up against his mouth, wanting, wanting,

wanting until she would have begged had speech not been beyond her. She begged with her body, with her hands in his hair, with the soft whimpers that escaped her.

Her body began to hum with impending pleasure, to rise and vibrate and sing with it, until it burst through her, finally—fast enough, hard enough, deep enough, and with his mouth and hands and will, he made it last long enough, pushing her onward ruthlessly when she would have accepted just a taste of pleasure, until she was moaning and undulating helplessly against his mouth.

"Westhaven." She ruffled his hair and said it again, her voice soft with the surfeit of pleasure he'd brought her.

"I'm here," he murmured, his face against her belly.

"Cover me," she said, and he reached for the sheets.

"No." She tugged at his scalp. "You, cover me. Please."

It was an odd request, but he rose up on all fours, crouched over her, and lowered his chest to hers.

"All of you," she said, eyes closed, hands drifting over his shoulders and back.

So he settled between her legs, giving her his weight, his erection resting snugly on her belly. When she sighed in contentment, he tucked her crown under his chin and matched his breathing to hers.

"Thank you," she whispered. "For all of it, but this, too. Thank you."

Twelve

"I CAN HEAR YOU THINKING," WESTHAVEN RUMBLED above her moments later.

"What you did," Anna said, too closely wrapped for him to see her face. "Is that…?"

"Is it what?" he smiled, in charity with all of creation. "Legal? Yes, unlike some other intimate pleasures. Is it biblical, absolutely not. Is it what?"

"Is it something you did with your mistress?"

"Ye gods, Anna." He levered up on his arms and frowned down at her. "What is this fascination you have with a woman you've never met?"

"Not with her." Anna met his gaze, her face crimson. "With you. Is that something men like to do—or you like to do?" A slightly different and more acceptable question, he decided, snuggling back down.

"As a young man," he said, brushing her hair off her forehead, "it's something you want to experience, as it's wicked and forbidden and said to delight those women willing to allow it. But no, I've not offered this to another. There is a whole invisible community of women whose job it is to educate university boys and I put them through their paces and they put me through mine, but not in this regard."

"So you enjoyed it?"

"What I enjoyed," he said, smiling at her, "was bringing you pleasure and learning your responses and feeling close to you when you let yourself go. Some women, Anna, go their whole lives without experiencing passion the way you do. You are lovely, and so, yes, I most assuredly enjoyed doing that with you."

She was blessedly silent while Westhaven anticipated her next outrageous, blushing question.

"I enjoy it, too," she said, "having you find your pleasure in my mouth. It is…intimate."

"There is trust involved," he replied, thinking about it for the first time in years. "On both sides." She nodded under him and closed her eyes.

You do trust me, he wanted to point out. Maybe not completely, but you do. He wanted her to admit it, to him, if not to herself, but wasn't willing to breach that intimacy she'd alluded to. Rather than start a lecture, Westhaven began kissing her, his mood still slow and relaxed.

"Would you like me to…?" she began. He stopped the question by covering her mouth with his then drew back.

"I'll do the work, such as it is," he said. "You relax. We don't want to make you sore."

He rocked against her, their bodies snugged tightly together. She was learning the way his body moved when it sought pleasure and subtly undulated with him. When she tilted her hips just a little, sealing them even more closely together, he buried his face against her neck.

In a very few moments, he felt his pleasure welling up, a thick, hot current radiating up his spine and out through his extremities. He didn't fight it, didn't hold back, but pulsed against her hard for a half-dozen thrusts, and then went still on a long, fraught sigh against her neck.

"God, Anna." He lifted himself off of her. "You utterly undo me." He walked naked across the room to his jacket, extracted a handkerchief, and used the water in the pitcher on the nightstand to wet it. He swabbed at himself thoroughly, rinsed the handkerchief in the basin, and wrung it out. He then sat at her hip, washed his seed off her body, and raised his gaze to hers.

"I am fond of you," he said, "and maybe more than that. If you are in trouble, Anna, I wish you'd let me help you."

"You can't help," she said, her expression unreadable.

He said nothing but climbed into bed beside her and lay back, his hands laced under his head. He should not have made that admission—fond of her, for God's sake—what woman wants to hear that? He was fond of Elise, fond of Rose's pony, George. It was as good as saying he did not love her, which he feared might not be true.

That is to say... He shied off that fence and turned his mind to Anna's virtual admission she was in trouble. That was progress, he decided. From bearing confidences, to being in trouble. Dev had been right, and it meant Westhaven had to take a little more seriously Anna's threats to leave him. What kind of trouble would a young, pretty, gently reared housekeeper have?

She had a brother, he recalled. It was a brother's

job to protect a sister, so where was that worthy soul now that Anna needed him? But even a brother had no rights where a husband was concerned.

"Please assure me," he said, glancing over at her, "you have no living husband."

"I have no living husband," Anna recited. But this time, the earl was paying attention, and he raised a skeptical eyebrow.

"That is the truth," Anna remonstrated. "We are merely fornicating, not committing adultery."

He cracked a dry smile. "My dear, we are not even fornicating."

"Not yet." She offered him the same smile back.

"Are you a convicted felon?" he asked, puzzling over it.

"I am not charged with anything that I know of," Anna said, "but you can cease the interrogation, Westhaven. I am fond of you, too."

She sat up, hugging her knees, and Westhaven had the sense she was fighting back tears. Surely there was no more damning testament to a man's seductions than that they left a woman in tears? He reached out and stroked his hand over her elegant spine.

"You are fond of me, but you are leaving me anyway." She nodded once, her back to him, and he felt her heart breaking. With gentle force, he dragged her back into his arms and held her while she cried.

❧

When the hamper had been repacked, Anna stood beside the earl in the stables, waiting for Pericles to be harnessed to the gig.

"Penny for them," the earl said softly. He was standing just a hair too close to her, but there was nobody save the young stable hand to see, and much to Westhaven's pleasure, Anna let herself drift back against him.

"It is lovely here," Anna said. "You are to be commended for taking such care with a sister's welfare."

He heard the wistful, almost despairing note in her voice, and knew with absolute conviction Anna Seaton's brother had somehow disappointed her or played her false. His mind turned back to those ideas, the ones he'd been formulating earlier about how to uncover Anna's troubles and assist her with them.

"I love my sisters. As any brother should love a sister."

"They don't all—brothers, that is," Anna said, stepping away from him. "Some of them love their gold more or their drink or their flashy Town habits. Being a sister is sometimes not much more of a bargain than being a wife."

"You simply have to choose the right brother"— Westhaven smiled at her gently—"or the right husband. I have enjoyed our time here, Anna. I hope you did, as well."

"Even when I cried," she said, a world of resignation in her tone, "I was glad to be here with you, Westhaven. Believe that, if you believe nothing else of me."

He handed her into the gig, puzzling over that comment. They were halfway back to Town, Anna tucked shamelessly close to him even in the heat, before his brain woke from its stupor.

What she had meant was: Even when I cried *because*

I must leave you, I was glad to be here with you... Believe that if you believe nothing else of me *when I find the courage to finally go*.

The hot, lovely day suddenly became ominous, and where Anna wasn't touching him, he was chilled.

※

Morgan stood beside Val when they'd left Viscount Fairly's townhouse and *listened*. Fairly had worked a miracle, gently and thoroughly cleaning her ears, explaining that she had scar tissue complicating the natural process and her hearing would always be impaired. She thought he was daft, as she heard everything.

"It's loud," she said wonderingly. "But sweet, too. Like your music. The sounds all go together to say something."

"Let's walk home through the park," Val suggested, offering his arm. "You can hear birds singing, hear the water in the Serpentine, hear the children playing... I never realized how happy the park sounds."

"There's so much..." Morgan took a deep breath and fell in step beside him. "I would never go anywhere I didn't know well, because I could not stop to ask directions. I was confined to those places Anna would take me or that someone else would escort me to. I could not get lost; I could not need assistance."

"That has changed. You may get lost several times a day, just to hear people give you directions. Are your ears hurting?"

"They are..." Morgan frowned. "Not hurting from the viscount's treatment but throbbing, it feels like, with sounds. I'm pleased beyond telling to hear your voice, Lord Valentine."

"Val," he said easily. "I'd like to hear you say my name."

"Valentine Windham." Morgan smiled at him. "Musician and friend to hard-of-hearing chambermaids."

"Did you ask Fairly if the cure is temporary?"

"It is. If I don't look after my ears, they can get into the same state, particularly if I let quacks poke at me and bring me more infections and bleeding and scarring. He gave me an ear syringe and his card, should I have questions. However did you meet such a man?"

"Mutual friends," Val said. "The circumstances were not particularly sanguine."

"This involves your papa's meddling?"

"Nanny Fran's been talking again." Val rolled his eyes.

"She talks all the time. I got much faster at figuring out what is spoken by watching the speaker's lips around her, and when people don't think you can hear, they often say things you ought not to overhear."

"What sorts of things?" Val asked, noticing Morgan's voice was already increasing in range of pitch, taking on the intonations and inflections of a woman who could hear.

"Footmen are a bawdy lot," Morgan said. "Nanny Fran and Cook are just as bad."

"Has anyone been talking out of turn to His Grace?"

"Not that I know of." Morgan frowned. "Mostly, the staff are very loyal to the earl, as he provided employment when His Grace was letting junior staff go, to hear them tell it. And I can." Morgan sighed and hung a little on his arm. "I can hear them tell it. I will be on my knees for a long time tonight and every night. I wonder if I will sing again someday?"

"You like to sing?"

"Love to." Morgan beamed at him. "I used to sing with my mother, and sometimes Anna would join us, but she was an adolescent just as my voice was becoming reliable, and singing was not her greatest talent."

"So you are related to her?" Val asked, but Morgan's hand dropped from his arm. "Morgan," he chided, "Anna brought you into the household with her, she has admitted to Westhaven she knew you when you could hear, and Dev has seen the two of you tête-à-tête over something serious."

Too late, Morgan realized the trap speaking had sprung on her. Deaf and mute, she could not be questioned; she could not be held accountable for any particular knowledge or intelligence.

Val peered down at her as they approached the park. "Dev says Anna has secrets, and I fear he is right. They are your secrets, too, aren't they?"

"It's complicated and not entirely my business to tell," she said, speaking slowly. "This is part of the reason you must not tell anyone I can hear."

"I do not like lying, Morgan. Particularly not to my brother, regarding people in his employ."

"The earl hired me knowing I could not hear or speak," Morgan pointed out. "He is not cheated when you keep this confidence for me. And if it comforts you to know it, I am not even going to tell Anna I can hear."

"You think she would begrudge you your *hearing*?"

"No." Morgan shook her head then grinned. "I can hear that, when I shake my head." She did it again then her smile faded. "Back to Anna and me... For the past two years, Anna is all that connected me with a world I had long since stopped hearing. I owe her more than you know, and yet, having me to look after has also meant she's had to look after herself. Were I not in such great need, Anna might have given up. She might have taken some options for herself that were not at all desirable. In any case, I do not want to disclose I can hear, not until I know it's going to last."

"That much I can understand," Val said. "How long do you think it will take to convince yourself you are back among the hearing?"

"Oh, *listen!*" Morgan stopped, grinning from ear to ear. "It's geese, and they are *honking*. What a wonderful, silly, undignified sound. And there are children, and they are *screaming* with glee. Oh, Valentine…"

The way she'd said his name, with wonder, and joy and gratitude, it lit the places inside him that had been going dark since his closest brother had died. The music rumbling through him when he watched her hearing the sound of childish laughter was not polite, graceful, or ornamental. It was great, bounding swoops and leaps of joy, and unstoppable, unending gratitude.

Brothers slowly wasted of terrible diseases; they died in asinine duels in provincial taverns; and sometimes, a gifted pianist's hand hurt unbearably, but Morgan could also *hear* when the children laughed.

He sat beside her for a long time in the sunshine and fresh air, just listening to the park and the city and to life.

❧

"Gentlemen." Westhaven addressed his brothers as they ambled back from a morning ride. "I need your help."

Val and Dev exchanged a look of quiet surprise.

"You have it," Dev said.

"Anything you need," Val added. "Anything. Anywhere, anytime."

Westhaven busied himself fiddling with the reins of the rangy chestnut gelding Dev had put him on. He might have expected ribbing from his brothers or teasing or idle curiosity, but their unconditional response caught him off guard.

Dev smiled at him, a smile more tender than humorous. "We love you, and we know you are all that stands between us and His Grace. Say on."

"Good to know one's sentiments are reciprocated," Westhaven said, eyeing the sky casually.

"I suspect whatever you need help with," Val chimed in, "we are discussing it here because you do not want to be overheard at home?"

"Perceptive of you," Westhaven said. "The matter at hand is Mrs. Seaton. She is not, as Dev has suggested, exactly what she appears to be. She tells me there is no spouse trying to hunt her down, nor is she wanted on criminal charges, but she is carrying some burden and will not enlighten me as to its nature. She claims the matter is confidential, and it necessitates her departure from my employ in the near future."

Dev quirked an eyebrow. "We are to find out for you what plagues her and make it go away."

"Not so fast." Westhaven smiled at his darkest brother, the one most likely to solve a problem with his fists or his knife. "Before we go eavesdropping in doorways, I thought we might first combine our knowledge of the situation."

When the brothers returned to the townhouse, they took their lemonade—cold tea for Val—into the library, and closed and locked the door. After about an hour's discussion, they boiled down their objective knowledge to a few facts, most of those gleaned from the agency that had recommended her:

Anna Seaton had come down from the North about two years ago and was on her third post has housekeeper. She'd worked first for an old Hebrew, then briefly for a wealthy merchant before joining the earl's household almost six months ago. At each location, Morgan became part of the household staff, as well. Anna admitted to having a brother and a sister, but being orphaned, had been raised by her grandfather, the florist.

"He had to be one hell of a successful florist," Dev observed. "Didn't you say Anna could speak several languages? Tutors, particularly for females, cost money."

"She plays the piano, too," Westhaven recalled. "That means more money, both to own the instrument and to afford the instruction."

"I wonder," Val said slowly, "if Morgan is not this sister Anna has mentioned to you."

"I suppose she could be." Westhaven frowned. "They do not look particularly alike, but then neither do many sisters."

"They have the same laugh," Val said, surprising his brothers. "What? Morgan can laugh—she isn't simple."

"We know, but it's an odd thing to notice," Westhaven said, noting his youngest brother was more than a little defensive of the chambermaid. "You're reminding me, though, Anna said her parents were killed when their buggy overturned and slid down an embankment. They were on an errand to look at a pony for her younger sister. Then you tell me Morgan lost her hearing after a buggy accident left her pinned in cold water. I think you've put the puzzle pieces together correctly, Val."

Dev drew a finger around the rim of his glass. "We need to send someone north who can find us a very wealthy elderly florist, perhaps two years deceased, perhaps still extant, with three grandchildren, whose son died in a buggy accident that cost one grandchild her hearing. How many of those can there be?"

"Don't rule out a title," Val said quietly.

"A title?" Westhaven winced, hating to think he might have been cavorting with some duke's daughter. That hit a little too close to home.

"Anna once teased me about my…public mannerism," Val said.

"You mean"—Dev grinned—"your mincing and lisping?"

"And so on." Val nodded and waved a hand. "She said something like: You are no more a mincing fop than I am an earl's granddaughter. I remembered it, because Her Grace is an earl's granddaughter."

"We can keep it in mind," Westhaven said, "intuition being at least half of what we have to go on. Anything else?"

"Yes." Dev rose from the sofa and stretched. "Suppose we find out who our housekeeper really is, find she's suspected of some wrongdoing, put the accusations to rest, and so forth. Are we going to all this effort just to keep you in marzipan for the foreseeable future? There are easier ways to do that."

Westhaven pushed away from his desk. "We are

doing this because the duke will soon be asking the same questions, and his methods will not be discreet nor careful nor at all delicate."

"And ours will be?" Val asked, coming to his feet, as well.

"Utterly. We must be, or there's no point to the effort. If anybody finds out we are poking around in Anna Seaton's past, then they could easily insinuate themselves into her present, and that I cannot allow."

"Very well." Dev scratched his ribs and nodded. "We find the elderly florist, et cetera, and do it without making a sound."

"Not a peep," Val agreed just as his stomach rumbled thunderously. "Not a peep once I get some breakfast."

"We can all use breakfast." Westhaven smiled. "We'll talk more about this later, but only when our privacy is assured." He unlocked the door and departed for the breakfast parlor, leaving his two brothers to exchange a look of consternation.

"So." Val looked to his elder sibling hopefully. "We're going about this stealthy investigation of a housekeeper's personal business, why?"

"Noticed he dodged that one, didn't you?" Dev rubbed his chin. "Smart lad. I would hazard a guess, though, we are abetting our brother's ride to the rescue of the fair damsel because for once, he's delegating the tedious work to someone else and keeping the fun part for himself."

"He picked an odd time to turn up human."

"I didn't think the housekeeper was to your taste." Dev grinned and slung an arm around Val's shoulders. "Thought you were more enamored of the quiet housemaid who—though is she *deaf*—sits in the music room by the hour—*watching* you play?"

"Let's get some breakfast," Val groused, digging an elbow into his brother's ribs to shove him away. Smart lad, indeed. Bad enough to have to dodge the duke's spies among the help, but he'd have to warn Morgan that Dev wasn't going to miss a trick either.

❧

Since their trip out to Willow Bend more than a week ago, Anna had felt the earl watching her the way one man might size up another in preparation for a duel or a high-stakes card game. He studied her but made no more mention of trips to the country or marriage. He kept his hands to himself, but his eyes were on her if they were in the same room.

She tried to tell herself it was better this way, with Westhaven keeping his distance and the household rolling along in its pleasant routine. The three brothers usually went out for an early ride then breakfasted together. Thereafter, the earl would closet himself with Tolliver for most of the morning, while Val repaired to his piano and Dev spent time in the stables or at the auctions. Occasionally, all three would be home for lunch, but more often, it was dinner before they joined each other again.

And occasionally, Anna had noticed, they would join in the library for a brandy before dinner, some three-handed cribbage after dinner, or just to talk. And when they did, the door was both closed and locked.

Since the earl hadn't even thought to lock the door when he was naked with her, Anna wondered what could be holding their interest that demanded such privacy. Something they did not want the duke to learn of, no doubt.

Still, it hurt, a little, not be in Westhaven's confidence—not to be in his arms.

But life went on. The agency from Manchester had written they did not place candidates from London unless or until said candidates were removing to the local environs. Bath had at least two openings, but they were for the households of older single gentlemen who enjoyed "lively" social calendars. Anna knew one by reputation to be a lecherous roué and assumed the other was just as objectionable. She waited in the daily hope of more encouraging news from the remaining possibilities and was thus pleased when John Footman brought her a letter.

One glance at the envelope, however, told her the news was not good. Another epistle from rural Yorkshire could not bode well.

I am most concerned for you. A man has been about asking pointed questions, and I am sure he was followed when he returned south. Use greatest caution.

A man asking questions… Dear God, she had caused this. With her reticence and mention of confidences and unwillingness to yield details to his bloody lordship, the Earl of Westhaven. He was resorting to his father's tactics and causing more trouble—more *peril*—than he could possibly imagine. The fear Anna lived with day and night boiled over into rage and indignation at his high-handedness. She barreled out of her sitting room, the letter still in her hand, and almost ran into Devlin St. Just.

"Where is he?" she hissed.

"Westhaven?" St. Just took a step back but kept his hands on her upper arms. "Is there something I can help you with?" His gaze traveled over her warily, no doubt taking in the absence of a cap and the utter determination in her eyes.

"You?" Anna loaded the word with incredulity and scorn. "With your strutting and sneering and threats? You've helped more than enough. *Where is he?*"

"The library." He dropped his hands, and stepped back as Anna stormed away.

"She upset with you?" Val asked as he sauntered out of the kitchen, cookies in hand.

"I did not get off on the proper foot with her, which is my fault," Dev said, "but it's Westhaven who had better start praying."

"Front-row seats, eh?" Val handed him a cookie, and they stole up the stairs in Anna's wake.

❧

"A moment of your time, my lord." Anna kept her voice steady, but her eyes were a different matter. One glance, and the earl knew a storm was brewing.

He rose from his desk. "Tolliver, if you would excuse us?" Taking in Anna's appearance, Tolliver departed with only a brief sympathetic glance at the earl.

"Won't you have a seat?" the earl offered, his tones cordial as he went to close and lock the door.

"I most assuredly will not have a seat," Anna spat back, "and you can unlock that door, Gayle Tristan Montmorency Windham."

An odd thrill went through him at the sound of

his name on her lips, one that made it difficult to appropriately marshal his negotiating face. He had the presence of mind to keep the door locked, however, and instead turned to assess her.

She was toweringly, beautifully, stunningly angry. Enraged, and with him.

"What have I done to offend?"

"You…" Anna advanced on him, a piece of paper fisted in her hand. "You are having me investigated. And thanks to you, *my lord*, what might have been a well-planned move to a comparable position will now be a headlong and poorly thought out flight. I cannot believe you would do this to me, behind my back, without saying a word to me."

"What does your letter say?" the earl asked, puzzled. Yes, he wanted to have her investigated but had yet to identify a sufficiently discreet means of doing so.

"It says there is a man asking questions about me back home." Anna waved the letter, keeping her voice low. "And he was followed south when he returned to Town."

"He was not employed by me," the earl said simply, still frowning in thought. "Though I am fairly certain I know who did retain him."

"You did not do this?" Anna asked, spine stiff.

"I am in the process of trying to identify means appropriate to assist you. I am aware, however, your circumstances involve confidences and have thus been unwilling to proceed until utmost discretion can be assured."

He watched the emotions storm through her eyes: Rage that he would admit to wanting to investigate her, shock that he would be honest, and finally, relief, that his better sense had prevailed.

"His Grace," Anna said, the fight going out of her suddenly. "Your thrice damned, interfering ass of a father, abetted by the toad."

"I will dismiss Stenson before sunset," Westhaven assured her. "I will confront my father, as well. Just one request, Anna."

She met his gaze squarely, still upset but apparently willing to shift the focus of her rage.

"Be here when I return," he said, holding her gaze. She huffed out a breath, nodded once, and dropped her eyes.

"Be here." He walked up to her and put his arms around her. She went willingly, to his relief, and held on to him tightly. "Do not pack, do not warn Morgan, do not pawn the silver, do not panic. Be here and try, just try, to find some ability to trust me."

When he was sure she'd calmed down, Westhaven whipped open the library door to find both his brothers lounging against the wall, munching cookies.

"You lot, look after Anna and Morgan. Don't hold the meals for me." He stalked off, bellowing for Pericles, leaving Anna standing shakily between Dev and Val.

"You are no fun," Dev said, passing Anna a cookie. "We couldn't hear a thing, and we were sure you were going to tear a strip off the earl. Nobody tears a strip off Westhaven, not Her Grace, not His Grace, not even Pericles."

"Rose could," Val speculated, handing his drink to Anna. "Come along." He put an arm around Anna's shoulders. "We'll teach you how to cheat at cribbage, and you can tell us what we missed."

"I already know how to cheat at cribbage," Anna said dumbly, staring at the drink and cookie in her hands.

"Teach that in housekeeper school now, do they?" Dev closed the library door behind them. "Well, then we'll teach you some naughty rugby songs instead. She's going to cry, Val. Best get your hankie at the ready."

"I am not going to cry," Anna said, shoulders stiff. But then she took a funny gulpy breath and two monogrammed handkerchiefs were thrust in her direction. She turned her face into Val's muscular shoulder and bawled while Dev rescued the drink and cookies.

❧

"Mother." Westhaven bowed over Her Grace's hand. "I should have listened to you more closely."

"A mother delights in hearing those sentiments from her children, regardless of the provocation," Her Grace responded, "though I am at a loss to divine your reference."

"You tried to tell me at breakfast the other week." Westhaven ran a hand through his hair. "His Grace is off on another wild start, isn't he?"

"Frequently," the duchess said. "But I wasn't warning you of anything in particular, just the need to exercise discretion with your staff and your personal activities."

"My housekeeper, you mean." Westhaven arched an eyebrow at her. "Somehow, the old bastard got wind of Anna Seaton and set his dogs on her."

"Westhaven." The duchess's regard turned chilly. "You will not refer to your father in such terms."

"Right." Westhaven shuttered his expression. "That would insult my half brother, who is an honorable man."

"Westhaven!" The duchess's expression grew alarmed rather than insulted.

"Forgive me, Mother." He bowed. "My argument is with my father."

"Well," the duke announced himself and paused for dramatic effect in the doorway of the private parlor. "No need to look further. You can have at me now."

"You are having Anna Seaton investigated," the earl said, "and it could well cost her her safety."

"Then marry her," the duke shot back. "A husband can protect a wife, particularly if he's wealthy, titled, smart, and well connected. Your mother has assured me she does not object to the match."

"You don't deny this? Do you have any idea the damage you do with your dirty tricks, sly maneuvers, and stupid manipulations? That woman is terrified, nigh paralyzed with fear for herself and her younger relation, and you go stomping about in her life as if you are God Almighty come to earth for the purpose of directing everybody else's personal life."

The duke paced into the room, color rising in his face.

"That is mighty brave talk for a man who can't see fit to take a damned wife after almost ten years of looking. What in God's name is wrong with you, Westhaven? I know you cater to women, and I know you are carrying on with this Seaton woman. She's comely, convenient, and of child-bearing age. I should have thought to have her investigated, I tell you, so I might find some way to coerce her to the altar."

"You already tried coercion," Westhaven shot back, "and it's only because Gwen Allen is a decent human being her relations haven't ruined us completely in retaliation for your failed schemes. I am ashamed to be your son and worse than ashamed to be your heir. You embarrass me, and I wish to hell I could disinherit you, because if I don't find you a damned broodmare, I've every expectation you will disinherit me."

"Gayle!" His mother was on her feet, her expression horror-stricken. "Please, for the love of God, apologize. His Grace did not have Mrs. Seaton investigated."

"Esther…" His Grace tried to get words out, but his wife had eyes only for her enraged son.

"He most certainly did," Westhaven bit out. "Up to his old tricks, just as he was with Gwen and with Elise and with God knows how many hapless debutantes and scheming widows. I am sick to death of it, Mother, and this is the last straw."

"Esther," His Grace tried again.

"Hush, Percy," the duchess said miserably, still staring at her son. "His Grace did not have your Mrs. Seaton investigated." She paused and dropped Westhaven's gaze. "I did."

"Esther," the duke gasped as he dropped like a stone onto a sofa. "For the love of God, help me."

❧

"He was working for some London toff," Eustace Cheevers informed his employer. "His name was Benjamin Hazlit, and he does a lot of quiet work for the Quality down in Town. He never discloses his employers by name, but it's somebody high up."

"Titled?" the Earl of Helmsley asked, mouth tight.

"Most like." Cheevers nodded. "Folk down south distinguish between themselves more. A fellow who works for the titles wouldn't want work from the cits or the squires or the nabobs. Hazlit's offices are top of the trees, his cattle prime, and his tailor only the best. I'd say a title, yes."

"That pretty much narrows it to Mayfair, doesn't it?" The earl's tone was condescending, as if any damned fool might reach such a conclusion.

"Not necessarily," Cheevers said. "There's a regular infestation of money and titles in Mayfair itself, but the surrounds are not so shabby, and there are other decent neighborhoods with quieter money."

An earl worthy of the title would have spent some time in Town, Cheevers thought, keeping his expression completely deferential. But this young sprig—well, this not quite middle-aged sprig—had obviously never acquired his Town bronze. Pockets to let, Cheevers thought with an inward sigh. The word around York was to get paid in advance if Helmsley offered you his custom.

It hadn't been like that when the old earl was alive. The estate had been radiant with flowers, the women happy, and the bills always paid. Now, most of the gardeners had been let go, and the walls had bleached spots where valuable paintings had once hung. The drive was unkempt, the fences sagging, the fountains dry, and nobody had seen the dowager countess going about since she'd suffered an apoplexy more than two years ago. Where the granddaughters had got off to was anybody's guess.

"So that's the extent of what you've learned?" Helmsley rose, his tone disdainful. "You can tell me the man's name and that he's a professional investigator with wealthy clients? Nothing more."

"It's in the file." Cheevers stood. "You will have his address, the names of those with whom he spoke, what they told him, and so forth. I don't gather he learned much of significance, as people tend to be leery of Town fribbles up here."

"That they do." Helmsley nodded, his expression turning crafty. Cheevers considered the earl and wondered what the man was plotting, as it boded ill for someone. Helmsley had the look of man who could have been handsome. He had height, patrician features, and thick dark hair showing only the barest hint of gray. Cheevers, expert at summing people up, put Helmsley in his early thirties. The man looked older, however, as the signs of excessive fondness for both the grape and rich foods were beginning to show.

Helmsley's nose was becoming bulbous and striated with spider veins. His middle was soft, his reactions slow. Most telling of all, Cheevers, thought, there was a mean, haunted look in the man's gray eyes that labeled him as a cheat and a bully.

Good riddance, Cheevers concluded as he showed himself out. There were some accounts that even the thriftiest Yorkshireman's son was happy to close.

Thirteen

"WELL?"

Wilberforce Hammond James, ninth Earl of Helmsley, carefully composed his features before turning to face the man who'd thrust open the interior door to the study. He did not face a pretty sight. Hedley Arbuthnot, Baron Stull, was nearly as round as he was tall, and he wasn't exactly short.

Worse, he was untidy. His cravat showed evidence of the chicken he'd consumed at lunch, the wine with which he'd washed down the chicken, and the snuff with which he'd settled his understandably rebellious stomach. That stomach, Helmsley knew, was worked incessantly.

But Stull, who was at least ten years Helmsley's senior, had two qualities that appealed, despite his appearance, lack of couth, and tendency to flatulence. First, he was free with his coin when in pursuit of his own ends, and second, he was as determined as a bulldog.

"Well, what?" Helmsley flicked an imaginary speck of lint from his sleeve.

"Where are the girls?"

"Mayfair," Helmsley said, praying it was true.

"Best get packing then," Stull said, sniffing like a canine catching the scent of prey. "To Mayfair it is."

❧

"He's been gone for hours."

Anna stopped pacing and pinned her gaze on Dev, whom she'd accurately assessed as the more soft-hearted brother. Val was sensitive and perceptive but had learned as his sisters' favored escort to keep some perspective around emotional women.

"He said we weren't to hold meals for him," Dev reasoned. "Meals, Anna, plural. Not just luncheon. He might have gone to talk with His Grace's investigator or taken Pericles for a romp."

"He romped Pericles this morning, when it was cooler," Anna pointed out. "I liked you better when you weren't trying to turn me up sweet."

"I'll go to the mansion and find out what's what," Val said. "When His Grace and Westhaven go at it, they are usually loud, ugly, and to the point. Anna's right—it shouldn't be taking this long."

He shot Dev a sympathetic glance but knew his brother would not have offered to investigate. Dev did not show up at the ducal mansion uninvited or unexpected, and Val wasn't about to ask him to break that tradition now. .

The library door opened, and Westhaven strode in, surprising all three occupants.

"What's wrong?" Dev asked. "Don't tell me His Grace got the better of you."

"Well, he did," Westhaven said, going straight for the whiskey decanter, pouring one drink, knocking it back, and pouring another.

"Westhaven?" Val asked cautiously. But it was to Anna the earl spoke.

"For once," he said, "His Grace was blameless. You were investigated by a man named Benjamin Hazlit, who is legendarily thorough and legendarily discreet. He was on the Moreland payroll, but at my mother's request, not the duke's. I did not become aware of this until I had shouted dear Papa down with every obscene expression of my petty, selfish frustrations with him. I ranted, I raved, I shouted, and I told him…"

A pin could have dropped while Westhaven stared at his drink.

"I told him I was ashamed to be his son and heir."

"Ye gods." Val went to the brandy decanter. "About time somebody set him straight." He handed drinks all around but saw Dev was staring at Westhaven with a frown.

"The old windbag got the last word somehow, though, didn't he?" Dev guessed while Anna waited in silent dread.

"I sincerely hope," Westhaven said, pinning Anna with a troubled look, "it isn't quite his last word. Just as Her Grace was explaining that Hazlit was her agent, the duke suffered a heart seizure." The silence became thoughtful as all three brothers considered their father's mortality, and thus their own, while Anna considered the earl.

"He's still alive?" she said, drawing three pairs of eyes.

"He was demanding his personal physicians at full

bellow when I left," Westhaven said. "I've sent Pugh and Hamilton to him and left very strict orders he is not to be bled, no matter how he rants and blusters."

"Are you sure it was real?" Dev asked. "I would not put chicanery past him."

"Neither would I," Val said, eyes on Westhaven's face.

"I am sure it was real though I am not sure how serious it was. I am sure *he* thought he was dying, and of course, he still might die."

"He will die," Val corrected. "We all will. What makes you think he wasn't faking?"

"I've seen him morose, playful, raging, and—with Her Grace—even tender," Westhaven said, "but in thirty years of memory, I cannot recall our father ever looking *afraid* before today. It was unnerving, I can tell you.

"I recall his rows with Bart," the earl went on, shoving back to sit on his desk. "I used to think Bart was half-mad to let the old man get to him so. Why didn't he just let it roll off him, I'd wonder. I've realized though, that there is a kind of assurance to be had when you take on His Grace, and he doesn't back down, doesn't give quarter, doesn't flinch or admit he's wrong, no matter what."

"He's consistent," Dev admitted. "Consistently exasperating."

"But he's always the duke," Westhaven said. "You never catch him breaking role, or doubting himself or his God-given right to be as he is."

Val took a thoughtful swallow of his whiskey. "If the duke falls, then what?"

"Long live the duke," Anna said, holding

Westhaven's eyes for a moment. "I am going to have dinner brought in here on trays. I am sure you will all be going to check on your father afterward. You might want to take Nanny Fran with you, as she's a skilled nurse and would be a comfort to Her Grace."

Westhaven just nodded, seeming relieved she'd deal with the practicalities.

The evening unfolded as Anna predicted, with all three brothers off to the ducal mansion to see His Grace—to watch Westhaven argue with the duke over the choice of physicians—and to offer the duchess their support.

Val elected to stay at the mansion, agreeing to send word if there was any change in the duke's condition, while Dev went off to inform their half-sister, Maggie, of the duke's heart seizure. When Westhaven returned to his townhouse, it was late enough that Anna had dismissed the footman at the front door and waited there herself for Westhaven to return.

She was dressed in only her night rail, wrapper, and slippers when she met him, and heedless of any prying eyes or listening ears she wrapped her arms around him as soon as he was near enough to grab.

"He looks like hell, Anna," Westhaven said, burying his face against her neck. "He finally looks old, and worse, Mother looks old, too. The girls are terrified."

"And you are a little scared, too," Anna guessed, drawing back. "Give me your hat and gloves, Westhaven, and I will fix you a tray. You did not eat worth mentioning at dinner, and Her Grace warned me you go off your feed when you have concerns."

"What else did Her Grace warn you about?" the

earl asked, letting Anna divest him of hat and gloves. She didn't stop there but went on to remove his jacket and his cravat, and then undo his cuff links and roll back his shirtsleeves.

"It is too hot to go about in your finery," Anna said, "and too late."

He'd stood there in the foyer like a tired little boy, and let her fuss with his clothing. She piled his clothing over one arm, laced her fingers through his, and towed him unresisting into the peaceful confines of his home.

꩜

The warmth of Anna's hand in his felt like the first good news Westhaven had heard all day.

"My grandfather died just a couple of years ago," Anna said as she led him through the darkened house. "I was so lucky to have him that long, and he was the dearest man. But he suffered some wasting disease, and in the end, it was a relief to see him go, but he held on and held on for my grandmother."

"I can see His Grace doing the same thing," the earl said, squeezing Anna's fingers slightly.

"I recall that sense of dread," Anna continued, "dread that every time Grandpapa dozed off, he was actually dead. He looked dead, sometimes, or I thought he did until I actually saw him pass. Three weeks after he left us, my grandmother had an apoplexy and became quite invalided herself."

"She suffered a serious blow," the earl said as they gained the kitchen.

"We all had," Anna said, sitting him down at the work

table. "I recall the way the whole household seemed strained, waiting but still hoping. We were...lost."

He watched her moving around the kitchen to fetch his lemonade, watched her pour a scandalous amount of sugar into it then assemble him a tray. Something in the practical competence of her movements reassured him, made him feel less *lost*. In the ducal household, his mother and sisters, the servants, the physicians, *everybody*, looked to him for guidance.

And he'd provided it, ordering the straw spread on the street, even though the mansion sat so far back from the square the noise was unlikely to disturb his father. The need was for the staff to do something—anything—to feel like they were contributing to the duke's welfare and comfort.

So Westhaven had issued orders, commandeering a sick room in the ducal chambers, sending word down to Morelands, setting Nanny Fran to inventorying the medical supplies, directing his sisters to pen notes to the family's closest acquaintances and extended family, and putting Her Grace to extracting a list from the duke of the cronies he wanted notified and the terms of the notice. He'd conferred with the doctors, asked them to correspond with Fairly on the case, made sure Dev was off to inform Maggie, and finally, when there were no more anxious faces looking to him for direction, let himself come home.

And it was home, he thought, not because he owned the building or paid the people who worked there, nor even because he dwelled here with his brothers.

It was home because Anna was here, waiting for him. Waiting to care for him, not expecting him—hell, not really even allowing him—to care for her, solve her problems, and tell her how to go on.

I love you, he thought, watching her pull a daisy from the bouquet in the middle of the table and put it in a bud vase on his tray. When she brought the tray to the table and set it down, he put his arms around her waist and pressed his face to her abdomen.

"I used to look at your scalp wound this way," Anna mused, trailing her finger through his hair to look for a scar. "I am lucky I did not kill you."

"My head is too hard," he said, sitting back. "I am supposed to eat this?"

"I will wallop you again if you don't," Anna said firmly, folding her arms. "And I'll tattle to Pericles, who seems to have some sort of moral authority over you."

"Sit with me," he said, trying to muster a smile at her words.

She settled in beside him, and he felt more at peace.

"What do the physicians say?" Anna asked, laying her head on his shoulder.

"Odd," the earl said, picking up a sandwich. "Nobody has asked me that, not even Her Grace."

"She probably knows, even if she doesn't admit it to herself, just how serious this is. My grandparents were like that, joined somehow at the level of instinct."

"They loved each other," the earl said, munching thoughtfully. Were he and Anna joined at the level of instinct? He thought so, or she wouldn't be sitting here with him, feeding him, and offering him company when his own family did not.

"They surely did," Anna said. "My grandfather

grew his flowers for *her*. For me and Morgan, too, but mostly for his bride."

"Morgan is your sister," the earl concluded as his sandwich disappeared. Beside him, Anna went still.

"I know you are related," he said, sipping his lemonade then offering it to Anna. "You care for her, and she is much more than a cousin to you."

"You know this how?"

"I know you," he said simply. "And we live under the same roof. It's hard to hide such a closeness. You were willing to murder me for her safety."

"She is my sister."

"Val guessed it," the earl said, biting into an apple slice. "He's a little in love with her, I think."

"With Morgan?" Anna frowned. "An infatuation, perhaps. I am guessing she symbolizes something for him, something to do with his music or his choices in life. I know she adores him for his kindness, but I trust them."

"He plays Herr Beethoven like a man, not a boy."

"You would be better able to decipher that than I." Anna accepted the apple slice he passed her. "His playing to me has lately become passionate, and brilliant as a consequence."

"That's well said," the earl responded, munching thoughtfully.

"You've dodged my question about the physicians," Anna said, rubbing her hand across his lower back.

"They can't tell us anything for sure. The duke's symptoms—the sensation of a horse sitting on his chest, inability to breathe freely, pain in the left side of his neck and down his left arm—are classic signs of a heart seizure. But the pains were very fleeting, and His Grace is a very active fellow. He has not felt particularly fatigued, is not in pain as we speak, and hasn't had any previous episodes of chest pain. He may make a full recovery and live another twenty years. The next weeks will be critical in terms of ensuring he gets rest and only very moderate exercise."

"But they also implied he may die tonight. Do you believe he's had no similar incidents, or has he been keeping up appearances for your mother?"

"Dev asked the same thing, and we decided if there had been earlier warnings, Her Grace might be the only one to detect it."

"And she would say nothing, except possibly to His Grace when they had privacy, which they will have little of."

"I can see they have some." The earl glanced over at her. "You learned this from your grandparents?"

"My grandmother. From time to time she shooed everybody away from the sick room and had Grandpapa to herself. It gave us all a break and gave them some time to be together."

"And to say goodbye." The earl sipped his drink again then handed the glass to Anna. "God, Anna, when I think of the things I said to my father today."

"You can apologize," Anna said simply. "It's more than he's ever been willing to do when it's time to mend a fence. And he has bullied his way through many fences."

The earl chuckled at her tart tone, despite his fears and guilt and fatigue. "You are a ruthlessly practical woman, Anna Seaton."

"Eat your marzipan," she ordered. "I've learned to be practical, and you've no one to talk sense to you tonight save me. A man of the duke's age is lucky to be alive, much less alive and getting up to all the mischief he does. You did not cause his heart seizure, Westhaven. Do not even try to argue with me on this." She leaned over and kissed his cheek then handed him a piece of candy. "Eat."

He obeyed, realizing the food, drink, and conversation had restored him more than he would have thought possible.

"The next week," he said around a mouthful of almond paste, "will be trying."

"Your entire existence as the duke's heir has been trying."

"It has," he agreed, fingering his glass. "But I'm getting things turned around, Anna. The cash flow will soon be reliable and healthy, the estate managers are getting better organized, the girls and Mama and even His Grace are learning to deal with budgets and allowances. By the end of summer, I won't have to spend so much time with Tolliver. I wanted my father to see that."

"You wanted him to offer some gesture of thanks, or perhaps you wanted to be able to brag on yourself a bit and see if he at least notices all your efforts."

"I suppose." He picked up the second piece of marzipan and studied it. "Is that such a sorry thing, for a grown man still to want his papa to approve of him?"

"The sorry thing is that there would be any doubt in your mind that he does." She kissed his cheek again, a gesture that felt comforting and natural to him, then rose and began tidying up the kitchen.

"In all of today's tumult, I'll bet you forgot to fire Stenson and also forgot that our new butler started."

"Sterling." The earl nodded. "I did forget. Have we counted the silver to make sure my choice was worthy? And yes, I have yet to speak to Stenson."

"Send him back to the mansion, then," Anna suggested. "Lord Val is there, and Colonel St. Just's smalls are all mended."

"He's probably told you to call him by name." Anna and Dev might never be the best of friends, but in her tone there was none of the latent prickliness Dev had engendered earlier.

"He is much like your papa," Anna said, pausing as she picked up the earl's tray. "Gruff and sometimes unable to communicate his motivations, but tender-hearted and fierce."

"A good description. He was a grown man, though, before he could even speak clearly among strangers."

"Lord Val told me of the stutter," Anna said, coming back to the table with a clean rag. She bent over to wipe down the table, and Westhaven seized her hand in a gentle, implacable grip.

"Anna?" She straightened slowly and met his gaze. "Spend the night with me."

❧

Anna detected an odd light in Westhaven's eyes, combining daring and ferocity, but behind that, a stark vulnerability, as well. "Spend the night with me," he'd said. Simple, straightforward words with a wealth of complicated meanings.

She closed her eyes, trying to brace herself against

his request and against her own raging desire to grant it. *Not now*, she thought desperately. Not now, when they hadn't even discussed that investigator and the urgent need for her to flee.

"I will behave," the earl said, dropping her wrist. "I'm too damned tired to really… Well, maybe not too tired, but too…" He fell silent and frowned. "It is an unreasonable request and poorly timed. Forget I asked."

Anna opened her eyes and saw he was no longer looking at her. He rose and stretched, then glanced over at her where she stood immobilized, the rag still in her hand.

"I've offended you," he said. "I just want… Will you be here in the morning?"

He hadn't wanted to put that question into words, Anna knew. Hadn't wanted to ask her to be with him in the morning.

"I will be here," Anna said, unable to listen to her common sense screaming to the contrary. "In your bed, if you want me there."

He just nodded and took the rag from her, wiping up the table while Anna finished putting away the dishes she'd washed. To her, the moment was resoundingly domestic and somehow right for them. He wasn't pretentious with her, wasn't always the earl. Sometimes, like now, he was just Gayle Windham, a thoroughly, completely lovable and worthy man.

He waited until Anna had finished tidying up, took a candle from the table, and held out his arm to her. The gesture was courtly and oddly reminiscent of Anna's grandparents. *Oh, to grow old with him…*Anna thought, wrapping her hand around his forearm.

When they gained his room, the sense of domestic peace came with them. Anna finished undressing him; he tucked her into his bed then set about using the wash water kept in ample supply by his hearth. The balcony doors were open, and a refreshing breeze wafted through the room. She watched his ablutions, finding him simply beautiful in the light of the single candle. It wasn't even an erotic appreciation but something more possessive than that. He was beautifully built, of course, but the pensive expression on his face was beautiful to her, too.

He is the way he is because he cares, and maybe in this, he and his father can finally find some common ground.

When he wrung out the wet cloth and straightened, Anna flipped back the lavender-scented sheets. "Come to bed."

"Your night rail, madam?" He held out a hand. "It is too hot for all that extra, Anna, and I promise I will not bother you."

"So you've said," she replied, pulling the night-gown over her head and handing it to him. "Did you lock the door?"

"Ye gods." He padded through the dark and took care of the lock, blew out the candle, then climbed in beside her.

"I cannot remember the last time I spent the night with anyone other than a cat in my bed, save for our night at Willow Bend." Anna settled on the mattress as she spoke.

"I could say the same thing." The earl punched his pillow. "It would have different significance. Sorry." He was apologizing for yanking inadvertently on her pillow, but Anna let the apology cover his teasing, as well.

Anna folded her hands on her stomach as they both stretched out on their backs. "What awaits you tomorrow?"

"I'll meet with His Grace," the earl said. "Deliver Stenson his orders, probably call on Maggie, and try to toss enough work at Tolliver so we don't get behind."

Anna reached for his hand, prying it off his own stomach and lacing her fingers through it. "You should send a note around first thing to your brothers and go for your regular ride."

"Instead of seeing if my father is still alive?" The earl's frown was evident even in the darkness, but Anna was more aware that his fingers were closed around hers tightly.

"If he passes in the night you will receive word immediately. Lord Val will see to it. You enjoy your rides tremendously," she went on. "Some days, I think it's the only time you permit yourself to do what you please and not what you ought. And Pericles will not be around forever."

"Using my horse's welfare, Anna?"

"And your brothers need to see that though the duke may be failing, the earl is not; nor is the earl spending every waking minute in anticipation of his father's demise. The earl is too sturdy to capitulate to anxiety like that and too well inured to his responsibilities. Death befalls us, and while it is sad, the duke has lived a very long and good life. Though he will be mourned, his passing will be in the natural order of things, as will the earl's, when the time comes."

He sighed and considered her point.

I love you, he thought, *because you are honest with me and because you are willing to speak the truth to me when others might seek to curry favor instead. I love you because you are in this bed with me, not trying to conceive the much-awaited next generation of Windhams, but just holding my hand.*

"I'll go riding."

"Good." Anna rolled toward him, and in the dark he felt her moving on the mattress. She kissed his forehead and sighed. "Now go to sleep, Gayle Tristan Montmorency Windham. I will be here when you waken. I promise."

She wrestled him then into the position she deemed best suited to his slumbers, leaving him lying in her arms, his face resting against her shoulder. She stroked his back in the same easy rhythm he often gave her, and Anna soon heard his breathing even out.

I will be here when you waken, she thought, *but for how much longer, I do not know.*

The investigator sent north had precipitated the need the leave, and now, when the duke lay so ill, any temptation to confide in the earl was put to rest. He needed to be looking to his own and not to the troubles brought to him by his housekeeper.

Anna wrapped her arms around the future Duke of Moreland and sent up a heartfelt prayer for his happiness and her own safety.

～✌～

The days and nights that followed saw shifts in the routine of the earl's household. His morning ride with his brothers, a casual habit earlier, became standard. Stenson's departure brought a sense of relief to everyone, and Sterling, a quiet older gentleman recommended by no less than the Duke of Quimbey, brought order among the footmen.

And the nights…

The earl rose each morning, well rested and ready to face the day, because Anna shared his bed. The need for her hovered in regions Westhaven could not articulate. There was desire in it, but not enough that he initiated any seduction. The simple comfort of her presence was far more precious than any fleeting pleasure might be.

And he had the sense Anna was granting him the boon of her nightly company only because she was more determined than ever to go, and go soon. His Grace had enjoyed four days of continued freedom from chest pains, and the ducal household was beginning to admit to some cautious relief.

Watching Anna sleep, Westhaven frowned as he realized that when the duke was deemed safe from immediate danger, then Anna would likely go.

He would not allow that. *Could not.* Mentally, he kicked himself for not making the time to meet with Hazlit earlier in the week. He'd meet with him today, he vowed, if he had to pursue the man on foot through Seven Dials to see it done.

"You're awake." Anna smiled at him, and he smiled back. Such a simple thing, to start the day with a shared smile. He leaned over and kissed her.

"No fair." Anna shoved the sheets aside. "You've used the tooth powder already." She heaved off the bed, shrugged into her wrapper, and made for the privacy screen in the corner.

She was not too fussy, his Anna. She emerged and made use of his tooth powder and toothbrush, then caught sight of herself in the dressing mirror.

"I look like I was dragged through the proverbial hedge backward. How can you not be overcome with laughter at my appearance?" In the mirror, he assessed her reflection: Her braid was coming unraveled and she had a wrinkle across her cheek from the pillow seam.

"You look very dear. Come back to bed."

"It is almost light out, your lordship." Anna eyed him balefully. "I am surprised you slept this late."

"Dev has to take his horses back to Surrey today, and Val made for a late night at Fairly's piano. No morning ride for poor Pericles, I'm afraid. Come back to bed, Anna."

There was something…implacable in his voice, and in the gray shadows of the room, Anna felt as if she were suddenly facing a life-defining moment. She could get in that bed, and this time—this time, finally—they would make love. She knew it as surely as a woman knows the scent of her lover, as surely as a mother knows the cry of her child.

Or she could smile, shake her head, and set about tidying herself up for the day.

Slowly, she unbelted her wrapper and walked naked back toward the bed.

"Your courses?" the earl asked as he watched her. "When will they fall?"

"In a few days," she said, not surprised at the intimacy of the question. In some ways, the past days had seen them become more intimate than lovers. They shared his toothbrush; he brushed out her hair. She helped him dress, and he was her lady's maid. At the beginning and end of each day, they held quiet conversations, holding hands in bed or holding each other.

And moment by moment, Anna stored up the memories. This man, this very wealthy, powerful, handsome, and singular man was hers to love for the next very little while. It was a privilege beyond any she could have imagined, and now he wanted to make these last few memories with her, as well.

She might have been able to deny herself, she thought, but she could no longer deny *him*.

"You still think to leave me, Anna," he said as she settled on the bed, "and I am telling you quite honestly, I will fight you with every weapon I can find, honorable or not. I don't want you to go."

It was the first time he'd said that out loud, but Anna sensed it was the essence of what he was trying to communicate by bringing her back to his bed.

"I don't want you to go," he said again more fiercely.

"I'm here," Anna said, meeting his eyes. "Right now I am here with you in this bed."

He nodded, his gaze becoming hooded. "Where you will stay until I have pleasured you within an inch of your sanity." She smiled up at him for that piece of arrogance and brushed his hair back from his forehead.

"Likewise, I'm sure."

He smiled, a wolfish smile that nonetheless held an element of relief. "No rushing," he warned.

"No promises," she countered, scooting her way under him. "And no more lectures." She wrapped her legs around his flanks and levered up to kiss him. He growled, wrapped his arms around her, and rolled with her across the bed.

"I'm going to fuck you silly," he warned, positioning her on top of him.

"I'm going to let you." Anna smiled down at him. "But not just yet." She tried to scramble away from him, but he caught her by the ankles, slapped her bottom twice audibly, and dragged her back to him, grousing the whole time about troublesome women and naughty housekeepers. This side of him—the playful, exuberant, mating male—fascinated and delighted her.

And she wasn't averse to his hand on her buttocks, either, particularly not when he was so considerately rubbing the sting from her flesh.

"Shall I spank you when you're naughty?" she asked when he had her caged beneath his body.

"Please," he murmured, dipping his head to kiss her. "Spank me as hard and as often as you dare, for with you, I want to be very, very naughty."

The talking was finished, she surmised, as his tongue began to forage at her mouth and his hand covered her naked breast. He was bent not on seduction, so much as arousal and possession. *You are mine*, his hands seemed to say. *I am yours*, his kisses echoed. *All mine*, the insistent press of his cock against her belly declared.

I am yours, Anna thought, wrapping her legs around him and bringing her sex to stroke over his erection. And for today, for these moments, *you are mine*.

"Easy," he breathed, his hand going still just as his fingers closed over her nipple.

"No promises," Anna retorted. "I will rush if I

please, sir." She glided her fingertips over his nipples and pressed hard with her hips.

"Jesus God, Anna," the earl whispered. "I want to be careful with you…but you…"

But she wanted him too desperately to appreciate his care. Heat was building below the pit of her stomach, in the place where worry and loneliness could make her feel so empty and desperate. It was the heat of desire, desire for him, and desire to give herself to him. He was bringing her fullness in places that had gone too long wanting and lonely.

"I need you inside me," she pleaded softly, framing his face with her hands. "Later you can be careful, I promise. Now, just please… I need you."

"Do not hurry me, Anna. I won't answer for the consequences if you do." But to her great relief, he brought the tip of his cock to the entrance of her sex and began to use it to nuzzle through her folds. He was content to explore that pleasure, lazily rooting and thrusting with little apparent focus, sometimes coming close to his goal, sometimes—deliberately, Anna thought—angling himself to one side, too high, the other side…

"You…are tormenting me."

"Then guide me, Anna," he coaxed. "Show me where you want me."

She was wet—he'd made sure of it—and he was wet as a result, as well. Anna's fingers closed around his shaft and drew him directly to her. She didn't withdraw her touch until he'd advanced enough to understand where she'd put him, snugged against her but not quite penetrating.

"You let me do this part," he cautioned, levering up on his forearms to hold her eyes. "I mean it, Anna. I'm not a small man, and you're… Oh, Jesus." The last word was said on a near groan as he pressed forward just the smallest increment. "God Almighty," he breathed as he lowered his face to her neck. "You are so blessedly fucking…"

He is joining his body to mine, Anna thought in wonder. Oh, it felt strange and wonderful and too damned slow by half.

"Westhaven." She arched her hips tentatively, only to have him go still.

"No," he ground out. "You damned let me, for once in your stubborn life, take care of you, Anna. Just…let me."

She liked his cursing and his foul language and the way he was so stern with her, but mostly, she liked the feel of him inching carefully into her body.

And then she didn't quite like it as much.

"Hold onto me," Westhaven urged. "Hold onto me but relax, Anna. I won't move until I feel you relax. Kiss me." He dipped his head and planted slow, easy kisses on her cheeks, her jaw, her eyelids. When her breathing was steady and she was kissing him back, he let a hand drift to her breast, there to knead and fondle and stroke, until Anna heard herself sigh and felt her whole body going boneless in response. Gradually he pressed his cock forward.

And again met resistance.

He slid a hand under Anna's buttocks, braced her, and without warning, gave a single hard thrust. She winced and stiffened beneath him but made no sound.

"It will go easier now," he assured her, moving much more gently. "Tell me if I'm hurting you."

He had hurt her, Anna thought, but only for a surprising twinge of a moment. It felt better now, and the more deeply he moved into her body, the better she felt.

"I like this," she said, pleased and breathless and bothered. "Don't stop, Westhaven. I do like this."

"Move with me now, Anna. The difficult part is over, and it's all pleasure from here. Fuck me silly…" he teased, but there was a desperate note beneath the tenderness in his tone even as his thrusts became more purposeful.

Anna tried to match the undulation of her hips to his, and that forced him to slow down, to give her time to catch his rhythm. But what he gave up in speed, he made up for in intensity.

"That's it," he whispered a few moments later. "Move like that, and…Anna. *God.*"

She was a quick study, able to move with him and send her hand wandering up his side to find his nipple, as well. Her thumb feathered across his puckered flesh in the same deliberate rhythm as he made with his cock, then she applied more pressure, actually rubbing him in a small, gratifyingly erotic circle.

"Anna…" He slipped his own hand more firmly around her buttocks. "Slow down… You've got to let… Ah, Christ. Don't stop, love."

"You either." She traced her tongue over his other nipple. "For the love of God, don't you dare stop."

She tried to quicken their rhythm, but he held firm to the more deliberate pace.

"Westhaven, please…" she wailed softly. "*Gayle*…"

His name, spoken in that hot, pleading tone, had the effect she'd hoped. He let the tempo increase until she was shaking and keening beneath him in the throes of her pleasure. Still he didn't stop but bent his head, took her nipple into his mouth, and drew strongly on her. She flailed her hips desperately against him, whispering his name over and over against his chest, her legs locked around his flanks.

He lifted his head, anchored a hand under her buttocks, and Anna felt a wet heat spreading deep in her body as his thrusts slowed and deepened. Westhaven groaned softly in her ear then went quiet above her.

"You," Westhaven rasped long moments later. "Sweet, ever-loving, merciful, abiding Christ."

He made it to his feet, carefully extricating his softening cock from Anna's body. She winced at the sensation of him leaving but made no verbal protest, merely watching him with luminous eyes in the soft predawn shadows. He used the wash water then brought the damp cloth to the bed.

"Spread your legs for me." She complied, unable to deny him in that moment any intimacy he wanted. Dear God, the things he had made her feel… The cloth was cool and soothing, and yet knowing he wielded it made it arousing, too.

"Take your time," she murmured. "No need to rush."

"Naughty." He smiled approvingly. "But you'll likely be sore, so no more marzipan for you this morning."

"And you won't be sore?"

"As to that"—he tossed the wet cloth over the rim of the basin—"I very well might be. You have much to answer for."

"Much."

"Anna?" The earl climbed over her, bracing himself on his forearms, and regarded her very seriously. "Weren't you going to tell me?"

"Do you need to hear the words?" She met his eyes, feeling sadness crowd out contentment.

"The words?" Guardedness crept up on the tenderness in his eyes.

"Oh, very well," Anna sighed, brushing fingers through the lock of hair on his forehead. "Of course I love you." She leaned up and wrapped her arms and legs around him. "I love you desperately. I would not still be here if I didn't. I would not be leaving you if I didn't. I love you, Gayle Windham. And I probably always will. There…now are we both thoroughly mortified?"

"I am not mortified," he whispered, burying his face against her neck. "I am…awed. Beyond words. You honor me, Anna Seaton. You honor me unbelievably."

He should say more, he knew, but his heart was pounding again, and she could probably feel that, so tightly was he clutching her to him. He should say that he loved her, for he certainly did, but he could not speak, could not contain with words the emotions rioting through him.

"Westhaven?" Anna stroked his back, her tone wary. "Are you well?"

"No," he said, feeling—merciful God—tears

thicken in his throat as he held her even tighter. "I am not exactly well. I am...fucked silly."

And he meant it in every possible way.

∽

"I tell you that was her," Stull hissed. "I know my girls, Helmsley, and that's my little Morgan."

"It has been more than two years since you've seen your little Morgan," Helmsley said with as much patience as he could muster. "Women change in those years, change radically. Besides, it can't be her. That girl was laughing and shouting and talking with her swain so the whole park could hear her. Morgan can't do any of those things."

"It's *her*," Stull insisted. "I bet you if we follow her and that callow buffoon on her arm, we will find my Anna, as well."

"You are more than welcome to go haring off in this heat after a girl who obviously is not my sister, though I will grant you a certain resemblance. Morgan's hair was not so light, though, and I do not think Morgan was as tall as that girl."

"You said it yourself," Stull shot back, "women between the ages of fifteen and eighteen will change, delightfully so to my way of thinking."

"So go on. If you're so convinced that's Morgan, trot along. Confirm your hunch."

Stull gave him the mean look a grossly fat boy will often show when taunted, then sighed.

"It is too hot," Stull conceded. "If she's in the area, she'll be back here. The park is the only decent air to be had in this miserable city. I'm parched—what say we find us a flagon or two of summer ale and perhaps the wenches that happily serve it?"

"A pint or two sounds just the thing," Helmsley said, knowing Stull, true to his two consistent virtues, would pay for it. "And perhaps we can find someone to watch for your girls in the park. I still have their miniatures."

"Good idea. Put the common man to work and let us do the thinking. What was the name of that inn where we saw the one with the big…?" He cupped his hands over his chest and wiggled his eyebrows.

"The Happy Pig," Helmsley sighed. It would be The Happy Pig. "I'm sure we can find a couple of sharp eyes there, maybe more than a couple."

⁓

For Anna, the week was passing too quickly. In her mind, the duke's health would be resolved in those seven days, giving him either a cheerful or a grim prognosis. Westhaven was gone during most of the days, spending time with his parents and sisters, tending to business, dashing out to Willow Bend, or riding in the mornings with his brothers.

But the nights…it had been two nights and three mornings since they'd become lovers in fact, and Anna had all she could do to stumble around the house, appearing to tend to her duties. She was swamped with Gayle Windham, her senses overwhelmed with memories of his tenderness, passion, humor, and generosity in bed. He insisted she find her pleasure, early and often. He talked to her before, during, and after their lovemaking. He teased and comforted and aroused and asked no questions other than what pleased her and what did not.

It all pleased her. She sighed, frowning at the flowers she was trying to arrange in the library's raised fireplace. Normally, she could arrange a bouquet to her satisfaction without thought, the patterns simply working themselves out. This morning, the daisies and irises were being contrary, and the thought of Westhaven's hand clamped on her buttocks was only part of the problem.

She heard the door open and assumed Morgan was bringing in fresh water, so she didn't turn.

"Now this is a fetching sight. I don't suppose the buttons of your bodice are going to get stuck in the screen?" Anna sat back on her heels and looked up at Westhaven looming over her. He stretched down a hand and hauled her up, bringing her flush against his body.

"Hello, sweetheart." He smiled then brushed a kiss to her cheek. "Miss me?"

She leaned into him and wrapped her arms around his waist.

"How is your father?" she asked as she always did.

"Improving, I'd say." But her unwillingness to return his sentiments bothered him, and that showed in his eyes. "I met with Hazlit," the earl said, letting Anna walk out of his embrace.

"You did?"

"I got nowhere." Westhaven sat down on the sofa and tugged off his boots. "He is an interesting man—very dark, almost swarthy. It is rumored his grandmother was a Jewess, rumored he is in line for some Scottish title, rumored he is filthy rich." He sat back and stacked his boots beside the sofa. "I'll tell you what is true: That man has the presentation of a cool demeanor down to a science, Anna. He gave away exactly nothing but told me to call again in a few days, thank you very much. He will call on Her Grace and hear from her in person that I am to be trusted with her confidences."

"Her Grace hasn't given you the substance of his investigation?" *I don't have a few more days to tarry*, Anna silently wailed.

"He does not write down his findings," the earl explained, "and he made the appointment to call on Her Grace, and then my father fell ill. He will reschedule the appointment, and Mother will receive him immediately."

"You could simply join that appointment."

"And give the appearance that I am coercing my mother?" the earl countered. "I wish it were simpler, but that man will not be bullied."

"One wonders how such an odd character would winkle secrets out of my dour Yorkshiremen."

"So you are from Yorkshire," the earl replied just as Anna's hand flew to her lips. "Anna…" His voice was tired, and his eyes were infinitely sad and patient.

"I'm sorry." Anna felt tears welling and turned away. "I always get like this when my courses are looming."

"Come here." The earl extended a hand, and Anna's feet moved without her willing it, until she was sitting beside him, his arm around her shoulders. For a long, thoughtful moment he merely held her and stroked her back. "I will meet with Hazlit in a day or two, Anna. What he knows will soon be known to me; I'd rather hear it from you."

She nodded but said nothing, trying to pick through which parts of her story she could bear to tell and how to separate them from the rest. She shifted to the rocking chair, and he let her go, which was good, as she'd be better able to think if they weren't touching.

"I can tell you some of it," she said slowly. "Not all."

"I will fetch us some lemonade while you organize your thoughts. I want to hear whatever you want to tell me, Anna."

When he came back with the drinks, Anna was rocking slowly, her expression composed.

"You're beautiful, you know." The earl handed her a glass. "I put some sugar in it, but not as much as I put in mine." He locked the door then resumed his seat on the sofa and regarded the woman he loved, the woman who could not trust him.

Since their first encounter several days ago, Anna had not repeated her declaration of love, and he had not raised the topic of her virginity. The moment had never been right, and he wasn't sure explanations mattered. Many unmarried housekeepers were addressed as Mrs., and the single abiding fact was that she'd chosen to give him her virginity. *Him.*

"So what can you tell me?" he asked, sitting back and regarding her. She was beautiful but also tired. He was keeping her up nights, and he knew she wasn't sleeping well in his bed. In sleep, she clung to him, shifting her position so she was spooned around him or he around her.

In sleep, he thought a little forlornly, she trusted him.

"When my grandfather died and my grandmother fell ill," Anna began, staring at her drink as she rocked, "things at home became difficult. Grandpapa was a very good and shrewd manager, and funds were left that would have been adequate, were they properly managed. My brother was not a good manager."

Westhaven waited, trying to hear her words and not simply be distracted by the lovely sound of her voice.

"My grandmother encouraged me to take Morgan and flee, at least until Grandmother could meet with the solicitors and figure out a way to get my brother under control. But she was very frail after her apoplexy."

"You came south, then?" The earl frowned in thought, considering two gently bred and very young women traveling without escort far, far from home. Morgan in particular would have been little more than a child and much in need of assistance when away from familiar surroundings.

"We came south." Anna nodded. "My grand-mother was able to provide me with some references written by her old acquaintances, people who knew me as a child, and I registered with the employment agencies here under an assumed name."

"Is Anna Seaton your real name?"

"Mostly. I am Anna, and my sister is Morgan."

He let that go, glad at least he was wasn't calling her by a false name when passion held him in its thrall. "You found employment."

"I took the job no one else wanted, keeping house for an old Hebrew gentleman. He was my own personal miracle, that bone the Almighty throws you to suggest you are not entirely forgotten in the supposedly merciful scheme of things."

"The old Hebrew gentleman was decent to you?" the earl asked, more relieved than he could say to realize whatever price Anna had paid for her decisions, she'd kept her virtue until such time as she chose to share it with him.

"Mr. Glickmann knew immediately Morgan and I were, as he put, in flight. He had scars, Westhaven, from his own experiences with prejudice and mean-spiritedness. He'd been tossed into jail on flimsy pretexts, hounded from one village to another, beaten... He knew what it meant, to live always looking over your shoulder, always worrying, and he gave us the benefit of his experience. He told me the rules for surviving under those circumstances, and those rules have saved us."

"And is one of those rules to trust no one?"

"It might as well be. I trusted him, though, and if he'd only lived longer, then perhaps he might have been able to help us further. But his life had been hard, and his health was frail. Still, he gave us both glowing characters and left us each the kind of modest bequest a trusted servant might expect. That money has been sent from heaven, just as his characters were."

She fell silent, and Westhaven considered her story thus far. Difficult, he tried to tell himself, and sad, but hardly tragic. Still, the what ifs beat at him: What if the job nobody wanted had been working for a philandering lecher? What if they'd been snatched up and befriended by an abbess upon their arrival to London? What if Morgan's deafness had meant no jobs presented themselves?

"Go on," Westhaven said, more to cut off his own lurid imagination than because he wanted to hear more.

"From Glickmann's," Anna continued, "I got employment in the home of a wealthy merchant, but his oldest son was not to be trusted, so I cast around and found your position. The woman the agency picked for the position was at the last minute unable to serve, as she was sorely afflicted with influenza. Rather than make you wait while they interviewed other more suitable candidates, they sent me over, despite my lack of experience and standing."

"Thank God they did," the earl muttered. Anna's fate was hanging by threads and coincidences, with social prejudice, influenza, and pluck standing between her and tragedy.

"What of your brother?" he asked, rolling back his cuffs. "I gather he is part of the problem rather than part of the solution?"

"He is," Anna said, the tart rejoinder confirming the earl's suspicions.

"And you aren't going to tell me the rest of it?"

"I cannot. Grandmother has bound me to silence, not wanting to see the family name dragged through scandal." The earl stifled the urge to roll his eyes and go on a loud rant about the folly of sacrificing one's name for the sake of family pride.

"Anna." He sat forward. "You have no idea—none at all—how lucky you are not to be serving men in doorways for a penny a poke, you and Morgan both, as the pox slowly killed you. Sending you south was rank foolishness, and I can only consider your grandmother devised this scheme because she considered the situation desperate."

"It was," Anna said, "and I do know, Westhaven. I have seen those women, their skirts hiked over their backs, their eyes dead, their lives already done while some jolly fellow bends them over to have a go before toddling home after his last pint."

If she'd been close enough to see that much, Westhaven thought… Ye gods.

"Let me hold you," he said, rising and tugging her to her feet. "When you are ready, I will hear the rest of it, Anna. You are safe with me now, and that's all that matters."

She went into his arms willingly, but he could feel the resistance in her, the doubt, the unwillingness to trust. He led her up the stairs, her hand in his, determined to bind her to him with passion if nothing else.

Each time they were together, he introduced her to new pleasures, new touches, new ways to move. Tonight, he put her on her hands and knees and had her grip the headboard as he sank into her deeply from behind. She met him thrust for thrust, and when her pleasure had her convulsing hard around his cock, he couldn't hold back any longer. And like a stallion, he let his spent weight cover her, resting along her back, his cheek pressed to her spine.

"Down," he panted, easing one of her feet back several inches to explain himself. Anna straightened her knees and slipped to her stomach as his cock slid wetly from her body. He followed her, blanketing her back with his greater weight.

"Are you all right?" He kissed her cheek and paused to suckle her earlobe.

"I am boneless," Anna murmured. "I like this, though."

"What this?" He nuzzled at her neck.

"The way you like to cuddle afterward."

"I am a rarity in that regard," he assured her. "I know of only one other person in this entire bed so prone to shameless displays of affection." His moved his hips partly off her but shifted only a little to the side to kiss her nape.

"You trust me," he said, biting her neck gently.

When she said nothing, he got off the bed to use the basin and water. He washed his hands and his genitals then came back and stood frowning at her for a long moment.

"You do trust me, but only in this," he said again. "You would let me take you in any position, anywhere I pleased, as often as I pleased."

Anna rolled to her back and hiked up on her elbows, wariness in her expression. "You have never given me reason not to trust you in this bed. I am safe with you."

"You don't believe that. You might believe you are safe from me, from the violence and selfishness that can make any man a rutting boar, but you do not believe you are safe with me."

There was such defeat in his tone, such resignation, Anna was almost glad this would be their last night together. In the morning, he'd ride off to meet with his brothers, and she'd gather up her sister and her belongings and board a coach for Manchester. She'd lie in his arms for this one final night, hold him close, breathe in his scent, and love him. But it would be their last night, and this time tomorrow, she'd be far, far away.

It was that simple to do and that impossible to bear.

Fourteen

"My lord! My lord, you must wake up!"

Shouts at the bedroom door had Westhaven struggling up from sleep as Anna shook him hard by his shoulder.

"Gayle," she hissed. "Gayle Tristan Montmorency Windham!" She had her fist cocked back to smack him when he caught her hand and kissed her knuckles.

"Please! You must wake up!" Sterling sounded near tears, but the earl only heaved a sigh, knowing he was going to hear himself addressed as "Your Grace" from that moment on for the rest of his life.

"Under the covers," he said to Anna quietly as he reached for his dressing gown. A small part of him was grateful he at least wasn't going to be alone when he got the news of his father's death.

"Yes, Sterling." He opened the door, his composure admirable—worthy of a duke.

"A message, my lord"—Sterling bowed—"from Lord Amery. The messenger says there's a fire at your new property."

Not His Grace, the earl thought with soaring relief. Not His Grace, not yet.

But there was a fire at Willow Bend.

"Have Pericles hitched to the gig," the earl said. "Pack a hamper and plenty of water. Send word to my brothers—Val should be at the mansion; Dev will be at Maggie's. Under no circumstances are Their Graces to get wind of this, Sterling." He hoped Dev was at Maggie's, but he might also still be at his stud farm or holed up with old cavalry comrades. He glanced at Douglas's note.

The Willow Bend stables are ablaze as I write; no loss of life thus far. Will remain on site until the situation is contained. Amery.

A thousand questions fluttered through Westhaven's head: How did the fire start, how did Amery come upon it, was the house safe, and why the hell was this happening now…?

"What is it?" Anna had risen from the bed, put on her wrapper, and padded over to him silently.

"There's a fire at Willow Bend. Just the stables, according to a note from Amery. I'm going out there."

"I'll go with you."

He sat on the bed and drew her to stand between his legs. "That won't be necessary."

"Fires mean people can get hurt. I can help, and I don't want you to go alone."

He didn't want to go alone, either. He had good memories of her at Willow Bend, and she had a point. Unless he brought medical supplies with him, there were none on hand at Willow Bend adequate to deal with the burns and other mishaps that could come with fighting a fire.

"Please," she said, wrapping her arms around him. "I want to go."

He leaned into her embrace, pressing his face to the soft, comforting fullness of her breast for just a moment. He was torn, knowing he should spare her this but also feeling a vague unease about leaving her side for any extended period.

Mistrust, it seemed, could go both ways.

"Dress quickly," he said, patting her bottom. "Bring a change of clothes. Fires are filthy business."

She nodded and darted for the door, pausing only long enough to make sure the corridor was empty before slipping into the darkness beyond. In her absence, Westhaven heard a clock chime twelve times.

✦

"At least we now know for sure where they are," Helmsley said over their rashers of morning bacon.

"We do." Stull smacked his greasy lips. "But who could have imagined the earl would snatch up his housekeeper to go to the scene of a fire?"

"She may be more than just his housekeeper," Helmsley said. Stull looked up sharply, his expression reminiscent of a dog whose bowl of slops was threatened.

"She damned well better not be, Helmsley," the baron with a snort. "I'll not pay for used goods, and if she's strayed, then she'll be made to wish she hadn't."

Helmsley kept his peace, wishing not for the first time he'd had some choice before embarking on this whole miserable scheme with Stull. But really, what choice had he had? A man needed coin, and a gentleman had few means of obtaining same.

Their time in London had been productive,
however. It had been Cheevers's suggestion to check
the employment agencies, and with others set to
watching in the park, Helmsley had taken his sisters'
miniatures and made the rounds. The third agency had
recognized Anna's portrait immediately, as her case
was memorable: Young, not particularly experienced
but obviously very genteel, they'd been able to place
her in the household of a ducal heir, no less, and she
had worked out there *beautifully*.

Not too beautifully, Helmsley hoped, as Stull could
be very nasty when thwarted. In the brief glimpses
Helmsley caught of his sister the previous night, Anna
had seemed comfortable with the earl but not overly
familiar. He hoped for her sake that was the extent of
the earl's interest in his housekeeper.

And Morgan, he realized, must have been stashed
somewhere else, perhaps absorbing all of Anna's wages
with her upkeep. The agency had been forthcoming—
for a price—with the information that his lordship was
again in the market for a housekeeper, this time for a
newly acquired property in Surrey.

Stull's plan had been to draw the earl out to
Willow Bend then hie into the city and snatch the
housekeeper from under his nose. With Anna in
their grasp, it would have been short work to extract
Morgan's location from her. It was, like most of Stull's
endeavors, clumsily done—and now they had the
King's man nosing about, looking for arsonists, which
was no small worry.

Arson, even if only the stables burned, was a
hanging felony, though they'd be tried in the Lords and

probably get transported instead. Helmsley wondered for the millionth time why *his* sisters had to be so stubborn, wily, and unnatural, but it seemed he'd soon be rid of the pair of them.

Stull, greedy shoat, wanted them both, and Helmsley had agreed it would be better for the sisters that way—and easier for him, than if he had to live with either of them when this debacle was complete. And deaf as she was, Morgan's options were limited at best, earl's granddaughter or not.

Stull patted his lips with his napkin, chugged his ale, and belched contentedly. "What say we check in with those fellows watching the park, and perhaps find one of their confreres who might keep an eye on this Westhaven's townhouse, eh? Sooner or later, a housekeeper must go to market, run her little errands, or have her half-day. We can snatch my Anna then, and the earl will be none the wiser."

"A capital idea," Helmsley agreed, rising. It had actually been his idea, proffered as an alternative to torching the earl's country retreat, but Stull was not the most receptive to another's notions once he'd got the bit between his teeth.

Stull rubbed his hands together. "And then we can have a lie down through the worst heat of the day, before turning ourselves loose on the evening entertainments, what?"

"Splendid notion." Helmsley dredged up a smile. In London, the better brothels kept out the likes of Stull and himself. Titled though they were, Helmsley had never taken his seat, and Stull had probably voted exactly twice since coming into his title. They were not…connected. They were instead caricatures of the sophisticated lordlings on the town, having neither savoir faire nor physical appeal.

With any luck, they would soon be in possession of both of his sisters and on their way back north. Helmsley's pockets would be heavily lined with Stull's gold and his conscience numbed by as much alcohol as a man could consume and remain alive.

❦

"I tell ye, guv, the bird ain't there." The dirty little man spat his words, disdaining his betters with each syllable.

"She has to be there." Helmsley threw up his hands in exasperation. "You set men to watching both the front and back of the house?"

"Lads, not men," the man replied. "Lads be cheaper, more reliable, and not so fond of their ale, nor as apt to wander off when they's bored."

"And in four days," Helmsley went on, "your… boys haven't left the place unattended once?"

"Not fer a bleedin' minute. No bird, at least not the one in yer little paintin'. Maids and laundresses and such, but no lady bird like you showed us. Now where's me blunt, guv?"

"Stull!" Helmsley bellowed, and the baron lumbered out of his room into their shared sitting room. "The man wants his blunt."

Stull frowned, disappeared, and reappeared, a velvet bag in hand. Too late, Helmsley realized the cretin they'd hired to manage surveillance of Westhaven's townhouse was eyeing the velvet bag shrewdly.

"Your coin." Stull counted out the payment

carefully and dropped it into the man's hand from a height of several inches above his palm. "Now be off with you. She's there, and we know it. Your job is to tell us when she leaves the house."

"Not so fast," their hireling sneered. "You pay us for the next four days, too, guv. Unless you want me sorry self gracin' yer 'umble abode again."

Slowly, Stull counted out another fistful of coins.

"My thanks." The man smiled a gap-toothed grin. "If we see the bird, we'll send a boy."

He took his leave, and Stull shrugged, much to Helmsley's relief.

"We'll find her," Stull said. "She's got a decent job, probably making enough to look after Morgan, for which we must give my Anna credit, and when she pokes her nose out of that earl's townhouse, we'll snatch her up and be gone. I'm for a little stroll down to the Pig, Helmsley. You can come along and put in a good word for me with Wee Betty?"

Helmsley smiled thinly and reached for his hat and gloves. He was of the mind that Anna had once again given them the slip, just as she had in Liverpool a few weeks after leaving Yorkshire. He was damned, *damned*, if he'd spend another two years haring all over England, drinking bad ale and screwing dirty serving maids in Stull's wake.

Anna had given her word, in writing, and Helmsley was going to see she kept it—or died trying. Either way, the result was the same for him: His troubles would be over, and so would hers.

Fifteen

"I TELL YOU, IT'S TIME TO GO HOME," HELMSLEY SAID for the fourth time.

"Not when we're so close," Stull argued in a whispered hiss. "The lads in the park saw that girl again, the one who looks like Morgan, and they trailed her to Mayfair, just a few streets over from the earl's home. I'm telling you, we've found them both."

"Morgan is deaf and mute," Helmsley shot back. "No deaf mute is going to be coddled in the great homes of Mayfair, not in any capacity. Even the footmen have to be handsome as lords, for chrissakes."

Stull glared at him sullenly. "I am beginning to think you don't want me to find your sisters. You'd rather have them wandering the slums of London with no protection whatsoever, when their every need will be met in my care. What kind of brother are you, Helmsley, to abandon the chase now, when they're almost in our grasp at last?"

He was an awful brother, of course. The question was ludicrous coming from Stull. But he wasn't a stupid brother, particularly, and if he was ever to get out of debt, he needed to find Anna and Morgan, hand them over to Stull, and let them make shift as best they could. They were damnably resourceful; their haring all over the realm for two years on little more than pin money proved that much, at least.

But did he really want to be there when Anna realized what he'd done? When Morgan dissolved into tears? When they realized the extent of his betrayal?

"What aren't you telling me, Helmsley?" Stull's look became belligerent. "You threw in with me when the old man died, and don't think you can turn about now. I'll go crying to the magistrate so fast the Lords won't be able to protect you."

Lie down with dogs, Grandpapa used to say, and you wake up with fleas.

"I'm not like you, Stull." Helmsley tossed himself down in a chair, affecting a manner of dejection. "I have been nothing but a burden and an expense to you on this trip. One has one's pride." He managed just the right ashamed, glancing connection with Stull's eyes and saw the baron's ponderous mind catching the scent.

"You found those fellows to watch the park and the earl's house," Helmsley went on. "You thought of drawing Westhaven out to the country with that fire, you provide all the blunt for the whole scheme, while I merely stand by and watch."

"I could spare you for a bit," Stull said. "If you want to head back north, I can manage things here and send word when I have the girls. Might be better that way."

His porcine eyes narrowed as he circled back to his earlier thought.

"You aren't thinking of peaching on me to the magistrate, Helmsley? You're the one who's pissed away your grandpapa's fortune and your sister's dowries. Don't think I won't be recalling that if you turn on me now."

"I know better, Stull." Helmsley shook his head. "You know my dirty business, and I know yours, and we both know where our best interests are served."

"Well said." Stull nodded, chins jiggling. "Now, what say we nip downstairs and grab a bite for luncheon? You can't leave today, old man. Too deuced hot, and you must make your farewells this evening to that bit of French muslin we came across last night."

"I can spend tonight in Town," Helmsley agreed. "I'll go north first thing in the morning and leave this matter entirely in your capable hands."

"Best thing." Stull nodded. "I'll send word when I have the girls."

⁂

"The prodigals return." Dev smiled as Anna and the earl trundled in the back door from the townhouse gardens. "Westhaven." He extended his hand to his brother, only to be pulled into a brief hug. Over Westhaven's shoulder, Dev shot a puzzled look at Anna, who merely smiled and shook her head.

"Good to be back," Westhaven said. "My thanks for keeping an eye on things here, and Amery and his neighboring relations send their felicitations."

"By that you mean Greymoor recalled I outbid him for the little mare he wanted for his countess and has decided to let bygones be bygones."

"He sent his felicitations," the earl repeated, "as does Heathgate, who as magistrate provided us most gracious hospitality these past days while the fire was being investigated. Have we anything to eat?"

"I can see to that," Anna said. "Why don't you wash off the dust of the road, and I'll have your luncheon served on the terrace."

"Join us?" the earl said, laying a hand on her arm.

Her eyes met his, and she saw he would not argue, but he was *asking*. She nodded and made for the kitchen, trying to muster a scold for giving in to his foolishness. At Willowdale, she'd been a guest of the Marquis and Marchioness of Heathgate, as Heathgate served as the local magistrate. There she'd been treated as a guest and as the earl's respected…what? Friend? His fiancée? His…nothing. Certainly not his house-keeper. Anna had allowed the fiction out of manners and out of a sense it was the last chapter in her dealings with Westhaven, an unreal series of days that allowed them a great deal of freedom in each other's company.

And at night, he'd stolen into her room, slipped into her bed, and held her in his arms while they talked until they both fell asleep. He'd told her stories of growing up among a herd of the duke's offspring on the rambling acres of Morelands, of his last parting from his brother Bart, and his suspicions regarding a second ducal grandchild.

She told him what it was like to grow up secure in her grandparents' love, surrounded by acres of flowers and hot houses and armies of gardeners. But mostly, Anna had listened. She listened to his voice, deep, masculine, and beautiful in the darkness. She listened to his hands, to the patterns of tenderness and possession they traced on her bare skin. She listened to his body, becoming as familiar to her as her own, and to the way he used it to express both affection and protectiveness. She listened to his mind, to the discipline with which he used it to provide for all whom he cared for.

She listened to his heart and heard it silently—and unsuccessfully—plead with her for her trust.

❧

"And there be our bird," the dirty little man cackled to an even dirtier little boy.

"So you'll tell the fat swell we seen her?" the child asked, eyeing the pretty lady with the flower basket.

"I will, but happen not today, me lad. He pays good, and we're due for another installment when I call on him tonight. Too hot to do more than stand about in the shade anyways—might as well get paid fer it, aye?"

"Aye." The child grinned at the soundness of his superior's reasoning and went back to getting paid to watch.

"You tell old Whit if the lady goes out, mind, and be ready for yer shift again tomorrow at first light."

❧

"You use the same employment agency as Her Grace," Hazlit began, his eyes meeting the earl's unflinchingly. "So I started there and eventually found copies of references your housekeeper brought with her two years ago. They all came from older women, ladies of quality now residing in York and its surrounds, so I went north."

"You went north," the earl repeated, needing and dreading to hear what came next.

"On her application," Hazlit went on, "Mrs. Seaton put she was willing to work as a housekeeper or in a flower shop, which caught my eye. It's an odd combination of skills, but it gave me a place to start. I took her sketches and what I knew, and wrote to a colleague of mine in York. Some answers essentially fell into my lap from there."

"What sketches?"

"Mrs. Seaton goes to the park occasionally, the same as most of London in the summer," Hazlit said. He opened a folder and drew forth a charcoal sketch that bore a striking resemblance to Anna Seaton.

"It's quite good," the earl said, frowning. Hazlit had caught not just Anna's appearance but also her sweetness and courage and determination. Still, to think Hazlit had sketched this when Anna was unaware rankled.

"It is your property." A flicker of sympathy graced Hazlit's austere features.

"My thanks." The earl set aside the portrait, and gave Hazlit his full attention. "What answers fell into your lap?"

"Some," Hazlit cautioned, "not all. There are not charges laid against her I could find in York or London, but her brother is looking for her. Her name is Anna Seaton James, she is the oldest daughter of Vaughn Hammond James and Elva James nee Seaton, who both died in a carriage accident when Anna was a young girl. Her sister, Morgan Elizabeth James, was involved in the same accident and indirectly lost her hearing as a result. The heir, Wilberforce Hammond James, was the only son and resides at the family seat, Rosecroft, in Yorkshire, along the Ouse to the north-west of the city."

"Granddaughter to an earl," the earl muttered, frowning. "Why did Anna flee?"

"As best my colleague and I can piece together," Hazlit replied, "the old earl tied up his money carefully, so the heir was unable to fritter away funds needed for the girls and their grandmother. The heir managed to do a deal of frittering, nonetheless, and I took the liberty of buying up a number of his markers."

"Enterprising of you," the earl said, reaching for the stack of papers Hazlit passed to him. "Ye Gods…" He sorted through the IOUs and markers, his eyebrows rising. "This is a not-so-small fortune by Yorkshire standards."

"My guess, and it's only a guess, is that Anna knows of the mishandling of her grandfather's estate perpetrated by the present earl, and she made the mistake of trying to reason with her brother. Then too, the younger sister, Morgan, is very vulnerable to exploitation, and if a man will steal from his sisters, he'll probably do worse without a qualm."

"You manage to imply a host of nasty outcomes, Mr. Hazlit," the earl observed, "though nothing worse than my imagination has concocted. Any advice from this point out?"

"Don't let them out of your sight," Hazlit said. "It is not kidnapping if you are a concerned and titled brother looking for sisters whom you can paint as flighty at best. He can snatch either one, and there will be nothing you or anyone else could do about it. Nothing."

"Can he marry them off?"

"Of course. For Morgan, in particular, that would be simple, as she was arguably impaired by her deafness, and marriage is considered to be in a woman's best interests."

"Considered by men," the earl replied with a thin smile. "Well, thank you, Hazlit. I will convince the ladies to remain glued to my side, and all will be well."

Hazlit stood, accepting the hand proffered by the earl. "Better yet, marry the woman to someone you can trust to look out for her and to manage Helmsley. The situation could resolve itself quite easily."

"You are not married, Mr. Hazlit, are you?"

"I do not at this time enjoy the wedded state," Hazlit said, his smile surprisingly boyish. "I do enjoy the unwedded state."

"Thus sayeth we all," the earl said, escorting Hazlit to the front door. "Those of us in expectation of titles sometimes particularly enjoy the unwedded state—while we can." Something briefly shone in Hazlit's dark eyes—regret? Sympathy?—it was gone before the earl could analyze it.

"Good day, my lord," Hazlit said, his eyes drifting to the huge bouquet on the table, "and good luck keeping your valuables safe."

The earl retreated to his study, penned a note asking Val to return to the townhouse at his earliest convenience, and another thanking Heathgate for the recent hospitality. For all Hazlit had been informative, though, Westhaven had the sense there were still answers only Anna could provide.

So he sat for a long time, sipping his sweetened lemonade, contemplating the bouquet in the fireplace, and considering how exactly he could keep Anna Seaton—Anna *James*—safe when her valise was packed and sitting on her bed, just as it had been the night they'd been called out to Willow Bend.

When darkness was beginning to fall, Westhaven was pleased to see both his brothers would be joining him for dinner. Val, with music books, wardrobe, and horse in tow, had rejoined the earl's household, claiming the duke was bloody well enough recovered to drive anybody to Bedlam.

Dev was clearly trying to contain his questions about the fire out in Surrey, but when the meal was consumed, sweets and all, the earl asked his brothers to take an after-dinner stroll with him to the stables. Once there, away from the house and its balconies, he explained what Hazlit had told him and enlisted his brothers' support in seeing to it Anna and Morgan were kept safe.

"But you can't keep them under surveillance every minute," Dev protested. "They are intelligent women, and they will soon know we're up to something."

"I'll talk to Anna tonight," the earl said. "She has to be made to see reason, or I'll bundle her off to Morelands myself, there to be confined until she'll marry me."

Val exchanged a look with Dev. "So the ducal blood will out, and you're taking the Roman example of seizing and carrying off your bride."

Westhaven sighed. "I am no more willing to force a marriage on Anna than she would be willing to take her vows on those terms. I would live down to her worst expectations were I to even attempt it."

"Glad you comprehend that much," Dev said. "Best of luck convincing her she needs bodyguards. Morgan, at least, can't argue with us."

"Don't bet on it," Val said, his expression preoccupied. "I have missed my piano though, so I'll leave you, Westhaven, to reason with Anna, while I bare my soul to my art."

"Damn." Dev watched his youngest brother depart and smiled at the earl. "And here I've been baring everything else to the wenches at the Pleasure House. Which of us, do you suppose, has it right?"

"Neither." The earl smiled. "When it comes down to it, I'm having to admit, in the things that matter most, it's the duke who has gotten closest to the mark."

Devlin cast him a curious glance then ambled off to tuck in his horses. Westhaven was alone in the darkened alley when he heard the barest thread of a whisper summoning him farther into the shadows.

❦

"This is short notice, your lordship." Hazlit studied the Earl of Westhaven by the light of the candles in the man's library. It was a handsome room, and Hazlit had noted at their earlier meeting the whole house appeared well cared for. The bouquets were fresh, the wood work polished, the windows sparkling, and not a speck of dust to be seen.

"I apologize for the lateness of the hour, Hazlit," the earl said. "May I offer you a drink?"

"You may." Hazlit accepted the offer, in part because the quality of the drink served told him about a man's character, but also because he had the sense the earl was offering not in an attempt to manipulate but out of sheer good breeding.

"Whiskey or brandy?"

"Whatever you're having," Hazlit replied. "I assume we meet to discuss the same matter?"

"We do," the earl said, handing Hazlit a generous tot of whiskey. "To your health."

"Yours." Hazlit sipped cautiously then paused. "Lovely, but I don't recognize it."

"It's a private label." The earl smiled. "Heathgate owns the distillery and calls this his bribing vintage."

Hazlit nodded. He *had* sampled this vintage before but not often, and it wasn't something he'd admit about one client to another. "My compliments. Now, how can I assist you?"

"Shall we sit?" The earl gestured to the long, comfortable-looking leather sofa, and Hazlit sank into one corner. The earl took up a rocking chair, his drink in hand. "I have become aware my house is being watched, front and back. I had a very interesting discussion last night when I went to bid my horse good night. I was accosted by an urchin loyal to David Worthington, Viscount Fairly, who was picketed in my mews unbeknownst to me."

Hazlit merely nodded, his eyes locked on the earl.

"More significantly," the earl went on, "I was informed my house is also being watched by the minions of one Whit, who is in the employ of two gentlemen from the North, one of whom is obese." The earl paused to sip his drink. "I recently purchased a modest property a short distance from Town, Willow Bend by name. The stables there were burned last week, and other buildings were soaked with lamp oil. By chance, acquaintances happened to see the stables burning and summoned help before the rest of the property could be set ablaze.

"Fortunately, the place was not yet occupied, and only the stables were lost. I hired a runner, who was able to deduce that two men, well dressed, one quite portly, bought a quantity of lamp oil the day before my stables burned, from the last likely source before one leaves Town for the Surrey countryside."

"You suspect these men were sent after Mrs. Seaton," Hazlit suggested.

The earl met Hazlit's eyes. "I suspect one of them of being her brother, the earl. Is he reported to be portly?"

"He is not." Hazlit fished in a pocket of his coat, and brought out a small pad of a paper. "Have you a pen?"

The earl got up and went to his desk, setting out ink, pen, sand, and knife on the blotter. Hazlit brought his drink to the desk, assumed the earl's wingback chair, and with the earl looking over his shoulder, sketched a figure of a man.

"Helmsley," Hazlit said tersely, tearing off the sheet and starting another sketch, this one of the man's face. While Hazlit sketched, the earl studied the little ink drawing.

"Helmsley has bulk to him," Hazlit said as he

worked. "He's close to six feet, and bad living is going to ensure middle age is a short interlude before the man's shoulders are stooped, his gut sagging, and his face lined. There."

Hazlit tore off the second drawing. "He bears a slight resemblance to your housekeeper around the eyes and perhaps in the texture and color of the hair."

"He does." The earl frowned. "He's older than Anna?"

"He is. He is not your portly man, though. He qualifies as well fed but not obese."

"Can you take this picture to the man who sold the lamp oil?" the earl suggested, picking up the second drawing. "And maybe get a description of the other fellow?"

"I can. I can also go back north and ask around regarding the portly man."

"That will take some time." The earl leaned against the arm of the sofa. "I hardly need tell you to spare no expense." He appeared lost in thought, and Hazlit waited. "Do you think Anna's grandmother is well enough to travel?"

"She hasn't been seen much off the estate since her husband died," Hazlit replied. "That does not suggest good health, but it might also mean she's a virtual prisoner."

The earl looked up sharply, and Hazlit had the sense his casual comment snapped something into place in the earl's mind.

"If we cannot establish Anna's brother is here in London," the earl said slowly, "then I want you to go north and figure out just where the hell he is. I believe he is the primary threat to Anna's welfare, and his leverage is that he holds her grandmother's welfare in his hands."

"And the fat man?" Hazlit rose. "We know he's in Town and that he's probably lying in wait for Mrs. Seaton."

"But waiting for what?" the earl mused. "For the brother to come to Town and have the legal right to reclaim his sisters, perhaps?"

"Good question," Hazlit agreed. "Let me take the sketches with me, and maybe by tomorrow, I can have some answers for you."

"My thanks," the earl said, showing his guest to the front door.

Westhaven sat in the library for long moments, sipping cold tea and staring at the first sketch. When Anna came in, he slid the drawing into a drawer then rose to meet her.

"You are up late," she observed, going into his arms. He kissed her cheek, and Anna squealed. "And your lips are cold."

"So warm them up," he teased, kissing her cheek again. "I've been swilling cold tea and whiskey and putting off having an argument with you."

"What are we going to argue about?" Anna asked, pulling back enough to regard him warily.

"Your safety," he said, tugging her by the wrist to the sofa. "I want to ask you, one more time, to let me help you, Anna. I have the sense if you don't let me assist you now, it might soon be too late."

"Why now?" she asked, searching his eyes.

"You have your character," he pointed out. "Val

told me you asked him for it, and he gave it to you, as well as one for Morgan."

"A character is of no use to me if it isn't in my possession."

"Anna," he chided, his thumb rubbing over her wrist, "you could have told me."

"That was not our arrangement. Why can you not simply accept I must solve my own problems? Why must you take this on, too?"

He looped his arm over her shoulders and pulled her against him. "Aren't you the one telling me I should lean on my family a little more? Let my brothers help with business matters? Set my mother and sisters some tasks?"

"Yes." She buried her nose against his shoulder. "But I am not the heir to the Duke of Moreland. I am a simple housekeeper, and my problems are my own."

"I've tried," he said, kissing her temple. "I've tried and tried and tried to win your trust, Anna, but I can't make you trust me."

"No," she said, "you cannot."

"You leave me no choice. I will take steps on my own tomorrow to safeguard you and your sister, as well."

She just nodded, leaving him to wonder what it was she didn't say. His other alternative was to wash his hands of her, and that he could not do. "Come up to bed with me?"

"Of course," she said and let him draw her to her feet.

He said nothing, not with words, not as they undressed each other, not as they settled into one another's arms on his big, soft bed. But when communications were offered by touch, by sigh and kiss and caress, he told her loved her and would lay down his life to keep her safe.

She told him she loved him, that she would always treasure the memories she held of him, that she would never love another.

And she told him goodbye.

❧

The next day started out in a familiar pattern, with the earl riding in the park with his brothers and Anna joining Cook on the weekly marketing. The women took two footmen as was their usual custom. Unbeknownst to Anna, the earl had taken both men aside and acquainted them with the need to serve as bodyguards and not just porters.

When the earl and his brothers were safely away from the mews, he wasted no time informing them of recent developments.

"So as long as this Whit is content to bilk his employers and draw out his surveillance contract," the earl concluded, "we have some time, but it becomes more imperative than ever that Anna not be left alone."

"Where is she now?" Dev asked, frowning at his horse's neck.

"At market, with a footman on each arm, both ordered not to let her out of their sight."

"Let's ride home by way of the market," Dev suggested. "I have an odd feeling."

Val and the earl exchanged an ominous look. Whether it was Dev's Irish granny, his own instincts, or mere superstition, when Dev got a hunch, it was folly to ignore it.

They trotted through the streets, the morning crowds thinned by the heat. The market was bustling, however, with all manner of produce and house-hold sundries for sale as women, children, and the occasional man strolled from vendor to vendor.

"Split up," the earl directed, handing his reins to a boy and flipping the child a coin. "Walk him."

Val and Dev moved off through the crowd, even as the back of the earl's neck began to prickle. What if Fairly's guardian urchin was wrong, and Whit had gotten tired of watching in the heat? What if Anna had chosen today to slip out of his life? What if the fat man was a procurer, and Anna was already on her way to some foul crib on the Continent?

A disturbance in the crowd to his left had the earl pushing his way through the throng. In the center of a circle of gawking onlookers, Anna stood, her wrist in the grasp of a large, seriously overweight man. Westhaven took one step back then set his fingers to his lips to emit a shrill whistle.

"Come quietly, Anna," the fat man crooned. "I'll be good to you, and you won't have to live like a menial anymore. Now don't make me summon the beadle, my girl."

Anna merely stood there, resistance in every line of her posture.

"We can collect little Morgan," the man went on, happy with his plans, "and be back to York in a week's time. You'll enjoy seeing your granny again, won't you?"

The mention of Morgan's name brought a martial light into Anna's eye, and she looked up, fire in her gaze, until she saw Westhaven. She sent him a heart-rending look, one it took him an instant to decipher: *Protect my sister.*

"Morgan isn't with me," Anna said, her tone resolute. "You get me or nothing, Stull. And I'll come quietly if we leave this minute for York, otherwise…"

"Otherwise," Stull sneered, jerking her arm, "nothing. You are well and truly caught, Anna James, and we'll find your sister, too. Otherwise, indeed."

The earl stepped out of the crowd and twisted the fat man's hand off Anna's wrist. "Otherwise, bugger off, sir."

Stull rubbed his wrist, eyeing the earl truculently. "I don't know what she's told you, good fellow"—he tried for an avuncular tone—"or what she's promised you, but I will thank you to take your hands off my wife and leave us to return peaceably to our home in Yorkshire."

The earl snorted and wrapped an arm around Anna's shoulders. "You are no more her husband than I am the King. You have accosted a woman for no reason and treated her abominably. This woman is in my employ and under my protection. You will leave her in peace."

"Leave her in peace?!" Stull screeched. "Leave her in peace when I've traveled the length and breadth of this country seeking just to bring her home? And she's dragged her poor, addled sister with her from one sorry scheme to another, when I have a betrothal contract signed and duly witnessed. It's no wonder I don't have her sued for breach of promise, b'gad."

The earl let him bellow on until Dev and Val

were in position on either side of the ranting Stull, a constable frowning at Val's elbow.

"Sir," the earl cut in, his voice cold enough to freeze the ears off of anybody with any sense. "You have produced no such contract, and you are not family to the lady. I do not deal with intermediaries, and I do not deal with arsonists." He nodded to Dev and Val, each of whom seized Stull by one beefy arm. "I want this man arrested for arson, Constable, and held without bond. The lady might also want to bring charges for assault, but we can sort that out when you have him in custody."

"Along with ye, then," the constable ordered Stull. "His lordship's word carries *weight* with me, and that puts you under arrest, sir. Come peaceably, and we won't have to apply the King's justice to your fat backside."

The crowd laughed as Dev and Val obligingly escorted their charge in the constable's wake. The earl was left with Anna in his arms and more questions than ever.

"Come." He led Anna to his horse and tossed her up, then climbed up behind her. He was on Dev's big young gelding, and the horse stood like a statue until Westhaven gave the command to walk on. Anna was silent and the earl himself in no mood to hold a difficult discussion on the back of a horse. He kept an arm around her waist while she leaned quietly against his chest until they were in the mews.

When the grooms led the horse away, Westhaven tugged Anna by the wrist across the alley and through the back gardens, pausing only when Morgan came into sight, a basket over her arm.

"Morgan!" Anna dropped the earl's hand and rushed to wrap her arms around her sister. "Oh, thank God you're safe."

Morgan shot a quizzical look over Anna's shoulder at the earl.

"We ran into Stull in the market," the earl explained, watching the sisters hugging each other. "He was of a mind to take his betrothed north without further ado. I was not of a mind to allow it."

"Thank God," Morgan said quietly but clearly. Anna stepped back and blinked.

"Morgan?" She eyed her sister closely. "Did you just say 'Thank God?'"

"I did." Morgan met her sister's gaze. "I did."

"You can hear and speak," the earl observed, puzzled. "How long have you feigned deafness?"

"When you went out to Willow Bend, Anna." Morgan's eyes pleaded for understanding. "Lord Val took me to see Lord Fairly. He's a physician—a real physician, and he was able to help. I've not wanted to tell you, for fear it wouldn't last, but it's been days, and oh, the things I've heard…the wonderful, beautiful things I've heard."

"I am so happy for you." Anna pulled her close again. "So damned happy for you, Morgan. Talk to me, please, talk to me until my ears fall off."

"I love you," Morgan said. "I've wanted to say that—just that—for years. I love you, and you are the best sister a deaf girl ever had."

"I love you, too," Anna said, tears threatening, "and this is the best gift a deaf girl's sister ever had."

"Well, come along, you two." The earl put a sister

under each arm. "As pleasing as this development is, there is still a great deal of trouble brewing." As both sisters were in tears, it clearly fell to him to exercise some rational process, otherwise the lump in his own throat might have to be acknowledged.

He ushered them into his study, poured lemonade all around, and considered the situation as Anna and Morgan beamed at each other like idiots.

"Don't forget your sugar," Anna said, turning her smile on him. "Oh, Westhaven, my sister can hear! This makes it all worthwhile, you know? If Morgan and I hadn't fled York, she might never have seen this physician. And if you can hear and speak…"

"I cannot be so easily declared incompetent," Morgan finished, grinning.

"Unless…" Anna's smile dimmed, and she glanced hesitantly at the earl. "Unless Stull and Helmsley convince the authorities you were feigning your disability, and that would be truly peculiar."

The earl frowned mightily. "Rather than speculate on that matter, what can you tell me about this betrothal contract Stull ranted about. Is it real?"

"It is," Anna said, holding his gaze, her smile fading to a grimace. "It is very real. There are two contracts, in fact. One obligates me to marry him in exchange for sums he will pay to my brother; the other obligates Morgan to marry him in the event I do not, for the same consideration."

"So your brother has sold you to that hog." It made sense enough. "And you were unwilling to go join him in his wallow."

"Morgan was to have come with me," Anna added,

"or I with her. Whichever sister he married, he agreed to provide a home for the other sister, as well. Even if I married him, I could not have kept Morgan safe from him."

"He is depraved, then?"

"I would not have rejected a suitor out of hand," Anna said, her chin coming up, "just for an unfortunate fondness for his victuals. Stull makes the beasts appear honorable, though."

"And you know this how?"

"Grandmother hired on a twelve-year-old scullery maid," Anna said wearily. "The girl was nigh torn asunder trying to bear Stull's bastard. The baby did not live, but the mother did—barely. She was not"— Anna glanced at Morgan—"mature for her years, and she had no family. Stull preyed on her then tossed her aside."

"Who is he? He comports himself like a man of consequence, at least in his own mind."

"Hedley Arbuthnot, eighth Baron Stull," Anna said. "My betrothed."

"Don't be so sure about that." The earl looked at her, frowning. "I want to see these contracts, as in the first place, I don't think a conditional betrothal is enforceable, and in the second, there is the question of duress." And a host of other legal questions, such as whether Helmsley had executed the contracts on behalf of his sisters, and if Morgan was a minor when he did. Or did he sign on behalf of Anna, who was not a minor, and thus bind himself rather than her?

And where in the tangle of questions did the matter of guardianship of the ladies' funds come into it?

The earl looked at Morgan. "You are going to let my brother escort you to the ducal mansion. Stull does not know where you are and does not know you have regained your ability to speak and hear. It is to our advantage to keep it that way."

"You"—the earl turned an implacable glare on Anna—"are going to go unpack your damned valise and meet me back here, and no running off. Your word, or I will alert the entire staff to your plans, and you will be watched from here to Jericho unless I am with you."

"You have my word," she said quietly, rising to go, but turning at the last to give Morgan one more hug.

She left a ringing silence behind her, in which the earl helped himself to the whiskey decanter, pouring a hefty tot into his lemonade.

"So what hasn't she told me?" The earl turned and met Morgan's gaze.

"I don't know what she has told you."

"Precious bloody little." The earl took a swallow of his cocktail. "That she was keeping confidences and could not allow me to assist her. Christ."

"She was. My grandmother made us both promise our situation would not become known outside the three of us. Anna and I have both kept our word in that regard, until now."

The earl ran a hand through his hair. "How could this come about? That Anna could be obligated to marry a loathsome excuse for a bore—or boar?"

"It was cleverly done." Morgan sighed and stood, crossing her arms as she regarded the back gardens through the French doors. "Helmsley sent

Grandmother and me off to visit a friend of hers, then took Anna aside and told her if she didn't sign the damned contract, he'd have me declared incompetent. In a similar fashion, he told me if I didn't sign the contract, then he'd put a pillow over Grandmother's face. Anna doesn't know about that part, and I don't think he'd do it…"

"But he could. What a rotter, this brother of yours. And lousy at cards, I take it?"

"Very. We were in hock up to our eyeballs two years ago."

"So he probably told your grandmother some Banbury tale, as well," the earl said, staring at his drink. "What do you think would make Anna happy now?"

"To be home," Morgan said. "To know Grandmother is safe, to see Grandpapa's gardens again, to know I am safe. To stop running and looking over her shoulder and pretending to be something we're not."

"And you, Morgan?" The earl shifted to stand beside her. "What do you want?"

"I want Anna to be happy," Morgan said, swallowing and blinking. "She was so…so pretty and happy and loving when Grandpapa was alive. And the past two years, she's been reduced to drudgery just so I would be safe. She deserves to be happy, to be free and safe and…" She was crying, unable to get out the rest of whatever she wanted to say. The earl put down his drink, fished in his pocket for his handkerchief, and pulled Morgan into his arms.

"She deserves all that," he agreed, patting her shoulder. "She'll have it, too, Morgan. I promise you she'll have what she wants."

When Val and Dev joined him in the library less than an hour later, Anna was still unpacking while Morgan was busy packing. The earl explained what he knew of the situation, pleased to hear the magistrate had agreed to delay Stull's bond hearing for another two days.

"That gives us time to get Morgan to Their Graces," the earl said, glancing at Val. "Unless you object?"

"It wouldn't be my place to object," Val said, his lips pursed, "but I happen to concur. Morgan can use some pampering, and Her Grace feels miserable for having set Hazlit on their trail. This will allow expiation of Her Grace's sins, and distract His Grace, as well."

"Creates a bit of a problem for you," Dev pointed out.

"How so?" Val frowned.

"How are you going to continue to convince our sire you are a mincing fop, when every time Morgan walks by, you practically trip over your tongue?"

"My tongue, Dev, not my cock. If you could comprehend the courage it takes to be deaf and mute in a society that thinks it is neither, you would be tripping at the sight of her, as well."

Dev spared a look at the earl, who kept his expression carefully neutral.

"You will both escort Morgan to Their Graces later this afternoon," Westhaven said. "For now, I'd like you to remain here, keeping an eye on Anna."

"You don't trust her?" Dev asked, censorship in his tone.

"She gave her word not to run, but I am not convinced Stull was the only threat to her. Her own brother got her involved in this scheme with Stull, and he's the one who benefits should Stull get his hands on Anna. Where is Helmsley, and what is his part in this?"

"Good question," Dev allowed. "Go call on Their Graces, then, and leave the ladies in our capable hands."

Val nodded. "His Grace will be flattered into a full recovery to think you'd entrust a damsel in distress to his household."

The earl nodded, knowing it was a good point. Still, he was sending Morgan to the duke and duchess because their home was safe, a near fortress, with servants who knew better than to allow strangers near the property or the family members. And it was nearby, which made getting Morgan there simple. Then, too, Anna saw the wisdom of it, making it one less issue he had to argue and bully her through.

He found Anna in her sitting room, sipping tea, the evil valise nowhere in sight.

"I'm off to Moreland House," the earl informed her, "to ask Their Graces to provide Morgan sanctuary. I will ask on your behalf, as well, if it's what you want."

"Do you want me to go with her?" Anna asked, her gaze searching his.

"I do not," he said. "It's one thing to ask my father and mother to keep Morgan safe, when Stull isn't even sure she's in London. It's another to ask them to keep you safe, when I am on hand to do so and have already engaged the enemy, so to speak."

"Stull isn't your enemy," Anna said, dropping her gaze. "If it hadn't been him, my brother would have found somebody else."

"I am not so convinced of that, Anna." The earl lowered himself into a rocking chair. "The society in York is provincial compared to what we have here in London. My guess is that there were likely few willing to collude with your brother in defrauding your grandfather's estate, shackling you and Morgan to men you found repugnant and impoverishing your sickly grandmother into the bargain."

"That is blunt speech," she said at length.

"I am angry, Anna." The earl rose again. "I fear diplomacy is beyond me."

"Are you angry with me?"

"Oh, I want to be," he assured her, his gaze raking her up and down. "I want to be furious, to turn you over my knee and paddle you until my hand hurts, to shake you and rant and treat the household to a tantrum worthy of His Grace."

"I am sorry." Anna's gaze dropped to the carpet.

"I am not angry with you," the earl said gravely, "but your brother and his crony will have much to answer for."

"You are disappointed in me."

"I am *concerned* for you," the earl said tiredly. "So concerned I am willing to seek the aid of His Grace, and to pull every string and call in every favor the old man can spare me. Just one thing, Anna?"

She met his gaze, looking as though she was prepared to hear the worst: Pack your things, get out of my sight, give me back those glowing characters.

"Be here when I get back," the earl said with deadly calm. "And expect to have a long talk with me when this is sorted out."

She nodded.

He waited to see if she had anything else to add, any arguments, conditions, or demurrals, but for once, his Anna apparently had the sense not to fight him. He turned on his heel and left before she could second-guess herself.

Sixteen

"I HAVE COME TO SEEK ASSISTANCE," WESTHAVEN SAID, meeting his father's gaze squarely. The duke was enjoying his early afternoon tea on the back terrace of the mansion, and looking to his son like a man in a great good health.

"Seems to be the season for it," the duke groused. "Your dear mother will hardly let me chew my meat without assistance. You'd best have a seat, man, lest she catch me craning my neck to see you."

"She means well," the earl said, his father's response bringing a slight smile to his lips.

The duke rolled his eyes. "And how many times, Westhaven, has she attempted to placate your irritation with me, using that same phrase? Tea?"

"More than a few," the earl allowed. "She doesn't want to lose you, though, and so you must be patient with her. And yes, a spot of tea wouldn't go amiss."

"Patient!" the duke said with a snort. He poured his son a cup and added a helping of sugar. "That woman knows just how far she can push me, with her Percy this and dear heart that. But you didn't come here to listen to me resent your mother's best intentions. What sort of assistance do you need?"

"I'm not sure," Westhaven said, accepting the cup of tea, "but it involves a woman, or two women."

"Well, thank the lord for small favors." The duke smiled. "Say on, lad. It's never as bad as you think it is, and there are very few contretemps you could get into I haven't been in myself."

At his father's words, a constriction weighting Westhaven's chest lifted, leaving him able to breathe and strangely willing to enlist his father's support. He briefly outlined the situation with Anna and Morgan, and his desire to keep Morgan's whereabouts unknown.

"Of course she's welcome." The duke frowned. "Helmsley's granddaughter? I think he was married to that…oh, Bellefonte's sister or aunt or cousin. Your mother will know. Bring her over; the girls will flutter and carry on and have a grand time."

"She can't leave the property," Westhaven cautioned. "Unless it's to go out to Morelands in a closed carriage."

"I am not to leave Town until your quacks allow it," the duke reported. "There's to be no removing to the country just yet for these old bones, thank you very much."

"How are you feeling?" the earl asked, the question somehow different from all the other times he'd asked it.

"Mortality," the duke said, "is a daunting business, at first. You think it will be awful to die, to miss all the future holds for your loved ones, for your little parliamentary schemes. I see now, however, that there will come a time when death will be a relief, and it must have been so for your brother Victor. At some point, it isn't just death; it's peace."

Shocked at both the honesty and the depth of his father's response, Westhaven listened as he hadn't listened to his father in years.

"My strength is returning," the duke said, "and I will live to pester you yet a while longer, I hope, but when I was so weak and certain my days were over, I realized there are worse things than dying. Worse things than not securing the bloody succession, worse things than not getting the Lords to pass every damned bill I want to see enacted."

"What manner of worse things?"

"I could never have known your mother," the duke said simply. "I could linger as an invalid for years, as Victor did. I could have sent us all to the poor house and left you an even bigger mess to clean up. I guess"—the duke smiled slightly—"I am realizing what I have to be grateful for. Don't worry…" The smile became a grin. "This humble attitude won't last, and you needn't look like I've had a personal discussion with St. Peter. But when one is forbidden to do more than simply lie in bed, one gets to thinking."

"I suppose one does." The earl sat back, almost wishing his father had suffered a heart seizure earlier in life.

"Now, about your Mrs. Seaton," the duke went on. "You are right; the betrothal contracts are critical but so are the terms of the guardianship provisions in the old man's will. In the alternative, there could be a separate guardianship document, one that includes the trusteeship of the girl's money, and you have to get your hands on that, as well."

"Not likely," the earl pointed out. "It was probably drawn up in York and remains in Helmsley's hands."

"But he will have to bring at least the guardianship papers with him if he's to retrieve his sisters. You say they are both over the age of eighteen, but the trust document might give him control of their money until they marry, turn five and twenty, or even thirty."

"I can ask Anna about that, but I have to ask you about something else."

The duke waited, stirring his tea while Westhaven considered how to put his question. "Hazlit has pointed out I could protect Anna by simply marrying her. Would you and Her Grace receive her?"

In a display of tact that would have made the duchess proud and quite honestly impressed Westhaven, the duke leaned over and topped off both tea cups.

"I put this question to your mother," the duke admitted, "as my own judgment, according to my sons, is not necessarily to be trusted. I will tell you what Her Grace said, because I think it is the best answer: We trust you to choose wisely, and if Anna Seaton is your choice, we will be delighted to welcome her into the family. Your mother, after all, was not my father's choice and no more highly born than your Anna."

"So you would accept her."

"We would, but Gayle?"

His father had not referred to him by name since Bart's death, and Westhaven found he had to look away.

"You are a decent fellow," the duke went on, "too decent, I sometimes think. I know, I know." He waved a hand. "I am all too willing to cut corners, to take a dodgy course, to use my consequence at any turn, but you are the opposite. You would not shirk a responsibility if God Almighty gave you leave to do so. I am telling you, in the absence of the Almighty's availability: Do not marry her out of pity or duty or a misguided sense you want a woman in debt to you before you marry her. Marry her because you can't see the rest of your life without her and you know she feels the same way."

"You are telling me to marry for love," Westhaven concluded, bemused and touched.

"I am, and you will please tell your mother I said so, for I am much in need of her good graces these days, and this will qualify as perhaps the only good advice I've ever given you."

"The only good advice?" Westhaven countered. "Wasn't it you who told me to let Dev pick out my horses for me? You who said Val shouldn't be allowed to join up to keep an eye on Bart? You who suggested the canal project?"

"Even a blind hog finds an acorn now and then," the duke quipped. "Or so my brother Tony reminds me."

"I will get my hands on those contracts." The earl rose. "And the guardianship and trust documents, as well, if you'll keep Morgan safe."

"Consider it done." The duke said, rising. "Look in on your mama before you go."

"I will," Westhaven said, stepping closer and hugging his father briefly. To his surprise, the duke hugged him right back.

"My regards to St. Just." The duke smiled winsomely. "Tell him not to be a stranger."

"He'll come over with Val this evening," Westhaven said, "but I will pass along your felicitations."

The duke watched his heir disappear into the house, not surprised when a few minutes later the duchess came out to join him.

"You should be napping," his wife chided. "Westhaven was behaving peculiarly."

"Oh?" The duke slipped an arm around his wife's waist. "How so?"

"He walked in, kissed my cheek, and said, 'His Grace has advised me to marry for love,' then left. Not like him at all." The duchess frowned. "Are you feeling well, Percy?"

"Keeps his word, that boy." The duke smiled. "I am feeling better, Esther, and we did a good job with Westhaven. Knows his duty, he does, and will make a fine duke."

Her Grace kissed his cheek. "More to the point, he makes a fine son, and he will make an even better papa."

◈

"From this point on," the earl said, "you are my guest, the granddaughter and sister of an earl, and every inch a lady."

"A lady would not be staying under your roof unchaperoned."

"Of course not, but your circumstances require allowances to be made. Morgan is safe at the mansion, and you will be safe with me."

Anna rose from the library sofa. "And what if you cannot keep me safe? What if the betrothal contract is genuine? What if when I break that contract, the damned baron has the right to marry Morgan?"

"I can tell you straight out Morgan's contract is not valid," the earl replied. "She signed it herself, and as a minor, she cannot make binding contracts except for necessaries. Even if a spouse is considered a necessary, she can legally repudiate the contract upon her majority. The family solicitors are busily drafting just such a repudiation, though it would be helpful to see the contract she signed."

"You are absolutely sure of this?"

"I am absolutely sure of this," the earl rejoined. "I spend hours each day up to my elbows in the small print of all manner of contracts, Anna, and I read law at university, since that is one profession open to younger sons. Morgan cannot be forced to marry Stull."

"Thank you." Anna sat back down, the fight going out of her. "Thank you so much for that."

"You are welcome."

At least, Anna thought, he wasn't telling her he wanted to paddle her black and blue, and he wasn't tossing her out on her ear—not yet. But he'd learned what manner of woman she was, one who would sign a contract she didn't mean to fulfill; one who would flee familial duty; one who would lie, hide, and flee again to avoid security and respectability for both herself and her sister.

The earl took up the rocker opposite the sofa. "There is yet more we need to discuss."

Their talk, Anna recalled. He'd warned her they would be having a lengthy discussion; there was no time like the present.

"I am listening."

"This is going to come out wrong," the earl sighed, "but I think it's time you gave up and married me."

"*Gave up and married you?*" Anna repeated in a choked whisper. This was one outcome she had not foreseen, and in its way, it was worse than any of the others. "Whatever do you mean?"

"If I marry you," the earl went on in reasonable tones, "then the worst Stull can do is sue for breach of promise. As he was willing to pay for the privilege of marrying you, I am not sure there are even damages for him to claim. It is the only way, however, to prevent him or some successor in your brother's schemes from marrying you in another trumped-up circumstance."

"And if he sues, it ensures you are embroiled in scandal."

"The Windham family is of sufficient consequence Stull's paltry accusations won't be but a nine days' wonder. Marry me, Anna, and your troubles will be over."

Anna chewed her fingernail and regarded the man rocking so contentedly opposite her. Marry him, and her troubles would be over.

Marry him, she thought bitterly, and her troubles would just be starting. He'd never said he loved her, never asked for her brother and his nasty friend to descend like this. She wasn't raised to be a duchess, and polite society would never let him forget he'd married, quite, quite down.

"I am flattered," Anna said, staring at her hands in her lap, "but can we not wait to see how matters resolve themselves?"

"You are turning me down," Westhaven said. "Stubborn, stubborn, stubborn." He rose and smiled down at her. "But then, if you weren't so stubborn, you'd be married to Stull by now, and that isn't an eventuality to be considered even in theory. I've put you in the largest guest room, and you are dead on your feet. Let me light you up to your bed, Anna."

She hadn't realized he'd had her things moved, and so accepted his arm in a daze. She was tired—bone weary and emotionally wrung out. The day had been too eventful, bringing with it both joy, relief, and loss.

"You are my guest," the earl said when he'd lit the candles in her bedroom. "I will wish you sweet dreams and promise you again to see this entire matter sorted out. You will consider my proposal and perhaps have an answer for me in the morning."

He bowed—*bowed!*—and withdrew, leaving Anna to sit on the bed, staring unseeing at the hearth.

Since he'd learned she was betrothed to another, the earl had not touched her, not as a lover. He'd offered his arm, his hospitality, and his name in marriage, but he had not been able to touch her as a lover.

It spoke volumes, Anna thought as she drifted off. He was a dutiful man and he needed an heir and he was sexually attracted enough to her, despite her deceit, that he could get a child or two on her. She owed him more than that, though, and so her last thoughts as she found sleep were of how she could spare him the very thing he dreaded most: a wife chosen out of duty.

❧

Several doors down the hall, the earl lay naked on his bed, cursing his solitude, his houseguest, and his own lack of charm. *Give up and marry me?* What manner of proposal was that? He was tempted to get up, stomp down the hall, and drag her back to his bed, but desire on his part was not the same thing as capitulation on hers.

"Well, Papa," he muttered into the night, "I cannot see the rest of my life without her, but alas, I am certain the sentiment is not reciprocated."

A soft knock on his door had his heart leaping in hopes Anna was seeking him out. He tossed on his dressing gown and opened the door to find Dev standing there, smiling slightly.

"Saw the light under your door and thought you might want to know Stull is again at liberty."

"I thought we had at least a few days to catch our breath."

"The magistrate had to leave Town and moved up his hearings," Dev reported. "Somebody came along and made bail for the dear baron."

"Come in." The earl stepped back and busied himself lighting a few more candles. "Do we know who might have bailed him out?"

"One Riley Whitford," Dev said. "Better known as old Whit, late of Seven Dials and any other stew or slum where vice runs tame."

"You know the man?" the earl asked, settling on the sofa in his sitting room.

"He was involved in a race-fixing scheme just about the time I left for the Peninsula." Dev ambled into the room as he spoke. "Clever man, always knows how to put somebody between him and the consequences of his actions."

"He was the one managing the surveillance of my house." The earl scowled. "Stop pacing, if you please, and sit quietly like the gentleman Her Grace believes you to be."

"How she can be so deluded?" Dev rolled his eyes, looking very much like a dark version of His Grace. But he sat in a wing chair and angled it to face his brother. "What will you do with Anna?"

"I've proposed and proposed and proposed." The earl sighed, surprising himself and apparently his brother with his candor. "She'll have none of that, though the last time, she put me off rather than turn me down flat."

"Things are a little unsettled," Dev pointed out dryly.

"And marriage would settle them," the earl shot back. "Married to me, there wouldn't be any more nonsense from her brother, not for her or Morgan. Her grandmother would be safe, and Stull would be nothing but a bad, greasy memory."

"He is enough to give any female the shudders, though maybe Anna has the right of it."

"What can you possibly mean?" The earl stood up and paced to the French doors.

"You and she are in unusual circumstances," Dev began. "You are protective of her and probably not thinking very clearly about her. She is not a duke's daughter, as you might be expected to marry, not even a marquis's sister. She's beneath you socially and likely undowered and not even as young as a proper mate to you should be."

"Young?" the earl expostulated. "You mean I can get her to drop only five foals instead of ten?"

"You have a duty to the succession," Dev said, his

words having more impact for being quietly spoken. "Anna understands this."

"Rot the fucking succession," Westhaven retorted. "I have His Grace's permission to marry for love, indeed, his exhortation to marry only for love."

"Are you saying you love her?" Dev asked, his voice still quiet.

"*Of course I love her*," the earl all but roared. "Why else would I be taking such pains for her safety? Why else would I be offering her marriage more times than I can count? Why else would I have gone to His Grace for help? Why else would I be arguing with you at an hour when most people are either asleep or enjoying other bedtime activities?"

Dev rose and offered his brother a look of sympathy. "If you love her, then your course is very easy to establish."

"Oh it is, is it?" The earl glared at his brother.

"If you love her," Dev said, "you give her what she wants of you, no matter how difficult or irrational it may seem to you. You do not behave as His Grace has, thinking that love entitles him to know better than his grown children what will make them happy or what will be in their best interests."

Westhaven sat down abruptly, the wind gone from his sails between one heartbeat and the next.

"You are implying I could bully her."

"You know you could, Gayle. She is grateful to you, lonely, not a little enamored of you, and without support."

"You are a mean man, Devlin St. Just." The earl sighed. "Cruel, in fact."

"I would not see you make a match you or Anna regret. And you deserve the truth."

"That's what Anna has said. You give me much to think about, and none of it very cheering."

"Well, think of it this way." Dev smiled as he turned for the door. "If you marry her now, you can regret it at great leisure. If you don't marry her now, then you can regret that as long as you can stand it then marry her later."

"Point taken. Good night, St. Just. You will ride in the morning?"

"Wouldn't miss it." Dev smiled and withdrew, leaving his brother frowning at the door.

Dev was right, damn him to hell and back. In Westhaven's shoes, His Grace would have married Anna, worn her down, argued, seduced, and argued some more until the woman bowed to his wishes. It was tempting to do just that—to swive Anna silly, maybe even get her pregnant, lavish her with care and attention, and send Stull packing.

But her brother had tried to take her choices from her, and His Grace had made many efforts to take the earl's choices from him. It was not a respectful way to treat a loved one.

So… He'd solve her problems, provide her sanctuary, and let her go, if that was what she wanted.

But he'd resent like hell that honor—honor and love—required it of him.

❧

"I trust you slept well?" the earl inquired politely over breakfast.

"I did," Anna lied with equal good manners. "And you?"

"I did not," the earl said, patting his lips with his napkin. "Though riding this morning has put me more to rights. I regret you will not be able to leave the house today."

"I won't?" Anna blinked at him over her teacup. He was very much the earl this morning, no trace of humor or affection in his eyes or his voice.

"Stull has made bail," Westhaven explained. "I do not put it past him to make another attempt to abduct you."

"I see." Anna put down her tea cup, her toast and jam threatening to make an untimely reappearance.

The earl laid a hand on her arm, and she closed her eyes, savoring the comfort of that simple touch. "You are safe here, and he can't force you to do anything, in any case. You won't go beyond the back gardens, though, will you?"

"I will not," Anna said. "But what happens next? I can't simply wait here in this house until he gives up. He won't—not ever. It's been two years, and he's spent considerable coin tracking me down."

"I've had him arrested on charges of arson," the earl reminded her. "He is likely not permitted to leave London itself, or he will violate the terms of his bond, baron or no baron. You can have him arrested for assault, though if he does have a betrothal contract, that likely won't fly very far."

"He has one," Anna rejoined. "I was trying to recall its particulars last night as I fell asleep, but it was more than two years ago that I signed it, and my brother did not want me to read the document itself."

"I cannot wait to meet this brother of yours. My sisters and my mother know better than to sign anything—anything—without reading each word."

"You are a good brother. And they are good sisters."

The earl looked up from buttering his toast. "You would have been a good sister to Morgan by allowing Stull to marry her?"

"No"—Anna shook her head—"but I am hardly a good sister to Helmsley for having refused to marry the man myself."

The earl put down his toast and knife. "You had two choices, as I see it, Anna: You could have married Stull, in which case he was essentially free to take his pleasure of you or Morgan, or to use Morgan to control you. In the alternative, you could have married Stull and left Morgan in your brother's care, in which case he'd just be auctioning her off behind Stull's back. Those options are unthinkable."

He went back to buttering his toast, his voice cool and controlled. "You created a third option, and it was the best you could do under the circumstances."

"It was," Anna said, grateful for his summary. But then, why did he still appear so remote?

"Until you met me," the earl went on. "You had a fourth option, then."

"I could have broken my word to my grandmother." Anna rose. "And taken a chance you would not laugh at me and return me to Stull's loving embrace, errant, contractually bound fiancées not something your average earl is willing to champion at the drop of a hat."

He remained sitting. "I deserve better than that."

"Yes," she said, near tears, "you most assuredly do, and if we marry…"

She whirled and left the room, her sentence unfinished and her host unable to extrapolate her meaning. If they married…what?

"I see we're starting our day in a fine temper." Dev sauntered in.

"Shut up." The earl passed him the teapot. "And do not attempt any more advice so early in the day, Dev. I do not like to see Anna upset."

"Neither do I." St. Just poured himself a cup of tea and frowned at the earl. "I don't like to see you upset either. What is the plan for the day?"

"I have to meet with Tolliver, of course, and I asked Hazlit to stop by, as well. I've sent for a dressmaker to see to Anna, and expect that will keep us out of each other's way for the day. What of you?"

"I am going to visit with some old army friends," Dev said, getting to work on a mountain of scrambled eggs. "I should be back by midday and will make it a point to join Anna for lunch."

"My thanks." The earl rose, feeling none too pleased with the day before him. "Tell her…"

Dev shook his head. "Tell her yourself."

❧

The morning was interminable, with no Anna tapping softly at the door with a little lemonade or marzipan for him, no water for his bouquets, no anything but work and more work. He sent Tolliver off well before luncheon but was pleased to find Benjamin Hazlit had chosen that hour to call.

"Join me for luncheon," the earl suggested. "My kitchen is not fancy, particularly in this heat, but we know how to keep starvation at bay."

"I will accept that generous offer," Hazlit said. "My breakfast was ages ago and not very substantial." The earl rang for luncheon on a tray, sending up a small prayer of thanks he'd have a valid excuse for not joining Anna and Dev on the back terrace. When lunch came, it showed that Anna was not behaving herself exclusively as a guest: There was a single daisy in a bud vase on each tray, and the marzipan was wrapped in linen, a little bouquet of violets serving as the bow.

"Your kitchen isn't fancy," Hazlit remarked, "but somebody dotes on their earl."

"Or on their lunch trays," the earl said. He quickly brought Hazlit up to date regarding Baron Stull's allegations of a betrothal, and the need to secret Morgan with Their Graces.

"Good move," Hazlit said. "Divide and conquer, so to speak. When I got your note, I did some poking around regarding Stull."

"Oh?" The earl paused in the demolition of his chicken sandwich.

"He's a bad actor," Hazlit said. "Been making a nuisance of himself in the lower-class brothels, trying to procure young girls, and using thugs to spy on your house."

My poor Anna.

Hazlit went on to advise the earl Stull had been identified as the purchaser of a large quantity of lamp oil, "right down to the grease stains on his cravat." The tallish gentleman with him, however, had remained in the shadows. Hazlit further suggested there would be another attempt to kidnap Anna.

"Why won't the baron just take his lumps and go home?"

Hazlit's gaze turned thoughtful. "So far, the evidence for arson is all circumstantial. The charges won't stick. He has a betrothal contract he thinks is valid, and he has Helmsley over a barrel, so to speak, financially. He wants Anna, and he wants her badly. You haven't described him as a man who is bright enough to cut his losses and find some silly cow who will bear him children and indulge his peccadilloes."

"And she would have to be a cow," the earl muttered, grimacing. "I hate just sitting here, waiting for those idiots to make the next move."

"And they hate just sitting there"—Hazlit reached for a piece of marzipan—"doing nothing. You should probably prepare yourself for some kind of legal maneuvering."

"What kind of maneuvering?"

"Charges of kidnapping or alienation of affections, breach of promise against Anna, demands of marriage from Helmsley."

"Demands that I marry her?" The earl scowled thunderously. "In God's name why?"

"If Helmsley sees you are a fatter pigeon than Stull, he'll rattle that sword."

"Christ." The earl got up and paced to the window. Anna and Dev were on the terrace, and she was smiling at something he'd said. Dev's smile was flirtatious and a little wistful—charmingly so, damn the scoundrel.

"We can hope it's a moot question," Hazlit said, rising to his feet. "If Stull attempts to remove her from your property, then you bring the kidnapping charges, and that will be the end of it. Unless she's married to the man, she can testify against him in any court in the land."

"What was the extent of the old earl's estate?" the earl asked, staring out the windows. Hazlit named a figure, a very large and impressive figure.

The earl continued to watch as Dev and Anna laughed their way through lunch. "If Helmsley has gambled that away, then he is guilty of misfeasance?"

"He most assuredly is," Hazlit replied, coming to stand where he, too, could look out at the back terrace.

"So I need to prove Helmsley guilty of misfeasance," the earl said, "and foil the baron's attempts at kidnapping, and then Anna should be safe but penniless."

"Not penniless. There is a trust fund that simply cannot be raided, not by God Almighty or the archangel Gabriel, as it is set aside for Anna's exclusive use. Her grandmother has seen to it the money was wisely invested."

"That is some good news." The earl turned finally, as Dev was escorting Anna back into the house. "Do you know how much she has left?" Hazlit named another figure, one that would keep even a genteel lady comfortably for a very long time.

The earl turned, watching as Hazlit gathered up his effects. "If nothing else, I appreciate my family more, my siblings and my parents, for this glimpse into Anna's circumstances."

"You are a fortunate man," Hazlit said. "In your

family, in any case. I'm off to loiter away the afternoon at the Pig. I'll report when something warrants your attention."

"I will await your communication," the earl said, seeing his guest to the door. "But patience is not my greatest strength."

The earl had no sooner returned to the library than Dev appeared, Anna in tow.

"So who was that?" Dev asked.

"Who was who?"

"That handsome devil who eyed us out the window, the one who stood right beside you," Dev shot back.

"Benjamin Hazlit. Our private investigator." The earl turned his gaze to Anna. "He thinks you should marry me."

"Let him marry you. I think I should join a convent."

"Now that," Dev said, "would be an inexcusable waste."

"I quite agree." The earl smiled thinly. "Hazlit says we wait now and expect either the baron to try to abduct you again or your brother to bring kidnapping charges."

Anna sat down in a heap. "As a man cannot kidnap his wife, we have another brilliant reason to marry me to you."

"Sound reasoning," the earl said. "I gather you are not impressed."

"I am not impressed." Anna rose abruptly. "And what do you mean, Westhaven, by summoning a dressmaker here?"

"I meant you to have some dresses," the earl said.

"Dresses that are not gray or brown or brownish gray or grayish brown. I meant for you to enjoy, at least, the fashions available to you here in London and to spend some time in a pursuit common to ladies of good breeding. I meant to offer you diversion. What did you think I meant?"

"Oh." Anna sat back down.

"I believe I will check on my horses and maybe take one out for a hack," Dev said and headed for the door.

"In this heat?" the earl asked, incredulous. Dev was nothing if not solicitous of his horses.

"A very short hack," Dev conceded over his shoulder, leaving Anna and the earl alone in the library.

❧

Why are you ignoring me? Anna silently wailed. But she knew why: Westhaven was treating her as a guest, and not as a guest with whom he was in love.

In all her dealings with him, Anna realized, she had worried for him. Worried he would suffer disappointment in her, worried his consequence would suffer for associating with her, worried she wasn't at all what he needed in a duchess. In hindsight, she saw she should have saved a little worry for herself—worry that her heart would break and she would be left to pick up the pieces without any clue as to how to go about it.

Westhaven was frowning at her. "Anna, are you perhaps in need of a nap?"

"Like a cranky child? Yes, I suppose I am. Are you?"

He smiled at that, a slow, wicked, tempting grin that heartened Anna immeasurably.

I missed you last night, but she didn't say it. Couldn't say it, with his frown replacing that grin.

"Did you know," the earl said, "you're a wealthy woman?"

"I am *what*?" Anna shot back to her feet. "Your jest is in poor taste, Westhaven."

"You *are* tired." The earl shifted to sit in his rocker. "Sit down, Anna, and let us discuss your situation."

"My situation?" Anna sat as bid, not liking the serious light in his eye.

"You are wealthy," the earl repeated. He described her trust fund and her grandmother's stewardship of it. "You can do any damned thing you please, Anna James, and in terms of your finances, you needn't marry anybody."

"But why wasn't I allowed to use my own money?" Anna wailed. "For two years, I've not had more than pin money to spare, and you tell me there are thousands of pounds with my name on them?"

"There are, just waiting for you to claim them."

"Why wouldn't my grandmother have told me of this?"

"She might not have known at the time of your departure exactly what funds were available for what purpose," the earl suggested gently. "She was unwell when you came south, and solicitors can be notoriously closemouthed. Or she might not have wanted to risk Helmsley getting wind if she tried to communicate with you. You must ask her."

"I knew we had dowries," Anna said, shaking her head. "Of course my brother would not tell me I had my own money. Damn him."

"Yes," Westhaven agreed, pulling her to her feet. "Damn him to the coldest circle of hell, and Baron Lardbucket with him. You still look like you need a nap."

"I do need a nap," Anna sighed and looked down at his hand linked with hers. There was something she needed much more than a nap, but the earl was apparently not of like mind. Well, damn him, too.

"I'll leave you, then," Anna said, chin up, tears threatening.

"You will see me at dinner," the earl warned her. "And Dev and Val, as well."

She nodded, and he let her go.

Now what in blazes, the earl wondered, could make a sane woman cry upon learning she was financially very well off indeed?

For his part, the knowledge was more than justification for tears. When Anna thought herself penniless and facing lawsuits, she hadn't accepted his offer of marriage. How much more hopeless would his situation be when she had the coin to manage without him entirely?

Anna presented herself freshly scrubbed for dinner, but she'd slept most of the afternoon away first. She had not joined all three brothers for a meal previously and found them to be formidably charming, the earl less overtly so than Val and Dev.

"So what will you do with your wealth?" Dev asked. "The only suitable answer is: Buy a horse."

"She could buy your stud farm," Val remarked, "and then some."

"I will look after my grandmother and my sister," Anna said. "Nothing else much matters, but I would like to live somewhere we can grow some flowers."

"Will you move back north?" Val asked, his smile faltering.

"I don't know. All of my grandmother's friends are there; my best memories are there."

"But some difficult memories, too," the earl suggested, topping up her wine glass.

"Some very difficult memories. I've always thought it made more sense to grow flowers in a more hospitable climate, but the need for them is perhaps greater in the North."

"Will you grow them commercially?" Dev asked.

"I simply don't know," Anna said, her gaze meeting the earl's. "Until things are resolved, and until I have a chance to sort matters through with Grandmama and Morgan, there is little point in speculating. Shall I leave you gentleman to your port and cigars?"

"I never learned the habit of smoking," the earl said, his brothers concurring. "Would you perhaps rather join us in a nightcap, Anna?"

"Thank you, no." Anna stood, bringing all three men to their feet. "While your company is lovely, my eyes are heavy."

"I'll light you up," the earl offered, crooking his arm at her. Anna accepted it, taking guilty pleasure in even that small touch. When they were safely out of earshot, the earl paused and frowned at her. "You aren't coming down with something, are you?"

"I am just tired."

"You have every right to be." He patted her hand,

and Anna wanted to scream. She held her tongue though, until they'd gained her bedroom.

"Is this how it's to be, Westhaven?" She crossed her arms and regarded him as he lit her candles.

"I beg your pardon?" He went on, carefully lighting a candelabra on her mantle.

"I am suddenly a sister to you?" Anna began to pace. "Or a stranger? A houseguest to whom you are merely polite?"

"You are not a sister to me." The earl turned to face her, the planes of his face harsh in the muted light. "But you are under my protection, Anna, as a guest. You are also a woman who has repeatedly told me my honorable intentions are not welcome. I will not offer you dishonorable intentions."

"Why not?" she shot back, wishing her dignity was equal to the task of keeping her mouth shut. "You certainly were willing to before."

"I was courting you," he said, "and there were lapses, I admit. But our circumstances are not the same now."

"Because my grandfather was an earl?"

"It makes a difference, Anna." Westhaven eyed her levelly. "Or it should. More to the point, you are likely to be the victim of another attempted kidnapping in the near future, and your brother is guilty of misfeasance, at the very least."

"You can't prove that," Anna said. But more than fatigue, what she felt was the weight of the earl's withdrawal.

He walked over to her, hesitated then reached up to brush a lock of hair back behind her ear. "You are tired, your life is in turmoil, and while I could importune you now, it would hardly be gentlemanly. I have trespassed against you badly enough as it is and would not compound my errors now."

"And would it be ungentlemanly," Anna said, turning her back to him, "to simply hold me?"

He walked around to the front of her, his eyes unreadable.

"Get into your nightclothes," he said. "I'm going to fetch you some chamomile tea, and then we'll get you settled."

Anna just stood in the middle of her room for long minutes after he'd left, her heart breaking with the certain knowledge she was being *humored* by a man who no longer desired her. She desired him, to be sure, but desire and willingness to destroy a good man's future were two different things.

Still, it hurt terribly that while she missed him, missed him with a throbbing, bodily ache, he was not similarly afflicted. She had disappointed him then refused his very gentlemanly offers and now he was done with her, all but the wrapping up and slaying her dragons part.

"You are ready for bed," the earl said, carrying a tray with him when he rejoined her. "Your hair is still up. Shall I braid it for you?"

She let him, let him soothe her with his kindness and his familiar touch and his beautiful, mellow baritone describing his conversation with his father and the various details of his day. He lay down beside her on the bed, rubbing her back as she lay on her side. She drifted off to sleep, the feel of his hand on her back and his breath on her neck reassuring her in ways she could not name.

When she woke the next morning, it was later than she'd ever slept before, and there was no trace of the earl's late-night visit.

Anna slept a great deal in the days that followed. Her appetite was off, and she cried easily, something that put three grown men on particularly good behavior. She cried at Val's music, at notes Morgan sent her, at the way the odd-colored cat would sit in the window of the music room and listen to Beethoven. She cried when her flower arrangements wouldn't work out, and she cried when Westhaven held her at night.

She cried so much Westhaven remarked upon it to his father.

"Probably breeding." The duke shrugged. "If she wasn't one to cry before but she's crying buckets now, best beware. Does she toss up her accounts?"

"She doesn't," the earl said, "but she doesn't eat much, at least not at meals."

"Is she sore to the touch?" The duke waved a hand at his chest. "Using the chamber pot every five minutes?"

"I wouldn't know." The earl felt himself blushing, but he could easily find out.

"Your dear mother was a crier. Not a particularly sentimental woman, for all her softheartedness, but I knew we were in anticipation of another happy event when she took to napping and crying."

"I see." The earl smiled. There were depths to his parents' intimacy he'd not yet glimpsed, he realized. Sweet depths, rich in caring and humor.

"Mayhap you do." The duke's answering smile faded. "And your mother was most affectionate when breeding, as well, not that she isn't always, but she was particularly in need of cuddling and cosseting, much to my delight. If this woman is carrying your child, Westhaven, it puts matters in a different light."

"It does."

"I'm not proud to have sired two bastards"—the duke frowned—"though in my day, these things were considered part of the ordinary course. Times aren't so tolerant now."

"They aren't," Westhaven agreed, sitting down as the weight of possible fatherhood began to sink in. "I would not wish bastardy on any child of mine."

"Good of you." The duke smiled thinly. "The child's mother is the one you'll have to convince. Best not fret about it now, though. Things sometimes work themselves out despite our efforts."

The earl barely heard him, so taken was he with the idea of creating a child with Anna. It felt *right*: in his bones it felt right and good. She would be a wonderful mother, and she would make him an at least tolerable father.

Papa.

The word took on rich significance, and the earl turned to regard his own sire.

"Weren't you ever afraid?" he asked. "Ten children, three different women, and you a duke?"

"I wasn't much of a duke." The old man snorted. "Not at first. But children have a way of putting a fellow on the right path rather sooner than he'd find it himself. Children and their mothers. But to answer your question, I was fairly oblivious, at first, but then Devlin was born, and Maggie, and I began to sense my own childhood was coming to a close. I was not sanguine at this prospect, Westhaven. Many of our class regard perpetual childhood as our God-given right. Fortunately, I met your mother, and she showed me just how much I had to be fearful of."

"But you kept having children. Fatherhood couldn't have been all that daunting if you embraced it so frequently."

"Silly boy." The duke beamed. "It was your mother I was embracing. Still do, though it probably horrifies you to hear of it."

"No." Westhaven smiled. "It rather doesn't."

The duke's smile faded. "More to the point, you don't have a choice with children, Westhaven. You bring them into this world, and you are honor bound to do the best you can. If you are fortunate, they have another parent on hand to help out when you are inclined to be an ass, but if not, you muddle on anyway. Look at Gwen Hollister—or Allen, I suppose. She muddled on, and Rose is a wonderful child."

"She is. Very. You might consider telling her mother that sometime."

He shifted the conversation, to regale his father with an account of his time spent with Rose. It seemed like ages ago that His Grace had come thundering into the sick room at Welbourne, but listening to his father recount more stories of Victor and his brothers, Westhaven had the strong sense the duke was healing from more than just his heart seizure.

Westhaven took his leave of his father, so lost in thought he had little recollection of his journey home. Pericles knew the way, of course, but ambling along in the heat, the earl was preoccupied with the prospect of fatherhood. When he gained his library, he sat down with a calendar and began counting days.

He'd retrieved Nanny Fran from the duke's household, and he wasn't above putting the old woman up to some discreet monitoring of Anna's health. By his calculations, he had not been intimate with Anna when she should have been fertile, but women were mysterious, and he'd taken no precautions to prevent conception.

It hit him like a freight wagon that in that single act, he'd probably taken away as many of Anna's options as her brother and Stull combined, and he'd never once considered behaving any differently. He sat alone in his library for a long time, thinking about Anna and what it meant to love her were she carrying his child.

At the same time, Anna was sitting on the little bed in the room she'd used when she held the title of housekeeper, thinking what an odd loss it was to not be even that anymore to the earl. She had found it heartening that she could earn her own keep. Looking after the earl and his brothers had been particularly pleasurable, as they took well to being tended to.

She, however, did not take well to being tended to. Not lately. For the past several nights, the earl had served as her lady's maid, taking down her hair, bringing her a cup of tea, and spending the end of the day in quiet conversation with her. All the while, even on those nights when he rubbed her back and cuddled her close on the bed, she felt him withdrawing to a greater and greater emotional distance.

He wasn't physically skittish with her, but rather very careful. Anna wanted to think he was almost cherishing, but there was no evidence of desire in his touch. And she bundled into him closely enough the evidence would have been impossible to hide. She clung to him for those times when he offered her comfort but felt all too keenly the comfort he was no longer interested in offering, as well.

She was losing him, which proved to her once and for all that her decision to leave—her many, many decisions to leave—were the better course for them both.

Better, perhaps, but by no means easier.

～⁂～

"I am being followed," Helmsley said, taking a long swallow of ale. Ale, for God's sake, the peasant drink.

"You are a well-dressed gentleman on the streets when few are about," Stull said. "No doubt you attract attention, as I do myself. I want to know why you're back in dear old London town, where you don't fit in and you do depend on my coin."

Helmsley rolled his eyes. "Because I am being followed. Big, dark chap, rough-looking, like a drover returning north without his flock."

"And what would a drover be doing staying at the better inns, when they have their own establishments for that purpose?" Stull replied, draining his own tankard.

"You take my point." Helmsley nodded, glad he didn't have to explain everything. "I thought you should know."

"You thought I should know." Stull frowned.

"But you've been gone nigh a week, which means you probably made it halfway to York before turning about and deciding to tell me."

Helmsley studied his ale. "I had a delay on the way out of Town. Horse tossed a shoe, then it was too late to travel. He came up lame the next day, and rather than buy another horse, I had to wait for him to come right."

"And you waited for how long before realizing you had company?"

"A few days," the earl improvised. "I was traveling slowly to spare the horse."

"Of course you were." Stull scowled. "You're up to something, Helmsley, and you'd best not be up to crossing me."

"I am up to nothing." Helmsley sighed dramatically. "Except imposing further on your hospitality. Now, why haven't we collected my sisters yet?"

Stull banged his empty tankard in a demand for more ale and launched into a convoluted tale of arrests, accusations, and indignities. From his ramblings, the earl concluded Stull had yet to locate Morgan but tried at least once to abduct Anna almost literally from the Earl of Westhaven's arms.

"So where does this leave us?" Helmsley asked.

He had been followed, but he'd also been struck with an idea: Dead, Anna was worth more to him than alive. The difficulty was, she had to die—or at least appear to die—before she wed Stull, or all her lovely money would fall into the hands of the baron. The thought that the baron might procure a special license and start his connubial bliss with Anna before

Helmsley even saw her again had sent Helmsley right back down the road.

Of course, he should offer Anna the option of faking her own death and disappearing with a tidy sum, but working in concert with Stull for the past two years had left a bad taste in Helmsley's mouth. Partners in crime were tedious and a liability.

Once Anna had been dealt with, Morgan could be used to appease Stull. It would then be easy to arrange an accident for Stull—ingested poison seemed the appropriate remedy—and then as Stull's widow, Morgan would inherit a goodly portion of the baron's wealth, as well.

A tidy, altogether pleasing plan, Helmsley congratulated himself, but one that would require his presence in London, where the gaming was better, criminals for hire abounded, and Stull could be closely monitored.

"So how do you propose we retrieve dear Anna?" Helmsley asked. "I gather snatching her from the market did not go as planned."

"Hah," Stull snorted, then paused for a moment to leer at the young serving maid. "That damned Westhaven got to throwing his weight around and had me arrested for arson. The charges will be dropped, of course, and it gives me the perfect excuse to malinger in Town. The plan remains simply to snatch the girl. She's helpless when it comes to her flowers, and I have it on good authority she's out in the back gardens several times a day. We'll just seize our moment and seize your sister."

"Simple as that?"

"Simple as that." The baron nodded. "Trying to

nab her in the market, I admit, was poorly thought out. Too many people around. This time, however, I'm prepared."

"What does that mean?" Helmsley made his tone casual.

"If that damned earl makes a ruckus"—Stull wiped his lips on his handkerchief—"I'll wave the betrothal contract at him. And for good measure, I'll wave your guardianship papers, as well."

"Hadn't thought of that," Helmsley said slowly, though of course he had. "Why not simply send a solicitor 'round to the earl with the documents? If he's a gentleman, as you say, he should send Anna along smartly, and Morgan with her, assuming she's nearby?"

"You don't understand your peers, Helmsley." Stull leaned forward. "I'll wave that document around, but I'm not turning the earl's solicitors loose on it. The Quality don't engage in trade, and anything that smacks of business befuddles 'em to the point where they must bring in the lawyers. That will take weeks, at least, and I am damned tired of waiting for my bride."

"I'm sure you are," Helmsley said, as he was damned tired of waiting for Stull to pay off his debts. He also silently allowed as how any solicitor of suitable talent to serve a future duke would likely find holes the size of bull elephants in the contracts. "Your plan sounds worthy to me, so what are we waiting for?"

The baron smiled, an ugly grimace of an expression. "We are waiting for Anna to go pick her bedamned flowers."

Seventeen

"WHY THE FROWN?" VAL ASKED, HELPING HIMSELF TO the lemonade provided for the earl and Mr. Tolliver each morning.

"Note from Hazlit." The earl handed the missive to his brother, Tolliver having been excused for the day. "He began the journey north to track down Helmsley, and lo, the fellow was not more than a day's ride from Town, supposedly waiting for his horse to come sound. He rode right back into Town and connected with Stull at the Pig."

"So you have your miscreants reunited." Val scanned the note. "I wonder what the foray north was about in the first place?"

"Who knows?" The earl sipped at his drink. "They don't strike me as a particularly cunning pair."

"Maybe not cunning," Val conceded, "but ruthless. They were going to torch an entire property, for reasons we still don't know. That's a hanging offense, Westhaven, and so far, they've gotten away with it."

"The charges are pending, and I suspect if we catch

one of them, the other will be implicated in very short order."

Val sat on the arm of the sofa. "Stull hasn't implicated Helmsley yet."

"The arson charges are not likely to stick," the earl said, "though they do create leverage."

"Or unpredictability," Val suggested.

"Possibly." The earl noted that Val was being contrary, which wasn't like him. "How is Miss Morgan?"

"Thriving," Val said glumly. "She's blooming, Westhaven. When I call upon her, she is giggling, laughing, and carrying on at a great rate with our sisters, the duke, the duchess…"

"The footmen?" the earl guessed.

"The butler, the grooms, the gardeners," Val went on, nodding. "She charms everybody."

"It could be worse." The earl got up and went to the window, from which he could see Anna taking cuttings for her bouquets. "You could have proposed to her, oh, say a half-dozen times and been turned down each time. Quite lowering, the third and fourth rejections. One gets used to it after that. Or tries to."

"Gads." Val's eyebrows shot up. "I hadn't realized it had reached that stage. What on earth is wrong with the woman?"

"Nothing. She simply believes we would not suit, so I leave her in relative peace."

"Except you tuck her in each night?"

"I do." The earl's eyes stayed fixed on the garden. "She is fond of me; she permits it. She is quite alone, Val, so I try not to take advantage of the liberties I'm granted. I comprehend, though, when a woman doesn't even try to kiss me, that I have lost a substantial part of my allure in her eyes."

"And have you talked to her about this?"

"I have." The earl smiled faintly. "She confronted me quite clearly and asked how we were to go on. She wants comforting but nothing more. I can provide that."

Comforting and cosseting and cuddling.

"You are a better man than I am." Val smiled in sympathy.

"Not better." The earl shook his head. "Just... What the *hell* is going on out there?!"

A pair of beefy-looking thugs had climbed over the garden wall and thrown a sack over Anna's head. She was still struggling mightily when the earl, both brothers, and two footmen pounded onto the scene and wrestled Anna from her attackers.

"Oh, no you don't," St. Just snarled as he hauled the larger man off the wall. "You stay right here, my man, and await the King's justice. You, too, Shorty." He cocked a pistol and leveled a deadly look at the two intruders.

Baron Stull let himself in through the gate. "I say, none of that now. Westhaven, call off your man."

"Stull." Westhaven grimaced. "You are trespassing. Leave, unless you'd like the constable to take you up now rather than when these worthies implicate you in kidnapping."

"I ain't kidnapping," Stull huffed. "You want proof this lady is my fiancée, well here it is." He thrust a beribboned document at the earl, who merely lifted an eyebrow. On cue, Val stepped forward, retrieved the document, and handed it to a footman.

"Take it to His Grace," the earl ordered. "Tell him I want the validity of the thing reviewed, and it's urgent."

"Now see here." The Earl of Helmsley sauntered in through the gate, and Westhaven felt Anna go tense. "There will be no need for that. Anna, come along. Tell the man I'm your brother and the guardian appointed by our grandpapa to see to you and our sister. Grandmama has been missing you both."

"You are not and never were my guardian," Anna said. "I was of age when Grandpapa died, and while you may control some of my funds, you never had legal control of me."

"Seems the lady isn't going to be going with you," the earl said. "So you may leave, for now."

"Now, my lord." Helmsley shook his head. "Let's not be hasty. I, too, brought proof of my claims with me. Perhaps Anna would like to read for herself what provision Grandpapa made?" With his left hand, he held out a second document, rolled and tied with a ribbon. As Anna took a step forward to snatch the document from his hand, the earl noticed Helmsley's right hand was hidden in the folds of his coat.

"Anna, don't!"

But his warning was too late. As Anna reached for the document, Helmsley reached for her, wrapping her tightly against his body, a gun held to her temple.

"That's enough!" Helmsley jerked her hard against him, the document having fallen to the cobblestones. "Stull, come along. We've got your bride, and it's time we're going. Westhaven, you are free to call the magistrate, but we'll be long gone, and when it comes down to it, your word against ours will not get you very far in criminal proceedings, particularly as a woman cannot testify against her spouse." He wrenched Anna back a step, then another, keeping Anna between him and the earl.

A shot was fired, followed instantly by a second shot. Anna sagged against her brother but was snatched into Westhaven's arms.

"I'm hit." Helmsley's hand went to his side, gun clattering to the cobblestones beside the document. "You bastard!" Helmsley shouted at St. Just in consternation. "You just *shot* me!"

"I did." St. Just approached him, pistol still in hand. "As I most assuredly am a bastard, in every sense of the word, I suggest you do not give me an excuse to discharge my second barrel just to shut you up. Defense of a loved one, you know? Deadly force is countenanced by every court in the land on those grounds."

"Val…" the earl's voice was urgent. "Get Garner or Hamilton. Get me a damned physician. Anna's bleeding."

"Go." Dev nodded at Val. "John Footman and I will handle these four until the constable gets here."

❧

Anna was weaving on her feet, the earl's arm around her waist holding her up until she felt him swing her up against his chest. The earl was bellowing for Nanny Fran, and pain was radiating out from Anna's shoulder, pain and a liquid, sticky warmth she vaguely recognized as her own blood.

"Hurts," she got out. "Blazes."

"I know," the earl said, his voice low, urgent. "I

know it hurts, sweetheart, but we'll get you patched up. Just hang on."

Sweetheart, Anna thought. Now he calls me sweetheart, and that hurt, too.

"I'll be fine," she assured him, though the pain was gaining momentum. "Just don't…"

"Don't what?" He laid her on the sofa in the library and sat at her hip while Nanny Fran bustled in behind him.

"Don't go," Anna said, blinking against the pain. "Quacks."

"I won't leave you to the quacks." The earl almost smiled, accepting a pair of scissors from Nanny Fran. "Hold still, Anna, so we can have a look at the damage."

"Talk." Anna swallowed as even the earl's hands deftly tugging and cutting at the fabric of her dress made the pain worse.

"What shall I talk about?" His voice wasn't quite steady, and Anna could feel the blood welling from her shoulder and soaking her dress even as he cut the fabric away from her wound.

"Anything," she said. "Don't want to faint."

Her eyes fluttered closed, and she heard the earl start swearing.

❦

"Clean cloths," Westhaven said to Nanny, who passed him a folded linen square over his shoulder. "Anna, I'm going to put pressure directly onto the wound, and it will be uncomfortable."

She nodded, her face pale, her eyes closed. He folded the cloth over her shoulder and pressed, gently at first but then more firmly. She winced but said nothing, so he held the pressure steady until the cloth was soaked then added a second cloth on top of the first.

"Have we carbolic and basilicum?" the earl asked.

"We do," Nanny Fran replied. "And brandy by the bottle." She held her silence for long tense moments before peering over Westhaven's shoulder again. "Ain't bleeding so much," she observed with grudging approval. "Best take a look."

"Not yet," the earl said, "not until the bleeding stops. Time enough to clean her up later."

By the time the physician arrived—Dr. Garner—Anna's wound was no longer bleeding, and her shoulder had been gently cleaned up but no dressing applied.

"Capital job," the physician pronounced. "It's a deep graze, right over the top of the shoulder. Few inches off, and it would have been in the neck or the lung. Looks as if the powder's been cleaned adequately. You're a lucky girl, Miss James, but you are going to have to behave for a while."

He put a tidy dressing on the wound and urged rest and red meat for the loss of blood. He prescribed quiet and sparing laudanum if the pain became too difficult. He also pulled the earl aside and lectured sternly about the risk of infection. The doctor's demeanor eased a great deal when the earl described the initial attention given the patient.

"Well done." The doctor nodded. "Fairly will be proud of you, but your patient isn't out of the woods yet. She needs peace and quiet, and not just for the wound. Violent injury takes a toll on the spirit, and even the bravest among us take time to recover."

"And if she's breeding?" the earl asked quietly.

"Hard to say." The physician blew out a slow breath. "She's young and quite sturdy, generally. Not very far along and strikes me as the sensible sort. If I had to lay odds, I'd say the child is unaffected, but procreation is in hands far greater than ours, my lord. All you can do is wait and pray."

"My thanks." Westhaven ushered the doctor to the front door. "And my thanks, as well, for your efforts with my father. I know he hasn't been an easy patient."

"The old lords seldom are." The doctor smiled. "Too used to having their way and too concerned with their dignity."

"I'll try to remember that"—the earl returned the smile—"should I ever be an old lord."

When the doctor was on his way, Stull and Helmsley had been taken into custody, and the household settling down, the earl was surprised to see evening was approaching. He made his way to Anna's sitting room and the small bedroom beyond it.

"I'll sit with her, Nanny," the earl said, helping the older woman to her feet. "Go have a cup of tea; get some fresh air."

"Don't mind if I do." Nanny bustled along. "Cuppa tea's just the thing to settle a body's nerves."

Westhaven frowned at his patient where she reclined on her pillows. "I hate that you're hurt."

"I'm none too pleased about what happened either," Anna said. "But what, exactly, did happen?"

"Your brother attempted to abduct you," the earl said, taking the seat Nanny had vacated. "St. Just deterred him by means of a bullet, but the gun your brother had trained on you discharged, as well."

"You mean my brother shot me?"

"He did. I cannot say it was intentional."

"How is he faring?" Anna asked, dropping his gaze.

"He's gut shot, Anna," the earl said gently. "We sent him Dr. Hamilton, whom I believe to be competent, but his prognosis is guarded, at best."

"He's wounded and in jail?" Anna said, her voice catching.

"He's enjoying the hospitality of the Crown at a very pleasant little house St. Just owns, with professional nursing care in addition to armed guards. He is a peer, Anna, and will be cared for accordingly."

It was more than Helmsley deserved.

"Anna." The earl's hand traced her hairline gently. "Let me do this."

She met his gaze and frowned, but he wasn't finished. "Let me put matters to rights for you. I will take care of your brother and see to final arrangements if any need be made. If you like, I will notify your grandmother and have her escorted south. We can do this in the ducal traveling coach, in easy stages, I promise."

"Do it, please," Anna said, wiping at her eyes with her left hand. "My thanks."

"Anna." Westhaven shifted to sit at her left hip and leaned down over her. He carefully cradled her cheek with his left hand and tucked her face against his neck. "It's all right to cry, sweetheart."

She wiggled her left arm out from between them and circled his neck, pulling him close, and then turned her face into his warmth and wept. Unable to move much beyond that, her tears streamed from her eyes into her hair and onto the earl's cheek. He held her and stroked her wet cheeks with his thumb, letting her cry until his own chest began to ache for her.

Westhaven levered up enough to meet her gaze. "You must allow me to manage what I can for you now. All I want is to see you healed, the sooner the better."

"For now, have you a handkerchief, perhaps?"

"I do." He produced the requisite handkerchief and wiped at her cheeks himself before tucking it into her left hand. "And I am willing to read you Caesar, beat you at cribbage, discuss interior decoration with you, or speed your recovery by any means you please."

"I am to be served my own medicine," Anna said ruefully.

"Or perhaps you'd like to be served something to eat? Maybe just some toast with a little butter or jam, or some soup?"

"Toast and butter, and some cold tea."

"It will be my pleasure." The earl rose and left her. And Anna felt his absence keenly. Nanny Fran was dear, but she muttered and fussed and did very little to actually ensure the patient was comfortable. The earl returned, bearing a tray with cold tea, buttered toast, a single piece of marzipan, and a daisy in a bud vase.

"You brought me a flower." Anna smiled, the first genuine smile she'd felt in ages.

"I have been trained by an expert." The earl smiled back. He stayed with her while she ate then beat her at cribbage. When night fell, he asked Val to play for her, the slow, sweet lullabies that would induce a healing sleep. When she woke in the night, he got her to the chamber pot and back into bed and held her left hand until she drifted off. Nanny Fran shooed him out the next morning, but by early afternoon he was back.

When Dr. Garner reappeared to check the wound, the earl stayed in the room, learning how to replace the dressing and how to identify the signs of proper healing. For three more days, he was by her side, until Anna was pronounced well enough to sit in the gardens and move about a little under her own power.

On the fifth day, the duchess came to call with Morgan. While Anna and Morgan chatted volubly in the back gardens, the duchess took her son aside and pointed out some difficult truths.

Anna was the acknowledged granddaughter of an earl, and the danger of infection was diminishing with each day.

Morgan missed her sister.

The earl's offers of marriage had been rejected not once but several times.

The earl was running a bachelor establishment, not just for himself but for his two equally unmarried brothers.

Something was going to have to be done, the duchess concluded, her preferred *something* obvious to her son.

"Give me a couple more days," the earl reasoned. "Anna is still uncomfortable, and even a short carriage ride will be difficult for her."

"I can understand that," the duchess said, "and she deserves some notice of a change of abode, but, Westhaven, what will she do now?"

"We've discussed it, we'll discuss it some more.

Plan on receiving her the day after tomorrow before tea time."

"Morgan will be very pleased." The duchess rose. "You are doing the right thing." The earl nodded, knowing his mother spoke the truth. It was time to let Anna get on with her life and to stop hoarding up memories of her for his own pleasure.

Her convalescence had been pleasant. They'd spent hours together, mostly talking, sometimes reading. The earl worked on his correspondence while Anna slept or while she dozed in the shade of the gardens. They talked about the Rosecroft estate up in Yorkshire and the effect of her brother's lack of heirs; they talked of Morelands and how pretty it was. He apprised her of the rebuilding of the stables at Willow Bend and brought her correspondence from the Marchioness of Heathgate and Gwen Allen, wishing her a speedy recovery.

When those good wishes made her cry, he lent her his handkerchief and his sturdy shoulder and brought her bouquets to cheer her up, and still, they did not talk about what mattered.

༜

"Has my mother put you to rights?" the earl asked. He looked handsome to Anna, in shirtsleeves and waistcoat, his cuffs turned back as he wandered onto the back terrace where she was enjoying the sunshine on a chaise.

"She clucked and fussed and carried on appropriately," Anna said. "I am to make a speedy and uneventful recovery by ducal decree."

"Your grandmother will be here late next week,

you know, if all goes well." Westhaven sat on the edge of her chaise, regarding her closely. "You don't look so pale, I'm thinking."

"I don't feel so pale," she assured him. "I've not taken the time to just sit in the sun for more than two years, Westhaven. It's bad for one's ladylike complexion, but in the North, we crave the sun."

"Will you be going back there?"

Anna fingered the cuff of her sleeve. "I do not want to. I want to remember Rosecroft as it was in my grandfather's day, not in the neglect and disrepair my brother allowed."

"You don't ask about him," Westhaven said, taking her hand.

"I assume he is malingering."

"He is not doing well. It's to be expected."

"And Stull?"

"Made bond. But seems content to await trial at the Pig. I did bring trespass charges, just for the hell of it, and assault and conspiracy to assault in your name, as well."

"Will any of it stick?"

The earl smiled, and the expression had a lot of big, white, sharp teeth to it. "It's a curious thing about assault, but it's both a tort and a crime."

"A tort?" Anna frowned.

"A civil wrong for which the law provides a remedy." The earl quoted. "Like, oh, slander, libel, and the like."

"You are saying I can sue him personally, not just bring criminal charges?"

"You already have," the earl informed her. "On the advice of the duke, of course."

"Why would I do such a thing, when lawsuits take forever to resolve, and all I want is to be shut of that man immediately?"

"Civil matters are often settled with money judgments, Anna, and while you might think you have sufficient capital, Morgan might not be of the same mind, nor your grandmother."

"I see." Anna pursed her lips. "I trust your judgment, Westhaven. Proceed as you see fit."

"I will," he said and brought her hand up sandwiched between both of his. "There's something else we need to discuss, Anna."

"There is?" She watched him matching their hands, finger for finger.

"Your grandmother will be scandalized to find you dwelling with three bachelors, and my mother has reminded me Morgan is worried about you."

"Morgan just visited, and my grandmother will hardly be scandalized to find I'm alive and well."

"Anna…" He met her gaze. "I've made arrangements for you to remove to the mansion the day after tomorrow, where you will complete your convalescence under my mother's care."

"Westhaven…" He rose abruptly, and Anna came to her feet more slowly. "Gayle? Is this what you want?"

He looked up at her use of his name, a sad smile breaking through his frown.

"It is what must be, Anna." He kept his hands in his pockets. He did not reach for her. "You are a well-bred young lady, and I am a bachelor of some repute. If it becomes known you are under my roof without chaperonage, then your future will be bleak."

More bleak, Anna wanted to rail, than when Stull and Helmsley were hounding me across England?

"I will miss you," Anna said, turning her back to him, the better to hide her tears. God above, she'd turned into a watering pot since getting involved with the earl.

"I beg your pardon?" He'd stepped closer, close enough she could catch his scent.

"I will miss you," Anna said, whirling and walking straight into him. She wrapped her arms around his waist and clung, while his arms gently closed around her. "I will miss you and miss you and miss you."

"Oh, love." He stroked the back of her head. "You mustn't cry over this. You'll manage, and so will I, and it's for the best." She nodded but made no move to pull away, and he held her as closely as her wounded shoulder would allow.

∽

In the library, Val looked up from rummaging for a penknife and frowned at Dev.

"Are you peeking?" Val asked, moving to stand beside his brother at the window.

"Enjoying my front-row seat," Dev replied, scowling. "I do not understand our brother, Valentine. He loves that woman and would give his life for her. But he's letting her go, and she's letting him let her go."

"Could be a flanking maneuver." Val watched as Anna cried her heart out on Westhaven's shoulder. The couple was in profile, though, so when Westhaven bent his head to press his lips to her temple, the expression on his face was visible, as well.

"Come away." Val tugged at Dev's sleeve, and Dev left the window. "We should not have seen that."

"But we did see it," Dev said. "Now what are we going to do about it?"

"We will not meddle," Val said. "We are not the duke, Devlin. I have every confidence Westhaven will let Anna catch her breath and then approach her properly."

"Why wait?" Dev pressed. "They love each other now. And I have my suspicions as to why Anna cries so easily these days. I am years your senior, and I can recall the duchess's last few confinements."

"They love each other," Val said, "clearly they do, but Anna deserves to be approached as the wealthy young lady of quality she is, not as a housekeeper on the run from venal schemes. And I don't want to hear talk of confinements, particularly not when His Grace has ears everywhere."

"Westhaven's honor has gotten the best of his common sense," Dev argued. "Anna doesn't want to be approached later; she wants to be approached now."

"Then why does she keep turning him down?" Val said reasonably. "His efforts to woo her would be an embarrassment, were I not convinced he has the right of it."

"I don't know." Dev rubbed his chin and glanced at the window. "This whole business makes no sense, and I am inclined—odd as it might sound—to hear what His Grace has to suggest."

"I agree." Val sighed, closing the desk drawer with a bang. "Which only underscores that Westhaven isn't making one damned bit of sense."

◈

In the less than two days that remained to them, the earl and Anna were in each other's pockets constantly. They sat side by side in the back gardens, on the library sofa, or at breakfast. When Dev and Val joined them for meals, they affected a little more decorum, but their eyes conveyed what their hands and bodies could not express. Anna was again sleeping upstairs, and the earl was again joining her at the end of each day.

The earl drew a brush down the length of her dark hair. "I have asked Dev and Val to escort you to Their Graces tomorrow, Anna."

"I see. You are otherwise occupied."

"I will be. I think you will enjoy my mother's hospitality, and my sisters will love you."

"Morgan adores them," Anna said, her smile brittle. "Mourning has left them in want of company, and Morgan is lonely, as well."

"And you, Anna." The earl's hand went still. "Will you be lonely?"

She met his eyes in the mirror above the vanity, and he saw hunger there. A hunger to match his own.

"I am lonely now, Westhaven." She rose and turned. "I am desperately lonely, *for you*." She pressed her lips to his, the first they'd kissed in weeks, and though his arms came around her briefly, he was the first one to step back.

"Anna, we will regret it."

"I will regret it if we don't," she replied, her expression unreadable. "I understand, Westhaven,

I must leave tomorrow, and in a way it will be a relief, but…"

"But?" He kept his expression neutral, but his breathing was accelerated from just that brief meeting of lips. And what did she mean, leaving him would be a *relief*?

"But we have this night to bring each other pleasure one last time," she said miserably. "What difference can it make how we spend it?"

He had been asking himself that same question for days and giving himself answers having to do with honor and respect and even love, but those answers wouldn't address the pure pain he saw in Anna's eyes.

"I do not want to take advantage of you," he said. "Not again, Anna."

"Then let me take advantage of you," Anna pleaded softly. "Please, Westhaven. I won't ask again."

She desired him, Westhaven told himself. That much had always been real between them, and she was asking him to indulge his most sincere wish. That it was his most sincere wish didn't mean he should deny her, didn't mean he should assume, with ducal arrogance, he knew better than she what she needed.

"Come." He tugged her by the hand to stand by the bed and slowly undressed her, taking particular care she not have to move her right shoulder and arm. When she was on the bed, resting on her back, he got out of his own clothes and locked the door before joining her.

"We will be careful, Anna." He crouched over her naked, his erection grazing her belly. "You are injured, and I cannot go about this oblivious to that fact."

"We will be careful," she agreed. Her left hand cradled his jaw and then slid around to his nape to draw him down to her. "We will be very careful."

He remained above her, his weight on his forearms, even as he joined his mouth to hers and then his body to hers.

"Westhaven." Anna undulated up against him. "Please, not slow, not this time."

"Not slow, but careful."

"Not that either, for God's sake."

He laced his fingers through hers where they rested on her pillow and raised himself up just enough to hold her gaze.

"Careful," he reiterated. "Deliberate." He slowly hilted himself in her and withdrew. "Measured." Another thrust. "Steady." Another. "But hot," he whispered, "hard...deep..."

"Oh, God, *Gayle*..." Her body spasmed around his cock, clutching at him just as hot, hard, and deep as he'd promised her. She buried her face against his shoulder to mute her keening groans of pleasure, and still he drove her on, one careful thrust at a time.

"I am undone," she pronounced, brushing his hair back from his brow. "I am utterly, absolutely undone."

"I am not." The earl smiled down at her, a conqueror's possessive smile. "But how is your shoulder?"

"You can even think to ask? My shoulder is fine, I believe, but as I am floating a small distance above this bed, I will have to let you know when I am reunited with it."

"You are pleased?" he asked, lacing his fingers with hers. "This is what you wanted?"

"This is what I needed," she said softly as he began to move in her again *carefully*. "This is what I sorely, sorely needed."

"Anna… When you leave tomorrow…?"

"Yes?" She closed her eyes, making it harder to read her. He laid his cheek against hers and closed his fingers around hers, needing as much contact as he could have.

"When you leave tomorrow and I am not there, this will be part of it," he said, turning his face to kiss her cheek then resting his cheek against hers again.

"I don't know what you mean."

"I will be thinking of you," he said, "and you will be thinking of me and of this pleasure we shared. It's…*good* is the only word I can find. Joyous, lovely, beautiful, somehow, even if it can't be more than it is. I wanted you to know how I feel."

"Oh, you." Anna curled up to his chest tears flowing. "Gayle Tristan Montmorency Windham. Shame on you; you have made me cry with your poetry."

He kissed her tears away this time and made her forget her sorrows—almost—with his loving, until she was crying out her pleasure again and again. He let himself join her the last time, his own climax exploding through him, leaving him floating that same small distance above the bed, until sleep began to steal his awareness.

He tended to their ablutions then stood gazing down at Anna where she dozed naked on her left side. It was time to go, he knew, but still, dawn was hours away.

"Don't go." Anna opened her eyes and met his

gaze. "We will be parted for a long time, Westhaven. Let us remain joined just a little while longer."

He nodded and climbed into bed, spooning himself around her back and tucking an arm around her waist. This night's work was pure, selfish folly, but he'd treasure the memory, and he hoped she would, as well.

He made love to her one more time—sweetly, slowly, just before dawn, and then he was gone.

⁓

Anna slept late the next morning and considered it a mercy, as the earl had told her he was off to Willow Bend for the day. Val and Dev had ridden out, and so she had breakfast to herself. Her shoulder was itchy, and it took her longer to pack than she'd thought it would, but before long, she was being summoned for luncheon on the back patio.

"You look healthy," Dev said. "If I did not know you were sporting the remains of a bullet wound, I would think you in the pink."

"Thank you." Anna smiled. "I slept well last night." For the first time in weeks, she truly had.

"Well"—Val sat down and reached for the iced lemonade pitcher—"I did not sleep well. We need another thunderstorm."

"I wonder." Anna's eyes met Val's. "Does Morgan still dread the thunderstorms?"

"She does," he replied, sitting back. "She figured out that the day your parents died, when she was trapped in the buggy accident, it stormed the entire afternoon. Her associations are still quite troubling, but her ears don't physically hurt." Dev and Anna exchanged a look of surprise, but Val was tucking into his steak.

Dev turned his attention back to his plate. "Anna, are you ready to remove to the ducal mansion?"

"As ready as I'll be," Anna replied, her steak suddenly losing its appeal.

"Would you like me to cut that for you?" Dev asked, nodding at the meat on her plate. "I've pulled a shoulder now and then or landed funny from a frisky horse, and I know the oddest things can be uncomfortable."

"I just haven't entirely regained my appetite," Anna lied, eyeing the steak dubiously. "And I find I am tired, so perhaps you gentleman will excuse me while I catch a nap before we go?"

She was gone before they were on their feet, leaving Dev and Val both frowning.

"We offered to assist him in any way," Dev said, picking up his glass. "I think this goes beyond even fraternal devotion."

"He's doing what he thinks is right," Val responded. "I have had quite enough of my front-row seat, Dev. Tragedy has never been my cup of tea."

"Nor farce mine."

❧

She didn't see him for a week.

The time was spent dozing, trying on the new dresses that had arrived from the dressmaker's, getting to know the duke's daughters, and being reunited with her grandmother. That worthy dame was in much better form than Anna would have guessed, much to her relief.

"It took a good year," Grandmama reported, "but the effects of my apoplexy greatly diminished after that. Still, it did not serve to let Helmsley know I was so much better. He wasn't one to let me off the estate, but I was able to correspond, as you know."

"Thank God for loyal innkeepers."

"And thank God for young earls," Grandmother said. "That traveling coach was the grandest thing, Anna. So when can I meet your young man?"

"He isn't my young man." Anna shook her head, rose, and found something fascinating to stare at out the window. "He was my employer, and he is a gentleman, so he and his brothers came to my aid."

"Fine-looking fellow," Grandmama remarked innocently.

"You've met him?"

"Morgan and I ran into him and his younger brother when she took me to the park yesterday. Couple of handsome devils. In my day, bucks like that would have been brought to heel."

"This isn't your day"—Anna smiled—"but as you are widowed, you shouldn't feel compelled to exercise restraint on my behalf."

"Your dear grandfather gave me permission to remarry, you know." Grandmother peered at a tray of sweets as she spoke. "At the time, I told him I could never love another, and I won't—not in the way I loved him."

"But?" Anna turned curious eyes on her grand-mother and waited.

"But he knew me better than I know myself. Life is short, Anna James, but it can be long and short at the same time if you're lonely. I think that was part of your brother's problem."

"What do you mean?" Anna asked, not wanting to point out the premature use of the past tense.

"He was too alone up there in Yorkshire." Grandmother bit into a chocolate. "The only boy, then being raised by an old man, too isolated. There's a reason boys are sent off to school at a young age. Put all those barbarians together, and they somehow civilize each other."

"Westhaven wasn't sent to school until he was fourteen," Anna said. "He is quite civilized, as are his brothers."

"Civilized, handsome, well heeled, titled." Grandmother looked up from the tray of sweets. "What on earth is not to like?"

Anna crossed the room. "What if I said I did like him, and he and I were to settle here, two hundred miles from you and Rosecroft? When would you see your great-grandbabies? When would you make this journey again, as we haven't a ducal carriage for you to travel in?"

"My dear girl." Her grandmother peered up at her. "Yorkshire is cold, bleak, and lonely much of the year. It is a foolish place to try to grow flowers, and were it not the family seat, your grandfather and I would have removed to Devon long ago. Now, have a sweet, as your disposition is in want of same."

She picked out a little piece of marzipan shaped like a melon and smiled encouragingly at her grand-daughter. Anna stared at the piece of candy, burst into tears, and ran from the room.

❦

"Anna." Westhaven took both her hands and bent to kiss her cheek. "How do you fare? You look well, if a bit tired."

"My grandmother is wearing me out," Anna said, her smile strained. "It is good to see you again."

"And you," the earl responded, reluctant to drop her hands. "But I come with sad news."

"My brother?"

The earl nodded, searching her eyes.

"He passed away last night but left you a final gift," the earl said, drawing her to sit beside him on a padded window seat. "He wrote out a confession, implicating Stull and himself in all manner of crimes, including arson, misfeasance, assault, conspiracies to commit same, and more. Stull will either hang or be transported if he doesn't flee, as deathbed confessions are admissible evidence."

"My brother is dead." Anna said the words out loud. "I want to be sad, but no feeling comes."

"He was adamant he wasn't trying to shoot you. Dev spent some time with him, and though your brother considered murdering you for money, he couldn't bring himself to do it. He insisted the gun went off by accident."

"And Dev?" Anna looked troubled. "Will charges be pressed, and is he all right?"

"It is like you to think of St. Just. But Anna, your family's title has gone into abeyance. You might lose Rosecroft."

"Dev served on the Peninsula for nearly eight

years," Anna said. "He brought two peers of the realm to justice when they were bent on misbehavior. Let him have Rosecroft. Grandmama has just informed me it's a stupid place to try to grow flowers, but it's pretty and peaceful. Horses might like it."

"Then where will you live? I thought you were going to bow to the wishes of your family and remove to Yorkshire?"

"My family." Anna's lips thinned. "Morgan flirts with everything she sees, and Grandmother is suddenly tired of northern winters. I am related to a couple of tarts."

"Even tarts have to live somewhere."

"Will you sell me Willow Bend?" She looked as surprised by her question as he was, as if it had just popped into her head.

I'd give it to you, he wanted to say. But that would be highly improper.

"I will, if you really want it. The stables are done, and the house is ready for somebody to live there."

"I like it," Anna said, "very much in fact, and I like the neighbors there. It's large enough I could put in some greenhouses and an orangery and so on."

"I'll have the solicitors draw up some papers, but Anna?"

"Hmm?"

"You know I would give it to you," he said despite the insult implied.

She waved a hand. "You are too generous, but thank you for the thought. Tell me again St. Just is not brooding. He took a man's life, and even for a soldier, that cannot be an easy thing."

"He will manage, Anna. Val and I will look after him, and he could not let your brother make off with you. The man did contemplate your murder, though we will never know how sincerely."

"Dev knew"—Anna frowned—"and I knew. Helmsley wasn't right. Something in him broke, morally or rationally. It's awful of me, but I am glad he's dead."

"It isn't awful of you. For entirely different reasons, I was glad when Victor died." He wanted to hold her, to offer her at least the comfort of his embrace, but she wasn't seeking it. "Are you up to a turn in the garden?"

"I am." Anna smiled at him, but to him, it was forced, at best an expression of relief rather than pleasure. When they were a safe distance from the house, he paused and regarded her closely.

"You aren't sleeping well," he concluded. And neither was he, of course. "And you look like you've lost weight, Anna. Don't tell me it's the heat."

"You're looking a bit peaked yourself, and you've lost weight, as well."

I miss you terribly.

"Are my parents treating you well?" the earl asked, resuming their sedate walk.

"They are lovely, Westhaven, and you knew they would be, or you wouldn't have sent us here. I am particularly fond of your papa."

"You are? That would be the Duke of Moreland?"

"Perhaps, though the duke has not been in evidence much. There's a pleasant older fellow who bears you a resemblance, though. He delights in telling me stories about you and your brothers and sisters. He flirts with my grandmother and my sister, he adores his wife, and he is very, very proud of you."

"I've met him. A recent acquaintance, but charming."

"You should spend more time with him," Anna said. "He is acutely aware that with Bart and Victor, he spent years being critical and competitive, when all he really wants is for his children to be happy."

"Competitive? I hadn't thought of that."

"Well," Anna stopped to sniff at a red rose, closing her eyes to inhale its fragrance. "You should. You have brothers, and it can't be so different from sons."

Tell me now, Anna, he silently pleaded as she ran her finger over a rose petal. *Tell me I could have a son, that we could have a son, a daughter, a baby, a future—anything.*

"How soon can I remove to Willow Bend?" she asked, that forced, bright smile on her face again.

"Tomorrow," the earl said, blinking. "I trust you to complete the sales transaction, and the house will fare better occupied. It will please me to think of you there." She stumbled, but his grip on her arm prevented her from falling.

"I have been dependent on the Windhams' kindness long enough," Anna said evenly. "I know Morgan and Grandmama will be glad to settle in somewhere."

"Anna." He paused with her again, knowing they would soon be back at the house, and Anna had every intention of moving out to Surrey, picking up the reins of her life, and riding out of his.

"How are you really?"

The bright, mendacious smile faltered.

"I am coping," she said, staring out across the beds of flowers. "I wake up sometimes and don't know where I am. I think I must see to your lemonade for the day or wonder if you're already in the park on Pericles, and then I realize I am not your housekeeper anymore. I am not your anything anymore, and the future is this great, yawning, empty unknown I can fill with what? Flowers?"

She offered that smile, but he couldn't bear the sight of it and pulled her against his chest.

"If you need anything," he said, holding her against him, "*anything*, Anna James. You have only to send me word."

She said nothing, clinging to him for one long desperate moment before stepping back and nodding.

"Your word, Anna James," he ordered sternly.

"You have my word," she said, smile tremulous but genuine. "If I am in any difficulties whatsoever, I will call on you."

The sternness went out of him, and he again offered his arm. They progressed in silence, unmindful of the duke watching them from the terrace. When his duchess joined him, he slipped an arm around her waist.

"Esther." He nuzzled her crown. "I find I am fully recovered."

"This is amazing," his wife replied, "as you have neither a medical degree nor powers of divination."

"True." He nuzzled her again. "But two things are restored to me that indicate my health is once again sound."

"And these would be?" the duchess inquired as she watched Westhaven take a polite leave of Miss James.

The duke frowned at his son's retreating back.

"The first is a nigh insatiable urge to meddle in that boy's affairs. Devlin and Valentine dragooned me into a shared tea pot, and for once, we three are in agreement over something."

"It's about time."

"You don't mind if I take a small hand in things?" the duke asked warily.

"I am ready to throttle them both." The duchess sighed, leaning into her husband. "And I suspect the girl is breeding and doesn't even know it."

"St. Just is of like mind. He and Val all but asked me what I intend to do about it."

"You will think of something. I have every faith in you, Percy."

"Good to know."

"What was the second piece of evidence confirming your restored health?"

"Come upstairs with me, my love, and I will explain it to you in detail."

&

"I am here at the request of my duchess," Moreland declared.

"Your Grace will always be welcome," Anna said. "I'm sure Grandmama and Morgan will be sorry they missed you."

"Making the acquaintance of that scamp, Heathgate." The duke shook his head. "I could tell you stories about that one, missy, that would curl your hair. His brother is no better, and I pray you do not allow me to stray onto the topic of Amery."

"He loves your granddaughter," Anna countered,

"but have another crème cake, Your Grace, and tell me how your duchess goes on."

"She thrives as always in my loving care," the duke intoned pompously, but then he winked at Anna and reached for a cake. "But you tell her I had three of these, and she will tear a strip off the ducal hide. Seriously, she is doing well, as are the girls. I can't say the same for old Westhaven, though. That boy is a shambles. Were it not for his brothers, I'd move him back to the mansion."

"A shambles?" Anna felt the one crème cake she'd finished beginning to rebel.

"A complete shambles." The duke munched away enthusiastically. "His house is in no order whatsoever. Old Fran is running things any damned way she pleases, and you know that cannot be good for the King's peace. Tolliver has threatened to quit, St. Just is back to his drinking and brooding, and Valentine has taken to hiding from them both in the music room."

"I am distressed to hear it. But what of the earl? How does he fare?"

"Forgets to eat." The duke sighed. "Not a problem he inherited from me. Rides his horse every day, but otherwise, it's business, business, and more business. You'd think the boy's a damned cit the way he must read every paragraph and negotiate every price. Mark my words, the next heart seizure will be his."

"Your Grace," Anna said earnestly, "isn't there something you can do? He respects you, more than you know."

"I've reformed." The duke reached for a fourth crème cake. "I do not meddle. I've learned my lesson;

Westhaven needs to learn his. He did seem to manage better when you were on hand, but no matter. He'll muddle along. So"—the duke rose, brushing crumbs from his breeches—"my duchess will want to know, how fare you?"

He leveled a lordly, patrician look at her.

"I am well." Anna rose a little more slowly.

"Not fainting, are you?" The duke glowered at her. "Makes no sense to me at all. The lord plants a babe in a woman's womb then has her wilting all over. I can understand the weeps and the constant napping, but the rest of it… Not the way I'd have arranged it. But the Almighty is content to make do without my advice for the nonce, much like my children."

"I am well," Anna repeated, but a ringing had started in her ears.

The duke leaned over and kissed her forehead.

"Glad to hear it, my dear," he said, patting her arm. "Westhaven would be glad to hear it, too, I expect."

"Westhaven?"

"He's an earl," the duke said, his eyes twinkling. "Handsome fellow, if a bit too serious. Gets that from his mother. Lonely, if you ask me. I think you've met him."

"I have." Anna nodded, realizing she'd walked her guest to the door. "Safe journey home, Your Grace. My regards to the family."

The duke nodded and went smiling on the way to his next destination.

～

"Not managing well, at all." The duke shook his head. "Your mother was concerned enough to send *me*,

Westhaven, and I am barely allowed off the leash these days, as you well know."

"You say she looked pale?"

"Women in her condition might look a little green around the gills at first, but then they bloom, Westhaven. Their hair, their skin, their eyes… She isn't blooming and she's off her feed and she looks too tired."

"I appreciate your telling me this," the earl said, frowning, "but I don't see what I can do. She hasn't asked for my help."

The duke rose, snitching just one more piece of marzipan. "I am not entirely sure she understands her own condition, my boy. Grew up without a mother; probably thinks it's all the strain of losing that worthless brother. You might find she needs blunt speech if your offspring isn't to be a six-months' wonder.

"A six-months' wonder," the duke repeated, "like Bart nearly was. He was an eight-months' wonder instead, which is readily forgivable."

"He was a what?" The earl was still frowning and still pondering the duke's revelations regarding Anna's decline.

"Eight-months' wonder." The duke nodded sagely. "Ask any papa, and he'll tell you a proper baby takes nine and half months to come full term, first babies sometimes longer. Bart was a little early, as Her Grace could not contain her enthusiasm for me."

"Her Grace could not…?" The earl felt his ears turn red as the significance of his father's words sunk in.

"Fine basis for a marriage," the duke went on blithely. "What? You think all ten children were exclusively my fault? You have much to learn, my lad. Much to learn. Now…" The duke paused with his hand on the door. "When will your new housekeeper start?"

"My new housekeeper?"

"Yes, your mother will want to know and to look the woman over. You can't allow old Fran to continue tyrannizing your poor footmen."

"I haven't hired anybody yet."

"Best be about it." The duke glanced around the house disapprovingly. "The place is losing its glow, Westhaven. If you expect to resume your courting maneuvers in the little season, you'll have to take matters in hand, put on a proper face and all that."

"I will at that," the earl agreed, escorting his father to the door. "My thanks for your visit, Your Grace."

The earl was surprised witless when his father pulled him into a hug.

"My pleasure"—the duke beamed—"and your dear mama is probably relieved to be shut of my irresistible self for an hour or two, as well. Mind you don't let that old woman in the kitchen get above herself."

"I'll pass along your compliments." The earl smiled, watching his father trot down the front steps with the energy of a man one-third his age.

"Was that our esteemed sire?" Dev asked, emerging from the back of the house.

"It was. If I'd known you were home, I would have made him wait."

"Oh, no harm done. Did he have anything of merit to impart?"

"Anna is not doing well," the earl said, wondering when he'd lost all discretion.

"Oh?" Dev arched an eyebrow. "Come into the library, little brother, and tell me and the decanter all about it."

"No decanter for me," the earl demurred as he followed Dev through the door, "but some lemonade, perhaps, with lots of sugar."

"So the duke called on Anna and found her in poor spirits?"

"Poor health, more like. Pale, tired, peaked…"

"Like you." Dev stirred sugar into his lemonade.

"I am merely busy. As you have been busy liquidating Fairly's stables."

"And flirting with his fillies." Dev grinned. "They are the sweetest bunch, Westhaven. But did His Grace intimate Anna had that on-the-nest look about her?"

"And what would you know about an on-the-nest look?"

"I breed horses for a living," Dev reminded him. "I can tell when a mare's caught, because she gets this dreamy, inward, secret look in her eye. She's peaceful but pleased with herself, too. I think you are in anticipation of a blessed event, Westhaven."

"I think I am, too," Westhaven said. "Pass me the decanter." Dev silently obliged and watched as his brother poured whiskey into the sweetened lemonade.

"I promised you last week," Dev said slowly, "not to let you get half seas over again for at least ten years."

"Try it." The earl pushed the decanter toward him. "One cocktail does not a binge make."

"Very ducally put," Dev said, accepting the decanter. "How will you ensure my niece or nephew is not a bastard, Westhaven? I am prepared to beat you within an inch of your life, heir or not, if you don't take proper steps."

The earl sipped his drink. "The problem is not that I don't want to take proper steps, as you put it. The problem is that it is Anna's turn to propose to me."

Eighteen

Dev eyed his brother. "I wasn't aware the ladies got a turn at the proposing. I thought it was up to us stalwart lads to risk rejection and to do the actual asking."

"We can take first crack," the earl said, his finger tracing the rim of his glass, "but I took first through fifth, and that means it's her turn."

"I'm sure you'll explain this mystery to me, as I hope at some point to put an end to my dreary bachelor existence," Dev murmured, taking a long swallow of his drink.

The earl smiled almost tenderly. "With Anna, I proposed, explaining to her she should marry me because I am titled and wealthy and so on."

"That would be persuasive to most any lady I know, except the lady you want."

"Precisely. So I went on to demonstrate she should marry me because I am, though the term will make you blush, lusty enough to bring her a great deal of pleasure."

"I'd marry you for that reason," Dev rejoined, "or I would if, well... It's a good argument."

"It is, if you are a man, but on Anna, the brilliance of my logic was lost. So I proposed again and suggested I could make her troubles disappear, then failed utterly to make good on my word."

"Bad luck, that." Dev sipped his drink. "Her troubles are behind her now."

"And she has neither brother nor family seat to show for it," the earl said gently, "though if I haven't thanked you before, Devlin, I am thanking you now for pulling that trigger. Helmsley was a disgrace."

"I was aiming for his hand, though. I grabbed your pistol, and I've never shot with it before. I apologized to Anna and Morgan both, but they just tried to make me feel better."

"I am ordering you to feel better. Anna herself said Helmsley was morally or rationally broken somehow. Could you imagine selling any one of our sisters to Stull?"

"No," Dev said, "and that perspective does put it in a more manageable light. But back to your proposals, as the tale grows fascinating."

"Well, I blundered on," the earl said. "She was to marry me for legal reasons, if all else failed, to prevent kidnapping charges, since I hadn't prevented the kidnapping attempt. She was to marry me to spike Stull's guns and so forth. One has to be impressed at the single-minded focus of my proposals, particularly when juxtaposed with their consistent failure to impress."

"Juxtaposed," Dev mused. "Very ducal word. So you fell on your arse."

"I did, and my sword. Shall we have another drink?"

"One more"—Dev waggled a finger—"and that's it." He did the honors, even remembering to sugar the lemonade heavily first. "This is a delightful summer concoction, though it needs mint or something."

"It needs a taller glass."

"So you are done proposing?" Dev sipped his drink.

"I am. I forgot to propose for the one reason that might have won the prize."

"That being?"

"She loves me." Westhaven smiled wistfully. "She cannot bear to think of the rest of her life without me."

"That reason." Dev nodded sagely. "I will remember that one, as it would not have occurred to me either. Do you think it will occur to Anna?"

"I hope to God it does." The earl took a long pull of his drink. "I cannot make a move at this point unless she invites it."

"Why not? Why not just ride out there, special license in hand, and lay down the law? You haven't tried that approach. You can name it after me, the Devlin St. Just Proposal of Marriage Option Number Seven."

"Dev, I fear you are getting a bit foxed."

"A bit, and I am not even the one trying to drown my sorrows. Am I not the best of brothers?"

"The very best," the earl agreed, his smile carrying a wealth of affection. "But I cannot exercise option number seven, as that option was preempted by the lady's late brother. She did not tolerate attempts to lay down the law."

"He's dead," Dev observed. "Not much appeal to that approach. So what now?"

"Wait. Sooner or later, Anna's condition will become apparent even to her, and then I can only hope she will recall who it was that got her pregnant."

Dev lifted his glass. "Another good reason for having a candle lit when you're swiving one you want to keep. I think our little brother would benefit from such profound wisdom. Where has he got off to?"

As if summoned by magic, Val strode through the door, his expression bleak, his gaze riveted on the decanter.

"There's good news and bad news," Dev said as he slid his drink into Val's hand. "The good news is we are going to be uncles again, God willing. The bad news is that so far, Westhaven's firstborn will be taking after me rather than the legitimate side of the family."

"And this is bad news, how?" Val asked.

Dev grinned. "Is he not the best of little brothers?"

"The very best," the earl agreed, pouring them all another round.

Fortunately for Westhaven, Anna's note did not arrive for another two days. By that point, he, Dev, and Val had sworn not to overimbibe for the next twenty years and endured the hangovers required to make the vow meaningful.

Westhaven,

I am bound by my word to seek your assistance should I find myself in difficulties. The matter is not urgent, but I will attend you at Willow Bend at your convenience.

My regards to your family, and to St. Just and Lord Valentine most especially.

Anna James

PS - You will soon be running out of marzipan. Mr. Detlow's sweet shop will be expecting your reorder on Monday next.

Being a disciplined man, the earl bellowed for Pericles to be saddled, barked an order to Cook to see about the marzipan, snatched up the package he'd been saving for Anna, and was on his way out of Town at a brisk trot within twenty minutes of reading her note. A thousand dire possibilities flitted through his mind as Pericles ground up the miles.

Anna had lost the baby, she had mismanaged her finances, she had decided not to buy the place, but rather, to move back north. She'd found some hapless swain to marry, the neighbors were not treating her cordially, the house had dry rot or creeping damp, or the stables had burned down again.

Only as he approached the turn to the lane did he realize he was being needlessly anxious. Anna had sent for him about a matter that wasn't urgent, and he was responding to her summons. Nothing more, nothing less. He brought his horse down to the walk, but for some reason, his heart was determined to remain at a gallop.

"Westhaven?" Anna greeted him from the drive itself, where she was obviously involved in some gardening task. Her dress was not brown or gray but a pretty white, green, and lavender muslin—with a raised waistline. She had on a floppy straw hat, one that looked to have seen better days but was fetching just the same, and her gloves were grubby with honest Surrey dirt.

"You certainly got here quickly." Anna smiled at him.

He handed off his horse to a groom and cautiously returned the smile. She looked thinner, true, but there were freckles on her nose, and her smile was only a little guarded.

"It is a pleasant day for a ride to the country," Westhaven responded, "and though the matter you cited isn't urgent, delay seldom reduces the size of a difficulty."

"I appreciate your coming here. Can I offer you a drink? Lemonade? Cider?"

"Lemonade," the earl said, glancing around. "You have wasted no time making the place a home."

"I am fortunate," Anna said, following his gaze. "As hot as it has been, we've finally gotten some rain, and I can be about putting in flowers. Heathgate has sent over a number of cuttings, as have Amery and Greymoor."

They would, the scoundrels.

"I've brought along a few, as well," the earl said. "They're probably in the stables as we speak."

"You brought me plants?" Anna's eyes lit up as if he'd brought her the world.

"I had your grandmother send for them from Rosecroft. Just the things that would travel well— some Holland bulbs, irises, that sort of thing."

"You brought me my grandfather's flowers?" Anna stopped and touched his sleeve. "Oh, Westhaven."

He glanced at the hand on his sleeve, wanting to say something witty and ducal and perfect.

"I thought you'd feel more at home here with some of his flowers," was all that came to mind.

"Oh, you." Anna hugged him, a simple, friendly hug, but in that hug, he had the first glimmering hope that things just might come right. She kept his arm, wrapping her hands around it and toddling along so close to his side he could drink in the lovely, flowery scent of her.

"So what is this difficulty, Anna?" he asked as he escorted her to the front terrace.

"We will get to that, but first let us address your thirst, and tell me how your family goes on."

He paused as they reached the front door, then realized her grandmother and sister would likely join them inside the house. "Come with me." He took her by the hand and tugged her along until they were beside the stream, the place where they'd first become intimate. She'd had a bench placed in the shade of the willows, so he drew her there and pulled her down beside him.

"I told myself I'd graciously listen to whatever you felt merited my attention," he began, "but, Anna, I have been worried about you, and now, after several weeks of silence, you send me two sentences mentioning some problem. I find I have not the reserves of patience manners require: What is wrong, and how can I help?"

A brief paused ensued, both of them studying their joined hands.

"I am expecting," she said quietly. "Your child,

that is. I am…I am going to have a baby." She peeked over at him again, but he kept his eyes front, trying to absorb the reality behind her words.

He was to be a father, a papa, and she was to be the mother of his child.

His *children*, God willing.

"I realize this creates awkwardness," she was prosing on, "but I couldn't not tell you, and I felt I owed it to you to leave the decision regarding the child's legitimacy in your hands."

"I see."

"I don't gather you do," Anna said. "Westhaven, I'd as soon not raise our child as a bastard, so I am asking you to marry me. We do suit, in some ways, but I will understand if you'd rather choose another for your duchess. In fact, I've advised you to do just that on more than one occasion. I will understand."

Another pause while Anna studied their joined hands and Westhaven called upon every ounce of ducal reserve to keep from bellowing his joy to the entire world.

"I must decline," he said slowly, "though I comprehend the great honor you do me, and I would not wish bastardy on our progeny either."

"You *must* decline?" Anna repeated. There was disappointment in her tone, in her eyes. Disappointment and *hurt*, and even in the midst of overwhelming joy, he was sorry for that. There was no surprise, though, and he was even more sorry for that.

"I must decline," the earl repeated, his words coming a little faster than he intended, "because I have it on great good authority one accepts a proposal of marriage only when one cannot imagine the rest of one's life without that person in it, and when one is certain that person loves one and feels similarly in every respect."

Anna frowned at him.

"I love you, Westhaven," she reminded him, "I've told you this."

"You told me on one occasion."

Anna held up a hand. "I see the difficulty. You do not love me. Well, I suppose that's honest."

"I have not been honest," the earl corrected her swiftly, lest she rise and he give in to the need to tackle her bodily right there in the green grass.

"At the risk of differing with a lady, I must stand firm on that one point, but I can correct the oversight now." He slipped off the bench and took her right hand in both of his as he went down on one knee before her.

"I love you," he said, holding her gaze. "I love you, I cannot foresee the rest of my life without you, and I hope you feel similarly. For only if you do feel similarly will I accept your proposal of marriage or allow you to accept mine."

"You love me?"

"For God's sake." He was off his knee in an instant, dusting briskly at his breeches. "Why else would I have tried to keep my bloody paws off you when you were just eight and twenty feet down the hall? Why else would I have gone to my father—Meddling Moreland himself?—to ask for help and advice? Why else would I have let you go, for pity's sake, if I didn't love you until I'm blind and silly and…Jesus, yes, I love you."

"Westhaven." Anna reached out and stroked a hand through his hair. "You are shouting, and you mean this."

"I am not in the habit of lying to the woman whom I hope to make my duchess."

That, he saw, got through to her. Since the day she'd bashed him with her poker, he'd been honest with her. Cranky, gruff, demanding, what have you, but he'd been honest. So he was honest again.

"I love you, Anna." His voice shook with the truth of it. "I love you. I want you for my wife, my duchess, and the mother of all of my children."

She cradled her hand along his jaw, and in her eyes, he saw his own joy mirrored, his incredulity that life could offer him a gift as stunningly perfect as the love they shared, and his bottomless determination to grab that gift with both hands and never let go.

She leaned into him, as if the weight of his honesty were too much. "Oh, you are the most awful man. Of course I will marry you, of course I love you, of course I want to spend the rest of my life with you. But you have made me cry, and I have need of your handkerchief."

"You have need of my arms," he said, laughing and scooping her up against his chest. He pressed his forehead to hers and jostled her a little in his embrace. "Say it, Anna. In the King's English, or no handkerchief for you."

He was smiling at her, grinning like a truant schoolboy on a beautiful day.

"I love you," Anna said. Then more loudly and with a fierce smile, "I love you, I love you, I love you, Gayle Windham, and I would be honored to be your duchess."

"And my wife?" He spun them in a circle, the better to hold her tightly to his chest. "You'll be my wife, and my duchess, and the mother of my children?"

"With greatest joy, I'll be your wife, your duchess, and the mother of all your children. Now please, please, put me down and kiss me silly. I have missed you so."

"My handkerchief." He set her down on the bench, surrendered his handkerchief with a flourish, and wrapped his arm around her shoulders. "And my heart, not in that order."

And then he bent his head and kissed her silly.

Epilogue

ANNA WINDHAM, COUNTESS OF WESTHAVEN, WAS enjoying a leisurely measure of those things which pleased her most: peace and quiet at the end of the evening, and anticipation of her husband's exclusive company in the great expanse of the marital bed.

"I can wait, Anna." Her husband's voice shook a little with his mendacity, and behind those beautiful green eyes of his, there was both trepidation and heat. "It's been only a few months, and you must be sure." He stood beside the bed, peering down at her where she lay.

"It has been eternities," Anna said, "and for once, your heir appears to have made an early night of it. Come here." She held out her arms, and in a single moment, he was out of his dressing gown and settling his warmth and length over her.

"Husband, I have missed you."

"I'm right here. I will always be here, but we can't rush this. You've had a baby, given me my heir, and you must prom—"

She kissed him into silence then kissed him into kissing her back, but he was made of ducally stern stuff.

"Anna, I'll be careful. We'll take it slowly, but you need to tell—"

She got her legs wrapped around his flanks and began to undulate her damp sex along the glorious length of his rigid erection.

Take it slowly. What foolishness her husband spouted.

"We'll be fine," she whispered, lipping at his earlobe. "Better than fine."

As they sank into the fathomless bliss of intimate reunion, they were fine indeed, and then much, much, *much* better than fine.

For more from Grace Burrowes, read on for an excerpt from

The Soldier

Available now from Sourcebooks Casablanca

DEVLIN ST. JUST, EARL OF ROSECROFT, PREPARED HIS own tea and took a cautious sip. "What is your relationship to the child?"

"One might say I am her cousin, of sorts, though it isn't common knowledge, and I would prefer to keep it that way."

"You don't want the world associating you with the earl's bastard?" her host asked, stirring his tea slowly.

Emmie met his eyes. "More to the point, Bronwyn does not realize we are related, and I would prefer to be the one to tell her."

"How does that come about?" The earl regarded her over the rim of his teacup even as he sipped.

"My aunt was kind enough to provide a home for me when my mother died," Emmie said, lips pursed, as the recitation was not one she embarked on willingly. "Thus I joined her household in the village before Bronwyn was born. When the old earl got wind of that, he eventually sent me off to school in Scotland."

"So your aunt brought you here, and you were then sent off to school by the beneficent old earl."

"I was, and thereafter, my aunt became the young earl's mistress. I suspect his grandfather sent me off to spare me that fate."

"And Winnie is the late earl's by-blow? Your aunt must have been quite youthful."

"She was ten years older than Helmsley but said, since his mama died when he was young, she suited him."

"Did you know the late earl?"

"I knew him. When the old earl grew ill about three years ago, I was retrieved from where I was governessing in Scotland, with the plan being that I could help care for him. When his lordship saw I was subjected to unwanted attentions, he established me on a separate property."

"In what capacity?" The earl topped off her teacup, a peculiarly civilized gesture, considering he was leaving her no privacy whatsoever.

"I support myself," Emmie replied, unable to keep a touch of pride from her voice. "I have since I returned to Yorkshire. On the old earl's advice, I never rejoined my aunt's household in the village, hence Winnie doesn't understand we are cousins. I'm not sure it ever registered with Helmsley, either."

"Did it register with Helmsley he had a daughter?"

"Barely." Emmie spat the word. "My aunt did well enough with Winnie, though she was careful not to impose the child on her father very often. Helmsley was prone to…poor choices in his companions. One in particular could not be trusted around children, and so Winnie was an awkward addition to her father's household after my aunt's death."

"And now she's been appended to your household?"

"She is…she finally is." For the second time that evening, Emmie smiled at him, but she teared up as well, ducking her face to hide her mortification.

"Women," the earl muttered. He extracted his handkerchief and passed it to her.

"I beg your pardon." Emmie tried to smile and failed, but took his handkerchief. "It was difficult, watching her grow from toddler to child and seeing she'd had no one to love her since my aunt died."

"One must concede, you seem to care for the child." The earl regarded her with a frown. "But one must also inquire into what manner of influence you are on her. You aren't supporting yourself as your aunt did, are you?"

"I most assuredly am *not* supporting myself as you so rudely imply." She rose to her feet and tried to stuff his damp hankie back into his hand. "I work for honest coin and will not tolerate your insults."

"Keep it." He smiled at her slightly while his fingers curled her hand around his handkerchief. "I have plenty to spare. And please accept my apologies, Miss Farnum, as your character is of interest to me."

"Why ever is it any of your business how I earn my keep?" She resumed her seat but concentrated on folding his handkerchief into halves and quarters and eighths in her lap rather than meet that piercing green stare of his again.

"I am interested in your character because you are a friend of Miss Winnie's, and she has become my concern."

"About Bronwyn"—Emmie rose again and paced

away from him—"we must reach some kind of understanding."

"We must?"

"She is my family," Emmie pointed out, then more softly, "my only family. Surely you can understand she should be with me?"

"So why wasn't she?" One dark eyebrow quirked where he sat sipping his tea. Emmie had the thought that if he'd had a tail, he'd be flicking it in a lazy, feline rhythm.

"Why wasn't she what?" Emmie stopped her pacing and busied herself straightening up a shelf of books.

"Why wasn't she with you? When I plucked her off that fountain, she was filthy, tired, and hadn't eaten all day."

"I couldn't catch her." Emmie frowned at the books.

"I beg your pardon?" The earl's voice came from her elbow, but she was damned if she'd flinch.

"I said, I could not catch her." Emmie did peek then and realized the earl wasn't just tall, he was also a big man. Bigger than he looked from across a room, the scoundrel.

"And I could not run her off," the earl mused. "It might comfort you to know, Miss Farnum, I am the oldest of ten and not unused to youngsters."

"You do seem to get on well with her, but I have an advantage, my lord. One you will never be able to compete with."

"An advantage?"

"Yes," Emmie said, feeling a little sorry for him, because he really would not be able to argue the point much further. "I am a female, you see. A girl. Well, a grown woman, but I was a girl, as Bronwyn is."

"You are a female?" The earl looked her up and down, and Emmie felt herself blushing. It was a thorough and thoroughly dispassionate perusal. "Why so you are, but how does this make yours the better guidance?"

"There are certain things, my lord…" Emmie felt her blush deepening, but refused to capitulate to embarrassment. "Things a lady knows a gentleman will not, things somebody must pass along to a little girl in due course if she's to manage in this life."

"Things." The earl's brow knit. "Things like child-birth, perhaps?"

Emmie swallowed, resenting his bluntness even while she admired him for it. "Well, yes. I doubt you've given birth, my lord."

"Have you?" he countered, peering down at her.

"That is not the point."

"So no advantage to you there, particularly as I have attended a birth or two in my time, and I doubt you've managed that either."

"Why on *earth* would…" Emmie's mouth snapped shut before she could ask the obvious, rude, burning question.

"I was a soldier," he said gently. "And war is very hard on soldiers, but even harder on women and children, Miss Farnum. A woman giving birth in a war zone is generally willing to accept the assistance of whomever is to hand, regardless of standing, gender, or even what uniform he wears."

"So you've a little experience, but you aren't going to tell me you're familiar with the details of a lady's bodily…well, that is to say. Well."

"Her menses?" The earl looked amused. "You might have some greater degree of familiarity than I, I will grant that much, but as a man with five sisters, I am far more knowledgeable and sympathetic regarding female lunation than I had ever aspired to be. And surely, these matters you raise—childbirth and courses—they are a ways off for Miss Winnie?"

"Bronwyn," Emmie muttered. Standing so close to him, she could catch the earl's scent, and it managed to combine both elegance and barbarism. It was spicy rather than floral, but also fresh, like meadows and breezes and cold, fast-running streams.

"She *answers* to Winnie," he said, "and she got away from you."

"She did." Emmie's shoulders slumped as some of the fight went out of her. "She does. I've lost her for hours at a time, at least in the summer, and nobody has any real notion where she gets off to. It wasn't so bad when my aunt first died, but it has gotten worse the older Bronwyn gets. I was terrified…"

"Yes?" The green eyes steadily holding hers bore no judgment, just a patient regard with a teasing hint of compassion.

"I was terrified Helmsley would take her south, or worse, let that cretin Stull get hold of her; but Helmsley was her father, so I'd no right to do anything for her, nor to have any say in how she goes on."

"And had your aunt lived, the law would have given Helmsley no claim on the child, nor any obligation to her either."

"Oh, *the law*." Emmie waved a dismissive hand. "The law tells us the better course would have been to allow the child to starve while her dear papa gambled away the estate. Do not quote the law to me, my lord, for it only points out what is legal and what is right do not often coincide where the fate of children is concerned."

"Legalities aside then, I am in a better position to assist the child than you are. Just as the old earl gave you an education to allow you to make your way as a governess, I can provide every material advantage for Winnie, too. If it comes to that, I can prevail upon the Moreland resources for the child as well."

"But I am her cousin," Emmie said, feeling tears well again. "I am her cousin and her only relation."

"Not so, though the reverse might be true. The child's Aunt Anna is now married to my brother, which makes me an uncle-in-law or some such, and I am one of ten, recall. Through her aunt's marriage, Winnie has a great deal of family."

"But they don't know her," Emmie quietly wailed. "I am Winnie's family. *I am.*"

"Shall we compromise?" he asked, drawing Emmie's arm through his and escorting her to the sofa. "It seems to me we are considering mutually exclusive outcomes, with either you or myself having Winnie's exclusive company. Why can't she have us both?"

"You could visit," Emmie said, warming to the idea. Maybe, she allowed, he was an enlightened barbarian, though his arguments for leaving Winnie in his care were sound. "Or perhaps Winnie might spend time here, as she considers this her home."

"I do not *visit* my responsibilities, Miss Farnum,"

the earl replied, resuming his seat across from her. "Not when they require regular feeding and bathing and instruction in basic table manners that should have been mastered long ago."

"So how do we compromise?" Emmie ignored the implied criticism by sheer will. "If Winnie lives here with you, how is that a compromise?"

"Simple." The earl smiled at her, a buccaneer's smile if ever she saw one. "You live here, too. You've said you have experience as a governess; the child needs a governess. You care for her and hold yourself out as entitled to assist with her upbringing. It seems a perfectly feasible solution to me. You remain as her governess until such time as I find a replacement, one who merits your approval and mine."

"Feasible." Emmie felt her mouth and eyebrows working in a disjointed symphony of expressions, none of which were intended to convey good cheer. "You want me to be a governess to Bronwyn?" She rose, and the earl watched her but remained seated. "There's a difficulty." She hoped her relief did not show on her face.

"Only one?"

"It is formidable." Emmie eyed *him* up and down. "I am qualified to supervise a child of Bronwyn's age, but I have always been more a friend to her than an authority figure. I am not sure she will listen to me, else I would not find myself fretting so often over her whereabouts."

"Having not had a papa to speak of and having lost her mother, the child has likely become too self-reliant, something that can only be curbed, not entirely eradicated. And while the child may not listen to you, I have every confidence she will listen to me."

"*Every* confidence?" Emmie arched an eyebrow and met his gaze squarely.

"I got her into the house." The earl started counting off on his fingers. "I inculcated basic table manners, I engaged her in civil discussion when she was intent only on repelling boarders, and"—he arched an eyebrow right back at her—"I got her into the bathtub, where she was soaped and scrubbed into something resembling a lovely little girl."

"You did." Emmie scowled in thought. "May I inquire how?"

"Nelson at Trafalgar. One can only demonstrate sea battles under appropriate circumstances."

"*You* gave her a bath?" Emmie's eyes went wide.

"Soap and water are not complicated, but the tweeny is hardly likely to comprehend naval strategy. I'll provide the child the right bath toys, and my direct involvement shouldn't be necessary from this point out. You do, I assume, have a grasp of naval history?"

"Naval history?" Emmie all but gasped in dismay.

"Well, no matter. I can teach you a few major battles, and any self-respecting child will take it from there. So are we agreed?"

"On what?" Emmie felt bewildered and overwhelmed, perhaps as if a cavalry regiment had just appeared, charging over the nearest hill, and her all unsuspecting in their path.

"You will serve as her temporary governess until we find somebody we both approve to serve in that capacity. I shall compensate you, of course."

"I will not take money for looking after family."

"And how will you support yourself if you do not take money for services rendered?"

"That's the other reason I cannot agree to this scheme." Emmie all but snapped her fingers, so great was her relief. "I cannot let my customers down. If I stop providing goods for any length of time, they'll take their business elsewhere, and I'll get a reputation for being unreliable. It won't serve, your lordship. You'll have to think of some other compromise."

"What is your business that your customers would be so fickle?"

Emmie smiled with pride. "I am a baker, my lord. I make all manner of goods…breads and sweets especially."

"I see. There is no impediment, then."

"Of course there is." Emmie gave him a version of the local art-thee-daft look. "I cannot abandon my business, my lord, else I will have no income when we find a permanent governess for Bronwyn."

"You don't abandon your business," the earl informed her. "You merely see to it here. The kitchens are extensive, there is help on hand, and you were obviously prepared to look after your cousin and your commercial obligations at the same time, so you should be able to do it easily at Rosecroft."

"You would have me turn Rosecroft into a bakery?" Emmie all but squeaked. "This is an old and lovely manor, my lord, not some…"

"Yes?"

"My customers would not be comfortable coming here to pick up their orders. Helmsley was not on good terms with most of his neighbors, and you are a stranger."

"Then we'll have your goods delivered. Really, Miss Farnum, the measures are temporary, and I should hope the good folk hereabouts would understand Winnie has lost both father and mother. As her family, we must put her welfare before somebody's tea cakes and crumpets."

She met his eyes and sighed a sigh of defeat, because he was, damn and blast him, right. Nobody's tea cakes, crumpets, or even daily bread could be as important as Bronwyn's future. And he was also right that Bronwyn did so have family—powerful, wealthy family—who could offer her much more than a cousin eking out a living baking pies in Yorkshire.

"I'll want your apple tart recipe," she said, chin up. If she was to allow this man to take from her the child she loved most in the world, then she was owed that much compensation at least.

The earl's lips quirked. "Dear lady, why wouldn't I give out such a thing to everybody at whose table I might someday sit? I've never understood the business of hoarding recipes. Now, how quickly can we arrange for you to start?"

He was gracious in victory. She had to give him that. He'd also gotten Bronwyn into the tub, and he had the best apple tart recipe she had ever tasted. The picture wasn't entirely bleak. Moreover, the Rosecroft kitchens might need a thorough scrubbing, but as he led her on a brief tour, she saw the ovens were huge, the counter space endless, and the appointments surprisingly modern and well kept.

"My inventory will have to be moved, and I will need storage for it as well."

"Details, and ones I'm sure you'll manage easily." The earl put her hand on his arm as they left the kitchen. "As we've lost the light, Miss Farnum, I must conclude the hour has grown late. Will you allow me to call the carriage for you?"

"I am not but a half mile up the lane. It will not serve to bother the stables for so paltry a journey. I walked here; I'll enjoy the walk home."

"As you wish." He led her through the house to the front door, where her frayed gloves and ugly bonnet were waiting on a table. "Shall I carry it for you?" He held the bonnet up by its ribbons, her gloves folded in the crown. "It's not as if you need to protect your complexion at this hour."

"I can carry it." She grabbed for the bonnet, but his blasted eyebrow was arching again.

"I do not comprehend yet all the local nuances of manners and etiquette, Miss Farnum, but I am not about to let a young lady walk home alone in the dark." He angled his free elbow out to her and gestured toward the door held open by the footman.

Barbarian. She wanted to stomp her foot hard—on his—and march off into the darkness. She'd capitulated—albeit grudgingly and perhaps only temporarily—to his idea of sharing responsibility for Bronwyn. She'd put up with his sniping and probing and serving her tea. She'd agreed to move her business activities to his kitchens, but she would not be bullied.

"I know the way, my lord," she said, glaring at him. "There is no need for this display."

"You are going to be responsible for Winnie's first efforts to acquire a sense of decorum and reserve, Miss Farnum." He picked up her hand and deposited it back on his forearm, then led her down the steps. "You must begin as you intend to go on and set a sincere example for the child. She'll spot fraud at fifty paces, and even my authority won't be able to salvage your efforts then. A lady graciously accepts appropriate escort."

"Is this how you trained recruits when you were soldiering?" She stomped along beside him, ignoring the beauty of the full moon and the fragrances of the summer night. "You box them in, reason with them, tease, argue, taunt, and twist until you get what you want?"

"You are upset. If I have given offense, I apologize." His voice was even, not the snippy, non-apology of a man humoring a woman's snit. She hauled him through the darkness for another twenty yards or so before she stopped and heaved a sigh.

"I am sorry," Emmie said, dropping his arm. "I suppose I am jealous."

He made no move to recapture her hand, but put his own on the small of her back and guided her steps forward again. "You are jealous of what?"

"Of your ease with Bronwyn. Of the wealth allowing you to provide so easily for her. Of your connections, enabling you to present her a much better future than I could. Of your ability to wave a hand and order all as you wish it."

"Are we being pursued by bandits, Miss Farnum?" the earl asked, his voice a velvety baritone in the soft, summery darkness.

"We are not."

"Then perhaps we could proceed at less than forced march? It is a beautiful night, the air is lovely, and I've always found darkness soothing when I took the time to appreciate it."

"And from what would the Earl of Rosecroft need soothing?" She nearly snorted at the very notion.

"I've felt how you feel," he said simply. "As if another had all I needed and lacked, and he didn't even appreciate what he had."

"You?" She expostulated in disbelief, but walked more slowly and made no objection to his hand lightly touching her back. "What could you possibly want for? You're the firstborn of a duke, titled, wealthy; you've survived battles, and you can charm little girls. How could you long for more than that?"

"My brother will succeed Moreland, if the duke ever condescends to expire. This harum-scarum earldom is a sop thrown to my younger brother's conscience, and his wife's, I suppose. He and my father had considerable influence with the Regent, and Westhaven's wife may well be carrying the Moreland heir. Anna made the suggestion to see Rosecroft passed along to me, and Westhaven would not rest until that plan had been fulfilled."

"How can that be?" Emmie watched their moon shadows float along the ground as they walked. "A duke cannot choose which of his offspring inherits his title."

"He cannot. According to the Moreland letters patent, it goes to the oldest legitimate son surviving at the time of the duke's death."

"Well, you aren't going to die soon, are you?" She glanced over at his obviously robust frame, puzzled and concerned for some reason to think of him expiring of a pernicious illness.

"No, Miss Farnum, the impediment is not death, but rather the circumstances of my birth." There was a slight, half-beat pause in the darkness, a hitch in her gait he would not have seen.

"Oh."

"Oh, indeed. I have a sister similarly situated, though Maggie and I do not share even the same mother. The duke was a busy fellow in his youth."

"Busy and selfish. What is it with men that they must strut and carry on, heedless of the consequences to any save themselves?"

"What is it with women," he replied, humor lacing his tone, "that they must indulge our selfish impulses, without regard to the consequences even to themselves?"

"Point taken." For a barbarian, he reasoned quickly and well, and he was a pleasant enough escort. His scent blended with the night fragrances, and it occurred to her he'd already admitted to being comfortable with darkness.

And in his eyes, in odd moments, she'd seen hints of darkness. He referred casually to serving King and Country, and he admitted now to being a ducal bastard. Well, what would that matter? By local standards, he would be much in demand socially, and the squire's daughters would toss themselves at him just as they had at Helmsley once long ago—poor things.

She was so lost in her thoughts she stumbled over a gnarled old tree root and would have gone down but for the earl's arm around her waist.

"Steady on." He eased her up to find her balance but hesitated before dropping his arm. In that instant, Emmie gained a small insight into why women behaved as foolishly as her mother and aunt and countless others had done.

"My thanks," she said, walking more slowly yet. The heat and strength of him had felt good, reassuring in some inconvenient way. For twenty-five years, Emmaline Farnum had negotiated life without much in the way of male protection or affection and she'd been at a loss to understand what, *exactly*, men offered that would make a woman suffer their company, much less their authority.

And she still didn't know, exactly, what that something was, but the earl had it in abundance. The sooner they found Bronwyn a real governess, the better for them all.

"Why do you still wear black?" the earl asked as he ambled along beside her. "Your aunt died several years ago, and one doesn't observe full morning for years for an aunt."

"One doesn't have to, but my aunt was like a mother to me, so I dyed my most presentable ward- robe black and haven't had the coin to replace it since—nor much need to. Then too, wearing black made me less conspicuous to Helmsley and his cronies."

"You did not respect my predecessor. I suppose you don't respect many men, given your aunt raised you alone."

Another pause, but again his hand was lightly at her back, steadying her.

"She told me my father tried, but he became

restless and she could not find it in her heart to force him to stay."

"She did not care for him?"

"She did. I never want to fathom a love like that, a love that puts a loved one aside and says it's for the best."

"Did she know she carried his child when she wished him on his way?"

"No." Emmie sighed, feeling his hand at her back as she did. "She was not…she did not have clear indications of her predicament early on, and by the time she was convinced the unthinkable had happened, her fellow had shipped out for India."

"Be very, very glad she didn't follow the drum," the earl said, something in his voice taking on the darkness. "It is no life whatsoever for a woman."

"Particularly not when the man ends up dying in battle, and there you are—no man, no means, no home and hearth to retreat to, and babies clinging to your skirts."

"This is an abiding theme with you, isn't it?" The earl's voice was merely curious now, but he was identifying a pattern accurately.

"I have avoided the Rosecroft grounds as much as possible," Emmie said, her steps dragging. "Helmsley was an eloquent reminder of how dishonorable a titled, supposed gentleman can be."

He was a thoroughly disagreeable cad," the earl agreed. "A more disgusting excuse for a man, much less a gentleman, I have yet to meet, unless it was that porcine embarrassment colluding with him, the Baron Stull."

"So you met Helmsley?"

"I killed him," the earl said easily, taking her hand in his. "Watch your step. We've reached a rough patch."

EMMIE STUMBLED AGAIN, MORE HEAVILY, BUT HE caught her this time, as well. His left hand went around her left wrist; his right arm secured her to his chest by virtue of a snug hold about her waist. They stood for a long moment in an off-balance version of a promenade, while Emmie used the earl's height and strength to regain her balance.

"Well, good," Emmie said with a certain relish. "The man was in want of killing." Next to her, she heard and felt the earl exhale, a deep, slow breath, sending air fanning past her cheek. She had the sense he'd been holding it a long time. Weeks, maybe, months—his whole life.

"He was, at that," the earl replied. "Shall we proceed?" His voice gave nothing away, though Emmie thought he'd call his earlier words back if he could. Not because he regretted taking the man's life, but because announcing such a thing while escorting a young lady home through darkness wasn't at all the done thing.

Even a barbarian would know that.

"He made a few tries at me," Emmie said. She kept hold of the earl's hand as she walked along, then adjusted her grip as they negotiated more roots, so her fingers laced through his. "It was Helmsley's attentions the old earl sought to preserve me from."

"Did Helmsley ever… achieve his ends?" Rosecroft asked, the same foreboding in his voice.

"I am a baseborn girl, my lord. What difference would it have made if he had? He threw more than a good scare into me, and the lesson served me well

when I went into service. Beastly nuisance of a man.
I am glad you killed him. Glad and relieved. The
old earl, much as he loved his grandson, would have
applauded you for protecting his granddaughters."

It was safe, somehow, to speak so openly with him
in the darkness, even though holding hands with him
this way was also *not* safe. Not safe, nor smart, not
what a prudent woman would do. A prudent woman
wouldn't take such pleasure from it nor speculate
about what other behaviors Lord Rosecroft might
engage in on a dark and breezy night.

Emmie turned the topic to the details of moving
her bakery to Rosecroft, then prattled on about the
neighbors surrounding the property and the various
tradesmen and farmers in the area. She cast around
for topics that were pleasant, soothing, and even
humorous rather than make her escort dwell on a past
better left in silence. And she did not drop his hand
until they approached a stately two-story house, the
structure more grand than a tenant farmer's cottage,
but certainly not a manor in itself.

"The old earl put you here?" Rosecroft asked as he
led her up wide porch stairs.

"He did. He purchased it as a sort of dower house."

It was a pleasant place, or so Emmie told herself.
Flowers abounded, a small barn with adjacent paddocks
stood back from the house, and large trees afforded a
shifting mosaic of moon shadows. In sunlight, it was
cheery, airy, and gracious.

"This is a lot of property for one person to maintain," the earl said as Emmie settled on the porch
swing. He set her bonnet on the steps and turned to

look at the moonlit landscape. "You have a nice view to the river, though."

"I do, and I love my trees. The shade is lovely, and in winter they provide protection from both wind and snow."

"I missed the greenness of England terribly when I was on the Peninsula," her companion mused. "Missed it like some men missed their sweethearts."

"We English are basically homebodies, I think." Emmie set the swing to rocking gently with her toe. "We wander hither and yon for King and Country, but we come home and are glad to be here."

"I will take that as my cue to wander home," the earl said, holding out her bonnet.

"Thank you for your escort, my lord." She rose from the swing and retrieved her bonnet. "I will see you on Monday."

"Until then." He took her hand in his and bowed over it, a courtly gesture one might show a lady but not the daughter of a mere soldier, earning her living in some Yorkshire backwater.

"You can find your way in the dark?" she asked then realized the question was silly. What if he said no? Would she escort him back to the manor?

"I'll manage." His teeth flashed in that buccaneer's smile, and he waited as an escort should until she was safely inside her house. Before she lit a single candle, she turned and peered through her parlor window, watching him disappear into the shadows, his stride brisk, his sense of direction unerring.

Acknowledgments

It takes a village to transform a first-time author's aspirations into the lovely book you're reading now. At the risk of leaving out a few deserving villagers, I'd like to thank my editor, Deb Werksman, who has been patient and supportive over a long haul, and my agent, Kevan Lyon, who has been forbearing with an author who has more enthusiasm than industry expertise (for now!). The art department, marketing, and copyediting folks all deserve an enthusiastic nod, along with editorial assistants and numerous other contributors.

And first, last, and always, I must thank my family, whose emphasis on education and the life of the mind resulted in my having enough imagination to create *The Heir*. Enjoy!

About the Author

Grace Burrowes is the pen name for a prolific and award-winning author of historical romances. Her manuscripts have finaled or garnered honorable mention in the New Jersey Romance Writers Put Your Heart in a Book contest, the Indiana Romance Writers Indiana Golden Opportunity contest, the Georgia Romance Writers Maggie contest, the Virginia Romance Writers Fool for Love contest, and the Spacecoast Romance Writers Launching a Star contest. She won the historical category in both the Maggie and the Indiana Golden Opportunity contests. She is a practicing attorney specializing in family law and lives in rural Maryland. Grace can be reached through her website, graceburrowes.com, and through her email at graceburrowes@yahoo.com.

No Earls Allowed

The Wars are over,
but a battle of wills is upon them...

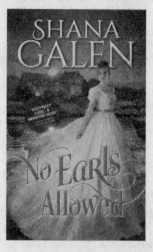

A veteran of the Napoleonic Wars, Major Neil Wraxall is as honor-bound as ever. So when tasked with helping the headstrong daughter of an eminent earl, he can't say no...

Lady Juliana will do whatever it takes to restore a boys' orphanage in her sister's memory. The last thing she needs is for a man to take over. But the orphanage and its charges need more help than she can give. And when Juliana pushes a local crime lord too far, she'll need a warrior. Good thing Neil never leaves anyone behind.

"Bright, funny, poignant, and entertaining."
—Kirkus Reviews

For more Shana Galen, visit:
sourcebooks.com

An Affair with a Spare

The Survivors

Regency romance full of flair and fun from
award-winning author Shana Galen

Rafe Beaumont, fifth son of an earl, uses his irresistible charm
with the ladies to glean dangerous war secrets. Now he's
putting those skills to the ultimate test: capturing an elusive
assassin by seducing his daughter. The problem? She's entirely
immune to Rafe's flattery.

Never before has Collette Fortier met a man as attractive as
Rafe. But her father's life is at stake, and succumbing to Rafe
would be disastrous. When Rafe turns the tables on her, offering support and friendship instead of a fleeting affair, Collette
finds herself tempted in ways she never could have imagined…

"A passionate, page-turning tale."
—Lorraine Heath, *New York Times* bestselling author,
for *Third Son's a Charm*

**For more info about Sourcebooks's
books and authors, visit:**

sourcebooks.com

Scandalous Ever After

Does love really heal all wounds?

After being widowed by a steeplechase accident, Lady Kate Whelan abandons the turf. But eventually her late husband's debts drive her to seek help in Newmarket amidst the whirl of a race meet. There, she encounters Evan Rhys, her late husband's roguish friend—whom she hasn't seen since the day of his lordship's mysterious death. Now that fate has reunited them, Evan seizes the chance to win over the woman he's always loved. But soon, long-held secrets come to light that shake up everything Kate and Evan thought they knew about each other.

"Romaine's elegant prose, inventive plotting, brilliantly nuanced characters, and refreshingly different setting make her latest superbly written romance de rigueur for Regency romance fans."
— *Booklist* Starred Review

For more Theresa Romain, visit:
sourcebooks.com

Lord of Lies

**His voice was low and rough. His eyes burned.
"You are not alone," he said.**

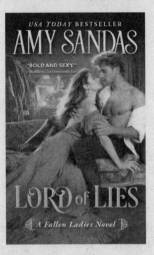

Portia Chadwick longs for a life of adventure. When a
dangerous moneylender kidnaps her sister, she dares to seek
help from a man known only as Nightshade. Soon, she finds
herself charging headfirst into his world of intrigue and
danger—and unexpected passion.

**"Riveting Regency romance...a dark hero,
strong-minded heroine, simmering sensuality...
and a few twists."**
— *RT Book Reviews* Top Pick

For more Amy Sandas, visit:
sourcebooks.com

Earl Interrupted

Pirate Earl Seeks Wife.
Squeamish Ladies Need Not Apply.

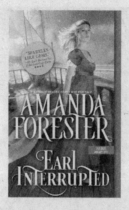

After restoring his fortune as a notorious privateer, Captain Robert Ashton, Earl of Darington, goes to London in search of a bride. Instead, he finds unexpected dangers and unknown assailants. He is shot and left for dead. Life on the high seas was far calmer.

Enter Miss Emma St. James. She may appear sweet and demure, but she quickly proves herself to be equal to any challenge, including saving Darington's life. Just when Darington is sure he has found his perfect bride, she reveals she's betrothed to another.

Now things REALLY start to get complicated…

"Forester's gift for humor and memorable characters sparkles like gems."
—*RT Book Reviews* for *If the Earl Only Knew*, 4 stars

For more Amanda Forester, visit:
sourcebooks.com

The Duke Knows Best

**They're wrong for each other,
for all the right reasons…**

Lord Randolph Gresham has come to London to find a suitable wife. Verity Sinclair may be intelligent, beautiful, and full of spirit, but her father knows a secret about Randolph that makes her entirely unsuitable as his bride. Not right for him at all. Never. Not a chance.

Verity knows that Lord Randolph lives in a country parish, and she wants nothing more than to escape to town. He may be fascinating, attractive, rich, and the son of a duke, but she'll never marry him, nor will she talk to him, flirt with him, walk with him, or dine with him. She'll sing a duet with him, but only this one time, and only because everyone insists. But one duet invariably leads to another…

"Jane Ashford absolutely delights."
—*Night Owl Reviews* Top Pick for *Nothing Like a Duke*

For more Jane Ashford, visit:
sourcebooks.com

Brave New Earl

The Way to a Lord's Heart

First in a brand-new Regency romance series from
bestselling author Jane Ashford

Widower Benjamin Romilly, Earl of Furness, has given up
hope of finding happiness. His wife died in childbirth five
years ago, leaving him with a broken heart and a child who
only reminds him of his loss.

Miss Jean Saunders doted on Benjamin's late countess,
and can't bear it when she hears rumors that the earl is too
bereaved to care for his young son. She arrives on the scene,
questioning his abilities. She simultaneously infuriates and
invigorates him, and she might be the only person who can
breathe life into his neglected home—and his aching heart…

"Filled with wit and charm."
—Fresh Fiction for *Nothing Like a Duke*

For more info about Sourcebooks's books and authors, visit:

sourcebooks.com

Also by Grace Burrowes